John Steel Collection

John Steel Collection

Books 4-6

Stuart Field

Copyright (C) 2023 Stuart Field
Layout design and Copyright (C) 2023 Next Chapter
Published 2023 by Next Chapter
Cover art by CoverMint
This book is a work of fiction. Names, characters, places, and incidents are the product of the author's imagination or are used fictitiously. Any resemblance to actual events, locales, or persons, living or dead, is purely coincidental.
All rights reserved. No part of this book may be reproduced or transmitted in any form or by any means, electronic or mechanical, including photocopying, recording, or by any information storage and retrieval system, without the author's permission.

Blood and Steel
John Steel Book 4

This book is for all the fantastic people who have supported me throughout this journey. To the people who have loved the series and have encouraged me to write more.

This is for you.

Thank you all.

Acknowledgments

I would like to thank
My Amazing Wife, Ani, and my family and friends for their constant support.
To my fantastic daughter, who always makes me proud.

Chapter 1

High above the Manhattan skyline, dark clouds clustered. Flashes of light illuminated the blackened mass as the storm brewed. There was a low rumble followed by more eruptions of light within the angry-looking clouds. The wind howled through the city streets like a wraith hunting for its prey. The storm was nearly over, pushed on by the easterly wind. The downpour of rain had left its mark, leaving lakes on the streets and sidewalks. Despite the sparks of electricity in the clouds, there had been no lightning, just a fantastic light show. Bellow in the sodden streets, there was more flashes of light, but these were from a 9mm. The loud cracks were not from the storm, but the bark from the Sig Sauer.

"Stay away from me, you freak," cried a man as he released another volley of hollow points into the dark. Mario, "the Shark" Brunetti, was afraid – scared shitless, someone was hunting him. The man was a mobster, loan shark, a piece of shit who would sell his mother for a profit. He was a short man with a receding hairline and a round figure. Too much of a good life, too much good food from blood money had shaped him and made him slow, vulnerable. Once a man that put fear into people, but now, he was running scared – or rather limping. He'd taken a bullet to the leg; he'd been lucky, his men had been taken out one by one, shot from a distance. All headshots, even the ones that had used walls as cover, however, bricks are no match for a .50 BMG calibre bullet. The M2 Armoured Piercing round was possibly overkill, but the shooter didn't care, he only needed one of them alive – Brunetti. 706.7 grams of full metal death travelled the short distance quickly, and quietly. At 856 meters per second, the bricks were vaporised, and so were the men behind them. One of the men sought refuge behind a steel beam, but the bullet just passed through it like it was made from butter. The hunter had used an AS50 from Accuracy International with a smart sight with multi-imaging, which included thermal and suppressor – no noise, no flash from the barrel. The .50 calibre monster took out the men in a blink of an eye, ten rounds in just less than a minute. Brunetti had run. Smart move – pointless but smart. He had run to his car, only to find a hole in the engine block, and a bloody mess where the driver had been. Brunetti had run back inside the building. It was an old factory in the Bronx built in the twenties and left to rot for years, but he had bought it at a discount, a good place to do business. Brunetti pulled out his Sig Sauer 320XL custom and held it with his chubby fingers. A nice gun, polished steel with rubber combat grips. Fifteen in the mag, one in the pipe. Nice long barrel. Nice if you're a sports shooter or a guy looking for a gun to intimidate. The Desert Eagle used to be the favourite, but gangsters soon learned that more bullets were far better than a few big bangs. If you're in a firefight, you want more bullets. Magnums are good for intimidation – very good, in fact, but it means you must carry lots of heavy magazines. Brunetti was smart, possibly learned the lesson the hard way. Unfortunately, a nice gun is no match against what he knew was coming for him.

He had run inside the building, hoping the deeper he went, the less likely those damned bullets would be able to reach him. A good plan. Brunetti was smart, but the hunter was smarter. Brunetti ran towards the door of his office; he had a secure room there. Three inches of reinforced steel with lead lining, nothing was getting through, not even him. Brunetti smiled as the door came into view. Six more feet, and then he was safe. His eyes widened with eagerness as if willing the room to come to him. His gaze fell to a red LED light on the door. His eyes squinted as he approached. Was it a new alarm system his tech guy had fitted? Brunetti slid to a stop, dropping to the ground as he did so. As the red LED turned green, there was a rush of wind, followed by a blinding flash of light. Brunetti was lifted off the ground and hurled across the open space. A massive explosion rocked the building, but there was no fire, just the blast. Brunetti looked over at the gaping hole where his office had once been, now jus smouldering bricks and twisted metal. The air was thick with smoke and the smell of burnt wood and metal, making his eyes sting and water. Brunetti wiped the tears from his eyes with his sleeve and coughed. He felt the urge to stand, to run, to get the hell out of there. As he stood, he turned towards the way he had come. He looked back at the hole in the wall. Two options, both could mean his death, but for some reason he wasn't, the killer could have taken him out any time, yet he lived. Working on this, Brunetti smiled. The assassin needed him alive. Brunetti laughed and ran towards the hole, confident that the killer was too far away after all the shooter would have to be quicker than an Olympic runner to get from the nest to the other side of the building, no, Brunetti had the advantage. As he ran towards the gap, he froze, there stood a figure in a long coat, the light from a nearby streetlamp showed only the outline of the man, but Brunetti didn't need to see the man's face, he knew exactly who it was – John Steel.

"Brunetti, where is SANTINI?" Steel yelled. Brunetti skidded as he struggled to turn and run. There was a soft sound of metal against metal, followed by a scream from Brunetti. He looked down to see blood streaming from the outer side of his left leg. Brunetti turned and released a volley of rounds at the hole in the wall, only to find an empty space. Steel had gone. Brunetti's eyes darted from side to side, hoping to catch a glimpse of the phantom, but found only darkness. He scrambled to his feet and headed towards the main entrance.

"Where is SANTINI?" Steel yelled out once again. Brunetti released another volley before the clicking sound of an empty gun. Brunetti replaced the magazine with a fresh mag and clicked the bolt release catch on the side, forcing the top slide forward, loading a new round into the chamber.

"Stay away from me, and you freak," Brunetti yelled, firing blindly into the dark.

"I'll only ask one more time Brunetti, where are they?" Steel yelled, his voice echoing around the empty space of the abandoned building.

"Go to Hell, ya freak," Brunetti screamed, then fired off another volley. As he turned to run, he bumped into something. His blood ran cold as he dropped to the floor. He raised the weapon, but Steel grabbed it with a swift movement, ripping it out of the mobster's hand.

"I am in Hell thanks to you and your friends, now, where is SANTINI?" Steel growled. Brunetti looked at Steel. He was a big man, six-two compared to his five-six. Steel's handsome square-jawed face was masked by a pair of military-style sunglasses, which hugged his face like a mask, his black hair styled with a side parting. He was dressed all in black with a long black wool and leather trench coat. Brunetti looked down at Steel's leather military-style gloves with the plastic knuckle guards, but Brunetti's eyes were more fixed on his own gun that Steel was pointing down at his groin area.

"Talk, or you'll never need that vasectomy," Brunetti shook with fear as he noted the emotionless expression on Steel's face as he spoke. "Where are they, talk, or I'll take you one piece at a time, starting with the smallest," Steel said, shoving the 9mm into Brunetti's groan.

"If I tell, I'm dead," Brunetti screamed, waving his arms about. Steel smashed the gun against Brunetti's head to calm him.

"Well, if you don't, I'll keep you alive," Steel said with a deep growl. Brunetti held a puzzled look.

"Don't you mean you'll kill me?" Brunetti laughed, thinking Steel had it backwards.

"No, you'll be alive, but I will make sure that every scumbag in the city knows you like kids – little kids, make sure the word is spread that you couldn't talk enough about every mobster in the city. You'll want SANTINI to kill you, you'll want me to kill you, but I won't, I'll make sure you stay alive – until I get bored of saving your arse," Steel said holding up the gun and releasing the magazine, which fell to the concrete with a clatter of metal. Steel pulled back the top slide enough to make sure to check a round was chambered, then released the slide. "You have three options, one – you say nothing and your life becomes a living Hell, Two – you tell me what I want to know, you live and take your chances, or Three – you tell me, and I leave you with this quick way out?" Steel said, his face half in shadow, half in the light coming from a top window.

"I don't see no incentive, either way, I'm dead," Brunetti moaned, holding his bloody leg.

"You have a choice, more than my family was given, more than you gave them," Steel said, this time the anger was starting to show.

"But I had nothing to –,"

"You told SANTINI that my family was having a party that day, you told them who was responsible for the raid on the warehouse and who was hunting them, you even provided the weapons used, so do not tell me you had nothing to do with it," Steel screamed and ripped Brunetti from the floor as though he was a rag doll. Brunetti gasped at the display of power. "I grow weary of your excuses, and I'll give you one more chance to answer, use it wisely." Brunetti stared into those damned sunglasses and his scared reflection. The question wasn't whether he was going to live or die; it was how he was going to die, horribly, or by his own hand? Steel had given him that choice, SANTINI wouldn't.

"What do you want to know?" Brunetti sighed, his body going limp, the fight, and fear had drained out of him. Steel smiled and placed the man onto the floor.

"You help me – I'll help you," Steel said, dragging Brunetti out of the hole in the wall and to a waiting vehicle. As the blacked-out Yukon drove off, the old factory was ripped to pieces by several explosions, leaving nothing but rubble.

* * *

Several miles away, deep under the city, in the depths of the Manhattan subway, Tara Burke looked out of the subway trains window. Raindrops had pooled onto the rubber corners of the safety glass, droplets of water rolled together like globules of mercury. They had collected from when the train had gone above ground. Her thoughts were a million miles away. Dreams of a different life, a better life. The cold glass felt good against her warm skin. The first time she had felt cool all day. The diner where she worked had been busy from breakfast up to the end of her shift. *Thank God for nine o'clock,* she had thought as she clocked out. The nights were getting warmer, but the season was bringing the rain. Sometimes she hated spring, sure it was getting darker later, and if she never saw another snowflake, it wouldn't be too soon, but the nights were still cold. Tara had one of those 'girl next door' pretty faces, which was framed with shorter hair. Weeks before it had hung along the length of her back, but she needed a change. Now her red locks hung on her shoulders. *New spring, new you,* she had promised herself the year before. A New York summer is not the best time to have long hair, especially if you work in a Diner.

She looked at her reflection in the nearby window. A sad face stared back at her from the black background of the unlit subway line. Tara stared into her large blue eyes, noting the sadness within them. That was going to change. She had plans that would make her dreams come true. Tara took a deep sigh as she thought about her life. She had just celebrated her twenty-fifth birthday and had nothing to show for her life. She had been nowhere, nor had she done anything special. Straight after school, she had gotten that stupid job in the Diner just so she could live. Her mother had skipped out as soon as she could, leaving Tara with the two-bedroomed apartment while she disappeared to God knows where not that Tara cared.

Good riddance, Tara thought as she remembered reading the note telling her she was on her own. That was the only thing her mother had ever given her apart from the beatings. Now, she was on her own, apart from the new roommate, who was only there to help pay the rent.

The screech from the train's brakes signalled that they were approaching the station on 50th Street. Tara took her face away from the glass. She felt the tingle in her cheek as the skin began to warm up. As the train came to a stop, the doors opened with a hiss from the hydraulics. She stood up and headed out into the chill of the night. It was almost quarter to ten at night as she reached Main Street. The walk home would take her five minutes—she knew this for certain after walking it for so many years. Down West 50th, then onto Ninth Avenue until she got to 48th Street. Tara took out her cell phone and checked her messages. She had forgotten about the vibration the phone had given off on the train. But then, late at night is not the time to pull out your cell phone on the subway.

Where the hell are you, we must talk...

She stared at the message for a moment, and her blood froze at the tone. Something was wrong. Tara put the phone back into her pocket and walked home. Her pace had quickened. Her heels tapped the concrete. The sound echoed through the streets like tiny horses' hooves on cobbled roads. The night appeared darker than usual, even though there were plenty of street lamps and lights from the houses as families stayed up to watch television, but it was a different dark. A fearful darkness that no one could see unless you were terrified by it.

To her left, there was a dark spot, a gap in the light, Clinton Community Garden, a nice place in the day, but it was bathed in darkness. She shivered again, and her imagination began to run away with her as she began to see and hear things, she was sure weren't there, or hoped. Tara looked at her watch. The digital display read twenty-one-forty.

She had worked overtime to help pay the rent until her new roommate moved in properly. Tara smiled as she thought about the fresh-faced girl who had answered agreed to move in. An old friend who needed digs, she had a good job so money wouldn't be a problem. The friend was a pretty woman in her late twenties, but hey, who was Tara to judge why a woman like that was single? All Tara knew was she had been in a bad relationship but was now single...of sorts. Tara turned on to her road; the apartment wasn't much further. A cold breeze met her as she started down the final stretch, making her shiver as though someone had just danced over her grave. She had that feeling again.

Something was wrong.

Tara walked up to the door at the front of the building. Stopping, she looked around to see if there was anyone lurking in the shadows. She shook her head as if to shake the silly idea from her mind; she was letting a simple text spook her. It was probably nothing. She smiled at her foolishness. The bad thing about texts is they don't convey emotion unless you want to lighten the tone, and you put the standard *LOL* at the end. Tara took out the phone again and re-read the text.

Where the hell are you, we must talk...

She had to admit that at first, it had looked bad, but then she looked at it again. She had pulled a double shift and not told him, plus he could get a little jealous what with her flirting for tips and all. Once, she had gotten a twenty for giving some guy a peck on the cheek because it was his birthday. A little harmless fun, she thought, plus it paid the bills. Tara smiled as she walked up the stairs to her apartment on the fourth floor, her *exercise for the day* as she called it. The sound of televisions filled the tight corridors, some people watching games shows, others watching police dramas. Music blared through the thin flooring above. There was a baby's cry from number 4.

She stopped outside number 42 and slipped the key into the lock. Tara pushed the door open and stepped inside the dimly lit room. An orange glow from the streetlights outside broke up the blackness. All she wanted now was her bed after a long day. Tara listened to the couple next door: loud moans of passion came through as if there was no wall between them at all. She smiled as she shook her head and shut the door behind her. A scream filled the building—a scream like no other. Then there was only the sound of the neighbours' televisions filling the corridors once more.

Chapter 2

Detective Joshua Tooms was woken by the sound of banging. He sat up quickly and listened more carefully, just in case it was coming from inside the building. His wife was about to speak, but he raised his finger to his lips as a signal for silence. At first, he thought the banging was from a neighbour's house, reasoning that the noise had travelled through the open bedroom window. He listened harder. The hammering was coming from downstairs. Someone was at his front door. His wife Barbara held on to his muscular arm for comfort. He patted her hand for reassurance. Tooms looked over at his clock: the display was blank, signifying a lack of power. Had someone cut the power to his house? Tooms rolled out of bed and stretched off his muscles, unwittingly showing off his large frame. Even though he was in his late forties, he was still in good shape. Years in the Marines had taught him to look after himself.

"Don't worry, it will be OK," he told his wife. "Just lock the door behind me and get ready to call 911."

Barbara nodded and watched as he turned to his bedside drawer and pulled out his service 9mm Glock 17 pistol. He didn't need to check it; he always had a full magazine of fifteen rounds and one in the chamber. The bullets were called *critical duty*—quite appropriate, he always thought. The 135-grain bullets were meant to put someone down, not just tickle them. He never turned as he heard the door close behind him; he just stopped and listened for the lock to be put on. Moving to the staircase, he saw his two daughters holding each other in fear as they looked down the stairwell, almost hypnotised by the banging. They looked up to see their father, who was now padding towards their rooms. Quickly they hurried away and locked themselves in, tears of fear running down their faces.

The downstairs was bathed in a vale of blue. Streams of moonlight flooded through the sitting-room window like the sun on a summer's day. Tooms was thankful for the illumination, realising he'd left the flashlight in his car. He stood there in his sleeping shorts, the moonlight glistening off his large muscular form, making him look almost like a black gladiator. The banging became more violent, but there were no voices to let him know who was there. Cautiously he headed for the door, the Glock raised up in his right hand, leaving his left free. Again, the person hammered on the door, always in blocks of three knocks interrupted by a brief pause. He put his back against the wall next to the door, then breathed in a lungful of air to steady his heart rate.

"Who the fuck is there?" he yelled, expecting the door to be shredded by gunfire. "I'm warnin your ass. I'm a cop. I'm armed, and I'm pissed, so you better answer up or get the fuck away from my house," Tooms's voice bellowed like a brown bear that had gargled a shot of whiskey.

"Tooms, it's Tony. Open the door, man!" came a voice from the other side of the door. Tooms opened the door to reveal a white guy with short brown hair, wearing jeans, and a black three-quarter-length leather jacket.

"Tony, what the fuck, man? Why didn't you call first? I could have shot your ass," Tooms said, exhaling the air he had been holding. Tony walked in through the open door and saw the three women coming down the stairs to see who was making all the noise.

"I tried calling, but some idiot who was higher than Armstrong ran into a transformer. Looks like the whole block has lost power. It must have affected the cell tower as well as the power lines, which means no phones," Tony explained. He looked past Tooms's large frame and, giving an embarrassed smile, waved at the now angry women who stood at the bottom of the stairs. Tooms reached over and tried the light switch near the door. He had tried the switch several times, to the point of not knowing whether it was in the on or off mode. The *clicks* filled the air, but no lights broke the darkness.

"You've come to check on me, man, now that's touching, bro, you know I can take care of myself?" Tooms joked as he shut the door, and Tony made his way into the sitting room.

"Yeah, you got Barbara to hold ya hand, just in case it's too dark," Tony laughed. Suddenly the television and the lights came on, making them all jump. Tooms and Tony laughed at their cowardly display in front of the women.

"So, what you doin' here, at...?" Tooms remembered that he didn't know what time it was.

"Eleven o'clock. Sorry, man, but we picked up a fresh one," Tony apologised. The two detectives were on call. The one thing Tooms hated about the job was that most people died at night or early in the morning. A social job this was not; however, compared to the army, it was a dream occupation. Being shipped off to God-knows-where at the drop of a hat wasn't great for family life either. Joshua Tooms left Tony to make some coffee while he showered and got dressed. The girls had gone back to bed after saying their goodnights, leaving Barbara Tooms to look after their unexpected guest. Tony looked around the house, feeling a touch of jealousy. Tooms had the package: a great family and a nice house in a nice part of town.

"So, Tony, what you been you to?" she asked with a warm but weary smile. "Apart from dragging my husband out of bed in the middle of the night."

"Not much, I am sort of seeing someone now ... Sort of," Tony replied nervously. He knew she would be firing a million questions at him, just because of that gossipy interest she had. He saw her eyes light up at the thought of meeting his girlfriend, and Tony could tell that she was planning a cosy dinner party to engineer it.

"So, what's her name? Where does she work?" Barbara was suddenly awake as if she had had too much coffee.

Tony looked up thankfully at the staircase as Tooms came down the stairs, pulling his jacket on as he walked. It hadn't taken him long, five minutes tops, but then he had had a lot of practice. Tooms crossed the room and gave his wife a kiss before heading for the door.

"OK, partner, you're drivin'." Tooms smiled as he opened the front door, and the two men stepped through into the fresh night air. Tooms looked around. He hadn't even noticed it had been raining. Tony had parked in the driveway next to Tooms's blue Honda Odyssey. As they got into Tony's red Challenger, Tooms smiled as he looked over towards his house. It wasn't a mansion or anything. It was comprised of just three bedrooms with a bit of a garden to make barbecues in the summer, plus a front porch where he could sit outside and watch the world go by, but most of all, it was home.

His parents had left it to them when they moved away. They had won on the lottery and decided to get that house in the Hamptons that they had seen once on holiday. It hadn't been' a big win, but it was enough for a couple of pensioners to live on.

"So, where we off to?" Tooms asked, taking a sip from his travel mug.

"Midtown, we got a woman found dead in her apartment." Tony stuck the car in reverse and powered out of the driveway. Tooms blew down the small hole in the mug's lid to cool down the coffee a little. His face held a saddened look, and he realised that this was going to be a long night.

Chapter 3

The trip to the crime scene was more like an interrogation. Tony had regretted telling Barbara Tooms anything about his new girlfriend because he knew that even if she couldn't ask the questions, Joshua would. Tony loved her like a sister, but she was too much into the 'need to know' group. She was a gossip, and her husband were worse because he fuelled her addiction. Tooms checked a message on his phone. It was from Barbara, Tooms smiled before replying to the message and tucked his phone away into his pocket. Tony felt nervous as Tooms adjusted his seating position to face his partner.

"So, who is she, and where did you meet?" Tooms asked as they passed another coffee shop.

"You're kiddin' me, right? Can't it wait until after we have solved the case?" Tony asked, knowing full well that Tooms would be badgered with the same questions when he got home. Tooms just shrugged and gave a little noise of disapproval.

"What?" Tony asked in response to the little 'Huh' that his partner let out. He knew what it meant—his mother did it every time she wanted to show her disapproval of a choice he had made—normally a girl he was dating.

"Nothing," Joshua Tooms replied. "Just you never mentioned her before, that's all. We have been partners for how long? And you keep this from me, man, I thought I knew you?" Tooms looked away in a childish manner as if turning his back on Tony.

"Barbara's gonna nag the shit outa ya if you don't bring back some gossip, ain't she?" Tony said, realising the real pain his friend was going through.

"You got that right. And it's all on you, brother, it's all on you," laughed Tooms, after he gave up trying to keep a serious face. Tony parked as close as he could to the building. Black-and-whites cordoned off the area, as well as the police barriers that were blocking off the building to people who just wanted to get a view of the crime scene. Tooms and Tony approached the building and showed their shields to one of the uniforms at the cordon. Even though it was late, 'rubberneckers' had gathered there, eager to feed their morbid fascination.

Inside the building, the two detectives spoke to another uniformed officer, who directed them upstairs to the fourth floor. To their dismay, they had to take the stairs as the elevator was in use, with the CSU – or Crime Scene Unit offloading in their equipment. The stairwell was only just wide enough for two. The walls were painted a sickly yellow, probably to hide the dirt, so that the owner didn't have to clean them too often. However, in general, the building was clean, with no apparent cracks or peeling wallpaper. This was a 'cheap rent' place, but the landlord had some sense of pride about his property, that much was obvious.

"So, this girl of yours, where did you meet?" Tooms smiled as Tony shot him a look.

"Seriously? We're on the way to a crime scene, and you're bringing this up now?" Tony asked, even though he wasn't surprised. Tooms shrugged and smiled as they reached the first floor.

"We met at a flower store, OK?" Tony said, feeling he had to give his inquisitive friend some information or the trip to the fourth floor would be unbearable. Tooms stopped and turned, placing a hand on Tony's chest to halt him.

"Wait a minute," the Tooms asked him. "you pick up a chick while you were getting flowers for another girl?" Tooms shook his head in disappointment. "That's ... cold, man. I don't know whether to be proud or disgusted, man, No wonder you're single!" Tooms turned and started towards the stairwell. Despite his words, he was impressed, but he didn't want to let Tony know.

"The flowers were.... for my mother. It was her birthday." Tony felt almost embarrassed to admit how it had happened. The sound of Tooms's laughter echoed up to the second floor.

"OK," Tooms stopped, his face cringed with disappointment. "I preferred to be disgusted and proud, now I just feel.... never mind," Tooms said, shaking his head as he walked, all manner of being impressed had crumbed.

"So, where does she live? What does she do?" Tooms grilled Tony once more.

"She has just moved actually. Moved in with an old college friend, she said. Better on the bills as her other roommate bailed on her," Tony explained. Tooms shook his head, for he could understand that kind of situation. It had happened to him once or twice before he joined the service. As they rounded the corner of the fourth floor, Tooms and Tony saw the circus getting ready. CSU were putting on their coveralls and opening aluminium cases that had their gear neatly packed inside. A young blonde CSU woman was getting her camera gear ready and attaching the special lens lamp onto the Canon 1d. As far as they could see, each member of the team of six had a task: fingerprint lifting, fibre collection, or laying evidence markers.

Tooms led the way into the room, which was empty apart from the ME (Medical Examiner), Tina Franks. The dark-skinned woman was crouched over the body, blocking the two detectives' view.

"What we got, Doc?" Tooms greeted her as he pulled on his surgical gloves.

"White female in her late twenties, I would say," Tina said as if she was reading off a menu. "Cause of death is undetermined as she has multiple injuries." The police's medical examiner wasn't being callous or unfeeling, and she was simply being focused on the job.

"Do we have a name?" Tooms asked as Tony walked around the ME to look at the body. Something about the corpse looked horribly familiar to him. He thought he recognised her clothes and the small silver pendant necklace that had a small dragon on it.

"Her name was Amber ... Amber Taylor," Tony announced, deathly calm. Both Tooms and Tina looked up at their pale-looking colleague. Tooms's stomach turned over as he had a horrible feeling.

"Don't tell me that she was—," Tooms began hesitantly.

"—My girlfriend. Yes, she," Tony's voice was a choking whisper, "was."

Joshua grabbed Tony by the arm and walked him out. Tony's face betrayed a jumble of confused emotions. Should he cry? Yell? Break something?

"Make a hole!" Tooms yelled, forcing people out of the way with his roar. Uniforms and techs parted like the red sea, allowing the two detectives through. They headed for the elevator, and Tooms barged past a couple of techs who were waiting to go in.

"Get the next one," Tooms ordered the two shocked men, letting the doors close in front of them.

Outside, the cold wind stung the two friends like a swarm of wasps. It was cold enough to see the smoky breath of passers-by. Tony was uneasy on his feet, his legs unable to support him. But his powerful partner held him long enough for them to make it to the wall next door. Suddenly Tony vomited in the bushes next to the building. Tooms stood watch over his partner as he hung onto the wall and screamed out in emotional pain. Tooms's massive hand hovered above his partner's back, ready to give him a sympathetic pat, but somehow it felt not so much wrong as not enough.

"No point tellin' you to go home, because I know you won't," Tooms said. "So, get your ass to the precinct, man. I will fill you in there." Tooms rested a gentle hand on his partner's shoulder. Tony stood up. His pain had turned to anger, and it showed in his eyes. Tooms looked over towards the crime scene as Tony sat down on the doorstep of the adjacent building. Joshua pulled out his cell phone.

"Yeah, McCall? It's Joshua. We got a bad situation here."

* * *

It only took fifteen minutes for McCall to turn up. Her arrival was signalled by the roar of her GT 500 Mustang. Tooms looked over from his spot next to Tony on the neighbour's front step. He stood up and looked down at his partner.

"Back in a bit, man," he told him. Tony, unable to talk, just nodded in response. Tooms smiled and walked over to the beast of a car. The motor purred as she let the engine idle before switching it off. Detective Samantha McCall swung her long legs out of her car and stood up, showing her catwalk model height. Her gaze was on Tony as she slipped on her black leather jacket.

"Hey, Joshua, how's he doing?" she asked as the large black cop approached her.

"Pretty much as you would expect," Tooms replied as they hugged as if they were close relatives. They made their way towards Tony, who was staring down at the pavement while his thoughts were elsewhere. The sound of the clacking heels of Sam's high leather boots caused him to look up at them. Samantha McCall gave him a comforting smile, then moved closer. She had shoulder-length brown hair and had an athletic form that was currently hidden beneath a pair of jeans that hugged her perfect behind and a black baggy T-shirt under a black leather jacket. In another life, she should have been walking catwalks or photoshoots in faraway places, but her father's death by gunshot had made a model's life impossible for her. Indeed, McCall had the looks and the body of a supermodel, but she also had the brains and the instincts of a first-rate cop, something she had always wanted to be after coming from a long line of police officers, detectives, and one lawyer. Detective Samantha McCall walked up to Tony and gave him a hug. She knew what he was going through, and if anyone did, it was her.

"Where's Steel?" Tooms asked, looking around and paying attention to the rooftops. "I figured he would have come with you?"

"Who knows?" She shrugged as she spoke. McCall didn't really care about Steel's whereabouts; she was too preoccupied with Tony's pain.

"You OK, partner?" Tooms asked as he watched Tony nod, then shrug with mixed emotion. He knew the answer, but he just wanted to hear it from him.

"No, not really. I just saw my girlfriend dead on the floor with bits cut out of her," Tony growled. He wasn't mad at Tooms. He was angry at whoever was responsible for the killing.

"You know the captain ain't gonna let you work this?" Tooms told him. "In fact, he probably won't let me be on the team either." Tony looked up at Tooms, confused.

"I am your partner, man," Tooms explained. "He ain't gonna let us work this." Tony knew he was right, but he wanted blood.

"I'll talk to the captain and make sure Steel, and I get the case," Sam said. Tony looked up and gave her a smile of gratitude. Sam simply nodded with that same sympathetic smile.

"Head back to the precinct and start digging up what you can about her," McCall ordered. Tony was confused.

"I thought we weren't on the case?" Tony stood up. He suddenly looked different, less angry, and more driven.

"You're not on the case, Tony, but you are the only one who knew her. For that reason, we are using you as our best source of information until someone better comes along. Is that a problem, Detective?" she asked in a stern voice. But Tony saw through her plan to keep him in the loop, despite the regulations.

"No, ma'am," Tony replied, trying to keep a straight face. However, the quick lift of the corner of his mouth gave him away. As Tooms and Tony headed back to their blue Challenger, McCall looked up at the building, towards the fourth floor. She took a deep breath to get herself in the right frame of mind.

* * *

McCall had ended up taking the elevator, having rejected the prospect of the long walk up the stairs. She felt a little lazy for doing so, but then it was far too early for a Stairmaster workout—besides, she hadn't had her coffee yet. The steel box elevator was small, and she wondered how the designated 'twenty people allowed' was even possible.

With a shudder and an alarming flicker from the lights, the elevator stopped on the fourth floor. The doors slid open to reveal the crime scene technicians getting to work on evidence collection. McCall could see through the open door her friend Tina, kneeling over the body, taking the liver temperature of the young woman.

As she approached, McCall tried to repress a sudden expression of disgust at the way the woman had been brutalised. Amber Taylor had been tall with long brown hair. Her blue eyes were open, and still registered the terror she must have felt. The rest of her face had been badly cut, and the jaw was broken. If she had once been a pretty woman, someone had clearly gone out of their way to hide it.

"Hey, Tina," McCall greeted the ME as she walked round to the side of her friend.

"Are we sure it's her?" McCall asked, almost daring to hope there might have been a mistake.

"Tony identified the clothing," Tina replied. "They had met up that morning, and she had worn the same outfit then, in fact, poor Tony showed me a photograph he had taken on his cell." Tina picked up a small evidence bag, inside which was a necklace. "The photograph also shows that this was around her neck." The doctor pointed to a purse next to a large beige handbag, which lay on the breakfast bar. McCall picked up the purse and found Amber's ID inside.

"I will still run tests, but I think we've got enough for an identification for the time being." Tina sounded as sad as she looked. McCall nodded as she placed the purse back onto the breakfast bar.

"Hey. How's our boy doin'?" Tina still couldn't forget the look on Tony's face when he had identified her.

"Too soon to tell, I guess," Sam said as she pulled on her surgical gloves. "I sent him back to the precinct to do a check on our vic."

"Are you sure that's the right thing to do? Why not send him home?" Tina's question made McCall give her one of those 'really' looks.

"If I send him home, then he goes stir crazy and does God knows what. Besides, you're a fine one to talk, lady. Did you stay at home after that trouble in the morgue?" Tina shot McCall a guilty look, knowing that her friend was right.

"So, what killed her?" Sam asked, taking out her small notebook to note down any facts the ME had.

"Well, I don't know for sure until I get her back to the office, but I'd say she was tortured. Possibly for hours," Tina said, jotting down another point on her report form.

McCall took a small camera from her jacket pocket and started to take her own photographs. This was something she had learnt some time ago, and it made sense because she didn't have time to wait for the CSU to produce their shots. Besides, she figured that she might pick up on something that they missed.

"By the look of things, they started at the feet and worked up. Some of the injuries I won't find till later, but others are obvious." Tina pointed to a hole in Amber's upper leg. "Someone took a corkscrew to this poor woman's femur. By the look of things, it went in deep." Tina pointed to the metal corkscrew that lay next to the body.

"They removed the skin from her fingers using a potato peeler. Sammy, I tell you we are lookin' for one sick individual." As Tina finished her sentence, she could see the look of horror in McCall's face.

"Could it be him – could he back?" McCall mumbled. A shiver ran down Tina's spine as she realised who McCall was talking about, a sadistic killer they had all encountered almost a year ago, a man who now called himself Mr Williams.

"But he has been gone for over a year now. In fact, I thought he was dead," Tina said, standing up. The two women looked at each other, terror in their eyes. A sudden noise from above made the pair jump, breaking McCall from her trance of concentration. Someone was in the room above. McCall turned to one of the two uniforms who were guarding the door.

"Officer!" she yelled to get their attention. The young cop immediately turned to face her.

"Yes, Detective?" he answered, but he did not enter the room for fear of contamination of the crime scene.

"Has anyone spoken to the neighbour's upstairs?" Sam asked as she looked up at the sound of heavy footsteps on the flooring above.

"I don't know, but I will find out," the cop replied and was about to head off to check.

"Never mind." She raised a hand to signal for him to stop before he disappeared to find someone.

"Go upstairs and talk to whoever is above us. They may have heard something. If they say they didn't, ask again, because we can hear everything that's happening up there," Sam said with a smile. The officer nodded then rushed away to go and find out what he could.

McCall turned back around to face her friend. Dr Tina Franks was busy watching two men in blue overalls with the words 'Coroner's Office' on the back in white lettering. The men were carefully placing the body into a black plastic body bag ready for transport back to the morgue.

Tina looked up and met McCall's gaze, which reflected her own look of concern. Previously they had known a man, an evil man, who had killed three women in the most horrible way. Now their thoughts went back to that person and hoped it was him because it was terrifying to think that there could be another who was as depraved as he was.

"So, where's your shadow?" Tina asked, looking around for the tall detective. McCall shrugged as if it was no big deal he wasn't there.

"He's probably off saving the world or something," McCall's words were uncaring. She had work to do, and he knew the address and the circumstances. She figured that if he wanted to be there, he would be.

But he wasn't.

The sound of the uniformed officer knocking on the door's frame caused both McCall and Tina to turn to face him.

"Detective, the couple above said they didn't hear anything until around ten o'clock. That's when they heard a woman scream." The officer almost sounded apologetic that he didn't have more. McCall smiled and thanked him before turning to Tina.

"That doesn't make sense," Tina said, shaking her head. "There was no way that she could have endured that much pain and not screamed out."

Sam had to agree. Amber must have wanted to scream out, if only as a way of attracting the attention of neighbours.

"Where's the roommate?" asked a voice that came from behind the young officer. McCall tried to hide her smile at the sight of the uniform, who had nearly leapt out of his skin at the sudden appearance of the man behind him. Detective Steel was standing close enough to the man to be his shadow.

"Where have you been, Steel? I texted you ages ago." McCall's words sounded hurt and angry.

"I met Tony and Tooms on the way. I was making sure Tony was OK." His British accent had a calm and gentle tone. The officer turned to face the tall detective; whose unorthodox appearance had made him nearly soil himself. At six foot two, Steel was taller than the officer by about two inches. Enough to make the young cop rethink the scornful look he was about to give him. Steel wore a black suit with a high-collared black shirt. Black Bugatti boots shone from being highly polished, but the uniformed cop only noticed two things: the strange leather-and-wool trench coat that stretched from Steel's broad shoulders to his calves, and the sunglasses. It was eleven at night, and he was wearing sunglasses!

"Good evening, doctor. Always a pleasure to see you, despite the circumstances in which we have to meet." Steel's words sang with an innocent flirtation, which made the attractive ME blush. Steel watched as one of the orderlies closed the body bag. He noticed the victim's face had been pretty before someone had gone to work on her. He wondered how Tony could have been so sure of her identity after such injuries. As the zipper closed, there was a silence from everyone, as if they had all lost a friend. In a way, they had, for she had been Tony's girlfriend, which made her family. Steel headed towards McCall, who was still taking photographs of everything she felt was important.

"Any idea where the roommate is?" he asked.

McCall stopped shooting and shook her head.

"We don't even know who she is or what she looks like. And in case you hadn't noticed, this place isn't exactly bustling with photographs," McCall said, waving a gloved hand around the room, pointing out the unusual lack of pictures of anything on the walls. "No pictures of boyfriends, family, or even of a pet. Nothing."

"Maybe she's camera shy?" Steel joked as he looked around the room, then headed for a stack of boxes that sat neatly in the middle of the floor near the breakfast bar. The boxes were full of Amber's stuff. Each one was neatly labelled, showing its contents like an inventory list. Steel found it strange that there were only around seven large boxes but then figured that the rest were in storage or en route.

"She had just moved in by the look of things," Steel pointed out.

McCall nodded, but he figured that she had already noticed that.

"Surely the building super should know what her name is, a neighbour even?" Steel said, shocked that there was nothing to show there was a roommate apart from a bedroom full of clothes and some personal items.

"We will speak to the super in the morning. Unfortunately, he picked tonight to see his kid in New Jersey," McCall added. "We called him, but he doesn't have a car, but he'll be on the first train tomorrow." Steel shot McCall a strange look, which she disregarded, turning away from him.

It was too late at night for stupid conspiracy theories.

"Do we suspect the invisible friend to be part of this?" Steel asked as he continued to browse through the boxes. McCall shrugged at Steel's question.

"Who knows? But you can be sure I will ask her as soon as we find her." Her voice was angry, but the fury was not directed at Steel. She was angry that one of their own had been hurt. Tony had not been physically hurt but emotionally harmed.

Tina Franks picked up the metal suitcase, which contained her examination kit, and turned to the two detectives.

"I am heading back to get her ready for the autopsy," she told the pair of detectives. "If you want to be there, I will be starting around eight o'clock."

McCall shook her head, although she was pleased to be invited.

"No, it's fine, you can just let us know when you're done," McCall replied.

"Sure. It looks like your vic died between eight and ten o'clock, but I will have more for you once I get her back to the lab," Tina said, pulling off her blue surgical gloves.

McCall nodded. Tina waited for the orderlies to finish strapping the body onto the medical gurney then followed them out. Samantha McCall looked back around the room, hoping to get some sort of clue as to why the girl had been tortured. The room was still immaculate. She could have understood if the apartment had been trashed, indicating a frenzied uncontrolled attack.

But everything looked as if nothing unusual had happened there.

Chapter 4

Back at the 11th Precinct, a distraught Detective Tony Marinelli sat in the quiet of one of the briefing rooms. The room was long—around twelve feet by ten—with a large window at the back, the walls were painted a putrid yellow, possibly to cover the day-to-day stains. In the centre was a large wooden table, which could comfortably accommodate twelve people sitting around it whilst being briefed on a case. Surrounding the heavy looking table sat twelve blue plastic chairs, six on each side. A large corkboard stretched the breadth of the short right-hand wall. This was placed to allow a perfect view for the twelve seated around the table so that visual exhibits could accompany the verbal briefings.

Tooms walked in, holding two coffee mugs. Using his heel, he closes the door behind him before handing over the mug of fresh coffee to Tony. The two men had been through a lot in the seven years they had worked homicide together. But nothing like this had happened before. Tooms looked at his partner as he struggled to make a list of anything which may help the investigation. He was listing everything he knew about his girlfriend – their murder victim. Where she worked, where she used to live. Family, her other friends. Her life was suddenly under a microscope, and he didn't like it, because now, so was his.

"You sure you want to do this now, man?" Tooms asked. "It's OK if you want a bit of time first?"

Tony gave Tooms a scowl, but Tooms knew it wasn't for him. Tony was hurting, and nothing mattered to him more than catching the bastard who did this.

Tony's expression changed suddenly as he realised his partner's meaning.

"Sorry, man, I know you didn't mean it like that. It's just—"

"—Hey, I get it, man. Don't worry. We are gonna get whoever did this," Tooms interrupted.

At that moment, Tony's words were as broken as his soul was. As far as he was concerned, no one knew what he was feeling.

No one could.

"So, where did she work?" Tooms asked, sitting in the chair across from Tony.

Tony tapped his pen onto the A4 legal pad. He had written as much as he could before realising; he didn't know that much about her. They had been together for a long time, but the fact was that he was privy to very few of the details of her life. The sound of Tooms clearing his throat made Tony look up from what he was doing. Tony tossed the pen down and sat back in the chair. He smiled at his partner, who waited patiently for an answer.

"Sorry, man, I was miles away." Tony laughed.

Tooms smiled and placed down his coffee mug onto the scratched surface of the table.

"I was just wondering where she worked. It might be an idea to go there tomorrow …" Tooms looked at his watch to check which side of midnight it was. "Better make that later today," Tooms corrected himself. Tony blew onto the hot coffee before taking a small sip. The smell of freshly brewed coffee wafted up to his sinuses. It was good coffee.

"She worked at some large shipping firm." Tony smiled and shook his head. "Which I found funny because it turns out they're just a delivery company. Sure, they use ships, but they haul the goods mainly by truck."

Tooms was glad to see his partner smile. He had gone through something no cop should have to go through losing a loved one. Joshua noticed the name of the firm on the yellow legal pad in front of Tony: 'Trent Shipping' stood out on the paper. It was written in big, bold letters and circled. The list also contained several names. Tooms wondered if they were the names of her family and friends.

"Did she talk about her family?" Tooms asked, almost hoping there was a family member so that Tony didn't have to grieve alone. "her parents, brothers or sisters?"

Tony nodded and pointed to a name that Tooms couldn't quite decipher properly.

"Her name is Brooke, Brooke Taylor. She lives in Washington." Tony's gaze drifted into nowhere. Tooms figured he was remembering some happy day shared with his girlfriend, and he wasn't contemplating the crime scene. A quick smile from the corner of Tony's mouth confirmed it, and Tooms was glad.

"Did you meet her mom and dad? Maybe some of her friends?" Tooms asked.

But there was no reply. Tony was still somewhere else in his head.

"Hey, Tony. Are you with us, man?" Tooms's voice raised its volume slightly. He wasn't shouting but had sharpened his tone just enough to bring his partner back to the present.

"Sorry, man. Just remembering ... never mind." The smile had fallen away from Tony's mouth.

"Did you meet any other family or friends? Perhaps, someone she worked with?" Tooms asked. Tony began to shake his head, but a quick recollection stopped him.

"Her parents are dead. They were killed in a car accident years ago. But I did meet one friend of hers. Tara, I think her name was." Tony looked worn out as he answered. Tooms wished he could let him go home, but he was afraid he would get some bad ideas if he was left by himself.

"OK, nice," Tooms went on. "So, have you got any ideas where this Tara chick lives?" His face had lit up at the prospect of a lead.

"We think she was the girl Amber moved in with," said McCall, who was standing in the doorway. Steel stood behind her like a looming shadow. They walked in and sat down, hoping to share in the findings.

"We found some bills in the kitchen addressed to Tara Burke. The question is, where is Tara now?" McCall said.

"Maybe she came home and found the body, then she bolted just in case the killer was still there," Tooms added. His voice almost sounded hopeful that might be the case, and that they weren't looking at two homicides.

"It's possible," Steel said, leaning back in the chair. "She may have come back and seen the body. The neighbours did say they heard a scream at around ten o'clock."

Samantha McCall saw the expression on Steel's face turn to stone. She knew that hardened look meant that he felt something was wrong.

"What's wrong?" she asked. Steel turned to face her. Her eyes sparkled with the reflection of the overhead lights. He smiled and shook his head.

"Nothing. Just a passing thought about something else, that's all," Steel replied. She could see through his white lie but said nothing.

"OK, you guys. Find out where Tara works, and we will go to where Amber worked," McCall suggested as she stood up. She had noticed the name on the yellow legal pad and figured that was first the place they had to go. Steel stood up as McCall approached the door.

"Road trip?" he asked with a smile.

"Road trip," she replied, rattling her car keys.

* * *

Tooms and Tony went back to the crime scene to see if there was anything that would help with finding the roommate. Before, they had only concentrated on the victim—Amber. But now, they might have a missing person or worse, another body.

Tooms didn't really want Tony in the apartment. He would have preferred to have gone alone and left him at the precinct, but his friend made out he was OK. Tooms didn't believe a word of it, but that was Tony Marinelli all over—putting his job first and his personal life second.

As they reached the front door to the apartment, a uniformed officer stood watch. The two detectives showed their shields. The young uniformed cop nodded, then watched as they went to enter. Tony froze as Tooms reached for the handle. Joshua sensed something was wrong and turned.

"Damn it!" Tooms cursed, patting down his jacket. "Hey, Tony, you couldn't go back to the car, could you? I forgot my friggin' camera." Joshua saw the relieved look on Tony's face.

"Yeah, no problem. Besides, it gives me time to check on that other thing," Tony bluffed. Tooms watched his partner walk away towards the staircase. Then his gaze fell to the young cop, who was trying to look as if he hadn't been taking it all in. Tooms turned the door handle and walked in. CSU had removed the yellow evidence markers, but back smudges remained from the fingerprint powder. The clean-up crew hadn't been in yet: it was still a crime scene. Tooms stood for a moment and looked down on the large red stain on the carpet. He was glad Tony was downstairs, for he didn't need to see this. Joshua pulled on a pair of blue sterile gloves as he moved towards the second bedroom. He stood back as he entered the missing girl's room. The walls were painted bright pink. The light from the small window reflected on the right-hand wall and seemed to turn it neon. A double bed rested against the left-hand wall next to which was a large cheap-looking closet. The room was small—ten feet by eight if that. Purple shelves were attached to the walls fixed with metallic right-angled supports. Books and stuffed toy animals sat neatly as if they were on display. A nightstand separated the bed from the wall. Its glossy white paint was broken up by pink swirls that Tooms figured she had done herself. A tall bedside lamp with a pink plastic shade sat next to a 'pink cat' alarm clock: the digital display was held in the smiling mouth of a pink-and-purple striped cat.

The detective looked around the room. Initially, it had reminded him of his girls' rooms, and they were considerably younger than Amber—thirteen and fifteen. Tooms made his way to the bedside cabinet, hoping to find something in its four drawers. He quickly closed the third one. He had no intention of prying in a woman's 'naughty' drawer. The top one was full of odd bits of junk and bracelets. The others contained mostly magazines and holiday brochures. He stood up and made for the closet. Joshua found it odd there were no photographs anywhere. No pictorial evidence of family, friends, snapshots from holidays, nothing personal like that. To look at the apartment, you would think it was a show house.

The curious officer then opened the closet door and there before him was a rail of neatly pressed clothes, on hangers: blouses, jeans and so on. He stopped and smiled as he reached in and pulled out a red-and-white uniform. The name 'Bob's Diner' was stitched into the white top in red lettering.

"Time to get some breakfast," Tooms said with a grin. He placed the uniform back in the closet and left the apartment.

Chapter 5

Steel and McCall arrived at the Trent Shipping yard. The whole place was in a massive fenced off area. Several large warehouses stood in rows, each of which had six trucks of different sizes parked with their trailers backed up to the loading bays.

A tall five-storey building sat in the centre of the industrial estate, with two large warehouses either side of it. Large billboards crowned their upper levels, advertising the company. The large building was the main office, the central hub. Its windows were blackened by the glare of the morning sun. McCall pulled up to the front gate, where a tall security guard waited. She had seen him get out of his booth as she approached. As she stopped, he smiled pleasantly. She noticed that the man was in his late fifties, but he looked as if he was in good physical shape.

Steel wasn't sure if his welcome was just natural courtesy, the fact an attractive woman like McCall was there, or if he was just happy to see someone new.

"Good morning, how can I help you folks?" the guard asked. His eye contacts never left McCall, even when Steel showed his shield at the same time as she did.

"We are with NYPD, and we would like to speak to whoever is in charge here," McCall said with a smile and a bat of the eyelids. The guard directed them to a parking lot next to the main building. McCall thanked him and left the guard with a broad smile that Steel suspected he wouldn't lose for quite a while.

She pulled up to the parking space the guard had instructed her to use. There were several other visitors' parking spaces, all of them empty. The front entrance was just around the corner from where she had parked her beloved Mustang. Steel got out and immediately looked up at the five-storey building. Cream coloured walls and smoked windows made the structure look more like a Manhattan office than a shipping headquarters.

The two detectives entered the lobby through automatic doors. The room was huge, with white tiled floors and cream painted walls. Small potted ferns and palms were dotted strategically around the place, breaking up the sterile colour. Steel and McCall stood for a moment taking in the layout of the place. Steel smiled as he gazed over at the front desk and the two attractive ladies at the reception. McCall gave him a quick look and shook her head in disbelief.

"Unbelievable," she groaned and headed for the two women who were sitting behind a long wooden information desk. On the front of the light wooden frontage was the company name in brass lettering. Steel reckoned it was more likely to be imitation 'stay bright' rather than metal. This would be more practical since brass needs to be cleaned regularly, what's more, it picked up every fingerprint and scratch. As they approached the desk, a tall woman met them halfway along the floor. She wore a light blue skirt suit and white blouse that was open at the neck, and she had a broad smile to match. She tossed her head, flirtatiously. Her long, wavy, fiery red hair brushed past her shoulders. McCall had wondered if she had popped a couple of buttons after seeing Steel: enticing his interest more as a distraction tactic than a 'come-on.'

"You must be the detectives," she began. "I am Helen Adler, Mr Adams's personnel assistant." Her voice was husky as if she had just had a glass of Jim Beam to gargle with.

"Of course, you are," Steel replied, raising an eyebrow. McCall rolled her eyes then smiled before shaking the woman's hand.

"This is Detective John Steel, and I am Detective Samantha McCall," she said.

The woman smiled back at McCall, but there was a different kind of smile on her face for Steel.

"If you follow me, I will take you to see Mr Adams," Helen Adler said in a sultry voice. They followed her to the brass-coloured elevator doors, whose surfaces had a strange texture. Small indents covered the bright metal, almost as if it had been attacked with a pin hammer. Steel walked behind the two women. His concentration was on checking the security and cameras. There were two large men at the main entrance and two more at the elevator. Each was dressed in a black suit with white shirt, black tie, and the bulge in their jackets indicated that they were 'packing.' He nodded to one of the men as they waited for the doors to open. The man nodded back after eyeing up Steel and McCall. The doors slid open, and Steel let the ladies enter first. As they closed, Steel saw the man he had greeted touch his ear, after which he shot Steel a glance before saying something into his wrist microphone. Suddenly, Steel had an uneasy feeling. The ride up was quiet. The only interaction was Helen checking Steel out in the walled mirrors. He smiled at her failed attempt to be discreet.

As the doors slid, open Helen walked out first with McCall and Steel following not far behind. Steel noted two more men at the elevator doors. A long corridor led them to another desk by a large window, next to which was a wooden double door. To the right was a corner couch, which Steel figured was in the waiting area. Helen smiled and nodded to another woman who sat behind the desk: this was Adams's secretary. The woman was in her thirties with black hair and a black skirt suit. Helen knocked on the door, then entered. McCall and Steel followed her into a large office. The whole of the right wall was made of glass and showed a fantastic view of the parking lot and the warehouse with the billboards. The only greenery in view were the trees that had been planted in the parking lot. To the left, there was a long cabinet that housed awards for industry and a couple of sport trophies. At the end of the large room sat a large metal and oak desk, behind which sat a man. He was a large built man with broad shoulders and a square head. His neatly cut grey hair was gelled and styled, and he wore a suit that probably cost enough to pay for McCall's rent for the next three months. As he rose to meet them, Steel noted that the shipping giant was all of five foot eight. But what he lacked in height he made up for with self-confidence.

"Mr Adams, may I present Detectives Samantha McCall and John Steel?" Helen's gravelly voice almost purred Steel's name. David Adams looked frantic and annoyed as he gathered up some papers and stuck them into a leather case.

"What's up, detectives? Has my chauffeur forgotten to pay her parking tickets again?" He growled the question whilst shaking his head.

"What?" McCall said, almost shocked at his abrupt manner. "No, we are homicide detectives, and we would like to ask you some questions about one of your employees."

"Well, it had better be about my overseas financial adviser. At least then she might have an excuse for not being here five minutes before a major deal!" Adams yelled, standing up and heading for the door.

"And who is that exactly, if I may ask?" Steel said, hoping his gut was wrong.

"Amber Taylor. The funny thing is, she has never missed a day's work until now," Helen Adler said. Her tone was filled with confusion, as well as a hint of worry.

"Look, can't this wait?" Adams barked as if the thought of two homicide detectives asking about his people didn't bother him. "I'm a very busy man."

"Actually, no, it can't," McCall said. "We're investigating the murder of one of your employees. Amber Taylor, to be precise." Samantha McCall's eyes were fixed on Adams's face, to try to gauge his reaction.

"What? Amber's dead? How? When?" Adams said, looking alarmed and shocked as he walked back to his chair and collapsed into it.

"Last night, someone attacked her in her apartment." McCall watched the businessman's face as she delivered the news. She could tell if someone was genuine or not, and he seemed to pass the test.

"What exactly was it that she did here?" Steel asked as he put back a glass award that was in the shape of an eagle that he had been examining. Steel turned slowly to face Adams, making sure he gave Helen a quick smile as he did so.

"She was one of my top financial managers, she handled a lot of overseas business, export and import, that sort of thing," Adams replied, but his gaze never left his large monitor that was on the right corner of his desk. Anyone else might have considered this as evidence that he was avoiding eye contact, but Steel knew that the man could see himself in the reflection.

"Do you know of any reason anyone would want to kill her? Any rivalry in the office, an ex-boyfriend perhaps?" McCall asked, knowing sometimes it was people the victims knew who were the most likely to be their murderers. Money, jealousy, and love were all good motives to kill.

"No. Everyone loved her. She got on great with all of us. As for a boyfriend, I'm afraid I couldn't say. She liked to keep her private life private," Adams said, shrugging his shoulders and raising his hands.

"I guess you could speak to Rebecca Miles, she worked closely with Amber," Helen said. Her gaze was on Adams as he just sat there staring at his monitor. "Maybe she knows something."

McCall nodded after jotting down the woman's name. Adams looked up at the two detectives then shot out of his seat.

"Miss Adler will help you with anything you need." Adams's voice trembled as he spoke. He grabbed his leather pouch bag and left the room, leaving Steel and McCall looking at each other in surprise at the man's strange behaviour.

"Please follow me, I'll take you to see Rebecca," Helen said, leading them out of the room.

"So, it's Miss Adler, is it?" Steel said with a playful tone. McCall rolled her eyes and wished she had come alone.

Rebecca Miles, or 'Becca' as her friends called her, was busy getting some files together. Steel could see by her demeanour she had not yet been told of her friend's fate. She was around five foot six with short hazelnut-coloured hair and was young and attractive – Steel reckoned she was in her late twenties. Becca was clearly a 'fresh catch' from one of the many prestigious universities – probably Stanford or Columbia. Steel smiled as they approached, seeing that she was singing away to herself. He noticed the earplug headphone in her ear as she danced around, sorting out the paperwork.

"Becca?" Helen shouted just as Becca reached a high note, or at least tried to. "BECCA!" Helen shouted louder, causing the young woman to jump. Paper was tossed into the air like confetti. Becca pulled out her headphone and switch off her music wired from her phone.

"Sorry, Miss Adler, I didn't hear you," she explained. "I've been trying to get all this paperwork sorted for the meeting." She knelt to retrieve the scattered documents, and Steel crouched down, joining her on the floor. She looked up at the gallant man dressed in black and smiled. He returned the smile as he gave her a handful of papers.

"Becca, these people are with the police. Something has happened to Amber." Helen's words were soft and full of compassion, almost like a mother giving a child some bad news.

"What? No! Is she OK?" Becca asked, her voice sounding dry as if all the moisture in her mouth had dried up. McCall always hated this part; the part of the interview when she could see the person grasping the hope that whatever had happened, it didn't involve death, at worst that it was just a bad accident. She hated the part where she had to crush that one hope.

"I am afraid she was found dead in her apartment last night," McCall explained. Becca stumbled back towards the office chair. Steel rushed forward and caught her as she dropped just short of her target. Sam McCall rushed forward and pushed the chair closer so that Steel could place her down comfortably. Becca's face was pale, her eyes were wide, and her mouth was moving but failed to produce words. Helen grabbed one of the bottles of water that was on a side table. She handed it to Steel, who cracked the top and placed the mouth of the bottle to Becca's lips. She took a small sip then her eyes looked directly at Steel. She saw her own reflection in his dark sunglasses. Becca smiled and thanked him. Steel stood up straight and moved back, giving the shocked woman some space.

"Are you alright now?" he asked. She nodded and took another sip before wiping her eyes with the sleeve of her blue blouse.

"So, what happened? Was it an accident?" she asked.

Steel shook his head and passed Becca a cotton handkerchief he had gotten from the inside breast pocket of his jacket.

"I am afraid not. Someone broke into her apartment and attacked her," he explained. He could see that Amber and Becca had been close. Hopefully, they'd been close enough to have shared some secrets.

"Who did this to her?" Becca's tone changed as she began to get over the initial shock.

"That's what we are trying to find out. I can see you two were good friends. Can you tell us anything? Did she have any problems with anyone? Work colleagues, old boyfriends, maybe? Is there anything you can think of?" Steel asked, his voice soft.

Becca shook her head after thinking for a moment.

"She was seeing some guy for a while. I think he was a cop or a security guard, I can't remember. That ended kinda bad. He used to call her up all the time, saying how she had used him." Becca looked away as if she was straining to remember details.

"This ex, did he have a name?" asked McCall with pad and pen at the ready.

"Tony, I think … Yeah, that was it. Tony. Medium build with dark hair. Had an Italian look about him."

McCall looked at Steel, who had the same unhappy expression on his face as she had.

"Oh bollocks," Steel said, knowing what they had to do next.

Chapter 6

McCall drove back to the precinct as fast as the midday traffic would allow. The sun was now hidden behind massive billows of white clouds. The thick traffic gave her time to reflect about what had been said back at the shipping company. Her thoughts were all heading in one direction.

And it wasn't a good direction.

Steel could see the frustration in her face. Samantha McCall and Tony Marinelli had worked together for a long time and been through a lot during that period. She was angry at what Becca had said: that Amber had a boyfriend called Tony.

Had as in past tense.

Had Tony lied about being with Amber? Had they broken up and he had taken it badly? Steel had not known the detective as McCall had done, but Steel normally had a pretty good take on people, and for him, Tony was one of the good guys. Someone you wanted watching your back.

"Maybe there is another guy called Tony?" Steel said, hoping to dilute the trail Sam's thinking. He held on to the seat belt as she put her foot to the gas after seeing a space to charge into. He shot her a look of disapproval as she raced through the traffic as though she was in the Indy 500.

"Yeah, right. And this other Tony just happens to look like him as well?" she growled, and her knuckles whitened as she gripped the leather-bound steering wheel.

John Steel had to admit to himself that the whole thing did sound all too much of a coincidence. The ex-boyfriend, whose name was Tony and the guy had the same build and hair colour as their friend!

"Maybe she has a type she goes for. It can happen." Steel kept his eyes on the road but tried to hide the need to jump out of the car in fear of his life.

Soon they would be back at the precinct, and he hoped that she wouldn't jump in with both feet by tackling Tony without asking him first. She was mad and wounded. Suddenly Steel realised they were heading back to the crime scene. He didn't question it. In fact, it was probably a better idea than going back to the office and her jumping all over Tony.

She pulled in next to the kerb, stopping near the junction and killed the engine. Steel turned to her slowly. She just sat there for a moment as if gathering her thoughts.

"Sam," he began, "when we get back, take it easy on Tony, just in case what Becca told us happens to be a coincidence. Don't forget he just lost his girlfriend."

McCall shot him an angry look as if he had said something to insult her.

"All I am saying is be careful. You can't 'un-say' something. If you're wrong, he may not forgive you."

McCall's face calmed as she took in the words. He was right. She was angry because of something that could be, not something which had been proven.

"OK, we let him know what was said. If he is hiding something, I will know." McCall smiled at Steel. He had saved her from making what might probably be a massive mistake that could have changed everything. Tony was a friend, and she didn't want to lose his friendship. Steel went to say something to McCall, but his mouth remained open as if dumbstruck by a thought. McCall looked at him curiously until she saw the reflection in his glasses. She turned to see a tall man standing outside on the sidewalk. He was wearing a white shirt, blue jeans, and was covered in blood.

They both jumped out of the car and rushed over to the man, who appeared to be in a daze.

"Sir, are you OK? Are you hurt?" Samantha asked. The man looked up as she finished her sentence. He looked at her with a confused expression.

"Sir, what's your name? Can you tell me if this is your blood?"

He looked around at his surroundings then back at McCall. He now had a panicked look on his face.

"I don't know," he muttered. "Oh, God, I don't know anything!" The man screamed out the words and then fell to the ground, unconscious.

"Well, this could complicate things," Steel said. McCall just shot Steel a look that said it all as she pulled out her cell to call for an ambulance.

Steel sat back in the comfort of the leather and cloth seats of the muscle car, while McCall followed the ambulance to the hospital. In a way, McCall hoped that this injured man was somehow connected to the Amber case, but then life was never that simple. The trip over was silent. Steel was thinking about a million other things; McCall's thoughts went back to Tony. The route to county hospital was anything but straight forward due to construction. Another new building was taking shape; for the moment, it was just the bare skeleton of the steel framework. John Steel was born and had lived in the country on his family's estate for most of his life. After that, he had travelled with the Army. In truth, this last year had been the longest he had stayed put in one place for most of his adult life, so the pleasant chaos of Manhattan was somewhat alien for him, the city of constant change. McCall found a parking spot near the hospital, placing the plastic-covered NYPD parking pass in the window she looked over at Steel.

"You check with the nurses, we need his clothes, I'll speak to the doctors," she said, Steel smiled as her request seemed to be more an order. She was a strong woman, tough as nails, he liked that, but he didn't take been ordered too well.

"Not a problem, but only because you asked so nicely," Steel said with a smile, his words rang with sarcasm. McCall scowled at him, and she didn't have time for his pride, antics, or him just been – well, him.

They got out of the car into a bitter wind. McCall pulled her coat tightly around her, Steel just stood with his head high, and his eyes closed, feeling the crisp wind against his warm skin before walking over to the hospital entrance. Inside had a mixture of smelts, the strongest of which was sterilising chemicals. Steel didn't care much for hospitals or doctors; he had uttermost respect for them but had no great desire to be near them.

While McCall chased after the doctors, Steel perched himself at the nurse's station and talked to the nurses behind the counter. At the station was two large black women in their mid-forties. Both had eyeglasses that hung from beaded chains around their necks, both held a dreamy look, and shoed away anyone that sought to interrupt their conversation with the British detective. Steel eased the request for the man's clothes into the conversation, hoping sugar would get more of a quicker response than an order. It took less than a minute to get the clothes along with several phone numbers. Steel just hoped that CSU could find something on the mystery man's clothes, knowing that they would be able to tell if it was Amber's blood he was covered in, or someone else's. While Steel continued to flirt, McCall waited for the doctors examined the mystery man. On the way to the hospital, McCall had phoned ahead to CSU, requesting a tech. She knew that they would need pristine samples. As McCall paced up and down the corridor outside the man's room, she chanced several glances inside the room. Inside, the doctors examined while a CSU tech took nail scrapings and brushed the man's hair for trace materials. If he wasn't their killer, they needed to find out where he had been to get himself so messed up, also whose blood it was that he was covered in.

McCall waited impatiently on the other side of the curtain. She needed to get in there to find out what the guy knew. McCall looked over to see Steel return from the CSU guys, who were walking around with several paper evidence bags containing the man's clothes.

"Is that all of his stuff?" her words sounded almost disappointed.

"Yeah, unfortunately, there's no wallet or cell phone," Steel told her. "I figure he had a jacket that he put all his other items in," Steel answered, he could tell she was anxious, this was the last thing she needed while there was a possibility that Tony could be incriminated in his girlfriend's murder.

"Are you still thinking about Tony?" Steel asked, almost knowing the answer. She looked over at him, her face filled with mixed emotion.

"Go, do what you have to do," he suggested. "I will take care of this, and you can sort it out with Tony." Sam knew that Steel was right. Besides, she realised that in her frame of mind, she wouldn't be much use now. She smiled and thanked him.

As Steel watched McCall disappear through the ward doors, his smile faded. He looked over to the curtains as they drew back. The guy was sitting on the side of the bed wearing a medical gown, his legs hanging over the side while the doctor looked at his eyes, searching for signs of concussion. Steel turned to the tech, who was busy packing away his CSU sample jars and swab containers.

"Did you get everything?" Steel asked quietly. The tech nodded as he closed the metalwork case and headed off back to the lab. Steel turned to the doctor and the man on the bed.

"Any ideas, doctor?" Steel asked, hoping for a simple answer. The doctor was in his mid-fifties with thick grey hair and a trimmed beard to match. His white coat covered a striped shirt and a stocky build.

"There was a nasty gash at the side of his head," the medical man told him. "It was bad, but not bad enough to explain his memory loss. If you want my opinion, he has probably suffered a great emotional shock." The doctor smiled and shrugged. Steel looked over to the 'John Doe'—the name police and the legal profession traditionally assign to an unidentified person. The man was in his late twenties, tall with a medium build. His thick strawberry-blond hair was all messed up from the recent medical examinations, giving him that *just got up* look. His blue eyes were bright but held a sadness. Someone had to get into this guy's head, and Steel knew just the guy.

Chapter 7

Doctor Colby Davidson walked into the 11th Precinct feeling full of mixed emotions. The last time he had worked with the Homicide division, it had nearly cost him a lot. His six-foot, thin frame was draped in a two-thousand-dollar blue pinstriped Armani. The tap of his black Christian Louboutin shoes was dulled by the noise of the precinct's lobby. The sound of the bustle made his body tingle. Uniformed cops yelled at criminals who refused to do as they were instructed, crying women who had been mugged or lost their kids, ringing cell phones just added to the chaotic melody. The desk sergeant's phone was ringing off the hook, while he gave 'directs' to a woman trying to give a missing person's report.

Davidson smiled as he revelled in the chaos. He believed that most of these problems could have been stopped if the wrongdoers had seen a good shrink. He stood in front of the elevator and pressed the call button. He caught a glimpse of his reflection in the dull aluminium fittings on the elevator's exterior. He combed a long-fingered hand through his greased back brown hair and smiled at what he saw. His face was long with a thin roman nose and pale skin, his deep-set large eyes were pale blue, with a menacing touch to them. He wasn't a handsome man, but he held a strange allure.

The elevator opened, and he stepped inside and turned to face the heavy steel doors just as they were closing he sported the kind of wicked grin you would expect to find on a Cheshire cat.

As he rode the elevator, he noted the pungent mix of smells, most of which he decided not to try and think about what they could be. It stank of cleaning fluid, vomit, piss, body odour, not to mention the unknown ones. The box came to a stop with a shudder, and the doors slid open. Davidson lost the grin as he stepped out on to the department floor. Familiar faces looked up from their desks, watching him as he stepped off the elevator and stopped to look around the room. The other detectives remembered him.

He wasn't welcome.

Davidson headed for McCall, whom he had spied from the elevator. Steel was with her in a small conference room, along with another man he did not recognise. As he walked across the busy floor of the bullpen, people stopped and stared, remembering what had taken place the last time he had worked a case, what his brother had done – the man that was now known as Mr Williams. The doctor knocked on the door and then stood in the doorway, almost as if he was waiting for a friendly invitation to step inside.

"Doctor Davidson, good to see you again," McCall said with a smile. They shook hands while Steel stood behind her with his arms crossed.

"Hello there, doctor, good to see you again," Steel said, then paused and moved closer for a better look. "It is you – isn't it?" he added jokingly.

"And if it wasn't, do you think I would say so?" Davidson replied with a smile. Steel laughed and shrugged as if to agree with the statement. Davidson turned towards John Doe and smiled a greeting. "Don't worry, it's a private joke," he explained to the amnesiac man. "Someone once impersonated me."

"Yeah, your twin brother did," McCall pointed out. "A guy who was, let's face it, a little *off*," McCall said diplomatically.

"A little *off*? Really the guy was a bloody psychopath," Steel butted in.

John Doe just sat there with a bewildered look on his face, up until the point when the doctor approached to shake his hand.

"Sorry for ignoring you, sir. I am Doctor Colby Davidson," he said, stretching out a pale palm. John Doe just stared up at this strange-looking man, noting his tall thin body, his long fingers, and *that face*. But it was the large blue eyes and the mouth that wore the most terrifying smile he had ever seen. Naturally, red lips curled up at the sides in a menacing grin, exposing rows of pearly white teeth. John Doe just stared, hypnotized by the doctor's unnatural smile. He imagined a shark having the same expression just before devouring someone.

"Doctor Davison is a psychiatrist," McCall explained. "He is here to hopefully help you with your memory."

John Doe's face looked almost shocked at the revelation that this guy was here to help him, and not to kill Batman.

"Don't worry, he is good at what he does," Steel said, trying to sound convincing. "We worked together before, a long time ago."

The man with no name seemed calmer at Steel's reassurance, but there was still something about the newcomer that he didn't like.

"Right then, shall we get started?" Davidson said, placing an aluminium briefcase onto the desk. He stood in front of a chair as he unpacked a block of plain pieces of paper, a large yellow jotter pad, and a tape recorder. He took out of his pocket a gold pocket watch and placed it onto the table. Steel stared at the watch. Memories of that first case came flooding back.

"What's with the watch, doc?" Steel asked, slipping his hand under his jacket to the small of his back.

Davidson picked up the watch and dangled it brieflyso that it swung back and forth in a pendulum motion.

"It's so that I can hypnotise him and take him back through his thoughts," Davidson said with a straight face.

"Really? You can do that?" John Doe said, seeming uncomfortable at the idea.

"No, I am only joking. My watch is in the shop getting serviced. I bought this because … You know, I don't really know why. I just liked it." Davidson grinned and placed the watch back down. Steel saw the fear in John Doe's eyes, and he felt sympathy for him: being stuck in a room with this guy was enough to drive anyone nuts.

"You know I don't know what is worse. Having amnesia or having to see the good doctor," Steel joked as they walked out, leaving the two men alone. McCall slapped Steel on the shoulder then shook her hand in pain.

"You've been working out again, haven't you?" she joked, but all the while, she undressed him in her mind's eye. Suddenly she shook her head to stop the unclean thoughts before they started. They headed for Tony and Tooms, who were in the break room, draining the last of the coffee from one of the machines. McCall had a lot of questions, and Steel could sense her eagerness to ask them. As they entered the room, Steel walked in front of McCall and headed for Tony.

"So, Tony, we spoke to a work colleague of your girlfriend, or should I say your ex-girlfriend," Steel said bluntly. Tony looked blankly at him at first, then the look of confusion was replaced with one of clarity.

"I tracked down her sister, Brooke," Tony replied. "The captain asked me if I would break the bad news to her, thought it might be better coming from someone who knew her." Tony sighed deeply and closed his eyes tightly for a second, thinking back to the conversation, remembering how she had cried down the phone at the news. Tony didn't want to admit he had asked Brant if he could do it, feeling it was his responsibility to do so as her boyfriend. Tony had found Brooke's number on Amber's cell phone, which she never locked. "She cried for a while. Then she asked me how I knew her sister, asked me all sorts of questions about us, probably trying to avoid the inevitable conversation, I guess. We talked for a while, about her Amber's past, her friends from before, her boyfriends. It seemed kinda weird; it showed me how much we didn't know about each other," Tony shook his head in dismay.

"Tony, you were only going out for a short while, it takes time to really know someone, and sometimes, even then you don't know them as much as you thought," Steel said, his face was emotionless, but his words were bitter. Everyone looked over at Steel, wondering who he had been talking about.

"Did you learn anything new?" McCall asked, her gaze glancing back towards Steel who stood motionless with his arms crossed.

"She was seeing a guy before me, they had dated for about a year, Brooke said the guy was a real dooshbag, used to smack her around, treated her like garbage, they broke up about six months ago," Tony explained, massaging his knuckles as though he had thoughts about doing to this ex-boyfriend what the asshole had done to Amber.

"Did we get a name on this charmer?" Tooms asked.

"His name was Tony – Tony Russo," Tony said, leaning back in his chair. After hearing Tony Russo's name and getting his description, Tony knew that the coincidence was going to come back on him, from how Brooke had described him, Tony and the asshole could have been twins. Amber had a type, which didn't make Tony feel any better. "Brooke lives and worked in D.C. However, she said she'd be on the first flight out," There was a sadness in Tony's eyes as he explained what he had found out. McCall smiled and touched him on the shoulder.

"You OK?" McCall asked, sensing something new was gnawing at him.

"I have made that phone call so many times, but that was the hardest," Tony said, looking up at McCall. She nodded, then smiled at him and turned to Steel, who was staring at the murder board next to her desk.

"Any luck with the roommate?" she asked, looking at Steel for a moment before turning to face Tony and Tooms. The British detective's thoughts were a million miles away from the rest of them. His imagination was conjuring up images of what may have befallen the missing woman.

"The roommate was Tara Burke, as we thought. She is twenty-six, five-seven with red hair," Tooms read from his pad. Steel stood still staring at the board, unmoving and not uttering a word, but Tooms knew that he had taken everything in.

"Do we know where she worked?" Steel asked after a short while.

"Bob's Diner. It's in Harlem," Tooms explained, handing McCall a yellow post-it notes with the address on. McCall looked at the piece of paper for a couple of seconds as if to memorise the address. Then she opened her leather folio case and placed it onto the blank A4 pad inside.

"OK, you two take the ex-boyfriend, and we'll take the diner," McCall said, suddenly looking at her watch. It was nearly half-three, and she knew they were going to hit traffic on the way back. She shrugged. It wasn't as if she had anything better to do.

"Shall we go, Detective?" Steel said, raising an arm towards the elevator.

"Yes, we shall, and 'WE' are probably driving again," she growled as if to make a point. "Seriously, are you saying you don't have a car? Or does it have to come with a chauffeur?" she joked.

John Steel smiled and shook his head. "Oh, don't worry, Detective, I have a car, and I can assure you, you will want to play," John quipped.

Sam McCall walked off towards the elevator, shaking her head.

"No thanks, I got my pony." Her voice almost purred, and Steel laughed to himself. McCall and Steel stood at the elevator. Behind them, the boys were busy trying to locate the ex-boyfriend. As they stood in front of the heavy steel doors, Steel looked up at the LED display that showed that the elevator box was one floor above them.

"I hope this isn't going to take long. I have dinner plans," Steel said, giving a quick smile from the corner of his mouth as he bounced off his heels.

"Sorry if work is getting in the way of your personal life," she growled. "You could always quit, then you would have plenty of time for your bimbos." Although she was joking, she was still somewhat jealous that he had a personal life that didn't include her. The doors slid open, and he stepped inside and leaned against the back wall.

"And you're doing what tonight?" His words were playful, but they left a bitter sting. McCall stepped in after him but said nothing. She had to wonder though, what was he going off to do tonight? Dinner and dancing? Or chasing down the people responsible for his family's murder. Whatever it was, he would be having more fun than she would be having tonight.

Chapter 8

The Diner was on a busy corner of Adam Clayton Powell Jr. Boulevard and West 148th Street. Above the white-walled exterior of the building began the red-brick apartments. Steel noticed a 'For Rent' sign on one of the walls. Its green writing was bold, designed to catch the eye. The dinner was in the corner building. A double-door entrance was situated directly in view of the pedestrian crossing, giving good easy access for all customer needs. The place itself was clean, with PU leather upholstery in the booths and dark wood tables. The black-and-white checkerboard tiled floor glistened from the overhead lighting.

To the back of the diner was a long counter with glass showcases full of doughnuts and cheesecakes. Behind that was the delivery counter, where the waitresses collected the orders from a large angry looking man who was wearing a white T-shirt and a small chef's 'skull' hat. Steel was convinced that he looked more like a bulldog chewing a wasp, the hanging jowls and beady eyes just added to the picture. On a far wall, a small twenty-inch television set was tuned to the news. The customers just looked through the two cops as if they weren't even there. Steel sat at one of the padded seats that was in front of the counter. The stainless-steel pinion was bolted firmly to the ground a little too close to the counter for Steel, causing him to sit with spread legs. McCall shot him a look of disapproval, then did the same. McCall didn't want to stay and have lunch, they were there to deliver bad news and get information, something she hated to mix, but it was necessary given the fact it was a homicide investigation. Two waitresses rushed about frantically, like catchers in a ball game. Steel picked up one of the menu cards and checked the vast array of artery-blocking dishes on offer.

"I don't think they have caviar here," McCall joked, just as a pretty black-haired woman in a red-and-white uniform appeared behind them, her pad and pencil at the ready.

"Hey there. Welcome to Bob's Diner. So, what can I get you folks?" the waitress asked, sporting a bright smile.

"We are with the NYPD," Sam said, flashing her shield. "We are here about one of your waitresses. Tara?"

The woman's mouth fell open as if to say something.

"That bitch better be in hospital or dead!" yelled the man who wore a grease-stained T-shirt and jeans. "I am down three waitresses, and she decide to not come in!" A dirty white chef's cap covered most of his large fat head.

"I take it you're Bob, the owner?" McCall said. Her tone had changed, her voice now sterner and more authoritative as she spoke to him. He stayed behind the wall and just blew hot air and waved his spatula about.

"Yeah, I'm Bob, what's it to you, lady? Look, I am busy here, so what do you want?" he yelled. Sam McCall could feel her blood boil at his apparent lack of manners or respect. It wasn't so much that she was a cop; she felt his disregard was more because she was a female cop.

"So, what's happened to her?" asked the waitress, her voice full of genuine concern.

"She's gone missing," Sam said softly. "Her roommate was found murdered, and we are worried about her safety."

The waitress looked shocked, and her face blanched as she stumbled backwards. Steel was already up and had caught her before she fell any further. He led her to a booth, where they all sat down.

"Hey! No sitting down on the job, you hear me?" came Bob's angry voice from behind the counter, but everyone just ignored him.

"My name is Detective Samantha McCall, and this is Detective Steel." McCall smiled as she spoke.

"I am Kim, Kim Washington. She was ... She *is* my best friend." Kim's eyes shone with fresh tears.

"You don't think she could have done this murder, do you?" Kim asked, her voice sounding dry and scared at the possibility.

"We don't know. She isn't in any trouble, we just want to talk to her," Steel said reassuringly. Kim looked up at him and smiled.

"When did you see her last?" McCall asked. Kim looked up at the clock above the door as if she was trying to remember.

"It was around half-eight, nine, I guess. She had pulled a double and was heading home. It had been a long day for everyone," Kim explained.

"Are you open all night?" Steel asked, looking around the room, but paying special attention to Bob, who was sneaking brief, worried looks from his area beside the grill.

"No, four until midnight. Unless we know something special is on, then we are open twenty-four-seven," Kim told them. Steel sat back and continued his unobserved scan of the place. There were around twenty people sitting in various places. Most of them appeared to be drivers who were just passing through. He looked out of the window at the traffic that was beginning to build up outside.

"Did she have any problems with anyone that you know of?" McCall asked—she was almost hoping that Kim would say that her boss was causing problems. The thought of getting him in the box was making her salivate.

"No, not really. Everyone liked her. She didn't have time for a boyfriend or anything," Kim added, expecting the usual question about personal relationships.

"What about Bob? Any problems there?" Steel asked. He noticed Bob look up suddenly at the mention of his name. Kim shook her head but said nothing.

"How did she seem when she left?" the British detective asked.

Kim looked puzzled at this strange cop's question. "She was distracted, but then she was tired. Why?" Kim said, still wondering about Steel's question.

"We are just trying to piece everything together," Steel said with a smile.

McCall passed across her business card. "If you do see her, can you get her to contact me, please?"

Kim looked at the card and placed it in a breast pocket of her uniform. Steel looked up angrily towards Bob, as he hammered a brass call bell. Kim stood up. She knew that was her signal to get back to work.

"Are you OK?" Steel asked as he noticed the strange eye contact Bob was giving Kim.

The young waitress turned towards Steel and smiled quickly before nodding. "Sure, I'm fine. Look I've got to get back to work. If I see her, I will let her know."

Sam nodded in appreciation. "Thanks for your time," she said, shaking Kim's still trembling hand. As they watched Kim return to her station, the two detectives became uneasy. Something was wrong, and whatever it was had nothing to do with their case.

Bob dragged Kim into the kitchen so no one could see, and then he slapped her hard.

"What did they want to know about that silly bitch?" Bob growled; his voice toned down so as not to not draw any attention.

"Nothing. She has disappeared and they—"

Bob slapped her again, hard. So hard that his finger marks were visible on her face.

"You don't say anything, you hear me?" he screamed, his voice breaking its strained tone. He raised his hand again to give her another shot just in case she didn't understand. Then he looked around suddenly, shocked to feel the firm grip around his wrist. He turned to find Steel holding him back.

Bob swung with his other fist at the British man, but he failed to connect. Steel wrenched down Bob's arm and pulled it behind his back. As he did so, Steel added a bit of force, bouncing Bob's shaven head off the stainless-steel preparation table. There was a metallic thud as skull met metal, making Steel feel a little better.

"Bad move, jackass," McCall said, almost with a hint of pleasure as she slapped the cuffs on the bruised Bob's wrists.

"OK, you're both coming with us," McCall growled as they dragged Bob to the door. Kim followed sheepishly. As they left the place, the second waitress stood watching the scene, open-mouthed. There was a helpless look across her long face as the double doors swung closed. She was alone with twenty customers, all of whom had just ordered food.

* * *

Steel and McCall headed back to the station. McCall had collared a passing black-and-white to take the dazed Bob to lock-up, whilst they escorted Kim Washington. The journey to the 11th was quiet. They had to take the FDR back to East Village where the 11th Precinct was based. It took nearly an hour and a half due to a three-car pileup, but Steel didn't mind, McCall's Mustang was more comfortable than a squad car. He had never asked her why she was banned from using police vehicles; a mystery he thought he would leave for his imagination. That said, the way she had treated her own car – namely the car before they one they were enjoying the comforts of, had led to many questions for him. Sure, she had sacrificed her beloved car to save him from a situation, but he was sure they could have been another way to have done it? Of course, his gratitude for saving his arse came in the form of a new car, and what a car.

Warm sunbeams broke past the gaps in the towering buildings filling the car like strobe lights. The only sound came from the police radio, and the daily commotion as everyone headed home. The local radio station was on low and was more background noise than anything. McCall looked in her rear Kim Washington, who was doing something on her cell phone to pass the time.

"I hope you ain't putting this on social media!" McCall said, looking around at Kim; who shot her an angry look.

"Yeah, I can see it now "Having a fun day stuck in a police car on the FDR," that will get loads of likes," Steel laughed turning to McCall, Kim giggled, and McCall shot him a burning gaze.

"You're such an ass," McCall said with almost a whisper.

"No, just bored, and hungry," Steel said, looking over at the street food vendors. McCall looked back at Kim, who was sitting in the back with her earbuds in, listening to music or watching a film on her phone. McCall had questions for her, but they could wait until they reached the station. Steel had plans for later, plans that could not wait.

On the way to the precinct, they had taken Kim Washington to New York-Presbyterian Hospital to get her checked out. She had taken quite a beating from Bob and McCall wondered what other wounds she had sustained since she had worked there. McCall had gotten a female uniformed officer to stay with her to make sure she was safe. When Kim was finished, the uniform would bring her to the precinct. McCall didn't want to wait; she was afraid what the doctor might find and give McCall to lose control and beat the shit out of the owner. Steel convinced McCall to go back to the station, for her good and Bob's.

The 11th Precinct was busier than usual. Hordes of people filled the entranceway, yelling and screaming – mostly abuse. Steel smiled as they entered, think that the last time he had seen this kind of chaos, he was waiting for a flight out of Germany. As Steel and McCall stepped off the elevator onto the department floor, they saw John Doe still in the room with Doctor Davidson. Steel opened the door to the small briefing room slowly and entered almost unnoticed. Steel felt that John Doe looked nervous and uncomfortable, but then, how else would anyone look after losing track of everything they ever knew, their entire life gone in a moment. In a way, Steel envied him, wished he had no memories, especially of that day he lost everything, and everyone. Unfortunately, he couldn't change being inquisitive, and Steel knew that if he had lost his memory, he would do everything to find out who he was and what had happened. Surely that would be worse, to find out that way rather than having the memories – or rather, nightmares?

"How's he doing, Doc?" Steel asked, his gaze firmly resting on John Doe. Steel heard the door open behind him. But he didn't turn as McCall entered the room and stood next to him.

"Well he has his muscle memory," Davidson replied. The two detectives shot him a blank look. Davidson smiled and nodded as he realised what pleasure he would take when he explained.

"Muscle memory is something you do every day, for instance, signing your name, tying your shoelaces," the doctor explained. "This man's memory for those actions is intact. However, his long-term memory is gone, or at least hindered." Davidson directed his lecture to Steel in particular, behaving almost like a teacher explaining something simple to a stupid child. Steel prodded the bridge of his sunglasses with his middle finger to adjust them and smiled, knowing full well what the doc was doing.

"So, what could cause this?" McCall asked. "A bump on the head?" She took a seat opposite John Doe.

"There are many possibilities. Head injury or a stroke, substance abuse, or the most likely thing, since we haven't found any relevant injuries, is a massive emotional event. You know? Something like a serious car accident—that sort of thing." Davidson smiled as he answered McCall's question.

"Will he get his memory back?" Steel asked, his tone dry and distracted.

"Nobody knows. He could get it back in an hour, five days, a year, or never. It is a waiting game," Colby Davidson said, shrugging. John Doe suddenly looked alarmed at the last part. *Never getting his memory back.* It was a lot to take in.

Steel nodded as if he understood, but his mind was elsewhere. He had questions of his own, such as: who was this man, and why was he covered in blood? Not forgetting, who the hell's blood was it?

"OK. So, is there —" McCall froze in mid-sentence. She was about to ask if there was someone they could call, or if he needed dropping off somewhere. Her mouth slammed shut, and she gave John Doe an embarrassed smile.

"Don't worry, Detective, this is a first for me as well," John Doe said to her, smiling. Steel had left the room and was on his cell whilst they spoke.

"OK. So, we need to find you somewhere to stay. I will speak to my captain and try and arrange something." McCall knew there was no budget for dealing with lost people who had amnesia but decided she could spin it as a 'protective custody for a potential witness'.

"Don't worry, I got it covered. I think he has been through enough, so I have got him a hotel room," Steel said, with a broad grin on his face.

"OK, so where is the hotel?" McCall asked, suspicious of Steel's intentions.

* * *

McCall's mouth dropped open as they walked into the suite at the five-star Manhattan Hotel. There were panoramic views and marble bathrooms. The two-bedroom suite even had a small dining table. Sam shook her head at the sight of a hotel room that was bigger than her apartment and probably cost more to build.

"So – uhm, John, I hope you will be comfortable. There will be two policemen outside for your protection, so there is no reason to worry." Steel smiled.

John Doe shot him a confused look. "Do I need protection?" he asked. His tone sounded almost angry at the thought of being watched. Steel smiled reassuringly.

"Sir, you were covered in blood, and you were not hurt," Steel explained. "Which means that you either saw something you shouldn't have—"

"—Or I did something I shouldn't have done. In which case, this is my prison." John Doe scowled at Steel, who nevertheless kept his smile. The British detective reached into the inside pocket of his jacket as his cell phone began to vibrate. He checked the message and smiled at the text from the desk sergeant.

The babysitters should be there now.

Steel sent a 'thank you' reply, then placed the phone back into his pocket.

"So, sleep well, and we will see you in the morning," Sam McCall said reassuringly "Hopefully you may have remembered something by then."

"I will come around tomorrow to check on him, detectives," Dr Davidson, who had come with them, butted in. "I am sure you have other things to attend to," Davidson said as he opened the refrigerator to check its contents.

"You take it, you buy it doc," Steel said with a smile, as he saw Davidson take out a small bottle of sparkling wine. Davidson reached into his pocket and pulled out a wad of bills. "It's OK, first one is on me," Steel smirked before walking off. McCall rolled her eyes at the show of testosterone. McCall headed for the front door, where Steel was already waiting. Outside in the hallway stood two officers, who were dressed in plain clothes. Steel smiled as he recognised the two men. His previous encounters had left the guys unnerved, to say the least. One was tall and thin, the other shorter with greying hair and had a 'veteran cop' look about him. As the two officers saw Steel their mouths dropped open. They, too, had recognised him and instantly had a bad feeling.

"Gentlemen, the task is simple," John Steel told them. "One man is to be on shift out here, while the other acts as back-up inside the room behind you. You work out the shift change between you, but someone is always out here. Nobody is to come in or out of that room except us and the good doctor there." Steel opened the door so that they could see the tall strange-looking doctor in the grey suit. The two men nodded.

"Any questions?" Steel asked, almost trying not to grin at the confused look they both wore. The two officers shook their heads. Steel smiled and turned for the elevator.

"Right then, see you all tomorrow." Steel said with a smile then checked his watch. McCall followed, leaving the two men to argue about who was going to take the first shift.

As Steel pressed the call button, he heard McCall approach. He could feel her almost agonizing need to get the millions of questions off her chest. The doors slid open, and they stepped inside. He just looked forward at the doors and towards the two cops in the distance. He looked contented as McCall stood patiently for the doors to close before she opened on him.

"Steel, just what the hell is going on?" she screamed as the doors closed, and the box began to move. He just smiled and took in the rant. She was pissed and had every reason to be. McCall regarded amnesiac John Doe as a victim, perhaps even a witness. But Steel saw something else. There was something about the man that set off every alarm bell in Steel's head.

Chapter 9

After Kim Washington had been released from hospital, she was taken to see McCall at the 11th. Kim didn't like police stations at the best of times. In fact, the only times she had been in one was to pick up her mom, something that happened too often.

McCall had spoken to the doctor's and found she was in perfect health considering a slight case of malnutrition. If the chef had beaten her, he had hidden it well, or it had been some time since the last one.

Kim Washington stepped off the elevator at the third floor – the Homicide Division of the 11th precinct. She stood for a moment and looked around as if hoping to find a familiar face in the sea of people. Detectives were either on their phones or darting around after getting that "hot lead." She felt alone as eyes stared at her, judging her. Kim could feel their questions, "why was this woman there, what had she done, was she a criminal or a witness?" Kim felt like turning around, getting back on the elevator and going. Did she really need to be there? She went to leave, but a familiar voice called her name, "Kim, over here," said the voice. It was detective Samantha McCall. Kim looked back towards the voice, McCall was stood next to a room – a briefing room, or so she thought. Kim walked over slowly, dragging her heels, feeling the eyes on her once more.

"Thanks for taking the time to talk to us," McCall said, ushering Kim into the room. The room was small – ten by ten with a large window, a square table and two chairs. The room – despite being scares of furnishings, was friendly, or more so than an interrogation room. On the white plastic covered top of the table was two mugs of coffee. There were no recording devices, no cameras. Defiantly not an interrogation room. Kim sat and looked around the room. No double mirror, just a mug of coffee.

"Did I have a choice?" Kim replied as she took her seat.

"Sure, but then we would have had to talk to you again, at home or at your work, I just thought this would be easier," McCall said with a comforting smile. In truth, McCall wanted to get Kim out of her comfort zone, away from distractions or intimidations.

"What do you want to know?" Kim finally asked. McCall smiled inside.

"Tell me about Tara, what kind of person was she?" McCall asked, picking up her mug of coffee.

"She's nice, the kinda gal that would give you her last dollar if you were in trouble, which is weird considerin," Kim said before blowing on her hot beverage.

"Considering what?"

"Considerin her past, her poppa died when she was young, her momma was a real piece of work," Kim explained, her Southern Georgia accent broke through her Brooklyn. "Her Momma took off when she was in her late teens, poor thang had to survive by herself since she was a littlun, not right, not right at all," Kim shook her head.

"Did she have a temper?" McCall asked, taking note of Kim's reaction.

"You mean, could she have killed her roommate, her best friend?" Kim scowled. "No ma'am, Tara was the sweetest thang, sure, don't get me wrong, the gal stood up for herself, took no shit from nobody, includin that piece of shit boss of ours," Kim smiled, a distant memory slipped into her mind. "One time the bastard tried somethang with one of the new girls, Tara wasn't havin none of that, put him in his place she did," Kim's expression changed as if she had just said something she shouldn't have. McCall saw it and leapt on it.

"How did she – handle it?" McCall asked, leaning forward. Kim swallowed hard.

"She... she, look you gotta understand, she was just savin the girl from a beatin," Kim spurted the words, trying to un-ring that bell, but it was too late, it had been well and truly rung.

"How did she handle it?" McCall repeated the question.

"She put a knife to his balls and told him next time he'd lose them," Kim explained, her head tilted with shame of giving up her friend. "She looked after us, protected us, I guess the only reason the boss did what he did today was because he knew she wasn't there," Kim's voice trembled, the sudden realization that Tara wasn't going to be there to look after them hit home. McCall saw the panic in her eyes, and she knew in that instance how big a roll Tara played in their lives. Tara had been their bodyguard against an abusive boss; now, she was gone.

"If you are worried about your boss, you could press assault charges?" McCall said, but her words were met by a frightened, tearful gaze.

"Yeah, and then what, he gets out after, what, a month. Then he'll really do some beatin. And what about my job, he goes away, I got no work, whose gonna pay my way, you?" Kim growled. She was bitter and terrified.

"I have no answer, I wish I did, but I don't, all I can do is promise to keep an eye out for you and the other girls," McCall's voice was soft but held a power to it. Kim smiled and nodded.

"Maybe, you gonna cook as well, we ain't got no chef no more?" Kim laughed. McCall smiled and shrugged.

"Sorry, I can't help you on that one, I mostly get takeout," the two women laughed. McCall's smile faded. She knew that they had lost the momentum. "About Tara, did she have any boyfriends?"

"No, she didn't have much time for those, not the hours we were pullin," Kim shrugged. "She had a couple of casual pick-ups, but nothin serious." McCall nodded and made a note on the yellow pad.

"Did she have any problems with customers, anything like that?" McCall asked, trying to get a picture of the missing woman.

"Nah, she was friendly to everyone – well, everyone except that asshole, but he wouldn't do nothin," Kim explained. The picture that McCall was getting was of a bright, friendly, caring woman, who by all accounts could hold her own. So, did this make her and victim or the killer? The questions continued for a short while longer. While McCall was busy with Kim Washington Steel decided to make some calls. He knew a man in the room would just make Kim clam up, mostly through embarrassment, besides, McCall had told him to stay the hell out.

It wasn't long before the door opened, and McCall and Kim stood at the entrance. Steel looked over at the two women and smiled. They looked calm in each other's company, and that was what McCall was good at, getting through to people.

"Thanks again for speaking to me Kim, I will do everything to make sure your boss stays away for a while," McCall said handing over her business card. "if there is anything you ever need, call me." Kim smiled and held the card in both hands before tucking it away in her pocket. "I'll get uniforms to bring you home," McCall offered.

"No, that's OK detective. Unfortunately, I don't need the neighbours seein me gettin out of a police car. In my part of town, only two kinds of people get out of a police car, snitches, drunks and the cops themselves. Unless of course, you're the lady from number seven, this old gal always got a lift because she was always too drunk to drive herself home," Kim shrugged. "I'll be fine detective, thank you." Kim turned and faced Steel who was sat at McCall's desk with his feet up on the desk talking on his cell phone. Kim smiled and nodded to him. Steel returned the gesture and watched her walk to the elevator.

As Kim headed for the elevator, she smiled to herself. Bob was in lockup as a result of the assault on her and the attempted assault on a police officer. Kim had smiled when she saw her pig of a boss take a swing at the big cop. Kim was shocked at how fast the cop had moved and remembered that he'd been dressed completely in black clothes. She could still hear Bob's head impacting with the metal table. He had swung at a cop, and that would cost him a good couple of years. As Kim waited for the elevator, she hatched a plan, and she would keep the diner running, after all, she had done all the accounts and orders because Bob couldn't. She was already running it anyway, not that he had paid her any more for all those extra duties. In a way, it was her diner now, or at least it was until he got out of prison, by which time she would be long gone. While the place was running, she and the other waitresses had cash coming in.

Two subway rides later; she was nearly home. Kim had checked up on the diner before leaving. Fran's cousin, Carl, had taken on the cooking after she and Bob had left with the police, and Fran had done a hell of a job after they had gone. The night shift had come in, and so had Stan, Carl's boyfriend. He had offered to be the night shift chef. The place would run OK; indeed, it would probably run better now that Bob was out of the picture.

It was late, and her watch said it was half-past nine. She cursed the time, as she had missed her favourite TV show. Her street was at least two blocks from the station, but she began to hurry. Kim would be on early shift tomorrow and needed some sleep. The night air had a bite to it, and dark clouds covered the heavens from view. She turned onto her road and hurried towards her home. The sound of her heels echoed through the avenue of buildings.

She saw nothing around her, only the screen from her cell as she searched for missed messages. Even as she made her way up the stairs to the third floor, her vision never left the mass of messages from her social media pages. Her corridor was poorly lit, as though some of the bulbs had blown, but she was chatting to some guy on Twitter. Even as she opened the door with her key and nudged it open with her foot, she was away in another place. She never saw the hand cup her mouth or the person who thrust her into the apartment and slammed the door behind them. The corridor was silent apart from the sounds of the television sets behind closed doors.

No one had seen it happen. No one knew what had happened.

Inside Kim Washington's apartment, the darkness made the situation seem a thousand times worse. She had seen the movies: the ones where a girl gets attacked in a dark apartment, and they never ended well. Then she remembered what the cops had said about Tara's roommate, found dead in her apartment. Was she next, she wondered?

Suddenly the lights came on, and Kim shielded her eyes from the sudden brightness. This suddenly made it worse. With the lights off she could say she hadn't seen anything but now! She kept her hand over her eyes, but this time it was to shield her view of her attacker. She didn't want to see them; she didn't want to die.

"Kim put your hand down. I am not gonna hurt you," said a familiar voice. Kim ripped her arm down to her side.

There before her stood Tara Burke.

Kim's terror subsided as she saw the look of utter panic in Tara's eyes. Tara was scared, alone and hungry.

The scared waitress sat down on her brown fabric-covered couch and hoped that Tara would do the same. Slowly, Tara sat. The dazed look in her eyes made them seem larger than normal. This was a woman running scared. But from what, Kim wondered. Of the killer? Or of the cops?

"Where have you been, Tara?" Kim's voice was soft and soothing, but the tone rang with a hint of weariness. "The cops have been lookin' for ya."

"Amber … Amber … is—" Tara raced to the bathroom and threw up. The shock of what she had found still burned in her memory. As Kim walked into the bathroom, she found Tara on the tiled floor, holding her legs against her body for comfort. Tears ran freely down her pale cheeks. Tara looked up at her friend with large scared blue eyes.

"They butchered her, cut her up. Why, Kim? Why?"

Kim didn't have any more answers than Tara did. Kim helped her friend to her feet then led her back to the couch. As Tara crashed down onto the cushioned couch, Kim headed for the kitchen. She needed a drink—hell, they both did.

She passed Tara a glass with two fingers of scotch in it, then sat down next to her friend. Kim sipped the golden liquid whilst Tara just cradled the glass and stared into nowhere.

"Hey, it's OK. You're safe now."

Tara looked over towards her friend and smiled. She was hoping that Kim was right. She hoped she was safe here.

"Why didn't you go to the cops?" Kim asked, before taking another hit from the glass.

"Don't know, I was scared, I guess."

Kim nodded as though she understood, but then the sight of Tara's pink suitcase made her wonder. If she was so scared, why had she packed a suitcase to leave?

"You leavin' the city?" Kim asked, her eyes now fixed on Tara, who just shrugged and took a sip of the golden liquid.

Tara coughed as the whisky hit the back of her throat. Kim smiled to herself as she watched her friend wave a hand in front of her mouth.

"Not a whisky gal then." Kim laughed, and Tara joined in, almost forgetting her troubles for a moment.

"The police came around the diner looking for you," Kim said.

Tara just nodded as if it was expected.

"What did you tell them?" Tara asked before trying another sip from the glass.

Kim shrugged. "What could I tell 'em? I didn't know anything." She smiled wickedly. "One good thing happened, though. Bob took a swing at a cop." She explained what had happened, and Tara's mouth fell open.

"Did he get him?"

Kim shook her head to the question. "Nah, the cop was too fast, the man moved like lightning, put Bob right down on his fat ass!"

The two women laughed, but Tara's laughter died, and she stared into her glass.

"I keep seeing her lying there in all that blood. I keep thinking that should have been me!"

Kim gave Tara a puzzled looked. "What do you mean?" She suddenly had a bad feeling about what the answer might be.

"Kim, she wasn't supposed to have moved in for another two days. She shouldn't have been there!"

Kim shuddered at the revelation. Was her friend being stalked? And if so, would they come here?

* * *

Steel entered his park view loft apartment and was greeted by the orange glow of the city. The large three-bedroom apartment's trio of huge windows allowed a panoramic view over the skyline. A huge sitting area gave way to a kitchenette and two staircases. One of these went to the gallery, which was also his bedroom, and the other led to the spare rooms. A long corridor next to the kitchen was home to the bathroom and two other rooms: an office and another which was at the end. The door to this room looked heavier than normal and could only be opened by using a security pad.

John Steel walked to a small drinks cabinet that was next to the breakfast bar and poured himself a glass of Johnny Walker Blue Label. He took off his jacket and tossed it gently onto the large L-shaped brushed-leather couch. Steel signed, at last, he had quiet. Even though he liked working with the cops, he found it too noisy. Steel looked over to his answering machine which was blinking with a red glow. He had messages, the last thing he needed. He walked over to the machine and noticed that seven missed calls showed up on the LED display.

He pressed the 'play' button and walked slowly towards the window to take in the view. Two messages were from the CEO of his father's company, Steel Industries, or Kyoi Industries as his father had named it. The other one was from some woman from a charity who was wondering if he was attending an event in September. More people after money for a good cause that they possibly didn't give a shit about, but it made them feel better every time they did their taxes.

Steel smiled and shook his head. September was a long way off, and he never planned anything further than two weeks ahead. The rest of the messages were from people who were wanting to talk to 'Lord Steel' rather than 'Detective Steel'. He liked it like that, gave him a little sense of home.

As a beep sounded, the machine told of the time and date of the next call. It was from a man called Laurence. Steel turned his head slightly to hear better. The message was simply to tell him of his resupply. Steel smiled and walked towards the locked door at the end of the corridor.

Stopping at the door, he punched in the code and placed his hand of the scanner that slid out of the wall. A red light turned to green on the keypad, and he entered. As the door closed, the machine's voice told him: 'No more messages.

Steel returned to the sitting room wearing a new watch. He topped up his glass and headed for the leather chaise longue that was in front of the windows, with their spectacular view. He liked it there: the view, the silence. He sat down and stretched out along its full length. John took a mouth full of the whisky and let it warm in his mouth before allowing it to trickle down his throat rather than swallowing it in one go.

He closed his eyes and hoped for a peaceful sleep, but he knew that would never happen. His memories haunted him, but strangely enough, he found strength in the pain.

Images of a bright summer's day broke through the darkness of his thoughts. His return home from nearly a year overseas with his SAS Regiment. He had done his tour and was returning home. With the war still in his head, he needed rest, quiet and most of all his beloved wife.

Steel's eyes creased together in mental anguish as the memories unfolded in his head. The memory of his homecoming. The bright summer's day, the marquee on the back lawn. The people lying dead: all of them had been family and friends murdered by gunmen—the mercenaries he had taken out. He could almost smell the cordite, feel the heat from the explosions. His body tensed up as in his mind he was back in the attic. The dimly lit place of his death and rebirth.

The sound of laughter, the six shots, the image of his poor dear love in his arms and her lifeless eyes.

The darkness.

The plastic glass fell from his hand and bounced on the wooden floor. Steel sat up and screamed. He looked around, confused and disorientated. His cold emerald-green eyes appeared almost black in the dull light. Cascades of sweat flowed down his forehead. He swung his legs around as he sat facing the room. Tilting his head back, he sucked in the conditioned air.

Standing up, he headed for the bathroom. He had at least an hour before his car would arrive. He stripped the shirt off his back and tossed it onto the couch. On the underside of each step of the staircase to his bedroom, there was a metal bar. This created the perfect facilities for a workout, and they were almost like monkey bars that led upwards. Steel moved up and down the twenty-bar construction at least five times. He could feel his muscles tighten. Sweat poured down his chiselled form as he moved quicker and quicker. Steel felt the pain in his shoulders and arms. His forearms burnt from the grip.

Finally, he just stood, his hands on his knees, sucking in the air. He stood up straight and leant back as far as he could, feeling his midsection stiffen. Steel grabbed the whisky glass from the breakfast bar and headed for the shower. In less than twenty minutes, the car would be there. He stripped off the rest of his clothes and stuck them into the hamper, before turning on the shower. There was a whoosh of water that sounded like rain on the glass divider. Steel looked at himself in the mirror. His large dead green eyes stared back at him. He tested his stubble growth with his left hand, weighing up whether to shave or not. His stubble was rough; it felt like he was stroking sandpaper. He couldn't really be bothered to shave, but then he realised that he had an appearance to maintain. Tonight, he would be attending as Lord Steel, not as Detective Steel.

The warm water cascaded over his muscular form, soaking every inch of his powerful body, washing the soap lather from his overworked muscles. After shaving in the shower, he just let the water run over him. He placed his hands on the side and let the shower pound his tight flesh. The alarm on his phone alerted him that he had ten minutes in which to change into his clothes. He grunted in disapproval of leaving the soothing waters, then got out.

After drying off, he slipped into his all-black tuxedo and Bugatti shoes. He checked his reflection: he had to admit that he looked good, just did not look happy about where he was going.

He looked at the hands-on his new Military style smartwatch. The carbon-fibre face was illuminated by the luminous dials. It was nearly eight o'clock. There was a benefit on at The Museum of Modern Art, and the Mayor and the Governor had insisted that he attend.

Steel stood in front of a long Elizabethan mirror and checked his attire. He had put his blue contact lenses in and set his phone to vibrate instead of ring.

He was ready to go but not willing. He looked around at the comfort of his sanctuary. Suddenly his house phone rang. Steel picked it up and listened to the concierge, informing him that his car had arrived. John opened the drawer and looked at his Barretta Storm bulldog 9MM sub-compact pistol, then closed it. He feared that if he took it out, he might end up using it on himself.

"Oh well, for Queen and country," he said, opening the front door.

It would be a long night of rubbing shoulders. A night he could do without. With people, he could do without too.

Chapter 10

At Four in the morning, the garbage men and cops doing their own kind of patrol. Sirens wailed as fire engines, and ambulances travelled to emergencies around the city. The city that never sleeps was right; there was always something going on. Yellow cabs made their way with tourists fresh from JFK or businesspeople heading for that early meeting. The city was bathed in a mix of bright multi-coloured lights from stores, delis and restaurants. It would be hours yet until the sun would brake over the horizon. Soon the dullness would be replaced by bright ochre, and the city would come alive. The day before the weather girl had predicted: "Sunny spells and highs in the fifties." Joggers got an early start, and so did the paper delivery service.

McCall's alarm let out its usual loud serenade of *BEEP, BEEP, BEEP*. Her arm snaked from under the covers like a mythical beast, then slammed down on the off button before disappearing back under the covers. There was a three-minute pause before the second alarm went off. She groaned disapprovingly, then crawled out of her warm bed. She needed coffee and a shower. Sometimes she wished someone would invent a showerhead that would give out coffee instead of water for those early mornings. But soon changed her mind as she smelt the aroma coming from the kitchen as her coffee machine switched on, using the timer.

She poured the first cup of coffee and headed for the bathroom. McCall leaned in and switched on the shower before slipping out of her shorts and T-shirt. She stood there looking at her slightly tanned firm figure. She had the body of a supermodel from *Sports Illustrated*. She kept fit by training with her kickboxing instructor every Tuesday and Thursday.

Men dreamt about her, and so they should—that was her power over them. But she was a damn good cop, and she would never let her looks take precedence over her abilities as a detective. She had worked hard for her position and then she worked even harder and got the due respect for it. Sure, she had been passed over by others she had joined with because they were men, but she didn't mind because they ended up riding a desk and doing what they were good at kissing ass.

Sam reached up to her left shoulder and touched the scar she had got a year ago. A mercenary had shot her, for him to draw out Steel. McCall could still hear the screams of the man after Steel had gotten hold of him. It had been their first case together and what a ride that was.

McCall stepped into the shower and let the warm water cascade over her athletic body. She closed her eyes and leant against the tiled wall with outstretched arms. The water was relaxing to the point where she wanted to stay there all day. But she had work to do, and she owed it to Tony to find his girlfriend's killer.

She dried off and dressed in a grey trouser suit with a blue blouse. Her Gabor boots were almost flat-bottomed with a slight heel, which enabled her to run. She had tried heels, but they just slowed her down.

Pulling on the suit jacket, McCall headed for the front door and the dresser next to it. Opening the right-hand drawer, she pulled out her custom Glock 17 and her shield. Tucking the brushed steel pistol into the holster under her jacket, she grabbed her keys and headed out.

* * *

Walter T. Hobbs walked out of his apartment building. He was a small man with a large balding head that had tufts of black hair clinging to the sides. A pair of gold-rimmed glasses perched on a fat nose, giving him the appearance of a school physics teacher. He wore a black suit with a green tie and brown brogue shoes.

Behind him, he dragged the wheeled suitcase towards the curb. The doorman raised a gloved hand to flag down an approaching cab. Walter pulled out a ten-dollar note for the man's trouble, which was snapped up and tucked away before anyone else saw it.

"Where you goin, buddy?" asked the cabby as Walter sat on the long back seat. The doorman shut the door behind Walter and doffed his hat as the cab sped away. At that moment Walter noticed two large men in black suits enter his building, and he knew they were there for him.

"JFK if you would, please hurry," Walter said, taking note of the man's credentials that were on the dashboard. His eyes scanned the driver for a moment. Walter noted the man's lumberjack shirt and blue padded vest, which resembled a life preserver.

He smiled happily to himself then let his gaze fall to the outside, the passing streets and pedestrians, his thoughts a million miles away.

"So, you are going anywhere nice?" the black cabby asked, his dreadlocks dangling from under his multi-coloured woollen cap.

"What – sorry, I was miles away, I'm off to see my aunt in Portugal. She is very ill, poor dear," Walter said convincingly, almost as if he had rehearsed it a thousand times just in case the line was needed.

"Wow, Portugal," the cabbie replied, shouting back through the plated dividing screen. "Never been there myself but I have heard it is very beautiful."

Walter took a handkerchief from his inside pocket and removed his glasses to clean them. Beads of perspiration were beginning to form on his forehead.

The cab's passenger used the white cotton handkerchief on his moist forehead, then put his small spectacles back on. He took a deep breath, exhaled and sat back in the seat. He glanced out through the window again. He knew the turn-off for the airport would soon be coming up and then he would be home free. A panic ran through his body as he noticed they had gone past the exit. Walter leaned forward and tapped on the safely glass that separated them.

"Hey, you missed the exit!" Walter screamed.

The driver shook his head and smiled. "No, man, I saw it. It's just that Mr Williams said he wanted to say goodbye before you left."

Walter's head began to spin. He tried the door handles, but the deadbolt was on.

He was trapped, and he was on the way to see a madman.

The worried man knew at that moment that he would be going on a trip, just not the one he wanted. The cab's interior began to spin, and he fell into darkness as he lost consciousness. The cabbie mumbled curses to himself as he tossed his Taser to one side. He had been waiting all through the trip to use it and then that loser of an accountant had gone and fainted. He picked the Taser back up and Tasered Walter anyway, just out of spite.

He smiled and drove on into Brooklyn. Walter had an appointment, and Mr Williams didn't like to be kept waiting.

* * *

Walter T. Hobbs awoke to the sound of voices. Voices that seemed to be muffled, as if they were far away, or on the other side of a door. Everything seemed blurred and distorted, and everything seemed dark.

He tried to lift his hand to check his glasses but found that he could not move. He was being held down by something. His senses had been shot as a result of an electric shock. He tried to struggle but gave up after a few minutes. He was strapped to a table, a cold metal table.

Walter's heart began to race as he realised where he was. He stopped moving and listened. The room was silent, but he knew he wasn't alone. Heavy impacts struck the floor as someone large entered the room.

"Mr Hobbs, our employer, would like to know where it is," said a deep angry voice.

"I don't know what you mean. Where is what?" Walter screamed, tears of fear running down his face. He was glad of the darkness, for he didn't want to see anything.

"Some merchandise came in a couple of days ago, very important merchandise. Now it's missing, and unfortunately, only a few people knew about it. So, you see my problem … Well actually, your problem right now," said the voice.

"I don't know! Really, I don't. If you mean Tuesday's shipment, I made sure it was secure," Walter answered.

"So why were you in such a rush to get out of the country, Mr Hobbs?" The mystery voice sounded calm but authoritative.

"My aunt, she's sick. I was—"

"—Blah, blah, blah," the voice interrupted. "You really expect me to believe the coincidence that your aunt is sick the same week that information goes missing?" The man was now yelling loudly, and Walter knew that his time was up.

"Look, tell us what we want to know, or else Mr Williams is coming in, and believe me you don't want that." The man's voice almost sounded cheerful at the prospect.

Walter had heard things about Mr Williams: bad things. He would perform unspeakable acts on people that weren't even worth thinking about. He wasn't a butcher. He was a surgeon, an artist some said. Either way, if you ended up on his table, your experience would be long and painful.

"Please! I don't know anything," Walter cried out.

The footsteps walked away, and Walter began to shake.

He heard a door open, and then after a time, it closed again. Then he heard something. A sound that chilled him to the bone. Music, soft music from a music box or … a pocket watch.

Mr Williams was there.

Walter began to shake uncontrollably. The music grew near, and the sound of metal-tipped shoes on a tiled floor echoed around the room.

Both sounds were moving around him, as though he was being circled. He wanted to cry out to ask who was there, but in another part of his mind, he didn't want to know. The tapping grew slower until finally, it stopped, and so did the music. There was a silent click as the watch was closed and put away. Then came a voice that made Walter nearly soil himself: it was a voice like knives on violin strings:

"Hello, Mr Hobbs. My name is … Well, they call me Mr Williams. I don't know why, but for what they pay me they can call me Susan and stick me in a leather corset for all I care."

Walter felt puzzled at the man's apparent joviality. Mr Williams was softly spoken, but his tone raised and lowered with each word. However, his voice ground like nails on a chalkboard.

"I don't know anything!" Walter pleaded. "I did what I was asked, and then I locked it away."

The footsteps tapped slowly, as though Williams was thinking as he walked.

"My colleague said you were fleeing the country," Williams spoke softly.

The sound of metal sliding against metal filled Walter's ears.

"My aunt is sick, she has cancer. I was off to see her." Walter's voice was filled with fear and defeat. He knew whatever he said they would not believe.

"Oh, I am sorry. I had no idea. There must have been a terrible mistake, I do apologise," Williams said, and the tone of sincerity rang in Walter's ears. But he felt more afraid than ever. He felt the sudden weight of someone on top of him, but the darkness revealed nothing.

"OK, so can I go now?" Walter said, taking a chance in that moment.

A long thin pale face emerged from the blackness and loomed over Walter. Williams had high cheekbones and large maddening eyes, and a long Roman nose under which was a smile. Pearly white teeth behind ruby red lips. His blond hair was brushed back to reveal a large forehead.

Williams leered down at Walter like a tiger looking at its prey.

"Well, Walter … I can call you Walter, can't I?"

Walter nodded quickly to the question so as not to antagonise his captor.

"It seems the powers that be feel that you're a bit of a fibber and a thief, which is good. I mean, that's what we do, isn't that right?" Then Williams's tone changed; his voice went deeper. "But we don't appreciate it when we get this treatment from one of our own. It's kind of takes you off the Christmas card list," Williams growled.

Their eyes met. Walter wanted to look away, but Williams's eyes were strangely hypnotic. Williams drew closer so that his nose rested on Walter's.

"I have been asked to come down here and find out if you're lying or not. So far—"

Walter held his breath. He waited for the words: 'No you're not lying' or 'I believe you'.

But Williams said nothing more. He just sunk his teeth into Walter's nose and bit down hard.

Walter screamed in pain. Williams jumped down from the table and spat the bitten off chunk of flesh back at Walter. There was a small burst of light which illuminated the operating table from above, then a scrape of metal. Suddenly Walter found himself moving as the table was being repositioned. To the side of him was a large mirror.

"This is for you, Walter, because I don't want you to miss anything," Williams rambled. "It is very rare that I get an audience so I can't wait to share my performance with you. That is until you either die or blackout. Whichever comes first, I guess."

Walter felt the warm urine flow down his leg, making Williams smile.

"Oops a little accident, oh well, never mind," Williams joked as he moved back into the darkness.

"OK, Walter, last chance. Where's the goodies?" Williams asked again as he pulled on some long surgical gloves, then pulled at a metal stand covered with various bottles of fluids. Williams clearly had enough chemicals and drugs to keep Walter alive and conscious. Tapping the side of Walter's neck, Williams found an artery and stuck in a needle.

"Normally we would use an arm but … Well, you get the picture." Williams laughed as he began to walk off to fetch more equipment.

"Please don't—"

The torturer turned and slammed a gloved hand over Walter's mouth.

"Dear Walter. Here's the thing. If you say that sentence once more, I will rip out your teeth. You'll need your tongue to tell me the truth later. So, tell me the truth or don't say anything, OK?"

Walter nodded frantically.

"Smashing!" Williams said, clapping like a child who had won a prize. He moved to a small table that contained some bottles of water. He wiped his forehead then cracked open a bottle. As he moved the opened drink to his lips, he stopped and turned towards the bleeding Walter.

"Oh, dear me, where are my manners? Walter, you must be parched. Do forgive me, won't you?" Williams walked over to Walter, who opened his mouth to receive the cool liquid, his mouth feeling drier than a sandstorm. Williams took care to pour a bit at a time into his victim's mouth, so as not to choke him.

Walter nodded a 'thank you', careful not to speak after the last instruction. Williams smiled, pleased that he understood.

"You see, Walter, I am not such a bad guy. All I want is the truth, that's all." Williams smiled again and pulled up a chair that was at the far side of the room. He placed it next to Walter's head and sat down.

"I got the information from the courier and proved it was the real thing," Walter explained for what he thought must be the thousandth time. "It was then sealed in the safe, and then I gave the keys to the night watchman—Donald, I think his name was. Anyway, after that, I left. That's it. That's all I know."

Williams sat and tapped an index finger on his lips. "So, your aunt is ill, you say? Sorry to hear about that."

Walter looked at his captor in some confusion.

"What?" the powerless man answered, surprised to see the compassionate look on the other man's face. "Yeah, I got the call this morning. The hospital called to let me know."

"I believe you, Walter, really I do. In fact, the hospital confirmed your story just a while ago," Williams explained.

Walter exhaled a lungful of air in relief.

"So, am I free to go?" Walter felt a huge surge of relief at the thought of his ordeal being over.

However, Williams's sympathetic expression changed to a callous grin.

"I believe your story about your aunt, my dear Walter. But I never mentioned anything about the other matter."

Walter's face fell, and his fear returned with a vengeance.

"You said you sealed it in the safe, but the safe was empty. You said you gave the keys to the watchman Donald. Tell me, who the fuck is Donald? WE DON'T HAVE A DONALD; YOU ARE LYING PIECE OF CRAP!" Williams yelled.

He lost control, and in one swift movement he turned, picked up a meat cleaver from the instrument table and smashed it down onto Walter's right wrist. Blood erupted from the wound as his hand was separated from the wrist.

Walter screamed in shock and pain as he looked in the mirror. Williams stood back in disgust at the screaming Walter. He had been a trusted member of the organisation. Suddenly the door opened, and a guard rushed in, holding a cell phone. Williams looked over at the guard with a disapproving look.

"What is it?" Williams simply said, not in the mood for chit chat on the phone. The guard sheepishly held up the phone.

"It's the warehouse, sir," the guard said, sweating.

"What do they want? Oh, never mind, give it here before you give yourself a friggin' heart attack." Williams took the phone and held it to his ear. The guard's eyes were transfixed by the sight of the meat cleaver that Williams was playing with as he listened. Williams nodded to the guard, indicating that he should silence the still-screaming Walter. The scared guard put his hand over Walter's mouth to dull the screams.

"Yes … Uh … Yep … R-right. OK then, thanks." Williams pressed disconnect on the phone and smiled at the guard.

"Oh dear, this is s-so embarrassing. Really it is," Williams said, laughing and passing the phone back to the guard, who reached for it.

Quick as a flash, Williams grabbed the man's hand and swung the cleaver, neatly slicing through his wrist, severing the hand entirely. A cascade of blood-drenched the poor confused Walter.

Williams threw the freshly amputated hand at the guard, who was cradling his wound, the shock so fresh he hardly realised what had happened.

"So, tell me. How long did you wait outside before you gave me the phone?" Williams said calmly.

The guard turned to face the madman, still dazed. But as he began to reply, Williams's fury peaked once more. He threw the cleaver so hard that it embedded itself deep into the man's skull.

"Well, you know what they say. Don't shoot the messenger. Thankfully they didn't mention decapitation or the severing of limbs," Williams joked. He looked down at the still-bleeding Walter. Williams grabbed the clothes iron that he had been saving for later and slapped its red-hot soleplate directly onto his gaping wrist, thus cauterising the wound. Walter screamed even more, and Williams rolled his eyes and stuck a rag into his mouth to silence him.

"I am sorry, Walter, it appears there was a bit of a mistake. They found that apparently there *was* a guy called Donald working there that night. A Donald Soap. Apparently, he was a sick relief for the regular man. Anyway, it looks like we were all duped and now I have egg on my face."

Williams headed for the door and called for a guard. A large man walked into the room. He seemed to have virtually no neck, and his bull-like appearance probably matched his IQ.

"Mr Hobbs has been, erm … injured. Make sure you take good care of him, OK?" Williams said, keeping his voice level down. The guard nodded and smiled, revealing bad teeth, a sight that made Williams jump backwards in repulsion.

Williams left the room and started marching down a long corridor. Suddenly he heard a gunshot. Williams stopped and stood still. He looked at the ground and shook his head.

"How can I soar like an eagle, whilst working with turkeys?" he wondered.

Chapter 11

McCall met Steel outside the precinct. She noticed he wasn't wearing his usual suit. Today he was in black jeans, T-shirt, a pair of Bugatti boots and a pea coat. The body of it was made of wool, but the sleeves and collar were padded leather.

"Going for the sporty look today?" she joked. Steel shook his head and smiled.

"I've got to go to the range, apparently I have to qualify," he said, shrugging.

"Oh, you qualify for lots of things, Steel, believe me," she answered with a large grin. She didn't have to drive him, but she wanted to see what he could do. In all their time together, she had never really seen him shoot. McCall was itching to see 'Supercop' mess it up, or at least miss the target a few times. In fact, it so happened that McCall was the department's 'best shot'. Her dad had taught her to shoot when she was in her teens, and her natural aptitude had caused her to improve over the years.

They arrived at the outdoor range. It was a wooden construction, arranged into individual 'pens' that denoted each shooter's firing point. Several staff were on standby to assist and to monitor the firers. Before heading to his position, Steel was briefed on the conditions of the shoot and the safety protocols. John nodded to the veteran cop and put on his ear defenders and headed for his given lane. McCall sat at the back next to the rear wall and opened the box of popcorn she had gotten from the vending machine. She was going to enjoy this.

* * *

The pair's drive back to the precinct was silent, as was their elevator ride to the department's floor. McCall was pale and felt ill. As the doors opened, they found Tooms and Tony ready with some toy pistols and a large target, their joke in order to shame Steel for when he failed the shooting test.

Steel marched into the captain's office and handed him the folded target and the 'pass confirmation' paperwork. Tooms and Tony looked at McCall who was sitting at her desk, a strange haunted look on her face. Then they crept over to the captain's door, just in time to see the captain unfold the target. The 'ten ring' in the centre was completely gone, the hole in the target being around twenty millimetres in diameter.

"Holy shit!" yelped an excited Tooms, causing his boss, Captain Brant, to look up at him.

"Quiet!" Brant said, folding the target back up and filing the paperwork.

"So now you are qualified you can get your ass back to work, Detective," Brant said to John Steel. "And that goes for you two jokers as well," he yelled after Tooms and Tony, who quickly hurried back to their desks.

As Steel approached his office, he said nothing, nor did he smile. He could see that Sam McCall was pissed at him: he had beaten her previously unmatched score.

"Is there anything you're not good at?" she yelled after him.

He stopped and gave a small uncomfortable smile.

"Yes," he replied grimly. "Not letting the people, I care about get hurt or killed." His face was pained. Then he disappeared into his office.

McCall sat there with her mouth open, suddenly feeling shitty. She stood up and followed him into his office, via the break room.

Steel's office was an old storeroom he had commandeered and made his own. During a Christmas break, he had arranged for workmen to come in and turn it into something fantastic. The walls were covered with wooden panelling and burgundy velvet wallpaper. The same shade of oak that was on the wall panels was also that of the timber floorboards. Victorian furnishings filled the floor space, along with a large carved oak desk that was near the back of the room.

Two brown leather chesterfield armchairs were in front of the desk, and a red leather ship's 'captain's chair' sat proudly next to the footwell and the back of the desk. On the left-hand wall, a sixty-five-inch monitor acted as Steel's murder 'smartboard'.

McCall entered the room, brandishing two mugs of fresh coffee. Steel looked over at her and quickly tucked something away in a drawer.

"I thought you could use a coffee," she said apologetically.

He smiled and took the mug from her. Funnels of fresh steam drifted up from the fresh brew. McCall sat in one of the armchairs, and the creak of heavy leather filled the room as it took her weight. The smell of the room was intoxicating old wood and leather filled the senses. McCall was sure that if he could have done, he would have had a fireplace installed as well.

McCall liked it there, for it was almost like stepping back into time. The only thing missing was the Sherlock Holmes-style deerstalker cap and the briar pipe. It had a very Victorian feel to it all.

"Sorry about before," McCall said, swinging her legs over one of the arms of the huge armchair, with her head resting of the other.

"I was ... Well, I guess I was shocked, really, to be honest." She smiled at her own confession.

Steel sat back in his chair and cradled the cup into his hands.

"I have always been good at that sort of thing." His voice was soft, but there was a strange bitterness to it. "I don't know. Maybe it's a genetic thing. I joined the tactical combat engineer Regiment when I was seventeen," he explained, smiling as he thought back. "By the age of nineteen I was being poached by the SAS Regiment—they saw potential in me. Somehow I passed the entrance course first time—a lot of good men didn't." Steel's words almost sounded regretful of his past and the friends he had lost.

"I was with them for several years until ... Well, until something happened."

Sam McCall could not see Steel's eyes, but she knew if he could cry, he would be weeping right now.

"You mean your family?" she coaxed. "The massacre at your home?"

He looked shocked. But then smiled and nodded as if it was a relief that she knew already.

"After that, it was not safe for me to be in the SAS, so my father-in-law got me into the training for the SEAL teams. He is a senator with connections to the defence department, so all I had to do was pass." Steel smiled again as if remembering.

"I passed the training first time. Of course, when they learned of my past employment, they couldn't wait to give me a hard time because of it. I joined Team Five. A good unit with good men. In the first Iraq War, one of the helicopters carrying another team went down. Operations knew where they were, and they just needed a nod to get them out. We knew by dawn they would either be moved, or they would be dead before the extraction plan could be approved."

McCall stared at him; her eyes wide, almost afraid to hear the rest. But she felt a strange compulsion to know what happened too.

"The problem was they were being held in a small town, a well-fortified town that had been there for a couple of thousand years at least. It had high walls to see off invaders. The powers-that-be could have ordered heavy armour and a couple of squads, but that meant collateral damage. The town was historic, so they had to come up with some other idea. That night I went for a walk and found myself getting captured." Steel frowned as he remembered the details.

McCall's eyes were still fixed on him, her hands shaking with a mixture of excitement and fear.

"They tortured me for what seemed like hours. They had their fun until the commander came. I knew he would come eventually; that was why I waited." Steel took a sip from the coffee.

"I was hung upside down, like an animal ready for the slaughter. The commander laughed when I explained what was going to happen. About how I was going to kill them all. He seemed confused when I never mentioned killing him." Steel took another sip from the mug, and the hot steam fogged up his sunglasses for a few seconds before clearing.

"I have no idea how many men died that day, but I do know that twelve of my brothers walked out, including fifteen others from different nations. The commander realised at that moment why he had been spared: so that he could warn others of the 'green-eyed demon'. But rather than face the humiliation of losing all his men he shot himself." Steel shrugged as though it was nothing.

"After that, I got picked for LOAN WOLF missions."

Sam McCall lifted her cup with shaky hands, the dark liquid almost spilling over the sides.

"So … W-why did you leave?" she asked, her voice as unstable as the rest of her.

Steel smiled. "Something happened, and I lost a lot of friends. You could say that my past had found me. Later I was recruited by an agency to do … Well, *things*, shall we say."

McCall suddenly had an uneasy feeling. She knew he had a past but not one that was as colourful as this.

"So, then you left the agency and became a cop?" McCall asked, hoping that was the end of his résumé.

"You could say that." Steel spoke with an almost playful tone, which spooked McCall even more.

"Anyway, that doesn't matter. What matters is finding Amber's killer and finding out how our John Doe fits in, or if he indeed does fit into all this."

"Sure." McCall nodded and sipped her coffee. "So, what's the plan?" she asked.

"We break Bob. We find out what he knows."

McCall looked sceptical of Steel's idea. She wanted to watch the bastard squirm, and she wanted to be the one who made him talk.

Chapter 12

Owen Levitt was his real name. He told everyone it was Bob Gablonski just for the image. He was a large no-neck man with a bald head, and even shorter temper and a large bruise on his head above his right eye.

"Bob Gablonski, or should I call you Owen Levitt?" McCall said smugly.

The large man just folded his arms and looked away.

"You have been informed of your rights and your right to counsel," McCall said calmly. Bob just sat there and grunted whilst avoiding eye contact.

"I'll take that as a yes," McCall said, laying down an open yellow legal pad and placing a thick brown file next to that. She took a pen from her jacket and clicked the end revealing the ballpoint and then placed it gently onto the pad.

"So, when did you see Tara Burke last, Bob?" McCall asked, her voice calm but authoritative.

Bob smiled and shook his head.

"It wasn't me," he growled, a smug grin crossing his large face.

McCall shot him a puzzled look. "What wasn't you? It wasn't you who killed or kidnapped her?"

Bob suddenly looked panicked at McCall's accusation. "What do you mean, lady? Tara's dead? What do ya mean she's dead? Nah, nah, nah. You ain't pinnin' that on me!"

The detective saw genuine concern in the big man's eyes. "So, what do you think you're in here for? Apart from being an idiot and swinging at a cop of course," McCall asked as she leaned back. Behind the two-way mirror, Captain Brant stood with Steel, both taking in the show. Brant looked at Steel, who just shrugged at the statement McCall had just made.

"He took a swing at you?" asked Brant. Steel just shrugged and smiled broadly. Brant shook his head, thinking what a bad move that had been on the part of their interviewee.

"Here's the thing, Bob," Sam growled, whilst leaning on the edge of the table. "I am going to get a warrant, and we are going to search your home and your diner. And if I find anything to say you had anything to do with her disappearance, you're going down." McCall's tone left him cold. "So, what happened that night?" she continued. "Did you two get into a situation and she bolted?" McCall went on, bluffing as a ploy to make him talk.

"No, it wasn't like that. Some guy came in lookin for Tara. Didn't think much of it, just thought it was some guy hopin' she did 'after-work' stuff. They met up and took a seat in one of the corners, out of the way, like. Anyway, they start gettin' into it, so I kicked the guy out. Tara left soon after, 'cause her shift had ended," Bob was talking fast, leaving little time for a breath, he was nervous, and had the right to be, he was looking at a murder charge. McCall sat back, feeling a sense of fulfilment because she had brought this bully down.

"Do you think you can talk to a sketch artist to get a description?" she said, with an arm hanging over the backrest of her chair. Bob shrugged and nodded, hoping his cooperation would get him off the charges, unaware that McCall wasn't feeling that generous.

"So, what did he look like—this mystery, man?" she asked.

"Gee, I don't know. Average height, ginger hair, blue eyes. Kinda plain lookin'," As Bob described the man, Steel and McCall both had the same thought.

Bob had just possibly described their John Doe.

* * *

Tony and Tooms had tracked down Tony Russo, Amber's previous boyfriend, and sat him down in one of the interrogation rooms with a cup of coffee. The two detectives watched him through the two-way mirror. He was around five foot seven and weighed about two hundred pounds. He was broad-shouldered, and the muscles of his ripped body showed under his tight T-shirt. He was a security guard in the local mall but acted as if he was a top detective.

Russo's brown hair was styled and held together with enough grooming products to be a fire hazard. His pearly white teeth glinted in the bright lights of the small room as he checked himself out in the large mirror.

Tony shook his head. "What the hell did Amber see in this dork?" he said as he watched this player start to pat his hair in case one strand had fallen out of place.

"Beats me, man. Sure, as hell wasn't for his personality," Tooms noted as he bit into a snack bar, he had gotten from the vending machine. "I think I know who ended it though," Tooms added after swallowing down his snack.

Around half an hour had passed before they went into the small grey-walled room. They had checked up on their vain and preening friend, ensuring they knew everything about him before they went at him with questions. Nothing kicks off an interrogation more than a big fat surprise.

They found Tony Russo asleep on the table, his jacket nestled comfortably between his head and the cold metal surface. The two detectives looked at each other in a mix of surprise and anger, because to their way of thinking, this was an interrogation room, not a hostel. Tooms purposely slammed the door, causing Russo to stir and wipe the drool from the corner of his mouth.

"Get your ass off of my integration table!" Tooms growled like a hungry bear with a taste for dirtbags. Russo slid off the table and onto the chair. He yawned as he picked up the empty coffee cup and stared at its brown-stained bottom. He looked up at Tony and raised the cup.

"Don't even think about askin' for another one," Tony said angrily, beating Russo to the mark. Russo shrugged and placed the cup back onto the table.

"Mr Russo, do you know this woman?" Tony asked, sliding a photograph of Amber over to their sleepy interviewee. It was an old photograph that he had found in an album Amber had stored in one of her boxes. Russo looked at the picture but never picked it up. He sat back and smiled smugly.

"Yeah, I knew her, we went out for a while, but she broke it off." Tony could sense the bitterness in his voice, and that suited Tony just fine. Anger was always a good motive for murder.

"When was the last time you saw her?" Tooms asked. Russo shrugged and tilted his head as if this whole thing was a waste of his time.

"I am sorry, are we boring you?" Tony growled at Russo, feeling the blood boil in his veins. Russo shrugged again and sucked his teeth as if he was removing the remnants of his breakfast. Tooms slammed a fist onto the table and leant forward. "Look, Russo, this woman is dead and so far, you're the only suspect. So, unless you give us something, I am gonna lock your ass up. Have I got your attention now?" Tooms's eyes became wide with anger. The other man suddenly sat up in his chair, and a look of utter panic contorted his face.

"Wow now hang on, fellas! Look, I haven't seen her in, like, months. She found out I was trying to hook up with her sister, and she got a little mad and threw me to the kerb." Russo held his hands up as if to show that was all he had to say.

Tony shot Tooms a confused look.

"So, you were trying to hook up with Brooke?" Tony asked, drawing a big question mark on the yellow legal pad. Russo shook his head and gave the two cops a disgusted look. "Brooke? Nah, she's way too old for me. No, I am talkin' about Sharney, Amber's twin." Russo had a look of surprise on his face as though he was astonished that he was the only one who knew of the existence of this twin.

Problem being, of course, that he was the only one. Tooms leant forward with interest.

"Her twin? Are you sure?" Tooms looked into Russo's eyes to try to detect any hint of a lie.

"Amber had just got this job at some shipping place, International Removals or something. Anyway, she was always working and had no time for me. So, one day I am just walking down Park Avenue when I bump into Amber, leastways that's who I thought she was. She explained that she was Amber's sister and that she worked in Philadelphia."

Tony stood and picked up Russo's coffee cup, thinking that he had earned a refill. He opened the door and passed the stained cup to a uniform and asked him to fetch another.

"Go on," Tony said, closing the door and heading back to his seat.

"Apparently she had worked in one of the hotels there and was just back to get her stuff before heading off." Russo's eyes darted between the two detectives, hoping this was pulling him out of the grave he had dug earlier.

"So, you tried hitting on Sharney?" Tooms asked, already having guessed the answer. "So, what happened? Did she call Amber or something?"

"Yeah, the bitch called her sister, totally sold me out, Next day Amber kicks me to the kerb."

Tony detected the merest hint of remorse on Russo's face as he talked.

"Strange girl!" Tooms added sarcastically.

Russo's face lit up as if he had finally found someone who understood his pain.

"Yeah, right, she sure was," Russo said, his hands held out in surprise.

"So, what happened then? Let me guess. You got pissed and tracked her down. Thought you would make her pay, did you?" Tony's voice was gravelly from lack of moisture. His anger with this guy had made his mouth dry.

"Nah, sorry, cop. You got the wrong guy," Russo sat back and waved his palms at them as though to say "wow, stop." When did this all go down?" Russo asked, almost hoping he wasn't home alone at that point.

"Tuesday night, around ten," Tony answered, hoping that this scumbag had no alibi. He felt his soul die a little as Russo thought for a moment before a big smile came over his face.

"I was with some buddies. We had gone to Eddie's Bar on 3rd. We were there until closing time." Russo sat back, exuding an air of relieved smugness.

"OK, Mr Russo, we will need to know the names of your buddies, just so we can check your story out," Tooms said, almost as disappointed as Tony was.

As Russo got up to head out, Tooms saw the look on Tony's face. It was a lost, faraway expression.

"You OK, man?" Tooms asked his partner. Tony shook his head, then looked up at his friend.

"Tooms, if our victim wasn't Amber, then, where is she? And is she still alive, or are we going to be looking at a second body?"

Tooms felt a chill at his friend's words.

Because he was right.

Chapter 13

McCall had put a request into Traffic for any CCTV footage around the diner. The description they had gotten from Bob made no sense. If their John Doe had something to do with the murder of Amber, why was he walking around half a day later covered in blood?

This whole case was making no sense. She stared up at the murder board to see if there was something that they had overlooked. From the corner of her eye, something moved, causing her to look over. Steel approached with two steaming coffee cups. She smiled as he placed them down on the comical coasters that sat happily on her desk. Steel pausing slightly before covering the coasters, the yellow 'smilies' all had different expressions. There was a stack of them next to a photograph of her with her mom and dad. It appeared to be an old photo, judging by the age she seemed to be. The British detective stared at the photograph for a couple of seconds. McCall looked up at him with a curious stare.

"Anything wrong?" she asked.

He turned and smiled before sitting in the chair next to her desk. "You must miss your father a lot." Steel's voice had a soothing tone to it. She looked at the small eight-by-five photo and nodded.

"It's been eleven years this September. Eleven years since we got the call about his shooting in that hotel." A small tear had gathered in the corner of her eye, but she forced back the emotion. *Time enough to cry later*, she thought. McCall picked up her coffee mug and blew on the pale-coloured coffee before taking a sip.

Steel looked across towards the murder board. The collage of photographs and scribbles were all held together in their own little headings: SUSPECTS, VICTIM, PERSONS OF INTEREST.

At the bottom, a think black line denoted the timeline. A thick red bar reached from seven in the evening until ten o'clock in the evening, when she was found. McCall was aware that the ME had put 'Time of Death' at around eight to nine o'clock that night, but McCall liked to be more thorough and accurate than that generality.

The only picture in the 'Suspect' column was that of Tony Russo, and the likelihood of his guilt was looking shaky. Amber had been liked by everyone as far as they could see. But then who would stick their hand up and say otherwise during a murder investigation?

The door to the interrogation room opened, and Tooms and an angry Tony stepped out. Steel looked over to see the smug Russo sitting comfortably on his chair, waiting to be told to go home.

"So, what did you get from laughing boy?" McCall asked, not feeling hopeful when she saw Tony's burning eyes.

"He has an alibi which we are about to check out," Tooms told her. "But one thing he did say was that Amber had a twin." The Tooms sat at the desk next to McCall's.

Sam's jaw dropped open in surprise.

"So, what you are saying," Steel said grimly, "is that we have no clear idea who is in the morgue?" His expression was extremely serious.

McCall shot him a look of disappointment. "John Steel, did anyone ever tell you that you're a very 'glass half empty' kind of person? I was going for the hope of Amber being still alive, but of course, you're right," she said, keeping the scowl.

"What else did you get from him?" McCall asked, this time looking over to Tony.

"Not much," Tony spoke with a hint of disappointment in his voice. "He said he hadn't seen her for months. Apparently, he hit on the sister, and Amber found out and told him to hit the bricks. I will contact Brooke and see what she can tell me. Hopefully, she has an address for this sister."

McCall nodded at Tony in agreement.

"And what did you guys get from the meathead?" Tooms asked, hoping they had gotten more than they had.

"Well it appears that Mr Handy saw our runaway with a man a couple of days ago," McCall said with a hopeful tone in her voice.

"Did you get a description?" Tony asked with a newfound vigour.

Steel smiled and nodded.

"Sam has gotten Traffic to send footage from around the time, but from what Bob told us we may have a match." Steel pointed to the board with his thumb.

Tooms and Tony looked up at the general direction towards the 'Persons of Interest' section. They looked at each other, then in unison spoke loudly: "John Doe?"

Tooms shook his head in confusion. "So, your suspect is the guy with no memory?"

Steel nodded in answer to Tooms's question. "Convenient, don't you think?" Steel said with an almost evil grin, like the cat that got the cream.

"Well I hope it is him, I want to go home this weekend to see my mom," McCall said, looking at the photograph once more. "In the meantime, CSU have his clothes and are testing the blood, once they finish the backlog that is." She stuck out her bottom lip in disappointment at the situation. She looked up at the board for a second then stood up and grabbed her jacket.

"Where you are going?" asked Tooms, suspicious at the sudden movement.

"Off to the crime scene, see if we missed something." McCall watched Steel get up from his chair to get ready to go with her.

"Let me know when the footage comes in and if I don't see you guys, don't stay too long, and I'll see you in the morning," she ordered as she headed for the elevator with Steel.

"Come on, let's find that sister," Tooms said, patting Tony on the shoulder.

* * *

As McCall turned onto 48th Street, she groaned at the sight of the mass of parked cars. Then as she drove up to the crime scene, McCall saw the red-and-white hazard tape and orange cones as city officials marked their spots for making repairs to the pavement.

The sun was high, considering it was late in the afternoon, but the heat had burnt off hours before, leaving a cool breeze. McCall found a parking spot near to the junction. The narrow street was made more difficult to negotiate because of badly parked, or as McCall called them, 'abandoned' vehicles.

The two detectives walked the forty or so feet to the building. Steel welcomed the walk, it gave him time to think, or as he called it "walk the walk." A fresh gust carried Sam's hair upwards, and she closed her eyes for a second to enjoy the 'natural air conditioner'. Steel smiled at the sight and shook his head. If anyone had witnessed, her expression, they would have thought she was doing an advert for hair products or perfume.

"Come on, supermodel." He laughed.

She shot him a friendly scowl and pretended to walk the catwalk to the apartment building. McCall stopped suddenly. She looked over at the taped off area to see the workmen wolf-whistling and applauding her performance. She bowed and headed inside, leaving Steel to look to the heavens and shake his head in disbelief.

McCall had used Amber's keys to gain entry. The key chain was full of different sets of keys plus a small teddy bear. McCall had wondered if Tony had given her the bear as a present: perhaps a reminder from a date at a fair or just a simple gesture of kindness. The tiny panda looked worn, as though it had seen a lot of use or alternatively had been there awhile.

They ventured up to the fourth floor and stood in front of the yellow police tape. Using another of her keys, they opened the door and entered.

The afternoon sun acted as a spotlight. The sitting room was almost aglow with the natural illumination. CSU had taken what they needed, including the rug where Amber had bled out. On first impression, no one would have even consider there had been a murder in the room. Everything seemed as normal as could be. All perfectly straightforward, apart from the faint bloodstains on the carpet. The rug had soaked most of it up, but not all of it.

Steel stood in the middle of the room and stared into nothing. His body was solid, like one of the statues at the Metropolitan Museum. McCall watched him for a moment, a look of concern on her face. She knew what he was doing, for she had seen him do it before. He was re-enacting the movements of that night in his head. She also did the same when she got to a crime scene but seeing the way that he did it somehow scared her, and it was almost as if he could actually see the events taking place.

She had a good imagination for these things, but the imagination needed for this kind of work could only be gotten from experience. She dreaded to know what experiences John Steel had gone through in order to conjure up such nightmares. Steel moved his head slowly as if he was watching someone come through the door. He moved back as if to give them space to move uninterrupted.

John suddenly stopped and looked around the room. He had a confused look on his face as though something was wrong. Suddenly he dropped to the floor and searched the carpet, his hands gliding across the short fibres.

"Lost your contacts?" McCall asked jokingly. However, her smile faded as she realised, he was either ignoring her, or he had simply blocked out her existence. Steel stopped at one point before moving across the coarse brown flooring. His fingers swept another area. Then he stopped and stood up before turning towards her.

"Did CSU move anything?" he asked, his tone almost sounding excited.

McCall opened the report file and scanned the pages. She shook her head. "They only moved things in order to retrieve the rug, but they put everything back as they found it. Why?" she asked curiously.

"The couch and these tables have been moved." He pointed out the large blue fabric couch and the two nesting tables on either side. McCall knelt to find the set of indentations from where the couch's round feet had stood. Their shape and depth were consistent with how long the piece have furniture must have stood in that spot. By their look, McCall estimated it to be years—a lot of years.

"Someone moved the furniture!" she said, almost as puzzled as when she had watched him pat down the carpet. "Why the hell did they move the furniture?"

Steel looked around the room, then shook his head.

"I don't know. But one thing is clear," he said, helping McCall to her feet. "They were looking for something."

She shot him a confused look as she straightened her clothes out.

"They?" Her tone was as if she was unconvinced. She wondered how he had come to such a 'so exact' assumption that there had been more than one person present. Sure, they were waiting for toxicology to come back, but she was sure that Amber had been knocked out by something. Chloroform was a possibility.

"How do you know there was more than one person, just from seeing that the furniture has been moved?" She sounded unconvinced.

John raised a hand and pointed to the furnishings. "There are no drag marks for one thing. If you move something that has been there a long while it's going to leave a trail. Then there is Amber herself. How did 'they' or 'he' subdue her?" Steel could see the glint in her eye, as if to say that she had a theory, possibly a good one.

"Before you say chloroform, just ask yourself how they would have got it to her," he went on. "She has a peephole in the door. If the killer was a stranger, she wouldn't have opened it, which means she knew him or them. And if so, why would they do all this?"

McCall folded her arms in disappointment at his deduction. He had been right, and she hated to admit that.

"OK, Sherlock, what's your theory?" she said, waiting for some elaborate deduction, some grand scheme revealed.

But Steel just shook his head and shrugged. "Elementary," Steel started mockingly, causing McCall to scowl at him, "You see I don't think they were after Amber. I think they were after the roommate."

His statement shocked Sam McCall.

"In fact, I don't think Amber had just moved in. I don't think whoever did this expected her to be here. She shouldn't have been here." Steel pointed to the mountain of removal company packing boxes that were just visible through the open spare bedroom door.

"So, she surprised someone in here and paid for it with her life?" McCall suggested, looking around the room for more clues, but finding nothing but more questions.

"Yes, but she surprised them when they were doing what? They weren't searching for something; the place is spotless. They could have thought Amber was the roommate, but then if so, why did they torture her?" Steel shook his head. Something didn't feel right. In fact, something felt very familiar, and that scared him.

"Perhaps whoever did this didn't know the face of the person they had to kill, only their address? They figured that there was only one person living here, so poor Amber just happened to be in the wrong place at the wrong time." McCall voiced her theory as she was opening one of the removal company packing boxes and sorting through its contents.

"Which would lead us to another question," Steel continued. "Who sent them and why?" Steel caught a brutal look from his partner. "Hey, sorry, but it was your theory," he concluded, before turning and heading for Tara's room. Of all the rooms, this was the only one with photographs, making it seem almost as if she didn't want to share them with anyone else.

He stopped as he noticed a blank space where a photograph had obviously once hung. The lonely nail looked out of place, but the paint had not faded, meaning it hadn't been there long. The remaining photos were of Tara in the park, in which she seemed very happy. This suggested that she had been with someone special to her.

Sam McCall noticed that Steel was standing there at the wall, studying it as she closed the box.

"Is something wrong?" she asked, almost hoping that he might give her a clue.

"There is a photograph missing. And it looks like these were taken recently too." He said, his thoughts lost in theories.

"Maybe the killer took it?" she suggested.

He nodded and looked closer at the area in the picture, hoping to get an idea of where it had been taken.

"Maybe the killer was in the missing picture?" he said, taking one of the pictures down and showing it to McCall, who was making her way over to him.

The glossy six-by-four was of the fountain at Bethesda Terrace. McCall smiled. She knew that place had cameras all over it.

"If we can find out when it was taken, we might get lucky," he said, thinking the same thing as McCall. She opened the file again and looked at the crime scene photographs, observing the way that the body was positioned, the brutality. However, there did appear to be care taken in the undertaking of the deed. This wasn't just a brutal killing: this was a torture. She looked at the photographs again. A shiver ran down her spine, one of such intensity that she nearly buckled. McCall looked over at Steel, who just stood there with a solemn look on his face.

"You think he's back, don't you?" she said, the dreaded words almost creeping out of her mouth. He nodded slowly. She felt an anger towards him. She wanted to scream at him.

"How long have you known that it might be him?" she demanded.

He shook his head slowly. "I suspected more than anything really. It was ever since I first saw the crime scene photographs. I didn't want to say anything until I was sure." His words were soft and calming, but she maintained her pained expression.

"And are you?" she said, almost hoping he wasn't.

Steel shook his head again. "No, I am not."

He could see that this was not what she wanted to hear. He felt her sudden fear of that monster's return. The man who had unknowingly brought them together.

The man most knew only as … Mr Williams.

Chapter 14

Tara Burke awoke to the sound of a police siren wailing. She jumped up, confused at first at seeing her strange surroundings. Tara sat up, holding her beating chest through the T-shirt. As her breathing shallowed, her memory began to return. The frightened young woman reached for the bottled water and cracked the cap. Beads of sweat cascaded down her back, and her forehead looked as though she had just made good time running the hundred.

She heard a noise from the kitchen and knew that Kim was up and getting ready for work. Tara stood up and carried the water with her to the door.

She found Kim's ginger cat prowling the worktop for leftovers. It was seven in the evening, and Tara knew that her friend was heading off for the night shift at the diner. Tara sat on one of the tall stools at the counter to the kitchenette—not quite a breakfast bar, but it made up for a dining table. She smiled at the post-it that was stuck to a large mug with a smiley on it. *Fresh coffee in the machine, frozen lasagne in the freezer. don't leave the apartment, don't open the door to anyone.*

Tara stood up and walked round to the large coffee machine. She switched it on and waited for the sound and the aroma. The ginger tomcat came up and purred loudly as Tara picked him up.

"Don't worry, Mr Jinx, we're not going anywhere," she crooned. The cat let out a quick meow as if to answer. Tara smiled and placed him back down, then poured him some milk from the fridge into a small saucer. The coffee machine would take a while, so she decided to shower.

Tara stripped off her sweat-drenched clothes and wrapped the large red towel around her slimly built body. In the bathroom, she pulled the shower curtain, so it covered the cast-iron bath, then reached in and turned on the water. The bathroom was a comfortable size for one person. It had plenty of wooden shelving that housed folded towels and cosmetics. The walls were beige with white tiles in a half-and-half match, the pattern repeated on the floor, which had matching coverings.

She looked at herself in the mirror. She had that girl-next-door prettiness about her. Her pale skin showed disturbing echoes of her past. Thick, angry scars covered her back, evidence of her mother's abuse: a reminder of how worthless she was to her. But she had survived. She had outlived her drunken abuser.

Tara stepped under the hard torrent of water which came out of the large shower head like a bad storm shower. Tara leant against the cool tiles and just let the water run over her. She felt the hard-warm spray beat down on her skin, and it felt good. So good that she didn't want to leave.

The attractive woman had dried herself off and put on her blue pyjamas. She figured she wasn't going anywhere, so why change? She had poured herself a coffee and put the suggested meal into the microwave. Dinner in five minutes, he'd said, but she made it ten, just to be sure.

She picked up her phone and checked it for any new messages. She tossed it down onto the small coffee table which sat in front of the blue couch. She hadn't heard from him for a long time, too long in fact.

Tara didn't just think she was in trouble. She knew she was.

And they were coming.

* * *

Mr Williams sat in a large office that looked as if it had fallen out of the 1800s. Oak and brass covered the walls and furnishings. Even the computer's monitor had been dressed up to fit in with the antiquated surroundings. The oak panelling with brass touches and the stand looked as if it had once belonged to ancient lamp.

A large fireplace with a dark marble surround was to the left of a large ebony desk. Carvings of snakes and beasts were cut into the desk's heavy wooden panelling. The large windows to the right were in the original Elizabethan style.

On the wall opposite the desk was a large painting of a battle scene from the Vlad, the Impaler campaign of the 1400s. But the ink was false, and the image itself was in fact a high definition screensaver. The immense eighty-inch monitor blended into the room seamlessly. Suits of armour and swords guarded the corners and the walls.

Williams held a brandy bowl of cut crystal in one hand while he sat back in a thick padded, red leather chesterfield office chair. His feet rested upon the antique desk as he listened to a loud rendition of *Vesti La Giubba*—otherwise known as 'The tears of a clown'. His eyes closed as he held the glass under his nose. He inhaled the scent of the eighty-year-old brandy whilst the music grew to a crescendo. The psychopathic torturer waved his free hand as if he were conducting the masterpiece. He was in heaven: a good brandy, loud opera and his plans were going well.

Suddenly his desk phone began to ring. He opened one eye and stared at the wood and brass 1904 replica. He didn't want to answer it, for he knew it would be trouble. If someone was ringing him direct, it was a problem, and he didn't like problems. He reached over whilst trying not to lose his comfortable position. He kept the brandy glass held by the hand with an outstretched arm, using the other to reach for the receiver.

"This better be good. I am in the mood for giving someone a spinal tap," he growled as he used a remote to turn off the music, after finally putting his glass down. He listened to the voice at the other end. His eyes rolled with disappointment as the voice gave the report.

"So, did you find this Douglas fellow? OK, so – that's a no then. I take it you found the woman?" As Williams listened a wide grin crossed his face, his pearly white teeth on display, looking like a shark spying his next meal.

"When you get hold of her bring her to me UNSPOILT, do you understand?" he instructed. The voice on the other end confirmed the order and quickly hung up. Williams stretched over and replaced the handset onto the brass cradle. He was suddenly in a good mood again. Sure, two pieces of good news would have been great, but he could settle for just one.

He sat back in the chair and picked up the glass. He raised it to the large fake picture to salute it. He took a mouthful of the brandy to celebrate. Then he sat for a moment whilst a wicked thought crossed his mind. Williams reached for the small intercom next to the phone and pressed the button.

"Crystal," he said whilst swilling the brown liquid around in his glass. He stopped and looked at the intercom, on which he was trying to reach his secretary.

There was no response.

"Oh, Crystal," he said a bit louder this time.

But there was no answer.

"CRYSTAL!" he yelled down the intercom, almost losing his footing and the brandy from the glass.

"Yes … Yes, sir," a squeaky mouse-like voice came at last. Williams rolled his eyes again, knowing full well what was probably happening in the room next door.

"Be a dear and arrange for the operating room to be set up, will you?" he said, then took another hit from the glass.

"Yes, Mr Williams," she answered, her voice sounding breathless.

"Thank you, Crystal. Oh, and tell the young man with you that if he makes you late answering my call again, I will make lampshades from his skin, and he will watch me do it."

Williams smiled at the thought of the young guard suddenly soiling himself at the thought. The torturer reached over and turned the music back on, then returned the glass to its former position under his nose.

Chapter 15

Tooms and Tony decided to check out the hotels on West 59th Central Park South. They had been told about a hotel with a park view, of which there were many. They had tossed a coin as to where to start north or south. Heads had won the toss, so south it was.

As they entered the lobby of one of the hotels, they were met by a tall man with a broad smile wearing a blazer with the hotel's name on it. He was thin, with a pencil moustache, his black hair brushed back as though it should reveal a large forehead, but in the event all there was to see was a receding hairline. His whole demeanour was that of a snake—even his face had a serpent's aspect to it.

"Hello, gentlemen, may I help you?" asked the snake man, who was obviously the floor manager. Tony and Tooms showed him their shields and his smile quickly disappeared.

"I am Detective Tooms, and this is Detective Marinelli," Tooms said, tucking his ID back into his jacket pocket. He pulled out a photograph of Amber, and it was obvious that the man immediately recognised her.

"Has something happened to Sharney?" the man asked, almost panicking. Tooms and Tony looked at one another in surprise.

"Her sister was found murdered on the night before last. Sir, is there somewhere private we can speak?" Tony asked as he looked around the lobby at the other guests.

"Yes, of course. Please follow me." The man nodded and led them to a back office near the reception.

"Sorry, but who are you, sir?" Tony asked, taking out his notebook to jot down any details. The man was sitting on the edge of a small desk in a decent-sized office.

"I am Mr Tate, and I am the daytime floor manager," Tate said, still looking badly shocked.

"We are trying to track her down," Tooms said, with a stern look on his face. "To let her know about her sister."

"I didn't know she had a sister. I'm sorry," Tate said, sincerely.

"How well did you know Sharney?" Tooms asked, letting Tony take notes. Tate shrugged and smiled as he considered the question.

"She used to work here, part-time of course. She had a kid, so she could only work half days. But unfortunately, she had to go." Tony looked up from his notebook, his pen poised over the paper. He was shocked to hear about Sharney having a child.

"So why did she leave?" Tooms asked, folding his massive arms.

"She had a new job in Phoenix, or was its Philadelphia? I can't remember, sorry," Tate said and shot them a quick embarrassed smile.

"How long did she work here?" Tony asked, curious about the manager's strange demeanour.

"Oh, around six months, I believe. She was a cleaner here." Tooms noticed Tate's hand move a photograph in a stand-up frame, as though he was trying to hide the picture from them or from himself. Tate was obviously hiding something: he clearly had a little skeleton in the closet.

"Did you know her well?" Tooms asked, suddenly getting a bad vibe from the floor manager.

"No, not really. It was a manager/employee relationship. I told her what to do, and she did it." Tate's smile almost made Tony want to push his head in the fish tank that stood on the far wall.

"So, do you have this kind of formal relationship with all of your staff, sir?" Tooms asked, almost seeming to be polite. Tate's mind seemed to wander off, and his grin returned as if he was thinking about past employees.

"Yes, we have good working relationships here at the hotel." Tate's eyes began to sparkle. Tooms smiled before he spoke. "Thank you, sir, for your time. Would it be OK to speak to any of your staff?" He watched the smile disappear from Tate's face, to be replaced by a wary, nervous expression.

"Uhm, what for?" Tate's voice began to tremble, and he started to fidget with his hands.

"Because they may know Sharney better than you do," Tooms said, trying his best to sound reassuring. "After all, they were all work colleagues. It may give us a better picture, that's all." Tate smiled again; this time, it appeared to be more relieved, more like a friendly gesture. The two detectives turned to leave the office. Tate got up from his spot on the desk to look outside to make sure they were heading out of the building. Tooms said nothing as he opened the office door and stepped back into the lobby. As he did so, the guests all seemed to either hide their faces in magazines or suddenly start gazing out of the window. Tony smiled at their poor attempts to look casual. He wondered what stories would arise from this investigation. The pair headed for the door and stepped out into the street. It was three o'clock, and they were beat. It had been a long day. They both knew they wouldn't get any information from the other staff members. In fact, Tooms was certain that they wouldn't even remember Sharney. They climbed back into their car and headed back. But first Tooms needed to make a stop-off. He felt another chilli dog coming on.

* * *

McCall stood in front of her murder board with a marker in her hand. Tooms had called her with news of the sister. How people remembered her and that she had supposedly moved to Philadelphia or somewhere with else with a 'P' in its name.

Sam had contacted Philly P.D. to see if they could track her down. She didn't seem hopeful, though. Her gut told her that Sharney had never left New York. The truth was they didn't know a hell of a lot about either of the sisters. Financials had come back, and nothing had popped. Amber's records were clean. From what McCall could gather, she was well-liked and hard working.

Feeling frustrated, McCall sat on the edge of her desk and just looked at the board, hoping something would pop out at her. This was one of those cases she hated. The sort of homicide that would be investigated for a short while and then become a 'cold' case. She looked up at the clock. Tooms and Tony would be back soon, but from what Tooms had said on the phone, they had very little information to share.

McCall looked up at the picture of Tara Burke. She was now missing; the chances were that she was scared and running. A sane person would go to the cops for help. But McCall had seen the body, and she could understand how scared that might make anyone. *Run before they come back for you*, would have certainly been the first idea on Tara's mind. This was a puzzle with far too many pieces that were missing or lodged in the wrong spaces.

Captain Brant walked out of his office and just stood staring at McCall. He could almost feel her brain sorting through the evidence on the board. He could also feel the tension emanating from her.

"Trouble with the case?" he asked. She didn't turn around, just nodded slowly.

"There is something wrong here, Captain, and I don't know what it is." Her words sounded bitter, as though she was angry with herself for not having been smart enough to see the truth.

"What have Tooms and Tony found?" Brant asked, hoping to break her concentration.

"Not much. Apparently, there was a sister, but she moved away, possibly to Philly," she said, then shrugged as if to say she didn't believe it either.

"*Possibly?*" Brant said, almost surprised at the lack of uncertainty.

"Her old boss apparently didn't know her that well, but the boys think otherwise." McCall frowned at the thought of Tooms's description of the manager: *a snake-like weasel*, or something along those lines.

"They should be back soon," she announced, finally turning to face Brant.

"Any news on our missing waitress?" Brant asked, taking a seat in the chair of the desk next to hers. McCall shook her head as she bit her bottom lip.

"No, she's in the wind. Not that I blame her. Seeing that body made me gag, so God knows how she felt," McCall said, remembering her first case. It had been a mugging gone wrong. The perp had gone for the woman's purse. She must have struggled to give it up. She was shot point-blank with a .38. McCall had been a rookie back then, and she had been first on the scene. Someone had reported shots in the park. On seeing the scene, McCall had been frozen to the spot. Her training officer wasn't far behind, but it was unfortunate that he hadn't arrived first.

A .38 round at close range makes a mess. McCall had never realised how much blood could come out of a body so quickly, but it was a headshot. The back of the woman's head had disappeared. Fragments of skull and brain matter were spread over a large area, but it wasn't until she had hit the floor that the red plasma began to pool.

The ringing phone McCall brought her back to reality. Brant looked over to his office phone as the noise of the electronic ring bellowed out of the open doorway. McCall's boss got up and walked to his desk. He didn't run. He figured that if it was important, they would wait, after all, they wanted him. After a moment of nodding and hand gestures, Brant came back to where McCall was sitting.

"That was Traffic. They said there was no footage of that alleyway. So, they are going to try and find the cab to find out where else it has been," Brant said, not feeling hopeful they could actually find that particular needle in such a big haystack. He looked around for a second, a confused look on his face.

"So, where's Steel?" Brant asked, suddenly noticing the British detective's absence.

"He said he had some stuff to take care of. Hopefully, he'll bring me back a coffee and a bear claw," McCall joked.

Brant smiled and nodded. "Well, keep me posted, Detective," Brant concluded, almost tempted to wait for the phone to ring again.

"Will do, sir. Will do," McCall answered as she watched the large bear of a man head back into his office. It was almost three p.m. according to the clock above the elevator doors. Three o'clock and they had nothing. Forensics had a backlog, so the clothes that John Doe was wearing would have to wait their turn, according to their importance. *More time wasted*, she thought as she read the email from CSU.

She looked across at Tony's empty desk and wondered what he must be feeling. She had lost her dad when she was younger, but it would be nothing to compare to what he was likely to be going through.

For now, it was a waiting game to see what else might come up.

Chapter 16

A short man in a black suit and dark sunglasses sat on a bench in Washington Square Park. He was heavily built, as a result of spending too much time behind a desk and eating too many business dinners. Thinning black hair covered a large head, and a handmade suit from Chinatown covered his large frame. Even his shoes were a classy knock-off. But he didn't care. The fact they lasted longer than the original would have done, made them that much sweeter to wear.

The sun was high, and a slight breeze made the surrounding trees sway in unison as if they were dancing to the same tune. The large white marble arch was stained from years of weathering, which made it more magnificent. The park itself was a circular meeting place of grey concrete slabs that encircled a large fountain. Grass and wooded areas added to the pleasant setting around the two-hundred-year-old memorial.

Tourists walked around with their tablets and cell phones, taking shots to send to the web. The man shook his head as he bit into the sandwich, he had brought with him.

"Doesn't anyone own a camera anymore?" he asked himself. There was a squawk in his earpiece as someone gave a situation report, otherwise known as a 'sitrep'.

"We'll give him another five minutes. If he's a no-show we'll call it a day," he said, careful not to give away the presence of the microphone in his sleeve. He wiped his large brown head with a cotton handkerchief he had taken from his jacket pocket. He was nervous. Who wouldn't be?

The park was surrounded by three teams. They weren't here to arrest anyone. They were there for his protection.

The man looked at his watch. It was ten past three. "OK, people, he's a no-show. Shut it down." The disappointed man shook his head and gave the signal to collapse the operation.

He stood up and headed towards his car, which was parked on Thompson Street. The teams had broken off and disappeared into the mass of people. The man pushed through the crowds, his eyes scanning every face just in case. He was feeling the temperature, not from the sun, but from his own body heat, as his heart pumped the blood around his system like fuel for a rocket.

Then he saw the blacked-out GMC Yukon parked in a shady spot. The street was narrow, meaning there was not so much traffic. The man breathed a sigh of relief as he climbed into the back of the oversized SUV.

"OK, Tom, let's go," the man said, buckling up his seat belt and not really paying attention to the driver.

"Tom let's go!" he repeated, but the driver stayed still.

"What, you fell asleep on me again?" he said, tapping the driver on the shoulder. Tom's head fell to the side, with only the seat belt to stop it falling further. Suddenly the rear passenger door swung open, and Steel slid onto the seat next to the man. In one swift motion, Steel grabbed the gun from his holster and tossed it into the car's footwell. The bemused man was shocked by the speed of it all and sat with his back firmly against the car's door.

"Steel," he said in shock with his hand's half-raised.

"Hello there, Agent Hardy," Steel said with a broad smile on his face. "I've been waiting for you."

* * *

Agent Frank Hardy had finally calmed down after Steel's sudden and theatrical entrance. Hardy sat for a second whilst he gathered his breath. Steel handed him a bottle of water that was in the cup holder in the door. Frank Hardy snatched it from him and drank slowly. An angry look came over his face as he started to feel his heartbeat reach normality.

"We were supposed to meet outside, in public," Hardy growled.

Steel smiled and looked in the rear-view mirror. He found it amusing to watch the agents trying hard to blend into the crowd as they made their way back to their vehicles.

"Never been one for public appearances," John said, still holding on to the childish grin. Hardy reached into his inside pocket, pulled out a bottle of pills and flipped the lid off. He poured a tablet into his large hand and swallowed it down dry.

"Have you got an ulcer again?" Steel asked, sounding concerned.

Hardy shot him a look and smiled. "My ulcers have ulcers. All because of you." He laughed.

Steel nodded then shrugged. "What are friends for," Steel joked.

Hardy looked over at the unconscious body of Tom, the driver. "Did you have to slug him? I mean you could have made him go for a walk or something," Hardy grumbled, sounding worried about his driver. Steel knew enough to realise that all Hardy was bothered about was how he was getting home without a driver. The chances were the man would wake up on a plane heading for Iceland or some outstation in the middle of Alaska.

"Are you pulling me back, Frank?" Steel asked. His smile had faded, meaning that he was no longer joking.

Hardy gave him a shocked look. "God, no. Since you left the others have found that they must do some work," the agent joked. "This case you're working on now. What have you got so far?"

The British detective sat back in his seat and looked at Hardy for a moment. He said nothing, just sat and stared.

"Oh, will you cut that bullshit out?" Hardy yelled, his face going red. "You probably had the whole thing worked out before you got in the car."

"Amber was one of yours, wasn't she?" Steel asked, just to confirm his suspicions.

"Yes. She was investigating some strange things we had discovered about the shipping company. We were seeing strange shipments being taken in and out of the country. Large amount of goods was being shipped out and distributed around the globe," Frank explained.

Steel just looked at him, puzzled for a second. "You think someone was smuggling something out in large quantities? What? Drugs? Guns? Cars?" John was hoping to get some clue as to what nefarious activities Amber was investigating.

"Honestly, we don't know. All I do know is that whoever is doing it is using the shipping firm. Who knows, maybe they are in on it, or the company is paying a hell of a lot for them to look the other way?" Hardy sounded angry. Not because the bad guys were getting away with it, but because Amber had died trying to take them down.

"She was a good kid, John," Agent Hardy continued. "She didn't deserve what they did to her."

John Steel nodded slowly as if to agree with Hardy's words. But something was bothering Steel about the killing.

"Uh oh, I know that look. What's up, John?" Hardy spoke carefully as if he was unwilling to break Steel's concentration.

"The murder of Amber made no sense," he simply said after a while.

Hardy now had a puzzled look across his sweaty, pale brow. "What do mean, made no sense? The bastards tortured her, didn't they? It was just a killing, Steel. Hell, you've seen enough in your time to know that." The agent took another sip from the water.

"Yes, I've seen torture before many times, by different cultures. But this was different. This was as though they wanted to erase her existence. Her face was cut up, teeth extracted and the skin from her fingers removed. This was a *deletion* not just a torture." Steel bared his teeth as he spoke. He could feel the hatred welling up inside him for those who had done this terrible thing.

"OK, let's say you're right. Why leave the body?" Frank asked, hoping not to hear what he thought Steel may come out with.

"Maybe it was meant to be a warning to those who knew what she was doing. You know—back off." Steel looked his watch. He had nearly overstayed his welcome.

Hardy saw a look on Steel's face that he had come to know quite well. "You have an idea who may have done this, don't you?" he asked calmly, sitting back in his seat. "I was almost waiting for that, 'and the murderer is' moment."

"I … That is, *we*, think that Williams is back," Steel said, almost terrified to consider the prospect of that madman running around in the city.

"Williams?" Hardy thought for a moment. "Oh, yes, I remember. The psycho you were hunting before. He was the reason you joined the NYPD in the first place, wasn't he?" Hardy smiled at the irony of the situation.

"So, you think that the organisation is behind this?" Hardy asked.

Steel shrugged and shook his head. "In all honesty, I don't know. It could be SANTINI, but it seems too obvious to be him," Steel said, questioning his own instincts.

He wished it was the organisation, so he could take them down once and for all. Or at least hurt them badly enough to destroy them. But even that idea seemed wrong.

"So, what's your plan?" Hardy asked, hoping that his associate would suggest something simple.

"To carry on with the investigation. There's no point running blind. Just follow the evidence as we always do." Steel shrugged.

"OK, just keep me in the loop and by the way, Steel—be careful." Hardy smiled.

Steel gave a mocking look of surprise. "Why, Agent Hardy, are you concerned I may get killed or something?"

Hardy shook his head and grinned. "Chance would be a fine thing; you pain in the ass. No, I am just worried you're going to make a mess, the sort of mess insurance companies is afraid of."

Steel smiled and gave a quick joke-salute. As Steel went to get out the car the agent grabbed his arm.

"Remember, Major, you're *our guy*, not NYPD," Hardy said with a stern look on his face.

The other man just looked him until Hardy felt an uncomfortable feeling come over him. He quickly released Steel's arm without a word.

"That's funny, and I thought you had thrown me to the LONE WOLF operation." Steel smiled and got out of the car, just as a large bald agent came around the corner. Steel moved casually towards the corner of West 3rd Street. Hardy turned to see the agent approach.

"Is everything OK, sir?" his colleague asked, not noticing the unconscious state of the driver. Hardy laughed at the whole situation. "Well, son, I guess you're driving me back, my driver seems to be otherwise, let's just say, *out of order*." Hardy laughed, looking back at the junction where Steel had disappeared.

"See you around, Major," the detective said, smiling to himself as they drove away back to headquarters.

Chapter 17

Sunrays poured through the large windows of the suite of rooms that held John Doe. The luxury pad was high on the sixth floor. Steel had booked it, thinking it was safer than the usual kind of so-called 'safe house'. John Doe sat watching a rerun of an old movie on the large flat-screen television. He was sitting in luxury, but his mind was in hell. He had no idea who he was, what sort of life he had had before today. But the most disturbing thing of all was, he didn't know why he had been covered in blood, or even whose blood it had been.

So far, his only visitor had been Dr Davidson. He had been on a house call to check on John and to do some tests. The psychiatrist was still baffled by what had caused the amnesia. There was the head wound, certainly, but that didn't seem serious enough to have instigated such a harsh reaction.

Davidson had left at around three o'clock to get back to his practice. This left John Doe free to wander around like a caged animal. Sure, he was free to go, but to where, he wondered? He didn't know anyone.

The hapless man walked up to the window and looked out across the city. There were people, cars, tourists. Life. He turned and walked to the telephone and picked up the receiver. Suddenly his thumb paused over the keypad. He smiled and looked up as if to ask God what he was doing. He shook his head then placed the receiver back down.

John remembered the doc saying his problem might have been caused by a massive traumatic event. But what could have happened? He was covered in blood, so if such an event had occurred, the likelihood was that this had something to do with it.

Davidson had told him that he was sure his memory would come back in time. But *in time* was not a real definitive answer. John Doe looked across at a pile of books Steel had brought for him, just in case, he got bored. There was a mixture of sci-fi, mystery and even some Shakespeare plays. John smiled at the irony of seeing the stack of mystery novels.

"I sure don't need any more mystery in my life," he thought out loud, reflecting on things. He sat back down and flicked through the TV channels until he saw the local news. Suddenly he stopped and stared. The news station was reporting on a local murder: the murder of a woman called Amber Taylor. His jaw dropped, but he pulled himself together quickly before changing the channel back to the movie he'd been watching, his face now impassive.

John stood up and stretched. He turned and tidied up the couch's cushions before disappearing into the bathroom.

In the room next door, three men sat at desks wearing headphones and checking the monitors in front of them. The six screens showed images of the various rooms in the suite, plus the stairwell and the elevator.

Steel had put John Doe under strict surveillance.

Because Steel didn't trust John Doe. There was something about him that made the British detective nervous, and he didn't like things that made him nervous.

When he felt nervous, it normally meant trouble.

* * *

McCall walked out of the restroom. Too many coffees and hardly anything to eat had taken its toll on her. She returned to her desk and her computer, where she had been looking up anything she could find on Amber and Sharney Taylor. So far, there were only birth certificates, college information, and social security numbers that told McCall there were two of them. She turned in time to see Steel step off the elevator with a coffee and a bear claw. McCall suddenly had a strange look of mistrust as he handed her the coffee shop items.

"What?" he said abruptly, looking shocked at her lack of gratitude. "I thought you'd be hungry." He was looking hurt and somewhat confused.

"You're not bugging my desk, are you?" she asked, giving him a glare.

"Why would I do that?" He started to speak, but she just smiled and bit into the pastry.

Steel shook off her put-down and attributed her bad temper to her having low blood sugar. He looked at her monitor and saw the background check she was doing on Amber. He suddenly had that bad feeling of knowing something and not being sure whether he should share the information.

For he knew that Amber had been working undercover. But if he told anyone, that would lead to awkward questions. Questions he didn't want to answer, at least not right away.

The trouble was it was information that might help them to find her killer. If he was going to say anything, he was going to have to be discreet about it.

"So...have you had any luck in finding the sister?" Steel asked, waiting for a moment when McCall didn't have food in her mouth.

"Not yet. I don't think there was another sister. I think that Amber and Sharney are one and the same." She explained her theory with a sparkle in her eye.

Steel nodded as if he was going over her theory in his head. McCall scowled as she watched his bad acting skills.

"But then you've already thought of that, haven't you?" she growled.

It was true that he had—that was why he had met up with Hardy. He didn't want to give anything away to Hardy, not yet anyway. Steel had suspected that Amber had been with the agency. He also figured that she had taken both jobs at the hotel and the shipping company. What he didn't know was why work at the hotel? Sure, the shipping company was obviously a useful way to get information, but the hotel? There seemed no point.

Another question that bothered him was Tony's involvement, or indeed the lack of it. Was he just being used as a cover, a useful boyfriend to take her places, so she blended in with other people, or did she really care for him?

Steel watched McCall stretch off, her T-shirt clinging to her shapely form as she arched her back. He looked away, so as not to stare in admiration. McCall smiled at his almost-gallant display of restraint but knew he had seen enough before turning away. She smiled at the thought that she had put a sexy image into his head. It was almost a display of teasing on her part.

McCall knew that most men saw her as 'just a woman', so she had to work just as hard as her male colleagues to prove herself as good as they were. But she was smart and damned good at her job, and that's how she had got ahead. She had not used her looks or sexuality to get her shield, she had simply showed that she was just as good as any other cop out there, and Captain Brant had seen that.

She could have been anything in life, but she wanted to be a cop like her dad had been. Every male on her dad's side of the family had been a cop, but her mother had only produced two girls. McCall had been the tomboy of the family: as if she'd been chosen to hold up the tradition. In fact, it didn't matter to her grandfather that she happened to be a woman; what mattered to him was that the tradition of having cops in the family never died.

Steel looked up at the clock on the wall. "It's nearly five, are you going home for the weekend?" he asked McCall, sitting back in his chair. Sam McCall glanced up at the clock as if to confirm he was telling the truth.

"We've got so much to do here, and I shouldn't," she said, in an almost disappointed tone. Steel stood up and pulled the jacket from the back of her chair and held it up for her to put on.

"Don't worry. I'll cover the weekend. Besides I have a benefit, I must attend, so working here might give me an excuse not to go." He smiled.

McCall stood up and slipped her arms into the leather jacket. "Are you sure?" she said.

He scowled at her jokingly. "Go before I change my mind and I go in your place," he joked.

Sam didn't need to be told twice and bolted for the door. Brant walked out of his office and watched McCall almost skate across the floor to the waiting elevator.

"You said you'd cover for her, didn't you?" Brant said.

Steel nodded and leant back in the chair. "She needs some mother/daughter time. Time to clear her head." Steel was still watching as the door closed behind McCall.

Brant approved. "Yep, we all have to have some sort of outlet. So, tell me, Steel. What's your outlet?" Brant asked, not caring that he was invading the Englishman's privacy.

"Not this bloody engagement tonight, that's for sure." John Steel laughed to himself.

Brant placed a hand on his shoulder. "The Governor and the Mayor expect to see you there, Steel. You know? Shaking hands and smiling, taking one for the team and all that." Brant joined in with Steel's laughter.

"Yeah, well, I guess I will see you inside then, Captain," Steel said with a look of sudden distaste at the thought of all those false people he had to talk to.

"You're going to sneak in again, aren't you?" Brant asked, shaking his head. "I mean seriously, who sneaks into an event they have a ticket for?" Brant was confused.

"Simple," Steel told him. "Someone who sneaks in is the kind of person who doesn't want to world to know where he is."

Steel headed for the door.

* * *

The benefit event was a massive affair. Anyone who was anyone was there, as well as all the wannabes. Guests included actors, actresses and politicians. Of course, the District Attorney or the DA, and the Police Commissioner were hovering around, blending and rubbing shoulders with the great and the good. Outside the darkness was banished by the glare of outdoor lighting and camera flashes at the main entrance of the Waldorf Hotel. Park Avenue was full of limousines and state vehicles. News vans were parked down the street—out of view but close enough to transmit their signals. For the police it was a nightmare: security services were posted here and there, trying to blend into the crowds.

Steel stood across the street beside a prestigious looking bank and watched the chaos. He smiled to himself as he checked out the building. CCTV cameras hugged the walls, and there were tough-looking men in badly fitting tuxes at the entrances, checking purses and tickets. The main entrance was clear, but the other surrounding walls were under renovation. Scaffolding towered over everything, looking like a child's climbing frame.

To Steel, he regarded the practice of 'sneaking in', rather than entering in the usual manner, as good training as well as being a challenge. He had been trained to be a 'ghost', and lately, he hadn't had the opportunity to practise his skills. He wore an all-black tux and had rubber soles on his shoes: trying to sneak into a place while making a noise like horse's hooves didn't exactly work.

He headed for East 50th and the car parking structure. He noticed that one of the windows had been carelessly left open. He smiled as he brushed off the idea. *Too obvious. Besides you only leave the window open if you're in the room,* he thought to himself.

Outside, FedEx trucks were parked up, making deliveries for the party. Catering vans from various companies sat nose-to-nose on the side of the building, their logos bright and obvious.

Steel sneaked up to the furthest one, whilst blending in with a crowd of nosey tourists. He made his way to the truck and set off the alarm. Smiling, he blended back with the crowd then eased himself back to the parked trucks. Men with ill-fitting suits and earpieces rushed out to check out the commotion. Steel climbed up onto one of the trucks and hoped that the chaos had made the cameras zoom in on the guards' location.

On the third floor of the building, there was a flat roof. Steel clambered the structure like a monkey up a tree and made for the shadows, which the two towering parts of the building provided. There were a group of people huddled around a bucket of champagne: obvious escapees from the function down below. Billows of cigarette smoke caught the breeze. Steel smiled as he saw their escape route: an open window that led into one of the hallways. He left the group, who were having more fun there than the other guest's downstairs.

As he stepped out onto the carpet, he brushed himself off and headed for the elevator. He was in. Not quite in the way, he had wanted to enter, but he'd managed it.

The lobby area was full of wives in new dresses that probably would never be worn again, husbands in rented tuxedoes and staff holding trays with flutes of champagne. Steel headed down to the ballroom, where the event was being held. It was a massive room with a stage at the far end and balcony seats going up two levels. Above them, was a huge chandelier that was around sixteen feet wide. Below, round tables stood lined up like soldiers on parade, each one able to seat five people. The seats had been arranged so that they all faced the stage.

Music played in the background, courtesy of a small string quartet on the stage. Steel passed a young waitress who smiled and offered him a glass of champagne. He returned her smile and took one of the flutes before entering the swarm of wealthy people. He sipped the golden liquid and scanned the room for any friendly faces.

He saw Governor Alan Childs talking to Mayor Tom Lawson. Each of them looked as bored as the other but cloaked their lack of enthusiasm behind fake smiles. Childs saw Steel and called him over, looking as if he had finally found someone of interest to speak to. Steel downed the champagne in one and placed it on a nearby waiter's tray, before picking up a fresh glass to dull the pain.

"John, my boy, glad you made it," said the heavily built governor. Childs was over six foot three with broad shoulders and an ever-increasing waistline. He was in his late fifties and had grey hair and a bleached smile. From what Steel knew of him, he was a good man, an honest man.

"Governor, Mr Mayor," Steel greeted them both.

Childs scowled at Steel.

"Now come on, John, we're behind closed doors now," Childs said, laughing.

Steel nodded a gracious defeat. "Sorry… Good evening, Alan and Tom," Steel said, raising his glass to them. "So, Tom, has he bored you with proposal plans yet?" he asked the Mayor, who was clinging to his scotch like it was his last.

Tom Lawson nodded and rolled his eyes jokingly. Alan laughed and slapped the poor man on the back. Lawson, who was around two feet shorter and thinner than the others, stumbled slightly at the impact.

Mayor Lawson was in his late forties and had inherited a family nest egg that could choke Godzilla. He, too, was one of the good guys. Lawson was ex-military, which had seen him through to the rank of colonel in the infantry. He was smart and intelligent. But most important of all, his face fitted.

Tom Lawson was six feet tall and had dark hair, chiselled good looks and an eye for the ladies. He was the full package. The ladies were queuing to be the next 'Mrs Mayor', but he was happy enjoying the movie star lifestyle as a bachelor. The three men spoke for a while about nothing. That was until something caught Tom's eye.

"Oh, sorry, gentlemen, it appears that Miss New York has become free," Tom said, raising his glass as a quick salute before gliding off in the brunette's direction.

"Think they'll be in page six tomorrow?" Alan asked, jokingly.

Steel smiled. "Page two at the most."

Alan laughed. Steel rubbed his right eye, finding that his contact lenses were itchy from lack of use.

"Didn't think you liked coming to these damned things," Alan remarked, looking around the room at people raising their glasses to him as if they were old school friends.

"I don't, but I have been told to keep up appearances. You know how it is." Steel suddenly caught a glimpse of a familiar face near a white-clothed table full of drinks.

"However, tonight could be interesting," Steel said as he gazed through the crowd at a tall woman in a red cocktail dress. Her fiery red hair hung down to her shoulders. He had not seen her face, but he was sure that it was Helen Adler, the woman he'd met at the shipping company.

Helen Adler stood at the bar waiting for her drink while a small blacked-haired man with a weaselly face hit on her.

"Excuse me, but is this man bothering you?" Steel asked in a sympathetic voice.

The man turned around to face the person behind him. His angry look faded as he stared directly into Steel's chest. Slowly he looked up as if he was counting each button on Steel's shirt. A look of fear appeared across Helen's admirer's face, as he gazed upon Steel's emotionless features. He stumbled backwards, almost crashing into Helen Adler. He stopped and turned to face her before turning tail and moving away quickly, afraid that John Steel might be her husband.

"Why, Mr Steel, you *are* a pleasant surprise," she said, provocatively biting an olive off a cocktail stick. Steel made a 'two' gesture as the waiter brought her drink: a large martini with a splash of vodka served in a bucket-sized glass.

"So, are you following me, Mr Steel?" Helen asked. Those blue eyes moved slowly up and down his frame as if checking the cut of his tux. The waiter passed Steel his drink which he raised. "Cheers," he toasted. Helen raised her glass to return the gesture.

"I'm afraid not," he went on. "I am here on orders. They like someone from the precinct to come down and smile. It's good for PR apparently."

His words were a lie. But then, what could he tell her, a possible suspect? Could he really tell her that he was the poster boy because of his social status as Lord Steel? It was much simpler to leave her in the dark.

"Well here's to good PR," she said, raising her glass.

He gently clinked glasses with her, and their eyes locked on to one another. The music in the background was drowned out by the hum of conversation. Steel and Helen made their way to the far side of the room to a quieter spot, with her leading the way, deliberately, or so it seemed to him, but he wasn't about to argue. The dress fitted her as if it had been sprayed on. Steel had to admit that she really was a fantastic looking woman.

They sat at a table that probably belonged to someone else, but it was out of the way, conducive to quiet conversation.

"So, tell me, Detective," she began.

Steel shook his head. "Please, let's not be formal. Call me, John."

She smiled and nodded. "So, tell me, John, what other activities do you enjoy, to pass the time?"

He was about to answer when the lights began to dim, and a woman walked onto the stage. She was a tall blonde with a blue sequined dress. Her long blonde hair was arranged with fabulous twists and probably had been fixed with enough hair spray to be a fire hazard.

Showtime, Steel thought to himself. Everyone took to their seats, but Steel and Helen stayed put at the lonely table.

They talked for hours, finding time to dance whenever there was a break in the proceedings. Helen, like John Steel, was only there as a representative. For her boss at the shipping company, it was all about 'being seen' at the right places. It was a pity he didn't want to be seen himself, she thought.

However, on this occasion, she didn't mind. This time she was having fun. After one dance Helen led Steel out into the lobby. She turned and kissed him passionately. He kissed her back with equal enthusiasm. There was no room full of people, no music. Just them. They went up to her suite on the third floor.

"We're going to miss the dinner," Steel said as she pushed him through the door and into the room. He noticed a hunger in her, like that of an animal that has had its appetite suppressed for too long. She pulled off his tux jacket and let it fall. Her fingers passing over his shirt explored his body beneath.

"Why, Mr Steel, you do live up to your name, don't you?" she purred. Then she unbuttoned his shirt slowly as if she was unwrapping a special present, kissing every part of bare flesh as it was revealed. Steel pulled off his shirt and picked her up as if she was made of tissue paper. She gasped at the sudden use of his strength. They moved to the bed where he lay her down. Her eyes held that cat-like stare that she had noticed before. Steel moved on top of her, still half-dressed.

With a flip, she was now on top of Steel, and she could feel his hard body between her legs. Steel sat up, and they kissed again, their mouths and tongues exploring each other's. His fingers reached at the back for her zipper but found none. He pulled away from her with a confused look.

She smiled and stood up. "It's a side zipper, John," she purred seductively as she pulled the tag down and let the dress fall to reveal her stunning body. She stood there naked and gorgeous.

"I find underwear tends to get in the way," she explained.

Steel nodded, somewhat speechless, his mouth dry. Helen crept up the bed like a panther on the prowl and undid his trousers.

Their naked bodies were entwined in a passionate embrace, their hands holding onto one another as if never wanting to let go. Her face had a look of ecstasy as she felt all of him. His hard body brought her to the place that she longed to be, time and time again. Her painted nails clawed at his hard-muscular back as he slammed against her. Time meant nothing as their bodies became wet with perspiration and the heat of the moment. She grasped the bed covers as they lay on their sides, his body holding her close as he was lying behind her. She felt his powerful hands against her soft flesh. Just the feel of his tight body against hers was enough to bring her to a shuddering end. Her cries of passion were muffled as she bit into the pillow. They fell into each other's arms and laughed, gasping for air as though they had just run a marathon.

"I hope the diner's still on. I just worked up an appetite," Steel joked.

Helen slapped his bare chest and grinned pleasurably, like a cat that had gotten the cream.

Nearly two hours had passed before they returned and blended into the party, each going their separate ways. But they had not been missed. Steel headed straight for the bar. He was still sweating from their adventure's upstairs. A young waiter approached, and Steel ordered a large water with a double Johnny Walker Blue chaser.

"Thought you'd bailed out on us," said the familiar voice of the Governor. Steel turned after picking up the water and downing it almost in one. The Governor looked at him in surprise, saying, "You're drinking water?"

Then Steel picked up the double whisky.

"You had me worried for a minute, my boy," the Governor laughed. Steel raised the glass in a toast, and the two men drank.

"So, where have you been? You missed the dinner," the large man said, rubbing his belly. Steel's eyes scanned the room until he caught a glimpse of Helen standing with her boss and another white-haired man with a goatee. She looked around the room nervously until she caught Steel's gaze. Suddenly she looked back at her boss. Steel took out his cell phone and took a picture. As a precaution against losing his phone, he sent it to his desk as an email.

"Apparently, I was getting screwed over," Steel said. The Governor followed Steel's gaze then slapped him on the shoulder and laughed in a bellow.

"Well, my boy, it looks like you had a better meal than I did," Alan said, almost feeling jealous. As Steel watched, he noticed Helen's attitude towards her boss. It was not one of cooperation, and it was of antagonism and hatred. He could almost feel the loathing in her glare every time her boss wasn't looking.

At one in the morning, Steel decided to call it a night. The day before had been a long one. He was tired and just needed a shower and then bed. He had gotten a room for the night, so as not to waste time with taxis.

In the elevator, he noticed that his room number was just down the hall from Helen's. He held the brass tag tightly as if willing her not to be anywhere near. He felt used but didn't know why. Had she slept with him to achieve influence? He didn't know.

The doors slid open, and he found Helen sitting, crouched upon the floor outside her room, crying, looking as if she was ill or in trouble. The key was in the door. For a second, he felt like rushing up to her instinctively and consoling her. But he stopped himself and deliberately strolled up to her casually, not turning or attempting to look at her. Sure, she was a beautiful woman. But one that he didn't trust. Was her breakdown an act? But if it was, then how could she have known when he was coming?

He turned the key to her room and then looked over to her. Her whimpering remained a shallow piteous sound. If this was an act, it was a very good one. Steel cursed himself and his gallantry and moved over to her. He stood next to her, bent down and helped her up.

She was drunk. So drunk that she didn't even know he had opened her door. Steel picked her up and carried her to the bed and lay her down. She stirred slightly and tried to kiss him. Steel smiled and helped her back to her pillow.

He smiled and picked up the phone and dialled for room service. He ordered Helen breakfast and a bloody Mary for the hangover. He watched her as she slept a restless sleep. As he looked across, he suddenly felt some other emotion towards her. He thought back to the look of hatred she had given her boss. And the emotion she displayed in the office whenever she was around him.

He suddenly felt something. He felt pity.

He felt that Helen was in trouble and that she needed help.

Chapter 18

A deep burnt umber sky covered the city. The morning began as any other. The garbage men had already been on their rounds early, leaving the streets clear for the usual mayhem to ensue.

Steel had stayed with Helen until the early hours before heading home. She had been in no fit state to be alone. He had been out of the door before the sun had broken over the horizon.

He entered his apartment and locked the door. The whole place was bathed in a blazing orange with the light of the morning sun. He hadn't really slept, but then he never did. Watching over Helen had been a welcome change to his usual round of nightmares. He stripped off his shirt and headed for the shower. The twelve o'clock shadow had grown darker on his chiselled jaw.

The British detective ran the shower until a cloud of vapour rose, almost filling the room. *First shave, then shower*, he thought to himself. In the kitchen, the sound of the coffee machine let him know it was time to get up. Steel wiped the mirror clean of its misty shroud.

"Here we go again," he laughed, and then lathered up his face.

Showered and shaved, he stepped out into the coolness of his open-plan sitting room and headed for the kitchen. He poured a coffee from the machine and got milk from the fridge. There was a note on it held on by a magnetic 'smiley' that wore a pair of sunglasses.

New toy for you. Don't lose this one. Steel smiled at the note and sipped the coffee. He ventured down the hall to the room with the coded door. He punched in the numbers then put his hand on the scanner before entering.

Moments later, he came out holding a cell phone. He searched through the new applications while he drank his coffee. There was a strange app icon with a first-aid sign. He smiled and tucked the phone away.

"They think of everything, apart from making calls better," Steel joked to himself as he pulled on a shirt, he found on a hanger on the coat rack. He pulled on the leather-and-wool jacket and headed out. He would grab breakfast on the way to the precinct.

Steel stepped off the elevator onto the hard laminate squares of the department's floor. Most of the desks were empty. Detectives were either out working a case or off for the weekend. Apart from the odd phone call, the morning was quiet, but Steel had found that most people tended to be inconsiderate and committed murders in the middle of the night.

He headed for McCall's desk to check on her messages. Her password was easy: the date of her father's shooting. As he scanned through the mass of garbage and laughable chatter between Sam and her friend Tina, the ME, all of it was dull.

The seven o'clock sky was already lighting up the Homicide department through the large windows, as he watched other detectives started to return, and the phone lines got busy. But he had other things on his mind. Things like: who was Helen's boss talking to at the party?

Steel sat in McCall's chair for a while, as he looked up at the murder board. They still had no idea where Tara had disappeared too. She could be miles away or injured or dead. Also, he thought about John Doe. Who the hell was he and why was he covered in blood? He wasn't in the system and CSU were backlogged, so the report on the blood wouldn't be due until at least Tuesday, so they had promised.

After his conversation with Agent Hardy, Steel had wondered what the real motive behind Amber's murder was. Deep down, he knew it made no sense. McCall was convinced it was Williams's work, but Steel was unsure of that. Yes, Williams was a complete psycho, but there was just something wrong with the way that Amber's body had been left. Williams liked to make a 'statement' with his bodies. Amber's corpse had just been abandoned in her apartment.

Steel looked up at the picture of Tara on the board. His mind began to speculate on what her involvement could have been. Had she seen everything or just found the body? He shook off the thought. Tony and Tooms were on her trail, and he already had enough to do.

He stood up, leaving the comfort of McCall's chair. His first plan was to go and check up on John Doe. Or rather not so much to check on him, but to evaluate the surveillance team who were watching him.

Suddenly McCall's desk phone began to ring. Steel hesitated before picking up the receiver, just in case this was news of another murder that had nothing to do with Amber's case. He gave in and answered. It was Dispatch, telling him that there had been another murder in the Village. First responders thought it may be linked. Steel wrote down the address and replaced the receiver.

John Doe would have to wait. Morbidly, Steel hoped that this new body was linked to their murder so that they could move forward. So far, they had nothing but questions and theories. Hopefully, this might answer a few of those questions.

* * *

The morning sun was bright, but a cool breeze kept the heat at bay for the time being. In front of the apartment building, members of the press and nosey onlookers gathered to try and get a glimpse of something. Steel smiled and shook his head. The press he could understand, for they had a job to do. But Joe Public wanting selfies with a corpse? Please.

Steel had no love for having his photograph taken. Normally he would just let McCall deal with the press, and he would just sneak in while they were busy with her. Hell, she had the looks and the body of a model, so she was already media-friendly. Plus, it was good for her career. But talking to the media was something he could do without. Especially in this situation.

John Steel sneaked around the back of the building and found another entrance via a fire escape which he was nimble enough to get into. Inside he found that the main activity was on the third floor. Uniforms were gathered there to prevent any unauthorised access.

At the entrance to the room, two large uniforms stood watch. A large bouquet of flowers lay on their side adjacent to the next room. Steel took note but didn't pursue it. It could have been nothing, but then it could be everything. First, he wanted to see inside before making that call.

He walked into the apartment and came out again and stared at the arranged flowers before turning to the uniformed officer closest to them.

"The flowers there, make sure nobody touches them, would you?" Steel asked the large officer. The man turned and looked at the innocent flowers and nodded with a shrug.

Inside, the small angry ME was crouched over the body of a white male, or at least what used to be a complete body. Doctor Eliot Bauer was on call when Tina Franks was otherwise engaged – in this case; she was busy back at the morgue with a boatload of new cases due to an accident. He was a slight man, medium height with a thin frame. The man was in his late thirties but looked older, possibly the lack of compassion for the living, or humour had something to do with it. His ravel coloured hair was styled merely by brushing, but his clothes were immaculate with pressed creases in his shirt and trousers.

"Morning, Doctor Bauer," Steel greeted the weasel-faced man, who just grunted back. Steel looked over towards a large black cop, who just shrugged. Steel smiled at the situation and crouched down.

"Not to ask the obvious, but what have we got?" Steel asked, looking at the blood-soaked corpse.

"White male in his late thirties. Several gunshots starting at the ankles and working up to the shoulders. The final shot was to the liver." The ME spoke, all the time having a strange, passionate look on his face, which Steel found disturbing.

"This was torture at a high scale. I figure the killer used a suppressor on the weapon because the neighbours didn't hear anything, also the lack of powered residue you would normally find. At a close range you would have powder burns, stippling of some kind, these are lacking here," Bauer said, pointing out the entry wounds with his pen.

Steel looked confused at the doctor's theory.

"They didn't hear screams?" Steel asked, also noting that there were no signs of the man having been tied up.

"He was drugged with the same stuff they used on your first corpse. Poor guy couldn't move but could feel everything. We still don't know what it is yet. But an impressive drug… don't you think?" The ME grinned.

Steel gave him a look of concern, then walked away towards the officer who had been first on the scene.

The cop was an average young-looking guy. His short black hair was cut with a military short, back and sides. Around him, CSU were dusting for prints and taking reels of film. Steel had noticed the place was untouched, meaning that there were no signs of struggle.

As Steel approached the young officer braced up, and this amused the detective. He remembered his days as a recruit in the army. Every sign of someone with command had made him flinch to attention. Several times he had incorrectly saluted sergeant majors thinking they were officers.

"Relax," Steel told the young man, smiling. The uniformed officer attempted to do so but waved his hands, not knowing what to do with them.

"If it makes you feel better, stick the tips of your fingers in your pockets." Steel smiled broadly, understanding the stress. The cop smiled too, nodded and slid them partially into his trouser pockets.

"So, tell me what you found," Steel asked the young cop. He closed his eyes so he could picture the scene as it was described.

"I got a call from Dispatch," the younger man explained. "The neighbours next door was fighting so I went to check it out. As I approached, I noticed blood on the door frame. I knocked on the door, but there was no answer. I got hold of the manager who let me in, and that's when I found—" The cop's face went white, and he held his mouth in a reflex action.

"Is this your first body?" Steel asked.

The cop nodded. Steel returned his nod and tapped a reassuring hand on the man's shoulder.

"You'll be fine. Now tell me what else did you see?" Steel asked as he turned away and looked around the room.

The officer looked puzzled as if Steel wasn't taking notice of him.

"Don't worry, I am still listening," Steel said, sensing the cop's puzzlement.

"I saw the body on the ground and so much—" Steel raised his hand.

"—Forget the body." Steel raised his hand. "What else did you see? Did anyone pass you in the corridor? Did any cars race off when you got here? Try to think of things that struck you in a split second when you first arrived," Steel explained.

The young cop thought for a moment, then shook his head. "No, sorry. Maybe I should have been more observant." The young cop was instantly feeling guilty.

"Trust me, that comes with practice," Steel reassured him. "Besides if there had been something wrong, you would have known it."

The cop nodded, and Steel walked away back towards the ME.

"Have you got a time of death, doctor?" Steel asked, hoping for a time frame that coincided with when most people were awake.

"I estimate between six and seven this morning. Oh, there is one more thing," the doctor said with a curious grin.

Steel noticed the two cups of coffee on the breakfast bar and the ladies' bag hanging on the high back tall stool.

"What's that?" Steel asked. "That he wasn't alone, and we have a missing person? Or that this missing person was the killer?" Steel noticed the crushed look on the ME's face.

"Something like that—yes," he answered, before hurrying after the body.

Steel shook his head and smiled as he watched the man scamper away. Steel grabbed one of the CSUs and told him about the flowers. Steel's gut told him that the flowers had been a decoy: a way in. He had seen it in the movies, so many times he wondered if people still fell for it. But he had to be sure.

The bag was a brown leather Gucci. The long strap held it just below the seat. Steel picked it up in his gloved hands. The blue latex almost matched the black of his suit.

Inside the bag were the usual hairbrushes, car keys, a day planner and her purse. Steel checked the name on the driving licence and cursed his luck. The licence was in the name of Brooke Taylor. Steel sat down on the highchair and sorted through the rest of the purse. Cash and credit cards were all there. She had been taken, and Steel guessed that the blood on the wall outside belonged to her. He bagged the purse and walked towards the door. The handle had blood on it, and there was a fruit knife on the ground.

Steel figured that she had opened the door to someone carrying the bouquet. The guy probably said it was a delivery so as not to draw attention to himself. Steel saw the images in his mind as he set the scene like a small movie rerun.

How the door had opened, and the man pushed his way in. She would have struggled, maybe even got in a couple of hits before being overpowered. How the other agent had rushed forward and probably been hit with a Taser before he could get to his piece.

Steel frowned as the movie in his head revealed possible new evidence. There had been more than one of them. Two to three at the most.

Brooke had purposely cut her hand to leave a trail. She was a smart woman. Without the blood trail, no one would have even known about her dead partner.

The question now was, why did they take Brooke? And more importantly, did they know who she really was?

Steel thought back to the first crime scene. How Amber had been tortured.

Someone was looking for something.

What Steel could not figure out was why Amber's apartment had not been trashed. Normally the place would have been tossed, but it hadn't been. However, the furniture had been moved. They had moved the couch back to make more room; however, there were no marks on the carpet to suggest a secret place in the floor. Steel stopped for a second and cursed his stupidity. They had checked underneath the couch. Whoever had done, it had tipped up the couch and checked underneath.

But they had not found it, and they figured that Brooke had gone. This then led to even more questions.

The key ones being: who were they? And what was worth killing for?

Chapter 19

Brooke Taylor opened her eyes slowly. The last thing she remembered was the man at the door. A delivery mans. Brooke had been slicing an apple as she had answered it. There had been no time to react, and the door had been rammed open just as she turned the handle. She had taken the brunt of the full force and had been thrown against the wall from the impact. A metallic thumping sound had rung in her ears as she had lost consciousness.

Brooke had slipped away into darkness. Now she had woken up in darkness. She looked around, but there was no light to even make anything out. Her head throbbed from where the door had made contact. Brooke tried to raise a hand but found she was unable to move.

A sudden fear came over her. She was tied onto something. Her arms, legs and middle were bound by strapping. She struggled, but the pain in her head became intense. Brooke lay there for a moment. She felt like shouting out, but who would hear her? Her captors presumably.

The sudden tap of footsteps on a hard floor filled her ears. Then she was suddenly bathed in light from a lamp above her. The illumination seemed intensely bright after so much time she'd spent in darkness. As her eyes adjusted to it, she looked around. An expression of terror crossed her face as she realised, she was on an operating table. The cold steel surface glistened, reflecting the light from above.

Then another sound filled her ears: the sound of music. Soft mechanical music from a music box or … Brooke felt her soul freeze over. She had heard the tales about Mr Williams and how he loved to play his tunes for those who were about to meet him.

He drew near, and she struggled to break free of her bonds. He stood there partially in the darkness—only his lower half was visible. Brooke could feel her heart racing in her chest. All the stories she had heard about Williams never ended well.

She wanted the music to play on forever. They said that when the music stopped, his fun started. A tear rolled down her cheek towards her ear. She could feel herself growing faint again. The music stopped, but he stayed there. Motionless. Silent.

"What do you want from me?" She spoke almost softly. She wanted to shout, but she had no idea how he would react.

Williams disappeared into the shadows again. There was a click, and the table began to rise so that she was sitting in an upright position. The fear grew stronger, and her breathing became heavy

What the hell was he doing? she thought. The motion stopped, and Brooke stared forward as she heard his approach.

Suddenly there was a buzz from a cell phone. She saw the illumination from the device as he pulled it from a jacket pocket.

He sighed heavily. "I am sorry about this," he apologised to her. "You try and add a little drama to things, and this happens. Please do excuse me while I take this call, will you?"

So, saying, he turned his back to speak, almost as if he was trying to hide the conversation from her. He walked into the light, and she saw him completely for the first time. The thousand-dollar suit hugged his tall, thin frame. He had an elegant yet disturbing look about him.

"Hello ... Yes, I am with her now." He turned to face her and smiled and rolled his eyes as if he was bored with the caller. "No, I haven't asked her yet. Because I have only just walked in and—"

Brooke watched him as he talked. His body language was almost like that of a schoolboy who couldn't wait to go out and play.

"Yes ... Yes ... OK ... Right."

She watched as he answered but wasn't really listening. She watched as he made a 'yap, yap, yap' hand gesture.

"What was that? ... orry ... ery ... ad ... s-gle ... our ... aking up," He said, faking a bad line, then he rolled his eyes before crushing the cheap cell phone in his bony right hand – just in case, they tried again. Williams let the broken device fall to the ground, then brushed off his hands. As he walked up to her, Brooke noted his almost embarrassed smile. He raised a hand to gently brush away the lock of hair that covered a slight cut above her left eye.

"I must apologise for your treatment, Miss Taylor. My employees do not know the meaning of 'gentle and unharmed'," he said softly, then raised a straw that was resting in a crystal cut glass to her lips.

She stared at the clear water. Williams smiled and took a sip from the crystal glass.

"My dear, if I wanted you dead, you would not be here." He smiled and raised the straw to her lips. Brooke drank. The water was cold and refreshing. Williams looked up at the angry bruise, and his smile fell away. He turned and walked into the shadows. There was a slight buzzing sound, and then the whole room was illuminated.

Brooke's heart sank as she saw that she was in an operating theatre. The white-tiled walls and floor made for easy cleaning. A small table to the side of her was filled with many different devices for surgery.

Williams walked towards a door at the far end and spoke to a guard who stood on the other side of the entrance. They were too far away to be overheard. Brooke had a bad feeling. Why was she here, in this place? The door closed, and Williams slowly walked back. He was calculating something in his head, but his gestures gave away his thoughts.

Moments later, the door opened, and a large man dressed in black walked in and stopped at the entrance of the doorway. Williams smiled and turned to face the man.

"Are you the one who brought her in for me?" Williams asked excitedly.

The man nodded proudly whilst wearing a dumb smile.

"Well I must say, you did a great job," Williams said, ushering the man to come over. "Please join us."

The newcomer grinned broadly and strolled over, feeling like he was a king's champion.

"Yes, indeed, a fantastic job. Just one thing though—"

The man's smile faded as he saw Williams's agreeable expression turn into a scowl.

"Tell me. How did she get the cut on her head?" Williams asked as a mean grin crept over his face forcing his mouth to widen like that of a Cheshire cat.

"I ... I don't know, sir," the man stuttered in confusion. "It could have been when we kicked the door in—"

The man suddenly stopped talking, realising what he had admitted. He stepped back slightly. He was at least a foot taller and much wider than Williams. But Williams had an air about him that could put the fear into anyone with just one glance.

"You see what I have to work with?" Williams said to Brooke, pointing to the man with a flat palm. "A simple task. Not much to ask of him, I thought. I told him to go and bring me the woman unharmed—that's what I said. Nothing too hard to do, or to understand, I would have thought," Williams said, his voice remaining calm.

"You do know what *unharmed* means, don't you?" Williams asked the large man.

"Uh, yes sir," the brute replied, almost puzzled by the question.

"Really? Are you sure?" he said, dragging the man towards the frightened young woman.

"*Unharmed!*" Williams said, pointing to the man. "Not *harmed!*" He pointed towards the cut on Brooke's head.

"Unharmed!" he said again, but this time pointing to himself. "Harmed." He laughed, pointing to the man. The man's face fell, and he suddenly realised where Williams was pointing. Williams laughed out loud as if he was joking, the big man laughed as well, mostly out of relief.

Brooke never saw Williams reach for the scalpel, but then neither did the man. Blood poured from the open wound at his throat. The big man grasped his neck in a futile attempt to stop the cascading red liquid. A gurgling sound came from the man as he dropped to his knees and then to the floor. Soon a lake of crimson had engulfed the man's corpse.

The terrified young woman remained still and quiet so as not to join the man on the floor. She had heard about Williams. Ever since he had made his first appearance on the triple murder case the year before she had heard his name mentioned. It was standard protocol to know about him. He wasn't governed by money or power. In fact, he had no real master. He enjoyed what he did, and that made him even more terrifying. Her body trembled with fear as he casually walked to the washbasin and began to scrub the man's blood from his hands. There was silence, but somehow the mood had lifted. He turned towards her, and he smiled as though nothing had happened. Williams moved up towards her and stared into her eyes. She saw a different man. His eyes were almost kind and surprisingly gentle. He stroked her hair and smiled. "Don't worry, my dear. No one will ever hurt you again."

* * *

Steel stepped off the elevator at the lower level of the coroner's office. He had decided before going to see how John Doe was doing, and he would see if Tina Franks had any new information. They had been waiting for the test results on John Doe's clothes. 'We've got a backlog', CSU had said. He was aware they had been swamped with work since a recent accident on the subway. Was it an accident or an act of terrorism? some had wondered, especially the press. A train had derailed and crashed into another one. There were hundreds of dead or injured. The papers were filling the public's minds with all sorts of tales of possibilities, most of which was heading down the terrorist route. The Feds weren't talking, and the police were under orders not to reveal anything either. The social media groups had spun their piece posing their opinion and asking for feedback. Some blamed the president for cutting costs, others the Mayor. It was a media circus. Unfortunately, it was one of those that would stay in people's minds for a blink of an eye until the next catastrophe happened. Steel thought it sad there could be a mass genocide in a faraway land, but nobody gave a shit, but if there was something at home...different story, the people wanted blood.

Steel stopped for a second and checked his cell phone for any messages. There was nothing, just junk emails. People selling things, service providers telling him of the latest deals. Steel put the phone away and looked over at a room full of sheet-covered bodies. He counted twenty at the most. He figured that these were only a few of the crash victims.

He shook his head and headed for the double doors of Tina's lab. An orderly came out of one of the other labs and passed Steel on the way to the changing room, his scrubs covered in blood.

Steel turned and watched the man as he strolled away as if he was just strolling down the street without a care in the world.

This got Steel thinking. How was it that nobody had noticed John Doe walking around in a daze and covered in blood? But then some people don't want to get involved with strangers, just in case of any trouble—especially strangers who were covered in blood. He pushed through the double doors and walked into the lab. He found Tina standing over her latest 'guest'. It was the body of a young male with a GSW – gunshot wound – to the midsection.

Steel noted that the kid was in his late teens or early twenties. Anyway, he was way too young to be where he was.

"Hi, doctor, you're looking as radiant as ever," he said.

She looked up at him with one of those *really* looks. She was wearing a full-body suit and a full facial mask ready for the 'cutting' part of the autopsy. She already had streaks of fresh blood on her, and her gloved hands were covered with tissue from internal organs.

He smiled and leaned against the steel table that contained some sample dishes and scales for weighing body organs. He watched as she slipped her hand deep into the cadaver's open chest cavity.

"What can I do for you, Mr Steel?" she asked, but already knew what he was going to ask for. "If it's the test results, I am afraid you're gonna have to wait. They are backed up pretty bad up here," she said, pulling out the boy's kidneys, and putting them in a large stainless-steel bowl on top of some scales.

"Anything on the guy from the hotel?" Steel asked, almost hoping for some good news.

"Not much. I have got a date with him after this poor kid. What I can tell you is he wasn't shot. He was stabbed with something round," she said shrugging. "I will know more once I have cut him up." Steel nodded and headed for the door. "Thank you, doctor, a pleasure as always." He gave her a small bow and then headed out through the double doors. She stood there for a moment with the skull cutter clutched in both hands and a dreamy look in her eyes. She felt her knees tremble at the indecent thought she had just had. Tina smiled to herself and then proceeded to saw the top off the kid's head.

* * *

Tooms got off the elevator and headed for Tony, who was sitting at his computer. Tony had sent photographs of the missing woman – Tara Burke, to all the hospitals, train stations and airports. Tony looked up at his partner, who was biting into a chilli dog whilst holding another. Tony smiled and shook his head.

"Hungry?" he asked as Tooms finished the hotdog and sat down, readying himself for the other one.

"You know she will kill you," Tony advised him.

Tooms shrugged and smiled. "Only if she finds out," Tooms said, grinning.

Tony smiled broadly. "Shouldn't be hard. All she has to do is check your tie." Tooms looked down at his blue tie to see chilli sauce in the dead centre of it. "Oh, great! This was a present from her, as well," groaned Tooms, taking off the evidence and stashing it in a desk drawer.

"Anything back on Tara Burke?" Tooms asked.

Tony sat back in his chair and stretched off. "Nah, no priors, nothing on the system apart from her birth certificate. Her mom bailed out on her when she was eighteen. Real piece of work by all accounts. Used to beat the crap out of Tara starting from when she was little. Then she just up and left." Tony looked over at Tara's photograph on the board. She was a pretty little thing with a touch of hardness about her. Tony thought back over the recent past and realised that he had never met her. He knew most of Amber's friends but not her. But then again there weren't that many friends to know. He reached down to the picture on his desk of Amber. It had been taken on a summer's day. She was wearing a white blouse, blue shorts and a beaming smile. He mapped her face with an index finger.

"You OK, man?" Tooms asked softly.

Tony looked up at him and smiled. "Yeah, I am fine," Tony looked back at the picture. "It's just that I miss her, man, I really miss her."

Tooms nodded slowly. He had no idea how his partner felt, and in truth hoped that he never would. Tony looked up to see Steel walk out of the elevator. He didn't look happy. Tony nodded over to Tooms, just as Steel ushered them to follow him into his office. The two detectives stood up and followed Steel inside.

Steel held the door open and watched them sit in the chesterfields opposite the large desk. Steel closed the door and headed for the desk and sat on its surface, facing them.

"I thought you were off to see Memory Boy?" Tooms asked, confused at Steel's manner.

"Doc Davidson is in with him doing some tests or something," John explained. "I stopped at the morgue instead, to see if they had anything. Looks like we will have to wait for the results a bit longer."

Tony nodded, but he was still curious. Steel was staring at him, and the British detective's face was like stone.

"What is it?" Tony asked, sensing bad news. Steel reached into his inside pocket and pulled out a small baggy with something like a piece of paper or a photograph inside it.

"Tony, I got some news today, but you aren't going to like it," Steel explained.

Tony sat back in his chair as if preparing himself for a punch.

"Amber wasn't who we thought she was," John elaborated. "Amber was an undercover agent. She worked for a government agency. Apparently, she was investigating something big." Steel watched Tony's reaction. He saw the look of searching, the familiar stare of trying to make sense of what had just been said.

"Did her sisters know?" Tony asked, then he took in the look on Steel's face. "Ah. I get it. There are no sisters? But wait, if that's the case, then who the hell is Brooke?" Tony asked suddenly.

"She was Amber's handler. But there's something else. She was abducted, and her colleague was killed. She was possibly the only one who knew what Amber was up to," Steel answered.

"So…someone found out what she was doing and killed her?" Tooms asked, confused. "But if that's the case, why kidnap Brooke? Why not kill her?"

Tony was having the same thoughts.

"Amber was tortured," John went on, playing the probable scene through in his mind. "I think someone was looking for something, and I don't think they found it. That's why they took Brooke."

"So how does Tara Burke fit in?" Tooms asked.

Tony looked over towards his partner. "She must have seen something or walked in on them. She is probably hiding." Tony put forward his own theory.

Steel considered it carefully, then shook his head. "You know I think that we have been looking at it all wrong. I think Amber shouldn't have been there. Don't forget that she wasn't due to move in until the Monday. She probably walked in just as they were looking for whatever it was, they wanted. If anything, I think that Tara is more involved than we think." The more Steel thought about it, the more sense it made.

An angry look crossed Tony's face. He had just remembered what started the conversation: the news that everything had been a lie.

"So, what about the ex-boyfriend—me," Tony Marinelli growled. "Was everything a cover?"

Steel picked up the plastic evidence bag and looked at whatever was on the front of it. "You have to understand that working undercover takes a lot out of you. It makes you forget who you are sometimes. You need an anchor. Family, boyfriend, girlfriend. Something you can come back to. You need something *solid*. I think you were that for her." Steel passed over the bag to Tony. Inside it was a photograph of Tony and Amber together.

"CSU found it in her diary," Steel explained kindly. "If nothing else, Tony, you have to remember that she cared for you."

Tony took the picture and held it for a moment. He looked up at Steel and nodded a 'thank you'.

"What now?" Tooms asked.

Steel's face became emotionless and cold. "Now, we find out why Amber had two jobs. And we find Tara Burke."

Chapter 20

Brooke Taylor was blindfolded, then led away. She had been taken up some stairwells and down others, and along straight and winding corridors. It was an old trick. Use disorientation, so that the person has no idea how large the building is, or whether they are up fourteen storeys or deep underground. If she had escaped, she would have had no idea where to run, meanwhile giving ample time for her captors to find her.

Eventually, they stopped, and she heard a heavy metal door being opened. She was led in, and then the door slammed behind her.

Brooke ripped off the blindfold and stood ready.

She was alone.

The sudden brightness of the light stung her eyes. Brooke closed them quickly and let them adjust. Slowly opening them, she saw the room properly for the first time. It was a large space that had been created to be like the luxurious bedroom of a six-star hotel. A large four-poster bed was draped in a maroon silk covering with a matching throw.

The furnishings looked European and antique. There were no windows, but flat screens behind wooden frames gave the illusion of the outside world. Oddly enough, the landscape was of a sea view. Possibly seen from an Italian villa. She was in comfort. The ensuite bathroom had black marble flooring and brass fittings. The cast-iron tub sat in the middle of the room with a shower curtain surround. The drawers and cabinets were of dark mahogany.

She sat on the bed and just lay back. Lying on the bed was like relaxing on a cloud. She felt herself slip away into a state of complete serenity. At that moment, nothing mattered.

Brooke looked over to the far side of the room. She stood up and walked over to the heavy mahogany door. Her hand remained just a few centimetres away from the brass handle. She had no idea what was behind this. It wasn't the way out, for she knew that was behind her. It was probably another bathroom, and maybe even a room joined to that of another prisoner. She turned the handle and opened the door.

Her mouth fell open at the sight of the massive walk-in wardrobe. Then it suddenly struck her. This wasn't just a sudden snatch and grab. This had taken time. This had been planned over a very long period, or else she was the only one who had spent time there.

* * *

Tara Burke sat, staring at the television set. The news broadcast told of some story about the pension problem of some big firm. She had flicked through the channels a dozen times and found this one to be the most interesting. Besides, she hoped they would have more information on Amber's murder. She still couldn't believe that her friend was dead, murdered in their apartment. The press had shown her apartment building on the newsflash. But that seemed a lifetime ago. Now they were showing fluff pieces and sports.

She sat in a comfortable curled up position on the couch, her head resting on a stack of throw cushions. She looked over to a few clothes Kim had sorted out for her. Luckily the two women were around the same size. There was nothing much—just some T-shirts and jeans. But it was something new to wear. Tara found the gesture sweet but unnecessary, as she had her own clothes in the pink suitcase. Tara figured it was some kind of 'big sister act'. Kim had always tried to look after her since her mom had bailed out on her. Kim was the big sister she never had.

Tara picked up her cell phone from the coffee table and checked her messages. Still no word from him. She re-read the last message: *Where the hell are you, we must talk...* Tara looked at the desperate-looking words. Had he known something about what had happened to Amber?

She closed the cell and placed it back on the cold wooden table. The weather girl came on TV to tell everyone how great the day was going to be—she was a bubbly blonde with a tight dress that some guy must have picked out for the job. 'Clear with bright spells' was the prediction. But Tara didn't care. She wasn't going anywhere.

Kim had advised her to 'stay in and don't answer the door to anyone', something Tara intended to do anyway. Someone had gotten into her apartment and killed her friend and roommate. The news reporter put it down to a 'home invasion gone bad'. Tara was not convinced. Not after what she had found out.

The weather girl's report finished with a close and a smile. When the programme resumed, Tara saw the time in the top right-hand corner of the screen. It was nearly eleven in the morning. She was scared and bored—a bad combination. Tara stood up and headed for the refrigerator. She had slept through breakfast. *Wow,* she thought, *I slept through breakfast, never done that before.* She smiled at the thought. She was on holiday. Tara suddenly felt a bounce in her soul.

Now that she thought about it, she felt hungry. First, solve that problem, she reasoned, then she could tackle the boredom issue. She opened the fridge door and peered inside. The cold air felt good on her skin. So much so that she closed her eyes and just waited for a moment. Tara opened them and grabbed the milk container. Cereals were good. Chocolate cereal was better.

Tara sat back down on the couch. The spot was still warm from where she had lain all that time. She crossed her legs and began to spoon the chocolate squares into her mouth. Her eyes darted towards the TV screen as she saw the report of a murder. Her heart began to race. Some guy had been knifed in the Bronx. Her eyebrows raised in anticipation and she held the spoon full of coloured milk and cereal in mid-air, just in front of her gaping mouth.

The picture of the victim was that of some poor Hispanic kid with a rap sheet if a roll of toilet paper. She breathed easy and shovelled the spoon into her mouth.

Tara was worried about him. Had they found him? Had he given her up? She shook her head at the very thought of it. Besides even if he had, they had no idea where she was. She suddenly froze again. They might know where she worked. They might hurt Kim to get to her.

The worried woman cursed her situation.

It had been a good plan. A sound plans. But they had become greedy and careless. Now the people they stole from wanted their stuff back.

They wanted revenge.

* * *

It was around one in the afternoon when Steel had decided to go and see John Doe. The hours of searching for anything on Amber or Sharney Taylor were proving to be a nightmare. Tony had gotten an old address from the hotel where Sharney had worked – someplace on the Lenox Hill. The boys said they would check that out after they had gotten a warrant.

Steel walked out of the elevator onto the floor where they were keeping John Doe.

The silence suddenly hit him.

There was no sound of a blaring television, and where was the guard? A sudden rush of panic rushed over Steel as he ran for the guard's room. With one swift movement, he sped up then dove at the door with his shoulder. With a crash, the door swung open, and Steel rolled, pulling out his Barretta as he hit the floor. Steel rolled behind the nearest cover, which was the sofa. Steel brought up the weapon over the couch and aimed. Silence filled the air, nothing but his breathing and a muffled sound coming from the bedroom. Steel stood quickly and headed for the noise. There on the floor were the two policemen, and both had been stripped down to their underwear and bound.

The men had been duct-taped together back to back, and the silver tape pulled tight around their chest areas, as well as around their arms and hands. Steel cringed as he noticed the older cop appeared to be the hairiest man he had ever seen.

"Oh boy, that's going to hurt when it comes off," Steel said to himself. He smiled as he reached for his cell phone to take a picture. But his childish thoughts soon passed. Steel turned and ran for John Doe's suite of rooms. He called out for him, but no answer came back.

There were signs of a struggle. Small tables lay on their sides with shattered vases spread across the carpeted floor. A large bookshelf lay on its front, its contents fallen onto the floor before it. An armchair had been turned over, and the glass coffee table smashed. There had obviously been a fight. A struggle.

Steel examined the scene. It looked as if possibly two or more men had been sent to collect him. But the more Steel looked at the scene, and the more something nagged him about it. He looked over to the wall and realised something. He ran out and headed for the room with the surveillance crew. The door was closed but not locked. The three men lay on the ground or were slumped over their desks. They were out cold.

The detective then noticed the empty food containers from a Chinese restaurant that was located down the road from the hotel. He reached into his jacket pocket and pulled out a pair of surgical gloves. Suddenly one question hit him: *Why did they order out when they had a room service tab?* Steel turned and took out his cell phone. He needed paramedics and CSU. As he entered the room with the bound cops, he noticed the same Chinese food containers. He would have to wait until the men regained consciousness before they could answer any questions, but one thing was clear: if they hadn't ordered the food, then someone else had.

John Doe had suddenly jumped up some notches on the 'important person' scale. At first, he was a possible person of interest, and now he was a definite one. Not many people would go to such lengths to get to someone. They only reason they would do so was if they had done something bad to the wrong people.

Someone had laced the food and taken John Doe, but how did they know he was there? More importantly, who wanted him and why? Steel finished the call and looked the photograph of the cops tied up on the floor. But he didn't feel in a mood for laughing. These people were smart enough to knock out cops and get to their possible witness. More importantly, they were smart enough not to kill cops. Whoever it was, they were organised.

* * *

Tony and Tooms had gotten a warrant to search Sharney's – or rather Amber's apartment. It was a large place on East 60th Street: Lenox Hill. The location was perfect, as it was not far from the hotel where Amber had once worked. The two-bedroomed apartment seemed a bright and happy place.

The front door opened into a slim hallway. Just off to the side was a sitting room and the small kitchen sat opposite. The white walls of the hallway displayed paintings of flowers and landscapes. Several photographs of Amber with her family and friends hung in framed eight-by-tens. Further down were the two bedrooms and the bathroom was at the end. The wooden parquet flooring resembled oak, but Tooms had laid enough of the stuff to know it was a stained wood imitation.

All the doors had been left open, allowing the sunlight to illuminate the hallway. A fresh scent of lavender hung in the air from the automatic dispenser that was plugged into a nearby socket.

Tooms headed towards the sitting room, which was a few feet from the front door. A dark green three-seat couch was perched up against the left wall, and was opposite a large teak unit, on top of which stood a forty-two-inch flat-screen TV and a Blu-Ray player. Above the flat-screen, photographs had been arranged in an arch formation.

Several potted plants had self-watering systems attached to their decorative pots. It was obvious to Tooms that Amber wasn't planning on moving out. In fact, everything in the apartment said to him that she was going to return.

Tony opened the large refrigerator. The steel sides glinted as they caught the afternoon sun. Inside there were no perishables. In fact, there was nothing with a 'Best By' date on it. However, the cupboards told a different story. Most of the food was in cans or packages.

"Hey, Tooms, I think this was home," Tony said, walking out into the hallway. Tooms stepped out, holding a pink silk nightshirt up in front of himself as he studied it.

Tony raised his eyebrows. "Something you want to share, partner?" Tony said, trying to keep a straight face. He only wished he had a camera. That would have been worth at least two months' worth of bribery.

"Yeah, yeah, screw you," Tooms said. "Come take look at this." Tooms thought quickly change the subject. Tony smiled and followed his partner into Amber's bedroom. The room was large enough for the double bed and some other furniture. As he entered, he saw the window was straight in front of him, and the bed was against the right-hand wall. A pine dresser stood in the middle of the left-hand wall. A small stand mirror and several jewellery boxes cluttered its top. The fourth drawer of the six-drawer dresser was pulled out. This held various types of nightwear. Tony noticed Tooms had left a gap where he had parted the garments. "Ain't nothin' here," Tooms said, placing the shirt back in the gap, then quickly shut the drawer.

"Were you hoping to find something?" Tony asked, almost wondering what Tooms's reply would be, given the fact he had been caught looking in the underwear drawer.

"I don't know. Guess I was hoping for a gun, a badge maybe. Something to explain what's going on," Tooms said, sounding frustrated.

"And you thought it would be in her underwear drawer?" Tony pointed out, hiding the grin of satisfaction.

"Hey, I had been through all of the drawers, you just caught me at that one," Tooms said, hurrying out of the room.

Tony smiled. He was glad that Tooms was there, not just to help with the case, but for support. Just being in the apartment and seeing the pictures was killing Tony. But he knew he had to carry on. He had to find Amber's killer.

They had swept through the rest of the apartment and found nothing out of the ordinary. Tony reasoned that if she had been working for a government agency, had they already been through the place and cleared it of anything that could tie her to them?

As the two detectives made their way back to the sitting room, Tooms noticed the answering machine. The digital display showed that she had ten missed messages. Tooms looked over at Tony. Tony walked over to the machine and looked down at the red LED display.

"Are you sure you want to hear this?" Tooms asked his friend, a sympathetic smile on his large face. "It could be disturbing."

"Probably no more disturbing than watching you holding my dead girlfriend's nightclothes next to you as if you were trying them for size," Tony said, raising his eyebrows.

Tooms scowled. He knew Tony wouldn't let this one goes for a very long time. But it was a worth suffering the taunts to see him smile.

The black officer pressed the 'play' button on the machine, and they waited. The first two messages were telemarketers selling stuff. The next, however, was from Brooke. Her voice was trying to sound calm, but traces of anxiety broke through the façade.

"Hey there, sis," the recorded voice said. "Sorry we haven't spoken for a while; things have been a little crazy here. Look, call me when you can. OK?"

Tooms looked at his partner, who just stared at the machine in disappointment, almost as if he was hoping the machine would spurt out clue.

The next few messages were from some insurance companies who were hoping to catch a score. Tooms and Tony both scowled with disappointment. They had come up empty. They turned and headed for the door. They had wasted precious time following this lead, and now they had to backtrack and find something new. The machine announced the last message just as the two cops were about to leaving the apartment. Tooms had barely closed the door as the sound of Brooke's voice echoed through the rooms.

"Amber. It's me. Whatever you do, don't go to the other flat," they heard.

The door burst open again, and the two detectives rushed back inside. Tony began to speak, but Tooms raised a large hand to signal for him to be quiet.

"Do you hear me, Amber? Don't go to Tara's apartment. Go straight to Alpha location and wait for extraction." There was a background noise. It sounded like a car's tyres screeching.

The call went dead. Tooms grabbed the machine. He had a mixed look of anger and relief on his face. This was their first piece of data.

"What now?" Tony asked as he watched his friend wind the loose cables around the small device.

"Now we play this for Steel and see what he has to say. The man must know something, or at least he'll have an idea," Tooms said with a hint of hope in his voice.

Tony nodded. "Let's see if we can trace the call as well. It may tell us where Brooke was, and who was driving the car that spooked her." He looked around the apartment for the last time. He frowned and then closed the door behind them.

Chapter 21

Steel stepped out into the warmth of the afternoon sun. A cool breeze brushed his face as he stood for a moment as if he was basking in the bright sunlight. The roads were full of traffic, and the sidewalks crowded with passers-by.

Upstairs CSU and the paramedics were doing their thing now that Steel had left. There was nothing more for him to do, and if he'd stayed, he would only have got in the way. The CSU report would take a while, possibly a day or two, due to the backlog.

Steel pulled up the collar on his coat, so it wrapped itself around his neck. Autumn would soon be here; he could feel it in the breeze. The leaves on the trees had already started to turn brown. Steel thought back to his days back home on his English estate. He remembered looking up at the geese as they made their yearly pilgrimage to avoid the winter weather.

He looked at his watch. It was two in the afternoon. He knew he had to get back to the precinct and assign the various jobs pertaining to finding their John Doe. He had more than enough to do, and they were short on manpower due to one of their number having recently quit his job.

Steel walked to the kerb and raised his hand to hail a cab. Several drove past as though no one was there. He stepped back as a yellow cab stopped. Steel noticed the attractive redheaded woman in the back. He opened the door for her and assisted her out onto the sidewalk.

"Why thank you, kind sir," she said to him. She had a soft voice, and deep brown eyes you could get lost in. She wore a white skirted suit with a black silk blouse that was open enough to distract you. Steel climbed into the back of the cab and froze. Something had set him thinking: a scent of perfume. One he had smelt before. Twice before in fact.

But where?

"Where to, buddy?" asked the cab driver.

But Steel was a million miles away, searching his memories to try to remember where he had smelt that perfume before.

"Hey, buddy, if you're thinking about that chick, I am afraid that ship has sailed, my man." The black cabbie laughed. The man's slight muscular build showed under his open sleeveless denim jacket. The sun shone off his shaven head, showing the beads of sweat that had begun to gather there. Steel got out quickly and looked at the crowd of people. The woman had gone, but he remembered where he had remembered that perfume before. The first time he'd seen her was on a cruise ship, and the second time was in the Precinct, the female officer who had guarded the Chief of Police.

Just before she put a bullet through his skull.

'Missy Studebaker', or at least that's what she had called herself, he remembered. Steel got back in the cab. His mind began to work overtime. Why was she here? He remembered seeing her shopping bags: they were all from the same store.

"The woman you just dropped off. Can you take me to where you picked her up?" Steel asked as he leant forward near the dividing window.

The cabbie smiled and winked. "Sure thing, boss," the man said as he wiped his brow with his sweatband that had the colours of Jamaica on it. Steel sat back and let the man drive quietly. He looked out of the window and took in the surroundings as they travelled to Brooklyn.

The half-hour trip was filled with odd burst of chatter from the cabbie. Steel didn't answer much, just sat and watched the world go by. He could have driven himself, but when you don't want to be followed, a car tends to make things difficult. With a cab, you can just jump out and walk or catch a subway train.

"This is where I picked her up," the driver said, nodding to a pet store. Steel pulled out his cell phone and typed in a search. He had noticed the name on the woman's bags as she left the cab. It was a boutique called *Le Bon Voyage*.

The search engine showed it was just around the corner from where the cab had stopped. Steel paid the cabbie and got out. The cabbie noted the generous tip and smiled, showing off a couple of golden teeth.

"You have a good day, boss, and I hope you find what you're lookin' for," he said. Steel waved him a quick salute and headed in the direction the map had sent him. The cabbie waited until Steel had turned the corner and then picked up his cell phone. He pressed the auto-dial and waited. After several rings, a man's voice answered in a dry tone.

"Yeah, it's Jamal," he said into the phone. "We have a problem. I just picked up a cop from the hotel. I think he recognised the asset." He sounded alarmed at the turn of events.

"Where is he now?" asked the voice on the line.

"He's headin' for the store. What do you want me to do?" The cabbie was still watching the corner; just in case, Steel came back.

There was a brief silence from the other end.

"Nothing. We have this covered."

The phone went dead. The cabbie put his cell away and drove on. He wanted to be as far away as possible.

One of the shops Steel was near was a boutique. The store was an old building, built in the late '30s, he judged. The three-storey building had large windows and a fabric overhang. The store next to it was a mattress shop, and they were taking delivery of some double mattresses.

He stood for a moment. His eyes scanning the building and the surroundings, taking note of anything unusual or out of place. Steel waited as two bulky men carried in a mattress before heading for the store next door.

The inside of the boutique was a mix of clothing and strangely decorated furniture. Natural sunlight was aided by a few dimly-lit lamps. The ground floor was mostly filled with women's clothing and accessories. Old revamped furniture was strategically placed amongst the items for sale: old chairs covered with mixed gold and silver paint, and dressers with the same touch. Large and small picture frames hung on the walls.

Opposite the door was a long glass counter which displayed silver and gold antique necklaces, brooches and watches. Behind the display, cabinet stood a stunning Asian woman. She had a gothic look about her, with her long black hair and dramatic make-up. Her athletic form was clothed in a tight black leather corset and trousers. These were topped off by knee-high black leather boots and a long thin fabric trench coat.

She looked up at Steel as he entered and cracked a smile. He smiled back before starting his wander around, making out that he was a lost shopper.

"Men's stuff is upstairs," she told him, her tone soft but at the same time forceful. "But I doubt if it'll be to your taste." Her voice made the hairs stand up on the back of his neck.

"Oh, I have very adventurous taste in clothes," he said, smiling.

She raised an eyebrow and smiled subtly.

Steel looked up at the stairwell to the next floor, which was of large dark wood boards that had recently been varnished. "Thank you, I am just browsing," Steel replied.

Her eyes widened with interest. "An Englishman in New York. You're on holiday, I suspect?" she said, almost purring the words as she looked him up and down with approval.

"Something like that. I saw your shop and thought I would give it a look," Steel said, picking up a wooden jewellery box.

"Are you looking for a present for your wife or girlfriend?" she asked, walking past the counter and moving beside a woman with red hair and wearing almost the same outfit, who appeared to be trying to blend in with the surroundings.

"Neither, I am afraid. I am very single," Steel replied, using objects with shiny surfaces to spy around the room for other shoppers.

The sexy woman smiled broadly at the news of Steel's availability.

"Upstairs, you say?" Steel said, pointing towards the wide opening stairwell.

She nodded and crossed her arms as she watched Steel climb the stairs which fluted at the bottom and the top like a grand staircase. This gave character to the store, almost blended its combination of 'old' and 'new' decor.

As he made it to the top, Steel heard the door open and caught a glimpse of a woman dressed in dark blue, with hair to match. The first floor was not as spacious as the ground floor, and every available space was packed with items. Along the left-hand wall, clothes hung in sections separated by size. On the right were the small changing rooms, with only a simple curtain to hide the customers from view. In the centre of the room, statues and busts were mixed with strange furnishings. Directly in front of him, two large windows let in a stream of warming sunlight.

Steel stood at the top of the staircase and looked at the strange mixture of people. A large mixed-race man in his mid-twenties stood at the racks arranging some clothes. He turned to Steel and just simply stared for a moment before returning to his task.

"Charming service," he muttered under his breath, not surprised at the lack of customers. Steel looked around, checking price tags and sizes, trying hard to look like a customer and not a cop.

"You lookin' for anything particular or are you just – looking?" The man's voice was abrupt and unfriendly.

The detective smiled as he looked through some shirts.

"Oh, just browsing. I am sure I will find something interesting though," Steel said, still holding the smile.

There was a sudden yelling coming from downstairs. It was the woman who was at the till. She was asking the man to come down to her. Her tone was composed for show, but he knew that the man was going to be given a lesson in manners.

Steel looked around the room. Something was off. There was obviously another floor above, so where was the stairwell? He walked over to the changing rooms. He opened one of the curtains and found a chair and a long mirror that almost filled the wall. Steel checked the inside but found nothing.

Quickly he checked the next one but to no avail. He was beginning to think his theory was just a bad idea until he reached the fourth one. He walked inside the booth and looked around. There was nothing out of the ordinary. Steel leant against the mirror out of frustration. There was a click as he pressed against the mirror, and then it moved away like a door.

Steel smiled. He could hear the conversation between the man and woman grow louder. *Good,* Steel thought.

It was the perfect time to check the upstairs floor.

At the top of the dimly lit stairwell was another door, and there was a mechanical sound emanating from within. Slowly, he turned the handle, opened it slightly and peered through the gap. The area appeared to be empty, so he crept in and closed the door behind him.

It was a large room, with only supportive upright beams to break up the floor space. The surrounding walls were painted white, and the floor was of grey plastic tiles. The mechanical sound was being made by rows of large counting machines.

Steel walked over to one of them. There appeared to be around thirty machines and mechanical stackers beside each one. Each machine was churning out ten-dollar bills. One machine would bundle them into stacks of ten, and the other would bind them. Behind all that were large metal containers, which Steel figured held the cash. It was a fully automated system, a large operation with few employees to know about it.

The detective took out his cell phone and took photographs of the presses. He went to call Tooms and realised that doing so may not be the brightest move, not while he was still in the building. There were a handful of women downstairs and a man with an attitude. Possible civilian casualties if it went wrong.

This was a major operation, so there had to be back-up nearby just in case things went awry. Besides, this was more in the Civil Enforcement Unit's line than Homicide. Steel waited until he was outside to make the call to a detective he knew: the guy he had in mind was a heavy-handed son-of-a-bitch named Walter Cobb.

Steel made his way downstairs to the changing stall. He hoped they hadn't been looking for him, for that could complicate things. As he edged out from behind the mirror, he heard silence. This was a bad sign. He had taken several shirts and trousers into the booth with him as a bluff, just in case, he was seen coming out of it.

As he stepped out, Steel found himself alone: the large assistant had gone. Music played downstairs—some sort of classic and rock mix of Beethoven's Fifth with orchestra and guitars in a mix.

Steel walked towards the top of the stairs to find five women standing there looking up. Each of the women had almost the same style of clothing, but each had her own colour.

Even their hair was dyed in the same shade as their clothes. Steel noticed the Oriental woman standing at the centre, dressed all in black. The others were of brighter colours: red, violet, blue ombre, pink and white. As well as wearing the same style of attire they all had the same concentrated stare.

They seemed to be unarmed, but he knew better than to trust his judgement about that. If he was inclined to arrogance, he might have decided that they were only weak women and pile in. But from what he had seen drunken soldiers' wives do, he knew better than to underestimate their fighting skills. One thing that did worry him was the missing assistant.

Steel suddenly felt the vice-like grip around his middle, as the man grabbed Steel in a bear hug.

"Ah, there you are," Steel said with a slight loss of breath as the man squeezed, apparently to show off his strength. Steel looked down at the woman in black as she placed her right leg on the bottom step and leaned in slightly.

"Did you find anything interesting?" she asked. Her voice had a hard softness to it, and her eyes stared at his face as if she was looking for a lie.

"Well the shirts were quite nice, but the other things were really an eye-opener," Steel said with a smile. The man squeezed again in defiance of Steel's mockery. But the man thought he was stronger than he was.

"Who are you…a cop?" his attacker yelled to show off his authority, of which he had none. The woman stared into Steel's face, but this time the look was different. This time she was sizing him up.

Steel suddenly got bored with the cuddling and scraped the inside of his boot down the man's shinbone. The hugger screamed and released his grip slightly. Steel leant forward and brought his head back. There was a scream of pain, and a loud cracking sound as Steel's head crunched against the man's nose. He released Steel and stumbled backwards before falling to the ground, blood pouring from the wound on his face.

Before Steel could react the woman in blue was already on him. She landed a roundhouse that he barely moved for, causing him to spin. She made several more kicks, which he was able to block. As she made another kick, Steel managed to grab her leg. A look of surprise crossed her face, and he just gave a quick grin before tossing her into the changing rooms.

As she flew from his grip, he received a sidekick to the back from the woman in red and then a sweeping kick from the woman in white. Steel hit the ground hard, making a dull thump. He looked up and rolled just in time before Red's heel came down where his crotch would have been.

Steel got up into a crouched 'ready' stance. This wasn't just five against one. This was five *highly trained ass-kickers* against one. The woman in red made a spin kick to either knock him off balance or distract him from seeing the woman in pink rush up behind him. Neither worked. He waited until the last moment and then dived out of the way. The woman in pink took most of the kick to the side of the head and was thrown to the side. The red woman roared in anger. Steel simply smiled and shrugged. This made Red enraged, and she lost her head. She charged, despite the woman in black's command to stop.

She made several impressive attacks with both feet and hand punches. But Steel blocked them all until he found the right moment, and then grabbed her leg and sent her flying into the booths along with her colleague.

Steel let out a muffled grunt as Blue let loose a hard kick to his midsection. He stumbled backwards slightly from the impressive power shot. Blue spun to make another hit, but Steel dropped to the ground in a press-up position, just as her leg passed over him. He spun around on the ground and swept Blue's legs from under her. Blue let out a brief cry of pain as her head met with the flooring.

Steel stood up, almost ready for the next shot. White and Pink didn't disappoint. The two women took turns in hammering at Steel with kicks and punches. The woman in black stood at the top of the stairs and watched as she realised something. This man was only blocking their attacks. He was doing everything he could so as not to hit her girls.

However, the detective knew he couldn't keep up his lack of aggressive tactics, and that had to do something. He had worked out that each of the girls appeared to wait for each other, and that they wouldn't both kick at the same time. He waited for Pink to kick, and then he suddenly backflipped out of the way and landed badly on his front.

Pink's kick landed full into White's stomach, sending her halfway across the room. Steel stood up but managed to drop backwards, just as the large mixed-race guy swung a mannequin's leg at Steel's head. This missed Steel but landed full onto the back of White's head. Steel watched angrily as the woman fell. Steel slid and managed to land under her to break her fall.

"Silly bitch got in the way, her own damn fault." Those were the man's last words. He grabbed at his throat, which had suddenly been pierced by a strange-looking throwing knife.

The much-battered detective stood up. Blood flowed from a couple of scratches on his face. The woman in black walked forward, and he moved back towards the window. The sun felt warm on his back. The sunlight poured in, turning the blood pools into white coloured liquid.

Steel and the woman in black started to circle one another, each ready for the other's move.

"So, you never answered the question," she asked him. "Are you a cop? A Fed even?" Her voice had something about it that made the hairs stand up on the back of Steel's neck. There was something about her that Steel found arousing. Maybe it was the look, the voice or perhaps just the fact that she was dangerous.

"I guess telling you that I was just a guy out shopping wouldn't wash?" Steel said with a smile.

The woman in black smiled back and shook her head. "Sorry, but you can drop the accent now," she said, impressed with what she thought was a fake accent.

Steel kept smiling, even as the two gunmen walked into the store and opened on Steel and the woman in black. She stood defiantly as the shots rang out, but Steel grabbed her and pulled her through the window.

As they crashed onto a pile of old mattresses from the store next door, they heard the gunfire and saw the wood and brickwork splinter away above them.

"How did you know there were mattresses here?" she asked with a surprised look on her face.

"Truthfully —" Steel said with an innocent look on his face.

Her expression changed to one of shock. "You mean you didn't know?" she screamed, as Steel dragged her off the mattresses just in time. A hail of 5.56mm rounds ripped the mattresses apart. Then there was silence, and two bodies fell to the concrete in front of them, each of them with a knife in their backs. The woman in black looked down at the men who had fallen from the window and spat on their corpses. She looked up to see the other girls standing in the window. She nodded at them; they returned the gesture and left.

"So, Mr Shopper, who are you?" the woman in black said, turning to face him, only to find an empty space. She looked around in shock. He had gone, and there was no way out of the courtyard but up or through the back entrances of the stores. She smiled to herself, looking forward to a better encounter in future with her mystery man.

Chapter 22

A blacked-out Bentley 'Flying Spur' limousine cruised down the gravel driveway which seemed to be a mile long. Tall ferns lined the way, ending in two sandstone lions on tall mounts which faced the oncoming traveller. The car pulled up to a two-hundred-year-old mansion. A relic from after the civil war, whose sandstone walls were tarnished with age, but held its magnificent appearance. Surrounding the structure was green lawns which were cut off by tall bushes and stone wall archways. Rose bushes sprung from ornate arched frames while smaller ferns sat in Grecian style plant holders.

The huge vehicle pulled onto the gravel driveway which encircled a fountain and a small grassed area surrounding it. The car stopped outside the front entrance, and the occupants waited for a moment before the doors opened. The driver got out and opened the passenger door on his side. Williams got out of the town car along with three of his large henchmen. The former straightened out his grey pinstriped suit as he looked up at the huge mansion.

The sun beamed down onto the grounds, giving the estate a friendly feel. But this was not a friendly place. Williams started for the steps, but his guard dogs waited outside. Company rules decreed that no weapons or 'gorillas' were allowed. He entered the main lobby and smiled at the splendour of the antique carvings in the woodwork, admiring the paintings and tapestries. The outside of the mansion had been altered a bit over the years, but its interior was maintained in its period splendour.

Williams could spend hours just walking around the old place, but duty called. He took off his black trench coat and handed it to the butler, or maybe it was just some guy dressed in tails who was collecting coats. Williams thanked the man and headed inside.

The left-hand corridor led down a long stretch. But he didn't mind, and it gave him time to study the art on the walls. Behind him, on the other side of the lobby, was the ballroom which was fitted out as the 'relaxation room': a place he loathed to go. It was tradition for all members to go there after business and just talk casually amongst themselves. The trouble was Williams disliked all the people he encountered there. He found them to be lacking in any sense of honour or actual purpose. In his opinion, they were all conmen, killers, thieves, spies and terrorists. An organisation who sought to gain power, control and money. They weren't after world domination, for that sort of aspiration gets you noticed. It makes you a target for the security agencies. This group preferred anonymity to hide in the shadows.

Williams appreciated the finer things in life, whereas these people just wanted the best for its own sake. He had worked for these people for many years. Back in the old days, the founder had given the organisation a purpose, had set rules that were never to be broken—a code, even. But the newcomers had come in and made it their own. Perverted what it meant to be SANTINI. Williams often smiled at the brilliance of the name. It did not spell anything, nor did it for that matter represent anything. The name was more of a distraction than anything. It was a deliberate ruse because it made the worldwide agencies think that they were looking for a person or a family, not something less trackable.

He walked down the long corridor and headed for two men. These big-framed guys were standing on either side of two large wooden doors. As he approached, they opened the doors to allow him entry. The huge room was long, with oak-panelled walls, and the floor was carpeted with a blood-red carpet with a thick pile.

Williams stood for a moment and took in the beauty of the room, admiring the white high ceiling and the works of art that adorned the walls, and the crystal chandeliers whose lights were reflected in the long oak dining table. The table's top was polished, so it glistened as if a layer of glass had been placed upon it. Twelve red velvet-backed dining chairs surrounded the table, six per side. At the far end, at the head of the table, was a sixty-inch monitor.

The psychopathic expert torturer looked around the room at his colleagues and gave a false grin. There was none of them worthy of his time or conversation, apart from one. Williams's eyes lit up at the sight of a new person at the table. It was a beautiful looking woman, who must have stood at six foot eight and who had the build of a Russian shot putter, or maybe one of the WWF fighters. She had long black hair and hands bigger than those of most men. Her black skirted suit covered a white blouse and an ample bosom.

Williams saw there was a free space next to her and hurried towards it before anyone else could, nudging others out of the way as he went. They all stood behind their chairs, waiting for the signal to sit. Various shapes and an almost gyroscopic view appeared on the screen, while lines of contrasting colours spiralled and danced across the black background.

"Good afternoon, everyone, please be seated," said a voice emanating from the many speakers around the room. Everyone sat and waited for the voice to speak again. Williams thought the whole thing was very theatrical, but it preserved the leader's identity, and, in some ways, it was kind of fun.

"Mr Forbes. Your report please," the voice went on in a British accent: an accent Williams considered to be fake—another 'hiding place' for the head of operations.

A tall thin man with blond hair and an expensive grey suit stood up. "Our operations in Africa have been a success," Forbes began. "Also, the crashing of the four aircraft over the past week have seen shares fall worldwide, and so we have made a nice profit from that." He waited for a moment for some sort of pat on the back. Then he looked around and sat down, confused at the silence.

However, Williams took no notice of him or anyone else, as he was leaning against the arm of his chair and staring deeply at the woman next to him.

"Mr Charles. Your report please." The voice was speaking more slowly this time, and his tone was filled with disappointment.

A short, stocky man with black hair and a blue suit rose from his seat. He took a sip from the water and wiped the sweat from his brow. His face was red with embarrassment. Or it could have been fear.

Charles swallowed hard before starting his speech. "Well … Uhm," he began. His gaze landed on Williams, who was oblivious, as he was too busy staring at the huge woman next to him, the adoration in his eyes like that of a smitten schoolboy.

"Well…uhm, what, Mr Charles?" demanded the voice. "Did you lose the package?"

As the words came from the speakers, the lines and shapes on the screen danced in tune with the tone.

Mr Charles began to panic. He knew he had to say something. In desperation, Charles pointed towards Williams, who was still lost in his lascivious thoughts about his Amazonian neighbour.

"No, sir," Charles floundered on. "Mr Williams lost the package, and he has failed to recover it." He was almost proud of his lie.

"Is this true, Mr Williams?" asked the voice.

At first, Williams did not react. Not until he had that burning feeling that everyone was watching him. He sat up and wiped the drool from his mouth.

"I am sorry. What was the question?" he said, confused. But his confusion cleared when his gaze fell on to Mr Charles's smug face. He knew at that moment that he had been set up.

"Is it true you have lost the package and have not recovered it yet, as Mr Charles has explained to us?" the voice said, in a tone that was strangely calm.

Williams also picked up on this apparent calmness, and he wondered why it was. After all, they all knew that failure was not an option.

He smiled and stood up quickly, almost forcing his chair backwards. He bowed his head to the large monitor, banking on the instinct that a sign of courtesy and a lack of fear would work in his favour.

"As our good friend Mr Charles has explained, the item in question was stolen, not lost," Williams explained succinctly. "However, steps have been taken to track down and recover it." He looked across at Charles, and his smile turned into an evil glare, his mouth opens wide, showing his teeth with every word.

"However," Williams went on smoothly, "I would like to point out the loss of the item was down to *someone else's* lack of judgement." Suddenly his arms flew about, and his voice was raised, as though he was delivering a sermon. "But I do not blame anyone, and I blame circumstances. I blame—" Williams glared at Charles for a moment before continuing, "—I blame sheer bad luck. And I also blame the person whose idea it was to put everything on a flash drive that was in the shape of a dog. That said, I expect to have the package back soon. Before next Friday at least." Williams looked around the room, then down at the neighbouring woman as she stared up at him. He smiled at her, which made her look away in disgust.

Feeling he had finished his statement, he bowed low to the monitor, like a conductor who had given the performance of his life. His bow was not given because of any great respect he felt for their leader, but as a ploy so that he could get a better look at the woman next to him. This act only resulted in the woman landing a giant paw across his face, causing Williams to disappear onto the carpeted floor below.

The meeting continued for another hour. A long hour, in which Williams just wanted to leave. He knew that afterwards, they would all have to go into the large 'relaxation room' and pretend to get along.

But tonight would be different. Tonight, he would have the large woman to use his charms on.

The meeting closed, and everyone bowed to the monitor. Williams didn't want to do so, because he felt it was quite a stupid thing to do. But then he remembered what had happened to the last person who had neglected to show respect. How could he forget? He still had the video on his cell phone. The guy was run through with a sword and then left to bleed to death. The thing about polished tables is that the blood seems to flow faster. Williams smiled to himself as he remembered everyone backing away at the sight of the oncoming red tide.

The two heavy doors opened, and the assembly began to retire to the relaxation room. Williams waited until the woman next to him turned to leave, and he followed, next to her. His charming conversation was one-sided. She had given her report earlier, and that's when he found out that she was German. Her accent had made him tingle. But now, standing beside him, she said nothing.

He liked the challenge. He knew that she was simply toying with him, or at least that was what he was telling himself. As they entered the lobby, a man with a silver salver stopped Williams.

"A message for you, sir. Most urgent," the tall thin man said. Williams watched in torment as his prize glided off to the room full of men and their hungry obsessions. Williams took the envelope and stared at the wax seal covering the fold. He thanked the man and opened it slowly. He knew these messages did not come very often. In fact, according to his reckoning, it had been at least ten years since the last.

He broke the seal and pulled out a folded piece of paper. The six-by-four sheet had a spider-headed emblem embossed into the paper. Williams began to smile wickedly as he read. His gaze moved across to where Mr Charles was standing. He was talking to another smaller man whom Williams did not recognise. Williams refolded the paper and placed it back into the envelope. Slowly he slid it into his jacket pocket and walked into the room as though he was floating on air.

Williams spied the woman sitting next to the bar, and she was very alone. To her amazement, he simply walked up to her and kissed her on the lips. Everyone looked at them for a moment and then carried on with their conversations.

She was about to slap him but stopped herself. She saw the menacing grin he wore, and she backed off slightly. She was afraid. There was a glint in his eye that she feared.

"My apartment, twenty minutes," she said. "You bring the champagne." She turned and marched out of the mansion. Williams danced towards the door, singing and kicking his heels as he went.

This will be a night to remember, he thought.

* * *

Steel walked into his apartment. His bloodstained hands left trails on the door as he moved inside. The bright light of the afternoon sun illuminated the area. He moved to the bathroom slowly, his body hurting all over from the beating and the fall.

He was glad that the mattresses had been there. In fact, it was probable cause to buy a lottery ticket after an experience like that. Steel walked into the bathroom, causing the automatic lights to come on. He looked in the mirror at his scratched face and shredded clothing.

Feeling every muscle in his body scream in pain, he removed his jacket and shirt. Blood flowed from a couple of wounds on his arms and chest. Opening one of the bathroom cupboards, he took out some tweezers and iodine. He dug the tweezers into his flesh and pulled out the mini shards of glass that were keeping the wounds open. He turned around and was amazed to see in the mirror that his back had not sustained any cuts.

Taking the bottle of iodine, he poured some onto a cloth and dabbed his wounds. He winced at the biting pain of the sterilising fluid. Steel reached inside the cupboard once more and pulled out a 'skin stapler'. Carefully pulling the skin together with the tweezers, he began to use the dissolvable stitches on the worst of the wounds.

He stood and looked at himself in the mirror. His body was full of taut muscle, and there were plenty of scars, six of which would never heal, either emotionally or physically. Steel turned on the shower and let it run for a moment to allow the hot water to flow. He stripped the rest of his shredded clothing from his muscular form and stepped inside the shower cabin.

The warm water cascaded over his body. He felt the strain in his muscles start to slip away. Even though he was fully trained in combat, the mileage always took its toll. He put his hands on the wall and leant forward, completely immersing himself under the hammering water.

Steel had sent Cobb a text and the incriminating pictures of the money-counting operation before he had left for home. By now the place would be swarming with cops in tactical gear and others on standby. But Steel was sure there would be no sign of the women. They were smart enough to be 'in the wind' by now. The money, however, was another story. There were thousands of banknotes there. Too much to move unless they had a truck hidden somewhere.

In a way, he was glad that the Oriental woman had gotten away. Sure, she was on the wrong side of the law, but she just had something about her that intrigued him.

The cab carrying Steel stopped outside the precinct. Steel paid the driver and got out. The warmth had been replaced by a crisp wind. Steel walked calmly inside and headed for the elevator.

He stepped out onto the dull floor of the Homicide department to see Tooms and Tony jokingly checking their watches. Steel adjusted the bridge of his sunglasses with his middle finger and smiled.

"Where you been, man? You've been gone most of the day!" Tooms barked. Steel checked his watch. It was nearly four o'clock.

"Sorry. I had to go home and change clothes after a spot of 'store assistant' trouble. They were looking to make a quick killing," Steel said the words with a straight face.

Tooms shot him a look. The sort of look that said, '*should I be looking for bodies?*' Tooms knew Steel had a way of attracting trouble, or else he just was good at finding it. He had a good track record for being in the wrong place at the wrong time, though the people whose lives he saved would probably disagree.

"But those are the clothes you went out in," Tooms remarked, looking at Steel's black attire. Steel looked down at his black suit and shook his head.

"Never mind, I don't want to know," Tooms said, giving up before something weird started.

Steel noticed the strange expression that Tony was giving him. It was almost a 'begging' expression.

"OK, what do you want? It's not the Ferrari, is it?" Steel asked curiously. The American detectives looked at one another with child-like expressions.

"You have a Ferrari?" Tony asked quickly, almost forgetting what he wanted to ask Steel.

The British man smiled and shook his head. "No, but it was interesting to see how quickly you would lose your attention span." Steel grinned as he quickly bent down and grabbed the answering machine.

"Don't tell me, the answer to everything is on this, and you want me to decipher it because you think no one but me can do it?" Steel said, waving the machine about.

Tooms and Tony looked at Steel with gaping mouths.

Steel's grin faded. "Really ... Look, I was just joking, guys. I thought it was just an answering machine from your home or something." Steel said, looking at the machine in his grasp. "So...you think there is something important on this?"

The two detectives stood up and gave Steel a serious look. Steel nodded and headed for his office. "I'm the only one who can find out, I guess," Steel said. Tooms and Tony raced for Steel's office and the comfort of his chesterfield armchairs. Once at his desk, Steel placed the machine on top and plugged it into a nearby socket. The leather of his 'ship captain's' chair creaked as he rested his still-aching body onto it. He looked at the two detectives sitting opposite him.

After he had listened to the tape, Steel sat back in his chair and tapped his fingertips together in a thoughtful gesture. His face held a concerned look.

"Who else has heard this?" Steel asked. Tooms and Tony looked at each other and shrugged.

"Nobody. Why?" Tony asked. Now he felt an uneasy feeling creeping up his spine.

"Keep it that way. In fact, if I were you, I would burn it and never speak of it again." Steel's face was like stone.

Tooms could tell that something was very wrong.

Tony started: "But—"

"—There is no 'but', Detective," Steel growled softly, interrupting him. "This tape never existed."

Tooms looked at the door behind him and then back to Steel. "Why, what does it mean?" Tooms asked in an almost whisper. Steel leaned forward over his desk, the others following his every move.

"You don't want to know what the truth is about this, Tooms. It is something ... Well, something terrible." There was fear in Steel's voice.

"You don't have a friggin' idea, do you, Steel?" Tooms asked, keeping the tone of fear in his words. Steel looked Tooms in the eye and shook his head.

"Haven't got a bloody clue."

Tooms sat back, catching his breath. "You're a real asshole, you know that, don't you? You nearly gave me a friggin' heart attack!" Tooms boomed.

Steel smiled and sat back, smugly.

"Hey, what can I say? It's been a bad day, I needed cheering up," Steel watched the two men scowl at him. The smile faded as he looked over at the large electronic murder board. He looked at Amber's photograph. She had been a looker: young and very good looking, which made Steel think.

Why was she in the agency? And how did all this mystery fit together? He turned towards the two detectives, who were still scowling at him.

"So, we know that Amber was working for the government, we also know that Brooke was her handler," Steel said, standing up and heading for his drink's cabinet. He grabbed three bottles of water from the small fridge and tossed two of them to his colleagues.

"How did you know she was an agent?" Tony asked, cracking the seal on the bottle.

Steel shook his head as he sat down. "The last call on this machine were instructions, not a warning as such. Plus, most 'spooks', as you like to call them, have someone watching their back. Getting intel, doing background checks, and so on, while the asset plays the part." Steel looked over at the picture of Brooke. He saw something in her eyes. She looked like a woman who had a lot of experience.

"We need to find out who took her and hope she's still alive," Steel said, looking at the hands-on his smartwatch. It was nearly four o'clock. He reached into one of the drawers of his desk and pulled out a yellow legal pad. Taking a pen from his pocket, he started to make a list:

Amber, John Doe, Brooke, Tara. Steel tapped his pen on the pad in frustration. Something connected them all. There was no way the murders and abductions had happened coincidentally. Steel lifted his arm and dramatically slammed the pen into the thick pad.

Tooms and Tony jumped out of their seats and reached for their weapons.

"What the…? Have you gone crazy, man?" Tooms yelled, still holding his hand over the pistol grip of his Glock. Tony had drawn his and was looking at Steel, waiting for more sudden movements.

"None of it makes sense," Steel growled as he stood up, his chair giving out a creak of protest.

"It's like a puzzle with most of the pieces missing and no picture to follow," Steel said, but his tone had calmed slightly.

Tony re-holstered his weapon with shaky hands.

"We have a missing John Doe."

"What…John Doe is gone, what the fuck, did he walk out or summit?" Tooms said in surprise.

"Sorry…" Steel started; his trail of thought broken by Tooms's outburst. "– no, he was kidnapped, someone drugged the guards and took off with him," Steel's words were casual as if it was a daily occurrence. Tooms and Tony just sat opened mouthed, wondering how he could be so calm. "OK, John Doe…we don't know who he is, or where he had been to get blood on him. We don't know whose blood it is because CSU is backlogged." Steel looked up at the murder board with his hands behind his back. The way he stood made Tooms think of his old platoon sergeant major.

"We have a missing woman, who was maybe a witness to something, and a government agent who is also missing," Steel said, almost chewing on the words as they came out. He was mad. Not that he was showing it.

"You asked me why I was late? The answer is, shall we say, painful," Steel said, rubbing his right shoulder. "Today, I was outside the hotel, where John Doe was taken. There I met a woman." Steel watched as Tooms and Tony leaned forward for some juicy details. He smiled and shook his head.

"I thought I recognised her. I didn't know where from at first. I got the cab driver who had brought her there, to take me to where he'd picked her up. It was a boutique in the Bronx. I did some snooping around and found the top floor full of counting machines." Steel turned to face the two men, who were taking in every word.

"Don't tell me you blew it up?" Tooms said, causing Tony to smile. The British detective tapped his pocket to check that his cell phone was still there.

"No, I called a friend in Task Force. They are probably in by now. Not that they will find much." Steel shrugged. Tony shot Steel a curious look.

"Let's just say, the people involved are ready for anything." Steel looked back to the board with a faraway look.

"So, where did you know the woman from?" Tony asked. "Was she an old girlfriend or something?"

Steel turned to them and shook his head, his face stern. "What if I told you she was the cop who was guarding the chief when she called herself 'Missy Studebaker' on that cruise ship last year?" Steel watched as his colleagues' jaws dropped.

"Now, you see why I followed her." Steel watched the two detectives nod, whilst wearing blank expressions.

"Don't worry," he reassured them. "We won't be chasing her. We have enough to do. Besides, she is probably long gone by now." He knew that 'Missy Studebaker' was just a part of their mystery and finding her would waste valuable manpower and time: time that Tara and Brooke didn't have.

Steel wondered what her connection was with the store. He knew she wasn't working for SANTINI: that had been proven when she'd murdered the Chief of Police. However, there was another organisation that was working against SANTINI. One that was more power-driven—and more sinister for that matter. Steel tapped an icon next to Amber's picture, which was in the shape of a file. It opened and showed the crime scene.

Tony just stared before looking away. Tooms's eyes glared at Steel for his lack of compassion.

"Hey, man, you could have warned Tony before Poppin' that open," Tooms growled.

Steel turned slowly to face him, his face as impenetrable as stone. A shiver ran down Tooms's back.

"I am sorry. But I understood that we were here to catch her killer," Steel said calmly, but his tone had a hard edge to it.

"I'm looking at the pictures because there is something in them that is bothering me. What it is, I do not know." Steel said as he turned back to the board. He looked at Tara's furnishings in her living room. At first look, it appeared to be a normal single woman's apartment. Ordinary.

"How are we going trying to find Tara Burke?" Steel asked without breaking his gaze from the board.

"All patrols have a copy, so do people in public transport. It's a long shot, but someone might have seen her leave," Tony said, taking a mouthful of water.

Steel shook his head. "She isn't leaving. I have a feeling there is more to Miss Burke than meets the eye." A disquieting feeling tore at his gut as he stared at the photographs.

"She is in hiding. We've just got to find out where." Steel touched the photograph of Tara on the monitor, causing it to enlarge.

Tooms shot Steel an 'unconvinced' look. "What makes you say that?" he asked.

"Simple. We haven't found a body." Steel turned to look at them.

The two detectives knew he was right.

Steel checked his watch: half-past four. "OK, you guys, you can take off. It's been a long day. We hit it again tomorrow. With fresh eyes." He returned to his chair.

Tooms and Tony raised their bottles as if to wish him a 'goodnight' and headed for the door.

Steel watched them as they left the room and then waited for a moment. He took another hit from his own bottle and leant back in the chair. His gaze fell onto the enlarged picture of Tara. He looked at her eyes. They had a sadness to them. No, not sadness.

Pain.

Given her past, it was understandable. Her father had split when she was little, and her mother beat the crap out of her until she was old enough to take herself off. By all accounts, she was a good kid. Worked hard, paid her taxes. No criminal record whatsoever.

But still, something struck him that didn't fit right. In addition to the unexplained abduction of Brooke. Why take her? Steel took another sip from the bottle. The cold liquid felt good as it flowed down his throat. Steel tapped the bottle as if he were playing an instrument. A thousand thoughts cascaded through his brain.

Steel reached into his pocket and pulled out his cell phone. Finding a number in the contacts list, he pressed the autodial and waited.

"Yes, it's me. We need to talk," he said, sitting back and crossing his legs, feet on the desktop. He waited for a moment and then took a mental note of the address.

"Roger that. See you then." Steel closed the phone and sat finishing the rest of his drink. His eyes were fixed on Tara's image.

"What really happened that night?" he said to the picture, almost hoping she would speak.

Chapter 23

The next day brought a brilliant burnt umber-coloured sunrise. A fresh breeze carried gently on a westerly wind. Joggers and dog walkers had filled the park early to beat the masses that would soon congregate. It was seven o'clock on a Sunday morning. The sound of birds in full song blended with the background noise of early-morning traffic.

A young female jogger made her way around the lake. She had to beat the time it normally took her to get to the boathouse. Her effort wasn't being made for any other reason than a personal goal. Her grey-and-pink cotton shirt and shorts fitted well enough to show some form without being restrictive. Her long brown hair was held high at the back in a ponytail. The sound of her music from her cell phone blared in her ears via the wireless earplugs. Her feet hammered the concrete as she went.

She preferred this time of day to any other. It was cool, and most people were still in bed. Her view was locked forward, like a racehorse with an eye on its goal. Sweat began to collect and pour from her forehead. Her breathing was steady: in through the nose and out through the mouth. She had the boathouse insight. *Not far now, just a little more*, she thought. Her arms were pounding the air as she pumped out the strokes, matching her footwork. She ignored the pain in her thighs as she headed for the finish.

Finally, she ground to a sudden stop and put her head back and laid her hands on her slender hips. Sucking in the cool air, she walked around, shaking off her aching legs. The cool breeze tickled her bare flesh as it swept across the water. Pulling up her wrist, she checked her time. It was a good one: at least two seconds faster. As she looked down the path, a handsome man dressed in a blue T-shirt and shorts jogged past. He looked back with a smile as he continued. The woman's smile was lost to the back of him as he disappeared across the path and past some rocks and bushes. She scowled at the lost opportunity and jogged slowly on.

Taking a path from the boathouse, she headed for Azalea Pond, then reached a group of bushes, stopped and backed off. The mass of green was shaking as though someone was moving through it.

"Who's there?" she cried out, wishing she had her can of mace.

The bush continued to shake. At first, she thought it was the man she'd seen before. Something seemed very wrong. The bushes were in a small area under a tree. It was a good place to make out with a partner without being seen.

"Hello, who is there?" she said, creeping forward slowly, curiosity pulling her on. Her hands parted the bushes that were like a curtain of foliage. Her breath became shallow, and she could hear her heart pounding.

The branches parted and she was suddenly knocked back by what seemed to be a large black mass of sharp beaks and feathers. She screamed and fell to the ground as the huge flock of crows swarmed past her like a black cloud. She stood up and brushed herself off.

"Stupid birds," she said to herself. As she turned to leave, something in her head stopped her. That curious feeling had returned. Slowly she made her way back to the place and parted the foliage curtains once more.

Her scream was loud and piercing. People across the park heard it and came running. Her screams continued. She couldn't stop her screams any more than she could stop staring at what she had found. Her eyes were wide and fixated, unable to break free from the sight before her.

* * *

Steel had risen early. He had already been on his eight-mile run and was now in his building's gym. It wasn't quite Gold's Gym, but it held enough equipment for what he needed. Besides, membership was included in the residency package.

The gymnasium room was long with white walls and a wooden floor for easy cleaning and to create a good visual effect. The right-hand wall was virtually all mirrors, in front of which were some of the machines. To the left were twelve bike machines and five units for 'rowing'. At the far end was a stand with the free weights and loose weights for the bars. In the centre, a couple of benches sat ready for use.

The well-muscled detective sat on the bench and finished the last of his reps with the free weights. He had done around two hours in there to stretch out the discomfort in his muscles caused by the beating. He let the dumbbells drop from his fingers and onto the padded mat. As he dabbed the sweat from his brow with his towel, two young women came in and debated which piece of equipment to start using, oblivious to anyone else in the room. One of the women had short brown hair. She saw Steel in the mirror and tapped her friend on the shoulder. They watched as Steel started his second set of exercises with the fifty-kilogram weights.

The second woman brushed her long black hair with her fingers as she watched him in the mirror.

Steel paid them no mind. His thoughts were a million miles away, and the pain from the workout was aiding his concentration.

He finished his final rep and stood up. His T-shirt was soddening from the sweat that clung to him, showing off his muscular form underneath. As he put the equipment back, he turned and saw the drooling women, who were still standing at the machines. He walked past and bowed slightly.

"Good morning, ladies, wonderful day isn't it?" he said. He caught their reflection in a mirror. They just stood nodding as their eyes followed him. He smiled to himself as he waited for the elevator. All the while, he could feel the women's stares upon him. It felt good.

The doors opened, and he stepped inside. The only thing on his mind was a cool shower and a good cup of coffee. The doors closed, and with a small shudder, he started to ascend.

Steel caught his reflection in the elevator's mirror. He turned and looked at himself. He was almost unable to understand the attraction he seemed to have for women.

As far as he could judge, he was an average looking man who had turned into a freak. Steel looked deep into his own eyes. The blue contacts covered his cold, lifeless emerald-green eyes: eyes that most men could not bear to investigate. He also noted the wounds on his body from where he had been shot all those years ago—six holes in a strange 'V' pattern.

'The mark of the phoenix', his old mentor had called it. 'The mark of a dead man walking' was what Steel called it. Six 'through and throughs', each of them narrowly missing a major artery or organ. Either the shooter had been a bad shot, or the lack of a lethal shot had been done purposely. Steel reckoned that the shooter had just wanted him to die slowly.

No one had known that the gardener had been nearby to save him.

He looked at himself and remembered what it had been like to be normal. To have a family life. Things like that had been taken away from him. His master told him that everything happens for a reason. That everything has a purpose. Steel couldn't understand that. He refused to believe it.

The elevator came to a stop, and he ventured out into the hallway and headed for his apartment. One day he would understand everything, but for now, he had work to do.

Steel had showered and changed into a black suit but didn't wear a tie. He pulled on the quarter-length suit jacket and headed for the kitchen. The coffee machine had stopped making the unhealthy 'choking' noise, meaning that his brew was ready. On the refrigerator was a post-it notes. He smiled as he read the message: *New suit is ready. Look after it. G.*

Steel made his way to the room at the end and punched in the code and entered. Moments later, Steel came outstretching his arms and shoulders, as though he had tight-fitting underwear. He wore a big smile and new glasses.

There was a buzz, and his cell phone danced across the kitchen's breakfast bar as it vibrated. He picked it up and answered it.

"Steel… how fast you can get to the boathouse in Central Park?" the voice in his ear said. It was Captain Brant, and he didn't sound happy. Steel looked at his fresh cup of coffee and then at the wall clock.

"Twenty minutes, I guess, why?" Steel asked, hoping there'd been a break in the case.

"We got a fresh one for you," said Brant. "It may be connected."

Brant hung up, and Steel cut the connection and finished his coffee. He was almost afraid to find out what this new development might be.

It took him around fifteen minutes to get there, and he used the time to think, to review the case so far. He figured that the 'fresh one' that Brant had referred to was likely to be the body was one of the missing people and was assuming that was why he'd been summoned.

The ME's truck confirmed his suspicions that it was indeed a new body that had been found. The question now was, whose body was it? As he approached the yellow tape, he saw Tooms making notes in his notebook. Tony was talking to a pretty woman dressed in grey-and-pink jogging gear.

A uniformed officer lifted the tape as Steel approached. Steel nodded a thank-you as he pulled on a pair of black surgical gloves.

"What have we got?" Steel asked as he met with Tooms. Tooms nodded towards the bushes.

"A female jogger thought she was scaring off a peeper or creep. Hope you haven't had breakfast yet," Tooms said, leading Steel to a break in the foliage. As they pushed through the natural veil, Steel saw the ME and some of the CSU team. Tina Franks was kneeling in front of something he couldn't quite make out. But then his view was mostly engaged on the two CSU people who had their backs to him as they were trying to gather air. Tooms stayed at the entrance to the gap they had just come through.

Steel felt the hairs on the back of his neck begin to tingle something was badly wrong. As he approached, he saw something that used to be a person. The sex of the corpse was impossible to determine, as it had been badly burnt. Steel knelt next to Tina, who said nothing at first. He certainly wasn't going to push her either.

He took out his small camera and took some shots. *Always take a camera with you*, was one of McCall's unwritten rules, and Steel had always found it to be good advice, as it meant there was no delay whilst waiting for the lab to send up the photos. He could feel the emotion coming from Tina. Sure, she had obviously seen a lot of dead bodies. But none before quite like this one.

Apart from being burnt, it looked as if the body had had its skull smashed in to prevent any reconstruction. The teeth and the flesh on the hands had been removed. Even for the battle-hardened Steel, this was a bad one.

"Are you OK?" Steel asked, placing a reassuring hand on Tina's shoulder. She turned, smiled and nodded. He stood up and offered his hand to help her up.

"Sorry, Steel," she told him. "I can't give a TOD as the liver has been removed. DNA may be a problem because of the burning of the body." She shrugged and shook her head. "Someone went to a lot of trouble to hide this person's identity. The ribs have been smashed, and so has the pelvis." She pointed out the broken chest cavity and pelvic area.

"They didn't want us to know if this is a male or a female," Steel said, shocked at the depths of depravity the killers had sunk to. He turned to Tina with a hopeful look.

"But you can, can't you?" he asked, looking into her deep dark eyes. "You can find out who this was."

She smiled. "I will see what I can do but no promises." Her voice rang with uncertainty. It would take a miracle, or there was always the slim chance that the killers hadn't been as thorough in covering their tracks as it appeared.

The orderlies carefully bagged the remains and took the body away, leaving CSU to sketch, photograph and measure everything, while Tooms took the jogger's statement.

Steel stood for a moment and took more photographs of the small area. There were no scorch marks on the ground. No blood or signs of a struggle. Everything was undisturbed, apart from the immediate area where the body had been found. The British detective shook his head.

Something was wrong, very wrong.

Why go to the trouble of making ID impossible, but leave the body where it was sure to be found? It didn't make sense, just like everything in the Amber case. Steel was certain that this fresh body had something to do with the Amber case. He also had a suspicion of who it was. He didn't need tests to prove that it was most likely to be their John Doe, the amnesiac man who they'd done their utmost to protect.

They were being played with. Someone was purposely making them chase their tails.

And he was going to find them.

* * *

Back at the precinct, Steel sat at McCall's desk and sorted through the statement of the girl jogger and those of the officers who had been overpowered and drugged whilst supposedly babysitting John Doe.

There wasn't much information to be found. The jogger girl had not seen anyone, and they were still waiting for any footage from security cameras nearby. The cops had all said the same thing about the food delivery to John Doe's apartment, and that the delivery guy had told them that the precinct had sent the food. The delivery guy had disappeared, but according to his boss he often disappeared on his days off, probably blowing his earnings at a local strip joint.

If the body was that of their John Doe, why did they want him, and why did they try to conceal his identity? Steel looked over at Tony, who was calling Traffic to try and get the footage from outside the hotel. Tooms was yelling down the phone at some guy from the parks and recreation department for the CCTV footage, if any, of the whole area.

Steel could feel his head spin every time he thought about this case. It made no sense. None of it. A dead undercover agent who had two lives, and who got killed in an apartment of a now-missing waitress. Meanwhile, her handler goes missing, and a man who was walking around covered in blood may have been partially skinned and barbequed to conceal his identity.

The agency had no idea what their operatives had been working on – or at least that's what they had told Steel anyway. But one thing was for sure: the Trent Shipping Company was at the heart of it.

Steel stood up quickly, forcing McCall's chair to slide across to the next desk. Tony and Tooms looked up at him. Steel seemed calm, but they knew something was eating at him.

"Where are you going?" Tony asked, covering the mouthpiece of his phone.

"Off to clear my head," Steel said, rushing down the stairs.

Tooms and Tony looked at one another and swallowed hard.

Steel stood outside the precinct building and took in the warmth of the morning sun. The wind had died down to a pleasant breeze. The volume of foot traffic had increased. Tourists and families spending quality time hurried past. He stood and watched, hoping for an epiphany to strike. He smiled to himself, wondering what McCall was doing at that moment. Having brunch with the family, no doubt.

He recollected the painful memories of his own past summer holidays—or 'leave' as they called it in the service. Brunch on the patio whilst watching his little brother and sister play. Staring into those beautiful eyes of his darling Helen, whilst his father talked about work.

His thoughts were a million miles away. He was so distracted that he did not hear Doctor Davidson yell a greeting.

"Mr Steel…are you alright?" Davidson asked, staring at Steel, almost wishing he knew what the detective was thinking about.

Steel shook his head as if to bring himself back to reality. "What?" he asked. "Sorry, doctor, I was miles away. Good morning." He smiled. "What brings you to this neck of the woods?" He thought he already knew the possible answer.

"I heard about what happened at the hotel. Is everyone OK?" Davidson's tone was one of genuine concern. But Steel detected something else in his face. A tiny flash of fear was visible in his eyes.

"Have you found John Doe yet? Or do you know who took him?" Davidson continued.

Steel just stood there for a moment, quiet and motionless. Then he shook his head, with a grim look on his face.

"No, we don't know right now. However, we did find a body in the park," Steel explained.

Davidson's eyes widened. "Is it him?"

Steel wasn't sure if Davidson's question was one of concern for John Doe's safety or whether he was worried about how easy identifying the corpse was going to be.

The detective shrugged. "The body was … unrecognisable. We are waiting for the ME to do her magic." Steel looked down at the doctor. "If it is John Doe, it only means that he was involved in this case, as we suspected he was."

Davidson nodded as if to concur with the theory.

"Did he tell you anything?" Steel asked, hoping for any snippet of information the doctor could give him.

The psychiatrist investigated space, trying to compute the situation.

"Doc, did he tell you anything at the hotel?" Steel repeated.

Davidson shook his head. Then he shot Steel a look of horror. "I never met him at the hotel. I was … Oh, God. He's back, isn't he?" Davidson cried out, nearly collapsing to the ground. Steel managed to catch him before he hit the hard concrete.

"It would appear that he is back, yes," Steel replied calmly. "But why he's back I have no idea. Doctor Davidson, you might like to consider taking a short vacation far away from here. I hear there's a package deal to Mars." Steel smiled as he spoke.

"I may just do that, Detective." Davidson appreciated the humour and the advice, fussily straightening out his clothes after his near fall. "There happens to be a conference in Paris, and I was looking for a good reason to go." He smiled.

Steel nodded and looked across the sea of people. "To me, that sounds like a good enough reason to go. You might like to consider staying on for another week afterwards."

Steel's words were more than just a friendly suggestion, they were a warning, and Davidson knew it. The two men shook hands, and then Steel watched the strange doctor turn and hail a cab.

The detective knew that Davidson would be safe while he was out of the country. But better still, with Davidson out of the way, Williams would be unable to do his 'doppelganger' double act. Steel still couldn't believe that Williams and Davidson were twin brothers. But their futures had been sealed when their mother had sent Davidson away. Davidson had gone on to become a good man, a respectable doctor. His brother had become something else—something evil. On Steel's first case with the NYPD, he had seen first-hand what Williams could do, how he could pretend to be Davidson in order to gather information. Williams was cunning and a perfectionist. He also had an ego as big as a planet.

A yellow cab stopped, and Davidson got into the back seat without looking back. Steel smiled as he watched him, nodding to himself. He saw the cab take off and disappear into the mass of traffic. Then he turned and ventured back inside the station house.

Chapter 24

Tara sat in Kim's apartment, flicking through the channels on the television. She had vacuumed and dusted just out of boredom. She knew making the noise was a risk, but she had done it the same time the neighbours above had done theirs.

It was the longest she had been still that she could remember. Normally she was on her feet for twelve hours a day. But now she had time on her hands, and it was starting to get to her. Tara knew she couldn't stay there forever. At some point, she would have to make a break for it. Trouble was, where could she go, Canada maybe, Mexico? But then there was the question of how would she get there and what she would do for funds?

She picked up her cell phone and checked for any new messages. There was nothing, only the ones she had seen a thousand times before. He hadn't sent anything for days now, and she was worried. Worried they had found him, and he had ended up like Amber. Worried, he had given up on her.

The worried woman grabbed the cushion from behind her and hugged it tightly. She felt alone and scared. He had left her with the problem, and she would have to decide: to go to the cops or to go ahead as planned. Tara looked up at the front door as she heard a sound coming from the hallway. *Only the neighbours*, she told herself. Her eyes were glued to the door handle, waiting for it to turn.

The news came on TV with a top story: *Body found in Central Park* was the headline. Her eyes widened as she switched her gaze. The female reporter stood with the park behind her. Yellow police tape showed the area along with a dozen uniformed officers making sure nobody tried to get a closer look at the crime scene.

A sudden bad feeling flowed through her veins like lead. The reporter had said an 'Unknown person'. Why person? Not male or female but … *person*. Her imagination took hold, and she felt sick. What state had the body been in for its sex to be difficult to determine? Tara got up and went to the kitchen for a glass of water. Her nerves were shot.

She downed two glasses then leant against the aluminium sink, her head bowed.

If the body was his, what had they done? Was she going to be next? She looked back to the television set and watched the rest of the newsflash. As the reporter spoke, Tara could tell that the police hadn't divulged many details to the media and that the information she was giving was largely just speculation. The police had obviously blanked her efforts to find out more.

Tara sighed as her clear head was trying to make sense of it. Fear had begun to affect her thoughts. One thing was certain for sure: she had to get out. She had stayed here too long.

* * *

Steel stepped out of the elevator. He had just gotten off the phone with Alan Cobb. The police team had found cash, the machines and a dead black guy in the boutique premises that they had stormed, thanks to his tip-off. But the women were gone. Cobb told him that he reckoned there was at least around three to four million dollars on the premises. Steel had smiled when his friend had asked what had happened before they'd arrived. A room torn apart by gunfire often leaves a shocking impression. Steel had said nothing, just let his friend's imagination run riot.

The loss would hurt someone. Probably not for long but enough to pinch. Steel hoped it was SANTINI, the organisation that had murdered his family. The people who had hunted him for so long. The ones he was now determined to see burn in hell.

But something nagged at him. It was 'Missy Studebaker', or whatever her real name was. She was with the other organisation, so was the boutique theirs? Regardless, the money was off the streets, and someone had a bloody nose. If they were in the middle of an organisation 'turf war' the Feds knew about it. That part was obvious, and it would explain why Amber was working two cases. But why did Brooke have reservations about telling the company what was going on? Did she suspect someone in-house to be a mole?

He couldn't know the answers to any more questions without Brooke. If she was alive, there had to be a reason for her survival, since they had killed Amber.

Steel had put his phone away with mixed feelings. Sure, it was a good bust, but the perpetrators had gotten away. Whoever they were.

The detective looked across the field of empty desks. It was Sunday, and most of the team were at home or out on a case. He walked over to Tooms and Tony and sat on the edge of Tony's desk.

"Feel better now?" Tooms asked.

Steel nodded as he looked over at the murder board. It still made no sense. He shook off the negative feelings that were clouding his thoughts.

"OK, guys, go home. There is nothing more you can do today," Steel said, watching their mouths fall open.

Tony suddenly felt a strange, happy feeling. Had the great detective John Steel given up on the case? Tony smiled to himself, just waiting for him to admit it. This great man with the strange theories and the even stranger methods, who was now evidently stumped.

"So, are you just giving up?" Tony asked, trying to force Steel to admit it.

Steel stood up and shook his head. "No. I said there is nothing that you guys can do. It's Sunday. I am sure Tooms wants some family time," he said.

The Tooms didn't need to be told twice. Before Steel could say another word, he was halfway to the elevator. Steel smiled and shook his head as he watched Tooms disappear into the elevator before the doors closed.

Tony felt bad. Part of him hoped that Steel had given up. This great sleuth, the man with all the great ideas, was finally admitting defeat. But he hadn't done so, and that tore a little in Tony. Sure, he liked Steel but felt that there was something surreal about him. He was more like a comic-strip hero than an actual cop. What Tony really didn't like was that Steel had *everything*: money, the title 'Lord Steel', pertaining to some family seat in England, and great looks that made women fall at his feet. Whereas all Tony had was a lousy pension plan and a dead girlfriend.

Steel turned towards Tony. He could see something in his eyes. A sadness of sorts.

"You don't have to stay, you know," Steel pointed out, heading for the break room.

"I am not leaving until we have Amber's killer," Tony growled.

Steel cracked a smile from the corner of his mouth and nodded. "You and me both, Tony. Come on, I'll make you a coffee." Steel raised his cup and turned as he headed for the smell of freshly brewed beans.

Tony took a seat and watched as Steel poured the steaming liquid into two mugs.

"I heard that the Task Force made a big bust this morning. A boutique full of cash and counting machines," Tony began, smiling suspiciously as Steel passed him his coffee. "It wouldn't be the same place that you were talkin' about, would it?" Tony quizzed him.

The other man just smiled and blew on his hot coffee. Steel sat down on the chair opposite Tony. His head was full of possible situations, but without solid data, they were all only theories.

"We need to find Tara. She is the centre of all this, I can feel it," Steel said before taking a sip.

Tony nodded. He had the same feeling.

"If you're right and she is here, she's gonna make it difficult for anyone to find her," Tony noted.

Steel knew he was right, and he just hoped since they couldn't find her, maybe nobody else could either.

Chapter 25

Mr Charles lay on his back. He was enjoying the quiet of the pool as he lay on the inflatable, which looked more like a floating chaise longue. He smiled with his eyes closed, thinking about the meeting and the look on Williams's face.

He had stolen from his organisation and had gotten away with it: whilst they were chasing their tails busying themselves over the lost data stick, they had missed the money transfer from the people in Berlin. They would find out about it sooner or later, but he wasn't worried. Once Williams's credibility had been crushed, he could blame Williams for almost anything now. He could even blame Williams with aiding the man who had taken the stick. How else would the man have known how to get into the safe?

The pool was inside a large glass conservatory which was attached to his seven-bedroom mansion. He loved money but loved demonstrating his wealth to others even more. His garage was more like a parking lot for classic cars. Charles was unmarried. He loved wealth too much to share it with someone who might try to take it away.

He could feel the warmth of the sun as it glared through the glass ceiling. The cool water lapped at his fingertips as it splashed onto the buoyant chair. All was good, and the eight security guards would make sure that he was safe.

Mr Charles hadn't stayed long at the meeting. Listening to all the pointless pleasantries and watching Williams drool over the huge German woman had made him feel nauseous. Besides, he had other matters to see too. Much more important matters, such as tying up loose ends.

There was a sudden noise from the sitting room, which joined onto the pool room via a sliding door. Charles looked up and over to where the sound had originated from. It had been a slight metallic clatter as if someone had dropped a key or some other small object onto the wooden flooring.

Charles shook it off, reasoning that his ears were playing tricks on him. He closed his eyes and went back to his daydream.

He looked up quickly.

It was the noise again, but this time it was closer. Very close, in fact. His eyes became wide, and he scanned the room, searching. There was someone there. It could be one of the security guards, but generally, they stayed outside.

Charles's brown eyes found nothing to tell him that anyone else was in the room. Gently, he used his hands as a paddle and started to turn himself around in the water. Charles half expected to see a masked man with a weapon standing ready. However, he was alone. He breathed a sigh of relief and paddled over to the metal stepladder. Charles reached for the polished steel railings and froze. Paranoia crept into his mind. The sudden thought of Williams seeking revenge filled his thoughts. In his smugness, he had forgotten what sort of man Williams was.

That had been a mistake.

He stared at the shine on the polished metal: what if Williams had wired the bars? *Water and electricity don't play well together*, he thought to himself.

Charles snapped his hands back and jumped into the water, opting to climb out using the side. Unfortunately, lack of exercise and an overindulgent lifestyle made the climb more of a sight of amusement than an elegant escape.

The flabby man stood up and hurried over to his bathrobe, which lay on a sun lounger. The fluffy white cotton clung to his skin as he pulled it on. Charles looked through the open doorway into the sitting area. It was large and modern. The whole mansion was early 1900s, but he had modernised the interior.

The antique wood panelling and staircases had been replaced with bright white walls and gaudy furnishings. Expensive art hung on the walls, its sole function being to advertise his wealth rather than demonstrate his artistic preferences. The house was an extension of his own personality: large and empty.

Charles moved slowly into the house. His bare feet left wet impressions on the wooden floor as he crept forward. The place was quiet, too quiet. He wanted to shout out but held himself back. Doing so would only alert the intruder to his presence. That was, of course, if there was an intruder, which he doubted.

The unnerved executive could feel his carotid artery pulsate with every heartbeat. His hands trembled with fear. He didn't know why. He looked out through the sitting room window and saw his guards, who seemed calm and undisturbed. Nothing seemed to be untoward. Nevertheless, he had a gut feeling that something was wrong.

Charles moved quickly through the sitting room and into the hallway. He cursed the slapping noise his bare wet feet were making on the polished wooden floor. He stopped for a moment and took off his bathrobe and tossed it to the floor and stood on it. Charles rubbed his feet on the soft cotton then headed off towards his study, leaving the trampled robe on the floor.

He needed to get to his desk, where he kept his gun. Pool water splashed off his body as he moved, leaving droplets on the floor and nearby wall. He felt a surge of relief as he entered the room. Rushing over to his desk, he pulled out a nickel-plated Kimber Carry .45. Now that he felt the weapon gripped tightly in his hand, he felt safe, confident.

A large bang from the floor above made him look up in terror. Charles gripped the weapon, and his strength returned. The sound had come from one of the bedrooms upstairs. More precisely, his bedroom. Carefully he made his way out of the study and headed for the brass bannister rail of the marble staircase. His movements were slow. Each step was taken as if he had a lead weight attached to his ankles.

Beads of sweat began to form and mix with the pool water. Charles wiped his eyes as a few drops of the mix trickled into his eyes and began to burn like acid.

Charles stopped at the top of the winding staircase and looked towards his door. There was an eerie silence, which was only broken by the sound of his erratic breathing. He crept forward towards his door. He could feel the gun in his hand begin to shake the closer he got. He stopped suddenly.

Soft music was coming from within.

At first, he couldn't make out the tune because of its low volume. But it was definitely music. Slowly he turned the handle and opened the door. The curtains had been drawn, and the only light was from a few candles that had been arranged around the large bedroom.

He walked in, feeling slightly confused. What the hell was going on, he wondered to himself? In the darkness, he suddenly caught sight of a pair of long legs in black stockings. Red high-heeled shoes and a black-and-red Basque completed the picture. However, the woman's face and shoulders were bathed in shadow.

"Oh, I do hope you're Mr Charles," came a sultry female voice.

Charles couldn't stop himself nodding enthusiastically, almost as if he was making a special point of his identity. His eyes fixed on this vision of beauty in front of him.

"Who are you?" he asked, but he wasn't really interested in the answer. His jaw was slack, and his grip was slacker. The gun fell from his hand as his arms came to rest by his side.

"Me?" she replied. "I am just a present from the management for all your hard work." Her voice was like a siren's song, drawing him closer. He stumbled forward as though under a hypnotic spell. Charles watched as she moved onto the bed, her perfect form suddenly held in a dim light. He moved steadily forward, the drool starting to form in the corners of his mouth.

"Come on, Charles, I don't bite... well, maybe a little." Her voice and laugh were intoxicating.

"P-please call me Charlie," he said, fumbling his words and his steps. She patted the bed next to her, and he obeyed by climbing up like a small puppy. She opened her legs slowly and pressed the chest piece of the Basque together.

"Come to me, Charlie, show me what you have got!" Her words tingled down his spine.

He climbed between her legs and moved forward, a huge grin across his face. This was the stuff of dreams or those sexy 'fake' letters to men's magazines. Her body was gorgeous, and he wondered what her face was like. Why did she keep it hidden, he wondered?

But it didn't matter. He looked over at the hand, restraints on the bed's headboard. Devices he had used before on many a young woman! Indeed, he had a perverse taste in sex. He was a little man that liked to hurt women because it made him feel good. A man who liked to watch others 'feel the pinch'. He couldn't wait to see how this one would fare.

"Let me see your face, my dear, let me see where I will end this night," he growled with a sudden burst of authority.

Suddenly her powerful legs shot up and locked around his neck. He struggled, but she was far too powerful for him. He started to lose consciousness.

"What are you doing you bi—"

She applied more pressure, cutting off his words.

"A certain someone sends his regards." She laughed as she heard something crack in his body.

"Whatever he is paying you I will double it," Charles begged, hoping it would be enough for her to let him go.

"I doubt it. His fee was very high." Again, she laughed as she squeezed a little more.

Charles could feel the air leaving his body.

"I will give you anything!" he gasped with the minimal breath he had left. "What did he offer you?"

"He said I could take you down and kick your ass as a punishment for all the women you ever hurt your sick bastard." As she spoke, she squeezed his neck, ever more powerfully.

He tried to claw at her, but her legs were long. As he slipped into darkness, he heard something else: Music. But not from the stereo. It was from a pocket watch.

As the darkness took him, he prayed that this would be how he died.

* * *

Mr Charles awoke to blackness. Blackness and the silence of the grave. There was a chill in the air. At first, he thought he was outside. Then he felt the cold of the metal on his back, the restraints on his arms, legs and chest. Before he had been groggy from his ordeal, but now he was very much awake.

He struggled to break his bonds but to no avail. Charles stopped and listened. There was a slight tapping noise. He froze, his heart began to pound against his chest. And then it came the music. The distant sound of the musical pocket watch.

Charles knew what the music meant: it was the signature of a madman. The last sound a person would hear before he started his devilish work. Charles looked as small pools of light appeared as the madman approached. Finally, a large lamp came on over Charles's head, and he could see himself and his perilous situation in detail. He was bound to a special table with his arms and legs spread out. Tubes of medical chemicals had been inserted into his neck and just above his collarbone.

"You can't do this to me, you psycho!" screamed out Charles in a futile attempt to scare Williams. The latter said nothing, just looked down at the bound man and stroked his hair, as if to comfort him.

"The council will find out what you have done, and you know the rules," Charles yelled desperately. "No one member may hurt any of the others." The desperately scared man hoped that his show of authority would sway his torturer from doing something terrible.

Williams looked at Charles and gently smiled. "I guess you're right. There would be questions, certainly. But then I could always say you ran off to South America or something. Oh, I know how about Australia?" Williams said with a sudden excited look as if something else had popped into his head.

"You know I have always wanted to go to Australia," the crazy doctor continued in a conversational, friendly tone. "Kangaroos, the wide-open spaces."

Charles looked up at his tormentor with a confused look. "What?" he asked.

Williams looked down at Charles in some excitement and slapped himself on the forehead. "Sorry, I do apologise, I was away somewhere else for the moment. Silly me. Now, where was I?" Williams said, looking puzzled. Then that callous grin of cruelty came over his long pale face.

"Oh, yes, I remember now. I could lie to the council, but that's not my style. That's more … yours," Williams went on, his face only inches away from the other man's. Suddenly he shot upwards and walked backwards. As he did so, the circle of light grew bigger, and five women dressed in scrubs entered the circle. Each of the women had different coloured hair.

Two of them walked towards Williams, holding out a surgeon's gown, which he stepped into, and another tied it up at the back. Two others held out a pair of surgical gloves and pulled them over his long bony fingers. Charles realised with horror this was not a scare tactic: they were getting him ready for surgery.

"Williams, you maniac, when the council find out about this you are a dead man!" Charles spat his words. His misplaced overconfidence in his dire situation showed on his smug, fat face.

His enemy froze for a moment and looked as if Charles had struck on a valid point.

"You know, Mr Charles, you are absolutely right, they would find out. That leaves me no alternative, I guess," Williams said disappointedly, turning and walking away.

Charles grinned. He had beaten the executioner. The great Mr Williams had been denied his pleasure.

Suddenly Williams stopped and turned with a smile. "Of course, if I showed them what I had done, I guess that would be different. Don't you think?"

With that, all the lights came on, and Charles saw for the first time the dreaded 'operating theatre' that he had heard so much about. Above him was the viewing gallery, inside which all the members of the council were standing, watching the proceedings.

Two of the women pulled out a large table from the wall, on which was a large monitor. As Charles watched, he realised with horror that Williams had been given permission to do his terrible business.

They all watched as the strange dance of multi-coloured lines twisted and swayed with every pitch of tone.

"Mr Charles," came the words from the loudspeaker that accompanied the picture on the screen. "You know the penalty for stealing from us. Not only did you steal from the organisation, but you also tried to incriminate one of your own colleagues. You know the punishment for this. I found it only fitting that you should face the man you accused." The lines onscreen were hard and jagged to match the words.

"Let this be a warning to you all," the voice said in roar of displeasure. "Mr Williams, you may proceed."

The star of the show gave a low theatrical bow and then turned to the gallery.

"Ladies and gentlemen, there are refreshments at the back, and for those who are squeamish...and the bathrooms are down the hall," he said with a smile. Williams then walked back to the wriggling Mr Charles. Williams pushed the remaining air from his gloves and smoothed them out over his fingers.

"Don't worry. I am not going to hurt you. I give you my word," Williams said once again, stroking Charles's hair.

The tied-up prisoner looked up; half confused. "Then why am I—"

Williams placed his index finger onto Charles's lips to silence him and slowly shook his head.

"Do you remember those young girls you raped and brutalised?" the psychopath went on. "Some of them took their own lives, and some ended up in a clinic. And some, well, let's just say... I got to them just in time." Williams stood back and revealed the line-up of the five women who had been assisting him.

A look of utter terror-filled Charles's face. Each woman held a bone saw. Each of them also had a look of utter contempt on their faces.

Williams walked around to the other side of the table, his hands behind his back. Charles was too transfixed on the women.

"I would like to say this was not personal, but I would be lying," Williams said with a kind of pleasure, as each of the women took her place standing beside a limb.

The tall, black-haired woman stood between his legs and held what appeared to be a rusty kitchen knife with a serrated blade. She winked at Charles and smiled. "Oh, lucky me. I won the toss," she said, and as she spoke, the other women moved in.

Revenge burned in their eyes. There were a piercing scream, and all the people in the gallery looked away. All apart from the large German woman, who was now staring into Williams's eyes with a lustful hunger. He stared back with equal pleasure. He smiled wickedly and headed for the door.

Chapter 26

Steel and Tony arrived at the apartment where Amber was found. Steel took the keys from his pocket and headed for the lock. The guard was gone, but the police tape remained. He looked over at Tony, who had a wary look on his face as if he really didn't want to go in.

"If you can't do it, I will understand," Steel said in a soft, reassuring tone. Tony felt almost insulted at the accusation. But the more he thought about it, the more he realised he was angry with himself, for if he couldn't bear to go into his dead girlfriend's apartment, he was letting her down. Tony gave Steel a shallow nod. Steel cracked a smile from the corner of his mouth and nodded back. He slipped the brass Yale key into the lock and turned it until they heard the click of the bolt release.

"You think we missed something?" Tony asked as they entered.

Steel said nothing at first, he simply headed for Amber's room. As Tony entered, he saw the huge stain where the blood had soaked into the floor. He stopped and stared for a moment. Flashback images of Amber's mutilated body lying on that spot returned. Steel stopped and looked over at Tony. He knew what he was going through.

"Tony," Steel gently called over. He knew that the more Tony relived that moment, the less likely he would be able to stick around. Not that he should have been there in the first place.

"Hey, Tony," Steel yelled loudly: since the soft approach didn't work, he'd decided to play it rough.

Tony looked up at Steel with an almost dazed look.

"Listen, Tony. This time you're here for Tara. If we find her, it may lead us to Amber's killer. You take Tara's room I will check Amber's," Steel explained.

Tony shot him a puzzled look. "I thought you just said we were here for Tara. So why would we look in Amber's room? We never found anything last time," Tony said, missing the point.

"No," John went on patiently. "I said YOU'RE here for Tara. You said there was nothing at her other apartment, so the chances are there may be something here we have overlooked."

Tony nodded and walked over to Tara's room, opened the door and walked in. He didn't know why they were there. He had already checked the room days ago to try and find out who the roommate was. He pulled on a pair of latex gloves and started to search for anything he could find. There'd been no visible signs of her having a computer, so he hoped for at least a diary.

Steel entered what had been Amber's room. Most of her stuff was still in boxes that took up that main part of the sitting room. The room was decorated in a ghastly pink colour, and there was not much in the way of furniture. A double bed rested against the left-hand wall facing the window. The wardrobes were built into the walls to save on what little space there was.

There was a black canvas holdall and one of those armoured suitcases. Steel noticed that there was fingerprint powder residue on the lock. He smiled at the CSU's thoroughness. He looked around the room. Apart from the stacked boxes, it was tidy. Steel walked out and headed for Tara's room, where he found Tony with a handful of Tara's panties.

Steel coughed and raised an eyebrow. Tony turned quickly and looked at Steel, then realised what he had in his grasp.

"Not very appropriate, but needs must I suppose." Steel smiled.

Tony just stood there, his mouth opening and shutting like a carp out of water. He turned red then shoved the underwear back in the drawer.

"I didn't find anything, how about you?" Tony said quickly, hoping to deflect Steel's crude humour away from himself. Steel looked back at the sitting room then returned his gaze to Tony.

"The place has been searched, so if there was something here, it has gone."

Tony looked blankly at Steel, reflecting that his claim that the apartment had been tossed didn't fit. "How do you work that out?" Tony asked. "The place isn't trashed. It looks normal." He looked around the room for signs of tampering. Steel walked over to a small dresser and picked up a tiny music box with a figure of a ballerina on its lid. He turned the key and let the tune play.

"And that, Tony, my friend, is what worries me. There are two possibilities. One they searched the place while nobody was here. Or two, they did it after Amber had come in. They managed to leave everything where it was, and doing that after you've killed someone … Well, that's takes nerve." Steel put down the music box.

"You see, whoever did it was careful enough not to draw attention to the fact," Steel noted as he walked back into the sitting room. His gaze fell onto the blood pool, and his own personal memories came flooding back. He closed his eyes as if to hold onto the image of his wife's smiling face. Steel was glad of his sunglasses to hide his pain.

Unlike Tony, Steel had not revisited the scene where his loved ones had died, which was the attic in his father's mansion in England, where he had lost his mother and wife. Sure, he had been home, mainly to uphold the formalities of the estate he had inherited. But he had never once ventured up those cold-looking stairs. He had ordered that during the renovation the attic was to be left as it was. It was more of a shrine now than a storage space.

"Are you OK?" Tony asked on seeing Steel standing there motionless as if he was in a trance. Steel turned slowly and nodded. Tony noted something different about him. Something dark, as if a haunting cloud had passed over him.

"I am fine," Steel reassured his friend. "I was just remembering something from a long time ago. It doesn't matter." He smiled and headed for the boxes that were stacked near the kitchen. Tony shook his head and went back to searching the bedroom.

Steel had looked through most of the boxes and found nothing but everyday items. Each box was labelled for convenience. But he could not find anything worth dying for in any of them. He had hoped for secret compartments and hidden data sticks but came up empty. All she had were pots and pans and a load of clothes. Even the suitcase was just a suitcase: no false bottoms.

The British detective leaned against the door frame of Tara's bedroom and watched Tony rip the room apart. He had searched through books and jars of creams. Neither of them knew what they were looking for, but Steel figured it wasn't anything big. Only information or data was likely to attract the unwanted attention of scary people.

The chances were if the other organisation was behind it all, the mystery involved something worth a lot of money or that could be used as 'leverage'. Tony slammed the last drawer shut and looked over at Steel with an angry glare.

"There is nothing here, Steel," Tony growled. "We just wasted half a day lookin' for nothin'!" He wished that McCall was there: she was someone whom he felt something for.

"We have learnt nothing, Steel, so are you friggin' happy?" Tony barked.

The other man rocked his head from side to side. "Actually, yes. I am feeling quite good. However, I sense you are not." Steel moved away from the door's wooden frame.

Tony's mouth fell open with surprise. "How the hell can you feel good about this?" He walked around, trying to stop himself leaping over and strangling the smug Englishman.

"For one thing we know whatever it was they were looking for, they never found it," Steel explained, talking softly. "Secondly, I'd say that unfortunately your girlfriend was killed by accident."

Tony's tearful wild-eyed stare shot over towards Steel. A look of bewilderment was carved into that stout Irish/Italian face.

"How can you be sure they didn't find it?" Tony's voice was close to breaking. "Maybe they found it on her and killed her."

"No. If they had it, why take Brooke? And why is Tara missing? I think we have been looking at it all wrong. I think that Tara has what they are looking for, and Amber walked in at the wrong time. Remember someone telling us that Amber wasn't due to move in until Monday? I think they mistook Amber for Tara. I think Tara walked in after they had gone and now, she is running scared."

Tony investigated nothingness and weighed up what Steel had just said. It made sense, but it didn't change the fact that Amber was dead. In fact, if her death had been an accident, it made things worse.

* * *

Steel had told Tony to go home. It was Sunday and would be limited to witnesses he could talk to due to the weekend closures. Besides Tony was still shaken up after having been in the apartment. Steel had planned to go back to the precinct and wait for the ME's report on the body from the park.

The British detective stood outside in the warm sunlight and watched Tony's police-issue Dodge Challenger disappear into the mass of traffic at the crossroads of Ninth Avenue. He stood for a moment and looked up and down the street as he pulled on a pair of leather-and-neoprene gloves.

Tomorrow everyone would be back at work. There was a lot of investigating to do, and the body in the park meant even more activity. Neither was it helpful that the accident earlier in the week was tying up the labs with urgent tests. He started to head towards Eighth Avenue.

From the corner of his eye, Steel saw a yellow cab pull up. Curious, he stopped and turned just in time to see a fabulous brunette get out and start struggling with her shopping bags. Steel smiled and shook his head at the damsel in distress. As he approached, Steel took note of the driver: a large black guy with dreadlocks and a strange knitted hat.

"May I be of assistance?" Steel asked politely.

The woman giggled and nodded. Steel noticed that she kept her face away from him or else blocked it from view whenever possible.

"Oh, thank you so much," the woman said in a southern accent as Steel placed the bags on the ground.

All the while, his alarm bells were ringing.

"Hey, do you need a taxi, man?" asked the driver in a joyful tone.

Steel stepped backwards to give the woman space to sort her bags out, but all the time, he took care to never look at her directly.

"No, thank you," Steel said to the cab driver. "I don't have far to go." He had not noticing the air-powered dart gun that the cabbie had just aimed out of the window. There was a dull thud of gas being released as the weapon was discharged. Steel grabbed his neck and pulled out a small dart.

"Oh, bugger," Steel said, looking at the small projectile. Immediately he started to feel the effects of the drug, but he grabbed for the cabbie, nonetheless. Steel still had some fight left in him, and he intended to use it on the driver. The cabbie yelped as Steel approached and wound the window up. Groggily Steel made it to the cab's door and raised a white-knuckled first. The safety glass of the driver's window exploded into small fragments and Steel began to drag the screaming cabbie out before the woman hit him three more times with the dart gun. Steel lay on the ground, with the bleeding cabbie pulled halfway out of the window.

"We stickin' this crazy motha in the trunk, man," yelped the driver as he fell out of the broken window. "I ain't riskin' him wakin' up and killin' me!"

The woman smiled and took off her wig: it was the black-haired woman Steel had encountered at the boutique. She knelt close to the unconscious man at her feet. She smiled and kissed two fingers and then placed them onto Steel's ruby lips.

"Sweet dreams, my white knight. Dream well," she crooned to him.

Chapter 27

Steel awoke slowly. He felt coldness on his skin. That was when he realised; he was naked. He was bound to something cold … Something metal. He didn't try to struggle; he could feel it would be pointless. He was bound with his arms and legs out to the sides. Everything was black, and there was a clinical smell in the room.

Above him, a bright light came on, followed by the tap, tap, tap of expensive shoes. The single light on above him revealed he was bound to a strange metallic construction, shaped into the letter 'X'. He was upright and exposed, in more than one way. The tapping came closer until the walker stopped and he heard a whispered discussion. Suddenly all the lights came on, and there stood Williams and the black-haired woman from the boutique.

Williams took one look at Steel and turned to the woman. She just shrugged and smiled broadly.

"Keres, my dear, I asked for him to be unharmed… not undressed, but I see now why the ladies think so much of him," Williams said, laughing and raising an eyebrow.

"Why of course, sir," Keres said, fumbling over her words as she grinned. "After all, there is so much of him … I mean, he is very muscular, sir."

"I also had to make sure he wasn't armed," she said almost innocently.

Williams rolled his eyes and walked up to Steel with an embarrassed look. "I must apologise, John, it would appear, my assistant, Keres, has taken a shine to you. Once you've gotten dressed, please do join me upstairs." His voice was apologetic and sincere. This was not the man Steel was used to: the madman – the killer, no, this was a civilised man, the complete opposite from the man Steel had first encountered a year ago . Williams smiled and walked back towards the doorway.

"Keres, please ensure that our guest is well taken care of, and bring him to the study, will you?" Williams saw a glint in her eye as he spoke. Her gaze locked onto Steel's impressive physique.

"Oh, don't worry, Mr W, it will be my pleasure," she said and waited until she heard the door close behind her. As she approached, her metal high heels gave a loud tap as they impacted on the tiled floor. She moved slowly as if to enjoy the view for a moment.

Keres looked up at Steel. There was a purposeful glint in her eye. She moved close to him, almost nose to nose. Steel wondered what she had interpreted Williams's commands to mean. He felt something cold against his stomach but was unable to look down to see what it was. The brunette's hand moved across his muscular chest, her fingertips paying special attention to the scars from the bullets' exit wounds. She had a sad look as she touched them, almost as if she could feel the pain, they were a reminder of. Her other hand was held firmly behind her.

John Steel had found himself in many tight spots before, but none like this. By this stage, after his capture, he had usually devised a way out of the situation and was already making plans to carry out an escape.

But this time it was different. There was something sinister and oddly surreal about all this, and it was all her doing.

"I think your boss wants me alive," Steel said, confused about the whole situation.

"He also said that I have to take very good care of you," she purred. There was a clicking sound, and then Steel felt the X-shaped contraption he was attached to begin to move down to a horizontal position.

"And, my white knight, I intend to take vvveeery good care of you indeed." Her words were followed by the sound of a zip being pulled down, followed by the soft flapping of clothes hitting the floor.

* * *

Williams sat in one of the red leather chesterfields that faced a large marble fireplace. He took out his pocket watch and checked the time. They had been gone for over an hour – almost two. Normally he would be worried, knowing what he did about Steel and what he was capable of. However, Williams also knew that Steel was curious, and Williams had sparked Steel's curiosity by bringing him there.

He was about to get up and find out what was keeping them when the two oak double doors opened and in walked Steel and Keres. Williams noticed Keres wore a particularly wide smile and walked with a swagger.

"I hope Keres didn't give you a difficult time, Mr Steel?" Williams said, walking over to a large drinks cabinet that was housed behind a wall panel. The mirrored back glistened as it reflected the small lights above.

"Oh, there were a couple of hard moments, but I'll live." Steel smiled and Keres bit the nail on her right index finger. Williams looked at them both in the mirrored back of the wall panel and shook his head with a smile. Picking up two large-bowled brandy glasses, Williams turned and walked towards Steel.

"You may leave us now, Keres, thank you." Williams's words were soft and gentle. Keres nodded and swaggered out of the room, closing the double doors on her way out.

"Please, sit down," Williams said, handing Steel a glass. Steel took it, and both men sat before the roaring fire.

"We're drinking Domaine des Forges, bottled over three hundred years ago. Preserved since the eighteen hundred. The cost, astronomical," Williams said, before putting the glass under his nose and inhaling the aroma. His eyes closed as he savoured the strong hard smell.

"Such a thing should be savoured and enjoyed." Williams looked over at Steel, who was admiring the golden colour in the firelight. Williams smiled comfortably, reassured in his estimation of Steel's character. He knew from their first meeting that John Steel was much like himself – a different side of the same coin.

"This is all very nice, Mr Williams, but can we get to the point? I don't think you brought me here because you wanted to catch up on old times." Steel lifted the glass to his lips and sipped the ageing cognac. He had noticed a woman's handbag on Williams's desk, meaning that Steel's arrival had interrupted something.

Williams smiled and raised his glass. "Quite so. To the point then," he said, crossing his legs underneath him and sitting like a child. As he did so, Steel noticed that Williams was wearing odd socks. One was black and red stripes, and the other was yellow and blue.

"John, you're investigating the death of Amber Taylor… yes?" Williams asked, wriggling around on the chair, trying to find a comfortable position.

"I can't really say. Why, what's your interest?" Steel asked, suddenly getting a bad feeling.

"Well, if any of your colleagues are investigating the case, tell them to be careful. It isn't at all what it seems," Williams explained, leaning forward.

Steel sat back in his chair and looked suspiciously at Williams. This wasn't what he had been expecting from Williams. He had been anticipating a very different sort of warning.

"Why the concern? Surely having us killed would be a very good thing from your point of view, wouldn't it?"

Williams looked mortified. "John! How can you say that after all, we've been through together?" Williams raised his bottom lip over his upper one and gave Steel a sad look, like a disappointed puppy.

Steel laughed and took another sip of brandy.

The psychopath's face became serious, and he uncrossed his legs and leant forward. "Let me explain. The other 'organisation' you are following in this regard, the ones I told you about before, well, they are dangerous and out of control. You know our methods, but them ... Let's just say they have no rules, only objectives and no one ever gets in their way. They need to be stopped. And unfortunately, fate has chosen you to stop them." Williams appeared to be talking matter-of-factly as if he was describing the finer points of an ordinary business. His usual maddening tone had gone.

Of course, Steel had seen first-hand precisely what the 'organisation' could do, and he could see that Williams was nervous.

"So, what do you want us to do, stop investigating this murder?" Steel asked, smiling and shaking his head.

Williams's face, however, was like stone. The orange glow of the fire reflected in his corneas, giving them a demonic look.

"No, Lord Steel. I want you to watch your back and prepare for war."

* * *

Steel woke up with a strange taste in his mouth and feeling slightly disorientated. He blinked several times as his vision started to return. He found himself lying on his side, looking at what appeared to be a television screen. The smell of fake leather and the sensation of movement beneath him told him he was in the back of a car.

He sat up and immediately felt as if he had been out all-night drinking bad cocktails. He touched his brow: it felt cold and clammy. His vision came and went, almost as if his eyes could not focus. He knew something was wrong. Steel had already figured that they would knock him out for travel purposes, but this was something else.

It appeared to be almost dawn. As he looked out of the window, he saw everything had that blue tint of pre-dawn light. As they travelled through the nearly empty streets, Steel noticed small orange shards of light breaking through between the buildings.

"What time is it? And where have I been all this time?" Steel demanded. The driver in front of him said nothing. He just shot a smile at the rear-view mirror and cupped his ear, as if to signal that he had not heard what Steel had said.

The detective felt something roll against his thigh. Looking down, he could make out it was a bottle; however, the label was a blur. He picked it up for a closer look.

He could feel the refreshingly cold moisture on the clear plastic. Cracking the lid, he carefully put the neck to his lips. The liquid was cold and still, and he hoped it was water.

Steel went on inhaling the liquid until the plastic screwed together under the vacuum, as he sucked out every drop of the contents.

"Where are you taking me?" Steel yelled, angry at himself for letting his abduction occur.

"I was told to take care of you. Don't worry, I have the address," the driver said.

Now wider awake, Steel realised that he was in the back of a yellow cab. As Steel listened to the cabbie's voice, he thought he recognised him, but couldn't place where from.

"Who put me in here?" Steel asked. He didn't really want to know. He just wanted to hear the man's voice again.

"Some pretty lady. She gave a good tip as well."

Steel smiled as he worked out it was the same cab driver who he'd met before, but why was he been so secretive? Surely, he would realise that Steel would recognise him. Unless of course, he had something to do with his present condition.

Without the cabby noticing, Steel took off his watch and pressed a button on its side. The hour marks started to glow green and Steel stuffed the watch down the back of the seat. Slowly, everything began to spin. He knew he was in trouble. Reaching for his phone, Steel pressed the 'medical app'. From its base, a small pin shot out. Quickly, Steel stabbed himself in the chest with it. His breathing became laboured, and his chest began to burn.

"Let me out," Steel growled. He still had strength but very little. The cabbie looked in his rear-view mirror and saw Steel pull out his Berratta Storm Bulldog. The cabbie's eyes widened as Steel aimed it at him.

"Let me out now, or you won't be around to spend the tip," Steel growled.

The taxi screeched to a halt and Steel opened the door and fell out. Steel could hear the scream of brakes from the other surrounding cars and could feel the wind from the river. He realised that he was on the Brooklyn Bridge.

Slowly he stumbled towards the metal railing. As he reached the edge, he stuck his fingers down his throat and then vomited hard onto the concrete walkway. As he held the rail, he felt a bit of metal bright against his skin. Quickly, he used the sharpness of it to cut his hand and then clenched his fist so that the blood would ooze from the wound. A cascade of fresh blood flooded over the railings.

Steel knew he didn't have much time. There was a peeping sound from his cell phone. He smiled, climbed up over the rail and let himself drop. People rushed over, and women screamed.

But all any of them saw was a man in black disappearing into the murky depths of the East River.

Chapter 28

Detective Lewis Coreman was new to Homicide; in fact, he was a new detective altogether. The last detective in his job had quit because of personal reasons. Coreman was ambitious and full of himself, and for some reason, the brass saw fit to promote him to detective.

Some said he was promoted on posting: a cunning ploy by his D.C. captain to get him away from the other cops. But he didn't care; he had gotten it.

He was of medium build and medium height. He wore styled brown hair and a grey Armani suit. He dabbled in stocks, but his main money came from Daddy. He was a rich kid whose encounter with a judge, made sure he was given a choice: go into the military or the police. The army had rejected him, but luckily his father had pulled some strings and got him into the police academy. His only saving grace was that he was a computer whiz, and he liked everyone to know it.

Coreman checked his reflection in the monitor. He smiled and nodded, admiring his own idea of good looks. His clean-shaven round face was proportionate to his stocky bulk. The floor was clear because most of his colleagues had not come in yet. He had been there since five a.m., and most of the night shift had already headed home or were out on cases.

He sat back and stroked his desk as though it was made from gold. He smiled and looked around, but there was no one to brag to. Suddenly one of the night shift detectives walked up to him and handed him an address.

"You're up for this, newbie," the tall, thin, ageing detective said as he slung his jacket on.

"Where we are going?" Coreman said excitedly.

The ageing Tooms laughed. "Well, I am going home to my wife, and you are going to check that out. It's a possible suicide. There are lots of witnesses, so I would hurry your ass up before they all go home," laughed the veteran.

Coreman sat open-mouthed for a moment before looking down at the address. *One times white male, possible suicide. Brooklyn Bridge.* Coreman stood up. If he waited around, witnesses and evidence would be lost. He smiled nervously and headed out. This was his first case, and he sure didn't want it to be his last.

* * *

Coreman had taken a cab to the scene—it was quicker than filling out the paperwork to take a vehicle, he could do that later. What's more, driving there would have been his first time driving in New York—after all, he had been a cop D.C. The three lanes of the bridge had been put down to two so that the forensic teams could do their work in safety. He got the cabby to pull up close to the scene. He sat for a moment to gather his thoughts. Coreman looked at the chaos of the situation: uniformed cops trying to wave on curious onlookers in their cars.

There wasn't much press, just a couple of freelancers trying to get something to sell. It was an old story, so why should there be? It was just some guy who woke up hating himself and took a dive. It would have been hot news if he had gone on the rampage with a weapon. Coreman spotted the ME's wagon and the CSU's vehicles. There was a huge blacked out SUV parked up next to the railings for easy access to their equipment.

Beads of sweat started to collect around his collar. He was in charge. The thought had just sunk in. This was his mess to sort out. His eyes were fixed on the situation. His hands gripped his A4 organiser until his knuckles became white.

Suddenly there was a loud knock on his window, causing him to jump. He looked over to find a veteran uniformed cop staring in. The cabbie wound down his window and faced the officer.

"Good morning, sir, I am afraid you're going to have to move along, this is a crime scene," the cop told him. He was polite, but his tone rang with authority.

"Don't blame me, officer, I am just droppin' this dude off," said the ageing black cabbie.

"I am Detective Coreman," said Coreman, showing his shield. His voice was stern and almost arrogant. He got out of the cab and passed the cabbie a twenty-dollar bill. The driver took off quickly, assuming he'd been given a big tip. Coreman scowled at the misunderstanding, but he had other things to worry about.

Coreman walked briskly, heading for the ME and the CSU, who were camped out together, with people busy taking samples.

"I'm Detective Coreman, so what have we got?" he asked, hoping for a quick end to his first case.

"I'm Tina Franks, the ME," replied the busy medical professional. "As for what has happened, well, Detective, that's your job. All I know is we have blood and a missing body. A man was seen jumping into the East River early this morning." Tina gave him a look that said, 'your turn'.

Except he didn't have one, he was clueless. He cursed the other detective for landing this one in his lap. He looked around for a moment, gathering his thoughts. *Eyewitnesses*, he thought, after all, someone had phoned the cops. He thanked Tina and hurried off to the uniformed officer near their squad car.

"Who called it in?" Coreman asked the veteran cop. The cop smiled and took out his notebook. Coreman felt the man toying with him as he slowly flicked through his notes.

"We were just finishing our patrol early this morning around six when we got flagged down by a couple in a car," the officer readout. "They had just come off the bridge. They said that there was some guy getting ready to jump off the bridge after getting out of a yellow cab. There are some more eyewitnesses over there, next to the other squad car."

Coreman looked over to another squad car at the other end of the cordon. Beside it, there was two officers and two couples, each officer interviewing one of the couples, keeping away from each other as to get individual accounts. Coreman looked around to see if there were any close circuit cameras, and he spotted at least two. He made a note in his book: *Contact Traffic for any footage they may have.* There had been plenty of cell phones with footage which the CSU teams had taken in. Tina Franks was all done picking up her samples of vomit and blood, which she needed due to fact that the witness had said the man had thrown up before jumping. Coreman put it down to a drunken jilted lover who couldn't let go. When he had spoken to the first responding officer, it turned out that he hadn't seen much, but had just responded to someone flagging him down. Unfortunately, by the time they had gotten through the traffic, the man had gone.

The keen new detective smiled to himself: his first case alone, and he was breezing through it. This was one way of getting the captain's attention. He walked back to Tina Franks like a man who had already cracked the case.

"Well, Dr Franks, you and CSU have taken samples. Seems to me to be an open and shut case. A man gets drunk after been dumped by his girlfriend; he can't take the disappointment, so he jumps," Coreman said confidently.

Tina just looked at him and said nothing. She looked around the scene. To her mind, something was wrong. The vomit and the blood. Sure, she could understand the throwing up if it was the result of a drunken last moment. But the blood? Her gaze halted on one spot at the railings. She found the place where whoever it was had apparently slashed themselves and took another sample. It was a small piece of metal that was sticking up out of the rail. It was only a tiny thing but was enough to cause a nasty scratch.

The ME looked at it for a moment, realising that their 'jumper' must have slashed themselves on purpose because of the whereabouts of the piece of metal. She said nothing at first. As usual, she would test things first then inform those in authority of her findings later.

* * *

Coreman had made it back to the precinct and was going through some of the footage from the cell phones. By the time Tony and Tooms had arrived, he had watched around twenty images.

Tooms and Tony walked over and introduced themselves. Coreman greeted them politely and told them of the suicide case he'd attended. The three detectives gathered around Coreman's computer as he began to watch the next footage. This was the best one yet. It was clear and close. Close enough for Tony and Tooms to recognise the jumper as Steel.

"I mean seriously what sort of moron decides to jump off a bridge?" Coreman laughed. "I mean really, what a loser!"

Tooms ripped the man out of his chair and pinned him against the back wall. "That 'loser' happens to be one of the best detectives that we have," said Captain Brant as he walked up to the group. He had just seen the same footage on the news. Tooms let the man drop to the floor, and he backed away before he did something, he would later regret.

"Son, you have a lot to learn," Brant said softly. "Right now, lesson one is don't be here when McCall gets here. Because if she finds out what you just said, she will shoot you." Brant held his hands tightly together so that he couldn't shoot him himself.

Coreman nodded and ran for the elevator. Tony looked over at Brant. "I want this one boss."

Brant said nothing at first, he just stared at the frozen image of Steel on Coreman's computer.

"I got a better job for you, Marinelli," Brant said with a lump in his throat. "Figure out how to tell Sam that Steel is dead."

* * *

For McCall, Monday morning brought a grey skyline and a cold biting wind. She had left her mother's house in Boston early, in order to beat the traffic. Plus, she wanted to get an early start on the case. Some German pianist called Richter was blaring from her stereo. Steel had lent her the CD a week ago, but she kept forgetting to give it back for some reason.

She pulled into her usual parking lot and eased the Mustang into her parking spot. She had been such a good customer the owners gave her a nameplate. It was a simple thing. A licence plate with *SAM McCALL* stamped on it.

McCall turned off the engine and just sat for a moment. The weekend had been great, fantastic even. However, now it was time to go back to work. McCall stared into her own eyes in the rear-view mirror. She had to get back into the mind step. Time to be a cop again.

McCall closed her eyes and took a deep breath. As she exhaled, her eyes shot open. She was back, and she was ready. She locked up her car and clicked the remote again for the alarm. The lights flashed twice to indicate the activation.

As she headed towards the precinct, she couldn't help but wonder how far the boys had progressed with the case during the weekend. McCall was hoping she hadn't missed anything important. She smiled at the thought of Steel having already wrapped up the whole case and the dirtbag being in a cell. McCall laughed and shook her head at the stupidity of the idea. Nothing could have happened, because he hadn't blown anything up, as he had a habit of doing.

As she walked into the precinct, she picked up on the mood. It was like she had walked into a wake. Every cop either looked angry or lost. McCall waved at the desk sergeant and smiled as she always did. But he just stared at her and shook his head.

Something turned in her gut. Something bad had happened, and she should have been there. McCall didn't bother waiting for the elevator; she rushed the stairs. As she reached the top, she saw Tony and Tooms talking with Captain Brant. She froze for a moment. She was confused. Everyone was there, so what was the problem?

Everyone was there except for Steel.

As she walked towards the three men, she felt her legs grow heavy. Tony looked up and caught sight of McCall. His eyes said it all. She went to sit at her desk but missed the chair completely. The men rushed over and found her just sitting on the floor, her eyes moving from side to side as if searching for something. Tony and Tooms grabbed an arm each and helped her into her chair. She looked over at Steel's office door, expecting him to walk out with a smile and a coffee mug. Except he didn't. She looked up at Brant with watery eyes. She wanted to do something: scream, yell, smash something. But all she could do was sit and look at Brant.

Outside the clouds were getting greyer, and the wind was picking up. There was a storm coming. McCall had gone from the emotion of shock to anger. She was now pacing up and down the floor of the large briefing room. Brant, Tooms and Tony were sitting at the long desk waiting for Tina to arrive back from the morgue. Detective Coreman hung around by his desk, almost afraid to say something, in fear of the wrath of McCall.

"So, what happened?" McCall asked.

Tooms looked over at her as she paced up and down with a face like thunder.

Joshua Tooms leant forward, using his elbows as support, saying, "From what Detective Coreman explained—"

"—Who the hell is Coreman?" McCall interrupted.

All three men turned and looked at the stocky detective who was cowering at his desk. Coreman felt himself being watched and looked over with a slightly panicked look. Brant waved him over.

"Detective Coreman is Jenny Thompson's replacement, the 'apparent suicide' was his case," Brant explained as Coreman walked in sheepishly. All of them stared at him with an almost hateful gaze.

"Tell them what you found, Coreman," Brant said in a soft calming voice. Brant knew what the kid was going through; they all did. But at that moment all their memories of his first day had been clouded by hate. Not for him personally, but that wasn't to say that if he now said the wrong thing, his life would become unbearable.

"Well, early this morning, I was given the address of a possible suicide. On arrival, I saw that the first responding officer had—" Coreman stopped talking, finding that everyone was staring at him with menacing eyes.

"Oh … Right." Coreman gulped. "Well at around six this morning, a yellow cab was seen to make an emergency stop on the bridge, and the passenger got out. Eyewitnesses and several cell phone videos have film of the passenger throwing up, and then he purposely seems to cut his hand. After which he jumps from the bridge." Coreman's eyes darted around from person to person, hoping for a response.

"I looked at the best footage, and it was Steel," Brant said sorrowfully. He looked into McCall's eyes as they turned red but refused to tear up.

"The ME found traces of blood and vomit at the scene," Coreman continued, aware that all eyes were upon him. "She suspects that whoever the jumper was, purposely threw up and the cut was a result of the climb over the railings." Beads of sweat started to collect on the back of his neck. McCall's glare was the worst; her eyes searing like laser beams. He chose not to identify the jumper as Steel. It was Brant's idea not to say his name, and now he knew why.

"Traffic is sending over any footage to and from the bridge for around that time, also any footage around the area. Harbour patrol are sweeping the area, but due to the current this morning they are not feeling hopeful." Coreman looked at his notes. He couldn't bear to look up at them with their scowls of judgement.

Coreman had thought being the newbie would come with some sort of unpleasantness—having to get the coffee, being the guy who bought the takeout food, doing that sort of menial job to earn their respect. But he never imagined that his first case would be the death of one of their own, and it sucked.

"Did we find the cab, the driver? Have we found…?" McCall started to say but quickly stopped as Brant gave her the famous 'be quiet' stare that most parents must use.

"In spite of this, we still have cases to finish," Brant went on grimly. "Now I know it's a blow and it is a lot to take in. However, we've got to carry on." He looked around the room at the pained expressions. He was feeling the pain as well but couldn't show it. He had to be strong, to set an example.

"Coreman, you will remain on this case," Brant said calmly. He could feel McCall's disappointed look but ignored it. "Tony, you stay on looking for our runaway witness."

Tony nodded and got up to leave, but Brant raised a large index finger and made a downwards motion. Tony smiled and immediately sat back down.

"McCall, you and Tooms have the Amber case and the body in the morgue. Find out if Steel is … was … right, and whether the body is indeed our John Doe." Brant looked around at the gathering of detectives. He wore a doleful expression instead of his usual angry one. Sometimes, McCall thought, to be captain, you had to have a good 'angry' face. *No one fears a happy captain*, she thought.

McCall stood up slowly. She looked over at Coreman, who was trying to stand up to look tall. She moved towards him and extended a hand. As he took it, her hand closed around his in a vice-like grip. She looked into his eyes.

"Welcome aboard, Detective Coreman," she told him. "However, if you mess this up, I will make sure you spend the rest of the year in vice, undercover." McCall released her grip and walked away without turning around. Tooms smiled and put a massive arm around the young detective's shoulder.

"Welcome to the team, man," he simply said then went to work.

Coreman just stood there and felt his stomach turn.

This sure is a bad first day, he thought.

Chapter 29

Tara paced up and down the apartment. She had been there for days with no contact with the outside world apart from Kim, and she had to honest – as much as she loved Kim as a friend, it was beginning to wear thin. It had been far too long since his last message, far too long without a word. On several occasions, she had almost sent him her address but had deleted the message every time. She kept remembering the newsflash about the body at the park. She knew it was him. She didn't want to believe it, but it had to be. Why else wouldn't he have called? Yesterday Tara had taken the battery out of her phone after watching some cop show: in the drama, the bad guys had caught up with the witness using the phone's GPS.

She was street smart; she had to be. She grew up alone in a bad neighbourhood with only a few friends. Tara knew she would have to leave soon. She thought the best time was when Kim was at work. She couldn't risk any questions.

"Where will you go, what will you do?" Tara could hear Kim's voice now asking the sort of questions that would get her into trouble. She would leave a note, that was the simplest way. The less Kim knew, the better.

Tara went to the kitchen and looked for some paper and pen. It took at least fifteen minutes before she found something, an A4 pad and pen in an old sideboard, which had probably a result of Curb mining – the art of finding furniture on the street that you need. She closed the drawer to the sideboard in the sitting room and carried the A4 pad and pencil over to the couch. The note was simple: *Thanks Kim for everything, I will be fine just need to get away for a while. T.*

The worried young woman folded the paper in half and wrote Kim's name on the front to make it stand out and left it on the coffee table. Tara got up and headed for her bag, which lay in a corner next to the television set. Washed clothes lay folded next to the pink case. Tara looked down at the case and thought for a moment. No one knew where she was. She was safe. Then she looked up at the flat-screen TV as the news came on. It was a recap of the 'body in the park' story.

She bent down and set to packing up her stuff. It was nine in the morning, so she had plenty of time. Luckily Kim wouldn't be back until late.

It took only minutes to find and pack her stuff away. Her clothes had been washed and freshly ironed. Given the amount of time she'd had to kill, she could have redecorated Kim's apartment. Tara took one last look around the room, almost as if she was saying goodbye to her family home. Suddenly she caught her reflection in the glass of a photograph that hung on the wall.

Tara raised her left hand and touched her beautiful red hair. A tear rolled down her right cheek and hung onto her chin for a moment before falling onto her black T-shirt. She headed for the bathroom and searched the lower cupboards. Finding what she was looking for, Tara Stood up straight, she investigated the mirror and then at the package of hair dye.

She smiled for a brief second before thinking: *well, they say blondes have all the fun.*

* * *

Early that morning, nobody had seen the small black hovercraft speed towards the bridge. Its matt black shell and blacked-out windows, along with its sleek space-age look went unnoticed.

Nor did anyone see it slowly and silently pull up and snatch Steel's limp remains from the black depths of the murky waters. Even though people were looking down at the blackness, they never saw anything. Not even the ripples in the water.

The craft slipped away down past the Governors Island and then past Gravesend Bay. Once it had hit open water, the beast opened and headed north towards Southampton and Mecox Bay. The trip took an hour. By the time the hovercraft had reached the bay, the sun was just rising over the horizon. The vessel turned towards Mecox Bay and headed towards the beach and onto the strait. The craft sped across the sand without leaving a trace of its actions.

As the sun broke free from the horizon, the craft was on Hayground Cove and moving fast. As it reached the large boathouse, it slipped inside, and the automatic doors slid down.

An old Oriental man in a white suit watched silently for a short time while another man approached.

"We have him, sir. Where do you want the—" The man stopped talking suddenly, and the Oriental character shot him a stare. The man swallowed hard and stepped back.

"Take him to my office, I will take care of things there." The Oriental guy was in his late fifties and had an air of fear about him. The man bowed slightly and walked away with some urgency.

Well, Johnny, what have you gotten into this time? the man thought to himself, smiled and shook his head before heading towards a large mansion in the distance.

Tara walked out of the bathroom, drying off her new styled hair. It wasn't the best job in the world, but then it wasn't green either. She had cut it shorter just to add to the disguise. She looked in the mirror to check the result. She smiled. Somehow, she preferred the new look to the old.

Out of the corner of her eye, she caught another newsflash on the TV. The report was that of someone jumping from the Brooklyn Bridge earlier that morning. Tara turned to watch. The grainy footage appeared to be from a cell phone. It showed a man falling from the bridge into the river. The reporter said it was thought to be a detective who was working on the Amber Taylor case. Tara froze. She felt faint and nauseous. She sat for a moment and just watched as they played more footage. The female reporter's tone was full of played emotion – possibly to enhance the report, people loved emotional stories. Tara stood up suddenly. She knew she had to go, but first, she had to get back to her apartment. She needed the money she had saved and her passport. Tara picked up her suitcase and headed for the door. *Time to go,* she thought to herself. Tara knew she had to leave for Kim's sake. If they could kill a cop, what would a waitress's life matter? She placed her hand into her jacket pocket and pulled out some crumpled bills. She didn't have much money, only a few dollars. Tara looked over to the small kitchen and the china cat cookie jar that sat happily on a shelf next to a basilikum plant. She knew Kim kept some money aside for that rainy day. Tara took down the large white cat and stuck her hand inside. There was around six hundred in various bills. Tara took a hundred and slipped an IOU into the jar before placing it back. She had enough for a cab to take her to the nearest subway. Tara knew she couldn't afford to be seen on the street, so a taxi made sense. She was alone, and she was scared. However, she had to be strong to see it through. She still had a chance to make it out alive.

The scared young woman walked out into the sunlight and slipped on the sunglasses. She pulled her jacket's hood up over her hair and headed off. Next stop, back home.

* * *

Williams sat in a small, darkened room. There was only the light from the twelve flat-screen televisions to illuminate the space. It was a ten-by-ten area with nothing but an old cloth chesterfield armchair, a small side table and the twelve different-sized television sets which had been arranged to make huge screen. Mr Williams watched as the news reporter told of a detective who had jumped to his death earlier that morning. He watched the footage that had been shot on a dashcam. Williams watched as a yellow cab screeched to a halt, and a man dressed in black got out. The man stumbled, then made himself throw up before jumping over the rails into the water.

Williams's eyes squinted in displeasure. The remote in his right hand made a loud cracking sound as he squeezed the life out of it. He sat for a moment and tossed the crumpled plastic remains into a shadowy corner, with the others that had suffered the same fate.

"I really must stop watching television," Williams grumbled as he reached over to the small side table to where an intercom unit sat beside a crystal glass decanter set.

"Crystal," he said into the intercom, his gaze still on the arranged televisions. No answer came.

"Oh, Crystal," he said again, as he sung the words in a mocking tone. Still, there was silence. Williams rolled his eyes, stood up and headed out of the room.

Williams opened the heavy wooden door and walked out into Crystal's large secretarial office. The whole place was redolent of a 1960s British government office, with wooden wall panelling and red leather on the doors. Various potted plants sat on top of grey metal filing cabinets. She had chosen the style of furnishings herself when she first started. A stack of books by authors such as Le Carré, Ian Fleming and Graham Greene lay lined up on wall shelves above a deep burgundy leather couch.

Crystal's employer stood in the doorway for a moment, unnoticed by the pretty blonde secretary or her tall visitor, who at that moment was sitting on the antique oak desk whispering in her ear and grinning. Williams watched and gave a little smile at the delightful display. *Ah, young love*, he thought to himself. Then his face became serious and had a touch of displeasure.

"Obviously you are working for free or have very little to do," Williams's tone was full of wrath, but the volume didn't break above his normal speaking pitch. The man shot up onto his feet and stood rigid, as though a pike had been inserted through his body – Vlad the Impaler style.

Williams walked around the scared man, looking up at him as he did so. The man stared forward, his line of sight above Williams's head. He had heard things about Williams and didn't want to end up like Mr Charles.

"Do you have something to do, Donald?" Williams asked. His tone had become softer but still rang with disapproval.

"Uhm, well, sir—" the man started, his mouth opening and shutting in a panic, almost as if his brain was censoring any stupid words that were about to come out.

"Well here's some good news, Donald, I have a job for you. Find the cab that took Mr Steel to the bridge and bring the driver to me. How's that?" Williams smiled.

The man smiled awkwardly and set off for the door. "Uhm ... Just one thing, sir," he stuttered, "my name's not—" The man's sentence was cut short, for he realised that Williams didn't care. If he told him that his name was Donald, his name was Donald.

"What cabbie and who is Mr Steel?" 'Donald' dared to ask. But then he saw a look in Williams's eyes, then noticed the watch had been drawn from Williams's pocket. He decided there should be no more questions. "OK, no problem, boss, I am all over it." And with that, he was gone.

Williams opened the watch and checked the time. He wore a large grin as he sat on the corner of Crystal's desk.

"I do like him. Nice catch for you, my dear." He grinned at her and planted a small kiss on her left cheek, then he stood and headed for his office. On the way out, he raised a hand as if he was going to speak.

"—No problem," Crystal spoke first. "We have a batch of spare remotes heading in tomorrow. In the meantime, you have a spare next to your coffee, Mr W, sir." She grinned smugly.

Williams said nothing. He didn't need to. It was as if she knew already. He returned to his office and sat in his leather-bound chair, and it creaked with age. As he looked over at the two chairs facing the fireplace, his smile faded.

Even though Steel was an adversary, a thorn in his side, he was ultimately the only person he could call a friend. The only one who would not lie.

Williams thought back to their conversation that had lasted most of the night. They had talked about everything apart from work. That night they had been just two men enjoying a quiet drink by a blazing fire and sharing confidences.

The distracted man unknowingly picked up the remote and snapped it into two. Suddenly the door opened, and Crystal stood in the doorway, an angry glare on her face. Williams looked down at the carnage at his fingertips.

"Oops," he said shamefully.

Crystal walked over, carrying a strange-looking doll and placed it onto the desk. Williams looked at the ugly looking thing, then at Crystal.

"What the hell is this, my dear?" he asked with a panicked look, almost afraid to touch it.

Crystal picked it up and pulled the head off it. "It's called a stress doll. It's cheaper than a remote, and you can put a face on it." She pointed to the small plastic window where the face should be. Williams picked it up and pulled off its arms and then smiled.

"My dear, what would I do without you?" he said with a childish grin. Crystal left him alone with his new device and sat her desk. She smiled at a naughty thought that had just entered her head and then got back to work.

* * *

McCall and Tooms were heading for Bob's Diner. Something Steel had said had stuck with McCall. Perhaps they were looking in the wrong place. Maybe Amber simply had been in the wrong place at the wrong time.

The sun was high and blazed through the windshield, making driving difficult in some areas, because all she could see was the bright light and nothing else. She turned onto the FDR to avoid the brunt of the sunlight which was now behind them, but despite this, as they passed the mass of glass-fronted buildings, the sun reflected into the collage of windows causing a blinding a strobe effect, making McCall to close one eye. Traffic was its usual nose-to-tail gridlock, and Sam was sure that she had hit every traffic light they had come across. Steel's death had pissed her off, and the traffic wasn't helping settle her temper. Tooms had offered to drive, but the knifepoint stare she gave made him back off.

Steel had always maintained that the waitress was the key, and maybe he was right. They had been blindsided by Amber's agency job. It made everything make sense: *undercover agent killed on duty*. However, she knew things were never that simple – that neat.

Amber had been ripped apart to get answers from her. The problem was, maybe she didn't know what those answers were.

"Do we know who Tara Burke's previous roommate was?" McCall asked, breaking the silence. Tooms looked over at McCall with a blank expression which suddenly changed as he caught on to her trail of thought.

"The people who broke in were looking for someone – or something," Tooms said, pulling out his cell phone.

"What if they just got the wrong one? What if they didn't know the old roommate left?" McCall completed Tooms's thoughts. Tooms pressed the speed dial for Tony. After a short wait, Tony picked up.

"Tony, can you find out who the previous roommate of Tara's was?" he asked his friend. "Thanks, man, later." Tooms put the cell away and made himself comfortable in the Mustang's leather seat.

"He should have an answer in a couple of hours."

McCall nodded a response. Her concentration was locked onto the old lady in the Hummer SUV in front of them.

"Seriously, couldn't she have found anything bigger?" McCall said, shaking her head as all they could see through the rear window was a pair of arms and the bob of her hair.

Tooms finally let out a laugh, which made McCall take her eyes from the road for a second.

"What?" she asked, trying to get rid of the urge to stick the siren on. Tooms just shook his head and smiled at the situation.

"You're not gonna put your lights on, because that old gal will panic, and we'll have a whole lot of shit to explain." His humorous reaction wasn't so much because he knew what she was thinking; it was the fact that he had had the same idea.

Eventually, the old woman pulled onto a side street and disappeared into the traffic. McCall cracked a smile: she had to admit that the image was quite amusing. She looked over at the Sat Nav on the display screen of the all-in-one media centre. The diner wasn't far, only around fifteen minutes away.

McCall parked on the other side of Adam Clayton Powell Jr. Boulevard, next to some electrical supermarket. The crossing led straight to the diner's front entrance. *Great access*, McCall thought. They got out of the car and headed over. Tooms's belly let out a growl, almost as if it knew they were close to food. McCall gave Tooms a surprised look, to which he just shrugged and smiled.

"Didn't you have breakfast?" McCall asked, then stopped and looked at her watch. It was quarter to twelve. She smiled and shook her head.

Inside the diner, it was starting to get busy. Three waitresses were running about taking orders, while a new chef tossed the burgers in the back. Kim was at the till making up some old guy's check. Her smile was broad and accentuated by the ruby red lipstick. McCall had to compliment her on her tactics: *big smile, big tip*.

The diner looked fuller and cleaner than the last time she was there. The staff even had new uniforms. McCall headed over to Kim, who was busy shoving a five-dollar bill into a glass jar that had a slit in the lid and had a handwritten sign held on with tape. *Tips are always welcome* was written in thick black ink and fancy lettering.

"Miss Washington, the place looks great, where did the money come from?" McCall asked suspiciously. Kim smiled as the two detectives approached.

"Detective McCall, are you guys stoppin' by for a free lunch? It's the least we can do after you got rid of that nasty son of a bitch." Kim said, passing some menus over. McCall could see Tooms eyeing up the three huge burgers that one of the waitresses was taking to a city worker and his crew. Tooms held his stomach as it rumbled into life. Kim smiled, and McCall gave him a swift elbow to the side.

"Well, our dirtbag boss made the mistake of putting everything he had stolen off of us, and his suppliers in a kitty," Kim explained. "Unfortunately, he named it 'Diner petty cash'." Kim shrugged and raised her hands.

McCall gave her a confused look. "So, how did you get hold of it?" McCall watched her closely as she prepared another check, this time for a couple sitting at the back. The detective was impressed that Kim knew they were ready to pay without them even telling her.

"As smart as he thought he was, he wasn't." Kim had a skip in her voice. "The restaurant is actually in my name. If something happens, I take the fall. Nice of him, don't you think?"

"I didn't find out until he got locked up," the waitress continued. "That's when a guy from the bank came around here. It appears that our boss had wanted to put this place up for his bail, but he couldn't because he had forgotten about what he had done. The bank guy explained the situation. Later, I found the checking account details and checked it out. Even that was in my name. I mean, what an idiot." Kim laughed, passing over the check to a brunette waitress.

"I paid off all the restaurant's debts and got new help. Now we are rakin' its in." Kim smiled broadly as a middle-aged priest came in and sat in one of the stalls. He waved and smiled back.

McCall's smile faded, and she pulled out her notebook. "Kim, have you seen or spoken to Tara since the last time she was on shift?" McCall spoke softly but with a serious tone.

Kim shook her head. She didn't pause to think about it. "No. Sorry, but the last time I saw her was on that horrible day. I take it you have no leads on her roommate's killer?" She suddenly scowled at McCall. "You're not thinkin' she did it, are you?" Kim looked angry.

"No," Sam reassured her. "But we think she may be in a lot of trouble, and we would like her to come in for her own safety." McCall's tone and facial expression was full of concern.

However, Kim shook her head. "Look, I am sorry, Detective, but I have no idea where she is. I would love to say she has family someplace, but she ain't." Kim's face lit up as she had an idea. "Did you try her old roommate?"

"No, not yet, do you have a name? Maybe an address?" McCall said calmly, not wanting to give away the secret calculations she was making in her head.

"Sorry, Detective McCall, I don't have an address, but his name is Jake … Jake Harding," Kim told her, smiling again.

"I don't suppose you could give us a description of this Jake Harding?" Tooms asked, his eyes darting back and forth to the kitchen.

Kim thought for a moment and disappeared to a noticeboard that hung on a back wall. It was full of photographs of the staff with tourists, and a couple of famous people who had dared to eat there. She returned, holding a photograph to her chest.

"Here, this was taken last Christmas," Kim said, smiling as she looked at the photograph briefly and handed it over to McCall, who took it and smiled graciously.

However, Sam's smile faded as she recognised the man from the photograph.

"And this is Jake Harding, her former roommate?" McCall asked. She passed the photo to Tooms.

"Yes, why?" Kim shot Sam McCall a confused look, suddenly feeling her legs begin to shake. "What's happened?"

The look on McCall's face turn to one of those you see just before giving bad news. Kim thought she was going to puke.

"The man in the photo was found wandering the streets. He had lost his memory." As McCall spoke, Kim's eyes lit up.

"Unfortunately, he was covered in blood and had no memory of whose blood it was," Sam continued. "He wasn't far from where Amber was murdered." McCall watched as Kim's legs became unstable. It struck Tooms that for some reason, she was overly concerned. Was its fear for Tara or fear for their John Doe?

"He was taken from a safe house and possibly killed, most likely by those who had killed Amber," Tooms said, hoping for a reaction, and he got one.

Kim threw up before she fainted. All the patrons looked over suddenly, more concerned about getting their food, than Kim having received bad news.

"It's OK, folks, she got some bad news, that's all," Tooms explained to the worried-looking customers. They all grumbled at the lack of excitement, and those who had stood up to look retook their seats. Two of the waitresses came to her aid, one holding a glass of water while the other helped her to a seat. McCall took the glass and smiled at the small Hispanic girl.

"Here, drink this," McCall said, holding the glass to Kim's mouth. She was still shaken up and slightly dazed from the shock. Kim took a couple of sips before pushing McCall's hand away.

"Are you sure it's him?" Kim asked, her voice full of emotion. Tooms looked down at McCall, interested in what she would say.

"We don't know yet. We are still waiting for Forensics to make an ID. But at least now we have a name, so thank you." McCall's smile was gentle and warm.

The unhappy waitress stared into McCall's large gentle eyes and felt almost at ease.

"And what about Tara. Could she be—?" Kim looked away. She didn't want to say those words, the words nobody ever wants to hear. McCall held Kim by the shoulders and squeezed slightly, a comforting trick her father had done so many times.

"We don't know, but I have the feeling that she is somewhere safe. She seems to be a smart woman. So no, I don't think she is dead."

Kim looked up at McCall and smiled as she wiped away a small tear from her left cheek.

McCall stood up and looked down on Kim. "Please, if she contacts you, get her to call me. We can keep her safe." McCall turned just in time to see Tooms pick up a wrapped burger. She scowled at him as they made their way out.

"When the hell did you order that?" she asked him, confused. Tooms just smiled and opened the door for her.

"Hands quicker than the eye, McCall, hands quicker than the eye!"

Chapter 30

A cool westerly breeze skipped across the lake. There was a calm silence in the air. High above, wandering seagulls hovered in the warm sunshine, scouring the land for their next meal. Anglers sat on the riverbank; carbon-fibre rods held on stands as their masters sat idly. In the distance, cars hurtled past on the freeway that led back to the city. Southampton was green and open. As part of the Hamptons, it smelt of money as much as it did of fresh air. There were large estates with long drives—some were so long they almost seemed like freeways.

Some people had moorings on the lake: long wooden piers that held expensive weekend playthings. Long-nosed powerboats, with shiny white hulls and padded seating. One large estate had a helicopter pad; its dull, grey concrete was adorned with a large yellow circle and a large painted *H* in the centre denoting the helipad. A black Dauphin helicopter sat proud on its grey concrete. The shine of the gloss frame made it glow as brightly as the midday sun. A man on a sit-on lawnmower powered past, paying the world around him no mind. He seemed content on his red machine.

A pair of blue dungarees covered his red-and-blue chequered shirt. A blue Yankees baseball cap hid most of his features. A black beard with streaks of grey made him look older, probably older than he really was. He drove on, lending his gaze to the TV show on his tablet that sat on a handlebar mount. The sound of the blades trimming above the acres of grass was the only noise for miles. The house itself was late 1900s: a large sandstone building, with tall windows and a grey tiled roof. A gravel turning circle for the drivers encircled a statue of Eros. Rose bushes and small hedgerows broke the lines between gravel and grass.

The inside of the house had been kept to its original design. The walls were half white plaster above, with the lower part covered with dark wooden panels. Sometimes there was just the panelling. Polished brass fittings and works of art were scattered throughout the place. Thick, heavy maroon carpeting stretched across the public room areas and winding staircase to the upper floors. The hallways and corridors remained bare wood, with only a thin layer of wax as cover.

It had more of a 'stately home' feel to it than that of a private dwelling. Above the main entrance, a stone coat of arms sat proudly: a shield with a chevron centre. To the left was a crown, to the right a gryphon. Below was a strange-looking eagle. Some may even have called it a fiery bird of prey. The same crest was etched into the wood of the thick bannister rails. But there the words stood out. Written in a deep engraved scrolling script were the words: *In Causa, Invenire Vires*, meaning *In Cause, we find strength*.

The house was seemingly quiet. Staff moved about following their daily routines. The sound of a radio from the kitchen was only a murmur. A man in a black suit exited the kitchen, stopping halfway to converse with the two women chefs inside.

"You know I only have eyes for you, ladies," he said.

They laughed, and he went on his way, leaving the door to close slowly on its hinge. The middle-aged man was of average build and height. His expensive suit fitted well, and his stay-bright shoes glistened as they caught the light from the windows. He carried a large tray that held a coffee pot, milk and sugar in silver set. A large domed food cover sparkled, polished to perfection. He headed down a corridor that seemed to have a hundred windows. He felt the warmth of the sunlight, and it felt good. To his front was a doorway to the dining room. To his right, there was another door that resembled one of the panels. The man pushed the door open with his foot and took the stone staircase down to the old cellar.

The cellar was strangely warm. Not a humid, stifling warm, but a comfortable warmth. Its thick heavy walls were straight with six rooms on either side. The doorways were arched with heavyset wooden doors. Several of them housed wine in environmentally controlled conditions: one room was for red wines and another for whites and champagnes.

He headed casually for the last door on the right. He stopped in front of a heavy steel door. This had a keypad entry, which was embedded in the wall next to the door. The man balanced the tray while he typed in the numbers. He should have put the tray down and stood ready for any eventuality. He should have remembered who was inside.

Everything happened lightning fast. The man looked up in surprise as the door was ripped open. The tray was thrust upwards into his face. He yelled as the hot coffee covered his left side, the scalding pain making him cringe. Then the heavy tray came back at him, this time under control. Its impact sent him hurtling against the opposite door. He was dazed and confused. Two powerful hands grabbed his jacket and threw him into the cell. The door slammed shut with a metallic thud that echoed around the cellar.

The newly imprisoned character in the black suit sat on the floor against a small bed. He tried to stand but found his legs could barely hold him. A shaky hand checked his forehead for damage, and he sighed with relief at the absence of blood. He took a moment to get his head straight, then sucked in a lungful of air, kept it for a moment then released it slowly. Carefully, he stood up, using the wall as support. He smiled as he stood confidently. The smile faded as he noticed the control panel at his side had been destroyed. Quickly he checked his pockets: his wallet, sidearm and car keys were missing. The man sat down heavily on the bed. He had no contact with upstairs, and his guest had just broken out. Looking at the tuna sandwich on the floor, he just shrugged. Knowing he would be there a while, he decided to tuck in.

Almost an hour had passed until someone came down. It was a waiter who had sounded the alarm. He had noticed the signs of struggle as he went to get the wine for the evening meal. The tray that was leaning up against the wall had a strange imprint on the metal. The coffee set was strewn across the concrete floor, shattered. They found the man on the bed, with his arm folded underneath his head. His face was swollen, and the signs of scalding on his skin told them the story of what had happened.

Later, an old Oriental man sat in a high-backed chair. It was almost a throne, made of gold-coloured wood, with red velvet cushioning. He was in his mid-sixties, possibly older, as his healthy complexion hid his years. His office was huge, a twenty-by-twenty space with dark wood bookshelves covering the walls. To the left, a large blue marble fireplace with a brass guard broke up the dark wood and the blood-red carpet. His desk was made of ebony and had Oriental carvings. The telephone was made of brass and green marble, and the desk lamp was designed as an ebony dragon curling around a woman, whose outstretched arms held the silk shade. A strong smell of incense hung in the air, plus there was the scent of flowers and some sort of wood aroma. The old man sat with his eyes shut. His index fingers were pressed together and held against his lips, almost as if he was meditating, or contemplating.

The door to this office opened, and an injured man stepped in, limping, a cold, damp cloth held close to his face. The Oriental man said nothing. He just sat there with his eyes still closed.

"Uhm sorry, sir," the unfortunate guard fumbled with his words. "Lord Steel … Lord Steel, he—" He was nervous at having to deliver his news.

The old man opened his eyes and smiled. "It's not your fault," he told his servant. "We underestimated his will. Something is driving our boy. At least we know he has all his instincts back. He knows friend from foe." The old Oriental man stood up and walked over to the injured guard and rested a small hand on the man's shoulder.

"How do we know that, sir?" the man asked his employer.

The old man smiled again. "Because, if he didn't, you'd be dead."

The guard swallowed hard.

* * *

Tony had waited in line for a hotdog for what seemed like forever. Even though the sun was giving off a pleasant warmth, standing around almost motionless made him aware of the slight crisp wind. Five people stood in line, and he was number four. Impatiently, the crowd looked over at the woman who getting served. Tony looked over at the cart and noted the way her food was being stacked up. She was a short, thin lady, somewhere in her late eighties Tony estimated. Her long fake leopard-skin coat was old and had seen better days. She paid and left with her arms full of food. Tony turned and watched her as she headed towards a group of other pensioners, who were sitting across the road in a large eight-seater cab.

He smiled and shook his head as he heard the suddenly raised voices about who got what. The next woman was quick: 'a dog with onions' was all she wanted—a small, but simple request, that took less than a minute. Tony smiled as he neared the stall. He didn't need to order, for the tall man behind the counter smiled and pulled up one large dog with 'the works. Tony paid as well as sticking a five-dollar note in the tips jar before saying his farewells. He stopped before entering the precinct and looked around at the busy life before him. People and traffic were moving at different paces, but all had the same sort of purpose. As he watched, he saw someone in the distance. The figure looked like – Steel. It was just a shape of a person because it was far away, but it looked like the detective. As the figure grew closer, Tony grew excited as he saw the figure walk past on the other side of the street. Tony went to call out but stopped himself as he realised his mistake, remembering his friend's demise. Tony remembered the footage he had seen from the cameras. There was no doubt it had been Steel that had plunged from the bridge. Despite this, the hooded figure had Steel's build, even the way he carried himself had something familiar about it. Tony remembered that Steel liked to disguise himself, but this wasn't him, not this time, he was gone. There had been witnesses who had seen him jump – or fall!

The stranger was just a tall guy dressed all in black with a long black coat with a hood. The hooded figure was scruffy, his clothes worn and dirty. Tony shook his head to clear his thoughts. Why was he seeing the ghost of Steel and not that of Amber? Why was he missing John Steel more than his deceased girlfriend? Tony shrugged and stepped inside the large old building of the 11th Precinct. The hooded figure stopped and looked across at the precinct, almost as if the man was deciding. The cowl of the hood placed the man's face into shadow, and the long cut of the coat covered all but the military-style boots. The figure just stared for a moment. Passers-by just seemed to move through him as though he wasn't there. A tour bus hurtled past, and he was gone.

Inside the building, Tony sat at his desk just as there was an electronic *ping* from his computer. He placed the hotdog down on a clear space of his desk and searched for the email he had just gotten. He smiled as he saw that it was a message from Traffic, with five attachments: it was the CCTV footage from the bridge—five views from different cameras. Three were street views, and the others were from the bridge. Coreman was at the ME's trying to get anything from CSU on any of the cases. Tony had sent him because he was a new face, a face that hadn't pissed them off – yet.

He played the footage in turn. The street views seemed uneventful: just lots of early-morning traffic. Then he opened the next attachment and sat back to watch. Grabbing his meal, he settled down for another hour of nothing. Tony went to bite into the bread and sausage when he stopped. His mouth was still open as he saw the yellow cab stop suddenly and a darkened figure got out.

Tony leant forward and placed the hotdog back down as he watched. He saw the figure bend forward and throw up, and then climb up onto the ledge. Tony stopped breathing. His eyes were wide as he was watched the final moments of Steel's life. He moved closer to the monitor, still holding the same breath as if he was afraid to exhale. His unblinking eyes focused on the darkened figure until it vanished from view.

Detective Tone Marinelli sat back in his chair, feeling as though he himself had felt the impact of Steel's body hitting the water. He looked around, almost panicked at what he had seen. He wiped the moisture from his eyes: tears that had formed from staring for too long. Finally, he released that stale breath that he had been holding onto.

His eyes went back to the screen. Now the taxi had gone, and people had started to gather. Tony couldn't do anything but watch. His instincts told him to stop watching and find that cab. But he was frozen. He had just watched his friend jump to his death, and he was lost as to what he should do.

Tony's desk phone began to ring. The sudden alarm made him jump, bringing him back to reality. It was Tooms. Just a quick call to say they were going to Kim Washington's apartment. It was a friendly check-in, but Tony knew that Tooms had other motives for calling. Tooms was worried about him. Ever since they had found Amber, he knew he had been different, unfocused. By rights, he shouldn't have been on the case, but everyone had managed to convince the captain that his relationship to the victim wasn't a problem—everyone, including Steel.

The phone conversation was short. Tooms had asked if he had anything new. Tony had lied and said, "No." Not so much a lie, as a holding back of information for the right reasons. He couldn't risk them being unfocused if there was a situation. He could see McCall had taken Steel's death badly, even though she tried to hide it. He would wait until his two colleagues were back.

Tony looked back at the monitor. His head had lost its muzziness. He was thinking clearly again. He picked up the mug and drained the last dregs of the hour cold coffee.

"OK, Mr Cab Driver, where are you, and who are you?" Tony muttered, going back to look over the footage again. This time his focus was on the cab. The driver had been the last person to see Steel alive. The cabby knew where he'd picked up Steel from, and thus where he had been. If they could find the driver, maybe they could find the killer.

The process was long. He had to send the footage to the Tech department so that they could look for anything they might have on the cab. On his monitor, all the images were too small to see things properly, and he didn't have the software to enhance the views. A young guy in a grey suit and yellow T-shirt and white deck shoes had worked on his computer. In the half-hour Tony had waited he had looked hard at the street cams, trying to detect the direction from which the cab had come from.

Tony looked up to see the tech guy approach with a brown folder in his hand. Tony almost forgot about the pencil that he held in his mouth, making him look like a dog with a bone. As he began to talk, the yellow HB fell to his desk with a small clatter. He ignored it and stood up.

"Did you get anything?" Tony asked, almost excitedly.

The man smiled and handed over the file. Tony opened the flap and flicked through the pictures.

"Thanks, they'll be a great help," Tony said, looking up at the man and smiling broadly.

Tony retook his seat and began to search through the blown-up stills. The smile faded as he saw that it was Steel getting out of the cab. Then he froze at one of the stills. He could see what appeared to be Steel forcing himself to be sick, by sticking his fingers down his throat. Had he known something?

Tony shook off the thought and concentrated on the cab. There in one still was a shot of the cab's rear. He had the licence plate and the medallion number from where it was sprayed on the trunk. Tony put the pencil back in his mouth and ran the medallion number through his system. It didn't take long before it spat out a name and DMV photograph.

"OK, Mr David Kidd, let's see where you're at." Tony's voice was muffled by the stick of wood and graphite. The cab belonged to a company on the West Side. Tony grabbed his gun and his badge. Taking his jacket from the back of his chair, he swung it on and headed for the elevator. Tony took his cell phone from his pocket and pressed the fresh number on the speed dial.

"Coreman? It's Tony. Meet me at this address."

Chapter 31

The afternoon sun began to cool, and the traffic in Harlem began to build up. For most, it was time to head home, and for others, it was nearly time to start the late shift. New York – like so many other cities, was always on the move: alive and active. Shift work and tourists kept the city in momentum. But for a few of them, it was never-ending, such as double shifters, or those with too many jobs and not enough time to do them. The economy was in a bad place, not enough cash for people to live but the government asking for more. Cuts to police, the military and small business had left its mark.

The sea of yellow metal washed down the busy streets as taxis carried their fares. The sidewalks were awash with people walking hurriedly for *that* station, to catch *that* train. A movement of people oblivious to others, who were busy in their own little worlds. What better place to hide?

The hooded figure moved amongst them almost as if he wasn't there at all. He moved with ease through the crowds of people, moving no quicker than a normal stroll. His body would twist and turn gracefully to avoid those awkward shoulder impacts.

This lone character made his way to a darkened alley. Clouds of white steam rose up from the subway vents, successfully concealing his entrance into the passageway. The passage he walked down was long, the breadth of the two adjoining buildings, which also gave him plenty of shadows to disappear into.

Eventually the alley it led to took him to a group of old warehouse buildings, one of which had three roller doors. It was an old building, built in the late '40s. The doors were new, but it seemed as if the green of the paint was faded and weathered camouflage for the untrained eye. The figure hurried up to the building and climbed the fire escape to the roof, before disappearing. The red brick construction stood four storeys tall and was untouched by graffiti. The street itself had an unloved feel about it. Bits of paper and a couple of paper cups danced across the concrete, carried by the wind like an invisible child was kicking them around. The breeze was a slight and from the west. The apparent normality of the place was broken by one of the roller doors screeching open. As it reached a good height, a blacked-out Aston Martin Lagonda SUV nosed out as the door began to come down again. The car's heavy, snub-nosed front made it look angry and foreboding. Its thin, almost *peering* headlamps added something animalistic to the vehicle. The paint finish was a strange matt black. There were no chrome or bare metal parts. This vehicle had been built for stealth and power. It took off into the distance with a throaty roar of its V12 engine and a scream of tyres.

The street was silent once more. The breeze picked up again, chasing more garbage down the street.

* * *

McCall had forced her car through the maddening traffic. She had parked the Mustang at the nearest available spot, which was halfway down the street. The street itself was calm compared with the main highways. But the volume of parked—or in some cases abandoned—cars discouraged people from staying long. McCall pulled her coat tightly around herself as the westerly breeze picked up. Even though the buildings acted as a windbreak, the cold air always found a way.

McCall was hoping for some good news from Tony after the phone call. He had said something about a breakthrough on the cab, but she had learned not to get her hopes up. She had found out far too often that life often has a wicked sense of humour.

She rechecked her notebook for the address of Kim's apartment. The red-brick building looked like all the rest, apart from the fact that the fire escapes were painted dark green.

The detectives made their way up the small steps and towards a wood-and-glass door. The door was also green but not wide. Tooms held the door open for a young blonde-haired woman who was struggling with her luggage. As she finally managed to pull her pink suitcase out from the doorway, she nodded at them. Tooms smiled back and entered the hallway while McCall stepped to the side to let the woman drag her case down. The woman smiled at McCall. She wore overly large sunglasses that covered her eyes and part of her face. McCall returned a sympathetic smile, feeling almost jealous of the woman, who was obviously going away on a trip.

As McCall entered the small lobby, she stopped dead. She turned slightly, almost as if a voice in her head had just called to her. McCall ran out, just in time to see the woman get into a yellow cab. Everything seemed to slow down, almost as if she were watching a movie. The woman turned slightly before getting in, and her face had turned pale with the fear of being caught.

McCall had reached the bottom of the steps, just as the cab's door closed. That's when she saw the driver, who was smiling at her. She felt a chill as she realised this was a victorious smirk and not an expression of friendship. His dark skin seemed to shine as the sunlight reflected off it. His long dreadlocks were falling over his shoulders, the multi-coloured beads matching his woollen cap. The driver stepped on the gas just as McCall's hand was near to the door handle. She began to run after the cab but lost it as the driver turned onto the main street. McCall went to reach for her gun but stopped herself in time. She could see the headlines now: *Cop shoots cabbie*. The press would have a field day. She just stood and watched the exhaust fumes until they faded into nothing.

Tooms came running out. He wore a confused look as he followed her gaze down the street.

"What's up?" he asked, looking around to see what the problem was.

"I think that was our girl. She's dyed her hair, but I know it was her." McCall cursed herself. She looked up at Tooms with a frown. He knew that expression meant that things had just gotten worse.

"What...what is it?" he asked, almost afraid to know.

"I think we just found the cab that dropped Steel at the bridge. The problem is, she's in it," McCall said, turning back to the main street. Their only hope now was that Tony did indeed have something. If not, then they might be looking for another body sometime soon: the body of Tara Burke. McCall felt her jacket pocket vibrate and pulled out her cell phone. It was a text message from Tina Franks at the ME's office.

"Tina's got something for us," McCall said, showing the phone's display to Tooms. He nodded, and they both headed back to her car. There was no point trying to chase the cab. It and the girl were long gone. Tony said he had something on the driver. McCall felt a ray of hope. Even though things seemed bleak, they were starting to look up. Now they had leads to follow.

* * *

Tara rearranged her seating position and put on her safety belt. She didn't look back. She didn't want the cabbie to think there was anything wrong. Tara looked out of the window. Watched the world go by.

"So, where'd you wanna go, miss?" the man shouted back through the intercom system in the dividing safety glass, his gaze directed firmly on the traffic ahead. Tara noticed the man was completely secure. She figured he had been held up too many times. Tara had heard about cabbies getting rolled over by bogus fares, some of the many stories she had heard at the diner.

"Grand Central, please," she replied, leaning forward to make herself heard. The driver nodded, and she saw him smile in the rear-view mirror.

"Good time for a holiday. Going somewhere special? Jamaica or Hawaii, perhaps?" He laughed, a tone of jealousy in his voice.

She smiled broadly and shook her head. "No, just visiting family upstate," she lied, but she concealed the truth well. Almost as if she believed there really was someone out there for her.

"Family is very important. I myself have a wife and three beautiful daughters," he said proudly, pointing to a photograph that was taped on the dashboard. It was of a pretty woman with three young girls. The eldest must have been around fifteen and the youngest five. Tara smiled at the photograph. She had dreamed of having a family with the right man someday. A home with a white picket fence and lots of kids playing in the yard.

Her smile faded, and she stared out of the window. From then onwards, the only conversation was from the cabbie. She couldn't believe a man could talk so much. She just stared, but not out of the window, but into her dreams. She saw only those white picket fences.

The vehicle hit a small pothole which crashed Tara back to reality. She pulled out her phone and checked for any new messages. The inbox only held the last message, one she had received days ago. She closed the phone down and looked up at the driver, who was checking something on his phone. Curiosity got the better of her. Tara leant forward as if to check something in her case. That's when she saw the display on his phone. Luckily the thing was massive, and the words were clear: *Package on route.*

Tara sat back in a panic. Something was badly wrong. She reached for the door handle, but the deadbolts were on. She tugged frantically at the opening handle, but nothing happened.

She was trapped. They had found her.

Tara looked over at the driver, who was smiling proudly. His head was rocking side to side as if he were singing to himself.

Tara took off her seat belt and leant back to kick out the windows. This made the man laugh even harder. Her shoes struck the glass, but the window just rocked with the impact. Now she was sweating with fear. Beads of fresh perspiration poured out of her with every effort. She started to feel faint. The world began to spin. All the while, the cab driver's voice boomed through the intercom.

"Don't worry, miss. You give them what they want, and I am sure everything will be fine." His voice had a skip to it—as though he was getting off on her dilemma.

"Who are you? Who are they?" Her words began to slur, and she slipped into her dreams.

All she could see were those kids and the picket fence.

* * *

A throaty wail filled the corridors as the sound of James Brown's music blared from one of the rooms at the city morgue. McCall and Tooms stepped out of the elevator and was greeted by a chorus of "You gotta, gotta, give me some..." as they walked briskly towards Tina's door. Tooms looked down at McCall, who was grinning and shaking her head in disbelief.

"I guess she's done with her backlog," McCall announced, recognising the tune as a victory announcement. As they entered the room, they found Tina pouring a coffee from her small machine that was on a long table next to her desk. She hadn't noticed the two detectives standing in her office's doorway, watching as she shook her shapely rear in time with the music.

"I thought it would have been champagne you were drinking," McCall shouted over the din. Tina turned and smiled happily before turning off the stereo. Tina looked fresh, but there was a sadness in her eyes that didn't match the smile. The smile faded.

"Backlog done, CSU and this office have done the impossible again." Tina's words sounded victorious. However, there was something in her body language that didn't match her apparent joy.

"OK," she began. "First we got the blood work from the shirt. It's a match to Amber." Tina passed a brown file to McCall, who opened it up and held it so Tooms could read it as well.

"So, he killed her?" Tooms said, almost disappointed and confused.

"No. It just shows he came into contact with her, but he was there." Tina picked up another file. "This is the report on Amber. She was drugged. She had high doses of some weird cocktail. A mix that renders the patient conscious but unable to move. She was completely awake while they butchered her." Tina was almost in tears as she explained the way she figured they had done it. "They had started at the feet and worked upwards. Taking their time so that she didn't pass out."

Then she picked up another file. Her hands were trembling as she handed it to McCall. As McCall took it, she felt Tina's grip on the thin brown card, almost as if she didn't want to show her. McCall looked into Tina's glassy eyes.

"I am sorry," Tina spoke with a soft broken voice. McCall opened the file and just stared at the figures and long words.

"We checked the vomit and blood found at the scene on the bridge. I think he did it on purpose so that we would have something to work on. He knew he was going in the river and knew the chances of us getting anything if his body was found," Tina tried to explain without hurting McCall's feelings. She could see McCall was rocking on her feet before Tooms pulled round a chair for her to sit on.

"From our analysis, we found that Steel had snake venom in his system. I can't say how he got it, but there was traces of bottled water in the vomit. My guess is he drank a laced glass of water. The dose was high, so without treatment, he would have been dead in minutes, maybe an hour." Tina sat on the stainless-steel operating table. She could see the pain in McCall's eyes.

All the time, McCall had found comfort in the fact that Steel's body had not been found. She had almost been expecting him to turn up in some damned disguise like he had done on their first case together. McCall shook her head as if denying it would make it untrue.

"I am sorry, Sam. He's gone, and he's not coming back." Tina fought away the lump in her throat.

McCall nodded and shot her a quick sympathetic smile. Apart from her red eyes, she was solid. Her mind was on the job and if that meant grieving later then so be it. Tina walked over to a table on which lay the body of the agent from the hotel.

"This guy, however, is a different story. Gunshots starting at the feet. We thought this was a slow and methodical job." Tina voice sounded as if there were more questions than answers. "The gunshot to the head was first," she said, pointing to the medium size bullet hole in the man's skull.

McCall shot her a puzzled look. "If he was already dead, then why do this?" McCall asked, suddenly wishing she hadn't come here. She looked over at the peaceful-looking corpse. Even after so much suffering, he still looked at ease. McCall closed her eyes for a moment, trying to take everything in. Sorting it all out like a murder board in her head. Suddenly her eyes opened. There was a shocked look on her face.

"We ran his prints, he worked for the Feds, but nobody's saying who else he was working for." Tina's words rang with a hard tone. She was sick of the body count on this case.

"This was a cover-up," McCall said, thinking as she talked. "They wanted Brooke, but they wanted someone else to think they had interrogated the agent as well. Someone grabbed Brooke while she was in a safe house. They thought she knew something because she was Amber's handler." McCall paced about like a tiger in a cage, her mind computing all the new data. Then she looked up—the scared look was back.

"The question is…who's got her?" her words trembled as one name sprung to mind, and she just hoped to God she was wrong.

Mr Williams.

Chapter 32

Tony pulled up outside the taxi company's premises. The once pale blue sky was becoming a darker, with streaks of purple gathering on the horizon. Cloud formations had begun to taint the once clear heavens. The evening would be a cold one, but the night had been promised to be dry. The front passenger door opened, and Coreman got in. Tony said nothing at first. In fact, he didn't even look around to acknowledge the new detective, for his gaze was on the cab company's garages, and he was watching the vehicles coming and going.

They were looking for a Checker Sedan: a big old car used back in the '50s through to the '80s. The sort of car you expect to see in an old movie or cruising around Cuba or some other place south of the border. Tony didn't need a picture. He had one firmly in his mind, but he needed something to show around.

Tony took out a picture of their suspect and passed it to Coreman to look at. Coreman took the piece of paper and looked at the DMV photograph. He had to admit that the man did look serious, but then, with the restrictions made on what identification photographs should look like, everyone looks like a criminal. No smiling, no glasses, you just must glare at the camera. The older of the two detectives had spoken with Tooms earlier after he had found the right taxi firm. Tooms had told him to stay put until he and McCall got there. Smiling to himself, Tony had remembered the three-way conversation. Tooms had been the relay for McCall, passing messages back and forth. He had reckoned McCall had been driving at the time.

Tony leant forward, his fingers gripping the leather of the Dodge's steering wheel impatiently. They had sat still for a long time and had seen vehicles come and go. Some of them three or four times. But there had been no Checker insight.

"Come on," Tony said, getting out of the car. Coreman looked at him strangely, almost speechless at Tony's action.

"Sorry, but Tooms told us to wait," Coreman said nervously. Tony looked at Coreman who was still sitting in the car.

"I'm just going in to get a look, maybe get an idea where this asshole might be," Tony growled. He was regretting having Coreman there. The man was green, but that was only the 'first-month blues. That awful first month when you don't know how to act, or what to say. The first month of getting coffee for everyone and being looked at with suspicious eyes. *Will he make it? Will he be able to handle himself?* or more importantly, *has he got my back?* Tony's regret was more a question of *has he got my back?* the other questions were, at that point irrelevant.

The two detectives crossed the busy road and headed towards the cab office. Tony resisted getting his shield out: the last thing he needed to do was to spook anyone. Looking around, he guessed that most of the drivers were there illegally, without the correct permits, but that was someone else's problem. Tony put a strut into his walk and hoped the new guy wouldn't fuck things up.

The cab company's garage was large, with enough room for around twenty-five vehicles. There was a small office in the corner with two large windows and a blue wooden door between them. The whole place reeked of exhaust fumes and fuel. A couple of drivers were heading for another room next to the office. Tony figured that was a restroom or locker room.

Tony could see inside the brightly lit office. A woman with sky-blue hair and a love for doughnuts sat at a control desk. There were two phones, a stick microphone and a computer with three monitors on a long pale wooden desk. Behind her sat a smaller man at another desk. This also had a phone and a monitor. He was in his late fifties, wearing a bad Hawaiian green shirt and an even worse comb-over. The little guy appeared to be the boss. He wasn't the owner, merely the ringmaster.

The senior detective had around fourteen steps to walk in which he had to come up with a good cover story. He knew it was a risk not waiting for McCall and Tooms, but he knew he had to do something, and sitting in the car wasn't getting things done. As they got to five feet away, Tony was happy, for he had a plan. However, time would tell if it was a good one.

Tony knocked on the door and waited for permission to enter.

"Come in!" yelled a surprisingly deep voice—presumably it was the only man they'd seen in the office, or so Tony hoped. He opened the door, and the two men entered, both smiling broadly.

"Yeah, what do you want?" the small fiftyish man in the Hawaiian shirt said, shoving half a Cuban cigar into his mouth. He had a Rolex and enough gold on his fingers to open his own pawn shop.

"Sorry to trouble you, but we are looking for one of your drivers, we need to talk to him," Tony began cheerfully.

The man gave the two detectives a suspicious glance. His eyes were large, and so was his dome-like head, from which miserable black strands of hair hung down.

"Sorry, don't know him," the man growled, leaning back in his chair.

Tony shot the man a confused look.

"But we—"

"—We were hoping he would be here," interrupted Coreman quickly. "We have the badge number for him, you see. We had just come back from our honeymoon and left something in the cab. We have looked all over, and yours is the last one to check. Please!"

Tony shot Coreman a shocked look, then smiled and put his arm around the new guy in a loving gesture. The small guy shook his head in disgust and waved them forward.

"So, tell me, what you two lovebirds got?" the man asked. The woman smiled at the two men affectionately. Coreman passed over a scrap of paper that had the cab's medallion number on it. The man took the paper and typed the number into his computer.

"8Z56, yeah, that's old David Kidd's rig." The man looked up at the clock, noting that it was nearly five. "He should be back any minute now." He chewed on the hand-rolled tobacco.

Tony smiled and thanked him before leaving the office. Coreman gave a quick, friendly wave and followed.

"Nice job in there, newbie," Tony said, heading for the way out. Coreman just smiled and nodded. He was almost afraid to speak in case he ruined the moment.

They waited for another fifteen minutes. Both men leant against the wall like schoolkids waiting to see the headmaster. The crisp wind forced both men to pull their jackets tightly around them, but all the while, they didn't falter from their observation of the street. Tony looked over to see a yellow cab approaching. He looked at the licence plate and the illuminated sign on the roof. *8Z56* stood out on the freshly washed vehicle. Tony looked at the car for a second, puzzled. Behind him, on the street, McCall had parked. Both she and Tooms were heading his way fast.

"What we got?" McCall asked as she ducked in with the rest of them.

"We got eyes on the taxi, were just waiting for the coast to clear," Coreman said proudly.

"Have we got a name for our guy?" she asked. Her voice was hard, with a hint of blood lust.

"David Kidd," Tony answered, his gaze fixed on the group. McCall looked over at a group of cars and their drivers, who were laughing and joking at shift change, sharing stories of their busy day. McCall walked in. The others followed close behind.

"I am Detective McCall; we're looking for David Kidd." She spoke firmly, with not a hint of emotion. If she hadn't bottled everything up, the next move could be her last as a cop. McCall looked at all the men who were just standing there. Their expressions had faded into stone.

"I am David Kidd, what's the problem, Detective?" one of the men said to her. McCall shot a look at Tony, then back to the man who called himself Kidd.

"Sorry, is your cab number 8Z56?" she asked, confused. Kidd looked at her, puzzled.

"Yes, that's my number, and my cab is over there." He pointed to a yellow Ford Crown Victoria.

"Thank you, sir, sorry for the inconvenience," McCall said, before turning and heading off. Tony looked at the drivers and then at McCall, a look of complete confusion on his face.

"Hey, McCall, what's going on? We got the guy!" Tony yelled as he chased after her. McCall stopped and looked round to face Tony.

"Tony, we saw the guy today on film. He was driving a yellow Checker Sedan, and this guy has a Ford Crown Victoria. Also, I know it's not our guy because the person we saw was a black guy with dreadlocks, while your guy is a three-hundred-pound Hawaiian," she growled before heading back to her car.

* * *

Tara Burke began to stir. Her eyes felt heavy, and her vision was blurred. She could feel the movement of the car as it thumped along the busy streets. If anyone was to look inside, they would think she was drunk or tired. The world around her seemed to move slowly, the sounds muffled as if she was listening to them from underwater. Her eyes felt heavy, and all she wanted to do was sleep. Slowly her eyes closed, and she was under.

The vehicle hit a large pothole, causing Tara to stir. She had no idea how long she had been under or where she was. She felt the cramp in her extremities and the muscle tension in her fingers and toes. She needed to move them, or she would scream out in pain. Careful not to make any sudden movements that would alert the driver, she tried to move her fingers first. One by one, she made slow movements that were luckily unnoticed. She felt a slight relief as she felt as if the blood began to flow once again.

Her body felt heavy, as though her clothes were made from lead. Whatever he had given her had played havoc with her muscular system. Maybe that was the idea so that if she did wake up, she couldn't do anything because her muscles wouldn't work. But somehow, she could move. It was painful, but she could do it, and what's more, her vision was improving. Unfortunately, all she could see was the rear seat of the car. Either he had moved her, or this was how she had fallen. She smiled to herself. She remembered those cop programmes, where the guy had got to the trunk by burrowing through the back seat. She thought about getting inside the trunk and then popping it open.

Tara stuck her hand between the backrest and the seat. Then felt a surge of disappointment as she hit a hard metal surface. Moving her hands slowly, she felt something else: something cold and round. Slowly she pulled it out. It was a Military style smartwatch. It was mostly made of carbon fibre, including the face. However, what stuck out most was the fact that the hour numbers were glowing themselves instead of being constantly illuminated.

Suddenly the sounds from outside the car had changed and so had the lighting. The whole car grew dark as if they were in an alleyway or inside a building. Quickly she tucked the watch into her pocket. The car began to slow down.

Her hastily conceived plan was simple. When he opened the door, she would roll onto her back and bend her knees. As he leant in to grab her, she would kick him as hard as she could and escape. Tara knew that she would have only one shot at this, so it would have to count. She got herself ready. Her breathing started to become erratic, and her pulse began to race. Tara didn't know if it was because of the drugs in her system, or if she was just plain terrified.

Tara felt the weight shift as the driver got out. She closed her eyes and took a deep breath. She heard the slam of his door and the crunch of his footsteps as he approached. She swung herself around and got herself into position. The movement of him leaving the car and walking to her door only took seconds, but for her, it seemed like hours.

She heard the click of the door handle. Quickly, she opened her eyes and mustered all her strength to go into her legs. If she was going to die, she would die fighting. Her eyes fixed on the door, waiting for the man's face to come into view. Suddenly she thanked all those hours on her feet at the diner, it had given her strong thighs, and she was going to use every inch of power she had on that face. She saw it in her imagination, the door opening, the cry of pain as her small heels encountered his nose and mouth, Tara envisaged the man falling back grasping his bloody wounds, possibly spitting teeth. She was psyched up, her body tensed like a coiled spring. She was ready for him. Tara gasped in horror as the door behind her opened. He had come in from the other side. She looked up at his grinning face. She wanted to scream, but she knew it would do no good. If anything, it would only make him feel more powerful.

"We have some talking to do… Questions and answers," he told her, laughing as he bent down to talk to her.

"I agree," said another voice.

She saw the sudden panic on the man's face as he looked around. She watched the driver stand up from his crouched position. As he did, so there was a scream, and the man were ripped from the ground and disappeared.

Tara lay there for a moment, wondering if the beast was coming back for her. Her breathing became more erratic. She closed her eyes and calmed herself slowly. Something she had taught herself to do as a child: a method of calming the fear of when her mother came home drunk. She slipped into happy thoughts. Her imagination led her away, on a beach somewhere. Probably somewhere she had seen photographs of once. She was listening to the sounds of the water on the sand, and the seagull's overhead. Tara's opened one eye. A look of confusion crossed her face, for the cries from the birds was strange… Almost like sirens.

Her eyes snapped open. Painfully she sat up and saw the approach of two black-and-whites. Flashes of red and blue filling the alleyway.

She smiled softly. She was safe.

For now.

The alleyway was becoming dark with the setting of the sun. Shadows that had once kept to the edges were now growing. Draping everything like a grey cloak.

* * *

McCall pulled the Mustang up to the garage where she usually parked when they got the call. Uniform had picked up a young woman in an alleyway. The cops had checked the plate number, and it had flagged up as McCall's suspect vehicle. It had taken her twenty minutes to get to the scene, hoping the driver was with them. She had left Tooms at the precinct. He said he had stuff to do, but she figured he just wanted to check on Tony. She didn't object to going by herself. It gave her time to think.

McCall had parked the black GT 500 near the mouth of the alley. People had begun to gather. They reminded her of hyenas near a kill. Most had cell phones on long poles, normally used for those ever-popular 'selfies. She pushed her way through the crowd, her jacket pulled tight around her, holding off the sudden chill of the evening. A female uniformed officer lifted the yellow crime scene tape and nodded a respectful greeting. McCall returned the nod and headed for the alley.

The dark of the passage was disturbed by the headlamps of the black-and-whites and flashes from the roof-mounted lightbars. This had no real purpose, apart from the fact that it made it difficult for the public to take photographs. McCall smiled at the officers' ingenuity.

McCall found the four first responders. Two of them were at the other end of the alleyway holding off those members of the public who had nothing else to do but make their lives difficult. McCall thought back to when she was a uniform. People didn't have smartphones with photographic options back then; all they had was cameras.

She always figured that if people would just do as they were told and move off, police wouldn't need to guard crime scenes so heavily. For her, the worst type of 'rubberneckers' were the souvenir takers: the morbid ones, who collected items from scenes of murder and carnage. For them, getting some souvenir from a scene was like having an autograph from a famous star, and for the cops, it was a nightmare. Most of the time, what they took was something insignificant—for instance, a bottle or a magazine. However, sometimes it might be a key piece of evidence, and that was the problem.

She thought back to the case of a serial killer who was almost not convicted because some interfering idiot had taken vital evidence from the scene. The killer found out about this and baited the man. In fact, the souvenir hunter, Henry Corp, nearly went down for the murders himself because he was in possession of the incriminating items. Unfortunately for the real killer, he had been so keen to set up Henry that he had left his fingerprints behind, assuming Henry would also be careless enough to leave his own. But Henry had been careful and worn gloves. So, the killer got the lethal injection, and Henry got a suspended sentence for hindering a police investigation.

McCall headed for two uniforms who were standing beside their black-and-white. The male officer was tall and medium built with short black hair. The woman cop was just a couple of inches shorter, with red hair and a slim build. They were both in their late twenties but had lost that 'rookie cop' that some young officers just couldn't get rid of.

"Detective McCall," the officers greeted her with a fond welcome.

"Hi, Wellman, Osborne," McCall greeted them back. Detective McCall had worked with them before and knew that they were good cops, with bright futures. She had hoped that Karol Osborne might have made it upstairs to their department as a detective, but they got Coreman instead. Wellman was one step away from SWAT. McCall had no idea why he wanted to join that crack division, but then it was his personal goal.

"What have we got?" McCall's gaze shot around the scene. There was a taxicab, its doors wide open. CSU were all over it, taking fingerprints and photographs.

"We received an anonymous tip that someone was about to get murdered in a taxicab," Officer Wellman explained. "They gave a location and a plate number. After what had happened with Detective Steel, we thought it may be connected. When we got here, we found a woman on the back seat, but no cab driver."

"We figured he took off when he heard the sirens," Osborne added, but McCall saw some doubt in her eyes.

"But?" McCall pressed.

Osborne looked around and then over towards the cab.

"The woman said he was…" She paused as if she was searching for the correct words to use without sounding crazy. "…That he was *taken away* by something."

"Taken away?" McCall asked. "What? You're saying that some guys tackled him or what? What do you mean taken away? How exactly?"

She looked at the two officers who both had the same expression. It was one of those looks that said, 'I knew you wouldn't believe me'. Then almost together, the two detectives looked up, up to the rooftop. McCall followed their gaze, and then her mouth fell open. Quickly she slammed her mouth shut and shook her head.

"Where's the witness now?" McCall asked, pulling on a pair of latex gloves.

Osborne pointed to an ambulance that had been reversed in, that was almost acting as a second barricade to stop onlookers getting too close. McCall nodded and headed for the taxi. At first, she didn't know what to think. Was the driver just a serial killer and had nothing to do with their case? If so, it meant the worst scenario imaginable: two cases running parallel—the odds of which were more than Mr Spock could predict.

As she came closer, she saw the taxi's medallion number on the trunk: *8Z56*.

McCall's heart skipped a beat.

It was the taxi she'd seen taking Tara away earlier that day. She looked over into the back of the ambulance. There sat a woman with short blonde hair.

There sat Tara Burke.

Chapter 33

The taxi driver woke up with a start. There was a searing pain in his feet. Below him was a bright light. So bright, in fact, that he couldn't see anything else. His head throbbed as if he'd woke from a massive hangover. He didn't remember much. Just the sensation of been ripped from the ground. After that, there was nothing.

The driver tried to move but found that he couldn't. He was bound tightly. Then, with horror, as his head began to clear, he realised he was upside down. He was strung up like meat heading for the slaughter.

He looked forward and saw blackness. The only light was that of the single bulb socket above his feet. The blackened-out lampshade was made to channel the light downwards in a column of light. His arms were stretched downwards, held tight by a chain that bound his hands together, and was secured to the floor via a heavyweight.

Sweat poured out of his body, mostly caused by fear. The room was silent apart from the driver's frantic breathing. His body was shaking from all the adrenaline that was being pumped through his veins. He tried to look around, but there was only blackness beyond the pillar of light that surrounded him.

"Who's there?" he yelled out. "I know someone is there… Come out!" He was trying hard not to show his terror. The silence continued until it became unbearable. The driver thought he would start bleeding from his ears as he strained hard to pick out a sound.

"What did you want with the girl?" asked a deep gravelly voice. The driver spun his head around as far as he could, hoping to get a glimpse of whoever was talking. But there was only darkness.

"Sorry, man, she was just a fare. I picked her up, and I drove her to her destination." The man's lies were almost convincing…almost.

"What did you want from the girl?" the male voice asked again with a hint of anger.

"Look, man, I don't know what you mean! The chick asked for a cab, told me to drive to some alleyway. I thought she had something goin' on," the driver cried out as sweat poured into his eyes, the salt causing them to sting.

"The girl. Tell me the truth please," growled the voice. "And I won't ask again."

The cabbie started to panic. His courageous attitude had washed away with the oceans of perspiration.

"I don't know, man, I am just the driver, that's all! I get a call, and someone picks them up or drops them off," he yelled, foamy spit spluttering from his desperate mouth.

"What do you mean, them?" asked the voice from the shadows.

The cabbie then realised that he had just crossed that line you should never cross. The line between ignorance and just plain 'covering your ass'. He swallowed hard.

"I get a call. They tell me to pick someone up, and that's what I do. They normally give me an envelope with cash and a picture of the person and instructions. That's all I know, man, honest!" He was almost in tears.

"The cop. Why did you kill the cop?" asked the voice. This time the words seemed to be delivered more calmly.

"You mean the guy on the bridge? No...no, that wasn't me, man. I just picked up the dude and drove him to his hotel. The man started raving and waving a damn gun. I stopped and let that crazy motha go, man." He shook his head as if to convince the stranger of his story.

"Who do you work for?" asked the deep, hard voice.

The cabbie said nothing.

"Who do you work for?" the voice asked again.

A thousand things went through the cabbie's mind. Most of his thoughts were about his death. Once his employer found out about this, he was as good as dead.

"Who are you?" the cabbie yelled out of frustration.

Was it the cops? The Feds? The local nuns' choir.

"I am Batman," said the voice. The cabbie investigated the blackness with a confused expression.

"What...Really?" he asked, then kicked himself for falling into the trap to make him look stupid.

"No, you idiot. I am something much worse," came the voice.

And then from the shadows walked a man in an ankle-length trench coat. The figure pulled back a cowl to reveal a stony face and a pair of sunglasses. Fear gripped the driver as he stared at Steel. He wanted to scream. To yell out for help. But his mouth quivered and flapped and gave no sound.

"Now, tell me about the girl and why you tried to kill me," Steel told him, his voice growling with satisfaction.

The cabbie looked over at the menacing form of Steel. He felt the warmth of his own urine flow down over his naked body. The driver spat and gagged as it passed over his face and into his mouth and nostrils.

Steel just stood there, his long black coat almost reaching the ground. The light from the lamp was reflecting in those damned sunglasses.

* * *

McCall drove Tara back to the precinct. She had decided that the thought of nearly a thousand cops in the building might make her feel safe. McCall could see that Tara was well shaken up, but she guessed it was because of something other than her recent abduction.

Detective McCall sat in the chair next to Tara's in one of the briefing rooms. Tara sat nursing a fresh cup of black coffee that McCall had just brought in. McCall let her just sit for a while in silence. There was no point getting straight to it. Firing questions at her at this stage would just make her distrust McCall and clam up. This was another reason why they weren't in one of the interrogation rooms.

The colour had returned to Tara's once-pale cheeks. Her eyes were less bloodshot, and she had that 'human' look about her once more. Tara was scared. Her edgy movements as someone walked past the windows spoke volumes. What she wasn't saying, was why she was scared. Of course, her fear could easily be attributed to being abducted by a madman. But McCall thought differently. Tara was troubled by more than the abduction, something even more terrifying than the death of Amber.

"How you doin'?" McCall finally asked. Tara looked up at her with innocent, frightened eyes.

"I'm a little shook up, but I am fine thanking you," she responded before taking a sip from the hot coffee. McCall gave her a reassuring smile and placed a comforting hand on hers.

"Are you ready to tell me what happened back there?"

Tara thought for a moment at the question. Then nodded slowly.

"Well, you saw me get into the cab," she began. "The driver asked me where I was going. I thought he was just a regular cab driver; had no idea he was some psycho killer. As we were travelling, he must have drugged me or something because I passed out..."

McCall nodded as she listened to Tara's account of events.

"...When I came to, I felt as if I couldn't move, there must have been something in the drug. I don't know. He parked up and got out. I planned to kick him when the door opened, but I wasn't figuring on him coming from the other side. I can still see his sickening smile as he looked down on me. Then suddenly someone said something to him."

McCall shot her a puzzled look.

"Someone else was there?" the detective asked. "Did you see them?"

Tara shook her head. "No, I couldn't see anyone. But I don't think it was *someone*. Sounds crazy I know, but it was more like a *something*." Tara spoke, looking slightly bashful.

McCall sat back in her chair and gave Tara a disappointed look. "More like a *something*? So, tell me, Tara, what did this *thing* look like?" McCall was disappointed, half expecting a monster story from this woman, who she realised had to be deranged.

Tara shrugged and shook her head. "I don't know. All I know is that whatever it was, it took him away." Tara felt stupid admitting she'd something so patently impossible. She knew that any second McCall would be standing up and walking out, and Tara wouldn't blame her if she did.

"So, someone drags away your attacker, but you don't see anything. Really. How's that possible? How could you *not see* the man being dragged away?" McCall said, her tolerance wearing thin. "OK. So which way did they go?" She leaned forward, resting her arms on the desk.

Tara simply looked up and pointed. "He went... Up." Tara held her upwards gaze. She gave a little smile as she recalled the man's screams as he disappeared.

"What are you thinking about?" McCall asked curiously, thinking that Tara's reaction was somewhat suspicious, to say the least.

"The man. As he was being carried up, he screamed like a girl," Tara said, her gaze falling back on McCall.

McCall said nothing at first, just sat back in her chair, her thoughts racing to one conclusion. She decided: *if you're going to hit her with it, do it now.*

"Tell me about that night with Amber," McCall dived straight in.

Tara didn't know why she suddenly felt herself looking shocked. After all, she had been waiting for the question ever since they had sat down.

"I had just finished a double and was heading home. It may sound strange, but I was looking forward to one last night alone," Tara started to tell her.

McCall leant forward, a confused look on her face. "So, you didn't know she would be there?" McCall quickly made a notation in her notebook.

Tara shook her head and took another sip from the coffee. "I wasn't expecting her until Monday. She said she had stuff to sort out before she could move in," Tara explained.

Sam made some more notes before laying the pen next to the notebook. "Sorry, you were saying you'd just finished work?"

"That's right. I got my usual train. It was around ten when I got to my final stop. I remember getting a text from my boyfriend. He was asking where I was. I figured he had tried the house phone and had gotten worried when nobody had answered."

McCall made a quick note of the times Tara had just given. She sat back in her chair, taking the pad with her. She crossed her right leg over her left, using her knee as a support for her yellow legal pad.

"When I got to the building, everything seemed normal," the witness continued. "Well, until I got inside the apartment anyway." Tara looked down at the steaming dark of the coffee, but all she could see was her own reflection.

"Is that when you saw Amber's body?" McCall asked gently.

Tara looked up at McCall and shook her head. "No, the lights didn't work. I thought there had been a short or something. The great thing about living alone is you know where everything is. We get a lot of blackouts in my building. Normally because of the gamer freak upstairs who sucks so much juice. I know where every table, chair, even lump in the floor is because the floors are coming apart. I headed for the side dresser for a flashlight. When I tripped over something, I knew there was trouble." Tara stared back at her coffee.

McCall could see how painful it was for her to remember that night.

"The floor was wet. At first, I thought the guy upstairs had left his bath running again." She looked back at McCall with a smile. "He gets so involved in his damn games he forgets stuff. Do you believe the landlord has put twelve fire alarms in the guy's apartment?

McCall returned the smile, reminded of her own occasional difficulties with neighbours.

"I ... I remember the front door opening and my boyfriend coming in. As he opened the door—" Tara closed her eyes tightly, as if she was trying to delete the memory.

"That's when you saw the body?" McCall finished; almost sensing Tara would be unable to say it.

Tara nodded. The tears began to stream down her cheeks. "He pulled me up and held me tight. It wasn't until later that we realised we were covered in blood. My boyfriend—"

"—Jake Harding?" McCall said as if to confirm the name Kim had given to them.

Tara nodded, looking somewhat confused that she knew his name.

"Well, Jake told me to get changed and to pack a case. He also told me to lay low. He thought you guys may think I was guilty and burn me for the murder. So, I packed a bag and disappeared." Tara took another sip from the coffee. She watched McCall as she scribbled down some notes.

"And what about Jake, what happened to him?" McCall asked, knowing full well that he was at the morgue.

"I don't know. That was the last I heard from him. I thought it had all been too much for him and he had bolted." Tara shrugged and then for the first time set down the coffee mug. She frowned and shook her head.

"You know it's funny when I heard there was a body found in the park. I hoped it was him." Tara looked over towards McCall, who just sat there with an expressionless face.

"You were hoping for closure. If he was dead, you knew he hadn't left you alone with this."

McCall's words caused Tara to nod as she wiped away another flood of fresh tears.

"Tara, do you know why anyone would want to kill Amber?"

McCall had successfully managed to place Tara in that comfortable spot. She had persuaded her to talk about that night. Tara felt at ease, unpressured. If she was ever going to get answers from Tara, now was the time.

Tara shook her head. "She worked for a big shipping firm, overseas stuff. It was a shipping company, not the CIA." Her voice trembled. It could have been because of tiredness, stress or emotion. Or more likely avoidance.

"OK," Sam went on gently. "So, Amber had no enemies that you knew of. How about you?"

McCall had been saving this question. Tara pushed her hands underneath the table out of sight. The unsure shrug and the biting of the bottom lip spoke volumes. Tara said nothing more. She just stared into that coffee cup and dreamt of that beach house. Just her and her man alone together.

McCall stood up and walked out of the room, leaving Tara to her thoughts. Captain Brant was waiting outside near her desk.

"You get anything?" he asked, popping some gum into his mouth.

McCall stopped and looked back at Tara, who hadn't moved. "Well, I think I know why our John Doe—or should I say Jake Harding—was covered in blood. They were a couple."

Brant raised an eyebrow at the revelation.

"She says he came for her at the apartment. The lights were off, and she must have fallen into the blood. When he picked Tara up off the floor that's when the blood was transferred," McCall explained.

Brant nodded. It was a good theory and would explain why he had blood on him. What it didn't explain was were had he been from ten that night until McCall had found him the next day.

"Well, she's a witness, where you gonna put her?" Brant asked.

Sam McCall shrugged and shook her head. She was out of ideas, or more precisely, she was busy trying to figure out what Tara was into.

"Use the safe house that Steel set up, it's already paid for. But don't tell her about her boyfriend having been there. If she knows something, she will spill it eventually. When she feels safe enough." Brant spoke with the benefit of years of experience, making McCall wonder how many times he had used the same tactics.

Brant and McCall looked over towards Tooms, who was approaching fast. He wore a childish smirk, looking like a child with a secret.

"Guess where our John Doe used to work?" he asked, his glances bouncing from McCall to Tara.

"I don't know where?" McCall asked impatiently. Tooms nodded towards where Tara was sitting.

"He worked at the diner?" Brant asked.

Tooms smiled and shook his head. "No, better than that. He worked at the same shipping firm as Amber did. In a different department but for the same company."

McCall looked over at Tara, who was still staring into her coffee. "Funny she left out that part of the story," she growled.

* * *

As the hour hand of her watch moved towards the five, McCall stared at her murder board.

The information was getting better. Thanks to Tina's time of death—more usually referred to as TOD—she was able to make a good timeline. Photographs of the scene were accompanied by lines and scribbles of information. Jake Harding was still a suspect. Sure, he was dead, but that didn't make it any less likely that he could be their killer. It just meant someone was 'cleaning the house'.

Tooms walked up behind her. She could smell the mixed aroma of the hotdog and the fresh coffee. She turned as he handed her a freshly filled cup.

"Where's Tara?" Tooms asked, afraid of losing anyone else connected to the case.

"Tony has taken her to the hotel." She saw his sudden look of concern and smiled.

"Don't worry. There will be two female officers inside with her all the time. Plus, four men outside in the hallway. Also, no take-outs allowed!" Her words were confident. But after all, last time they had been taken by surprise, they weren't expecting anything to happen. He was only a John Doe at the time, and they weren't aware of his importance. Tara, on the other hand, was different. They knew there was a real threat to her life, and they would be ready for it.

But something was bothering McCall. Tara had said there was no power to her apartment. McCall picked up the desk phone and called CSU. She spoke to some young guy. She requested someone to go to Tara's apartment and dust the fuse box for prints. It was a longshot, but sometimes longshots paid off.

"Anything on our flying taxi driver?" McCall asked with a smile.

Tooms shook his head. "Not for the moment, but I got the uniforms to look. Who knows, maybe the Batman left something behind?" Tooms smiled. He, like McCall, thought Tara's account of the cab driver's disappearance had to be a tall tale. She had probably seen the driver run off when the cops arrived but was too scared to say so. McCall looked over at the clock. It was late, and they were both tired.

"OK, that's enough for today. We'll pick it up tomorrow," McCall said, pouring the coffee into her thermos mug.

Tooms headed for his desk. Home time always sounded good.

"See you tomorrow, Sammy," Tooms said, pulling on his jacket.

"See you tomorrow, big guy," McCall answered as she watched him head for the elevator. She looked at the empty chair next to her desk.

"Good night, Mr Steel," she whispered, almost hoping he could hear her.

Chapter 34

Steel walked out into the darkness. He had left the cab driver dangling like a piñata. He hadn't learnt much from the man apart from the discovery that he had terrible bladder control and he was indeed just a driver, not otherwise part of the organisation.

It was a simple set up. He gets told by cell phone who or what to collect and he does so. He then knocks his passenger out with some drug, then leaves them in the alley where Steel had caught him. The cabbie didn't even know who he was working for; he just got paid a lot of cash to drive and not ask questions. Looking at the man, it was no wonder that they never told him anything. If he'd added just a touch more pressure, he would have sung for longer than Mick Jagger in a live performance.

The enigmatic British detective had made an anonymous 911 call to the police and ambulance services, telling them the driver's whereabouts. The cops could have him now. McCall would certainly love to talk to the guy.

Steel made his way through the darkened streets of the city. He couldn't risk being seen. In a way, the killers had done him a favour, for they had made him invisible. There is a certain freedom in being dead. Nobody is looking for you or expecting you for that matter.

Of course, he couldn't return to his apartment or go back to the station. He was now officially a ghost. He was back to doing what he was good at being a shadow.

Steel headed for his other safe house. It was an old abandoned power plant in Glenwood. A place he had seen about a year ago while working on another case. The machinery had been stripped away, leaving the rusted metal skeleton and the graffiti-covered red brick walls. This massive structure had been left abandoned. Now, he had a use for it. It was in a convenient position, close to the Hudson River. Everything of any value had already been ripped out and sold for scrap. New windows had been fitted on the inside; the old ones left on the outside. This gave the place the appearance of being abandoned. New, heavier doors had been fitted but made to look like the old ones.

Inside it was a different story. On one of the split levels, he had three computers and five large monitors. One room had been made into an armoury, another a bedroom of sorts. There was a shower room and a wardrobe. This was a safe house wearing the disguise of a ruin. The Aston Martin SUV was parked in one of the special bays next to several other vehicles, including a motorcycle. The power was from several generators that were stored in a larger room that once held the building's own generators. This electricity was completely off the grid.

When he first came over to the States, John Steel had acquired several places that no one else was interested in. Of course, his name wasn't connected to them, just in case, he needed a bolthole. They were places he thought would come in handy. Places that the agency didn't know about.

It had taken nearly a year to renovate this one. All that time plus a lot of money to turn the power plant into a base of operations: his own personal 'bat cave'.

Steel headed for the split-level section. This large area was set out as a war room. As well as the five computers and large monitors, there was a long metal table with a coffee machine and a couple of mugs, next to which was a grey fronted refrigerator, mainly used for milk and bottled water. Opposite a large flat-screen television was an old brown leather couch.

He took off his long trench coat and hung it on an old wood-and-brass coat stand that stood next to the metal staircase. Steel prepped the coffee machine then switched it on. There was a bubbling noise and then the whirring of motors, as the water was being passed over the ground coffee. He filled one of the cups with coffee, milk and sugar, then headed for the couch. As he fell onto the leather, it squeaked under the sudden pressure. He stretched out, using the armrest as a cushion. Closing his eyes for a moment, he inhaled the fresh smell of caffeine.

He let himself reach that comfortable place, that moment before slipping into a deep sleep: something he often didn't have time to do. He opened his eyes again and sat up. Taking a well-deserved sip of coffee, he stood and headed for one of the computers. He downloaded the picture of the cabbie who'd abducted Tara from his phone to the computer and started a search. The facial recognition software kicked in and started running, using all the standard databases. Steel took another sip before stripping down to the waist.

Steel stepped into a long room which had once been one of the main halls. To the side, there were walkways on many different levels. But now it held a strange assault course: eighty feet of multi-levels which came back on itself so that the start point was eventually the finish. There were long thin walkways, ropes, large jumps and long drops. It was a combination of an urban cross training track and a military assault course. Some of the latter, he had taken from the British Parachute Regiment's 'piece of terror'. This training area was punishing, but good for keeping you agile.

Steel strapped on a sports watch and started the timer. He bolted off to a ramp that went up around twelve feet at a ridiculous angle. He attacked each jump and apparatus with ease. His movements looked fluid, as though he was making no effort at all. His tight muscular body felt alive again, he felt the blood flow to his taut frame, and it felt good.

Finally, he dropped around eight feet and grabbed a horizontal bar. As he did so, he swung off and landed with a roll. As he came up, he threw two throwing knives at two targets, each one on either side of him. Steel stood up and stopped the watch. The whole thing had taken him five minutes. *Not bad for a dead guy*, he laughed to himself. But it was not his personal best. The knives had struck home. One was in the guy's head, and the other target had got it in the throat. He smiled, crunched his neck from side to side, rolled his shoulders and headed for the shower.

The water from the shower felt like tiny bullets hitting his skin. The mix of the hammering water and the steam from the heat was almost therapeutic. He turned the water from hot to cold: skin shock treatment.

He dried himself off and then changed into another set of clothing that was hung up ready. Black BDU trousers, a black long-sleeved top and military-style boots. They fitted well and were comfortable as well as practical. Steel made his way back to the couch and the coffee he had left. It had cooled to the right temperature. Steel headed over to another computer which was piggybacking from his own at the precinct. This held all the footage that the precinct had collected from that morning at the bridge.

He knew he had been poisoned; the question was when? Williams hadn't done it; he had made it clear he needed Steel alive. It wasn't the taxi driver, for he didn't have the stones for it. Then he remembered the driver saying that he 'just picks the people up'. They wouldn't trust him enough for him to pick Steel up at the house, for then he would have to know their location. It must have been at the drop-off point. Steel took a sip from his coffee as he moved over to the murder board he had recreated on a large smartboard.

Steel had to go back to the start, to Amber's murder. Everything that had happened was as a result of that. Abductions, bodies in the park, even the attempt on his own life. *Find out the why and you will find out the who*, he thought to himself. As Steel took another sip from the coffee, one thing dawned on him. The driver wasn't working for Williams, but what if he worked for the other organisation? It would make sense. If this was the case, where was Steel dropped off for the cabbie to get to him?

His head began to hurt with all the questions, or it could have just been the anti-venom and other medications rushing through his system. He sat down hard on the couch and stretched out once more. He needed rest, if only for a little while. He had to let his body recover. As he slipped into a deep and troubled sleep, one thought came to the forefront of his mind. Who was the girl in the cab?

And what did they want with her?

* * *

The next morning brought an early shower. Dark clouds hung in a blackened sky. McCall had got up early to take a run. A three-miler, just enough to blow away the cobwebs and give her brain a kick-start. The rain was light, not even heavy enough to get the store windows wet. But it was cool to the skin, which helped her to pound out the miles. Her plan was to do a quick run and then a workout at the station gym.

Despite everything, she felt good. They had Tara, and she hoped that would be the start of the good things to come. They had an ID on their John Doe and a location of where he worked. Tony was checking out the man's apartment that morning to see if there was anything relevant to the case, but even with all the progress, it still felt hollow.

It was nearly five by the time McCall reached the precinct's gym. Today was 'bag work' to relieve some tension. She felt that kicking the shit out of a four-foot bag was therapeutic. If she didn't hit the bag, then some other poor bastard was going to get it.

Sweat ran down her back, halted by the skin-tight Lycra bodysuit. Her hair was bunched up in a ponytail, giving her the look of a warrior. As well as relieving stress, the exercise helped her to think. One person that kept coming to her mind was Tara Burke and her statement. She was either lying about something or just holding back. McCall knew she would have to speak with her again, but she needed something that would tip the scales.

Tara was a smart woman. That had already been proved. She had been smart enough to hide out, and she had been smart enough to know it was time to run again.

Unfortunately, the bad guys were smarter.

McCall landed one final upper kick to the bag and grabbed her water from her own equipment satchel. The water was still cold. She smiled as she peeled away the sides of the sock which encased the bottle: a trick that Steel had taught her. Put a cold bottle in a sock, and it acts as a thermos. She had scoffed at the idea at first. In fact, she had no idea why she had done it now.

She took a mouthful of the liquid and swallowed hard. The cold fluid left an almost burning sensation, but it was simultaneously refreshing.

The glamorous woman detective showered and changed at the precinct—there was no time to travel back home. She sat at her desk and put her favourite coffee mug down on her coaster. The white china mug had an 11th Precinct logo on one side and on the other was her name printed out using a print label maker. The two-inch strip simply read: *McCall's Mug. Hands off.*

She opened her emails. There was still no word from CSU about whether there were any prints on the fuse box at Tara's place. Tooms was waiting to hear back from the uniforms, after their house-to-house questioning of the people in the apartments near the rooftops close to where the taxi driver had disappeared. McCall was still having a hard time with the whole 'flew away' business—Tara telling them that the cabbie had been spirited into the sky—but then she supposed that anything was possible given the right equipment. Tony had just walked in and was heading for the break room. He looked angry, but she knew it was a thing him and Tooms had going last one in gets the coffees.

She waited until Tony had sat down and checked his email before approaching him. It was pointless asking the guy what he had before he had checked. McCall closed her messages. The long list of mind-numbing trivial items could wait—she had more important things to look out for. McCall rose from her chair and wandered over to them, coffee cup in hand.

"So, what have we got?" she asked, sitting in the chair next to Tooms's desk.

"CSU are working on the taxi, no hope of any pictures, all the surveillance cameras in that area had been vandalised ages ago," Tony told her, rocking in his chair as he spoke. "The lab did come back to us. The blood on Jake Harding's clothes was Amber's. Which confirms the story Tara told you?"

"Let's look at that alley again, anything you can pull up," McCall had a lively bounce in her voice as if she thought things were looking up. "He must have taken her there for a reason. My guess is he has used that location before." She felt as if they were on a roll, and she hoped it was just the beginning of the breakthroughs.

"Tooms, you look more closely at Trent Shipping. It appears that our Mr Harding also worked there."

Tooms raised his eyebrows at McCall's revelation.

"Funny, they never mentioned that they had an employee missing when Steel and I spoke to them," she commented, smiling deviously. The people at the shipping company were all a little too smug for her liking.

"Pleasure to rip 'em a new one for you, McCall." Tooms smiled before taking a bite from the bear claw; he had brought in. Loose almonds fell onto his desk as he tucked in.

McCall smiled. It was like watching her nephew eat, and he was eight years old.

She looked across to her murder board, concentrating mainly on the picture of Tara. Tony noticed the long stare.

"I am heading off to Harding's apartment later," Tony told her. "The manager said it wouldn't be a problem; actually, he was asking how long before he could re-rent the place." Tony shrugged miserably. "All heart, eh?"

McCall smiled and shook her head. "I'll be with Tara this morning. She's got some blanks that need filling." McCall's voice had a stiff tone to it. Tooms knew that tone all too well. His wife had it whenever the kids weren't telling the truth about something.

McCall stood up and stretched off. Her body ached from the workout. *No pain, no gain*, she thought. She'd have preferred the gain without the pain, but hey.

She headed for her desk and pulled her gun from the top drawer, then relocked it, then pulled on her jacket and left.

"Call me if something comes up," McCall shouted as she headed for the elevator. Tooms just gave a quick salute, knowing she wouldn't be listening for an answer anyway. She bypassed the elevator and took the stairs. *Today will be a good day, but not for someone*, she thought and smiled as she headed for her car.

* * *

Central Park was full of life. Joggers, strollers, people taking that scenic route from one side to the other. The sun hung high in a picturesque blue sky. The only evidence of the early morning shower was a light film of water on the parked cars. The air smelled fresh, and the grass appeared greener than usual. The park was full of motion, of people hurrying around. All except one. It was a man in a hooded long leather-and-wool coat, who strolled along a path next to a lake apparently without purpose. To his left was a row of green benches, which curved round, following the contours of the path and grass verge. Steel stopped at the last one of a row which was next to an old-style streetlamp. Using a gloved hand, he wiped away the dampness from the bench, then sat and looked out over the lake.

The morning light made the blue still waters glisten. A family of ducks swam past in single file and dragonflies skated low, close to the water. Behind him was a mass of bushes and then a tree line. To his left was Bow Bridge, with its white arched cast-iron walls and six flowerpots. Each urn held an explosion of colours. He had a straight line of sight of the path to his right and the bridge. The running path that branched behind him, near the bridge, was no concern. If his view was blocked, so was theirs. But nobody was looking for him, and it was just his own paranoia that made him pick the spot: a very public place with good fields of vision.

Sure, he was dead, no one was looking for him. However, he was looking for someone. Steel pulled out a paper bag from his pocket and picked at the loaf of bread inside. He tossed the pieces towards some hungry birds. The pigeons happily pecked away at the free meal.

"I prefer ducks myself," said a low husky voice. It was the sort of voice that came as a result of using whisky as mouthwash and having alcohol breath as a result.

"Really? I am a swan person myself," Steel replied.

He wasn't moving, apart from the slow tossing of the bread. "They're majestic birds. Calming to watch."

The homeless guy sat next to Steel and offered a bottle in a brown paper bag. Steel didn't react, just carried on tossing the bread.

"There's a warehouse you might be interested in. Someone is providing weapons to small-time street gangs. Selling them cheap to flood the system. Someone wants to cause some trouble, methinks," Crazy Gus said, handing over a small piece of paper discreetly.

Gus looked to be in his seventies. But he probably just looked old because of his filthy appearance and the chemicals he poured into his body. He wore an old US army M65 combat jacket. The 'Screaming Eagles' insignia was dirty but intact. But the name shield had been removed, almost as if he wanted to forget who he used to be.

"Any ideas who this *someone* might be?" Steel asked, almost for confirmation of his theory.

Gus just looked at Steel and laughed, knowing full well that Steel had the answer. Steel smiled and nodded slowly, feeling almost foolish at having tried to trick the old-timer.

"Is there any word on the street about why someone wants a woman called Tara Burke so bad?" Steel asked softly, tossing another piece of bread at a fresh batch of birds.

Gus looked up for a second, almost as if he was asking permission from God to answer the question. "No, but I can ask around. Maybe there's some chatter on the East Side." Gus took a swig from the bottle. Steel had no idea what his friend was drinking, but the smell made him wince.

"Gus, I am surprised you remember anything at all after pouring that stuff down your neck," Steel joked.

Gus just laughed and went back to his drinking. Steel tucked the piece of paper away into a pocket and pulled out a folded hundred-dollar bill.

"You look after yourself, Gus," Steel said, shaking the man's hand and passing the bill in the palm. Steel stood up and straightened the long coat.

The old man watched as Steel walked away, making sure he was near crowds of people, trying to mask his escape. He smiled and tucked the note away without looking.

* * *

The warehouse was tucked away in Gowanus, Brooklyn. The red-brick monster was once a powerhouse, and now it was a disused shelter for the homeless and junkies. It overlooked a canal and the 3rd Street Bridge.

Inside the building were fifteen men who were all dressed in black three-quarter-length leather coats, jeans and black T-shirts, standing around impatiently. Mr James was the leader of the merry band. He was a large man, with a military-style haircut and a bulge in his jacket from the twin .45. It was a strange weapon, comprised of two 1911s put together, creating one beast of a gun.

He looked at his watch as he chewed on a toothpick. They were late. The deal was meant to have happened twenty minutes ago. His men were scattered around in tactical positions, armed with Heckler and Koch 416 assault rifles and SFP9 pistols. James touched the earbud in his right ear. It was the 'overwatch' on the roof sending a report.

"Roger that," he spoke into his sleeve, then looked over to the two men at the main doors. "Open her up, our guests are finally here."

There was a scrape of metal on metal as the massive doors were opened. Then a roar of engines which echoed throughout the structure, as two blacked-out GMC Yukon SUVs tore inside. With them was a box-body truck designed for house removals. It was a rented vehicle that they had no intention of returning.

The vehicles stopped, and fifteen black guys got out. They were an up-and-coming street gang, hoping to make a name for themselves. To do that, they needed what the big man had. The gang leader stood around six foot one, and he had broad shoulders. He wore a pinstriped suit and white Nike trainers. A blue baseball cap covered his shaven head, and round sunglasses hid his eyes. With him, as he approached were two massive hulks of men, each one standing at around six foot four and with the massive build of giants.

James said nothing at first. He just stood and sized up the men. He smiled to himself. The muscle that the man had with him was more useful for scare tactics than action. Their frames were too large, which made them slow moving. Sure, if they got hold of you, they could do some damage, but he knew he could have those men on the ground and screaming in no time at all.

"You're late, Mr DX," James said, spitting out the toothpick. "We have a schedule to keep, and you are messing with that."

"Relax, man, we got de money, yam got de goods, so everyone is happy." Mr DX spoke with a slow Jamaican accent. He smiled and waved at the driver. The man got out of the SUV and walked over with two aluminium briefcases and laid them flat on the bonnet of the SUV. DX clicked open the catches and opened each of them up, revealing three million dollars in cash.

"So, you got sometin' for me?" DX's smile was smug.

James waved behind him, and two men moved to the truck and opened it up. The vehicle contained large military cargo crates. There were enough automatic weapons, grenade launchers, grenades and ammo to start a small war.

DX smiled broadly and nodded. "Very nice, man, very nice."

The black guy's smug grin bothered James. His instincts told him it was a set-up. The voice inside his head told him to put a bullet into every one of the assholes. But that was not the plan, and those were not his orders.

"So, man, what if I told you I am walkin' out with me money and de guns. I know you can't stop me. I know dat yam boss has told ya to just deliver de stuff." DX held a Desert Eagle semi-automatic handgun up towards James's head, and his men had already pulled out their own automatic weapons. But James just stood there, saying nothing. Just staring at DX and his smug grin.

"You could kill us all and take everything," James told him calmly. "You could just leave us alive and take everything. But I also know that you're a smart guy and the last thing you want to do is to upset my boss and his organisation. Because you know that if you become a problem, he won't kill you and make you disappear. He will make your death public and very messy." James put another toothpick into his mouth.

DX's smile changed slightly. "Hey, man, you know I was just messin' with ya, man! We're cool, man, we're cool!" DX tried to hide the slight wobble in his voice. He stood tall and opened his arms, as though everything was on the level. His men put their guns away and went to load up the weapons. James tossed the keys of the truck over to one of DX's men.

"Let's just call it a gift," James said, chewing on the new stick of wood. He knew cross loading the merchandise would take time and the sooner he was away from the vermin, the better.

DX smiled again, and his driver handed over the case.

James watched as DX and his men drove out of the building. He hoped he would see DX again, just before he put a bullet into his brain. DX and his men sped along the road, along 3rd Avenue, and back to their own little hideout. The sun was cool, and a fresh breeze made what little vegetation there was sway.

They had their prize and, unknown to them, they also had a stowaway. A figure blended in with the darkened underside of the truck. For the gang, it was a good day that was going to turn bad.

Chapter 35

DX and his crew pulled into an old abandoned warehouse in Brooklyn that served as a distribution centre. The multi-level complex had offices on two levels, and the centre was open spaced with a clear view all around. The place was barren, apart from some office furniture and the odd leftover crate. Scratches of paint hung onto rusted metal, and glassless frames were caked in dust. Power was stolen from a nearby transformer, giving light via the only working lamps. Above, a glass skylight held off the elements. The one reason DX had scouted the place, was that it had a working roof and it was miles away from prying eyes.

As the vehicles rolled in, there was a cheer as if it was from a pack of animals. Armed men covered most of the levels, while the rest of them stood on the main floor. DX's SUV pulled up near a staging area. He got out and raised his hands to quieten everyone down.

"Today we have the power to take this town, tomorrow we take the city," he yelled out. As he raised his hands, the two mountains of men opened the back-shutter door to the boxcar to reveal the weapons. The mob howled again, the sound echoing all around. Then the music started to play from a huge stereo in a corner. There were speakers positioned all around, the sound system creating a massive din.

This noise was a distraction that Steel welcomed. High above on the roof, the resourceful ex-soldier had wondered how he was going to open one of the movable skylight panels so that he could get in. The squeak of rusted metal would certainly have got the attention of the guards below.

Carefully, he opened the skylight. He winced at the first metallic screech. He stopped for a moment, looking down at the guard who seemed to hear it. Slowly he moved the skylight a little more, chancing to go a little further. There was another screech followed by powdered rust falling onto the guard. Steel looked down, his heart racing, expecting the guard to look up and see him at any minute. But the man stayed firm, and his gaze fell to the party below. Steel opened the skylight enough to get through, and then clambered down, using the building's metal frame for hand and footholds. Now he had a clear view he could make out where everyone was.

There was a guard at every corner of the top floor, just as there was on the second. The first floor would be easy to break into. Using the offices as cover, he could take out the guards. However, the second floor was more open, and there was much more danger of being seen. Luckily all the lighting was from the skylight, and this created shadows and dark corners, which were good enough to disappear into. Good enough to allow him to wait patiently for that right moment.

The guards were lackeys, totally untrained. Just thugs with guns told to stand and cover them from above. Sure, if most men came in and found so many guards in position, they would think twice. However, Steel wasn't most men.

* * *

The guard called Laurence stood, rocking on his heels, listening to the party that was in full swing below. He didn't even have his gun in his hand. He had just slung it from its strap across his back. He felt the cold metal of the MP5 machine pistol against his back through his thin shirt. He leant on the railings and looked down. There were several women who had been dragged in with promises of cash, but most of them were here for the drugs. Each one would be given a free sample, after which they would be easy pickings. Laurence pushed himself off the rusty metal and paced about for a while. He was dying for some action, ready for something to happen. He walked over to the dark corner and stopped. His overexcited imagination stopped him from going closer. The movie he had watched the night before had given him a sudden fear of the dark. It had been some weird zombie flick about the last man on earth or something. He smiled at his foolishness and turned around to walk back to the railing.

He didn't have time to scream. Something grabbed him from behind. Something strange and leathery covered his mouth to prevent him from screaming, just before he was dragged into the shadows.

* * *

The second guard – a man called Jamal, stood at his post, this was to the right of where Laurence had once been guarding. He leant on the railings and looked down at the party, as did the other guards. They had nothing to fear: any attack would come from the main door. So before reaching them, they would have to get past the two heavies guarding the main entrance.

Jamal never noticed Laurence disappear. Nor did he see his two other colleagues fall to the same fate: something darting out of the shadows and ripping them into it. He smiled as one of the men below started dancing with one of the drugged women. She hung in his powerful arms like a ragdoll.

"Man, I am missin' the friggin' party while I am stuck up here," he complained to himself, sucking his teeth in annoyance. He wasn't a big man – eighty pounds at the most. He wore a pair of army cargo trousers, a white vest and some over-sized sport shoes. A red-and-blue bandana covered his head as if he was some guerrilla fighter of the '70s.

"Well, we can't have that, can we?" came a voice from behind him.

Suddenly he was being pushed over the side. The rushing wind caused by his fall pulled at his cheeks. His eyes widened, as all he could see was the dusty concrete rushing up towards him. At the last moment, he closed his eyes, as if not seeing it would make it hurt less. His screams made everyone clear a space. Then he felt the tug on his leg. He had stopped moving. There was no pain, just a swinging sensation. Carefully, he opened his eyes. The ground was close enough for him to clear the dust with his breath. He felt dizzy, nauseous. He vomited before he passed out.

Everyone stopped and just stared at Jamal as he swung like a broken builder's plumb line, his face covered in puke. Steel used the distraction to get to the first level. He was hoping most would venture upwards to the second floor, to find out who had done this.

As he tucked himself into one of the offices, Steel watched a stream of armed men rush upwards. He noticed some familiar-looking crates that had been piled up. Ammunition, 5.56, 9mm Lugar and 7.62. There were pine crates stacked up separately. One had black stencilling on it that said: *S4GIA Handle with care*. These were military pineapple hand grenades. The other had *M18, smoke grenades* stencilled on them. Steel smiled cunningly as he hatched a plan.

There was only one way up. The other staircase had fallen down years ago and was lying on its side on the ground floor. This left a large hole and a long drop. The floor above was a grated metal walkway that served no actual purpose apart from providing access to the crane that once straddled the walkways.

Steel had found a powerline that had once given life to the crane. Now it was held above the metal flooring at the other end of the walkway. A thin wire held it firm. A wire that was also threaded around the railing and attached to the wall. All it needed was a foot to kick it.

The armed gunmen ran about checking the upper floor, making their way down towards the other side. Steel looked at his watch. The second-hand quickly approached the twelve. He smiled wickedly.

The men on the level stopped and looked towards a sudden noise—a strange singing coming from the far corner. Three of the men ran towards the sound, their guns at the ready.

There was a flash of blue and sparks sprayed down from the upper levels. Light bulbs exploded from the power surge. Steel watched the chaos from the safety of the concrete office. Women screamed in panic, and the rest of the men yelled orders from the floor below. Gunfire rang out as the electrocuted men involuntarily squeezed the triggers on their guns as their muscles tightened. The others dived for cover, some of them too late as they caught the stray rounds. One man caught two in his body armour, hurling him through a window and into an office. There was a burst of light as he fired back out of anger, but all he managed to hit was an old fire extinguisher on the wall. There was an explosion of a white cloud and the sound of coughing. Steel smiled at the pandemonium he'd orchestrated and moved in towards the downed man, giving him a swift punch to render him unconscious.

DX was angry, confused and frightened. He thought at first that the attack had come from the mercenaries, who were coming back for their weapons. The women that was able to ran out of the main door, causing the guards to run in. There was a clatter of metal as if tin cans were hitting the concrete. Seconds later there was a hissing noise like air escaping, followed by thick smoke rapidly filling the room from the smoke grenades Steel had thrown. DX let out a spray of automatic fire onto the first floor. Sparks flew as 9mm bullets impacted with hard concrete and steel supports.

The eight men below were now enveloped in the thick white smoke. The air was too thick to breathe, causing them to cough and splutter. Steel knew he only had a small window of opportunity to do what he had to do. He adjusted his sunglasses and jumped into the fray.

He moved quickly. The noise of the shouting and jostling men gave him cover, so there was no need for him to sneak about. Each one of them was expertly taken out, knocked unconscious by using the quickest method: either a neck holds or a punch.

That only left DX.

The smoke had stopped pouring from the now-empty grenades. The thick clouds were starting to thin. To disperse enough for DX to see a figure approaching him, but not giving him enough time to do anything about it. It only took one punch, square in the face. He was unconscious before he hit the floor.

* * *

The police had received an anonymous call, that there was reports of gunfire in an old warehouse. It didn't take long for SRU to get there. Uniformed patrol units in the area had also been tasked with securing the area. The orders 'hold but do not enter' were very specific. Police helicopters were there in minutes, circling above, ready to give orders if need be. Thermal scanners were hot and ready. Tactical ground teams headed for the entrances while the second team prepared to abseil down through the roof.

The plan was to get inside the place quickly and easily. The anonymous tip had told them about the weapons, and the SRU teams were ready. 'Flashbangs' were fired into the building. After the first set of explosions, the teams moved in single file, one man on the other, like some Roman legion battle stance. The glass above shattered as the aerial teams swooped in.

The cries of 'CLEAR' soon died down, and the teams looked down at the men lying on the ground. All were zip-tied and had duct tape fastened over their mouths. Everyone looked down, astounded to see what had been done, all of them intrigued.

"What the…?" one of the men in the unit said, looking upwards. The others were just as shocked and amazed. There were twenty-eight men all lying down in a row, all except one of them. DX was hanging upside down from the ceiling. A rope had been tossed over a high beam, and he had been pulled up and fastened to the rear of the truck. The teams searched the area. It was a massive haul that would soon make the evening news. It was a good bust. One that the police commissioner would be getting his best suit pressed for. The only information that would be missing would be that the violent gang of hoodlums had been found neatly gift-wrapped.

From a distance, Steel observed the bust. He watched as the gang members were led into secure vehicles, ready for transport. Ambulances were also present to take care of the women.

Steel smiled. It was a fantastic sight. He had shaken the tree.

Now all he had to do was wait to see what would fall.

* * *

Tooms and Tony went back to the alley. The place where they'd found Tara and the cabbie had been spirited away. This time they took to the rooftops. They wanted a bird's-eye view of the situation. High above, they could get an idea of entrances and exits. The place they were above was a fast-food joint, which suited Tooms just fine. The stench of burnt oil and fats made Tony want to throw up and caused Joshua Tooms to drool. Tony had wondered how his partner wasn't suffering with a weight problem but remembered that Tooms hit the gym as much as he could, so none of the food turned into flab.

Being at roof level brought with it a biting wind, but the overview was perfect. It was a straight line past the main street to the next row of buildings. There was no way the cabbie could have been taken either way by road without being seen. Tooms and Tony stood at the edge and looked down. They were directly above where the taxi had been, and ultimately where the cabbie had vanished.

"Any ideas?" Tooms asked, leaning over the drop just that little bit further before pulling himself back.

"I may have one," Tony replied, crouching down and inspecting a spot where the concrete had been scraped by something.

Tooms looked down to look at his partner. "What you got there?"

"Not sure." Tony looked towards where Tooms stood. "Check over there, see if there are any more scuff marks, would you?"

Tooms looked around and immediately found the same sort of marks near where he was standing. "What the hell are they?"

Tony shook his head – he had no idea. He pulled out his phone and called CSU. Hopefully, they would come up with something.

"Let's get CSU to rip this place apart. Hopefully, they'll be able to find something. But I bet my badge this has something to do with the driver's flying act." Tony waited for someone to answer his call. Tooms smiled and headed downstairs to get something to eat before the CSU arrived. Tony shook his head as his partner disappeared down the stairwell.

When he got through to the CSU call desk, Tony spoke to some young woman with a bubbly voice. He told her the address and the exact location they were at. He could hear music in the background, possibly from a MP3 player or phone's headset. The conversation was short but to the point. Moving back to the scrape marks, he decided to take some photos of his own. If he had to leave before the crime lab got there, he would have a record of what he saw. Just in case.

The sun was high, but there was a haze which blocked out most of the heat. It was still the morning. He knew that by one o'clock it would start to get warmer.

Tony pulled out his cell phone again and sent a quick text to McCall with an update. As a small gust of air swept past him, he closed his eyes briefly. A sudden memory of a day in Memorial Park filled his mind: a Sunday morning with Amber. They had just been on the ferry to Liberty Island. He smiled as he saw her face. Saw her fantastic smile and those ruby lips. A sudden buzz from the cell phone in his hand woke him from his daydream. It was McCall. CSU weren't coming.

A patrol unit had found the cab driver.

* * *

The cabbie's body had been dumped in the river, and a river patrol had found him. McCall stood behind Tina as she examined the body. Uniforms were taking statements, and Coreman was with the patrol unit. McCall just stood there, looking down on the corpse. The man's eyes were open and held a look of fear. McCall took secret pleasure to think that he had suffered before he'd died.

She was ashamed of feeling that way. Almost. She had seen that look in people's eyes before. A long time ago, on another case. There was only one man who could scare anyone that much – Mr Williams. This turned out to be a double revelation. Firstly, it confirmed her fear that Williams was back. And secondly, this body told her something else: that the cab driver wasn't working for him. McCall noted the wounds on the man's body. He'd had information ripped out of him. If Williams was his employer, why would he do that? He would already know the man's secrets.

"So, what's this guy telling you?" McCall asked, kneeling next to her friend, Dr Tina Franks.

"Well, someone went to work on him that's for sure," the ME told her. "I will know more when I get him back to the shop. I would say he's been dead less than twenty-four hours. As for the cause of death. Um..." Tina looked closely at the body, which was covered in cuts. She shrugged. "Sorry, Sam, that I will have to get back to you on. Whoever did this knew what they were doing." Tina Franks's voice held a terrified wobble. McCall knew then that her friend had come to the same conclusion: that this had been the work of Mr Williams.

Tina's assistant helped bag the body and carted it off to the ME's wagon using the gurney. McCall stood and watched her friend climb into the black van and drive away. She said nothing at first, just took time to take in the scene. A sudden cold breeze brushed past, carrying her hair upwards. With a gloved hand, she brushed her hair from her eyes. The choppy water looked cold and unforgiving.

She found it curious that the body hadn't been weighed down, merely tossed into the water like the piece of trash that he was. It was almost as if it was a message for someone.

* * *

The midday weather had changed. The wind had brought dark, unwanted clouds. The breeze had become stronger and constant. There was a storm coming.

Steel sat in his lair, working busily on the computer. He was pulling up what he could on recent gang incidents, especially those involving weapons. At the power station, he had enjoyed a nice talk with DX. He was surprisingly chatty, but then Steel had learnt that most people would rat on their grandmothers if they were under the right powers of persuasion to talk. Someone was supplying gangs with weapons. Steel didn't know why, and DX wasn't much help, even though he had told him when the next shipment was meant to be.

The computer gave some reports on gang activity: a couple of robberies and shootings, all of them involving handguns. Steel was looking for something else. The weapons that DX had bought were military grade. If the gangs were using these sophisticated weapons, they might aim to attack banks or money transports.

Steel sat back in his chair and took a sip from his mug of Yorkshire tea. His cold emerald green unshielded eyes scanned the pages, only to find nothing useful. Steel pulled DX's phone from his pocket and plugged it into the computer. The plan was to copy the phone's memory and leave it somewhere for McCall to find. He smiled at the thought of his colleagues' reactions. They had been through a lot together recently. He only regretted his decision to remain dead to the world for their sakes, and he would have let his friends know he was alive, but the risk of his cover being blown was too great. It was a choice he had made with regret but also a sense of ease. He knew the pretence wouldn't have to be for long – just long enough for whoever was responsible for all these things to make a mistake.

He looked over at the screen, to see the message: *Transfer complete*. He unplugged and re-pocketed the phone. The data would have to wait. He had people to see. Standing up, John Steel took his long coat from the coat stand and pulled it on. Given its bulk and size, it was surprisingly light. He took the sunglasses from the wireless charging station and slid them on as he headed for the door. He needed to find out if DX had been lying about the other drop with another gang. If it was indeed going ahead, he had to shut it down.

***

David Adams sat behind his desk. He was busy writing an email to a client. He stopped, picked up his whisky glass and downed a mouthful of Jack Daniels as he read it through. His eyes suddenly darted over to the heavy wooden door of his office, as it burst open, and a small thin man walked in with two larger men. Adams's secretary ran in after them.

"Sorry, Mr Adams," she apologised, "I tried to stop them—"

Adams just raised a gentle hand and nodded with a smile. Reluctantly, she left the room and closed the doors behind her. Adams sat back in his chair, and the leather squeaked under the shift of his weight.

"What do you want?" Adams growled as he looked the man up and down.

The short man was in his mid-fifties. His blond brushed-back hair was hidden by a grey fedora, round-rimmed glasses matched his oval face, and a grey handmade double-breasted suit emphasised his slimness. His two henchmen looked like a couple of bouncers from a bikers' bar, with their shaven heads and short beards. Leather gloves hid whatever tattoos they may have had on their hands.

"Our employer is not happy with you, Mr Adams, not happy at all," said the man, who was known as Mr Kidd. He poured himself a drink from Adams's private bar. Mr Kidd chose the Napoleon brandy, filling the small bowl glass up to halfway.

"Why?" Adams asked. "The shipment went out today as ordered. Those kids should be getting ready, if they haven't shot each other, that is."

"Yes, I know it went out today. But it was also found by the police. The men and the weapons are in custody now. This is only one of several mistakes you've made." The sinister Mr Kidd spoke softly, but there was something about him that terrified Adams.

"You're talking about the disk, right?" Adams blustered. "Well we know who's got it and we're tracking her down right now." Adams's voice was filled with a mixture of confidence and fear. Kidd shot Adams a look that made him sit back in his chair, almost as if he had been punched.

"The woman you are referring to is also in the hands of the police. Oh yes, and while we are on the subject, who ordered the death of the cop?" Mr Kidd asked with a sneering tone. The door opened, and Mr James from the warehouse exchange walked in. There was an expression of confusion on his face as he expected Adams to be alone. Adams scowled at Mr James, almost as if his Number Two had been keeping secrets from him.

"Do you know anything about a hit on a cop?" Adams yelled at Mr James.

Mr James smiled smugly. "Oh, yes, sir. He was the boyfriend of that Amber woman. I figured she may have said something to him about the disk."

Kidd nodded and smiled. The man's smug grin broadened as he felt he had got one over on his employer.

"Interesting idea," Kidd told him. "But wrong."

Mr James suddenly looked shocked at Kidd's revelation.

"You see, firstly, that was the wrong cop," Kidd explained patiently. "And secondly, Miss Taylor had nothing to do with the disk. You, my dear boy, have made a grave error. One that could cost us dearly."

Before he realised what was happening, Mr James was suddenly picked up by the two men and thrown out of the second-storey window. His body hit the ground just in front of an eighteen-wheeler that was coming around the corner. His screams lasted a second or so, quickly terminated when there was a screech of brakes.

"Sort out your mess, Mr Adams. Get the woman, get the disk and get rid of the *correct* cop." Kidd tossed a piece of paper onto the desk. Adams picked up the small scrap. Written on it was an address of a bar.

"How do you know he'll be there?" Adams asked, confused.

Kidd said nothing, just headed for the door with his men behind him. Adams blew out a lungful of air and sat back in his chair as if a great weight had been removed from his chest. He thought for a moment, then picked up his cell phone. He searched the contacts on the display and pressed the autodial and waited.

"It's me," he said when he got through. "We've got trouble. Get your ass back here. We have to talk." Adams threw down the phone and rocked in his chair while he combed his hair with his fingers out of sheer frustration.

High on a rooftop of one of the warehouses, Steel knelt in cover. Massive billboards that advertised the company covered the flat roof. It was the perfect nest for him to set up. There was a foot-wide gap between the roof ledge and the bottom of the billboard, where Steel had secured a folding parabolic microphone. 8k digital cameras were also located on the roof, capturing images from the office and the surrounding areas. A small laptop with an external hard drive had recorded everything: including the criminals' plans to get Tony.

Steel waited. The bottom of his long coat spread around him and covered the ground below him; his cowl pulled tight over his head. He was invisible, just the way he liked it.

Twenty minutes later, a car pulled up into the parking lot. Steel looked over at the car, but only made out the nose of the Camaro. Steel looked over at Adams's office through a pair of special binoculars which were also connected to the laptop. Everything he saw was being recorded. Suddenly the door swung open, and Adams stood up, blocking his view of the visitor.

"This cop will be at this address tonight. Make sure it looks like an accident," Adams told the man.

"Well, bars can be rough places, especially if you've had too much to drink," replied the visitor.

Both men laughed.

"Just get it done." Adams's tone turned serious. He knew this job couldn't be messed up, for if it was, he would be joining his bag man under a truck.

"Don't worry. He's as good as gone."

The sound of the door closing signalled the man's retreat. It also told Steel that he had to find Tony immediately and shadow him all night. He could have warned McCall, but if his plan was going to work, he needed to stay dead, just a little while longer.

The resourceful detective plugged in the cell phone to the laptop and closed its weatherproof case. Now he could watch the feed from his lair. It had already been risky, just getting down there once. Coming and going would only tip someone off.

Besides, he had eyes and ears on the compound.

Now, he was one step ahead.

Chapter 36

McCall sat at her desk and re-read the case file. To most, it would seem like a Lee Child or Micheal Connelly novel. Undercover agents, assassin taxi drivers. But it wasn't, and it was reality. A harsh reality. It was also one of the hardest cases they'd had. Not because of the complexity of it but because of what they had lost.

McCall thumbed her notes on the yellow legal pad. For every opening, they found they also encountered a brick wall. Their John Doe had wound up crispy in Central Park, Brooke Taylor was missing, and the taxi driver had ended up as fish food. Their only lead was Tara, and McCall wasn't taking any chances there.

She took out a copy of Amber's reference from her previous employer: top of her class at NYU and a master's in business administration. The write-up was everything an employer could want, which of course screamed a cover story to McCall. For her, there was a bit too much icing on the cake. Most of Amber's life was a fabrication, not so much a lie as a deception. But McCall had to wonder, how did Tony fit into that aspect of her life? Was their relationship also a fabrication?

She looked over at the empty desks where Tony and Tooms normally sat. They were still out trying to locate any eyewitness of the body dump. She knew it would be pointless, for the people were pros. They would have got rid of the body late at night in a darkened spot. CSU were doing their thing with current shifts and so on. This might give them a location of the dumpsite, but then it might just be another diversion to head them off down another road.

Sam lifted her cup to her lips and took a sip. The aroma of freshly brewed coffee carried into her nostrils. It was strong and pure. No milk and no sugar. After a while, she tossed the paperwork back on to her desk, then stretched off her annoyance. McCall looked up at the wall clock above the captain's office door. She had worked through lunch, and now her blood sugar was punishing her for it. She stood up and headed downstairs to the street.

The sun was bright, and the buildings blocked most of the breeze. She pulled her jacket on and headed for a hotdog vendor. She had never seen him before, but she was glad he was there. She stood in the queue of four people. A young couple were at the front. McCall noted their body language and figured it was their first date. Next was a short woman with a Chihuahua dog sticking out of a large handbag. Its large eyes glared up at McCall with cruel intent.

The next few people didn't take long as the dogs were already practically ready. The maintenance worker directly in front of her ordered a dog with all the trimmings. The smell of the food made her stomach growl with impatience.

"Just a dog with onions please," she ordered as she reached the front of the queue that had built up behind her. The vendor smiled and nodded.

"Coming right up," the man told her cheerfully. He was in his late fifties, with a large, stocky build. His black hair was neatly cut, and underneath his apron, he wore blue jeans and a chequered shirt. The front of the cart was colourful, and *Vince's Hotdogs* was written in gold lettering on a red background. Small US flags on wooden poles blew in the breeze on top of the food stall.

"There you go, Detective, it's on the house."

McCall smiled and headed for the precinct. Suddenly she stopped and turned back. How did the man know she was a detective? Her shield was in her pocket, and she doubted he had seen her come out of the building. Even so, that didn't mean anything. McCall looked over at the stall. The older man was gone, and a man in his mid-twenties was now serving.

She scanned the area, hoping for a glimpse of him, but he was gone. She looked down at the food in her hand. A sudden look of suspicion crossed her face. Who was he and why the act? McCall decided to toss away the hotdog in case it had been laced with something. As she headed for the wastebasket, she noticed one of the napkins had writing on it. She removed the napkin and noted a message that had been written in ballpoint pen: *We need to talk. Come to the zoo at 18.00, come alone.* Alarm bells sounded in her head. This could be – and most probably was – a trap. On the other hand, who wanted to talk to her? And about what?

The alarm bells remained, but her intrigue was greater. The best possibility was that he was a witness; the worst scenario was that he was the killer. Either way, she needed to know, but she wasn't going alone—she was curious but not stupid.

She shrugged and ate the hotdog before heading inside the precinct. She figured there was nothing wrong with the food. What would be the point of send a message in a hotdog if you're going to poison it? As she bit into the dog, she rolled her eyes with pleasure. There was nothing wrong with the hotdog; in fact, it was perfect.

McCall returned to her desk, feeling her light-headedness subside. The food had filled a small gap, but she still felt unhappy about something. She looked at the murder board with its lines and photographs, but one thing stuck out to her: Trent Shipping. There was something about that place that didn't sit right with her. Everything seemed to revolve around that place. If it had been a thriller on TV, the set-up would scream that its connection was too obvious. But this wasn't a television show, and so what if it seemed too obvious a link? It was a start.

She grabbed her badge and gun from the top drawer and threw on her jacket. It was around three o'clock. She had time. After leaving Tooms a quick note on his desk, asking him and Tony to meet her at the statue in front of Central Park at five, she headed for the elevator and moved out into the busy streets.

* * *

Becca sat at Amber's old computer, arranging the files for the meeting that was due to take place later that day. She felt uncomfortable with the task, as it was normally Amber who did it. But Amber was gone. All the information she required had been put into specific folders on the desktop, making her life a lot easier. Amber had been a thorough person, someone who liked to ensure that everything was user-friendly and easy to find. Just in case she wasn't there for some reason.

Becca printed off page after page. Graphs and charts, world plans with route markers and locations. Becca arranged the folders she was creating for the meeting so it would follow the protocol for a PowerPoint presentation. She opened file after file. Becca was amazed what Amber had set up. Everything the company shipped abroad through their office was catalogued, and charts had been made ready for just an event. As she searched, she came across a strange-looking file. Curiously she opened the file that had no name, only a question mark. At first, she thought it was a miscellaneous folder. A place Amber may have junked the unknown, or just the unimportant files.

The young woman's mouth fell open. The files were of imports to Eastern countries that had trade embargos or that were involved in civil wars. The logs said it was mostly machine parts and farming equipment involved, but her gut told her otherwise. The more she read, the more she was convinced that Amber had been using the company to smuggle weapons. Her heart sank at the thought. Her best friend and mentor was an arms dealer, and she had had no idea. A sudden thought made her feel ill. She had unknowingly become part of it, whatever 'it' was.

Becca made a copy of the file because she knew she had to show this to Adams. Had she just discovered the reason why Amber had been killed? She looked at the telephone on the desk. Her thoughts were all over the place. She needed to talk to someone, she needed to share this horrible secret, but she didn't know who she could trust.

She caught sight of a small business card next to the phone under a piece of clear plastic sheeting. Even though it was with many others, this one stood out because of the police badge. She remembered the handsome cop who had given her the card. She took the card from under the sheet and picked up the handset and dialled the number. The sound of ringing seemed to go on forever until it went to voice mail.

"Hi, Detective," she dictated to the answering machine. "This is Becca from the Trent Shipping Company. Look I've found something disturbing, could you please come down here or we could meet somewhere? I think I may have found out why Amber was killed."

She held onto the receiver for a moment, her eyes still glued to the computer screen. She felt alone. The meeting would be on in thirty minutes, and she had to get the room ready. Becca put down the receiver and stood up, grabbing the files and heading for the door.

As she left the room, the door swung shut on its automatic closer. The computer screen still showed the open file. Suddenly the taskbar came on and showed the files that were being downloaded. The screen flashed and then showed the message: *Files deleted.*

Becca headed for the second floor. The conference room was down a long corridor on the left with a fantastic view of the car park. As she approached, she saw Adams enter with someone she couldn't make out. She took a deep breath and headed for the entrance with a sense of purpose. Becca stood in front of the door and raised a clenched fist, ready to knock. Her hand froze just inches from the timber as she heard Adams's raised voice.

"I told you to clean this mess up!" he ranted at somebody. "Find that disk and take care of the woman!"

Becca's heart stopped. Had she been so wrong about everything? She felt as if she was frozen to the spot, her legs grounded and unable to function. A tear of terror rolled down her cheek as she saw the doorknob begin to turn. Adams would see her there. He would know she had heard everything. She looked down at the stack of files, on top of which was the report she had found. If she was discovered with that, she was as good as dead.

The latch clicked, and the door began to open. She began to shake as the adrenaline began to surge through her veins. The last breath she took, she was holding onto, almost afraid to let it go in case he heard her. Her top half was as good as down the corridor and already in the car park, but her legs held fast onto the same spot. Sweat from her brow was cascading down her forehead. Her eyes stared at the door with utter fear.

Suddenly from within the room, a desk phone rang. The door closed, and the next sound was that of Adams asking: "What?"

Becca almost stumbled as she was released from her anchor. She had control over her legs once more, and she used them. As fast as she could, she hurried to the lobby and the car park. She needed to distance herself from this place and from him. She needed the cop; the handsome one they had called Steel.

The terrified woman stared at the sea of vehicles, but only saw hers: a small red Datsun that was parked next to one of the several large lamps designed to help drivers find their cars in winter months. She strode along at a fast walking pace, the paperwork clutched to her chest. She was running on autopilot, not hearing or seeing anything but her car.

When she reached her vehicle and tried the door handle, she remembered that the car was locked, and the keys were in her handbag, which was upstairs in her office. Becca fell to her knees and screamed to herself, shocked she had made it this far, only to fail now. Then she heard a voice calling her. It was Brad, the security officer, a stocky man with a doughnut belly and beady eyes behind round glasses. He was in his late fifties with more hair on his body than on his head. He was Adams's 'suck up', guy.

"Becca," he told her, "Mr Adams is looking for you. He wants to see you right away."

Becca stared up at the man who just stood there with his hands on his hips, trying to look important. It was as if he didn't care why she was on the ground: his lack of interest in others was a trait he was renowned for.

She stood up and wiped her eyes. She knew she was done for. The way back would seem long, but it would also be the last journey, she knew that.

"Do you know what he wants?" she asked, almost as if her breakdown had never happened.

He just shrugged and pointed towards the main entrance. He was a man of few words and a lack of personal hygiene. As they neared the building, there was a roar of a Ford Mustang and a screech of tyres as McCall brought her car to a quick stop. Becca turned quickly and recognised Detective McCall. Suddenly Becca ran for the Mustang's passenger side door, to the guard's amazement. Brad rushed around to Becca as fast as his legs would take him.

"Drive, Detective! Please, just drive!" the scarred woman yelled.

In a flash, McCall picked up on the mixture of fear and relief in Becca's eyes as the guard tried to open the passenger door that Becca had just slammed shut in his face.

The Mustang's engine roared again, the tyres spitting gravel as they zoomed out of the car park.

Brad looked up at the second-floor window to see Adams looking down at him. The guard swallowed hard and looked away as he re-entered the building.

* * *

McCall had put Becca into the safe house suite. She could see that the Trent Shipping employee was terrified about something, and the way she was grasping the documents, meant that they were part of her problem.

Detective McCall took Becca to the empty bedroom in the suite, where she curled up and fell asleep. The confrontation with her employers had been too much for her system and had worn her out. McCall would leave it for now. Tomorrow she would press Becca for the answers. Tomorrow, she would find out what was so damned important about the paperwork she had fallen asleep holding. But right now, she had a meeting to get to.

* * *

The sky had turned a deep purple as the sun began to creep into the horizon. The traffic was heavy as people travelled home after a hard day. The zoo had been closed since half-past four, but the park itself would be open until one in the morning. Sam McCall stood at the large, bronze statue of General William Tecumseh Sherman. She looked up at the glinting metal representation of the Civil War hero and smiled. It was more than a statue that she loved: it was a reminder of courage in the face of adversity.

Tooms and Tony had already signalled that they were set up and out of sight. They never made contact directly just in case they could be seen and communicated with her via quick text messages.

The entrance to the park was full of people, and the traffic on Fifth Avenue was stacking up, almost to a standstill. The whole place was a tactical nightmare. If someone wanted to take her out, this would be the time. Car horns blared wildly, and engines revved impatiently. McCall headed down the path towards the zoo, passing several nannies pushing expensive prams, as well as people who were out for an evening stroll.

The entrance was in sight. Green gates barred the way, and billboards in wooden frames showed timings and prices. Many people were passing, but no one was loitering. A tall black guy with a string shirt and baggy jeans was trying to sell off his music CDs—ten dollars was the asking price. A professional-looking cover was on the insert, but that didn't make his music worth it, that's if there was anything on it in the first place. He approached McCall with a smile. A smile that faded as she moved her jacket to show the shield on her belt. He raised his hands in a comical surrender and backed off.

She didn't have time to harass him, not that she would have done anyway—after all, the guy was trying to make a living. McCall stood by the entrance and looked around. There was nothing that looked off. Mainly joggers and dog walkers. She looked at her watch. It was now ten past the hour.

"I would say he's a no-show," McCall said quietly into the hidden microphone.

"Oh, I wouldn't say that," said a voice behind her. She spun around quickly, one hand on the pistol grip of her custom Glock. Her eyes widened, and her mouth fell open.

"You!" she yelled.

"McCall, who is it?" screamed Tooms from his hidden position. "McCall! McCall." He moved quickly the moment after he had lost sight of her. Tooms and Tony came running, only to find a blank space where she had been standing, talking to the black guy who was selling CDs.

"Are you the cops?" asked the CD seller. Tooms scowled at him and showed his shield.

The man held his hand out. On his open palm, he held McCall's microphone and earbud.

"The guy said he wanted to chat to her alone," the black man said, shrugging. Tooms grabbed the gear and pulled the man in close, practically dragging him off his feet.

"What guy?"

* * *

Williams wore a black pinstriped suit with stay bright shoes, and a blue tie with tiny pocket watches embroidered into it. In his leather-gloved right hand, he held a silver-tipped cane, for no other reason than he could. McCall walked alongside him, still unnerved by his presence. She could have brought him in, but he knew she wouldn't do so. She was curious as what he wanted from her. McCall wanted answers, and confinement in a six-by-four would have made him as mute as a monk.

"My dear Samantha, you are looking positively radiant. Have you done something with your hair?" Williams had a skip in his voice and a grin on his face.

"What do you want?" McCall said, cutting to the chase.

Williams's grin broadened. "Ah, always straight to the point, no foreplay. Very well. I want you to catch whoever killed Miss Amber and our Mr Steel." McCall was slightly taken aback by his interest in the deaths of both Amber and Steel.

"Frankly, I thought you were the killer," McCall admitted. "If so, it would have made things easier, but then things are never that easy are they?"

Williams shook his head. The smile had gone. "No, I am afraid that was someone else's doing. Steel was a great adversary to the point of him being a friend. Amber was ... let's just say she was an old acquaintance. Someone whose company I will miss and whom I wish I had known sooner."

McCall shot him a curious look. Had Williams had a crush on Amber, she wondered? Already the conversation was beginning to make her head hurt.

"It's funny," the psychopath went on, "the night Steel met his fate we had a chat. I had warned him to take care. And I'm giving you and your team the same warning. You see, there is an organisation who would like nothing better than to see the world burn. It is them I ask you to be wary of."

Williams stopped talking for a moment and looked across the green of the park's open space. An ocean of grass with large oaks was spread out, bordering the concrete pathways. The fingers of his left hand fondled something in his waistcoat. She knew it was his pocket watch. Something she had longed to forget.

"Detective, you need to watch yourself on this one," he continued. "Miss Taylor was an undercover agent at the shipping company, that I know you are aware of. We—or rather I—believe she found something out, and for that, they killed her. The organisation wants nothing more than to keep their plans secret. Something is about to happen and what she found out confirmed this." Williams pulled his fingers from his pocket and smiled at McCall.

"I know this is a strange situation, Detective, and I know you don't trust me," Williams told her. "And I know you want nothing more than to arrest me or shoot me. But I also know that your instinct is telling you that I am right."

McCall scowled at him. He was right on all accounts, most of all the 'wanting to shoot him' part. However, everything he had said made sense. She looked into his eyes and saw a kind of almost sadness. Somehow Steel's death had affected him as well. If that were true, she pitied the person who had killed him.

"After Mr Steel left the other night, he found himself in a cab," Williams revealed as they set off walking again. "I found this curious, as a limo had been arranged to bring him home."

"Yes, we found the cab driver. Someone had taken him for a swim."

"So, I heard. I also heard that you found a woman." Williams's tone growled at the mention of her.

McCall suddenly became uneasy. "It was just someone of interest in Amber's murder, a witness," she said as if to dismiss her importance.

Williams stopped abruptly and grasped both McCall's arms in a vice-like grip at the wrists. His eyes were burning with redness. "Detective, that woman has something I want. If I have it, I can end this business before it starts."

McCall stared into those menacing blue eyes and froze. In her mind, she was back to that terrifying day, the first day they had met.

Williams released her and stepped back, his arms out to his sides, and his head bowed in an almost regretful gesture. "Forgive me, Samantha, I am sorry for the outburst." His voice was calm and apologetic. "There is a war coming, and your city is caught in the middle of it. You need to choose aside. Is it not better to do battle with one enemy and ally with the other? Is the enemy of my enemy, my friend – or my enemy?"

She thought for a moment. What he was proposing was unthinkable, but also frighteningly logical. If there was a war, the police couldn't possibly fight both organisations. For a start, they didn't even know who both were. Suddenly from behind her, she heard Tooms yell out her name. She turned and yelled back: "Over here!"

When she turned to face Williams, she found he had gone. She looked around at the expanse of the park and couldn't see him anywhere. Tooms and Tony caught up with her and looked around, confused and wondering what she was searching for.

"Where the hell did, he go?" McCall asked.

"Where the hell did *who* go?" Tooms replied, confused.

"Williams," she told him, leaving the two men with blank expressions.

Chapter 37

The night sky was made darker by the blanket of cloud cover. The chill breeze had turned into a biting wind. Tony had been in the Irish bar on East 4th Street since nine o'clock. He had been in there every night since Amber's death. He had gotten a favourite spot – a quiet table in a corner where he could sit, virtually undisturbed.

It was an old place with bare brick walls, oak fittings and fixtures, as well as dim lights and the smell of Guinness and stale beer. The tavern had been around since the late '90s and Tony had spent most of his youth in there. It was his second favourite place in the world, of which he'd seen plenty since he'd been in the army – the first being his childhood home, which his parents still owned. By half-past ten the tavern's capacity had swelled, and this for him was a cue to leave. Sure, he wanted to drown his sorrows, but then again, he didn't want to risk losing his badge. It was all he had. The fresh air was sobering as the wind hit his bare skin like a thousand needles.

He headed towards Lafayette Street and past the strange multi-storey car park. It was a towering structure that placed vehicles into mechanical booths that held each one and stacked them upon one another securely. A man sat in a pay booth, which was a grey metal box at the entrance to the small lot. The attendant was a young guy who was busy watching a film on his laptop while he waited for someone to pick up or drop off. The lot itself was dimly lit, but the illumination was enough for the man to see the vehicles.

Tony pulled his coat tightly around him as he turned the corner. He headed towards the parking lot. The alcohol had thinned his blood and made him feel woozy. Probably too woozy. As he walked, he found himself beginning to sway, and his vision became blurred. He didn't remember having anything more than his usual three double shots and a coffee. As he neared the lot, he looked at the reflection of a passing car.

The four men behind him had been standing at the bar near the door. Now they were behind him. It could have been a coincidence, but he didn't believe in those. He began to open his pace. The footsteps behind him hammered on the concrete, meaning they were matching his sudden burst of speed. In a sudden quick movement, he headed into the lot, hoping the man in the booth would see him, but he was engrossed in a film on his laptop.

Tony stood his ground but was unaware of the two men who had come up behind him. It was now six against one, and the one was in no condition to punch a feather, let alone six men. Suddenly the lights of the lot flickered. The six men looked around to see what the problem was but detected nothing but shadows. The man in the booth looked up from his laptop in time to see a darkened figure move from man to man, knocking each of them down and then disappearing into the blackness. The men screamed as they were being dragged into the dark. In the end, only one man stood alone – Tony Marinelli – that was until he fainted.

The lights went out for a few seconds. As they came back on, the drunken man was gone, and six bound men remained. The attendant looked back at the superhero movie he'd been watching to see the same type of scene in the film. His eyes rolled, and he fainted in his chair.

* * *

The next morning Tony woke up with a massive headache as if hammers were banging at his brain. It took a moment until he realised that the banging was coming from his front door. He got up slowly and headed there as quickly as his body would allow. His mouth was as dry as a dessert, but his eyesight had improved. He opened the door, and Tooms stamped into the hallway wearing an angry look.

"Tony! Man, you look like shit!" he told him.

"And good morning to you too, Joshua," Tony said, turning and heading for the kitchen.

"Is this a problem I should know about?" Tooms asked, picking up Tony's newspaper from the mat in the hallway.

"I didn't get drunk if that's what you mean."

"Really? So, you had a bad pizza then?" Tooms said, taking a seat at the breakfast bar.

"I think I was drugged last night."

"Drugged? What the hell for?" Tooms asked, looking suspiciously towards Tony's ass.

"No, I wasn't raped, asshole. But six guys tried to take me out last night."

Tooms raised an eyebrow at Tony's revelation. "Did it happen in a parking lot on Lafayette by any chance?" Now it was Tony's turn to raise an eyebrow, before downing a bottle of water.

"Come on, Rambo, we got a crime scene to check out," Tooms said, standing up. Tony looked closely at his watch and groaned.

"Tooms, it's five in the morning!" Tooms just shrugged and smiled.

"Yup. It's breakfast time. You can buy me a coffee on the way."

Tony wore his sunglasses on the way to the crime scene, even though the weather was overcast, and it looked like rain. For him, everything was as bright as a summer's day. He was on his second cup of coffee and his second bottle of water. Tooms was on his third bear claw. Tony's apartment was on Broadway, so he had to take Spring Street and go up on Lafayette. The traffic was already getting heavy, despite the early hour. They found an open spot to park and decided to walk to the parking lot. Tooms thought the cold air would mask Tony's already pale complexion. Yellow crime scene tape and plastic barriers held the public back. Tooms shook his head at the thirty or so people who had congregated around with cell phones held high, taking photographs. One of the uniforms recognised Tooms and Tony and let them through. The lot was almost empty apart from the CSU techs, the ME and a couple of detectives. The parking lot attendant was busy giving his statement and didn't notice Tony's approach. The lead detective was a man called Sam Cryer, a good detective from the 8th Precinct. He was a huge man in his mid-fifties with broad shoulders, a huge barrel chest, grey quiffed hair and a moustache to be proud of. The man looked like one of those small-town sheriff types, from somewhere in Texas in the 1900s. Tooms went up to the man, and they embraced like the old friends that they were.

"Tony, I'd like you to meet my old training officer, Sam Cryer. Sam, this is my partner, Tony Marinelli." Tooms spoke proudly. The two detectives shook hands. Tony had trouble keeping hold of Sam's giant hand in a grip, so he just let the other man do all the work.

"What brings you down here, boot?" Sam said, laughing. "Are things so slow uptown you gotta come down here?" Tony looked over at the ME, who was kneeling beside six covered bodies. Lakes of deep red covered the concrete but were largely restricted to around the upper part of the covered bodies. Tony had figured that they had all taken shots to the head.

"So, what you got, Sam?" Tooms asked, trying not to reveal all his cards just yet.

"Someone decided to tie these guys up and then give 'em an extra eye socket," Sam said, pointing to his own forehead. "Bit of an odd place to do it, but I guess someone was trying to make a point." Tooms looked over to the attendant, who was sitting sideways on to them. The man looked shaken and drained from the night's activities. He was wrapped in an emergency blanket and nursing a cup of something that Tooms could only presume was coffee. A female uniformed cop was taking his statement. She was a cute black woman with high cheekbones and large glistening eyes. Short compared to Tony, minute compared to Tooms. She had two bars on her sleeves – obviously a veteran to the streets.

"Did he see much?" Tooms asked, fishing for information. Sam smiled at his old rookie's attempt to get information.

"Yeah, a ghost. Could have been a big bat, might possibly even have been Dracula."

"What?" Tooms asked in an insulted tone. Sam nodded towards the attendant.

"The guy was watching some superhero flick when some drunk guy walks in, followed by six other guys. The lights flicker, and before he knows it, the guys are gettin dragged away into the night. Of course, he faints and wakes up early this morning to find six fresh ones in his lot." Sam made circles with his index finger at the side of his head.

"If you ask me, he saw the whole thing, and he doesn't want to join them," Sam added, chewing on his cigar.

"Well you may have another witness," Tony said, his gaze not leaving the covered bodies. Sam stepped back slightly, surprised at the news. He looked around, briefly hoping to see someone lurking, waiting to make an appearance.

"OK, where are they? In your car?" Sam asked, looking towards their vehicle. Tony shook his head and opened his mouth to speak. He had no idea how to even start with an opening. Not only was he a witness, but he was also going to be a suspect.

"That's the guy!" the attendant yelled suddenly, pointing at Tony. "That's the drunk from last night!"

Sam stood open-mouthed at the news. "So, do you want to explain what the hell you were doing last night?" he asked suspiciously.

"Don't worry, Sam, he couldn't have done this," Tooms said confidently. Sam scowled at his old partner.

"Whoever did this was highly trained and nimble," Joshua Tooms added.

"Yeah, so? Isn't he highly trained and nimble?" Sam growled out his words. Tooms shook his head.

"Trained yes, but nimble? No. He said he was drugged last night, probably to make him an easier target. Besides, I've seen him fight, and I tell you a handcuffed guy of ninety could take him out."

Sam laughed, partly at Tooms's theory, but more so about Tony's inability to fight. Sam looked Tony up and down and nodded.

"Yep, guess you're right, but we're still gonna need a statement," Sam said before spitting the loose bits of cigar that had collected in his mouth. Tony nodded, struggling to remember as much as he could.

"Well, there's not much to tell. I had a couple of drinks at the Irish bar around the corner until it started to get full, then I left. As I got outside, I started to feel off, like I'd had too much. That's when I realised something was wrong. As I headed home, I noticed the four guys who were standing at the bar, but who were now on my tail."

Tony watched as Sam made some notes in his brown-backed notebook.

"So why come here?" Sam asked curiously.

"I knew there was a watchman at night. I figured he would help or call the cops. Boy, was I wrong?" Tony nodded towards the shivering kid who was beside the medics.

"So, you took them down yourself instead?" Sam asked, almost hoping to trick Tony into a confession.

"In truth, I only saw the four guys, and I never saw the two behind me. I stood my ground, hoping to intimidate them."

"I guess that didn't work out for you either?" Sam joked. Tony didn't smile. His gaze fell back to the six men who were now being placed into the coroner's body bags.

"The last thing I remember is the lights going out," Tony admitted.

"That's when you fainted, you mean?" Sam nodded and made a notation.

"No. That's when the lights went out. They flickered and then went out. I'll never forget the screams those men made as they were being dragged off." Tony spoke with venom in his voice. He could tell this friend of Tooms's had already made his mind up about what had happened, and it didn't involve some ghostly phantom.

"I woke up this morning at my apartment," the unfortunate detective went on. "I have no idea how I got there or what happened to the men. For all, I know the attendant could have done it." They all looked at the cowering man and, almost as one, shook their heads and said, "Nah!"

Sam thanked them and gave Tony his card, just in case something came back to him. Tony and Tooms took off back to the precinct. They had a case of their own to solve, and this one was all down to the 8th and Sam Cryer to sort out. Tony didn't doubt that they would be stopping for coffee. Tooms's stomach had already growled twice, so it had to be close to breakfast time. Tony took one more look at the lot's entrance, hoping for some inspiration. But he could remember nothing more. Only those screams of the men as they were dragged away.

"What are you thinking about, partner?" Tooms asked, popping a stick of chewing gum into his mouth.

"I'm thinking we need to see that roof. I think that our taxi-driver-grabber is back."

* * *

Steel sat at his computer with a large glass of something green. It was blended vegetables and fruit with three raw eggs added for good measure. He was checking out the feed from the monitoring devices pointing at the shipping company's main building. All the phones had been tapped, and Adams's computer hacked and cloned. If Adams got an email, so too would Steel. The whole of Steel's lair had been rigged for security just in case of unwelcome guests. Outside cameras had been set up with motion sensors and lasers. Williams had warned him to watch his back, and he had been right to do so. The other organisation – SANTINI's rival, had tried to get rid of him. Tried and failed, but so far, they didn't know that. Steel still wondered why Williams was helping him. He reasoned that maybe the psychopath thought it was a good way of getting rid of the competition without being involved. If it all went wrong, Williams's organisation would be blameless. But there was something else. The way Williams had spoken to him was almost full of admiration, no, he had talked to him as if Steel was a friend. Steel couldn't rule this out; after all, they had many encounters together. Maybe a strange relationship was forming. A kind of Holmes and Moriarty complex.

John Steel turned in his chair and faced another screen. It was a computer monitor, on which was Amber's records. He was unable to ask for them officially, so he had hacked the system instead. She was born in Virginia in 1982. An only child who had never known her father, raised by her mother until 1998, when her mother had died of cancer.

Tara Burke's life was not much different, apart from the abuse. Tara's mother was an alcoholic with a hatred for the world – and Tara. According to her file, Tara was 'accident-prone'. Back then, child abuse within the family had been a taboo subject, something to ignored rather than dealt with as it is today. Tara had slipped through the cracks in the system. However, Tara was a survivor. Now, she had her place and a job, which made her a winner. More than her mother ever had. Steel noticed that McCall had put her in John Doe's old room. It made sense; the place was paid for, so why not? Steel took a mouthful of the putrid looking cocktail as he opened a file on Trent Shipping. It had photographs from newspapers as well as copies of personnel files. One photograph was of a fundraiser for a children's home. Six men stood together, proud smiles on their faces, while in the background were several of the staff who had helped to make it possible, including Amber. Steel had seen several of the people when he had set up the surveillance gear, but two he had not. All of them were business types with nothing on their minds but money. Nothing in the files told him anything much, but he was hoping the file he had taken from Becca's computer would do so. He had deleted it for her safety. If Adams found out she had it, or indeed had even seen it, she was as good as dead.

Steel started to close the picture when something in Tara's open file caught his eye: a photograph of a Christmas at the diner. Quickly he picked up the ten-by-eight and held it next to the monitor. He leaned in closer to make sure, and his mouth fell open.

"Well, I didn't see that coming," Steel gasped, then gave a smile.

Chapter 38

McCall got off the elevator on the floor that had been specially secured. Two cops stood at the elevator and another two near the suite's door. Captain Brant had boosted the security due to what had happened to the second witness. The sound of McCall's footsteps echoed down the hallway due to the ferocity of her pace. She was mad, and it was written all over her face. So much so that the plainclothes cops never stopped her. She held her shield up for all to see, and her eyes fixed on that door to the suite. The door swung open just as Tara was coming from the shower with nothing but a towel around her middle and another round her head. There was a large selection of breakfast dishes laid out on a glass dining table.

"You could knock?" Tara said sharply, shocked at Sam's sudden entrance.

"I could also throw your ass in jail and let some tattooed thing make you her bitch," McCall snarled as she slammed the door behind her. "So, save it."

The angry detective walked over to the breakfast table and lifted the silver domed lid on one of the plates: eggs Benedict sat there, steaming with freshness. The other plate contained a 'full English' breakfast.

"Glad you're enjoying your stay," Sam McCall told her sarcastically.

"Is something wrong, Detective? Maybe you could use some breakfast? After all, the department is picking up the tab." Tara smiled smugly.

McCall rushed across and grabbed her by the arm and thrust her into a nearby chair. "The tab for this was paid for by a cop who died trying to find you, so think about that while you're ordering your next meal!"

Tara sat back into the chair as if she was trying to hide within its cushioned back.

"Sorry ... I ... I didn't know." Tara was trying to sound sincere but failing. McCall had the urge to toss her and the breakfast out of the window, but she wouldn't feel any better for doing it—after all, it would have been a waste of good food. Besides, McCall believed that Tara had no feelings because she'd always been hard. Her mother probably taught her that feelings get in the way.

"So, are you going to tell me what is really going on?" McCall said, her tone had calmed as she moved the plate with the bacon towards her.

"I told you everything, I swear," Tara said.

"Why don't I believe you? Why is it I'm getting the feeling that you're missing something out?"

Tara shrugged and shook her head, a look of confusion and innocence on her face, but McCall knew she had practised that one, possibly since birth. McCall reached into her jacket pocket and pulled out her cell phone. She checked the display and then her messages.

"I've got to go, but we'll continue this discussion later." McCall had a worried expression on her face as she slid the phone back into her jacket pocket. She turned and headed for the door. McCall didn't turn back as she left; she just let the door click shut behind her. Tara moved quickly to the dining table and picked up her cell phone. After looking around, she typed a text message, then hurried into her bedroom.

Meanwhile, McCall entered the room next door where the surveillance team were sitting. The large monitors showed the suite, each of the rooms, the hallway, stairwells, and elevator. McCall stood behind the two operators and leant forward.

"So, what was it, a call or a text?" She smiled wickedly.

"A text, then she went to her room," said one of the men.

"How long before we get the text?" McCall asked, feeling smug.

"A long time. We don't have it cloned. It's not her phone," the technical man answered.

McCall stood up and gave the man a puzzled look. "So, who the hell's phone is it? And how did we miss it?" McCall growled, looking back at the monitors. Then she saw Becca lying peacefully as she slept. "Tell me you cloned Becca's phone when she arrived?"

The two men looked at each other and simultaneously shook their heads.

* * *

Across the street, the hooded figure of John Steel crouched on a rooftop like some strange gargoyle. The leather arms of his long trench coat glistened in the morning sun. The lower half was splayed out, almost blending into the treated roofing. His rangefinder binoculars peered through the un-curtained windows, taking in the view of Tara. A beeping sound from his cell phone made him look down at the screen.

Suddenly a message came up, saying: *I have what you want. Fifty Million. Shipping yard, one hour.* Steel nodded to himself, filling in the blanks. The number she had sent the message to, it had belonged to the Trent Shipping Company. He knew something had bothered him about Tara. It still did, but he didn't know what it was. Something he had found on the computer didn't help his gut feeling. Slowly he sneaked off down from the rooftop and slipped away to the street. He couldn't risk telling McCall anything, not yet. This one was going to be messy, so much so he wanted his colleagues far away from the whole business until the end. He wanted to get more intel before calling in the cavalry. McCall had good instincts, but this was bigger than she could possibly have realised.

The same thing applied to Tara. The young woman thought she held all the cards because she had something they wanted. What she didn't realise was that she was up against an entire organisation, not just one person.

She wasn't in control; they were.

And there was no way that they were going to pay.

* * *

McCall made it back to the precinct. The techs said they would get back to her as soon as they had anything on the text message. She found Tony and Tooms in the break room making coffee. Tooms was finishing off a hotdog. He screwed up the wrapper and just missed her with his long shot. The ball of paper went into the waste bin effortlessly, to his delight. Tony raised a cup at McCall, and she nodded. She still wore the pissed-off look she had brought back from the safe house.

"So, how's our runaway doing?" Tooms asked. Her look said it all, but she answered anyway.

"She's living it up at someone else's expense. She sent a text to someone, and the techs are trying to track it down. The clever bitch used Becca's phone." She took the cup from Tony and sat at the table. "She knows more than she is saying, that's for sure." Tooms nodded in agreement. He had had a bad feeling about her since the first time he had seen her. "Tara is up to something. I can feel it." Tony passed Tooms his coffee and then joined them at the small table.

"How's Becca coping?" Tony asked as he dropped two lumps of sugar into his coffee.

"She was sleeping," Sam replied. "I didn't have the heart to wake her, not yet anyway."

Tony kept looking over towards Brant's office. He was waiting to brief him on the things that had happened last night and this morning before One Police Plaza could. Tony had already spoken with Brant briefly, so he had a heads up. But Brant didn't have the full facts because Tony himself didn't have them either. McCall could sense that Tony was uneasy but didn't push him for details on the incident, though she planned to do so later.

McCall got up and moved back to her desk. Her thoughts were of Becca and the way she had run away, terrified and jumped into McCall's car. Becca hadn't said anything, just looked petrified all the way to the hotel. She was still clutching the bunch of company documents when she fell onto the bed in her new room.

Sam decided to wait until the surveillance team told her that Becca was up and awake before talking to her. In the meantime, she had other work to do. Coreman was busy downtown. They were out of Steel's special coffee, so he was given the task of getting some more. She thought it was a bit much to make him run errands like that, but then he was a rookie detective after all, hell, when she got her shield she had to put up with all sorts of crap.

McCall had hoped to ask Adams some questions, but Becca had ruined that plan. If she went back to the shipping company now, she'd be questioned herself for abducting one of his employees, and she had no time for that. As far as she could tell all roads led to that shipping company. Either they were very bad at covering their tracks, or someone wanted the police to look at them closely.

Samantha McCall looked up from her desk as she watched Brant head to his office. Tooms and Tony were waiting outside, like school kids waiting for the principal. She leant back in her chair and watched with strange curiosity as they went in and partially opened the door. Through the window, she saw the two detectives waving their arms around in explanation. Brant seemed calm. He merely sat in his chair and listened, but McCall knew him to be the man who often listened quietly first to what you had to say, and *then* tore your head off.

Brant picked up the receiver of his desk phone and dialled a number, while the two detectives took a seat on the couch in his office. Brant put down the receiver and waved them out. His face was full of anger, but Sam knew that their boss wasn't mad at the two detectives.

"What's up, guys?" she asked as the door opened fully and they came out. "You didn't crash the car again – did you?"

"Nothin' much," Tooms told her. "Tony just had some trouble last night … Wait… What do you mean, crash the car again?" McCall smiled at Tooms's shocked expression.

"Trouble," she asked them. "What trouble?"

"Some guys tried to jump me last night that's all," Tony said, trying to make out it was nothing.

"Two on one, not very sporting. I hoped you kicked their asses," she said proudly. Tony just shot her an awkward look and walked towards his desk.

"Don't worry about it, and he just gets easily embarrassed," Tooms joked and followed his partner. Tooms felt bad about not saying anything to McCall in explanation, but Tony had asked him not to. At least, not yet.

McCall looked back at the notes on her desk. She was still waiting for Tina's report on all the bodies. The crash had caused a massive backlog, which had put everything on hold. They had even got extra help from the FBI labs to try and sort through the evidence for the hundreds of cases that were still waiting.

Sam looked at the empty chair next to her desk and suddenly felt utterly alone. She missed Steel sitting there and rattling off his strange theories. Smiling, she looked back at her notes. After the meeting with Williams, things were starting to seem more complicated than she had at first thought. This wasn't a random killing of an undercover agent. This was something much more.

She checked her messages on her phone. Tina had left a text, saying: *I need you here ASAP*. McCall stood up quickly and slipped her jacket on. Tony and Tooms looked up at her as she headed out.

"Tina has got something, I'll be at the morgue," she yelled back without turning around. She had a bounce in her step. She figured that Tina might have found something that could break the case. She might even have found something that could lead to Steel's killer as well.

* * *

Steel walked through the streets as though nothing was amiss. His long black coat was carried by the wind, causing it to flap like a ship's colours. Even though the hood of his coat was covering most of his face, he blended in with the crowd, almost as if he wasn't even there. Tara's text bothered him. Even he knew it would take longer than an hour to get that much money together. That was unless she knew that Adams had that sort of cash available. A meeting at the company was the worst idea in the world: one woman alone on their home turf. He knew they would have her in seconds. Snatched and never heard of again.

He knew the place, but he didn't know all the players, including the organisation's hitman, the man who had killed so many people to cover their tracks. Whatever information it was that she had, it was big. Fifty million was a big chunk of change. Steel was heading back to his lair. He had blueprints to look at. If he was going in, he had to have a plan. There was too much cover, too many places to put snipers. With a compound that size, they didn't even have to be good shots to kill efficiently.

All he had to do was identify the right spots and take out the men before the confrontation even started. These were amateurs, merely workers with guns. However, he couldn't afford to take any chances. Even the worst shot in the world just needed that one lucky hit. He had to be ready.

Steel threw off his coat to the side. It landed onto the office chair, causing it to turn slightly. He touched the huge touch screen monitor, which came to life in the blink of an eye. He touched an icon that had *Plans* written underneath it. The screen changed into a blueprint-type sketch of the compound. Around the side were several areal photos. Each photograph was alined with specific areas on the blueprint.

In the centre was the main building with the parking lot to the front. To the left and right was a row of five large warehouses, each standing lengthways. To the back were the heavy cranes and the loading area. Huge metal ISO containers stood ready for packing or unpacking, behind this was a rail track next to a loading station. Steel took note of several buildings that would be handy for getting bird's-eye views. The main building itself looked as if it could be a fortress. Once lockdown was initiated, not much would be able to get through. He would have to move quickly, which meant travelling light.

Anyone could go there with guns strapped to every part of their body, but that meant carrying a lot of weight and webbing gear makes a lot of noise. A simple two-weapon choice with plenty of ammo was always a good plan. Steel looked over the plan again. He would need 'eyes on' first. The thermal vision would be good to pick out the hidden few. Steel walked over to a gun rack and picked up a custom-built Desert Tactical Arms SRS sniper rifle. The .338 Lapua Magnum's magazine was a rear fit, which meant there was a place for a swivel foregrip. The barrel was just one long silencer. The Bullpup weapon was compact and easy to move with. It was also an upgrade from the original version which was bolt action; this new type was semi-automatic with a ten-round magazine. Steel smiled and tucked it into a kitbag, along with a silenced Heckler and Koch VP9 pistol and several magazines for each weapon.

He was hoping his surveillance gear would go unnoticed on the roof of the opposite building. The build boards next to the nest hadn't changed in years, so the chance of that happening now were slim. However, it was a good vantage point for a rifleman. Steel had camouflaged the equipment well just on the off chance, but he had to assume the equipment could be compromised at any time. "Always have a plan B, sometimes a plan Z could be an option," Steel's old Army instructor used to say. "Never assume, always secure." Words to live by, and Steel had. As well as the nest by the build boards, Steel had set up a secondary nest with equipment. Plan Z.

Since McCall had picked up Becca, Steel had to imagine Adams was desperate and would cover all his bases. Steel walked over to a rack of clothing equipment and picked out some more appropriate clothing to wear. Something more tactical and bulletproof. He picked out a tight-fitting bodysuit that had magazine pouches enlaced into the thigh parts of the legs and a belt unit that looked like a bat belt because of the pouches. Steel grabbed a small rucksack – ammo bag for the .338. He had to be ready for anything.

He just hoped that they weren't.

Chapter 39

Tara paced up and down in her room, unaware of the surveillance team who were watching her. She had to think of a way to get out. She looked at her watch. Twelve minutes had gone since her call. She picked up her rucksack and grabbed a chair. Standing on the chair, she pulled out a small disposable lighter and held it under the fire alarm. She winced in pain as the thing began to get almost too hot to hold. There was the loud shriek of a fire alarm. She smiled and tossed the red-hot lighter onto the floor, just as the door suddenly burst open.

The security detail gathered the two women and hurried them out towards the back stairs, knowing full well that the elevators would be shut off automatically. As they hit the lobby, there was a mass of hysterical people pushing and shoving to get out. Rational people suddenly turned to self-preserving animals rushing to leave the building. Security staff were standing at the door working hard to calm and marshalled the people out in a single file, through the entrances.

Tara saw her chance to escape as a large surge of women collided with the detail. As the detail made it outside to safety, the men looked around hurriedly.

Tara was gone.

Upstairs in the surveillance room, one of the men made a call to McCall.

"Detective?" he told her. "Yes, you were right. She's made a break for it."

* * *

Williams stood outside Brooke's room. He knocked and waited for an answer. Even though she was officially a prisoner, he somehow made her feel like she was a guest.

She answered with a, "Come in", and waited to see who would enter. Brooke smiled as he entered and gave a small bow with his head.

"I hope you'll forgive this intrusion," he said softly. He stepped aside to allow two women to enter. One carried a dress of red lace and silk, with high-heeled shoes to match. The other had a make-up bag and hair styling equipment.

"I believe you like opera?" His words had a mix of pleasure and anticipation of the answer.

"Yes…yes, I do." Brooke looked around at the women as they made themselves busy arranging the equipment, ready to get to work.

"I have a small engagement, after which I am hoping you will join me at the National Opera House," Williams told her. Brooke was taken aback by the gesture. Confused, but flattered.

"Aren't you afraid I will try to escape?" she asked with a childish grin. Mr Williams just smiled and shrugged.

"I think I would be disappointed if you didn't at least try," he spoke softly. She thought for a moment, before giving a large grin and nodding.

"Then thank you. I would love to go."

"Good, it's settled then. I will leave you ladies in peace." Williams bowed again and left, locking the door behind him. Brooke smiled, calculating that it might be a way to break out. The National was a great place to draw attention. But she knew that he would find some way of keeping her quiet. Perhaps he'd use the threat of snipers, or the murder of her family. She knew he was anything but stupid, which made her wonder why he was doing all this. Was she a prisoner? Or just a heavily guarded guest?

Williams headed down the long corridor slowly, his hands tucked behind his back. He was strangely quiet, almost as if he had received grave news. Halfway down the long corridor, beside a photograph of a woman and a baby, he stopped and pulled out his cell phone and pressed the speed dial. His eyes locked onto the picture on the wall. It was at least twenty years old, if not more; the texture was old and grainy, no high-end high definition camera was used. The ten-by-eight lay in an ornate gold frame. It was next to several other pictures, these being of the same baby as a child and then as a young woman at school.

"It's arranged," he muttered into the phone. "Now it's time for your part."

Slowly, he tucked away his cell phone and carried on back down the unlit corridor, whose only illumination was the stream of light that flooded through the French windows. Williams went along like a man in his nineties, his movements weak and feeble as if he had to drag himself across the wooden flooring.

Soon he reached his office. He poured a large brandy then sat down hard in his office chair. Williams's eye transfixed into space, as though something had appeared in the empty corner of the room. His gaze went far beyond the confines of the room.

There was a knock on the door. Williams's silence caused the caller to knock again. Williams said and did nothing, merely stared into the golden liquid in the glass. The young friend of his secretary walked in with trepidation, the look of fear for entering without being summoned evident on his face.

"Did you find the taxi driver?" Williams asked, his gaze still fixed on the aged liquor.

"Uhm… yes sir," the nervous young man replied. "Unfortunately, it was while the police were pulling him out of the Hudson."

"I see. So that's a no then really… isn't it? You found a corpse that used to be him but was not really… him."

The man squirmed where he stood, almost terrified at giving the only answer he could.

Slowly, Williams turned to look over at the pale, shivering man. Williams's eyes held a callous, unnatural look. Angry, but at the same time touched with playful excitement, almost like a cat who was having a psychotic moment.

"I gave you a simple task. Not much to ask, I would have thought. I asked you to bring the taxi driver to me." Williams sighed, the brandy swirling in the glasses as he rotated the crystal with his hand as he sat back into his chair. He looked over to the roaring blaze in the fireplace. The flames leapt up from the crackling, over-seasoned wood.

"Find me the waitress, alive and unharmed. Can you do that?" Williams asked.

"Yes … Yes, sir, no problem." Instantly, the man cursed himself, as the promise slipped from his lips, realising that what he had just said had sealed his fate.

Williams peered around the side of the tall back of the chair, a broad grin on his face.

"Oh, I do hope so," Williams's voice tore through the man's soul, almost causing the man to piss himself where he stood.

Mr Williams sat back into his chair, the sound of his cackling laughter continuing even after the door had been closed. The man was sweating buckets as he left. He knew if he messed this one up there wouldn't be enough left of him to be found in the Hudson. The sound of his running filled the corridors as he sprinted.

He had to find that waitress.

* * *

Tara needed to get up to town and had less than an hour to do it. The Metro was the best way, but not the safest. Muggers were the least of her problems. Not that they had ever been a problem in the past. The people who had killed Amber were after her and most probably knew where she was. If she took the train, she would have to ride it until the end, allowing plenty of time for someone to do something. She would have to keep an eye on all the passengers, see who stayed and rode the train. See who was looking suspicious and who just stuck out as different from the norm.

The worried young woman hurried down to the subway station. She soon blended with a crowd that had gathered at the turnstiles. It was a large group of fifteen people, probably students at NYU mixed in with people trying to be on their way. She waited her turn as the tickets slid into the slots of the waist-high turnstiles. Green arrows on the top of the scanner flashed as each ticket was approved. Tara looked at her watch: she had a good forty minutes to get to the compound.

A disapproving beep signalled that the man in front's card was either damaged or had just run out of credit. His friends laughed at him and waved mockingly. Tara rolled her eyes. She couldn't afford to make a scene or be identified, just in case the cops had put out an alert for her.

Then a nearby Metro cop took the man's ticket and checked it. Slowly he entered the piece of card into the slot. The light showed green, and he thanked the cop with an embarrassed grin. As the man's friends heckled him, Tara moved through the stall. She knew her card was new and hoped for no dramas. Tara faced away from the cops as she tried her travel card. The light turned red and spat the card out. Calmly, she repeated the process only to have the same response. She grabbed the card and rubbed it between her hands as if she was trying to warm up the barcode. For a third time, the scanner beeped angrily and returned her card. Tara felt the cop approaching behind her.

"Trouble, miss?" asked the same cop. Tara turned slowly and handed the card over, all the time trying to keep her head down so he wouldn't recognise her later. He took the card and checked the date. He slid the card in slowly and smiled at her as it showed green. She thanked him and scurried off towards the green line. Immediately, the cop lost his smile and pulled the radio mike on his shoulder towards his mouth.

"Control, this is Two-Zero Charley. We have a positive ID on the woman. She's heading uptown on the green line."

"Copy that, Two-Zero Charley," a woman's voice responded. The cop went back to his post, his eyes turning to the next horde of people.

Tara moved quickly onto the platform and looked around for a place to blend in with the crowd. She knew that if she just stood around, she would be picked out instantly. Her best bet was to join a group. She smiled as she spotted the group of students that had gone through before her. Carefully, she nuzzled next to them enough to appear to an outsider as if she was one of them. The group was so large that even they never noticed the extra member amongst them. Hiding in plain sight was always the best camouflage.

There was a rush of air and the sound of metal wheels clattering on iron rails. The train was on approach, and soon she would be rich. She smiled to herself as the train screeched to a halt and the doors slid open. A crowd of people pushed past, their eyes mostly fixed forward, looking at nothing but the stairs, down, and avoiding all eye contact whatsoever.

Tara had often wondered why everyone on the Metro avoided looking at one another. It was almost as if giving someone the wrong stare would get you into trouble. It was the same with elevators. Whenever she had gone into one of those mysterious boxes, she found everyone suddenly backed onto the walls, almost as if the sides had been magnetised.

The ride was a long one. Every time the train stopped and exchanged passengers, Tara would make a mental note of who was new and who had stayed put. From what she could see, everyone was getting off, all except two men. One was a young guy in his twenties, medium build with red dreadlocked hair and a goatee. The other was in his forties, tall with black styled hair, and wearing a blue pinstriped business suit. Neither of the pair paid her any notice. The suit was busy reading the *Financial Times* and the other guy was playing some game on his cell phone.

Tara looked out of the window. Flashes of electricity lit up the darkened tunnel. She rested her head against the cool glass and stared into the nothingness of her mind. Her memory slipped back to that fateful night when this whole thing had started. That cold, wet night when she had found her friend dead on the sitting-room floor.

There was a screech of metal on metal as the train began to slow. The walls began to get brighter from the lights of the approaching station. Tara's weary gaze rested on the glass and the reflections of the people gathering to get off. Tara's eyes wandered from person to person. She was spying on them as the shuffled about, eager to find a spot. Suddenly, Tara felt her heart almost stop; she had caught a glimpse of what she thought was her boyfriend's face. An image that lasted but a second, caught in the reflection of the glass. She turned quickly, only to see a woman with a child in her arms. Tara's gaze shot back to the window and hurriedly, scanned the crowd for any sign of him, hoping that using the reflective surface wouldn't draw attention to her.

Tara's heart began to pound in her chest with excitement. A sudden feeling of hope rushed over her as her eyes checked out every person who had gotten off. The feeling slowly faded as the train pulled away. He was gone – dead, the police had said so. Her imagination had given her false hope, or indeed may be false hope had tricked her imagination.

She looked up at the map on the arched information boards on the upper walls. There were another five stops to go. She sighed and looked back out of the window. She was tired of running. She was tired of being scared. All she wanted now was to disappear and have a good life.

The journey took another fifteen minutes. Each time the train came to a station, Tara checked the people's faces. The suit and the red-haired guy had gone two stops ago. Now only a fresh batch of faces kept her company. Finally, the train came to her station. She rose from her seat as the train came to a grinding halt. As the doors slid open, she was carried by a wave of people to the bustle of the platform. The smell of diesel and warm metal filled her nostrils. The overpowering smell of too much perfume emanated from a large older woman in front of her. Tara pushed her way forward, wading through a sea of men and women who were all desperate for the freshness of the outside air.

The bright light of the morning sun was welcoming. A breeze carried the smell of the city with it: a mixture of the traffic and food stalls. Tara checked the time. It was a quarter-too, and she still had a way to go. She had no money for a cab and hitching wasn't going to happen.

Her plan had been too hasty, and Tara wished at that moment that she'd thought it through properly. Tara knew that she should have called while she was getting closer. However, it was too late now. She had to see it through. She let out a determined grunt and pressed on. Tara reckoned that she had at least a forty-minute walk. *Too late now*, she thought to herself.

A large black SUV pulled up beside her; the window was down. She stopped for a second and looked over. At first, she thought it was some rich tourist looking for a monument or a hotel. She leant in and spoke with the driver and then got in. She smiled to herself at her good luck. The driver was going her way. Now, at last, things were turning around.

Chapter 40

McCall was pissed. The last report she had gotten was at the subway where Tara had got off the train at East 143rd Street. The techs had come through and traced the text. The message was obvious, but even before that, McCall had a gut feeling about the woman. The 'tail' had lost Tara at the top of the stairs, and now it was up to Traffic to find where she may have gone.

The cynical detective knew that Tara was travelling light on cash, so that removed the possibility of her taking a cab. Unfortunately, the techs could only find the text. The number she sent it too was taking time to find. McCall paced up and down, growling under her breath at another stroke of bad luck.

She stopped and looked at the murder board. There were too many bodies on there for her liking and not enough suspects. The few there were, all had alibis. She looked at each picture once more, hoping something would leap out her, something she had missed before. They were all linked somehow. Her eyes moved over towards the photograph of Adams. He looked smug and arrogant even in his six-by-four photograph. McCall turned and headed for her desk. Her coffee had gone cold by now, but that didn't bother her. Coffee was coffee.

McCall stood in front of her desk and flicked through her notes while drinking her hour cold coffee. Just as she lifted the cup to her lips, the desk phone gave off a dull electronic ring. She picked up the receiver and waited for the next big bit of bad news.

"McCall... Homicide," she said, then listened as one of the security guys for the witnesses explained about the documents Becca had brought with her.

McCall had thought they were just every day meeting presentations for the board. She sat down hard as the other cop explained what the documents meant.

"Are you sure about this?" she asked. "Why didn't she... Never mind. We need those documents sent to Financials ASAP," McCall said. She listened to the person on the other say their " will do's" McCall sighed before speaking again. "Don't let her out of your sight. Great, thanks." McCall shot up out of her seat and pulled her gun and shield from the top drawer of her desk. She clipped on the gun holster and shield onto her belt and arranged them, so they sat correctly. Tooms and Tony looked up in surprise at her sudden movement.

"What's up?" Tooms asked, getting up and hurrying over to her, his jacket already in his hand.

"Get your stuff together. We're going to pay Mr Adams a visit." She looked over towards Tony, who was getting out of his chair.

"Tony, see if you can get a warrant to search the Trent Shipping Company."

Tony gave a quick salute to the order and started filling out the request form on his computer.

"What's it for?" Tony asked as he opened the form.

"For all the records and data in Amber's office. Computers, hard copies, you name it. I want it. Also, get SRU to meet us there."

Tooms noticed her eyes sparkling with joy.

"I think we've found a motive," she told them, "and I think I know where Tara is heading." She said nothing else, just headed for the elevator. As Tooms caught up with her, he could see her satisfied grin.

"So, what's the plan?" Tooms asked. "Bust in with loads of cops and scare the hell out of him?"

"Sounds like a plan. Get some uniforms to come with us just in case the bastard causes any problems." Tony could see in her eyes that she hoped that Adams *would* be a problem. She was blaming him for Steel and Amber's murders. A guy with that much money wouldn't do time; he'd probably get off with a fine and community service.

As the elevator doors opened, they saw Brant looking his usual gloomy self. He saw the excited looks on their faces and chose to ride down with them. McCall and Tooms stepped inside the elevator and stood either side of their huge captain.

"I take it you have something?" Brant asked while facing forward, his body rigid.

"Becca, the woman who worked with Amber, she had some documents that implicate the Trent Shipping Company in smuggling," Sam McCall explained.

"Smuggling what?" Brant asked her.

"By the look of things, just about anything, to anyone. Mostly containers to Africa or Middle Eastern countries. Usually places with trade embargoes. Could be guns, drugs, even people. He doesn't care. If it makes a profit, he's into it."

Brant nodded but kept his statue-like stance, almost as if they weren't having the conversation. "So, you think Amber stumbled onto this?"

McCall shook her head. "No, sir, I think it was her job to find it. We know she was working undercover. She must have found something when she was working at the hotel, and that's why she changed jobs."

"So how does Tara Burke fit into all this?" Brant asked as he watched the numbers on the panel illuminate, showing the floors they were passing.

McCall shook her head and shrugged. "In truth, sir, I have no idea. Maybe they were friends. Remind me to ask her when we find her again," she said awkwardly.

Brant shot McCall a look that made her step back slightly. "What do you mean, find her… How the hell did you lose her?"

"They lost her at the Metro," McCall told him. "We're checking traffic cams now, just in case she got picked up." Brant gave a usual scowl and nodded.

"What's your plan for Adams?"

"We're gonna sit on the place until the warrant comes through. Make sure he doesn't disappear anywhere." McCall's voice almost purred at the thought of taking Adams down. Williams had warned her of the potential danger, that's why she was taking back-up. Tony was also on the phone with SRU. If it was as bad as Williams had explained they needed plenty of firepower.

"Watch your back you two, and make sure you get that son of a bitch," the captain told them. The doors slid open, and the two detectives strolled out. They never looked back as Brant watched them walk away. As the door slid shut, he suddenly had a bad feeling that one of them wasn't coming back from this one.

* * *

The SUV dropped Tara off on the corner near the entrance to the compound. The driver hadn't said much. Normally she wouldn't take rides from strangers, but there was just something about this driver that felt right, safe. He had worn a black suit that must have cost more than she made in two years, and the SUV must have cost a bundle as well. And since he didn't have 'axe murderer' written all over him, she took a chance.

But she did wonder why he had stopped to pick her up and why he just happened to be going that way. Those questions had only just come to her, questions she should have asked before getting into the car. However, she was there, and she was safe.

The wind had begun to pick up, blowing loose dust into the air and creating a funnel. From where Tara stood, the yard looked empty. Everything was still, no movement of any kind. No people were wandering about, no trucks moving – nothing. In fact, the only movement was that of the large cargo train that had just pulled in at the back of the compound. Tara shuddered as she had the feeling someone had just crossed her shadow.

Her eyes took in the surroundings, scanning the buildings for any signs of life, but she found nothing. Slowly, she moved forward, the wind pressing against her, almost as if it was trying to push her back. Even though she managed to walk casually towards the large main building, she was terrified inside, wondering if she had thought this through properly.

Tara moved past the security gate. Peering inside she saw the small one-person box was empty. The wind howled as she moved across the large empty parking lot. She looked around, constantly turning as she went, hoping to see someone – anyone. Tara began to get a bad feeling in her stomach, but there was no going back – not now.

She arrived at the entrance of the main building. Its towering walls cast a huge shadow which covered most of the buildings behind it. She tried the main doors, but they rattled in her hands. Both doors were locked. Her feeling of uneasy was now screaming for her to run – and keep running. Tara looked at her watch. It was now noon. She tried the doors once more, before cupping her hands to block out the daylight as she peered through the glass doors, but all she saw nothing but emptiness.

She was about to head back to the parking lot when she heard a noise: the sound of metal banging against metal. Slowly, she edged around the main building and headed for the warehouses. Tara felt alone, and her body trembled with emotion. As she neared the corner of the building, she saw the rows of warehouses, in front of which stood columns of ICO containers, stacked up ready to be shipped. They were laid in three rows, each was three high, with each row was seven containers long. She looked down one of the lanes to see the door of one of the warehouses swinging freely with the breeze.

It was like a bad horror movie. Tara knew she shouldn't go there, but she felt drawn somehow. Slowly, she headed for the door; her back held firmly against the cold metal of the containers as she steadily made her way.

High above her, on the roof of the main building, a sniper had her in his sights. The bolt-action hunting rifle was made more for hunting game, but the .303 full metal jacket bullet would do the job regardless. His fingertip paused on the trigger as he waited for the signal. His target was a good two hundred metres away. At that range, he couldn't miss. He held his breath and waited.

He smiled at the thought of taking her head off. The crosshairs of his rifle were following her figure, resting on different parts of her body. He could go for a kidney shot, or maybe just take her apart piece by piece. However, he had his orders: shoot to kill but only on the signal. He was already loaded and ready to go. He smiled again, disturbing thoughts rushing through his mind.

The sniper never heard Steel come up behind him. Steel's gripped the shooter's chin and the back of his head. It was a swift motion. A quick lift and twist-action followed by a sudden crack as the head separated from the Atlas bone in the neck. Tendons broke and ripped. There had been no sound; it had been a quick and silent death.

Steel swung the sniper rifle off the dead man's shoulder and lay down next to the fresh corpse. Using a pair of laser rangefinder binoculars, he scanned the area, searching specifically the places he had noted on the plans.

The two snipers on the far warehouse roofs each took a headshot: a simple kill at four hundred metres. The next two were on the roofs of the containers. Each one of them was lying down flat until the signal was given. A quick shot to the base of each of the heads made sure that they stayed down. The SRS sniper rifle made little noise, a meer sound of the metal on metal as the action worked and a gentle sound like gas escaping from the suppressor. No sound, no mussel flash.

With the snipers gone, Steel knew he was going to have to move. The containers would provide cover and plenty of shadows. The top cover had been taken care of, so now it was a matter of minimising the numbers. Steel slung his rifle and took the sniper's 9mm Glock 17 and a couple of spare magazines he had found in the man's jacket pocket. Steel slid out the magazine from the pistol grip, pushed down on the top bullet with his thumb. It was stiff with little give, a good spring, little chance of feed jams. The clear magazine showed the clip had the full fifteen shots. Steel replaced the clip then slid back the top slide on the pistol enough to see the glint of the top round in the chamber — fifteen in the mag – one in the pipe.

Steel made his way down using the outcrops of the building, such as window ledges or anything that gave enough grip to hold onto. He didn't have time for staircases.

As he touched down onto the hard concrete, he rushed over to where Tara was going. The warehouses were large and multi-levelled: good for a killing ground. Steel made it to the middle one and clambered up the side. He had to get high, and he knew the best vantage point was the roof. When he made it to the sheet roofing, Steel moved quickly and silently. His goal was the open window near the centre. It was a maintenance hatch as well as part of the skylight. He looked around at the other warehouses. They all lined up, with enough room between them all for the large forklifts to go about freely. At the far end, the train that had pulled in stood motionless as the crew waited for it to be unloaded. It was a long snaking thing with a mix of boxcars, containers and fuel pods.

Steel neared the small window hatch and looked inside. One guard was right below him – a small, stocky man, who was probably one of the workers and not a gun for hire. His long black hair and beard fell onto his red-and-blue chequered shirt. His arms, covered with tattoos. He was a rough-looking guy who looked more at home with a knife rather than a gun.

The black-clad intruder slowly opened the hatch, holding his breath as though it would help. A sudden squeak of metal made Steel freeze the motion, but luckily the man below didn't flinch. Slowly, Steel carried on until the hatch was fully open. He couldn't understand how the man had not heard the noise, for it had been loud enough. That's when he saw the earbuds. The guy was probably listening to the ball game. Steel smiled at his good fortune and eased himself down behind the guard. Steel could tell that the man wasn't interested in being there, he'd probably been told he'd get a bonus in his wages if he just stood there with a gun.

Steel threw aside palm at the man's neck. He watched as the man's knees buckled and then caught him before he slammed onto the metal flooring. Steel stayed in a crouched position; his long coat splayed out over the grated metal. He looked around for more gunmen. There were two more, and they looked as uninterested in their jobs as the first. The man at his feet carried an MP5K—the short 9mm weapon had a double magazine and a red dot sight. It was a fine weapon for close quarters but wasted if you didn't know what you were doing with it.

John Steel took off one side of the shoulder strap and pulled it from the prone man's body. Picking up the machine pistol, he reattached the strap and slung the weapon. If he were correct, the men would do one thing if challenged: run. He looked down to see Tara heading across the floor towards the exit. The men on the other side of the building just looked down at her and did nothing. Steel had begun to wonder if Adams had any real fighters with him. If he did, they were probably as close to him as possible, and he was as near to a getaway plan as he could be. Adams was in it for the money, nothing else. If there were any wet work, he would get someone else to do it. He watched as Tara exited the building. Quickly he headed across the walkway to a pile of crates. These were only stacked, thus forming a perfect step way.

As he hit the cold concrete, he looked up at the men who just stared down on him as though nothing was amiss. These men were bait: a reason to make someone to open fire and alert the others. But he wasn't going to give them that chance. He wanted to catch them unawares.

Slowly, he edged out of the building and ran across the open ground towards the next warehouse. This time a perfectly parked truck gave Steel the boost he needed to climb to the roof. Carefully making his way to the apex, Steel noted the buildings around him. There was nobody, the place was quiet and still. This worried him because it meant that if there were men out there, they were taking cover. As Steel reached the apex, he suddenly hit the deck as a large blade came flying overhead. He rolled as the blade came crashing down, creating sparks as metal hit metal. Steel looked over to see a huge thin man wielded the huge machete.

The man was around six-foot-five, large hands with long fingers gripped the massive blade. The man was slightly bent at the shoulders, giving him a ghoulish appearance. His face was long with a pointed nose; his eyes were sunken and dark, and rat-like teeth protruded passed thin pinkish lips. His naked upper half was covered with scars and tattoos on pale, leathery skin.

He smiled at Steel, who just shot him a surprised look back. The blade came down again and again. Each time, Steel rolled, and the sparks flew. The blade smashed down, and Steel rolled back onto the blade, locking it into position before landing a double-footed kick onto the man's chest. The man flew back but landed on his feet. A menacing grin crossed the man's face as he pulled out another blade from the sheath on his leg. Its blade was long and brutal. The eighteen-inch length glistened as the sunlight caught its polished sides. Blood grooves in the shape of a dragon were cut into the solid frame. The jagged teeth of the top serrations looked animalistic.

Steel could have shot him, but the noise would carry and alert them to the invasion if they didn't already know about it. Steel picked up the dropped machete, and the two men circled each other. The larger man lunged forward, and with a rear spinning motion, brought the blade around. Steel rolled and gave an upwards kick, catching the brute under the chin. The man didn't even flinch, instead carried on the movement, spinning like a tornado. Each time Steel did the same but targeting different parts of his opponent, trying to find his weak spot.

As Steel kicked up once more, but the man grabbed Steel by the leg and swung him like a ragdoll. Steel skidded across the roof, sliding towards the edge. Panicked, Steel drove the blade into the metal to try and stop his descent. There was a loud squeal of metal on metal. As Steel got to the edge, he brought the blade down again, and he felt it plunge deep into a weak spot.

The man looked down at Steel angrily, disappointed at his opponent's luck. Slowly he strode over to Steel, who was half hanging over the edge, fighting to clamber up. The man reached down and picked Steel up by the knife arm. He held Steel high and smiled. Grabbing Steel's other arm, he began to pull. Steel felt his arms being pulled out of their sockets and let out a cry of pain. This made the man grin even more. Steel pulled all his strength together and brought his arms inwards. A shocked look covered the brute's face, stunned as he was at Steel's power. That second of amazement and lack of concentration cost the man dearly.

Steel pulled his knees up and hooked his feet on the man's belt. Leaning back, Steel broke free from his grip and at the same time delivered a double chin-kick. The knifeman stumbled backwards, disorientated. Steel quickly jumped up and gave him a double flat kick to the chest. The brute stumbled and hit a weak spot in the roof. There was a loud scraping noise as the section of roofing gave in, and the man fell, screaming. Large, heavy sheets of metal followed, crashing down on the man, burying him under the debris.

The detective didn't stop to find out if his attacker was alive or not. Tara was walking into a trap, and she didn't know it. He knew the tell-tale signs. The way everything was laid out, the lack of innocent people, in fact, the lack of anybody apart from the odd few.

He raced to the roof's edge just in time to see Tara approach a covered walkway that was surrounded on either side by stacked wooden crates, ICO containers and large cargo containers. Steel guessed that this was the load-on and load-off point for the trains. Two large cranes loomed overhead; their thin-looking frames silhouetted by the afternoon sun.

Tara moved slowly towards the strange walkway. The wooden construction would have looked more at home on the side of a lake, rather than in a haulage company's backyard. She stopped around twenty feet shy of the entrance. Her stomach was telling her to run right now and get the hell out of there. But she had business to attend to. Down the centre of the eight-foot-wide path, wooden crates no more than four feet square had been stacked up to form an L shape. These zigzagged all the way down, forming a chicane. The lack of wind or even a slight breeze gave her an uneasy feeling. It was almost as if the world was holding its breath in anticipation.

Everything that had happened had led Tara up to this point. Her choices were clear: stay or leave – it was simple. But each choice had consequences. Either she could leave and run for the rest of her life, always looking over her shoulder, or she could move on down the path, and it ends. One way or the other, it ends today.

She felt alone and tired. The strength she had displayed over the phone at the hotel was almost gone. The emptiness of the compound was designed to do one thing: to smash her confidence, instil fear into her heart, and most of all, make her feel utterly alone.

Then she saw something. Someone was moving forward. The person was cloaked in so much shadow that delineating its gender was impossible. There was just the hint of movement heading her way.

Tara stood frozen to the spot. Her body pushed her to start running, but her legs were as firm as the Statue of Liberty.

Suddenly the stranger stepped out of the shadows but remained on the wooden decking of the walkway.

Tara's eyes widened, and her mouth fell open.

"You!" she yelled out. "But… but you're supposed to be dead!"

Chapter 41

Tooms held on for dear life in the front seat of the Mustang. McCall was driving as if she was in the Indie 500. The busy streets gave way to the weaving GT 500 as if she had dynamite strapped to the sides. The hidden police lights in the grill flashed to give a warning, and the horn did the rest. Over the roar of the engine, the sound of the car's media system kicked it. The Bluetooth feature on the system had picked up an incoming call. McCall looked down quickly at the caller's ID. It was Tina's work number.

"Hi, Tina, sorry I didn't make it down. What you got?" McCall said as she forced the Mustang past two other cars.

"Well, I just finished doing a DNA check on your Mr Crispy to see if it is John Doe, or whatever his name is now," the ME told her.

"Nice. And is it him?"

"I found skin fibres on a piece of rope that had been used to bind the hands. Somehow the body had prevented it from catching fire and preserved it. We tested this, and it was a match to your John Doe." Even over the phone, Tina could almost sense McCall's look of disappointment. A witness had been kidnapped and killed on her watch, and Tina knew McCall wouldn't take that well.

"So, it was him. Oh shit."

"Uhm, well…" A note of uncertainty was in Tina's voice.

"What… *uhm*?" McCall asked impatiently, swerving fast, and thereby forcing Tooms's face against the door's window.

"I found a piece of undamaged flesh at the back of the throat; this, however, didn't match. In fact, he hasn't matched to anything yet," Tina said gingerly.

McCall suddenly felt as if she'd been fooled. Was John Doe alive and part of this? Or was someone playing games? Either way, they were going to confront Adams because she was sure he was behind all of it. Tina had hung up after getting another call, and this suited her friend fine. She wasn't in a talking mood.

"What the hell is going on, McCall?" Tooms screamed, more at the near crash with the VW Golf in front of them than anything else.

"You can ask Adams when we get there, preferably while hanging him out of his office window," Sam snapped back. Tooms shot her a look, but she didn't register it. She knew where Tara was going, and she hoped she was wrong. All roads led to Trent Shipping.

"Do you think he had Steel killed?" Tooms asked his boss.

"Probably. Who knows? I can't see him doing it himself though, more likely he'd contract out a hit on him or get one of his goons to do it. Adams is a businessman, not a mobster."

"So, do you think John Doe is still alive or is someone just messing with us?"

McCall shrugged at the question. Then after a short while shook her head. "I honestly don't know, Joshua. One thing is certain, we've got a corpse in the morgue that someone has gone to a lot of trouble to disguise." Suddenly she thought back to the conversation with Williams. He had warned her about the threat. But she still didn't know why he had done so.

"But there's one thing for sure. I know who *isn't* in the morgue," McCall said confidently.

* * *

"Hello, Tara, you're looking … different," said Amber as she stepped out of the shadows. Tara could feel her legs begin to buckle under the stress of the situation. Amber was the last person she had expected to see there.

Distant sirens made Amber look over towards the cluster of buildings. She smiled and walked back down the walkway as though nothing was wrong.

Tara was still frozen to the spot. A mixture of fear and anger washed over her. She screamed loudly and rushed forward, chasing after the disappearing shadow of Amber.

Steel had made it to the roof's edge just in time to see Tara standing there like a statue. She appeared to be talking to someone, but part of the roof hid the other person from view. A sudden burst of sirens made him turn and look towards the gated entrance. Six black-and-whites and an SRU van were being led into the premises by a blue Mustang. He smiled as he watched the metallic beast skid to a halt, kicking up a cloud of dust and loose gravel.

The van emptied, as did the patrol vehicles. The SRU teams got into formation as they prepared to take the main building. They formed up in single file with the point man carrying a ballistic shield. The man behind him held his FN SCAR-L high, the barrel held above the shield for covering fire. They moved as one, each arc of fire covered, including the rear.

Simultaneously, the uniformed cops got out of their vehicles. Black Kevlar vests covered their torsos, and they were armed with M4A1 assault rifles and Mossberg 590 shotguns. As the SRU entered the main building, the uniforms split off in pairs and made for the warehouses. Steel knew he had to leave. The sight of an armed man on a roof would only add to the stress of the situation, and most probably get him shot.

Steel knelt quickly as he saw McCall head for the corner of the main building. She wasn't going in. He probably thought she would leave the chaos to everyone else. As she grew near, he could see the look on her face, that 'something's not right' look.

As she got to the corner, she began to run. Steel looked down to see she was heading for the covered walkway. He figured she had seen Tara and was now heading after her. He got up quickly and headed forward, towards McCall, using the containers as if they were steppingstones. He had seen how everything was laid out, and it screamed set-up.

McCall got to the start of the walkway. She held her custom Glock tight in a double grip and pointed at the ground in front of her, a standard safety precaution. It meant that if Tara were to come around the corner suddenly, McCall wouldn't blow her head off by accident: better a bullet in the ground than an innocent life taken. That was something she had experienced long ago, and she had no intention of making the same mistake twice.

As she got to the first set of arranged boxes, two men appeared from nowhere and opened on her. The few seconds she needed to raise and fire the weapon were not enough — a hail of 5.56 impacted with the boxes, turning them into matchsticks. Something hit McCall hard, throwing her to the ground just as a volley came her way. Stunned, she checked herself over. Confused, she looked down, finding that her hands were covered in blood. She checked herself again, but she found no wound.

"I am not hit, thank God, I am not hit," she thought out loud, then her eyes moved from her bloodied hands to where she had been standing. Her mouth fell open in surprise. There, leaning against another set of boxes, was Steel. He was busy inspecting a nasty looking wound on his left shoulder. She didn't know whether to be angry, happy or just plain astonished. Her thoughts and emotions were being tossed around like rocks in a concrete mixer.

"Steel?" she said, stunned. "But you're – !"

" – bleeding. Yeah, just a little but don't worry, it's nothing."

"What…?" McCall shot him a confused look. After all this time letting her think he'd died, and that's all he could come out with?

Another spray of loose gunfire shredded the box above McCall's head, causing her to keep low. She returned fire but was quickly made to dive to cover. Steel pulled out the 9mm Glock that the sniper had been carrying and dropped the magazine from its housing. There was a full clip. He slid the magazine back into the housing, leaned out and opened fire on his attackers. He caught one of them in the shoulder, which sent him spinning. The other one concentrated his shooting on Steel's position, which gave McCall a chance to open fire. Four of her rounds impacted with the man's cover and the other two caught him full in the chest. The man stumbled back and swore loudly.

"Shit, they've got vests on!" she growled with disappointment.

"I do love well-trained bad guys, don't you?" Steel said as he found shelter behind a group of large crates.

"Why's that?" McCall yelled out, annoyed at his childish grin. Three bursts of single-shot tore into the wood above them.

"Because they use the same weapons and they only fire the necessary number of rounds," Steel said, getting comfortable.

"And that helps us how?" screamed McCall as she slapped in her final magazine into the Custom Glock 17.

"It means more guns and ammo for us when we take them down," Steel said before disappearing behind some crates. Sam McCall shook her head in amazement. She had forgotten how she had missed him, yet right now, she wanted to shoot him herself.

There was a mass of gunfire. Stray rounds went wide and impacted with the stacks of crates and cargo storage on the outside of the walkway. McCall sat with her back against the cover and waited. In the distance Tooms and Tony ran towards her, using as much cover as possible on the way. Tony dived for cover where Steel had been sitting, while Tooms's massive form joined McCall.

"Well, I see you found the bad guys," Tooms joked as the whistle of stray 5.56 bullets made them lean away from the noise. McCall could see the shapes of the SRU teams heading towards them. Rounds impacted with their ballistic shields, forcing them to move slowly.

"McCall, are you hit?" Tony asked, looking at the blood on his hand.

"No. It's Steel's blood. He got hit when he rescued me." She smiled awkwardly, knowing exactly how it sounded.

"So, Steel rose from the dead to save you. Did you hit your head or something?" Tooms asked, checking her head for wounds.

McCall slapped his massive shoulder playfully. "No. It appears our Mr Steel didn't die after all, well not yet anyway," she said angrily. She opened her mouth to speak again, but the sudden silence stopped her. All three detectives slowly stood up, their weapons trained forward, ready to take down anyone with a gun. McCall and Tooms looked at each other, both utterly confused.

"Do you think we scared them off?" Tooms asked jokingly as the SRU teams rushed forward to meet them.

The three detectives took up the rear as the tactical teams swept past them. Slowly they moved as one, each covering the other. There was a strong smell of freshly fired weapons which hung in the back of their throats.

Next, the point man threw up a clenched fist, signalling everyone to stop. He turned to the man behind him and pointed to one of the men who was lying on the ground. The third man moved forward while everyone covered him. The SRU man checked for a pulse then gave the thumbs up. Quickly, he zip-tied the injured man and checked him for hidden weapons and knives.

As he rejoined the group, they swept forward until they got to the next man. He, too, was searched and restrained.

"Where are we going, Detective?" asked the SRU team leader.

"Follow the bodies." She shrugged.

"Sounds like a plan," he answered, shrugging back as they all set off down the walkway.

* * *

Steel had used the cargo containers as cover as well as a walkway. He was positioned too high up for the enemy to see him, and what's more, they were fully occupied by laughing and shooting. They weren't guns for hire or a couple of mercenaries. They were just two guys that probably worked at the company driving forklifts or vans. Either way, they had been given a couple of extra bucks and were enjoying the chance of shooting at some cops.

Both men were in their late thirties, with bulky figures and shaven heads. The guy on the left had a black goatee, and both his arms were covered with tattoos. The other was a no-neck with a nice big scar on his left cheek. They both wore body armour and used M4 assault rifles. The belts around their waists were full of magazines for both the rifle and the 9mm Glocks they were packing.

Steel sprang from one stack to the other. His long coat carried up by his movement. The loud clatter from the unsuppressed gun barrels drowned out any noise. He stopped and crouched down to get a better view. He judged that these weren't bad men, just idiots having some fun. Steel headed for a stack that was close to them and hurried over. It would have to be quick, for he couldn't risk the other guy getting the drop on him. Steel felt the adrenaline course through his veins. He took a deep breath and made his move.

In one swift movement, he had dashed across the stacked cargo and jumped for the roof. Like an athlete, he leapt up and caught the roof's edge, his legs swinging up, and at that moment he released his grip and double-kicked one of the men in the side. His victim was thrust into the crates behind him, impacting hard onto the wood, knocking him out cold.

The second man turned, a look of utter surprise on his scarred face. This expression was wiped away by a blow from his fallen comrade's Glock.

In one fluid movement, Steel had kicked the first man. As he rolled, he'd picked up the loose 9mm pistol from the ground and tossed it at the second man. The top slide of the weapon met the man's skull on the bridge of his nose and above his left eye. The stricken man saw stars for about a second as he stumbled about, then he crashed to the ground unconscious.

The first guy was out cold as he lay in a pile of splintered wood. Steel didn't know whether his comatose condition had been caused by his kick, or from the apparent masses of alcohol that was probably oozing out of the man's bones. The spent roll-ups, and empty beer cans on the ground next to his firing position spoke volumes. These guys were so high they probably thought zombie hordes were coming, not cops.

Steel looked down towards where Tara had made off too. There were six more possible firing positions, which was five too many. Steel headed out and back to the tops of the containers. He had been lucky this time. Next time he might be up against mercenaries.

The next two guards turned out to be more of a challenge. These were weekend warriors: the guys who had all their combat gear. The first guy was in his forties, stocky, with a camouflaged baseball cap. The tattoo on his right arm said *Ranger*, but Steel figured he had failed to get into decent military units, let alone Special Forces. He had probably used his apparent 'Ranger' status several times in the past to get laid.

Since this man was bulky, a kick wouldn't work, not a kick in the chest anyway. However, he screamed in pain as Steel's double kick landed perfectly on his left knee. His gun hand gripped the pistol grip tightly as he fell, letting loose rounds cascade down the walkway and towards McCall. Steel quickly stood on the man's wrist, forcing his hand to open. The detective then quickly kicked the weapon up towards the second, skinnier man, who dropped his weapon to catch the empty M4. Shocked at what he had done, the second man looked down at the weapon and then at Steel. Those few seconds cost the man the contest. He was not Ranger material: A Ranger would have never dropped his weapon, and even if he had, he would never have taken his eyes off the enemy.

The second man dropped to the floor. His nose was bleeding from where Steel had roundhouse his head straight into the nearby boxes. The first man got a pinch to the neck just to stop him screaming.

Then it was back to the silence. Back to the shadows.

The walkway led out into another open area. Three large warehouses stood lengthways, and behind them was the train yard. This area was predominantly for the loading of large goods for rail travel. There was a massive fifty-foot gap between the walkway and the warehouses: a perfect kill zone.

Steel looked up at the warehouses, taking note of their apexes. These would provide perfect cover for even an average sniper. However, Steel knew that this was where Adams's best men would be. Taking the sniper rifle from his back, he used the scope to search the rooftops. The meshed lens cover Killflash extension would hide the scope flash when the sun hit it. The gauze construction had saved his ass many times in the past. The whole point of being a sniper is not to be seen, and it isn't solely to kill. It was something his employers had spent a great deal of money on training him to do.

The Englishman spotted six men, two on each rooftop, each one spaced out at either end of each building. It made firing back and hitting them almost impossible. Or almost impossible. Steel got himself into a comfortable position before firing. The shot was complicated, as all he had was the weapon sights and not much of a view of the men's heads.

They were good. Now it was time to see if he was better. Steel knew he would only have a couple of seconds before they registered his muzzle flash and returned fire. Even with a suppressed weapon, the flash is visible, denoting the small explosion when the bullet leaves the gun's barrel when all those burning gases that force the bullet out are suddenly released.

Steel knew he would be able to get at least two, maybe three, of them before he was spotted. The distance between each man was large, making moving the weapon and staying on target a bitch, especially with the cover he had. The best thing about this shoot was the lack of wind. Just a sudden breeze could make all the difference between a hit and a miss. Millimetres on the scope was inches on the ground. Add a gust of wind, and it could be feet.

The marksman lined up his first shot. He adjusted the sight. He had a good line on the top of the man's head, but he chose the scope instead. If it went high, he would get him either way. Steel's breathing became shallow, almost non-existent. He would have to fire between breaths, for each inward breath would make the weapon rise. Breathe in ... Hold ... Fire ... Breathe out.

Steel rechecked his first target. Everything was perfect. His finger paused on the trigger, ready to take the slack, waiting for that first click before pulling and holding. Everything was ideal.

Suddenly there was an ungodly scream and Steel suddenly felt himself being picked up and thrown. As he hit the warm concrete of the open area, he rolled on his side to allow himself more breathing space. He looked up to see the thing that had crashed through the warehouse roof. The beast of a man was blooded and scratched. Bits of broken metal stuck out of his body, but he seemed unaffected by them. There was a loud crack as one of the snipers open fire, but Steel had moved just as the beast had brought down a massive boot where his head had been. The sniper's round hit the beast in the left shoulder. He screamed in pain and looked up at the shooter.

Then the beast's attention rested on the men on the roof. The sniper went pale as the beast began to climb the side of the building as if it was a child's climbing frame. Steel saw the opportunity and took it. He didn't have time to play. Tara was in danger. He had lost sight of her at the walkway, but there was only one place she was heading, and that was the train.

So, Steel rushed for the gap between two of the furthest warehouses. Above him shots rang out, followed by deathly screams. But he didn't stop to look. If he was right, whoever she was meeting wanted her on that train. If that happened, she would never be seen again, and Amber's killer would also be long gone.

As Steel made it to the corner of the building, more shots rang out. Two men stood by a carriage doorway, and their MP7 machine pistols sang a deadly tune. Streams of automatic 4.6 x 30mm rounds shattered the wall next to him, causing Steel to dive for cover behind a steel cargo container. The sound of hollow banging filled the air, like a wild beast trying to get out of the metal box. Steel waited until they had stopped firing. A few seconds was all he had before they could reload, depending on how good they were. Quickly he leant out and shot both men in the left kneecaps and fired another into their right shoulders. The men dropped, screaming in pain just as the train's whistle blew.

Steel's eyes searched the carriage windows and found Tara walking with two other people. The glare from the sun on the windows made the view to the interior almost impossible. However, one thing was sure: he had to get onto that train.

The monstrous EMD GP50 locomotive began to move. Its blue painted sides sported the Trent Shipping logo and a sign he had seen somewhere before: a red horse's head on a white background. There was a loud bang, and a screech of metal as the haul was suddenly being heaved forward. The snaking line of carriages and flatbeds began to move slowly, but they were picking up speed. Steel grabbed onto one of the railings and pulled himself up before the whole thing lumbered down the track.

Chapter 42

The engine made a slow start, which was all that Steel needed as he pulled himself to the top of a baggage car. He needed to get to the car where he had seen Tara. The gunmen had slowed his boarding but had not prevented it. However, there was a problem, a big one. Between him and Tara, there were ten carriages. Two carried steel ISO containers, and three were baggage cars. To the centre were two long oval fuel containers, and their polished outer casings glinted in the midday sun. In front of those were three more passenger carriages. Steel knew that these would be filled with Adams's men.

The wind began to pick up, as did the speed. The monstrous locomotive was underway. The blast of oncoming gusts dulled the clitter clatter of metal on metal. Steel knew he had to get inside, out of the blasts of wind somehow. Being outside was going to slow him down. Also, the threat of been blown off was increasing all the time. If he lost his footing, Steel would be blown back several feet – or worse.

Steel moved to the back of the carriage and climbed down. There was a small window in the door. Carefully he peered in. The car was full of armed men. He counted at least twenty before giving up. There were too many for close-quarters combat. Even if he disarmed one and took his weapon, getting all of them without injury was highly unlikely. Unlikely but not impossible.

He took out the 9mm pistol he had taken from one of the guards. Releasing the clip, he checked it: a full magazine of fifteen hollow points. He pressed down on the top round with his thumb. The spring was forced back on his pressure. He took another quick look, marking where everyone was. Most of the men were sitting down, chatting away. Others were rechecking their equipment. Seven men were standing up. One of the men was hanging off the baggage rail talking to two others. Two were standing next to the end doorway to the next car, making hand gestures as they talked. Another man was a monster who was probably standing because there was no room for him to sit. Even the momentum of the train failed to move him.

Three others stood and chatted with a group that was seated. But the one Steel was interested in, was the one who had just gone to the small toilet. As the man came out, Steel tapped on the window. The guy stopped and turned but didn't move forward. Steel tapped again. The man covered the pistol grip on his Glock with an open palm. Slowly, he moved forward. Looking out, he saw nothing, only the sight of the tracks they had left behind. He turned and began to walk back to his seat. Suddenly the door swung open, and Steel grabbed him and held him in front of him as a human shield.

Some of the men reacted instantaneously and opened fire. Losing a volley of 9mm bullets that ripped into the man's body and his body armour. Fountains of blood tossed into the air as the hot copper-jacketed bullets met flesh. Steel held the dead man and pushed him forward. As he grew near, he quickly put a round into each of the first two groups' kneecaps. Tossing the empty weapon aside, he grabbed the man's Glock from his holster. The pistol barked, and ten more men screamed in pain. There were five rounds left, but he knew it wasn't enough. On one of the seats, a guard's Heckler and Koch 45ACP UMP machine pistol sat ready. As he reached for it, a huge man, who appeared to be larger than a bear, suddenly ripped the blooded human shield from Steel's grasp.

What was left of the man smashed against the back wall, leaving a red stain on the window and wall. Steel fell to the ground before he could grab the weapon. A thick beard and facial tattoos covered the monster's massive, leering face. His grin revealed yellow, badly fitted teeth. His brown eyes that appeared to be almost black were wide with bloodlust. The man leapt towards Steel with malicious intent. Steel managed to roll backwards in time to avoid the giant's grasp. As he landed on his knees, Steel picked up one of the weapons that lay on the ground and fired into his shoulder. Steel's face dropped as the bear of a man bellowed and powered forward. The 9mm rounds just had the effect of pissing the man off. Steel looked at the pistol and then at his attacker before groaning with disappointment.

The man swung a massive open palmed hand, hoping to either catch or smash Steel in a sideward blow. Steel dropped to the ground barely in time, as the massive paw sailed over his head, and he felt the breeze scrape his scalp as he fell. Steel lay on his back and elbows for a second, looking up at the giant, wondering how he was going to get out of this one. The giant lunged again. Shocked at the man's speed, Steel double kicked upwards, hoping to catch him in the crotch. But the man was too quick and grabbed Steel's legs and swung him towards the windows.

Steel impacted with the large window and cracked the glass. As he fell, the remaining two guards ran for him. Steel reached over to a pistol that lay next to one of the injured men. He grabbed it and put one round into each of the men's right knees. Screaming, they hit the ground and cradled their wounds. The giant ran for Steel, his hands raised, and fingers extended, looking like a monster from the old black-and-white movies. Steel spun round on his back and let off two rounds into the man's right foot. There was an explosion of red, and the man screamed and fell hard, nursing his foot, and his missing toes.

The detective jumped to his feet and grabbed one of the assault rifles from a bench. He smashed the butt of the weapon into his enemy's face several times. Blood flowed freely from his mouth and nose, but he kept coming. But his movements seemed laboured, as though he was trying to grab Steel by instinct rather than rational thought. Steel landed another blow, splintering the plastic grips of the rifle. This time the giant fell to the floor, spark out. The weapon was twisted and bent from the impact, and he tossed it away and picked up another that was lying next to one of the unconscious mercenaries.

Pulling off the double magazine, he checked that both were full, then slid it back on until it clicked home. Steel headed out of the railway car, leaving the injured men to their wounds.

The next car wasn't as full, but they were ready for him. As he opened the door, he dived inside. Automatic gunfire ripped into the door and surrounding walls. The men were in two groups and two ranks, each of which was using the seats as cover. Steel fired back but was quickly edged back by the onslaught of bullets. The first rank would fire, followed by the second as the first row reloaded.

Bits of timber from the bench flew up in the air. There were flashes of light as metal on metal gave short flaming sparks as the bullets hit railings and parts of the structure. Steel fired a quick burst from his FN SCAR, and five men were pulled down with shoulder wounds, while the others dived for cover, their ranks were broken. It allowed him enough time to move forward. As he went, he picked off any unlucky soul who was too quick to return to his post. The weapon was held high, and the butt fully pressed into his shoulder, his cheek resting on the guard, his eye trained on the red dot sight.

Four more of the enemy stood up. Steel fired only single shots, each one aiming for a hit in the shoulder. Another four stood up, but this time they were firing. Windows shattered, but each shot was a miss. Steel returned fire. Sparks flew as rounds impacted with the metal posts as the men took cover. They fired back, hoping to pin Steel down.

Their ears rang with proximity gunfire, and the overpowering stench of spent black powder hung in the air. Steel fired again, first towards the men on the right. The rounds missed. But he knew the men on the left would be breaking cover, and his weapon was already pointing in their direction. Each of them was too slow to fire, a single shot to their shoulders putting them down screaming, with blood oozing through their fingers as they held their wounds. Steel re-aimed his weapon just in time to catch the men on the right. Steel's gun roared, and the men fell with wounded shoulders.

Satisfied that the train carriage was secure, Steel knelt and relieved the men of their weapons and magazines, tossing what he didn't need under the wheels of the train.

The next carriage was empty, apart from the piles of military equipment boxes. Weapons, ammo and explosives were arranged in three different stacks. Steel opened the door he had just come from and took several shots at the carriage link. Sparks flew and a there was a scraping sound as the carriages separated. He didn't need soldiers coming up behind him, injured or not. He would have enough to contend with as he moved forward, so he didn't want to have to watch his back as well. Steel slipped in another double magazine into the weapon, cocked it and moved forward.

The next two cars were fuel containers, each one around twenty feet long and made of oval steel. Steel couldn't go over them. At the speed they were moving it would be like walking on ice in a wind tunnel. He would have to go alongside or underneath. Moving along the side would be slow and leave him vulnerable while clinging on underneath would mean he'd be hanging on for dear life. One slip and it would be game over: hitting the tracks at high speed would grind him into the unforgiving steel, where he would be chopped to pieces.

All his options had risks, and all were as crazy as his being on the train in the first place. He looked at his choices again, standing with a foot on each carriage, weighing up the pros and cons.

Suddenly the window behind him shattered and he looked up at the guards on the far fuel carrier. Steel dropped between the carriages and grabbed hold of whatever he could, clinging on underneath the train's chassis, just as a barrage of bullets came down from the two men above. As he held on to his assault rifle, he felt it begin to drag as it became caught on the tracks slipping past him at speed below.

Steel managed to hold on as the weapon began to pull him from his handhold. With all his strength, he managed to pull himself up, hoping to create some more distance between his body and the ground beneath. He knew he wouldn't have a chance with the weapon on his back, so he unclipped it and watched it disappear under the train. Sparks flew up as the heavy wheels gnawed at the rifle. Breathing a sigh of relief, he looked towards where he had to go. Underneath the train, all the undercarriage looked identical, making it hard to see which direction he was moving in. There were no slivers of daylight from above to set a marker as to where the next break in the carriages was. All he could do was gaze forward and begin moving.

Steel dragged himself along the undercarriage of the train, easing himself along the grease and grime-covered underbody. Stones shot up like bullets, thrown up by the wind and wheels. The stench of fuel and hot metal nearly choked him, making him look down at his feet to gasp for air because it was clearer than the oncoming gust. The clatter of the wheels on the track was deafening, but he knew he had to carry on. Tara was in danger – they all were. Steel dragged himself along to the next car. He had no idea what was there, who was waiting for him – possibly no one, or a boxcar full of mercenaries. Either way, he had to get from under the train and detach the cars – separate Adam's from his men. As Steel came up to the edge of the carriage, he waited to ensure his enemies weren't waiting for him. Steel held on as the train snaked its way along the miles of track. As quickly as he dared, he moved under the next carriage and headed onwards, using the underside as cover, hiding his approach. A risky manoeuvre for sure, but less dangerous than staying above, and visible.

The next car was a fuel carriage. It was a large cylindrical container held in an open metal construction. On each upper corner of the open crate knelt four guards. They waited for their prey to make a move. They waited for the first sign of Steel, anticipating his movements, waiting for him to move along the carriages. There were two of them on either side, each guarding a corner. They were well placed; each man had an arc of fire that would cover the front or rear of the container. Each man had a throat microphone and headset so that they could talk over the din, as well as ski goggles and a face mask against the wind and dust. They figured that Steel wouldn't be foolish enough to go over the top of the boxcars and wasn't crazy enough to try going underneath. They hoped he would go through the cars, using up his ammunition as he went. As they waited, they never noticed a figure emerge from between the carriages. They weren't aware of Steel removing the securing pin that held the carriages together. The men thought that the judder of the car was just the track. As they held on, they swore at the driver because of the rough ride.

"Shit…tunnel," screamed one of the men. All four guards made themselves small as not to slam into the oncoming stone construction. They laughed as the darkness passed, and they were once more in the open.

"That was fuckin close," laughed the man on the rear right.

"You got that right, look out next time you bastards," yelled the man on the rear left to his colleagues at the front using the small communications set they had to talk over the noise of the train.

"Maybe next time we'll just let the fuckin bridge smash you off ya perch, might improve ya looks," laughed the man on the front left. The man on the rear left replied with a sharp upper thrust with his middle finger.

"Hey…?" asked the man on the rear right, looking around puzzled. "are we slowing down?"

"Nah, it's just your brain," laughed one of the men. They all laughed. Suddenly their laughter stopped; they all started looking around. Something was wrong.

"Shit…we are," yelled the man on the front left, confused. The men looked over at the car in front, just in time to see the train disappearing into the distance. The men at the rear guard opened fire at the last car indiscriminately. Hot copper impacted with the sides of the far fuel tank.

"Ceasefire, you idiots!" yelled the men at the front as they dove for cover. The men at the rear guard stopped firing and let out a cry in anger.

"Are you trying to blow us to kingdom come, you bunch of dumb asses?" he screamed. One of the men stood up and ran over to the man at the front right, squaring the man off. "Who you callin' dumbass?" the big man said before spitting a gob of saliva onto his boss's boot. There was a hiss as one of the control panels on the carriage began to spark. Their eyes widened with horror.

"Oh, shi…"

The shockwave from the explosion downed some of the trees and ripped up the track. Loose stones were hurled in every direction, impacting against the cart above him. Steel smiled to himself as he watched the red-and-black plume of fire and smoke. He turned and climbed up the cargo containers. The roof of the containers was flat with hook holes for the cranes, which he gladly realised he could use to crawl along the top of the container. Steel's body was flat against the cold metal as he dragged himself along, the gusting wind doing its utmost to rip him from the surface.

Steel reached the end and peered over the top. The area below the freight cars seemed unguarded. Slowly he climbed down, fighting against the torrent of wind. The carriages had no windows, only a pair of heavy steel doors on the sides for loading and smaller doors for access from one car to the other. The walls had a strange patterned surface, with one-foot-square sheeting. To most people, it would just look like an elaborate pattern, like some type of old Japanese armour.

He tried pulling at the handle as slowly as possible. It turned easily, making no noise. All the while, Steel had a bad feeling about what was going to happen. So far, the operation had been too easy.

Finally, there was a click, and the latch was released. Steel carefully opened the door and peered in. His mouth fell open at what was in front of him.

"Well that could certainly be a problem," he said almost casually, before closing the door again, equally as carefully.

* * *

Amber walked through the carriages with purpose, her head high. Her back was straight, and her long legs strode out as if she was a model on a catwalk. She wore a black business suit with only a waistcoat but no blouse to cover her bare chest.

Tara followed the other woman until they reached the furthest carriage. Inside it was set out like a modern office, and ceiling lights brightly lit the interior. It was a long room filled with a wall cabinet on the right-hand side and a couch on the left next to a long cabinet. All the furnishings were of black hard plastic that glistened with an unnatural glossy finish. Two leather armchairs with stainless steel legs sat side by side, and a huge black desk made from the same material was at the end of the room.

Behind the desk sat Adams. His face was emotionless and cold.

"Thank you for joining us, my dear," he said graciously. "Please sit down." He ushered Tara towards the seat opposite him. Carefully, Tara moved over to the high-backed leather chair and sat. The leather creaked under the sudden pressure. Amber moved away to the side of the room.

Two medium-built men dressed in black suits with black, high-necked T-shirts, stood either side of Adams's chair: bodyguards with short-cropped hair. Two other men of the same build stood guarding the door, their hands crossed in front of them, like bouncers at a club.

The long cabinet held a silver ice bucket and five champagne flutes. Large cubes of ice surrounded a bottle of Bollinger Special Cuvée. Amber picked up an already half-filled glass from the tray. Moving to the long black leather couch, she slowly eased herself down and relaxed. Adams smiled as if everything had gone according to some strange plan. Tara suddenly had a bad feeling, a feeling she couldn't explain, almost as if the situation was about to get worse. She could feel the beads of sweat beginning to form at the back of her neck and brow. She was glad she was sitting, for her knees had lost their strength out of pure fear.

"So, do you have it?" Adams asked before taking a sip from his champagne flute.

She said nothing, just nodded quickly.

He smiled and eased back into his chair. "Do you know what you've got there, young lady?" His words were soft and calm. Tara shivered at the question and the tone he was using. She would have preferred it if he had yelled at her. In her experience, good news was never given in such a deadly calm tone.

"It's just some bank accounts or something," she suddenly bit back, feeling a sudden rush of adrenaline. The more she looked at Adams, the more she felt anger swallowing up her fear. She began to loathe him as he sat in his fancy chair, behind his fancy desk, wearing his expensive clothes.

"You have no idea, do you?" Adams said smugly but also sounding curious. "Why on earth would you steal something if you did not know what was on it? What were you hoping to achieve?" His voice held an undertone of mockery. Tara watched as he took another sip from his glass.

"Maybe because she wanted to get back at you?"

A familiar voice rang out. Slowly from the shadows, stepped Jake Harding.

Tara's eyes widened at the sight of him, but not with joy. Her expression was one of disdain.

"You shit!" Tara growled. "I thought I'd killed you back at the apartment. I should have finished the job!"

Adams looked at her and then at Harding, who was moving towards the glasses of champagne.

"So, what connection do you have with her?" Adams asked, clearly confused.

"I was her boyfriend, I helped her to steal the stick," Jake Harding went on. "It was simple, really. She makes food delivery and grabs the stick. If she's caught, it doesn't come back on me, and if something was to happen to her afterwards—"

"—There's nothing to tie her to you. I get it." Adams's voice grew deep with disappointment.

"And why did you want the information? To blackmail me?" Adams gripped the desk with both hands to stop himself leaping forward to attack the smug Harding.

"Don't be stupid, Mr Adams, blackmail really! My sister asked me to get it. Personally, I don't even know what's on the damn thing, nor do I care." Harding smiled and looked over Adams's shoulder. There was a loud thumping sound followed by a piercing scream from Adams. Behind him stood Helen Adler holding a builder's industrial nail gun.

Harding paused before taking a sip from the champagne. "You didn't bring that with you, did you?" Harding asked her, almost afraid of the answer.

Helen looked at the gun and then back at her brother. "No, I found it at the yard, thought it would come in handy." She laughed, throwing it to the floor.

Tara had stood up, shocked at these revelations. Adams was still screaming in pain. Blood flowed freely from his hands, which Helen had nailed to the table, palms downwards.

"What are you doing, your crazy bitch?" screamed Adams, tears of pain gushing down his red face. Tara just stood and looked around at the people before her. She watched Helen as she walked past the desk and headed for the champagne.

"Don't worry, Mr Adams; I'm just finishing what we started. There's nothing for you to worry about…" Helen paused, then shot Adams an apologetic look. "Although actually, that's not true. You have a lot to worry about, you see, Adams, you're getting blamed for everything. Amber's murder, the kidnapping of dear Tara here … and, Oh yes, the SANTINI organisation wants its disk back. Apparently, you stole that as well. You naughty boy."

Adams scowled at Helen, who just smiled and blew him a kiss. He stood up suddenly in anger, but screamed in pain, momentarily forgetting about the nails embedded in his hands.

"You'll never get away with this!" he yelled at her. "The organisation will learn the truth, and they'll come for you." Adams spat his words as if they were venom.

Helen laughed out loud, clearly uninterested in his threats. "My dear Mr Adams, by the time they work out what's going on we'll be out of the country and far away." Her smug smile almost made him flare up again, but the bite of the metal in his hands soon stopped him.

Tara turned to Amber, frowning. "I…I don't get it, you…I saw your body at the apartment…you're dead?" Tara said, her words broken out of confusion. Amber looked shocked at first, almost as if she had no idea what Tara was talking about.

"Just a nobody we found in the street one day," Harding supplied the answer with a grin. "Her resemblance to Amber was almost uncanny Amber here was meant to watch you, that's why she moved in."

Helen took up the story. "It was all part of the plan, you see. I was to make sure you went through with picking up the disk and handing it over. Gaining your trust was easy. You are a sucker for a sad, hard times story. My dear brother, here was just another part of the plan, get you off balance. At first, I didn't think you would go for it, with your trust issues and whatnots, but well fuck me, if you didn't fall for him,"

Tara looked from Helen to Amber, who just shrugged and took a sip from her champagne.

"I thought you were going to kill me, that's why I hit you," Tara said, looking at Harding.

"Knocked me the hell out, more like it," Harding groaned, rubbing his head, remembering the pain from the blow from the heavy lamp.

"Yes, Tara, he was supposed to kill you," Helen continued. "It was one of the reasons we staged dear Amber's death, to make it look like a homicide robbery, then we planned to hack into medical records and swap them so that the 'Jane Doe' – the nobody whose body we left in the apartment – would come up as Amber Taylor. Unfortunately, you were quicker than he was. But all things considered, it worked out nicely." Helen chuckled callously.

"And the body at the park?" Tara asked Jake Harding. "The police said they'd found your body at the park, burnt and unrecognisable?"

"That was another unfortunate soul," Helen replied. "He had crossed the wrong person and got himself torched. Jake lent a bit of his skin and so, hey presto, we had the corpse of Jake Harding." Helen's words danced out of her mouth as if she was enjoying explaining the details of their devious scheme.

Tara felt confused and lost. She had been set up to take the fall when they hadn't succeeded in murdering her. Tara thought she had all the cards, but she soon realised she had none. They had played her like a fiddle, and she had let them.

"So, where's the disk?" Helen asked, sitting on the edge of the desk in front of Tara.

Tara's hand reached into her jacket pocket and felt the USB stick there, tucked into a corner.

"I don't suppose you're going to let me off the train if I give it to you?" she asked.

"I promise you'll leave the train at the next station," Helen said with a broad grin. Her eyes were open wide at first and then closed slightly in a snake-like manner.

Suddenly Tara knew that her enemy was lying. She had the feeling that the train would still be moving when they passed the station and threw her off.

She had the feeling that this was the end of the line.

Chapter 43

Steel moved slowly over the top of the carriage. Inside were ten large canisters, each of which had a biohazard warning sticker. Red blasting cable stretched between each barrel like a spider's web. Several large, green wooden crates sat in the middle of the room. The boxes had military markings and the words *C4* marked in thin black stencilling.

There was no way through it, and he had no intention of going underneath the train again. He didn't know where they were all heading, but he knew one thing – *Terminus* was going to have a new meaning. The sound of the wheels clattering on the tracks was rhythmic, mixed with a whooshing noise as the train hurtled along, completing the concerto of deadly speed. Steel looked up at the roof of the carriage and knew what he had to do. Slowly he began to climb. Using the small maintenance ladder on the side, he ventured up. At the top, he slowly peered over the edge of the roof to ensure that he was alone. The curved metallic surface was empty. Along the top, Steel noticed several hatches that stuck out in a zigzag form. He smiled at his good fortune, for these would be good as both foot and handholds, making his crawl across that much easier.

As he ventured over the top of the carriage, the wind blew hard into his face. Steel felt the skin being forced away from his features, practically baring his skull. He slammed himself flat against the rough hard metal surface, hoping the hatches would cancel some of the drag. His movements were slow and deliberate. Using the top rail of the ladder as a foothold, he edged forward towards the first hatch.

The wind was deafening as it howled in his ears. Steel winced in pain, feeling that crawling over this roof was like dragging himself over a badly repaired road. The non-slip paint seemed to have small rocks in it, which dug into his hands and knees as he relentlessly dragged himself along. As he reached the middle, he stopped and looked over towards the edge, which seemed miles away from his position. He rested he head on his right hand for a moment, gathering his breath. While in training for the army, he and the other new recruits were forced to leopard-crawl under barbed wire obstacles in deep mud. But compared to what he was doing now, it had been a walk in the park.

As Steel continued his slow crawl across the rail car, he was unaware of a helicopter approach. The blades of the Airbus H145M cut through the air, making a heavy thumping sound. The gloss black finish of its hull contrasted nicely with the tinted windows. On one side was the side spur: a 12.7 mm machine-gun pod. On the other side was a 20mm cannon pod. The helicopter was no ordinary bird: this was one of the organisation's 'attack' helicopters.

The wind blast and *clickety-clack* from the speeding train dulled the noise from the rotor blades. Steel lay on the roof, oblivious to the bird's approach. Suddenly the side door of the helicopter opened, and a beast of a man edged out. The machine was about twelve feet from the rooftop when Steel felt its downdraught. The sudden blast sent him sliding towards the edge. His hands grasped at nothing until he managed to grab onto one of the hatches.

The giant of a man jumped down and landed hard onto the roof, leaving a dent from his impact. Steel looked over, noticing that the giant was so big and heavy, he seemed almost unaffected by the wind. Each step the huge man took was slow and deliberate – it was almost as if the man had a pair of diving boots on. Steel fought to pull himself up and tried diving for the next hatch. As he did so, the giant brought down a mighty boot where Steel's head had been moments before. The wind carried Steel far from where he wanted to be, but he didn't care, for at least he wasn't anywhere near the giant.

As Steel watched the man's movements, he tried to formulate a plan. If he was to defeat the man, he couldn't do it by using his usual tactics. This character was solid, almost as if he were made of iron. No, he would have to find a way to tackle him and fast. The man came forward again, slow and deliberate, but moving quicker than Steel was able to because the wind was virtually pushing him down onto the roof. Steel was too far from the end of the carriage to climb down. His only option would be to go over the side and climb along the walls.

Steel started to jump again, but the giant grabbed him in mid-air. The big man pulled Steel up to eye level. The man snorted, like a bull in an arena. Steel felt the massive hand gripped around his throat begin to tighten. Steel kicked out as he felt his air was being cut off. The giant smiled as he watched Steel squirm in his death throes. Steel couldn't figure out how this giant was staying upright against the wind. Sure he was big and heavy, but it didn't explain how he wasn't blown off the roof despite his size.

As Steel kicked, he felt his foot impact against something had, not the man's midsection. It was more metallic. Steel kicked again, this time harder. The man suddenly began to slip and lost grip in his left leg. There was a loud thud as they both hit the metal surface. The man gave a panicked look as he pushed some buttons on a small control pad on his belt. A sudden look of terror filled the man's face as both his feet locked down onto the metal surface, followed by a puff of smoke from the pad. Steel's would-be killer looked up from the pad and just started forward. Steel followed the man's gaze just in time to see the low tunnel ahead.

Steel immediately hunkered down and spread himself low and waited until he saw daylight. The tunnel lasted only a few minutes before the bright sunshine replaced the darkness. Steel looked over to see a pair of massive black boots and a blood trail leading from them. Pieces of shinbone protruded from the footwear. The small control unit was waving around, tethered by a six-foot cable.

Steel rolled over to the boots and grabbed the control unit. Using the control buttons, he pushed one of the boots forward and then tried the other. Using them as an anchor, Steel pulled himself over the edge of the roof and slipped down onto the small gantry over the couplings. Steel took a moment to get his breath back, Smiling to himself.

He had one carriage to go, and then he would arrive at the one that held Tara. The carriage behind him had no windows, only a heavy door like the other one. Steel knelt and got to work on the couplings, hoping to split the train from one of its carriages, as he'd done before. As he was working to free up the connection mechanism, the door opened behind him, and a man's voice bellowed out. The man was looking back into the carriage, yelling obscenities to the other guards who he'd been playing cards with inside. The man was smaller than Steel but stocky, his red hair almost hidden by a black skullcap. The man walked forward, unzipping the flies on his trousers as he went. Steel turned slightly just in time to see him.

"Thanks for the offer, but sorry, I'm not that sort of passenger I am afraid," Steel joked with a shrug. The man spun round in shock and went for his 9mm Glock, but he wasn't quick enough. Steel grabbed the man and spun him around and shoved him off the train. The man's pistol clattered onto the deck in front of Steel. Four of the other men inside the carriage had watched Steel throw their comrade from the train, and they raced forward. Steel picked up the abandoned Glock and put a round into each men's right kneecap.

Screams and blood filled the carriage. Gunfire ripped at the doorway, forcing Steel to the side. Bright yellow ricochet sparks lit up the doorway, as the men's Heckler and Koch UMP's opened. The tinkling of spent .45 ACP ammo chimed out as the spent cases hit the hard metal floor. Steel slid out the clip from the magazine housing of the pistol grip. The small holes at the back showed that he had half a magazine left. Steel cursed he had been forced to ditch the assault rifle because of his ride under the train. He waited for his attackers to stop firing, knowing that they wouldn't waste ammo on something they couldn't see. Taking out his cell phone, he took a quick photograph of the carriage's interior.

The photo showed six men, each of them packing a .45 machine pistol. They were spaced out at different firing positions, making returning fire difficult but not impossible. Steel checked the photograph for anything else that may help him, but he had taken it too quickly, the background was blurred. Quickly he reset the camera and took another. This time it showed three of the men approaching slowly.

Steel quickly knelt and instinctively punched at the door. There was a sudden groan of pain as Steel realised that he had unwittingly rearranged a man's groin. In the blink of an eye, Steel had the man held in front of him as a shield. The man jolted as his comrades opened fire at Steel. The guard twitched as bullets impacted against the human shield's body armour, absorbing most of the impact. Steel had also managed to grab the man's weapon that hung by his side and was firing back, firstly at the two who had followed. The men yelled out as they were hit in the back before they could dive for cover. One of the men flew forward, hitting his head on a handrail. The other was pushed in front of another man's gunfire, the bullets ripping into him like a knife through butter. Steel fired at a fire extinguisher that hung on the left-hand wall. A sudden blast of a white cloud of foam covered the remaining men. Grunts of pain followed coughing as Steel took them out by hand. Swift kicks to the knees brought them down, followed by uppercuts and blows from the butt of his weapon. Steel took another Glock pistol and tucked it away and found two magazines for the UMP from pouches on a fallen man's belt. *No point turning up empty*, he thought to himself.

Moving out of the carriage, Steel used the .45 to blow apart the cup links. A full magazine of thirty rounds ripped into the metal until it broke free. Jumping over, Steel looked back as the carriages began to slow down. He slid out the gun's empty magazine and replaced it with a fresh one, tucking the half-full Glock into his belt at the small of his back. Taking off his trench coat, he rammed it into one of the storage bins for safekeeping. He took a deep breath and waited for a moment, pausing so that his heartbeat could settle. This next part of the operation wasn't going to be about blazing guns: what he had to deal with next was ultimately a hostage situation.

He was going in blind. Not just because he had no idea how many people were in the room, but because he had no idea who was friend and who was foe.

* * *

Still pinned by industrial nails to his desk in the train carriage, Adams groaned in pain, and the sweat poured down his pale face. Helen smiled as she walked past Tara, her long fingers glide over Tara's shoulders. Tara shuddered but didn't dare move or push her away.

"So, tell me, Tara," Helen spoke as if to taunt her. "When did you learn that Mr Adams here was your father?" Adams looked over at Tara with wide eyes. He tried for a smile, but the pain was too much.

"My mom kept a picture of him in her dresser. He was just some man in a photo until I saw him in the paper a couple of years ago." Anger filled Tara's words. Her hatred for the man who had left her alone with a brutal, abusive mother. Anger at the man who had everything while she had nothing. The man who had tossed his family aside.

"So, you wanted to make him pay, make him suffer? I can understand that," Helen said as she refilled her glass and then took a sip from it.

"Is that why you used me to get the disk for you, or rather get *him* for you?" Tara's words were cold and angry as she turned towards Harding.

"The plan was simple, really. The file goes missing, and I recover it along with the opposition's disk. Adams is disgraced, and I get his job." Helen grinned wildly at the thought of it all.

"I guess I messed that up for you, didn't I? Sorry about that," Tara sneered. She smiled at the thought of causing so much trouble. After all, they had tried to kill her.

"Actually, plan B is much more ... let's say *delicious*." Helen's smiled.

Tara felt a sudden shiver down her spine as she looked around at the people in the room. Something wasn't right. Helen could have killed Adams, but she was keeping him alive for some reason. Tara looked back at Amber, who was still sitting on the couch. She was quiet and still, but still alive.

"What's plan B?" Tara asked.

"Where's the disk?" Helen parried with her question.

"It's somewhere safe," Tara lied, hoping Helen would buy it.

"So, you didn't bring it?" Helen asked.

"Do you think I am stupid? Yeah, right. Someone tells you: 'come alone and bring the disk'. I ask you! Who would fall for that?"

Helen smiled at Tara's grit.

"It's a pity we have to kill you. I could certainly have used someone like you in my team." Helen sighed and pulled out a nickel-plated Walther PPKS.

"Helen, it's almost time," Harding said, walking up behind Helen, his hand resting affectionately on her shoulder. Helen closed her eyes and raised the shoulder, pulling his hand towards her face.

Tara wanted to be sick at the unnatural display: this was *much, much* more than brotherly love.

"So why keep us alive?" Tara asked, trying to take Helen's mind off her schedule.

"Let's just say that when they find your bodies, they need to be intact. A good ME can tell if you were alive or dead at the time of the crash, and a bullet to the head would sort of put a hole in that plan, wouldn't you say? I need people to think you have set off the bomb and not just become victims of it." Helen smiled and took another sip from the flute of champagne.

"What bomb?" Adams yelled in a rage of pain and anger.

"Why, the bomb that you two are going to deliver to Washington of course. Why else do you think you're in an armoured carriage? Live or die; you'll be classed as guilty. Oh, and yes, the District Attorney is on our payroll." Helen was so exhilarated that she almost sang the words. Tara's head began to spin wildly at the very idea of what was being planned.

"OK, so let's get down to it," Helen went on, all business now. "Where is the disk? And don't say you didn't bring it. Just remember it's easier to search a dead body than a live one." Helen raised the gun and pointed it towards Tara's head.

"You can't kill me. You need me alive, remember?" Tara's voice rang with panic.

"Don't worry, sweetie, I am not going to kill you now. Maybe I'll shoot you in the stomach. After all, some type of wounds would be expected when a bomb goes off. But don't worry, we know how to cover things up." Helen smiled wickedly.

Tara reached into her pocket and pulled out a data stick. Helen's eyes widened. She reached out to grab it.

Suddenly there was a bright flash of light as the door was opened, and it blinded everyone inside the room. It was quickly followed by two shots, each of which hit the guards at the back of the room.

The guards at the door raced forward, and their pistols held ready. The bright sunlight behind Steel blinded the men for a second, making them shield their eyes with pain. Steel fired again, putting a bullet into each of the guards' knees. They hit the solid flooring with screams of pain. Then there were two more shots, one of which hit Harding in the right shoulder, while the second hit the ground in front of Helen. The bullet ricocheted off and smashed the bottle of champagne. Glass and sparkling wine ran across the floor near the desk. Helen quickly grabbed Tara and pulled her in front as a shield. Steel had Helen dead in his gun's sights.

"Drop the gun, Helen," Steel ordered. "It's over." His gaze switched from her to Harding.

"No, Mr Steel, *you* drop it!" said a voice from behind him.

Amber had leapt behind the door as he came in, and she had been on his blind side. Now she had stolen the Glock he had placed in the small of his back and was pointing it at the back of his head.

"Oops!" Helen laughed, pushing Tara to one side and walking up to Steel. He dropped the gun and raised his hands just above his head.

"Well, this will look good!" Helen announced cheerfully. "The missing cop is also found. I can't wait to see the headlines on this one." Helen howled with laughter as she picked up the data stick from the floor.

"At last, we've got it!" Helen said exultantly, raising the tiny item as if it was a mighty trophy.

"Uhm … Not quite," Amber said, now pointing the Glock at Helen.

Helen's smile melted into an expression of confusion, then to anger as she realised, she'd been played all along. Steel just smiled and shook his head.

"Take the data stick from her, Mr Steel, if you'd be so kind," Amber ordered.

John Steel walked forward and stretched out an open hand. Helen slapped the stick into his palm, her face distorted with anger and disgust. Steel turned and walked towards Amber, the smile still on his face.

"I would love to know what you are smiling about, Mr Steel?" Amber asked him curiously. "After all, I have the disk, and you have nothing."

Steel handed over the stick, noticing that her hands were clammy and warm. He could see in her eyes that she was nervous, her act of being hard and ruthless betrayed by her large trusting blue eyes.

"Turn around, Mr Steel," she ordered. Amber knew that he had seen something. Steel turned around; his hands still raised in the air.

"I am afraid, my dear Amber, that unless you are jumping off the train soon, you will die with the rest of us," Helen said, laughing nervously as she looked at the wall clock.

"What do you mean?" Amber asked, clearly confused.

Helen put her hands down and sat on the edge of the desk, all the while gazing at the other woman with mild amusement.

"She has put a bomb on the train next to some fuel containers," Steel explained. "I figure that it's not fuel in those containers but combustible aerosol or something else that's quite nasty." He looked directly at Helen, who just shrugged and smiled as if she was perfectly relaxed.

"Once we reach the Capitol, it will go off," Helen went on. "It'll be a large explosion, and the fallout should cover most of the area. Once that is done, our 'gang' friends – several lawless groups of people whom we've supplied with plenty of arms – will begin to cause havoc with their new weapons. New York will fall, L. A. will burn, and five other major cities will erupt in chaos." Helen laughed, still confident that she'd be able to get off the train before it reached its destination.

"But why?" Amber asked, almost numb with horror. "Why would your organisation want to do such a thing?"

Steel slowly put his hands down and moved to the side of the room, where the champagne had been. He picked up a full bottle and checked the label before opening it.

"Because they are probably getting a lot of money from a foreign government to do so," Steel told her, pouring himself a glass and taking a sip.

"Not quite, Mr Steel," Helen told him calmly. "Actually, the money is going to be coming from our government. Do you realise the vast amount of money that will have to be spent on contractors, improvements to the police forces and the military? This will see all our armed services boosted no end, equipped with better equipment to tackle possible future problems. What's more, our people will make sure that terrorists will be blamed for the bombs, and then of course plans for retaliation will begin. Do you realise the money involved when there are wars?" Helen's heartfelt words sounded as though they were part of a speech she was delivering to Congress or some other important world forum.

"And of course, your organisation will be right there ready and willing, with all the necessary aid and equipment to rescue the country from its crisis." Steel's words were delivered sarcastically, but all he was saying was nevertheless obviously true.

"How perspicacious you are, Mr Steel," Helen commented, smiling as she pushed herself off the desk and strolled over to a large map of the United States that hung on the right-hand wall.

"All this will soon be ours," she explained, waving her hand across the map. "We don't want to be in the hot seat, that's not where the power is. The power really comes from the biggest companies who have the biggest wealth. The companies that can make or break a nation. Let some well-meaning idiot be president, that's just some public relations guy sitting in a big house who makes speeches to pacify the masses. We hide in the shadows and control everything. We will be unstoppable. We will be—"

There was a massive explosion that pushed the remaining carriages off the rails. The armoured carriage bounced from one set of wheels to the other, almost as if it was trying to right itself. Then there was another explosion, and this was larger, more powerful. The blast heaved the armoured carriage right from the track and set it tumbling down a grassed embankment.

Inside the carriage, Steel tried to find a handhold as furniture smashed against the sides of the interior. Broken glass and wood flew past them. The heavy desk splinted into deadly pieces of debris. The others screamed as they were tossed about like shoes in a tumble drier, somehow missing the flying broken furniture. Adams screamed as he was ripped from the desktop that he'd been nailed to, his hands virtually torn to pieces. The carriage rocked as it finally came to rest in a stream below them. The box of steel lay on its side and water was beginning to seep in from broken seams. Its interior was partially bathed in darkness, broken only by tiny pockets of cool orange illumination, some of which came from small ambient ceiling lights that were now under the water.

Helen pulled herself up. Small cuts on her face and arms were her only visible wounds, but a sudden wince of pain warned her of possible broken ribs. She looked around and saw Amber slumped over one of the armchairs. Was she unconscious or dead, Helen wondered? Not that she cared, for her, Amber should have died in the crash. Only the data stick in Amber's pocket was of importance. Helen searched wildly to try and find the small device.

When she couldn't locate it, she splashed about in the ankle-high water that was rising all the time. She turned suddenly at the sound of someone's slow approach. It was Harding, who was also visibly wounded. His hand pressed tightly to his left side, and blood oozed through his fingers. She looked at him for a moment, tears in her eyes, upset that her beloved brother was hurt. But then her expression changed as some dark and selfish driving force came over her. She turned back to her search and left her brother as he stumbled forward, using whatever he could find as support.

"Helen, help me… I need a doctor," her brother gasped.

"Shut the fuck up whining and help me look for that data stick. It's in here somewhere," Helen said, her efforts focused solely on the location of the item she was so desperate to find.

"Sis, *please*, I need help! I ... I think I am dying."

There was a series loud explosion, which caused Helen's ears to ring. She looked over to see that her brother been ripped from the ground into the air. As he hit the water, the dim orange light turned the colour of red wine.

Helen looked over to the side and saw Adams, somehow managing to hold the Glock in his bloodied fingers. His face was twisted by pain, anger and satisfaction. He turned the weapon on Helen. Her face went pale, and her body froze with terror as she stared down the pistol's barrel.

Adams moved around slowly, high on adrenaline which seemed to anaesthetise his agony to some extent so that he appeared oddly unhurt by the tumble. Of course, blood was pouring from the mangled mess that his hands had become, but he didn't care. The adrenaline was doing its job, and his pure unadulterated hatred of the woman in front of him was giving him the strength to wield the weapon.

"Move over there!" he ordered, pointing his gun at the door they had all come through. The water was now up to their mid ankles and pouring in slowly.

Helen raised her hands and looked up at him, bewildered. "But what about the data stick?"

"Don't worry. My salvage crew will find it. In case you haven't noticed, no water is running out of here, it's only coming in. Now ... Move!" He spat the words between his bared teeth.

Helen obeyed, turning and heading towards the door, and clambering over the furnishings that now lay smashed and piled up. The large cabinet lay in a hundred pieces, and the two guards who had been stationed at the door now lay impaled on debris.

As Adams and Helen neared the door, they stopped. Light poured through the open hatch. They looked around in the dimly lit room.

"Where the hell is Tara?" demanded Adams.

"Screw that, where the fuck is Steel?" Helen exclaimed.

They both froze for a moment. Fear ran through their bodies like a rush of ice-cold mercury. Adams pushed the weapon into Helen's side, ushering her out first. She shot him a look of panic, but Adams just grinned and pointed.

"Get your treacherous ass out that door," he growled, almost hoping Steel had a 'shoot the first person he saw' policy.

Helen struggled out of the door, while Adams waited as she walked out into the daylight. He almost seemed disappointed at the silence. Slowly and painfully he then made his way out, pulling on the tilted doorframe to haul himself up.

The air outside was heavy with the stench of hot metal. The warm sun seemed so much brighter after spending so long in the dimly lit carriage. He closed his eyes for a moment, then gradually opened them, allowing them to adjust to the bright light.

Slowly, he clambered up the embankment. His body ached in pain from the tumble. Adams looked around at the burning carriages that lay on the side on the grass. Thick black smoke billowed from the twisted metal. Smouldering pieces of metal and shattered trees littered the landscape. Thick plumes of blackened smoke could be seen around a hundred feet from him as another carriage lay halfway across the tracks. The side panels were gone, blown away, leaving a burning shell.

The train's engine lay down the other side of the embankment. On its side, the wheels were still turning, spitting up grass and dirt as it continued to slide downwards. Adams looked both ways along the tracks. Helen lay on her back, holding her ribs on her right side, a look of agony on her face. However, Steel and Tara were gone. Adams walked over to Helen and stood over her, his weapon still pointed at her.

"You're finished Miss Adler," Adams told her. "When the council hear of this, they will hunt you down." He took great pleasure in watching her face twist with a mixture of emotions. Adams turned when he heard the subtle thump of a helicopter's rotor blades in the distance.

"It appears my ride is here," he said, smiling and looking away for a second.

"You mean, my ride," Helen said, picking up a razor-sharp shard of metal and embedding it into Adams's stomach.

His eyes bulged, and he bent forward and spat thick dark-red blood. Helen stood up and laughed as the black war bird approached.

"So long, old man, don't worry, I'll take care of your company and your seat on the board of directors!" She laughed out loud until the broken ribs made it too painful. Helen left Adams to bleed out as she limped her way to the helicopter as it touched down. As the wheels hit the deck, the side gunner lept out and helped Helen aboard.

"Any more survivors ma;am?" he yelled. Helen shook her head. As she took her seat, Helen smiled. She had made it. They hadn't. She could tell whatever tale she wanted, and there was no one left to dispute the facts. The downwash pushed the smoke all over the area, creating the perfect smoke-screen for her. Just as they began to climb, the machine rocked suddenly.

"What was that?" Helen asked, looking out into the black fog.

"Could have been a sudden crosswind," the pilot told her. "Nothing to worry about."

As they climbed out of the smoke, Helen looked down at the burning debris from the crash. For her, the hellish scenario was a thing of beauty: a wonderful medley of nature and chaos. Helen reached into her pocket and pulled out a data stick. The small aluminium case just looked like nothing at all. However, she knew that this tiny object would change everything.

She smiled wickedly.

She had done it.

She had won.

Chapter 44

"Bitch!" Adams said, watching the black warbird fly away, but he was smiling. From the carriage they had just come from, Tara was helping Amber out of the doorway. The two women walked over to where Adams lay, watching the helicopter disappear into the distance.

"Father!" Tara screamed, running over to Adams, leaving Amber to fall onto the grass from exhaustion. Tara hugged Adams, and he hugged her back. Amber smiled at the touching scene. She stood up and walked slowly towards them.

"Are you OK, Mr A?" Amber asked. He nodded as best he could, with Tara's shoulder in the way. Tara quickly released him after feeling a sharp object pressed against her. She looked down in horror at the sight of the metal shard sticking out from his stomach.

"You're hurt!" Tara protested.

"Only a little, and it's all thanks to your friend Mr Steel," Adams said, successfully managing to pull the vicious-looking shard of metal from his mid-section.

Tara looked confused for a moment. Adams took his shirt off to reveal a thin vest of black weaved material.

"John Steel told me that I might need some security." Adams laughed at his narrow escape while Tara looked confused. "a present from Mr Steel, some kind of bulletproof weave," Adams admitted, punching his midsection in some kind of a display.

"But you're the bad guy! You work for the organisation, why would he – ?"

" – for you, my dear, for you. He figured I was been set up. Yes, he could have let me die, probably would have enjoyed doing it as well. But he said you'd suffered enough. He made me promise to look after you." Adams's voice and eyes boiled over with emotion.

"But you tried to kill her! You ordered her to be captured?" Amber said as she walked towards them. She was still confused by the events.

"The thing is, Amber, everything changed when I found out she was my child," Adams explained. "I may be a bad man, but I am not a monster." Adams stroked Tara's face with a bloodied hand, tears streaming from his eyes.

Amber nodded as she too shed a tear.

"And you, Miss Taylor, a government agent, and quite the role you played. You had me fooled, who were you looking into, the organisation or me?" Adams said with a courteous smile.

"You at first, we didn't know about the organisation or SANTINI until later, Mr Steel filled me in on the details later," Amber admitted.

"So this whole thing on the train…?" he asked.

"Steel's plan, he knew there was someone playing both sides, he just had to be sure his hunch was correct, as it was, he was right," Amber shrugged.

"What about Helen, she got away, and she has the data stick," Tara yelled, looking at the sky where the helicopter was disappearing. From a distance came another thumping of rotors. Another helicopter was on approach. The three people covered their eyes as a black Osprey landed. Its rear ramp began to lower, and from the darkness of the interior, someone stood there ready. There was a whoosh of the downdraft, and then the military craft touched down. As they watched, the figure began to approach the tailgate. There were gasps of surprise from the survivours, less for one. Amber Taylor. Shew stood up and waited for the man to come closer.

"Hello, Father, it's been a long time," Amber said to the man with a dull smile, brushing the dust from her clothes.

* * *

The black warbird flew to Adams's home in the country, a large estate in Rye. Rye was a quiet place on the East Coast that is an offcut from Harrison, New York. The place is full of tall trees and lawns that are so green you would think they had been painted. It was a sliver of land that was chock full of large estates and the stench of money.

The house was modest compared to some of them in Rye. It had beige coloured wooden walls and a stone-and-mortar chimney stack. A large outdoor pool fitted in well with the lush garden. Flowerbeds burst with colour, and tall oaks lined the borders. It was a modest place in which Adams had spent a lot of time alone since the death of his wife some years ago.

Now a new owner strutted into the house; her head held high as she paraded about, heading for Adams's study. She swung the door open and walked towards a large oak desk that sat next to a set of large windows: windows from which Adams had spent many a morning watching the sunrise, turning his garden into a blazing orange. Helen sat in the high-backed red-leather chair and rocked, taking in the splendour of the room. The walls were half wood and half white-plastered brick. Heavy oak bookshelves held leather-bound encyclopaedias, and volumes from literary giants, such as Dickens and Shakespeare. The heavy desk was clear apart from a computer monitor and keyboard. A brass captain's lamp sat at a corner, under which there was a picture of Adams's late wife.

A portrait in oils hung over the fireplace. It was of an older man, who was perhaps in his mid-seventies. But he had a strength about him: broad shoulders and high cheekbones.

Helen figured it was probably Adams's father or perhaps his grandfather. It didn't matter, for soon it would be put on a large bonfire and burnt, along with the rest of his stuff. She looked around until she spied a wooden globe of substantial size. She smiled and stood up and crossed the thick red shag pile carpet.

Finding the catch on the globe, she slid the top half down, to reveal the hidden drinks cabinet. She smiled and picked out a bottle of Jack Daniels and poured herself a glass.

Helen returned to the chair and sat, wincing with pain from her side. She raised the glass to the portrait and drank. The booze was a good painkiller, but she knew she needed to go to a hospital. She sat for a moment, her eyes closed, feeling the adrenaline fade, but the alcohol was beginning to kick in. She put down the glass and reached into her pocket, feeling inside until she found the data stick. She took it out and held it up at eye level.

It's amazing, how such a small thing could cause so much trouble, she thought as she smiled and placed it down on the desk. She was tired, weary from the day's excitement. But she had work to do.

Helen tapped the space bar on the keyboard, and the monitor activated immediately. She knew Adams's password was *Victoria*, after his dead wife. She typed with her left hand, to avoid using her right arm, which was giving her pain.

She clicked on an icon of a horse's head. The screen quickly went onto another, presumably secret, site, which also required a password. Helen thought for a moment and then typed in *Faith and Honour*. She knew that this was something Adams strongly believed in. She smiled as the page opened and revealed an online conference mode. Eleven people, men and women, sat around a table, and the empty place there was reserved for Mr Adams. All the other conference members looked shocked to see Helen's face appear at the conference mode.

"Ladies and gentlemen of the board, I have grave news," she started to say. She bowed her head as if to show sorrow. "I have uncovered a plan by Mr Adams to give a copy of our accounts to our enemies. He also constructed a plan to set off an explosive device in Washington. An ex-soldier, Mr John Steel, currently working for the NYPD, was also an accomplice to the plan." She listened to the murmur of voices as the board began to chatter until there was a loud hammering on the long table.

"How do you know all this?" asked the chairman, who was a thin man in his early sixties.

"They kidnapped me and forced me onto the train," Helen replied. "Fortunately, there was an accident. The train was derailed, that's how I managed to escape." Helen made her voice tremble, injecting a false tone of fear.

"Miss Adler, how do we know you are speaking the truth?" came the chairman's voice. "What proof do you have?"

Helen lifted the data stick with a trembling hand. She watched the nodding heads of the board, their faces full of sympathy for her. She felt warm inside, *wanted*. She felt the need to smile, but she knew she couldn't, not yet.

"How do we know you have, what you say you have?" asked the chairman, his voice deep and serious.

"I shall prove it to you," she announced confidently, and then placed the stick into an empty USB port on her computer.

The file started to download. But suddenly the screen started to flash red, and a virus warning came up. Screens containing images of people's bank statements began to appear, and words saying *Data deletion* came on screen too, along with images of files were deleted and, huge amounts of money were transferred into another account.

The members of the board at the conference began to panic, as did Helen. She ripped out the data stick and hit every key on the keyboard, trying to terminate the programme.

Suddenly on the monitor, she saw a man walk up to the chairman and give him a piece of paper.

"What have you done, Miss Adler?" yelled the chairman. "Do you dare to steal from us?"

Helen shook her head frantically, confused and scared by what had happened.

"No!" she screamed desperately. "No, it wasn't me, I swear!" She was still tapping the keys, hoping her actions might bring everything back as before.

"Miss Adler," the chairman's voice growled. "The money had been transferred into an account – your account!"

Helen stood up suddenly, knocking the chair to the ground, her face ashen.

"Oh, and by the way, we know what happened on the train," the chairman continued. "Our late friend Mr Adams was more cautious than you thought. He had an emergency camera installed for such – unexpectant eventualities. We saw and heard everything."

Two men appeared in the doorway to the room where she stood trembling, with 9mm silenced Berretta 9's in their hands.

"We await your arrival, Miss Adler," the chairman concluded.

Helen began to tremble, and sweat began to pour from her forehead. She wanted to run, but she knew that would be futile.

As she to stepped out of the front door, she stopped suddenly. Adams stood there at the rear of a large black Mercedes. As she approached, he opened the door for her and smiled.

They gave each other a silent venomous glare as they passed one another. One of the armed men forced her into the back of the car and then followed her in. Adams closed the door, his grinning face reflected in the car's tinted glass windows.

There was a spit of gravel as the car accelerated away. As Adams watched the car disappear, Tara joined him, holding onto his arm for comfort. Amber and Steel walked up slowly and watched with them.

"Tell me, Mr Steel, how did you know it was her?" Adams asked.

"There was a picture of a staff party at the diner, and something bugged me about it," Steel explained. "Harding was in the background, almost as if he was trying not to be part of the group. Then I saw a picture of Helen at a fundraiser you'd had – for a children's care unit or something I believe."

Adams thought for a moment before nodding as the memory of that day came back to him.

"She was part of the group who helped arrange it all, or so the internet said," John Steel continued. "Anyway, that's when I saw the resemblance: how alike Helen and Harding looked. I mean, they seemed to be far too similar for some random coincidence: these were almost identical twins. I did some digging on Helen and Harding and found that they had been separated as kids and sent to different homes when their parents died. They must have met up years later and re-bonded. She must have seen you, and wanted revenge. After all, it was your family that was to blame for their family's death."

Adams looked confused for a moment, not knowing how he was at fault.

"Their father worked for your father, both employed at a coal mine," Steel continued. "One day there was a cave-in, and most of the miners were killed, including their father. When their mother asked for help, your family brushed them off, denying any responsibility for the aftermath of the accident, saying they were not liable or something. Because she was desperate for money, the mother tried to find work at a factory owned by your family. Two years later the factory burnt down because of faulty wiring. Their mother, along with twelve others, burnt to death in the fire. Having no other family, the kids were taken into care. That's when the siblings were separated."

Adams's gaze fell to where the vehicle had disappeared. A look of shame crossed his face.

"As I looked harder at the photograph, I noticed something about you two," Steel said, smiling at Adams and Tara. "It wasn't something as obvious as Helen and Harding's facial similarity, but you two were alike too. The eyes, the mouth, just little things like that. I also checked on you, Mr Adams. You went to Princeton with Tara's mother. In fact, you dated her for a while. I guess you had a great time, and emotions ran wild?"

Adams nodded with a sense of sadness as he thought back on his previous life, the life he left behind.

"It was a love that wasn't meant to be," he told Steel. "Our parents never approved of it, especially my father. One night after a party we ended up making love at a small hotel. It was the best night of my life. We made plans to run away together, elope to another state. But that evening when I returned home, I was told I was going to be studying business with one of my uncles in London for a year. I met her the next day to explain. She said she understood and that she would wait for me. But when I returned, your mother had gone. Years later I tracked her down, hoping we could start anew, but unfortunately, she was married to the man you knew as your father. It wasn't until yesterday that I found out about you from Mr Steel." Adams hugged Tara, holding her tight, and she hugged him in return.

"But everything else?" Adams asked Steel. "How on earth did you know about it?"

"I bugged your office and Helen's. Luckily she does a lot of business at work." Steel shrugged. "It loses the magic when you know how's it's done, doesn't it?" Steel joked.

"Oh, don't put yourself down, Jonny, I thought you did splendidly," came a voice from behind them. The four of them turned to see Mr Williams standing in the doorway.

"You know this will take some explaining with my superiors. How our enemy saved my life?" Adams joked.

Williams shrugged and smiled. Next to him was a young man holding a silver tray of champagne glasses.

"Oh, I wouldn't worry about that," Williams assured him. "They already know. We struck a truce while things got sorted out. She was doing the same to us. She was the one who hired the taxi driver and poisoned you, John. She put a bottle of poisoned water on the back seat. Apparently, it was laced quite nicely. The driver had no idea, of course, the poor man." Williams handed out the glasses.

"What about Brooke? Is she still alive?" Steel asked.

Williams shot him a dirty look before smiling. "Please, John, don't remind me, that hurts." He put a gloved hand over his heart. "I was asked to keep her safe, and I did so. The trouble is I don't think she wants to leave." His face crumpled with annoyance. "She's so bossy, and eat … my God, for such a slim woman, she can eat so much!"

Everyone laughed as they headed inside the mansion. Steel stood outside with Amber, waiting for the others to close the door.

"So, what now?" Steel asked.

"Go back to the agency, I guess. My mission is over," Amber said, but she knew exactly what Steel meant.

"You hurt Tony; do you realise that?" Steel said, looking down at Amber.

She nodded, a tear trickling down her face.

Steel smiled softly. He could see she had feelings for him also.

"Well," he said to her, "it may take some explaining, but I am sure he'll understand."

"Do you think so?"

"Are you kidding? Tony is half Irish and half Italian. One half will try and kill you and the other half will try and romance you to death!"

They both laughed. Amber wiped away her tears and nodded.

"I will have a word with him, see if I can get you pair back together," John Steel promised.

Amber smiled and nodded in approval. "I'd like that. Thank you, Mr Steel. Thank you for everything." Amber kissed him on the cheek.

Steel smiled and handed over the champagne glass and breathed in a lungful of air. "I'll see you around, Amber. Keep out of trouble if you can," Steel said as he turned and started walking down the gravel driveway. The door behind her opened, and Williams walked out to join Amber, champagne bottle in one hand and a full glass in the other.

"A remarkable man, that," Williams said, downing the champagne in one. "Pity he's on the wrong side."

"Oh, really? And which side is that?"

"The most dangerous side. His own," Williams said, refilling his glass. "Come on, drink up," he said.

"Yes, Daddy," she said, smiling and watching the man in black disappear into the distance.

* * *

Streaks of lightning illuminated the night sky. Black billowing clouds approached across the water, bringing with them the storm. It was around seven in the evening by the time McCall had got back to her apartment. CSU was still at the shipping yard, and the derailed train.

It had been a hell of a day. Probably too much for her head to take in all at once. Tooms and Tony had been at the precinct for an hour or so. They had taken the train wreck. But as far as CSU was concerned, it was an accident. The explosion had pretty much evaporated any evidence of foul play, or at least that's what they had been told to say. Sure, it was a cover-up. The news of a faction war in New York would have caused all sorts of panic if it had been made public.

McCall sat on her couch with a glass full of red wine and just sat and stared into nothingness. Steel was alive. She didn't know whether to be angry or happy. Both emotions were erupting through her at the same time. She leant over and grabbed the remote for her stereo and turned it on. The silence was starting to become annoying; She needed something loud – she needed music.

The CD began, a mixed artist album was full of eighties music. McCall stood up and headed for the bathroom. She had good music, great wine and all she needed now was a deep bath, candles and lots of bubbles. She stripped down to her underwear and ran the water into the cast-iron tub, then poured in a mixed concoction of several different bath oils. McCall danced around with the wine glass in her hand while she waited for the water to foam up.

There was a rumble outside, and then the rain started. Suddenly one of her large windows blew open, and the lights went off as a clap of lightning brought everything into brightness for a second before the darkness became almost complete. Several candles around the room gave enough light to move by as she rushed to close the window.

McCall stood half soaked, watching the flash of lightning reflected off the buildings. It was a terrifying yet beautiful sight. She turned and headed back to her bath. Since the power had gone down, the sound of running water was the only noise. Ten large candles burnt brightly in the bathroom, creating shadows and an eerie reflection in the bathroom mirror, sliding a toe into the water she tested it for temperature. It was the right depth and warmth.

She slid out of her damp underwear and into the steaming bath. Her eyes rolled back as she felt the soothing water caress her body. All her troubles began to slip to the back of her mind. The scent of the bath oils and the warmth of the water was making her relax. She tilted her head back onto the bath pillow and closed her eyes.

McCall didn't know how long she had been in the bath, nor did she care. All she knew was that the water was now cold, and her wine was getting warm. Bubbles clung to her body like a strange bodysuit. She towelled off and headed for the living room. The place was still in darkness, which she found strange, as everything outside her window had power. She stared out of the window for a while. The storm had left lakes of water in the street, and several loose items lay there. She smiled at the beauty of the city at night. She sighed and turned. She let out a little yelp of fright as Steel stood behind her. She slammed a fist into his chest.

"Steel, you scared the shit out of me!" she said, trying not to seem glad to see him.

"Sorry. I did knock, but you were asleep in the bath." He smiled.

McCall suddenly blushed.

"I was not. And why were you watching me bathe? And how much of me did you see?" she asked, pulling the towel tighter. Steel stood closer and looked down on her. She could feel his warm breath on her wet skin, and it sent a shiver down her spine. As he moved closer, she could feel her knees begin to buckle with anticipation. He smiled gently. No words were spoken at first. She just wanted him to grab her and kiss her. Suddenly all those dreams she had ever had of this moment were coming true. She closed her eyes and angled her mouth upwards towards his. The feeling of electricity and tension was thick enough to cut with a knife. Suddenly there was a loud banging on her front door. McCall rushed over to the door to see who was there.

"Who is it?" she yelled in annoyance behind the closed door, not wanting to open it because she was still half-naked.

"Miss McCall? Hi, ma'am, it's the building superintendent. Just to let you know that the power will be back on in a minute," the man yelled through the closed door.

"Great, thanks." She tried to stop the anger in her voice because of the timing of the interruption.

She looked over to where Steel had been standing a moment before, only to find the window open and a blue rose on the table next to the wine glass.

McCall sat and picked up the rose and brought it to her nose. The flower's perfume was rich. She looked out into the night and promised:

One day, Mr Steel. One day...

Maltese Steel
John Steel Book 5

*This book is dedicated to all the fantastic people of Malta.
To all the people around the world who work to keep us safe and to all my family and friends who have supported me.
Thank you.*

Acknowledgments

I would like to thank

The Grand Hotel Excelsior in Valletta, Malta. For allowing me to include their fantastic hotel in this book.

To the US Embassy Malta.

And a special thank you to my good friend Malcolm Ellul and his family for all their advice.

And to Miika and the Next Chapter team for all their hard work.

To my editor Gail Williams.

Chapter 1

A cold March wind brushed Lucy Foster's cheeks as she plummeted from the top of the Azure Window. Once a rocky arch that stretched out from the Maltese Island of Gozo. Now just rock face with the broken pieces of the massive arch buried under the waves.

It was said to be one of the wonders of the world, but after a tremendous storm wreaked havoc on both islands – it was no more. The craggy archway lost to the deep.

The midnight sky was black and a freezing chill hung in the air. But it was nothing compared with the icy waters of the ocean below. Lucy would not feel it. The velocity of her fall masked the smell of the sea air. Around her, the sounds of the wind were dulled by the crashing of the waves.

However, Lucy did not feel or hear anything.

There was no light from the moon for the waves to reflect, which would have made the fall from the cliff seem endless – as if it was a nightmare.

Lucy's body slammed against the ocean as if the water were made from concrete. Her neck snapped back, and her ribs shattered. Her right arm was dislocated and pulled towards her back.

She had felt nothing.

The waves tossed her fragile body up like a piece of driftwood. The wind howled, and the waves roared. Towering waves crashed against each other. Pounded relentlessly against Lucy's limp body again and again. Giant, claw-like waves reached up and grabbed her, pulling her down to the depths. The ocean surrendered her battered body to the surface once more as if tired with its prey. The waves crashed as the wind howled.

Finally, Lucy's body vanished beneath the surface, dragged down into the blackened depths as she was swallowed into the abyss.

Chapter 2

At the same time, over four-thousand miles away from Gozo's coast, John Steel sat in his office at the NYPD's 11th precinct. The room had been an old storage room that he had commandeered. The walls were a mix of half red-painted plaster and a lower half made from dark wooden panels. The hardened concrete of the floor was now hidden under a polished wood. There were brass lamps and Cambridge style bookshelves. The whole place looked as though it should belong in a stately home.

John Steel sat behind a long oak desk. The top was covered with green leather. On the desk was a computer monitor to his right and a landline pushed far to the left. The computer keyboard and mouse were in front of the monitor, leaving the centre of the desk free. To his right hung a large, lifeless flatscreen monitor, which showed nothing apart from the room's reflection. His eyes glanced over the report he had just written and was about to file.

Steel sighed profoundly and tossed down the file in frustration. He had been assigned to the NYPD to monitor and – if necessary – hinder the operations of an organisation called SANTINI.

SANTINI was an underground organisation that dealt in murder, assassinations, arms smuggling, anything that would serve its purpose. However, unlike organisations such as the Italian Mafia, Yakuza, White Russian Mafia, SANTINI remained in the shadows. Carrying out assignments that would be profitable and draw no attention to their existence.

But Steel knew of them. His entire family had been murdered by them, and he had been gravely injured while trying to save his family. Steel looked over at his reflection in the powered down the desktop monitor. He gazed into his dark soulless green eyes, which were just another scare had had to remind him of that day. His once pale blue eyes had somehow turned to this dark unnerving dark emerald colour after his life-saving operation. For years he had thought that the old Japanese gardener had saved him, healing his wounds at his home. But Steel had found out later that the very people Steel worked, for now, had saved him.

Like his father before him, John Steel was British Secret Service – or MI8. He had been recruited after his time with the SAS. However, after the murder of his family, MI8 thought it best that Steel went into hiding until the organisation responsible had been identified, or at best, eliminated. So, Steel joined the US Navy SEALs. Whitehall suspected putting an ocean between Steel and the organisation would take them out of their gaze for a while. Also, the training would do him good for what he needed him to do.

But now, he was stuck behind a desk doing paperwork for a murder investigation. Steel felt nauseous, claustrophobic. This was not him. He was a soldier – an agent of the British Secret Service, not a cop. Sure, he had thwarted the plans of SANTINI on several occasions, but for some reason, they had gone dark. Were they laying low because of him? Possible. But then SANTINI did not just have him after them. There was this Trojan Group. Trojan was also a criminal organisation, but they – Steel's eyes – were more of a threat. They sought power, control and would do anything to get it. However, these had also disappeared from his radar. Steel found it curious but at the same time disturbing. One he could understand – but both, surely that couldn't be good?

But despite this upset, Steel had done his job and was ready to come home as far as he was concerned. He was prepared to do the job he was hired for, and that wasn't being a cop, that was for sure. John Steel grabbed a pair of sunglasses that sat on a wireless docking station and slipped them on. He saw a blink of red light in the corner of an LCD HUB in the right-hand lens, then the words *Retina scan complete. Identification confirmed*. Steel heaved himself out of the comfort of the padded leather office chair, grabbing the file and then headed over to the door. The report was done, all the eyes were dotted, and Ts were crossed. Despite his reluctance to be there, he knew he still had to do the job correctly. He opened the door. Suddenly, the silence of the office was shattered by the chaos of the homicide division's bullpen. Phones were ringing, and voices grew louder. As Steel looked out across the sea of busy people, the small screen in the right lens ran a diagnostic and quickly analysed them. John Steel smiled to himself at the gadget that had saved him and others live so often, but he also knew he could not be reliant on it. It was just an aid. Steel knew he had to rely more on his skills and own intuition.

Steel was looking at the people of the night shift. His shift had left hours ago. He had just stayed over to make sure there were no discrepancies in the report. The last thing he wanted was the guy's lawyer picking something out and get the scumbag off with. Steel walked over to Captain Alan Brant's office and knocked. Steel wasn't surprised he was still there.

Alan Brant was a bear of a man. He was in his fifties but still had the build of a quarterback. Steel looked over at the shaven football of a head. The light from the overhead light gleamed off his dark shin. To Steel, Brant always looked angry – even when he wasn't. But this time, those cold brown eyes scowled at Steel as he entered after knocking. Brant sat back in his chair, his massive form leant back against the PU leather, causing it to creak.

'Take it you done writin that report?' Brant said. His thick-lipped mouth curled as though every word had a bitter taste to it. His voice was deep like you might imagine a grizzly or brown bear to have.

'Yes, I'm done,' Steel said. His tone was emotionless. Despite being British, he had no accent to speak of. There was no hint of a regional accent, just British. Brant gave Steel a curious look. Steel wondered if Brant picked up on what he had said – or indeed, how he had meant it, 'Yes, I'm done.'

Steel placed down the file in front of Brant and ran his fingers through his raven-coloured hair. It felt longer than he would have wanted it to be. It was possibly time to visit that barbers shop in the morning, Steel thought, catching his reflection in the long window that separated the Captain's office from the bullpen. His black suit and shirt did not reflect too well in the window, making it appear as if he was a floating head without a body. Steel smiled to himself but did not show it.

'McCall is pissed at ya after what you did,' Brant said, rocking in his chair. The sound of the metal joints squeaked with the subtle movement.

'She will get over it. Besides, it got the job done, didn't it?' Steel said. His tone was cold and unemotional.

Steel did not care for their rules anymore. He found them tiresome. Rules that kept the allowed the bad guys to go free and hurt the innocent. Rules that with the slightest loop whole could be undone. He preferred his rules, the rules her was governed by. There is your target; investigate and take whatever action is necessary. He lived in a black and white world, with the only red been his enemies' blood.

'You threw the man outta the window, Steel!' Brant growled. His eyes bulged from their deep-set sockets. A slither of spit formed in the corner of Brant's mouth a was held by the hairs of his circular beard.

'And if I hadn't, you'd have several officers in the morgue or hospital right now – including McCall,' Steel said with an angry tone.

Brant sat back and sighed deeply. 'Yeah, I know, but still, these cowboy actions of yours are getting outta hand.'

'Understood,' Steel said calmly. 'don't worry, they won't happen again,' Steel said and turned to leave. Brant looked over at Steel. A look of concern filled his face.

'What do you mean by that?' Brant asked. He had read Steel's innuendoes and body language. Brant was the only one in the precinct who knew what Steel was, who he worked for. Sure, Steel had closed some exceptional cases, but now Brant felt Steel was just treading water.

'I mean –.' Steel paused and looked over at the commendations and photographs on Brant's wall. It was impressive, but Brant was a cop, and Steel wasn't. 'I'm going home, I'm tired,' Steel said and left the office, closing the door softly behind him.

Captain Alan Brant watched Steel cross the bullpen floor and wait for the elevator, and wandered. Had Steel just said goodbye or only good night?

Chapter 3

Dwejra sea birds hovered overhead. Their baby-like calls hung carried on a refreshing sea breeze which hurried across the coastline. The sun began to gather warmth over the Maltese Islands though it was still early morning.

The surrounding landscape had a dangerous beauty, like something from another time or planet. Yet, the image was broken by the parking spaces and shops.

Special Agent Marcus Foster stood near the rocky ground where the Azure Window had stretched out into the ocean. An enormous craggy arch that had been created by weather and stormy waters. Now, just a strange rock formation remained to mark where the arch had stood.

Some people would swear that there was a face in the rock if looked at from a certain angle. Set in the San Lawrenz district of the Island of Gozo. The window had been a magnificent natural structure that Foster had in years gone by brought his family to see.

Now, he was there for a very different reason.

He had received the call around six that morning. Pat and Michael Fabri, who owned the ice cream store close by, had found a young woman's body while walking their dog at the Blue Hole, a tourist trap and diving ground. They always walked their little terrier, Skippy, there before getting ready for the tourists. Skippy had alerted them to the woman in the water. She had been too far for either of them to swim out, so Pat had called the police on her cell phone. The police boat had found only the body, no purse or form of ID. However, the sergeant in charge had recognised her as Foster's daughter. Despite her broken body, her face was somehow mostly undamaged – enough for her to be identified at least.

Foster was a tall man with massive shoulders. Six-foot three and a haircut any Marine would be proud of. The fresh sea air brushed across his face as he looked out across the ocean. Trying to think of why his little girl would take her own life. For him, there was only one answer: She wouldn't.

'Marcus, the medical examiner, is about to take her away,' said Sergeant Gann Burlo. Burlo was a friend of the family since Foster's arrival five years ago.

Foster starred out at the serene beauty of the ocean and nodded silently. Burlo moved to speak – but felt awkward breaking the silence.

He turned to head back to the police Land Rover that waited for him.

'Gann, are you putting this down to suicide?' Foster asked without turning to look at his friend.

'I will wait to see what the medical examiner finds, but everything points to that, or just an accident. Why? Something we should know?' Burlo asked curiously.

Foster turned slowly and shook his head.

'Just so I can tell Martha. An accident would be better, knowing her little girl took her life would destroy her,' Foster said.

Burlo gave a sympathetic smile and nodded slowly. 'I'll let you know. But I think it was more likely to be an accident, but it's not for me to say I'm afraid. That's down to the medical examiner. But, out here late at night, and last night was pretty dark,' Burlo said.

Foster turned back to the view and sighed while Burlo returned to his car. Foster pulled out his cell phone and pressed a speed-dial number.

'Hi Janis, it's Marcus Foster. Can you find me John Steel's number in New York?'

Chapter 4

It was eleven o'clock in the morning when a cell phone rang in a secure office. A man waited before answering the burner phone. He was sat in the dark – he preferred it that way. It helped him to think – and he had a lot to think about.

'Yes, what is it, Beta?' His voice was deep and emotionless. His voice rang with a hint of a Boston accent.

'He called someone – just now. He's getting outside help,' said the muffled voice of a man on the other end.

'Do we know who?' asked the man called Alpha.

'No, not yet.' Beta paused for a moment before speaking again. 'Could be that old army buddy he keeps talking about?'

'What – the cop?' asked Alpha before pausing for a moment as if weighing up this new information. 'It's possible, I guess. Keep tabs on the airlines. If his name pops, put a detail on him.'

The man known as Beta did not immediately reply – a response wasn't necessary. There was a moment of silence, then Beta broke it. 'And what about the other thing?'

'You know what to do – so, take care of it,' Alpha said and placed the handset back onto the cradle.

Chapter 5

John Steel had taken a cab back to his apartment. The ride was quiet and uneventful. The cabby had talked of most of the way, not that Steel had not taken much notice and had replied with some friendly-sounding grunts. As the yellow Ford pulled up outside the address, Steel paid then climbed out onto the sidewalk. Steel watched the cab car's taillights disappear into the mass of traffic that was moving slowly like some cumbersome beast.

Steel entered the vast brick monstrosity built in the 30 – all Redbrick and windows.

Steel considered it had more class than the modern steel and glass buildings. It had character. Like the Cromwellian mansion he had lived in back home in England. Unfortunately, Steel was the son of an Earl since his parent's murder years ago, which had passed to him and the family company. But Steel was not one for titles. He wasn't a businessman; he was a soldier, an investigator, and now a cop.

Steel was greeted by a doorman who tipped his cap to Steel and opened the door for him. Steel nodded a greeting and entered. He was home.

Inside, the lobby was filled with a white marble floor and high arched ceilings. The reception desk was topped with black marble, and the front was polished oak.

Steel walked over at the two men behind the desk, said his good mornings and retrieved his keys. Steel had thought that taking his keys may be a bad idea if things went wrong. Luckily, his instinct had been correct, and he saved himself a hefty fine for losing them. He took the elevator up, using the time to think.

Steel lived on the top floor, with a terrace view of the park and the city. As he opened the front door, the crisp conditioned air felt good against his skin. He closed his eyes for a moment and enjoyed the temperature change.

He slipped off his jacket and hung it on the coat rack near the door. As he did so, his eyes scanned the open-plan loft, and he gave a comfortable smile.

It was good to be home.

The loft was spacious, with polished oak flooring and a mix of modern and antique furniture. The white-painted walls held various works of art but no family photographs.

To the right, a staircase wound upwards to a mezzanine that was Steel's bedroom. Behind the twisting staircase was the open-plan kitchen, which lay beneath the mezzanine. Next to the kitchen was a long corridor which contained a bathroom and several other rooms.

Steel poured himself a large whisky from a drink's cabinet in a corner near a large panoramic window, a virtual wall of glass. After the night he'd had – he needed it. Steel stood at the window and watched as a shifting orange-watercolour sky bathed everything in a dark umber. He looked down at the view of Central Park and the city. It was possibly the only time he was thankful for the family money. It gave him the freedom to do what he wanted without restrictions and also guaranteed the best rooms of seats on flights. But it was also a reminder for him. Steel had survived the attack on the family estate. His family had not. He was alone in the world. But his pain gave him purpose. Steel had gone to New York to find those responsible. An organisation called SANTINI. But they had gone underground. Disappeared. But he knew he would see them again. It was just a matter of time. Steel thought about one of SANTINI's agents – a man called Mr Williams, who he had encountered on his first Mission with the NYPD, not that the cops were aware it was a mission. Mr Williams was – for Steel, the epitome of the term, *the bad guy*. He was as sadistic as they came but somehow had a sense of honour and charisma. Somehow, through their encounters against each other, they had formed strange mutual respect. Steel knew that Mr Williams had nothing to do with his family's murder, possibly, Williams only saving grace. Mr Williams had also disappeared from the limelight. But Steel knew they would be back.

Steel felt tired. Drained. He took a sip from the whisky and stared out across the horizon.

He had been in one place too long, and it was starting to get to him.

Steel sighed. He loved the city and working with the team.

But it wasn't him.

This wasn't his life.

It was a mission that had gone on for too long.

Steel walked towards the kitchen to switch on the coffee machine. The machine gave an electronic whir before it began processing the mix of coffee grinds and hot water. It would take ten minutes before the brew would be ready – time enough for him to shower and freshen up.

It was five in the morning. Steel knew he had a couple of hours before he had to be back at the precinct. The truth was, Brant would be happy if he did not show, and as it was, Steel did not feel much like going in anyway. He had risked his neck again and not gotten so much as a thank you for it. Sure, Steel wasn't a glory hound. He did not care if that asshole Addams got the credit for it. But, all he had gotten was shit for it. And that was beginning to wear thin.

Steel downed the whisky and headed for the corridor and the bathroom.

He had to freshen up before heading off to the precinct.

Steel pulled off his shirt as he headed for the bathroom and kicked off his Bugatti shoes, leaving them lying at the bathroom door entrance.

It had been a long night, from which he was still hurting.

Flying into a guy at was going to leave a mark – it had, several in fact. He was bruised and scratched – but alive.

Steel pushed the door open and stumbled inside the bathroom.

It was a big room – possibly the size of most people's bedrooms. Gold Antique Limestone covered the walls and floor. Oak vanities with brass fittings made a perfect addition. The walls and flooring had an Egyptian feel, inspired by the tales of Cleopatra. At the far end of the room was a bathtub made for two, and a double window next to it, with a fantastic view of Central Park.

Steel took off the rest of his clothes and draped them over the wicker clothes hamper next to the door. He looked out of the large window as he headed to the entrance of the wet room. This was a long narrow 6x5 foot space, with staked slate wall panels covering the inside walls and slate floor tiles. Above, a foot square showerhead hung from the ceiling and seven small LED lights zig-zagged across the top. The dividing panel was a foot-thick false wall, with a voice-activated thirty-two-inch monitor built into it.

A little treat he had installed so he could check on the news and watch movies. It also showed the view from the several cameras he had installed in the apartment, just on the off-chance Steel had uninvited guests while he is freshening up. There were two monitors fixed back-to-back so that Steel could watch from both sides.

'Check emails,' Steel commanded in a raised voice. The screen blinked, and the display showed his email account. There was the usual junk mail; others were invitations to A-list parties. Parties that he had no time nor feel the need to attend. The remainder was from a man called Hendricks who in charge of Steel's company back in Britain while he was in the States. A company Steel's father had founded, and he had inherited. It was a billion-pound company that made everything from watches to the general public to weapon systems.

'Screen off,' Steel ordered. The screen went blank. He had neither the time nor the patients to respond to the emails. Steel knew they would wait a bit longer. Just until he was in a better frame of mind.

Steel walked to the shower controls, turned it on and stood back, waiting for that perfect temperature. Steam filled the area, and Steel moved to stand beneath the flow with his hands against the wall, his head down, letting the water slam against him, massaging his tight muscular but scared body. Steel's frame came from athletics and special assault courses more than gym work. He figured he needed to be flexible and nimble rather than a bulk of muscle, flexibility that had saved his life more than once. His thoughts were a million miles away. Back to another time, another place. Memories of that terrifying day in the garden of his own ancestral home when he lost everything. He could still hear the gunshots and feel the bullets' burning as they passed through him. Images flashed in his mind, but one lingered, the face of his wife as the life faded from her eyes.

The sound of his apartments phone ringing pulled him back to the present but left him slightly disorientated. He shook his head and stared at his reflection on the monitor.

'Phone,' Steel said. Then turned off the shower.

'Hi John, it's Marcus,' Steel listened as he walked out of the shower and wrapped a towel around his waist. Marcus Foster. A name he hadn't heard for years. The two men had been in the service together, the best of friends. More than friends, more like brothers. But something had forced Steel away, and they had lost contact – until now.

'Marcus, it's been a long time,' Steel said as he sat on the edge of the bathtub.

'Too long, man,' Marcus replied. His tone was trying to be emotionless, but there was a hint of sadness.

'Look, Marcus, I'm sorry about disappearing, something from my past....it.'

'Hey, I get it. I read the file. Shit, I would have done the same thing,' Marcus said.

'We good?' Steel asked.

'Always, man,' Marcus replied.

There was a moment of silence. Steel fought to find what to say next. He had to say something. The guy had tracked him down after all those years – then it hit him. Why? After five years, why had Foster decided to call?

'So, what's new at your end?' Steel said. He did not want to come straight out with the question he had on his mind. Steel thought it best just let Foster tell him.

'Oh, not much. I was going through some old photographs of when we were in the TEAMs together. Found one of us when we were in Serbia, you, me, Taylor, Baker, even Dickson was in it, you remember Dickson? Man, that was a shitty war,' Foster said. His voice trailing off slightly as though he remembered something.

'Yes, but we managed to have a laugh from time to time,' Steel replied. Waiting for Foster to get to the point.

'Yeah, so, I saw these and thought I'd look you up,' Foster's tone was trying to be calm and happy, but Steel could tell he was hiding something.

The mention of Serbia was the key. They had lost a couple of men back then, but there was one called Dickson that they had named their little sister because he was the youngest of them all.

He had been killed on a mission. There had been an intense firefight with enemy troops in the mountains. They had taken a few casualties, most of which were flesh wounds. After the firefight had ended, the team and re-organised. All except Dickson. After a search, they had found Dickson's body at the bottom of a nearby cliff.

Steel said nothing.

'Heard you become a cop in New York, you taking it easy or something?' Foster said.

'It has its moments. Besides, I heard you pulled a sweet deal and got a post in Malta. Who's arse did you have to kiss to get that?' Foster laughed. But Steel picked up on something in the shortness of his laughter.

Why did he mention Dickson? Why was he calling?

'You should come over; the sun would do you good. The family – .' Foster paused for a moment, leaving a second of awkward silence. 'The family would love to see you; I know Martha would.'

Steel felt a tightness in his chest at the mention of that name. His fingers touched the round scar on his left shoulder just under the collar bone. But something nagged at Steel. What had made Marcus Foster call him after years of silence. Steel rewound their conversation in his head, listened to every word once more in his head.

'Marcus – what's happened?' Steel asked, his voice was filled with concern.

A moment of terrible silence filled the air, then Steel heard Foster sob.

'Lucy…my little girl,' Foster began to talk but faltered at the last moment.

'Marcus, what is, what's happened to Lucy?'

'Steel, my little girl – she's – she's dead.'

'How? Was it an accident or –?'

'Can you come over? I know you're busy -' Foster's voice rang with urgency.

'Never too busy for family, I'll be over when I can,' Steel said. He would have asked more, but he knew it would be too painful.

'I'll see you when you get here,' Foster said. 'And Steel…thanks.' There was a click, followed by dead air.

Steel sat, staring into nothingness for a while. His fingers still feeling the rough edges of the scar. Steel's thoughts wandered to another time – a happy time.

The Foster's had been his second family. After the murder of his, family Steel had joined the SEAL's to disappear. The organisation knew Steel was still alive. The news had confirmed that. So, the best he could do was vanish until he was ready. Sure, he had been recruited, but he had passed all the tests. Steel had been placed on Foster's team, and they had just bonded. And they had been like brothers. But SANTINI had found Steel, and he knew he had to run before his team or Foster's family got caught in the crossfire.

Steel stood up and looked at his reflection in the mirror. He was six-one of taught muscle. His cold deep, emerald green eyes locked onto the six angry-looking scares where the bullets had gone through. It was a strange configuration that the assassin had made. Steel's old mentor had called it the mark of the phoenix. Steel just thought it looked ugly, like his eyes. Whatever they had done to him to save him had changed many things, including his eye colour. No one was sure what had happened to cause it to happen, but now, instead of pale blue, he was left with dark soulless green eyes.

Steel thought back to how the intruders had stormed the house and grounds, killing indiscriminately. Steel had taken out most of the intruders as he moved through his family home. Eventually, his search for his family led Steel to the attic.

One of the men had shot Steel six times, each round perfectly placed, not to kill him but to cause him the most pain before he bled out. But the old Japanese gardener had saved him, pulled him out of the attic and to safety. Steel remembered the operating room, the sounds of the machines that were keeping him alive. It had been a new memory. Before, he had just remembered waking up in the old gardener's Japanese style home. But now, his memories were returning slowly.

He had been recruited during his time with the British special forces. But the incident with SANTINI at his home had intervened. It had been Joint Operations that had sent Steel to the SEALs. Primarily for training and to keep him out of the way until he was ready. Now, Steel was British Secret Service and undercover with the NYPD. His time with the 11th precinct had begun with a triple murder about a year ago. MI8's curiosity with the case had been aroused because it had SANTINI's mark all over it, so Steel was sent in.

But there had been no sign of the organisation recently. So, for Steel, it was time to move on.

There was a gentle beep from the coffee machine to signal that the function had finished. The aroma of freshly brewed coffee wafted through the apartment. Steel turned to face the monitor. He knew what he had to do.

'Phone. Captain Brant,' Steel ordered. There was a moment of silence, then the sound of the auto dialling system. The noise of the phone ringing could be heard in overhead speakers before Brant eventually picked up.

'Steel, what's up? What you gone an' done now?' Brant's gruff voice bellowed over the intercom.

'Captain, I'd like to take some time off?'

'Sure...when?'

'Now,' Steel said. 'End call.'

Steel did not need questions; besides, he was only attached to the NYPD. It was only a courtesy he had asked in the first place. Steel stood up and walked to the washbasin, and began to pack his wash bag. He looked up at his reflection in the mirror. His eyes fell upon the six-round scars that marked his body. He had been told that the shape resembled a bird – or Pheonix.

Steel had said they were full of crap.

Some said Steel was lucky, six shots and all of them missed vital organs. All of them were through and throughs, each left scar in its wake.

He hadn't felt lucky at the time. The mercenary had been right behind Steel when he had fired. But even at close range, the shooter was a good shot. He knew what he was doing – he wanted Steel to suffer, probably did not expect him to survive.

Big mistake.

Steel went online and booked a last-minute flight from JFK to London and then a flight from Gatwick to Malta. It did not take Steel long to pack. He wouldn't need many clothes as he wouldn't be there long. If he did need anything, he'd just buy new there. A simple small-wheeled cabin bag with a few essentials was enough for now.

'Only pack what you need,' was what the British Army had always taught him. Steel smiled at the thought of his instructor at Hereford drilling that idea into their heads as they got ready for a training exercise in the unforgiving Welsh Brecon Beacons. But that seemed a long time ago now. Steel was thirty-six years old, but he'd been through a lot in a short space of time. Steel had done two years with the Commando Royal Engineers of the British Army before passing selection with the SAS. He had done four years with the SAS, with plenty of overseas tours. Unfortunately, his last tour of duty, which had been in Bosnia, had been the best and the worst. It had been his homecoming from that tour that had seen the slaughter of his family. The reason he had been in hiding for six months in Alaska. But an incident had brought him face to face with his next commanding officer – Colonel Grant of the US Navy SEAL teams.

Life had thrown Steel about, that was for sure. But he survived.

In his five years with the teams, he disappeared again. SANTINI had found him, and MI8 was waiting to snatch him up. He was ready.

As much as he did not want to admit it, it was beginning to tell on his body. But trained as much as he could, keeping himself fit and nimble.

Steel pulled on a black T-shirt, black jeans. And slipped on a pair of military-grade short boots. In a small case, he packed extra t-shirts and enough underwear to tide him over and a black shirt and suit, just in case the hotel restaurant had a dinner dress code. He figured he could buy clothes as he needed them, thinking Malta would have some decent stores to shop at.

He left the bedroom and headed for a room at the end of the hallway. Next to the door was a keypad. He punched in a number, and the door clicked open. As he entered, the light came on automatically. It was a twenty-foot-by-twenty-foot, sterile white room. There were no windows and only one entry. Shelving ran along the left-hand wall; this was made from black metal with green felt cushioning. The shelving held pistols and rifles of different calibres laid out. There were electronic devices, cell phones and watches. Several pairs of sunglasses sat on wireless charges along with containers with contact lenses inside. Gadgets of the trade. All of which had saved his arse more than once. The sunglasses did not just hide Steel's menacing green eyes from the world, but they were also connected to an MI8 HUB via his watch and cell phone. The right had wall held unique clothing, one of which had a temperature control so he could endure heat or cold. But despite all of the toys, Steel relied on his wits and training. He could not always rely on the gear. If it broke down or was lost, he would have to adapt.

Steel picked up one pair of glasses, a cell phone and packed a set of contact lenses into his bag. He checked he had everything, then closed the door and sealed the room.

Steel took a black leather jacket from the coat rack and pulled it on. He looked around at his apartment and smiled as he pulled on his sunglasses. Steel knew he had to inform Whitehall as to what was going on sooner or later. Steel pulled out his cell phone and texted the office.

Gone to see Marcus Foster in Malta, please send a welcome pack. Back soon.

Chapter 6

Forest travelled south-east on the long and winding road from the San Lawrenz, stopping in Victoria's city at the heart of Gozo. As he drank deeply from a newly purchased bottle of water, he looked around the town. Time could have stopped here in the 1930s. If only time could have stopped before Lucy died. The air thick and humid. Foster was reminded of bringing his daughters here when they were little girls and felt the loss deeply.

Foster remembered the day trips they used to take to Gozo when they first came here. He smiled, clinging to the memory. The horn of a car pulled him back, and the smile faded.

With another bottle of water in hand, he returned to his car, headed to the quaint coastal village of Mgarr and the only route to Malta. As he drove onto the ferry, he could feel the temperature change. The coolness of the interior was a blessing; Gozo had been hot.

The ferry took around twenty-five minutes to reach Cirkewwa on Malta itself. Just enough time to grab a coffee from one of the onboard kiosks.

The sun was unforgiving, and the lack of a cold breeze made it worse. Foster used to laugh how the guy he replaced would complain about the heat. Foster knew what twenty-five degrees felt like in New York. It was nothing. But on Malt, even the heat was different. Twenty-five in Malta could feel like fifty.

Foster opened his car door and left it open for a moment, allowing some of the dry heat to escape from the vehicle before he got into it. He wasn't in a rush; his boss had given him time off, given the circumstance. He leaned against his car and took a draw from a cigarette, anything to calm him for the drive home. It was that or drink. Smoking seemed the safer option.

He stuck the cigarette in his mouth, climbed into the driver's seat, and started it. Foster waited before moving off, allowing the sweet, cooled air to circulate from the car's air-conditioner. The drive back home would take a few hours over the harsh but beautiful countryside due to some narrow roads and bad drivers. Foster put the car into drive and headed off. He had no idea how he was going to break the news to his wife. Lucy was the eldest of his two daughters by ten years, but the two girls had always been close. He feared this news would crush Abby.

His mood made the journey back home seem longer. How could Foster tell his family what had happened when he didn't even know? He checked his watch. It was early afternoon, and the sun was high in the cloudless sky. He had stopped several times to gather his thoughts and to delay the inevitable.

Foster felt a sort of relief. Steel was on the way, and he would do what he could not. Foster would ask Steel to investigate what had happened to Lucy. This would be off the books, so he could not risk the Bureau finding out.

This was a difficult time, and he needed Steel here, someone he could trust. The two men had been in the same unit. They had been through hell and back. Steel had said he would catch the next available flight, but that could be anytime. Foster figured Steel would transfer in London and hoped for a quick turnaround, though flights did not always work out that way. He knew Steel would be here as soon as he could.

Foster knew Steel better than most. He could be a cold bastard. That's what made him good at what he did. Cold and calculated, but also as loyal and protective about his family.

Steel had saved Foster's life more times than he'd care to remember.

Which made Steel perfect as Lucy's godfather and Foster thought it only fitting. He knows what had happened.

Foster felt better when Steel had said he was coming over. Steel was always big on taking care of people who meant a lot to him. Since the tragedy of losing his own family in a brutal murder, Steel had come to think of the Foster's as family. As for the men who had killed his family, those Steel had found, Foster had imagined, went screaming.

Foster finally pulled into his driveway and parked. He turned the engine off and just sat. His gaze fixed on the large house. His large hands gripped the steering wheel, causing the covering to creak under pressure. He sucked in a large gulp of air and got out of the car.

It was time.

Chapter 7

The secure office phone rang. The Alpha waited, then picked up the receiver.

'Yes,' he said.

'We were right. It's the cop,' said Beta.

'When is he leaving?'

'He already left. He'll change in London then getting a direct flight. He should be here tomorrow,' said Beta.

Alpha said nothing. He breathed slowly, letting his brain calculate.

'Is the detail ready?' Alpha asked at length.

'Yes, they have the flight number,' Beta replied.

'Tell them not to engage. We don't want to draw unnecessary attention. If he's here for the girl, we can work around it,' said Alpha.

'And what about our orders, I thought —'

'I make the decisions here. If it comes to it, then yes, but we can't risk unnecessary action, not until we know.' Alpha's voice was stern. How dare Beta talk to him like that? He was in charge.

'Sorry, I – misspoke,' said Beta.

'Very well. You know the plan. That is what matters when we-.' Alpha paused for what did not need saying. '-The mission comes first. You can deal with the policeman later.'

'It will be my pleasure,' said Beta.

Chapter 8

'Anyone can rough it,' his old sergeant had always told Steel.

Words to live by.

It was going to be a long flight, so he knew he might as well make the most of it.

Business-class all the way.

The plane was a Boeing 777. A big old bird with seats he could relax into and not require a shoehorn to get out of. Steel was not one for pomp and ceremony, even though his father, the Earl, would insist from time to time. Given that it was a long flight and needed to be fresh when he arrived, the business class suited him fine.

Most in his financial situation would have gone first class but on a different floor with no exits.

It was an enclosed bubble on top of the aircraft, with no means of a tactical advantage. And besides, Steel wasn't a first-class kind of guy.

Steel had taken a flight from JFK to London Gatwick. From there, he took a direct flight to Malta. For him, time was of the essence, but unfortunately, the airlines had their own schedule. Steel had sent Foster an email giving him timings and flight numbers. Foster had offered to pick Steel at the airport, but Steel had said he would take a cab. Give Foster some time with his family. In reality, Steel did not think Foster would be in any shape to drive, given the circumstances. No, he would get a local taxi and take the time to think things through.

Steel felt terrible that they hadn't spoken in a long time, and he blamed himself for that. But when Steel had found SANTINI had discovered where he was, Steel needed to distance himself for everyone he cared about. But he had done it too late, and his team was ambushed on a fake mission. Many escaped, but not all.

Once Steel was in the secret service, he was put onto missions all over the globe. But a lot of his time was spent hunting the group who had killed his family. It had almost consumed him – then he was integrated into the NYPD.

He'd never forgotten those he had left behind, especially the Fosters, who had been his second family.

When Steel had thought it was best to put as much distance between him and them, hoping what had happened to his family, he wouldn't happen the Foster's.

Steel made himself comfortable and waited for the plane to take off. Once airborne, the passengers were free to use the internet. He needed to know what he was walking into. First, he would email the office in Whitehall, give them the facts, ask for any information relevant to Foster or his family. Next, he would check the local Maltese papers online, find out what was what.

This could be an accident or murder. Either way, Steel needed facts.

There was a roar from the engines as they began to taxi. One of the flight attendants was bringing round glasses of champagne or wine. Steel chose the champagne and sipped it slowly. Soon they would be in the air, and Steel's investigation could begin.

The flight landed late afternoon at the Malta International Airport the next day. The sun was high, with a few wisps of clouds covering the perfect blue sky. As Steel edged to the door, he braced himself for the sudden change in temperature. They would be going from air-conditioned twelve degrees to a roasting thirty-five in less than a second. Steel adjusted his wraparound sunglasses. He smiled at the attractive black-haired stewardess by the door.

'Enjoy your stay, sir,' said with a voice that made Steel week at the knees.

'Oh, I'm sure I'll find something to amuse myself,' Steel said, still wearing the seductive smile. The airport was large – nothing compared to JFK, but big enough to accommodate the thousands of tourists. Steel took out his cell phone and sent a message to Foster that he had arrived safely and the name of the hotel he would be staying in.

Foster just gave a simple emoji of a thumbs up. Steel cracked a smile, then place his phone away.

Stepping out into the blazing afternoon sun, a warm breeze swept across Steel's face as he scanned the faces of the waiting drivers. Some held up name cards, and others indicated the holiday service they were there for.

Near the exit was a booth with a sign for *Taxi Service*. Next to it was a board with different locations and the set price. Steel located the price for Valletta and took out a twenty euro note. He paid his money to a woman with long black hair, a beautiful face strained by the pressure of her job. She took the cash, passed Steel a ticket and told him to wait until his number came up. The woman was calling out numbers, and tourists moved to their waiting transport. After a short while, another number was called over a tannoy. 'Number twenty.' Steel checked the number on his ticket and ventured into the brightness and warmth of the outside.

Steel looked around until he saw a man leaning against the wall of the airport. The man was peeling an orange into a waste bin and whistling an unidentifiable tune. Steel walked past the local drivers who were pitching to him, calling out 'cheap taxi, cheap taxi', Steel kept on walking until he reached the man with the orange.

'I take it you're my ride?' Steel asked, watching the man shove a large piece of the fruit into his mouth.

'How'd ya figure that'?' the man replied in an East London accent.

'Because you're the only one whose not bothering me, which means you work for the firm,' Steel said with a smile. 'or I might be wrong, and your just some bloke eating fruit.' The cabbie laughed and ushered Steel to follow. Steel followed the man to the parking area – which wasn't too far from the terminal.

'I'm Stan,' the man said, offering Steel a handshake.

'John,' Steel replied, shaking Stan's hand. 'Pleased to meet you, Stan.'

'So, where we goin?' Stan asked before sticking another slice of orange into his mouth.

'The Grand Excelsior in Vallette.' Stan nodded as if complimenting Steel on his choice.

They walked in silence, measuring one another up.

Stan headed towards a red minibus. Though a few years old, it looked in good condition. Well cared for and maintained.

Steel thought the passenger windows had a smoked tint on them – for the passengers' comfort. He just hoped it had an air-conditioner.

'What, no black cab?' Steel asked with a grin.

'Na, they wouldn't let me bring one,' the driver replied with a disappointed look.

Steel could not be sure if the man was joking or not - but smiled all the same.

Stan looked at Steel and the small bag he was carrying.

'Not stayin,' then?' Stan said.

'Don't know yet, could be… life is full of surprises.'

'And you don't like surprises, I take it?' Stan laughed.

'Depends on what they are?' Steel shrugged and got into the bus, placing the small case next to him. Stan smiled to himself and climbed into the driver's side, then started the engine.

Stan was a short man in his late fifties. He had a shiny, shaved head with gold-rimmed sunglasses that perched on a button nose. He was slightly paunchy from too much good food, most of which was hidden beneath an awful Hawaiian shirt.

'Where you from?' Stan asked, looking in the rear-view mirror. However, before Steel had a chance to answer, Stan was interrupting with fun facts.

The rest of the journey was quite the same, a question followed by a fact or reference to something. Steel smiled, a London cabbie in Malta, acting as a London cabbie.

Steel was glad he did not have to talk. All he wanted was to get to the hotel, grab a refreshing shower and possibly a cold mojito.

The main roads winded up and down, left and right – like a long concrete roller coaster. The road narrowed in places and hugging the sides of hills while huge drops on the sides. The snaking routes followed the landscape's contours, taking them past breath-taking rugged scenery and small villages.

The air was thin and hot despite the vehicle's aircon.

Steel noticed the change in scenery the closer they got to the city. How houses that fitted into the early thirties blended in with the modern golf club and horse racing track. Olive groves and vineyards sat next to roads, adding a bit of green to the dry, arid landscape. It was a beautiful medley that he looked forward to seeing more. Steel also noticed Stan was texting a lot, which was possibly nothing, so Steel put it to the back of his mind.

They travelled along the Triq Nazzjonali highway, which then turned into the Triq Sant' Anna and Valletta, the capital city. Steel looked in fascination at the mix of old and new architecture, but everything had the same style regardless of age. Some of the streets that went through the towns narrowed to being suicidal, but they soon opened out to give a fantastic view.

Stan turned off Triq Sant' Anna and followed Triq L-AssedJu L-Kbir towards the coast and the hotel entrance. Through the bustling city, full of tourists and shoppers. The view from his window getting more fantastic.

There were parks, ancient buildings, palm trees and the never-ending blue sky. Steel looked at the street name, which read 'Great Siege Road.' And he wondered what had happened in the island's history to warrant such a name.

Steel had to admit he wasn't the greatest when it came to the history of a place. The truth was he never needed to do that kind of research. Most of Steel's research pertained to a job, or a person, never the past deeds of a country or city.

The realisation that he knew very little about the places he had visited saddened Steel. He knew the city's tactical layouts, the best and fastest routes in and out, entry and exit strategies. Where the police stations were, how far to the airport or harbour.

But he never studied the history of a place.

Steel promised himself, while he was on the trip, he would change that. If he had time.

Perhaps, once he was sure Forster was safe, he would stay longer and have an actual holiday. Steel knew he wouldn't be missed at the 11th Precinct. Captain Brant would be the first to encourage Steel to stay away for as long as possible. McCall, however, would be a different story. Steel had grown fond of their love-hate relationship, but he knew once he was gone, he'd be forgotten.

The cab turned left onto Triq Vincenzo Dimech. Then Stan took a sharp right and onto the hotel's driveway. This continued down a driveway until it came to the large circular courtyard of the Grand Hotel Excelsior Malta's main entrance.

Steel sat for a moment and looked out of the passenger window at the grand structure. Its looming white walls towered high above. Stan had parked at the entranceway under a colossal veranda, which sheltered them from the overwhelming sunlight.

Steel got out of the minibus and leaned through the open window of the passenger side. Steel handed the Stan fifteen euros tip and nodded with a smile. Stan returned the smile and gave a short salute before skipping back to the driver's side.

'You got a card just in case I need you again?' Steel asked, leaning on the open driver's side window. Stan took a card from a stack that was in the cup holder next to the gear shift. Steel took it and looked at the business card. *Stan Falan Taxi*, and below that was the telephone number. Steel placed it into his jacket pocket and stepped back from the vehicle as Stan took off. Steel grabbed his case and headed inside via the large glass entrance doors.

Inside was crisp with a fresh breeze provided by the air-conditioner, causing Steel to shiver slightly with the temperature change.

The hotel lobby was large and elegant, a long red carpet stretched across a polished marble floor. The ground level looked as grand as its name. Above, two lavish chandeliers sparkled overhead as the light was reflected through a thousand cut glass jewels. To the left was the concierge's desk, and the check-in desk was around the corner from that. Two arched red-carpeted stairways led to the first floor. Beyond where the staircases met were the bar, seating area, and the downward stairwell that led to the dining room, which sat parallel with the front entrance.

As Steel stood in the lobby, he took note of the people. Most were rushing here and there, while others sat staring at their electronic devices, making the most of the free WIFI. An elderly couple sat near the entrance clutching camera bags, eyes wide with anticipation of the tour bus's arrival.

A doorman wearing a grey waistcoat, the hotel's logo on the breast pocket, took Steel's bags and followed him towards reception. As they approached the desk, Steel noticed two men stepping out of the elevator.

The men both looked in their fifties. The taller had the look of wall street about him, the other, the bearing of a company man, CIA, or one of those three-letter agencies. The grey suits were similar, but Steel would bet there was a hefty price difference between them.

Steel noted a laminated pass hung around the tall man's neck. It bore the man's photograph and *ArmourCraft Industries* in bold red letters. The left side held a graphic representation of a black horse's head.

Steel figured this was the firm's logo – a simple design that had an ancient Greco-Roman feel. The kind of design found on a shield or banner.

As Steel stood in the line of people waiting to check in. The two men passed close by. Close enough for Steel to catch a small part of their heated conversation.

'Everything is going to plan. Don't worry. It's all taken care of,' said the smaller man.

The large man had an angry, bore a disbelieving look.

'We have a lot of money riding on this. If we go down… so do you,' the tall man threatened.

Steel turned slightly to his left and watched the two men head for the bar, committing them to memory. Something was obviously amiss and had the potential of being an exciting eavesdrop. Still, Steel had other things on his mind and did not need that kind of distraction.

Steel turned back to the queue of people. In front of him, a German couple waited impatiently. The man was in his late forties, with a beer belly and broad shoulders, dyed-brown hair sat upon a bloated, red face from either too much sun or anger. His wife was a tall brunette in a tight leopard print dress. She looked high maintenance. The woman looked at her watch every five seconds as if that would hurry things along. Steel looked over at the desk, and the young woman behind reception was tending to a young couple. Steel smiled as the couple's young boy and the girl began to fidget and annoy each other. The boy, who was around eight, was teasing his maybe-six-year-old sister. To the annoyance of the mother – and the waiting German's behind them.

As Steel waited, he took the time to check the lobby's layout. The position of the three elevators to his right, stairwells, and entrances to the restaurant and bar. He mapped the open space, a tactical layout in his head. Steel saw every pillar as cover, every fire extinguisher as a weapon.

Or a distraction.

As the family wrestled their children towards the elevators to get to their rooms, the German couple rushed forwards

While he waited, Steel checked his cell phone for missed calls but only had the usual greeting from the Maltese cell company telling the rates. Steel closed down the cell phone and tucked it back into his pocket. He watched as the German couple finished checking in and were now headed after a porter with a loaded brass luggage trolley.

As Steel stepped towards the desk, he smiled at the attractive raven-haired woman. She returned the smile.

'Hi, I believe you have a reservation for me. The name is John Steel,' he said. Passing her his credit card and passport.

'I'll just check for you, sir,' she held the cheeky smile as she checked for the reservation. Her smile became almost cat-like as she saw what he had booked.

'So, Mr Steel, we have you for ten days in the Presidential Suite,' she handed him a check-in card to fill out and prepared his key card.

'There is a possibility that the date could extend. Is that a problem?' Steel asked. Thinking that he might actually have a vacation after he sorted Foster's problem out.

'No sir, that shouldn't be a problem at all,' she replied, seeing that there were no reservations for that suite until the next month.

'Thank you,' Steel took back his credit card and passport and took the room card keys from her. He headed for the elevators.

The Presidential Suite was huge, with two bedrooms and a fair-sized bathroom. There were a dining room and a large sitting room with a big flat-screen tv and a writing desk. The sitting area had a long sliding window that led out onto a large terrace.

The room was pleasantly cool due to the air conditioning working throughout the suite. Steel explored, smiled and shook his head at the extravagance.

It was pricey, but then 'anyone can rough it.'

Between the long couch with its expensive covers and two armchairs with the same style covering, the lounge area had a small coffee table holding champagne on ice. Two flutes stood to the side. The silver bucket was drenched with condensation. Peaking from underneath a carefully arranged napkin was the neck of a bottle of champagne. Steel smiled as he uncorked the bottle then filled one of the flutes on the silver tray.

He took the glass and stepped out onto the terrace. Looking over the fantastic view, Steel raised the glass to salute the city.

Chapter 9

Foster sat at his desk in his small office at the back of his house. His wife had taken Valium and was lying on their bed, crying, Lucy's favourite teddy bear, a tattered brown thing with one eye, clutched in her arms.

He knew she needed to be alone, time to work through her grief, to come to terms with what had happened. It was her way. He had learnt that through twenty years of marriage.

So, he sat at his desk, a large glass of Jack in one hand and a family photograph in the other.

The alcohol did not help. If anything, it made things worse.

He went to take another sip but paused and looked at his computer screen. A message alerted him that he had mail. A quick scowl almost scorned the machine for the interruption.

He placed down both the whisky tumbler and the photograph, then leaned forwards to operate the keyboard. He had several emails, most of which he had known but left for later. But one was new.

An email from a friend.

He opened the email, and a broken smile crossed his face as he read the contents.

Steel has arrived. He's at the Excelsior. Foster picked up the glass of whisky, leaned back in the cream leather office chair, and took a mouthful of the golden liquid. Feeling the warm tingle at the back of his throat, he swallowed.

Foster figured with traffic and the roads, it was a good twenty minutes' car journey from the hotel to his house. That depended on if Steel was unlucky enough to get a taxi driver who wanted to show him the sights instead of route direct.

Foster leaned forwards, placed the whisky glass down onto the desk and took a burner phone from his desk drawer.

He paused for a moment, eyes fixed on the phone.

He placed the cell phone back in the draw and picked up the cordless phone from his desk with a head shake.

The years he'd served with the SEAL's and the agency had taught him to cover his tracks – to watch his ass. A simple thing like a new burner phone was subtle but effective.

However, the best way to hide something is to put it in plain sight. After all, as far as anyone knew, Steel was an old friend here on vacation.

'Grand Excelsior Hotel,' said a man's deep voice.

Foster pictured a tall man with a barrel chest and a beard on the other end line. 'Mr Steel's room, please,' he asked before taking another sip from the whisky.

'One moment, please,' replied the baritone.

Foster stood up and carried his almost empty glass to an antique rosewood drinks cabinet. He added a measure.

'Putting you through now, sir,' said the deep voice, making Foster smile as the image crept back into his mind.

'What's up, Marcus? Checking, I got here, OK?' Steel's voice rang with a touch of dry humour.

'No. Checking you ain't got a chick with you already,' Foster said. There was a brief moment of silence – both of the men choosing what to say next. Steel broke the silence.

'How are you doing, old friend?'

'Not great, better now you're here,' Foster said.

'Martha and Abby?'

'Martha's in bed. She's taken something to help her rest. Abby's…well angry,' Foster explained.

'Sorry bud, I know it's hard.'

'Yeah, I know you do. You've been there. Shit, you had it worse,' Foster growled.

'I come over in the morning, give you guys time.'

'That's ok. Look, get a cab and come over. You're having dinner with us tonight. Say around six?' Foster said. 'I would pick you up, but I'm kinda…'

'Yeah, I get it,' Steel said sympathetically. 'Give me the address. I'll be over soon.'

Chapter 10

James Calver sat at his computer, tracking a fishing boat coming from Tunisia and travelling fast. Calver had zoomed the satellite image in as far as he dared.

A few crew members were visible on deck, each dressed in waterproofs and going about their business. But something seemed wrong. Calver used the computer to check the vessel out. A fishing boat out of Egypt called the Al-Thar. Calver dialled a number and placed on a headset.

'Charlie two-four, we have a vessel on approach to sector fifteen from La Goulette. Be advised the vessel is on a fast approach,' Calver said.

'Roger that,' a voice said. 'Charlie two-four, two minutes. Out.'

Calver smiled as he watched as three small shapes leave the USS Nemesis, the aircraft carrier on operations in the area. They would have to wait until the ship was in Maltese water before they could do anything. The vessel held a steady course for the west side of Malta.

Possibly one of the quiet beaches.

Calver's suspicions were confirmed.

The vessel was undoubtedly a drop-off boat. Probably the ship Intel had warned of. A group of radicals hoping to get into the US, through Malta via the UK.

Unfortunately, the source had failed to provide pictures or names, so the whole crew was suspect. Guilty until proved innocent was the way things went since 911.

After the influx of people pouring into Europe, claiming to be Syrian refugees, security measures had gotten tighter everywhere. Before, it had been easy to spot a possible infiltration. Now, it was a damned nightmare. That's where the new system would come in.

Brand new facial recognition software would be linked to every country. It was fool-proof for spotting known terrorists in seconds. Even if they had a facial disguise.

The new system had proven to be ninety-nine per cent accurate. However, the bad guys were getting smarter. And that was a problem.

The new system had been trialled by all the agencies. In four days, it was due to come online. Until then, the people of Section G would have to stay alert and be on the ball.

Calver leaned back in his chair and ran his fingers through his blonde hair as the black hawk helicopters approached the ship.

Calver was twenty-five and working for the man. Snatched up from MIT for being a computer whiz. He remembered the day the Agency poached him. Remembered how the sound of being an agent gave him visions of working overseas, sipping vodka martinis and beautiful bedding women. They never mentioned being stuck nearly fifteen stories underground in a nuclear blast-proof rabbit hole.

His blue eyes fixed on the screen as the helicopters hovered above the ship. The orders from the team leader rang in his ear like running commentary. The yells and shouts of command, 'Let's go boys and keep it tight and by the numbers. Kowalski and Dicks, you got point.' There was zipping noise as the commander used the abseil rope. Then the sound of military boots hammering on steel deck flooring made it sound like a radio sketch. On another monitor, he had the helmet camera feeds. Live footage was reordered for playback if required.

'Zero, this Charlie two-four, the target is secure. Zero casualties. Awaiting escort for pickup of the package. Zero, be advised package is full. I repeat, the package is full,' said the voice.

'Roger that Charlie-two-four, good job and nice catch,' Calver said. Relieved at the lack of casualties, he sat back in his chair and blew out a sigh of relief. He stood up and stretched.

The five hours sat on his ass had taken its toll.

The shift was twelve hours, with an hour break in the middle. Janis would come around with a drinks trolley, offering refreshments so that they did not have to leave the desks.

The section chiefs had at least been generous and said they could make their workspace their own. Calver had several comic book superhero bobbleheads and a plastic cactus on his desk. Whereas others had pictures of their families or cars. The bosses had figured that a homely feel improved working conditions. The idea was fewer people went sick, and morale would be better, making the place more efficient.

Calver shook off his five-foot-nine frame and did some short arm and back exercises. He could feel the pain in his lower back subside as he touched his toes. But it came back as he straightened out. Twelve hours sat down sounded dreamy, but it had its downsides. For some of Calver's colleagues, it was too much junk food and a lack of exercise. For others, it was the absence of quick smoke breaks.

In his two years here, he had seen people come and go, but he stuck it out. His transfer applications had gone through to an office in Washington weeks ago. Now, it was a case of keeping his mouth shut, do a good job, and wait.

Calver looked at his screen and saw the patrol boats surround the ship, then the Black Hawks left. The destroyers wouldn't be too far away.

Mission accomplished.

The ship would be searched by bomb disposal units. They would do a sweep with sniffer dogs for explosives and traps. The crew would be kept on board the vessel until it was deemed necessary and safe to transfer them onto a holding facility. He tried to imagine what full was. Apparently, his interpretation and the team leaders differed. Amount and content mattered to the people upstairs. It mattered to him because a big score could get him noticed. However, the section chief wasn't there; he had to have some personal time apparently. Today was not the day for him to be nursing his kid's flu. Today of all days, he should be there to witness Calver's glory.

Chapter 11

Steel showered and changed. He slipped on the black suit and the black polo shirt he had packed. The refreshing shower had done the trick, but he feared the air-conditioned room gave his body false hope for what awaited outside. Reaching into his jacket pocket, Steel pulled out the cabbie's business card and phoned the number. There was something about Stan that intrigued Steel. It was one of those feelings he would have but could not quite put his finger on it. So, Steel decided to keep the man close. It was probably nothing, but he had to be sure.

'Be there in twenty minutes was the promise. Steel went down to the bar and had a quick double Jonnie Walker Blue. Steel looked out through the panoramic windows. The sparkling lights of the town across the water offered a hypnotic sight.

Steel checked his watch, then finished his drink before heading for the hotel entrance.

As the British cabbie pulled the minibus up in front of the hotel, Steel smiled. The guy was there with five minutes to spare.

Not bad.

'I hope you didn't run any red lights to get to me?' Steel joked, but Stan just rocked his hand from side to side, as if to say 'maybe.' The cabbie laughed as Steel climbed into the cab and clicked on his seat belt. The cabbie started the engine, then put his foot down. The engine screamed like a small, wounded animal as the vehicle took off, leaving a cloud of black, oily smoke.

'Where too, guvnor?' Stan asked, his mouth still full of whatever foul-smelling thing he was having for his supper.

'This address,' Steel said, passing the address to Stan. 'Also, I need to pick up wine and flowers on the way.' Foster lived in a town called Attard which was to the north, which Steel had discovered using the map search, was also close to the American Embassy.

Stan grumbled to himself before putting the destination into his navigation system.

Extended by the shopping trip, the journey through small villages, open country roads gave Steel time to think.

Why was he really here? What was the purpose of Foster's invitation after all these years? The guy worked for the CIA if they were hunting down terrorists. He had unlimited resources without Steel.

No, whatever it was, either off the books or personal – or worse – both.

It was five-fifty-five when they arrived. 'Five minutes before a parade,' Steel could hear his old drill sergeant scream.

Sometimes that five minutes made all the difference.

It did back then.

Two things Steel learnt from his days in the British Army.

One; never volunteer for anything.

Two; Five minutes before a parade, that way you'll never be late.

Words to live by.

Steel took in the scenery as Stan wound through the small towns, often getting stuck behind a tourist who had a rental car and had no idea where they were going. Just outside, Attard Stan pulled up next to a store he knew so Steel could get the flowers and wine. While Steel paid, he noticed that Stan was on his cell phone texting again. The man had been texting with someone almost the entire trip. Steel put it down as nothing to be concerned about, just a guy who liked to keep in touch, maybe a girlfriend or something?

Steel got back in the minibus cab and closed the door, all the while wondering what Foster's invitation was really about.

The cab wound through the dusty streets full of mixed looking houses before pulling up to a long driveway between two buildings.

'Here you go, sir. If you need me to pick you up…' Stan said, making a telephone gesture.

'Yeah… I know, just call,' Steel smiled and gave the cabbie twenty-five euros before getting out and taking his shopping bags with him. He shut the door and moved out of the way before Stan took off at speed, spitting loose gravel and pebbles everywhere. Steel paused for a moment, looking up both sides of the street as if he was unsure about what he was about to do and was weighing up an escape strategy. But Steel was checking for anything he considered strange – out of place. Just like the shiny blue mini down the road with a person sitting in it. Steel had seen it on the way down. He had seen the person had a paper map and a navigation system out. They could have been lost, a tourist who did not know their way around. Possible. Steel added it to memory, just in case.

Steel began to walk down the path. The houses on either side did not have much in plants and no lawn in the back gardens. He could tell the island was on some water allowance that did not cater to greenery. Some houses had pools for those who could afford to fill them.

Foster's house was large but humble, not the fancy white picket fence and big garden he had always dreamt of having. The house was three stories, with off-white walls and a terracotta tiled roof.

Steel found the Mediterranean look pleasant – quaint even. Out front, there were two cars parked. One was a large black Range Rover, and the other a massive white Mitsubishi four-by-four. Steel noticed the adjacent garage had been converted into an extra room.

Steel took a moment as he walked up to check the place out. Motion-activated cameras covered the front door and driveway. As he stood at the door, he looked across to the window to his right. The inner framework had a three-centimetre strip of aluminium next to the glass. A piece of obsolete metal to some, but Steel recognised it as laser meshing. A calibrated net of beams connected to an alarm, which sounded when the window was struck. The glass was probably bulletproof.

Why?

Steel did not understand.

As far as Steel knew, Foster was a section chief in charge of monitor watchers. They were the eyes for the Navy and passport control.

Maybe Foster thought his past might catch up with him. In all the years they served in teams, Steel never knew Foster to be paranoid.

Careful, yes – but never like this.

The door swung open, and a fifteen-year-old girl stood in the doorway. She was a cute kid who had her mother's looks. She wore jeans and a band T-shirt, her long brown hair fell straight down. Steel was shocked. The last time he'd last seen Abby, she was knee-high.

'Yes,' asked the girl with an unfriendly attitude.

'Abby? I suppose you don't remember me. My name is John, and I used to work with your father,' Steel said. Hoping for some reaction apart from a shoulder shrug.

'No,' she replied before slamming the door, followed by a loud sorrowful cry.

Steel smiled and shook his head. He remembered when she was a little girl, all freckles and braces. Now she was grown up. Cute innocence replaced by an angry teenager.

'Why's the door shut? Didn't you ask him in?'

Steel heard his friend yell out after his kid.

The door opened, and Foster stood there. He still stood tall, but his black hair had been replaced by a silver –Steel thought it suited him. The years of good food and desk work had added a couple of pounds. Despite that, Foster still looked in good shape.

Foster's eyes widened with relief at the sight of his old friend.

'I don't think much of your maid service,' Steel joked.

'Probably thought you were a beggar in those rags,' Foster shot back, pointing to Steel's thousand-dollar suit. The two men laughed and embraced like brothers.

'How you doing?' Steel asked. He saw the look of dismay on Foster's face. His were red from too much crying.

'Better... I guess. Hasn't really sunk in yet.'

Steel nodded; he knew that pain all too well.

'Good to see you, buddy,' Foster said.

At first, Steel said nothing; he just hung in the large man's vice-like grip. Steel just stood there, trying not to lose hold of the wine or the flowers.

'Come on, let's get you inside,' Foster said and led Steel inside.

Steel followed Foster through the house to a large kitchen and then to the backyard. There was a small, dried grass patch at the bottom of the square-shaped grounds, only a wall of high hedges enclosed space with a large pool and a patio. Between the house and the pool stood a long metal table with a marble effect plastic top, surrounded by eight wicker chairs.

Several small trees in terracotta pots lined the garden and other potted plants that had blossomed into various blues, reds, and yellows.

This added some life to the otherwise dry garden.

A black and white cat walked along the poolside before finding a shady spot in the corner of the back yard.

Martha Foster was a stunning woman. She had been then and even more so now. He remembered long golden locks that used to flow over her shoulders. But now, she wore her hair short. It suited her – but then everything looked good on her.

Even with the loose-fitting white dress, her figure was still that of a model - a career she had given up, to be with Foster. She may have given up the catwalk, but boy, could she still turn heads.

Martha was busy putting wine glasses on the long table, ready for his visit. Her movements were slow and laboured, like she had no energy.

Steel stood silently in the kitchen doorway and just looked at the vision before him. Waiting to see her reaction.

It seemed like a lifetime since their last meeting.

Foster coughed subtlety as if to get her attention.

Martha Foster turned with a broken smile to look at her husband. As she looked up, her gaze fell upon a familiar sight.

'Hello Martha,' Steel simply said.

Martha cried as she rushed forwards. Martha threw her arms around him and held him tight. 'Thank you for coming. It means a lot,' Martha said. Her voice was soft, but something about her tone made Steel uneasy.

'These are for you,' Steel said, handing her the flowers. Martha smiled and thanked him. Taking the flowers, Martha searched for a vase, and Marcus took the wine.

Steel watched Marcus and Martha as they busied themselves with opening wine and arranging the flowers. But all the while, Steel got the feeling there was more to his being there than just helping to morn poor Lucy. Steel had seen the redness of Martha's eyes, the drawn look in her face. She had been crying. Abby was angry, and Foster was attempting to put on a brave face for his family.

Chapter 12

Somewhere in the harsh lands of Tunisia, a man sat alone in semi-darkness. A low glow of light was coming from two standard lamps. These stood opposite each other in the large square room. The light was enough to break up the darkness at one end of the room. But failed to illuminate the twenty-twenty room completely. He sat on a claret leather chair in front of a large desk carved from olive wood. On the desktop was a large monitor, a cordless phone, and an old brass desk lamp.

The room itself had little in the way of furnishings. Two leather armchairs sat on a large Persian rug, between them a small oval oak coffee table. Along the right-hand wall was an antique bookcase to the left, a large painting of a battle scene set in the first Afghan war. The image was called *The Last Stand*, the final fight of the 44th Regiment at Gundamuck in 1842. Men on a rock platform surrounded by incoming hordes.

The man sipped green tea from a Turkish glass teacup. The weak light masked his face. However, his white cotton shirt stood out from the shadows. His hands were large and bore signs of hard labour. His short-sleeved shirt revealed a tattoo of a crescent moon under an open star on his left wrist, where a watch face would sit.

There was a knock on the single wooden door, then a young bearded man walked in and stood in the centre of the room. Waiting to be called forwards. Even in his loose-fitting khaki clothes, his trembling was apparent.

He was in the presence of The Master.

A man that governments had sort but never found, a man that would bring death to the invaders.

The man in the chair moved, only a beckoning hand. The young man approached and whispered something into his master's ear. The Master waited until the young man had finished and then pushed the glass cup into the boy's right eye with a quick, upward thrust. The boy screamed before the man grabbed him and smashed his head onto the table. There was a crunch of glass as the wooden desk drove the glass deeper into the boy's head.

The screams stopped, and The Master sat back in his chair. The body slid off the desk and fell into a bloody heap on the bare concrete floor. In the open doorway stood a tall, bearded man in a dark suit.

'I thought you might take the news badly,' said the man in the doorway. 'Don't worry, the other plan will be active soon. There will be no mistakes.'

'There better not Aamir. There better not,' The Master said. His voice was deep and ancient. Aamir bowed and then waved behind him before moving out of the way. Letting two large built men into the room to retrieve the blood-soaked body of the boy. As Aamir closed the door, The Master opened a desk drawer and pulled out a picture of a woman and a little girl.

'Soon, my darlings.... Soon.' His voice was as deep as his anger. He put the photograph away again and locked the drawer. The Master pulled himself out of the chair and walked towards the door.

There was much to do.

Chapter 13

The sun had kissed the horizon leaving a canvas of deep orange, reds and a wash of purple. The open sky and an easterly breeze had brought a crispness to the evening.

To Steel, it was still warm.

All through the meal, the conversation had been limited to chit chat. As if avoiding talking about Lucy. But Steel did not expect anything else.

They had asked what Steel was doing now.

Steel had answered but knew they weren't really interested. Abby had stayed in her room. The thought of food and guests was somehow wrong in her eyes.

The meal had been cleared just moments before. Steel had almost forgotten how good a cook Martha was. She had presented traditional Maltese food, including a tasty macaroni bake with a cheese topping. There were olives, bread, different cheeses and plenty of wine.

After the substantial meal, Foster helped Martha clear the table and bring out the coffee. Foster placed down a long wooden tray onto the table. He then off-loaded the large crockery coffee pot, three mugs, a sugar bowl, and a milk jug of the same design.

'What happened?' Steel said bluntly.

'They don't know. Local PD is investigating. Sergeant Gann Burlo has the case,' Foster said.

'What did the Medical Examiner say?' Steel asked before taking a sip from the coffee.

'He hasn't done the autopsy yet, tomorrow, I think,' Foster replied.

Steel watched as Martha stood up.

Martha said she was going back to bed and did not have the stomach to hear about her daughter's death. She said goodnight, and with a gentle kiss on the cheek, thanked Steel for coming.

It was almost as if she had already asked him to do something. He was just fearful of what it was.

Foster led Steel into his study, which turned out to be the renovated garage. Foster's workplace, away from work.

The overpowering stench of cigars and strong coffee hung in the air. By looking at the full ashtray on the desk and the empty crystal whisky glass, Steel knew that Foster had been there most of the day.

'Talk to me, Marcus,' Steel asked as he placed himself down on one of the leather armchairs.

'Yesterday morning...' Foster paused as he closed his eyes. The apparent pain of running through the events etched onto his face. 'Lucy's body was discovered at a place called Blue Hole Divesite. It's near Azure Window on Gozo Island,' Foster murmured. As if not wanting to be overheard by the rest of the house.

'She jumped?' Steel asked.

'No... I mean, I don't think so... I ...I don't know.' Foster said, tears in his eyes.

'Hey, it's fine.' Steel said. Trying to calm and reassure his friend.

'Jonnie, I don't even know what she was doing there. She was supposed to be at a friends house. Or that's what she told us,' Foster said. Suddenly realising how much he did not know his daughter or what she had been doing.

'So, the police are calling it a suicide, and you don't want to believe it? It happens. Kids go off the rails about all sorts of crap nowadays,' Steel asked bluntly.

Foster shot Steel an angry look.

'What do you need me to do?' Steel said.

What do you want me to do? To Foster and to Steel meant the same thing.

To everyone else, it was a simple request.

What do you want me to do? This wasn't just a simple request in Steel's or Foster's eyes. This was asking for permission.

What do you want me to do? Or rather – do I have Carte Blanche?

'Investigate, find out what happened over there, and if some bastard is responsible-' Foster's eyes were bloodshot with anger. His voice rumbled with a vengeance.

'We do things my way. If I don't like the situation… I walk,' Steel said. He stood up and placing his brandy glass down on the small coffee table which sat between the chairs.

'Agreed,' Foster said.

Foster shook Steel's hand and nodded.

'OK… tell me everything, and don't leave anything out,' Steel said.

Chapter 14

Around nine that evening, James Calver arrived back at his flat. His ginger tom, Percy, was curled up on a throw blanket that protected Calver's brown fabric couch.

Naturally, Percy was too busy licking at its left leg to notice Calver.

Calver walked into the kitchen and placed the shopping bags onto the work surface. His cupboards and refrigerator were almost empty.

The kitchen was big enough for one – in fact, the whole apartment was perfect for a single person. It was a two-bedroom apartment, but one of those rooms was now a small gym

The kitchen and sitting room was open-plan, with only a breakfast bar to separate them. A large Ultra High Definition television hung on the right-hand wall so he could watch tv from the kitchen. The walls were painted off-white. It was also light enough to reflect the sun's rays – making it bearable in the summer, which got up well into the high thirties.

He turned on his computer and pressed the button on his answering machine to check his messages. 'You have seven new messages,' said the electronic female voice.

One was from his mother. The others were just marketers, and another was from a girl who realised she had the wrong number. Calver smiled to himself as he listened to her voice. She sounded hot, but she was also drunk and wanting to kill some guy called Mike.

Lucky Mike, he thought.

Calver packed away a carton of eggs, some cheese, packs of cut meat into the refrigerator. Then he grabbed a beer to celebrate.

He had food in the apartment – yey!

The computer monitor showed a picture of a red moon setting over the ocean, with the Azure Window in the foreground. It was a photoshop picture, but he did not care. It looked great on the thirty-two-inch monitor. Calver typed in his password and waited the few seconds it would take to boot up.

He had around a hundred emails in his inbox. Most of it was junk and some links from several networking sites. He sat in his black office chair, sipping his beer and began to delete the unimportant ones. With a simple click of the mouse, and they were gone. He spotted an email from the Harley Davidson shop he had been to in Attard. They had sent him information on a Softail he had asked about the week before.

It was a luxury he could not really afford, but things were about to change for him in a big way. He would have enough to quit his job and live on a small island somewhere when that happened.

Seven more emails went in the trash. However, the next made Calver stop and sit up, his eyes fixed on the heading. Calver's hand tighten on the mouse.

I know what you did on Gozo, it read. The email had probably come from a public place like an internet café, with no natural way of tracking the sender even if he found the computer.

Those few simple words could ruin everything he had started.

Calver wrenched himself from his seat, forcing the chair to slide away to the side, teeth and fists clenched in anger.

This wasn't supposed to be happening; it was meant to be easy.

An evil grin crept across Calver's face.

He knew people.

The sort who made problems go away.

The sort of people who weren't squeamish – and did not ask questions.

Calver sat back down with a smile and finished going through his emails.

'It will all be OK in the morning,' he said to himself as he took another hit from the bottle.

Chapter 15

It was five the following day when Steel woke from his troubled sleep. He decided to go for a run. Hoping to shake off the effect of the long flight and too much wine the night before. Steel had taken another taxi home from Foster's. Thinking Stan could have used the rest, considering it was nearly eleven at night when he had left.

The sun had not yet risen. However, the sky was already dark purple. Steel had left the hotel and headed south from his location. He was heading for the other side, towards Valletta's waterfront. The run would take him at least thirty minutes because he did not know the lay of the land. He was used to the streets of Manhattan. The broad long, straight roads with towering buildings.

Here, he had narrow, surprisingly steep streets to contend with, more like San Fransico. The city was compact and beautiful.

But even in the early morning, it was warm.

The run would give him the chance to learn the roads and acclimatise.

The high twenties in Malta was far different from the high twenties in NYC. Luckily, he was there in March when it was not so warm as July and August – the hot months.

Steel noticed how much the streets were clear of traffic. Almost as if he was the last person on earth. He made his way down the picturesque Triq L-Assedju L-Kbir – one of the main streets that ran from the hotel.

Steel was amazed at the amount of strange, old buildings on the route. One of which was a C-shaped hotel surrounded by trees. A chilled wind nipped at his face as he went, taking in the sights as he went. His feet pounded the concrete as he pushed the pace. A police car passed him, followed by a taxi and a guy on a scooter. Across the road, he saw a couple of joggers heading in the opposite direction. He smiled to himself, glad he wasn't the only one fool enough to be up and running so early.

All seemed safe and yet surreal. Steel was in Malta trying to find what had happened to his friend's daughter, a friend he had not seen for years. He still wondered, why him? After all, Foster worked for the CIA. A Section Chief no less, so why get Steel involved? Why was this off the books? Foster had explained a few things the night before. How she was seeing some guy from the firm, Foster did not know who, she wouldn't say. *Kids and their secrets*, Steel thought to himself as Foster explained the relationship. But they had broken up weeks before.

To Steel, that did not matter; it was a place to start. After all, there was nothing like an angry lover. Then Foster told Steel about Lucy's work with the conservation community. 'A bunch of hippies who want to protect a lot of old rocks,' one angry developer had said in an interview with the local paper. His million dollar deal to build a shopping mall on top of an ancient ruin was thrown out. Lucy and her colleagues had also received threats from angry film companies who wanted to shoot scenes on protected sites.

Steel had a list of people to talk with, starting with the ex-boyfriend and then the developers. Steel had also considered it may have been something to do with Foster and his job, but Foster had shrugged that theory off. Foster was in charge of people who stared at computer screens all day checking facial recognition at the airport; he had nothing to do directly with the operation. Foster was just a figurehead if something went wrong. Despite what Foster had told him, Steel was still going to check.

Steel had made it back to the hotel as the sun was breaking the horizon. He spent an hour in the gym before showering, then headed to the restaurant and a hearty breakfast.

Steel did not know when he would eat again.

He opened up the map of the island he had purchased from the airport. It was detailed, showing all the major routes and places of interest. More importantly, it fitted in his pocket.

Steel sometimes considered paper better than electronics. Small, convenient, and if need be, you can burn it, and you don't have to worry about having a signal with a map.

He folded the map so it showed the island of Gozo. That would have been his first port of call. Foster had said they had found her near a place called Azure Window – whatever that was, but the ME wouldn't be available to see him until later in the week. That left Steel open to check out Lucy's apartment and workplace first. Steel hadn't seen her since she was young. Now he had to try and get inside her head.

Steel needed to see where and how Lucy lived before he saw where she died. He downed the rest of his coffee, then stood up to face the ocean view. The sun was high but not yet at full strength.

Foster sat at the breakfast bar drinking coffee from his *Best dad in the world* mug. It had been a gift from the two girls for his promotion to Section Chief.

That seemed like a lifetime ago now.

Foster had been in the Washington office then, chasing bad guys the old fashioned way. But he was now classed as old school, a relic. The new post wasn't so much a promotion as being put out to pasture. Foster was in his fifties, the truth was he always felt like an old man next to Steel, but he still had plenty to give. Hell, he could outrun most of the new guys on the track, and he could still beat the crap out of them.

He had forgotten more about been an agent than most of the newbies had or would ever learn. He looked around at his wife and little girl and smiled. The new job may be taking him out of the crosshairs, but he gained more time with his family. For that, he wasn't angry, however much the system made him mad.

The little tv on the counter next to the microwave showed the latest news on the island. There had been a car bomb in Rabat. No one was hurt, but many had been injured.

Foster shook his head in dismay.

This once peaceful place was becoming as dangerous as the rest of the world.

Foster finished his coffee and put on his grey suit jacket. His gaze stayed on the news channel. The first thing he would have to do is find out what sort of threat the bombing was.

Was it a terrorist, or just some guy who had cheated on his wife? He had seen it before in Miami. Some asshole life insurance salesperson caught with his pants down by his wife. She had been military, part of the bomb squad unit. One day the man said he was going on a trip out of town and would be gone all day. She had followed him to his girlfriend's place. It had been some big beach house with a long drive and four garages. She had seen them through a window, and he sure as hell wasn't selling her insurance.

She'd rigged the car.

It hadn't been quick; she had made sure the car caught fire first before exploding. She had made sure she could see him squirm before he was blown to pieces. The explosion was immense, destroying the car, and it took half the house and the mistress with it.

Foster kissed Martha and Abby goodbye and headed off to work. He had been offered the chance for compassionate leave, but he needed to work. Foster needed to be doing something. Besides, Martha had said Foster would be more beneficial to Steel if he was at the Embassy. Foster knew she just wanted him out of the house. He pulled out his cell phone and pressed the speed-dial for the office. Foster knew Edward Bryce; his second in command and floor chief would be there. Foster waited for a few moments, allowing Bryce to get to the phone or spit out whatever he had just taken a bite of for breakfast.

'Morning, boss?' said Bryce, almost choking on his breakfast.

'Edward, sorry for disturbing your meal,' Foster said.

'No problem, boss,' lied Edward. 'What's up?'

'Car bomb in Rabat, what do we know?' Foster asked, walking towards his vehicle.

'Not much yet, there hasn't been any chatter, so this is a bit of surprise. Chances are it's just local, but we're looking into it none the less,' Edward said.

'Roger that, I'll be there in twenty, make sure we have eyes on. I want to know what the cops know,' Foster ordered. Hanging up, he placed the phone in his pocket and got into his car. Leather moaned under his weight. Foster waited for a moment before turning the key and put the Land Rover into drive. His gut and head were in different places.

His gut told him to cancel the secret operation he was about to set into motion. An operation that had been planned for months. Now they were ready to activate it. The section chief had told him to bring it online and watch them all burn. A phrase that Foster had found odd, considering there was no burning to be done, just identification. However, Foster kept thinking about Lucy. In a way, he hoped she had jumped because the alternative would be far worse. But Foster knew deep down there was something not right. He knew his little girl. She was too full of life to have done that. Suddenly, Foster feared the worst.

Foster had given Steel Lucy's address in the district of Lija. John Steel used the spare key that Foster had given him to open the front door. It was a quaint place, simply furnished, a one-bedroom apartment, bedroom, bathroom, and kitchen. He stepped inside a small t-shaped hallway. The entranceway was littered with pictures of Lucy with family and friends.

Stretching in front of him was a hallway. It was painted white with laminate flooring. The only light was three single bulb lamps, and the sunlight poured in from the rooms' open doors. There was a door to his right, which led to the kitchen. This was small but modern, with all the essentials. Steel began to look through the fridge and cupboards, taking note of the bare minimum in crockery and cutlery. If anything, there was two of everything.

On his search of the cupboards, Steel found tea bags and coffee granules. He picked up the kettle to test how much water there was.

Half full.

Steel tipped out the water and refilled it. Not wanting to make a drink with stale water and goodness knows what else inside. He placed it back onto the charger and switched it on. While he waited for the kettle to boil, Steel opened the refrigerator and checked to contents. He had learnt that you could tell a lot about a person by what they eat. And by all accounts, Lucy was a careful eater.

It mainly was healthy foods with a lot of fruit and vegetables. The freezer compartment had a lot of fish and chicken. He wasn't surprised at the lack of red meat. But, Steel bet she liked the odd rib-eye at one of Foster's barbecues; if they were still as good as what Steel had remembered from the old days. As he looked around, he noticed that the kitchen was neat and organised. Lucy had been as house proud as her mother. A sudden click from the kettle caused Steel to turn to see the mist rise from the kettle's spout. Steel grabbed a mug, the instant coffee and made himself a black coffee. He wandered through to the next room along the hallway, which had been Lucy's bedroom.

He tapped the door open with his boot. It opened slowly, revealing a brightly lit room as the sun poured through a single window, illuminating the room. There was a double bed made up for one, along with a wardrobe and a dresser. On the dresser were boxes filled with a mix of cheap and what appeared to be expensive jewellery. Steel checked the bedside cabinets and wardrobe. The room held more pictures of Lucy on adventures; scuba-diving of some corral, mountain biking by the edge of a cliff, with a fantastic sea view. The drawers held nothing much to help with the case, only clothes.

By all accounts, this was a young woman who liked to live alone. Steel knew there was a boyfriend in the picture but figured he never spent the night here. The way the place was set out, this was her sanctuary.

Leaving the bedroom, he entered the sitting room. Despite the compactness of the space, it was arranged as both an office and a living room. On a back wall, a long wooden unit held books and glass sculptures. In another corner was a large standard lamp next to a potted plant.

A long brown couch stretched in front of a medium-sized tv. In the back corner was a large monitor next to a desktop computer. On a wall next to the desktop computer hung a corkboard. It was three-by-two feet with a thick dark brown frame. Steel noted the collage of notes and stickers to remind her of things to do that week. There were food shopping lists and a reminder to take food to the cat sanctuary.

Steel sat at the computer and switched it on. The monitor flashed, and there was a beep from the tower. Steel was hoping Lucy was comfortable enough in her surroundings that there was no password. He sneered at his misfortune as the system asked for the password. Lifting the keyboard, Steel checked underneath for evidence of a reminder but found nothing. Steel rocked in the chair and looked around for signs of anything she may have used but saw nothing.

While he pondered over the password, he checked the small set of drawers under the desk for anything important. There were bank statements, paychecks from the *Presidential Gardens*. Steel had remembered Foster had said she'd had a day job in one of the gardens.

He continued to search about, finding data sticks by the dozen and memory cards for a camera. Steel stuck them in his pocket and closed the drawers.

The screen still held the taunting message. '*Please enter a password.*' Steel sat, sipping black coffee. Hoping for the insight to crack the password.

Steel shrugged and just typed in *PASSWORD*; more out of frustration than anything. He looked up at the screen as there was another beep, and the operating system kicked in.

'You got to be kidding me,' Steel said. He did not know whether to be impressed at his luck or disappointed at her choice. But the more he thought about it, her decision made sense. After all, she lived alone, so why pick something difficult.

Steel checked the files on her desktop, but they were just working calendars and things related to the conservation group. Then he studied the files on her hard drive, concentrating on recently downloaded files.

Lucy had thousands of photographs and music files. The movie file was also quite large, mostly romantic comedies and action films. Steel checked further at her archives, trying to find anything that might explain why she would have taken her own life or, worse, someone took it from her.

As Steel searched through the rest of the folders, he came across one that had been created only a few days before her death. It was a video file; from a cell phone or camera. Lucy and some guy were walking across a massive cliffside, with the ocean on their left. The land looks different from what he had seen on Malta, harsher but strangely beautiful. Lucy was narrating as they walked, explaining some of the plant life and animals, almost like a documentary. The man with her was trying to do an impression of David Attenborough or some other wildlife presenter, making Lucy laugh at his lousy imitation.

Steel watch intently, searching for something he would recognise in the background for future reference, a cliff face or rock formation. As he watched, the camera panned across to the man and glimpsed another island. The ground around the man was jagged, limestone rock, dark green bushes, and sun-scorched grass. It had been a quick coastal shot. The camera action had been more on the man and the scenery. But, what there was gave Steel something to work on. All he had to do was find out where exactly it was.

Steel closed the file and checked how many more she had.

Too many to copy, and he had the feeling he needed to leave. Steel closed down the computer and headed back into the kitchen. He hadn't found a screwdriver on his search, so a knife would do just as well. Steel took out the holding screws and slid off the side of the computer. After locating the hard drive, he unplugged it and tucked it into his jacket pocket. Steel put the computer back together and placed it back on the desk as though nothing had been disturbed. He stood up and looked around one last time, then left. Locking up on his way. As Steel stepped back into the busy streets, he pulled out his phone to check the next thing on his to-do list. *Check out the ex-boyfriend.*

Steel hailed a passing cab.

Chapter 16

The phone in the secure office rang, and the man known as Alpha picked up.

'Yes,' said Alpha.

'Where the hell have you been?' Beta asked. The tone was full of anger and panic.

'Who do you think you are talking to?' growled Alpha.

'Fine – sorry, sir, but we have a situation for now,' said Beta.

'The cop?' said Alpha.

'He went to the girl's apartment. I think he's going to find the kid next?' said Beta.

The was silence. Alpha was thinking.

'We can be at the location and good to go in twenty – we just need the green light. Sir?' said Beta.

Alpha nodded to himself. It was a reasonable plan. 'Do it, but see if you can get anything on him. I don't need a trail,' Alpha said. He hung up and smashed his fist onto the desk. Then he sat quietly in the darkness of his room, planning.

Chapter 17

The sun hung in a cloudless blue sky, and flocks of birds darted here and there on a warm breeze. Steel was in a taxi heading for Mosta, a large city to the north. Steel took out his phone and flicked through the notepad app. Foster had given him a list of people he thought would be necessary to the investigation. One was that of Lucy's best friend, Zoe Keen. Another was a guy called Brad West, Lucy's ex-boyfriend.

The cabbie drove as if he was in the Dakar Rally. Steel held on in the back of the old Ford as it skidded about on the dusty tarmac roads. Steel smiled to himself as he listened, to what could only be an argument with the man and his wife. The man was yelling in Maltese – and very loudly over the phone's wireless earpiece.

The cabbie's driving got more erratic the louder he shouted. Steel grabbed the handgrip on the door as the cabbie overtook a woman on an old scooter and just missed an oncoming truck. Steel grinned childishly. This was both entertaining and thrilling. A feeling he hadn't gotten much of recently.

Zoe Keen worked in a Pharmacy as a chemist assistant. According to Foster, she had worked there for a couple of years. Before that, she was at another store in Victoria on Gozo. Before leaving his hotel, Steel had done some background work on Zoe. However, nothing of great importance stuck out. Father, a man named Albert Keen, worked at the embassy at the same time as Foster. In fact, they were good friends. The mother, Sue, died two years ago of cancer. Soon after, Albert took to drinking and lost his job. Last year he perished when his car went off the road and crashed. The ME at the time concluded it was accidental death due to driving while intoxicated. The story of Zoe was sad, but not one he hadn't heard before.

The more Steel had read into Zoe's past, the more he understood the bond between her and Lucy. According to Foster, Lucy was always there for Zoe.

If anyone knew Lucy well, it would be Zoe.

The taxi stopped abruptly on Constitution Street. There were cafes and restaurants, a cell phone repair place and a couple of shops sporting handbags and shoes. Across the road was a colossal domed cathedral – or the Mosta Rotunda. It reminded Steel of the Pantheon in Rome.

But he hadn't been to Rome for the view. And now, just as he had been then, he had a job to do.

Steel looked up at the magnificent structure. Massive limestone pillars stood proudly at a pinnacled main entrance. Either side bell towers loomed, each displaying a large brass bell and a clock face. Large groups of tourists began to gather outside on the walled forecourt leading up to the building, snapping photographs and taking in the view. Steel paid the cabbie with a ten euro tip. He was barely out before the cab sped off.

Steel stood for a moment, taking in the massive structure and the surrounding buildings, then turned to the buildings behind him. Seeing all the coffee shops and restaurants, he started to feel hungry. The breakfast seemed a long time ago after that terrifying taxi ride. Steel gaze darted from cafes to a place that advertised as 'Take-out and Pizzaria.' He felt his stomach give a grumble and gave it a gentle tap, a promise of a hearty meal later. Then he turned to look down to his right and smiled.

He had found the pharmacy.

Steel noticed the strong scent of healing creams, teas, and something he could not identify on entering the store. The store was quite large, with wooden shelves and glass cabinets. Two people stood at the front in white medical coats.

One was a short man in his fifties, the other a dark-haired woman around the same age. They stood chatting to customers while two younger women rushed about doing the work. One of the women was tall with short blonde hair. Steel remembered seeing her picture in Lucy's apartment, the unkempt hair, the smile, the hummingbird tattoo on her neck. This was most definitely Zoe Keen.

Steel waited until the pharmacy was empty of customers before approaching the chemist. The man looked up from a handful of small boxes he was putting away into a drawer behind the counter. Steel had noticed the man's name tag, *Mr Apap* engraved in thick black letters on a gloss white backplate.

'Yes, sir, how may I help?' the chemist said with a deep, friendly voice.

'I'm looking for Zoe Keen,' Steel said. 'I was told she works here.'

'And you are?' the chemist asked suspiciously.

'I'm her friend's uncle,' Steel said. Looking over at the backroom door as it slid open slowly. Zoe Keen stood in the doorway for a moment, then nodded as if to confirm she was the one he was searching.

'I'm Zoe. You must be Uncle John?' she said.

Zoe had spoken to the chemist and had taken a break. Stepping out onto the street, Zoe turned right, led Steel to a nearby café so they could have a little privacy.

'Why here? What was wrong with the other café down the road?' Steel said.

Zoe shrugged. 'I like the cakes here, and I get a discount.'

Steel said nothing, just sat there, silent, waiting.

She began to fidget.

He kept his face was cold, emotionless.

Zoe seemed pale, sick. Understandable Steel had thought, Losing someone could have that effect on a person – or was it something else?

They were sitting outside in the shade. The sun was high but on the other side of the building. A fresh breeze made its way down the busy streets, blowing up the skirts of unsuspecting women and lifting up hats like some mischievous spectre.

A tall, thin waiter came and took their drink orders. Zoe ordered a cappuccino, Steel went for a Café American. Steel could feel the lack of caffeine in his system.

'I don't get why she did it,' Zoe said, choking back a tear.

'Why she did what?' Steel asked.

'Killed herself, of course... jumped off Azure Window,' Zoe answered, almost puzzled by Steel's question. 'What else would I mean?'

Her tone was nervous, almost as if she thought he had discovered something.

'I don't know. What else would you mean?' Steel asked.

At first, all Steel wanted to know was Lucy's state of mind before the accident, now Zoe had let something slip, and he wanted to learn more.

Zoe's eyes widened, and tears began to flow. It seemed to be more out of fear than remorse. But fear of what?

As Steel looked into her eyes, he saw something. A secret.

'You don't think she jumped. In fact, you know she did not,' Steel said, sitting back in his chair.

Zoe looked terrified. 'What? No! I was nowhere near there, I swear,' she said. Fear rang in her voice – loud and clear.

'But you have an idea who was,' Steel growled, leaning forwards like a predator ready to strike.

Zoe looked around to make sure nobody could hear her. Her mouth flapped open and closed like a fish gasping out of the water. 'Lucy was on Gozo with Brad. He found something he wanted to show her,' Zoe explained, a look of relief crossed her face as if a massive weight was lifted from her shoulders.

'Do you know what he found?' Steel asked calmly. His face still stern.

'No, but I do know Lucy and Brad had split up. Something had happened between them. Lucy never said what, but she wasn't the same again after. Whatever it was, it was bad,' she explained, leaning forwards, closing the gap between them. Steel took a sip from the coffee that just arrived while he took in the new information.

'Do you know where Brad is now?' Zoe went to shake her head but stopped. Her eyes fixed on something behind Steel.

'Yes,' Zoe's eyes widened in surprise. 'He's right behind you,' she said, pointing over Steel's shoulder. Steel turned to see a young man dressed in jeans, a black t-shirt, and a bikers jacket. The mousey haired man stood on the other side of the street. He was in his mid-twenties, and from his hairstyle and the way he dressed, he thought highly of himself. He was busy checking something on his cell phone, which meant he had not seen Zoe or Steel.

'Zoe, it may be a good time for you to go back to work,' Steel said, as he stood up slowly, ensuring he placed himself between Zoe and Brad. Steel did not want to risk Brad suddenly looked over and saw Zoe talking to someone he might mistake as a cop. Steel told her to stay still for a second until it was safe to move. Steel was waiting for a crowd of people to pass next to them. As the tourists walked by, Steel nodded to Zoe, giving her the signal to move. A moment later, she'd disappeared in with the crowd.

Steel smiled to himself as he turned to face Brad. 'OK, Mr West, let's see what you have to say.'

Chapter 18

The Airbus A320 landed safely and headed towards the designated area.

It was the six o'clock flight from Tunisia.

The sound of turbines powering down filled the plane as they came to a final stop far from the terminal building. Outside baggage trucks and the mobile stairs moved forwards to get the passengers off as quickly as possible. Two buses came to a halt just short of the stairs, waiting to carry the two-hundred people safely to the terminal.

Stepping out of the plane, Aamir looked around for a second. Taking in the warmth of the sun and the view of the surrounding landscape. As he made his way down the stairs, he switched on his cell phone and typed a quick message. *Hi mom, got here, OK.*

He pressed send then switched off the phone completely. Aamir made his way through to the baggage claim and waited for the carousel to start moving. He stood near a back wall underneath a security camera. One of his colleagues had done reconnaissance days earlier and noted where all the cameras were.

Aamir pulled, put on his sunglasses and waited. He wore a beige suit with a blue shirt, thinking a baseball cap and hoodie would draw too much attention. He needed to fit in, not stick out. Just be an average guy.

In fact, there was nothing extraordinary about him. He was the average guy, average height, average build. This worked well for Aamir. It meant he could blend in – or disappear.

There was a loud clunk as the baggage conveyor began to move, and a red hazard light started to flash above a monitor that showed the name of the flight.

Aamir waited patiently as the first of the suitcases began to circle. There was a large crowd forming near where the suitcases were coming from a hole in the wall. But Aamir waited. He knew the attention would be on the crowd and not at a quiet spot near the end. Aamir was good at reading people. After all, it was essential to his job. Aamir shook his head, laughing to himself at how utterly predictable passengers were.

He saw his bag slide out, a large black armoured suitcase with a strange grey swirling pattern. On the top was a sticker of a red Trojan Horse's head. Aamir had put it on earlier, making sure the case was easy to spot. He waited until it was close by, then walked over casually and grabbed it. Aamir made his way through the airport without any trouble. He was dressed well and walked like a tourist. He was invisible.

As he stepped out of the airport, the warm air and blazing sunshine hit him. He closed his eyes to soak in those beautiful rays. For him, it was cold. The weather back home was much more intense. Aamir looked over at a car that was approaching. The old Mitsubishi SUV used to be red, but was now, the paint had faded to near pink, and the edges were full of rust.

It was better than a shiny new truck that would stand out.

The vehicle stopped, two men got out and embraced their friend. There was a short man, the driver, and a much taller man who was obviously the muscle. The tall man grabbed Aamir's suitcase and placed it into the wagon's trunk as Aamir got in the back of the SUV.

'Good flight, brother?' asked the small man as he sat behind the wheel.

Aamir said nothing; he just nodded with a gentle smile.

'Everything you requested is ready at the safe house,' the small man added.

Aamir reached into his pocket and pulled out the cell phone, and turned it on. 'Let's go,' he ordered. The small man nodded and put the car into gear, and drove off. Aamir sent a quick text to the safe house to note his arrival, then placed it back in his pocket. The small man switched on the local radio station it was playing some oldies. Aamir rolled up his jacket and put the makeshift pillow against the window.

A mixture of late nights and an early flight had taken its toll. Aamir had much to do once they reached their destination, but for now, he would try to sleep and dream of what was soon to come and the glorious battle ahead.

Chapter 19

Steel weaved in and out of the crowds of tourists, trying to blend in, attempting to be invisible so he wouldn't be seen by his quarry.

Steel did not rush in his pursuit. He was tall enough to see over most people's heads, but at the same time, he wasn't so tall he stood out.

Steel kept Brad in his sights. Twenty-feet out. Far enough to not give off that sixth sense people have when they think they are being followed.

The trick is not to make himself noticeable. Suddenly turning around to look at a magazine rack makes someone look suspicious. If the person turns around, you just keep walking, even if it's straight past them. Steel was mixed in with a group of tourists, the perfect cover, and in this city – there was plenty to make a person stop and look at the architecture.

And that's what Steel did. He walked a little, took some photos with his cell phone of the scenery, then moved on.

Steel wanted to see where Brad was going, what he was doing, and more importantly, who he spoke with.

Zoe's reaction to Brad's arrival made Steel think, why was the man there in the first place? Was he innocent, just a piece on the board, or was he in it up to his neck? Steel remembered Zoe saying that Brad had found something on the other island and that he and Lucy had broken up after that. Which led to the obvious question – what did Brad find?

Unfortunately, Brad wasn't doing much of anything. He just walked around. Brad walked about in silence. Steel was starting to think Brad wasn't a person of interest – or even interesting for that matter.

That was until Brad stopped.

The young man stood looking at his cell phone then began moving around strangely. The more Steel watched, the more he realised Brad was using an online map search. Brad suddenly looked over towards Zoe's place of work and started to move forward.

Steel hung back slightly. Allowing the gap to grow, so he would go unnoticed, but close enough to get to Brad in case he tried something.

Steel thought it strange Brad should be there. Foster had mentioned that Brad lived and worked in Valletta, but it could be a coincidence.

Only Steel wasn't big on coincidences.

He watched as Brad stopped in front of the pharmacy and stared through the window. A bad feeling ran through Steel as he watched Brad smile as Zoe appeared from the backroom. As Brad reached into his jacket pocket, Steel rushed forward, hoping Brad wasn't armed.

'Hi…Brad West, we need to talk,' Steel call, hoping to scare Brad from doing something stupid. Brad turned open-mouthed, fear painted on his face. Steel was only a few feet away when Brad took to his heels.

Steel rolled his eyes. Why did they always run? Brad set off quickly, his arms pounding out the pace. He yelled at people to get out of his way. Steel took off after him, dodging onlookers as he went, hot in pursuit down the main street.

Steel had to catch Brad quick. Brad knew his way around. Steel did not. Looking over a map of the cities wasn't as good as having the quarry's local knowledge. Brad was fast – but so was Steel.

Mosta was a maze of streets, but, unfortunately for Brad, not too many alleyways. Steel was thankful this wasn't New York or London. All the houses were built together, cutting off any quick escape. Steel figured Brad would try for one of the frequent buses or somewhere familiar to hide.

Steel was closing in. The many groups of tourists made things difficult but not impossible to get through. They slowed Steel down - more importantly, they slowed Brad down.

Steel wasn't far behind, but fear kept Brad going. When the adrenaline kicked in, a person could be as fast as an Olympic sprinter. The trouble with adrenaline is, it does not last that long and left a person cramped up.

That was all Steel had to wait for.

He was waiting for pain signs to see Brad on the ground holding a calf muscle or upper thigh.

But he never did. Brad just kept on running. The clip-clop of his shoes echoed off the cobbled street.

They were heading north on Constitution Street, a long straight road. Perfect for keeping track of Brad as he ran. But Brad had been clever. The street was full of shops and tourists. Steel had kept up with him and inched closer. Pushing past groups of people, missing dogs on leads that barked and snapped.

Still, Steel pursued.

Closer and closer.

Now Steel was just inches away, close enough to reach out and grab Brad's collar.

Soon it would be over, and Steel would have his answers.

Steel was so close now he could feel the heat from Brad's body on his figure tips.

Just reach out and grab the bastard, Steel thought. Stop fucking about.

Steel's heart pounded in his chest. The air seemed thin from the heat of the day. Steel made a lunge forwards, his hand outstretched.

Steel was suddenly ripped off his feet as a car knocked into him. Intent on his pursuit, Steel hadn't noticed they were crossing the road. Steel growled at the driver and launched himself off the hood of the car, and took chase. Now, he was mad.

Brad looked behind down the street to see his pursuer bounce off a car. He slowed to watch, a broad grin spreading on his face.

'Jackass,' Brad shouted at Steel. But the smile faded, and a look of utter fear replaced it. Steel was up again, coming for him, and he looked murderously angry. Brad turned and took off.

Panic clouded his judgement.

The car should have stopped the guy, but the man kept coming. He wasn't just a man. He was a killing machine, a Tank.

They must have sent him.

Steel ignored the pain in his side, set his sights on the frightened Brad, and ran. The two men hurried down the street, tossing people out of the way as they went. Steel could see something was driving Brad, and it had to be more than just fear of him.

'Brad, stop! I am a cop, you idiot!' Steel screamed forwards. But Brad either did not hear or did not trust him. Steel looked past his quarry.

Further on was a bridge and then another part of the city. Steel had wondered why Brad had not taken one of the many other side roads, tried to lose Steel in that part of the town. The bridge was long with no room to hide, no good cover.

Or was he planning to jump?

Steel needed to catch Brad, and he needed to do it now. Sweat poured out of Steel. He felt the burning sensation from his legs and side from where the car had struck him, but he dug deep and powered on, fighting the pain. The bridge wasn't far now. He could hear Brad yelling something, but it was drowned out by the beating of his heart in his ears. Then Steel saw it as Brad reached the bridge, something that changed everything.

The river was dry, probably had been for nearly a hundred years by the look of the trees and bushes growing there. Now Steel understood why Brad wanted to get to the bridge.

Below, in the dried-up stream, it was the perfect cover. With plenty of undergrowth to get lost in, and Steel would have little chance of finding him. Brad turn, his smile got broader, he moved as if to give Steel the bird, but he never got the chance.

Brad suddenly spun around, knocked off his feet like he had just been hit by a bus.

As Steel ran towards Brad, there was a crowd starting to gathered. There were people taking photos with their cell phones. Others were trying to hold people back. At the same time, some struggled to get closer, including an elderly couple. Steel heard screaming, then he saw the blood pooling from the body. Steel pushed his way through the gathered crowds and saw Brad's twisted body. Steel pushed everyone away and began compressions. As he pushed down, blood fountained from a wound in Brad's chest, forcing the people back. Steel looked at the wound, confused at first. Why hadn't he seen it before? The hole was tiny, possibly five centimetres in diameter, possibly from a .22 calibre weapon.

'Call for an ambulance,' Steel yelled as he put his hands on the wound to try and control the bleeding. That's when he felt the boy's body grow still.

Brad's heart was no longer beating.

Steel looked down at the body. Brad's brown eyes are staring up into space, cold and vacant. As Steel checked Brad's pockets, he made it look like he was searching for other wounds. A little trick he'd picked up over the years. He had found a cell phone, bits of junk, and a wallet. But Steel only needed Brand's cell phone.

'Did someone get an ambulance?' Steel shouted to the crowd. He looked up to a mass of blank faces.

His temper boiled.

'Idiots!' he shouted. 'Instead of filming this, why don't you try calling for help? And you can forget the ambulance. He's already dead,' Steel growled angrily, pushing through the crowd and making his way down the road, back to the restaurant.

At the restaurant, Steel ordered a coffee and asked to use the toilets to wash up. Steel had figured someone would have mentioned what had happened, which saved him a long drawn out account of the events. Just that the blood belonged to the victim and that Steel had tried to save him – hence the blood-stained clothes. Surprisingly, the man behind the counter seemed happy with Steel's account and even told him that the coffee was on the house for his efforts. The man behind the counter was short. His black hair was thinning and parted to one side. There was a pencil moustache above his thin-lipped mouth and deep-set dark eyes.

Steel thanked the man and headed for the bathroom, hoping to clean off as much of the blood from his hands and clothing that he could. After about ten minutes of scrubbing with soap and paper towels, Steel had removed most of Brad's blood, but there were still traces on the sides and in the folds of the fingers. He felt anger, anger that someone had taken a man's life so coldly.

Steel made his way outside the restaurant and found a small corner in the shade so he wouldn't put off future customers. The man from behind the counter had brought Steel a small black coffee with a glass of water. Steel thanked the man for his generosity and waited until the man had left before pulling out Brad's cell from his pocket. Steel switched the phone on but found it was password-protected.

Something Steel had expected. He pulled out his own phone, pressed an icon on display, and switched on a cloning programme. Steel could copy all the information on Brad's phone, but it would take time depending on how much crap Brad had on his. A picture came up on Steel's phone that showed two phones and a long bar in the middle. This would show how much was had been copied. Steel sat and enjoyed the coffee, all the while playing through what had happened on the bridge. Each time he thought it through, something irritated him. Something was off. Someone or something seemed wrong.

By the time the police arrived, Steel had was on his second small coffee, and the programme had finished copying. Steel had been just looking through a navigation app that Brad had been using when the cop arrived.

Steel had figured there was no point disappearing and drawing the police to the wrong conclusion. Besides, he would have to talk to them soon enough anyway, if only to find out what they knew about Lucy's death.

The cop who came to see him was young but seemed experienced. He was tall with an athletic figure. He had a natural tan and thick black hair. The blue of his shirt matched the black tie and peaked hat. He had his notebook in his hand as he approached.

Very professional.

Steel just sat near the door and watched the commotion near the body.

'Hello, sir, I am Constable Gatt,' said the police officer in a surprisingly deep voice.

'Hi,' Steel rose up out of his chair. 'John Steel.' Steel went to shake the guy's hand but paused. Despite washing his hands in the bathroom of the café, it did not seem enough.

'Witnesses said you tried to save the man, is that correct?' said Gatt. Steel nodded as he looked past the officer to the men from the coroner's office as they loaded the body into the back of a black government van.

'They also said you were chasing the man just before he was killed,' Gatt said, as he straightened himself out as if to make himself look bigger.

'His name was Brad West. He had information I needed. He was the ex-boyfriend of my God-daughter,' Steel's voice gave off no sign of emotion. His words were as stone as his expression. 'Her name was Lucy Foster, if that helps.'

The cop looked up from his scribbling in his notebook and stared into the black lenses of Steel's sunglasses. 'Lucy Foster, you say...?' Gatt said, puzzled.

'Yes, she died a few days ago up at a place called Azure Window. A friend asked me to come over,' Steel said. The constable wrote it down in his notebook.

'I'm staying at the Grand Excelsior Hotel if you have more questions, Constable,' Steel said.

Gatt made a note in his book.

Steel saw Gatt took down everything in that book.

Very efficient.

Very professional.

There was a buzz on his radio. Someone in the control room gave a message in Maltese.

The cop looked over to Steel and smiled.

Steel returned his look with one of confusion. Was he in trouble?

'Mr Steel, Sergeant Burlo, would like to see you. At the station,' said the cop. Steel thought for a moment. Sergeant Burlo was the cop Foster had mentioned. He was the one in charge of Lucy's case. Coincidence? He did not really believe in them.

'OK,' Steel replied. 'Where is it?'

'I'll take you. I don't want you getting lost on the way, do we?' Gatt said sarcastically.

Chapter 20

The police department wasn't too far away from the scene. Just a couple of minutes walk, and Steel was at the Mosta Rotunda. Steel felt the curious eyes on him as he was led to the station. He was a man covered in blood being escorted by the police. Steel thought of the many images that might have sprung into peoples minds. Was he a killer or a victim?

The blood had dried into the material and was now ruined. Steel doubted even an excellent dry cleaner could do any with it apart from burning it.

Mosta police station wasn't hard to miss. It was a two-story building that stood right next to the Rotunda. Outside there were flags on poles and a strange honeycomb statue. A palm tree sat in a small garden area. But what made Steel smile was the red British telephone box next to a park bench.

'Nice touch,' Steel thought.

Steel walked into the main lobby of the station. The cold air from its air-con smacked him in the face like a wet towel. It felt good, but with all this hot-cold-hot-cold, he was chancing to catch something. Steel saw there was a male uniformed officer behind a long wooden counter. The three bars on his epaulettes indicated the guy was a sergeant. Probably the desk sergeant, Steel figured. He was an older guy, possibly in his late forties. He was tall and lean with a short army-style haircut. Steel thought this guy must have been in the Force when the Brits had the island. Steel saw the nameplate on the guy's shirt. It said Mamo.

'This could be good, or this could be bad,' Steel thought. He wasn't sure of the situation with the Brits and the Maltese people, especially the cops.

Steel did not know. All he knew was that as soon as he opened his mouth and that British accent came flooding out, the guy behind the desk would do one of two things. Greet him with kindness or find an excuse to lock him up.

'He's here to see Sergeant Burlo,' Gatt said. Mamo nodded and pressed a buzzer to release the door catch. There was an electronic whine, and the door to the secure part of the station clicked open. Gatt opened the door wide and let Steel go in first.

Steel was led through one dogleg corridor after another. The walls were a very light grey colour, which was well illuminated by the long halogen strip lights above. The Battleship grey vinyl floor shone with cleanliness but still revealed black scrapes where fresh boot polish left a mark.

Steel was led down a left-hand corridor with doors to the left and right – each one with a distinctive shield on them.

Interrogation Room and a number.

Steel was led to number *five*.

Why? He had no idea.

Maybe the others were full, perhaps whoever was going to talk to him, their favourite number was five.

But it did not matter.

Whatever the case. Steel knew then, and there this wasn't going to be a friendly chat.

Steel knew interrogation rooms. He'd seen a lot of them – worked in a lot of them, been a prisoner in a few of them. He'd been in Police ones, military ones – terrorist ones, all kinds. But they all were designed to do one thing – intimidate the person in them.

Steel took a seat facing the sizeable two-way mirror. The room was small, ten-by-ten feet at the most. In the centre of the room was a small oblong table and four chairs. There were cameras in each corner and the microphone in the middle of the medal table. The walls were a putrid yellow, and the floor was the same grey vinyl as the hallways. It was a standard interrogation room.

And Steel was in it.

The door opened, and a small framed female officer brought a mug of coffee and a hand full of milk and sugar in sachets. She smiled and placed them in front of Steel. She stared him straight in the face.

Her eyes searching. For what Steel did not know. It wasn't a 'stare a psycho in the eyes and see why he did it,' look, it was more 'what do I make of this guy' assessment.

She was an attractive woman, but not his type.

His type right now would be tall, slender and holding the keys to the place, saying, 'let's get you out of here.' But she'd brought him coffee – whether it was her decision or not, it didn't matter.

He needed coffee, and they'd at least done that – or at least or whatever it was. The dark brown sludge reinforced Steel's thinking all police stations bought from the same crappy dealer.

The milk and sugar they had given him did not make it taste any better. If anything, it was worse.

Steel leaned back in the chair and stared into the mirror as he ran through things in his mind. Rewinding the events in his mind, searching his memory for a clue to the shooter. The calibre was too small for a long shot, and too many people in the way. Plus, there was a hell of a lot of bridge. Whoever had shot Brad had been facing him. There were plenty of pedestrians, and the only vehicles were travelling past Brad, not towards him. So a drive-by was out of the question. And besides, Steel would have seen such a shooter.

The door opened, and a big, plainclothes cop walked in and sat down in front of Steel. Steel noted the white shirt with the thin blue stripes that ran down it, together with his blue trousers and brown shoes. He imagined there was a casual suit jacket to match the pants somewhere in the building. Burlo was a detective and so had an appearance to maintain. Steel imagined his cars were pristine, both work and off-duty. He had short black hair and Greek God facial features most Western men would kill for.

Steel had noticed that about Malta, all the women were beautiful and all the men relatively handsome. Still, he had seen the same thing in most Mediterranian countries.

Burlo placed a paper carryout cup from a local coffee shop next to a tan-coloured file.

Good choice, Steel thought, looking at the coffee mug in his own hand.

'So Mr Steel, or do you prefer Lord Steel,' Burlo said. 'Or, how about Detective Steel of the NYPD?'

Steel said nothing.

'I'm Sergeant Gann Burlo,' the guy said. He opened a leather organiser and placed a chrome ballpoint on the white legal pad. 'You got a lot of titles, makes a man wonder,' Burlo growled the words. His voice was deep, not gravelly like a blues singer, just deep like it came from his boots rather than his throat. Steel could imagine the guy in the local choir singing all those deep notes. The thought of Lee Marvin singing 'wanding star slipped into Steel's head and made him smile inside.

Good song, great movie.

Steel said nothing.

Steel looked over. His eyes were thankfully hidden by his sunglasses. He could see Burlo was pissed, and probably with good reason. After all, Steel was pissing in Burlo's pond.

'So, what the hell you doing here, sir. I sure hope it's a vacation and not an… investigation?' Burlo looked Steel over.

Burlo had pulled Steel's records, not that there was much there. Time in the British Armed Forces emigrated to the US and joined the SEAL teams. After that, he was working homicide with the NYPD.

It was enough to worry about him.

'A friend invited me over. He had a death in the family. He asked me to…' Steel paused for a moment as if finding the right words that wouldn't land him in jail. '…Have a look. To see what may have happened. He knows I work with the NYPD and hoped I could assist.'

Burlo rolled his eyes and sat back in his chair.

'And the name of this friend?' Burlo asked. The tip of the pen hovered over the blank sheet of paper, ready to scribble down any relevant information.

'Marcus Foster,' Steel said, his voice was cold. Steel had already had enough of this guy. Burlo was just doing his job, but he was wasting Steel's precious time.

Burlo stopped writing and looked over at Steel. 'Marcus Foster…as in the Lucy Foster suicide?' he said.

'If you say so,' Steel shrugged.

'There is nothing to investigate, accident or suicide. No foul play, as you New York cops might say,' Burlo said. Tossing the pen onto the pad, and sat back in his chair.

Steel felt the irritation from Burlo. Which Steel considered reasonable. He wouldn't like anyone pissing in his pond either. 'What makes you think otherwise?' Burlo said.

'I don't know, I haven't started yet,' Steel lied.

'You know it's a waste of time,' Burlo said, rocking on the back legs of the chair.

Steel watched him for a moment. Wondering if Burlo meant it or if he was fishing?

Cop tricks, they were all the same. Lead someone in a false sense of security. Maybe they'll let their guard down, let something slip.

The funny thing was, Steel was doing the same to Burlo.

Stalemate.

'It's my time to waste,' Steel said.

'Don't you have bad guys to chase in New York?' Burlo laughed.

'I thought I'd give them a little vacation. I thought I'd work on something here.' Steel's voice was cold, detached, emotionless.

'OK, Mr Steel, what have you found out about Lucy?' Burlo asked, the veins in his temple throbbing. He knew that Steel had something, and that irritated the hell out of him.

'You were there… you attended the scene?' Steel asked.

Burlo nodded slowly.

Steel took a sip from the coffee just to put some moisture back into his lips.

'I spoke to Lucy's friend, Zoe Keen, asked her if she knew anything or if there were any problems with anyone. That's when she pointed me in the direction of Lucy's ex-boyfriend…literary as it happens. I followed him as he was heading for Zoe's place of work. For some reason, he appeared to be tracking her on his cell phone. When I approached, he bolted. He was afraid of something… and it wasn't me,' Steel explained. 'I chased him to the bridge, and that's where it happened. I did not see a shooter, and judging by the hole, it was a low-calibre bullet, probably a .22 or something similar,' Steel said.

Burlo saw the puzzled look on Steel's face. He could see Steel was struggling with something.

'What is it?' Burlo asked.

'If it had been a sniper, he would have needed to get into position and set up. That takes time. So if not a sniper, who? There was traffic about, but it was going in the wrong direction. So it could not have been a drive-by shooting, plus the traffic was moving too fast, so there was no clear shot. There were plenty of people about…' Steel stopped in mid-sentence. Searching his memory of the bridge for clues to the shooter.

'What is it?' Burlo asked, leaning forwards intently.g

'On the bridge,' Steel said, replaying the scene in his head. 'People were stood around, taking photographs. There was a woman with a pram. She was getting the hell out of there. Also, an old man and what I presume was his wife, they were trying to get to Brad,' Steel added.

'Maybe she used to be a nurse, wanted to help?' Burlo said. Steel shrugged.

'Possible, but there was something strange about them,' Steel said. His mind straining to reconjure the image.

'Strange how?' Burlo asked.

'The way they moved and held themselves, it was almost like you see on tv. Like a young person playing the role of an older one.' Steel said. His gaze locked into space as though all he could see were his memories. Burlo made a note of the people hoping to get a view on CCTV camera of them.

He looked up at Steel, who sat almost in a trance; his hands rested on the table as if he was steadying himself. Suddenly Steel looked up at Burlo and smiled.

But Steel's smile faded as he took a large mouthful of the coffee – and regretted it.

'So, what, the old couple were the assassins, you can do no better than that?' Burlo scoffed, tossing his pen onto the pad. 'Come on. You know something.' Burlo said, sitting forwards, his arms outstretched, grasping the sides of the table trying to be intimidating.

'When I was chasing Brad, he carried on down that street, he could have gone at least twenty different ways, but he carried on down that road. At first, I thought it was because of the bridge, he knew he could lose me in the undergrowth, but now…' Steel said.

'You think someone told him to go that way?' Burlo finished Steel's thought, but he still wasn't convinced by it. 'So how would they have contacted him, and who are they?' Burlo said.

'When I first saw Brad, he was checking something on his phone, I thought it was an online map or something, but he knew the area. That's when it led him to Lucy's friend Zoe. It was almost as if he had a tracker on her,' Steel said.

'That's a great story, Mr Steel, but we never found a cell phone on him. So I guess you're going to say the killers took it after they had dumped the wheelchair?' Burlo said, shaking his head unconvinced.

'No, of course not. I took it,' Steel replied with a grin. Steel took out the cell phone and placed it onto the metal table between them. Burlo gazed at the phone, then looked up at Steel.

'And were you ever going to give this to the police?' Burlo asked. Steel thought for a moment.

'Eventually,' Steel shrugged.

Burlo smiled at Steel's honesty.

Burlo left the room, leaving Steel to drink his coffee. Moments later, Burlo had returned with a latex glove and a clear plastic evidence bag. After stretching the blue glove over his large hand, he took the phone and then placed it into a clear evidence bag. He sealed it and filled out the details on the bag.

'I have no doubt you had a look what was on it?' Burlo asked bluntly.

Steel nodded, but his expression had changed. It was now cold and stone-like as before.

'From what I can tell, Brad was trying to blackmail someone, with what I don't know,' Steel said. 'The drop-off point was the bridge by the look of things. He had tried tracking the other person's phone using GPS tracker software, but that, unfortunately, sent him to Zoe's place of work…' Steel stopped for a moment.

Had he been that blind?

After all, Zoe had given Brad up without hesitation. Hell, she virtually gift-wrapped him. He'd tracked her to the café, not her place of work – but the café, and then the chemist. Brad had been tracking Zoe.

'We need to speak to Zoe Keen; she could be—' Steel said urgently.

'No, Mr Steel. *We* don't need to talk to her. I do,' Burlo said. He stood up and headed for the door. Burlo opened it wide and stood to the side. 'I've got a good hold on this case, Mr Steel, so there's no need for you to investigate further. Enjoy your holiday,' Burlo said, ushering Steel out.

As Steel reached the door, Burlo stopped him. 'And stay, out of trouble, Mr Steel. You're not a policeman here.'

Steel glared at Burlo, but even though he wore his sunglasses, Burlo could feel Steel's eyes burning into his soul.

'No, I'm not a cop here… I'm something far worse,' Steel said and walked towards the exit.

Burlo stood for a moment. A shiver ran down his spine.

What the hell had Foster unleashed on the Island?

Chapter 21

The midday sun was warm and appealing to James Calver. It was much more satisfying than the image from the fake windows down in the blockhouse. The hive building was a five-story complex that was over a hundred feet underground. Each floor contained a long central corridor with various sizes that branched off from the main hallway. Each floor had its own bathroom and breakroom facilities. Each floor was assigned to a different department; NSA, CIA and Homeland. All the offices had a function. There were satellite surveillance, command coordination, laboratories.

Two lifts ferried the workers from the surface down to the blockhouse. However, a stairwell went to each of the floors of the Blockhouse hive. This was considered more practical as it freed up the elevators.

The corridors were bright, with white walls, floors and ceilings. The place had a sterile feel to it. So much so, the designers had installed fake windows with images on high definition screens of the surrounding landscape. Psychologists had discovered that merely having a view to look at stopped a person feeling Closter phobic.

Calver thought the experts were full of crap and should spend twelve hours down a hundred feet underground. Besides, smoking was forbidden down below.

The experts hadn't thought about that.

Calver had come up to have a cigarette break. Twelve hours looking at monitors was enough to drive anyone to stir crazy. In quiet moments, he would sneak a read of a new book from his favourite author.

He sucked in a breath of fresh air, then lit up the cigarette. It was a quiet place to reflect on things, away from the operations room's incessant noise.

He looked up in time to see a swarm of playful swallows dance across the clear blue sky. The morning had been uneventful, to say the least. Shipping traffic was quiet, possibly too quiet, but it gave him a chance to finish the book he was reading.

Calver took another draw of nicotine. Letting the taste fill his mouth, hoping it would last him for the next six hours. He stood with his back against the brickwork of the long building, dreams of the weekend filling his mind. He had big plans for the weekend, things he had been planning for a very long time.

Calver looked at his watch and grumbled. It was time to go back down and finish his shift. He was already halfway through his twelve-hour stint, but it was still halfway. He snubbed out his cigarette in the box ashtray was attached to the wall, then headed in.

As he entered the building next to the embassy's pool house, he felt his phone vibrate. He took out his cell phone to check the message.

He stopped dead in his tracks as he read it. A look of relief crossed his face, followed by a broad grin. Calver placed the cell phone back into his pocket and headed for the elevator.

His uneventful day had just got interesting.

Calver reached the third floor of the blockhouse. The brightly lit hallways made his eyes hurt with the unnatural light. He made his way through the maze of corridors until he reached his section. He used a keycard on a side panel and punched in a four-digit code. There was a hiss of hydraulics, and the door slid open. The room was much darker, with only the light from monitors and desk lights to break the darkness. The room was a fifty-foot square with twenty work booths in the centre. The floor supervisor's office was to the left of the room's entrance, with a long window for the man inside to keep watch. He had to react to an arm raise from his staff. This would indicate a problem that they had discovered that he needed to respond to.

Calver slung his jacket over the back of his chair and sat down hard on the cushioned seat. He pulled himself towards the desk and got to work.

The map of the Maltese Islands panned out slightly. Then the image zoomed in on the Island of Gozo. Using his mouse and a couple of keys, the picture zoomed in onto a large building just on the outskirts of a small town.

He smiled as he watched the real-time feed. Two men loading a white van, both dress almost the same. Calver rocked in his chair as he watched and tapped his fingertips together. Out of the corner of his eye, he saw the approach of the floor supervisor. Calver leaned forwards and pressed the escape key, bringing the screen back to its previous feed.

He looked at his watch again. It was ten past twelve.

Six hours to go, and the next stage in his plan would begin.

Chapter 22

Steel had left Mosta police station and located a clothing store. He had bought a new black suit with a short-sleeved black shirt. After changing, he'd placed his old clothes in a plastic bag he had gotten from the store and dumped the ruined clothes but kept his boots. Steel had found a cab and headed back to his hotel. He needed a shower and to check some things online.

It was around two o'clock by the time Steel got back to his hotel room. Steel picked up his cell phone and sent a message to the office in Whitehall.

Find out all you can on Brad West. Thanks. Steel knew it would take some time before the information was found and sent to him. John Steel used the coffee machine while checking the rest of his emails but found nothing much of interest. Steel rolled his neck and shoulders. His bones were still aching from the car's impact and the morning's activities. Steel headed for the bathroom and switched on the shower. Waiting for the water to reach the correct temperature. The coffee machine stopped making the unsavoury gargling noises meaning his drink was ready. Steel grabbed the mug and headed for the bathroom, taking sips as he went.

Steam had filled the shower cabinet, and the bathroom mirror was clouded with mist. Steel stripped off his new clothes and stepped into the shower. He stood with his head down, letting the soothing water run over his head.

After leaving the police station, two things had struck him.

Firstly, who was Brad in contact with? And why did they kill him? Unless, of course, that was the plan all along?

Perhaps the blackmailer? But then why kill him so publicly? It would have made more sense to pick a quiet rendezvous somewhere than kill him. With the amount of wilderness available on Malta, it might take days – weeks even – until he was found, if he was at all.

The second thing, the blue mini that had been following him since he had dinner at Foster's house. Who was driving, and what did they want?

Friend or foe; witness or killer?

Steel thought back to Burlo and the interview – or the warning, it was all in perspective. He figured Burlo was just sizing him up. Getting a feel for him. From what Steel could see, Burlo was a good cop.

But great?

That was yet to be seen, but Steel doubted it.

But Burlo had a file full of information on Steel. He had had a background check on someone from another country – in minutes?

Burlo must have known he was coming, possibly days in advance. Steel found out about Lucy seventy-two hours ago. He'd only been in-country and working for a day, but yet this cop had all that information ready in minutes? It seemed unlikely.

Steel had an idea who had tipped him off, possibly by accident. Foster.

It made sense.

The two would have been at the scene. Burlo would have been telling Foster what they thought had happened. Emotions would have been high. All Foster had to do was swear he would get whoever did this or something along those lines.

Burlo would have told Foster it was a suicide. Which would have pissed Foster off. Steel paused in his soaping action. His hands resting on his chest.

The phone call – Foster would have gotten his secretary or someone to track Steel down. Hell, it was the CIA. They had probably known where Steel had been since the New York harbour incident. Burlo perhaps overheard the conversation, heard Steel's name being mentioned? Foster said that Burlo was a family friend. Maybe Steel's name had come up in a conversation over dinner or something? Perhaps Foster's wife had told Burlos's wife he was coming?

It would make sense.

Steel just hoped that was the case. If not, he had more to worry about.

Steel was glad he'd copied the data on Brad's phone before handing it over to the cops. Usually, he would be surprised if the local police would investigate further. Still, he had a good feeling about this Criminal Investigation Division Sergeant Burlo. However, Steel had to be careful.

Like Burlo had said. He wasn't a policeman here.

Steel stepped out of the large corner shower and stood in front of the mirror. Picking up the glass, he downed the rest of the whisky. He felt the tingle of the malt caress the back of his throat.

Steel grabbed one of the handtowels and wiped the mirror clear of condensation.

It had been a hot shower.

Lots of steam. Just the way he liked it.

He checked his body for bruises where the car had hit him. Luckily, there was nothing serious, more the bruises to his pride and a couple of superficial scratches on his hands and his forehead but nothing life-threatening. Steel was glad the car had been going slow.

He could not believe how careless he had become.

How did he not see a damn road? Steel put it down to the fact Brad had pissed him off so much he was focused on Brad and nothing else.

Steel thought about Zoe. How was she connected, or was it just pure coincidence the signal was coming from her chemist? Steel made a mental note to go and see Zoe again. Hopefully, this time he would get more out of her.

Steel's fingers touched the six-round scars on his upper body. All reminders of when he was shot years ago. A reminder of all he had lost that summers day.

He looked up into the mirror and stared into his dead, dark, emerald green eyes.

Another scar from that day. Steel shook off the memory that was just about to take him away. He did not have time for painful memories.

He had a job to do.

Besides, he was hungry, and he'd be no good without any energy.

The first rule of business. Eat when you can, you never know when your next meal will be.

Steel walked to his wardrobe. The clothes he had weren't practical for what he was about to do. Steel hadn't packed for an active investigation. He had packed for a practical one. He needed to go shopping.

Steel walked the short distance into Valletta. He was amazed at the medley of old and new. The ancient high walls of the city were married with modern shops and bars and restaurants. He found a clothing store and purchased two black polo shirts, two black cotton cargo trousers and a black military-style jacket. He thanked the woman behind the counter and headed back to the hotel to change. As he headed back to the hotel and tried not to notice the Mini parked discreetly around the corner from the complex. He had no idea how many blue Minis were on Malta, but then he was back to not believing in coincidences.

Back at his room, Steel set the coffee machine to task while he slipped into the new clothes and pulled on his military boots. He figured these would be more appropriate than a suit. Steel checked himself in the mirror then took a black military-style jacket from the bed.

Sure it was warm outside, but he needed pockets.

He drank his coffee while he checked his messages. Whitehall had said that Brad's family was wealthy, and he turned his back on money to do conservation work. This fact puzzled Steel. If Brad was blackmailing someone, it wasn't for the money? What the hell was it? And who was he blackmailing? Steel had sent a copy of Brad's phone data to the office. He hoped they could find something useful, possibly check the caller information, see who he had called or who had called him recently. He had also sent a situation report, letting them know how the investigation was proceeding. He knew he had to treat this as a proper investigation and not something personal. MI8 was not going to splash out funds for his personal mission, but he had to use the system a little.

Steel clicked onto Malta's internet map search and studied Malta and Gozo's satellite images to feel the place. Picking out landmarks or buildings so he could orientate himself on the ground. But a feeling in the back of his mind told him he had to go. He was getting too comfortable, and he had work to do.

Steel took the elevator to the lobby with five other people who stood silently. Steel did not mind the silence. He was busy playing that damned Lee Marvin tune in his head.

On the third floor, the elevator opened, and a new couple got on. The woman was a tall redhead with a small pasty looking husband. She wore what appeared to be a black bathing suit or just scraps of cloth.

She was attractive, and she knew it.

As the doors opened, she made sure she got out first, so everyone got an eyeful. Steel just smiled to himself and shook his head, wondering how the poor bastard of a husband could be so calm. Lots of vodkas, or valium, probably.

The elevator stopped at the lower ground floor, and Steel exited the elevator. He looked around the poolside for the first time. The sun was high and exceptionally bright. The cloudless sky was broken only by birds dancing and swooping in the blue heavens. The hotel grounds were extensive, including a small harbour and a large pool with surrounding seating areas.

His hawk-like gaze stopped over by the pool and the outside bar. The small rotund building made it look like a tropical beach hut.

'That'll do,' he said to himself, looking over at the bar, and set off to have lunch.

Steel chose a table with a straw canopy that faced both the small harbour. A refreshing sea breeze carried across the embankment, making the menu cards sway in their holders. Steel looked out across the two views before him while sipping the mojito he'd ordered and awaiting a BLT sandwich.

He needed to find Brad's apartment. He knew it wouldn't be with his parents. A guy like that would want his own pad, but not too far away from mom and the occasional laundry trip.

He'd seen the type before.

The kid would have been a complete nightmare for everyone but his mother. In fact, the more Steel thought about it, the more it made sense. Brad's father had probably insisted that he leave home.

He would avoid speaking to the parents. It would only make the kid's parents nervous. Having the police called was one thing he did not need. He opened up the tablet he had brought down with him to check the data he'd copied onto a data stick. There was plenty of music files and lots of photographs. He had managed to copy the text messages from the phone but not the call logs. The tablet displayed all the different files he had retrieved from Brad's phone. Some were junk, while others could be useful.

Steel was looking for anything that may help find who shot Brad and why. He was sure it was blackmail of some kind. The kid needed cash, and he did not seem the type to get his hands too dirty.

Foster had told him Brad lived and worked in Mdina, which was about twenty minutes in a taxi. He did not have an address, but Steel did have an idea where Brad worked.

While he waited, he opened up the photograph file and braced himself for what might be there. Usually, a young guy with a camera meant plenty of junk shots, and that's one thing he did not want to see, not on an empty stomach.

Surprisingly enough, they were all pictures of places from both islands, as far as he could tell. Buildings, churches, and waterside caves. Steel was just beginning to change his mind about the boy when he found pictures of the American embassy and someone getting into a four-by-four SUV.

Steel could not make the face of the man because of small branches that blocked the view. Steel stared at the photograph and hoped it wasn't Foster.

He flicked through the rest of the pictures. There was plenty of shots of the vehicle, but no more of the person inside. Steel sat back in the chair and took another sip from the cold drink. The smell of rum hung in his nostrils.

It was a stiff drink and just what he needed.

The following picture in the set was a small jetty and a sizeable fenced-off building that looked half-built. He thought he had studied all of the islands' wharves, but this one proved difficult to identify.

However, one thing he did notice was the large black superyacht in the background.

After the late lunch, Steel telephoned his new friend, Stan, the cabbie, to pick him up. Stan had joked Steel should put him on a retainer, something Steel had considered beforehand. Stan would make a helpful guide, and besides, there was something about the man that made the hairs stand up on the back of his neck. But then, Steel was suspicious about nearly everyone.

In some of the photographs, Brad had a local florist shop in the background. It wasn't much to go on but then how many florist shops could there be? Steel showed the photographs to Stan in the hope he recognises the place. Unfortunately, Stan did not. Stan got out his navigation system and typed in the keyword *Florist*. Steel sat back and made himself comfortable. He had faith there would be at least two. Stan turned around and smiled.

'Well, it's your lucky day. Apparently, you mentioned only one in the area,' Stan said with an excited grin.

'OK, let's go.' Steel fastened his seat belt and waited for Stan to speed off in his usual manner. As Stan drove, Steel flicked once more through the pictures, hoping to find some clue about what he had discovered.

And what was worth killing two people for.

Stan drove at a relatively leisurely pace. Steel had insisted on it. It was not out of fear but to allow him to see the terrain better and get a feel for the land. Travelling at eighty miles an hour and everything is a blur. At fifty – he saw just about everything, including an extensive golf course and a race track. Somewhere for the rich folk to spend a little of their free time, Steel had thought.

He saw the old stone walls that separated fields and vineyards and peoples gardens. He saw the roads as they wound up the side of the hills. Steel gazed at the plant life that sprung from the dry ground. He saw the endless blue sky without a single cloud. It was a beautiful but somewhat harsh land. Not dessert harsh, but an unforgiving landscape of high mountains and hills with jagged rock formations.

It appealed to Steel. Not the harshness, but the absolute hypnotic beauty of the place. As they wound their way through the countryside, Steel took the time to take in the fantastic views around him.

Stan had taken the Triq L-Imdina Road, which held plenty of mixed views on the way. A large town on the left and an arid country on the right. Brownfields mixed with the occasional green of a tree line. The aircon in the minibus taxi was on full to counteract the blazing heat from outside. Steel had once been used to such weather, but being in New York had softened him slightly. He figured in a day or two, he would have climatised again.

'So what brings you to Malta anyway?' Stan asked with interest.

Steel kept his gaze out of the window, taking in every point of interest, just in case something were to happen. It was easy to navigate with a reference point, sometimes better than having a map.

'I am here to see an old friend. Take in some sites while I am at it,' Steel said, wary of sharing too much. The Triq L-lmdia road hit a roundabout. Suddenly, they were on the TelghaTas-Saqqajja road heading west towards Mdina.

'So this flower shop, has it got anything to do with your friend, or you just hoping to buy something?' Stan asked with a curious tone of a man pressing for gossip.

'You ask a lot of questions, don't you, Stan?' Steel said in a deep, ominous voice.

Stan looked into the rear-view mirror and caught Steel's stony gaze staring back at him. Stan's smile disappeared, and his eyes stayed on the road and his mouth glued shut. Steel smiled to himself, amused his almost childish scare tactic had worked. The less Stan knew the better, Steel had thought.

Stan followed the TelghaTas-Saqqajja road until they hit another roundabout and the Is-Saqqajja road. Stan headed north on the road and U-turned the minivan after spying a shaded area on a large parking area.

'Sorry, guv, I can't go any further. You're going to have to foot it from here. I am afraid that road bottlenecks after a bit. No cars can get down, not where you're headin' anyway,' Stan said. He turned and pointed down one of the streets. 'It's just down there about two hundred metres.' Steel turned and looked at the road the cabbie was referring to. It seemed big enough to drive a vehicle down, but then most of the side roads Steel had seen in Valletta had been quite tight in places.

Steel got out and stretched out his muscles after the inactivity of being a passenger. Steel looked at Stan and then back at the street.

'Wait for me here, will you? I shouldn't be long,' Steel said. Stan just gave a quick salute and got comfortable in his seat.

Steel walked towards the road. It was busy with tourists who took up most of the street, a mass of people blindly following their guides.

Steel watched as one group waddled by. It was a group from France, Steel figured, or somewhere that spoke French anyway. The guide was a tall woman in khaki shorts and tight-fitting t-shirt, and brown walking boots with white socks, which broke the boots' tops. Her long black hair was tied off into a ponytail. Steel smiled to himself as he watched, hoping to get her name, or at least the name of her tour company.

Who knows, when I'm finished with the case, he thought to himself. The woman looked over and saw Steel watching as he leant against the wall of a nearby building.

She shot him a quick smile and purposely lifted her folder of information up. Steel noted the on a sticker on the back, which read *Malta Island Tours*.

Steel watched as the group wandered off. With their cameras clicking and cell phones beeping, as endless photos and selfies were taken. All of them stood open-mouthed in excitement, waiting for the next exciting piece of cultural information.

Steel just wanted her number. He sighed deeply as they disappeared from view. Steel knew that chances of seeing her again were slim to none. But then he wasn't on vacation – not yet.

That would have to wait.

Steel stared into the middle distance, his thoughts a million miles away. Ideas of what she would look like in something less formal – or even, just, less.

The sound of a bicycle bell startled him from his daydreaming. The sharp cling-cling made him jump slightly. He smiled as a little girl of about six years old struggled with a bike that seemed too big for her.

Steel's gaze fell back onto the street – and the flower shop.

The florist was a small shop in the middle of a long street so narrow it could be mistaken for an alleyway. Green shutter doors were locked back against the wall. An old-style security system that hid the display windows when the store was closed for the night. It was a tiny place compared to what Steel was used to. It had a single display window with a selection of net hanging baskets and what appeared to be miniature porcelain tea sets. Beyond this were containers containing fresh flowers waiting to be arranged for the customer requirements.

This was no grand window like on 5th Avenue, that was for sure. But he considered it quaint, with a lot of character.

Steel thought how much his wife would have loved to have seen all this. How she would have lazed by the pool at the hotel or explored each of the cities. Steel felt his pulse begin to race. His temperature was rising – he was getting angry. Angry at the people who had stolen everything from him, transferring the anger to something useful, he refocused on getting mad at Lucy's death.

He saw a woman in the store, busy sorting out a bouquet for someone. As he stared, he caught a glimpse of his reflection in the window. His face was full of anger, hate. His fists were clenched as if he was ready to pound away at the glass. The image shocked him. He wondered who else had seen him and thought he was there to do harm.

Steel watched almost in slow motion as the florist began to turn in his direction.

She would see him for sure.

Steel could still feel the anger consuming him. It must be still etched on his face, in his stance.

She stopped.

Steel felt blood rushing back into his fingers, his fist was starting to unclench, but he still bore that menacing glare.

Her eyes started to look up as if aware someone was at the window. Steel saw the smile beginning to form at the corners of her mouth. She would look up and greet a potential customer, and all she would see was a terrifying man dressed in black, looking at her with venom.

Steel traced her eyes as they moved slowly up towards him.

Her smile broadening.

Steel looked to see a kitten that had just walked into the window and curled itself around the tea sets, knocking one of them slightly, causing it to make a noise like the tink of a bell. A smile crossed his face.

'Saved by the bell,' Steel said, still watching the kitten.

He looked up quickly, shook off his cold demeanour and smiled as her gaze met his.

Steel cursed himself, angry he had once more allowed his feelings to let his guard down. What the hell was wrong with him?

Was it Lucy? Had her death affected him so severely? But that made no sense. He hardly knew her – wrong, he did not know her.

Could that be it?

He had let his own tragedy and selfishness drive away from the only other family he had. Sure he claimed he had done it to keep them safe. But had he actually done it to save himself?

'If you are alone, no one can hurt you or use someone against you. You are stronger alone…untouchable,' someone had once told him.

And Steel had believed them at the time. But now Steel thought it was all crap.

Trouble was now. Steel enjoyed being alone.

Steel entered the shop, looking around the store as if browsing. The shop was long and narrow. The walls were painted white and red tiles made up the floor. Above, a single strip halogen bulb illuminated the interior, making the inside glow with light.

Along both walls, wooden shelves stood three high, stacked with arranged bouquets in small metal buckets ready to buy. There were ornaments and hanging baskets. The air was thick with the perfume of flowers and the tang of greenery.

Now he was waiting for the two women to pay for the flowers they had just purchased and leave. The shop assistant was in her mid-fifties and had a china doll pretty face. She was a short, chubby woman with styled short black hair. She smiled at Steel and adjusted her black-rimmed glasses as he approached. Her dark eyes were large with long lashes.

'Looking for something special?' she asked, walking closer to the counter.

'My name is John Steel, I…' he paused; Steel knew telling her he was a cop would just make her clam up, especially if she'd been in trouble with the law before – which seemed unlikely, but he'd been wrong before. Or she was just sick of the police coming around because of Brad. Either way, he had to be careful.

'….I was Lucy Foster's Godfather. I came here hoping to speak to Brad about what had happened to her.' The woman nodded, a sympathetic look on her face.

'Yes, lovely young woman, I heard they had some trouble, poor kids. But I'm sure they will work it out,' The woman said confidently.

Steel was about to say something when it hit him. She did not know. The press hadn't confirmed it was Lucy's body that had been found at Gozo. Steel thought for a moment. Trying to find the right moment to say something. Before, he would just be telling her about Brad. Now, he would have to say to her about both Brad and Lucy.

'I understand he worked here?' Steel asked.

The woman shot him a curious look. 'What's that boy done now… was he found dead drunk again?'

'I'm afraid I have some bad news regarding Brad,' Steel's words were soft. He could see the woman had warm feelings for Brad. Hopeful that was the key to getting some answers for both of them. The woman struggled on her feet and grasped for a nearby chair. Her face had turned pale, and tears began to pool in the corners of her eyes.

'I'm sorry for your loss.'

The woman grasped at a handkerchief from her pocket and wiped away her tears, and blew her nose.

'I am Anna Bonello. I have known Brad for many years. You know Brad was a little bastard at times, but I loved him like a mother, probably better than his own mother,' she said with a sad smile as she thought back.

'Yes, he was a good boy, but a ladies man. Don't get me wrong, he cared a lot about Lucy, but he was a big flirt. Got him into trouble plenty of times that did,' she smiled sorrowfully. Her voice was scratchy, her eyes red and bellowed.

'Miss Benello, where was Brad last Saturday night?' Steel asked.

Anna looked up at him strangely. Her suspicious expression suggested the alarm bells had started to ring. 'Why?'

'Lucy's body was found a few days ago at a place called…'

'The Blue Hole in Gozo…' Her eyes flickered from side to side, thoughts began to weave a web of terrible possibilities. 'That was her – the body, that was poor Lucy?'

Steel nodded slowly.

'You think that Brad could have?…No, not true, not possible.' Anger filled her voice, and she stood up sharply. 'I'd like you to leave now,' she said, wiping away her tears.

'Miss Benello, I believe someone killed Lucy, and that person also killed your boy. I need your help to find out who did this and why,' Steel said before the police do. His tone was firm but compassionate, urgent, but calm.

Anna looked up at Steel again, this time with a puzzled look on her face. 'Sorry? I thought you were a policeman,' her tone rang with emotion as if relieved at the revelation.

'I am… in New York,' Steel shrugged. 'but here… I am just a man on vacation trying to find who killed my God-daughter…and your boy.'

'Brad was gone all day,' she said. 'I saw him again until the next morning. I did not know what was going on. You see, for the past few days, he'd been acting strange… secretive even, which wasn't like him.'

'When did it start… this change of his?' Steel asked with genuine concern.

'It was a few days before Lucy was killed. They'd all had gone to Gozo to make a documentary for a blog or something…. They did that a lot,' she said.

Anna looked over at the front door. Almost as if hoping to see Brad standing there. 'When he got back, he wasn't the same. He seemed scared. I don't know why.'

'That's what I am hoping to find out, Miss Benello.' Steel smiled reassuringly at her. 'Thank you.'

She nodded again in response.

Steel turned to leave, thinking there wasn't anything more she could tell him. He stopped for a moment and looked up at the ceiling.

'Miss Benello,' Steel said. 'Did Brad live near here?'

'Yes, he was renting the apartment upstairs. Would you care to look?' Anna said.

'Yes, yes, I would. Thank you,' Steel said.

John Steel used a set of stairs that ran along the shop's side. The store and apartment were accessed separately. He unlocked the door using the key Anna had given him. The key slid into the lock with little effort.

Steel stepped inside and found himself in a narrow corridor that doglegged out to the left. Immediately in front of him was a compact kitchen, with no room for even a tiny table.

Steel went inside and opened the refrigerator. The shelves held only beer, cans of soft drinks and day-old pizza. Steel opened up cupboards and drawers. The place was almost devoid of food or anything to eat on or with. It was almost as if Brad had moved in that day straight from leaving home.

Steel checked the cupboards over the sink. His face soured.

'No coffee, what sort of bloke was this?' Steel grumbled.

Steel reached inside the fridge, took out one of the cans of soft drinks, and opened it. There was a sudden hiss as the gases were released. He took a small sip of the can. He felt the refreshingly cold liquid on his tongue and the back of his throat.

Not the best, not the worst drink, but it was cold and wet.

Steel walked out of the kitchen and ventured down the corridor to the next room. Giving the door a gentle tap with his military-style footwear, it opened to reveal a tiny bedroom.

The bedroom was a shoebox. There was just enough room for a single bed with some cheap covers, which sat next to the right-hand wall. On the left were a wardrobe and a chest of draws. Steel checked the dresser, the closet, and the bed, even under the mattress. Steel did not find anything except a couple of dirty men's magazines and some photography magazines under the bed.

Steel left the bedroom and stepped out, back into the long hallway. He looked around at the bare walls. There were no pictures nor even a mirror.

Steel shrugged and put it down to the lack of space. Even he had to walk sideways as not to scrape his arms on the sides. Any pictures would have continuously been knocked off the walls every time someone walked by.

The last room was an ample sized sitting room. Steel stood in the doorway for a moment and assessed the layout.

The sun shone directly in front of him through two 5x3 sized windows. These were separated by a thick, stained wood audio-visual stand. Steel noticed the 65-inch flatscreen television and brand new games console sat on the display unit.

'Nice,' Steel thought. At the far end of the room to his right was a dark imitation-wood cabinet filled the wall. This was full of model cars, DVDs, movie action figures, and games for the console. All neatly displayed, even the DVDs and games, were in alphabetical order.

But still – no photos.

Against the wall next to him sat a long green velvet couch. Some parts were worn thin with use, probably second-hand. Between the sofa and tv was a small coffee table, a massive wooden thing from the eighties. Perched on top were the remotes and controllers, along with more magazines.

These were yachting magazines. Not Brad's style – or price range. Hell, the guy did not even have food.

Steel began to move about the room. Taking everything in. Seeing if anything did not fit. Steel had to admit this guy's overly neat way of arranging everything made his search easier.

The more Steel looked, he could only conclude this was just a place for Brad to crash and store his clothes.

No one really lived there.

The furnishings looked like they had come with the apartment, judging by the nineteen-eighties styles.

Steel started to look through the drawers of the wall unit and opened every cupboard. Checking under the cushions, as well as behind any easy to move pieces of furniture. Steel was convinced there had to be a clue in the apartment.

Brad had found something that he was blackmailing someone with, which meant there was proof of whatever this thing was. The photographs were the only logical thing worth blackmailing someone for. So that's what Steel searched for. Brad had found something on Gozo, something he had seen, so photos or a video was the only option. What Brad had on these people wouldn't be documentation, so it had to be digital.

However, Steel had found nothing on Brad's cell phone that had to mean he had been clever and transferred it off his phone onto something, just if he lost his phone. So there was a memory card somewhere. One Steel had to find.

Brad wasn't a criminal mastermind, but he was smart enough not to keep everything in one place. He would have made copies of whatever he had. Smart money would be on Brad, splitting them up. Possibly, giving the copies to someone he trusted. Brad had perhaps seen too many spy movies and was going down the whole if-something-happens-to-me thing.

Steel stopped his search and sat on the sofa. What if? If Brad had given the evidence to someone, who better than the daughter of a CIA section chief?

Was Lucy killed because someone believed Brad had given her the proof?

It would explain a lot.

Steel's gaze took a long scan of the room. The question was if Lucy had Brad's evidence, and Lucy was now dead, did that mean that the evidence was now in the hands of the bad guys here? Steel was praying it did not. If they had, it was going to make tracking the bastards that much more challenging.

But not impossible.

Steel thought for a moment. Trying to put himself into Brad's shoes. If you were going to hide something you considered that important, where would you go? He started with the CD cases and games boxes. Checking behind the disks and in the inserts. He checked behind the tv and under the games console. He checked lampshades and plant pots. But found nothing.

Steel took one more look around, almost as if waiting for something to catch his eye. But the room, like the rest of the apartment, was virtually empty. If Brad had hidden the evidence, then he had stored it well. Now all Steel had to do was find it.

Chapter 23

Steel left the apartment and handed the key back to Anna. He'd thanked her again and warned her that the cops may come round asking questions – he asked her not to mention that his visit, but also told her not to lie if they asked directly.

Steel walked back along the narrow street back to where he'd left Stan, who he hoped was still waiting. As he wandered down the narrow streets, he felt eyes watching him.

He was being followed.

But who, and how long for? Since the hotel?

Then he got thinking about Anna Bennello. Was she safe? Had they seen him enter the store – the apartment?

Steel wanted to turn around, confront his shadow, see what they knew. But Steel knew he could not turn around or even do the old movie's trick of tying a shoelace. If someone did it, the tail would know – or at least suspect he had been made. Besides, Steel was better than that – he was trained better than that. He needed to know if someone was back there.

Unfortunately, he could not use the store windows as a mirror. They were too flat, lacking the angle needed to show him his tail. And none opportunistically faced towards him.

God, he missed New York. The place was full of possible viewpoints.

Steel knew that further down the street widened and became a small junction where it came to a T-junction. Steel also knew that there would be parked cars, lots of them, and with cars came mobile mirrors angled to see behind.

Steel walked casually. Taking his time and looking in the shop windows, at the architecture – playing the tourist.

He did not need to rush.

Besides, it would drive whoever was following him nuts with anticipation.

Moments later, he saw the junction – and the many parked cars.

'OK. My turn,' Steel said to himself as he headed for the nearest vehicle, a parked UPS truck. Steel took a quick glance into the window of the open door.

The glass gave a reflection so clear it was almost like a mirror. All Steel saw were families and a small group of kids. He wasn't really surprised. His brain had been messing with since he'd arrived in Malta, so why not now. Then Steel saw them.

It was a black BMW with two men in the front. The driver was bald with a black goatee. The passenger was a large man too big for the vehicle, so much all Steel could make out was the bottom of his bearded chin. The smaller man shot Steel a glance then returned his gaze forwards. Not the most suspicious of actions, possibly nothing, then the guy nodded slightly to the big man next to him, the signal of his action was saying, *That's the guy.*

As Steel passed them, he took note of the licence plate, a simple three-digit, three number combo. He kept going until he was far enough away to dare another glance. Steel smiled as behind a crowd of kids. Then, another man appeared from the direction Steel had come – this had been Steel's tail in the alley. The man stopped and spoke to the men in the BMW. Steel sighed with relief. He wasn't losing it after all. He watched the man and the car for a moment longer while he stood amidst a crowd of tourists who had just gathered. Perfect camouflage – until they moved away, which Steel hoped wouldn't be for at least two minutes more. Luckily an elderly woman was probing the tour guide with questions he did not even understand.

He did not care what she asked. She was buying him time.

From where Steel stood, he could see both the short guy and the men in the car. Hand gestures were as clear as day through the windows. At least the bad guys had been curious enough to have reversed into the parking slot. What had been their perfect vantage point had now become his.

Steel was growing weary of watching the men. They hadn't moved or done anything to chase after him. They just talked. The medium-sized guy in the passenger seat had spoken briefly on his phone.

Steel was beginning to wonder if he'd gotten that all wrong. Perhaps they were just three guys, sitting and talking. Maybe the small guy hadn't been following him.

Steel headed towards the junction of the road he was on and the main TelghaTas-Saqqajja road and the parking space when Stan was possibly sleeping. Steel had just turned the corner when he heard the rev of an engine. Big, meaty, full of horsepower, the growl of a twin-pipe exhaust.

The BMW.

They were making a move.

Steel ducked quickly around the corner of S. Wistin street, where he had come from, and TelghaTas-Saqqajja road. Hoping to put at least some distance between him and them. There was a loud noise of voices behind him – It was the next tour, and they did precisely what Steel hoped they would do. They blocked the exit.

Steel walked quicker, not quite a jog, but a very brisk walk. Enough for him to get the lead he needed. The road was full of traffic and pedestrians that ran across at a whim, causing the traffic to stop or slow. The sound of horns been activated in anger. The gap between him and them was opening.

Misdirection.

They had seen him turn right and onto the next street. Steel needed them to follow him onto the road – and keep going.

He had no plan apart from disappearing from sight.

And that was just what he did. He disappeared.

Another tour was coming in the opposite direction. It was a larger group than the others he'd seen, thirty people at the most. But more importantly, it was filled with people from Texas.

Tall people from Texas.

Even at six-two, Steel felt a dwarf to some of the men in the group.

Steel smiled and ducked in amongst them, getting lost in a sea of tall people.

Perfect camouflage.

Steel watched as the BMW driver beeped his horn continuously while yelling angrily out of the window. The pedestrians blocking his path gazed at him in bewilderment. Steel smiled at the anguish of the men in the car – they were losing their quarry.

The tourists hurried out of the way. There was a screech of tyres as the men set off after their prey.

As the car had passed him, Steel had seen the small guy hadn't been in the car. Steel figured he had stayed behind to go back to await instructions.

No matter.

Steel's interests lay in getting rid of the two in the car. And he had.

Steel stood at the same junction, where he had seen the French tour guide. He leant back against the brickwork, arms folded across his chest, gaze fixed on the disappearing taillights of the BMW. He sighed, pleased with himself. He was a happy man, but he still hadn't gotten that coffee.

He was just about to leave and head back to the taxi. His head clearing from the adrenaline rush of the chase. And then, just as his gaze was about to leave the street.

He saw it.

He saw a familiar car.

There was a blue mini - travelling away from Steel but travelling towards the same direction as the BMW.

The question now became, who was following who?

Steel stood for a moment. Weighing up what he'd seen at Brad's apartment – which had basically been a bust. There was nothing there apart from crappy furniture.

That bothered Steel.

There had been nothing there. It was void of anything of interest.

Not even a computer. The guy was an internet freak who loved to post videos for the cause – so where was it?

Then he thought about the men in the car and the short guy who had tailed him. Steel had been on the island long enough to get a good feel and sense of the place, of what the local people looked like. A white guy from England looked different from a white guy from, say, Texas, just like a Black guy from Jamaica looked different from a black guy from Africa. Similarly, the Maltese people had a different look to those from the Middle East or North Africa. And Steel was sure that the guys from the car were not local. If he had to guess, he'd say Tunisia or Lybia.

If that was the case, why the hell were they following him? Was it something he'd done in the past? Steel had to admit in his long career – both in the Army and with the Agency, he'd made a lot of people unhappy. But if that was the case, why would they wait until now?

It did not make sense. The only logical conclusion was that the men were there for anyone who had checked out Brad's apartment. Or possibly left with something from there.

Steel reached Stan's minibus taxi that was still where he'd left it. Steel found Stan asleep on the back seat of the minibus. Snoring happily, content with life. Steel's gaze fell back onto the TelghaTas-Saqqajja road that both the BMW and the Mini had taken. The Beemer chasing its tail, the Mini chasing them? All the while, one thought came to Steel; *Is the enemy of my enemy, my friend or my enemy?*

Steel wiped his brow with the back of his hand. He was sweating. Little wonder, the sun was high and hot, that was normal here, but for the last two hours, he'd been too occupied to notice. He was done in Mdina for now. Steel weighed up the time he had left and the things on his mental list. One of which was heading back to the hotel, see if there was anything from the office, but first, he needed to see Foster.

Steel looked down at Stan while he slept. Stan was fast asleep, alright. He'd had heard the man's snores from just outside the vehicle.

Steel gently cracked the door open and slipped in behind the wheel. He started the engine and adjusted the mirrors using the internal setter. He pulled the safety belt across his chest and clicked it into place. He reached over and set Stan's navigation system to take them back to Foster's house. Steel figure the address would still be in the navigation system memory, so all Steel had to do was press the 'Go-To' button. As Steel fought with the settings, he noticed that Stan had taken someone over to Gozo a day before Lucy died. Hardly a coincidence, after all, Stan was a taxi driver. Maybe the person he took had offered a hell of a tip to ferry them around. A thick blue line showed up on display, showing the route. Steel put the vehicle into gear and headed back towards the road they had come to Mdina on, heading east. Then, at another intersection, head north towards Attard.

As Steel pulled onto the road and drove, Stan carried on sleeping, oblivious that they were moving.

As he navigated the busy streets, Steel began to think about Lucy. If she had gotten something from Brad, she would have hidden it well. She had been a smart kid who, from what the Foster's had told him, had watched far too many cop shows and spy movies. Not to mention her dad had been one hell of an agent.

Hours later, Stan was woken up by the sound of Steel slamming the driver's door. The panicked cab driver looked around, confused by where he was, and what time it was, and how the hell they'd gotten there in the first place.

Steel had driven to Foster's house. He wanted to update Foster on progress – which in truth, was very little. Steel was leant slightly into the vehicle, with his crossed arms leant on the open driver's door window. Stan sat up and rubbed his eyes, waiting for the bright blur to disappear and his vision to return.

'Thanks for the ride Stan,' Steel said with a smile. 'And go home. You look tired,' Steel joked. Steel stood up straight and tapped the roof once, making a hollow, tinny sound. He turned and walked towards Foster's house.

As Steel approached the house, he heard Stan leave, blasting eighties music that faded away mercifully quickly, then the front door opened. Foster stood in the doorway, a glass of whisky in his hand.

'Travelling in the style I see,' Foster joked. Steel smiled back at his friend then stepped inside, grabbing Foster's drink as he did so.

'Please, come in, have a drink,' Foster looked down at his empty hand. 'You know I spat in that?'

Steel took a sip, swirled the liquid around in his mouth like it was mouth wash. 'Adds to the flavour,' Steel replied before taking another sip.

'You Brits are gross, you know that?'

Steel shrugged with a childish grin, took another sip from the glass, and followed Foster into his office. Foster walked over to the drinks cabinet and poured himself a fresh drink, then raised the bottle of 18-year-old whisky as if to ask Steel if he needed a top-up. Steel shook his head and headed for one of the chairs which faced Foster's desk.

'Lucy's ex-boyfriend, Brad West, what do you know about him?' Steel asked before taking another hit from the whisky.

'Not much,' Foster shrugged.

Steel looked up from the glass, a look of disbelief etched all over his face. 'Well, that's a load of bollocks for a start, and you know it. If I remember, you vetted all of your nannies before you took them on,' Steel asked. 'So you would have vetted the shit out of a boyfriend. So… who was he?'

'Was – ?'

Steel saw something in Foster's face, something he did not like. Fear.

'Marcus, what the hell is going on here? I've got people tailing me, Brad got blown away in the middle of a town, and your daughter's death, so, tell me what the fuck is going on, Foster? Start talking, or I'm on the next plane home.' Steel growled.

Foster looked up at his old friend. His watery eyes confirmed something was going on, and it had gotten Lucy killed.

'Brad and Lucy were inseparable. They'd been together forever, or so it seemed. Known each other since we came over, hell, that's two years now.' He smiled and raised a shaky hand that held his glass to his lips and took a mouthful of the eighteen-year-old whisky. 'They were always on that damned island, trying to save the plants or the rocks, or the bugs. Anything to stick it to the man, I guess,'

Foster smiled again, this time with a sense of pride. Steel knew that he'd always taught his kids independence and their own way of thinking.

Steel sat and listened, let the story unfold. Allowing Foster to think back at memories of Lucy.

'Brad was a wild card, but he was good to her, so I allowed a little leeway as far as their relationship was concerned. Besides, if I'd banned her from seeing him, she would have just left anyway,' Foster continued.

Steel smiled and nodded. 'So, what happened that day?' Steel asked. He sat back in the chair. His left leg was crossed casually over his right.

Foster took a large mouthful this time. Malt caused him to wince and almost cough. 'They went to Gozo one day, some new project, save the damned birds or some crap like that, anyway when she came back to see us the one day, she was all secretive. I asked what was wrong, but she asked me...' Foster pause. Pain and confusion marked his face.

'She asked you what?' Steel said. He planted both feet on the floor and leant forward. Foster had his full attention.

'She... she begged me not to ask what was going on. She begged me, Jonny, my daughter begged me not to ask, nor to interfere,' Foster sat back in his chair and tossed his free hand about as though he was swatting away a fly. 'How could I interfere when I had no idea what the hell was going on in the first place. At first, I thought they'd had a fight, and it was all over, and she thought I was going to go make Brad change his mind. Hell, if that had been the case, I would have thrown a friggin party,' Foster laughed. The smile fell swiftly away. The solemn look came back.

'That night, we stayed up and talked, mostly about what she had been up to, catching up. Having the whole father-daughter thing. It was nice,' Foster said. 'Before that, we hadn't seen much of her. Her job at the gardens and her voluntary work took up a lot of her time. She'd phone each week to say hi, speak to her mom,' Foster's eyes began to fill with tears, and a small smile cracked at the side of his mouth.

Steel guessed that was the last good memory Foster had of Lucy.

'It was about two in the morning when she said it. She'd been drinking. We both had. We'd cracked open that bottle of Glen I'd been saving. Man, it was smooth,' Foster said, his gaze fell over to a drinks cabinet to a bottle of eighteen-year-old GlenGrant. Steel figured there must be no more than three fingers left in the bottle.

It must have been one hell of a night, Steel thought.

'She told me that Brad had given her something the day they broke up. She wouldn't say what it was, just that he had said it was insurance if something went wrong. Brad had found something when he had been on one of his exploration trips, she'd said. That Brad liked to go cave diving and all that shit. But this time, he'd found something, something that had scared the crap out of him,' Foster explained.

'Do you know what he found?' Steel said. He pulled himself out of the comfortable chair and dragged himself over to the drinks cabinet. Steel was impressed by the selection of fine malts on offer. He figured most had been birthday and Christmas presents. Steel chose Jonnie Walker Blue label and uncorked the top. The smell of herbs and the smooth malt filled his nostrils. Steel poured two fingers into his own glass before taking the bottle over and topping up Foster.

'No, Lucy never told me what it was or what he'd found. Apparently, I would find out when the time came.' Foster took a mouthful from the freshly topped up glass.

'I think it was an SD card or a data stick. Possibly full of photographs or a video,' Steel said.

Foster looked up at him, confused. 'How do you know, did you find it?' Foster asked.

Steel shook his head.

'No, but I am pretty sure it was. The SD card in his phone was new, had hardly anything on it, strange for a young bloke who likes to take pictures, don't you think? I believe he was blackmailing someone, the only way he could do that was with photos of something he'd found.' Steel looked over at Foster, weighing up his reaction. Foster remained still and almost emotionless at Steel's theory. 'I believe he had made a copy and gave Lucy that copy. That's what the insurance was,' Steel said.

Foster drank as he processed this new theory. 'I can't get my head around Brad blackmailing anyone.'

'I don't think it was for money,' Steel said. 'I spoke to a couple of people who knew him, and the impression I got was he wasn't the sort of bloke to do that kind of stuff. Besides, if he needed money, his dad was also doing well in the NSA, and his mom was an heiress,' Steel said. Foster raised a curious eyebrow. He wasn't surprised Steel had the information. Just wondered how he had gotten it so fast?

'And yes, Marcus, I did a check-up on Brad and his family.' Steel smiled to himself as he watched Foster's face contort with curiosity. 'No, this was more power over someone to do something,' Steel said. Then retook his seat in the armchair. The leather creaked with newness rather than age. Steel arranged himself in the chair, finding that sweet spot. Once he was comfortable, he took a sip from the malt and let his mind play through the facts.

He thought for a moment, then shook his head, almost doubting a theory he'd just had and quickly dismissed.

'What's wrong?' Foster asked.

'Why kill him in broad daylight? Why not wait until night time, wait for him in his apartment? If he had this proof, why kill him before getting it and the copy?' Steel said. He looked over to Foster, who was still processing the thought his daughter could be involved in such a thing and not tell him.

'Why didn't she come to me? I could have helped.' Foster started. 'I could have….'

'What could you have done? We don't even know what they had. You always kept your family in the dark about things because you thought it would keep them safe. Perhaps she was doing the same,' Steel said.

Foster nodded slowly. Understanding made it no less painful.

'All we can do is find the proof and get the bastards who did this,' Steel said.

Foster said nothing, just raised his glass to salute Steel. Steel returned the gesture, and both drank in silence. Steel had left Foster's place around midnight. The long day and booze had taken its toll. Steel had taken a taxi back to the hotel and had slipped into bed after a cool shower and had fallen into a deep, troubled sleep.

Chapter 24

The following day Steel woke early. It was still dark outside, and the air held a damp chill. The clock next to the bed showed it was half-past four. Steel found it an excellent time to go for a run. He'd gone out the same time the day before, and the conditions had been just right. He pulled himself out of the comfortable bed and headed for the bathroom.

Moments later, Steel walked back into the room and headed over to the windows. As he pulled open the drapes, he stared out across the ocean view. The sun had not yet broken the horizon, and the sky was a royal blue and purple watercolour on a dark blue backdrop.

It had rained during the night, cooling the air and leaving small puddles on the sidewalk and streets, not to mention his terrace.

Still, the view was spectacular, and he'd got coffee. It was a small Café Americano from the machine next to the minibar. Steel sipped his coffee as he stared out across the bay, passed the small island with the old fort, and onto the lights of the next city, which made an orange glow on the dark canvas of the morning sky. Steel made his way to the sitting room of the suite. He had noticed a large parcel had been left for him. The box was 2 foot-long, a foot wide, and a foot deep. It was wrapped in plain brown packing paper, and sellotape held the folds together. Steel smiled at the address of the sender. *Steel Grange, Kent, UK.* Steel tore open the parcel and opened the box. His trusted friend and butler had packed a hooded tracksuit and a set of decent running trainers, and a laptop with a 15-inch screen.

Along with some other luxuries, there was a note. *Just cause you're on holiday, no slacking off the training, ye bugger.* Steel smiled. His butler had once been his sergeant in the SAS. A tough bastard, to be sure, but a hell of a good man. Steel had offered him employment after the Sarge – as Steel affectionately called him, had gotten his cards and was let out into the world. The Serge had excepted after he had found out the conditions of his duties, which primarily was to look after the estate and any affairs that needed taking care of. He was also Steel's armoury consultant, picking out weapons and gear that Steel might require.

The Sarge had been there five years now, and the estate had never looked better, and the wine and whisky cellar never so full, most of the time.

Steel took out his tablet and pulled up the photos he had taken from Lucy's hard drive. It mainly was a mishmash of selfies or pictures of Brad. But Steel was interested in unusual ones. Ones that were of places of scenery, photos that just did not fit with her everyday work. He had found several pictures of harbours, including one in Vallette. This one was to the east of his hotel. It was part of an old fort complex, catering for large ships such as tankers or cargo ships. Steel went to another screen and pulled up the internet map search. He found an excellent spot to observe from, a nearby park that overlooked the place. Steel plotted the route he would have to take and closed down the device.

Steel pulled on the tracksuit and stretched out. His muscles ached from inactivity. He left his room and ventured down to the lobby to hand in his room key, figuring it would be safer in reception than his pocket.

Steel jogged at a steady pace. He was heading south-east along Great Siege Road, and passed the 'C' shaped The Grand Pheonix hotel, Passed the parking lots on both sides, passed the Statue of Independence. But all the while, he had the feeling he wasn't alone. He had noticed he had picked up a possible tail just after the Grand Pheonix. Two men in tracksuits. Possibly other joggers that preferred the early mornings? A possibility, but he committed their faces to memory, just in case.

The roads were quiet, making it easy to cross the junctions without stopping. Steel avoided the puddles on the pavement that last night's downpour had left. In a few hours, everything would be dry, as though it had never happened.

It had only taken him twenty-five minutes to reach the King George V Recreational Grounds. This was a small park with a kiosk and a fantastic view of Boilers Wharf across The Grand Harbour. The wharf was the business end of the island, with massive oil tankers and cargo vessels. All of which lay anchored and lifeless, only the docks' blinding lights made it look alive and busy.

To the left of the port was Fort St Angelo. A colossal limestone emplacement built back in the days of the crusades and then built-upon throughout the ages, and now a fascinating museum. The two men remained behind him. No longer a coincidence.

Steel looked upon the high angled walls and the low set buildings within the compound. He imagined the armies that had tried and failed to invade the island, including the Nazi's in the second world war. Steel looked over to a pier that stretched out from the fort. And the large, expensive yachts lined the pier almost like a showroom for the super-rich.

Steel took in the lay of the land, looking for something out of the ordinary. Unfortunately, he had no idea what was ordinary or what was unusual. The whole of Malta was a fantastic medley of old and new and ancient. Of high tech and no tech. Massive cruise ships and small fishing boats. He half-imagined Noah docking the Ark here, then the starship USS Enterprise would come into view in the sky.

A road curved ran along the ancient walls below him to another small pier full of powerboats of different shapes and sizes. The white of their hulls stood out against the still blue ocean. Steel looked down at his watch. He would have time enough to run back and have breakfast before another day of the investigation.

He wanted to get to the other island early before crowds of tourists filled the place.

Turning, Steel started to sprint back. He wanted to see if he could beat his time and see if he could lose the people tailing him.

Four men. Two teams. One was a small bald man in a blue and black tracksuit, taking a look at the same view near a set of benches. Next was a tall, thin man with black hair and a beard. He wore jeans and a sports jacket and carried a newspaper. Steel smiled to himself as the man sat down on one of the benches. It was so cliché; it was laughable, John Steel had thought. Steel saw the next team later as he passed by a kiosk. Two joggers dressed alike, pretending to have a coffee. Steel shook his head as he jogged on.

Now he could have some fun.

On his arrival, he had researched streets and possible escape routes, just for such occasions. After sizing up the men, Steel assessed the only one who may give any problems was, in fact, the thin guy with the paper. The other three were bulky – perfect for dishing out damage, but no good on their feet. They hadn't been the guys from Mdina. Still, they bore similar facial characteristics. They were also from North Africa, definitely not from Maltese.

As he headed for a fenced-off football ground, he noticed a woman jogging past him. She was tall, and her skin-tight outfit showed off her athletic form. Her long black hair was tied up in a pigtail that swung against her back with every step.

Steel could not help but stare. She was stunning and had an elusive, attractive air of danger about her.

And for Steel, that was enough.

He thought about pursuing her but remembered the two teams. As Steel took one last look back to hopefully catch one last look at her perfect form, he noticed the teams had gone.

Steel stopped in his tracks. He was puzzled, felt cheated at not having the chase after all. He thought about it for a moment.

These must have been a forward recognisance team. Observing precisely what Steel did. Which road he took, where Steel had stopped if he had done so – which of course he had. They were looking for a pattern. Steel knew this was how forward planning worked. Find out if there is a pattern in the way the target moved, was there a favourite place the target liked to frequent, did they prefer track to concrete, long mileage to short. Did they prefer scenic to none scenic?

Steel wondered if there had been other teams on different routes. If so, that meant a more extensive organisation than he had initially conceived.

Was it SANTINI or maybe the other organisation? If so, what the hell were they doing on Malta?

Steel shook off any thoughts about the other groups. This did not have their style. If Mr Williams had wanted Lucy and Brad dead, it would have been more… theatrical. And for the others, there probably wouldn't have been bodies to find – unless they wanted them found. And shooting in the middle of a city? A hit like that was more KGB, or CIA, or MI6, even the MI8.

Steel returned to the hotel. Showered, changed into black cargo trousers, a black T-shirt, and a black army-style jacket. The thin ripstop material would keep him fresh in the heat of the day's sun. Steel knelt down and fixed the laces on his military-style boots as he watched the news on the large flat-screen. The US had some weather issues, storms and blizzards. The UK had the worst flooding in years. India had launched a spacecraft. At the same time, in a village not far away, a building collapsed, killing hundreds. The world was in chaos. It always was, and probably always would be. He was starting to feel depressed by the programme. Then an advert came on for holidays in Barcelona. He raised an eyebrow and placed it on his list of things to do after the case.

'Who knows when this is all done?' Steel said to himself. He walked over to the desk, reached down for his unique sunglasses and synchronised the watch, phone and glasses. There was a bleep from all three, and a message of all three screens said *Sync complete*. Steel put on the watch, stuck the cell phone in the inside left jacket pocket and placed the sunglasses over his blue coloured contact lensed eyes.

He took breakfast in the restaurant with a sea view and a strong cup of coffee.

Steel thought back to the woman jogger. Wondering who she was? Would he see her again if he returned to the same spot tomorrow?

Then the thought of the two teams shattered those idle plans. If they had been a reccon team, Steel had two choices. He could go back on the same path tomorrow – hoping they would think he would change his jogging route, or indeed, he could change his route and see if his gut feeling was correct and there was another team.

If that was the case, he was looking into something bigger than blackmail. Steel checked at his watch as he walked into the lobby and thought about bringing his plan to go to Gozo forward, despite the ME having planned to see him the next day. He needed to see the place where they had found Lucy and also try and find that damned jetty he had seen on Brad's pictures. Of course, he'd keep an eye out for his new shadows. They were not discreet about making it known they were there, but their presence made Steel nervous.

He remembered what someone had once told him about wolves. 'It's not the one that you can see you should worry about. It's his twelve brothers and sisters behind you that you can't.' Maybe it's arse backwards this time. It's not the eight assholes that you can see but the one dangerous bastard you can't. Usually, that was Steel himself – the guy in the shadows you don't see until it was too late. If you saw him at all.

The events of the morning had made Steel later in his departure than he had hoped. Never the less he had to go. The main entrance was full of tourists. No doubt the groups were waiting to go on some guided tour of the island or hopefully Gozo itself. Steel excused himself passed an enthusiastic group of elderly women, and headed for the concierge's desk. He needed a taxi to take him to the ferry port in Cirkewwa, and he knew just the man to take him.

Suddenly, from the corner of his eye, he spotted the female jogger he had seen that morning. She was leaning against a wall next to the grand staircase. But despite his pleasure at her unexpected appearance, he could not help but wonder why she was there, in his hotel?

Was she there for the tour? A possibility. But there had been far too many of the coincidental meetings. Steel's mind began to spill all sorts of theories. The more interesting idea was that she was also a guest at the hotel, but what were the chances? In his experience – nil.

This time instead of the skin-tight jogging suit, she wore beige shorts and a white short-sleeved blouse with black ankle boots. She had the body of an athlete and the face of a goddess. Steel saw she was talking to a man, a local man, but not a guest. Steel caught the sheen of a plastic pass holder, which hung around his neck as reflected in the light from the chandeliers. Their conversation had been brief but had an effect on the man judging by his solum reaction. He walked away and left her standing alone. Steel felt himself taking a lingering look at this strange, possibly complicated woman. He touched the side of his glasses and took a photograph. He knew the picture would be sent to his phone, where he could send it off later to Whitehall for analysis. Steel wanted to know if there were any more players in this game and what hands they were holding.

The woman's hair was tied up at the back like before. Steel wondered what she would look like with it down and flow past her shoulders. He realised he was staring but did not care. His sunglasses were always a perfect cover for such things.

Steel remembered the greek tale of Odysseus. How he had tied himself to the mast of the ship so he could hear the songs of the sirens. The ocean temptresses. Sea creatures of beauty ready to drag down the unsuspected and entranced.

Was she a siren? Was she there to tempt him and drag him into danger.

He most certainly hoped so.

Steel smiled and nodded at the woman, but she just returned the nod without the smile. He laughed to himself as he made his way to the front desk.

She was definitely a tease, that was for sure.

As he turned to face the woman again, she was gone. Lost in the crowd, or at least from his view, causing Steel to smiled to himself as he stood in front of the concierge desk.

'Yes, sir, how may I be of assistance?' the concierge said with a broad grin.

'Yes, I would like to get to Gozo,' he explained, glancing back to where the woman had stood. But she was still nowhere to be seen.

'You want Gozo, why don't you come with us? We'll be going to Gozo,' came a loud, excited voice from behind Steel. Steel turned to see a tall man with long black hair, a beard, tanned skin and brown eyes. He wore a T-shirt with an emblem on the front from a television series and cut off jeans. He had a pair of Ray-Ban sunglasses perched upon his head, ready to be brought down to his face like a visor. Steel took note of a small badge pinned to his T-shirt. *Kane De Marco, Movie Tour Guide.*

The man had an element of coolness about him, which the women would find appealing. Steel approached the man, who was a couple of inches smaller than himself. The man who was called Kane looked Steel up and down, then casually slid his sunglasses over his eyes.

'So my friend, are you with us? Are you ready to learn what you've always wanted to know?' Kane said, raising his hands like a mad preacher.

'All I need to know is if you're going to Gozo?' Steel asked, unconvinced. Kane smiled broadly and put an arm around Steel's shoulders, and led them all to the bus. Steel asked about the cost of the tour. Oddly, Kane waved the question away, said that Steel could pay later. Steel just hoped there would be a later. Steel knew he shouldn't go, that he should decline and phone Stan. But something compelled Steel to go. Curiosity? What he did know was if those idiots from the park were following, he might have the chance to catch up with one of them.

The bus began to fill up, almost as if it was the last bus to anywhere. It was a medium-sized vehicle with enough places to seat eighteen people. It was cool inside, thanks to the vehicles air conditioning. The windows had a slight tint to them, which stopped the sun's glare but did not hinder photographs been taken. The seats were in pairs down the central aisle, with seat belts and pullout footrests. It was clean and comfortable.

Steel could feel the excitement of others in the air. Which puzzled him slightly. The last time he saw someone excited about getting on a bus, it was his squad as they were heading home after a tour or R&R.

Steel smiled to himself as he thought back to what his old sergeant major used to say, 'Don't consider this as havin got a two-week holiday. Think of it as you've got two weeks to get your arses back here.'

A small woman sat next to Steel. She was in her late fifties, with bottle-blonde hair and a hint of makeup. She wore all black, a sleeveless blouse and a pair of shorts that showed off her pale white legs. The woman seemed pleasant enough and excited for some reason that Steel did not understand. He was hoping this wasn't some shopping excursion, but Kane's pass had said movie tour. Unfortunately, Steel was oblivious to such things. He did not really watch films and definitely not TV if he could help it. If anything, it would be documentaries. Although he was fascinated by the Sherlock Holmes series, only because he enjoyed the novels.

As the last person took their seat, Kane stood near the driver and picked up a microphone.

'High everyone, My name Kane De Marco, and I'll be your tour guide on this fantastic journey,' Kane said. Steel leaned over to the woman. He was still curious at the excitement of the people on the bus.

'So, tell me, what tour is this? Grand tour of the islands or a historical tour?' Steel asked. Hoping to gain some local knowledge.

'No silly, it's a movie scene tour,' said the woman, as she bounced up and down with excitement.

'A… film tour, we're off to check out movie sights. You've got to be kidding me?' Steel snarled, giving Kane an evil glare. There was a shunt as the bus lurched forwards, and then they were off towards the city.

'As well as being a guide for these tours, I also work for the Maltese film and television industry. I have worked in many movies and tv shows as an actor, stunt man, or stunt coordinator. So, we are going to go around as see some of the places. And I'll share with you some of the things that have happened during filming.' The bus was filled with excited screams. Steel's murderous scream he kept to himself.

As the bus disappeared towards the intersection, the mystery woman walked out of the hotel. She smiled and nodded as if a plan had succeeded.

'That should keep him busy,' she said with an amused chuckle. She walked over to the hotels parking lot and got into a blue Mini Cooper.

Chapter 25

The man in the secure office sat patiently. He was thinking about the plan and the things yet to do. The pieces were put into place, and everything was going as it should.

The phone rang.

He waited until the third ring then picked up the receiver.

'Yes,' he said.

'The cop is taking a bus tour. Guess he's taking the day off,' the voice said.

'But?' the man said.

'We have people on him, just in case, and yes, they know to leave him alone,' the voice said.

'This better not be a problem.' said the man.

'It won't be,' said the voice.

'Do we have to be worried about the cop?' said the man.

'No, he is busy with the woman. He is no threat to us for the moment,' said the voice.

'At the moment?' said the man.

'Plan for the worst and all that...' said the voice.

'Very true,' said the man. 'Very true.'

Chapter 26

Steel looked out of the window as they travelled in the opposite direction to the one he wanted. They were heading deeper into Valletta. Despite Steel's anger at being dupped, he could not help but stare at the beauty of the city. A medley of old and new.

Kane was explaining the history of the island to pass the time. But Steel had other things on his mind. For a start, who was the woman at the hotel? Steel checked his watch; it had felt as if they had been travelling for hours. Steel let out a disappointed sigh when he realised it had only been twenty minutes.

Eventually, the bus came to a stop, and the door swung open to let the tour begin. Steel watched as Kane looked at his watch and waited for a moment. Steel found it curious but then shook it off, figuring the trip must have timings for each location. Which made sense, mainly if they were to get a ferry over to the other island. Kane smiled and opened the door, ushering the flock of tourists off the bus. He pointed to a flat area that had once been part of the city's defence system.

'Make your way over there, and please wait for everyone to get off the bus,' he called with a broad smile, showing off his white teeth. As the last person got off the bus – who was Steel, followed by Kane, who was placing his sunglasses over his eyes.

Kane moved through the crowd of people and stood with the view behind him.

This overwatch held a magnificent view of the port, and small island and fortress Steel had the same view from his hotel. Steel's interest suddenly perked up when he discovered the Manoel Island was out of bounds to the public.

'Now, that is interesting,' Steel said.

'See, told ya,' said the bubbly woman from the bus.

Kane spoke in a loud voice, so everyone could hear. Steel could tell he had done this many times and was enjoying every minute.

Kane pointed over to the island directly behind him, a place lost in time. With structures that belonged to the fifteen-hundreds. He explained that the island had been a fortress and a quarantine island due to an outbreak of plague. Later it had been a port for the British in World War 2. But now, the fantastic looking fort was a film set for movies such as the Assassins Creed action movie.

Steel stared across the blue waters to Manoel. His imagination started to run riot, with the notion that it was a perfect place to hide something – or indeed someone. Steel smiled and shook his head at the absurdity of his theory.

While the tourists snapped pictures of the surrounding buildings and the view before them. Steel used his cell phone to take photos of the Isle. As absurd as his thoughts had been, he did not want to take any chances. As he snapped two more pictures then closed down his phone

From the corner of his eye, Steel caught Kane check his watch once again. *Possibly time to go,* Steel thought, almost thankful to be moving on. As he took one last look at the island, he saw a large black superyacht from the Msida Yacht Marina. The large craft cut through the water with the grace of a predator. Its shape was slick as if it had been formed by nature. It was a three-deck, hundred-and-fifty-foot craft that probably had a tens-of-millions price tag. Steel took out his phone and took several pictures of the vessel before she disappeared into the open sea.

'OK, everyone, back on the bus,' Kane shouted enthusiastically. The women in the group giggled like schoolgirls on a field trip as they made their way back to their seats, with their husbands in tow. Steel looked back at the island and the horizon where the vessel had disappeared. He felt the hairs stand up on the back of his neck. Something was wrong, but he could not put his finger on it.

Starting with this trip, why was he here anyway? As far as he could tell – from speaking with the others, they weren't even going off the island? Why was the guide so insistent that Steel went on the damned trip? Why did he say they were going to Gozo? Also, who was the woman at the hotel? Was Kane working with her? He had seen them talking in the hotel lobby. Perhaps this trip was her idea. If so, to what end?

'Come along, Mr… sorry, I didn't catch your name before?' Kane said with a cheerful grin.

'That's OK,' Steel replied, walking straight past the guide and stepping on the bus, 'I didn't give it.'

Steel found himself intrigued by this whole cat and mouse game that he had thrown into. Sure, he wanted to go to Gozo, but the ME wouldn't be ready for him until the next day, so he had time. If these people had anything to do with Lucy or Brad, he would have to let this play out.

They drove for a short while. Kane continued to talk about the films that had been made there over the years. The busload of people sat drawn in by the information, taking it all in.

Everyone but Steel.

His thoughts were elsewhere. He was thinking about the woman and the men he had seen in Mdina and the park. He thought about Lucy and Brad. What the hell had they found?

As the coach drove on through winding streets, Steel's gaze fell onto the tinted windscreen of a parked car. A black four-by-four suddenly caught his interest. He'd seen the car before. It was outside the airport when he arrived, and then again outside Foster's place the night he went to visit and behind that had been the blue Mini.

Who was following who?

Is the enemy of my enemy, my friend – or just a pain in the arse who's sending me on wild goose chases?

Steel looked back quickly; the vehicles were now following. They had pulled out just as the bus had gone past them. Along with blacked-out SUV's, there was a blue VW transit van Steel had never seen before. This was a new addition.

The coach stopped, and Kane ushered everyone off in his enthusiastic way, asking everyone to wait until the final person got off. As Steel stepped onto the pavement, he used the time to look back casually. Both the four-by-four and van had parked. He smiled to himself as the group moved off.

'Maybe this trip will be worth it after all,' he thought to himself as he followed the crowd.

'OK, everyone, stay close,' Kane shouted, waving a folder he had brought with him. The file was about two inches thick and full of movie sets photographs. The walkways were narrow with dog-leg streets, and many had a steep vertical climb using ancient stone steps. Steel knew his mystery followers would have trouble trying to remain inconspicuous without a crowd or shop doorway to hide behind. The only possible way would be rooftops. Most of the buildings had flat roofs with a jumping distance between them.

At that thought, Steel felt uncomfortable and vulnerable.

The group followed Kane through the winding streets, taking photographs as they went. Steel held back from the group, just until they were within earshot but out of view. He needed a better angle on things. Most of the houses had crafted bars over the windows; others had stone balconies on the first floor. These made for a perfect climbing frame. It took him less than a minute to get on to one of the rooftops. He stood for a moment and took in the view. The breathtaking sight almost made him forget why he was up there.

Sprinting and jumping, Steel traversed across the rooftops, following the bellow of Kane's excited voice below. He stopped for a moment and looked down carefully.

Not far behind the group was the woman from the hotel. She could not be part of the tour, or she would have taken the coach with the rest of them. Her distance to the group showed she was shadowing the tour.

Or him.

Steel was just about to leave his position when he saw the two men from the van. Steel smiled, thinking how ironic it was. She was following someone, and they were following him. Or perhaps, they were all following him? Either way, it led to one question. Why?

The woman from the hotel and the park was the Mossad agent Samara Malka. She was twenty-eight and had been with them a few years, most of which was training before being in the Army. She had proven herself more than capable more than once while in the army, possibly why she had been chosen by the secret service. And now, she was on an intelligence-gathering mission. Nothing she could not handle, but her orders had been minimal. *Observe and do not interact.* Samara had the name of her target, and she was to gather information on anyone who interacted with her mark.

Samara watched the tour group from afar, paying particular interest in the man dressed in black. She had to be careful. Her intel had said that he was called John Steel. He was an ex-British Special Forces Soldier, now a New York cop – a homicide detective. The rest of his dossier was vague, to say the least. She had seen him trailing behind. Steel could have been bored by the tour. He had, after all, been forced to travel with them under false pretence. But the way Steel moved said to her that he knew. He knew that he had been tricked. The man knew he was being followed. But yet, he stayed. Perhaps he had questions for either the men or herself. She knew that Marcus Foster had telephoned with him after the death of Foster's daughter. It did not take much investigatory work to figure out that Steel was on Malta to find out what had happened to her.

She did not even know why she was there, but then she was a damn good soldier and did not question, just did what she was told to do. Which, in this case, was to observe and report. And from what she had seen at the park, that was something she did not mind.

She had been following him since he landed. He'd gone to visit Foster, his old friend who worked at the US Embassy no less. Then the next day, he'd go for a run in the morning. He'd visited Mosta and Mdina. So far, he was just a bored tourist. She had thought he may get all giddy about witnessing a shooting on the Mdina bridge, but then, why was he chasing the guy in the first place?

She had been sent on a mission with little to no intel.

Observe and report.

She had also wondered why he needed a cover story?

Really, Lord John Steel? Unless it wasn't a cover, and he actually was a Lord – or whatever those aristocratic bastards called themselves. She had to admit, a story like that would open a lot of doors.

But all she could see was a cop on vacation. However, looks can always be deceiving, unlike the blue VW transit van that had been hanging back. He, of course, was tailing someone – that someone – was the cop. Not exactly the most discreet mode of transport, to be sure. Especially with an advert for drain cleaning on the side.

It was a different vehicle from before, but the two men in the front were the same she'd seen since day one. The question was, why were they following the cop?

They had seen the old city, the former British bars, and the place where some actor had stood and nearly tripped over. Where this movie had been filmed and so on and so forth. The people had lapped it up.

All, except Steel.

He had just stood there and looked up at the roofs. Why the hell were the roofs of the buildings more critical than what the guide was saying?

Samara followed the group as they made their way back to the bus. Suddenly, the cop was gone. She hadn't seen him leave. Had it been when they'd gone past the old drug store? She looked around franticly. She could not believe she'd lost him. This explained the warning her director had given her about Steel before she left for Malta.

'Be careful, this is a slippery one,' the Director of Mossad had said. Samara remembered the smile of admiration her boss wore as he spoke of John Steel.

'Slippery? The man is like a frigging eel,' Samara swore under her breath. She decided to follow the others, thinking that he would need to ride the bus with the others – or at least she hoped so.

Her plan had been to force Steel onto the tour bus just so she could keep a better watch on him. When he was alone with the taxi driver, it was unpredictable, whereas the tour was scheduled. She would know where he was – apart from now.

Then she caught sight of Steel, coming down from another building, and slipping silently in with the group.

'Gottcha,' she smiled.

Samara knew that the next step would be a trip to the old British barracks.

This was a dangerous place to be caught in, with lots of excellent hiding places, not to mention there was only one way in and out. The gaggle of people returned to the bus and got inside, ready for the next part of the tour.

She sat behind the mini cooper's wheel, the engine was on, and she was ready to pull out onto the road and followed close behind. She watched the bus indicate and then pull out. She waited, letting at least one car pass, giving them space, so she wasn't directly behind the bus. She sat in silence, thinking the music from the radio would disturb her concentration. She pulled out onto the road.

The bus was in her sights, and the SUV was in her rearview mirror.

Behind her sunglasses, her eyes glared at the sight of the team behind her. It was undoubtedly a six-man snatch team – two men in the front and at least four in the back.

Standard Operational Procedure, or SOP for short.

The driver would stay put, the leader – who undoubtedly was the ugly guy sat next to the driver, would coordinate. He'd stay put too. The four guys would surround the person – two at the front – two at the rear. They might follow the subject, wait for the perfect time to strike. The best option, one would have a syringe with something to render the subject unconscious. Better to handle them that way – no chance of yelling or screaming or fighting.

It would be quick and quiet.

Professional. Or at least that's how she'd been taught. These guys could be a different matter. They looked like they did not care who saw them.

She looked in her rearview again. The van was at least two cars behind and hanging back. Something in her mind told her this was all wrong. Why only one team? There should be at least two? Unless, of course, they had no idea who this John Steel was.

She smiled. After reading his file and actually seeing the guy, she hoped she got to see that confrontation.

She watched as the tour bus pulled up near the entrance to the makeshift gate to the barracks. She found a spot some distance in front of the bus, pulled in and waited before getting out. She checked her rearview. A sudden uneasy feeling overtook her; where the hell was the blue van? She used the rear-view mirror, waiting for the last person to get off the bus. As the group disappeared through the gate. Pulling a 9mm Masada Striker from the holster at the small of her back, she slid out the magazine, checked it. The seventeen hollow pint rounds sat neatly. The top bullet glinted as the sun reflected off the copper.

Seventeen in the mag and one in the pipe.

SOP.

She slid the magazine back into the slot in the pistol grip and waited for the click. Tucking the weapon back into the polymer holster, she got out of the car and locked it.

The street around the entrance to the old barracks was busy. There was lots of foot and road traffic. She smiled to herself, knowing it would be difficult for the snatch team to do anything here.

She slipped through the gate and quickly mixed with a crowd of twenty-year-olds. She hoped nobody would notice one extra person.

The man called Steel was walking by himself most of the time. But he had talked with the others around him. She had to admit it did seem as though he was having a little fun.

Though he had the bearing of a soldier, back straight and shoulders back. His hands would fidget as if he did not know what to do with them. Possibly due to all those years been told not to put hands in pockets.

She smiled and brushed away a strand of hair that had broken free from its confined position behind her head. There was a slight breeze which did little to bring down the temperature, but she was used to it. For her, it was a lovely day.

Samara had seen Steel take note of the exits, possible cover options, and kill zones. His head movements were slight, but she knew what he was doing. Casualty, attack and retreat risk assessments. She knew what he was doing because she had done precisely the same. Steel may be a cop now, but his military instincts were ablaze.

For some reason, he was keeping a careful distance from the tour guide. Marking him as a possible threat, maybe? But then, Kane had lied about them going to Gozo, which had been stupid but necessary if only to get Steel on that damned bus.

The British barracks entrance was through an arched doorway, but the original door had long been replaced by a chain-link fence. Samara followed the group through the gateway, and everything opened out. To the right was a massive stone wall that possibly held the headquarters. There was a doorway and high above a small domed tower or lookout post. To the left was the old and unkept barrack blocks, battered from age and weather. In front of her was a steep ramp. This slopped down to an open area and more high walls and walkways.

As they walked down the steep ramp to the ground level, she looked back. There was still no sign of the men from the van. That began to worry her even more. If they weren't the snatch team, what were they doing there?

The old barrack block was a three-level Accommodation building, with rusted metal bannisters clung to the sides like scaffolding. The crumbling building had been used in many movies and tv series. All Samara saw was a perfect place for a sniper or kill team. She looked around again. There was still no sign of the men. She figured whoever they were, killing innocent people wasn't part of the mission. No matter how much they did not care about being seen, making front-page news was apparently not the plan. No, if they were there, it would have to be somewhere confined, indoors.

'Next, I will show you where the soldier's hand got chopped off in the zombie movie *World War Z*,' called the Kane to the excited people. Samara's heart sank. She'd been there before. If anywhere was perfect for an ambush, that would be the spot. There were lots of dark places to hide in.

Kane ushered the group to follow him. They turned back on themselves as the flat courtyard carried on to the side of the ramp, to another set of buildings – which, in effect, was just one big building. It was a two-story limestone building with archways and stone staircases. The buildings had no windows or doors, just holes in the walls where they should be. To look at them, they seemed to belong in Jerusalem or Bagdad, or any other Middle Eastern or North African city in the time of the Roman empire. The only give away was the mass of litter film crews had left behind. Kane wandered forward alone, kicking at large pieces of rock. The group held back slightly, the sound of the clicking of cameras.

Steel kept to himself.

The tour had, inevitably, split into two groups: the quick and the slow. Steel had placed himself between the groups.

As the group moved up the worn stone steps, past a pile of stones, past discarded beer bottles, and headed into the building. They followed Kane up old concrete stairs. People groaned at the sudden change from bright light to shadow. They laughed and joked about it. All the while, she stayed as close to Steel as she could without been spotted by him.

If anything was going to happen to Steel, the other men would have to wait until he was alone. Or something grabbed his curiosity. Either way, she had to be ready.

Observe and report.

As she moved with the crowd, an old woman in front of her dropped her small backpack, the contents emptied out on the stairs, bottles of water bounced down past her as she struggled to see where Steel had gone. She'd helped the others pick up the old woman's stuff, then quickly pushed forwards.

She scowled in anger.

Steel was gone, and if she wasn't mistaken, he'd knocked the backpack off Samara himself. But he would only cause a distraction if he'd known she was there.

But how? She'd been careful – or so she had thought.

Her scowl turned to a smile of admiration.

They were right. This man Steel was good.

Samara began to wonder how long he had known she was there. Since the first stop at the street tour, perhaps he had seen her car when they left the last stop? But none of that mattered now. Steel was gone, meaning the men from the van were indeed after him.

Kane waited patiently for the group to gather on the first floor of the building. The space was sizeable, though more of a large corridor than an actual room. It had doors that branched off as well as the stairwell they had just used. To one side was a large archway with a view. Kane explained the scene from the movie while he held up the file and showed a collection of stills taken on set. All in vibrant colour. A professional job.

They gasped and took more photos. The murmur of chatter echoed around the confined space of the building.

Click, click, was followed by gasps as he explained further. Kane pointed out the fantastic view from one of the archways, a panoramic view of the courtyard and barracks.

More, *Click, click, gasp.*

Kane looked at his watch. Time to leave. They were on a schedule, and the bus was waiting.

Samara watched Kane usher the people out and nodded slowly with relief. Good, Samara thought, get these people the hell out of here.

Kane waved his hands and beckoned the people to follow him. Warning them to take care as they walked down the worn stone steps.

She waited until the group had made their way back down before she made her move. Kane looked up at her from the stairwell. Their eyes met for a brief second.

She nodded to Kane, he returned the gesture. He knew then, something was about to happen.

Kane's attention shifted onto his party. He quickly ushered the group down, back to the central courtyard and the ramp. His voice echoed through the foundations as he continued the tour.

Samara looked down the empty staircase lit by natural light from the open doorway below. Steel hadn't been with the group. He had disappeared. The last time she had seen him was on the stairwell.

Samara wondered where Steel had gone. Was he hiding, or was he after something? Had her appearance spooked him and forced him into the shadows?

Or worse – had *they* found him?

She hammered a clenched fist onto the stone stairwell wall, cursing the situation. Her eyes fixed on the place where Samara had dropped her backpack. Trying to picture what she had seen last before the crowd intervened. All she remembered was Steel looking back at her, smiling.

She smiled softly to herself, reassured by the fact Steel had left by his choice, not someone else. A cold shiver ran down her spine. The snatch team would be waiting for him as he left the area. She wondered, how slippery was this eel? Or was he a cobra, waiting to strike?

She set off down the stairwell, but she was suddenly grabbed from behind. Powerful arms locked her in a bear hug, arms pinned at her side. Samara was overcome by the potent scent of body odour and lousy deodorant. She lashed her head backwards, hoping to catch her captor on the chin, but the brute was several inches taller, and all she was hitting was his solid chest.

The man laughed callously, knowing he could squash her like a piece of fruit. Samara gagged as his stench became overpowering. She wondered how long the guy had been stuck in the car or if the windows worked? Then she felt his grip loosen slightly.

She stomped a heel onto the man's foot, making him release for a second in pain and surprise. That second was all she needed. His arms widened slightly as though he was about to grab his foot. Giving her a chance at a second strike. Jumping as if skipping a rope, she launched herself directly up. The top of her head impacted the guy's bottom jaw.

A yelp of pain and a cascade of blood spat out as the man bit deeply into his tongue. He tossed her across the room like she'd burst into flames and stumbled backwards, both hands clutching his bloody maw. Samara could see he was still stunned and tried for a third strike, knowing that once he recovered, she wouldn't get another. Samara delivered a double kick to the stomach, forcing him back towards the open window. His bear-sized hands shot out to the sides at a terrifying speed. A speed that she had not conceived possible from the brute. His massive hands clutched the sides of the window frame and stopped his fall.

As he straightened himself out, he gave a bloody grin. His beard was damp with a glistening, blood looking almost black in this light. She realised this was the guy who had driven the BMW in Mdina.

A second-team?

It was the only explanation. Because the guy trying to squeeze her like toothpaste wasn't with the others.

'The others? Shit.' She thought out loud.

Then it struck her. The second team must have been in the barracks all along. The first team relaying Steel's position to these guys. So what was she, collateral damage because she was following Steel? Her mission was to collect information on Foster, and Steel was now part of that equation, and so had the men in the car after she had seen them at the airport.

It was supposed to be a simple data gathering mission, now it had exploded into something else.

She swallowed hard. The man was at least six-three and three-hundred pounds of mostly muscle. He had a short stubble haircut, a blood-soaked long beard, and no neck. He wore a checkered flannel shirt over a red t-shirt, baggy blue jeans and white deck shoes.

He rubbed his massive paws in anticipation as he watched her. Clearly, he had no qualms about hurting women.

He spat blood and wiped his mouth, his eyes full of bloodlust that made her shiver.

'My turn,' said the brute, crouching with open arms, like some kind of sumo wrestler. He was going to rush at her. After the surprising speed of his reactions, she acknowledged she had no idea how quickly he would be on his feet.

'What do you want with Mr Steel?' She asked, hoping the conversation may take his mind off, ripping her apart.

'Who the hell is Mr Steel?' asked the brute, his lustful eyes still trained on her.

'The tall British guy you've been following. You know, black hair, black clothes, sunglasses?' she said. Her breathing was steady, but she could feel her heart thumping against her chest. Adrenaline pumping through her veins, her muscles ached from the readiness for sudden activity.

The brute thought for a moment. Then shook his head, a puzzled annoyance twisted that round face. She figured he must have thought she trying to stall him with stupid questions.

She could see he was getting mad. The veins in his neck started to throb. Perhaps he thought her questions were to stall him – in which case he was correct. But his answer was terrifying.

Who the hell is Mr Steel?

Six simple words.

Six terrifying words because now, the game had changed, and she did not know the rules.

'The guy you've been following since the airport?' she said, her voice growing angry; he was pissing her off.

The brute shook his head again. His eyes had calmed slightly. The blood lust wasn't entirely gone.

'We haven't been following a guy – we've been following you,' the brute grinned.

And then that menacing, bloodlust look was back.

'I don't suppose coming quietly is still an option now?' she asked, still hoping to make it out alive. The man's evil grin spoke volumes. Even if she lay down and cuffed herself, he was going to hurt her, the way she had hurt him – and probably more. He seemed the sort who enjoyed beating up women, liked hurting people.

She knew fighting this mass of muscle wouldn't achieve anything, apart from her getting hurt or killed. Logically, she had to get away. Jumping the stairs was a good bet because she was nimble and quick. His reflex actions were sharp, but maybe on his feet, he was as slow as a sloth due to his bulk? Or worst still, perhaps he was built like an American football player and moved like one as well?

She was about to find out.

The man grinned like a wild beast and rushed towards her. He was quick for his size. She had to give him that, but he was slow enough for her to make a move. She rolled out of the way at the last possible moment, waiting for him to grow near before she moved, hoping momentum forced him on. The hunch had been correct. She smiled as he smashed against the stone bannister. He impacted hard against the old stone wall, let out a 'humph' as he knocked the wind out of himself. A cloud of dust that plumed from the wall that coved the man.

His gaze shot over to where Samara had rolled, just as she disappeared out of the window. He roared like an animal. The noise echoed around the room, through the passageways, across the courtyards. She heard as the man ran down the stairs after her. The sound of his puffing and panting echoed through the small narrow stairwell. This was a building made for smaller, slimmer people, not bulky, muscular brutes.

She heard the clatter as his feet slipped on steps worn to uncomfortable, unsafe angles.

Samara heard the man growl obscenities, threats of what he would do to her once he caught her. But, the misshaped stone steps forced him to lose time and footing.

She found an old piece of boarding on an old pile of old stage props. She picked it up and tested its strength, all too aware of the footfalls coming towards her. She put her back to the wall of the building.

As he ran out of the building, the blinding morning sun must have taken him by surprise. The shock of coming out of the shadow into bright light blinded him for a second, forcing him to clench his eyes shut and raised a large hand to block out the glare of the sun.

With a grin, she swung the boarding like she was hitting a home run. The makeshift weapon smashed against the man's face.

There was a loud crack, a grunt of pain. He stumbled backwards, holding his nose and looked at her with angry eyes, blood gushing from between his fingers. She swung the piece of wood once more, but this time it swung upwards between his legs. The man doubled over and a low moan all the winding would allow before he fell to his knees. Samara spun and landed a kick directly on his jaw.

She smiled as his unconscious bulk slammed against the ground, sending up a brown cloud of dust. That was one less to deal with. She knew his friends wouldn't be far behind.

The attack, the realisation that she'd been the target all along were stunning. But why follow her? She was nothing, a nobody. She was there to collect intel. *Observe and report.* Nothing more. And yet, there she was, battling with the people she was ordered never to make contact or interact with.

No interaction! She'd just laid one of them out, and she was sure his buddies wouldn't be too far behind.

Samara knew she had to get out of there fast before the others found her. The main entrance was out of the question. The other team members would be waiting. She would be drugged and tossed in the back of the van quicker than a blink of an eye. Samara looked over at the bottom of the ramp the tour had gone down and smiled. As a child, she used to sneak into the old barracks with her friends. She knew the best hiding places and also the best way to get out without being seen.

The old fort was in two parts. The upper level was now the military museum, and the lower barracks had been left to wither. At the end of the long doglegged ramp was an ornately carved limestone fountain with three large spheres on top. The fountain's base was overgrown with long grass. Behind the fountain was a curved Greek looking structure with large columns. It was old and worn but still inspired a sense of awe as though it did not belong with the rest of the barracks. As though the whole place had been constructed around the fountain and the arched columned structure.

Both exits to the museum and the barracks would indeed be watched, and she had to slip away quickly and quietly. She knew her only way out was behind the columned structure and over the wall.

Samara clambered past the old structure, through some high grass and towards an old stone wall, which had possibly been part of a building. Beyond that were trees, lots of trees.

Camouflage.

Cover.

Wild undergrowth and bushes blocked her way, but she continued towards her target.

The sudden burst of loud voices made her stop and turn.

It was the other team.

She figured they had probably become suspicious at how long it was taking the man to grab her and come to investigate.

Using the old buildings as cover, Samara moved low through the undergrowth. Samara would be able to handle these men, her training had been as good as it got, but she had also learnt that it was sometimes better to retreat, regroup, and assess than act. Samara had no idea the number of people she was dealing with, who they were or why they were after her. She could not take anything for granted.

Observe and report.

Yeah, those orders have gone to hell, she thought, fighting through the long grass.

Samara moved quickly but stealthily up the other side of the ruins of the old fort, to a climbing point she had used as a child, and hoping it was still there. Samara could not risk being caught; there was too much at stake.

Samara stopped and dropped to her knees. The voices began to get louder. They were heading in her direction. Using the large bushes as cover, she moved slowly, an inch at a time. She could not risk the movement of the vegetation giving away her position. She could hear their voices. They were at the wall she had just passed. Samara remained still. Her breathing became shallow and steady.

The bushes made it hard to see the men, making her more comfortable about her hiding place. *If I can't see them, they can't see me.*

One man shouted an order for the others to search the old barrack building and the courtyard, thinking she had hidden in one of the rooms. She smiled and moved slowly backwards, heading towards the climbing spot.

Slow and easy, she thought to herself. Slow and easy.

She listened to the men yelling back to the leader each time they cleared a room. It was undoubtedly a scare tactic to let their prey know they were closing in.

All the time, they unaware the quarry was heading for her exit. Samara began to move quicker. Hoping the cries from the men would cover her escape through the dense undergrowth. She could feel her blood racing, her heart beating so fast it might burst out of her chest. But it wasn't through fear; it was exhilaration. This chase excited her, but the sight of the climbing place excited her more. She smiled and moved forwards. This game was nearly over.

As she had passed a group of trees, a small flock of birds took to the sky, screeching as they went. Sure they had given away her position, she froze and dropped to her knees. Her heart was in her mouth. Samara listened carefully for the sound of footsteps or movement as the undergrowth was disturbed. She knew he had seen the birds –he was coming for her.

The question was, was he alone?

The leader of the group turned and faced the startled birds. A menacing grin crossed his face as he headed up the stone steps; towards her. He did not alert the others. He sniffed at the air, trying to catch a scent from perfume or deodorant. His movements were slow and deliberate. He was enjoying the hunt.

Chapter 27

Aamir stood in front of a map of Malta and the island of Gozo. It was a massive ten feet by ten feet, full-colour, topographical map, gridlines, and interest points. It was the kind of thing a person would expect to see in a military command post.

It was fixed to sheets of cardboard, making it easier for pins to be stuck into it. And the whole thing was attached to the wall using long nails on the four corners and along the edges. It wasn't the best of jobs, but it would do.

Behind him, several collapsible six-foot tables lay two wide and five long to create one large table. On this table were computers, files, and radio equipment. Sat against the wall next to the front door were rifle racks, full of automatic rifles and submachine guns. A room branched off on the right. This was full of sturdy green weapon and ammunition boxes, all neatly stacked.

Next to a far wall stood another of the tables. This was four monitors, each showing three of the twelve security cameras that guarded the building's outer walls. All windows had been boarded up to stop light escaping at night, making it seem no one was inside.

Aamir was pleased with the command centre. The men had done well in following his instructions. They were in an old house on the outskirts of a town.

It was a three-story building with a cellar. Here, they were safe from prying eyes. Movement in and out of the building had been restricted to one or two at a time. Too many people coming and going would draw unwanted attention. As per Aamir's instructions, everyone was wearing the same outfit. Jeans with brown working boots, a red checked shirt, and a blue baseball cap. Each of them had black hair and a beard. To the quick observer, they would appear to be the same person or at least family.

Aamir looked at the plan of the island. Cities, towns, ports. For the moment, it was a clean slate in which to place pin markers; safe houses, drop-off points, emergency extraction points. The whole plan had taken over six months to get to this point – half a year of watching and waiting. Aamir smiled confidently as he placed the first pin into the map. The large red pin sat neatly over a small drawing of a building he had sketched himself. Above the picture, the words *US Embassy* stood out.

All the other men looked at Aamir as he stuck in the pin with force. The room fell silent as they all stared, waiting to see what he would do next.

'Now brothers, it begins,' he said, still looking up at the map. Behind him, the men cheered with hateful lust and ambition.

Chapter 28

Samara edged slowly back towards the fort's rear wall. On the other side of this was the busy main street. She knew that her pursuer would have to go through an old derelict building until he got to the overgrown courtyard. His best bet was to wait for his men to return before breaking cover, then assess the situation before taking action. She could take them all, but not together. Samara was proficient in Krav Maga, but in a large group and all at once, even she would have difficulties. Maybe after a few more years of training, but not yet, she was only a year out of the academy, and this was her first actual assignment.

She had expected it would be an easy mission. *Observe and report.* How hard could that be?
Now all she could do was get the hell out – and fast.

The man moved slowly through the building. Pieces of rubble and old wooden furniture littered the floor. The stench of stagnant air hung in each room, causing the man to cover his mouth and nose. He searched the whole building and found nothing. He went to go back the way he came, then he stopped. He turned at the middle and looked back at the broken windows and the trees beyond them. He smiled to himself and moved towards a large window, which was more like a doorway than a window. Certainly big enough for a person. A bottom wall reached up about two feet from the ground, and there were signs of where the frame hand was fixed in.

The man stretched out his right leg slowly. Inching his foot through the hole in the wall as he could not see the other side. Placing his right foot gently on the ground, he pulled his body through slowly.
Inch by inch.
Slow and methodical.
Profesional.
The man found himself in a small wooded area. It was a perfect place to hide. He smiled wickedly as he tucked away his pistol and drew out a long, evil-looking blade. The blade was around ten inches in length and two inches wide. The long blade had a serrated top that ended in a double-edged tip which was at least two inches in length. The handle was made from carved redwood. The hilt and pommel were stainless steel, which glinted in the sun. It was a wicked blade for sure, a hunting knife.

He crouched down slightly and crept as low as he could, trying not to disturb the stones and rubble on the ground. He would stop and look around, listen, then move forwards again. The man did that for several paces.
Stop, look, listen, move. Stop, look, listen, move.
He had his orders, and she was in the way. Something to his left caught his eye. Something had moved quickly but quietly. He turned to look but found nothing. Had he imagined it? Could it have been a bird? He knew he had seen something, and he doubted it was Samara.

He shrugged it off as just been his overactive imagination and turned back towards where the birds had flown. From behind him, he could hear the muffled chatter of his colleagues, dulled calls to find him. But he did not want to risk answering, not with Samara so close. He would wait, let them come to him. The man figured with all his men back there, Samara could not double back and escape. She would be trapped. And then they would have her.

He smiled, thinking everything had come together, sure, though not as planned. Still, mission accomplished. He began to turn to face the way he'd been heading. The man gripped the hilt of the knife tightly, ready for anything.

A kick to the right knee took him down. A roundhouse kick to the head surprised him, cost him. But he did not go down. She went for a second kick, but this time he was ready for her. He caught her leg. The man sneered with glee and swung her by the leg, straight into one of the nearby trees. The man laughed as her body slammed against the trunk. He had plans for her, and he could not wait to see her face as he tortured her.

The man's grin broadened as he slowly approached her. Behind him, his men shouted, called for his location. They would soon be there, and then the fun would start.

'I've been looking forward to this,' he sneered, holding the knife in one hand and undoing his trousers with the other. 'We're going to ride you, and then we're gonna slice you,' he said.

In Samara's eyes, the man saw the anger and pain as she held her back, from where she had impacted the tree. He knew she wasn't about to show fear. She wouldn't give him the satisfaction of seeing that. She wanted to show him his knife sticking out of his gut, but given the circumstance, that wasn't about to happen.

'I'm over here; I've got the girl,' he called back to his men.

But no answer came.

'Hey, you sons-of-bitches! I'm over here,' the man shouted again.

Silence.

Only the murmur of the traffic beyond the wall and the chatter of the birds filled his ears.

'Where are you, you stupid sons-of-bitches? I'm over here?' The man called. A sudden panic ran through him. He turned sharply around with the knife in one hand and his trousers around his ankles. He was expecting an attack. But all he saw was the building, the trees, the grass. And through the window, he saw something. A pile of rags, no – his men. They were all laid in a heap on the broken ground. The man swung around quickly, the knife ready to strike in his hand. The blade held sideways, ready to slash whoever had done this.

But there was no one there.

The man turned back to Samara, only to find she was gone. The man cursed loudly and set off after her, forgetting about his trousers. He lunged forwards, but his restricted legs could not move. He lost his balance. He struggled to reach out for something, but there was nothing there but air. The man felt the rush of wind as he tumbled straight down towards the earth.

The man grunted as his face smashed against the dry earth. His mouth filled with blood as the impact loosened some of his teeth. He went to stand up but was forced down by something hard smashing against his back. Then it was followed by two more blows, one of which was to the back of his head. Everything went black.

Samara had seen the man fall. She had savoured the moment as his face smashed against the ground, the spat blood and teeth. Samara also knew she wouldn't get a second chance. He had to stay down. She found a broken branch and had brought it down on her attackers back. Samara had seen Steel take out the men. She was amazed at how quick and silent Steel had moved.

The man groaned and began to move. His movement was slow and painful – but he was awake.

Samara walked over to the man and looked down. She could have hit him again with the branch, but how many times would be enough? Samara picked up the knife and knelt on top of him. She had one knee pushed into his back while the other rested on the ground. Grabbing his forehead, Samara pulled back his head and exposing his throat. Calmly she drew the sharp blade across the taught flesh and listened as his blood filled his mouth and he started to drown on his own fluids. She did not slit the carotid. She would have been covered in arterial spray. This was slow and painful. The bastard would feel his life slip away.

She felt the body grow limp. The life had left the man's body. It was done. He was done.

Samara ran over to the wall and began to climb. It had been a long time since she had done this climb. Somehow, it had seemed easier when Samara was a child. She stretched her right arm out for the top ledge but found she did not have the reach. Her boot slipped from its foothold, and she slipped. From nowhere, a strong arm caught her. Fearfully she looked up. Almost expecting it to be one of the men. The sun glared from behind her captor, making it impossible for her to see who it was. Samara began to panic. Then she thought about the man she had just killed, had this man seen it? Did he belong to the other team, and now he would do the same to her? Giving her a slow, painful death in retaliation?

'OK, you bastard, let's get this over with,' she said. Knowing the first opportunity she had, her new captor would get a kick in the balls, followed by a punch to the throat. Samara knew it wouldn't be the big guy before. He was possibly thrown in the back of the van. It did not matter. Whoever he was, this guy would get it first, then she'd hunt the others down, and she'd kill them all.

The figure laughed and pulled her up slowly. As she neared the top, she pulled her arm back, ready to launch an attack. She knew a flat open palm hit could cause a lot of pain, and she was ready. She held her breath and prepared herself. She was ready. Suddenly as she neared the edge, she stopped. As Samara dangled for a brief moment, she wondered what was coming next. Was he going to drop her, leave her hanging until the others arrived? Then she heard an electronic click. He'd taken a photo of her.

What for?

Proof?

'OK, you can grab the ledge now,' her captor said. She looked up at the stone edge of the wall. She threw up her free arm and held on just as her other arm was released. Samara pulled herself up and over. As she stood, Samara looked up at her savour, John Steel.

'You know, there is a door,' Steel joked, watching her brush stone dust and undergrowth from her clothes.

'Sorry, I don't speak to strangers,' Samara said.

'Strangers? I think we are way past strangers, don't you? I mean, we do keep running into each other – so to speak,' Steel smiled and extending a hand to shake.

Samara looked down at his hand and then back to his face.

'It's a small island. We are bound to bump into each other. It happens all the time,' she said unconvincingly. A sudden commotion from the museum gate caught her attention. Two men looked down the road and straight at her. It was the other snatch team.

'Friends of yours?' Steel said.

Samara shot him an angry glare and ran off across the street with Steel fast behind her.

'By the way, my name is Steel – John Steel,' Steel yelled at the fast-moving woman.

'Not interested,' she lied.

'You know we would be a lot safer if we rejoined the group if we could find them,' Steel suggested. He felt his smartwatch vibrate, and he pulled out his phone. As he looked at the message he had just gotten. It was from the office in Whitehall with a quick background check on Samara. Steel smiled broadly before putting his phone away.

Now he knew who she was - Agent Samara Malka, of Mossad. The big question now was why she was following him?

Samara agreed with Steel that rejoining the tour was their best option. Thinking it was, if anything, a decent hiding place. Samara had suggested going back to her car, but Steel had figured whoever was after her would-be staking out her car just in case. No, the tour was the best option for now – safety in numbers. Steel doubted even these goons would have the gall to open up in broad daylight. But the more Steel thought about it, the more dubious he became of his own plan. Because he had no idea where Kane and the tour would be at that moment. Plus, there was also the threat that the tour bus was no longer in the city. After all, this was a movie tour. And there had been a lot of films and television series made on the island. Also, at least four cities there that he knew of, which meant there were probably more, he did not. And that did not include the small villages between them.

They would be looking for a small needle in a vast haystack.

But Samara insisted that finding them wouldn't be a problem and that she knew the tour's route backwards. Steel found that curious in itself.

Was Kane also under surveillance?

If so, why? He was just a tour guide, or was there another reason? A personal one, maybe?

Samara led Steel through the streets, which became narrow in places. There were lots of dog-legged streets with lots of sharp turns and long alleyways. Some roads went up at almost thirty-degree angles, and others then naturally went down the same gradient. The air was thick. The wind wasn't getting through the city's build-up, and the circulation of air was almost zero. It had felt like a million degrees in the sun, in the shade, it was cooler being out of the direct sunlight, but there was very little air.

Steel imagined the big guy that Samara had taken out with the plank trying to keep up. He imagined the guy keeling over as soon as they had hit the first incline, then rolling down to the next street, unconscious.

Steel smiled.

He would have loved to have seen that.

But he had got to see something better. Samara kicking seven shades of shit out of the guy. Which technically was all his own doing. It wasn't classy, but she'd made her point.

They reached the old part of town, with tall grey buildings which had a dark feel of the nineteen-twenties about them. These streets had once bustled with off-duty soldiers and townsfolk. The noise must have been loud and vibrant in such a closed environment, Steel thought as they passed what appeared to be an old tavern.

Now, the streets were quiet, with fading painted names of stores on the weathered walls. As they turned a corner, they saw the tour group at the top of a steep-stepped alleyway.

From where Steel and Samara were, they could see Kane's back. Kane was stood at the head of the path facing his audience. His arms were busy waving about, pointing here and there. His actions were erratic and full of drama and energy. The group were entranced by both his tales and his performance.

'And on this street, they filmed the famous zombie chase,' Kane said. He explained the scene and held up the folder again, showing more stills from *behind the scenes*. All Steel had caught of the talk was that Brad Pitt was the star and not much else.

Not that Steel knew who Brad Pitt was – or cared.

As they snuck back into the group, Steel realised nobody had missed them. All eyes were fixed on Kane, pointing down the main street to some old woman's house.

Samara looked down the street and the many stone steps they had just run up. Steel saw the confused and worried look on her face.

They had made it back without a tail.

Samara shook off the thought and smiled as she turned to face Steel, but her smile faded as she looked at his expression. It was cold and emotionless.

She did not need to ask. Samara already knew what he was thinking. Steel turned to face Kane as he hurried everyone back down the steep steps.

They were going back the way they came. Steel suddenly felt uneasy. He had hoped they were heading to another pick-up point and not going back to the car park near the old barracks. Steel looked over at where Samara had stood, only to find she had disappeared.

He smiled with admiration at her skills. She had slipped away, and why not? She knew the city better than anyone. Hopefully better than the people chasing her.

Steel mixed in with the group as they ventured down the steps. He looked back at the street and smiled to himself.

She would be safe for now.

The question was, what did she, or rather Mossad, want from him?

As the tour group got to the bottom step, they turned left and headed back down the narrow street. Kane stood with his arm pointing the direction they should take. Kane smiled with a broad grin, showing off pearly white teeth as he ushered them forwards. As Steel strolled past, he felt Kane's eyes stare up at the stairwell and then back to him.

'What you looking for, Kane?' Steel wondered as he continued to follow the crowd.

As the group lined up to enter the bus, Steel took photographs of the area, making like he was a tourist. In reality, checking if more of the men from another team had followed on behind. Steel suspected Samara had taken a cab back to a safe house or bureau. He noticed the blue mini was in the same spot. It would have been too much risk for her to come back for it. Besides, if they wanted her dead, he supposed that they would have plenty of opportunities.

They had been on her tail when she'd started on his several days ago, so why attack her now? What had changed?

Steel climbed onto the bus and headed for his seat, three rows back on the left-hand side. He found that the same woman he'd sat next to before was there and had already taken her aisle seat.

She wore the same silly, excited grin as before, all ready for the next phase of the tour. Steel smiled and took his seat. Politely declined the boiled sweet offer as she produced a packet and shoved them under his nose. Steel smiled and raised a hand, making the excuse that he was full. The smell of artificial fruit and starch dust filled his nose, bring back memories of childhood. Good times, happy times. He had to admit he did like them, but that wasn't the time or place – for sweets.

Steel gazed out of the tinted windows taking in the harbour's view and the other bay's new buildings. He massaged the side of his hands, which were sore from the encounter. He was glad that he was able to take down the men quickly. The last thing he needed was to walk around with torn clothes. However, he would have to live with the dust on his trousers for the time being.

If he was there under any other circumstance, he might enjoy himself. But today, he was on edge. A million thoughts rushing through his calculating brain. Steel began to wonder if there would be time to grab a coffee, or at least a quick drink, on this tour.

As the bus pulled away and Steel took in the view, he could not help but wonder who Samara really was. Her moves on the men in the fort showed she could handle herself.

Krav Maga seemed to be her choice of fighting technic, which did not surprise him as it was the favoured fighting skill of Mossad. Which also bore the question, what was a Mossad agent doing there?

They headed out of Valletta towards Mdina. A city he remembered for all the wrong reasons. He could still see Brad's lifeless face as he lay on the pavement. Someone had killed him for something, and Steel still had no idea what. The same people who had murdered Lucy.

The same people he was going to put in the ground.

Steel took in the fantastic but sometimes harsh looking countryside. Winding roads clung to the sides of steep hills, with a mix of green and craggy rock faces. Lush vineyards backed onto the rough ground. For him, the whole place was a beautiful paradox. There wasn't a simple walk from one location to another. You had to have transport, of which there was, thankfully, plenty.

Steel checked his cell phone for any missed calls. He was half expecting Foster to keep in contact just to see what he had found. But nothing.

Chapter 29

Director Walter Sloan of the Malta section of the FBI sat quietly in his office. He was in his fifties but didn't, look it. The Malta weather seemed to agree with him. He was of average height but an ego to rise above all else – way, above. He wore a brown cotton suit with a white short-sleeve shirt and blue clip-on tie. His brown Oxford shoes were highly polished, mostly with the help of the machine in the lobby. It was one of those automatic jobs that cleaned and polished your shoes while you still wore them.

Ingenious.

The embassy had installed it to stop people from treading dust into the carpets. Still, it also gave an excellent impression to visitors. Taxpayers money well spent.

Sloan's office was a twenty by twenty feet box, with a large window to the left, along the wall behind him. This 6x3 window had a clear view of the rear of the embassy. His desk was large and locally made by craftsmen. Constructed from a thick piece of teak that had been carved and stained to give it an aged effect. Along the left-hand wall near the bureau were three small grey filing cabinets. On these stood two potted plants and a picture of him shaking the President's hand. Behind his desk, two American flags hung from ash poles, the poles crossed at the base, pointing the polished metal tips outwards. The room was painted white with black skirting boards bordering a blue carpet.

Everything else in the office was dull and official-looking. The best that tax dollars could buy. Along the right-hand wall was a tall black cabinet. The shelves were filled with numerous styles of books and photographs of Sloan's family. The left-hand wall held only two paintings from a local artist. In front of the desk sat three armchairs arranged at a semicircle, so they faced the director.

Sloan had been excited when he received the posting. It had been a promotion. However, they had forgotten to mention his office would be around thirty feet underground. The window's view was an image relayed from cameras on the south wall, just like in the hallways.

'Damned psychiatrists,' Sloan said as he glanced at the fake window.

Sloan sat patiently in his thickly padded brown office chair. He found himself looking at his Rolex wristwatch every few minutes.

The others were late.

He had no doubt it was on purpose.

The section chiefs of the CIA, Homeland and NSA Malta section were coming at his request. And because of that, they were dragging their heels.

Sloan looked up as the door opened and his secretary walked in. She was a slim woman in her late forties. Stepping machines, yoga and other forms of workouts had done their job to keep her looking good. She had long black hair held back with a white clip. Her toned figure clad in a beige skirt suit and matching pumps. The suit had been a Christmas present from her soon to be wife. Sloan did not mind that she was, as he called it, 'one of those', and she did not care; he was a dinosaur that should have been made extinct after the cold war. Janis Fletcher had been with Sloan for years. She was a good secretary.

'Sir, your visitors,' Janis said, holding the door so the three could enter. She waited until Sloan gave her the nod and then quietly closed the door as she left.

'So, Walt, what's this all about?' asked Charles Tipp, Director of the NSA. Sloan did not answer. He just watched as Tipp sat in the right-hand chair. Tipp was around six-two and in his late forties. He wore a brown double-breasted suit and a sky-blue shirt that covered his stocky build and brown Oxford shoes, also highly polished. Tipp had a square head, all cheek muscles, a flat nose, square jaw, and flat ears. On top of this square head, he had a crown of blonde hair that should be on a hair products advert. He looked like a cartoon character from a kid show, with a big top half and spindly legs.

Lloyd Bolton of the CIA was an inch shorter than Tipp. He was a quiet man in his fifties, with hair as black as coal and quality grey suit but no tie. Bolton said nothing. He just walked over to the left-hand chair and sat. Leaving the middle chair free.

Sloan waited while Alison Price of Homeland Security sat at the window side and sipped her English breakfast tea she had brought in with her. Preferring her own company than sitting between the two men.

Sloan smiled at the display. Three agencies were sent to work together, but they could not stand to be sat near each other.

Price was a tall woman with an athletic figure and a blonde bob haircut. She wore a dark grey skirt suit that had a crossover closing jacket. She wasn't particularly attractive, but something about her drew men like a moth to an inferno.

'We need to talk about the project,' Sloan started. 'How sure are we that it's tamper-proof?'

Tipp rolled his eyes in disapproval to the question. 'We've been over this, Walt; it is a hundred per cent tamper-proof when it's downloaded.' Tipp had a Louisiana accent. His voice was deep but clear and had all the signs of a good education.

'Yeah – when it's downloaded, but what about now?' Sloan asked. His voice was gravely like he'd been using cheap bourbon as a mouthwash. The other two men looked at him in surprise.

'What do you mean, Walt? The disk is secure,' said Bolton with confidence. 'Nobody can get to the disk drive without us present, so what's your worry?'

'I always worry, Lloyd; it's my job. So, answer the fucking question.'

'Trust me, Walt. The disk is secure. Nobody is getting near it,' Tipp said, leaning back into the chair confidently. His thick arms sprawled over the arms of the armchair, he crossed his left leg over his right.

But despite all their confidence and reassurances, Sloan could not relax – not until the damned thing was installed.

Deep down on the sixth level of the blockhouse, a figure moved about, avoiding the cameras as it went. Dressed like the others in a black suit, blending in with moving groups of people, the figure approached a green-painted door near the end of a long corridor. Quickly the figure stopped and started to pick the lock. There was the sound of the tumbler turning, and the latch was undone.

Immediately, the figure moved inside, quick and silent, then closed the door behind them. It was cold and pitch-black inside. The figure fumbled about on the wall. Brushing their hand up and down the brickwork until finally, they found the switch. One-click, and the lights came on. There was no dust or dirt, but it felt grimy. The room was long, possibly twenty-by-ten feet, with mustard-coloured walls and industrial shelving. The shelving stood six sections high by three sections broad, each around three-by-two feet of dark grey metal sheeting. It was a regular army bolt-together system, cheap but effective.

The illumination was provided by three single bulb lamps, which hung on long cords. Their green metallic lampshades created pools of light on the grey concrete floor.

It looked like something from the Cold War.

Old cardboard boxes marked with serial numbers filled the ageing metal shelving. The room did not fit with the rest of the building, where everything was new and bright. It was as though this was the place where things got filed and forgotten.

The figure moved quickly towards the empty wall at the end of the room to run gloved hands over the brickwork. It was looking for something hidden. The figure stopped. Its right hand froze over what appeared to be some repaired damage to the wall, a set of three bricks that did not quite fit right, as if they had been inserted after the rest as part of a repair. The stranger pressed the uneven piece of wall and waited. There was a click and then a grind of gears before one of the shelving section swung out. The figure moved to the revealed door.

A sterile white room.

Chapter 30

Steel sat back in the coach seat as it headed for Mdina. The sun beat down relentlessly.

Steel had been to many places that had been hot and quite a few freezing. So, he was accustomed to weather and temperature change. However, being accustomed did not mean that his body liked it any better. The air-conditioner was working hard to bring the temperature down. Some of the older ladies cooled themselves with waved magazines. Others carried small battery-operated fans.

Steel gazed at a map of the island on his cell phone, switching between the satellite view and the map view. All in high definition, so good he could see a cat sat in a shop window – or at least he thought it was a cat. He was making mental notes of a few possible places of interest and distances between them. Which hilltop went somewhere, and which just led you to a sheer drop. Was there a village or farm or vineyard close by? He checked the small red dot on the map, which showed their location on the map. They were on Route 7, the Triq L-lmdina Road. Steel watched as the landscape wheezed by, the ploughed fields, the old stone walls, the trees and bushes that lined the road. He saw a bright red *FOR SALE* sign attached to one of the walls but missed whether it was for a house or a plot of land. He liked Malta. The people were friendly, the weather was great, and the scenery was breathtaking. He sighed deeply. Thinking about what could have been the holidays that he and Helen could have taken on this island.

Helen would have loved it here. Steel's lonely gaze went back to the window and the landscape. Samara next to him was taking photographs out the window. He had no idea what, possibly random things to show some poor unsuspecting friend when she was back home. A bottle of cheap chardonnay and four hours of holiday snaps awaited some poor bastard, Steel thought.

He smiled as the image came into his head.

Steel looked at the tablet and the image of the red dot moving closer to its destination. They had just passed a place called Misrah Kola, and now they were heading out into more countryside and towards a place called Attard, which would be on his right according to the map. But Steel wasn't interested in the place. He was more interested in what he had just seen on the map.

'And to our right…somewhere,' Kane said, trying to point something out, but all everyone could see was a high wall, trees and bushes.

Nothing of real interest. Nothing everyone hadn't seen before.

'… is the American Embassy,' Kane announced. His tone dulled as if giving up the search for visual confirmation but carried on the explanation all the same. Steel looked over with interest. He had seen it on the map. It wasn't a single building, not at all like what he had seen in places like London or New York. This was a large complex within a fence. At first, he had thought it was a military installation until he had seen the name. *EMBASSY OF THE UNITED STATES OF AMERICA.*

Steel looked over at Kane, who returned the glance. And Steel had to wonder again, who was this tour guide?

The coach parked up in front of a grand hotel in Mdina, and Kane ushered the group off.

Steel waited to be last.

He needed time to think about his next move. Kane seemed to have something he wanted to share. Perhaps the timing hadn't been right for Kane to say anything yet. Which given the circumstances, Kane, being surrounded continuously by inquisitive tourists, made sense.

Steel was in no rush. All he had to do was wait.

The group moved away from the bus, following Kane's direction towards a small restaurant that overlooked the rolling hills and diverse landscape. Kane had hung back slightly.

Steel walked alongside Kane, watching the group in front of them open the gap between them.

'So,' Steel said. 'When do we get to Gozo?'

Kane said nothing but glanced about nervously. His eyes darting left and right.

'OK, so if we aren't going, why did you convince me we were?' Steel asked. 'Was it Samara's idea?'

Kane looked over to Steel as they approached the restaurant.

'Not here. Not now,' Kane said laughing, as though they were chatting about the tour. Kane gave Steel a business card from his wallet. 'Please, come around tonight, dine with my family and me, and we will discuss this further.' Kane hurried off, take charge of the group, who were piling into the restaurant.

Steel stood for a moment and looked at the card. It was a dull-looking thing with Kane's address and phone number in bold lettering. Defiantly not his business card. Steel imagined that to have Kane's picture on it, a colourful logo of some kind. This was plain and simple.

Steel watched as Kane disappeared into the restaurant, laughing and joking with the owners. All Steel could do was how Kane was connected to what was going on.

Chapter 31

The phone rang in the Master's office. The telephone was what most would consider a relic from the sixties. It was lime green with a clear plastic dial in the centre, and the receiver connected to the base via a coiled plastic cable.

A simple operation. The clear plastic had ten holes on the outer rim, each hole at rest over a printed number. There were no buttons, no electronic touch screen, no voice-activated function. Just stick your finger in a numbered hole and dial, wait for the disk to rotate back, select the next number and repeat. The Master was in his sixties, but his body was broken from the years, making him appear much older.

This was as old school as it got.

But the Master was happy with that. After all, he was old school. The boy who stood to his right lifted the receiver from the cradle and nervously passed it over. All the while wondering if it was the others reporting bad news. Would he become the same fate as the other boy?

The Master took the receiver in his bony hand and placed it against his left ear. He said nothing, just listened in silence.

The boy heard nothing but muffled sounds over the earpiece. Someone was explaining something. The boy watched as the Master's grip on the receiver tightened.

They had failed.

The Master said nothing. He handed the receiver back to the boy calmly. The boy let out a gentle exhale of breath as he placed the receiver back onto the cradle.

The Master remained silent and still.

The boy wanted to run for the door or at least move slowly out of reach. But he knew that he dared not move, just in case, he should set the Master off.

'Leave me,' the Master eventually said.

The boy bowed and moved away slowly towards the door. The flickers of candlelight guiding his way. He was expecting to be called back, or a knife to be thrown, or a shot in his back.

But there was none of these.

Just silence.

The boy opened the door and left the Master alone in the dark.

As the boy began to close the door, he heard the telephone being dialled. *Click-whir, click-whir, click-whir* as the dialling drum was being turned.

'We have…a problem,' the Master said. His voice soft, calm. But behind all of that, the boy knew – he was angry.

Chapter 32

Calver sat in his booth, watching the small shapes of ferries and cargo boats on his monitors. Most of the traffic was commercial aircraft bringing in the latest batch of excited tourists. The island was getting busier.

All in all, it was a quiet day at the office. But after the raid the other day on the cargo ship, Calver was hoping for more. Unfortunately, all he had was what he considered to be 'every day, humdrum.' Even the bad guys must have a rest day, he had thought to himself.

He rocked in his chair and drank from the bottled water he had fetched from the vending machine. The wrappers from the two candy bars he had brought with it lay twisted in the waste bin under his desk. He had thought about the sandwich he had seen in the machine, which was the last tuna salad. He did not know why he was thinking about it or even wanted it. Perhaps because it had been the last one? He shrugged and opened a bag of crisps. The waft of salt filled his nostrils.

There was a blip on the screen, but that had been in Tunisia. Well, out of their area. But he wondered what it had been. An aircraft of some kind? He was not sure. He thought about switching to satellite, taking a look in real-time. But he knew if he got caught looking at anything other than his designated area without just cause, he would be dragged up before the director.

'Not worth it,' he thought.

Calver looked at his watch and then around the room, almost as if he was expecting something. Anything. Samara with the food trolley, a frigging brass band, anything to break the monotonous hours.

But there was nothing - just the quiet of the room. Calver did not count the background drone of radio chatter, the bleeps from machines, the whir from the computer's fans. He did not hear these sounds anymore. He remembered one guy had bought a Newton's Cradle. It had lasted about twenty minutes before someone ripped it off his desk and smashed it to hell.

Calver had to admit that he enjoyed the brutal way that Sandra had stormed over from three booths back. In an utterly brutal attack, she had smashed the metal balls from the frame using the edge of the guy's desk.

Calver had seen her in a different light after that – been attracted even. But she was in a relationship with someone in the NSA.

Calver sighed loudly and yawned. He needed to do something. The boredom was killing him.

Nobody moved, said or did anything. It was as though they had been assimilated into the machine, their brains connected to the web. His mind began to wander again, thinking about sci-fi movies.

Man and machine combined. The new race, the rulers of the world, the galaxy, the universe. But then he thought that it never really worked out very well for the machines. Mankind always came up on top.

Calver took another sip of water, and with a disappointed look, glanced around again. Hoping for something to be there.

Anything. But it never came, and Calver doubted it would.

'What's up, man? Looked like you were expecting something.' yelled Arnold Tanner from his booth to the left of Calver. Tanner was a short, overweight man with a severe sweat problem, the problem being he could not sweat. Poor bastard was born with no sweat glands.

Tanner was a round guy. He had a large round head, atop a circular body, and small round glasses perched on a button nose. He wore beige chinos with a white shirt and a mustard-coloured waistcoat that he never did up.

A nice enough guy Calver thought. In fact, he reminded Calver of the professor from the Muppets.

'Only looking for something to happen, Arnold, only for something to happen,' Calver smiled.

'Yeah, I hear ya,' Arnold laughed and got back to work. Calver looked at his watch again, then stared back at the monitor, his gaze fixed on that dot that kept blinking all the way over in Tunisia.

The secure doors opened, causing Calver to look up, then Foster walked in, and their eyes met. Calver quickly looked away, trying to make out it had never happened. Calver sneaked another look. This time Foster had his back to the workers, talking to the floor chief.

Edward Bryce was the floor chief. His face was like the rest of his body, which was long and thin. Bryce would often scrutinise the workplace with his dark sunken eyes. Glaring down his hawk-like nose. He looked like a Halloween caricature.

Long grey trousers with military-sharp creases covered his thin legs down to brown, highly polished shoes. His eggshell blue short-sleeve shirt was ironed to razor-like creases on the arms covered by a mustard-coloured waistcoat cardigan.

Calver had always thought Bryce looked more like a librarian than the head of the day shift in an intelligence agency. Even down to the cardigan and the glasses that hung around his neck on a cord.

Calver looked over at Foster and Bryce, intrigued by what the men were saying. So interested in fact, he was halfway out of his chair. Arnold tossed a ball of scrap paper at him. Hitting Calver in the eye.

'Hey, what you doin, man?' Calver asked angrily.

'Stopping you getting canned,' Arnold laughed.

Calver smiled and nodded. As he sat, he tossed the paper ball back at Arnold, hitting him in the chest. It rebounded and landed in his coffee. Arnold shouted friendly abuse, and he pulled out the soaked piece of paper and tossed it in the trash.

'Asshole,' Arnold said, flicking the liquid from his fingers.

'You love me really,' Calver replied, going back to his screens, but keeping an eye on his two bosses.

It was nearly five o'clock, and Calver was eager to get the hell out of there. He had things to do, people to see.

Calver watched as Foster gave the floor chief a pat on the back and left the room. Bryce turned to head for his small office. His head hung low.

Something had happened, and Calver assumed it wasn't good, well not for the asshole boss anyway.

Calver smiled at all the things that may have happened. 'Maybe the garbage men finally ran over that stupid dog of his,' Calver had muttered to himself.

But then he saw the look on Bryce's face, and Calver stopped smiling. Bryce looked shocked. The sort of look when you find out someone close to you has died. But there was no one close to him, just that stupid dog. A million solutions whizzed around in Calver's head. Had he been canned? Had they finally gotten rid of the ghoulish moron?

No. That look was something else, more like heartbreak – remorse even.

Something terrible had happened.

And it wasn't about a stupid dog.

Chapter 33

It was around five o'clock when the tour bus had dropped Steel back at the Grand Hotel Excelsior. It had been a more exciting day than he'd expected, but he still hadn't made it to Gozo. Which made him suspect whatever was on that island was important? As Steel walked into the lobby, he took out Kane's business card and flicked the edge with his index finger. The conflict inside his head and gut wasn't resolving.

To go or not to go, that was the question?

Unfortunately, it wasn't the only question, just one of many. Like who were those guy's trying to snatch Samara, and why were they after her?

Yet one question had started to nag him louder than all the others. Why was Lucy out on Gozo that night? Had she gone to meet someone? Without seeing the place first-hand, he could not get an idea of possible circumstances.

What the hell had Brad seen on Gozo?

Gozo.

Everything seemed to revolve around that small island. All Steel knew about the island was it had prehistoric ruins that predated the pyramids. It had a wonder called the Azure Window. The place where Lucy had jumped.

Steel had seen satellite pictures and photos of the Azure Window. A fantastic natural arch that had reached out into the ocean but collapsed a few years ago. Something that nagged at Steel. Something felt wrong about the whole thing.

Steel looked once more at the business card: the plain white card, the cheap print. He thought about what Kane had said near the restaurant.

'Not here. Not now, Please, come around tonight, dine with my family and me, and we will discuss this further.'

Steel remembered the look on his face. Not so much frightened as secretive.

Steel's gut told him it was probably another waste of time or perhaps even a trap, but his curiosity shouted far louder. He wanted to know what Kane knew – if he did indeed know anything.

Steel headed for the elevator. The overhead lights reflecting on the polished floor, like moonlight on the ocean. The lobby was full of people checking in and out. The bar area full of people grabbing a drink before heading downstairs to dine. Steel smiled and nodded to a tall woman behind the check-in desk. It had been the same woman that had checked him in days before. Her smile was warm and full of interest. Steel had returned the gesture, and a cat-like look suddenly crossed her face.

The cat that got the cream or the cat that saw the bird?

Steel smiled to himself. The game they were playing made for a pleasant distraction.

But he did not need distractions. All he needed a clear head, a drink, and a shower.

Steel stripped off his clothes and placed them on a chair. He would send them to get dry-cleaned in the morning. He walked across the carpeted floor towards the drink's cabinet. Letting the crisp air-conditioned air sweep over his naked body. Steel poured two-fingers of an eighteen-year-old malt into a glass and sipped it slowly.

He headed into the bathroom, his thoughts a jumble of ideas, facts, conclusions, and questions. He started to think about New York and the team, about McCall. He had left under a cloud.

He had not even said goodbye.

Was it?

Was this goodbye?

In truth, he had no idea. The whole NYPD thing was meant to be only for one case, and then the ship thing happened. Steel had to admit he missed the gang there, especially Detective Samantha McCall, his partner at the 11th precinct. He respected McCall. She was tough, savvy, funny, annoying, and beautiful.

But he did not really see that part of her. There were women, and then there was McCall. Every man's dream. The full package.

But not for him, despite what people may have thought.

Steel was not looking for anything permanent. Sure casual came up now and then. But in his mind, he was still married. There had only been one woman for Steel, and she was gone.

Taken from him.

Steel was as broken a man as there ever was. That day at the shooting, everything was ripped away from him: his parents, his brother and sister, his dear sweet Helen. SANTINI had destroyed his life, left him scarred emotionally and physically.

It had been meant to be his homecoming, a celebration of his returning from a tour of duty. One that had itself had been bad.

He had come home to gunfire, dead bodies of family and friends. The intruders had relentlessly gunned down people in the garden, not caring who they were or how old they were. It was a massacre. Steel had hunted the intruders through his home. Killing them one by one. Justice – revenge – anger – hatred? All the while, he searched for Helen. Steel had made it all the way to the attic of the old mansion. There, amongst the hidden away items of his youth, Steel had found his wife. She lay quiet and still on the dusty floorboards.

Steel closed his eyes tightly as the memory resurfaced.

As he held her in his arms, she turned and looked at him.

Their eyes met.

She was alive.

Boom. The ground shook, his ears rang with the noise. A handgun, close range in a confined space, is loud like an explosion, like sitting next to a ship's cannon when it's fired. But somehow, he did not hear it or feel the pain. All he saw was his wife's eyes. Large pale blue, searching – scared.

Boom.

The handgun sang again, five more times. Steel's felt the bullets hitting his body, like a prize fitter using him as a punching bag. Each hit in an aimed location. The last one hit his midsection. His eyes continually staring into Helen's as if he was using his body to keep her safe. He felt her head nudge to the side. Her eyes went cold. A single tear ran down her cheek. She was gone.

He had failed her.

Steel roared like a beast and tossed the empty glass. Blood lust coursed through his veins like fire. He grabbed the side of the washbasin. And breathed.

In and out.

He looked up at the long mirror. His soulless green eyes stared back at him.

He breathed again deeper.

In and slowly out.

Steel wished he could cry. But that was another thing stolen from him. Emotionally, he could not cry – not anymore.

Suddenly, he was calm, as though the fire inside of him had burnt out. Steel looked up at the mirror and sighed. Then a puzzled look crossed his face. He looked around quickly.

'Where the bloody hell did I throw that?' Steel said, looking up at the long, wide, huge – expensive mirror, which was still intact.

Steel found the glass embedded in the sofa. It had travelled the full breadth of the hallway, missed quite a few other objects – including the wall and the expensive wallpaper and had nestled safely into the cushioned back cushion of the sofa.

'Why can I never do that at home?' Steel groaned with a broken smile.

He retrieved the glass, poured himself another, which he took to the shower.

Steel changed into a black suit with a black shirt and military shoes. If Kane was setting a trap, at least he would be overdressed for it.

Steel walked onto the terrace and sat for a moment, looking out over the small harbour at the hotel's rear. The sun was just beginning to set. Flocks of seagulls swooped and dived in a show of aerial acrobatics. He smiled as three ducks swam happily in the large outdoor pool. He had to admit he loved it here. It was peaceful, serene. But he mustn't let the beauty of the place cloud his thoughts. He had a job to do.

Steel cracked open a bottle of water from the minibar and took a long draw as he watched the world go by. A cool breeze blew in from the ocean and ticked his skin while he listened to the haunting sound of the Scopoli's Shearwater, a native sea bird that sounded like a baby crying.

At that moment, life was good.

Possibly the best it had been for a long time. But Steel knew he could not relax into the mood. He was no closer to finding out what had happened to Lucy, but something was going on. It had got Brad killed, and Samara had almost been grabbed by a bunch of thugs. And then there was Kane. For some reason, Kane didn't want Steel going to Gozo. Why? Steel was hoping Kane would clear up that and a few other things that evening. He had wasted enough time on goose chases and dead ends.

Steel went back inside to the suites writing desk, a beautiful piece of furniture in a Victorian design. Steel's laptop and phone sat neatly on top of the desk, both charging and loading updates. His unique sunglasses and contact lenses sat upon a loading platform, also charging and loading updates.

Field equipment his handler had called them. Expensive was what Steel had called them. But necessary. They had helped him out of a lot of situations.

Steel checked himself in a long mirror. Ensuring he looked good, that his tactical shoes did not clash with his attire. He stared at his reflection, looking past the clothes and looked at his reflection.

The son of a British Earl, an ex-soldier and now worked for something bigger than he had imagined actually possible. There was MI6, CIA, FBI, the French DGSE, The German BND, and then there was – them.

Steel had been recruited after his time with the SEALs. It was plausible that they had their eye on Steel for a long time, possibly since a young age. MI8 was beyond a secret service. Formed after 9/11, just like the OSS soon became the CIA. MI8 was considered beyond black ops, beyond the red tape. And they had sought him out.

The perfect candidate.

The fact that Steel's father had also been a member of MI8 for many years may have helped tip the scales in his favour. Maybe it was the fact that he wanted revenge, or they did. Whatever the case, he did not care.

Steel checked himself in the mirror. He had found dark clothes suited him better, plus dark clothing had that look about it. He did not consider himself good looking or even anything special, regardless of his heritage. All he saw was a damaged man with talent – a talent for ending up alone because it was better that way.

If you love something, it will be taken from you. Steel had learnt a lesson years ago, and now being alone was as normal to him as being with a partner was for most others.

A sharp beeping noise from the desk broke his concentration. Steel turned to see the updates were completed on the phone and laptop. He unplugged the phone and placed it in his inner jacket pocket. The laptop had automatically switched off, the small blue LED power light faded. Steel took the computer and slid it into a slipcase before he put it in the wall safe. Steel wiped clean the touchpad if someone tried to check his prints to work out the combination. Not that it mattered, they would just use a code breaker device. But why should he make things easy for them?

Steel looked at his watch. It was nearly six o'clock. Steel picked up the receiver from the house phone and dialled the number on the card. It rang several times before being picked up.

'Mr Steel, I've expecting your call. I will meet you in your lobby in twenty minutes,' Kane said confidently.

'Sure, why not, nothing on TV anyway,' Steel said, picking up his sunglasses and placed them in the other inside pocket of his jacket. He heard Kane laugh before the phone went dead. Steel smiled and put the receiver onto its cradle. Steel grabbed the contact lenses and made his way to the mirror. He hated wearing them, but he found that his soulless, dark green eyes spooked the hell out of people. A useful tool sometimes, but something he liked to keep undercover. Besides, the lenses had a useful tech in them.

Just in case.

'Plan for the worst, hope for the best and anything in the middle is a bonus,' Steel's instructor used to tell him. Steel still had no idea what the '*anything in the middle*' part was about. But then the guy had been weird - even liked Marmite on his chips. Sick bastard. Steel knew he had time to kill, so he checked his messages. Several from his company, which he had replied to, used the digital signature app to sign off on a couple of documents. Steel hated this. He wasn't a businessman, though he knew the ins and outs of the company. His father had schooled him in that. Steel hadn't seen it at the time, but now, Steel was convinced his father knew something could happen, and Steel had to be ready to step into those big shoes.

After fifteen minutes, Steel stood up and closed down the tablet. It was time.

'OK, let's get this over with,' Steel sighed and headed out the door of the suite.

Steel found Kane sat in the lobby on a two-seater couch with ornate carving. It looked antique, as did all the furniture of the bar area beyond the double staircase. It was a classy finish to the hotel's exclusiveness.

Steel stood by the elevator. He looked at Kane and suddenly felt over-dressed. Kane wore half-cut jeans, a long white linen shirt, and training sandals.

Steel approached but said nothing. He just watched as Kane checked his phone.

'Twenty minutes, huh, so how long have you actually been waiting?' Steel looked down at the French reproduction table and saw scattered sugar granules. 'How about ten to fifteen?' Steel said.

Kane just rocked a flat palm from side-to-side in a 'so-so' motion and put his phone away as he stood up. 'About that – yes,' Kane smiled and offered a welcoming hand. Steel completed the handshake.

'Come,' Kane said and headed for the hotel's entrance.

Steel was a little wary about Kane, but there was something about this guy he liked. Probably because he was as mad as a hatter, but Kane reminded Steel of a good friend he'd had in the SAS.

Steel had lost a good friend after his life fell apart, and he knew he had to disappear.

The trip to Kane's house did not take long. Mostly because Kane drove like he was late for something. For Steel, it had the bonus of losing any tails they had picked up. Steel sat looking unnerved by Kane's driving; he had an image of toughness to uphold, but all the while, he was discreetly holding on to the door handle.

Kane pulled up to a modest two-story house and switched off the engine before getting out. Steel followed slowly; his gaze fixed on the house, waiting for something to happen.

'Welcome to my home,' Kane said proudly and headed for the front door. Steel followed while checking around him, looking for any new vehicles, decided to make a stop. The street was empty, but all the time, his gut was warning him something was off.

Inside was bright and homely. Pictures of his family filled the walls of the hallway. Documenting all the trips that they had taken. Steel could see Kane and his family loved to travel and work for the local film industry. The hallway was long, with a staircase to the left and a room to the right. At the end of the corridor was another door. Steel guessed that was the kitchen.

Steel followed Kane as he went through the door on the right. This led to the sitting room and dining room. It was a large open planned double room that led off to the left to an open-plan kitchen making an L-shape. The sitting room and dining room were bright with cream coloured walls and a stone fireplace which heated both rooms. The sitting room was twenty by fifteen, with a window with a view of the front garden.

There was a sofa against the right-hand wall and above the fireplace was a forty-inch flatscreen television. Steel noticed there were ornate cabinets with old porcelain miniatures. Steel figured these were an inheritance from a parent or a grandparent. The dining room was half the sitting room's size, with a sliding patio door leading out to the garden. In the centre was a small, highly polished dining table with four chairs. Steel guessed that this could extend, and there were extra leaves and chairs somewhere.

As they made their way through the sitting room, Steel stopped at a group of photographs on a wall. These were famous actors with Kane or his wife. Steel nodded, impressed at this family's history.

'An upside of the business,' Kane laughed, noticing Steel's interest in the photos. They headed for the kitchen. The smell of freshly cooked fish and meats filled the air in a delicious aroma. Steel felt his stomach growl in anticipation. As they passed near the fireplace, Steel froze. He looked down at one picture of Kane's wife with a white dress and flowers in her hair. The photo pulled at a memory of Steel's wife. Years ago, Steel had taken her on holiday in Bavaria. Helen had looked like Samara in the picture before him, happy, loving. A good memory - but one that brought him pain.

Steel touched the scar at his waist. A wound he could never forget and never wanted to.

'Oh, that,' Kane said. 'That was taken four years ago, in the Black Forest in Germany, beautiful, isn't she?' said Kane proudly.

'What?' Steel said in surprise. Kane's words bringing Steel back to reality. 'Yes, you're a lucky man,' Steel replied, pulling back his emotions with a smile.

'However, as beautiful as she is, my wife hates when her well-prepared food gets cold. Not a good thing to see, believe me,' Kane joked in earshot of his wife, who was busy in the kitchen.

'Don't believe him,' she said, giving Kane a stern look, 'I would wait until you have left.' She winked with a smile. Kane's wife was tall and slender. She had raven-black hair that fell past her shoulders and down her back. She wore a white wrap dress that revealed well-trained calf muscles. Brown t-strap shoes and a gold cross on a gold chain complemented the outfit. Steel followed Kane into the kitchen. It was a large room with plenty of windows, and white coloured walls matched nicely with the grey colour of the modern fittings.

'Mr Steel, this is my wife, Maria,' Kane said, indicated his wife, who was just about to take something out of the oven.

'Pleasure to make your acquaintance, madam,' Steel said, bowing slightly from the waist. Maria returned the gesture with a head bow and raised hands in oven-mitts. 'But please, call me John,' Steel said.

'Pleased to meet you, John.' Her voice was warm and soft. 'I hope you are hungry?' Maria said, tossing a green salad in a wooden bowl.

'Come, John, we shall get out of the kitchen before she makes us do something,' Kane laughed. Maria reacted by throwing a dishcloth at him, which landed gently onto his right shoulder. As they passed by the sink, Kane dropped the cloth onto the side.

Steel followed Kane into the garden where a long wooden table had been set with a white table cloth, wine glasses, and candles in small silver and glass candelabrum. Wooden bowls with different salads, bowls of olives, plates of bread, cold meats, and fish filled the table's centre. It was a feast for what appeared to be for many, not just three adults and two children. Then Steel noticed there were six chairs.

'Someone missing from the party?' Steel asked suspiciously.

'No, we're all here,' came a familiar voice from behind him. Steel turned and saw Samara in the doorway, holding two wine bottles, one red and one white. Steel turned to Kane and scowled. He had suspected something was wrong, and now he knew.

'John, I believe you know my sister,' Kane said with a broad grin.

Chapter 34

After twelve hours of monotony, Calver left the embassy, his brain was fried, but he wasn't heading straight home. He did not have time to crash out, watch TV and drink beer. He had things to do, people to see.

Calver was on a tight schedule. He'd brought everything he needed with him. A change of clothes and his bag was in his car. He had to be on the next ferry to Gozo, and he had little time to get there. The journey, on paper, would take around half an hour. But Calver was a practical guy. He knew that shit happened when you did not need it to. He would have to head Northwest on the Triq l-ldward towards Vjal L-lstadium Nazzjonali. The road would take him towards Mdina, and then at the roundabout, he'd have to head North until he hit the route 16 and then up towards Cirkewwa.

He could see the roads being clear at that time of the evening, something he desperately needed. Every second counted. The sun had not yet entirely set, for that he was thankful he hated driving in the dark. Also, he would have to take his chance on the roads, put his foot down and hope the cops weren't around. He could not afford to be pulled over, not just because of the time it would take, but he knew it would get back to the office. And there would be questions. Questions he could not answer.

He checked the clock on the dash of his Range Rover. According to the display, he was making good time. But he could not be complacent and assume it was going to last.

Against the odds - it did.

The roads remained clear, and the lights stayed green.

It was completely dark by the time he reached the port in Cirkewwa. Calver had made it and with time to spare. Good, he thought, time to load up and hit the onboard kiosk. The trip over to Gozo would take around half-hour tops; then, the road trip would take him twenty minutes due to the winding roads in almost complete darkness.

He found a seat on the passenger deck and sat with a fresh coffee and a sandwich from the kiosk. It wasn't a feast but all he had time for. Once his meeting was done, he would have time to have a proper meal – which would probably be breakfast in Victoria, Gozo's capital.

Calver checked his second phone for messages. His work phone was back at the car, turned off, battery out; no need for anyone to know where he had been, especially the Company. Calver grumbled to himself at the lack of new communications, *but then no news was good news,* he thought reassuringly. Calver placed his disposable phone back into his pocket and took a sip from the hot coffee. The potent beverage made him wince. He'd had weaker trucker coffee, but then he was used to the good stuff at work.

The crossing was calm and quick, which for him had been a blessing. He was a computer geek, and the closest he wanted to come to water was a shower in the morning. Taking the ferry, it was necessary, so he bore it.

The ship made an anchor at Mgarr Habour. The vehicles started to disembark through the small fishing village and make their way up Victoria's winding road. From there, he headed towards Hondoq Bay.

The bay was a great place for swimmers and people with boats during the day, with its clear blue waters and a small jetty. However, it was deserted at night and was the perfect spot for what Calver needed, dark and secluded.

Despite single lane roads close to deadly drops, Calver arrived at the slipway. He waited patiently with his lights off, but the motor is running. He looked at the digital clock on the dashboard. It was now ten-to-nine. He was early, but better that than being late. These weren't the sort of people you kept waiting for. Besides, he had a reputation to uphold and not being punctual would damage that.

He took out a pair of night vision binoculars and scoured the ocean for a vessel. Through the military-grade scope, everything was bathed in light emerald green. The Rongland Night vision binos had a fantastic x 5 magnification, making them perfect for his needs. Except he saw nothing but the ocean. He looked back at the clock. It was two minutes too. He raised the binos to his eyes for another look and again, nothing but ocean. Calver was suddenly sickened by betrayal.

Had he been set up?

Were the police or worse waiting back up the hill for him? Calver chanced one more look, his heart in his mouth.

Calver smiled as he saw a small dingy with three men aboard, the waves lapping up at the sides as it cruised towards the shore. It approached slowly, then halfway, it stopped. Calver watched and waited. He knew there would be a signal, one he would have to respond to, or the boat would turn and go back the way it came. Then he saw it. Three bright intermittent flashes, possibly from a flashlight. It was big enough to see, but the beam wasn't so intense it would alert the rest of the island.

Calver got out of the car, flashed his own small torch twice. There was a whirr of an outboard motor, and the craft raced towards the jetty.

One of the men tossed up their guide rope. Calver caught it and tied it off.

'Gentlemen,' Calver said with a smile. 'You had me worried.' He laughed and helped one of the men onto the pier.

Chapter 35

The Master handed the receiver back to the boy. Gingerly the boy placed it onto the cradle of the telephone. He had just received a phone call that made him happy. Things were finally moving forward.

The Master's men on the island had reported that the cop and Samara were in the house of a man called Kane. They had seen the cop arrive. The man called Kane had driven him. They knew Samara was there because the blue Mini was parked a couple of places away. Close enough to get to in an emergency, far away enough to keep someone guessing which house she was in.

So far, the Master's men had been blessed with good fortune, despite their incompetence at the old barracks. Their orders were clear, *grab the woman and bring her to Aamir*. Unfortunately, they had underestimated her abilities and the cop's involvement. Before, he was just a person to be aware of, nothing to worry about. But, since his participation at the bridge at Mosta and his interference in Valletta, he was now a threat.

The Master stood slowly, grasping the arms of the chair to push himself up. He wasn't an ancient man, but his bones hurt from too much conflict, the years had not been kind, but he was a fighter regardless.

He headed towards a large map that lay spread out on a sturdy wooden table. The boy followed the Master, carrying a candle with him. His youthful features lit by the glow of the flame. The old table was plain and functional. It had been used for many things; dining, food preparation, an operating table, and even laying out a body before burial.

The table, like the Master, had seen many things – good and evil, but they had always been together. He figured one day he too would be laid out on the table on his death. Family, friends and comrades would say their farewells. He would be gone, but the table would go on to serve its next Master.

Long boney fingers brushed against the top's uneven wood, then moved slowly over to the map. He smiled as he looked at the plan marked out with red and blue crosses and lines. Point A was their base in Tunisia, point B was Malta, point C was lost in the room's dark. Soon all would be illuminated, soon the world would know their name.

Chapter 36

The meal at Kane's home had been pleasant, with lots of local wine and excellent food. Kane told stories about his film career and the parts he and his family often played. Steel took an interest in the tales of the stars who visited, the stories he could not share on the tours. Steel looked around at Kane, his wife, and two sons. He had what most would consider a perfect life, a great family and a career doing what they love.

'So, John, do you have a family back in Britain?' Maria asked with a broad smile.

Steel shook his head, a hidden look of sadness masked behind a fake smile. 'No. I'm…alone, no family,' Steel said before taking a sip from the wine glass.

Maria looked over at Steel curiously, feeling his pain but not understanding it.

Samara leaned forwards and said something in Maltese. Steel did not understand. However, Maria's reaction spoke volumes as she turned to face Steel, her large glazed, hazel coloured eyes filled with sympathy.

Steel had heard the tales people told of his family's murder, and he was aware that most of the account was missing. Actual reports had been mixed in with Chinese whispers, and before he knew it, the story got watered down or blown out of proportion.

But he knew the truth of what happened. Steel still did not understand why they had attacked. He had been chasing the criminal organisation called SANTINI for what seemed like a lifetime. However, there was another organisation out there that could have orchestrated the murder.

He just did not know which had given the order.

'I am sorry about your family, your wife and parents. I did not know, forgive me,' Maria said with a sympathetic smile.

Steel smiled back and shook his head. 'There is nothing to forgive Maria. It was a long time ago. I have learnt to live with it and move on,' Steel lied.

Samara gaze suggested she saw through his lies, but she said nothing.

'So, apart from sending me on wild goose chases, what else you been up to?' Steel asked Kane, causing him to choke on the large chunk of bread he had just put in his mouth. Kane's children laughed as their father's face turned red.

Kane swallowed the bread and drunk some wine to clear his throat. Steel smiled at his small and simple revenge. Plus, it was an excellent way to shift everyone's thoughts from his past onto something else.

'It wasn't my brother's fault,' Samara said softly. 'Today's distraction was my fault. I asked Kane to do it. I thought those men were after you, and Gozo is… well, shall we say a not so public place in areas'.'

Steel had to admit Samara was a beautiful woman. Her eyes were large and inquisitive, deep hazel liquid pools that he could stare into all day. He thought back to Helen of Troy and Cleopatra's stories and could envisage Samara looked the way they might have. Her dark hair shone in the light spilling from the house. She was perfect in body and mind, and she could kick ass. He liked that.

'Nice place for accidents – or people going missing, I take it,' Steel said, reading between the lines.

'Exactly, I thought the tour might force them to make a move,' Samara said.

'So, why were they after you?' he asked.

'Who knows?' She shrugged. 'I am Mossad. It could be anything to do with that, a faction against us or someone in a panic because I'm here.' Her voice was calm, and she seemed unaffected by the thought that someone was after her. 'All I do know, John, is they seem interested in you. And that could work out to be useful,' she said, leaning back in her chair and smiling, as she remembered the big man's face as she gave it a massive roundhouse kick.

'What do you mean – *interested* in me?' His tone bit sharply at the realisation that they – whoever they were – had no idea who he was. All along, he thought he had been a target, but it wasn't so. Now they did know about him, what were they going to do about it? 'What is there to know? I'm just here on vacation and to visit a friend who lost his daughter?'

Samara shot a desperate glance at her brother; mouths gaped open as if struggling for words.

'Samara, why do you think I was here?' Steel growled, tossing the linen napkin onto the table. Maria hurried the children away to their rooms, sensing Steel's frustration.

'Your friend. He is Mr Foster, correct? One of the section chiefs at the Embassy?' Kane said.

'Yes, he called me a couple of days ago. His daughter Lucy had been found dead by the Azure Window. She was my Goddaughter.' Steel replied.

'Yes, it made the local news. I'm sorry for your loss,' Samara paused. 'But we have been watching your friend for some time. You see, someone in the Embassy has been contacting a terrorist group. And… shall we say his movements have been very…' Samara's voice drifted away.

'Questionable?' Steel finished the sentence.

Samara nodded at the choice of word.

'You know his kid just died?' Steel said, picking up the glass of wine.

'Yes, but we were watching a while before that,' Samara said. Her eyes had grown sharper, searching him for hidden answers or tells, or maybe she was just interested in him?

'Really, what's a little? Three months?' Steel said, placing the wine glass against his mouth, ready to take a sip.

'A year,' Samara finished.

Steel scowled at her omission. 'A year?' Steel said. Almost lost for words, not believing what he was hearing. Then it struck him like a hammer. Steel scowled at Samara. 'Well, if you were watching him, who else was?' Steel asked. Surely the CIA had to know. They always did. It was their job.

'Why the hell have you been watching him for a year?'

Samara said nothing. 'Mossad has been watching him for a year, not my sister. She only got this assignment a week ago,' Kane said. His gaze switched to Samara. She smiled back at Kane softly. Always the big brother wanting to protect her.

'And you, Kane? Are you also Mossad?' Steel asked sharply. He began to wonder what he had suddenly walked into, worst of all, willingly.

Kane smiled and shook his head.

'No, John. I was born in Malta, whereas Samara was born in Israel. Our father is an Israeli, and our mother is Maltese. They met when our father was stationed here during that time. They met, they dated, they fell in love, and I was the result. Soon after they married, our father was sent back to Israel. For some people, a possible strange combination, but no more than British soldiers marrying German women,' Kane shrugged. 'Samara and I are only separated by a few years, but some say I look older – it must be the beard,' he laughed.

'But you have different last names?' Steel said, somewhat intrigued.

'Ah, yes. The price of show business, I'm afraid. I changed my last name when I became an actor. My agent thought it would be best,' Kane explained.

'So, how is it you came back to Malta?' Steel asked, trying to figure out this families complex tale.

'My mother wanted me to grow up in the way of the Maltese people, to carry on our family heritage. I was sent over at a young age to live with my grandparents. I guess our mother had already seen that our father wanted us to be Mossad, but I was already an outsider. So, the decision was made, and well – here I am,' Kane said with outstretched arms.

'Weren't you a bit pissed-off you didn't get to be Mossad?' Steel asked before taking a sip from his drink.

'Not at all. Besides, I have enough action in my life,' Kane laughed. 'Sure, in my films, I do stunt work, shoot guns and exciting stuff like that, but the thought of actually risking my life?' Kane shook his head and cracked a smile from the corner of his mouth. 'no, I'm quite happy where I am, thank you.'

'So, what makes you think it's Foster that's the mole?' Steel said, returning his gaze to Samara.

'I'm just here on an intel-gathering mission, observe and not interact. That's it,' Samara's face held a neutral expression. Even her large brown eyes gave nothing away.

'Well, I'm impressed by your idea of *non-interaction*.' Steel smiled softly.

'They attacked me, I retaliated.' Samara shrugged. 'What's your excuse, Mr John Steel?' she growled. The words were drawn out.

'Damsel in distress.'

Kane smiled at Steel's quick reply.

'Was Foster the only one you're looking at?' Steel asked, hoping for a negative.

'I can't discuss a secret operation, especially one you are involved in,' Samara said. Her tone was stern but also playful.

'Hey, you brought me into this,' Steel said.

'When?'

'The moment you started following me.' Steel sat back in his chair. His gaze fixed onto her.

Samara smiled and combed her fingers through her hair.

'Fair enough, no, he wasn't the only one.'

'Wasn't – as in, he is now?' Steel said, sitting forward.

'He is the only one who was acting out of character, even before his daughter's death,' Samara insisted. But Steel saw something in her face. Uncertainty.

'But –?'

'But – nothing fits. Everyone else was clean except Foster,' Samara said. Her neutral expression had returned.

'You think the Agency is funding this terrorist group, don't you?' Steel asked, sitting back in his chair. He held the wine glass but rested it on the armrest.

Samara remained silent as she stood up and carried some empty plates inside. Steel stood up and did the same. He needed answers.

Was this why Lucy had died, and it had nothing to do with what Brad had found? Or had what Brad had seen something to do with what Foster was up to?

Or worse still – had Foster had Brad taken out because of what he'd found?

Steel followed Samara into the kitchen.

'I am sorry about your friend,' she said, hoping to smooth the situation.

'Foster's no traitor. He's too lazy for that,' Steel said, but he still nagged him why they were looking at him for the leak. 'Foster always liked the quiet, comfortable life. Heck, he spent most of our Op's sleeping.'

'Just because we were looking doesn't mean it was so,' Samara admitted.

'No, but either way, I'm going to find out. I am here to find out what happened to Lucy, so far, all I got is some kid called Brad and a blackmail scam,' Steel said.

'Did you talk with him?'

'Unfortunately, not. Someone shot him on a bridge in Mosta,' Steel said.

'So, what's your plan now?' She asked.

Steel leant against the side of the breakfast bar, feeling slightly uncomfortable in the presence of this beauty. Her eyes burnt into his soul, his emotions, his primal urges. He looked away and coughed.

Samara smiled softly, knowing that Steel had felt something for her – love, lust? She did not know, but there was something.

She had won this round. One point to her.

'Well, considering you dragged me into, this I guess we could work together,' Steel said as innocently as he could manage, his gaze crept back onto her's.

'Guessing or hoping?' she said, moving closer to Steel. She moved hypnotically like a snake dancer.

Steel swallowed hard but maintained his stance against the counter.

'Yes, of course, I mean someone's got to keep you out of trouble,' Steel laughed, looking down into her deep brown eyes.

They stood for a moment. Locked in one another's gaze. Two people trying to find that hidden something.

Steel wondered only one thing – could he trust her? He looked deeper into her eyes. Perfect white surrounded deep pools of hazel, with a hint of yellow. He started to wonder if he had been wrong about her likeness been that of Helen of Troy or Cleopatra. He wondered if she was more like the Medusa or the sirens. These beautiful monsters dragged the unwary to their doom.

'So, who wants coffee,' yelled Kane, striding in and switching on the coffee machine. Oblivious of the moment, he had just disturbed.

Steel and Samara both jumped at the sudden noise and smiled awkwardly. They moved apart casually as if nothing had been happening.

Chapter 37

Steel woke around three that morning, needing the bathroom and a bottle of water. He had watched the rain from the balcony window for a while as he sipped the water. It had come down heavily, making a lake on the terrace. He looked over at the small island and the old fort at Manoel island. Something was still nagged him about that place. It was too quiet, serene. What was it Kane had said? 'It was out of bounds to the public.'

He finished the water and headed back to bed. It was still early, and he had a long day ahead of him later.

Weather permitting.

He crawled back under the sheets and sighed heavily. The bed was still warm and very comfortable –too comfortable.

Steel breathed in and out.

He closed his eyes, hoping his nightmares wouldn't return.

He breathed in and out.

The image of Samara walking over to him, those hypnotic moves of her's burned in his memory. Steel smiled. Hoping that this time he would have pleasant dreams. Who knows, maybe Samara would be in them – perhaps in a bikini.

He breathed in and out, then fell into another haunted sleep – the nightmare of his wife's death had returned for another night.

The sound of pounding rain had woken him. The storm was still going, the downpour continued. He opened one eye and stared at the window. It was not going to be a dry and warm day as the days before. He stared at the window a little longer and gathered the sheets around him like a shroud of defiance. He did not want to get up. The bed was warm and far too pleasant to leave for that weather.

Steel looked over at the clock next to the bed and groaned. It was six in the morning. He'd forced himself to lie in – after all, he was on vacation. The unyielding sound of rain hammering against the bedroom window suddenly made him regret not getting a standard room with a balcony overhang.

Steel wasn't a great fan of rain. He would seek to avoid going out in it when he could. He'd spent too much time in the rain while he was in the Army and the Teams.

Steel gave a deep sigh and forced himself from the comfort of the warm bed. He had slept, despite the ever-recurring nightmares.

'Right ya fucker, get your arse in gear,' Steel said to himself, in a deep voice imitating his old training sergeant from the British Army.

By eight o'clock, Steel had spent an hour in the hotel's gym before having breakfast in his suite. He had chosen the continental breakfast, a somewhat impressive mix of fruits, bread, cold meats, fish, cereals, and lots of coffee. After he poured his fourth coffee, he left the breakfast table and headed for the sitting room. The morning sun was trying to break through, now and then, there would be a break in the clouds, and seamless blue could be seen, and then it would be gone.

Steel sipped the coffee. It was strong and rich.

A good coffee.

Steel sat in an armchair. He was wearing just a pair of pyjama shorts and a complimentary bathrobe.

After all – he was on vacation, allegedly.

Looking out across the small terrace at the grey weather outside made Steel wonder about his plans for the day. But it could not be helped. He had a job to do regardless of the damn weather. The rain showed no sign of stopping or letting up, which was perfect for the plants, crops and wildlife of the island.

Steel looked at his cell phone for messages, but there was nothing new. He looked back at the storm and drank his strong coffee. He needed a new plan.

The rain has stopped play, he thought to himself.

Something he could not afford. Steel needed to shower and change before committing to a plan. He rechecked his phone, just in case, then headed for the bathroom to shower. Steel hoped by the time he came out, the storm had passed.

If not - well, he'd just have to go and get wet.

Samara sat in her Mini and watched the Foster residence from across the road and a few cars back for cover. Samara had figured that now she had contacted John Steel, she could return to her original assignment. John Steel's arrival had derailed her from her assignment, but only briefly. Now, Foster had his full attention.

The rest of the family had left minutes before, leaving Marcus Foster home alone. She had been there for two hours. There was no need for an overnight stakeout.

She looked at her watch out of boredom. It was two minutes since she last checked at eight o'clock. Samara shook her watch just to make sure the hands hadn't frozen in place. She sighed and stretched her muscles, accidentally knocking over her coffee as she did so.

'Shit,' she cursed, grabbing old napkins from the back seat or anything back there to soak up the cold caffeine. As she leant over to the back seat, she missed the blacked-out Land Rover pull up outside Foster's house, or the four men get out and head for the residence.

Two went to the front, while the other two took the back.

Her cell phone rang, causing her to straighten from her mopping up. She looked over at the display panel of the minis onboard entertainment system. The cars Bluetooth system had picked up her phone, and the call rerouted. The display told her it was Steel calling.

'Yes – what?' she growled, wanting to end the call and get back to cleaning her passenger seat.

'Good morning to you too,' Steel said lightly, 'So, where are you.... what are you wearing?'

'At home, I just got out of the shower,' she snarled, still trying to mop up the liquid from the cloth seat. Suddenly, her gaze fell onto the blacked-out Land Rover. She cursed the fact she had missed it and quickly exited her car. As she headed for the other side of the road, she heard heavy footsteps behind her. She turned to see Steel running fast towards her.

'What's wrong?' Steel asked as he saw her pull her 9mm Masada Striker from the holster in the small of her back.

'Trouble,' she said, nodding towards the Land Rover. Slowly, with her pistol gripped tightly, Samara made her way around towards the passenger's side of the vehicle. At the same time, Steel crept towards the driver's side. If there was a driver, he would either drive off or bolt out of the door and start running. If Steel was in position, he could take him down silently. Steel waited at the door, checking the wing mirror, but he saw no driver. Samara swung the weapon around, the barrel targeting the driver's side – but it was empty.

'There's no one there,' she said loud enough for Steel to hear.

'They must all be inside. Did you get a look at them?' Steel asked. Samara felt embarrassed for a second. She had taken her eyes off the house for a second, but that had been enough.

'No…I, never mind, come on,' she ordered.

'You got a backup gun?' Steel asked.

'Why? You scared?' she mocked.

'Of you shooting me in the arse? Absolutely.'

'No, sorry,' she lied and pushed forwards towards the front door.

'Got a plan?' she asked. Steel remembered the layout of the house, possible exit points.

'Take the back, and be careful', Steel ordered as she came up beside him.

'You sure? They could be armed. Maybe I should take the front?' Steel shook his head.

'It won't matter either way whether you are front or back if they are armed,' Steel said. 'If someone is in there, they would be in the sitting room or bedrooms by now. We'll just have to go steady. You clear the ground floor, I'll take upstairs.' Samara nodded and headed for the rear of the house; her weapon gripped in two hands ready.

Steel reached to the front door to find it had been kicked open. The door frame splintered, and pieces of wood and metal littered the floor. Steel moved inside slowly, hugging the corners as he went. He did not know what to expect, but if these were the same people who tried to grab Samara, they would be armed and dangerous.

Steel stopped at the bottom of the staircase and slowly followed it up. Steel knew Samara would be clearing the lower levels while he took the first floor. He clung to the wall and kept his feet to the sides of each step where it was strongest. The last thing he needed was a creak from a floorboard to alert the invaders.

He would take each step slowly and carefully. Then he would stop and listen.

Step, stop, listen.

Step, stop, listen.

Adrenaline seeped through his body. Still, his heart rate was regular. He was transfixed on what he was doing. Years of training was being engaged, set into motion.

Step – stop – listen.

Step – stop… his gaze fell through the bannister on the upper floor. The long corridor, a straight line down to the end room. Four doors on either side, bedrooms, and bathrooms. Steel's sunglass covered eyes scanned for any signs of the goons or Foster.

Steel froze and ducked down. A large hulk of a guy came to the top of the stairs. Steel could feel his heart start to race. The man was muscular but small in height than to Steel, but it did not matter. It was either too much time in the gym or a chemical cocktail. Either way, the man wouldn't be going down easy. Steel crouched lower, hoping to make himself seem smaller and lower to the ground. Steel could not afford for the guy to signal his partners. He did not know where Samara was. She could be coming up on one of the others, ready to strike. An alarm now could blow the whole show.

Steel waited for the man to spot him, possibly pull out a gun or leap at him. A million scenarios raced through Steel's mind. Could he get to the man before anything happened, where the others just behind him and he had not yet seen them?

Steel braced himself. Hoping just staying still would make him unnoticeable until the last second.

The man took his post at the top of the stairs, and then Steel saw it. The cell phone in the guy's hand. He was too busy texting on his phone to have seen Steel. The guy was laughing at whatever he was reading or possibly a video someone had sent him.

Steel only cared that the guy was busy, and he had not seen Steel.

Steel exhaled carefully and moved slowly, trying to keep out of the man's peripheral vision.

The man stood solid at the top of the stairs. His legs were shoulder-width apart, while the back of his heels rested on the edge of the first step. He looked like a bouncer at a club. His concentration was on the video someone had sent him on his phone. The men were not expecting anyone to be in the house. They would have seen the family leave or have struck earlier. No, these men were looking for something, and they did not need a witness. Which would explain their relaxed nature. They probably figured they had all the time in the world.

Steel loved overconfidence. It was one of those double-edged traits. If you were selling something, or a reporter, or chatting to a beautiful woman, it was perfect. However, if you were a bad guy who did not account for a counterattack, leave someone at the door or have proper surveillance on-going – it was deadly.

Yes, he really loved overconfidence – and these guys had it by the bucket load.

Steel smiled as he crept up behind the man. Steel knew grabbing the man's shoulders and pulling him back would work. However, if he got the timing wrong, it may well be him who got flung down the stairs. Steel inched forward, his gaze switching between the guy's head and his feet – or rather his ankles that were at the edge of the first step.

Steel moved slowly, inch by inch. He made his breathing shallower, in through the nose out through the mouth.

Steel was getting closer. So close, in fact, he could smell the guy's body odour. Steel turned his head and sucked in a breath of clean air. He was convinced the big guy hadn't showered before they had come out – possibly for days before.

Steel found a good foothold and slowly reached towards the guy's legs. Steel figured it wouldn't take much effort on his part. The guy was standing legs wide apart, he was off-balance, and besides, he wouldn't be expecting it.

Steel grabbed the man's ankles – and yanked.

The big guy's face smashed against the top step and then bounced off the steps as gravity dragged him down, leaving a bloody streak. The brute was out cold and need some dental work when he woke, judging by front teeth embedded in the wood.

Steel couched near the top step. He listened for any sound. Waiting for the others to come rushing out. Half expecting goons to rush out into the hallway, guns and knives ready.

But there was silence, and nobody came.

Steel went back to the big man and checked him for weapons but found nothing apart from a cell phone. Steel grabbed that and stuck it into his pocket. Looking back up the stairs, Steel could hear a cry of pain.

Foster.

Steel clenched and unclenched his fists, prepared to move in. His friend was in trouble, and there was no knowing what the hell they were doing to him in that end room. Foster's screams grew louder; the closer Steel got. But he did not lose focus. He had closed off his emotions. These would just cloud his judgement. Steel needed to be cold and unemotional.

There were unknown numbers of people in that room. There could be only one guy, which meant there were two loose in the house, or all three men could be in the room. Which then led to a more interesting question, where the hell was Samara? She should have made it to him by now. So, if she wasn't kicking the shit out of a bad guy, what was keeping her?

Steel moved slowly down the corridor, following the sounds emanating from the room at the end. He knew there were only three men left. He figured there were at least two guys in with Foster. Which then led to the question of where the third guy was.

Steel would have preferred taking down one man at a time. It made the situation easier to control. Fighting more than one at a time was always difficult. Because they never fought one at a time like in the movies, they would gang up, surround, use weapons. Steel could handle himself for sure, and he had taken several people down at once but never come out ungrazed. He'd lost many a good suit and gotten plenty of bruises and stitches due to dirty fighting.

As Steel moved down the hallway, he froze. Someone who had just used the bathroom was behind him. But the door had been slightly open, and there had been no sound. Had the guy gone for a leak sitting down? There was a bronze statue of a man on a small table in front of him. Steel grabbed it. He could hear the man whistling to himself. Apparently, life was good – but it wouldn't be for long. Steel swung the figure as he twisted at the waist, catching the guy coming out of the bathroom across the forehead, forcing him back into the wall and knocked him out cold. Steel noted the two lines just above his nose, where the square base had impacted.

Steel checked the guy, but he had nothing except a bone-handled penknife and a cell phone. Puzzled, Steel left the man and turned to face the room where they were torturing Foster.

Now there were only two – and still no sign of Samara.

As Steel moved closer, he could hear the voices, yelling questions, screams of pain. Steel's heart began to race as the adrenaline pumped faster through his veins. The cries of pain grew louder, and Steel knew he needed a plan and fast.

He knew there had to be a weapon of some kind. There was no way Foster would have willingly gone anywhere with these guys, not even upstairs knowing he was going to be tortured. So, there had to be a gun. A knife would have been child's play for Foster to take away from the guys, even though he had been working a desk for years.

No, it had to be a gun.

With that in mind, Steel knew he would have to move quickly and quietly. Any sudden noise would spook them, and it could cost Foster his life. Steel reached the door and held his back against the wall.

His breathing shallow, his heart rate steady.

He raised a fist and knocked.

'What is it?' came a voice, Steel replied but muffled his voice.

'What... just come in,' said the voice. Steel again spoke in a muffled voice. Steel heard a grumble and the sound of heavy footsteps. Steel hid the best he could around the corner. His back against the other door and waited. He had no idea what to expect. He had seen what extremists, terrorists, freedom fighters and maniacs could do to people. Both Foster and Steel had seen their fair measure of the aftermath. Steel's mind ran ahead of him. There were two men down and possibly one in the room and one downstairs. The man heading towards the door was undoubtedly the leader, possibly an interrogator of sorts.

Steel looked over at the bronze figure he had left with the bathroom guy. Maybe it hadn't been such a great idea to have left it. But it did not matter now. It was too late. The person was coming closer. Steel could hear the creak of the floorboards, the *impact* of shoes.

Suddenly the door opened, and out stepped Foster. Steel stared at him blankly. Foster was unhurt, unbound, ungagged.

'Foster?' Steel could not believe his eyes. 'What the hell's going on?'

The door behind Steel opened. He felt the bite of the taser, then everything went black.

Chapter 38

At eight-thirty, the Master had finished speaking on the phone. The call itself had lasted only moments, but it had been enough. At last, he had gotten good news instead of constant excuses. Aamir was doing well. The Master wore a smile of contentment on his haggard face, the wrinkled contours etched with cracked skin.

But the good news did not make him any less concerned.

How had it gotten to this stage in the first place?

Who was this cop, and what was he doing there – with her? The Master could not see how Mossad and the NYPD were connected. And even if they were, the cop was out of his jurisdiction, so in fact, he was just a civilian – not a policeman. The contact had said that the cop had revisited the man, Foster. But this was to be expected as they were old friends.

The Master sat and contemplated the events and the facts. He sipped on his hot tea, letting the aroma of the herbs and honey waft gently against his nose. He breathed in the vapour and closed his eyes.

The only link the Master could see was Foster and the cop. The Cop hadn't met Samara until later – In fact, Samara had been following him. It was a puzzle. But one he no longer had to be concerned with.

Steps had been taken.

They were back on schedule.

Chapter 39

At eight-forty, the phone in the secure office rang. Alpha picked up the receiver and sat back in his office chair. It creaked with age.

'Yes,' Alpha said.

'The cop went to the house,' said Beta.

'And?' said Alpha.

'They secured him and the girl,' said Beta.

'Why was he there – for Foster?' asked Alpha.

'They are friends – but I think it was more for the woman. They seem to spend a lot of time together,' said Beta.

'It was a mistake to involve him,' Alpha said.

'The cop – or my second?' asked Beta.

'Both. But we both know your second has a problem with this Samara woman,' said Alpha.

There was silence.

'What is the plan for the cop?' said Alpha.

'They want to talk with him. Personally, I'd finish him. It's safer,' said Beta.

'You're probably right, but it isn't either of us who makes the call. Command said they had plans for him,' said Alpha.

'What about Foster?' said Beta.

'It's time for him, I think. But stick with the plan,' said Alpha.

Chapter 40

Steel groaned as he woke slowly. Everything was black, and he felt the restraints pull on the skin of his wrists. He tried to move his legs but found them bound as well. But he did not struggle or kick, yell or scream. He just lay still to get a sense of his situation. The floor was cold but not damp, which could mean he was underground, possibly a cellar. But he was basing his assessment on pre-existing information, and he did not know that much about old structures in Malta. For all, he knew he could be in a tower of one of the ancient fortresses. The truth was, he had no idea.

Steel moved his hands about slowly, trying to ascertain what the binds were made from. Steel felt the bite from thin plastic against his wrists, possibly plasticuffs. Steel moved his legs, but they were locked at the ankles.

It same deal as his wrists.

Steel thought about it. Why plasticuffs? Simple, a person could carry plenty of them without drawing attention. But Steel figured there was another reason – they weren't expecting him. They needed something quick and easy. Whoever did this may have just had a supply in their vehicle for another job? Whatever the case was, he was tied up in god knows where and they undoubtedly had Samara too.

Steel's hands had been tied behind his back, which wasn't a problem. Steel moved so he could move his hands past his legs and then to his knee. From there, he could break his restraints using his knees. It was a simple hit and pull-apart motion, standard training for three-letter agencies, special forces or anyone who could use the internet. Steel lay on his back, passed his bound hands over his arse, then threaded each leg through until his hands were in front of him. Steel took a moment. The exertion on top of the shock from the taser had drained him slightly. John Steel used his fingertips to find his right boot's laces and untied the laces after getting his breath back. He passed one part of the lace through the cuff and locked the other one down with his other foot, so the lace was taught. Then he began to saw. Steel winced as the plastic bit against his flesh. But he bit down and carried on sawing. He could feel the heat from the plastic, but he carried on. Steel was thankful he had replaced the standard laces with the re-enforced round laces. He could feel the sweat pouring down his face as he worked the cuff up and down against the lace. The plastic felt red hot against his skin, but he knew he could not stop. He could not let the cuff cool down. There was a snapping sound, and Steel flew backwards as the plastic cuff broke. Steel lay on the ground for a second, sucking in the air. Steel sat up and wiped the sweat from his brow. Surprised at how thick the cuffs had been.

He reached down and inched his fingers over his trouser material towards the binding around his feet. Steel was surprised to find it wasn't plastic that bound his feet but duct tape.

They really hadn't planned on an extra guest, Steel realised. Using the tips of his fingers, he began to strip away the duct tape. It was taking time – time he did not have.

Time Samara probably did not have.

She was in trouble, and Foster was going to find himself dangling out of a window by his ankles until Steel got her back and understood what was going on.

Steel felt the give as the last piece of tape was ripped from his legs. First things first, he checked himself over. They had taken his watch, sunglasses, wallet, and phone. He reached down and put his boot back. The last thing he needed after all his trouble was to tread on something that could damage his foot.

Steel had no idea where he was, how big the room was – where the ceiling was. The last thing he needed was to launch himself off the ground and find the gap between the floor and ceiling was shorter than he was. Reaching up to his hands, he tested for the ceiling as he rose slowly. Steel found himself stood upright with plenty of space still above his head. He stamped his left foot hard on the ground, but there was only the clap from his shoe on the floor – stone or concrete. *OK, no echo*, he thought to himself. Which meant he was in a small room. Which also said it wouldn't take long to find a wall and hopefully a door. He had gotten in somehow, so logic dictated there must be a way out. Then Steel froze and looked up. He could not see anything.

'Oh, crap, what if they've stuck me in a sodding hole?' Steel said. 'Huh. Oh, well, even a hole has walls,' Steel said as he stretched his right arm in front of him and his left out to the side. Then he started to move slowly forwards. The hope being at some point to find a wall.

Steel did not want to shout out. He did not think they would have brought him somewhere public on the off chance he did scream out for help. He hadn't been gagged, suggesting screaming wouldn't help him. And besides, there was no need to let them know he was awake.

Where was the fun in that?

Steel thought back to his time in the US Navy SEALs. It had been about seven months after his family's murder that he went for selection. It had been an opportunity given to him by someone he came to trust, a man called Major Avory Dickson.

Steel figured saving the guy's ass in Alaska counted for something.

No one there knew Steel's past. No one cared. The truth was that nobody really wanted him there.

He was an outsider, a loner. Not very good for someone looking to join a team. But he did OK.

Steel had done two years with the teams. One of his jobs had been prison infiltration and breakouts. It was a risky job, but he was crazy enough to do it, plus he had nothing to lose. If he died – he died, Steel did not care. It had been a dangerous job, but he perfected the art. Get captured, kill the bad guys, get everyone out.

Simple.

That was until his team were led into an ambush, and most of them got taken out. Steel found out the SANTINI organisation had murdered his family that summers day so many years ago. They had somehow found him and tried to take him out. But the day his team got hit, he was three thousand miles away on another operation for the CIA.

It's good to know even the bad guy's get bad intel, he had thought at the time. Steel realised it was time to leave the SEALs for the safety of the teams.

Time to disappear until it was time to take the fight to them.

And he had.

Now he was making them hurt. He was breaking the SANTINI organisation apart piece by piece. But oddly enough, he did not feel anything about that. No pleasure, no sense of revenge, no justice.

Nothing.

He was empty. They had made him that way.

His fear was that he would never feel again.

Suddenly, Steel's right hand brushed against the rough brickwork of a wall. He had only gone ten steps before he had reached that point. Steel used his palms to search for a light switch or door handle. He knew the chances of finding such things were slim, but then this had been a quick abduction, so they would have had to find a temporary place to put him.

Steel's thoughts went back to Samara and what had become of her. He hoped she had gotten away, gone to call for the Cavalry – whoever the hell that might be. What part did Foster play in this? If he was dirty, why did he bring Steel over in the first place?

Steel's mouth was dry, his tongue stuck to the roof of his mouth. He figured they had used a drug to knock him out, which would account for the thirst because the room wasn't hot or even warm. It was cool. So he wasn't dehydrated because of the temperature. Steel checked his neck for sore spots of pin-pricks. He hadn't been knocked out. He would have remembered that. Then he flinched slightly as his fingers found a place near his carotid. It stung like he'd been attacked by a bee or wasp.

Instinctively, Steel licked his fingers and rubbed the liquid onto the injection wound. It had been more muscle memory than anything, a sort of comforting trick a mother would teach a child to make them feel better.

But he did not feel better.

In fact, he was madder than ever. They had tasered him and taken Samara.

Why was he still alive? They could have simply tossed him into the ocean, been rid of him? Or maybe, they couldn't afford for him to die? Perhaps they were holding him to interrogate him later, so they would have questions. He knew he would have done the same.

Instinctively, Steel felt that this was not the decision of the men who had been following Samara. Someone was giving them orders.

Steel took a moment and gathered his thoughts and breathed in the cold air. The room was so dark he had to rely on smell, touch and ….Steel stopped. His trail of thought had switched.

Why hadn't he thought of it before?

The most obvious question.

Why was it so dark? Was he in a dark room that had no windows, or it was night time already? If so, how long had he been out, and what time was it?

Steel continued to search in front of him but only felt cold bricks and some sort of powder. Steel rubbed his fingers together, feeling the gritty texture and smelt it. Was he in an old building perhaps, and the mortar that held the bricks together had turned to dust with age?

It would account for the musty smell. Steel took off his right boot and placed it on the ground. He needed a reference point, so he did not keep going around in circles, then put his hands back on the wall and resumed the search. If there was no door, then a ceiling hatch would make life difficult if impossible to find in the dark.

As Steel continued his search, he found nothing but brick, his fear of the overhead hatch was becoming more a reality. But he had to wonder how high the ceiling was. If they had thrown him down with his hands strapped behind him, he would have sustained injuries, bruising or broken bones, maybe even a head wound, but he was unhurt.

Then, just as he was starting to give up hope, his fingers brushed against something. Not stone, it was wood – a door. A reassuring grin crossed his face. He mapped the edges of the doorway carefully. It was small and low down, which was possibly why he hadn't found it before. The door was about five feet by three feet. And old door Steel figured because everyone, for some reason, was shorter back then. But it did not matter. It was a way in – and out.

Steel cursed he never put his contact lenses in. The electronic systems within them would have made this situation thousand times easier. Still, he'd gotten out of worse problems without them. In a way, Steel was glad for losing his gadgets for a while, yes, they were useful tech, but he was becoming too reliant on them, lazy. This situation would blow off the cobwebs, force him to use his instincts again.

Steel felt around for the door and the frame again. He needed to find out if it was an old or new door he was dealing with? The difference between the two would be whether he got out quickly or not at all, not without light anyway.

His finger brushed against the rough, prickly texture of the wood.

It was old – ancient.

Which would mean this door was probably over a century old, meaning it would be at least three inches thick, with heavy, well-made hinges that would be made from solid iron.

Doors built to hold off invaders.

In other words, it's something that could not be kicked through like a modern door. But the locks on an old door would be simple, and the chances were if it was an old building and the old door was still there, it hadn't been maintained. Steel began to hope that where the hinges had been seated into the wall was no longer sturdy, that years of use and weathering had decayed the mortar, and the door could be forced out. Steel moved his hands from the frame to the door, half expecting the feel of thick oak.

But he did not.

He was feeling something else. It was weathered paintwork of a modern door. At some point, someone had replaced the old door with a new one, but now, even that was old. Steel guessed it had been done twenty or more years. Perhaps it dated back to the nineteen-sixties when the British were on the island.

Excitedly, Steel searched and found the door handle. By the feel of it. Steel figured it was a solid plastic-coated handle like the ones used in factories. Still, more important, it was a new lever handle. Steel smiled and put his muscular shoulder to work.

The door gave way quickly, making splinters of the ancient frame. Steel had held onto the door handle to ensure the door did not crash open and alert anyone who may be in earshot. He inched the door open just a crack to get a feeling of what light was outside the door. The corridor was poorly illuminated, but there was a light source from somewhere. Steel inched the door open a little more and listened for anything; radio chatter, footsteps, even someone clearing their throat.

But there was nothing, just silence.

Steel chanced to open the door a little more and peered out into what was an old corridor. The illumination was coming from poorly boarded up windows which let in shards of dusty light. There was a long hallway with a door at either end, and more importantly, he appeared to be alone.

Steel went to one of the windows and tried to look through one of the gaps. The bright light from outside was like a laser in the eye. John Steel reeled back in pain and closed his eyes tightly.

He shook his head, cursing his stupidity, then went back to the window. He needed to see outside to find a landmark, anything to tell him where he might be. Steel grabbed one of the boards and pushed with all his strength. There was a screech of metal against stone before the board came free in his hand. A sudden blast of cold air swept over his skin. It was crisp and salty –sea air.

But where?

Malta was an island, which meant he could be anywhere in one of the many old seaports. Steel hurriedly looked out. He could feel his anxiety growing. He did not know most of Malta, only what he had seen on the map. And there were two other islands, Gozo and Comino, about which he knew as little.

As Steel gazed out of the window, hoping to see a harbour, or a city, even a damned goat header. But all he could see before him was the ocean and bright sun, high in a cloudless sky.

Steel figured he hadn't been out that long, judging by the sun's position. It was still morning.

Steel swore to himself as he thought things through. He needed to get his stuff back, and rescue the girl, break them both out. Steel smiled and nodded to confirm the plan to himself.

A solid plan. If only he knew where the hell *here* was to escape from.

Steel looked around the room as he did up the bootlace. The light from the removed window board illuminated the room slightly. It was a large room, possibly an old barrack that could sleep up to twelve guys on bunk beds from what he could make out. But now it was empty of everything.

Steel went back out into the long stretch of corridor. He hadn't had a chance to properly look it over before. His concentration had been more on who might be in it rather than the construction itself.

The corridor was about thirty feet long, with windows on the one side and five rooms. The floor was flat concrete, the walls were uncovered limestone. There were light fittings on the ceiling, but without the bulbs, they were just decoration. Steel thought this had initially been an old fort of some kind. Possibly dating back centuries from its construction. But like most fortifications on Malta, it had probably been added to by each defending force that occupied it.

Steel looked up and down the hallway and noticed doors on either side of his former cell. Each one evenly spaced, giving Steel a rough estimate of the size of the rooms. He figured his equipment had to be in one of them, assuming he had been snatched at Foster's place but searched here. Both doors looked equally worn and uncared for. Which meant this was just temporary. They had not expected to bring prisoners here, or the doors would have been secured better. Steel looked at both doors. It was a 50-50 chance of getting lucky or finding a room full of bad guys.

And he was in no mood for a room full of assholes.

Steel reached for the left-hand doors handle. About the froze, considering an entrance strategy. Quiet or loud? The soft option would give him time to check out the room if no one came to check on him. If he was, they would react instantaneously, and the chances were one or two might respond by opening fire. On the other hand, the loud option would render them shocked for a second, a second that he could use depending on who was stood where and armed with what.

He broke through the door. As the door swung open, it revealed another room that looked as if it had been empty for some time. It smelt of dust, damp and old wood. Suddenly he heard men's voices. Laughter. Steel rushed to the last door.

If Samara was anywhere, she might be there. It was the last room. Suddenly, he heard a woman's voice, it was muffled by the walls and the door, but she had let out a scream.

Suddenly the clock was on a short count down. If Samara weren't dead, she soon would be. He imagined her, strapped to a chair, bloodied from beatings. Brutal looking men taking pleasure in hurting Samara. All of them hoping she would remain silent so they could continue with their torture.

Steel had seen the bloodlust in the men's eyes at the old barracks, the one who had been ready to rape her. He did not want to imagine what they were doing to her now for the fun of it. These men would continue their beatings, and god knows what, even if she cracked and gave them everything, then they'd carry on just because they wanted it. Steel charged at the door leading with his shoulder, the impact of his full weight shattering the door frame into splinters. As he emerged on the other side, he rolled to avoid any gunfire. Ready to take on these men. Ready to rip them apart.

Steel knelt in a crouch and looked around.

But he wasn't in the same room as the others. There were no men. There was no Samara tied to a chair. Steel found himself in the open air. The sun was over the horizon, the start of a new day. Birds danced in the heavens, the crisp sea breeze brushed against his skin. It was going to be a glorious day.

And then he saw them.

Twenty bewildered actors. All staring at him.

Steel bounced up on his feet and brushed himself off.

'Morning,' he said as if nothing was wrong. 'Lovely day,' he said and strolled off down a gravelled hill, leaving the actors stood, speechless. Steel looked over at the main fort, which was bustling with film crews. It would be too risky for the men to have Samara stashed up there where she might be found. Steel figured his abduction wasn't planned. That's why he had just been dumped there. The state of the place Steel had been left in showed it was never used so they could leave him there, possibly to return later to pick him up. He was confident Samara wasn't there. Whatever the reason, they had transported Steel to Manoel Island and taken Samara somewhere else. Possibly, for the same reason, they had wanted to grab her at the old barracks.

It was a stupid move by them, but fortunate for Steel as it was just across the water to his hotel. However, it was two miles of the rough ocean filled with yachts and smaller crafts. Failing that, he would have an hour walk back to the hotel.

Steel weighed up his options and dove into the water closest to the hotel's pier. He was already dirty from the dusty room, had no tech and no cash, so he did not think a little water would hurt.

The lobby of the hotel was full of guests and a very soaking wet John Steel. He could feel the eyes on him as he crossed the marble floor to the concierge's desk, leaving puddles behind him. Steel stood at the counter, patiently waiting for the man behind the desk to finish a phone call. The staff member laughed politely with the person on the other end of the phone, and Steel looked around as if nothing was wrong – just another day. At the same time, he looked up something on his computer, oblivious of the dripping guest before him.

'Yes,' The man paused as he looked at Steel, who was smiling as though nothing was wrong. The man placed the receiver onto its cradle at his desk, utterly shocked at what was before him. 'How may I help you, sir?' the concierge asked, his tone remained neutral, as though there was nothing amiss.

'Good morning, it would appear I lost my wallet, and it had my room key with it. Could I possibly get another one?' Steel said casually.

'Lord John Steel isn't it, the presidential suite?' asked the concierge, knowing he had committed Steel's name to memory as an essential customer.

The man smiled and produced a new key card.

'There you go, sir. Do you require the police to assist with your stolen wallet?' the man asked, concerned now he had a rich man, not just a wet man before him.

'No, it's OK, thank you. I think I know where to look for it,' Steel said darkly. At least he knew where to start.

With Marcus Foster.

Chapter 41

Calver had gotten to work early. He had misjudged the morning traffic and had time to spare, so he sat on the sixth-floor breakroom and ate his pastry breakfast. Calver wore a broad smile. His joy was partly because of the deal he had made the night before but more to do with new software coming online for the weekend. Software that would change everything, particularly for Calver personally.

His deal had gone well, sure they were Russians, but he was a businessman and not a government, not really. He just worked for them. Calver did not consider himself a traitor, just a man with products that people were willing to pay a lot of cash for.

The breakroom wasn't busy. Most people had brought in coffee and went straight to their desks. They'd had breakfast with their families. He, on the other hand, had no family. He hadn't even been home to change. He had brought fresh clothes with him. As he suspected, the ferry over had been later than he had imagined. It had been his own fault. Calver had never crossed over at that time in the morning before, he had usually stayed over, but he had work this time. So, he had caught the first ferry over and raced to Attard for work. Picking up a coffee and a couple of Pastizzi – a traditional pastry filled with cheesecake, on the ferry.

There were two other guys from the second floor in the breakroom, and a guy Calver thought was from the third floor but wasn't quite sure – not that he cared. And then there was the cute redhead, Wendy from Foreign Accounts. She was short and slim, wore a black skirt suit today, which he considered suited her better than yesterday's grey one. Wendy had an oval face with long wavy scarlet red hair. Her large blue eyes gave her a doll-like appearance. Calver smiled, and she smiled back before returning to reading something on her tablet. He had often seen her about but never dared to speak to her.

Calver smiled at the tragedy of it all. He could chat with arms dealers and scumbags all day but cowered at the thought of talking to Samara from Room 14.

He took little glances, taking note of how her white blouse fitted well enough to define her slender form. How the first couple of buttons were left open to show her gold crucifix. She looked up again and met his gaze and smiled. Did she know he had been staring? Calver smiled back shyly before looking down at his coffee cup.

Wendy got up and straightened her black skirt; most might liken it more a belt than a skirt and left the restroom, offering Calver one last triumphant smile. Calver gave a moment, then followed. He loved to watch her walk, the way her hips swayed.

To him, she was perfect.

Wendy turned a corner, but Calver paused before following. He looked around, then moved after her. Calver turned and saw the corridor empty; Wendy had vanished. Slowly he walked down the hallway, wondering where she had gone. He began to feel anxious; had she realised he was following and taken off. Maybe she would tell his supervisor. Calver started to move quickly towards the offices. He hoped he was wrong, and she was just quick on her feet.

Suddenly, the door to a janitor's cupboard swung open, and he was grabbed and pulled inside. Calver felt soft lips press against his and arms locked around his body in a passionate embrace. The room's lights were not on, but he knew exactly who it was.

'So, how did the deal go last night?' whispered a voice.

'Like clockwork, once they've seen the test, they'll wire the money,' Calver said. There was a click of a light switch, and Calver stood looking lovingly into the eyes of Edward Bryce, the floor manager.

'God, I can't wait to get back into regular clothes instead of this grandfather crap you got me wearing,' Edward moaned. Calver kissed Bryce hard on the lips and smiled. Just a couple more jobs, I promise. Besides, they haven't found out were not the real Calver and Bryce yet, so let's just enjoy it, shall we?' Calver said, grinning.

'Are you sure they won't find them? That kid was snooping around on the island?' Edward said anxiously.

'Yeah, and look what happened to him, look, we are safe, OK, don't worry. Just a couple more tasks, and we're done, I promise.'

'So, what are you going to do when she asks you out?' asked Bryce.

'Who? Oh, Wendy. Nah, she won't. It's just attention for her. Besides, she's already hoping someone else will ask her, that bloke from Flight Control,' Calver said reassuringly. Calver had done his homework down to the last detail; Wendy wasn't available, that's why he chose her. A married woman would be too risky. Especially long-term married with kids, they might be up for a bit of adventure. Newly married women was always a bad idea; they'd still be in the honeymoon period and not interested. And too single was deadly, too clingy and too much bother. Besides, he just needed the illusion of the chase.

Bryce smiled, and the two men embraced.

'OK, now get outta here,' Calver said, almost pushing Bryce out of the door.

As Bryce left, the smile wiped from Calver's face. This assignation was a risk. Had Bryce become a liability? Calver switched off the light and waited in the dark, gathering his thoughts, planning, scheming.

Chapter 42

At twenty-past ten, the Master's phone rang. He knew who it was. He knew Aamir would be reporting in.

'Yes?' the Master said.

'The Mossad woman and the cop went to Foster's house. He took out two of our men, nothing too serious though,' Aamir said. His voice cracked over the line like he was talking from another planet.

'And now?' The Master said.

'They did not find what they expected. We have him trapped on Manoel Island. We will have a chat with him later, find out what he knows,' Aamir said.

'And the woman?'

'She is secure.'

'We have come too far for mistakes, Aamir.'

'I know, Master. However, the appearance of the cop was unforeseen,' Aamir said.

'Do we know who he is yet?' The Master said.

'His name is John Steel. He's a British policeman working with the NYPD. He is staying at the Grand Excelsior, pretending to be a Lord or something. A strange cover considering he is saying he's just here because of Foster's little girl,' Aamir said.

'What has he to do with Foster?' the Master said.

'Steel was her godfather. He and Foster are old friends. So, it makes sense for him to come. But to have such an elaborate cover story, for who? He only came because his goddaughter jumped to her death,' Aamir said.

'Which, we both know to be untrue,' the Master said.

There was silence from Aamir's end, just the crackle of a bad connection.

'No more complications, Aamir, or I will deal with you personally,' the Master said. He hung up the phone.

The Master sat and stared over at the map table. He thought about all the planning that had gone into their mission. They were close now, close to their final goal, and for him, it wouldn't just be his last, but it would be his most glorious.

Chapter 43

Steel took the spare cell phone and glasses from his case and downloaded the updates while he showered. He wasn't worried about the lost items. They all had a suicide chip installed. Once the new equipment was updated, the others would burn themselves out, plus they were only compatible with Steel's biometrics. The sunglasses were just sunglass to everyone else, and the cell phone was useless. The credit cards were automatically cancelled, and the new ones he already had, activated.

As Steel stood in the shower, he began to run through things in his head, arranging them as a murder board in his mind. Had his old comrade betrayed him and possibly murdered his own daughter? He downed the two-fingers of whisky and placed the empty glass onto one of the glass shelves in the shower cabin.

He could not believe Foster would have done that. He wouldn't believe it. Regardless, his primary goal now was to find Samara and get her to safety, and if Foster were involved, then Steel would deal with it – and him.

Steel stepped out of the shower and dried off. His mind was abuzz with the details of this puzzle. Unfortunately, he did not know what picture he was making. He walked around with a towel to hide around his hips, letting the ambient temperature dry him off. As he walked past the mirror in the sitting room, he saw the bruises from his tumble with the parachute guy had nearly healed.

He had to admit he'd had a rough couple of weeks, but he enjoyed them. It kept him active. He thought he'd be riding a desk all the time when he was integrated into the 11th Precinct Homicide Department. As it turned out, he hadn't done that much, just made a lot of arrests and caused a lot of mayhem. His mind began to wander, thinking about McCall and the team. Not that he missed them as such, just the banter, the laughs, seeing how much he could annoy McCall before she snapped. Then he looked out across the bay to Manoel Island.

Why had they taken him there? Malta was big enough if you wanted to lose someone. So, why did they bring him there? They knew where he was staying, but yet they took him within, as it happened, swimming distance of the hotel?

He did not know whether these men were utterly incompetent or if there was a more practical reason. Then he thought about the black superyacht. Why had Brad had a photo of it? Was it the uniqueness of it? From what Steel had seen, there was only one of those about. Did that make seeing it significant? There was a limited number of harbours on the island suitable for a craft like that. So the appearance of the vessel wouldn't be a surprise.

Steel took out fresh clothes from the wardrobe. They were identical to yesterday's outfit, black cargo trousers, an Under Armour shirt and a lightweight jacket. He had bought three of everything. He wasn't the type of guy to shop around and try on this and that. He was the sort of person who knew what he wanted. He would go into a store, grab what he required and was out again. For many years he had worn green or DPM - disruptive patterned material – combats. His civilian clothing was limited to jeans, a t-shirt and boots, something Helen made out she hated. But, he knew she secretly found them kind of sexy, her piece-of-rough.

Steel opened up the safe, took out his spare wallet and checked the contents: credit cards, cash, and ID.

'Prepare for the worst, hope for the best and everything in the middle…' he said. He smiled softly, put the wallet into his jacket pocket, and strapped on his backup watch. Unfortunately, the 'everything in the middle was a bonus' end to the advice did not apply here because there was no middle. They – whoever they were – had seen to that. Before he was curious, it was a puzzle, a mystery. Now, they had made it personal.

Steel looked over to his laptop. The downloads were complete. Steel grabbed the phone and sunglasses and left the contact lenses for later. He closed down the computer and packed it and the contact lenses away. He secured the room as he always did. If someone had gotten in, he would know, and he'd have pictures of just who he would be looking for.

He closed the door behind him and wiped the door handle and the door, so if there were any prints, they wouldn't be his. And placed the *please clean my room* notice on the door.

He wanted to see how creative they were.

Steel took the bag of dry cleaning and headed for the elevator. It was going to be a fantastic day. He was going to get Samara back and get some answers along the way.

Steel had called for a cab to take him to Foster's place. It was around quarter-to-twelve in the morning. His daughter would be at school, and Martha Foster would be at the market getting groceries.

The house would be empty.

The cab had dropped Steel a few doors down from the house. He did not need to announce his arrival; in fact, he needed it to be tactical. Before he had been sloppy, he had thought Foster was in danger.

Now, all bets were off. He was going in quiet and deadly. This time he would keep a clear head, regardless of what he would hear. He had to be cold and emotionless. He had to get his head back in the game.

Using the neighbour's gardens, Steel checked the rear of Foster's house. It was quiet – possibly too quiet. Steel hoped his escape wasn't yet known, and he had a bit of time. But like the Sarge said, *Plan for the worst*.

Samara sat plasticuffed to a wooden kitchen chair. She had been beaten, but she was alive. The curtains had been drawn to block out any light or prying eyes. They had kept her in a room with no windows. So, she had no idea of time, let alone whether it was day or night.

Two men had taken their turns beating her, but not so much as she passed out. They needed her awake, if she was unconscious, that was as good as sleep, and they wanted to deprive her of that. They were to keep her tired, physically and mentally. When she wasn't being beaten or shaken awake, Samara had to endure white noise from an old pocket radio.

Samara had no idea where she was, but that was the point. If you don't know where you are, you can't formulate an effective escape plan. She wasn't blindfolded, which was always a bad sign, meaning even if she saw them, Samara wasn't getting out of there alive to tell anyone who had done this.

She looked around the room with an off-yellow glow from the two small lamps in two corners, illuminating the room just enough to know she wasn't at the Ritz Hotel.

The building was old. The walls were limestone and not brick. They weren't painted or wallpapered. There were two small windows, but even with the makeshift curtains covering them, Samara knew they had been boarded up. There was one door which she had her back to. And a person. But every time she went to turn her head, she was yelled at.

'Face forwards, don't turn around,' came a voice. But not always the same voice.

Intimidation and scare tactics, don't let the subject know who's there, she thought to herself. Nothing gets under a person's skin, as much as someone stood behind them when they can't see who it is. Probably a thing man had learnt millions of years ago, like the fear of dark places and shadows: a natural instinct – self-preservation.

But every so often, she would turn her head, and sometimes there would be no voice. Maybe there weren't enough of them to continually watch her. After all, between her and Steel, they had made a dent in their numbers. Or perhaps they were that confident she was secure and tired they did not have to anymore, or maybe they were just bored of beating her, and the thrill had worn off.

Whatever the reason, she needed to formulate a plan.

Samara struggled with her bonds, but they had double cuffed each arm. Her best bet was to break the chair, possibly use the broken pieces as weapons. Samara tried moving the wood. The construction was solid, but she knew that she could work it free given the right amount of force. She thought of falling back and using the drop to shatter the chair, but this wasn't the movies. Samara knew she was too light for that. The chair would just bounce off the floor.

Samara sat for a moment to gather her strength. The beatings combined with her lack of sleep had taken their toll. However, she still had a fight left inside of her. All she had to do was keep it stored until the right moment. Samara sat and breathed in. There had to be something she could do; this could not be the end….could it?

Later on that day, Steel had Stan drive him to Foster's house. He had gotten out at the end of the street and told Stan not to wait for him as he did not know how long he would be.

The street was busy with people going about their daily routines. Steel walked up to Foster's place and found the front door was closed, but the lock was still broken. Whoever had taken them and closed the door firmly enough, so the door appeared to be intact from a distance. Steel nudged the door and stepped inside after making a cautionary glance up and down the street to make sure he wasn't observed. Steel stepped inside and immediately closed it behind him.

Steel walked in gingerly. Despite his instinct telling him he was alone and the thugs had gone, he did not wish to prove himself wrong. He had survived one abduction. A second might turn out somewhat different under the circumstances. He might be seen as more of a threat, or worse, unnecessary to their cause. He stopped and listen. Silence filled the stale air. He was alone. He was sure of it. And, he hadn't seen the usual vehicles outside on his arrival.

Moving cautiously, Steel proceeded to go room to room. Not just to find if he was correct, but to search Foster's house for clues as to why he was working with these men. The downstairs was clear, so Steel headed for the staircase. As he got to the bottom step, he rubbed to wound on his neck and scowled. Remembering the bite from the electronic device.

Steel climbed the stairs, his eyes alert and always moving from side to side like eager searchlights. He wasn't going to get caught out again.

Steel started with Abby's room. It was bright, and everything seemed to be white or light pink. Steel noticed the closet door was open, and there was a group of empty coathangers on the rail. The house was empty, and Martha and Abby were out of town by the look of things.

Steel smiled. Foster had been smart enough to convince his family to take a vacation, possibly to see Martha's parents back in the States who were too sick to travel.

It was a good time to do stupid stuff when the families not there to worry about. Foster was using Steel's philosophy: 'Being alone is the best defence. If there is nobody there you care about, they can't get to you.' Foster was preparing for war. But that still didn't answer the question of what

Foster was doing when Steel was taken? Steel headed for Foster's room. He had to make sure that Martha had also packed. He hoped he was right and that they had left for a short while.

Steel moved to the door Foster had stepped from. He raised a wary hand and nudged the door open. It swung effortlessly, revealing Foster's bedroom. A large room with a king-sized bed and plenty of dressers. The walls were painted light pink, and the ceiling was white. The carpet was light beige, and the furniture was gloss white with gold patterns. The wardrobe had a long mirror that covered one of the doors.

The bedroom was clean, with no damage or signs of a struggle. In fact, it looked like it hadn't been used for days.

Steel gritted his teeth with anger.

Foster had betrayed him, for what reason Steel did not know, but he'd have pleasure beating that truth out of the man.

There was a noise. Steel's reactions were fast, too fast for the person behind him to react. Steel had grabbed them and tossed the person over his shoulder and onto the bed. Steel raised a mighty fist, ready to strike but held off the move.

There, sprawled on the bed, was Kane. He had spread-eagled, and his widened eyes were transfixed on that white-knuckled fist above his head.

'Kane, what the Hell are you doing here?' Steel asked suspiciously, his fist still ready to strike.

'I followed you from your hotel.' Kane paused. A look of fear crossed his face. 'Samara… she's… she's disappeared,' Kane's eyes were fixed on Steel's bruised knuckles.

'Yes, I know. I'm sorry. Someone took us both this morning from here. I came to… extract some information from an old friend.' Steel said, backing off, rubbing his fist.

'Who? The American whose house we're in? I passed him on the way. I think he's heading north,' Kane said, confused.

'North, what's in the North?' Steel asked, almost shaking the life out of the frightened tour guide.

'Uhm… I don't know, nothing really,' then Kane froze, and a strange look came over his face. 'The ferry. The ferry to Gozo!'

Steel grabbed the keys to Foster's Range Rover from the key holder in the hallway, and the two men hurried to the garage via the kitchen. Steel got into the driver's side of the Range Rover Velar and pressed the electric doors' clicker. As the door opened wide enough to let the vehicle through, Steel put the car into reverse and floored the gas pedal. The mighty V8 supercharged petrol engine roared as the Five-hundred and forty-two horsepower at Steel's disposal was engaged.

And he was going to use every single one of them.

Once they were on the street, Steel slapped the shift into Drive before pressing the gas pedal hard to the floor. Steel drove with a purpose. He needed to catch Foster, not just for Samara's location, but the truth about why he had brought him to Malta.

Steel swerved, avoiding pedestrians and other vehicles; all the time, Kane was in the front seat getting tossed about while he tried putting his seat belt on.

'Which way?' Steel kept on yelling to Kane, who had finally clamped himself down. Kane gave exact instructions, as well as pointing the left and right turns. Steel had no hope of catching up with Foster, as there were too many routes that would get to the port. Two main roads and several smaller ones, and he had no way of knowing which Foster had taken. All Steel could hope to do was to beat Foster to the ferry and question him there. Possibly threaten to throw him off the side. Maybe he would anyway, even if Foster answered all the questions.

Steel had taken Kane's advice and headed for a town called Burmarrad; Kane had thought it to be the quickest route and the more likely option for someone in a rush.

The traffic was thick with tour buses and commuters, slowing Steel down. But Steel hoped it was doing the same for Foster. Steel passed the traffic in front of him when he could, causing the oncoming traffic to beep their horns or swerve. Steel hoped that Foster was taking the journey casually, that would buy Steel some time. All the while, Steel was on the lookout for Foster's blacked-out Range Rover Discovery.

If he could catch Foster before the port, all the better. There would be fewer people to see him beat the crap out of his old friend.

'How far are we now?' Steel yelled backwards to Kane, who was busy looking at road signs.

'About fifteen minutes,' Kane shrugged, making an estimated guess. Before, they were a large round-about. Steel did not have time to read the signs before Kane began to yell instructions.

'Take a left here, first left,' Kane shouted. Steel did not look. He just obeyed and hoped Kane was right. As they turned onto the road to Dawret San Pawl Road, Steel smiled. Ten cars on, he saw Foster's blacked-out ride as it swerved side-to-side to avoid parked cars. The road was long and winding. On Steel's right side was the city of Bugibba. On the other, lush green farmland. Steel floored the gas pedal and switched to the second lane of the dual carriageway. Foster was near, and he wanted him.

Steel had Foster's car firmly in his sights as he passed the other vehicles, weaving in and out of the traffic, the tires spitting grit and leaving a dust cloud behind them. Soon Steel was right behind the large Foster with only one thing in his mind.

Get Foster off the road as quickly as possible.

Steel had to wait for the right moment; the last thing he need was a massive pileup on the freeway. Steel smiled as Foster's car moved out to overtake another vehicle. Steel saw his chance and took it. Steel sped up right behind the Discovery and rammed the right-hand side, causing it to veer off the road into a nearby field. Steel took off after him and powered into the back of the Discovery, hoping the crash had shaken Foster and caught him off guard. The two cars danced as the lead vehicle tried to swerve away, but Steel could foresee every move that Foster would make. Steel pushed the pedal harder, and the two cars locked together. Steel used all of the car's power and pushed forward. Neither knowing nor caring where they were going.

'When are you going to stop?' yelled Kane. As he looked at Steel with utter panic.

'When something stops us,' Steel said, grinning. Kane screamed something in Maltese and crossed himself furiously in hopes that God was listening.

'Saying a prayer for us?' Steel asked.

'For one of us, John, only for one of us,' Kane scowled as he held onto the dash and the grip above his door.

'Well, here's hoping he's listening, shall we,' Steel replied as he kept on the power to the anger of the engine. There was a sickening squeal of plastic and metal been torn and ripped apart. Suddenly Steel hit something hard and span out of control until the car stopped. The car enveloped by a cloud of dust, But Foster sped off out of control. Steel's brutal attack had done something to the steering, and it ploughed on forwards. Anger boiling, Steel got out of the car and listened. Expecting to hear the roar of Foster's engine disappear into the horizon. Steel went to turn and get back into the car. The engine was still running, and a quick inspection of the wheels and tyres on his side gave him confidence in this beast who continue the case. But Steel stopped because he heard a new sound. It was a loud crash and then the sound of water.

Steel grinned as the dust settled, then sprinted forwards with Kane close behind. There was a mass of noise, yelling and screams from a woman and children. Steel raced forwards over a small embankment to find Foster's car in some guy's pool. Steel jumped down into the pool and dragged out the driver.

The man was wearing Foster's suit and even looked like Foster – but it wasn't him. Then Steel realised this was the man he had seen before he was tasered. This was the guy he had seen at Foster's house. Steel felt a mix of relief and fear. Relief that Foster hadn't betrayed him, but also fear as to what had happened to Foster. Had it been a set up to get him and Samara into the house where they had been ambushed? Had the women seen leave the house also decoys? That's if they had been women in the first place?

'Where's the woman?' Steel growled. The man just smiled and said nothing. Steel dragged him out of the pool and looked up at the shocked family who were sat huddled at the poolside on deck chairs, shocked expressions on all their faces.

'Sorry about the mess, learner driver,' Steel quipped, forcing the man back over the wall. Steel dragged the man back to his car and tossed him hard against the side of the vehicle. The man's face impacted against the safety glass. His nose broke, leaving a bloody mark on the tinted window.

The man fell to the ground, dazed. Steel dropped down and went through the man's pockets. No wallet or ID, only a cell phone, and a silenced 9mm Heckler and Koch P8 A1 handgun. Steel clicked out the magazine and checked it was full. Steel pulled back the top slide enough to see the glint of brass from the chambered bullet. Steel slid the magazine back into the weapon and held the silencer against the guy's right knee.

'Who are?' Steel asked again, only to be met with silence and that sickening grin. 'Where's the woman?'

'You don't scare me, go ahead, kill me,' laughed the man.

'Seriously, you think this guy is going to kill you?' Kane said, shaking his head and casually crossed his arms, almost in an attempt to raise the tension of the situation.

Steel smiled and pulled the man's face closer to his own. 'Oh, I'm not going to kill you, I'm going to hurt you, but I am not going to hurt you,' Steel growled. The man smiled and shook his head.

'You're a cop. You're not going to kill anyone,' the man laughed. Steel looked at Kane, and Kane returned the puzzled look.

'You do know this isn't New York – right?' Kane said. His words trailed for effect. 'He isn't a cop here, and you kidnapped him and my sister, So – .'

'So, this is good cop bad cop, right? I get it.'

'No, you really aren't,' Steel said, shaking his head. His face was expressionless. 'He's not a cop, and neither am I, so I'm just going to hurt you until you say something or die. The choice is yours,' Steel shrugged.

The man continued smiling.

'I don't think he understands English. That might be the problem,' Kane said. Steel thought for a moment and nodded.

'You know, I'm an outstanding teacher.'

'Really?' Kane said with a curious grin.

'Absolutely, watch.' Steel pulled the man to the rear of Foster's Ranger Rover and tossed the guy to the floor. The man was the same build and height as Foster but had more muscle.

'Watch him, if he moves, shoot him in the knees,' Steel said. Giving Kane the gun and forcing the mussel close to the man's right knee.

'Now, my friend here has never used a gun before, and he is very nervous, so any sudden moves and who knows what he may hit instead,' Steel warned the man. Steel stood up and began to search through the back of the Velar. As Steel suspected, Foster still prepared for everything, he found plasticuffs and a tow rope. Steel held up the objects so the man could see and smiled.

'It's a pity it rained last night. The ground isn't as hard as what I would prefer – but it'll do.' Steel put the tow rope around the man's ankles. The man's eyes widened as he worked out what was going to happen. The man went to move but felt the silencer's tip in the ball socket of his knee. He watched in horror as Steel started to fasten the other end of the rope onto the vehicle's towbar.

'OK, dickhead, last chance. Where's Samara?' All emotion had left Steel's face and voice. He was as cold as ice.

The man was too terrified to talk, his mouth flapped open and shut, but no words would come out.

'OK, Kane, get in. We're going for a drive,' Steel said, getting into the driver's side. As Kane headed towards the passenger side door, the man began to scream.

'She's kept on the Gozo island,' the man yelled over and over. Steel got out of the car and walked around to the man.

'Gozo Island?' Steel asked calmly, waiting for the man to lie. The man stayed silent.

'Gozo, you're sure?' Steel asked. The man nodded erratically.

'You believe him?' Kane asked. Steel looked at the man for a moment. As if pondering what to do next.

'Nah, he's full of it, let's go,' Steel shook his head and headed for the driver's side. The man's eye widened as he heard the engine start.

'OK – OK, She's on Manoel Island. They've got her on Manoel Island. They took her there later today.' The man yelled in a panic, hoping they would hear him over the noise of the engine.

'Manoel island – are you sure this time?' Steel said. The man nodded furiously so much Steel thought the man's head would fly off.

'But I checked it out after you had left me there. There was no one there?' Steel asked, a searching look on his face.

'We brought her there later after the film crew had left.'

'But why was I taken there and not her?' Steel asked as he knelt down in front of the man.

'You weren't meant to be there. We assumed you had gone for a run like always. It was meant to be only the woman. We did not have room for both of you. Besides, it was only the woman we needed.' The man explained.

'Wow, that's got to sting. You were collateral damage?' Kane mocked Steel.

'It's fine, I've been called worse,' Steel cracked a smile and brought the side on his flat hand crashing down on the man's neck, knocking him out.

'Now, we go and get your sister,' Steel said, tucking the pistol away into the small of his back.

Chapter 44

The unconscious man lay in the boot of the Ranger Rover. Steel had used the plasticuffs he had found while searching the man for the identification or more weapons, to which there were none. Steel figured they must be in the car that was now in the bottom of the pool.

Steel had secured the guy's hands and feet in a hogtie position. Steel secured his mouth with duct tape he'd also found in the trunk's storage compartment to ensure the guy stayed quiet.

Steel thought the man may still be useful. Besides, Steel knew he could not leave him on the side of the road where he might be able to get to a phone and worn his colleagues.

Steel had driven back to Valletta, easing in with the rest of the traffic. He did not need to draw attention to himself – not with a guy in the trunk. Even though the car's front end was torn up, there were worse looking vehicles on the roads.

Steel figured they had time. If they were going to kill Samara, they would have done it already. No, they needed her for something.

She would be safe – for now.

It was a good hour drive back to Valletta and the daytime traffic hindering progress. Even Kane's quick routes turned out to be slow ones. Steel felt the Gods were against him on this one, but he cruised on, putting his foot down when an open space became available.

He had no idea who he was dealing with. It could be any number of terrorist groups or just someone Samara had pissed off in the past. It was evident to Steel they were only after her and had zero interest in him. After his part at the old Barracks and Foster's house, they would now consider him a threat. They needed her, but not him. He was an anomaly, a casualty of war, a bug on the windshield – disposable. Thye could kill him with impunity.

At the old barracks, Samara had tried to warn him someone was after her. And now they had her, all because he had been blinded by the misconception of a friend in need. A mistake he would not repeat.

Steel sighed with relief at the first road signs that signalled Valletta's direction and distance.

Steel was on the clock.

Samara had just had her second visit that morning. A large man with short-cropped hair and a tribal tattoo on his face. He did not have much to say; he just threw buckets of seawater over her. Samara licked her lips and tried not to puke. Out of all of her visitors, this was the only one who never hit her. In fact, he'd minimised all actual tactile contact with her. She figured he had a soft spot for her. Possibly he had a sister who she resembled or an old girlfriend or favourite niece. Either way, she had an in with one of them.

Samara looked up at the large man and stared deeply into his eyes. Her gaze was full of pain and terror. He went to turn away, but her gaze caught him. He seemed absorbed in her large brown eyes.

'Thank you,' Samara whispered, voice drew him in like a siren's song.

She had him. All she had to do now was to reel him in.

He came closer and closer.

Their gazes locked. He was under her spell. He pulled in so close, Samara could feel his breath on her skin.

His face was close to her's, his lips almost at hers.

Samara smiled up at him.

He returned the expression.

There was a noise of breaking wood, and then the muffled cry from the man as Samara brought the arm of the chair to bear on the man's temple. He stumbled back slightly, but she had managed to free her legs once she had broken the arms from the seat.

Their mistake had been their complacency, their overconfidence in the situation they were convinced they had under control. The men had stopped checking on Samara hours ago. They had not inspected her at regular intervals but at irregular timings to set a pattern. But worst of all, they had not made sure she was still bound. That had been her cue to start her escape plan. Now, she had means of getting out – now she had a key.

The man looked up, just in time to receive another blow to the face with the other broken chair arm still was attached to her arm. Samara looked like a gladiator, waiting for the next fighter. Samara spun and landed a roundhouse kick directly on the man's jaw, knocking him out cold. She was smaller than the man, but she put power behind every kick and punch. Samara fell to her knees for a moment, gathering her breath and strength. The over-use of energy that she did not have had taken its toll. But Samara felt good. She was almost free, and he was bleeding and unconscious.

Samara felt a little bad for the guy. After all, he hadn't done anything to her. But he was an opportunity she had been given – and she had taken it. Samara breathed in and blew out hard through her mouth. She did this several times, building her strength, her anger. She stood up and stood ready, the wooden make-shift weapons still attached to her arms. Expecting the door to swing open any minute and a dozen men to rush in to take her down. She welcomed the chance to return some of the beatings. Part of her wished they would. She was ready to give back some of the pain. Sure they were only doing as they were told – simple foot soldiers, but some had enjoyed it a little too much. She stood for a moment in the dimly lit room and listened.

There was nothing.

Then there were screams.

Samara raised an eyebrow. She had thought she had been alone; then she remembered Steel – they could have taken him as well. Was it him she was hearing? The cries grew louder as if they were moving towards her, but they changed as if it was from different people.

Samara shook her head. She was tired and dehydrated, and now her mind was playing tricks on her.

There was a screech of old metal hinges as the door opened, and then bright light filled the room. Samara felt a rush of adrenaline as she took a fight ready pose. She did not know how many she could take before they finally beat her down, but Samara was prepared. Suddenly a figure stepped into the light and made for her. Samara screamed a war cry and lashed out, knocking the man to the ground with a single blow.

'Anyone else wants some?' she cried fiercely.

'No… not really, and I don't think your brother did either, but I did warn him. Silly bastard,' said a familiar voice. Samara moved cautiously forwards and saw her brother sparked out on the floor. Samara dropped to her knees and cradled her brother's head in her still bound arms.

'I suggest we leave before any more people want to join the party,' Steel said, walking into the room and opening a large bladed knife with one hand. As he cut her free, she looked into those damn sunglasses, wishing she could see those blue eyes of his.

'What kept you?' she laughed.

'I thought I'd stop for a coffee, found this really nice place around the corner,' Steel joked, picking up the half-unconscious Kane and dragging him out of the room.

'You know, I had it all under control,' Samara said.

'Really, 'anyone else wants some?' is having it under control, is it?' Steel replied, their arguing voices fading as they hurried down the corridor.

'Are we there yet?' yelled Kane in a drunken voice, just before the sound of a door closing led to silence.

Chapter 45

An easterly breeze cooled the heat of the morning sun. Plans had been made ready, and assignments are given out. Aamir and his men were prepared. After nearly a year of planning, they had finally come to the day of judgement. The other team in Tunisia were on standby. Soon they would rain holy fire on their enemies, and it would be glorious.

Aamir sat and conversed with the Master over the phone, giving updates on their situation. In two days, everyone would know their name and tremble. Aamir had known they were not coming back. That was inevitable. He and his men were ready to die for the cause, and it was good. The Master had given them a holy task, and none questioned it. In fact, many had volunteered to carry it out.

Aamir looked closed down his cell phone. The Master had hung up after praising his men for their achievements and giving thanks to God. The Master was happy, and that was enough for Aamir.

He stood up and walked to the map that hung on the wall. Red pins marked points on Gozo and Malta. He smiled and nodded to himself. Everything was as the Master had predicted. Soon he and his men would be going into glorious battle.

Taking out his cell phone, Aamir pressed for speed-dial and waited. He heard the electronic ring and began to pace. Why wasn't Falcon picking up? Aamir stopped walking and waited. The phone still rang.

Something was wrong. Aamir closed down the phone and began to tap the concrete floor with his foot out of frustration.

He had told all his men to have their phones with them at all times and pick them up straight away. Aamir did not need problems, not at this point. He did not have time to go to Malta to find out that the idiot was busy with some hooker or dead.

Aamir growled and tried the number again. It rang and rang and rang.

No answer.

They were not there.

Aamir yelled in anger and tossed a coffee mug from the table next to him. Brown liquid followed the cup like the tail of a comet. The ceramic mug smashed against the wall, shattering into a thousand pieces and scattered across the floor. A hugely built guy rushed in. Concerned at the sound of Aamir's yelling and the sound of smashing.

'Go to Malta, find Falcon,' Aamir said, breathing heavily. The look of anger covered his face. The large man bowed slightly at the waist with his right hand over his heart before backing away.

Aamir looked at his cell phone once more, pondering whether to dial again. Falcon had always been a hothead, not like the others. But the Master liked him for some reason and insisted Aamir use him.

Aamir had sent Flacon to Malta, away from everyone else – away from him. Falcon was a liability. Aamir hoped someone had killed Falcon. It would save him the bother of doing it himself later.

Aamir walked over to the small bed in the corner and sat on the oversized mattress. As he lay back. A woman's arms and legs wrapped around him like a sea creature, pulling him close.

He closed his eyes and exhaled as a dark-haired beauty unbuttoned his shirt and lightly clawed his chest, her perfect white teeth biting at his neck.

She moved around until her naked body was on top of him. She purred like a kitten as she straddled and hardened him, took him to heaven.

Chapter 46

It was business as usual at the US Embassy. Information was passed back and forth through secured nets to Langley via the London office. Even though it was a few days until the new software was going online, there was a buzz of anticipation in the air. This unique programme would change everything - if it worked, of course. The contractors' production team had run test after test, and each one passed with flying colours. However, that was in a lab. Director Sloan wasn't sure this new wonder programme would work, no matter how many test results and reports they had given.

People lied, test results could be falsified.

And that was enough for him to know.

It was a billion-dollar contract that had plenty of contractors fighting for that place. But SteinTech Industries were the ones who secured it, possibly due to a backhander somewhere. But Sloan did not care about that; He would not let the infidels kill good American citizens. If it worked great, if not, the systems would be down for hours while they rebooted, and that was a window when all manner of shit could hit the fan. He preferred the old system. It worked, sure it wasn't a hundred per cent, but it worked.

Sloan was nervous, but he did not know why. He put it down to anticipation and nerves, the kind of sick feeling of waiting for test results. Sloan took a Robusto cigar from his inside jacket pocket and used his cutter to snip off the end. Sloan placed the thirty dollar cigar under his nose and inhaled the scent from the leaves. Sloan smiled wickedly and shoved an unlit cigar into his mouth, and chewed on the end as if it were alight. It wasn't the same, but he knew the rules about smoking in the blockhouse; after all, he'd made the damn law.

Sloan contemplated jumping in the elevator and heading outside to manage his craving. Instead, he settled for a dry smoke. Sloan sat forwards and leaned his elbows on the desk. Sloan needed something to do before the wait drove him crazy. He looked at his watch; it was only eleven, another hour then lunch. Sloan grumbled to himself and picked up one of the holiday brochures his wife had conveniently stuck in his briefcase. He smiled as he flicked through the many options, especially the ones his wife had drawn a star next to. Subtle she was not, but that's what he loved about her. She was straight down the line.

'Jeez, woman, could you pick anything more expensive?' Sloan laughed as he noticed one hotel in Hawaii she had earmarked. 'I could buy a friggin new car for that,' he grumbled, tossing the brochure in the waste bin next to his desk. It was true, he did need a holiday, but if this programme went south, the rest of his life would one big holiday - without the fun.

It hadn't been his decision, but it sure as hell was his ass and his career. People in the right places had made damned sure the buck stayed with him. It was undoubtedly a kick in the balls if it failed, but if it went well, if all systems functioned, he would get a pat on the back, and they would get the praise and the pay rise for a job well done.

Friggin politicians and bureaucrats.

Sloan lost his fight with the unsmoked cigar and stormed off to the elevator. He needed fresh air, the sun on his face and the smoke of the thirty dollar cigar on his breath.

Besides, there was nothing Sloan could do. In fact, sometimes Sloan thought he was just a figurehead for when the shit hit the fan. True, it opened many doors to those important dinners and garden parties, but he missed the States. Sloan had done an excellent job getting the blockhouse up and running. He picked a good crew to make it work. He knew that he'd done an excellent job and continued to do so. 'If a manager can sit back and do nothing, that means he's already done a good job,' Sloan's dad used to tell him, and he was right, of course. A well-oiled machine takes care of itself. Sloan smiled to himself as he stepped into the elevator, the cigar still stuck in his mouth.

As the elevator reached the ground floor, the doors opened, and Sloan stepped out with a broad smile in anticipation for that first breath of hand-rolled tobacco. The sun was high in a light blue backdrop. Sloan leaned against the wall next to a wall-mounted ashtray and lit up the fat cigar. The first draw was like heaven, a smooth taste with a hint of burnt cocoa.

Typically, his cell phone started to vibrate. Sloan took it out and checked the message. He had at least six missed calls, all from the same number. Sloan smiled and placed the phone back into his pocket; he would deal with it later, for now, he was enjoying his moment.

Chapter 47

It was late afternoon by the time Steel and Samara had gotten back to his hotel suite. Steel had insisted that she came with him back to the hotel, arguing that it was safer for her than her apartment.

Steel said he would order room service. He had other business to attend to, so she should get cleaned up, then he'd showed her to the bathroom. The only time she'd seen anything approaching this size before, it was a communal shower. Samara stood under the cascade of water, letting the water wash the filth and grime away. She winced as the droplets of water fell against her wounds.

But even though they hurt at first, Samara felt the pain ease as the muscles relaxed. Her body was full of bruises. Her face had only a couple of cuts, but her captors had mostly concentrated on hitting her upper torso. Apparently, they had other plans for her face and wanted it unspoilt.

Samara smiled as she combed her fingers through her hair. Thinking about the scene at Manoel Island, six men sprawled out in various rooms. She figured Steel hadn't killed them but made sure that they were out of action for a long time. One guy was in what appeared to be a kitchen. He was slumped over a square wooden table. Another guy had his right leg broken, another his left arm.

She was slightly disappointed she hadn't seen it, or better still, participated. But Samara was grateful and surprised that Steel had come for her.

She remembered the reports on Steel from Mossad. They had made him out to be a ghost –wrath. But after seeing him first-hand, he was so much more – definitely a force to be reconned with.

Steel looked at his watch; it was late, and he had things to do. Sleeping was a luxury he could not afford, but Samara could do with a rest after her ordeal. He remembered the second of his old sergeant's orders, *sleep when you can. You never know when you'll be able to next.*

Always excellent advice, Serge, he thought.

A noise made Steel turn. It was Samara. She was out of the shower and heading for the second bedroom he'd said she could use. Even in a bathrobe and a towel wrapped on her head, she looked good. She stopped and looked over at Steel.

He smiled, and she smiled back. The air was warm, but there was an uncomfortable tension. She stood rubbing the towel into her wet hair. Her eyes were large and welcoming, her skin glistened with dampness.

Steel walked over to her slowly. She looked up at him. She looked amazing. He looked like shit. Steel had put his contact lenses in, feeling she would need to look him in the eye rather than the sunglasses. Something he had learnt over the years. But he had to agree there were times for the glasses, and then there were times, like this, where it would be – inappropriate.

Samara looked deeply into his eyes. Her big brown eyes were full of emotion and sensual – intelligent.

A smile cracked from the side of Steel's mouth. He could feel the electricity between them, the attraction.

In the silence, her breathing became heavier.

They drew closer, slowly. Samara allowed the towel to drop from her hand as she inched forward. *Damn, she smells good,* he thought. He could see that the bathrobe was slipping open naturally as she stepped towards him. Showing just enough naked flesh. They were inches away from each other. But neither rushed, savouring the anticipation of the moment. Thriving off the thrill, like a kiss about to happen, lips that are close but not touching.

'You dropped your towel,' he said softly.

'Did I?' she said.

'You'll catch a cold,' he said.

'I better do something to warm up then,' she said, closing the gap slightly.

'I hear that the Eskimo people have a good idea how to keep warm,' he said. Their eyes locked together, unblinking.

'So I've heard,' she replied, her voice was soft.' body contact isn't it, recommended for in extreme cases?' she said.

'Absolutely,' Steel said, pulling her to him. Her body warm and hard. Steel ran his fingers gently across her skin which was as soft as silk. He wound his arms around her, and she did the same. Steel leant down and kissed her softly on the lips. She kissed him back hard.

'Shit,' she screamed, holding her mouth, pushing slightly away.

Steel stood confused for a second. Then he noticed the wound on her lip had opened up and was bleeding again. They had kissed too hard too soon.

'Typical,' she said, looking around then grabbing the towel and holding on to her lip.

'I'll see if I have something with me,' Steel said. And headed for his case. He pulled out what looked like a wash bag but was actually a small first aid kit. He took out an antiseptic and brought it over to her.

'This is gonna hurt,' he said. Sammara nodded as if to give him permission to apply the fluid. Steel placed the antiseptic onto the cut using some toilet paper. Samara winced but managed to mouth a thank you as best as she could.

'I'm off for a shower, give you time to rest after today,' Steel said.

Samara smiled and nodded. The moment had passed, possibly for the best.

Steel headed into the bathroom and turned on the shower. While waiting for the water to reach the correct temperature, he stripped off his clothes and tossed his dusty garments to the side. Hoping that dry cleaning could do something other than suggesting Steel should burn them.

Staring into the big mirror, Steel checked his frame for injuries. Apart from a couple of new scratches and bruises, he was in good shape. He stepped into the shower cabinet and let the water run over his body. The water was hot and felt like tiny ballbearings massaging his skin. It felt good. Steel stood there with his hands against the shower wall, letting the water wash over him. He thought he could stay there all day.

Steel's thoughts went back to Lucy. Trying to work out why she was at the Azure Window so late the night she died, and what had Brad found? It was like having a jigsaw puzzle with no picture for reference and half the pieces missing. Whoever killed Brad was a professional, not like the assholes who had taken both Samara and himself. Those guys were as subtle as using a cruise missile to open a pickle jar. The people responsible for Bran and possibly Lucy were different. They had been professional.

Steel used the hotel provided shower gel and lathered up his aching body. He knew dinner was on the way. But his thoughts weren't on food. There was too much going on in his head. Then his thoughts went back to what had almost happened with Samara. Maybe it was the excitement of battle or just the emotion of seeing her alive. Despite his undeniable attraction to her, he had to remain focused.

That thought lasted about a minute.

Because as he turned around to get the shampoo, there stood Samara. Her firm naked frame was more than he had imagined. Her body was as perfect as if it had been sculpted by the Gods.

Samara stepped forwards and wrapped her arms around his neck, and pulled him towards her. They kissed gently. He pulled her close, let their hands move tenderly over each other. Exploring every curve. Steel cupped her small, firm breast him his hand while she bit on his earlobe. She pushed him back against the wall and eased her way down his body, kissing her way down. Samara licked and bit at his hard flesh as she moved to her knees. Her long short nailed fingers clawed at his chest as she went.

Steel bent down and scooped her up in his arms and carried her to the bedroom. He laid her down on the cotton sheets. Her wet skin glistened as the droplets of shower water shone like tiny diamonds from the light of the lamp. Samara lay on the soft cotton sheet. Her perfect form and large brown eyes beckoned for him to come to her. Her fingers clawed at the bedsheet with wild passion, like a cat, while being stroked. She was everything that Steel had imagined and more. Steel slid onto the bed next to her and pulled her close. He kissed her hard, his hand on the back of her head, while his other hand ran across her body, caressing her breasts and taught behind. He felt her hands on his back, the tips of her fingers following the curvature of his back. She pulled him onto her. He felt her warm breath on his skin, their bodies entangled in a mix of arms and legs. He felt her legs lock around him and hold him in place as Steel moved slowly, his hips grinding against hers. Their bodies moved together. Hungry for one another.

Steel felt Samara's body convulse, her muscles tightened. He followed her over the edge. Panting for breath, they collapsed, exhausted but happy. They showered together, which was followed by more lovemaking, but they remained in the shower this time. By the time their meals had arrived, they had worked up an apatite. After dinner, they fell asleep satisfied, and for that moment, without a care in the world.

Chapter 48

A call at five in the morning woke Steel from his recurring nightmare. Steel reached over to his bedside cabinet and answered the call.

'Steel, where the hell are you?' asked a panicked sounding Foster. Steel sat up and paused before answering. Trying to work out what he was going to say, tell Foster everything or just see what Foster had to say.

'I'm in bed,' Steel said.

'How quickly can you get to the embassy?' Foster asked.

'Depends – what's up?' Steel answered with interest.

'We....I've got a problem.'

Steel thought for a moment, was this for real or another trap? But then the original ambush was meant for Samara, not him. And as they had found out later, it hadn't been Foster at the house, but the guy Steel had dragged out of the pool.

'I'll get there as soon as I can,' Steel said, getting out of bed and moving towards the bathroom. Samara woke and watched Steel through the open bedroom door as he crossed the carpeted floor, her gaze fixed on the scared muscular frame. She thought he looked more like a gymnast with his taught frame. She smiled with satisfaction as he disappeared into the bathroom. But the smile faded as she looked over at his cell phone that he had left on his dresser.

She swung her long legs out of bed and onto the soft flooring, strode over the dresser and picked put Steel's phone to check the last call. Samara smiled at seeing Foster's name. She quickly headed for her room and picked up her cell phone, and pressing a speed-dial app. All the while, her gaze fixed on the bathroom door. I hoping Steel was taking another shower.

'Yes, it's me, get a trace on a number. I want to know where Foster just made a call from,' Samara gave the number from Steel's phone. She had a feeling it would pay off. Wherever Foster had told Steel to meet him, Samara suspected Foster wasn't. She did not trust the notion that someone who just happened to look like Foster was at the house that morning.

In fact, she did not believe or trust Foster at all.

Just the thought of him made the hairs on the back of her neck stand up. For her, that was a bad sign. There was just something about Foster, something she could not put her finger on. Steel had explained about the man from the pool looking similar to Foster. At a quick glance, maybe, be she did not see it personally, and even more with the duct tape and the broken nose. Steel had left the man for the police to find. However, he was no longer bound or gagged, but he had been unconscious. Steel had crashed the car and placed the man in the driver's seat next to a bottle brandy Steel had bought from a local shop. Of course, the police would find him and go through the motions, mostly due to the man being covered in booze and because Steel had made sure it crashed into an empty police vehicle.

But that did not change her feeling about Steel's friend. She just hoped Steel wasn't blinkered. Sure, his loyalty leant towards his friend was commendable, but that wasn't important at this time.

As the door closed behind her, Steel walked out of the bathroom. He wore a confident smile. He knew she wasn't the type to just sit back. She had been sent to the island to do a job, and he respected that. In truth, he would have been disappointed if she hadn't carried on.

The sunglasses he had left on the table had caught everything and displayed it on Steel's watch. The security function had come on automatically as the built-in motion sensor activated. At first, he was just going to watch her naked form as she crossed the room. An innocent mistake, with benefits he had thought. But then she picked up his phone, then hers.

The phone's camera and microphone had activated after Steel's command, and he had heard everything.

He began to wonder if she just used him to get to Foster? Possibly. But in truth, would he have done anything differently? The hours in the bedroom with her had been spectacular. But had that too be a ploy, or had the events of that day and forced their bodies together. It was known that near-death experiences can enhance the need for lovemaking, or at least a momentary affectionate gesture.

Samara, or at least Mossad, had been watching Foster long before Steel had turned up. Steel could imagine his appearance had been a temporary annoyance – just someone else to keep an eye on. Still, hopefully, she now regarded him as a friendly – or, something more.

Steel picked up the concierge phone and dialled for the front desk. After a while, a friendly female voice answered.

'Hi, Mr Steel here from the presidential suite. I wondered if you could get me a couple of things?'

Steel went back in and showered, hoping the soothing water would help him to think straight. He started to run through what he knew, hoping a pattern would appear. Steel knew all the events fitted somehow, but how? There was a critical piece missing.

Why Lucy? Why the Azure Window? What had Brad seen? Was there a significance to the superyacht photo? If so, what was it?

Steel had phoned for a taxi before his shower. That way, it would be there by the time he had got to the lobby. Steel had a quick shower. He did not have time to luxuriate. He was in a rush to get to the Embassy. As Steel rushed out of the shower and headed for his room, he picked up the cup of coffee he had poured before he showered. It was lukewarm but still drinkable. He walked out onto the terrace and looked out across the water, and took in the view. He still could not get over how beautiful this place was. He just wished he was there to enjoy it – he wished Helen was with him to enjoy it.

Twenty minutes later, a knock on the door and a man entered with a large shopping bag for him. Steel signed a bill and tipped the man generously.

Steel had a plan, a surprise. Things were moving forwards, and he needed as much back-up as he could get.

He considered Foster's call. Foster sounded frustrated, which in all honesty, Steel expected. He still had no idea what had happened at Foster's house or why he had seen Foster and his family that morning. The man that Steel had dragged from the pool had been a good double for Foster, enough to fool someone at a distance or just before some bastard stuck a taser in the neck. The man had been a decoy for the neighbours. But Steel did know if Foster was at the Embassy like he had said, he was safe.

Steel poured himself another coffee and had picked a piece of toast before pulling on a black polo shirt and a pair of black jeans, and a leather jacket from the coat rack next to the door. Putting on the sunglasses, he looked around the room, ensuring he had secured his laptop and anything else. As he was about to close the safe, he stopped and smiled to himself. Picking up a piece of paper from the stationary, he wrote a note, slipped his keycard into the folded note, slipped it into the safe, and locked it.

Steel knew Samara was just doing her job, and now he had to his. He also knew he could not investigate alone. She wasn't giving up, and so, he might as well use her as a source of intel. She had more extensive resources.

He closed the door to the suite and headed towards the elevator.

While he rode down, he called Stan the cabbie, arranging a pickup. Stan assured Steel he'd be there in five, a promise that made Steel smile. Steel had seen the heavy traffic, and he knew it would take longer than five minutes.

Twenty minutes and a second cappuccino later, Stan parked his red minibus outside the main entrance and found Steel sat next to the stairs that led up to the main road. Steel looked at his watch mockingly, causing Stan to shrug.

'Five minutes? What did you do stop for breakfast?' Steel joked. Stan smiled and bit into a burger he had picked up on the way. Steel shook his head with a grin and got into the passenger bench just behind Stan's seat.

'So, where to chief?' Stan asked.

'To the US Embassy, please, Stan. I've got an old friend to kick the shit out of,' Steel replied with an intense look on his face.

'Uh, righty-oh, then. Embassy and arse kickin' it is then,' Stan said. He shrugged and took another bite from the burger.

The trip to the Embassy did not take long. Despite the traffic and the tight streets of the town on the way. Stan the cabbie had driven in his usual, get-out-of-my-way manner. Charging headlong down narrow streets, forcing other drivers out of his way, making up time as he went. Steel wasn't sure this was because of the generous tips he had given the driver or if Stan was just a maniac behind the wheel.

Stan pulled up to the main gate of the embassy. A security guard stepped out of his control box and stopped them at the barrier. He was a small guy in his forties, Steel figured, but he was lean and looked like he could handle himself. A local guy, probably. He'd possibly answered one of those ads online for, 'Locals wanted to work at US Embassy Malta.' He wore a light blue shirt and blue trousers with a red stripe down the side, his highly polished shoes glinted in the sun. His hair was cut short, and he was clean-shaven.

Very professional.

The security guy walked to the driver's side and stood far enough away. To the vehicle's side near the engine block – just in case the driver decided to kick the door open. But at the same time, he was close enough to hear and be understood.

Very well trained professional.

'I'm here to see Section Chief Foster,' Steel said, flashing his NYPD identification. The security guy took Steel's ID and went to make a phone call. Steel spent the time making a note of the security cameras and fencing, along with layouts of buildings. It was more habit than curiosity. They had quite a good set up he had to admit.

The security guard returned his attention to Steel. 'The Chief is expecting you, sir. He's over by the main building right over there,' the guard said, pointing out a large limestone building. 'However, your cab will have to wait outside or drop you here, I'm afraid, sir.' Steel smiled and took his ID back and put it away.

'I might be a while, so you can drop me here, Stan,' Steel said, passing over thirty euros to Stan's delight.

'You got my number, chief, just call us when you want us,' Stan said, shoving the cash away.

Steel stepped out of the red bus and slammed the door just in time as Stan reversed back out of the entrance, and handbrake turned it like a pro. Steel and the guard just watched as the red van disappear again down the road, leaving a trail of black smoke and dust from the road. The guard had told Steel he had to go through a reception building first and pointed out a new looking red brick structure. He thanked the guy and walked past a large area with small trees and low bushes. A path of concrete slabs headed directly from the security box to the building, straight and true, all the way to the front door. Aesthetically, it made the front of the main gate of the embassy pleasant to look at.

Inside the reception building, it was crisp and fresh from an air-conditioner and brightly lit. The walls have painted an off-white, and grey ceramic tiles made covered the floor. There was a long reception desk with three people behind it. The side near another glass door was four metal detectors with x-ray machines and conveyors for personal items. It looked like a checking-in area of a small airport. There were posters, and notice-boards showed pictures of local sites and a place on a wall that held flyers, which showed all the many tours that could be booked. Including Kane's movie tour.

Steel strolled over to the desk and headed for the woman. From her whole demeanour, Steel could tell she was in charge. She was higher up than the others, whether she was taller or how the seats were arranged. She also had that look in her eye, the one that said: 'I'm the boss.'

Steel went directly to her.

The woman's smile was broad and showed off pearly white teeth. She was around five-ten and slender. Her long black hair was tied up into a ponytail. Her make up gave her an almost oriental look with pale skin, dark eyeliner and brilliant ruby red lipstick. She reminded Steel of the women from a Robert Palmer video re-run he had caught once on tv. Her black and white outfit, closing the deal on the image.

He smiled back and took out his NYPD badge and his passport. He knew from experience that military bases and government installations did not regard an ID as a valid form of identification. It was a passport or nothing.

'So, you are here to see Director Foster, correct?' she said. Her voice was like silk, smooth and soft. There was a warmth about it that made the hair stand up on the back of his neck. She was the full package.

Very sexy and great voice.

She should have been an interrogator. Most men would admit anything after five minutes with this woman. He had seen that too. Sure there had been the hard-ass ones that would yell and scream, but they either scared you too much or just pissed you off, and you kept quiet. But a woman like this would have a guy selling out his mother after just hearing her voice.

The woman behind the counter clicked a few keys on the keyboard and checked Steel's ID and passport photo by holding them up in line with his face. She was thorough. He gave her that. Most people would have concentrated on is the photograph of a male, yes, name and date, but no one studied that hard on a picture.

She was competent, very professional.

'Here is your visitor's pass. Please wear it on display the entire time, and the director will meet you outside the main building,' she said. Pointing over in the direction of the massive limestone building. Steel went to leave but paused for a second.

'Yes, is there anything else?' she asked.

'No, that's fine, thank you,' he said before headed for the x-ray machines and the way into the main building.

Steel passed through the metal detectors after emptying the contents of his pockets into a small grey plastic tray and placed it on the conveyor. As he took off his glasses, he was glad he had remembered to put his contacts in as well as having the sunglasses. He did not worry about the x-ray machine and the sunglasses. They would just register as a gadget with headphones in the arms. There were plenty of those on the market.

Steel walked through without setting off any alarms and reclaimed his items from the conveyor belt. Steel put his belt back on, and placing his things into his pockets, Steel ventured out of the security building and into the sun.

Steel paused for a beat and slipped the sunglasses back on. It was a fantastic day, with blue skies and wisps of white cloud.

Steel looked over at the main embassy building and the surrounding grounds. There was a tall concrete wall that surrounded the area, along with tall lamposts, fences. It was a great set up he had to admit.

He headed over to what he knew to be the embassy building from the online photographs. He had been surprised that they had their own social media page. It was a magnificent structure all limestone bricks and tinted windows. The same limestone blocks were used to create two columns supporting a glass overhang for the main entrance. Palm trees lined a mosaic pathway, and in the centre a brass badge of the office of the US Embassy. The two-story building was a grand sight to behold.

As Steel approached, he saw Foster waiting impatiently at the entrance. Steel exercised his fists, getting them ready if he had to start using them. Foster looked over, shot Steel a look of anger. Steel's pace quickened, he wanted answers, as well as breaking every bone in Foster's body, but that would have to wait.

'What the hell have you been doing? I said to be discreet in your investigation, keep under the radar?' Foster mumbled, grabbing Steel by the arm and attempting to haul him around a corner. But Steel did not move, his feet suddenly anchored to the floor.

'Foster, some goons kidnapped a woman and me this morning from your house?' Steel said, his voice growled. 'One of them was made out to look like you.'

'Why were you at my house and with a woman?' Foster asked, stunned at the revelation.

'Her name is Samara Malka, she's Mossad, and we went there because we thought you were in danger, as it turns out, they were laying a trap for Samara,' Steel said. Foster shook his head as if trying to comprehend what Steel was saying.

'Steel, what the fuck are you talking about? and why the hell is Mossad involved?' Foster pulled at Steel's arm, urging him around the corner out of sight.

'Where's your family now, Foster?' Steel asked. Trying to get back on point.

'They went back to the States. They are stayin at Matha's folks because they are too sick to travel.' Foster paused for a moment, gathering his thoughts and emotions. 'I thought it best under the circumstances, the coroner hasn't released the body yet. He is still doing his checks. Something about a backlog.'

'So why didn't you go with them?' Foster shook his head and sighed.

'I've been here, working. It stops me from thinking about what happened. I think without really knowing how Lucy died, I won't be able to rest. So, I've been here, burying myself in this damned project that's going online this weekend.'

Steel said, looking over at the Embassy building. 'Foster, it's time you told me everything.'

'Project?' Steel voice sounded grave. 'What project?'

Foster's eyes widened in panic. 'The new software.'

'How big of a deal is it?' Steel asked.

'Big enough,' Foster said. Steel felt that Foster hadn't brought him there just for a scolding, and his wife and kid weren't just out of the country for a family visit.

'Steel, how much do you know about facial recognition?' Foster asked, leading Steel to the quiet of the pool house.

Chapter 49

The sun beat down relentlessly on the island. Some found beaches to bask on, like seals. Others sought refuge in hotels or restaurants, unaccustomed to the dry heat.

It was seven in the morning, and the sun was high in an almost cloudless sky.

A perfect day – for some.

For others, it meant sitting and watching and doing not much of anything – except planning.

Aamir sat in the back of the large, white Toyota SUV. The two men in the front wore the usual jeans and check shirts, but this time they had large pilot style sunglasses, somewhat to Aamir's amusement. To him, they looked comical, almost like they were trying to be the FBI or something.

If they had turned up in a blacked-out vehicle, Aamir did not think he would have been able to contain himself.

They had driven using several different routes, seeing which one was quickest, which one was more likely to be full of parked cars at a specific time. Which one had a line of sight to and from the target? Every route had a worst-case scenario, but ultimately they all converged onto one place – the target.

Planning and preparation.

They had made a note of everything.

The driver had taken more interest if there were any fast food places close to their base of operations.

The driver went to scratch his nose but winced in pain. He owed Samara a broken nose from when she had rearranged his at the old barracks. The big man's pride was hurt more than his nose, and she would pay for that as well.

He still could not believe she had taken him down with a plank of wood. When he had told the story, he had made it out to have been a huge plank made from hardened timber. But his colleagues – who loved to ridicule him, said they had seen this monstrous piece of wood, and it had been nothing more than a stick. And not only that, but the big man had been beaten by a little girl.

They pulled up close to the address the driver had been given and waited. They had been driving for some time. The driver was happy for the break but continuously complained he was hungry – to the others' annoyance.

Aamir pulled out a pair of binoculars and scanned the area while pressing the speed-dial on his phone. The electronic ring continued, giving Aamir an uneasy feeling.

Then a soft voice answered.

'Yes?' the voice said. Aamir could sense the arrogance of the person on the other end, just by their tone.

'Are you sure we are on schedule? You're sure that they were able to do what you promised?' Aamir asked.

'Yes. It's all taken care of. Everything you asked is done. Now, just make sure you hold up your side,' said the stern voice. Its tone was cold and rang with distaste. As if the person on the other end held Aamir and his group with contempt.

Aamir snarled at the phone.

How dare they speak to him like that? Had they no idea who he was? Who he represented?

Aamir placed the phone back in his pocket. The person, on the other end, had left the call without another word. Almost as if they could not be bothered to speak to this great man.

Aamir took another look through the binoculars. Checking the lay of the land, checking for weaknesses in the surrounding area. He knew that it would be easy if he wanted to get in, not covert, but manageable.

But then stealthy wasn't part of the plan.

'OK, let's go. There is nothing we can do here…not yet anyway,' Aamir said, giving the driver the next location to go to. As they sped past, Aamir took note of the sign on the side of the road. It was engraved on a long block of stone.

The Embassy of the United States of America.

Chapter 50

Steel watched as Foster sparked up a cigarette. Foster did not bother offering Steel one. He knew Steel's feelings on smoking. Steel sat under the shade of the pool house while Foster paced about nervously.

Steel said nothing.

He just left his old friend to gather his words. Whatever was going on had him hopping like a cat on hot bricks.

'We have a programme going online on Friday, one that will change the way we control the movement of terrorists and criminals. It is a full proof system that will enable us to catch a terrorist on our database anywhere. If they fly, sail, take a train, wherever there is a camera, we will find them,' Foster started.

Steel sat in silence, letting Foster unburden himself.

'This is unique software will do damage to every group we know. Their freedom of movement will cease to exist.'

'But...?' Steel asked, forcing Foster to cut the chit chat.

'I believe someone is plotting to change the software. I don't know how they'll get to the programme to do anything, but... I think – believe it's a real threat,' Foster said.

'Change it – how?' Steel asked. Not understanding how the whole system worked, he had never really taken much interest. He just knew that facial recognition existed.

'Put a glitch in the system somehow, so it doesn't pick something up, or not at all,' Foster replied.

'Is it a credible threat? Are they able to do it?' Steel asked. Foster shrugged.

'That's the problem. It's locked away and guarded. There should be no way of getting to it.'

'But?'

'We hear a whisper, and we have to react to it. After 911, I've learnt nothing is impossible and all threats should be treated as possible.'

Steel nodded as Foster took another draw from the cigarette. Steel watched the smoke twist rise from the tip of the cigarette, the red embers glow as Foster inhaled. The world was suddenly moving in slow motion. His trail of thought was slowing everything down, slotting pieces of data into specific places, like a child's puzzle.

Square block – square hole, round block – round hole... But the triangle was the problem because there was no triangle slot. There was only a square.

'So, let me guess, ' Steel said. Anger oozed from his tone. This new bit of information placed another piece into the puzzle, which Foster should have told him days ago. 'This group threatened you. You said no, they killed your daughter to show you they mean business, so... you called me to sort your problem out,' Steel said.

Foster's jaw dropped at the accusation and flew at Steel with fists raised.

'Sit your arse down, Marcus,' Steel barked abruptly, not even bothering to budge from his chair. Foster stopped, shocked at Steel's order. Steel gazed at Foster, his mind placing all the information into order. Starting from Lucy's death to Brad, then the attack at Foster's place and now this information. All the while, Steel thought about what Samara had said. Someone in the embassy was dirty. And the goons that had taken Samara and himself. There appeared to be many players in the game, but still, there was someone on the bench waiting to come out at the final inning to play. Steel looked over at Foster.

'So… if they did not get to you – who did they get to?' Steel asked. He watched as Foster fell into a seat next to him.

'I don't know,' Foster said, shaking his head. 'I just heard a whisper from a confidential informant, and yes, I still have CIs,' Foster smiled smugly. 'The chatter is a group from Tunisia is trying to get over here for something. What, I don't know. I thought it might be the EU conference next week, but my gut says it something bigger.'

Steel nodded. Taking in the information that Foster was giving him.

'So, why keep this from me? It may have aided my investigation?' Steel said.

Foster shook his head, 'No, this is something else. I didn't want you to follow false leads and forget what you are here for. It's my job to sort out this business. You're here…'

'To find out what happened to your daughter, yes, I know… but what if the two are related, which I bet they are?' Steel asked.

Foster smiled and shrugged. He had calmed down from his sudden and somewhat overreaction towards Steel's accusation. He took another draw from the almost finished cigarette.

'Then I guess we'll be working together again,' Foster grinned at the prospect.

'I'm off to see the coroner in Victoria today', Steel said. 'See what he can tell me about what happened.' Foster nodded.

Foster felt guilty he hadn't been back over to the island since the police had called him that fateful morning. Foster had identified Lucy's body so his wife wouldn't have to. He wanted to at least save Martha that pain. If she was to see Lucy, it would be at the funeral – not like that. Foster remembered what Lucy had looked like laid out on the rocks at the blue pool. The image of her broken body still blazed in his mind every time he closed his eyes, an image he wanted to spare the only two women left in his life.

'Find who did this to my little girl, Steel. You make them pay… every last one of them,' Foster said.

Steel said nothing. He nodded, then watched Foster disappear into the secured building. Steel sat and pondered over what Foster had said. He'd known Foster was keeping something more from him. He just hadn't known why.

Now he knew.

However, Foster was right about one thing. Steel could not get sidetracked, thinking this software had anything to do with it. Steel was there to find Lucy's killer – simple.

Nothing more.

Steel was sure Foster had the IT issue in hand. But Steel had the feeling they were connected somehow. All he had to do was wait. If they were connected, he had a feeling he would find out soon enough. In the meantime, he had Lucy's death to investigate.

Steel looked at his watch, half-past three. He would catch the next ferry over and stay the night if he had to. Either way, he was going to Gozo. He needed to see the crime scene in the day and in the dark. That way, he could get a feel for what may or may not have happened. He had learnt that sometimes you had to 'walk in their shoes'.

'See what they would have seen, combat the problems that they would have had to combat,' the friend had told him. And they had been right. Sometimes you had to think either as the killer or the victim – or both. No crime scene is perfect. There is always something that the killer never thought about, usually the slightest thing, that did not become apparent until it was time.

All he had to do, was find that square peg – or that triangular hole.

Steel pulled out his cell phone and pressed the speed-dial number.

'Stan,' Steel said with a broad grin when the cabbie answered. 'Question, how well do you know Gozo?'

As Steel headed back to the gatehouse, Alison Price sauntered over to Foster.

'Who's your friend?' Price asked. Her eyes fixed on Steel's form.

'Just an old army buddy, he was Lucy's Godfather,' Foster said.

Price did not say anything at first. She just sized up the big man dressed in black before he disappeared from view.

'Yes, we're all sorry for your loss Foster, truly,' Price said. Her eyes were warm and compassionate. The sun reflected in her eyes and the lipstick, giving both a watery sheen.

'Thank you. That means a lot,' Foster said.

'I'm sure if you need time away, we could…'

Foster shook his head. 'Thanks, but the work keeps me going,' Foster said. He smiled before looking away – the sound of a plane high above distracted him for a moment. 'I'm all alone now. Martha and Abby have gone to her mom's. It's better that way for a bit,' Foster said.

'Yes,' she said. 'It probably is for the best.' She smiled gently.

Section Chief Bolton leant against the wall of the blockhouse. He had seen Foster talking with the big man, and now he was talking with Alison Price. He sipped his coffee. Taking his time, observing, taking everything in. He looked at his watch. He would have to leave his perch pretty soon. He had a call to make.

Bolton knew who John Steel was and why he was there.

He also knew of Steel's reputation with New York cops – but he did not know if he should be worried or not.

Bolton took another sip from the ceramic mug. The coffee was strong. As he watched Foster and Price talk, he felt someone come up behind him – it was Tipp.

'What ya doin?' Tipp asked.

'Watchin' Foster and Price. He was talking to his friend before,' Bolton said.

'What, he's old buddy from the service?' Tipp's voice rang with amazement.

'Yeah. The cop,' Bolton said.

'I didn't know he was a cop,' Tipp said.

'And you call yourself an agent?' Bolton smiled.

'No – I'm a section chief who don't give a crap about Foster's old army buddies because I have more important things to worry about,' Tipp barked sarcastically.

'What – like crawlin' up Sloan's ass you mean?' Bolton smirked. 'Nah, I think you got that covered,' Bolton said as he walked away. Leaving Tipp to gaze over at Foster and Price.

Chapter 51

The phone in the secure office rang. Alpha, as always, picked it up on the third ring.

'Yes,' he said.

'The cop went to see Foster,' said Beta.

'I know,' said Alpha.

'The cop is on his way to Gozo. I think he's going to Victoria to see the body of the girl,' said Beta.

'It was to be expected,' said Alpha. 'Keep tabs on him, make sure he is only going in that direction. We don't need him messing up any plans.'

'We have someone on it,' Beta said.

'What, like at the Manoel island – yeah, that ended well,' said Alpha. 'stop underestimating this guy. He needs to keep on investigating the Foster woman's death, not us.'

'It was a mistake – I know. People have been told,' said Beta.

'Good, no more fuck ups,' said Alpha.

'And Foster?'

'Kill him.' Alpha said coldly.

Chapter 52

It was late afternoon when Stan had got to the ferry port at Cirkewwa. For Steel, the drive had been exciting, to say the least – if not slightly terrifying. Stan had proven himself to be a complete lunatic behind the wheel once more, causing angry drivers to beep their horns or shout abuse. But the old London cabbie seemed to enjoy it.

The ferry was due to depart at quarter past. Leaving them plenty of time to get the taxi aboard and grab a seat near the onboard kiosk. Stan had found a small shop on board and had taken off to top up on magazines and snacks. Steel grabbed a coffee, a bottle of water and a sandwich from the kiosk, thinking he would need them later.

The twenty-five-minute crossing was calm and uneventful. The ferry was full of tourists, unhappy babies, and locals. There were monitors dotted around the sitting area showing a documentary on the islands and their wildlife. Steel watched with interest, even though he could not hear the narrator over the crowd's noise. Steel thought of Lucy and her work, trying to save the creatures living in and around the islands.

Stan returned from his shopping trip, laden with bags in both hands.

'Sure you left anything for the others?' Steel asked with a grin.

Stan scoffed and sat down in the empty seat Steel had saved for him. Stan grabbed at the pile of sugar and milk sachets, took two of each, and poured them into his coffee. After a vigorous stir, Stan lifted the paper cup and blew on the drink, cooling it down before taking a sip.

'So where are we going to on Gozo?' Stan asked.

'The morgue in Victoria, it's at—'

'The hospital, yeah, I know where it is,' Stan interrupted. 'Might not be open when we get there, may have to stay over,' Stan said.

Steel smiled. He had already found a suitable place on the internet and arranged for rooms at a local hotel.

'Sure your boss is OK with you driving me, staying overnight?' Steel asked curiously.

'I told him you were paying me well for it. He just sees a profit at the end of the day,' Stan said with a curious smile. Steel nodded and took a sip from his coffee. He was glad of Stan's company and local knowledge.

Steel looked around at the people in the seating area, then turned his gaze out of the full-plated windows.

They were coming up on Gozo.

He had a beautiful, seductive view of craggy cliff faces and naturally bored caves along with secluded beaches. The waves crashed against the rocky surface of the cliff faces, and Steel began to wonder about Lucy and that fateful night. There was a roar from the ferries engine as it began to turn, moving with the current and heading for the harbour.

'So, what's first, the morgue?' Stan asked with a mouthful of a sandwich he had started. Steel's eyes locked on the island, which was now on their left, and nodded. The ship turned to follow its course.

In the distance, Steel watched as more craggy rock formations came into view.

Stan pointed to a cliff face to the left of them. 'Somewhere past them cliffs is San Lorenz. Technically, the other side of the bloody island,' Stan laughed with a mouth full of food. 'That's where Azure Window used to be, until we had a massive storm, knocked the bloody thing into the water, the rest of it is still there, underwater of course. Bloody shame, people used to flock to see that,' Stan said, then took another bite from his sandwich.

'Is it hard to get too?' Steel asked. His gaze still fixed on the point and that strange face like feature.

'Nah, pretty easy. More winding roads and stuff, but easy enough. Aye, and a bloody good coffee shop there as well.' Stan took a sip from his coffee.

'Good, that's where we're going tomorrow, so get some rest at the hotel,' Steel's gaze still fixed on the impressive sight. 'You can drop me at the morgue. I've got some things to do there; meantime, you can sort out things with the hotel.'

Stan nodded eagerly. The thought of spending time with cut up dead people turned his stomach.

'No arguments from me, boss,' Stan mumbled with a mouthful of sandwich.

Steel sipped his cooling coffee. His mind was processing a thousand thoughts, slotting those pegs back into their holes. He was still missing a peg and a hole. But only one thought stood out from the rest.

What was Lucy doing at that secluded place late at night?

The ferry docked at the small Mgarr harbour, which was full of small boats and water taxis. There were bars and restaurants on the front. The main road reached up to the right, and stretching with it were more bars, a petrol station, an ATM, and eventually overlooking the harbour, the local homes. Steel noticed on a hill was a magnificent looking church. A towering structure that seemed to glow with the reflection of the sun. Steel had to admit it was a quaint village and had enough to entertain someone until the next ferry arrived. Even if it was sitting at a bar watching the boats and the sea birds.

Stan drove off the ferry with his usual finesse and onto the winding road towards Victoria's city. The road was a steady upward climb, allowing for a fantastic view of the coastal town on the right and the majestic church on the hilltop to the left – The Church of the Madonna of Lourdes.

Stan's minibus almost sounded in pain as it climbed the steep road. Steel gave Stan an anxious look, wondering if any moment the engine would explode. But Stan just sang along to the music from his stereo as if nothing was wrong.

The trip to the capital city was long or felt that way after the sixth rendition of *Waterloo*. Steel was thankful he did not have a gun by the time they reached the hospital. Between Stan's lousy singing and the lack of effective shock absorbers, Steel was ready to kill something.

'Well, here we are. You sure you want to do this now?' Stan asked, looking at his wristwatch. 'How do you even know there's someone there? They could have all gone by now,' There was a scared tone in Stan's voice, and his irritability shouted to Steel.

'There's someone there, it's a morgue, the dead don't stop turning up after six,' Steel said. 'So, what is it, morgues or hospitals you don't like?'

Stan did not answer. He was too busy checking out the large building's front with a terrified expression.

'Hospitals it is,' Steel said to himself as he got out of the vehicle. Steel went to say something to Stan, but Stan had already put the bus into gear and was heading away at speed. Steel ventured inside the new looking building.

Chapter 53

Samara had broken into Steel's suite and accessed the safe. She laughed to herself as the thick security door swung open, and she saw the folded piece of paper, which stood upright. *Hi, Samara, make yourself at home, the extra room key is in the safe. If you're bored, I suggest you check out Marcus Foster's team; something is fishy there.*

Samara took out the key card and tucked it away. She was slightly disappointed with herself, to be that transparent. Then Samara thought back to the phone call she had made while she thought Steel was in the shower. She frowned, knowing that she had made the mistake of making the call while still in the suite. Steel must have overheard everything.

But what was done was done, and she could not undo it.

She glanced at the note again. If Steel had been mad at her, it did not show. In fact, it was just the opposite. Samara looked over at the desk telephone, and a wicked grin crossed her face. She picked up the receiver and waited.

'Hello, room service. I'd like to order some dinner,' Samara said. Plotting her payback, 'Oh... and, how much is your best champagne?' She sat back in the office chair and put her feet up on the desk, waited for a reply while hacking Steel's laptop. It was an easy enough code, which in itself made her suspicious. From what she knew of Steel, she expected more. If anything, multiple passwords and retina scan, but a simple code! As the laptop kicked into life, she got her answer from room service. She ordered the Grass-fed rib-eye with fried onions, café de Paris. and a bottle of Moet & Chandon Brut Imperial to accompany it. If she was going to do a background check for him, she wanted to be comfortable.

The main screen opened to reveal a new message, *Here's your new laptop, and I hope you enjoy the steak and the bottle of Champagne. Xx.*

Samara sat up straight and leaned forwards to re-read the note just to make sure she had read it correctly. 'Oh, he's good,' She laughed.

She was sure she wasn't that transparent, so he must be as sneaky as she was, and he would have done the same in her position.

Samara checked the desk for anything else he may have left, possibly a list of names to aid her search. But there was nothing except the hotel's information pack. Her eyebrows raised at the sight of the beauty and spar treatment menu but thought charging that was going too far.

Steel had given her a lead, and she had to follow it. Samara opened up the internet explorer and began to search for anything on Foster, failing that she would have to call in some favours. She knew Steel was there on Foster's request to look into what had happened to his daughter. He had mentioned it at Kane's house. She also knew that Steel and Foster had been friends from way back, long before Foster had joined the CIA.

Samara figured that's why he had dropped Foster's name. Steel could not look into him or his staff without being objective when the two had been friends. On the other hand, Samara could. She had no ties with Foster, so it would be easier for her to see if Foster or someone in his department was dirty.

Samara stared at the screen. Her thoughts were miles away. She was about to look into the CIA, generally not a big deal, a pass-the-time exercise of who can hack who. She had done it several times before for laughs, and her opposite number had done the same. It was a game.

But now…

Now, this was something different.

This was something that could cause a major shit storm. Samara took a deep breath and began to type. First was a message to an old friend who owed her a favour. This guy was a wizard and could find anyone or anything. After she had gotten the names of Foster's team, it would be a case of records. Email, bank, cell phone, the whole package.

She had no idea how long it would take him to find what she needed. It could be an hour, five minutes, a day even. One thing was for sure when she started looking; she needed to be mobile, untraceable. Steel had known this, which explained the laptop. It was a small machine; a beautiful 15-inch screen, light enough to carry, large enough to see everything on the monitor, and it could not be traced to her. And if someone checked and found Steel had bought it, Steel could say it had been stolen. That's if he hadn't already done so.

Now all she had to do was wait for her contact to get back to her.

The question was, what would come first. The information, or her dinner?

Chapter 54

The temperature had dropped slightly with the slow setting of the sun. The big day was drawing closer, and Aamir had to contain his excitement. Soon their day would arrive, and they would show the world of their might. Moments before, he had spoken to the team leaders and confirmed all was ready. Aamir was still unsure how the master had required the C-130 transport aircraft. But then, he never questioned anything their leader said. He was, after all, the man who knew everything.

Aamir walked over to the large map that hung on the dimly lit room wall, which was ripe with the stench of stale coffee, sweat, and take-out food. He hated the quarters they had been given. A small, cramped house in the middle of nowhere, even though it wasn't. It just felt that way because they could not contact the village, which was just down the road. Except for the odd trip down the local shop for supplies, they stayed away.

He looked at the map and its strategic layout—photographs and notations of timings pinned next to locations. The plan was coming together. All Aamir needed now was confirmation from the inside man to say that it was ready to go. Aamir smiled and nodded with satisfaction. He did not know who the inside man was or if he was, in fact, a *he* at all. The master had never told him for obvious reasons. 'If you're captured, you can't tell what you don't know,' the master had told him once. But all Aamir knew was there was a new software going online on Friday that could ruin the lives of many of his brothers. The insider's job was to make sure it never went online.

Aamir had to admire this patriot's courage, but he figured they were only in it for the money and not the cause. If that was the case, so be it. Either way, he did not care as long as it was done before their mission was to take effect.

Aamir walked back to the small desk on the other side of the room. His cell phone had pinged and alert of a new message. Aamir picked up the device and read the text.

Plane ready to go, device and cargo on board. Awaiting your arrival. He gave a wicked grin as he closed down the phone and placed it back on the desk. Soon chaos would rain on this small island, and then death would take flight. Everything was going as planned, and the Americans wouldn't know what had hit them.

Calver stood with his back against the pool house's brickwork and watched the sun sink into the horizon. The sky was deep with reds, orange, and purples. It looked as if the sky was on fire.

His eyes desperately search for anyone in the area who may have seen him. He looked around to ensure he was alone, then switched off his phone. He took out the battery and SIM card, then snapped it in half, tossed it in the nearby garbage bin. He looked up and made one more scour of the area. He was alone. Calver took another SIM from his pocket and slipped it into the device, placed the battery back and then the cover. Confident nobody had seen him, Calver smiled smugly as he put the cell into his pocket. All had gone to plan. Soon it would be all over, home free and rich.

He returned to the main building, just one hour to go before the end of his shift. Calver walked without a care in the world. His plan was going smoothly, and all parties were playing the game.

A figure stood at one of the windows on the top floor of the main building. The figure looked out across towards the pool house. The figure's features were hidden by the sunset reflecting on the dark glass.

Carver had not seen the figure.

But the figure had seen him and everything he had done.

As the bright orange of the sun's reflection sank from the window, the figure slipped away, leaving nothing but an empty corridor.

Calver entered the main building and headed for the elevator to the blockhouse. He took note of the others waiting for the same elevator. Several were from the cyber division. Most of them were ex-hackers who had been given a legal way of carrying out their hobby. The powers that be found the best way to find or beat an expert – was with an expert. It had been a kind of 'use a thief to catch a thief' way of thinking. Or, in this case, 'use a hacker to catch a hacker.'

There were also two from financial – small men who never seemed to smile much, or not in public from what he had seen.

Calver yawned at the prospect of a silent ride down. In some way, he preferred that to a lot of pointless chatter. The doors opened, and the group before him parted, allowing room for the people who had just come up to get off. Each of them looked pale and haggard.

It was a clear sign of an eight-hour-straight shift.

Calver got in last, making sure he stood directly in front of the door. This served no purpose, of course, only a form of irritation to the others. He was blocking the door; it would be him who chose who got off in time or just at the last moment. In his mind, it was a fun game to pass the time. He had the power, the control. But he knew deep down, they did not give a shit and would just shove him out of the way.

The elevator stopped on three, and Calver got off. He could feel that nobody had even registered someone had gotten off, only there was suddenly more space. Calver grumbled to himself at the lack of acknowledgement of his existence.

Soon everyone would know him and cower in fear.

Soon he would be someone they would never forget, even if they wanted to.

Calver headed for his cubical and put on the headset. Nothing had happened while he was away. No alarms had sounded, no chatter from anywhere. Calver smiled and thought that the time was drawing near when all that silence would change.

Foster watched as Calver took his seat. Recently there had been something about Calver that had made Foster uncomfortable. He had become smug and over self-aware. This wasn't a bad thing, but many strange things had been going on since the arms company had unveiled their new software. The death of his daughter, Steel's kidnapping, and now the floor chief had gone sick, something he'd never done in the two years he'd worked there. This new software wasn't a gift; it was a curse, and he wished that the damned thing had never been created.

Foster left the room and headed for his office. His meeting with Steel had left him rattled. Foster trusted Steel without question, but he knew Steel was holding something back, possibly for his own good. But it did not matter now. Steel was on Gozo, and the investigation into Lucy's death was moving forwards. All he had to do was keep his head and make sure his department had done their jobs before that damned software went online. The question was, would the software work? Or would it be the biggest mistake since the freedom of movement in Europe? Foster liked the idea of borders and checks. The thought that someone could travel from Italy to Oslo without showing a passport struck him as frightening. But then, in his line of work, he saw terrifying things. Most of which the public had no idea about.

Chapter 55

The General Hospital in Victoria was a modern complex of different sized buildings. Some were old with the limestone brickwork. Others more recently added new red brick structures with large tinted windows. The complex was divided by a road that traversed straight through, which would take visitors from one public street to the other. At each entrance of the hospital, the road was a barrier and a guard. Whose primary job was to restrict access to the road and ultimately to the hospital.

Visitors and hospital staff only said a sign at each security post. A large metal board painted white with discernible black letters, each letter being about two inches high.

Steel figure that they must have had problems with people using the road as a short cut because of the secondary school at the north end of the road.

Stan pulled to the security booth, and a small middle-aged man stepped out to greet them. He wore a sky-blue short-sleeve shirt and black trousers. His boots were military-style. He had pilot style sunglasses that perched perfectly on his roman nose. His head was shaved, so it gleamed in the sun, but a thick black moustache sat above a friendly smile.

'Good afternoon, visitor or patient?' the guard said. His voice was surprisingly high pitched, like his underwear was too tight.

'My name is John Steel. I have an appointment with Doctor Bondi, ' Steel said, passing over his passport. The guard took the passport and headed inside the small hut to check his paperwork. He soon returned, still wearing the smile.

'Yes, sir, you're on my list. The morgue is in that building over there,' the guard said, pointing to a second large building. Stan drove in slowly. Almost as if he was petrified to be there. That made Steel smile, enjoying Stan's awkwardness.

The hospital grounds were full of small bushes and palm trees, and seating areas gave it a pleasant appearance.

There a large visitors parking lot at the north of the complex, and he knew Stan would be dropping him there.

'You got the name of the hotel?' Steel asked. Stan tapped the side of his head as if displaying it was fully inputted.

Steel got out of the red bus, and Stan took off quickly, leaving Steel in a cloud of oily smoke.

Steel found the correct building and walked in slowly. The building was modern, with a large lobby and reception area. The walls were painted a cream colour, and the floor was the same grey tile as the embassy. The reception was a thick glass window of a small room. Inside sat two women, both in their mid-thirties and both with short brown hair, differently styled. The woman who greeted Steel had a slight perm with blonde highlights. She wasn't thin nor fat but had a glorious warming smile and large blue eyes. A white plastic name tag said her name was Miss Doe.

'Please, don't tell me your first name is Jane?' Steel asked.

'No, it's Tracy,' she replied with a confused look.

'Oh, well. Had to ask.' Steel replied. 'My name John Steel. I have an appointment with Doctor Bondi.'

'Ah, yes, Mr Steel, we got the call earlier,' the woman said, then directed him to the left door. 'Get to the elevator, then take it all the way down. After that, you will see a long corridor in front of you. The doctor's office is the last on the left.' Steel thanked her and strolled towards the elevator.

He found the elevator at the end of a long passage lined with offices – the dull metal of the elevator doors stood out against the petrol coloured wall.

Around him, he could hear the usual intercom chatter, calls for doctors or patient instructions. There were screams of pain coming from further down the hallway or whimpers from a waiting room he had just passed. Steel felt uncomfortable in hospitals. The only time he had been in them was to visit a wounded colleague or say goodbye to someone. He was thankful that MI8 had their own medical facilities.

The walls were bright with wipe free paint. Nurses passed by with emotionless smiles, something learnt from years of working the job. Steel knew those smiles; he had seen it enough on the army medics.

These were brilliant people doing a thankless job.

Steel had great respect for the doctors and nurses the angel's people hoped never to see, were grateful for in crisis and forgotten in normality. Steel smiled at a group of nurses who passed him by. They smiled back with that same standard smile.

'Thank you,' he said, causing one of them to stop.

'For what?' she asked, puzzled.

'For all those who never actually said it,' Steel replied and stepped into the elevator as the doors slid open.

The morgue was as cold and foreboding as Steel had expected it to be. Tiled walls and floors filled the corridors, giving it a clean but eerie look. Overhead, bright strip lights reflected off of the polished surfaces.

The first thing Steel noticed was the silence, then the smell. He had expected something foul. Instead, he found it to be a sweet fruity smell. Steel moved on, following the strange aroma. Then started to hear music. It was an upbeat sort of tune like something from the charts. He had heard it before but was unable to place it.

As he drew near, the melody became more apparent, and then he had it. One of the young women on the ferry had it blasting in her earbuds on the crossing, a catchy tune made to make you feel good.

Steel pushed the doors open and stepped in. He half expecting a twenty-something-year-old. But instead, found a large overweight man in his fifties. He was dancing and singing along to the music that was blasting from the stereo system.

Steel stepped back into the hallway and checked at the name on the door. *Doctor Henry Bondi. Medical Examiner.*

Steel just stood there for a moment taking in the strangest sight he'd seen in a long time.

'Well, that's definitely someone who loves his work,' Steel said to himself with a broad smile. The man is utterly oblivious to his presence in the room as he carried on dancing and singing. The medical examiner was about six feet tall and had an appetite for good food, judging by his girth. He wore brown trousers and a white shirt which had fine blue lines down it, on top of which he wore a disposable bloodstain apron. Black curly hair clung to the sides of his bulbous head, having deserted the top. He had a Roman nose and big ears with big lobs that swayed when he moved.

He looked like a cartoon character.

Steel dressed leaned against the wall next to the door with one foot resting against the wall and his arms crossed. As the song reached a high point, the coroner spun around to see him. With only his eyes moving, the man froze, almost as if he was looking for somewhere to dash off and hide suddenly.

'Well, I thought you nailed it perfectly, Doc, especially the bit at the end,' Steel said, kicking off from the wall and walked over to the troubled, blood-soaked man.

'I am John Steel, a friend of-'

'Marcus Foster, yes. He said you'd be coming over. Sad business, unfortunate such a young thing should go like that,' the Henry Bondi said. The smile falling from his face. Bondi walked over to the stereo and switched off the music.

'Uhm, doc, it's not my place to say, but isn't it slightly disrespectful to be dancing about while you're working?' Steel asked. Hoping he hadn't squashed any chance of help from Bondi.

'It's my office, not the autopsy room. Besides, I'm stuck down here by myself for nearly twelve hours a day. What can I say? It keeps me sane,' Bondi shrugged. Steel could see his point.

'Marcus was wondering if you'd found anything? He would have come, but work has him tied up,' Steel said.

'Ah, yes. The Lucy Foster case. This was an unpleasant case because I knew her. Well, that's to say I met her once or twice when I would go up to the Azure Window,' Bondi's face was filled with empathy. 'She was severely beaten about by the waves; it was a rough sea that night,' Bondi explained.

'So what're your thoughts, suicide, accidental death...murder?' Steel asked with interest. The coroner looked Steel up and down with a curious smile.

'Foster said you'd be direct.'

Steel shrugged one shoulder in response.

'Have you been to the Azure Window?' Bondi asked.

'No, just got over today, there were some – complications, which prevented me coming earlier,' Steel said with a gentle smile.

'Marcus told me who you were and why you are here,' Bondi said, and then his smile came back for a brief second. 'Tell you what, I'll give you what I know and see what you think.'

Steel could see that this doctor was more interesting than he looked. He was a man up for a challenge—possibly a chess and crossword enthusiast. Steel had noticed the chessboard in the man's office, halfway through a game, the newspaper on the desk which was folded to reveal the crossword.

Steel saw the pleasure in the man's eyes because he suddenly had someone to play with. The trouble was, Steel was finding this game interesting as well.

'OK, doc. What you got?' Steel said with a broad grin.

Chapter 56

Samara had gotten most of the files on the people in Foster's team. Not that she expected anything less than another fantastic rush job. Samara wondered if their wager of who buys dinner next had anything to do with it. The files were detailed. Showing everything from where a person was born to how much they had in their bank accounts. Flicking through the files, Samrara wondered. How much of her life was on display to anyone who might dare to investigate her? The files in her possession just proved that each side knew more about the other than they would care to admit.

She settled down with the files with the bottle of champagne she had gotten on Steel's tab.

Most of the files read as she thought they would. They came from good homes, excellent schools, never been in trouble with the police, somewhat boring people on paper, but she never believed print anyway. If these people were that good, nine times out of ten times, their whole world was fabricated. Good people have good thoughts. However, agencies such as the CIA, FSB, MI6, or Mossad, for that matter, need good people who could think like bad people – a thief to catch a thief as it were.

Samara read on, file after file. Nothing stood out to her. She looked over at the rest of the files on the laptop. She figured that she'd gone through only half of the forty records, and she felt depressed at the thought of going through the rest.

Samara took another hit from the champagne glass and grasped the next file. As she pulled it across, the one underneath snagged and fell to the ground. The pages spilt on the carpet.

Samara cursed. She had to move out of her comfortable spot to pick up the pages. She rolled out of her place on the couch and began she reach for the file. She stopped, her hand stretched out, ready to pick up the next piece of paper, but something had caught her eye. Samara noticed the front sheet of the file, which contained a photograph and personal details.

She sat down hard and stared at the picture. Her expression fell away, and a look of contempt took its place.

'What are you doing working for the CIA. You son of a bitch?' Her words, bitter and full of contempt. Samara stood up and headed for the door. As she went, she pulled out her cell and pressed the speed-dial number.

'Kane, how quickly can you get me to Victoria on Gozo? and bring something big and heavy. Your car will do.'

Chapter 57

Outside the small desert village, the wind howled like a wounded beast from the depths of hell. The sand storm was just about to hit, but the Master's people were safe from the unforgiving weather. They had been there for many years and had endured more than the weather. Every man, woman and child was a fighter. They would endure, even after he had gone.

The Master sat quietly in his room while the noise of the oncoming storm hammered outside. He was undisturbed by it. If anything, the Master found the sound of utter chaos and destruction soothing.

The Master smiled as he opened the link on his computer. A blackened silhouette of a figure. It was the man only known as *HE who* appeared on the video chat screen. The Master found the name curious, but then people called him the Master, so who was he to judge?

The man known as *HE* was responsible for the operation, the funding, the plans, the information on the target. It was *HE* who had procured the C-130 aircraft and left it in Tunisia for them.

The Master did not know what *HE*'s ultimate goal was, and the Master knew not to ask.

The man known as *HE* had delivered.

And now, so must the Master.

The target would be in place, ready for the conference, just as *HE* had said. It had seemed like years since the man known as *HE* had contacted the Master. He had warned the Master of an attack on his people, troops had stormed the old camp looking for them, but they had found only innocent farmers. The forces had killed the farmers and their livestock.

From that moment a relationship had been born, *HE* would give details on convoys and areas of interest. It was as if *HE* had been sent to the Master from the Gods. But the one known only as *HE* never asked for anything in return. *HE* would just call and lead the Master to something that helped their cause.

And then one day, *HE* called and told the Master of a Great Plan, a way to hurt the people of the West.

Everyone would know their name – Hisan Khashabiun – and tremble.

The plan had taken months to get ready, but most of it had already been done by the one known as *HE*. The Master had been suspicious at first, at how much had already been organised. But then, it had saved them time in the long run and money – to which the master had little compared to this new investor. *HE* had promised fire, blood and revenge. The Master had asked what *HE* was getting out of it? *HE* had simply replied, 'an opening.'

And now, the time was almost upon them.

Their time was almost at hand.

'I see your people are in place, and everything is going to plan,' said an electronically distorted voice. The silhouette didn't move. The Master looked shocked for a moment. How did this man know all these things, had his eyes everywhere like he claimed?

'Yes, that is correct. We will be ready to go at the appointed hour. I have a whisper of a man causing trouble on the island, a friend of one of the CIA agents-'The Master said.

'This is not your concern. He will be taken care of. At the moment, he is serving a purpose. If I were you, I would be more worried about the attack going off without a hitch.'

The man known as *HE* was calm, and if anything – emotionless. The voice was constant and unrattled by the Master's report.

The Master nodded as if displaying his understanding.

But the man known as *HE* was right. The cop on Malta was no concern of the Master's, not yet anyway. But he had a feeling that this man was trouble, and trouble had a way of getting in the way.

'This will be our last communication until after the mission. It is… safer that way. Make sure your people are ready and where they are meant to be on Friday. I want no mistakes. Do you understand?' growled the voice, sending a shiver down the Master's spine.

There was something about that voice that felt – evil.

To some, the Master was a powerful man, he was God-like, and he feared nothing or no man. But this mysterious *HE* was something different entirely. *HE* was no mere mortal. The resources he had given were bountiful, more than the Master could have dreamt.

'We will be ready,' the Master said. His voice was stern and commanding, but inside he feared what was to come. *HE* had given everything but asked for nothing in return. That was…not yet. Deep down, the Master feared the price *HE* would be asked for was his very soul. The screen turned black as the signal was lost. The Master pushed down the laptop's top as if concerned. He could still be seen through the small camera. The Master sighed profoundly and smiled to himself. They were ready, and nothing could stop them.

Later that day, Aamir had spoken with the Master, and all was well. Once again, Aamir had proven to the Master he was worthy. Soon, if Aamir survived, he would be given a proper command of his own.

Aamir had known that the Master was getting orders from a higher power, but he did not care. It was the Master he followed.

Everything was in place.

They were ready.

Aamir closed the lid of the laptop and stood up. He touched the roof of his mouth with his tongue; it could not have been drier. He walked over to a small refrigerator and pulled out a can of soda, and stood with the door open. The air was cold and soothing. The light illuminated a portion of the room.

Aamir reluctantly closed the refrigerator door and headed towards another room at the back.

The room was small with a boarded-up window. It had possibly been a small workshop a long time ago. The walls were painted dark beige, and brown smears went at angles and up and down. Almost as if someone had used a paintbrush to put them on with. It smelt of old walls, and old wood, and cigarettes, and body odour. The small room was now a radio room, or as they liked to call it, The Communications Centre. A man sat with a headset perched on one ear, and the other ear was free, so he could hear what was going on in the house. He was a big, heavyset man with a long beard and a large scar down his left cheek that went from his fringe to his chin. Somehow, it only scratched past his eye, missing it altogether. He had fought many battles with many brothers before finding these. But now he was older and wiser, smart enough to make him a cautious man, one who like to be able to hear someone coming as well as listening to the broadcasts.

He had been with the group almost as long as the Master. But the Master had a name, even if it was just *the Master*. The big man had no name. Or, at least, not one worth telling anyone else.

They did not need to know it.

'*If you have no name, you have no past, future. But most of all, no one can rat you out,*' was the man's philosophy.

However, Aamir wanted people to know his name. He wished for people to tremble at the very mention. Soon he would go down in history; soon, everyone would know his name.

Far across the water in the camp in Tunisia, The Master's turned to his aide, a young man in his twenties, tall and slim with an aristocratic bearing. The assistant pulled out the Master's chair and watched his master rise. The Master was tall, around six-three in height, white cotton robes concealed his slim build by giving the illusion of bulk to the shoulders. But his head remained uncovered, so his bearded face was there for all to see. The aide bowed as the Master walked past him.

'Come, boy; we have much to do. The time of history and revenge is almost upon us,' the Master said in a bellowing voice.

The aid smiled and bowed again.

'Yes, my Master, revenge is upon us.' The two men disappeared into another part of the building and began to start with the plan. Outside, the sandstorm was like a hungry predator, hitting the small village hard, devouring anything that the people had failed to secure.

Howling as it went.

Chapter 58

Darkness had fallen, and the small towns and villages of Gozo sparkled like fireflies in a field. High above, a million stars twinkled and blinked in a cloudless sky. In Victoria's city, people wandered the brightly lit streets quaint city, sitting in restaurants or frequenting cafes' bars. Tourists sauntered dreamily, taking in the warmth of the night and the big sky above. The aroma from the restaurants filled the air, along with music and laughter. But Steel had chosen not to stay in Victoria. Instead, he'd found a hotel in a town called Xewkija. he had found it online and booked the rooms straight away. It seemed a decent place, best of all, out of the way of the main road and the capital city of Victoria. If someone was looking for him, they would no doubt suspect he would be there.

Steel had worked on the theory that if they got over to the island too late, they could at least go straight to the hotel, then go to the morgue in the morning. After which, they'd then head off to Azure Window.

In front of the hotel was a large plaza. Which was caught in the middle of two main roads. The Triq San Bert, which ran along the local church's side, and the hotel's side, and the Pjazza Sang Wann Battista – which later became the Triq L- Indipendenza. Steel figured the plaza wasn't just used as a parking area. It was probably a market place, possibly at Christmas, or perhaps there was a Sunday market? The local church – The Rotunda St. Johns Baptist church, was to the left of the hotel, and directly in front were bars and restaurants. Down from the restaurant and bar was the local police station. Steel took particular note of a tall stone cross, which had probably stood there since the late sixteen-hundreds.

Steel stepped out of the cab that had brought him there and paid the man plus a decent tip. As Steel watched the taxi disappear, he could hear a television. They were watching football in one of the bars.

Steel found Stan. He was sitting outside a restaurant opposite their hotel. Stan was tucking into a juicy steak, along with a cold beer.

Steel sat but said nothing at first. Stan was unable to because of the food in his mouth. A waitress came over and gave Steel a menu card, but he just pointed to Stan's plate and smiled.

'I'll have what he's having,' Steel said.

The waitress smiled back and headed back to the kitchen. The beer did not take long coming, and Steel thanked her and watched her walk away. All the while, he could not help but think about poor Lucy.

What the hell was she doing out there at that time of night?

Tomorrow they'd head out to Azure Window nice and early, but for now, Steel was hungry and tired. The last decent meal he'd had seemed like days ago, and his stomach was giving him a painful reminder.

Steel watched Stan happily tucking into a thick rib-eye and using a Merlot to wash it down.

'You seem to be settling in,' Steel said curiously, picking up the bottle and examined it. The steak wasn't cheap, and he figured the wine was a good forty bucks a bottle. Stan just smiled with juices flowing down his chin from a broad, exhilarated smile. 'I take it this is part of your expenses?' Steel asked, waving at the waitress to bring another glass. She smiled shyly and scampered away.

'I figured why not, I'm on vacation,' Stan laughed.

Steel smiled back. 'Yeah, why not? After all, I did drag you here. Kicking and screaming,' Steel said, taking the glass from the waitress and filling his glass. Steel watched as Stan eat. He remembered seeing a film about the old kings and their banquets and how they used to eat the meat from the bone – long before table manners were apparently invented.

Stan bleched loudly and undid his belt notches.

'More mead, my Lord?' Steel said sarcastically. Stan replied with a dumbfounded look. 'Never mind,' Steel grinned and took a sip from the wine.

It did not take long for the steak to arrive. It was a large slab of meat that filled the plate with a side of mixed vegetables. Steel closed his eyes and inhaled the scent of the meal.

He hoped it smelt like it tasted – excellent.

They drank more wine and talked – or rather, Steel listened to Stan babble about the old days.

The hours drew on, and Steel could feel the fatigue of the day and the wine kicking in. He looked at his watch, 20:15. Making Steel wonder how long Stan had been drinking. Had he started as soon as he got to the hotel? The man was utterly intoxicated.

Steel had asked if he could settle up later as they stayed at the hotel across the road, and he would be over from breakfast. The waitress smiled and said it wouldn't be a trouble, and if he needed anything, she would be more than happy to bring it over – any time of night.

Steel was tempted to leave Stan nursing a fresh bottle of beer he'd just gotten and head over to the hotel. Steel needed a shower and to get a couple of hours of sleep. He knew that he needed to be fit for the next day. Especially if something happened. If the last couple of days had taught Steel anything, it was – be ready for anything.

Steel stood and watched Stan for a moment, wondering how much the old guy had drunk? And knowing that he would be doing most of the driving in the morning while Stan recovered. Which Steel didn't mind? It would be a good exercise, plus Steel had always found he learnt more about a route as the driver than as the passenger.

'I'm off to bed, see you early tomorrow,' Steel said.

'Come on one, have one more, what are you…a lightweight?' Stan laughed.

'When I need to be,' Steel shrugged. 'Besides, someone needs to keep a clear head for tomorrow,' Steel smiled.

He knew the state Stan was going to be in the next morning – unless, of course, he ended up in the local police station first, which was in spitting distance of the restaurant.

'Tomorrow…I will be – wait – what's happening tomorrow?' Stan said, then fell off his chair. The beer bottle hit the concrete but somehow did not smash.

Steel picked up Stan and slung the man over his shoulder in a fireman's carry. Stan was surprisingly light, but he stank from lack of deodorant, too many cigarettes and too much booze.

Steel carried the drunken driver over to the hotel and made his way to the front desk, hoping that Stan had actually gotten the rooms before hitting the bar.

He had.

Rooms 21 and 23. Steel naturally had gotten the balcony suite, and Stan was across the hall. Steel checked himself in and got his key. Stan's had fallen out of his pocket, relieving Steel of a body search he did not want to do. The fireman's carry was bad enough.

Steel took the stairs to the first floor and located Stan's rooms, and opened the door. Stan was still singing – or what could be counted as singing. The room was small but comfortable with a double bed, an ensuite bathroom, a desk and a chair. A small flat-screen tv sat on the desk, along with some flyers about what to do on the island. It was quaint and more than enough for Stan.

Steel dumped Stan on his bed and toss the man's room key beside him, then closed the door and headed back down to the lobby to arrange an early call for Stan at five in the morning.

They wouldn't be leaving until around seven. Still, Steel needed him to have a clear-headed for the drive, and maybe there was a small element of payback for the meal he had witnessed Stan devour.

Steel made his way to his room. He checked the flat circular white plastic tag on the room key for the number and then the small brass tag on the door.

Room 23 was a little to the right of Stan's, and Steel just hoped it was far enough away not to hear his snoring.

The room was homely with what appeared to be antique furniture. Steel suspected they were well-made reproductions. Opposite the bed was a green cloth couch, and next to that was a desk with a 30-inch flatscreen. The floor was covered with white marble tiles, and the walls were coated with a cappuccino colour. There was a blue rug on either side of the bed with soft cotton sheets and a blue throw blanket at the foot.

Steel sat on the bed to test the mattress's firmness and found it comfortable, not the usual stiff bed that left him feeling he'd spent the entire night on the floor. Steel unpacked his small bag and placed his toiletries in the bathroom. It was spacious. Grey tiles covered the floor and continued halfway up the wall. The other half was the white walls like the rest of the suite. It was clean and modern, and that shower looked very inviting.

Steel put his spare clothes away then headed to his window to check out what sort of view they had given him. The balcony was nothing more than a metal guard on the other side of the double doors. He smiled as he looked down at the street that lay between the parking lot and the restaurant. He was precisely where he'd asked to be when he pre-booked the room. Before they had left Malta, Steel had researched the hotels in Gozo, particularly those near the hotel and, more importantly, those that were out of the way but had direct access to the main road. The hotel he was in had ticked all the boxes. He had checked its location using a satellite view on a web page. He had noted the exits in and out of the square. Another reason he chose it was that they were utterly confined despite the road in and out.

If someone was to try something, the small road would have to be clear of traffic or parked cars. And with a police station nearby, such an ambush would be suicide for any would-be attackers.

Steel looked down at the plaza. Despite the only thing to see were the car park and the restaurant, it was a view and not the wall of someone's house – which was precisely what Steel had made sure Stan had gotten.

Steel stared at the restaurant and then the road. The road went down between the buildings, then narrowed to one lane, and even then, parked cars would make a concertina, Forcing cars to slow. But more importantly, it led straight to the main Triq L-lmgarr road and onto the north, to San Lorenz and the Azure Window.

Samara had checked with the Grand Excelsior Hotel's front desk to see if Steel had made any reservations or asked about Gozo's hotels. She was about to either try and bribe the man behind the desk or tell him she was Steel's fiancé. As it turned out, Steel had left a phoned through and left a message that if Samara asked, she should be given the details.

The tall, broad shoulder concierge smiled and passed over a card with the hotel's address in Victoria that Steel had booked.

Samara did not know whether to be impressed or annoyed at Steel. She took the card and made her way to the main entrance. Samara had only waited five minutes before one of her colleagues pulled up in a new black Mitsubishi Outlander.

'Thank you, brother,' Samara said, looking over to Kane.

'What's going on? Did your boyfriend get kidnapped again?' Kane asked with a broad grin.

'I just need the car. I won't ask you to come,' Samara said. Kane returned her suggestion with a grievous look.

'No, Samara, I'll drive you. That way, I can hopefully prevent either one of you from getting into trouble. Besides, I've seen you drive,' His playful mockery caused her to smile.

Samara did not smile. She just got into the passenger side and buckled up. Her thoughts were of Steel and the ex-fixer she had uncovered. The man who now called himself Calver was on the islands, and that meant trouble.

It also explained a lot.

It was why they were interested in her and not Steel. All they knew about Steel was his appearance of being some wealthy Lord playing detective.

Steel was here because of Lucy Foster's death.

She, on the other hand, was seeking out a terror threat.

'What's this all about, Samara?' Kane asked. Samara showed him the photograph of Calver. 'You got to be kidding me, wasn't this one of bastards you said used to work for Mossad before they got canned for making money on the side? ' Samara nodded silently. 'but Clive Denton, on Malta – now?' A look of anger crossed his face; then it turned to determination. The engine roared, and the tires spat dust as the Kane floored the gas pedal.

The Mitsubishi Outlander headed out of Valletta and headed north towards the ferry port at Cirkewwa. The beams from the LED headlights cut through the blackness of the evening, giving him a clear view of the oncoming street.

Kane had driven in the Dakar, and other rallies, including the Isle of Man, so this was child's play. Unfortunately, all his skills were no match for other drivers on single track roads and through towns who drove slowly and had no concept of *hurry up*.

They arrived in time to see the eight-fifteen evening ferry leave the port. Samara bared her teeth in anger. She knew Kane had gotten them there as fast as possible, but Fate was against them. Samara knew the next one would leave in forty-five minutes. Samara sighed her acceptance of the situation and turned to Kane.

'Coffee?' Samara said.

'Ah – why not,' Kane said. 'There's nothing we could do until the next ferry arrives,' Kane said.'Do they have cake?' Kane asked, just as Samara was just getting out the passenger door.

Samara laughed and shook her head. Kane was the only man she knew who could eat like a trucker and still keep his figure.

'So, what's the story with you and Steel?' he said as they walked over together.

'Nothing. We're just working the same case, that's all,' Samara said defensively.

'Mmmh, yeah, right,' Kane said with a teasing smile. Samara slapped her brother on the arm playfully.

They killed time with lots of coffee, and Kane found his cake before the ferry returned. They boarded and in the large seating area by the time the motors kicked in, and they were away. The sun was just setting as they left the harbour. The sky was ablaze with deep orange and grey smudges of cloud against the ochre backdrop. The ocean had turned to gold as the sun melting into it.

Samara looked out of the window at the glistening lights from Malta behind them. It was a beautiful sight, for sure. It also meant they would be driving unfamiliar roads in the dark. Samara checked the navigation app on her phone to see if it was working. The red dot on the map moved slowly across the blue background.

   Samara was glad Kane was driving. It would give her time to plan, something she could not do well if she had to concentrate on the roads. She was good at multi-tasking, but sometimes her mind drifted. Samara looked at the map and sighed with relief. There was only one road to Victoria, and Steel was somewhere on that road. The question was? Who else knew she was coming, and did they know Steel was already there?

Chapter 59

Across from John Steel's hotel, people had started to gather by the restaurant. Greeting one another with ' Hey's' and 'tajjeb li narak.' The music's sound grew louder. It was apparent to Steel that the people here ate late, rather than the typical fed by six and in pyjamas by nine that he had been accustomed to as a child.

The night air was warm despite being almost nine o'clock, but the cool breeze took the edge off the heat. Steel stool quietly, holding a glass of local red wine he had gotten from the hotel bar. He listened to the city's sound – which was more of a gentle hum – instead of the vibrant sound of a city like New York or London. Those sounded busy. This was almost soothing. Steel had seen of Victoria. He figured most of the traffic was made up of people on foot, heading to local bars or the other restaurants nearby. Steel had a feeling of tranquillity as he enjoying the dry, fruity wine. A subtle hint of wood and berries filled his nostrils. Steel closed his eyes and breathed in the fresh air. For a moment, he was tempted to just stare out of the window and take in the moment.

But he had work to do.

Steel finished off the rest of the wine and walked over to the complimentary tea and coffee facilities. Taking one of the free bottles of water, he poured the liquid into the kettle and switched it on.

Steel had relaxed and recharged his batteries slightly, with a pleasant evening – despite Stan's display of being a complete neanderthal. The food and wine had been excellent, as was the service.

But now, Steel had work to do before he could consider getting any sleep. He would need buckets of coffee and a clear head, knowing he would be sifting through his research and the new information from the medical examiner.

Steel had to be ready for the trip to Azure Window. He needed to know all the facts. Where they discovered Lucy's body and where they thought she had jumped. What else was nearby? And where was Lucy's film shot?

Steel looked over to the small desk in the right-hand corner of the room. The top of the antique-looking was full with a crockery based lamp, a telephone, and an information folder provided by the hotel. Next to the desk was an ornately carved wooden chair. It was made from the same wood and had the same style as the desk, with maroon coloured padding on the seat and backrest. The wood was dark like rosewood and polished to a shine.

The chair was pulled out to accommodate Steel's black canvas bag with outside pockets. Inside he had all the files on Lucy's case on his tablet along with some paper files he had managed to made up or picked up on the way.

The central part of the bag held Steel's laptop. The outer pockets had the loading cables and charges for his equipment.

He picked up the bag and unpacked the items onto the polished wooden top of the desk.

Since he had arrived in Malta, he'd not had a chance to sit down to sit and think, put things into perspective. His simple case had turned into something far more sinister and intriguing.

Steel thought about Foster's advice – which he had almost made an order.

'Find who did this to my little girl, Steel. You make them pay… every last one of them,' Foster had said. Something had puzzled him about that statement '…every last one of them.'

How many people did Foster think was involved? Foster had asked Steel to concentrate on Lucy's death and not to worry about the software, and that's precisely what he planned to do. This software was housed in a secure facility, and from what Foster had explained, it was better guarded than Fort Knox.

Steel was there for Lucy, and like Foster had said, if their interests crossed paths, all the better. The kettle clicked off, Steel poured in the water into a cup and opened one of the all-in-one sachets. The power hit the water and turned it a caramel brown. He preferred black coffee, but beggars could not be choosers. It was coffee, and that's all he needed.

Steel pulled out the chair and sat at the desk. The wood creaked. He picked up the porcelain coffee cup and took a sip from the boiling hot liquid.

After arranging the files in order, he pulled out a large notebook he'd bought at the ferry shop and got to work.

First, he wrote down the police report's details on when they had discovered Lucy's body.

- *Body in Blue Hole.*
- *Mr and Mrs Fabri while walking the dog.*
- *6 am.*
- *The body later identified as Lucy Foster.*

Steel tapped the end of the ballpoint pen over his writing. Something was bothering him.

He re-read Burlo's report.

It was the sergeant who had identified the body. Burlo had admitted to knowing Lucy and Marcus – how did he put it? An old friend of the family?

So it would explain how he had known it was her. Plus, Lucy's face hadn't been damaged too much by the waves. Even Steel had recognised her from her photos he had found in her apartment.

The body of a female found in Blue Hole.

Steel re-read what he had written. Again something felt off, but I did not know why. Steel opened up his computer and got a birds-eye view of the area. The Blue Hole was a body of water encased by a weathered rock enclosure used by drivers. Its sky-blue waters stood out from their limestone surroundings. Steel re-read the report; *The victim may have fallen from Azure Window, and body carried into the pool due to rough seas.*

Steel looked closer at the image but could not confirm from the small picture if it was possible. He looked at a photo of the sight on a beautiful clear day, not a stormy night.

He took another sip from the coffee and placed it back on the table. Steel drew a giant question mark next to the incident report.

Tomorrow he'd have a better idea.

For now – Steel needed to press on.

The medical examiner placed the time of death between one and three in the morning. Water temperatures made an approximate TOD impossible to determine for now. Awaiting a more thorough report later.

The victim sustained internal haemorrhaging; the left leg has compounded fractures.

The right arm dislocated at the socket.

There was server head trauma, which included massive damage to the frontal bone and zygomatic bone. The nasal region also suffered damage.

Several ribs had been broken, and skin lacerations possibly due to impacts on hard surfaces.

Steel made a note of the injuries and the time.

The more Steel read, the angrier he became. He wanted to get up to Azure Window as soon as possible.

He took another sip from the cooling coffee. He wished it was dawn, and they were heading away already. Steel looked at the satellite picture of the area again. Something was nagging at him, but he did not know what. All he had was an Arial, so he had no propper image of the area. Steel knew he had to see the scene for himself to get the right perspective. To get the lay of the land.

To see what obstacles a person may face. To walk the walk, get an idea in his head of what may have happened that night.

At twenty-past-nine, John Steel received a text from Samara. He was still going through the reports and satellite images of Gozo to plot routes from Azure Window to possible places where Lucy had taken the photographs. His bed was covered with files, maps he had bought at the airport and his tablet. Steel was on his third coffee. He'd had enough wine. He needed a clear head to think.

Which hotel are you in? The text message had read.

Steel smiled and replied. That's when he stopped and looked at the cell phone he had just placed back on the desk.

Steel thought for a moment. He had left the address with the concierge back at the Excelsior, just if she needed to get hold of him. But Steel knew then that she wasn't randomly asking for the address – she was there – on Gozo.

What had changed? What new bit of information was so important she had come to the island to pass it on? He doubted that she missed him so much she could not keep away. He had expected her to be doing background checks on Foster's team.

Perhaps that was it?

If she had found something, why didn't she just call to let him know? Whatever it was, it must be bad news.

That excited him.

Because information like that could push this whole investigation forwards – possibly both of them, despite Foster's assurance the business at the blockhouse was none of his affairs.

Steel tapped the desk with his fingers, making tiny drumming sounds of indecision.

If she had sent a message asking which hotel it was, that meant she was close.

Steel stood up and headed for the small mini-bar but found it to be an empty fridge. He closed his eyes as he felt the crisp air coming from the open door. Begrudgingly, he closed the door and grabbed his wallet and room key. He needed something to drink for when Samara got there. A couple of cans of something cold would be enough, possibly a bottle of wine.

Steel returned to his room with a bottle of champagne and a couple of bottles of water. As he tucked the water into the fridge. Steel smiled as he heard the screech of tyres and the slamming of the doors.

'This is going to be a long night,' he said. Steel went into the bathroom and took out the coloured HUD contact lenses. The last thing he needed was for Samara to see how his eyes really looked. Carefully, he slipped them in but did not activate them using the cell phone or watch. For now, they were just ordinary, blue contact lenses.

Suspecting that she was going to be angry or worried about something when she got there. Steel hadn't made a reservation for her simply because he did not expect her to come over. Steel thought about going downstairs to see if there were any rooms available. But a knock on his door stopped him.

Steel opened the door and found Samara and Kane stood there. Both looked equally unhappy. Samara seemed pissed about whatever she had discovered, and Steel figured Kane hadn't eaten yet.

'Oh, this is going to be a very long night,' Steel said, as Samara barged into the room. Steel just stood there and looked at Kane waiting in the hallway.

'Evening,' Steel said to Kane.

'Evening,' Kane said, an awkward tone in his voice.

'The restaurant across the road, I've…' Steel looked over at Samara and smiled. '… got a tab,' Steel said.

Kane did not reply. He did not need any more information. He was halfway down the stairs by the time Steel had closed his door.

'You really should pack a lunch for him or have treats in the car,' Steel smiled as he walked over to the small fridge.'Drink?' Steel picked out the bottle of champagne. Samara smiled and grabbed for water.

'So,' Steel said. 'How bad is it?'

'Not sure, but it could be very bad.'

Steel nodded silently as he closed the door. He sat on the bed, and she followed. Samara looked into the blue contact lensed eyes. They were warm and welcoming.

'What did the coroner say?' Samara asked as she took a sip from the water.

'He doesn't think it was an accident, but he's not going to hang his career on it.'

'What now?' Samara asked. She was beginning to calm down, relax.

'I'm off to Azure Window tomorrow. Check out where they found Lucy. I need to see it first-hand. Photographs are no good. I need to get a feel for the place,' Steel said. 'And you?'

'I have – a problem to find, make sure that it isn't one,' Samara answered, her words drawn out as if she was unsure about something.

'Well, that's cryptic,' he said. Samara looked up at Steel and smiled softly.

'No more than half the shit you spill to me.' Steel shrugged.

'I better see about getting you a room,' Steel said as he went to stand up. She touched his hand and gazed into his eyes.

'Maybe later, maybe, not at all,' Samara grabbed Steel's shirt and pulled him down as she leant back onto the bed. Their lips met. Steel kissed her hard. She kissed him back. Her hands pushed off his shirt and clawed into his back with her fingers. Steel's had one hand nestled on the back of her head while the other fought with tiny buttons of her blouse. As he undid the last one, he pushed the cloth to the side, revealing her breasts and the black lace bra. Samara pulled Steel close, biting his neck and earlobes. Steel eased her onto her back and watched as she took off her trousers and underwear, just as he took off the rest of his clothes. Samara smiled at the sight of his tight muscular frame, even his scars. She lay there naked, her tanned skin glistened with sweat. She was beautiful with her athletic form and welcoming eyes. Steel eased himself down on top of her, but she pushed him onto his back and straddled him. Samara ground her hips into his, her tight butt rubbed against his upper thighs. She leant back and placed her hands on his legs for support as her movements became more intense. Steel reached up and took her breasts in his hands. She was warm and soft and in control.

Steel had no idea why she was really here, she could have just phoned, but he was just glad she came.

Samara ground herself against him, ridding him like a rodeo horse. She leant forwards, her hands grabbing his shoulders. Steel pushed upwards with his hips. Suddenly, they both cried out with release and collapsed side by side, panting. Steel looked over at Samara, she had her eyes closed, her breathing heavy, but she wore a smile. Steel laid back onto the bed, the sound of paper under his back. He had forgotten to clear the bed, but he did not care. He'd worry about it later. For now, he was in bed with an amazing woman.

The rest could wait.

Chapter 60

Foster had worked late. For him, there wasn't much reason to rush home. Lucy was gone, and Martha and Kim were back in the States, and he had nothing but microwave meals in the freezer and cold beers in the fridge to look forward to. And after Steel had explained what had happened to him and Samara, Foster was even less willing to venture home. Foster had phoned with a locksmith and general handyman he knew to go to the house and make it secure. The last thing Foster needed right now was more uninvited guests.

The night shift had come on hours ago, and he had remained. Foster had tried phoning Edward Bryce, but it went straight to voicemail. The guy lived alone and was probably resting.

But Foster had a bad feeling.

It was another hour before Foster decided to head home. He considered stopping off at Bryce's place. A quick detour to make sure the guy was OK. Foster looked down at his watch, nearly eleven. Foster shook off the idea but made a mental note to go around before work the next morning.

Foster walked along the long stretch of corridor. The light from the fluorescent tubes above and the sterile paintwork made everything bright and clinical. It was like being in a hospital or a laboratory.

Foster started his routine of bidding everyone a good night. Which consisted of a friendly wave as he wandered past the partition windows of each section.

Most did not respond. They were too busy or just did not care.

Foster stopped at the elevator and pressed the call button. The round button glowed white, and Foster waited. There was no display to show the floor. The designers probably did not think it necessary. After all, who the hell wanted to be reminded about how far deep in the earth you were?

Foster started to hum to himself, a little tune he had heard earlier but did not know where – or what it was.

He stepped alone into the steel box and watched the door close. It wasn't an unpleasant place to be, there were red marble tiles on the floor, and the side was half wood, and the top was a brass metal polished so much it was like a mirror. Foster did not mind being alone. In fact, at that moment, he preferred it. He wasn't in the mood for polite conversation.

Foster sighed as he looked at his reflection in the metal. He looked tired and worn down. He wondered how Steel was getting on.

Foster leant against the cold metal, and his mind drifted. He started to remember times with Lucy. He remembered their last words together. There had been an argument over something trivial. Her last words had been unkind. 'I hate you,' she had said before, slamming down the phone. A tear ran down Foster's cheek.

Foster took out his cell phone. He hadn't checked his voice messages for a while.

He had been too busy. The truth was he was beginning to think that he was always 'too busy.' He had become too busy for his family.

He wondered when he had become *that* person. Before, his family always came first, and now – he had no idea. Sure, he was still the loving husband and father, but not like before.

He missed the old him.

Maybe when this was all over, he would ask for a transfer.

He looked at the display and saw there was a voice mail from Lucy. Received the day she had died. How had he missed it? But then it had been lost in a sea of other voice messages, mostly from other people or the States. Foster would average twenty messages a day from various people. Most of the time, it was like spam mail on his computer.

As he looked at the caller id and the date, a shiver ran down his spine.

Foster started to hammer at the main lobby button, like hitting it would make the elevator work faster. As the buttons began to light up, showing the floors, his feet began to dance with agitation. Mumbling to himself that the thing should move more swiftly. The doors slid open, and Foster rushed for the door, knowing there was no chance of a cell reception within the building due to the signal dampeners.

Foster ran to the pool house, which was near the Blockhouse entrance building and paused. His finger poised over the play button. Almost frightened to hear the recording. What if her actual last words were even more hurtful, they would be stored forever for him to listen to? But what if she phoned to make up, to arrange time together, the time he would never spend with her?

Foster tapped the cell phone against his head and cried. He gazed back at the phone and swallowed hard.

Then with a shaking index finger, he pressed the button.

There was a clicking sound, then a faint background noise.

Foster swallowed again. His mouth was dry.

'Hi Daddy, it's me…I'm sorry…' Lucy's voice was sad but not distressed. A simple, heartfelt apology.

Dropping to his knees, Foster screamed in anguish. Embassy staff and Marines looked on, but no one interfered. They had heard of his loss, and they left the man to greave.

Foster picked himself up and wiped away the tears. He smiled gently. Relieved that the message Lucy had sent was something he could treasure.

Foster looked at his watch and wondered how Steel was getting on in his investigation.

Had he found anything?

Foster smiled to himself. If Steel were anything like he used to be, he'd probably be sat somewhere sipping champagne with some woman he'd just met in a bar. He never judged Steel for it. Foster understood. In fact, he was one of the few people who knew everything from Steel's past, and not just the stuff that could be found on the internet. How a team of invaders had butchered his family during a welcome home party. How his wife had died while he held her. He understood why Steel never committed to a relationship after that. *If you're alone, nobody can use someone you love against you.* Foster remembered Steel's words clearly. At the time, he pitied Steel and his choice to remain alone.

But now.

Now – he really understood.

Foster stood for a moment. Taking a cigarette from the packet with his teeth and using his Zippo lighter to ignite the tobacco.

It was quiet, less for the usual sound of nearby traffic. It was, for a better word – tranquil.

The usual guards stood watch of the inside while another two made their patrol of the perimeter. Foster sucked in the fresh warm air. Foster looked at his watch again. It was getting late, and the pizza restaurant would be closing soon. Foster could almost taste the fresh salami and melted cheese as he walked to his car. A quiet night with the Baseball games he had missed on one of the internet sports channels and a large pizza was all he had on his mind.

Foster clicked the button on his electronic key fob to open his car. Suddenly, a blinding flash followed by a powerful blast wave knocked Foster and the nearby soldiers from their feet. The ground heaved, car alarms wailed. Windows smashed, nearby cars began to burn. Foster had been thrown through the air and landed on the hood and windshield of a vehicle seven feet from where he'd stood. His bleeding body, still and lifeless. The guards scrambled off the ground and ran back to the cover of the embassy. They kept low as red hot shrapnel flew in indiscriminate directions. They all watched from the safe distance as the red and orange flames billowed from the wreck that was once Foster's Range Rover.

Alarms whirred, and soldiers ran to their posts. Armed with M4 assault rifles and wearing body armour. A squad of soldiers rushed to Foster in single file. Each man covering left, right and forward arcs. The soldier at the back of the column, turning to cover the rear every five steps.

They moved fluidly, each man knowing where he or she should be covering, each soldier with a designated arc of fire.

First man front.

Second man-front-left.

Third man-front-right.

It was a well oiled and professional team. There was no sound – no verbal orders. When there were commands, they were given by hand signal.

Smooth and professional.

The gates were shut and locked. Emergency lights came on, lighting up the grounds like a football stadium. Soldiers poured out with sniffer dogs, each one having its own designated areas.

The embassy on lockdown.

Nothing in, nothing out.

The sound of Blackhawk helicopters circled overhead. Two circled the perimeter using night vision and thermal. A third hovered just off from the scene, close enough, so its powerful floodlight illuminating the area. Still, far enough away, so the downdraft did not affect the scene of the explosion. Medics from the embassy's infirmary raced towards Foster carrying medical bags, and two others pushed a gurney.

Flashes of blue lit up the area from light bars, and the glow of orange covered reflected off surfaces. The monstrous plume of heat and smoke radiated from the remnants of Foster's car.

From a window, a figure watched.

The figure's features were hidden by the reflection of the carnage below. There was an electric buzz from a cell phone. The watcher took a device from an inside pocket and answered the call.

'Everything is in place – now it's your turn.' The voice of the Master. The voice of anger and impatience.

'You'll get everything you have ever wanted,' said the figure before closing down the cell and placing it back in the pocket.

The figure stood and watched.

Not moving, just observing.

The beam of the helicopter searchlight lit up the side of the building as it moved position. Suddenly the corridors were illuminated – and the figure was gone.

The Master placed his cell phone down on the desk and stood up. Twelve men stood before him, each dressed in USAF flight uniforms.

'Soon, my brothers, we will strike fear into the hearts of our enemies. Soon everyone will know our name and tremble.' The Master said. 'After so much planning, the day was almost upon us.

Tomorrow we head for the transport – and our destiny.' The men burst into a roar of chants and yells of jubilation. The Master smiled at the sight of his flock.

A nod to his aide and the man ushered the others to leave. The noise of their war cries dulled as they left the room.

'It seems all is going well, Master,' the aide said, pouring a cup of green tea for his lord.

'Yes. Soon we shall have our revenge and our greatest hour,' the Master's tone was soft as he picked up the photograph of his family. 'Soon, they will weep for their lost ones.'

The aide laid the glass cup down on the table and waited. The Master picked up the cup and took a small sip from the hot beverage.

'You may go. Take time for yourself. I wish to be alone with my thoughts tonight,' the Master said.

The aide bowed and left the dimly lit room going directly to his small room where he locked his door. Breathing out a heavy sigh of relief, he walked to a small dresser and pulled out one of the top smaller drawers, and carried it to his bed. Quickly he turned it upside down. Socks and underwear fell out onto the thin mattress. On the underside was a cell phone taped to the wood. The aide pulled the device from its hiding spot and turned it on. He waited until it had booted up, then pressed a number on the contacts list.

He waited while it rang.

After a few moments, a voice answered with a simple 'Yes.'

The aide waited for a moment. His nerves shot to pieces. 'They're all ready to go here. Tango is due to leave the location tomorrow. Estimated time of departure to be confirmed.' The aide ended the call and taped the cell back to the wood. He packed his clothes away, then placed the drawer back.

The aide was sweating hard. He did not know what was making him sweat more. The warmth of the tiny room, or the fact if someone heard his transmission, he was as good as dead.

Chapter 61

Steel woke early. Too early, even for the usual chorus of bird song. Not that he had really slept. The sky was dark purple with a blanket of stars. Steel looked up at the enormous full moon, and a shiver ran down his spine. The moon had been a bright white the night before; now, it was a dark orange. So dark, it was almost blood red.

Steel thought back to his old nanny, who had been from Scandinavia. A tall blonde woman with broad shoulders and hands like a lumberjack. Despite the fact she had been in her fifties when she was his caregiver, she was still a handsome woman. She had shown Steel pictures of when she was younger. By all accounts, she could have been a model by today's standards. But she lived on a farm and had to work with the rest of the family. She would often tell him the tales of Beowulf, Thor, Draugen and many other stories. He remembered her looking up at the blood moons and whisper something to herself, almost as if it was a secret prayer. She had told him once that legends said whenever there was a blood moon, blood had been spilt that night. Steel smiled and shook off the superstition.

Steel decided not to shower. He would do that later when Samara was awake. For now, he needed fresh air. Her surprise visit had taken up most of the night, so he hadn't had time to read through the files and notes properly.

He figured, taking a quick walk around the block before breakfast would give him the quiet to think. He also needed coffee, but that wasn't going to happen. He doubted that anywhere was open to serve it.

Steel headed for the door, pulling on his jacket as he went, looking over at Samara, who had taken over the bed. It was a mass of arms, legs, and bedcovers. Steel smiled at the sight of her. She had woken in the night and put on one of his shirts that were long enough to act as a nightshirt. They had talked for a while. Steel had told her what he had found at the morgue and about Foster. Samara told Steel that while she was doing the personnel check, she had come across someone who used to work for Mossad until he left under a cloud.

'We knew him as Clive Denton,' Samara explained. 'But now, he works for the CIA, where he goes by the name James Calver.' She spoke with a hint of surprise. 'He's good, but he is also – how do you say – as slippery as a fish?'

Steel smiled at her attempt at the phrase. But it also made him wonder. How the background checks not come up with anything? John Steel picked up his cell phone and sent a quick text to London.

Run Background check on one Clive Denton, a.k.a. James Calver.

Steel put down the phone then Samara had told him about what had happened and why the Denton had been expelled from Mossad and the country.

They had talked for a while, drank wine then, made love again. He had gone to the couch, telling her it was best as he wasn't a sound sleeper. As he had settled himself on the couch, he had also seen her stuff something under the pillow. He did not see exactly what, but he guessed it was her gun.

The couch had been comfortable enough, but then he'd learnt to sleep anywhere. If you can sleep in a C-130 transport, you can pretty much sleep anywhere, he thought to himself with a smile. Besides, Steel knew he was going to wake up early. He always did. It wasn't insomnia, more the fact he could function quite well, even after a couple of hours of sleep. It wasn't a thing he had learnt in the army – it was his nature. It was something he had always done, even as a child. The guy's in his squad loved him because they could get more shut-eye – not that that ever happened because they never got time to rest that much.

It was always one dumbass mission after the next. The more successful they became, the more chance his team got picked for the next mission. But that was the army way. If you were terrible at something, you did it and kept doing it until you got it right. If you were excellent at something, you always got picked.

So, Steel liked being the grey man, the guy who no one noticed. But he got to be very good at that. But someone had noticed.

Steel had put Kane in with Stan – not that Stan would mind, but Steel felt a little sorry for Kane. Not knowing how long they would be on the island, Steel made a mental note to reserve another two rooms later in the day if necessary.

It could be hours – or it could be days. There was no way of knowing.

Steel still could not believe she had come all that way to warn him about a former fixer. A phone call would have been enough, but he felt there was more to it than what she was telling him.

However, this was the last thing on his mind. This fixer wasn't a problem at that moment, and if it had anything to do with the embassy, it wasn't his problem. He was there for one reason. To find out what happened to Lucy.

He had a job to do. Unfortunately, the investigation up to this point had been fraught with distractions he did not need and one he really was glad about. But Steel was doing this investigation, not for Foster, not even for himself – but for Lucy. If it was foul play, Steel wanted to know.

Steel slipped out quietly, letting the door click behind him. He thought they'd all have breakfast around seven o'clock before they set off to the crime scene. This Azure Window held the answers, and he would find them. Even if it meant ripping the island apart to find them.

Steel gazed up at the sky. It was still a dark blue, with no signs of the dawn. The shimmering stars were bright, and the moon had lost its red shroud, leaving it massive and glowed intensely. Steel looked at the streets bathed in shadow, the crisp breeze carrying down from the other street. Steel began to think.

He closed his eyes.

Suddenly he knew what he had to do, but someone wasn't going to be happy about it.

Stan lay as if he had been thrown onto the bed from a great height. His arms and legs looked contorted; his head lay at an angle. His mouth wide open, with a pool of fresh drool stretching from it.

Suddenly he opened one eye.

His dreams of supermodels and him sat on a yacht in Msida Marina faded as he had a feeling, a feeling he wasn't alone. Stan searched the blackness with one eye open. He dared not move. Stan's visions of models soon became a big angry thief with a lust to shut up witnesses.

Stan thought about sliding onto the floor and leopard crawling to the door. He had no weapons and had no desire for conflict, knowing he would come off worse. Stan began to move, thinking his movements were stealthy and unnoticed.

That was until Stan miss judged the fall to the floor and landed with a sickening thud.

'Stan, what the bloody hell are you doing, man?' said Steel, trying to contain himself from laughing. Steel reached over from his seated position and turned on the small lamp on the desk. Stan just lay for a moment, both angry and confused.

'What are you doing in my room…wait?' Stan said, looking around quickly. 'How did you get in my room?' Stan said as he stood up and brushed himself off.

'You took your phone off the hook and refused to answer your early morning call. Get dressed – we're late,' Steel said, standing up and heading for the door. Stan looked at his watch and grumbled at the hour.

'It's not even five in the morning. Why are we going so early?' Stan said.

'I want to see Azure Window in the dark,' Steel said, with a severe look. 'You got five minutes, or… you can head back to Malta?'

Steel had everything planned out.

Places – timings.

Steel was on the job and in the zone. From this point, everything had to go as he planned. And he would do it with or without Stan.

Stan stood up and held his head and smacked his tongue against the roof of his mouth. The fury texture was unpleasant, to say the least. There was a sudden, loud grunt, followed by a loud throaty snore. Stan turned to see a man on his couch.

'Who the bloody hell is this? How did he get in my room,' Stan bellowed.

'Be quiet,' Steel whispered, clamping a hand over Stan's mouth until he shut up. 'He and Samara came in last night. They are here to help.' Stan went to say something, but Steel forced his hand down over Stan's mouth once again. 'just get your arse downstairs, I'm leaving in five minutes, and don't wake him up,' Steel said and closed the door behind him. Stan stared at the door and the man on the couch.

'Well, this is bloody great.'

It took Stan all of ten minutes to get downstairs; he found Steel waiting with two coffees that Steel had gotten from a local bakery. Stan smiled awkwardly and took a cup from Steel.

'So, where am I driving you to?' Stan said, blowing on the fresh brew to cool it down slightly.

'You're not driving, not in that state anyway,' Steel said, watching Stan rock from side to side.

'Hey, only I drive my cab,' Stan argued, then burped loudly.

'Good, that means I didn't rent this in vain then.' Steel walked out with Stan in close pursuit. Parked on the road was a brand new BMW four-by-four. The black paint and tinted windows sparkled under the street lights. Stan's mouth fell open in excitement.

'You rented a brand new BMW X6?' Stan said, then stopped suddenly and looked at his watch. 'when did you rent this? Nothin is open?' Stan said, puzzled.

'I have contacts. They dropped it off early this morning while you were still snoring,' Steel exclaimed.

'Nice of them to led you this mota,' Stan grinned, thinking about the soft leather of the seats.

'No,' Steel said, shaking his head. 'we need something that blends in,' Steel said. He glared at Stan as if he was an idiot. 'I got this.' Steel smiled wickedly and walked over to an old Army 110 Land Rover and got in. Stan's mouth remained open, this time in horror. The extended wheel-based version with back seats went along the sides rather than straight across, the safari version. It was military green, and someone had tinted the back windows. A long black plastic exhaust snorkel snaked from the engine compartment, making river crossings less troublesome. It was a massive beast of a vehicle with thick off-road tyres.

'Where did you find this? A museum?' Stan cried out with disappointment. Looking over the dents and touched-up paintwork. Steel just smiled and started the engine.

'No, I'd made some calls while you were sleeping, they do…shall we say last-minute deliveries, and, we need to blend in. Besides, when this gets trashed, it won't hurt as much,' Steel said.

Stan thought about it, then gave a quick nod of understanding, sat on the passenger seat.

'Wait! What do you mean *when* it gets trashed?' but Stan's words were drowned out by the roar of the engine as Steel pressed hard on the gas.

The roads were dark and lonely. Steel was almost sad; he could not see the landscape around him. There was a single road heading towards San Lawrenz. Either side was fields of blackness through which wound the Triq l-Ghab road. The 110 Defender lights were like candles in a jam jar compared to a modern car, but they did well enough.

The ride was rough due to solid shocks and lack of power steering, but Steel was in his element. He knew he could have had any vehicle, but this was more nostalgic. In his years with the British Army, he'd experienced rides in many vehicles. Most of the time, they had cut down Land Rover Defenders equipped with Browning heavy machine guns and Minimi light machine guns.

Steel powered down the twisting road towards San Lawrenz. The tires are gripping the used roads as he cornered the hairpins. Steel could feel the exhilaration of the night drive – the thrill of not knowing what either side of him or how the darkened road traversed before him.

It took an hour to reach the last small town before the road turned left and travelled south towards the coast. The sun hadn't broken the horizon, but the sky was getting lighter. The dark purple held streaks of blazing orange. Steel could now make out the road and the countryside around them.

The trail began to incline, and the view grew more spectacular. The road swung west, and Steel noticed to his left a massive limestone quarry. Its cut sides made it look like an accident ruin.

Stan did not pay it much heed. To Steel, it was beautiful but commonplace. He must have seen it a thousand times, and the novelty had worn off, but he had to admit, seeing it with dawn colours gave it a whole new beauty.

As the sun rose, it draped everything with a living orange, making the landscape appear on fire. They drove down a track to a car park, large enough for coaches and buses to make their drop-offs.

Steel parked the ageing vehicle next to a small church path that sat off to the parking area's side. To his right was the divers training area, which was a large pool of water called Inland Sea. The pool spilt out into the ocean via a tunnel the weather and ocean had carved out. Surrounding the pool was several buildings and jetties for small crafts for the drivers.

The drop-off point's circular road held a central parking area for cars and a limestone building, the education centre and a restaurant. The car park was virtually empty but for a couple of vehicles that held people who had stayed over to see the sunset.

Steel got out of the Land Rover and walked over to where the parking area finished, and the natural rock started. Steel was still dark enough to get the image he needed but light enough to make out the loose ground. He looked over the Mediterranean sea. The waves crashed angrily. The surrounding area before the ocean looked like the landscape of another world. Steel had to admit in this light it had a savage beauty about it.

Stan joined him as they watched the sun break the horizon. Steel looked over to a high craggy cliff face.

'So, this is the Azure Window?' Steel said, looking over the impressive view.

'Yes…I mean, no. That is, well, that was,' Stan said, pointing to the cliff face.

Steel gazed over at the twenty-eight-metre wonder and gasped. 'How do we get up there?' Steel said, searching for a path.

'Follow me,' Stan said, sucking in a breath.

Steel followed the cabbie up towards a small church; The kappella Sant' Anna. It was a small smooth-sided building with very few windows from what he could see. The entrance was a single heavy wooden door, with Venetian-style stone handrails on either side of the steps.

There was a small bell tower above the entrance. It reminded Steel of the churches he had seen in the old spaghetti westerns.

To the church's right were sets of old steps, little more than pieces of long stone rammed into the earth, to the left flat open ground that led to another cliff face.

'What's over there?' Steel asked.

'The Blue Hole, divers, use it a lot,' Stan said.

Steel nodded. He noted its position and followed Stan, who was heading for the church's right steps. The stone steps become sparser until they had disappeared entirely, leaving just a dusty path. Steel noticed all the way up from the church. There were arrows spray-painted on the ground, showing the direction up – possibly a safety feature for unknowing tourists. He started to notice signs tell the public there was no entry. Steel figure that the mass number of people venturing on top of the once-grand archway did not help much with its demise. Steel started to feel saddened by the loss. He had spent so much time going around the world he had never really stopped to appreciate the landmarks, and there was one he had missed. He wasn't sure whether he was getting old or sentimental, or both.

Steel got halfway to the top of the hill and stopped.

He was a fit guy, but the change of altitude and the rough terrain made him stop and look around.

'What's up?' Stan said. He was breathing like a locomotive and resting his hands on his knees, welcoming the quick break.

'Where's the Blue Hole from here?' Steel asked.

'Over there,' Stan pointed down and across towards the ocean. At least twenty feet from where they stood.

Steel walked over to where Stan had indicated. It was an overhang that gave a perfect view of where the Azure Window had once been and the Blue Hole. Steel took out a small pocket camera and took several photos of the pool and the Azure Window's remains. Then, Steel headed back to the path and took more photographs. Stan lit up a cigarette and inhaled deeply, watching Steel as he took more pictures and made notes on his phone.

Steel clicked an icon on his cell and opened up the crime scene photos he had saved to the device. Steel looked around and tried matching each picture with the place, always moving to see if there was one.

Stan walked back to the parking lot and found a place to sit while Steel looked for what he needed.

Steel looked at the Blue Hole picture where the report said Lucy's body had been discovered and walked over to a large flat area that sat just above the pool. A safe place for tourists to take in the view. Steel looked down at the ocean-filled hole, took photos for himself, and then jotted observations in a notebook app on his cell.

Steel walked back towards Stan, who was still smoking.

'What's up?' Stan asked, noting Steel's confused expression.

Steel looked back at the view but said nothing. All Steel saw were puzzles, questions. He took out his phone again and searched for the film Lucy had made. Steel handed the phone to Stan, then pressed play.

'Any idea where this is?' Steel asked, knowing it was a long shot the half-drunk cabbie would be able to see anything, let alone recognise a view from a home movie. Stan brought the device closer and squinted at the image.

'I am not sure, but it could be Hondoq Bay,' Stan said, shrugging.

'Really… Hotdog Bay?' Steel said disbelievingly.

'Not Hotdog – it's Hondoq,' Stan almost annoyed at Steel's mispronunciation.

'OK, sorry. So where is this Hondoq Bay, and what's so special about it?' Steel said.

Stan thought for a moment as if checking the route in his head, then looked up and smiled.

'I don't know what's so important about it, but I do know where it is,' Stan said excitedly. Stan stood up quickly and turned with enthusiasm, the passion that died when he saw the beat-up Land Rover.

'OK, Stan, which way,' Steel said. Grinning as he walked past the disappointed cabbie.

'We need to drive back to Victoria, I'll tell you the way, and you can drop me off. I feel the need to stay drunk after riding in this tub,' Stan said.

Steel laughed and got in the driver's seat. As Stan crawled in, Steel started the engine. The turbocharged engine gave a choking cough and a whir like a massive hairdryer, then the engine roared to life.

'Oh good, there's no aircon in here,' Stan noted as he watched the sun come up, and the sky became a light blue. He could already feel the heat warming his face.

'Mr Steel?'

'Yes, Stan.'

'You ain't paying me enough for this shit,' Stan said, trying to get comfortable.

Steel laughed and swung the car back onto the road and back up the way they came.

Chapter 62

Clive Denton – A.K.A – JamesCalver arrived at the embassy early, only to find an increased security level. At first, he thought it was to do with the new software, then he saw the emergency services spread out near where he and his colleagues usually parked. There was the usual guard checking identifications, along with two Marines in full tactical gear standing guard.

'What happened?' Calver asked as he handed over his plastic-covered ID.

'Someone blew up Agent Foster's car last night. The camp's been on alert since late last night.'

Calver checked his cell phone.

No new messages.

He blew out a sigh of relief. The last thing he needed was to find a missed call from the night before for him to come in.

'Oh God, that's...that's terrible,' Calver said, sounding like he meant it. In truth, Foster being dead would make Calver's life less stressful. The guy was like a pit bull. With Foster gone, Calver could move about more freely. Calver could carry on without feeling Foster's eyes permanently watching his every move. But then, he wouldn't wish anyone dead, possibly hospitalised for a spell, but never dead.

'Was he badly hurt?' Calver asked, hoping for the bad news.

The guard shrugged and passed back Calver's ID. 'Can't say, nobody tells us nothin' here. All I can say is his car was blown apart,' said the guard.

Calver took back his ID and waited for the guard to raise the barrier. As Calver drove past, he gave a quick wave salute and went to the park.

The main parking area had been cordoned off at the crime scene, with armed guards and FBI forensic teams, which meant he had to drive past the vast parking lot. Then past the older parking lot with the solar panel roofs, between two larger buildings and towards the pool house. Calver wasn't sure if he was early or the rest of the staff had been encouraged to park elsewhere. He knew there was a parking area outside by the park. That would have been used by the embassy staff more than the hive staff. Others may have been informed to carpool due to the lockdown and the minimum allowance to vehicles. The parking lot that was now a crime scene was new. Years before, the US Embassy had been given permission to place the lot in a grassed area. It had taken nearly a year to complete and had provided jobs for that year.

Calver thought it strange nobody questioned why they needed so much space. But he figured they had gotten away with the deception by putting a helipad sign in the centre. This wasn't just a parking lot but an emergency helipad.

Calver looked around. The cordon had made parking difficult because the cars – that were possibly from the night shift had filled most of the allotted space. He drove slowly while looking around.

Searching for that elusive parking spot.

The sunrise had bathed everything in deep orange. Making the scene look surreal. The bright glow from the sun reflected in the passing cars' windscreens, causing a blinding deep umber strobe effect. Calver had kept his window down, letting in the crisp morning air. But instead of the usual scent of fresh, unspoilt air, he was greeted with a pungent odour of burnt metal, rubber, oil, petrol and asphalt. He coughed and pressed the button to close the window, hoping to keep out the stench, but the cars ventilation system just sucked up the air from outside and pumped it inside. Calver struggled with the controls and turned it off completely, figuring he would rather cook than suffer the stink.

As he wound through the chicane of badly parked vehicles, he caught the first glimpse of the scene. Calver could not see it before due to the surrounding cars and armed soldiers, but now he had an unhindered view.

His mouth fell open as he stared at the carnage.

The sight of Foster's car froze his heart.

The Land Rover had been sixteen feet long and six feet high – now it was just a crumped hunk of twisted metal with angry-looking claws. The twisted metal mass looked as if some giant beast had chewed it up and spat it out. The ground underneath had bubbled asphalt where the intense heat had melted it.

Calver slowed his vehicle to a crawl. It looked like something from a war film. He stared with wide – despairing eyes at several tangled pieces of metal. Next to them were the same yellow markers – 102 and 105 stood out against the bright yellow in bold black letters.

He looked over at what was once a wheel. The rubber of the tyre was gone – melted away, the alloy was dented and deformed. Calver figured this one had been close to the device as it had been thrown upwards, not sideways. It had landed around thirty feet from the vehicle, a kind of straight up-straight down momentum – this was 106. On the other side, another wheel had embedded itself into the door of a car, which had been a good fifteen feet away – this was 67.

Those vehicles which were unlucky enough to be parked nearest Foster's car had been blown on their sides. Others had landed on their roofs. Some had been ignited by the blast or burning debris – the luckier ones who had been slightly further only had smashed windscreens and side windows. Nearby trees stood scorched with blackened bark, and leafless branches reached skywards as if they were in pain. Several of the solar panels on the old parking spaces had shattered.

Suddenly all of Calver's evil thoughts towards Foster melted.

The sight of the mangled mess that used to be Foster's car made Calver rethink. He then thought of Foster's family. They were just getting over losing the eldest daughter – and now this.

Calver pulled up to the pool house and found a spot next to a VW flatbed truck and three Ford pickups. Some of the cars parked there had smashed windscreens of dents, but Calver figured that they had nothing to do with the incident unless they had been discounted and told to move.

Calver imaged that the forensic teams had worked from the outside inwards. A way of eliminating what was relevant and what was not. To ensure they weren't adding to their workload with something that could have been done days or months ago and had nothing to do with the crime scene.

He parked, then switched off the engine, listening to the *tick-tick-tick* as all the pistons and gears settled and the engine started to cool.

He sat there for a moment.

Things were getting out of hand.

He was paid to do a job, and he was doing it, but the murder – or from what the guard said, attempted murder of a section chief? That was something else, and he did not care how much they were paying him. He was done. Calver realised if these people are willing to do that to someone for just snooping around, what would they do to a loose end which was ultimately what he'd be?

Calver walked past the pool and over to the main building. As he drew near, he saw two Marines in full tactical gear stood either side of the door. The guard on the right asked for Calver's ID.

His ID was on a neck chain that had tiny bat signals all over it. Calver pulled the ID from over his head and showed the laminated identification. The guy looked at the picture and then at Calver.

This guy was a professional. None of the usual 'yeah that will do' quick check. The guy even raised it up to see if the picture and the man matched.

Calver did not know whether to be impressed or scared.

The soldier gave Calver his ID back and waved him inside.

Nobody spoke.

There was no 'Good morning sir' or 'how are we today'. The soldier had his game face on. Someone had committed an act of terror on American soil, and that made him and everyone else in the place mad because, in the soldier's eyes, they had let it happen. They had not been vigilant enough.

Calver said nothing.

The last thing he needed to do was to create animosity. After all, he was just an employee. He wasn't really one of them – he was only a citizen.

Calver entered the building in silence. He was looking forward to getting in and sitting down, and drinking coffee. He slipped his lanyard back over his head and looked up.

Calver stopped dead.

He felt his heart skip a beat in terror.

They're near the entrance were three portable metal detectors and a handful of Marines checking bags as people went through.

Calver froze to the spot.

He could feel people looking at him, eyes glaring with suspicion. He wanted to turn and run out of the door. Run to his car and speed away, but that would make him seem guilty of something.

Pulling out his cell phone Calver, pretended to take a call. He turned and headed back towards the door with a finger in his free ear – as if he could not hear over the noise of the lobby.

Calver carried on his fake phone call until safely out of view. He was cursing the situation as he walked over to the pool house. He did not know whether to be angry, scared – or both.

The bombing could not have come at a worse time. Calver patted the inside pocket of his jacket; as if reassuring himself, something was still there. He paced up and down, hoping a plan would form. Calver stopped and sat down on a small wall, and took out his cell phone.

Calver pressed the speed-dial and waited.

He heard the electronic chirp of the ring tone emanate from the cell phones speaker. He was starting to sweat – more from fear than the heat. He would have to phone it through. All Calver could hope for was that they would understand.

Calver and Bryce had everything planned out. Calver would make the exchange, and Bryce would be ready with the boat. After the swap, they would contact the man who had hired them then disappear wealthy people.

It was a simple plan.

They were assured nothing could go wrong. But it had, and now Calver was left hanging on a phone waiting for instructions. After tomorrow it would be too late. The exchange had to be today. Calver went to cancel the call when a man's voice answered.

'What is it?' said a man. His voice was deep, emotionless, accentless.

'We got problems,' Calver said. 'someone set off a bomb in the parking lot last night. We're all getting patted down. They've even got metal detectors,' Calver explained.

'So?' said the voice. 'I paid you to get it done, so get it done,' the voice was cold.

'You said it would be easy, a straight swap. This is messed up, man. No way it can be done now,' Calver said, trying not to shout down the phone.

'Was anyone killed?'

'Foster, I think, not sure, nobody's saying anything,' Calver explained.

'Why did they target Foster?' asked the voice. For the first time in the conversation, there was an emotion – puzzlement.

'I don't know, because he's an asshole, I don't know. Look, I can't get past the guards with this thing, not with this level of security,' Calver explained. There was silence for a moment. Then the sound of voices in the background, as if the man was on the phone with someone else.

'If you complete the job, we're willing to give you double for your trouble,' said the voice calmly.

Calver paused. For a brief second, he was about to rant and scream, telling the voice it was impossible.

But he did not.

He stood for a moment and thought. The whole perspective had changed. Now they were offering double the price. What they had offered to start with was insane, but double?

Calver smiled to himself. His mind on the money, not the task at hand. The phone went dead, and Calver just stood, grinning to himself, almost pleased with his negotiation skills. Then he stopped and turned to face the building, and the smile fell from his face. How the hell was he going to get fake System Drive into the building without anyone noticing? Calver started to sweat again - the realisation that he was a dead man walking if this went wrong.

Chapter 63

Samara ran the shower, playing with the hot and cold to get the perfect temperature. She could hear the noise from the kettle as the elements started to heat up, and the water gave a gentle *blup-blup-blup* as bubbles began to form and rise.

Samara began to gather her clothes together, laying them out on the bed, ready to slip them on once she was done with the shower. There was a gentle electronic buzz from her cell phone. She watched it dance across the bedside table. It acted and sounded like a may bug that had landed on its back. Samara picked it up and tapped the touch screen to check the message.

'Crap,' she said, then sent back a quick reply before closing down the cell. She placed the phone back on the bedside cabinet and went into the bathroom to shower. The noise from the kettle was getting louder.

He had knocked, and she had replied with a friendly 'Come in, Kane.' Kane found Samara dressed and cleaning her gun when he entered the room.

She was just putting the top slide back onto the weapon as he took a seat on the couch. He did not ask her how she knew it was him at the door. It would have been a futile question. He thought it was the way he walked, the sound of his footsteps, or it could be something as simple as he was the only one there. Why would anyone else feel the need to knock on her door so early in the morning – it was too early for housekeeping.

There was a silent pause while Samara placed the pistol back into its holster in the small of her back, and Kane got up to make himself a drink. He'd seen the steam rising from the lip and figured it had just boiled. Samara picked up her cup and took a sip from her freshly made coffee.

'Where's Steel now?' Kane said while he tore open a sachet with his teeth and poured the powder into a cup.

'Azure Window, he is working on the girl's death for Foster. He has nothing to do with my investigation by all accounts,' she said.

Kane nodded as he filled the cup with hot water. 'What time did he leave?'

'Five-ish, at a guess.'

Kane rechecked his watch. 'That's plenty of time to get there, have a good look around, and come back.'

Samara nodded. 'But if he found a witness, maybe he's getting more information.'

'Seems unlikely he'd find a witness the police haven't.'

'Depends how hard they tried.' She looked up at her brother. 'I told him about Calver.'

Kane nodded as he stirred the beverage with a cheap, flat aluminium spoon.

'In truth, we shouldn't have left Malta,' Samara said.

Kane shot her a confused look.

'Why not?' Kane said as he walked over to the couch. He stopped and changed direction. He was now walking over to her. Samara stood with her cell phone in her hand. The display screen held vertically so he could see it better. The message was in bold writing, black script on a white backdrop speech box.

Kane peered at the text. It was from one of Samara's colleague back in Malta.

Kane's mouth fell open as he read it.

'Crap,' he said.

'That's what I said when I read it,' she said with a shrug. The message was about Foster and the car bomb at the Embassy.

'That's not good…' Kane said. 'I vote you tell Steel,' he shrugged.

'Wow, thanks. Some brother you are.' she laughed.

'So, what do you want on your headstone?' Kane said, with a mocking look.

'You know, I sometimes wish I was an only child,' she said.

'Oh, yeah, then who would you get to drive you in the middle of the night?' he said.

Samara said nothing. She just smiled while she sent Steel a message.

Where are you? We need to talk.

She placed the cell onto the bed and looked over to Kane, who was sipping his coffee. Samara looked over to the cell phone as it gave a two-note burst, signalling a received message.

She picked up the device and opened the post.

It was Steel. He had sent the name of the place he and Stan were heading to.

'Kane, we have to leave, now,' Samara said. Kane looked up, his lips pursed together, ready to take a sip of the hot coffee.

'What's wrong?' he said.

'I think Steel may be heading into trouble,' she said.

Kane put down the cup and stood up.

'Right then, where are we going?' he said.

Samara smiled.

Kane could be a pain in the ass, but he was as loyal as a puppy. Kane just took whatever she said on faith. He never questioned why.

'Hondoq Bay. We're going to Hondoq Bay,' she said.

Kane saw the worried look on her face. He knew that look, and now he was feeling scared.

Kane opened the vehicle and started the engine. Simultaneously, Samara programmed the car's built-in navigation system, typed in the *HONDOQ BAY*. After a few moments, the device had plotted the best route. They were ready to go.

Kane pressed the gas pedal, and the Land Rover's V8 growled. There was a blowing sound as the turbo kicked in. They set off, heading south. The navigation system had said it was a fifteen-minute journey. They would have to get back onto the Triq L-lmgarr road and head east.

As they hit the exit and were on the Triq L-lmgarr road, the sun was high in the cloudless sky, and they were driving directly into it. The tinted glass made everything look green from the bright, unyielding sun. Kane was cursing the lack of cloud cover, squinting as cars approached, the blazing sun reflecting off their polished skins. Even though he had his sunglasses on, the glare was unbearable – and often dangerous, blinding him. They had thought about stopping, pulling over and waiting, but it wouldn't have made a difference. It would be hours before the sun moved into a more desirable location. They did not have hours – possible, neither did Steel.

Calver headed back inside the main building. He knew he had to do something, but what? He could not get the image of Foster's burnt-out wreck of a car out of his mind. A black, mangled mass of twisted metal. When Calver had seen it, he was convinced Foster was dead.

How could anyone survive such a blast?

Even if he wasn't close to it, the shock wave would have been tremendous, not to mention the flying shrapnel. The nearby vehicles were a testament to that. Windows had been blown out, and tyre marks on the ground showed the blast had forced cars sideways. Foster's car's engine block ended up in a field next to the embassy wall.

But why?

Killing Foster served no purpose, especially to Calver's real employers. In fact, it would have been the last thing they wanted because of the resulting added security measures. A lockdown would have – had - made it virtually impossible to carry out the actions he was being paid to do. Besides, if they wanted Foster dead, why did not they just do it when he was home. Car bomb in his driveway.

BOOM.

Game over.

But this? It made no sense.

Calver looked back at the queue of people waiting to pass through the heightened security. He could not help wonder who would want this lockdown to happen, but he had nothing. One thing was sure; they could not find Calver with the system drive had in his pocket, or it would be all over.

That's when it hit him. Someone wanted the disk drive found. He was just a patsy.

Calver froze on the spot.

His job was to exchange the drive that held the new software.

Or was it?

What if he was supposed to get caught swapping them over?

Calver turned and walked out of the main door.

He was in trouble, and there was only one thing to do. Find this friend of Foster's and tell him everything, or else he was a dead man.

Chapter 64

It was almost eight o'clock when the old Land Rover drove past the town of Borg Gharib. The Triq Borg Gharib took them on the outskirts of the town and but through it – which Steel was thankful for. The last thing he needed was more hold-ups. He looked at the map on his tablet to try and get his bearings. Making sure he was, in fact, heading in the right direction. The map was in the satellite setting, so he could see the buildings and surrounding area. It also informed him of places of interest, restaurants, gas stations, even a quad hire place. The map automatically changed the scale to a zoomed-in view so he could see his driving route better. That when he realised that south of the town was Mgarr harbour where they had arrived the evening before.

The Land Rover was now heading East on the Triq ll Kuncizzjoni Road. The town and ferry port behind them.

The sun was still rising, warming the air, and there was a crisp morning breeze blowing in from the ocean. It wouldn't last. By midday, the sun would be high above the island, and according to the weather, it would be a beautiful day.

For Steel, that meant damned hot and uncomfortable.

The Triq ll Kuncizzjoni road took them through open scenery. Steel fought his way through the narrow streets of Qala, the town bursting with bars and restaurants. He tried to avoid tour buses, taxis and the general population. Steel had noticed that all the houses on Gozo and Malta were of similar style. As if some law insisted they had to be built that way to preserve the aesthetic. They left the town still heading east. They passed more open ground, fields, and stone walls.

It had all become quite generic.

Steel came to a T-junction. A tall pillar with a stone cross on it formed an exciting roundabout.

'You been here before?' Steel asked. Stan squinted as he peered through the windscreen and shook his head.

'Nope, sorry, not seen this place before. I normally stick to the normal touristy spots.' Steel nodded. It was feasible the cabby had never been here before, but his response had been a bit too quick for Steel's liking. Steel put it down to Stan's hangover, which he well deserved.

Steel checked the online map on his tablet and turned right, south. He followed the road with his finger until he reached his location. Luckily this stretch of road was quiet for the moment, giving him time to plot his course.

Steel drove on while Stan slept off his condition. Steel took note of a cemetery they had just driven past, which backs onto open fields and farmland.

The scenery was breathtaking. The only annoyance, however, was Stan snoring loudly on the back seat.

The day was getting hot and stifling. The old truck had no air conditioning, only windows. Steel was beginning to wish he had rented the BMW or at least something that wasn't from the last century – or saw action in the second world war.

As they passed the cemetery, Steel saw the ocean to the right ahead. With a sharp turn, the road began to snake downwards towards the bay. Only stone walls would prevent a crash into a field. In places, the driving was made more difficult by parked, possibly abandoned, cars.

The view grew more spectacular with the suns warm glow of the ocean. Large yachts glinted, reflecting the sun's rays off their polished skins. All Steel wanted to do was park up and take in the view.

To do nothing just – gaze out and enjoy the moment.

Stan snorted and coughed on the back seat, then there was silence. Steel was beginning to hope that was the cabbie's final breath. Then Stan started snoring again like a bull elephant in pain. Sleeping off his over-indulgence the night before.

Steel was beginning to wonder why he had thought he needed the man in the first place – so far, he'd done nothing. He was useless as a guide. He had done none of the driving. All he had done was drink and complain. But there was something about Stan, something that made his gut twinge. What was that saying? 'Keep your friends close, but dodgy bastards closer.' Or at least that was Steel's interpretation.

Steel glanced over at a set of tall ancient-looking stones on top of a hillside. He figured nobody would find Stan's body there for a while. The birds, animals and bugs would make short work of him.

Steel smiled, shaking off the idea as he drove on, taking in what little view the drive would allow him. Soon they were on the open road and heading East. There were plenty of smaller roads, but he did not have time to turn back if they failed him. Steel stuck with the main roads and the map from his tablet.

Each bend tested Steel's metal, as well as the vehicle's brakes. In the distance, Steel could see the deep blue of the ocean was getting closer.

They were nearly there.

Hondoq Bay was made up of a concrete jetty, a lengthy parking area, and a café with wooden booths.

There were adverts for ice creams and beer and food items, all readily available over the counter. Giant umbrellas displayed beer company logos and offered shade to the people in the booths. There was a beach area nearby and a couple of old disused buildings, possibly from the British involvement on the island.

Steel pulled into a parking area near a café with a view. The car park was full of cars and boats. Across from the café was an old building that looked as if it had been a school long ago. A large steel mashed fence surrounded it – to keep out curious eyes.

Steel parked up next to a red VW camper and turned off the engine. He sat for a moment, took off the lid of his water bottle and took a mouthful. Steel swilled the liquid around inside his mouth like mouthwash – trying to rehydrate his dry mouth then swallowed the water.

He finished the rest of the bottle, tossed the empty bottle behind him, striking Stan gently on the forehead. Stan just snorted and brushed his nose with his hand as if a fly had landed on it. Steel smiled and shook his head in disbelief.

Picking up his cell phone, Steel began to search for the video Lucy had made. He was hoping this would lead to something, and he wasn't wrong about this place – about the island, and it turned out to be just a big waste of time.

As the video started, Steel stepped out of the car, his gaze switched between the home movie and the view before him, hoping to match the two images. Steel swung around and looked back at the road they had driven down.

Steel looked at the image on the screen once more and closed one eye. Hoping the restricted view would help. He looked back at the landscape before him, it was the right landscape, but the angle was wrong – and so was the surrounding area. The screen's image hadn't been taken in the parking area. There were too much foliage and rocks. The parking area was virtually flat.

Steel moved back up the road and tried again. He raised the cell phone and viewed the image both on the screen and the landscape. He looked around at the nearby untouched patches of land. The ground was full of loose stones and jagged rocks, knee-high bushes and cactus, there were old stone walls, there were buildings in the background – and the parking lot was in the distance, not directly in front of them.

Lucy had stood in a field next to a cliff face and not in a concrete parking lot.

He was in the wrong place.

Steel froze the image on the phone that held the small island in the backdrop and noted vital points; the contours rose and fell at specific locations, the ancient watchtower in the distance. Steel moved away from the car, passed the old building and on to a narrow road. Excited, Steel rushed forwards, the feeling he was close to something spurring him on.

The two images began to come together.

He stopped and compared the two views, but something was wrong. Steel had the correct area, but it had been shot from some sort of field. Steel ran the video for more clues to the location.

Suddenly he hit pause.

He noted the unique features of the senary on the screen. There was a road below and an old limestone wall to the left. Steel turned to look up the hill and smiled.

'Oh, there you are,' he said, spotting the limestone boundary wall. Quickly, Steel made his way up the rough terrain, orienteering the image of the phone to where he was. Stopping only to move the phone around until the two views matched.

'OK,' Steel said. 'This is the spot.' He started to look around, searching the area for the reason why this video had been so dangerous that Brad had to hide it.

Steel had to admit that it was a fantastic view. But, found nothing worth killing the kid or anyone else over. He replayed the video and watched intently for anything that stood out. He was about to give in when something caught his eye. It was a Zodiac – an inflatable craft used by the special forces.

Steel cursed himself for not noticing it before.

Steel had been too busy concentrating on the location at not what was on the ocean. He'd probably seen the boat but hadn't registered what it was. Because all he could see was Brad posing and the surrounding area – the sea had only come into view a couple of times. So, Steel had discounted it.

Steel re-played the clip but enhanced the picture. The boat was moving fast and had several passengers aboard – all of whom were wearing black. Steel tried to enhance the image to get a better look at the men, but the picture just got more pixellated as he zoomed in. Definitely not good enough to make faces.

Steel followed their route until they went off-screen. He pressed the screen, which created a viewing bar, a quick way of rewinding or fast-forwarding to the clip's point. He moved the highlighted dot to the left. The images moved quickly, making it almost comical to watch.

Then he let the button go and rewatched the scene again.

He did this several times.

Rewinding and watching.

Rewinding and watching.

He wasn't interested in the craft or the people in it. But he was interested in which direction they had come from, and more importantly, where they were going.

Steel checked the footage once more and followed the course of the boat. Plotting the movement of the vessel in relation to where he was standing. Steel moved down, along a dirt track and towards where the craft had disappeared in the footage. He followed the small path down until he came to a hidden jetty.

Steel placed the cell back into his pocket before making his way down to the wharf. He wanted to check for any indication that a craft had been there recently.

As he walked down, Steel figured that this was mostly used by people with large yachts, sending their small boats to shore to get supplies.

Steel saw families sunbathing nearby. It was a great spot if you wanted to get away from the bustle of a regular beach, quiet and secluded.

The jetty was a simple construction, a length of concrete with rusty steel tie-off points. In fact, there wasn't anything that struck Steel as being out of the ordinary. Steel looked back at the people basking in the hot sun. If these men had landed here, someone would have noticed. A Zodiac isn't exactly a tiny craft at fifteen feet long. Seven men would stand out considering what they were all wearing black jeans and jackets. The seventh man would naturally have taken the boat back after dropping the others off.

Steel watched the footage again, this time taking in every detail. The sky in the film was overcast, with dark, angry clouds and violent crashing waves. Birds fought to glide against the coming wind. Steel noticed that the wind was picking up, judging by Brad's hair and jacket being blown to the side.

The storm was coming.

Steel watched the film twice over, just to be sure he hadn't missed anything this time. He was still mad at himself for being so unprofessional. Usually, he would have seen every detail. He would have been able to tell someone how many birds were flying and the registration numbers of all the vehicles. No detail had ever escaped him before – but there was just something nagging at him.

Was it because of Foster or Lucy?

He did not know. But something was making him slip up – and it ended now.

Steel switched off the video, tucked the phone away, and headed back to the parking lot. Steel made his way to the bar. If someone had arrived, that night Steel was hoping the people there might have seen something. Steel walked in and was greeted by a man behind the counter.

'Hi there,' said the man. He was a small round man in his late fifties.

'Hi, nice place you got here,' Steel said, looking around.

'It pays the rent.'

'I'm looking for some people that may have arrived on a boat. Sunday afternoon, there was about six of them, all wearing black,' Steel said.

The man thought for a moment as he polished a glass. 'Yeah, I remember, odd-looking bunch. All dressed the same carrying grip bags, thought they were army at first,' the man said. Steel nodded towards the coffee machine and pulled out thirty euros from his pocket. 'and two bottles of water, please.'

'Did they meet up with anyone?' Steel asked as the man poured the coffee into a carryout cup.

'Yeah, they were picked up by an SUV, big black Mitsubishi, didn't see the driver though,' the man said. He passed steel his coffee and the bottles of cold water. Steel waved off the offer of change, so the guy slipped the cash into the till.

'Have you seen any other men like that arriving?' Steel asked before taking a sip of the coffee.

'Yeah, a couple of weeks before that. Six more arrived. We all thought it was a training exercise or something. We get soldiers and navy around here from time to time,' the man explained.

Steel nodded. He went to leave but stopped suddenly and turned. 'Are there any farms or buildings nearby that have been up for sale or rent recently?' Steel asked.

'Couldn't say, but there are plenty of old disused farms near Qala, could try there,' the man said. Steel raised the cup in thanks. The man nodded.

Steel walked out to the parking lot and took out his phone, and used the internet to look t properties close by. He was looking for a farm or an area with plenty of buildings to use for storage. Preferably something that had been disused for a while and now had occupants. Steel's search came up with a few options, but only one was close by. Steel pulled out his tablet and used the navigation system to plot a route to the property, then used the software to zoom in. It looked like the place he was looking for. A place he might use if he was using it as a base of operations.

Steel looked up at the sound of an approaching vehicle. He recognised it as Kane's Outlander. As the car came to a stop, Samara got out. She looked stunning with the sun reflecting off her skin and hair, but she looked sad and a touch angry.

'What is it? What's wrong?' Steel asked.

'It's… It's your friend. Foster. There was an explosion at the embassy…' Samara's tone was sombre.

'Any casualties?' Steel asked.

'We don't know how many so far, reports are still coming in.'

'And Foster?' Steel asked. Samara looked at the ground as if she wasn't able to look Stell in the eye.

'I… I don't know. I am still waiting for confirmation. But reports say it was Foster's vehicle that had exploded…. I'm so sorry, Steel,' she said. As she caught a glimpse of her own reflection in his sunglasses.

'Why are you, sorry?' Steel said. His tone full of anger, but his expression was neutral and cold.

'Because we were meant to be watching him, you told me to look after him. Instead, we came here to warn you about Calver,' she said.

Steel shook his head. His expression was like stone.

'It's not your fault Samara, there was no way you could have prevented it. It happened at the embassy. You can't get in there. So there was no way you could have done anything.' Steel said reassuringly. Samara nodded, she knew Steel was right, but it did not stop her feeling like she had failed somehow. 'But we know one thing,' Steel said.

'What's that?' Samara asked.

'It was someone at the embassy itself, maybe even this Calver bloke.'

'It does make some sense. But Calver was never the type to do such things. He was a fixer – or rather – tech support, but never a killer.' Sammara said.

They walked towards the driver's side of Steel's hire car. 'What now?' Samara asked.

'Well, I need to find out what happened to six men who arrived here on the day Lucy was killed. Meanwhile, you try and find out what happened to Foster and also, find what your friend Calver is doing here,' Steel said, opening his door and leaning on the frame. 'Oh, and see what you can find out about this new software that goes live tomorrow. Foster did mention something about it last time we spoke,' Steel said.

Samara nodded. She was going to enjoy digging up Calver's dirty little secrets.

'You think it could be linked with what happened to Foster?' Samara asked, watching Steel climb into his vehicle. She could see he was the sort of man that when they showed no emotion, they were at a dangerous level. Samara knew people like that. But none scared her as much as what Steel had at that moment. Samara almost pitied the people responsible for this mess – nearly, but not enough.

'At this point, Samara, anything is possible. I don't really know. Look, see what this Calver bloke has to do with any of this. Tear his life apart, dig up every little secret. If he does know something, I want you to squeeze it out of him,' Steel said. Samara nodded.

As Steel started the engine, they stared at each other for a moment in silence.

Steel smiled at Samara, and she returned it. He slapped the gear shift into first and sped off up the road towards Qala.

Samara watched Steel drive away. He was the sort of man that, when showing no emotion, was at his most dangerous. Samara knew several people like that. But none scared her as much as Steel did at that moment. Samara almost pitied the people responsible for this mess – nearly, but not enough to stop Steel. She climbed into the driver's side of her car, and Kane turned to her and smiled.

'So, what did Steel say?'

'He said we have work to do,' she replied, her face expressionless, her eyes filled with revenge.

Chapter 65

As the sun rose to its pinnacle over the island of Gozo, so did the temperature. The hope of cloud cover had been carried away by a wind from the west. The once cool breeze had become warm and stifling. Even though it was late in the morning, the heat to come was apparent.

Aamir sat in an old Mitsubishi flatbed truck and looked out of the window at the diverse landscape. The rest of his men were in four other vehicles, two at the front, the other two to the car's rear.

They were heading for the ferry and then the US Embassy.

This would be the ultimate strike. Destroy the eyes and ears of the crossroad between North Africa and Europe. The people at the embassy would be taken by surprise – they would have no idea what had hit them.

Everything was going as planned.

Everything the Master had promised would happen, had happened.

Their source inside had arranged everything, the house, weapons, intel, and the plane in Tunisia. The Master had been right to trust this hidden HE. Soon, the Master would be on the plane, taking the fight to the United States.

Aamir closed his eyes and rested his head on the headrest, letting the breeze from the open window brush his face. He thought about his family, friends, everyone he had lost in the war in the old country.

Aamir had fled to Tunisia from his village. He had seen everything and everyone destroyed by missiles. Death from afar had taken everything from him. He had made it alone on foot. Surviving the perils of the desert. He had heard stories of a better life in the city.

His old life was gone – ripped away from him.

It had taken him nearly a month to get to the city. Aamir had taken on jobs for food and shelter at farms. He had stolen to eat when he had to.

And then he met the Master. He was in a village Aamir was passing through. The Master had this aura about him. He was a big man, tall and straight-backed, his head held up high. His hand's hand long boney but powerful-looking fingers. To Aamir, this was the most impressive looking man he had ever seen – almost god-like. The Master had seen Aamir – who was only a boy at that time. Twelve years old and alone in the world, with only hate to carry him through.

The Master had walked up to Aamir. They stared at one another in silence – each one sizing the other up. The Master had just smiled and looked over at the men with him. Then returned his gaze to Aamir.

No words were spoken – they were not required. The Master returned to his group, and Aamir followed gingerly behind.

From that moment on, his path was clear. He would take the battle back to those who had taken everything from him. Aamir had been trained and schooled. He had learnt how to read and write in both English and Arabic. He had become an excellent student and had the admiration of the others. The Master had regarded him more like a son than a soldier, his right hand.

A tear rolled down Aamir's face but was quickly taken by the wind. He wept for the family that he had lost, but soon they would be avenged. He raised his right wrist and looked at the battered timepiece – it was nearly eleven in the morning.

The second safe house was southwest of Attard. It was an abandoned farmhouse – another gift from *HE*.

It was a ten-minute drive to the port at Mgarr and then a twenty-minute crossing to Cirkewwa harbour in Malta. The ferry crossing would give them time to eat and drink. The first rule of any soldier – eat when you can. They had no idea when the next time would be at the other end, and the last thing Aamir needed was the men fatigued for what they were about to do.

He needed them fit and functioning.

When they got to Malta, it would be a good half hours drive to the safe house. If all went well, they should be there by two o'clock. They had time. There was no need to rush.

Once at the safe house, the plan was simple – they would wait there until the signal. The Master would call them when all was in place, which would be the last call they would receive.

Aamir stared out of the window as they passed the parish church in Qala. He stared at all the people happily taking photos. All of them completely unaware of the chaos Aamir and his men would soon bring.

Chapter 66

Steel drove into the small village and stopped at the fork in the road. He had passed the church with the cemetery. To the left, he would be back in Qala. To the right, he would be heading north. Steel checked the maps on his tablet. Steel looked over at his cell phone. A quick electronic ping told him he had a new message. From Samara, her contact had come through. Foster was ok. He was injured but alive, and he was resting in the embassy's medical centre. Steel sent her a thank you, then placed his phone into his pocket. He felt slightly better, definitely relieved at the good news.

There was nothing much, no big towns or villages, just open fields and a limestone quarry to the north. Steel smiled, then swung the vehicle off to the tight right turn and headed for the Triq ll Fortin Sant Anton Road.

Stan was woken as Steel revved the engine and hit the road hard. Sending Stan upwards from his seat, and landed just as hard on the floor.

'Sorry,' Steel said, glancing back over his shoulder. Stan sat up on the back seat, rubbed his back with one hand, and held onto the other's front passenger seat. Steel steered erratically, hoping the wheels were moving in the same direction. The lack of power steering often meant he moved the steering wheel but was lucky if the actual wheels moved with it – or at all.

'Did you find what you were looking for?' Stan said. 'At Azure Window, did you find what you wanted?' Stan said again, his hand still nursing his back.

'Yes, and more at Hondoq Bay,' Steel said. Glancing back at Stan, who was placing his cell phone into the top pocket of his shirt. The pocket was illuminated by the light from the screen.

'So, you found the place on that film you showed me – cool,' Stan said. He looked around for a moment, taking the time to get his bearings. He did not recognise anything, so he looked over the passenger seat at Steel's tablet and saw where they were going.

'Where you are going, there's nothing up here, just a couple of farmhouses, nothing unusual.' Stan said. His face creased as he slapped his tongue against the roof of his mouth.

Steel looked at Stan using the review mirror and grinned to himself. The overindulgence was getting to the cabbie. Revenge was sweet – or rather a foul sickly taste in the mouth.

'Precisely, if you're going to hide, you're not going to be in the middle town. You need somewhere out of the way – but, at the same time, close enough for access to supplies,' Steel said.

Stan wobbled his head in no particular direction, an indecisive movement, whether to agree or not – he looked like a bobblehead on a dashboard. Then his look changed to one of confusion.

'Wait, who's hiding?' Stan asked. Slipping on his seat belt and clicking it into place.

'The men on the boat,' Steel said.

'Oh, yeah, right,' Stan nodded. Then the puzzled look returned. 'Wait… hang on… what boat? What men?' Stan looked around, confused. 'And where the hell are we?' Stan looked about in a panic as if he hadn't actually studied the map on the tablet.

'We're… Never mind, go back to sleep,' Steel said. Stan bleched loudly, releasing fumes that could be weaponised. Stan sat back and closed his eyes, his head rested on his shoulder, and he began to snore. It had taken an impressive four seconds for Stan to have fallen asleep – Steel wasn't entirely convinced the man had been fully awake to start with. Many a time in the Army, Steel had seen men so tanked up they had no recollection of what they had done, but still, they had continued on throughout the night like sobberish men. It was possibly the lizard brain had kicked in – or muscle memory.

Steel had forgotten how many times had he gone downtown and gotten so drunk he had no idea of anything. But still managed to go to the local chip shop, order fish and chips, walk back to camp – all with an alcohol content that should have killed him.

He'd let Stan sleep it off for now, and then, Stan would earn his keep.

The sun beat down relentlessly. The lack of an air-conditioner made the inside of the vehicle a furnace. Steel had opened the windows in the hope to get a cold breeze, but he was rewarded instead with warm air and dust. The last time he had driven like this was in Iraq.

Steel stopped the car at a junction and looked at both routes that led off into the distance. He grabbed the cold bottle of water and cracked the top, and drank. It was still cold, condensation running down the sides. Steel picked up the tablet with his free hand and looked at the satellite image. The map showed Qala and the coastal line, but the picture was too big to get an idea of where he was. He tapped the screen twice, and it zoomed in to that point showing a road, but not the one he was on. He placed the tablet onto his lap and played around with the image, sliding the frame back and forth, up and down until he reached the crossroads where he sat.

The road to his right followed the Triq ll Fortin Sant Anton Road. This led to the quarry and, from what he could see, not much else for at least a few miles, far too much distance between Hondoq Bay and what lay further up. The quarry was out of the question as it was still active, with no chance of hiding there.

However, the road that went left seemed more promising. There were several farmhouses, and it wasn't too far from the bay. He would start there, and if he was wrong, he would head back and take the road to the right. Steel took another sip from the bottled water and put the gear into first, turned the wheel and headed down Triq AndarlX Xaghari road, which was little more than a dusty track. Steel figured this was the perfect route the people he was looking for would take. He'd passed another road further back – the Triq ll Wileg Road, but it was a decent asphalt road, which meant it was the main route with plenty of people using it. Not the sort of road you would want to use if you did not want to be noticed. Steel was looking for people who had smuggled themselves onto the island and were hiding out. They wouldn't be in plain sight or anywhere. Many people might find them suspicious.

He'd always had a knack for spotting a place people would hide. The other kids used to refuse to play hide and seek with him because it would take him minutes to find them, but they could never find him. He had learnt to think like the people he was tracking. It was a natural skill he had always had, but the army had perfected it.

'If you want to find the enemy, you gotta think like um,' said one of his instructors.

Steel was looking for a large enough place to house twelve or more men. He thought back to the idea that *something big was going down* – and something big wasn't going to take seven men. It was more than likely that there was at least twenty or more. And they would possibly split into two teams – a group in the north and the second in the south. If something happened to one of the units, the other could move in within minutes.

The operations building would have to be a place to stash vehicles and equipment for a length of time, which meant somewhere with a large capacity to sleep and feed a section or company of men.

Luckily, the part of Gozo that Steel was searching held little in the way of options. It was mostly fields and hills of low bushes and rocky terrain.

Steel wiped the sweat from his brow. He figured it must be at least fifty degrees in the truck, even with the windows open. From time to time, there was a cool breeze from somewhere, making him close his eyes briefly and praying it would last. However, it was soon replaced by more hot, unforgiving air.

Steel followed the road and checked the map on the tablet, making sure he wasn't driving past anything. Some of the tracks were old, just two groves carved out by vehicles, with long grass growing tall and untouched in the centre, making it difficult to assess when the last car had used the track. He was driving down a single lane track with low stone walls on either side. He had farmland to his left, the ocean to his right, and the unforgiving sun above him as they headed north along the track. Steel stopped the old Land Rover and took another sip from the water.

He had parked next to a strange-looking old limestone building. It had a doorway and steps on the outer wall that led up to a second doorway. The building was square and looked almost like a tiny fort or watchtower – only it was far too small for either. Steel figured it was a resting place for the farmers when the weather got too much, possibly the lower level was for animals – goats or sheep.

He sat and drank for a while longer. His thoughts wandered to Foster. He wanted to call and find out how what had happened, but he knew Foster would just tell him it wasn't part of his mission. And Foster would have been correct – Steel was just there to find out what had happened to Lucy, nothing more. But Steel kept on having the nagging feeling that what Foster was working on and Lucy's death weren't entirely exclusive.

Steel fought with the gear leaver to put it into first. After a couple of seconds of mechanical crunch and screams from the gears, the vehicle lunged forwards, and they were back on the road. As he drove, Steel noticed a short track and an old farmhouse at the end of it. Steel went a bit further and found an excellent spot to pull in without blocking other users' narrow path. The last thing he needed was a load of farmers or locals beeping their horns at him, attracting the people he sought. He may as well hold up a sign saying 'I'm here.'

Steel parked the vehicle so it could not be seen from the farm. If they happened to see the car, they would think it was just another local parking up. Also, Steel was suffering by driving this ancient Land Rover and not a brand new rental. A new rental would be too obvious, never blending in. Steel searched his pack and pulled out a set of binoculars. They were simple things, about twenty bucks from a store he'd been to in Valletta, but they did the trick.

Unfortunately, where he sat, Steel had no clear view of the property due to the old walls, trees and contour of the ground. This meant he had to get out of the car and find a decent reconnaissance point. He checked the image on the tablet for any stone walls he could use as cover. Steel mapped out a route in his head to what he considered to be an ideal spot. He could follow the limestone wall line to another one of those square buildings he had seen previously. The building would be perfect as a cover.

Steel closed down the tablet, tucked it back into his backpack, and then took another sip from the water, which was now lukewarm. But it was wet, and his mouth was dry from the dust and heat.

Steel watched as Stan sat up and stretched off, belching loudly as he did so. Steel said nothing, just shook his head in amazement at the man's lack of social graces.

'Why 'ave we stopped?' Stan asked, looking around.

Stan did not know what was more disappointing, the heat and lack of air-conditioner or the fact Steel had brought them to the middle of nowhere with no sign of a café.

'We're not far from a town called Qala,' Steel said. He took out a paper map and followed it into a neat square, making it easier to read.

'Qala, yeah, I know it.' Stan said, twisting himself in the middle. Steel nodded and passed Stan the map.

'We are here,' Steel said, pointing at the track on the map, which was nothing more than a dotted line. 'If you follow this road, it will take you back to Qala,' Steel said.

Stan stared at the map and looked around at the landscape, getting his bearings.

'So, where you goin'?' Stan said, with a puzzled look, as he suddenly realised he had just been given an exit strategy.

'You stay here. I'm going to check something out,' Steel said as he checked the items in his backpack. 'If I am not back in ten minutes, go find Samara, don't try and come after me, just find Samara,' Steel said.

Stan nodded, his eyes wide with fear. 'what bloody sort of trouble you expectin?'

'Oh, you never know,' Steel shrugged as he looked back at the direction he would be taking. 'but, if there is any, get the bloody hell out of here.' Stan nodded and watched as Steel crossed a nearby field to avoid the line of sight from the farmhouse. Staying low and keeping to cover. The sun was to his right, meaning any shadow he may have a cast would be hidden by an old limestone dividing wall, bushes, and trees. Steel headed for the small square building not far from the main building. He could easily observe what was going on without being seen from there. All the while, he checked for movement or hidden cameras. If he had been in charge of the location, he would have set up wifi cameras all around, covering the grounds for intruders.

However, he did not see any.

Steel got to the square building and snuck up to the roof. The door to the upper floor was unlatched, so he gingerly inched it open. Steel found it was somehow cooler inside. But he was out of the direct sunlight, making it feel a whole lot better. Inside, the air was thick with dust and sand, Steel coughed into his sleeve. The room was small and had the signs someone had used it, but not recently. Whoever had stayed there had made a small fire near a tiny window – which was more a hole in the wall and perfect for covert reconnaissance.

Steel found a spot where he could observe without being seen. He took out the cheap binoculars and a pair of ladies nylons. He took one of the nylons out of the package, and using a knife from his backpack, he cut out two small pieces of the fabric. He reached inside his pack and took out two elastic bands. Steel stretched each of the pieces of cloth over each of the large lenses of the binoculars. Then secured them with the bands. A trick he'd learnt from his time as a sniper in the army to avoid glare giving his position away.

He could see them, but they could not see him.

The farm was made up of a small group of buildings. A two-story building which Steel figured was the farmhouse. This was made of limestone with grey roof tiles. The windows had green wooden shutters, and the front door was also green with flaking paintwork.

There was another long building with twin double sliding doors at one end. It had several small windows at the top of the structure and a flat roof. Steel thought this had to be the barn for tractors and other machinery. Between the track leading into the farm and the farmhouse, he spotted a small stone building. This was square – about forty-by-forty, with a flat roof with one door and no windows. Steel figured that had to be a generator room because there had been no power cables coming down the track, and they had to be getting power from somewhere.

Steel observed the buildings for signs of life or for anything that would suggest anyone had been there.

The grounds were still and lifeless.

If someone had been there, they weren't home now.

Steel edged forwards, using any form of cover he could find to not be observed on he approached. He was unarmed and unprepared for a gunfight.

His only hope at this point was to strike unseen, take them out one at a time. At the same time, he had to be sure that his gut wasn't wrong, and he wasn't going to burst into the home of an elderly couple.

Amusing as it would be – and not the first time it had happened to him – it wasn't what he needed right now.

A black and white cat ran happily from the barn to the main house. Steel followed eagerly.

The animal obviously knew a way into the building.

Steel had no idea what to expect, a broken board in the window or even a partially open door. Anything that would afford him a look into the place would be welcome.

As he moved to the rear of the house, Steel stopped. On top of the generator, the object looked more like an upsidedown umbrella on legs. Steel recognised this as a military SAT communications dish. The dish was made from a pliable material, making it easy to erect and disassemble. It was the kind mostly used by special forces on reccon or infiltration operations.

The question was, how did they get hold of one, and who the hell were they?

The dish faced southwest. Steel figured it wasn't used as an expensive satellite dish to pick up North African TV.

He watched the cat as it jumped up onto a barrel and then in through a gap where some boards had come loose and moved across, giving the cat the perfect entry point and Steel a means to see inside.

Inside was dark. The only illumination was from natural light shards that broke through the shutters' gaps. Steel could make out a large table and some chairs in the middle of the room. In the corner, a dozen large boxes were stacked up along with several smaller, long boxes. Steel made his way around to the front of the house and tried the door.

The handle turned with ease, and then with a click – it opened.

Steel tried to keep the door from opening too much as he passed through. The last thing he needed was flooding the entrance with sunlight and alerting anyone to his presence.

He found himself in a small corridor that opened out into a larger room. The hallway was twenty feet long and dark, with a concrete floor and smooth walls. It was too dark to see what colour the walls were, but he guessed it was an off-white or cream. Most buildings here picked those colours. His boots scrapped on the floor from the thick sand that covered it. It was apparent someone had had the door open to try and get as much fresh air into the building.

It wouldn't take much. A door or window upstairs and the front door would be left open. This would create a through draft carrying fresh air through the building. Perfect if you could not afford for all the windows to be seen left open – if you did not want prying eyes knowing anyone was there. If someone was to see a door and a window left open in an abandoned building, they wouldn't think anything of it. Maybe a nosey tourist had gone for a quick investigation or some homeless person taking shelter.

Steel remembered when he was a sniper for the SAS, and he had a target that needed taking out. He would reccon the area. If there were animals nearby, he would set himself up days, even weeks before, so the animals would be used to him. The serge had taught him, 'you can have the best camouflage in the world, but if the animals and birds avoid you, you may as well be painted pink with a sign on your head.'

Chapter 67

Steel walked through the hallway and into the large room and was greeted by the stench of dust, body odour and take-out food. Steel gasped at the lack of air and covered his mouth with his arm. Whoever had been staying there had been for a long time. And had no thought for taking out the trash. Another ingenious idea Steel had thought. If someone did make it through the door just out of curiosity, they wouldn't be staying long.

The more he learnt about these men, the more he appreciated that these weren't just some half-assed assholes. These had training.

But he could not put together the idea that the men at the old barracks in Valletta and these men were part of the same group. Unless it was the commander that was the intelligent one, and these men were just… necessary.

He walked through slowly, taking each step heel-to-toe, desperate not to make a sound. A sudden noise to his left made Steel turn, only to see the cat dining happily on day-old pizza.

'Bon appetite,' Steel said with a smile and continued his way through what appeared to be a dining room for a large number of people, possibly fifteen to twenty. With six long picnic tables and benches as seats. The tables were arranged in a U shape confining the dining area to the centre, giving plenty of room to the room's sides. Beams of light bled through cracks in the window shutters, giving Steel enough light to make out things in the room.

Steel stopped and looked around, taking in what they had left and the marks on the floor where the dust hadn't had the chance to settle. Some of the gaps were long and wide – possibly rifle cases. Others were smaller – ammunition or hand grenades, perhaps.

Someone was getting ready for a fight, he thought – but where and who with?

The large room had four other rooms branching off from it. There were two on the left and two to the right. At the back was a stairwell leading to the upper floor.

Steel walked over to the first room on the right. Carefully he nudged the door open with his boot and peered inside.

The room was long, with a window at the far end. Steel imagined it had possibly a storage room with shelving.

There was shelving – but no food. Steel found shelves stacked with Sig Sauer SIG516 assault rifles, Sig P320 9mm pistols, sniper rifles that range from 7.62 to .50 calibre. There were boxes of ammunition, grenades and claymore mines lined the left-hand wall, along with crates of plastic explosives. Steel thought this might be a safe house or just a facility to store weapons until needed.

'Wow, someone's planning a party,' Steel said. Taking in the armoury before him. Slowly, Steel backed out and headed to the next room and found the door to be open. This was the kitchen and larder. There was a camping gas stove on a table connected to a twenty-litre gas bottle by a thick orange hose. There were five clear jerry cans of water laid in a row on the floor. The shelves were full of tinned and packet food, as well as pots and pans. There were cans of cooking oil and big bags of flour and sugar stacked up along the left-hand side. On the right, bottles of water and soft drinks lined the wall. He figured there were enough rations there for at least twenty guys for three weeks – maybe a month, depending on the food's rationing. He guessed the reason for the takeaway food was because they'd never had it before. And if that were the case, Steel had just learnt something else about the people in the house – they were from somewhere barren, possibly a desert or a mountain region.

The food store was impressive, he had to admit. It had everything you could want – except a window to let the foul air escape through.

Steel turned away from the kitchen. The sun was starting to pour through another set of windows shutters – the sun was moving. He expected by the time it reached due south, temperatures would rise further. Not a prospect he was looking forward to. Because they would be driving south – and towards the blistering sun.

Steel looked around the large room. The light was now pouring down the staircase, proving his point about a window or door being open on the upper level. The new illumination filled the rear of the room. Where he stood was still bathed in shadow. He looked over at the last two rooms.

If this was a safe house for soldiers or terrorists, they would need several things: communications and a war room for etching out each part of the plan. If the kitchen and armoury were behind him, that would leave the other two places for comms and a command post. Steel walked past the U shaped tables, across the dusty floor. He could hear rats scurrying about on the level above him. He noticed the footprints he had left in the dust, but it did not matter. The chances were the men were long gone, possibly leaving a couple of men to guard it. It was also possible this was just one of many places they had.

But Steel had a bad feeling about the site.

It was as if it had been set up for them, and they hadn't brought the equipment. Someone had provided it.

He remembered back to the footage. The boat they had arrived on was no way big enough to have brought all the rations and armaments Steel had just found. And how would they know this place was empty?

He supposed that there could have been a forward recce party, just to scope out suitable accommodation. But to find something like this farmhouse in this country – they would have needed months, possibly years. Steel thought that could be possible – and highly unlikely. Someone was financing these guys.

Then he thought back to what Samara had said about something big going down.

More and more, Steel was beginning to think that this software and the men following Samara were no coincidence, no matter what she or Foster said.

Brad had seen the Zodiac and the men aboard, possibly when he was rewatching the movie he had made. Perhaps he had posted it, and someone had seen it? It would explain why they came after him.

Or maybe, he saw the footage and wanted to know who they were and found more than he bargained for? Steel looked back over at the cat, who was still enjoying the pizza. He smiled softly to himself. It was possibly the best meal the poor animal would be getting for a while. Steel heard the howl of a breeze rushing down the stairwell. But, it only kicked more dust and sand into the air. Steel coughed and covered his mouth with his arm. Nestling his face into the crook of his elbow. He was glad of his sunglasses to shield his eyes from the particles hanging in the air.

Steel walked to the door frame of the left-hand room. He needed to be sure he was alone and that some half-assed asshole wouldn't try and stick a blade into him from behind. He sneaked a look inside, checking the corners for anyone hiding in the shadows – or behind the door itself. Then he checked the right-hand room. This, too, was empty. The staircase had thick dust on steps. Nobody had ventured up there for some time.

The footprints that were there had started to fill with sand and dust. So much so there were hardly visible. Steel figured the last time someone had used these steps had been at least the day before.

There was nobody upstairs.

He was alone.

Steel went back to the left-hand room. He had only had a quick glance to see if anyone was dumb enough to hide in there but not taken any real notice. He knew he'd be going back to study it later.

It was a decent sized room – twelve-by-ten, with one window at the far end. There were tables around the sides and two canvas folding chairs – military and available at every army navy store or online. The tables along the back wall and near the window all had radio equipment and laptop computers set up like a proper communications room.

And all the equipment was on – and running, it was still in use.

Someone hadn't left for the party, Steel thought.

Another table at the back, near the door, had weapons and ammunition ready to issue out.

He was starting to get a bad feeling, like any minute twenty guys armed to the teeth were coming crashing through the door, guns blazing.

Steel walked around the room until he reached the map nailed to the wall. The thing was huge, at least ten feet by ten feet. It was a blowup of a local map – a map of Malta. The map contained positions, safe houses, routes – and a target.

Steel froze as he saw the red pin marking the location of the American Embassy.

Steel ripped the cell phone out of his pocket and started to make photographs of the map. He knew the embassy needed this information as quickly as possible. Without it, many people – including civilians, would perish. Steel looked at his watch; it was half-past-eleven. He had to get the information to someone as soon as possible.

He typed a message to Samara, knowing that she would be in Malta by now. He just hoped she would get the information in time.

Take pictures to the embassy, urgent, Attack imminent, numbers unknown. Steel wrote, then put the images as an attachment and pressed send.

No networks found, was the response.

Steel growled at his bad luck. He looked around at the radios, thinking that they were blocking the signal. He made for the dining room, knowing he needed to get outside to resend the text, hoping that the building was blocking the cell signal. He was using a unique network to get a signal in the middle of the Atacama desert if he had to.

As Steel rushed into the large room with the dining tables, he was greeted by three men. They were all the same height, build. It was like looking at triplets as they stood next to each other. They all wore the same unwashed look, and all held MP5K submachine guns.

'I just moved in next door and was wondering if you had some sugar?' Steel said and raised his hands with a shrug.

The men stared blankly at him.

Steel wasn't sure if they did not understand or they did not care. Suddenly a noise at the front door made them turn, and Stan walked in. Steel went to warn him to get out, but it was too late. The men parted and let the cabbie walk in and took his place in front of them. In his hand, Stan carried a polished steel Desert Eagle .50 AE pistol. The foot-long handgun looked massive next to his slight frame.

'I tried to stop you,' Stan said with a disappointed look. 'I tried to make you turn back and head for the hotel, tried to get you drunk last night to hold you up too,' Stan said, shaking his head in disappointment. 'So, now, Mr Steel, we have to do it the hard way.'

Stan smiled, then raised the cannon towards Steel and fired.

Steel was already diving out of the way. Although, he had to admit he hadn't seen Stan being a bad guy. Lazy – yes, but not of this band of assholes. The wall behind where Steel had stood exploded from the impact, leaving a golf ball-sized hole in the wall. The other men opened fire. Blinding light flashed from the weapons' barrels, so much, so the men were now shooting blind.

Steel had rolled into one of the other rooms and slammed the door shut. It had been more out of instinct than anything. He knew with that much firepower, the door would be in shreds in moments. There were several massive *boom-boom-booms* as Stan fired into the wall. Each shot was horizontal, moving from right to left. He was trying to force Steel to move away from the door.

'That's four out of you're your seven,' Steel said. Counting off the rounds of the canon. A magazine change on a .50 AE isn't as quick and fluid as with a 9mm – or even a 45. The weapon was hefty, nearly five pounds in weight, meaning the gun can't remain in the firing position. It has to be lowered. This would take time for a guy like Stan in his physical condition.

Steel figured that Stan hadn't used the gun that much because he was using both hands to fire with, and the first shot nearly slammed the top slide into his face from the recoil. This meant he wasn't used to the weapon – add another minute.

The magnum's bullets passed straight through the wall and slammed into the wall opposite. Shattering the wall and pieces of old stone fell away, leaving huge tea saucer size dents in the wall.

Grabbing a chair next to the door, Steel slammed it under the door handle, jamming the door in place. Steel smiled smugly at his quick escape from the hail of bullets and turned around. His face dropped. He thought he had aimed for the armoury but found himself in the kitchen. He picked up a saucepan and slapped it against his hand as if testing its density. The handle snapped, and the metal pot clanged to the dust floor. There was another burst of fire, and the high calibre 7.62 NATO rounds punched through the wall. Hammering squash ball-sized holes through to the kitchen wall.

Wall dust and fragments fell all over him as Steel dove for cover as the limestone shrapnel filled the air. Steel looked around, hoping to find weapons or just something he could use against the men, but found nothing useful. Even the cooking knives were blunt.

Steel knew it wouldn't take long before they started to shoot more rounds through the walls and the door. Ammunition wasn't a problem. All they had to do was go to the room next door. He turned around at a strange *glugging* noise from behind him. A can of cooking oil had been struck and was leaking. Steel looked back at the holes the .50 calibre pistol had made. Big menacing holes that Steel could quickly search through like a spy hole in a door. Then Steel noticed one of the bullets had been fired at an angle. This had gone through the kitchen wall and straight through to the armoury. Leaving a fist-sized hole into the weapons cash.

In the dining room, Stan was yelling through the barricaded door. He was giving some grand speech about their cause and how everyone would burn.

Steel ignored Stan's ramblings. He was too busy making a funnel and piping the cooking oil into the next room. As Steel watched the liquid disappear into the next room, he hoped the wall between him and the munitions would be strong enough to take the blast. Steel hunted for some matches he had seen earlier when he searched the larder when the can was empty. He smiled as he picked up the matchbox and shook it to make sure it was full. Steel knew a match alone wouldn't ignite the oil, but he had seen some dish clothes on a shelf. He grabbed a cloth and stuck it through the whole, just leaving enough out for him to light. As more bullets pounded against the wall, Steel struck a match and lit the cloth. At first, the fabric did not take. He held it to the end, but the match went out. Steel struck another, but this broke. Steel swore as brick dust fell around him. He took another match and lit it. The flame burnt brightly. Slowly Steel placed the match next to the corner of the cloth. At first, there was nothing, but then it began to smoulder. Steel waited until it was happy it was alright, then poked the burning cloth through the hole using a spatula's handle and ducked.

'It's a shame it has to end like this, Steel,' Stan said. His voice rang with admiration. 'We could have been allies, you and I. Just think of the glorious things we could have accomplished!'

'So, who do you work for?' Steel said. 'Looking at all this equipment, it's not some bunch of arseholes who woke up one morning and decided to take over the world.'

'No,' Stan said. 'We are the word of the Master, the followers of truth. We are the Hisan Khashabiun, and this is the Falcon,' yelled one of the men.

'Nice – catchy,' Steel said as he emptied the can of oil into the funnel.

'You mock us?' yelled another of the three men. 'We are chaos. We are fire. We are…' The man continued.

Stan turned to see smoke rise from under the armoury door. The man who had been on the far right of the three saw it as well. Confused, he walked over and went to open the door.

'No, wait!' Stan yelled, but it was too late.

There was a whoosh of flame as the man was engulfed in a backdraft. He yelled in pain and fear. His grip tightened on the trigger of the MP5K as he screamed. A burst of automatic gunfire ripped through the building as he writhed in pain. 9mm parabellum bullets shattered the brickwork, and several stray rounds found their mark in one of the men's back and legs as he ran for cover. The man was now completely engulfed in flame. Still screaming. Stan could only watch in horror as the man ran blindly into the armoury – and directly into the stacks of ammunition and explosives. The building was rocked by a loud explosion as some of the plastic explosives detonated. Thick smoke and searing heat filled the air in the building.

The through draft from the open window on the first floor and the open door forced the inferno upwards and engulfed the ceiling in an orange and red ocean. Stan looked back at the two downed men and then at the front door – his and Steel's only exit. If he could get there first, he could cut down Steel as he ran blindly out. Stan stood ready to make his retreat but was forced to duck behind one of the upturned dining tables. Smaller popping sounds were followed by the noise of stray bullets flying indiscriminately as the ammunition heated up by the raging fire.

Inside the building, there was a deafening roar from the inferno. Thick black smoke filled the room, and the blaze from the armoury was intense. There were more popping sounds as more bullets exploded from their casings. But the sound of their travel was lost by the animalistic roar from the flames. There was a moaning sound – like the building was in pain, just before parts of the ceiling came crashing down, smashing onto the tables and the bodies of Stan's men. Stan looked around in anger and panic.

He knew he had to get out, and his only hope was the front entrance, a good twelve feet away. Each foot towards the door had the potential of either the roof caving in on him or one of the damned loose bullets taking him out. But it was a chance he had to take if he was going to get out alive. Stan began to run, plotting his course, getting ready to move at a seconds notice whenever he heard the sounds above, indicating the ceiling was coming down. He dodged and weaved like a ballplayer. Avoiding parts of the ceiling that came crashing down in front of him in a blazing heap. He could feel the heat against his skin, the hairs on his arms had gone, and he could feel the hair on his head being to burn. Stan ran as hard as he could.

He fought through the heat and the pain and ran.

Stan conjured up ideas of the terrible things he would do to Steel – if he survived this. The man had to pay for what he had done. His eyes fixed on the prize, the old wooden door.

Stan was near the door – so close he felt he could almost feel the fresh air from outside. He was practically out – almost home free.

Almost.

The blast from the gas bottles sent brick and metal shrapnel flying and smashing and shredding. It blew Stan forwards and through the open door.

Stan rolled on the ground. The momentum of the blast had smashed him against the door and across the open ground of the farmyard. He was stunned, and his ears were bleeding.

At first, Stan did not know whether he was alive or dead. Had he survived the blast, or was he suddenly going to look down on his burning body in a spectral form?

The burning sensation on his right arm told him he was very much alive – and on fire. Stan ripped off the jacket and tossed it to one side. His face scarred from the heat, his eyes burnt with hate.

Stan looked over to the fallen side of the building. Stan wanted Steel dead if he wasn't already. Stan would see Steel's head on a pike. Stan walked towards a body that was lying on the ground face down. It's black clothes, smouldering from the inferno the man had escaped from. Stan raised his pistol and pulled the trigger, emptying the magazine into the body. Grinning wildly as he did so until he heard the *click click click* of the empty magazine. Stan reached to his jacket in the hope to find more magazines for the canon but discovered his pockets were empty. His maddening grin remained as he kicked the body over, hoping to see the great Mr Steel lying before him.

Stan's smile fell away.

His eyes began to search all around him.

The man at his feet was the third man on his team. His body lying still, half-burnt and full of fist-sized holes.

Stan let out a cry of anger. 'Steel!' He roared and shook his fists to the air.

A small explosion was followed by an enormous blinding flash, and then a blast wave ripped Stan off his feet and hurled him across the farm's courtyard. The explosive had detonated along with the mines and grenades. The farmhouse building was torn apart, with brick and glass and wood sent reeling in all directions. The barn next to the farmhouse was smashed by the burning debris. The large barns door was decimated by burning limestone and metal from the ammunition boxes.

Flying metal shards and the ball bearings from the anti-personnel claymore mines embedded themselves into the nearby buildings. The old stone wall was sent crashing sidewards onto the adjacent field.

Steel stood up from behind an old wall some ten feet from the burning building. The sound of the final bullets being set off was more like firecrackers after the decimating explosion. Steel had made it out through a hole in the fragile wall at the side of the house. Stray bullets from the man who had been on fire had loosened the brickwork. It had been enough for Steel to push the wall with his legs while he lay on his back. It was a risk. The wall could have fallen on him, or it could have refused to budge. But, as Steel pushed with all that he had, a part of the wall fell away. It wasn't massive, but Steel did not give a damn. It was enough for him to crawl through and get the hell out of there. Steel pulled out his cell phone and pressed resend on his last email.

Steel smiled slightly as the words, *message sent*, appeared. Now it was down to Samara to convince embassy officials something was going to happen.

Steel looked around at the carnage around him. The two buildings had all but vanished. Only a burning shell remained and a large crater where the ammunition room had been. Steel sat hard on the ground. His body hurt from the beating of the blast and the building dropping on top of him. Steel knew he would be a walking burse by the end of the day. Maybe, when it was all over, he would take that holiday.

Steel sat for a moment and watched the farmhouse burn and hoped the photos he had taken had been enough. There had been a lot of information in there, but now all of it destroyed. Even the hard drives of the laptops would be useless. Hopefully, someone at the embassy could figure out who had planned all this and what their plan was.

But one thing was for sure if his theory was correct, this had only been one team of many. Possibly even, not. Perhaps the men Steel had seen were merely a rearguard to watch the equipment until the others returned. Given the numbers, that would make more sense – after all, there had only been four of them – that he knew of.

Steel sighed as he rested. He was tired, tired of getting close and then it all been taken away.

A sound from behind him made Steel drop and roll to the side and stood half crouched. His limbs taught, and a fresh blast of adrenalin pumped through his veins.

Stan stood a few feet from Steel; his body was full of wounds from the last blast. His flesh, blackened and angry, cuts showed muscle and bone.

'Help me,' Stan mumbled, his hand reaching out.

Steel's face was cold and emotionless. Steel could see the irony. Stan was taken out by the same weapons he had brought to cause death and destruction.

A part of Steel wanted to leave him there to rot, but he had a better idea. Stan had information, and judging by his present state, he wasn't going to need truth serum.

Chapter 68

Samara had phoned the embassy to warn them, but the person on the other end had put her on hold for the best part of fifteen minutes, listing to some crappy music. Using Kane's cell, Samara tried Foster's number, but there was no answer. Samara had suspected there wouldn't be – after all, the man was in the hospital.

' OK, new plan,' Samara said. Kane stared into her eyes and trembled slightly as if he had read her thoughts.

'You want me to drive there?' Kane said.

'Nope, I'm driving. You're handling the phones,' Samara said, lept into the driver's seat, and started the engine. Kane got in and fastened his seat belt.

'You know this is going to be a really bad idea?' he said. Samara just shrugged, smiled and hit the gas.

They were heading south towards Attard when Kane got Steel's text on Samara's cell.

'We still need to get to the Embassy and warn them,' Kane said. Samara nodded silently, her brain calculating the route.'Stay on this road until the roundabout at the Kapelle of San Pawl,' Kane said. Samara squinted, unsure of his route, but then he knew the place better than she did.

The Outlander sped down the highway, heading towards Attard. Kane had tried calling Steel, but it just went to voicemail. Now Samara and Kane were getting worried. What if something had happened to Steel? What if that was his last message?

Kane looked around, hoping the scenery would calm him. But it was all blurred passed. Then he looked at his side mirror, hoping the seeming still image of traffic would help him to feel less motion sick. Kane shot Samara a concerned look, but she kept her eyes on the road, she had a job to do, and by God, she wasn't going to let Steel down.

'Uhm…Samara…' Kane said. His voice rang with a concerned tone.

'Not now,' she barked, concentrating on the road ahead.

'Uhm – Samara –,' Kane yelled, his voice filled with purpose.

'What?' Samara screamed back, trying not to take her eyes away from the busy road.

'Behind us,' Kane said, thumbing behind them.

'Yes, I know, I saw them a while back,' Samara said confidently.

Samara rechecked her rearview mirror and saw the four black Yukon SUV's speeding up behind her.

'Hold on,' she warned. Kane nodded and braced himself as Samara began to dart in between traffic. Kane looked back through the rearview. The lead vehicle was flashing its lights as if trying to get their attention.

'I think they want us to stop,' Kane said.

'I bet they do,' she said, her eyes transfixed on the road ahead. 'Besides, we don't know who they are.' Kane had to agree with her logic. After all, she had kidnapped a couple of days ago.

'Try Steel again,' Samara insisted. I hoping Steel had contacted someone at the embassy. As she looked in the rearview mirror, Samara saw the lead vehicle speed up behind them.

'They could be friendly?' Kane said, with a hopeful tone ringing in his voice. Suddenly the sound of gunfire rang out, and the back window shattered. 'Or not,' Kane added, trying to crawl down into the footwell. The phone still to his ear. Samara swerved the vehicle, hoping to not give them something to aim for. More shots rang out, stray bullets began hitting other cars, causing them to swerve erratically.

Samara manoeuvred the Outlander, like a rally driver, swerving between vehicles and racing ahead. The highway they were on only had two lanes that headed north, and on the other side of the partition, there were two lanes southbound.

More shots rang out. This time the windscreen took a hit, shattering the glass centre. The spider's web effect was making it hard for Samara to see the road. She moved her head side-to-side, up and down until she found a small spot where she could navigate a safe route, but it meant she had to slow the vehicle.

'Shit.' Samara cursed their luck and the assholes behind them. 'I can't see anything.'

Kane sat up, and with his feet, he pushed on the splintered safety glass and forced it out onto the bonnet. The next shot hit the rearview mirror, sending it into the wild.

'OK – I have had enough of these bastards,' Samara growled, 'Hold on, brother.' Kane looked over at Samara. He noticed the corner of her mouth was raised.

She was smiling.

He knew this could not be good, whatever she was planning.

'Oh, no,' he said and pulled his seatbelt tightly across his chest.

Samara slammed on the breaks and slipped the car into reverse. The vehicle squealed with disapproval at the sudden change of direction, then powered backwards. The deadly convoy's first car did not have time to react before the heavy Outlander slammed into the front end, destroying the front grill. The two gunmen who were leaning out of the rear passenger windows were thrust backwards. Their bodies slammed against the steel of the window frame, almost cutting them in half.

Samara slipped the car into gear. The Outlander lunged forwards, the rear of their vehicle damaged, but so was the lead vehicle's cooling system.

There was another loud crash behind them as the middle two SUV's managed to avoid the leader, but the fourth wasn't so lucky. The rear vehicle was moving fast, and a dust cloud from the first two vehicles compromised the driver's vision. The rear car ploughed into the back of the rear of the front vehicle. There was a massive *bang* as the two cars became almost one. The rear vehicle hit with such force it punctured the leader's fuel tank.

There was an explosion which resulted in a fireball. As fuel began to seep out onto the road, and this too caught fire, creating a wall of flame.

Samara smiled again and pressed down on the gas. Behind them, the two remaining vehicles pursued at speed. Samara looked back past her shoulder quickly to check the distance between them and the two cars. The gap wasn't large enough. The SUV's were closing. Samara needed to get them to the US Embassy and warn them of the attack. There they would also be safe from the guy's in the SUV's, even for a short time.

'Who the hell are they?' Kane growled. Samara pulled out her gun and handed it to her brother.

'You'll have to shoot back Kane.' Samara yelled.

'How much ammo have you got?' Kane asked.

'Not enough for you to miss all the time – so make them count,' Samara said, swerving the car to avoid another volley of shots from behind. 'I just hope all that time with the film set firearms guys was worth it?' Samara said. Kane scowled at her. 'I did OK,' Kane said as he shot back twice, hitting the lead car windshield.

'Yeah, baby,' Kane said, praising himself as the glass splintered, causing their vehicle to swerve, enough for Samara to push forwards on the other side of the road. Cars beeped their horns as she hammered forwards. The rear vehicle went to overtake the blinded car but was forced to slow as the traffic bunched up in place due to the chaos. Samara was now in front of the eighteen-wheeler, and the roads ahead seemed empty for the moment. She knew if the cars made it past, they would soon catch up with them.

'What's your plan now?' Kane asked, sliding out the pistol's magazine and checking how many rounds were left. Twelve bullets and one in the pipe. Enough rounds for one vehicle, but not if more turned up.

Samara looked at her side mirror; there was enough gap between her and the artic lorry. Enough space for what she needed to do.

'I hope I have this right,' she said with a grin.

'Have what right?' Kane asked, looking behind them, noticing the large truck.

'Oh, you're not…?'

'Yes, I am.' With that, Samara braked hard, leaving a smell of burnt rubber in the air. There was a squeal of tyres as the truck went from eighty to zero in seconds. Suddenly there was a collision and explosion from behind the truck.

Samara turned on to the Triq Buqana road at the roundabout instead of heading for the Triq Durumblat road, meaning they were now heading South and not East. It was a two-lane highway where both lanes travelled north. The southbound route was on the other side of the partition. Meaning there was no oncoming traffic to navigate against. Samara wove in and out of the other cars in front, her eyes darting at the rearview mirror to check for any new pursuers. Then she saw it – the last SUV far behind but still too close for them to relax. The trick with the eighteen-wheeler had slowed them, but not enough. Kane looked over at Samara. She was calm and focused. He was crapping himself – possibly more about her driving than the men behind them. Samara kept her foot on the gas. The car wasn't steering correctly, causing it to sway out slightly every time she accelerated. But it had been worth damaging the vehicle somewhat just to get the number of pursuers down. Now they were one-on-one. But they only had one magazine for the Masada 9mm, and she figured their opponents would probably be fully stocked with weapons and ammunition. But she also hoped that she was wrong.

Samara got Kane to try Steel's number again. If someone was after them, he might also be in danger – if he wasn't already. She knew it wouldn't be long before she would be turning at a roundabout and then turning onto the Vjal L-Istadium Nazzjonali road. This would take them straight to the Embassy's main gate – and hopefully, safety.

Samara looked into the side mirror for the other car but found it had gone. She looked around nervously. She did not believe that they would give up. If anything, they would fall back and regroup. Samara's senses were now off the chart.

Every new vehicle on the road was a possible threat.

Kane redialed. The voice from the speakers was that of the answering service. Kane ended the call and stuck the phone away in his pocket.

'Maybe there's no cell reception where he is?' Kane said, trying to reassure Samara. She just nodded and bit her bottom lip. She was worried about him. He was this stranger in paradise, a man in search of the killer of his Goddaughter.

'He'll be fine,' Kane said with a smile, almost as if he was trying to reassure himself more than her.

'He better be because we're not,' Samara growled as she looked in the mirror and found the next team almost upon them. She saw the last SUV and four motorcycles coming up – fast. Behind them, a mass of blue light bars from the police patrol units.

'Where the hell are they all coming from?' Samara yelled.

Samara put her foot down hard on the gas and gripped the steering wheel. Shots rang out, and bullets whizzed as the hot projectiles flew past them. The back seats took most of the damage, along with the back door. Samara was happy that Kane had bought the six-seater model, each seat having more protection from the incoming fire.

'Stop shooting my car, you assholes,' Kane yelled as he fired four shots at the lead vehicle; each one hit the windscreen and grill. As he went to fire again, but a volley of 9mm ripped into the back of his headrest, pushed him back into safety.

Sparks flew as the centre console's entertainment centre took a direct hit, leaving a distorted picture on the LCD display. Samara swerved just in time to crash into one of the men on a motorcycle, launching him over the centre partition and onto the other road. The man screamed and raised his hands in a futile effort to stop what was going to happen next, just as a dumper truck smashed into his body and carried what little there was away.

Samara swerved the other way, but that biker was quick and braked in time. The driver of the SUV behind the bike wasn't so quick. Metal and plastic screeched sickeningly as the two vehicles collided.

The bike and rider were hurled into the air.

Both came down hard.

The bike smashed onto the front of the SUV, splintering glass and plastic shards across the road. The metal buckled and twisted as the SUV ran over the top of the bike.

The rider came down straight through a nearby car's windshield, causing the vehicle to swerve and stop side on to the traffic behind him. There was another screech of breaks as another biker crashed straight into the front panel of the car, sending him volleying over the car and skidding onto the road.

Samara took the turn at the roundabout, and then another left. Now they were on the Vjal L-Istadium Nazzjonali road.

She smiled – they were getting away.

They were on the main road to the embassy – by her estimation, another fifteen minutes. Samara did not notice as her gaze was more on the two men on motorbikes cutting through the parking lot and heading for the junction.

Samara knew they were trying to force her down one of the side roads where there would be a roadblock – a kill zone. But Samara stayed firm. If they wouldn't move, she'd move them. More shot rang out, but this time, they aimed at the local police giving chase. One of the police cars roared off after being riddled with bullet holes; the others swerved to miss the incapacitated vehicle, which lay motionless, steam spewing from the radiator. The two bikers had stopped at the junction and drawn their weapons.

'Get down,' Samara ordered, just as the men opened fire with their full-auto Glock 17's. Samara and Kane got down as much as they could, the tops of their seats ripped apart by gunfire.

But their car kept going despite the bullet holes.

Samara slowed until the bikers were close then slammed on the breaks. From behind them, the vehicle shunted forwards as the bike smashing against the back of the Outlander. The rider was propelled over the car and landed on the other side of the street. The biker stood, dazed by the impact, and walked straight in front of an oncoming vehicle as it went to overtake. The car's windshield fragmented as the rider smashed against it. The vehicle swerved blindly and ploughed directly into a flower store window.

The second bike braked and swerved, missing the rear of the Outlander by inches. As it came up close to Samara's door, the biker opened fire. Bullets spat, ripping at the rear seats. Samara wrenched at the wheel and collided with the biker, sending him hurling into one of the pursuing police cars.

Kane yelled as something hot hit his leg.

'Kane, are you OK?' Samara asked, a tremor in her voice.

'Never better, look what they left us,' Kane smiled as he showed the pistol one of the bikers had lost in the crash.

Samara smiled with relief, he was alright, and now they had another weapon. The police sirens' noise was drowned out by gunfire and the screech of tyres from behind them, but Samara kept her foot down.

Samara caught a quick glimpse of Kane from the corner of her eye as he aimed the new pistol and fired at the SUV. Sparks flew wildly as bullets struck the hood, and the windscreen shattered as a line of bullet holes pearled up the glass.

'Nice shot,' She said after seeing the aftermath of his shooting in the rearview.

'Thanks, but it's not over yet,' Kane yelled back over the noise of the engine.

The others were close now, so close Samara could hear the roar of their engines. She knew what they would do. They would attempt to box them in and then open fire. Not subtle but effective.

She had other plans.

Samara saw the last of the bikes coming up on her left. At first, she did nothing – it was too early to make her move. Soon they were level with the rear passenger door, but her eyes were fixed on the road and the sudden turn off on the left. Quickly, Samara turned the wheel, and the massive Outlander veered to the left, causing the bike to veer off, crashing into a parked van.

Samara smiled. It wouldn't be long now before they were safely at the embassy. All they had to do was stay alive long enough to pass on Steel's warning.

Ten minutes down the Vjal L-Istadium Nazzjonali road – at the US embassy's main security gate, the Marines stood ready – alert. Samara had seen the circling helicopters, no doubt ready, just in case there was another attack.

It was twenty-eight degrees in the shade for the three men and the security guard and hardly any cover to shelter in. The three marines were in full tactical gear. Body armour with ballistic plates, Kevlar helmets, webbing gear, camel packs full of water – and hot as hell. They had spent time in Iraq and Afganistan, so the Maltese heat shouldn't have been any different, but it was a different kind of heat. Just as twenty-eight in New York is different in, say Arizona. But the men were professional and dug in and got the job done – besides, their shift was almost done, and the promise of ice cream at the canteen egged them on.

The three men had been there since ten o'clock and could not wait for a break. Two of them stood as overwatch on either side of the strip. While the other had eyes on the security guard who was busy checking the identifications.

They were officially on lockdown. This meant 'nobody in and nobody out.' But that had been relaxed by the base commander, so only essential workers were allowed in.

Lance Corporal Dickson stood ready at the gate. His M4 assault rifle pulled to his chest and his hands on the pistol grip and foregrip. The other two, Cooper and Sanchez, chatted about what cars they were going to get when they went back stateside. Dickson stood near the security guard but not too close. He needed enough distance to watch the guy work but not so close he could not use his weapon if necessary.

Dickson was tall and lean – they all were, lots of time to hit the gym kept them in shape. Dickson was in the worst of the three locations. He had the sun directly over him, while the others had found a little bit of cover. But Dickson had to move around – he had to move when the security guard moved.

He was dehydrated and starting to get a headache. The water in his camel pack was almost gone, so he had to take small sips.

Their relief was late, but given the situation, Dickson could understand – but it did not make him any annoyed. He watched as more cars came forwards. The sun reflected off the windshields, making him squint – despite the ballistic sunglasses he was wearing. Some of the drivers had been told to turn around and go home until the all-clear was given. Others were allowed through and told where they could park and where to avoid. Dickson looked at his watch. He was getting angrier the more this damned headache dug into his skull.

He could not wait to hear the excuses. 'Oh, sorry we're late, we had to do this or that,' he wasn't bothered as long as they got there soon.

Dickson looked up from his watch.

The street was empty.

The rush hour had passed. He figured that the heads of departments had gotten hold of their employees and gave them the good or bad news. He moved to the barrier. He stopped and listened hard. Some distant sounds had caught his ear. The noise was far of and muffled by the sound of the helicopters overhead. Cooper and Sanchez spoke loudly about the new Camero, figuring that they were free to raise the volume a little with the lack of people now coming through.

'Shut up a minute,' Dickson ordered, straining to pick out the sound.

'What's up?' asked Sanchez, pulling his weapon into the ready position.

'I'm not sure, kinda sounds like—'

A group of vehicles raced towards them. A battered black Outlander and a blacked-out Yukon all heading their way. Then Dickson caught sight of several police vehicles trying to get in front of the SUV. Blue and the red light flashed and winked. The vehicles hurtled towards them, sirens blaring, shots ringing out. Stray bullets impacted the walls and floor close to the marines and the security guard. Instinctively they all scrabble for low cover, ready for the next volley, unsure whether that was meant for them or someone else. Dickson lined up his rifle scope and checked out the view in front. His gaze started with the lead vehicle – the battered Land Rover. The red dot of the scope looked directly at a woman in the driver's seat shouting something and flashing her headlights. Dickson and Sanchez knelt ready while Cooper radioed it in.

'Zero, this is Two-Four Echo, we have a situation at gate Bravo, require immediate assistance, over,' Cooper said. His voice was calm, and each word slow enough and clear enough to understand.

'Roger that Two-Four Echo, QRF on route to your location. Over,' came the response.

'Zero – be advised, we have approximately six Tangos and shots fired north of our location. Out.' Cooper took a firing position next to a blast wall and waited. He wasn't waiting for a reply from command.

The Marines had no idea what was going on. Was it an attack? They did not know. But one thing was for sure. If they were fired upon, they sure as hell would fire back.

Each man picked a target, specifically the black Toyotas giving chase to the Land Rover. The other vehicles were doing all of the shooting, both at the lead vehicle and police – clearly making them the aggressors.

Situation – unknown hostiles were firing on a vehicle heading towards our location.

The three Marines waited for the Quick Reaction Force to arrive and handle the situation. In the meantime, they just had to wait and observe. At first, it looked like an agency vehicle firing on a Mitsubishi Outlander. But they were also firing on the local cops. Cooper held the first black SUV in his sights. Dickson had the Outlander, while Sanchez switched between both. Dickson looked down his scope at the car; as it grew closer, he saw the woman. She was stunning. She had a face he could stare at all day. Next to her was a man in his late thirties – a local possibly. He was full of panic and firing back blindly with what appeared to be a handgun. The bullets hit Yukon's front grill, smashing the headlights but not doing much damage. This guy was not a combatant – just some scared bastard who had gotten a gun. The men in the back of the Yukon turned their attention on the two police vehicles – their MP5's spat 9mm full metal jacket rounds into the wheels of the cop cars. The two police vehicles span uncontrollably. One swerved off to the right and ended up in a nearby grass area. The other cartwheeled down the road, flipping from its roof to its wheels, leaving smashed glass, oil and coolant in its path.

Dickson looked back at the woman. She had fear and anger etched on her perfect face. She was closer now, so much so he could see her perfectly in the scope. He did not know if it was dehydration or the headache, making him see things.

But she was talking – to him!

'What the…?' Dickson said, taking his eye away from the scope and shaking his head as if to reset his brain. Then he looked again. Yes – the woman who was trying to shout something. He went to reread her lips using the scope. Samara's mouth moved slowly as if she knew that someone would be watching. Suddenly Dickson saw a splatter of red mist as one of the rounds from the persuing vehicle hit her in the left shoulder. The Outlander swerved left and right before barrel rolling towards them. Dickson and his men gasped as the two-tonne car bounded towards them on its roof. Sparks flew as the vehicle skidded.

'Shit!' Cooper yelled as they all dove for cover. Suddenly, wood, metal and concrete exploded from the impact, sending splinters of red and white wood, raining down like badly cut confetti. To the side, there was a hollow *dong* as the unbroken half of the barrier bounced off the small security hut and clattered onto the ground.

The Outlander's front had careered into the barrier on its roof, shattering the multicoloured wood into a million pieces, and left a long blackened skid mark on the road's concrete.

Dickson and his men ran back to their post and aimed their weapons out towards the oncoming vehicles. They knew they wouldn't be allowed to fire out of the compound, but just the sight of three fully armed Marines made the vehicles turn and disappear. The cop cars had been incapacitated and lay across the road. Screams from injured officers filled the silent air.

Two Hummv's approached at speed from the main building, more Marines armed and ready to go.

There was a low groan of pain from the Outlander, followed by the sound of broken glass falling. Samara and Kane crawled out the front of the vehicle and collapsed on the ground, looking skywards. Samara looked up at the unspoilt blue sky, the dancing birds that swopped and darted, not a cloud in the sky. It looked like it was going to be a beautiful day. She breathed in but winced in pain as she exhaled. The wound from her shoulder hurt like hell. Suddenly twenty M4 gun barrels bared down on them as the Marines stood over them. Causing Samara to laugh.

'What's so funny, Miss?' asked Dickson, somewhat confused.

'I don't think my brother's insurance is going to cover this one,' She laughed.

Chapter 69

The building was gone.

If there had been anything more to find, it had been destroyed along with the farmhouse. There were still popping and the sound of stray bullets as the ammunition continued to burn. Steel just hoped all the explosives and grenades were spent. The farmhouse was now just a pile of limestone rubble. A flamming funnel of red, yellow, and black cloud rose up. The barn was burning, the roof had collapsed. The sound of the bricks falling into the inferno mixed with a crackle of burning lumber. There was nothing more he could do in the way of search for information.

Steel hoped his message had gotten through to Samara and that they could get to the embassy in time. The cell signal he had used had been weak – two bars at the most.

He had heard the cries of pain. It was Stan.

Steel would recognise his voice anywhere.

Steel sauntered over to Stan. He had many question's, and Steel would make it as painful as possible until Stan answered

Stan just stared at Steel. The image of this man clad in black with the blazing farmhouse behind made Steel look like he had just crawled from the pit of hell. Steel kept his movements slow, pondering what to do with Stan as he approached the trembling man. Steel crouched down in front of Stan.

There was silence for a moment.

'I have nothing to say to you.' Stan said. Spitting his defiant words.

Steel said nothing. He just smiled.

'Go on. Kill me. I don't care,' Stan said, his tone and facial expression wrought with pride.

Steel continued to smile. It wasn't a wide broad smile like he was happy. It was more a thin mouthed slither with just the sides curled up – it was more amusement, or – satisfaction.

'Oh, I'm not going to kill you, Stan, but you are going to talk.' Steel said, slowly taking off his sunglasses, revealing his cold, soulless, emerald green eyes. 'Believe me.'

The sound of Stan's scream was lost in a westerly wind. To the two fires behind them, reach up to the heavens like clawing hands. There was a roar of flame and the sound of bricks falling.

'Who do you work for?' Steel asked, holding the desert eagle that Stan had dropped. 'and don't give me that crap about being part of a terrorist group.' Stan glared angrily at Steel. Steel smiled and stood on a wound that Stan had on his upper thigh.

Stan screamed.'OK, OK.' Steel released the pressure and stood back.

'I work for a powerful organisation,' Stan groaned. 'I know you know them,' Stan bore his teeth with pain. The sweat poured down his pale, cut face. 'my associates were most interested in finding out you were coming here,' Stan grinned through the pain. Steel thought back to the hotel's lobby, the men with the id badges, the picture of the horses head that kept creeping up. At first, Steel thought it coincidence, but now it made sense.

'The trojan organisation, the people responsible for the Cruise ship bombing last year,' Steel said.

'Amongst other things,' Stan nodded, grasping his leg. Sweat poured from his forehead.

'So, what's it all about, why you working with terrorists? Not really your sort of thing, though you guy's stuck to the shadows?' Steel asked.

'A means to an end. These terrorists, as you call them, are fighting for a cause. We gave them the means to do so. In so doing, they served a function. It was all misdirection?' Stan moaned with the pain. 'All these incidents. Yours and the Mossad woman's kidnapping, the car bomb at the embassy, all planned to cause panic,' Stan said, licked his dry lips as if trying to put moisture onto them. 'Enough for the right people to look in the wrong direction, of course,' Stan said. His breath was laboured from the pain.

'And Lucy, why did she have to die?' Steel growled.

'That Brad idiot had tried to blackmail the wrong people. He had a damned video. Of course, we didn't know if he had given it to the girl, so we had a chat.' Stan went to smile and shrug. But Steel changed his mind as he stamped heavily on the wound once again with his heel and dug it in. Stan screamed out in pain and grabbing at Steel's leg.

Steel brought the desert eagle down, smashing the gun against the side of Stan's head, forcing Stan to fall back. He was exhausted from the pain, but Steel wasn't going to let up until he had answers.

'So, what is the Trojan group after?' Stan remained silent for a moment from the pain. Then Steel thought again to those men in the lobby. Foster had talked about outside the pool house that day when he talked about the recognition software project. 'this is about that damned software,' Steel said. 'This whole thing is about a friggin defence contract?'

'Not just a defence contract, but THE defence contract. Weapons, clothing, vehicles, ammunition, food, logistics. We are talking billions of dollars,' Stan said. His eyes were alive with passion at the thought of it all.

'But, you didn't get it. Someone beat you to it.'

'It happens. That's business for you,' Stan shrugged. Steel thought for a moment. This wasn't the sort of people to sit back and say, 'oh well, maybe next time.'

'So what was the contingency plan?'

'You, actually. Yes, we had a plan, but then you arrived and stirred things up enough, especially without Tunisian friends. Between you and Samara, I think you got a lot of people's attention. They wanted to kill you at Foster's place, but we convinced them it was best you were left alive.'

'Thanks,' Steel said.

'Oh, don't worry, we promised there would be another time, and they could do what they wanted with you,' Stan groaned in pain.

'So, how are you going to trash the other software? You can't swap it. It's too well guarded, from what I hear?'

'Oh, I wouldn't worry about that. I'd be more concerned about what our terrorist friends are up to next,' Stan said. Steel knew about the Embassy attack. He just hoped Samara had gotten his message in time.

'Don't worry, I think I got that covered,' Steel said. 'all you have to do is worry about the Feds when they get hold of you – or worse – your people.' Steel brought the pistol down onto the back of Stan's kneck hard, knocking him unconscious.

After making a quick call to Sergeant Burlo in Mdina, Steel had tied Stan up and left him for the cops to find. Steel had figured he would make the appropriate phone calls to the right people. He was in doubt the people at the US Embassy would be interested in hearing what Stan had to say, but Steel could not risk being caught with a bound man in his trunk.

Steel walked back to the old Land Rover. The smell of smoke was still lingering in his nostrils, and his mouth was as dry as a desert. He climbed and searched his pack for his cell phone. He saw the ten missed calls from Samara's phone. A shiver ran down his spine. Had something happened to them? Steel pressed the call back button and waited. The phone rang several times until a man answered the call.

'Yes?' A male voice, American.

'Is Samara there?' Steel said.

'Who's this?' asked the American.

'Odd – I was thinking the same thing,' Steel replied, getting a bad feeling.

'This is Director Walter Sloan of the US Embassy in Attard, and you are?'

'John Steel, I'm a friend of Agent Foster,' Steel said.

'Ah, Mr Steel, we've been waiting for your call. It appears you have some explaining to do. Why don't you pop in, and we can discuss it,' Sloan almost hissed his words.

'Happy too – got a helicopter?' Steel said with a grin.

'That we do, Mr Steel. That we do.'

The Embassy sent one of their two Black Hawk helicopters to pick up Steel. They were mostly used for transporting officials rather than troops. They could also be called on to help with casualties transport if the ambulance helo was too far away. The embassy thought it was in good relations between the two governments to lend aid when necessary.

The half-hour journey back made Steel feel better, and it did not hurt that he loved to ride in helicopters. Steel looked out of the side window. Everything looked small, like a model. It made him think back to a museum he had been to in Hamburg, Germany – The Miniatur Wunderland, or something like that. The whole thing was like a massive train set, but buildings and street lamps lit up with moving cars and planes. He found it quite fascinating. They had recreated London, Times Square, Berlin, amongst other places, all in miniature detail.

Steel gazed down, seeing the fields, streets and towns from three thousand feet. It looked even harsher than before – but at the same time more beautiful. He ignored the deafeing *thump thump thump* of the blades and the roar of the twin engines.

He heard voices in his headset, talking over the open channel, informing everyone of their location and how long they had until they touched down. But Steel just sat and stared across the woven blanket of colour below. His thoughts were a million miles away. Thinking about Helen and how much she would have loved this place. Foster in the hospital, and at his life in New York. Steel caught his reflection in the window. His emotionless gaze looked back at him.

Then he smiled slightly as the pilot announced they were getting ready for landing. Not because the trip was nearly over, but the mission was.

Someone had killed his Goddaughter – they had messed with his family.

Now, they were going to pay.

As the transport helicopter touched down, it seemed to bounce slightly Then, the turbos' sound screamed, and the rotor blades thumped at a different pace. The helicopter was idling. The downdraft was at a minimum but still enough to cast sand and dust across the landing pad. As the door slid, open Steel saw five men stood in line with ten Marines behind them. Each must have been six-four, weighed over two hundred pounds.

Big capable-looking guys, possibly there in case Steel caused any trouble.

Steel glanced over at a man who stood dead centre of the line of three men and woman. The man in the middle looked older than the rest. In his fifties, Steel thought. He oozed power. This had to be Director Sloan. Which meant the others were heads of departments – CIA, Homeland, FBI.

Steel gave a thumbs up to the pilot and the loadmaster as a thank you. Then he ducked down and moved away from the downdraft of the helicopter. He headed towards the group of men who stood patiently to the side. All of them were there told Steel that Samara had delivered the message – and that meant she was OK.

The downdraft from the rotor blades swept clothing and hair about.

'Mr Steel, I'm Director Sloan,' Sloan yelled over the noise of the helicopter. Sloan offered his hand. Steel took it. The man's grip was firm considering his size, which was three inches shorter than Steel with a thinner frame, but Sloan was still in good shape.

'Pleasure to finally meet you, director,' Steel lied as they shook hands.

'We saw the photographs. Thank you for the warning. Our computer techs are busy enhancing the pictures now,' Sloan said.

'Not a problem, oh, I also got a little present for you, back of the chopper. Someone, you guys, might want to have a chat with,' Steel said, pointing back at the Black hawk. Sloan signalled to two of the marines to go to the helicopter. Sloan's face dropped at the sight of this beaten man who was hogtied.

'And we didn't get you anything,' Sloan joked.

'Bring me a black coffee, and we'll call it quits,' Steel said.

'Deal.'

Sloan waited for the helicopter to leave and head back to its helipad. As the bird lifted off, Sloan introduced Steel to the others. As Steel had guessed, all department heads, all except one – Foster.

'This is Alison Price from Homeland, Charles Tipp from the NSA, and this intence looking gentleman is Lloyd Bolton from the CIA.' Steel shook each one by the hand and gave a curious head bow to each.

'So, do we call you Major John Steel or agent Steel of MI8, or as we know it IMIA?' Sloan asked.

'Glad you did your homework. Makes things easier,' Steel said.

'Well, you've done enough work with all of our agencies to be known to us. Glad you were here on this one.'

Steel just nodded. 'Any news on Foster, sir?'

'He's in the hospital. It could have been worse. Doctors are working on him now. They'll let us know,' Sloan said. 'He's a tough old bastard. He's gonna make it.'

Steel smiled and shook his head. 'Na, he's just too stubborn to die.'

'Let's hope we are both right,' Sloan said.

'Do you know what happened?' Steel said, looking about, noticing the crime scene techs doing their thing.

'Car bomb,' Sloan said. 'Must have been the same sorry sons-of-bitches who attacked your friends there,' Sloan said, pointing to the upside-down Outlander that sat in the place a barrier had been.

'Are they OK?' Steel asked.

'They're in a conference room, giving us a statement,' Sloan said, with a curious look in his eye, an almost distrustful look.

Steel experienced that bad feeling again. He could feel their suspicion burning into him. And, in their shoes, he might do the same. After all, they did not know him. He said he was Foster's friend, but what if Foster had never mentioned Steel to them.

As far as they were concerned, he was a British citizen who had sent a Mossad agent to a US Embassy. Steel had to admit if someone was telling him the facts, he might be inclined not to believe them either.

Foster was there to make it worse, so he had no alibi for being in the country.

'Shall we talk inside?' Sloan said, showing the direction to the main entrance with an outstretched arm. Steel could feel Marine's gather round as they walked. A wall of highly trained muscle was blocking his exit.

Steel checked out his surroundings. Exits, how many guards and where what type of weaponry they had. Steel noticed a row of photographs. All were high ranking officers, one Steel had seen before, a man called General Leyermont, but he had been a colonel when Steel first met him. Now the photograph showed a white-haired man with tanned skin and wide eyes. He had put some weight on since Steel had seen him last. Bains of a desk jockey Steel had thought.

Steel knew an escape plan might be in order, just in case this whole thing went south. The air was thick with the smell of fumes and burnt cars, making breathing harder than usual. It was nearly twenty degrees outside, and the sun was high and unforgiving. Despite the promise of conditioned air, Steel was a little anxious about going inside this secure building. All they had to do was go into lockdown, and he would be trapped. Sure he could get out. After all, that had been his job in the SEALs, but it would also mean innocent people would get hurt.

And he wasn't there to be the bad guy.

As they entered the building, Steel felt the sudden drop in air temperature, and it was glorious. The fact was, it was the coldest he had been all day – and it felt good.

Steel was searched for weapons, then asked to go through the metal detector. He was glad he ditched the pistol when he knew the helicopter was coming. These Marines would have been all over him in seconds. One-on-one isn't a problem. Three on one with space to manoeuvre wasn't a problem. But he had more than six nearby and another six who were armed with assault rifles, all ready to take him down if necessary.

As Steel passed through the detector, he noticed Sloan nodding to their heavily armed escorts, who saluted and took up posts in the lobby. Making Steel wonder if they had just been an intimidation tactic?

Sloan led the way through the building, assuring Steel that Samara and Kane were OK. But the feeling something has off stayed with Steel.

They all walked through long corridors, which had the same tiled floor and cream walls and overhead lighting as the lobby. The whole place was generic. Everywhere had the same doors, the same windows, the same sized rooms. It was like being in a New York office block. Steel followed Sloan as they moved deeper into the embassy until they reached a conference room. It had a single wooden door with brass fittings. Sloan opened the door and let Steel go into the room before him. Steel wasn't sure if it was a polite gesture, or he was going to find himself in a secure room, and the door suddenly slammed behind him. So Steel smiled and gestured Sloan should go first.

As if understanding Steel's concern and motive for the action, Sloan smiled and nodded. The room was surprisingly long. With pure white walls and not that annoying cream the rest of the building had. There was a red carpet on the floor instead of the grey tiles, and the lighting was provided by two brass chandeliers.

The room's centre was a long English oak wooden table, which had been highly polished to a mirror finish. Surrounding the table were twelve ornate high backed chairs, five on each side, and two sat on the ends. On the table were two conference phones and some bottles of water.

Steel took in the two flags on pikes at the end of the room. The American and Maltese Flag crisscrossed, and the base, in the centre, were two pictures, the American and Maltese Presidents. Steel thought it was a very diplomatic room. The room walls were decorated with paintings from both US and Maltese history, works of art in oil and finished with golden frames.

They all sat. Sloan sat at the head of the table with Tipp to his right and Bolton to his left. Price sat next to Tipp, leaving Steel to take the seat next to Bolton. Steel waited for someone to speak. He imagined lots of questions, most of which Sloan would use to paint a bad picture of Steel's situation.

'So, Mr Steel, tell me more about what this man, that you brought to us,' Sloan said.

'Stan Falan?' Steel said. 'The others called him the Falcon.'

'So, what did this Falcon say?' Sloan wore a neutral expression as he spoke.

Steel sat and nodded for a moment as if he was thinking about what to do next. Steel noticed a dark grey device on the table. It had three arched arms, each of which had built-in loudspeakers and a microphone. In the centre was a square plate around 12 inches in diameter. This was the device wifi function for accessing cellphones. This was linked to an overhead projector designed for conference calls. He smiled and stood up.

'How about if I show you?' Steel took his cell phone and plugged it into the nearest device. Grabbing the remote control, Steel started the film of the interrogation he had recorded. Then he picked up a bottle of water from the middle of the table and sat.

The group watched as they heard Stan's confession. About the defence company and how they had arranged everything for profit. How they had used a terrorist organisation to do their dirty work. They had all been betrayed for money.

'Who else has seen this?' Sloan asked.

Steel paused for a moment. The hairs on the back of his neck stood up straight. Taking a sip of water from the bottle before he answered. 'Nobody, only us,' Steel said, his eyes fixed on Sloan.

'Good,' Sloan said as he quickly pulled out a 9mm Sig Sauer P320 pistol. As Sloan took aim at the Tipp, who was on Sloan's right. Steel reacted and hurled the water bottle at Sloan's hand, knocking the weapon to the side. The shot hit the wall leaving a small hole in the wall.

Steel leapt over the table, knocking Sloan off his chair and onto the ground. Steel knelt over Sloan and punched him hard in the face before he grabbed Sloan's pistol hand, forcing the barrel of the gun away from Tipp, who had rolled out of his seat – or anyone else. The door burst open, and the Marine who had been standing guard reached for his gun. Sloan jerked his hands to the side, pulling Steel down enough for Sloan to react with a headbutt. The hit did not connect properly, but it was enough for Sloan to regain control of the weapon.

The Marine stood confused for a moment at what was going on. He pulled his service Sig Sauer P226 and went to aim, but Sloan saw the weapon and panicked. He fired to the side and shot the Marine in the left foot. The guard let out a cry of pain and dropped to the floor, nursing his wound.

Steel grabbed Sloan's gun hand and twisted. Sloan screamed out in pain as he felt his tendons and muscles stretch and twist out of place. He expected to hear the crack as his wrist broke. The pistol fell from his grip, hitting him in the shoulder. Steel reacted by elbowing Sloan in the face – giving him enough time to brush the weapon to the side. It skidded across the carpet but not far enough for Steel's liking.

Sloan slammed a punch into Steel's side, but his muscles took a lot of the impact. Steel punched Sloan's face then tossed the man over his shoulder and onto the side of the table. Sloan's back slammed hard against the wood, letting out a moan as the wind left his lungs. Bolton went for the gun, but Sloan had seen him and kicked a chair hard, which slammed into Bolton, causing him the fall over the chair, his face smashed against the floor. Sloan rolled off the table and kicked Bolton in the ribs' side. He doubled up in pain.

Sloan picked up the gun just as Tipp ran for the door. Steel picked up a nearby chair and hurled it at Sloan, but as it hit, Sloan fired, shooting Tipp in the side of the left arm. Sloan hit the ground, and the pistol slid across the floor. Steel moved over to the Marine. His feet slid on the carpet. He was tired from the fight and exhausted from dehydration. Steel reached down and grabbed the Marine's cuffs, then turned to Sloan, grabbed him by the wrist.

Sloan forced himself up, knocking Steel backwards. Steel lost his grip, Sloan dived across the floor to grab for the Marine's Sig Sauer.

Several shots rang out – which echoed loudly in the confined space, defending everyone in the room. Steel looked over at the open door, where a man stood with Sloan's gun in his shaking hands – it was Calver.

Sloan lay in a bloody heap on the floor. The hallway outside was full with the deafening sound of an alarm, which drowned out the heavy pounding from the Marines' boots as they ran for the door. Their weapons drawn, ready.

Sloan had taken several tight shots to the chest. Steel looked at Sloan and then back at the department chiefs, each of which wore a horrified look.

Calver let the pistol drop from his hand. He had no use for guns. The truth was he did not really like them unless it was on a computer game.

'Nice grouping, pity we needed him alive,' Steel said mockingly as he checked Sloan's pockets. Along with his wallet and ID, there were two cell phones. Steel cracked a smile. He knew one was for business, and the other was hopefully in contact with the Trojan organisation. Steel clicked it on, it was password-protected, but he could see one number had tried calling him. The caller ID said Beta.

'What for?' asked Tipp, who was nursing his wound.

'We needed to know what they have done. Stan mentioned the software. Something was going to make it fail. We need to know if it has been done or not.' Steel said.

'Both,' Calver said. Everyone looked over to Calver, who slapped a hard drive onto the desk. 'I was meant to swap it today, but then the car bomb went off last night, putting everyone on alert. That's when I realised; I was supposed to get caught with this, so when it goes wrong, I get blamed.'

'I take it that's a fake?' Steel asked.

Calver nodded.

'That's what they gave me,' Calver said. 'And before you ask, a courier gave it to me. I never knew who sent it.'

Steel nodded.

'What would you get from this?' Steel asked, taking a mouth full of water.

'These people knew things about me, my past. They had enough on me to send me to prison forever, and what they did not have, they said they would make up. I was scared,' Calver said. He had fear in his eyes. But Steel could not be sure why. The fact he had just killed a man or the fact he could be going to prison without trial. 'What would you have done?' Calver wondered about his friend – Bryce, and why he hadn't heard from him in a while. Then he looked at the bloody mess that had been Sloan and realised – Bryce was dead.

'They said it had to be done today,' Calver said with a terrified look on his face.

'Makes sense. The programme goes online tomorrow at midday,' said Alison Price. 'If there were to be a switch, it would have to be today.'

Steel looked at the hard drive with confusion.

'If the drive has been changed already, why send you to swap it for another fake?'

'I told you,' Calver said. 'So I would be caught and get the blame.'

'Yes, sure I get that – but what if you had succeeded, what if you had swapped them? From what you are saying you, would be swapping a fake one with a fake. It does not make sense…unless?' Steel paused as he let his mind work on a theory.

'Unless… what?' asked Tipps, who was sat down holding his arm.

'This software, what does it do again?' Steel asked as he went through his phone pictures until he got to the map's photograph and beamed it onto the back wall.

'It's a next-generation anti-terrorist software. We call it body mapping. It's a step up from facial recognition.' Bolton said proudly.

'OK,' Steel said, gazing at the map. His brain starting to put as many of the pieces together as he could. 'Here's a theory. If Calver has the original software, someone swapped it out for a fake because someone was paying big bucks for it to fail. That someone being the organisation. Calver has the original. He gets caught with it, so what would you do when you find out it was swapped out?' Steel asked the men.

'We'd check it and swap it back. But why do it in the first place? It makes no sense,' Tipp remarked.

'Actually, it makes perfect sense. It's a double dupe. Stan already said they were using the terrorists, so what if this software went online after they thought it had been sabotaged?' Steel said.

'They'd all be caught, but this guy Stan said they were going to be blamed for something…' Bolton said, then thought for a second. His eyes widened with clarity. 'The car bomb?'

'No, I got a bad feeling it's something else. The embassy strike I saw the plans for would only be the start,' Steel said, his gaze fixed on the sixty-by-twenty map. 'But we shouldn't worry about that just yet,' Steel said, turning to face them. 'You need to find the others. Before they kick down your front door tomorrow.'

'What are you thinking?' asked Price, her eyes following Steel's gaze to Calver.

'What is it you do?' Steel asked Calver with a cunning smile.

They all raced over to the blockhouse and took the elevator down. The Chiefs looked uncomfortable with Steel's presence, but after everything, they would waive it. The paperwork for keeping his mouth shut would come later.

'So what's the plan?' Calver asked nervously, hoping he would see daylight again after everything that had happened.

'You keep watch of the whole island, right?' Steel asked.

'Right,' Calver replied nervously.

'Ok, so, if you have Malta on satellite, it shouldn't be a problem to pick an area and go back on any activity happening at that point, correct?' Steel asked.

'In theory, yes.'

'Just try it. It might be a long shot or not. You won't know if you don't try,' Steel said. Calver shrugged and pulled up a screen on his monitor.

'What we lookin for?'

'Find the farmhouse in Gozo, near a place called Qala. Then re-trace anyone who had left there in the last hour before I arrived,' Steel explained as if he did it every day.

'What farmhouse?' Calver asked. His voice wrang with a mix of a question and fear he would be searching every farm on the damned island until they found the correct one.

'Oh – you can't miss it. It should still be on fire,' Steel said with a serious face. Calver shot Steel a look, then turned slowly back around.

'Oookkkaayyy,' Calver said.

Calver followed Steel's directions to find what was left of the farmhouse. Then used the downloaded data to track back.

'When do you want to start?' Calver asked.

'I'd say... yesterday afternoon, two o'clock,' Steel said.

'Why two o'clock?' Price said, raising an eyebrow.

'The ferries over from Gozo,' Steel said. 'They run, what? Every forty minutes? Our boys aren't in a hurry, but they also don't want to be caught in a rush,' Steel explained before taking another sip of water. 'Most tourists will want to go over in the morning or afternoon. That means most people will be going over to Gozo at around half one, and a half-empty ferry will be returning to Malta around two,' Steel said.

Bolton, Price and Tipps nodded. They could not find any fault in the logic, and it did make sense.

Calver typed commands into the computer, and a new picture came onto the screen. It was a picture of Gozo at two o'clock the day before. Calver played with the scroll mouse and zoomed in on the farmhouse. It was busy with box vans, cars and lots of small shapes moving about – people.

'We got them, four vehicles in total, unknown numbers of targets though,' Calver said. Bolton picked up his phone and called the watch commander while the Price phoned Washington.

Calver tracked the trucks to their new safehouse and wrote down the address. As he handed it to Steel, Tipp snatched it from Calver and read out the targets' location. Steel looked over to Calver and nodded with a subtle smile.

'Good job.' Steel patted Calver on the shoulder as he got up from the desk.

'OK, let's go,' Steel said, rushing towards the corridor which led to the elevator. Suddenly Steel felt a hand on his shoulder, and he stopped.

'Sorry, Mr Steel, we can't let civilians get involved. You've done a hell of a job, now let us do ours.' Steel nodded at Bolton's request. Sure, it was dangerous for civilians, but Steel wasn't a civilian.

'I take it you know who I really work for, and you just want me to – ?'

'We know who you are, Major, and who you work for, but this wasn't sanctioned by them, so this is our rodeo. Do we have a problem?' Bolton said. His words were hushed and angry. Bolton did not appreciate a Brit rocking their apple cart, especially their secret service.

'And just in case, there will be four Marines posted around the room. For your protection – of course,' Bolton said.

'But of course.' Steel smiled casually.

Steel watched as Bolton, Price and Tipp, with a medic trying to attend to his wound, rushed off to make phone calls and set up briefings – all except Steel and Calver.

Calver sat back on his chair and began to rock backwards and forwards. Steel picked up one of the bobbleheads from the desk and nudged the head – causing it to wobble back and forth.

'Thanks for saving my arse back there,' Steel said.

'No problem,' Calver said, as though it was nothing.

'I take it you didn't like him much?' Steel said, putting down the toy. Calver reached over and held the head of the figure, so it stopped moving.

'Why do you say that?' Calver said innocently. His gaze moving over to the computer screen.

'Because you shot the guy in the balls before the nice grouping,' Steel said, with a respectful grin.

'Like I said...nice grouping.' Steel patted Calver on the back.

It was twenty minutes later when Price, Bolton and Tipp returned. They had a game plan, and it would involve Calver. He was to give minute by minute intel to the ground forces. He had done the same thing for years, but under different names, working for lots of various agencies. He wasn't a double agent, just a guy who liked his work but got uncomfortable being in one place. The CIA knew his rap sheet, and if anything, it made him more attractive to them, or rather Sloan, who had hired him. Now Calver knew why.

Two Marines teams would back up the Maltese Rapid Intervention Units as they breached the building.

A sound plan typically.

However, Steel knew these were extremists, and they would do anything to take out US soldiers if they had the chance.

The infiltration of the safehouses would have to be swift and with no prisoners.

Steel grabbed a chair and pulled it over to calver's desk. Leaving Calver to do his thing.

The time moved on slowly.

They watched as the teams move into the safety cordon. Getting briefed by the team leader, discussing triangulations and positions.

Steel was forcing himself not to scream at how long it was taking. He drank the bottle of water dry, then tossed it into a nearby wastebasket.

'You got a coffee machine here?' Steel asked.

'Down the corridor, to the left, there's a break room,' Calver said, his gaze fixed on the monitor.

'You want anything?'

Calver shook his head quickly as though moving slowly would make him miss something. Steel got up and headed for the breakroom, all the while checking what the other screen watchers were doing.

Steel still had no clue what the group had planned. The embassy would be a big statement if it were they who were planning it. But it wasn't. They had outside help.

As Steel walked past one monitor with a big guy with a Punisher logo on his T-shirt. Steel stopped. His gaze fell on the monitor and appeared to be a familiar shape – it was a C-130 transport plane.

'Where's this?' Steel asked with fearful curiosity.

'Tunisia, why?' asked the man in the chair.

'How long has it been there?' Steel asked.

'I don't know… a couple of days…why?' the tech asked.

Steel's blood ran cold.

'Who's dealing with my photos?' Steel asked, suddenly looking around the room.

'Sarah, I think,' replied the T-shirt guy. His large football head full of nervous sweat.

'Imagine I have no idea who Sarah is?' Steel growled in a low, quiet voice. The man stood up and pointed to a pretty redhead in a far booth.

'Thanks, and nice t-shirt,' Steel said before rushing over to speak to Sarah. Sarah was slender with long thin legs covered by black and red striped long stockings that came up past her knees. She had cut off jeans that she had made into shorts and a pink and white t-shirt. Steel figured Sarah was in her late twenties, and from what he could see of her t-shirt and the gathered on her desk, she had a thing for fat unicorns.

'Sarah? Hi, I'm John. Those photos, have you done them yet?' Steel asked impatiently. He watched as she opened the image and showed it to Steel. Steel leaned forward, leaning on her chair for support while staring at this stranger next to her with large, curious, blue eyes.

The image on her screen had been enhanced and blown up. Steel moved forwards, and so did she. Steel looked over the map. He knew he had seen something in the room, something that had caught his eye, but never really took notice. Looking harder, he saw a bit of an island or some landmass on the corner of the photograph.

'Can you make it bigger?' Steel asked.

'Sure,' Sarah replied.

As the image enhanced, he saw one of the markers was in Tunisia – specifically an old airfield by the pictures he had seen on the monitor. Coming from the picture was a red piece of string leading upwards to the top of the map.

Steel kissed Sarah on the forehead and ran back to the T-shirt guy, who monitored the plane.

'Has anyone been to the aircraft recently?' Steel asked, hoping he wasn't right.

'Uhm...yeah. Yesterday,' T-shirt guy replied. 'They were loading crates. Probably medical supplies,' the T-shirt guy said. Steel shook his head and raced towards Calver.

'Calver, you need to let the chiefs know there is a plane leaving Tunisia and heading for the States. I think it's got a bomb board,' Steel said.

Calver shot Steel a disbelieving look.

'How could you know that?' Calver asked, excited by the explanation.

'These people want to make a lot of noise. They've got a large cargo plane, which means they are carrying something big. What do you think will happen if a military plane goes down in the US and explodes? Who will get the blame, especially if the US Embassy had been attacked?' Steel said. 'They will track it back to Tunisia, and as usual, they will put two and two together and get seven.'

Steel picked up Calver's cell phone, put his own number into it, and then made a note of Calver's number from his desk phone.

'In case I need you,' Steel said. 'Just pass the information on the Bolton and the others,' Steel said, tossing Calver's phone back to him. Calver thought about it, then nodded.

'OK, I'll let them know. Wait...where are you going?' Calver asked. Steel nodded over to the T-shirt guy who was watching the transport plane.

'Catching a flight,' Steel replied.

Chapter 70

Steel rode the elevator to the ground floor of the blockhouse. He'd had enough of being sidelined. That's not who he was. Besides, the others would be busy with the assault on the safe house. The doors opened, and he shielded his eyes from the sudden brightness of natural sunlight. Even with his sunglasses on, the sun's glare was still intents.

Steel stood for a moment and basked, taking in the warmth and sunlight.

'We were told nobody must leave,' came a voice by the main entrance. Steel opened his eyes and smiled at a young Marine guarding the entrance. Steel figured Marine was green, very green. Possibly fresh out of Boot Camp. He already looked nervous. Steel smiled to himself as he approached the man who was no more than 19.

'I'm here to pick up the two people who gatecrashed earlier. Can you tell me where they are?' Steel said, flashing his NYPD identification quickly.

'Sorry, that a need to know, sir,' answered the Marine. Steel walked towards the guard, still wearing his smile, hoping it would calm the man.

'Good answer Marine, however, I've just come from a meeting with director Sloan, and he's asked me to collect them,' Steel lied.

'Sorry, sir, I've had no orders to let anyone through,' said the Marine. Steel knew the man was just doing his job and doing it well. But Steel was pressed for time.

'That's fine, not a problem, it's just we've got the Pentagon on the horn, and they want to speak to the Mossad agent. But that's fine. I'll just go back and tell General Leyermont… What's your name, Marine?' Steel asked. Leaning forwards to check the name patch on the guy's uniform.

'Uhm. Over in the main building, sir, the first floor they're in one of the safe rooms there,' the Marine said nervously.

'Thank you, son,' Steel said, giving a quick nod and a well-done smile. Steel could sense the man had started to sweat the moment he'd mentioned the general. Steel was just glad he'd paid attention to some of the Generals' photographs and names in the lobby.

He walked out and headed across the parking area to the main building. There were two guards at the front and two roaming patrols. Steel felt safer already, but he'd feel a lot better when he had found Samara and Kane. Steel passed the guards unhindered. Steel figured they had seen him come out of the blockhouse, so he must have some sort of authorisation. As he walked in, he saluted the men, who returned it just as quick.

Steel smiled, remembering something his old sergeant used to say. *If you look like you should be there, people will assume you should be there.* Steel hoped that his battered appearance could be attributed to the car bomb if he asked Steel to say that he had been there all night. A flimsy excuse, but more feasible than trying to tell the truth.

Unfortunately, he referred to gate crashing big parties rather than infiltration – but it seemed appropriate for both cases.

The inside of the building was plush, with a more friendly feel to it than the outside. Rolls of red carpet covered a brown marble floor was by leading to the many ground floor rooms. A mix of antique and modern furnishings dressed the walls and offices. The place had the feel of a grand hotel.

Staff moved about, going here and there – their lives controlled by their tablets and cell phones. Steel walked towards a grand staircase that ran along the right wall, giving maximum floor space to the lobby. He walked up casually, nodding a greeting to perfect strangers. Most of which did not even register him. Steel figured that the people worked by the theory. *If you made it in, you must belong there.*

Of course, this made his life easy as he explored the building. Steel stopped and thought back on what the guard had said, 'on the first floor in one of the safe rooms.'

Steel proceeded down the long hallway. Which, like the rest of the interior of the building, looked more like a stately home. With luxurious rugs on wooden flooring. Antique furniture and an expanse of oil paintings. There were brass chandeliers with crystal teardrop, There were vases from China and ornaments from Malta and Gozo. Steel made it to the first floor, with no clue where Samara or Kane would be.

But he had an idea.

Unfortunately, there were plenty of rooms to choose from. Still, Steel was looking for only one in particular –one with a guard outside of it.

If Steel knew the three-letter agencies like he thought he did, Samara and Kane would be separated. Hopefully, on the same floor, and if he were in luck, they would be next to each other.

Steel turned on to another corridor where he saw the guard. He was a man in his twenties, tall and slim. His black hair was cut short on the sides but left a bit on the top to style. He wore a black suit, white shirt and possibly a Sig Sauer P226 in a belt holster.

Steel moved towards the guard casually. There was no need to spook him or give him cause to set off any alarms.

'Hi, I'm looking for the two Mossad agents you're keeping up here,' Steel said. As if he worked there. The guard shot Steel a concerned look.

'What two Mossad agents?' asked the man. His voice was deep and accent-free. 'We only have one, and he's in here,' said the guard opening the door. Steel looked over at Kane, who was lying on the table of the small room.

Steel walked over to the table and found Kane fast asleep. Steel poked him.

Kane did not move, just snored louder.

'Kane,' Steel said.

Kane continued to snore. Steel rolled his eyes and looked to the heavens, then tipped the table. Kane crashed onto the floor with a yelp. The guard at the door smiled to himself and looked away.

'What did you do that for?' Kane yelped, rubbing his back.

'Nice to see you too,' Steel said. Kane smiled and shrugged apologetically.

'Where's Samara?' Steel asked.

'I don't know. We got separated after they brought us in. They asked me a bunch of questions and then stuck me in here,' Kane said.

Steel turned to the guard, a look of urgency on his face.

'Where's the woman?'

'What woman, sir? I was told there was this guy, no woman,' said the guard.

'Fine, he's coming with me. The director wants to see him,' Steel lied, hoping the guard hadn't yet heard of Sloan's fate.

'Fine with me, I'm sick of his complaining anyway. I was thankful when he'd fallen asleep,' said the guard, who headed back down the corridor. Steel ushered Kane out of the room, then headed back out the way he came.

Samara was gone and possibly in danger. Someone wanted her out of the way. Now, Steel was afraid that they had finally got her. Kane followed Steel down the corridor to the stairwell, his expression worried. The two men moved quickly but casually, down the stairs and out of the main entrance. Now they were heading back to the blockhouse. Hoping someone could tell them where Samara was. As they approached Steel, they saw Lloyd Bolton coming from the blockhouse. He looked worried with a cigarette between teeth ready to light up.

'The woman, where is she?' Steel asked, catching the man by surprise.

'What wom…' Bolton started to speak, then saw Kane. 'Oh… the Mossad woman?' Bolton said, lighting the cigarette. 'She's in the main building, a couple of doors down from that pain in the ass,' Bolton said. He indicated Kane, who just smiled at the thought of being so much trouble.

'No, she's not,' Steel said. 'I found him, but she's missing,' Steel answered. Bolton thought for a moment. Then taking out his cell, he made a call. He waited for a while, then started talking. Bolton had turned his back and moved out of earshot.

Steel looked at Kane – who just shrugged. Bolton turned slowly and faced Steel, the look of horror on his face.

'What is it?' Kane asked. 'Where's my sister?'

'Sloan had her transported out of the embassy. She's heading to the airport,' said Bolton. Slowly placing his phone in his pocket. Steel looked at his watch; they could not have left that long ago, so he might be able to catch them up.

'I need a car,' Steel said urgently. Bolton pointed to the row of black Yukon SUV's.

'Keys should be inside, anything else you need?' asked Bolton.

'Yes – delay that software going online. I think this whole thing is about that going online,' Steel said.

'You got two hours at the most. After that, it's out of my hands,' Bolton yelled as he headed back towards the blockhouse door.

'Roger that,' Steel replied, heading off towards the row of SUVs.

Chapter 71

The safe house near Attard was still. Aamir's orders had been clear – no one was to be outside until it was time. No lights or loud noises, no television or music.

It appeared no one was there.

The house itself was out of the way, far from prying eyes. But Aamir wouldn't take any risks. All it would take was someone to see them bring them down. All contact with the Master had been severed to prevent the authorities from tracking either of them. It was a risk, but the Master thought it necessary, especially with the new software going online.

The Angel told the Master it was taken care of. But Aamir wasn't so sure; he trusted the Master but not the word of someone he had never seen.

Aamir watched his men get the weapons ready, magazines filled. He had a look of pride on his face. Many of his men would not be coming back, but they had prepared for the next life. Of course, he would be holding back with the second team once the assault had taken place and the blockhouse was taken. Team two would control the computers and send viruses over the net to all connected, causing a security panic like no other. The Angel had told the Master which computers to use and give them passwords.

A young boy ran up to Aamir. The boy had an innocent smile on his face, wide brown eyes and scraggly black hair. The boy was no more than ten years old, but he was a soldier.

This boy would lead the fight.

He would ride his bike to the gate and tell some tale about being lost. The guards wouldn't think twice about the school bag on his back. The explosives inside the bag would make a large hole and bring the guards running. That's when Aamir's men would hit the second gate. A decent plan if ever there was one. After all, nobody knew they were coming. Despite the incident at the main entrance, Aamir was confident the plan would still work. His men had been foolish to have not taken the Mossad woman out earlier as she and her companion drove to the embassy. But it did not matter now. Things had been set in motion, and the plan had to go ahead, no matter what.

The Marines and Maltese SWAT teams stood ready a few houses down from that which had been identified as the terrorists' safe house. The four mixed teams waited at their assigned points, while the entry team's had the lead. They would breach the front and rear entrances. The Marines were there as support, both with snipers and cover fire as required. The Marines did not like it, but they were on someone else's turf.

A simple job.

Aamir sat on an old kitchen dining chair the previous occupiers had left behind. He took a long draw on his cigarette as he watched his men. The boy had gone to bed. It was late, and he needed to be fresh for tomorrow. Aamir could tell his men wanted to sing. Let their voices fly and be carried on the wind for everyone to hear.

But that was not possible.

Not tonight.

Tomorrow they would sing, tomorrow they would roar like lions, tomorrow they would be more than men.

They would be legends.

Windows shattered as several flashbang grenades were shot through into the ground floor and the first floor. This was quickly followed by four explosions and blinding flashes as the flashbangs activated. Four loud pops sounded outside the safehouse as the breaching crew took out the front and rear door using a solid shot from Remington shotguns. The doors splintered at the frame and were kicked open. At the front of each breaching crew was a man with a ballistic shield, behind him seven men from the mixed force team. Two terrorists stood in the small hallway holding the sides of their heads, blind and deaf, disorientated. Both were quickly brought down. The front door breach team swept through the hall, checking rooms as they went. As they entered a large room on the right, sparks flew from the shield as four terrorists opened fire with their AK-47s. The team behind the shield paired off, moving to the right and left of the mobile cover. Then took out the four gunmen. The rear door crew encountered four men in the kitchen. One of the men from the local RIU team took one shot into the vest. But he returned fired as he lay on the ground, taking out his shooter. As the teams converged inside the building, the noise was deafening. The night air was filled with more roar of explosions from shock grenades, yelling and screaming.

Aamir stumbled about, half-blind and deaf from the flashbangs and stun grenades. His hands are waving about, hoping to find a wall or something stable to steady himself.

Gunfire rang out.

Bullets whizzed past Aamir, striking one of his men in the chest. Screams of pain sounded from all over the place. The smell of gunpowder and smoke from the grenades filled the room, stinging Aamir's eyes. He was half-blind, confused and dazed.

There were bursts of light as Aamir's men fired blindly. Their bullets impacting on the ballistic shields of the entrance team. There was more gunfire, but this time no screams as two of the terrorists were cut down instantly.

Aamir started to get his hearing and eyesight back. There was a noise from upstairs.

It was the boy with the explosives. Soon all would be consumed by fire, and the Master would be pleased. It wouldn't be the Embassy, but this would do.

The shouting stopped along with the gunfire.

Aamir looked up at the staircase, waiting for the child to do his duty. A tear rolled down Aamir's face as he saw the boy carried down the stairs by an RIU policeman. The boy held on to the armoured cop – he confused and scared.

Aamir burst with rage and ran at the child with a grenade in his hand. Suddenly Aamir was pushed to the side as if a gust of wind had blown into him.

But no sound of breaking glass, the sniper had shot through one of the broken windows.

Aamir fell before he could pull the pin.

Blood oozed a hole where his chest used to be. The .50 calibre round had punched through his body like going through butter, ripping a football-sized hole in his back.

The grenade rocked in Aamir's hand.

Then – stopped.

The RUI cleared out the injured and waited for the bomb squad to make the building safe.

The Marine team leader watched as the RIU men exited the building. With him, his opposite number in the RIU looked relieved.

'Good job,' said the Marine.

'You too,' replied the RIU Police Sergeant before he walked off to see his men.

The Marine pressed the switch to operate his throat microphone.

'Zero, this is Echo One-One. Threat eliminated. Seven injured, thirteen dead. No friendly casualties. Over,' said the Marine, team leader.

'Roger that. Good job. Return to this location. Out,' Bolton said, then leant back into the chair he had been hovering over ever since the operation started. Bolton and Price were sat in the operations room – they had been huddled around Calver's screen, watching the operation unfold. Tipp was back upstairs making calls to the Pentagon.

'What now?' asked Alison Price as she strolled over to another chair. Her black high heel shoes tapping on the polished floor as she went.

Bolton looked over at her and shrugged.

'That's in Steel's hands now, thank God he was here,' Bolton said, venting a breath he'd been holding onto for a while.

'Yes – isn't it? I just hope we don't have to kill any more of Steel's friends to nudge him to do things for us,' Price said with a smile. Bolton looked at her with a shocked expression on his face.

'What do you mean?' Bolton went to stand up, a confused look on his face.

Alison Price drew a Smith and Wesson M&P 9c nano pistol – and put a bullet into his left leg. The bullet hit the upper thigh, just at the fleshy part of the outer muscle. Bolton hit the deck with a scream of agony – grasping the hole in his leg.

The blood flowed freely between his fingers and pooled quickly on the shiny surface of the floor.

'Don't worry, Lloyd, I'm not going to kill you – not yet anyway,' Price said with a cold smile.

Calver rushed over to thee medkit and ripped it from the wall, then rushed over to Bolton. The rest of the staff screamed in a panic and rushed for the elevators.

'Now, don't you boys go anywhere,' Price laughed and left the room. They knew she would be heading for the elevator. They also knew they were trapped down there. Price could make up any story she wanted. She could even tell people to ignore any phone calls from the Blockhouse. She could say it was part of the lockdown. Price could even say that Bolton had killed everyone, and securing the elevator was the only way to contain him.

They watched and waited – making sure Price wasn't going to change her mind and come back to finish them off.

She did not.

The two men stared at the doors, each man holding his breath in anticipation.

The silence was deafening as neither of them spoke. The second ticked by.

'I take it that bitch has left us down here to die, then?' Calver said.

'Yeah, lucky us,' Bolton nodded. Sweat was pouring from his brow.

Calver used the medical kit's scissors to cut open Bolton's trouser leg to check the wound. Bolton winced in pain as Calver checked the back of the leg to find an exit point.

'It's a through and through. You're lucky.' Calver opened a packet containing a strange-looking syringe device which contained what appeared to be mini marshmallows.

Bolton looked at it and shook his head. 'What the hell's that for?'

'This,' Calver said, plunging the twelve-inch clear plastic tube into the wound and pressed the plunger, injecting the miniature blood soaking sterile sponges into the wound.

The container emptied, and Bolton passed out.

'Your welcome,' Calver smiled as he started to bandage the wound.

Calver's thought drifted to Steel and what he might be doing. Then his thoughts went to what Steel might do to Price when he found out what she's done.

Calver had read up on this John Steel character, and he was more than impressed. In fact, just reading the file had sent shivers of fear down his back.

To Calver, it was all fascinating, but what was more mysterious was the British military intelligence file on him.

John Steel was a spy – or agent – or something for the British Secret Service. Calver had seen his record sheet, the things Steel had done. Calver knew that Price was going to pay.

Far down the brightly lit corridor, Price ambled between the work sections and the fake windows. Two of the Marines who had stood guard down the corridor ran towards Price.

'What's going on, Ma'am?' one of them asked.

'It's agent Bolton. He's been shot, quick, you have to help him,' Price said in a panic. As they rushed past her, she shot them both in the back of the head. Price shook her head. A cold smile crossed her face as she walked down the series of doglegged corridors to the elevator. She found a group of people hammering at the elevator door. Screaming for it to open. Price raised the weapon and shot them, one bullet for each, one round either in the head or the chest.

Price watched with amusement as the light came on over the elevator doors showing it had arrived. There was a gentle *ping*, then the doors slid open. She watched as some of the bodies fell into the small metal box. To her, it was comical – like a scene from a comedy film.

She smiled to her self coldly, then began to pull the bodies from the elevator then stepped inside.

Chapter 72

Steel was back on the Triq L-Imdina road and heading southeast. The streets were full of afternoon traffic, making driving slower than he had hoped.

'So where are we going?' Kane said.

Steel shot Kane a confused glance. 'The airport... we're going to the airport, remember?' Steel said.

'Yeah, I get that, but which part?' Kane asked.

The happy, confident feeling Steel was having melted. 'What do you mean – what friggin part?' he growled.

Kane said nothing. He took out his cell phone and activated the *find cell* app. A map came up, and a tiny red dot showed Samara's cell phone – and her location.

'She's at the by the Lufthansa hangers,' Kane said, leaning over and putting in the new location into the navigation system. It took a few moments. The map swivelled and turned, zoomed in and out and recalculated a new route.

Steel shook his head in disbelief. The new route would force them south onto the Triq Ta' Hal Farrug road. He just hoped it wasn't a narrow street full of traffic and parked cars. Steel looked down at the dark blue arrow showing the direction. The computer voice was calming and set with an American accent.

Steel was happy with that – it could have been worse for him, and it could have been in Maltese, and he had enough on his mind besides driving. Steel just nudged vehicles out of the way – sometimes, on purpose.

Steel still could not believe Sloan was part of it all. Foster had spoken so highly of the man.

In the end, Sloan had betrayed Foster and the rest of his country. But, Steel had the nagging suspicion Sloan was only a pawn in all of this. Stan had confirmed that the Trojan organisation was behind this. Sloan had been an agent of the organisation that was clear to him now. Steel figured Sloan must have been the one who had provided the hardware. The C-130, along with the weapons and vehicles, the safe houses for the terrorists. Stan had been the go-between, giving the terrorist information. Steel had come across the Trojan organisation more than once. The organisation had people everywhere, and its main goal was power. Sure Steel's old enemy – an organisation called SANTINI was a bunch of high-level scumbags who worked in the shadows. They were into licence killings, money laundering, espionage gun-running. But they had no interest in power or ruling the world – not like Trojan. The Trojan organisation wanted absolute power and control, and they would use any means necessary. But Steel couldn't figure out what they wanted with the Blockhouse in Malta? Sure, there was a reason Sloan wanted the terror strike on the embassy. However, Steel did not know what it was yet. The truth was he wasn't thinking about that. Steel's full concentration was on Samara, and why Sloan wanted her on a plane?

Kane held on as Steel wove between moving vehicles, causing horns to sound in anger.

Steel did not care.

Samara was about to get on a plane with men who probably weren't even agents and go who-knows-where. Steel's hands gripped the steering wheel tight and drove like a manic. Despite all of his excellent skills – driving wasn't one of them. Steel had been impressed by Samara's driving. She was able to manoeuvre the car in and out of impossible situations.

His mind focused on the road and the distance yet to travel.

Kane let out a yelp and pointed at a sign for the airport – 5 miles to go.

That meant Steel had five miles to formulate a plan.

Plenty of time, Steel thought to himself as he turned the vehicle abruptly – throwing Kane against the window of his door.

'So, what's the plan when we get there?' Kane said, rubbing the side of his face.

'I'm working on it,' Steel said.

The road took them through what appeared to be an industrial estate with new buildings on either side of the street with trucks at loading bays. The voice on the navigation system told them in four hundred metres to turn left at the roundabout. Steel's eyes locked on top of the road, searching for the first signs of the roundabout. The turning was coupled with a long grassed roundabout with four palm trees and waist-high bushes.

Steel took the turn hard and forced the SUV down the road, smiling with relief. It was a double road and not a narrow street like many he had been used here.

Every chance Steel got, he floored the gas pedal. Overtaking cars that sauntered along in front of them. For them, time was of the essence, and there was no room for those casual drivers – not today. Once Samara was in the air, there was no telling where she would end up or what they had planned for her.

Steel saw a large group of buildings peeking from the top of a tall brick wall. Then the brick stopped and was replaced by a wire fence with razor wire spiralling across the top. Steel could see the airport and another set of buildings with the air company's recognisable dark blue decorating parts of the walls. Steel noted there weren't so many aircraft at this part of the airport. It was possibly reserved for smaller aircraft such as private jets.

Steel rechecked the position of Samara's phone on the screen. The red dot continued to blink in the same spot.

She hadn't moved.

Steel did not know whether to be happy or worried – but he had to believe she was OK.

'Where is this?' Steel asked Kane.

Kane checked the satellite view, using his fingers to zoom in.

'It seems to be a hanger next to that building,' Kane said. 'Pity this isn't live, I could tell you what was going on,' he shrugged disappointingly.

Steel said nothing. He was busy concentrating on the road and trying to form a plan. Whatever they were heading into, it wasn't going to be good – No handshakes and introductions.

'This could get messy,' Steel said.

'What? Messier than at the Embassy?' Kane smiled.

'Good point.' Steel continued to weave in and out of the traffic.

'There should be an entrance coming up,' Kane said, checking the satellite image once more.

'Seen,' Steel confirmed.

'You got a plan yet?' Kane said.

'Get through the front door and take it from there,' Steel said.

Kane swallowed nervously.

As they approached the airport entrance, the phone rang. Kane answered it and put it on speaker.

'Yes,' Kane said.

'Who's this?' said a voice. Steel recognised Calver's voice.

'Never mind Calver – he's with me,' Steel said. 'What's up?'

'Price just shot Bolton and the rest of the staff on my station,' Calver said. 'They're all dead – apart from Bolton and myself that I know of, I think she just wanted Bolton to bleed out or something.'

There was silence for a moment.

'Is he OK?' Steel asked.

'Yeah – we both are, thanks for asking,' Calver replied angrily.

'Yeah, sorry, forgot you were all sensitive.' Sarcasm oozed from Steel's tone.

'What about Price?' Steel asked.

'I spoke to the watch commander. She'd already left the embassy compound. All agencies have been briefed. The airports and ports have her photograph. She won't get far,' Bolton said confidently.

'I see you guys are at the airport,' Calver said, staring at his monitor closely. The receiver of the phone hitched between his cheek and his collar bone. 'You catching a flight?' Calver said, confused.

'No, hopefully – stopping one,' Steel said. 'Samara's been taken. We think whoever is behind this has her on a plane,' Steel said.

There was silence for a moment while Calver used the satellite to pinpoint any unusual aircraft.

'Well, there is an aviation display on at a hanger near you, looks like some firm pitching their latest aircraft to some people,' Calver said. He could see around thirty people walking around at the front of the hanger. Still, the only angle he had was from above, making confirmation impossible.

'Anything else?' Steel asked. He swerved to miss a car, then yanked the wheel until they were back on their side of the road. Kane sat with wide – terrified eyes, his back embedded into his seat. He knuckles on his hand, white as he gripped on to the handle above his head.

'There's a lear jet near there.' Calver's voice was hollow.

'Company jet or civilian?' Steel asked. Almost knowing the answer before he got the reply.

'It's one of ours – and Steel, they are loading people on,' Calver said.

'How long do I have?'

'Not long, so haul ass,' Bolton yelled from his position on the floor.

'It's the third hanger at the end, past the main building, you have to go through a security barrier, so you'll need a good cover story,' Bolton said, taking over the conversation.

'It's OK – I have an ID,' Steel said with a smile. 'Thanks, Bolton,' Steel said.

Bolton looked at Calver with a confused look. 'Where did he get an ID from?' Steel heard Bolton's confused voice over the speaker and cracked a smile. Suddenly there was a beep beep beep from the cell phone.

'Bollocks, we've lost the signal, must be interference from something close by,' Steel said, taking back his phone and placed it in his pocket.

As they pulled up to the security barrier Steel, saw the guard. He was a short, stocky guy in his late forties. He wore the same sort of blue-shirted uniform as the embassy. His clothes were neatly pressed, and he looked the part. His face was round, and black hair clung to the sides of his head. The guard wore a weary expression. Then he saw the vehicle and stared up at Steel – and the expression changed.

'Afternoon, gentlemen,' said the guard. His voice was low but friendly.

'Afternoon,' Steel replied. Reaching into a side pocket of his jacket, and pulled out a black ID wallet.

'You here with the other group?' asked the guard.

'Yeah, we are, sorry we're late, some idiot forgot itinerary files,' Steel lied in his best New Yorker accent. 'Where they at?' Steel asked politely. Steel showed the guard the ID, making sure the sun reflected off the clear plastic. But the guard just smiled and nodded. Steel figured the guy had seen enough of these vehicles come through that he knew the registrations off by heart.

'No problem,' the guard said. He stepped back slightly, giving himself enough room to point the directions out. He had been doing it all day, and now it was just like muscle memory. 'Just follow the road over there, past the main building, you'll see your friends.' The guard pointed. 'Have a good day, Agent Bolton,' said the guard, letting them through.

'When did you snatch that off him?' Kane smiled as he looked over at Steel. Steel just smiled silently as he grabbed the ID and placed it back in his pocket.

Steel drove past the main building, hidden by the three-story building casting across the concrete. Steel saw where the other Yukon was parked. It stood alone – abandoned near the third hanger. Steel looked over to his right to see the crowds of people looking at something in the first hanger. Then he noticed a banner for Sikorsky and a picture of something that looked like a helicopter. He shook it off, and his gaze locked back onto the third hanger. The lack of people around the car or the hanger was left him with a bad feeling – worst of all – there was no plane.

'Didn't the guy on the phone say there was –?' Kane said.

' – a plane – yes,' Steel said. 'He did, so, the question is... where is it?'

Steel parked by the hanger, and a man in a pair of blue overalls came out. He was small and thin, his face and hands dirty from oil and grease. He wore a blue baseball cap which shaded his eyes from the glare of the sun. Like the guard – he was in his forties, but this guy seemed to have aged better.

'There were some agents here? I was supposed to meet them, but the traffic was terrible,' Steel said, using his New York accent.

'Sorry, agent, you've just missed them. The plane just took off a few minutes ago,' the man said. Steel thanked him and drove off quickly to avoid any questions. Steel knew he could not ask for a flight plan because he said he was meant to be on the flight. Steel found an excellent spot to park and pulled out his cell phone. Steel checked that he had a signal. The display showed only one bar. He just hoped it was enough. He pressed redial and waited for Calver to pick up.

'You just missed them,' Calver said.

'I know,' Steel said. 'Is there any way of tracking the plane?'

'Yeah, we already have the tail number. Just give me a second,' Calver said. His fingers danced over the keyboard. He kicked the mouse and entered some numbers, followed by more clicks from the mouse. 'OK, got it.'

'Can you plot a route, possibly tell me where they could be heading?' Steel said.

The bad feeling was back again.

'Hold on. They're heading for...' Calver said.

'Tunisia?' Steel said.

'Yeah, how did you—?' Calver said.

'Remember that plane T-shirt guy was tracking?' Steel said.

'Yeah.'

'Well, I bet they are heading for that plane now,' Steel said.

Before, Steel could not figure out why they would need Samara. She was an inconvenience – a pain in their assess. But now he understood why they wanted Samara – she was Mossad. The perfect person to be found on the plane with terrorists makes it appear as though the Israelis were behind it. Tensions between the US and the Israelis had been tense these past couple of years. A bomb going off would be enough to sway public opinion.

Someone wanted the unthinkable – a war with the Middle East.

America against Israel. But it wouldn't end with America. There would be a call for NATO to get involved. Possibly Russia would back Isreal or even China? And the company that had the contract to supply the armed forces would make billions.

'Calver, what's the quickest way to get there?' Steel asked.

'Flying, I guess. Takes about an hour,' Calver said with a sorrowful tone.

'But – I won't make it will I?' Steel said as he did the maths. The plane would be ready to go as soon as their valuable cargo touched down. By the time Steel was even close, they would be halfway to Spain.

'No, sorry, we've got nothing that would get to you in time. Whoever it was, they took our only jet.' Calver's words rang with regret.

'Steel, you know what we have to do. I'm sorry,' Bolton said. As he forced himself to stand and looked over to Calver's monitor, which now showed the C-130.

'Yeah. I know,' Steel said before hanging up. He wanted to yell and toss the phone, but he kept it inside.

There had to be a way to catch them – but he knew deep down the only way to stop them was an airstrike on the plane. Steel could imagine Bolton on the phone to the Pentagon, explaining what had happened. Asking for permission for the USS Nemesis aircraft carrier to send its fighters. They would probably wait until it was in the air and over the ocean. Nobody knew what was on the plane, but whatever it was – wasn't good. And if they took it out while it was still in Tunisia, it could lead to the very problems that they were trying to avoid in the first place.

Steel looked over to the first hanger. He had remembered the poster they had seen on the way in – the helicopter.

Steel got back into the car, and Kane followed. Steel did not wait for Kane to buckle up. He just put his foot on the accelerator and drove towards the first hanger. As they grew near Steel, they hit the breaks hard, almost sending Kane through the windshield. Steel lept out of the car like the thing was on fire and ran over to the hanger. Inside, there were groups of men and women, all dress, ready for a meeting or a business deal. Steel looked around at several aircraft on display – future concepts. But Steel's interest lay elsewhere.

As Steel neared, he smiled as he recognised the silhouette of the latest concept of the Sikorsky helicopter. The machine was sleek and shark-like. The grey of the metal shone from the overhead lighting of the hanger. As well as the top twin-rotor blades, it had a single propeller at the rear. Two slit vented engine exhausts sat at the top near the rotors. The side loading door was open, displaying the plush interior. Steel figured this was the civilian version and not the military. The whole thing looked like something from a science fiction movie – yet, here it was.

Next to the machine stood three men. One was a pilot, and the other two were sales representatives from the aeronautic company.

'Excuse me, gentlemen,' Steel said. 'Is that the new S-98 Raider Mark 2?' All three men looked shocked – but also intrigued at this strangers question.

'Possibly,' said one of the suits, a tall man in his fifties.

'Are you with the Embassy?' the man said. The words were drawn out as if he was cautious about what he was saying – and who he was saying it to.

Steel smiled and flashed Bolton's ID.

'Agent Bolton, CIA. I need to commandeer your helicopter and pilot. It's an emergency,' Steel said, a stern look on his face.

'You've got to be joking, agent Bolton. We are getting ready for a grand unveiling,' said another suit.

'I'm afraid not, sir,' Steel said. 'We have a global situation. Just one question, is it fast enough to catch a C-130?' Steel smiled, moving closer to the helicopter. Steel needed to know, just in case, the terrorists had already taken off with the transport plane by the time Steel had got to Tunisia.

Steel figured it was the talk of a live field test that had sold them to the idea. The thought of the helicopter catching up with a C-130 had them working out their bonuses for the year. Of course, Steel had to agree to the pilot filming the whole thing.

Steel could hear the *thump thump thump* as the rotor blades picked up speed. Steel felt the pull as the helicopter lifted quickly. Then the electronic whir as the landing gear retracted into the main body. As they reached ten thousand feet, the aircraft pulled forwards, and the engines roared like a savage beast. Unstrapping himself from his chair, Steel moved forwards to the cockpit, his phones still tightly fixed onto his head. Before they took off, Steel had phoned Calver. The phone rang twice, and Bolton answered.

'Steel, what's going on?' Bolton asked.

'I'm borrowing a helicopter. See if we can get to the plane in Tunisia before they take off,' Steel explained.

'Sounds like a plan, but we got jets on standby to blow that bird out of the sky once it's in international waters, no need to worry, we got this,' Bolton said.

'Samara's on that plane, I've got to try,' Steel said, looking over at Kane, who silently nodded.

'Damsel in distress, huh. God, you damn limeys and your gallantry shit,' Bolton laughed at the thought of Steel on a white steed and shining armour.

'Something like that, but most of all, I owe her.'

Bolton remained silent for a moment.

'Look, I just need a safe frequency the pilot can patch through so we can talk, and Calver, I'm going to need your eyes on this. I need to know locations and directions.'

'Rodger that,' Calver said, typing something into his computer. 'We can chat on 134 megahertz,' Calver replied.

'Thanks, guys, speak to you soon,' Steel said before closing down his phone. Steel gave the pilot the frequency Calver selected. Steel figured he would need Calver to direct them to the C-130. There was a lot of sky out there, and Steel did not have time to guess where they would be.

Steel had left it an open channel, so the pilot would get the information directly and would be able to compensate quicker if needed.

'So, what happens when we get there?' asked the pilot.

A question Steel was dreading because up to now – he had been winging it. All his thoughts had been on getting to the plane before it took off. Now he would have to think about how they would get to the transport plane in flight. He knew there was no way they would get to it before it took off in Tunisia. They could not shoot it down – first off, Steel was in the civilian model – not a gunship. But more importantly – Samara was aboard.

'Calver you there?' Steel spoke into the microphone of the headset.

'I'm here.'

'How are we looking?' Steel asked, hoping for good news.

'That lear jet is already about twenty minutes in front of you, need to get a move on or change ya plan,' Calver said. Steel realised that his negotiations over the aircraft had cost them time. If Calver's computations had been correct, it was about an hours flight. The lear jet had a twenty-minute leed on them. That meant they would have to fly west until Calver gave them a course to move to. Not ideal, but it was the best they had.

'Got any parachutes?' Steel joked.

'Back there somewhere,' said the pilot. 'We were due to pick up some of your parachute display fellas after the presentation and do a display.' The pilot pointed backwards, using his thumb towards the rear of the craft. 'I think their gear is in the back already.'

Steel turned and followed the pilot's direction moving slowly, keeping low as not to get knocked over by the many small pockets of turbulence. He found a storage bin containing several parachutes.

Steel smiled.

Now, he had a plan. They would have to get close to the transport plane, and Steel would have to find a way inside. The C-130 had several hatches on the top he could use. The trouble was opening them.

'Calver, can you access the C-130's onboard computer to open a hatch?' Steel asked.

'Uh – yes – why?' Calver asked. His words were drawn out in fear of the answer.

'I'll get back to you on that,' Steel said and sat back in his seat.

Chapter 73

The CIA's Learjet aircraft touched down on the dusty tarmac of an abandoned Tunisian airstrip. The sun beat down hard, and the wind was dry and harsh.

The side hatch from the jet opened with a heavy *clunk*, then the steps extended towards the ground. Angry voices left the plane, and then Samara appeared at the top of the stairs. Samara raised a hand to shield her eyes. Blinded by the sudden, intense sunlight.

'OK – get going,' said a voice behind her. Samara walked down steadily, her hand still shielding her eyes while her other handheld onto the rail for support. Behind her was the giant man who had tried to take her to the old barracks. His nose was thick and purple, and dark circles surrounded his eyes. The rest of the team were behind him, each carrying M4 Mk 18 CQBR rifles with ACOG 4X32 scopes and tri-magazines. As Samara reached the foot of the stairs, she looked over at the massive C-130 transport plane. The four propeller engines' noise was deafening, and black smoke billowed from the exhausts at the four Rolls-Royce engines' side.

The man behind Samara nudged her forwards using the elbow of his gun arm.

'Go on you, your going for a little ride.' He grinned maliciously as he nudged her in the back again. Samara turned, anger burned in her eyes, her pearly white teeth bared into a snarl.

The man just laughed and pushed her again, harder. Samara looked at the hardware the men were carrying and decided against the move she wanted to make. The kick in the balls and the knife to the carotid artery could wait until later.

Samara looked around at the almost deserted airfield. By the look of things, it hadn't been used since the second world war. Around the plane were ten men, five on either side of the loading ramp. Then Samara saw another man approach. He was an older man dressed in white cotton garments and holding a strangely carved wooden walking stick.

Samara knew this man from his file. He was the one they called the Master. Even though he was in his sixties, the Master was as dangerous as they come. As his file read, the Master pulled no punches when it came to chaos, so this whole thing came as no surprise to discover he was behind this.

'Welcome, my dear,' the Master said as she approached. His voice rang with politeness and something some may mistake as fondness. 'It appears you will be joining us after all – I'm so glad.' The Master smiled. The old man stepped up to Samara and brushed the back of his scared hand on her cheek. Samara jerked her face away, repulsed at his touch.

The Master smiled gently.

'As you can see,' the Master said, turning towards the C-130, 'we have a little surprise visit planned for the good people of the United States.'

He pointed his cane towards several large crates that sat in the middle of the transport plane's loading bay. They were heavy wooden crates. Some were long, others short and box-like. They were a mix of wood and brown metal. Samara realised with horror what they were. They were hundreds of boxes and crates, full of weapons and ammunition, broken down and strapped onto pallets, tied down with cargo nets.

Samara had seen the same thing many times, but they had been for aid packages.

'Those are weapons, you're going to…' Horror and disbelief stopped her.

'Yes.' the Master said. 'We shall drop these in the heart of the Washington D.C and watch the people wreak havoc. We will rejoice as the country tears itself apart. Their country will burn, and their own people will be responsible for its demise,' the Master said. His voice was loud like it was a war cry. His followers cheered as the Master raised his arms.

Then the Master's gaze fell onto Samara, a wicked grin etched across his face. His eyes alight with passion and blood lust.

'But don't worry, my dear, you won't be making the journey alone,' the Master said. His voice returned to its calm and friendly tone.

Samara shivered at his unnerving presence.

'We have a friend of yours with us to keep you company,' the Master said, with a hideous smile, like a snake before it struck.

The big man pushed Samara in the back, urging her up the ramp to the aircraft's cargo hold. As she reached the top, she saw the silhouette of a man. He was sat on the canvas bench at the far end of the plane near the cockpit. His features bathed in shadow, but she could make out his hands and feet, which were illuminated by a console's red light. His back was flat against the fuselage or the plane. He was a big man, all dressed in black, which made the white plastic of plasticuffs stand out against his clothing's dark. His hands and feet were bound.

A tear of despair rolled down her face as hope left her. She did not know how, but Steel was meant to save her. He was supposed to suddenly appear like he always did and rescued her. Instead, he was bound and was sat in a darkened corner, the strength missing from his body.

She did not cry just for her but for him. The stories she had heard about him painted him as some mythical beast to be feared.

A green-eyed demon some had called him.

But all she saw from his place in the shadows was a man whose will had left him. The legends had been wrong. In some way, she pitied him. That he would go out like this.

A broken man.

Chapter 74

The S-98 helicopter travelled fast through the clear blue sky. The engines screeched like a banshee, giving it a distinctive sound. Steel could imagine the helicopter's military version, the shiny skin of this model, replaced by a matt anti-infrared green or black. The shape, coupled with the terrifying howl from the engines, would be enough to make an enemy crap themselves.

'Steel,' Calver's voice came over the headset.

'What's up?' Steel asked. Surprised at the sudden call.

'Looks like they are getting ready to take off, so – what's the plan?' Calver asked.

'You know that question?'

'What, the one about – ?' suddenly silence filled the airwaves as Calver figured out what Steel's next plan was. 'You know that's completely nuts?'

'Probably,' Steel replied as he started to pull on one of the parachutes.

'You know, as soon as I pop the hatch, the plane is going to lose control because of the lack of cabin pressure?' Calver asked nervously.

'Know it, I'm actually counting on it,' Steel said. 'can you do it, though?' silence filled the headset. 'Calver – Calver?'

'Yeah, I'm here, and yeah, I can do it.' There was a whistling sound over the headset as Calver exhaled.

'Thanks, the pilot will let you know when,' Steel said.

Silence.

'Catch you on the other side,' Bolton's voice crackled over the headset.

'Just make sure he does it, Bolton,' Steel ordered.

'He will just make sure that plane doesn't get stateside,' Bolton said.

Steel did not answer. He just let the crackle of the airwaves fill the void. Steel just hoped he was making the right decision. The futuristic new attack helicopter was pulling at two-hundred and seventy miles an hour. Possibly the fastest Steel had travelled in a helicopter. Steel looked out of the windshield at the landmass in front of them. Tunisia grew nearer. Steel knew if he did not bring the plane down, an F-22 Raptor aircraft from the USS Nemesis would make sure the transport plane did not make it across the North Atlantic.

Steel watched intently as they approached the two miles point. Steel and the pilot saw the Hercules C-130 travel upward then level off.

'So, what was plan B?' asked the pilot.

Steel scowled at the image of the plane getting away. 'Try and get close to it, will you.'

'Where do you want to be?'

'Inside it, before the damned thing took off,' Steel said, still using on the New York accent.'But, I guess on top just behind the cockpit of it will have to do for now.'

'I'll get you as close as I can,' the pilot said. He was both confused and scared. Whatever this man had planned was bound to be completely nuts – but would make great footage for the bosses.

Steel knew this could end in several different ways. One of which was him impacting the cockpit like a bug hitting the windshield of a car. Another was with him flying into the propellers and getting blended. Even with the parachute, he would have only one chance. He had to get on the aircraft somewhere in the middle. He knew they had several emergency hatches on the top – he just had to find one – and not get ripped off the plane or sucked into the propellers.

Steel hoped Calver was right, and he could get the hatch open once he got onto the plane. There weren't any latches he knew of, only the internal ones. Steel began to worry. If Calver could not, Steel would have to think of something else – and each moment, the Raptor was getting closer.

'There she is,' said the pilot, pointing to a distant aircraft.

'Get her up, as close as you can,' Steel said.

'Sure you wanna do this?'

'No, not really, but I've got no choice,' Steel said. His eyes fixed on the plane in front.

'You'll have to tell Calver when to open the hatch. Luckily, he's got three to chose from. I just hope he opens the right one,' Steel said.

They watched in silence as the rear of the transport came into view. It was getting closer and closer as the pilot of the helicopter pushed the craft to the limit. Once he was over the C-130 transport, the helicopter pilot match speed until Steel was inside.

The helicopter began to shudder as the pilot pushed it to the max. The helicopter pilot was hoping the C-130 wasn't going full speed. The pilot flew parallel but keeping a safe distance above the C-130.

Steel just hoped the transport pilot hadn't seen them. If they had, the pilot would start manoeuvring. But the transport plane remained true and steady.

The timing would have to be perfect, the helicopter would level off above the transport plane, and Steel would jump down. If they heard a bump, the people inside would think it was a bird or something. They wouldn't be expecting a crazy guy jumping on top of a moving plane.

The helicopter pilot moved over the C-130. They were at least twenty feet above. Steel got him to close the gap as much as he could. Steel could be blown straight off the roof of the plane without touching it if there was too much distance.

The helicopter lowered.

Ten feet. They began to feel the turbulence rocking the helicopter.

At five feet, the helicopter began to shudder and sway. Caught in the wake turbulence from the engines of the transport.

'If you are going to do it, it needs to be now,' said the pilot, who was now struggling with the controls.

Steel raced for the side door of the helicopter. His timing would have to be precise.

'Your friggin nuts – you know that?' said the pilot.

'I've been called worse,' Steel said, opening the door. There was a blast of air and the helicopter rocked from the change in air pressure. But the pilot kept the craft steady.

'Good luck Agent Bolton.'

'Ah, yeah, about that,' Steel said. His accent was gone. 'My name's not Bolton. It's John Steel.'

Steel grinned, shrugged, pulled off the headset – then jumped.

The pilot eased off the power, and the helicopter slowed slightly, inching back over the transport plane. He began filming with the HD camera, taking it all in like it was some action movie.

Steel hit the sheet metal hard just behind the cockpit. He was amazed the pilots hadn't noticed the helicopter that had been above them. The impact winded him slightly, but the air current had taken most of the damage away, but he was still going to have a bruise on his chest to show for it.

His target was one of the three emergency escape hatches on the roof of the plane. Steel was hoping that Calver could open one of them before he got ripped off the plane.

Steel lined himself up as best as possible as the downdraft pushed him, and the oncoming wind was ripping him backwards. As Steel began skimming the surface of the transport, he started to grasp at anything that would hold him. He had already passed two of the hatches, and now he was beginning to get nervous. It would just be his luck if Calver managed to open the hatch at the front of the plane, or even the primary loading ramp – underneath the tail. Steel was dragged down the length of the aircraft like a ragdoll, his hands desperately grasping at anything. Cursing the makers for their aerodynamic design – hell – even trains had handholds. There was a *clunk*, and the hatch opened. Steel quickly grabbed the sides. Steel could feel the muscles in his arms straining as he fought to hold on. The plane shuddered and banked to the side. The sudden loss of air pressure had done precisely what Steel had thought it might. Steel imagined the pilot struggling with the controls, fighting to bring it to five-thousand feet to level it off. The wind dragged him backwards while he gritted his teeth, and with all his strength, fought to pull himself down towards the hatch and drag himself inside – Calver had come through.

In the helicopter, the pilot sat stunned. His mouth opened closed like a bass out of water. Not believing what he had just seen and also hoping he had caught the footage.

The new helicopter hovered where it was, only turning to capture the shots. As the plane disappeared into the horizon, the helicopter pilot banked and headed home.

Calver and Bolton watched the monitor.

They had seen everything and still could not quite comprehend what they saw.

'Nice job,' Bolton said, patting Calver on the shoulder.

'I'm just glad it worked. You think I want that guy tracking me down cause I fucked it up?' Calver said with fear in his eyes.

'Yeah, you're probably right,' Bolton said. 'Crazy ass limey,' he laughed. Bolton went to walk away. He had a call to make upstairs. They needed the cavalry down here, and he needed a doctor, but he stopped and turned.

'Can you predict a route, a flight plan, I mean? Find out where these assholes might be going?' Bolton said.

Calver started to type and click the mouse. Bolton watched Calver work. His method was fluid, with no starting or stopping. It was only one motion. He was slightly jealous. His typing involved two fingers and a lot of swearing.

Calver stopped, and his eyes stared slowly at the screen.

'So…got anything?' Bolton said. Calver turned the monitor so Bolton could see.

'Shit…their heading for the States,' Bolton said. His voice was full of fear. 'What the hell are they carrying on that plane?'

Calver shook his head, unable to speak, and wore the same look of fear as Bolton.

Chapter 75

A call to the embassy lobby brought the troops down. The guards in the lobby of the blockhouse were told of the situation. As Bolton had thought, Price had given some bullshit story about how they were not disturbed because of the software. And because of the lockdown, anyone leaving the hive should be detained – regardless of who they were. And they had believed her.

And why shouldn't they?

After everything that had taken place over the past couple of days, it seemed feasible.

'Nobody in – nobody out,' were her orders. But Bolton had spoken to the watch commander, explained everything. Now the big green machine was in action. But Price was already gone.

The medics saw Bolton. He needed stitches and lots of whiskies. He had refused to go to the hospital. He needed to see this through. If not for all the people who had died – then for all those who would have – or still might.

Calver stayed downstairs, monitoring the feed and Steel's progress. He had watched what Steel had done on the plane via the satellite feed – then grabbed a wastebasket and thrown up.

Bolton sat in Sloan's office on the second floor, which was closer to the hive's clinic. It was just a small set up for slight injuries, but it was adequate for the medics that had come down to attend to the wounded. He was seated in Sloan's old chair, sipping a glass of eighteen-year-old malt. He thought if he had to bleed anywhere, it should be over Sloan's stuff and not his own. So far, this operation regarding the new software had been a complete clusterfuck.

Bolton still could not get his head around the fact they had Foster's daughter killed just to get Steel over to the island and that the section chief of the Homeland was dirty.

Foster was in the hospital after been blown up in the parking lot, and to top it all, terrorists were in a C-130 heading for the States with an unknown cargo. But it was unlikely to be gifts or medical aid.

Bolton took a large mouthful of the Balintines whisky and stared at the picture of Sloan's family that sat on the edge of the desk. Bolton was thankful the ambassador was out of the country for a visit to Italy.

That had at least been one less problem to worry about.

Now all he had to think about was the activation of the software. A programme he still did not know would work. The tech department had a look at the two hard drives and found that Steel was right. Calver had indeed had the original software. The other was a variant on the program. This would have had the opposite effect. It would have hidden know terrorists and shown all agents.

Bolton was still confused why anyone would have gotten Calver to try and swap them back. Still, maybe Steel was correct in his assumption. Someone needed Calver as a scapegoat. Calver was never meant to get in and switch them, and if something happened to him and the drive was found, he would naturally get the blame.

The question was, who?

Price? Or Sloan?

Even so, they were apparently working for someone, and that someone had significant resources.

Bolton had someone collect all the items on Sloan's body and put them on the director's desk. He wanted to search the office and Sloan's things to find out what the man was into. Bolton knew the best place to hide something was Inside a secure building, so there wasn't a chance of someone from the outside getting hold of anything incriminating.

Bolton picked up a black leather wallet and looked inside. Two-hundred and fifty euros in notes and seven in change, a picture of Sloan's family, visa cards, insurance emergency card, driving licence.

'Not much to work on,' Bolton thought as he sifted through the wallet. The other items from Sloan's person did not help much either. A zippo lighter from his time in the Marines, a ticket for dry cleaning, a large bunch of keys that included Sloan's house and car, and a packet of chewing gum.

Bolton sat back in the leather office chair and looked at the desk, at its many draws. Bolton considered his own desk, which was simply a six-foot sheet of glass on stainless steel legs. He hated his desk; the damn thing got fingerprints and smudges as soon as you looked at it. But this was an old Victorian oak desk or a fantastic replica.

Bolton tried the three thinner draws at the top. Naturally, the middle one was locked. He wouldn't have expected anything less. Picking up Sloan's keys, Bolton searched for one that matched the old-style lock in the desk. He found one that looked about right and tried it. There was a click, and Bolton smiled as he slowly slid the drawer open. Bolton hoped he wasn't going to find the man's porn collection.

He sighed with relief as he found the paperwork. Bolton began to search through, looking for anything relevant. There were work orders for Sloan's home and memos he had received from the head office – but nothing relevant. Bolton continued the search. There was nothing much, just a pack of unopened post-its and some pens. Bolton also found a business card. It was made from thick card, and the lettering was raised – black writing on a cream coloured background. The card was from one of the companies who were bidding for the new security contract. In the corner was a picture of a horses head, and the name Brian Slater was underneath the companies name.

Bolton figured this Slater character was some hot-shot at the companies sales department. But then, he'd have to be to try for this billion-dollar defence and security contract.

Bolton's right index finger tapped the side of the card, his brain telling him it was important somehow but not why. He took the card and slid it into his inner jacket pocket, hoping it would come to him later.

Looking up at the clock, Bolton saw it was nearly time to activate the software. There was no stopping it; every agency was plugged in and waiting to get the download, so it was active all over the world at the same time.

Bolton stood up and closed the drawer.

The rest could wait.

For now, he had to get everything ready for the installation. As he walked out of Sloan's office and down the corridor, one thought echoed in his mind.

I hope Steel pulls this off.

Chapter 76

There was a sudden rush of air, and the C-130 banked slightly due to the sudden loss of atmospheric pressure. Steel fell hard straight on top of one of the terrorists, smashing him into the steel metal floor. Instinctively Steel grabbed the man's head and twisted. He should have heard the neck crack, but the engines' loud drone drowned out any noise, including his fall. Steel lay for a moment, gathering his breath. His body hurt from his hard landing, but he could not worry about that now. The wind howled through the open hatch. Loose debris was being sucked up and out. That told Steel they were still too high. Steel felt the planes, erratic movements as it rocked from side to side until finally the nose came up and they were flying level. Steel looked around but was unable to see anyone, the stacks of containers was blocking his view. Steel smiled.

If I can't see you, you can't see me, he thought.

Steel searched the ground. He found the terrorist's M4 assault rifle and picked it up, holding it firmly with both hands.

Steel took a moment to get his breath back. The adrenaline was starting to wear off, and he could not afford to be light-headed.

He looked down at the guard he had just killed and searched him for anything useful. Steel found a candy bar and quickly ate it as he continued the search. The chocolate would give him a boost of energy. The man on the ground was tall and bulky. His tactical vest should be the correct size. Steel removed the guy's vest and leg holster and put them on the floor. Steel knew that if he was attacked on the aircraft, he'd need to move. The parachute would restrict that. So, he stripped off the chute and strapped on the vest and holster he had gotten from the man he had fallen on.

Steel took the pistol from the holster and slipped out the magazine. The twenty round magazine was full. Steel placed the magazine back into the housing of the Army issue Sig Sauer M17 and put its weapon back in the polymer holster.

As Steel peered around the cargo's right side, he saw three men sat on the canvas seats. They talked with another three men, who were stood next to another pile of cargo near the cockpit. The plane continued to shudder and rock from air turbulence, causing the men to hold on to the sides of the aircraft.

He moved to the left and checked down the side of the cargo. There were six men, all armed the same way. The men were busy talking. Two of the men were sleeping.

All oblivious to his presence.

Steel looked down to where the guy had smashed his head on the side of one of the boxes. He was surprised the hit hadn't broken the guy's neck in the first place. As Steel moved back around, he noticed something behind the box the man had struck. The crate had moved, dislodged by the man's head impacting on it. Steel looked around. Nobody was taking any notice of what was happening in his direction. They were busy laughing. Steel peered into the gap, hoping to learn more about the contents of the cargo. Steel had already seen the weapons cases and ammunition boxes.

That had been disturbing enough. But something else had caught Steel's eye. Steel looked in closer, inching some of the other boxes out of the way. Now he was able to see into the middle of the pile of boxes.

Steel paused for a second.

Instead of more crates, Steel saw Large silver-coloured barrels with bio-hazard stickers on them. Strapped to the barrels were wires and electronic detonators. This wasn't weapons cash, these were chemical bombs, and they were flying it to the US.

Steel had to think fast.

The simple answer would be to shoot everyone, grab the girl and reset the autopilot, so the plane crashed in the ocean. But they were heading towards the North Atlantic, miles from anywhere, and with no life raft. With that prospect, he may as well stay on board and go down with the plane.

No – he had to find another way.

Looking behind him, Steel looked at the door controls. It would be simpler to jettison the cargo and let them explode in water with no harm to anyone. But once it started, he would have no cover for the firefight that would soon follow. He could not risk blindly firing – he had no idea where Samara was.

Steel looked back at the cargo door controls. He'd had another idea.

He would bring them to him.

Steel snuck back down the aisle towards the controls and lowered the loading ramp. There was a massive rush of air, and daylight poured in like a flood. Lose items were blown out, including the man Steel had landed on. He shielded his face as the torrent of debris hurtled past him. Steel glanced over at the parachute he had stowed near one of the chairs – it was still there. He had at least that for an exit plan.

Steel snuck back to the pile of crates, and using it as cover, moved closer up the plane. The men started to move down. At first two, only two men came. Steel suspected they thought their guy had played with the door controls – possibly fell out the plane.

Steel leaned against the side of the first crate to remain invisible, waiting for them to pass.

The two men passed by, their guns held ready to fire if necessary. The men headed for the controls, hoping to close the door.

Bad idea.

The terrorists never saw the Steel creep up behind them. The first man took a kick to the back, which sent him rolling out of the open cargo door. His hands grasped at the floor of the plane in the hope to stop the inevitable. At the edge, his hands caught something, a ring from the loading straps. The man sighed with relief, but his legs were still over the edge. He wasn't out of danger yet. The man pulled himself over the edge, moving slowly towards the inside of the plane. Sweat poured from his brow.

Steel swept the next man's leg, who landed hard on his back, then Steel gave a swift smash to his jaw, knocking him unconscious. The rushing air carried the body off as if it were paper on a stiff breeze.

Steel moved back to the crates and planned the next attack. This time it wouldn't be so easy.

Knowing Samara was on board, he had to stay hidden and attack carefully. Guns blazing wouldn't do it. Besides, one stray bullet hitting the hazardous containers, and all their problems would be over. Even if they did not explode, the contents were bound to do something unpleasant. But dying wasn't in Steel's plan. He needed to stay alive to find the mastermind behind it all, and it wasn't these terrorists – Sloan had made that clear.

Steel checked on the left side.

The six men were moving down in staggard formation. They knew something was up now the door hadn't closed. Steel stuck to the shadows. He suspected the men on the other side would also be moving in a similar formation. They had probably gotten orders from the cockpit to see what was going on.

Steel waited for the men to move closer to the edge.

Four obliged him while the others stood fast at the sides. Steel chose to cut his losses and headed for the loading switch, and pressed the launch button. There was a metallic clang, and the cargo was jettisoned in seconds, pushing several of the men with it. The other men looked out at their colleagues, shocked at what had happened. Steel grabbed the parachute he had brought with him and opened the canopy. The wall of silk rushed forwards towards the men, engulfed them and dragged them out. Shots rang out as the men fired in panic. Sparks flew as the bullets struck metal and cables.

Steel turned quickly, hoping to see Samara safely strapped into a seat at the front. But all he saw was a monster of a man with a fire axe. Steel drew the Sig from the holster and raised it, but the man swung the weapon downwards with enough force that it would have cut Steel into two. But Steel rolled to the side, the sharp head of the axe slamming hard into the deck. Steel went to fire again, but the plane rolled hard to the side, sending everyone crashing to the side of the aircraft. One of the loose boxes smashed onto Steel, causing him to lose his grip on the weapon. Steel hed his injured shoulder, he did not think anything was broken, but it sure hurt like hell. Steel rolled again, this time to his feet. The beast swung after him but just missing Steel's middle. As the man swung once more, he left his face and the side of his body open. Steel took the chance and landed several punches, which had no effect but to anger the brute further.

'Really – does someone actually breed these for the bad guy's?' Steel groaned.

The man swung again at Steel's middle, just as Steel jumped back to avoid the weapon. The head's blade hit hard, embedding itself into the plane's side and was stuck fast in the wall. Steel picked up one of the empty rifles that had spilt out onto the deck as the cargo was dragged off and smashed the butt of the weapon against the man's left knee. The brute screamed in pain and dropped down long enough for Steel to land another hit on the other the man's head. Dazed, the man got to his feet and swung for Steel, but his sudden blurred vision was the only thing that saved Steel from his massive fist.

The man's fist impacted the plane's wall, making him cry out in pain as he smashed into the glass of the fire extinguisher storage box. Blood and cut flesh mixed with large pieces of shattered glass, making the wound to his hand look angry and painful.

Steel grabbed the fire extinguisher and fired a blast into the man's face, forcing him backwards. Before the brute could recover, Steel gave another blast from the extinguisher, which covered the beast of a man in a cloud of white fog. The man stumbled backwards, disorientated and hurt. Steel gave a final, more extended blast. The rear of the plane was covered in a white haze for a few seconds, but as it cleared, Steel saw with a sense of relief the brute had gone.

Steel tossed the fire extinguisher to the side and grabbed his painful shoulder. He looked over at the front of the plane and dragged his battered body there. He needed to make sure there were no more surprises. So far, he'd had more than he had expected on this trip.

Near the steps to the cockpit at the front, Steel saw two people strapped in and plastic cuffed. Steel froze for a second while he took in what he was seeing. Samara smiled at Steel with a broad, relieved look and next to her was – Foster.

His clothes were ripped, and he was bandaged up in places, but he was alive.

'What kept you?' Samara said, waiting for Steel to break her bonds.

'Sorry, got caught in traffic, and to try and find a cab...' Steel joked. He went back to the cabinet that the beast had broken and removed a shard of glass. Steel walked back to Samara and Foster and cut their bonds.

'I thought you were in the hospital?' Steel said, helping Foster out of the seat.

'I was. Well, +heading there anyways. One minute I'm in an ambulance heading to the hospital. Some medic gives me a shot, then the next thing I know, I'm here,' Foster said, still confused and in pain from his injuries.

The plane rocked as it hit a small pocket of turbulence, forcing them to grab hold of anything stable. Steel looked up at the ladders that led up to the cockpit. The door was closed and probably locked from the inside. Somehow he had to bring the plane down. Steel knew that Raptors were on standby to take action.

Lethal if necessary.

'You've got to get off this plane,' Steel said.

'Really, got a liferaft in that vest of yours? We're over the ocean. I don't think we'll last long, especially if no one is looking for us?' Foster argued. 'Any ideas?' Foster searched through the emergency bins for anything better than a life preserver and a flare gun. They had passed over Spain and Portugal around half an hour ago. They were now approaching Ponta Delgada and its surrounding Islands. Their only hope was to get as close to these as possible, which meant bringing the plane down.

Steel took out his phone and touched a couple of buttons and reset a marker on a map, then waited before putting the phone away in his pocket.

'If you're asking for a cab, I don't think they do this far out,' Foster joked. Steel grabbed the M4 from the floor and rechecked the magazine was full. Samara and Foster followed Steel to the right-hand side of the plane and a crew hatch.

As they peered out through the small round window, they saw the engines. Flames spurted from the exhaust, and black smoke billowed out and carried on the slipstream as the access fuel was being burnt off. The noise from the engines and the rattle of metal was deafening. Samara and Foster watched fearfully, wondering what he had planned.

'So… Steel, what's the plan?' Samara said.

'We are close to Porta Delgada. We need to land there,' Steel replied, his face emotionless – cold – calculating.

'Land or crash?' Foster asked.

'I would prefer land,' Steel said, still looking at the engines. 'But we can't let this plane enter US airspace. We don't know what else they have. I'd rather see this plane at the bottom of the ocean than crashing into a building in the capital,' Steel's voice was suddenly calm and focused. 'I need you to sit right at the back if we are low enough to water. I want you out of the plane via that ramp, put on the vests, the coast guard will pick you up,' Steel said.

'Pick *us* up, you mean?' Samara's words rang with emotion.

'We have to bring down the plane, and the only way to do that is to take out the engines,' Steel said, opening the small hatch, and the plane rocked from side to side from the pressure change.

'Go on – strap in, but be ready,' Steel yelled. Foster and Samara ran to the seats furthest back and strapped themselves in tight. Steel took the automatic rifle and emptied a magazine into the first engine. Sparks flew, and black smoke and flames billowed from the engines. Steel clipped on a fresh magazine and opened up on the next engine. Sparks flew as the rounds impacted the frame. Pieces of torn sheet metal fell away, leaving the exposed components. Then the engine exploded, sending chunks of steel and iron spiralling down to the ocean. Both engines were engulfed in red hot fireballs.

The plane started to bank to the side and fall. The other engines failing to keep the aircraft aloft.

Steel headed for the back of the plane to get ready for the sudden exit. Suddenly something hit him in the back, pushed him to the ground. He had been shot, but the vest had taken the impact. As Steel rolled over onto his back and looked over at an older man approached. He was dressed all in white cotton and wore an angry glare. He looked around at the empty cargo hold, and his anger grew.

'What have you done? You have ruined everything,' yelled the Master.

'Sorry, wasn't big on the idea of some loon crashing a chemical bomb into Washington, let alone two,' Steel shouted over the howl of the wind blowing through the hatch. The Master shot Steel a confused look. Something Steel had just said made no sense.

'What are you talking about?' said the Master, his anger building. 'We were dropping weapons for our brothers. We were going to watch America burn, and their people would fight amongst themselves. They would tear their country apart,' the Master said. 'But you have ruined that!'

'So, why were their two bombs in there?' Steel paused for a moment. The realisation of what was happening suddenly hit him. 'You didn't know. You had no idea they were there. Someone made it so you would take the fall for a chemical bomb. They needed you on this plane for DNA purposes,' Steel said. 'You were meant to die today, but not how you expected, I guess.'

The Master's eyes moved about, his mouth hung open. Steel could see the emotions racing through the man's eyes. Steel stood up slowly. Ensuring no sudden moves. The man in front of him was unstable as it was. Steel did not want to risk getting shot a second time. Who knows, the Master could hit something less protected next time – like Steel's head.

'Sloan was right. You have been set up to take the fall.' Steel thought for a moment and looked back at the Master. 'You never planned to go down with the ship,' Steel said.

The Master looked up at Steel. His pistol was now angled down as if it was too heavy for him. Steel did nothing. He did not rush to take the weapon away from him. If anything, he pitied the man at that moment. The Master's glorious dream had turned out to be a setup.

The Master's face fell as he realised he was just a pawn in someone else's game.

'You were going to drop off the weapons and then scarper back to whichever hole you crawled out of,' Steel shouted over the noise. All the while inching closer to the Master.

The Master nodded.

'But they needed a terrorist. They needed a face to be on television. They needed someone for the people to hate. Just like 9/11,' Steel's expression wained as a thought sprung into his head.

'I've just worked out what this whole thing is about, and I think I know whose behind it as well,' Steel said with jubilation. There was another shot, and Steel was pushed down again. The Master had fired again, but this time in the chest. Steel groaned as he felt the bruise the bullet had made.

'No! You did this,' the Master said, his eyes burning with rage. 'I know who you are, Mr Steel. I'm surprised you are still alive. I was assured you were dead, but no matter, you soon will be,' the Master raised the weapon once more and went to fire. There was a violent crash, and the plane shook violently. Steel and the Master were thrown about in the cargo bay as the plane went into free fall. The two men rolled like rag dolls in a tumble drier. The aircraft was out of control and falling fast. Samara raced towards the cockpit, fearing that there was no pilot. Foster followed after her.

Steel rolled close to the Master and released a punch that should have taken the man's head off, but the movement of the plane meant he just about reached the Master's jaw. However, It had been enough to send blood and teeth flying.

Samara and Foster entered the cockpit, only to find the empty seats of the pilot and co-pilot.

'You know how to fly one of these?' Foster asked. Samara shot him a nervous smile. 'Great, that's a no then.'

'How hard can it be?' Samara said, climbing into the pilot's seat.

'Well, there's good news and bad news,' Foster said, climbing into the seat next to her.

'What's that?'

'Good news is, we are close to land.'

'And the bad?'

'We are too close to land, and neither one of us can fly this puppy, let alone land the sucker,' Foster said, pulling at the controls to try and level the plane off so they didn't crash nose-first.

Samara heaved along with him. Suddenly the only working engines sputtered and died. The fire had burnt them out. The nose tilted down, and Foster and Samara heaved at the half-circle steering device. The nose began to rise slowly, they were no longer diving, but they were losing altitude. The island before them was growing closer.

'Any ideas?' Foster asked.

'No, but we still need to keep this beast away from land. If not, then at least away from a town or city. We need to put this in the water.' Samara said. Foster nodded. They saw a spot near a cliff face. It was away from a beach. It wasn't perfect, but it would have to do. Samara looked over at Foster, and he nodded.

'You done good kid, I just hope someone gets to know that,' Foster said. Samara smiled. Then as she looked over at their target, she gripped the steering column and prayed.

The Master raised the pistol once more and went to fire. But Steel had gotten to his feet, charged the man, and tackled him like a quarterback. The weapon flew out of the Master's hand as he was lifted off the ground and slammed hard into the plane's side. The Master let out a grunt of pain as the air left his body. The Master brought an elbow down onto Steel's injured shoulder, causing him to scream out in pain. The Master smiled. Steel looked up at this hideous grin from the man and headbutted him directly in the face.

'What you laughin at ya, bastard?' Steel said and tossed the man towards the other side. As the Master smashed against the wall, he fell directly on the Sig that Steel had lost. The Master gave a menacing grin and raised the weapon.

'Goodbye, Mr Steel.'

Suddenly, everything was thrown forwards as the belly of the transport aircraft hit the water. Steel and the Master were thrown forwards. Steel landed hard against the side of the wall, letting out an *oomph* of discomfort. The Master slid down the centre like a hockey puck. Water began to flood through the open loading ramp. The plane was tilting down the tail first, forcing the nose was upwards. The hold's contents began sliding down towards the water, coming up fast through the open loading door.

Samara and Foster sat in the cockpit. They were dazed but alive. The plane had come in straight like a glider. The nose had been slightly up, thankfully. Samara could feel a crisp sea breeze on her face, with droplets of water like a slight rain wetting her skin.

'Am I dead? Is this heaven?' she asked, staring up at the bright sunlight above. It all seemed surreal.

'Samara,' Came a voice. She smiled. Was it him, was, had she died, and now she was in the afterlife? 'Samara! Get up, we are sinking, kid, we have to go.'

Samara shook her head as if to wake herself from a pleasant dream. Foster was up and out of his seat. The bandages that the medics had put on him were covered in blood and oil. Samara crawled from her seat. The impact of the crash bruised her, but nothing was broken.

The plane was going down. It was now at a twenty degrees angle, and the aircraft's weight was pushing more in-depth into the sea. But the Master did not care. He wanted his revenge on Steel. The man had destroyed his plans, and so, he would destroy him. Steel began using the seats as a ladder to clamber up, heading for the hatch.

A massive wave smashed against the side of the plane, knocking Steel and the Master to the ground. All the while, the aircraft continued to sink. Steel headed for the hatch, but the Master had other plans. He shot at Steel again, clipping his shoulder, but the kevlar held.

Steel fell once more and grabbed at the impact point. It hurt like hell, and he was getting tired of the old man.

The Master raised the weapon again and fired. But Steel had anticipated the move and had rolled to the side and slid down. Steel stood up and ran at the Master, and rugby tackled the old man smashing his body against the lined walls.

The Master groaned in pain as the wind left him. Steel grabbed the Master's pistol hand and, with a twist, had disarmed him. The Master went to draw a knife, but Steel tossed him to the back of the plane. Blood dripped from an abdomen wound the Master suffered when the plane hit the water. The blood dripped into the water. The Master looked down at the pooling blood and saw something at his feet. He reached down and grasped a pistol that he had lost during the battle. The Master pulled it up out of the water, letting out a roar of anger as he did so. Bullets spat from the barrel as he fired indiscriminately.

Steel knew that was his cue to exit. The old man's aim was getting better, and he was nearly out of luck. The law of averages said that the old man must get lucky at some point, and he only had to do that once.

He'd already had three unlucky strikes.

Steel did not want to find out if four was his unlucky number.

The water was rising and was up to the Master's upper thighs. Defiantly, the Master swore in Arabic and raised to the weapon. The blood dripped from his hand. The water began to change colour around the Master.

'I heard you killed the one known as *HE*,' growled the Master.

'Who the hell is *HE*?' Steel said, confused.

'HE was the one who showed us the way, gave us these gifts,' the Master said.

'What – Stan, or rather the Falcon?' Steel asked, hoping it was, and there was some other guy out there he had to try and get rid of.

'No, *HE* worked at the embassy, the head of this pathetic gathering of infidels,' the Master said, bearing his teeth as he spoke. Steel sighed with relief.

'Sloan, his name was Sloan, and bad news dickhead, I didn't kill him,' Steel went to shrug, but the pain in his side stopped him.

'No matter. Still, I will have my revenge, Mr Steel!' screamed the Master. He fired, the bullet hit Steel in the side of the vest, probably bruising a rib or two. Steel fell to the cold metal of the floor. The water was coming in faster now.

The Master smiled and aimed. 'You shall all burn,' The Master said calmly. Suddenly the room turned a brilliant red as Samara fired a signal flare directly at the Master. He screamed as the phosphorus burnt into his midsection. His robes began to ignite. The Master's burning body began to stumble around, flaying his arms and screaming before dropping to his knees and falling to the metal floor. All three watched as his burn body slipped into the water and disappeared.

Steel, Samara and Foster clambered out of the hatch and hauled himself to the top of the craft. The plane had crashed on Vila Do Porto's island's southern tip and had anchored itself on jagged rocks to be battered by waves. The tail end of the transport plane was hidden under the swirl. Steel stood precariously on top of the wrecked plane, hoping not to slip and join the Master in a watery grave. He saw that the wing had snapped off at the joint to the main fuselage, leaving an angry mess of twisted metal framework and sparking cables.

Steel stood for a moment and closed his eyes. Letting the crisp, salty sea air and the crisp sea breeze envelop him. He took a moment to take in the fact they had survived. Against all the odds, they had succeeded.

Steel opened his eyes and took in his surroundings. Steel had half expected to find themselves on top of a sinking aircraft in the middle of the ocean. But Samara and Foster had made it to the islands. Steel stared down at the broken wing and smiled. It had fallen across the tops of a group of rocks, providing a bridge to safety.

Steel walked over the wing and looked over at the wreckage of the plane and the endless ocean. Smiling, Steel turned, admiring the view. Chaos mixed with beauty. Steel knew that Calver would be monitoring their movements while everyone else got ready for the software installation. Bolton had tasked Calver to keep watch and give reports.

At last, Calver had something good to say.

Plane down. Three survivors. Cargo lost at sea.

As they waited on the wing for rescue, Steel had told them everything. About the farmhouse, Calver, Price, Sloan – everything.

Chapter 77

While Price had been causing chaos in the Blockhouse, Tipp had been several floors above speaking with Washington. They had agreed on a delay in putting the software in action until it could be verified as untampered with and genuine. Tipp had told Bolton the news while they were stood in the operations room. At the same time, a computer technician from the company varified it using his secured laptop. The company sent the technician over with the software about a month ago. The guy was there just in case of any issues – not that the company envisaged any at the time. But Washington had insisted there was tech support on hand.

Bolton agreed the delay was for the best. Besides, nobody knew it existed. There would be nothing in the media to report on this breach in the security system. Bolton stood awkwardly against the wall. He had his leg bandaged by the medics, and he was forced to walk with a crutch.

Calver sat at one of the booths. He was nervous but at the same time relieved. He no longer had to look over his shoulder where Sloan was concerned. But Calver also knew he was either very unemployed or very unemployed and going to jail.

Bolton felt easier now he knew that the plane hadn't made it to the US, and Foster was still alive. Price was still at large, but a call the Bureau had sealed her fate. She would have three-letter agencies and law enforcement looking for her.

Tipp was on his fifth espresso, was in charge of the installation of the software.

Bolton had to admit he was happy someone else had that job. Being the one to flick that switch was too much of a risk. Bolton was in line for the directorship. He did not need any mistakes with the software. Besides, for him, it was a win-win. If it failed, Tipp would look bad. If it worked, he could claim the credit.

Two other men stood on the sidelines, representatives of the company that provided the software. They were both tall and stocky. One had a grey suit, the other brown. They were both in their early forties, and both had black hair.

While Calver coordinated the rescue of Steel, Samara, and Foster, Bolton had other worries. One of which was Sloan, who was dead, and Bryce was missing. Who had he and Price worked for, and who else was involved?

Bolton took a sip of coffee he had gotten from the machine in the break room. It was intense and dark with a thick texture. At this point, he needed the caffeine. Bolton looked at the watch.

One minute to go.

One minute, until they found out if it was all worth it.

A black hawk helicopter from the USS Nemesis aircraft carrier first took them back to the aircraft carrier to get medical treatment. The medics had wrapped a bandage around Steel's midsection and tented to his cut shot wound. Samara had escaped with minor cuts and bruises. At the same time, Foster became stitches and new dressings, both from the explosion and the crash.

They were now aboard a second Black hawk. This was taking them back to the embassy. Foster had spoken with Bolton over a secure satellite connection on board the Nemesis. He had de-briefed each other on what had happened.

The Nemesis had sent out hazmat crews to the crash site to evaluate possible contamination. While salvage crews tried and located the cargo that had been jettisoned from the back of the C-130.

Steel had closed his eyes in hope to sleep, or at best just to rest. He'd briefed Bolton and Tipp at the same time as Foster. Steel had also used the time to contact London and appraise them of the situation. His last communication had been days ago when he had requested a background check. Steel figured he would have to return to London and take the harsh verbal treatment from his Commanding Officer. Steel had found it amusing that the head Secret Service was called 'C.'. Still, the head of MI8 was simply called CO. not very original, but functional.

Samara spoke to Kane. Using the helicopter's communications system, letting him know they were OK. She figured he would be going out of his mind with worry, which he had been. But just hearing her voice had calmed him slightly.

The ride back seemed longer than it should. Which suited Foster. He'd have time to think about things, who played what part.

The black hawk cut through the sky with ease. Steel looked over at Samara, who was busy talking. Foster was sedated but awake. Steel had tried to sleep – the first rule of business, sleep when you can. But something was keeping him awake.

Samara felt Steel's eyes on her and turned towards him. She was still talking on the headset but gave him a gentle smile.

Steel looked at the city and the streets below. He saw the large domed church. He figured they were over Mgarr, and Attard wouldn't be far away. The sky was a deep purple. The stars were out and shining bright. The moon was already out, displaying a brilliant half full.

Steel nudged the cold pack between the body armour and his t-shirt. He felt the refreshing cold on his skin. He could not wait to get back to the hotel and take a long shower or even a deep, soothing bath.

He looked down and saw the lights of a vast city to his left – Mosta. He had to admit, seeing it from up above was impressively beautiful. He had seen most cities from above and during the night. New York still gave him chills.

As the helicopter touched down in the embassy's cleared parking lot, Steel saw Bolton and a hand full of Marines following him over. The side door slid open, and Steel got out first and helped Samara out while the Marines grabbed Foster's stretcher.

The transport waited until they were clear, then took off, returning to the aircraft carrier.

'Is it working?' Foster asked.

'Yes, it's working,' Bolton said with a surprised smile. 'The damn thing works.'

Bolton had always been a bit apprehensive about the software – they all had. The company had promised the earth, and they had delivered.

Foster smiled and nodded to himself.

As they all headed for the blockhouse entrance, Steel lagged behind. Thinking about the events of the past week. Reflecting on Lucy's death and the possible death of thousands more.

As the string of people marched into the elevator, Steel got a text message. It was from a friend he had reached out to.

'I'll catch you up,' Steel said, waving his cell phone as if to say he had to take this message.

Bolton nodded and pressed the button. The doors slid shut, and suddenly Steel was alone. Steel pressed the button to check the message. The office in Whitehall had done some digging for him.

They had reviewed emails, financials, and background checks on the names Steel had given him – including Price, Bolton, Tipp, Sloan and Calver.

The result raised Steel's eyebrow and made him tense with anger.

Steel pressed the call button and waited.

People passed by behind him. They were going here and there, none of them paying him any notice. He was invisible to them, a shadow, a figure in the corner of the eye.

The doors slid open, and Steel found himself face to face with Foster. He had ridden the elevator back up.

'We need to talk… alone – away from the others,' Foster said, looking around the lobby.

'Sure,' Steel replied as he stepped into the elevator. There was a silence as the doors closed. Each stood with their backs firmly against a wall.

Their gaze locked in front of them towards the door.

'Did you find what you needed?' Foster asked calmly.

Steel waited for a moment before answering.

Letting his anger subside.

'Yes, I'm still wondering why though,' Steel's voice was calm, but his fists were clenched tightly as if taking the strain.

The men remained still.

The air was full of tension.

'How did she die?' Foster asked. A simple question, Steel thought. One he would have thought Foster would have known – if he'd checked himself.

Perhaps that's why Foster had gotten Steel over, ask the questions he could not. But what father wouldn't want to do it himself, especially one with Foster's background?

But Steel already knew the answer. It was a plain and straightforward one that scared Steel to the bone while causing his blood to boil.

'She was murdered, possibly run down by a car with no plates. She was then taken to the Blue Hole and tossed off the edge,' Steel said, working his theory in his head as he spoke. Steel thought back to the pathologist and the report. He thought back to the broken bones and injuries that Lucy had sustained. They had been too severe for a simple fall off a cliff, and besides, she had not fallen from Azure Window. Steel had already proven that was impossible. Steel had tried it during the day, and it was hard going. So at night, carrying a body would have been impossible. It was probable that was the killer's first intention. Still, after seeing how difficult it was, they had chosen the easier option. But she had landed in the Blue hole, not the ocean.

'So, a car killed her?' Foster said, almost relieved at the thought it had been quick. But Steel remained silent for a moment, his mind a million miles away. 'Steel, did the car kill her?'

'I can't be sure,' Steel said. 'I'd like to think so. There was no water in her lungs, so she did not drown,' Steel's words were soft and calming, despite his hidden rage. In reality, after speaking to the medical examiner, Steel concluded it was more likely the shock of the fall that had taken her. However, Foster did not need to hear that.

It hadn't been quick because they did not want it to be – someone wanted her to suffer. And the thought of her crying alone, stuffed in the back of a car or truck while they drove her to her watery death, angered Steel.

'Do you know who did this?' Foster asked. He looked over at Steel, who just stood rigid. 'Do you know who killed my little girl?' Foster's words rang with anger and revenge, possibly too much emotion for some.

Foster watched as Steel just turned his head slowly and stared at him. Foster could feel the cold glare from Steel's dead, soulless dark emerald eyes even through Steel's sunglasses.

Foster had seen that very same stare once before, years ago in Bosnia.

A ruthless soldier was butchering innocent women and children. Until their SEAL team had caught up with him and his men, Steel's team had been sent in to rescue an American pilot who had been shot down. The enemy soldiers had seized him and were offering him for ransom. Five million dollars, or they would get him back in pieces, and they would send a film of the parts being taken.

The team had located the camp; Steel had gone in alone to recce the area; as he always did. *One person can disappear. A squad cannot.* This had always been Steel's way of thinking. It was in a small village. The soldiers were in the middle of a rape and slash rally on the women and kids. The men had left to fight in the war, leaving them defenceless.

When Foster and the rest of the team heard nothing from Steel, they moved in, only to find the soldiers dead and the commander injured and cowering on the floor. Steel, standing over him, drooling like an animal, covered in blood and scratches. And all Foster could remember were those eyes glaring back at his team. His body screamed with rage, but those cold, dead eyes just stared without emotion. Even when Steel tossed the man over to the women so that they could deal with him.

Foster still shivered at the thought of those chilling, soulless eyes he had seen that da, with the same anger that had now. Foster said nothing. He just shivered and looked away.

'Lucy died, for nothing, Foster. But I made sure that they died for something,' Steel said.

Foster nodded silently.

'I head that Stan had an accident,' Steel said.

'Must have been Price when she escaped, tying up tie up loose ends?' Foster replied.

'Maybe?' Steel said. His gaze was now fixed on the doors of the elevator.

'Shame, he could have told us a thing or two.'

'He did that already, but I think he only knew what he was required to,' Steel said. Nobody spoke after that. The ride down was silent. All the while, Steel had his doubts. Price did not have time. Also, he still had no idea who had transported Samara to the airport.

The software and transfer had worked perfectly. Bolton looked around the dimly lit room of the NSA operations room. Under the circumstances, he felt changing the venue was more appropriate as there was still blood all over the place downstairs. Washington had agreed. Bolton knew it was irrelevant on whose system it was launched because they would all have it using piggy-back shareware. Bolton watched all the operators who were cheering and clamping at the success. It was almost as if they had just landed a guy on the moon. Bolton smiled shook Tipp's hand again, a feeling of relief flowing through his body. He was a happy man.

As Bolton looked across the room, he noticed the two men from SteinTech Industries. One had a brown suit, the other wore grey.

They wore broad grins on their neatly shaven faces. Bolton could sense all they wanted to do was punch the air and scream out with joy.

But they remained composed – professional.

Bolton walked over and said his congratulations to the delegates. He felt he had to do something, the Director was now gone, and Bolton thought he was the best person to step in for the moment. Tipp wasn't really the people sort of guy. Come to think of it, Sloan had often sent Bolton to do the people thing. Bolton had spoken to Washington as Foster was travelling back on the Black Hawk, given a full briefing on the situation as he knew it. It felt good not being in the hot seat. Bolton felt the tension as he explained about Director Sloan and Agent Price.

They would need new people to replace them.

They would need a new Director In Charge.

Bolton had hoped his suggestion of using someone who already worked there would pay off. There were only two apparent candidates, himself and Tipp. Foster was a junior section chief compared to Tipp and Bolton. He would move out of the monitor room and get a senior position in the upper levels, if anything. It was a natural progression – dead man's shoes the army called it.

Besides, Foster's title of section chief was the only honorary. The old Director In Charge had been from the FBI, and with him out of the picture, Foster's position could be fully instated. If the CIA got the Directorship.

For Bolton, things were looking rosy. The programme worked, Sloan was out of the picture, and now a chance for promotion was in sight. Life was good.

Bolton looked over to Calver, who was sat in a corner, watching as everything unfolded. Bolton walked over, confused by the look on Calver's saddened expression.

'What's wrong?' Bolton said quietly. 'We did it. It's up and running, mostly due to your help.'

Calver nodded slowly, as if accepting the recognition, but the sadness remained.

'I can't help but feel we didn't win anything. People have died, and for what?' Calver said.

The elevator doors opened. Everyone looked over to see Foster step out onto the floor. He was greeted by loud clapping and shouts of congratulations. Foster's face was pale from shock, and his walk laboured. His body felt like he had been run over by a steam roller.

Bolton hurried over to his colleague just as Steel stepped out and onto the tiled floor. Bolton stopped as he looked at Steel's sour expression. Bolton stepped back slightly and composed himself before rushing forwards to shake their hands.

'Damned fine work, men. Washington sends their thanks. There's talk of a medal for you both,' Bolton said with a skip in his voice.

'Any sign of Price?' Steel asked, his gaze fixed on Bolton.

'No, she's completely vanished, but then, she was a hell of a spy back in the day,' Bolton said.

'So, Steel, you'll be flying back to New York tonight…tomorrow?'

'I can't go yet; my investigation isn't done,' Steel replied. He looked around the room, spotting Calver and stopped. Calver held Steel's gaze, unable to move.

'What do you mean you're not done? We got the disk, the software was downloaded, you stopped the attack, you got Foster and Samara back. What more is there?' Bolton asked, trying to understand the man's thinking.

'I didn't come here for your software or to stop terrorists from parking a bomb in the middle of New York. I came here to find my goddaughter's killer,' Steel growled.

'You mean two bombs? And it was Washington, not New York,' came a voice from behind them. Everyone turned to look at Tipp, who was still looking at the monitors.

Steel smiled as if his plan had worked perfectly.

'How did you know it was two bombs?' Bolton asked, a sudden fear running through his veins.

'Because I was there when Foster gave his report to you over the Satcom,' Tipp reached for a cover story.

'But he never said how many bombs or where they were heading. All we knew was it was stateside,' Bolton replied, hoping someone had called security.

'No… I'm sure you….' Tipp said. Then he froze.

'It's over, Tipp,' Steel said. He felt his blood starting to boil again. Tipp snarled and pulled out a 9mm M&P 9C nano pistol from his trouser leg and grabbed a female agent who was next to him. Tipp stuck the barrel of the weapon into her back next to her kidney.

'Oops,' Tipp said as he watched the man aimed directly at Steel. Tipp swaggered over to the elevator, the man with the weapon followed. The gun still trained on the people in the room.

'Everyone just stays where they are, and nobody gets hurt,' said Tipp, smiling a confidant.

Steel just watched them step into the steel box of the elevator, and the doors slide shut behind them. Suddenly, the room was busy with people on the phone to the main desks and the embassy's security division. But the phones were dead and the internet down.

'What the hell is going on?' Bolton shouted, tossing the handset of the telephone at the cradle.

'He's cut you off. It won't surprise me if he has a plan for the power supply down here as well. No, loose ends, no one to tell the world. He could make up any fact he wanted, including saying Price had done it,' Steel said calmly.

Panicked, Calver rushed over to the lift and pressed the button, but to no avail.

'He's locked off the elevator somehow,' Calver said, somewhat unsurprised.

'So what can we do?' asked Bolton, suddenly feeling powerless.

'Well, next time, make a place with emergency stairs, but for now, we climb,' Steel said with a grin. Bolton and Foster looked worried.

'We are about a hundred feet down, and you want to climb, are you nuts?' Bolton asked, looking up at the ceiling. Steel headed for the lift shaft and opened it with Foster and Calver, and a few others.

'Climb, yes,' Steel said. 'we'll get on the counterweights' Steel pointed to one of the counterweights on the side. 'You lot coming or what?'

'No, that's fine, we'll catch you up,' Foster said, looking up the long, dark shaft.

'Don't worry, I'm only kidding. There's a backup relay just in case things go wrong. The problem is, it's over there,' Steel said, pointing to a control box on the other side of the shaft.

'This will send down the elevator whether the doors are open or not, a safety feature they installed but didn't tell everyone.' Steel said. Looking at the massive gap between him and the box. While deciding if it was a good idea after all.

'How did you find it?' Bolton asked.

'I looked up the schematics of the place. I felt a little uncomfortable about been stuck underground without knowing the escape routes.

'Smart,' Bolton said. Wondering why he'd never thought about doing the same. But then he thought about all the great minds down there that could get them out, even if it meant hacking a system. Steel leapt out and grabbing a small service ladder on the side.

Steel moved around the shaft slowly, using the support structure as footing. Finally, he reached the box and opened the panel. Inside was lots of wires and switches. On the one side was a blue-lit console with an options panel. Steel went through the reprogramming menu and set it for the elevator car to return down. There was a metallic clang and a hiss as the motors started to work. The counterweight to the side began to move, meaning Steel had little time to get back before being stuck behind the elevator.

Steel chose to jump from one metal pillar to the other. The sound of descending metal got closer as Steel made his next jump just as the elevator came whooshing past him. Steel's body flew through the gap knocking over one of the female computer techs and landing on top of her. As he looked down at her face and large lens glasses, he smiled. She blushed and giggled.

'Hi,' Steel smiled.

'Uhm…hi,' she said back.

Steel pulled himself off her and helped her up on to her shaky legs.

'What now? Tipp's probably already left. How we are going to trace him?' Bolton asked. Steel turned to Calver, who smiled at Steel, knowing full well what he would ask.

'I take it Tipp didn't mess with the power then. That's nice of him,' Steel said.

'I have people going to the generator room now. Make sure he hasn't left any presents,' Bolton replied. 'Still can't believe Tipp was involved.'

'I'm still not sure you're not, given that nearly everyone else was,' Steel said.

'What makes you sure I ain't?' Bolton asked, wearing a stern look.

'You've only just got here by all accounts, the others have been here since the beginning, and they knew each other before that. Don't worry, I had you all checked out. I just got the information back,' Steel admitted. Steel turned to Calver.

'You get me the internet and the air vents back online, and I'll get you a location,' Calver said. Steel nodded and stepped inside the elevator.

'Anyone going up, do it now,' Steel said, but only Foster stepped in.

'We have work to do down here, Steel. Just get us back online, and then catch that bastard,' Bolton said. Steel nodded and stepped into the elevator.

As the doors slid shut, Bolton turned to his people.

'OK, people, let's get this place running again. I want to know what else they've done to our systems.'

Chapter 78

Steel and Foster took the elevator up to the ground floor lobby. As the doors slid open, they were greeted by a squad of Marines with their M4 rifles targeting the elevator door. Steel stood for a second with his hands raised until the sergeant recognised him.

'Ah, barn doors after the bolt – aye Sergeant?' Steel said.

The tall sergeant gave Steel an angry look. 'We're just following orders, Mr Steel,' the sergeant said. Steel nodded and rushed out of the elevator, then stopped suddenly.

'Where's the incoming communications relay?' Steel asked.

The sergeant pointed towards the building next to the pool house. Steel smiled and nodded a thank you and carried on running. Steel knew he had to get the power back up and running so they could check their systems. Steel wasn't convinced that the software installation was quite what they had made it out to be. Tipp looked positively ecstatic about the launch – that meant there was more to it.

Steel found the small box-shaped building. It was no more than twenty-by-twenty, with a solid metal door and no windows. Steel tired the door handle and found it to be open. He took a deep breath and slowly opened the door, waiting for a tug of a cable or the metallic thud of a grenade.

But there was nothing but silence, and the door pulled freely.

Inside was dark, less for the stream of light through the doorway which illuminated the generator. It was painted yellow, and next to it was lots of boxy control panels. The motor sat silently in the dark. Steel did not know that much about engines and generators. His only experience had been with the twenty-watt generators the army used and the bulky thing at his family cabin in Alaska. But he figured this could not be all that different. Besides, he knew that they wanted the software online, so Tipp wouldn't have done too much damage. If he made sure there was no power to the hive, it would defeat the object. Steel figured Tipp had just cut the power to the communications buy time. Which – in effect, Tipp had done. He was counting on Steel, or someone, to restore communications first before starting to hunt him down. Tipp knew this would buy him at least a fifteen-minute start. More than enough – or so Tipp had probably thought.

Steel searched around the metal beast until he found what looked like a starter button. It was a big green push button next to a big red button.

'Well, I hope green means go,' Steel said. Then slapped the green starter. The engine roared to life, and the room was lit up from a fluorescent strip light above his head. Steel rushed outside and watched as the compound lights started to flicker on. He smiled and exhaled the breath he had sucked in before pushing the green starter.

Steel rode the elevator back down to Bolton. He knew there was no way he was going to catch up to Tipp or find Price. The chances were they were long gone by now. However, their travel options were limited. The company jet was still in Tunisia. They would have to fly commercial or catch a ferry. Then a thought sprung into Steel's head. He thought about the superyacht – who did actually own it?

As the elevator doors slid, open Steel could hear cheers of joy as all the systems were back online, including the air ventilation.

Bolton met Steel at the elevator. 'Good job.'

The two walked together towards Calver.

Calver looked up from his computer, which was rebooting from the system shut down. Calver smiled as Steel approached.

'Who owns this big black superyacht? It's probably anchored in one of the ports around Valletta.' Steel said. Steel pulled out his cell phone and showed Calver a photo of the ship. It was a blow-up of the picture Brad had kept on his data stick. Calver looked at the picture.

Calver had seen the ship before many times but had never seen who owned it. He had just seen the men who had come over on the Zodiac – the men he was paid to bring to Victoria. He had been paid well – he just did not know who by – until now.

Calver figured either Price or Tipp had set it up on Sloan's orders. Calver figured they probably had photos of him taking them. Insurance if anything went wrong, he would get the blame, maybe even arrested for smuggling in terrorists. Calver had known why Sloan had recruited him. His past had caught up with him. Calver was hoping to use the money to disappear. Even for a little while before Sloan found him again.

'Uhm. Once this is rebooted, I can… you know… check,' Calver said nervously, his voice strained at every word as though they burnt.

Steel smiled. He knew guilty men. He had seen what they looked like, how they reacted, moved, talked. Steel knew that Calver wasn't a team player. He was always out for himself – Samara had said as much. But he was in it for a quick buck. Nothing more. Deep down, Steel knew Calver was a good guy, just a little broken.

'OK,' Steel said. 'Send what you got to my cell phone,' Steel said. He had turned to head back to the elevator when Bolton stopped him.

'Where you going?' Bolton asked.

'To break into Price's apartment,' Steel said and headed to the parking lot and the row of government-issue vehicles. 'I just need an address.'

Chapter 79

Alison Price had a house just outside of Mdina. The place was modern, with a large garden. There was a seven-foot wall that enclosed the grounds. From what Steel could tell, she was not the neighbourly sort. The driveway was bared by a twin metal gate that appeared to be electronic.

'Well, someone had cash,' Steel said.

He parked the black Yukon he had taken from the embassy parking lot and climbed out of the driver's seat. Steel looked around casually as he headed for the rear of the vehicle. He was hoping to find something more than a spare tyre in the trunk. Steel clicked the catch on the door and lifted it only to find it empty. But, Steel knew if they had any toys, they would be out of sight.

He grabbed the corner of the mat and lifted it. Steel smiled as he looked down at the weapons cache. There was a Sig Sauer 320 with a suppressor, an M4 CQB assault rifle and a Kel-Tec Bullpup shotgun, all stored in a foam casing.

Carefully, so no one could see, Steel removed the Sig from its compartment and checked the magazine was full. The top 9mm hollow-point round glinted in the sun as he pressed down on it to checked the spring. It was nice and tight, meaning there was less chance of a stoppage.

Steel replaced the magazine and tucked it into the small of his back before closing the trunk. He looked around once more. The street was quiet. Steel figured that's one of the reasons Price had chosen the area. Steel sauntered over to Prices house. He would need to look for a way in. Which in itself didn't appear to be that difficult for a man of his means? But this was a woman who valued her privacy.

Steel figured there was most certainly an alarm system, possibly guard dogs – most likely Dobermans or ex-special forces trained German shepherds.

Steel peered through the fence and waited. There was no barking or thundering of massive wolf-like paws on the lawn. There was nothing but the sound of the gentle wind.

Steel smiled and hopped the fence. Then he waited again.

Nothing.

He walked casually towards the house. Taking in the vulgar shape of the structure. It was square and modern, with white walls and glass sliding doors. The roof was almost one complete solar panel. Definitely not keeping within the local tradition or style. Steel walked on the grass and avoided the concrete tiled path.

Steel walked around the house and checked for a way in or any signs of life. The last thing he needed was to come this far only to have his nuts ripped off by a big angry dog. Steel had made it back to the front door and had found several possible entrance points but no signs of either two or four-legged occupants. There had been no doggy door of feeding bowls in the kitchen. While at the kitchen, he'd also had a clear view of the front door and hallway. The house was mostly open planned, which made his life a lot easier.

Steel was surprised to see no alarm system. He figured she was safe enough with the wall, or perhaps she was confident enough that if someone did break-in, the agency would hunt them down? Steel went back to the kitchen, thinking that was the best entry point.

He looked up at the large glass sliding door. It was well made, with a slight tint to the glass to minimise the harmful effects of the suns rays. Steel took out the Sig, and aiming at the top right-hand corner, fired a shot. There was a gentle *thump* as the suppressor silenced the shot. There was only the sound of the window as it shattered into a thousand pieces, sending tinted glass sliding across the tiled floor.

Even though it was night time, Steel was surprised how light it was inside, allowing him to move about freely. Checking draws and cupboards. He started in the kitchen and worked his way through the house.

The interior was like something from a dream house catalogue. It felt more showroom than a place to live, with modernistic furniture.

Steel moved into the sitting area where there wasn't much in the way of furnishing. There was a big tv on the wall, above a brick fireplace. An oversized brown leather couch sat in front of the tv, and in front of that was a long glass and wood coffee table. To the right of the tv was a wall cabinet, full of china ornaments and glass objects. There were no photographs but expensive-looking artwork hung from the walls. There was a drinks cabinet to the left, between a large window and the fireplace. Which made his job of finding anything that much more challenging. He was used to rooms with lots of hiding places, draws, desks, and filing cabinets, but nothing was here. He tried the rest of the house. The bathroom was big and fancy but had nothing of use. Steel was just about to throw in the towel and head back to the embassy with his tail between his legs when he found another room. This was on the first floor, down the hall from the bedroom. At first, he thought it was just a place for towels. But a gap in the wall panel made him think otherwise. Steel pushed the shelving, and it slid gently open to reveal an office. He stood in awe at what could only be described as a command centre. There were maps and photographs, blueprints and charts. Steel took out his cell phone and began documenting as much as he could. Then he found a picture that made his eyes widen. Brad and Lucy were near the cover in Gozo near Hondoq Bay. They were photographing men offloading weapons crates from a Zodiak.

Steel paused and stared at the photograph for what seemed forever. Steel blinked and forced himself, turned away. He could feel the hate rising within him again, so he took a deep breath to control his temper. Steel looked around at another board. This had more photographs, this time of Steel, Samara, Foster and Stan. He looked at some of the reports and background checks that they had produced. It was a thorough job, but thankfully a lot was missing from Steel's file. The fewer people knew what he really did, the better.

Steel moved about the room – which was small compared with some others, but it was still considerable. Steel figured it was at least twenty-by-fifteen feet, but with no windows and only one door, making it perfect for planning boards. In the centre of the room were a desk with a laptop and an old lamp. The office chair wasn't extravagant, just an old leather thing, possibly she had found it in a second-hand store. But he had to admit it was oddly comfortable. He eased himself down onto the padded caramel-colour leather and began to search the drawers of the desk. There were notebooks and data sticks as well as the usual pens and pencils.

Steel switched on the computer and waited. The seventeen-inch screen blinked, and the ever-annoying 'Please enter the password' popped up. Steel had been lucky with most people's passwords. Most had used the obvious things such as their birthdays or dogs name, even the name of their favourite movie star. But he knew there was no chance in hell he was going to get into this one.

Steel took out his cell phone and made two calls. The first was to Bolton, the second was to London. Each call lasted less than a minute. Each call contained vital information. The call to London had responded with a brief. 'They're on the way.'

Steel stood up and turned to head out the door. He did not need to be there when the cleaners arrived. He took one more look around the room to make sure he hadn't missed anything. Checking each of the six action boards that filled the walls. As he gazed at the second board, a photograph caught his eye. He smiled. It was the black superyacht, and Tipp was aboard it along with Sloan and someone else he had never seen before. The man was tall and thin. His head was shaven, but he had a long greying beard. He looked European but not from this area. He had a pale complexion and a flat nose. Steel figured he was at least six-two judging by the height difference between him and Tipp – who was six-foot.

'Well, now I know where you bastards went,' Steel said to himself. He nodded as a plan started to formulate and headed for the door. Then he stopped and stared at what appeared to be an old wood locker peeking behind where the shelving had stopped on its track. Steel moved around to the locker and opened it. Inside were two sets of clothing, one for an old man, the other for an old woman. Steel reached inside and pulled out the old man's cane. As he twisted the fashioned wood, Steel could not find anything sinister about it. The end had a rubber end cap, and the top hand a silver handle. Then Steel stopped admiring it, and his hands froze. The handle had a trigger? Steel searched the silver cap and found it twisted at the neck, revealing a barrel. This was a single-shot weapon. But then it only needed one shot in skilled hands. And because the .22 was a small calibre, the shot would be almost non-existent if the stick was just one big suppressor.

Steel tucked the stick back into the locker and closed the door. He wanted to smile, knowing he had found Brad's killer. But he could not. He still had no idea who had killed Lucy or how, even though the why was now evident. She had seen too much, and Brad had tried to blackmail Price.

Steel headed back downstairs. He had seen enough, but he knew he had to try the garage next to the house. The thing was wide enough for two cars, but he had only seen her drive one. The entrance to the garage was through the kitchen, and he found the door was unlocked. Steel pushed the door open and saw absolutely nothing but darkness. Gingerly, Steel moved his hand up and down the wall until his fingers found the light switch. He clicked it down, and two long strip lights blinked, and light revealed the interior.

The garage was huge, with cream walls and a grey ceiling. On the far side, there were sets of shelving containing tools and ropes. But at the far end was a green pick-up truck. As Steel walked over to the truck, he noticed the front end and bumper were dented – as if she had run into something – or someone. Steel looked over the damage to the front end. The damage was too high for it to have been a sheep, and as far as he knew, there were no deer on Malta. Steel thought back to Lucy's autopsy. The broken bones and the lack of water in the lungs. Steel took out his cell and searched his call log. He checked his watch. He just hoped he hadn't missed the crazy pathologist in Victoria.

The phone rang several times before someone picked up. It was a young voice, a man. Steel's heart fell.

'Is the Doc Bondi there?' Steel asked.

'He's gone to the bathroom, why... who's this?' answered the voice.

'My name is John steel. I spoke to the doc the other day. He should remember me,' Steel said. 'Can you ask him to recheck the Lucy Foster case? Ask him, is it possible that she was hit by a car?' Steel said.

'Sorry, what was your name again? I had to get a pen?' said the voice. Steel groaned with impatience.

'Get me the doc now before I come over there and feed you your own intestines,' Steel growled. Steel heard the kid yelp and the sound of running footsteps. In the distance, the shrieks of the guy's voice. Moments later, the familiar voice of the pathologist said, 'Yes.'

Chapter 80

As the superyacht pulled slowly out of Msida Yacht Marina. It glistened as the half-moon reflected off its sleek black curves. The hum of its engine and the sound of music broke the silence of the night.

Tipp sat on the deck sipping Dom Perignon from a crystal flute. He wore a nervous smile. Everything had gone to plan - until Steel turned up. He had ruined years of planning. They had escaped with their lives and from the threat of prison. But Tipp knew that the Trojan organisation would be displeased at the failure of the mission. Someone needed to be held accountable. Luckily for him, Price was a higher rank in the organisation, in effect, his boss. It was Price they would punish, not him.

Price had told him she'd given the ship's crew the night off, they had business to attend to, and the last thing they needed was fifty-odd witnesses. Only two guards and the pilot had remained. One guard had stayed at the front of the ship, the pilot upstairs in the wheelhouse. The second guard was below.

A noise behind Tipp caused him to turn. He smiled as Alison Price strolled onto the deck in a black bikini. She had mentioned her longing for the vessels hot tub. She was in her fifties, but her body was tight with slight muscle definition, a product of years of working out at the tennis courts' and gym hours.

As she walked towards Tipp, she picked up the champagne bottle and poured herself a glass.

'Where will we go?' she asked, sitting on the leather chair opposite his.

'We have to go and see them,' Tipp said. 'Seek favour. After all, it wasn't our fault. It went wrong. We never asked Steel to join the party,' Tipp said, taking a sip.

'No – they did,' Price said coldly. 'They thought we might be able to kill two birds with one stone. But your men ballsed it up, too busy trying to kill that woman, Samara,' Price said with a callous grin as if she sensed who the bosses would blame.

'And you never told me?' Tipp said. He was angry but also suddenly afraid. Had she set him up to take the fall? It would explain why he had had to source the terrorists.

'I did warn you,' Price purred. 'Several times, in fact. I told you to leave the girl, but no. Your obsession cost us, sorry - cost you,' Price said, her tone changing to one of contempt.

'But it doesn't matter. The software is installed as planned. No one will ever know its real purpose,' Tipp said.

'What, you mean the fact it masks all your agent's identities while at the same time picks out our agents?' Came a familiar voice from above them.

Price and Tipp turned quickly only to see Steel at the pilot's cabin high above them. Fear ran through their veins as they knew they had nowhere to run.

'This was all about misdirection,' Steel said. 'Sure, you knew you might not lose the contract, which would have made you billions, but you had a fail-safe, swap the software for the one you had doctored for your needs. It was a win-win either way,' Steel said, pointing Sig Sauer P320 pistol at them.

'OK, you caught us, bring us in, Detective,' Tipp said. His expression turned into a mocking smile. 'You do have proof, though, don't you?'

'You're right,' Steel said. 'There is no evidence, but then, I don't need proof, not where you two are going,' Steel said. With a movement of his pistol, Steel ushered them to the side of the ship. Forcing them away from him.

Steel moved slowly down the steps, watching for any sudden movements from the two agents. He was quite happy to put a bullet in each of them, but he knew people wanted to have words with them. As far as the agency he worked for was concerned, they were a font of information. And two was better than one – especially if you turned one against the other.

As Steel got halfway down, two hands grabbed his feet and pulled. Steel fell but managed to roll and hopped back onto his feet. Steel looked over and saw a man in white, the man whose nose Samara had broken. Steel re-aimed the pistol, but the man swung the pole and batted it out of his hand with a boat hook. The end caught Steel on the wrist, but it hurt like hell even though it did not rip the skin.

The pistol skidded across the deck, straight into the waiting hands of Tipp, who grasped the weapon and aimed it at Steel. Steel saw the gun and went to dive out of the way before Tipp took the shot. But as he moved, Steel found he was side on to the big man. As he moved, the big man brought the pole smashing sideways on Steel's back, sending Steel crashing to his knees. The wind had been knocked out of him. The big guy raised the pole, ready to do a downward swing, the metal spike aimed at Steel's head. Steel rolled as the pole came crashing down. Tipp went to fire, but the big man had moved in front of his target. Tipp's cursed, and Price giggled with a sick amusement. She wanted to watch as the life was choked out of Steel.

Steel was on his knees, crouched, ready for the next attack. The big man was swinging the pole, moved towards Steel, the hook whistled past, Steel rolled and perfectly timed his upward kick. Steel caught the guy full in the sternum, sending him flying and forcing him to release the pole. It clattered onto the wooden deck.

Steel went to reach for the pole. Tipp fired, sending a wooden splitter into the air, leaving a two-centimetre hole in the deck. Steel ripped his hand back, Tipp fired another round, just missed Steel's head.

Steel rolled to his feet, Tipp fired again, but Steel was moving, the bullet shattered a window. The tinted glass exploded across the floor.

'I thought you were a good shot?' Price said.

'Oh, shut up, woman,' Tipp barked back, holding the weapon with both hands, waiting for his next chance.

The man in white raced at Steel with the pole he had retrieved. The man was swinging it and stabbing as he went.

Steel moved to the side just as the spike swung past his head, then, in one swift movement, grabbed the pole and yanked it towards him. Ripping it out of the man's hands.

Steel spun the pole and smashed the blunt end against the man's head, dazing him slightly as the pole caught him directly on the side of his big, meaty head.

Tipp raised the gun and fired, but the dazed man had stumbled in the way and took a bullet to the left shoulder.

Angrily, Tipp aimed again and fired. This time the bullet flew past Steel and hit a scuba tank that Tipp had left next to the bar. Steel looked back at the tank and the escaping air. His eyes widen as the tank began hissed. Steel dove out of the way just as the tank exploded, sending shards flying indiscriminately. The fireball engulfed the interior of the craft, setting the seating area ablaze. Tipp held his shoulder of his gun hand. Blood flowed from where a glass shard had found its mark. Tipp roared in anger. He'd had enough of this nuisance. He fired again, but the pain in his shoulder restricted him from lifting the gun into the aim. Now he was firing from the hip while smoke from the fire obstructing his view. There was a sudden click of an empty magazine.

Tipp froze.

He did not see the punch, but he sure as hell felt it. His nose erupted under Steel's fist. Tipp reeled back and then dropped to the ground, blood gushing.

Price ran for the speedboat that was moored to the side of the yacht. She knew this fight was lost. Tipp was incompetent and deserved what he got. Smoke billowed from the burning bar. There were more explosions as more of the air tanks exploded. The roar of flame and the sound of metal shards impacting off the interior filled her ears. There was another explosion – another air tank had erupted, this time shattering nearby windows. She ran blindly, heading for the lower deck and the speedboat they had come over on. Alison Price screamed as another window shattered, showering glass in front of her.

She ran on.

She needed to get off the boat before Steel got to her.

The speedboat was large enough for six people, but she wasn't taking passengers. Price used the controls to lower the boat into the water. It was a slow operation, with the squeak of gears and the click of leavers and the winch system lowered the craft.

'Come on, come on,' she said, looking around, making sure she hadn't been seen. So far, all the action was happening on the deck above – she hoped it stayed there.

Soon, she would be home free and be rid of Steel at the same time.

As the speedboat hit the water, Price climbed down and unhitched the winch gear. Price smiled coldly as she powered the boat out and away from the yacht.

There was a roar of the outboard motor and a whoosh of spray. Price knew she had to get away as quickly as possible.

Flames leapt from the ship's top deck, small explosions as the liquor in the bottles began to catch alight. The yacht was caught in an inferno.

Price smiled as she swung the boat around and headed the other direction. She waved goodbye and blew a kiss to them all.

'Bon voyage, and burn in hell,' she cried out, hoping at least one of them would hear it. There was a blinding flash, and then a massive explosion of the gas and fuel tanks ruptured. Pieces of burning debris splashed into the water near the speed boat, covering the ocean in flame. Price smiled as she watched all her problems burn.

Alison Price moved the speedboat to a safe distance and powered it down. She moved to the rear of the boat and watched. Cursing, she did not have her cell phone, so she could take a picture. Price stared at the scene, thinking how beautiful it was, a fire on the ocean at night.

For her – nothing could spoil the moment. And there was nobody left actually to do it. She imagined Steel engulfed in flame. Possibly some of those metal shards from the air tanks had pierced his body. She imagined the pain he suffered, right up until the end. She hoped he hadn't died before the explosion. She wanted him to feel the full power of the ship being ripped apart.

Price never noticed the fuel spilling into the ocean. She had no cause to look. One of Tipp's erratic fire had punctured the gas tank on the speedboat.

As the debris fell, she looked up at what seemed to be red hot snowflakes. She smiled and just watched at the beauty of it all. It was like a thousand tiny lights floating down, each one an orange glow. She had never seen such a beautiful sight burning away her problems. She breathed in the crisp sea air and was pleasantly greeted with the smell of destruction. She smiled and hugged herself.

She looked up again at one of the embers. It seemed bigger than the others and glowed with more intensity. She followed the ember spiral down, then lift as it was caught on the breeze. The extra air caused it to glow brighter. Her eyes were transfixed on this tiny light. Wondering if it would fall into the ocean or fly forever. The ember began to descend once again. She gasped as just before it touched the water, another breeze carried it up. She smiled with excitement at her new game. Price watched open-mouthed as it began to fall once again.

Down it sailed, unhindered, uninterrupted. Alison Price's eyes widened in anticipation. Would it fall or fly? It grew near to the water. She leaned forwards, her hands clutched the sides of the boat. Down it went, further and further.

Its brightness was almost hypnotic.

Price sighed with disappointment as it hit the water, almost as if she had wanted the game to go on for longer.

Price shrugged and went to turn towards the boat controls. Maybe it had been for the best the game was over. She had to leave anyway before the coast guard arrived and started to ask questions. A sudden flare of light caught her attention.

She turned back slowly.

Her eyes widened in fear.

It wasn't just the yacht that was ablaze, but a stream of flame on the sea heading towards her.

Price went to scream, but it was too late, as the explosion ripped the speedboat apart.

Steel bobbed about treading water. He knew it wouldn't be long before the coast guard came to his rescue. As he watched the speedboat disappear under the waves, he could not help but see the irony.

From what Steel had pieced together, Price had killed Lucy Foster. Lucy had seen the black yacht and witnessed the terrorists given weapons at night in Hondoq Bay. Lucy had tracked the boat to the marina and found the weapons cash at Manoel Island. But Brad saw an opportunity to make money, not realising who he was dealing with – the Trojan Organisation. But what Steel could not understand was why Lucy did not tell Foster. He could have done something. Or maybe she had recognised Price or Tipp from the embassy. Perhaps she did not realise how big it was. Perhaps she thought these were a couple of agents making a quick buck? But it did not matter in the end. What did matter – to Steel – was the way she was killed. Steel had the pathologist in Victoria look at the legs again, and he confirmed Lucy hadn't just been knocked down by the car but run over. The result was internal haemorrhaging and broken limbs.

The news had made Steel feel sick and angry. He'd asked Calver to search the data banks to trace movements Price and Tipp had made lately. It had shown Price going to Azure Window the night of Lucy's death. Unfortunately, because of the weather, there was no image of her tossing Lucy over. But from what Steel had seen of Tipp and Price. Neither one of them would be physically capable of carrying a body to the cliff at Azure Window in the day, let alone at night. It did explain why they had used the Blue Hole and not gone all the way up to Azure Window – they physically could not. They weren't big enough to walk that path in the dark and carry a body.

Steel looked over at the sound of a boat approached. The strobe light on the life preserver he had managed to grab flashed violently. He was sick of drinking seawater – he needed a real drink – possibly lots of them.

Steel was taken to the local hospital for a check-up. He was slightly scarred, bruised and need a few stitches. He'd had an x-ray on his chest, but they had found he'd suffered bruising to the ribs due to being shot in the vest. But they had classed him as fit but said he'd have to be on light duties for a while. Steel phoned the Grand Excelsior Hotel and asked if a driver could pick him up and return to the hotel and also if there could be a bottle of 18-year-old Glen Grant put in his room. He was tired and just wanted a long bath, some good food, and to sleep.

After an hour's drive, the car pulled up outside the hotel. Steel had tipped the driver and thanked him before heaving his body out of the passenger side and headed inside the hotel. He felt like he'd been hit by a freight train, but Steel knew after a long sleep – if that was possible, he'd feel better.

Steel went to the front desk and got his key, and checked if there were any messages. The man behind the desk passed over a handful of message forms. They were all mostly from London or the family business. Steel thanked the man and headed for his room.

Inside the suite, on the desk, Steel found his wallet, watch, and other items he had thought lost from Manoel Island's encounter. There was a note with them. It was from Sergeant Burlo.

With kind regards, we found these in a car in a swimming pool, thought you would like them back. Burlo.

Steel headed over to the drinks cabinet and picked up a bottle of 18-year-old malt and half filled the glass.

Grabbing the glass, he headed into the bathroom and stripped off his battle scared clothes. His muscles ached from the ordeal, but he would survive. He took a hit from the glass and looked at his bruised, muscular frame. The past week had not been kind. His wardrobe had suffered the most. He took another mouthful of whisky and stepped into the soothing waters of the shower.

Steel slept until late morning. He had no plans, so he stayed in bed until eleven. He used the phone next to the bed to order brunch – eggs, bacon, mushroom – the works, along with a pot of coffee. Steel had made several calls. One had been to Whitehall. They had been briefed by the US Embassy on the events, so Steel's input had just dotted the i's and crossed the t's, but he was required to see the CO as soon as possible. Steel had then booked himself on the next available flight back to Britain, which was due out the next day.

The next call had been to Foster, who was on sick leave. Which meant he was home alone and bored. Foster had told Steel that there was a black-tie event at the embassy and that Steel, Samara and Kane were invited. Foster had also said that this was not an invitation; more a 'must attend.'

The next call was to Samara. She'd said that she had also received the invitation but felt uneasy about going back there. Oddly enough, her bosses in Mossad seemed most insistent, calling it a 'momentous occasion.' Which made her even more uncomfortable.

After breakfast, Steel decided to spend the day doing nothing. He walked around Valletta as though he was a tourist. He found a store and bought a tux for the evening's event. He wandered about, taking in the sights, stopping at coffee shops. But, it felt alien to him. He had never really been on holiday. He felt uncomfortable but at the same time at peace.

Later that evening, after showering and changing into his tux, Steel ventured down to the lobby. Earlier that day, Steel had arranged for a hotel to provide a car to take him to the embassy and a twenty-year-old bottle of Glen Grant as a present.

The car pulled up to the arched main entrance, and Steel crawled onto the Mercedes C class's back seat. The cab was clean and had a pleasant smell of air fresher and leather soap. The radio was playing a local radio station and some group he had never heard of – but then, Steel wasn't really that musical. He had met Jon Bon Jovi once and hadn't known who he was.

The cab ride was smooth and, without incident, a first for the trip.

The driver pulled up to the battered front gate, which still had Samara's car littering the grass area. The guard recognised Steel at once and swung up a grand salute. Steel saluted back, and they drove through. Outside the main entrance, Foster waited with Samara and Kane. Steel smiled at the sight of Foster, who was dressed in a tux with crutches under both arms. Samara looked stunning in a figure-hugging black dress, and Kane looked respectable in his tux. He saw Samara smile softly as Steel climbed out of the car, wincing slightly at the pain from his ribs. They all stood for a moment while they greeted each other with hugs. This merry band had been through a lot in the past week.

One they would never forget, that was for sure. Steel looked over at Foster, who was balancing on his crutches.

'I hear there's a party inside. Want to crash it?' Foster asked. Steel smiled and raised the bottle of whisky.

'I thought it was a *bring a bottle* gig,' Steel said with a smile. The four of them walked in. Inside was as formal as it got. There was a live band who were playing soft jazz or something. The staff walked about with trays of champagne and h'ordeves. There were people in cocktail dresses, or dress blues, or tuxedos. Steel was beginning to think he was back home at the estate at one of his father's damned suck up parties. Steel grabbed a drink for Foster and Samara, and Kane both took a glass from a nearby server.

'So, what's the party for? The fact we avoided world war three or that the damned software that nobody is meant to know about worked?' Steel asked.

'Probably both, but it was the ambassador's idea,' Foster said.

'Who is the ambassador anyway?' Steel asked, slightly embarrassed he did not know.

'Ambassador Moira Kent,' Foster noted that Steel had gone quiet, his smile had faded. 'You ok, bud?' Foster asked.

Steel nodded silently, then took a sip from his glass.

'I hate these things,' Steel finally said, with an uncomfortable look on his face.

'I know, that's why I organised it. So suck it up, soldier,' Foster laughed.

People laughed, drank and eat, but Steel wasn't in the mood to celebrate. He had no reason to.

Steel looked over to see the ambassador, a refined woman in her late fifties, approach Foster and shake his hand. She had short blonde hair and blue eyes like pools of ice. An attractive woman. A long blue sequined dress hugged her athletic form. Steel suspected this was mostly to make some of the other guests embarrassed about letting themselves go.

They chatted for a while before Foster introduced Samara and Kane. As Foster turned to Steel, he found an empty space.

'Sorry ambassador, he's...' Foster said.

'A little shy?' The ambassador said.

'Actually, I gonna say a pain in the ass – but yeah, we'll go with shy,' Foster said. The ambassador smiled and followed Kane's gaze to the door to the garden.

The ambassador found Steel in the garden next to a small table and a couple of metal chair. He held a glass, and the table took care of his bottle of malt whisky. She grabbed a glass from the conference table and slowly walked up behind him. Steel was looking up at the stars. Enjoying the solitude.

'So, is this a private party or you going to share?' Moira Kent asked, holding out her glass.

Steel smiled and poured her a drink.

'What are you doing out here, John, thought you aristocratic types loved these things?'

'No, that was my father's thing if you remember. I don't do functions. Not anymore... not after....' Steel looked down at his glass and smiled.

'Yes. Of course,' the ambassador said. 'But she would have been proud of what you did here.' the ambassador lay a gentle hand on his shoulder.

Steel smiled and nodded as he looked up at the brilliant display of stars.'She loved the stars,' Steel said softly.

'She loved you more. Never forget that' the ambassador replied.

'I'm sorry about Helen,' Steel said. 'I'm sorry I wasn't there for your daughter, Moira. I let you down, both of you,' Steel said, wishing he could at least shed one tear, but those had been denied him since that day.

'You were there for her. You were right there when she needed you most – at the end,' the ambassador said, choking back the tears. 'What you are now is because of that day. And what you have become is what saved so many lives. And don't you forget that, Earl Alexander John Leonidas Steel,' she smiled. 'And don't you let them forget that either – ever,' she said before clinking Steel's glass and downing the scotch.

'God, I hate that she told you my full name,' Steel groaned.

'You should be proud. You have a name of warriors – of kings,' Moira said. 'Now, stop being a sour puss and get your ass inside. There's a party going on.'

'Yes, ma'am,' Steel replied before finishing off his drink and picking up the bottle. As Steel returned to the building, he found Foster in the doorway, with a smile on his face.

'What did the boss want with you?' Foster asked.

'She heard you're a great cook – I told her it was a lie,' Steel smiled.

'Thanks, and thanks for finding out what happened to my little girl,' Foster said, giving Steel a big hug.

'You used me, Foster,' Steel said. 'You did it for revenge, not justice. You knew what I would probably do. You put me in a bad position,' Steel said, his voice rang with hurt and betrayal.

'Yes – I guess you're right. I did, and I am sorry, but I'd do it again,' Foster spoke with a thick tone.

'Yeah, I know you would, and I'd still probably help you,' Steel smiled and undid the top of the bottle. Foster tossed the champagne from his glass and offered it to Steel for filling.

'Don't mean you can share my booze, though,' Steel said, laughing.

The night continued until the early morning, and the sun rose in blazing orange. Samara found Steel sat on one of the garden chairs.

'Hey handsome, have you been avoiding me?' Samara asked, feeling slightly hurt.

'No, avoiding everyone, really. I just wanted some quiet for once. It's the first quiet time I've had since the prison cell on the island,' Steel joked. Samara smiled and nodded in agreement.

'I have to admit it had been a heck of a ride,' Samara said. 'So, John Steel, tell me. Are all your holidays like this?'

Steel thought for a moment, paused, then nodded with a quick shrug.

'On the whole, pretty much, yes,' Steel said.

Samara laughed, thinking he was joking. 'You know they want to give you a medal, don't you?'

'A raise would be better,' Steel joked. 'Want to dance?' He stood up. Samara followed close behind.

Steel's flight to New York was early, with a long stop off in London. Foster and Steel had said their goodbyes at the party, they had talked about getting together again soon, but Steel knew that wouldn't happen.

Samara drove Steel to the airport. Their final goodbyes were filled with promises to stay in touch. Deep down, Samara wanted to hear from him again, but she knew she wouldn't. But somehow, it was OK. The time they had spent together was one she would never forget.

Steel waved as he entered the terminal and watched her car disappear. He smiled and took one last look, then passed through the gate. His thoughts lay a million miles away as he walked through the security and into the boarding lounge. Steel sat and reached into his pocket and pulled out a black notebook with a diagram of a horses head embossed in the leather cover. Steel smiled as he flicked through Price's journal that he had taken from the boat, a little something to read before his flight.

Again, he was alone. But that was fine…he preferred it that way.

A Year Later

A crisp, refreshing breeze brushed across the hillside of the Azure Window. The early morning had seen a perfect sunrise in a clear sky. A woman stood on the top and looked out across the expanse of water and sky.

She could feel it was going to be a warm day later. She breathed in and closed her eyes. Letting the sounds of uninterrupted nature fill her ears. Soon the crowds would come and spoil the moment.

But she had waited.

And she had been rewarded with the silence of the moment.

The woman opened her eyes and softly let the breath leave her mouth. She turned to see a figure stood at the edge. She could have sworn he hadn't been there before. He was tall, but his face was covered by the hood of his long coat. It was a strange design, with a wool body with leather arms. The bottom of the coat was carried up by the wind. Causing it to flap like a flag in the breeze. She saw a pair of black trousers and some kind of military-style shoe.

The woman walked over to the figure.

'Hello,' she greeted the stranger.

'Good morning,' replied the stranger. The woman noticed the man was holding a bouquet of flowers with white lilies and blue roses. She drew closer and saw his eyes were covered by a pair of face-hugging sunglasses.

'Meeting a girl, are we?' the woman asked.

'No – they're for someone – someone I lost. A girl who died on here some time ago,' the figure replied.

'You don't mean that poor girl who was found washed up in the Blue Hole, do you, poor thing?' the woman said. Shaking her head at the thought of the story. 'She was murdered, you know. They never did catch who did it, though,' the woman said, almost saddened there wasn't more to tell about it.

The figure smelled the flowers and then tossed them into the crashing waves below. Then the man turned and left.

The woman turned towards the man and watched him climb into a black Land Rover and drove off.

The woman looked down at the flowers being consumed by the waves. She smiled at the man's gesture. Thinking how sweet it had been. She closed her eyes again. And went through the same ritual as before.

She breathed in and listened. But this time, instead of the sound of the wind, she thought she could hear something else…music. It was quiet, possibly distant or – small. It reminded her of an old music box her mother once had.

The woman opened her eyes in time to see a tall thin man climb into the back of a taxi – his features hidden underneath a large fedora. The woman shuddered, almost as if death had just walked past.

She looked back over the ocean and watched as the sun loomed out of the horizon.

Running Steel
John Steel Book 6

This book is dedicated to all the writers, both veterans and new.
Thank you for inspiring me on my writing journey, and may you continue to inspire others in theirs.
Thank you.

Acknowledgments

I would like to thank:
My darling wife, who had to endure being dragged on so much research while I wrote this.
And to Miika and the Next Chapter Team for all their hard work.

Chapter 1

Charles King was free, which didn't sit well with John Steel.

Steel was a British detective on loan from Scotland Yard, or at least that had been his cover story for the past year that he had worked with the NYPD.

The truth was Steel was a member of MI8, the British Secret Service. He had been sent to New York to hunt down a secret criminal organization. They specialized in arms deals, assassination, corruption, and blackmail, known as SANTINI—an organization responsible for the murder of Steel's entire family.

The investigation into SANTINI had led MI8 to believe that the organization had something planned in New York. So, of course, this meant Steel had to go undercover and work alongside the 11th Precinct. The cover story had been arranged, but a case involving a serial killer changed all that. But for Steel, it was the perfect way to integrate himself into the team because this case had SANTINI written all over it.

He had hoped to be on the first plane home once the case was done. But unfortunately, Whitehall and Washington had thought it a good idea if he stuck around, just in case the SANTINI reared their heads again.

But the organization had gone quiet. So now, he was left hunting down arseholes like Charles King when he should be in London doing what he was paid for.

Steel's interest in King had started when MI8 had contacted him and told him to investigate several buildings demolished courtesy of explosives. Something to be expected in an ever-changing city.

However, these buildings were not due to be demolished; the explosives used had been military-grade and not for civilian contractor use. Explosives that the SANTINI organization had been known to sell. This news had gotten London's interest.

Was the bomber working for, or had dealings with, SANTINI?

Steel had used his NYPD cover to carry out the investigation, and it all led to one man: Charles King.

King was the son of a billionaire construction tycoon. A man who had come up from nothing and built and owned half the city.

However, Charles King preferred to destroy rather than create. He had been arrested for destroying old buildings around the city using explosives. Even though the buildings had been empty didn't change the fact he had used explosives and had endangered life. Luckily, no one had been killed. However, four people had ended up in the hospital after Charles King's last job.

In Steel's eyes, the man was a menace to society, someone who had been caught and arrested and should spend the rest of his smug ass life in prison. But Steel had learned that people with money and power sometimes slipped through the net on technicalities. That was why, when Steel put this case together, it was watertight … or so he believed.

But somehow, the months of work, investigating, and gathering evidence was for nothing. Charles King sat with a broad grin as twelve lawyers surrounded him. Of course, he did. Charles was Edward King's son, the billionaire construction tycoon, a top dog in the city.

What should have been a slam dunk turned out to be a waste of time. Evidence had somehow been tainted, witnesses had changed their testimony or had just disappeared, and the lawyer from the DA's office seemed to be off her game.

The case had fallen apart.

The judge had torn the assistant district attorney apart for his lack of hard evidence and inadequate preparation. The case was lost, and King walked free.

Steel stood at the back of the courtroom, watching everything slowly crumble apart. But, as the judge told King, he was a free man. Steel clenched his fists. Hoping the act would help him run down to King and smash his face through the table in front of the judge. As the bailiff told everyone to rise, King turned to look at the door, almost hoping to see Steel's face, but found only a gap in the crowd. A roar of mumbles and mutters flowed as members of the crowd conversed over what had happened.

The lawyers ushered King and his father out the doors, and the inevitable media circus awaited. White blinding flashes from cameras lit faces as the media took picture after picture. Then, finally, Edward King spoke, thanking the jury's decision and condemning the police for trying to lock up an innocent man while the actual bomber was still out there.

Steel watched from afar, away from the crowds, blending into the shadowy backdrop of the courthouse. Steel knew King would do it again – it was inevitable. All Steel had to do was wait and catch the bastard in the act.

* * *

Two months had passed with no new incidents concerning Charles King. It was September, with longer days and soaring temperatures. Steel sat outside the King building, a massive monstrosity on West 42nd Street, waiting. Disguised as a homeless person, Steel peered from his perch. It was a decent enough costume that had fooled most. But Steel only needed to deceive one person, and by the look on King's face as he looked straight at him, Steel had done just that.

He first noticed how distant King looked, as though his mind were somewhere else. Steel smiled to himself as King waved down a cab and hurried inside. Steel got up from his perch and waved down another cab by standing in front of it to stop it.

'You crazy, man?' yelled the cabby.

'Look, I'm a cop; follow that cab,' Steel said, showing his shield and pulling off the fake beard.

'For real?' the cabby said with a curious look on his weathered face.

'Yes … for real,' Steel replied, watching in desperation as King's cab disappeared into the traffic flow.

'This isn't a TV show?' asked the cabby, suddenly excited.

'On a TV show, would they drag you out of your cab and beat you half to death for wasting time?' Steel snarled.

The man sat silently as a sudden sense of panic washed over him.

'Look, catch him, and you get this,' Steel said, pulling a hundred-dollar bill from his wallet.

The cabby smiled, faced the steering wheel, put the shift into drive, and put his foot hard on the gas. Steel was pushed back into his seat as the man sped after the other cab.

The cabby talked all the way—about how he'd seen so many cop shows and never thought a detective would actually say 'follow that car' to him for real. The man was ecstatic, but Steel's thoughts were elsewhere; for one, where the hell was King going?

The cabby drove for around twenty minutes; all the while, Steel got more nervous the deeper they carried down 11th Avenue.

'Where the hell are you going, King?' Steel said to himself, but loud enough for the cabby to overhear.

'Maybe he's going to a mall … to get his … wife a present?' the cabby suggested with a skip in his voice.

A sudden shiver ran down Steel's back. The mall—he's heading for the mall.

Steel pulled out his cell and tried phoning Samantha McCall, his partner, but there was no reply. Steel hung up and tried Captain Brant. The phone rang a couple of times before an angry voice came down the speaker.

'Where the hell you at Steel? Please don't tell me you're tracking, King?' Brant yelled angrily down the phone.

'He's heading for the new mall at Brookfield Place. I need backup,' Steel said. His brain had already calculated that he had to do this by the book, or King would walk again.

'He's probably going for a present or something. Look, Steel, I get it. He won, we lost … just leave it alone and get your ass back to work,' Brant growled.

Steel said nothing. He just hung up and put away the cell phone. King was off to do something stupid, and Steel couldn't let that happen.

King's cab stopped, got out, and slipped into one of the entrances.

Steel told the cabby to stop behind the other cab, passed over the promised cash, and then jumped out and followed King. He was close behind but far enough away to be unnoticed by King.

Even for a Tuesday, the place was heaving with shoppers. The mall was bright and modern, with an arched glass roof, brown marble floor, and white stone pillars. The top-level held fancy fast-food restaurants and shops for people with expensive tastes below.

Steel walked in and looked around quickly, hoping to catch a glimpse of King, but found no trace. So he headed amongst the shoppers, hoping his luck hadn't run out. From what Steel had seen, Charles King was nervous about something that couldn't be good.

Steel made his way to the next floor, which had most of the various food courts. The smell of Chinese, Italian, and another he couldn't quite place, filled his nostrils, causing his stomach to rumble. Steel could feel people's eyes on him, but then he remembered that he was still disguised as a homeless person.

A sea of people waiting for food made sighting King virtually impossible, but Steel couldn't give up. Something was off, and King was volatile.

As Steel stood near the top of the elevators, something caught the corner of Steel's eye. He turned to see what had caught his interest, just in time to see security guards on the ground level rushing towards him. Steel cursed his disguise choice and went to head off the guards so they could catch up to him and give him a chance to explain.

Then Steel saw King.

King was frozen to the spot. In his hand was a large black canvas bag. A bag that he'd not had before when he had entered the mall. King stood between Steel and the approaching guards. His terrified eyes were glued to them.

'How did they know?' King thought to himself.

Steel went to call out for them to stop, but it was too late.

King had ripped open the bag to reveal an explosive device, then took something from the bag and held it high in the air. 'Get back, I'm warning you, get back,' King screamed. His voice filled with panic.

Steel didn't have a good visual of what King was holding, but he knew it was a kill switch from the guard's expression.

Slowly, the guards backed off, their weapons still drawn and held in aim. People rushed about in a panic, tripping over one another to get to one of the many exits. Steel backed off and crouched so King wouldn't see him. King was spooked enough without Steel adding to it. The four security guards remained while others tried to calm people's hysteria and get them out safely.

Steel needed a plan of action that didn't involve being blown to pieces. As he watched, the floor he was on was slowly being cleared. 'Good,' Steel thought, his gaze slowly moving back to King.

Outside, the police arrived to begin cordoning off the area and setting up a Forward Command Post. Soon the bomb squad would be there along with fire and ambulance crews. Not forgetting the wave of press that would undoubtedly make things a thousand times worse with media coverage.

* * *

'It's OK, sir. We can work this out. Nobody needs to get hurt,' said one of the guards.

'Get back … stay back … I'm warning you,' King screamed, waving the kill switch about so the guards could see it, his thumb tightly on the button.

Steel remained crouched and watched everything. King's demeanour was all wrong. He was panicked, out of control … frightened. Perhaps because he had been caught, it made sense. People like him derived power from anonymity and the fear of others. Now that was over, he was cornered and out of options. But what was he doing in the mall with the bomb? It wasn't his MO.

'Drop your guns and kick them over here,' King ordered.

The guards complied, their hands raised above their heads, looks of fear covering their faces. King looked around to see the mall was emptying. A glimpse of realisation came over his face; he was losing hostages.

'Everybody on the ground, *now*,' King yelled, grabbing a gun from the ground and firing two shots into the ceiling.

Glass fragments fell from the shattered ceiling, smashing on the ground below; it stopped a group of people who had ventured too close to Charles King. They screamed in terror and lay on the tiled floor, trying to make themselves less of a target.

'You … get over here and join them,' King said, waving his gun towards the guards in front of him as if directing the twenty-five unlucky souls who didn't make it out in time where he wanted them. The people got up from the floor and quickly obeyed, running to the guards. Their eyes were wide with fear, women and children crying, thinking this would be the last day they would ever see.

'Now, everyone … get your asses on the ground … spread out so I can see you all,' King directed, wiping the sweat from his brow.

The weeping crowd of hostages complied. Then, sitting cross-legged on the cold marble floor, eyes fixed on King and that wireless kill switch in his left hand.

Steel moved around the upper floor, ensuring he was out of sight. The hostage situation made Steel's plan fall apart, but he had somehow expected it. King was smart, a survivor. Unfortunately, the whole situation went against everything that King was. Steel could understand taking a hostage at gunpoint, but using a large bomb to level a small building? It went against his character.

'You,' King yelled at one of the security guards, 'How do you lock this place down?' The guard went to mumble something but was stopped by another guard.

'He doesn't know; he's just started,' said an older guard.

'But *you* do, I bet?'

The man nodded.

'Then what are you waiting for? Lock it down, now,' King ordered.

'I can only do it from the security room,' lied the guard.

'Well … you better hurry. You have five minutes; if you're not back by then, I'll start shooting people,' King said, pointing the gun at different people, making them flinch in terror.

The guard quickly rose to his feet and ran towards the escalators.

Steel watched the display–King was getting bolder, more organized. He felt a sense of power, and once it was locked down, he would be damn right dangerous. Once those security gates came down, the police would have little chance of getting in without alerting King due to the alarm system.

Steel had to find a way of defusing the situation and get that trigger away from King. One mistake would put innocent lives at risk.

* * *

Outside, the media were already telling the story of how the recently acquitted Charles King had a bomb and several hostages. The media circus was filling up by the second, along with people with cameras and cell phones. Police cars and vans from the Hostage Rescue Unit created a boundary so the cameras couldn't catch any Command Post—or CP—footage. For now, the police were in charge. But soon, the Feds would arrive in their blacked-out vehicles, taking control, playing the whole *domestic terrorism playbook* thing. But in the meantime, snipers, spotters, and entry teams were put into place, awaiting orders. Everyone was looking for a peaceful solution. The press waiting for a story.

Steel noticed more and more people who weren't quick enough to get out moving around the top floor. More lives hung in the balance. Steel showed his shield and told them to get close to the other side of the mall and get out through any exit possible. Telling them to take others that they found with them. But Steel didn't have time to play shepherd to stray people—he had to get to the security room and talk to the guard.

* * *

Steel found his way to the security office. The guard was busy closing the shutters but ensuring he left the parking lot until last. A security monitor showed people still herding through the exit, the guard giving them time to escape.

'Nice job,' Steel said, causing the man to turn.

'Who the hell are you?' asked the guard, spinning around in his seat and looking for the crazy guy from downstairs.

'I'm NYPD,' Steel replied.

'But your British?' said the guard with a look of distrust.

'I'm on loan from Scotland Yard.'

'You got ID?' asked the guard.

Steel scowled at the man. 'Seriously, we are doing this dance while an arsehole is a downstairs, trying to hold everyone hostage with a bomb?' he growled. His accent was British, but his voice was neutral. It is a product of being in the Army, where all accents are made neutral after a time, sometimes making it hard to tell if someone was from Scotland or England.

'Look, I'm here to try and get everyone out,' Steel said.

'Thank God,' replied the guard, looking at the ceiling and making a prayer gesture.

'Oh, don't do that just yet … it's just me,' Steel said with a shrug.

'Wait …' The guard suddenly realized something. 'You're the bum we were told to toss out.'

Steel shrugged again. 'Guess it's lucky you didn't,' Steel said with a smile.

'How's that?' The guard had a confused look on his face.

'Because I'm going to get everyone out of this alive,' Steel said sternly.

He watched as Steel grabbed the first-aid box and began sorting through the bandages.

'Is someone hurt?'

Steel took one bandage and unrolled it with a smile. 'No ... this is for ... something else.' He rushed over to the monitors. 'How long do you have?' Steel asked.

The guard looked at his watch. 'Two minutes.'

'You better go and try not to let it slip you saw me. I don't want to get him any more agitated.'

The guard nodded in agreement and took off. Steel looked at the monitor just in time to see the final escape route close. He knew he had to get this right, for everyone's sake. Steel headed back to the overwatch and onto the ground floor. He needed a distraction to catch King off guard, something subtle ... but then, Steel never really did subtle.

He pressed redial on the cell phone's display, taking out his cell; he needed to talk to Brant quickly. Steel knew the police would want to take a shot at King the first chance they got, but they didn't know that King had a kill switch.

The phone rang for a minute before Brant answered with an excited voice. 'Please tell me you're *not* in there,' Brant said, his voice trembling as though expecting bad news.

'Would it make you feel better?' Steel replied calmly.

'Not really. What we lookin' at?' Brant was unsurprised by the answer.

'Well, King has around twenty-five hostages, a big black bag with a device of some kind in it and ... oh, did I mention the wireless kill switch?' Steel said in an amused tone as if trying to lighten the mood of the bad news ... but Brant wasn't laughing.

'A friggin' kill switch?' Brant asked, hoping he had heard it wrong.

'Look, captain, I have a plan, but I need a distraction.'

'What kind of distraction?' Brant asked, rolling his eyes, almost fearful of the answer.

'Fire alarm and sprinklers would be good,' Steel replied.

'I can't authorize that?' Brant declared, knowing full well someone would, but the city would get the bill for damages.

'Sorry, Alan ... I missed that ... it's rather loud here.' Steel spoke as if they had a bad connection.

'I can hear .... no...wait. Steel?' Brant yelled, but it was too late.

Steel pressed the fire alarm button and ran back over to the glass wall of the balcony. There was a sudden burst of an alarm; the noise was deafening. Orange strobe lights began to blink, and all the emergency lighting came on, showing the nearest exits.

King looked confused; then he gazed up as water began to cascade from the sprinkler system. He glanced at the people on the ground. None of them had moved. He then thought about the security guard, but he had returned just as it had started—so, who had set off the alarm? Then he heard a noise from above. He turned and looked just in time to see a homeless guy landing on top of him.

Steel rolled and was up on his feet in a flash.

King was dazed from the impact as if he'd been hit by a truck. Slowly, he forced himself to get to his feet. But Steel was waiting for him, watching the man rock back and forth like a drunk. Then, just as King was almost standing straight, Steel hit him—with a powerful clenched fist to the nose.

Everyone watched as King was ripped off his feet and landed hard on the tiled floor, making a dull, sickening thud. Before King could recover, Steel grabbed King's hand and started to wrap the bandage around it. Steel made sure the bandage was tight, fastening King's grip onto the kill switch, locking the thumb into place, making it impossible for King to release the trigger.

'Handcuffs,' Steel said to the security guards. The men tossed over their cuffs so Steel could secure King to a bench leg.

'Don't go anywhere,' Steel said to King.

King bared his teeth in contempt, his eyes red with anger. Steel looked over at the security guard who had activated the lockdown and nodded to him. It was a silent command. As though a prearranged signal had been given. 'All clear.' The man doubled back to the security room to release the security doors, giving the police and Special Reaction Team—or SRT—an entrance.

Steel smiled as he saw the guard disappear, and the other guards ushered the hostages back towards the nearest exit. No one was risking sticking around just in case King got free.

Steel looked down at King. He seemed small, no longer the big confident man he had been earlier. King lay there, his arms cuffed to the sides so he couldn't tear off the bandage. Steel had thought about breaking the fingers of his left hand, but some might class that as excessive force. So, Steel went for another option and knocked him out instead. It was another mighty fist to face, but from the side this time, it had the same desired effect of knocking King's head backwards with such force that he smashed his head on the wall behind him. Lights out.

Steel looked around; the guards were doing a good job getting people out. Soon, the cops and the bomb squad would be there. King was subdued, and the weapon would soon be disarmed; all was right with the world.

Steel walked over to the glass frontage and looked out across the bay. The sun was bright, and the sky a cloudless blue. A tiny sound like a stone hitting a windscreen was followed by a massive burst of energy from behind Steel, heaving him forwards through the window. Everything went black.

* * *

Brant looked at the cell phone in his huge bear-sized hands. Had Steel just hung up? He rushed to the command wagon; he needed to speak to the agent who had just arrived on the scene to take charge.

'My guy inside said King has a kill-switch and a big-ass bomb, so no snipers,' Brant said, moving in between the other people from the agencies.

Inside the command vehicle, a man sat at a communications desk and relayed the information to the teams.

The agent, who had identified himself as Headley, said nothing. He just sat there and looked at Brant with a cold expression and Ray-Ban sunglasses concealing his eyes.

The noise from the fire alarm made everyone look over to the mall.

'Um, that's my guy's distraction. He's going to try something,' Brant admitted.

The agent gave Brant the stare again before getting up and walking away to make a call. Brant closed his eyes and looked up to the heavens, praying it all went as Steel had planned.

The explosion rocked the mall and shattered the windows of nearby cars and buildings. Brant looked over in horror as a colossal fireball rose from the shopping centre. Fire trucks and ambulances raced over, as well as the police teams. No one thought of personal safety, only getting the people out. Brant followed, his heart in his mouth. Something had gone wrong. Had Steel missed his mark and paid for it with his life and the others?

Fire crews got to work to contain the fires while the HRT teams breached the building, searching for survivors and possible accomplices. Alan Brant moved around the front of the building where the blast had originated. If Steel had gotten out, he would be there, possibly sitting by the water's edge, waiting for a chewing out. Brant stopped suddenly at the sight of a homeless man's body lying amongst broken glass and burning debris. Brant yelled for help before rushing over. Brant rolled him over to find Steel in disguise.

Glass shards were embedded in the suit, and he had cuts to his face and hands. Steel was breathing but unconscious.

'Medic, I need a medic over here,' Brant yelled, then he looked at the burning wreckage of the mall. Bodies were mangled by the blast, and a crater where the device had once been. Brant looked at Steel and shook his head.

'What the hell did you do, Steel?'

Chapter 2

Two months had passed since the mall incident, and life had gone on as it always did. People went to work, school, and college. Tourists came and went. People went about without a plan, just their daily routine, except for the shadowy figure that held the woman in its gaze.

The Sentinel had been observing the woman for some time. Alison Kline, forty-two years old. A single, career woman, a lawyer. It was a dull day, with grey clouds looming overhead with a promise of cold winds and possible showers.

* * *

It was late November, and most of the trees had shed their golden foliage; winter was not far away, and bone-chilling winds and snow showers would come with it.

But today, it was a fresh twelve degrees with a slight easterly breeze.

Alison moved with the busy New York Street. Her brown Burberry coat wrapped around her tightly to keep away the chill. It was 12:22. Alison made her way to the coffee shop across the firm's road, her favourite place at this time of day. Inside, Alison ordered a caramel cappuccino with cream and a chicken wrap to go.

Alison didn't know she was being watched or had been for a week.

But The Sentinel saw everything she did. The way Alison ran her fingers through her long brown hair. How she wore the skirt suits to every meeting; today, it was grey with a sky-blue blouse and a pair of black Christian Louboutin platform shoes. And how Alison had slipped into that Victoria's Secret black lace number she'd gotten two days ago.

The Sentinel took note of everything Alison did. How she dressed, how she went to work, how she made love to all those men. Her life had been catalogued and studied like an experiment. But she was more than that to The Sentinel: she was a name on a list.

Alison took her lunch and left the coffee shop, heading back to her office across the street. The traffic that day was maddening as everyone rushed to get somewhere.

Alison used a crowded pedestrian crossing, holding on to her lunch as if it were made from gelignite. Avoiding the oncoming traffic of people by swerving and dodging the hordes of pedestrians.

Alison made it safely to her building with an exhalation of relief and headed inside. She said hello to the two security guards at the desk and used the elevator to get to the third floor. It was another quiet day at Alison Kline's office, the top attorney at a reputable law firm.

Alison placed her lunch and moved the mouse on her desk to reactivate her computer from the power-save mode. The screen returned, showing a calendar of appointments she had throughout the week. Today was Saturday, not much on, but Tuesday was full. Including preparation for a big case on Friday. This meant lots of working late at home during the night. Alison noted plenty of wine and takeout food from Tuesday onwards on the jotter next to her keyboard.

The Sentinel moved a small laptop around for a better view. The picture on the screen was Alison at work; the feed was from a camera hidden in one of her office's strip lights. The Sentinel zoomed in on the computer screen and then the jotter. Finally, The Sentinel took a screenshot of what was written on the yellow legal pad.

The final phase of a plan was coming together.

The Sentinel had cameras everywhere: Alison's work, home, and even her car. The Sentinel paid close attention to Alison and her lifestyle. *Very* close attention. After all, reconnaissance was crucial, especially if you were going to get rid of someone in public without ever being there.

* * *

Dark clouds loomed over the Manhattan skyline, and flashes of lightning flickered in the distance. The clouds appeared heavy, but not a drop of rain fell. Instead, the streets were full of midday travellers, tourists, and workers searching for that diner or fast-food stand to grab a quick snack. Long silver mobile dressing rooms and sound studios lined East 40th Street, setting up another big production, hoping the weather wouldn't break.

People walked past with interest, hoping to catch a glimpse of a movie star or at least find out what was about to be filmed.

The Sentinel was clad in a long black hooded trench with black cargo trousers and military-style boots. Black leather gloves met with black leather gauntlets. It had been quite a look in some places in Europe in the 1800s or even now.

The figure moved fluidly through the streets, almost as if they were made from the mist. The Sentinel didn't rush or push past other pedestrians but moved lithely and blended in with the masses.

The crowd walked past an alleyway, and the figure ducked in unseen as if it had never been there. The Sentinel moved through the alley, then got on to the next street before heading back up the street to a hotel. Looking around, The Sentinel ensured no one was following before ducking through the hotel entrance.

The inside was gloomy, but streaks of light from the windows revealed dust particles in the air. It was an old hotel, a pay-by-the-hour and no-questions-asked kind of place. Perfect for what The Sentinel needed. The figure moved to room 213. Faded, peeling wallpaper from the eighties barely hung on the walls, and what used to be red carpet was dark, stained, and walked flat. Despite all this, it was a place for low-rent people. Some people had made arrangements with the owner and had a lease. It was a steady, cheap income, so the guy didn't mind.

The Sentinel opened the door to room 213 and went in. Inside was a short hallway leading to the bathroom on the right. Down past, this was a big room equipped with a small kitchenette comprising a small sink, a tiny workspace that held a coffee machine, and a single electric cooking plate. This was next to a built-in wardrobe on the back wall of the bathroom. Directly in front was a long, dirty glass window with orange and white patterned curtains.

To the left: a desk and a small cheap flat-screen television. A double bed with a dated orange bedspread sat against the right-hand wall. The bed had two bedside cabinets; each had a snaking aluminium lamp that came through the side of the bedhead. It was clean but required updating. The wallpaper was from the late seventies, brown with orange cut-out triangles, and the carpet used to be cream but was now a greyish colour. It wasn't the Ritz, but it was all that was required.

The Sentinel moved towards a desk facing one of the back walls. On the workspace were a computer and printer. On the wall next to the workspace was a large board. Several photographs of Alison Kline, a map of the locations she frequented, timings at each site, and distance from one place to another. Alison was the perfect target. She stuck to a routine to the second. Her compulsive nature was part of her reputation; it would also be her undoing.

The Sentinel took a memory card from a camera and placed it into the computer. There was a gentle hum. It started to download Alison's surveillance photos taken throughout the day. Some included photos from the night before and the grey-haired man in her bedroom. With a mouse click, the printer started to spew out photographs.

The Sentinel stood, walked to the kitchenette, opened the refrigerator, and pulled out a carton of orange juice. Taking several mouthfuls, The Sentinel then placed the container back. Next, The Sentinel plugged the camera into a power socket and headed for the bed, moving back to the table.

It would be a while until Alison would venture out again. So, The Sentinel decided to get some sleep. And if Alison did make an unscheduled visit somewhere, The Sentinel had Alison's phone tracked so she would find her or at least learn where she had been. The gentle whir from the printer was soothing to The Sentinel, almost like those ocean machines to help someone sleep. But The Sentinel didn't have any problems sleeping; it was the nightmares that The Sentinel feared.

Chapter 3

It was several months later. After the incident in the New York shopping mall, London ordered Steel to take extended sick leave. This was to rest his injuries and give him space from the NYPD.

In his report to the head of MI8, a man known only as CO, Steel insisted that his time in New York was over with no further signs of SANTINI. Steel suggested that he should return to Britain for reassignment.

CO had agreed that his time was best spent doing his job with the Secret Service, not playing detective and eating doughnuts. London was satisfied with what had occurred, but they were still puzzled about how the bomb had detonated.

Steel had thought there might have been a second person involved, someone with an electronic detonator, just in case something went wrong. However, London had dismissed this theory and thought it more plausible that the device had a fault.

The skies above Barcelona were watercolour splashes of red and purple on a cloudless canvas. Barcelona's streets were filling with people, commuters heading about their business, and flocks of tourists who wanted an early start.

Freshly fallen leaves danced along clean pavements, and the fountain display roundabouts lay dormant and unlit until later that evening.

The city streets were filled with a mix of modern and turn-of-the-century style buildings—breathtaking architecture. Christmas lights hung from lamppost to lamppost across the streets, dressing up the roads and making fantastic photo opportunities during the dark of the evening. The cries of seagulls mixed with traffic sound as they swooped and danced in the perfect blue heavens.

Even though it was November, it felt like a British spring morning. It was nine degrees at seven in the morning, with the promise of high teens later in the day. So, the heat would be warm but not uncomfortable.

Steel had been up for hours; the truth was, he had hardly slept at all. His flight had gotten in around eight o'clock the evening before. After a fantastic meal in a local restaurant, he'd headed off to the casino to try his luck.

The modern casino had been loud, more Las Vagas than a quiet room, with people in tuxedos. Steel had played a couple of hands at the poker table and won around two grand, then lost a couple of hundred on craps. He was there to unwind and blow off some steam. His last case had been tough, and he needed some time alone.

He had left without warning. No goodbyes or news of where he was going; he'd just disappeared two months ago after being sent on sick leave. Steel had used the time to sort out his father's company back in Britain and recuperate from the shrapnel they had taken out of him. The costume he had been wearing was padded on the upper body, so he had taken several shards to the legs and arms. Just more scars and bad memories to add to his collection.

Steel could hear Captain Brant of the 11th Precinct yelling and cursing. But Steel didn't care.

At that moment, he felt nothing apart from the warmth of the sun and a fresh, subtle easterly breeze on his skin. Steel smiled as he walked off, the stiffness caused by the long flight and the lack of sleep from the night before.

Steel was dressed in black, the suit and shirt he had bought at a local store, which still blended in during the day without looking like he'd spent the night in it. He took off his jacket and slung it over his shoulder. Steel decided to take the route near the beach. It was over a half-hour walk, so he thought he'd make the most of it. The sea breeze continued to feel good against his skin, and the sound of the ocean was like soothing music to his ears.

The sidewalks near the seafront were almost clear at that time in the morning, less for joggers, dog walkers, and the occasional person who wanted to watch the sunrise. As he casually walked towards his hotel, Steel could feel the wondering gazes of women on him as they headed to their places of work. He had to admit that he did look good for a guy who had only had two hours of sleep on the plane. Steel put it down to the suit, tanned skin, and the twelve o'clock shadow he had going. He had left his cell phone and unique sunglasses back at the hotel but wore contact lenses to hide his green eyes.

Here he was, just Steel on vacation. He didn't even feel much of a British Lord. Let alone an NYPD Detective. *Lord* Steel. The title made him laugh every time he heard it. But, of course, he wasn't Lord Steel; his father had had that honour. As far as he was concerned, that died with him that fateful day. But Steel was, if anything, an honourable man. A man who believed in everything that people didn't want to get involved in, such as duty, code of honour, and keeping up tradition. For that reason, he kept the title he'd inherited and carried on the family business. So not only did the multi-billion dollar company give him a little extra capital but gave him access to some exciting toys.

Steel had to admit that the title did have some perks, such as the best hotel rooms and not waiting in line in busy restaurants, and of course, it proved a massive hit with the ladies. But as much as it was a blessing, it was a burden. His whole job was to blend in and disappear when required. He was trained to be a ghost, and someone shouting out his name and trying to photograph him could blow that whole thing out of the water. So, he kept to himself and indulged in the press a few photographs when he was back in Britain, dealing with the family business. But all that seemed irrelevant at that moment. Steel was hungry and tired. All he needed was coffee and a good breakfast.

Steel made his way past the harbour that housed expensive yachts and catamarans and headed for a footbridge that connected the main footpath with a sea view mall to his left. The building was a multi-level glass, concrete, and Steel construction, with wooden decking flooring up to the main entrance. Steel glanced at it and moved towards a towering statue of Columbus, which stood on a decorative column of stone and weathered bronze.

Steel was enjoying his first holiday. Sure, he had time off in the Army, but he had always spent that time with his dear wife, Helen. So, now, he was alone except for the people watching him. At first, he had thought it was MI8 keeping tabs on him. But these were different; these were company people. Steel figured CIA.

Steel hadn't done anything about them. Why should he? So far, all they had done was follow him. He kept checking his room for cameras or listening devices but always came up empty. So, were they there for him or someone else? Or was it a mere coincidence?

But Steel didn't like coincidences. He believed in them, but it didn't make them less tiresome.

Following the street, he passed several government buildings. Structures that, despite their unkempt state, still held a grand elegance. He was heading left, following the natural curvature of the sidewalk, past the World Trade Centre to a curved pale stone building near the water's edge: Steel's hotel.

About twenty feet behind him, a man in a blue tracksuit and black hair, pretending to jog, followed Steel all the way.

As he entered the lobby, he felt an invisible pull, as if his bed were summoning him. The lobby's ample open space was full of people checking in and out. Still, three people positioned on a long sofa caught his eye: two bulky men and a tall woman. One of the men wore a grey suit and had a serious look.

At first, Steel thought nothing of it. He was too tired to care. Besides, they would be there for someone else if they were suits from an agency. So, Steel put them down as private security for one of the many rich people staying at the hotel.

They couldn't be there for him because nobody knew he was there. Steel hadn't even known he would be there until he boarded the flight the day before. It was a last-minute decision, one he was enjoying.

Steel waited for the elevator while ensuring he kept the three in his line of sight using various reflective surfaces. They just sat there and looked ready to pounce at the first sign of trouble.

'Nice way to blend in, lads,' Steel said, joking.

The suite was lavish and modern, with a wooden floor stretching throughout the open plan. A small lounge area was doglegged to the right of the sleeping area. Directly in front of the bed was a balcony and a panoramic view from a huge arched window.

For Steel, it was more about the view than the price, something his mother had always taught him and something he still aspired to do. He tossed his jacket on the bed in the hotel suite before collapsing next to it. His eyes felt heavy, the bed soft ... and the next thing was inevitable ... as Steel fell into a deeply troubled sleep.

* * *

Three hours had passed when Steel woke to the sound of housekeeping entering his room. The woman was in her late twenties and quite attractive from what Steel had seen through blurry eyes. She had long raven-coloured hair, straight and unstyled. Her white uniform hugged her athletic figure.

'Oh, sorry, I didn't think anyone was in here,' the maid gasped. 'I'll come back later.'

'It's fine,' Steel said, heaving himself off the bed. 'You go ahead and clean. I am off to take a shower anyway.' He stepped into the large bathroom.

The woman thanked him and watched. Her eyes widened as he took off his shirt, revealing an athletic, muscular frame. But her gaze was fixed on the six-round scars on his back. Three formed an odd V-shape from his shoulders to his lower back. Three more were at the centre of his back in a curious design, almost like the number one. The door closed, and she shuddered to think what he had been through; then she smiled, considering that tight muscular back and wondering what the rest of him would look like naked.

* * *

Steel turned on the water, took off the rest of his clothes, folded them neatly, and placed them on the toilet seat. He looked in the mirror as it started to fog up due to the steam from the scalding hot water, noting how tired he looked, with bloodshot eyes and a day-old beard. Steel gazed into his soulless dark-green eyes, hoping to make the memory of the last case go away. Wishing he would wake up and find it was seven months earlier ... that London hadn't given him that case.

Steel closed his eyes tight and then opened them again slowly, gazing back into those lifeless eyes. From the other side of the door, he could hear the cleaner hoovering and a couple of knocking sounds which he put down to the woman hitting the furniture. He climbed into the shower and stood under the cascading water. Letting it hammer his tight muscular frame.

Chapter 4

After thirty minutes, Steel emerged from the bathroom. The room smelt of cleaning sprays, and a fresh breeze blew through the open window.

He didn't have much planned for the day, possibly a pleasant walk around the sites or a stroll along the beach. After all, he was on vacation. So, why should he have a schedule or plan?

That was until he looked over at his computer and saw the maid had left a brochure for the Montserrat Monastery. Steel picked up the thin folded brochure and opened it. A message was written in thick black ink: **15.00 today at the restaurant with a lower-level view**.

Steel screwed it up and tossed it into the wastebasket as he headed out the door. Before the door had time to lock, Steel returned and retrieved the paper ball and placed it in his pocket.

'I knew this trip was going too bloody well,' Steel cursed, heading back out the door. Walking down the corridor, he saw a maid cleaning a room four down from his.

'*Hola, bon dia*,' Steel said.

The woman turned around and responded with a smile, but it wasn't the woman from earlier. Steel smiled and made his way to the elevator. He didn't know who had sent her but was glad they had. It was nearly one o'clock, and there was a long way to go.

* * *

Because of his lack of time and local knowledge, Steel had to take a taxi to Placa de Espanya station, northwest of his hotel. The driver was initially from Nigeria but had settled here twelve years before. The man was chatty and friendly, pointing out local features and explaining which train to take to the Monastery.

They got to a massive roundabout with an ancient statue in the centre. To the left were two immense red-brick towers which came to a pinnacle, and beyond this, on a hill, was the MNAC, a grand-looking building reminiscent of a castle.

The underground station was bright and clean, with plenty of ticket machines; a woman in a red shirt darted from person to person, helping them get the correct ticket. After buying his round-trip ticket, Steel headed for the platform, towards the Aeri de Montserrat. The journey by rail and then the cable car to the top would take just over an hour, giving Steel time to catch up on the unread messages on his phone. He wasn't surprised that he hadn't any from the precinct. If anything, there would have been one from Brant telling him he was fired, but not even Brant actually had that power.

Steel had been assigned to the 11th Precinct. He wasn't even a cop as. He was something else, something the others didn't know about, nor could they.

After an hour, he looked up at a sign for his station. From there, it was a minute's walk through an underpass to the cable car station. Steel made his way out of the station and towards the platform.

The view before him was breathtaking; the grey mountain range loomed over a small village. A distant main road passed alongside the river that separated them.

The sun was at its highest point, and the heat was bearable thanks to a constant cooling breeze. Steel showed his ticket and climbed aboard the small yellow cable car.

Inside was like being in a greenhouse. The glass from the windows reflected the sun onto travellers. However, the magnificent view made them forget the heat, and cameras and cell phones took picture after picture. Steel just stood and held onto the rail. It was a remarkable sight, but his mind was elsewhere. Who was he going to meet, and what was the mission? The car swayed with the momentum of travel. The sound of metal-on-metal as the gears and winches pulled them along. Despite this, the ride up the mountain was tranquil. The chatter was minimal, less for the inevitable oohing and aahing.

Steel smiled as he thought back to the maid and hoped he would see her again, this time over dinner and drinks. Unfortunately, her poorly fitting uniform and the lobby suites made him suspect she wasn't a real maid. Steel wondered which agency she belonged to. He had sent a photo of her to a friend in Whitehall. He had taken with his specialised sunglasses when he spoke to her. He loved gadgets, but sometimes he missed the times when he relied on his own intellect, cunning, and ingenuity.

If she was CIA or FBI, he would soon know. He'd considered she was simply meant to go in, leave the brochure, and possibly go through his stuff.

Steel looked over as the car began to slow and creak, as brakes and gears worked to bring the vehicle to a halt. The passengers moved out of the small yellow box, stopping at the large opening of the station to take in the view.

Tiled steps led to the exit from the station house and onto a long winding pathway that led downwards to a long winding path; it ended on the main road leading to the Monastery.

Steel took a path that led upwards, around the side of the cable car house. The view on his left provided a fantastic view of the world below. To the front, surrounding the monastery, was a towering mountainside. These were reminiscent of looming mythological gods, giving Steel a strange and uncomfortable feeling.

At the top was the main street. This held another station for the monorail that led to the very top of the mountain. There was a restaurant with a gift shop, but neither was what Steel was after. The card had said *the restaurant with the view*, but this one was back against the mountainside with no real view.

Next to the road was a billboard map that revealed the location of a second restaurant. It was further up, on the mountain's edge, giving the customers a clear view of a vast landscape below.

The Monastery was a set of modern and ancient buildings that created a dramatic, awe-inspiring image. Steel stood and looked out across the vast, green expanse of Catalonia. The landscape was beautiful, but he didn't have time to stop and take it in; he had a rendezvous with someone. Who? He could only guess.

Steel followed the signs for the restaurant as he waded past tourists taking photographs and movies on their cell phones. But Steel was invisible to them, a blur in the corners of their eyes, which suited him just fine.

The restaurant was big enough to accommodate large groups. The place was modern with a tiled marble floor and brown compressed wood furniture on stainless-Steel legs. On first impression, it could have been a self-service restaurant anywhere in the world, but one with a view. Above was an outdoor seating option, but Steel thought this might be a little crowded for the sort of meeting that had been arranged.

He found a table with its back against a wall, facing the only door; he preferred to see what or who was coming while he enjoyed a cappuccino.

Steel watched people as they went here and there, some in large groups and others on holiday. But none stood out as being alone, only him.

'Is this seat taken?' asked a familiar voice.

Steel looked up to see the woman who had pretended to clean his room. He smiled and stood, beckoning her to sit.

'Thank you, kind sir,' she said with a smile.

She looked very different in black cargo trousers and leather-strapped boots, which came to the bottom of her knee. Her top was a thin cotton blouse with a crossover opening and long sleeves, and her black hair was tied in a ponytail.

'I take it the maid's job didn't agree with you,' Steel joked as he took a sip of coffee.

'I don't know; it had some perks,' she said, returning his smile.

'So, who sent you and why?' he asked with a curious smile.

'Straight to the point. He said you didn't mess around, well with words anyway,' she joked. 'Stanton sent me.' The smile and playful gaze became severe. 'There is a problem back home. After your little meltdown in New York a couple of months back, he wanted me to see if you were OK to do the job.'

'And am I in my right mind for the job?' Steel almost hoped she would say no.

'Mr Steel ... John ... if you weren't, you wouldn't be on holiday.'

'You say that like holidays are unusual.'

'For you, yes, very. Apparently, you've never been on one,' the woman said, wearing a look as though she had many questions.

'I went to Malta,' Steel shrugged and took a sip.

'Yes, I read the report. If that is your idea of a vacation, then it's lucky I'm taking you away from here,' she laughed.

Steel looked down at his coffee, then back at the woman. 'Forgive me. Can I get you a coffee? It appears to be all self-service here.' He hoped to change the subject and her mind ... and let him stay there to do nothing but enjoy himself.

She smiled. 'Coffee Americano, please.' She watched as Steel went to get the drinks, all the while wondering if he would use the opportunity to run off. But she could see he was curious because if he wasn't, why was he here?

Steel soon returned and placed her coffee in front of her before retaking his seat. They smiled at each other once more, wondering who would start first.

The woman started to say, 'I'm—'

'Kitty West, Virginia office, transferred from Boston two months ago. You grew up in Brooklyn in a foster home after your birth parents were killed in a car accident. You were only seven months old,' Steel said matter-of-factly, sitting back and rechecking the room for anyone who looked out of place.

'I see you did your homework. Thanks for proving my point,' Kitty smiled, covering up her shock and amazement upon hearing his quick background check. She glanced at her watch, then at him.

'I take it I'm leaving tonight then?' Steel asked.

'In two hours, actually. We've already packed for you, don't worry,' Kitty smiled cockily.

'How do you know you haven't missed anything? I may have something hidden away in a secret compartment?' Steel asked calmly, trying to draw her in.

'Then you can come back and get it when the jobs are completed, and you continue your vacation,' Kitty grinned.

'Oh, something tells me this place is the last place I'd come. A tropical island with no cell reception would be better,' Steel joked but meant every word.

One thing began to bother him as he finished off his coffee. Why had she insisted he meet her here? She could have just as easily met him at the hotel. And why was there another team there to back her up?

Steel had noted the couple to his left at eleven o'clock, a red-haired woman and dark-haired man both in dark suits, she with lots of jewellery. Another group, a team of four pretending to be part of some football team he'd never heard of, to his eight o'clock. At twelve o'clock were three nuns wearing traditional habits. One had forgotten to change her shoes, as he sighted sneakers when she walked.

'Looks like I have no choice,' Steel said with a weary smile.

Kitty smiled and nodded curtly to confirm his assessment of the situation.

'Shall we?' Steel stood and dropped a twenty euro note on the table next to his coffee cup.

'What's your rush? You didn't finish your coffee?' Kitty said smugly.

'Oh, it's fine. I think I've had enough drugs in my system with all this caffeine,' Steel said as he walked to Kitty's chair to pull it out for her.

'Always the gentlemen,' Kitty said with a surprised look.

'Oh, not always.' Steel tipped the chair forwards when she was halfway up, causing her to fall onto the table, spilling the hot drink.

Kitty yelped as the scolding liquid fell onto her trousers and arms. She spun around to call the others but found the other teams had already reacted and rushed over.

Steel was quick on his feet, dodging grasping hands. He vaulted over one table, and an agent went to follow. But as he lunged, Steel kicked the table, hitting the man in the gut and winding him.

Steel spun around and rushed for the door, but his gut told him to expect more agents to be ready for his exit. So, he took the second exit to the rooftop. When he reached the roof, he headed for the end of the building.

Agents ran after him, but Steel had already jumped from the roof and was heading down the street.

The nun with the sneakers was hot on his trail and nearly within reach as they raced down a long street. As she grabbed his jacket, Steel stopped suddenly and sidestepped, causing her to crash into a group of priests.

Steel smiled childishly and ran towards the cable car station.

He noted the time; a car should be ready to leave. All he had to do was be on it. As he made his way to it, he began to second-guess his getaway plan. He knew a team would be waiting at the cable car station, ready to grab him when he got off.

Steel knew this because it was what he would have done, but he also knew he had to get off the mountain and away from Kitty and her colleagues … and the only way might just be that cable car.

Steel ran into the small building, with Kitty's team only a few seconds behind.

As she entered the building, she saw the car had already left, full of people. She smiled as she watched it depart.

'Don't worry, Kitty, the team at the bottom will catch him,' said a tall agent standing next to her.

Kitty looked over at Agent Martin Brena, the guy in charge, a cool-looking customer with brown, styled hair and a charcoal-grey suit. A career agent whose arrogance made his decisions for him. Kitty looked back at the car and nodded.

'I'm sure they will,' she said, smiling as she walked away.

Brena looked down at the car and smiled confidently. 'We got you now, Major Steel; we got you now.'

* * *

The obvious choice would be to make it down the mountain using the train that hugged the mountainside, a safe way of travelling for those with height issues. Steel had gone through the cable car station, then jumped onto the rocks below before heading for the walkway that curved its way to the bottom.

Steel knew the team would be small, eight- to ten men strong, if that. A compact team did not stick out, but it was too small to cover everything.

The cable car and train were the better choices; they were perfect for a quick escape. However, Steel preferred things slow and structured—it was paramount to know where your enemy was, making them think they had you. That was just pure entertainment, and this was no different. Steel had doubled back and climbed to the parking area near a circular overwatch. Steel needed a vehicle to get down from the mountain; to do so by foot would take too long, especially for what he had in mind.

Steel smiled as a man on a Can-Am Spyder RT stopped to drop off something at a store. Moments later, the man came out laughing and whistling and made his way to where he had left his machine. He stopped and looked around as if puzzled. He was confused at the disappearance of his ride and tried to figure out what could have happened. Then he remembered he'd left the motor running while he made his delivery. In a rage, he tossed his helmet and cursed his stupidity … just as two nuns walked past. The man blushed and apologised as the two young, wide-eyed sisters hurried away.

* * *

Below, on the winding road, Steel opened up the machine. His hair was brushed back by the open air. He knew it wouldn't be long before the police stopped him for not having a helmet, or more likely because the man had reported his machine stolen. But Steel only needed the vehicle to get him as far to the bottom as possible … to the next town would be perfect. Either way, Steel had left Stanton's dogs barking, which felt good.

He had no idea why they were after him because he hadn't done any missions since the thing in New York had gone south—or maybe that was why?

Had the Charles King case come back to haunt him? But what had happened hadn't been his fault; it had been the system he had believed in that let them down. However, one thing was for sure. Steel had to speak with Stanton. Find out if Stanton had put these dogs on his tail, and if so, why?

This woman Kitty had tried to convince Steel he was coming in on a mission for Stanton. If that were the case, why had a snatch team been recruited? But the more Steel thought about it, it made sense. Stanton was a great one for giving as little information as possible. He made an agent do their homework. Was the target friend or foe? How much was necessary?

Looking back, Steel had no idea why he ran. After all, they were just taking him back to the States to meet Stanton. But there was something off about the whole thing. And who was the joker in the grey suit? He had tried to blend in but stuck out like an arsehole? He was a company man, probably in charge of the whole damn thing. Thinking about it, Stanton was a bastard, a good man, but a bastard nevertheless.

Steel remembered being given many missions with very little data to go on. 'Go and pick up this man.' Steel wouldn't know if the person was a friend, foe, or random person. Stanton was a trickster for his amusement but a hell of an agent.

Steel smiled to himself.

That was why the team was there.

They knew nothing about Steel apart from what was in the files, which wasn't much. Steel had read it once and had to admit it had been watered down. He thought about the guy in charge of the OP; he didn't understand the parameters or had a hard-on for Steel, and he wanted to prove a point. Either way, he had failed.

He had considered giving himself up, but where would the fun be in that?

No, if they wanted him, he would make them work for it. This wasn't arrogance on Steel's part. It was payback for trashing his holiday.

* * *

Steel followed the road down, ensuring he kept close to groups of bikers or coaches he could hide behind. He was good at blending in. After all, it had been the company that had taught him. Steel found a parking area with a scenic view and stopped, checking the back storage bin, hoping for a spare helmet. Instead, he found a couple of new Harleys in the parking lot, possibly rentals. Their owners had wandered off to see the sights, leaving their helmets strapped to the handlebars.

Steel rechecked the bins for a toolkit and found what he needed. Quickly he quickly removed the plates from the Can-Am, swapped them with one of the motorcycles, and took one of the helmets. Then, pulling on the helmet, he started up the three-wheeled machine. Then, he was gone with a rev of the throttle and a spit of gravel. At least the plates and helmet would buy him some time.

Steel figured returning to the hotel in Barcelona was out of the question. Besides, they would have his luggage by now, and the room would have been wiped clean.

Chapter 5

Agent Martin Brena was more than angry. This man he had been sent to bring in had fled, and no one knew where he was. The ground units had reported Steel hadn't come their way. The train and the cable car had both been cleared.

It was as if the guy had just vanished.

Brena was on a deadline; he had one hour, and then he went home empty-handed. The only thing they did have was Steel's luggage from the hotel. Brena had people looking through the guy's things to try and get an angle on him. Brena knew next to nothing about Steel. Sure, he'd read the file, ex-military, did some work with the agency, and then joined the NYPD. Apart from that, this man's life was nothing but a half-empty file.

Stanton had said to bring him in alive and unharmed by any means necessary but didn't say why and Brena's mistake was that he hadn't asked.

It had been hard to find the guy the first time, and from what Brena could see, Steel wasn't trying to hide. He felt that if Steel didn't want to be found, you wouldn't find him.

Brena scowled. Who the hell was John Steel? And why did Stanton want him?

* * *

Kitty West sat in a taxi heading for the airport. Brena had sent her to secure the plane and take Steel's belongings with her. She had changed at the hotel, dying her hair back to its original raven black, and slipped into a black trouser suit with heeled ankle boots. Kitty preferred the look she'd had at the Monastery, but these were work clothes, nothing more.

She looked through the window, watching the world whiz by as the taxi drove hurriedly to the airport. She caught her reflection in the window; a sad face gazed back at her. Kitty wondered about this guy John Steel. She had seen his file. They all had. But they had no idea what Stanton wanted him for. Sure, the briefing was to tell Steel he was needed on an urgent mission, but she had no idea why. What could Steel do that they couldn't?

Then she thought back to the café. This Steel guy was fast, quicker than anything she had ever seen. Kitty smiled as she thought back to Brena's face after he had learned Steel had escaped. Seeing the veins in his temple throb was delightful. Brena was her boss, but he was an ass … or rather, a kiss-ass.

Brena had sent her away because he blamed her, but at the end of the day, he had dropped the ball, but she had no doubt it would say otherwise in his report. Kitty looked at the approaching airport sign, and her heart sank. She was leaving Barcelona empty-handed, and she hadn't fully seen the city, but then it was work, not a vacation. Well, that was what Brena kept telling her anyway. This was odd because he always found time to slip away and do recon. It had been his idea that she poses as a maid, possibly his way of telling her that was all she was worth. Never mind, she had gotten the job done, more than what he had done.

The taxi pulled up to the tarmac and headed for the Gulfstream jet, the company's first-class ride.

The taxi stopped, and she got out. The driver popped the truck and helped her with the bags. Kitty smiled and tipped him after he placed down the last suitcase. Not only was she transporting Steel's items, but those of the whole team. Kitty looked at all of the bags and sighed. There were at least twenty bags and suitcases, four belonging to Brena.

'Don't worry, Señora, I will take care of the bags for you.'

Kitty smiled and thanked the man wearing grey coveralls and a white baseball cap that covered his face. Kitty climbed onto the jet and took a seat. She could hear bumps and bangs as the luggage was stowed in the compartment at the rear.

With a content smile, she closed her eyes for a second, relaxing in the comfortable leather swivel chair, unaware of the door closing and the engines starting. Kitty began to dream as the aircraft taxied onto the runway. As she slipped into blissful sleep, the Gulfstream headed skywards.

There was a screech of tires outside on the tarmac as company cars skidded to a halt. Brena got out and watched the aircraft disappear into the endless blue sky.

'What the hell just happened?' Brena screamed, tossing his sunglasses to the ground. 'That dumb bitch just left us behind.' He turned when one of his colleagues coughed as if trying to get his attention.

'That's not all she left,' said the woman wearing the nun's outfit earlier.

Brena looked over at the bags and suitcases and screamed again as he kicked the side of the SUV.

'It's OK, Brena,' shouted another man checking out the luggage. 'She only left yours.'

The others turned, hiding giggles, while Brena screamed under his breath and took his phone out of his pocket. He needed to reach the pilot or inform Langley to get another flight. Brena was bloody mad, and he would make her pay for this.

Chapter 6

A quick judder of the plane woke Kitty from her slumber. She looked around with sleepy eyes, half expecting Brena's disapproving look, but found Steel seated across from her with a glass of whiskey. Kitty sat up and looked around at the empty seats.

'Where are the others? Where am I ...?' Kitty grasped the arms of her chair and looked around. She turned back to Steel with a confused look on her face. 'Why are you here?'

'I killed the rest and shoved them out of the door,' Steel said calmly, leaning forward and staring at her through his sunglasses.

Kitty felt a shiver run down her spine. Had he really done that? Had he killed the whole team? Then she saw the side of his mouth arch as he broke into a smile.

'OK, so where are they?' Kitty asked angrily.

'Back at the airport and mad as hell, I suppose,' Steel said, taking a sip.

'What changed your mind?'

'The way you asked so nicely,' Steel said with a shrug and a smile.

'Really?' Kitty said, surprised.

'Nah, I figured if Stanton sent you, he only gave you part of the information. He does that to everyone. That bloke is a complete arse when it comes down to his sick sense of humour." He watched her expression change as she began to calm down.

'Why did you leave the others and only take me?' Kitty asked, suddenly feeling uncomfortable again.

'Because you show promise, the others just follow. You use your head. You were the only one who worked out that I never took the car down. I'm just wondering why you didn't tell Brena?' Steel poured a glass of eighteen-year-old whiskey for Kitty and handed it to her.

Kitty held it to her nose and smelt the mixed odour of wood, herbs, and something she couldn't put her finger on. 'Like you said, he's an ass.'

'I left the others because this Brena seems to be a real dick, and the others ... well, no reason apart from that it seemed like the thing to do at the time.' Steel grinned and raised his glass.

Kitty said nothing; she just shot him an angry look and peered out the window.

'So, what's next?' Kitty asked after several seconds of tense silence. 'When we land, I mean.'

Steel thought for a moment and stared into the dark liquid in the glass. 'We go see Stanton, find out what that fruit bat wants.'

'Fruit-bat?' Kitty asked, puzzled.

Steel shook his head, feeling it wasn't worth trying to explain, and went back to looking out the window.

* * *

The midday sun was high in the sky but a fraction of the warmth of what it had been. Pedestrians moved about like colonies of ants while the built-up traffic moved slowly. The Sentinel had gathered more photographs and data on the next target. Alison Kline would be next, but she wouldn't be the last. The Sentinel had a list of names and their crimes. Each would be observed, documented, researched and eventually taken out. Each would know the same terror the people had felt when faced with a simple device.

The television in the corner of the room was showing the news.

A reporter was talking about a bombing in a shopping mall that had happened months before. The man responsible had been killed instantly. It had been someone the police had suspected in previous bombings. Charles King had been the son of a multi-conglomerate billionaire, Edward King, a man with enough juice to make things disappear. But only one man had stood up and tried to do what was right, which cost him. In other words, the cop was 'on administrative leave' … gone, probably a mall cop.

The Sentinel had created a mission board. It was filled with maps, timings, and locations. The rest of the intel would come later. The Sentinel had time.

The reporter spoke about the bombing, showing footage she had dug up from last week's broadcasts. People sat crying in the streets, covered in blood and dust. Emergency services lined the streets, helicopters from TV stations landing to offer their services to help carry the wounded—for a price, of course. Others, because it was the right thing to do.

Slowly The Sentinel eased into the chair. Unblinking eyes stared at the screen as footage showed bodies being carried out. There was no fire. The blast had been massive and destructive, with plenty of shrapnel.

The bomber hadn't intended to be in there with the device. Instead, the idea was to be somewhere away from the blast but within the line of sight, watching it all happen.

But the cop had intervened. He was trying to disarm the situation. But something had gone wrong; the cop had stopped the bomber, but the device went off anyway, according to the witnesses who made it out at the last moment. Thirty had died, thirty people, and the cop didn't have time to save. But The Sentinel knew it wasn't a timer that had run out; the kill switch in Charles King's hand set it off.

The Sentinel found it interesting there was no television footage of the cop, almost as if they wanted him to completely disappear. But The Sentinel knew who the cop was and what he could do.

So, The Sentinel picked up a postcard from the desk and started to write. Finally, The Sentinel wrote the name and address: Detective John Steel, 11th Precinct Police Department, New York City.

Chapter 7

The Gulfstream landed at Ronald Reagan National Airport. The ride had been smooth but somewhat quiet. Kitty had spent most of the flight gazing out of the window, looking more like a kid who had just been grounded.

The plane taxied into a private hangar, where two GMC Yukon SUVs were waiting. The aircraft powered down, and the door hinged downwards, creating steps.

Steel let Kitty go first, giving the illusion the rest of the team wasn't too far behind. However, the welcoming party looked confused as Steel stepped onto the concrete.

'Who the hell is this?' asked a tall, broad-shouldered agent. 'And where are the others?'

'Nice to see you too, Stan,' Kitty said flatly.

Stan Norris was a veteran agent. Six-two with a military-style haircut. The brown was slowly greying at the sides. His features were rugged, a look he had gotten from his time in the Marines, that long stare from seeing too much action.

'So, what's the story?' Stan asked, confused at the situation.

Kitty looked over at Steel, who stood stone-faced and unwelcoming. 'Never mind, it's a long story. This is John Steel. Section Chief Stanton sent us to get him.' Kitty pointed to the moody statue dressed in black.

'This is *him*?' asked the agent, with a fascinated look on his face.

'Yes, we can do autographs later. But, in the meantime, can we go? I've got some questions for Stanton,' Steel said and strolled to the first Yukon and climbed into the back seat.

An electronic whir caused Kitty to look over at the plane as the cargo hold began to open.

'Well, at least you didn't forget their luggage,' laughed one of the other agents in the second vehicle.

Kitty scowled at Steel, who just sat calmly and looked out of the window.

* * *

The drive to Langley was long, but this gave Steel time to wonder what Stanton wanted.

The two men in the front of the car were no help; they were simply there to pick up the team from the airport. Steel had tried to make conversation, but it seemed they were told not to talk to him, or perhaps they preferred not to engage him.

Steel had found his luggage when he had loaded the team's bags onto the plane, disguised as the baggage handler. Now, he was wearing his unique sunglasses, which had built-in HUDs in one of the lenses and his smartwatch. Steel pressed an icon on his cell phone and waited as the watch, cell phone, and glasses were synced and ready to go.

He checked for missed calls and messages on his cell phone. There weren't any. Steel felt a little disappointed. Even his partner at the NYPD, Samantha McCall, hadn't tried to call. But maybe that was for the best. After all, they had let him down, not the other way around.

Steel slipped the phone back into his pocket and closed his eyes. There was still over an hour to go. So, he decided to sleep. That was if the nightmares would let him.

Kitty sat in the other car with the tall agent, who questioned her about what had happened. Possibly more out of interest than a debriefing.

'He stole the plane didn't he?' the agent asked with wide, excited eyes.

'Kind of. I must have fallen asleep. When I woke up, he was there, and the others were– well, you get the idea, Frank,' Kitty said, her voice full of shame.

'Don't feel bad, Kitty. I wouldn't have expected less from reading his file. One thing does surprise me, though,' Agent Frank Dorson said.

'What's that?'

'Why did he wait until you were on board? By the sounds of things, he could have taken off ages ago, but he waited for you. Why?' Dorson asked, giving Kitty the once-over.

Sure, Kitty was pretty, but not stunning. She was shorter than the others, around five eight if that. But there was something about her. Kitty was tenacious when she had to be. Also, Kitty had a problem with authority, meaning she was a perfect match for Steel.

Kitty had lost her parents in a major accident: wrong place, wrong time. Yet, despite all this, she was a good agent with a bright future. If she could get from under Brena's grasp, that was. That guy was a career killer at best. Brena would use new agents to make himself look good and toss them under the bus if they made him look bad. If he messed up, great; he'd just say it was their fault.

But Steel had seen that somehow, which meant he'd known the team had been there at the restaurant. So Steel had just waited for them to make their move.

Dorson smiled to himself as his theory unwound in his head. 'I think I know why Steel picked you,' he said with an enlightened look on his face.

'What do you mean 'picked' me? Steel had no idea we were there ... did he?' Kitty asked, looking dazed. Had he known all along? She shook her head, unable to accept that Steel could have known that there was a team watching him all that time.

'Did you find anything in his room?' Dorson asked.

'Nothing ... well, nothing of interest. There were no messages on his cell or laptop. Looks like he really was on vacation,' Kitty said. 'I heard stories about him, but you know the gossip, how things get blown out of proportion.'

'Don't worry. This guy is beyond anything you can imagine. That's why Stanton wants him on this one,' Dorson stated.

'On what? We haven't been briefed on anything new.' A sudden shiver ran down her spine like Spidey-Sense. Something was wrong, especially if they were bringing this guy back. They knew nothing about this Mr John Steel; his file was as mysterious as he was.

'Don't tell me. Above my pay grade, I take it?' Kitty turned to Dorson, who just shrugged.

'Both our pay grades, actually. I'm as much in the dark as you are on this one, but if they bring him in, it's bad,' Dorson admitted.

Kitty shot him a curious look and leaned forwards. 'Who is he? Why doesn't he exist?'

'His file is thin. I mean *paper-thin*. Probably because the work he did never happened. If you get what I mean,' Dorson explained. 'This guy worked black OPs back in the day. I had to pull some favours to get that much. Steel was in the British SAS and then the US Navy SEALs. After that, he falls off the map until he joins the agency as an asset. After that, it went cold until a few years ago when he joined the NYPD.'

He paused, then frowned. 'Believe me when I say this guy is badass. Apparently, he was shot six times or something. Nobody knows where or when, or even how the bastard survived.'

'His scars, right? I couldn't believe them when I saw … never mind,' Kitty said, stopping herself before she said more.

Dorson smiled and nodded. 'Yeah, the scars. One old Japanese guy said they were the mark of the Phoenix, rebirth or some bull like that. Steel is as badass as they come when he's in the zone; don't be near him. A buddy of mine in NYPD SWAT did a job with him, some bust on a ship or something. Anyway, this guy took on a whole Army of bad guys and sunk the friggin' ship.'

Kitty noticed how excited Dorson was, like a movie-star crush. But Kitty couldn't see it. This guy Steel couldn't be that good; no one could be unless they were in a book or movie.

She put the stories down to just what they were: stories. Steel had probably done some fantastic things, which had been blown out of proportion; it happens. Chinese whispers. Information to boost an ego or relate dangerous things—especially to people who counted on them being accurate when it counted.

The men regarded the sleeping Steel in the other SUV. Watching every hand movement and foot kick. Stanton had warned them about Steel's nightmares; no one knew what they were about, only that he woke up disorientated and angry. So, each of the men sat sweating and armed with a taser, hoping it would be enough if he snapped.

Steel was curled up on the seat, snoring happily. But he wasn't sleeping; he was reading the data on the small drop screen in his glasses. The information he had received was a copy of a case the CIA had just gotten.

A serial killer was targeting random people; there had been two so far. The latest one had been a lawyer in a prestigious law firm, a woman called Alison Kline.

Chapter 8

A storm brought in a new day. Black clouds loomed as torrential rains washed over the city. Forks of purple lightning streaked across the sky, and booms of thunder shook windows and set off car alarms. The lengthy warm weather had changed suddenly, bringing weather of Biblical proportions.

Water filled the streets, and storm drains choked on the water overflow. Traffic was at a minimum. It was a Sunday, so most people stayed home. Most people, but not Alison Kline. Alison had a case coming up, and she needed to be prepared for it.

She had left the house after the power to her house had gone down. A tree had fallen and taken out the power lines to that street. An accident, an act of God, most called it. But most hadn't seen the man with the detonation cord in the early morning. It was a string-like explosive used by a specialist for doing precise work–such as cutting trees or poles in half.

The rolling thunder and massive booms covered the explosion. Some kid had caught it on his cell phone and posted it on the internet. Over a thousand clicks of approval made him happy, unaware he had just shared evidence.

Alison, in her frustration, decided to get a cab to city hall to finish off her work. It was a long way to go from Upper East Side, but necessary. The taxi took twenty minutes to arrive, which topped her bad mood, but as she stepped into the bombardment of heavy raindrops, she felt she'd better not complain. Alison knew all too well one wrong word and he would refuse to take her. She bit her tongue and hoped they would get there in one piece.

The cabby drove slowly, but Alison was impressed he could see at all. From where she sat, all she could see was water. Alison could have believed they were on a boat on rough seas if she didn't know better. They headed south on Park Avenue and headed for Union Square. From there, they would take Broadway. Typically, it would be an hour's ride, but today, she would be lucky if it took only two.

Alison looked at the man's ID, pinned to the dash next to a Lego minion figure. The cabby's name was unpronounceable, for her anyway. She guessed he was from the Balkans or someplace like that, but he had a kind face from what she had seen in the photograph. Alison tried speaking to him through the gap in the safety window, but he gave no response. The man wore a thick jacket and a grey hood; leather gloves covered his hands.

Suddenly, Alison got a bad feeling. She had seen this movie before. She tried the door, but the deadbolt stopped her from leaving. She began to panic and banged at the window, but the streets were empty, and the car's window was streamed up. Her fear grew as the driver began to speed up, despite the lack of visibility. Her fists slammed against the glass so hard her hands hurt.

The more she screamed, the faster he went. Alison pulled out her cell phone and began to dial the police, but she had no signal. She felt herself cower into the fake leather seat and await what was to come. Closing her eyes, she began to pray, something she hadn't done since she was a kid. That was when the cab stopped.

Alison listened as the taxi driver got out and walked around to her door, her eyes clenched shut, fearful of seeing her end coming near. Then her door opened, and she heard a voice yelling at her in a tongue she didn't understand. Alison felt a pull on her arm, and she resisted. The driver pulled harder, and she resisted further. Then another voice spoke a woman's voice. Alison looked up and saw they were outside Cornell Medical Centre. The cab driver was speaking to a nurse.

Confused and shaken, Alison got out of the car and looked around. 'Why am I here? I asked for city hall?'

The nurse spoke with the driver in broken Croatian.

'He said that this was where he was told to take you. He was told that you were sick, and when you started to cry out, he was worried about you. So, he rushed here as soon as fast he could,' explained the nurse.

The taxi driver nodded and gave a thumbs-up as if in approval of his actions.

Alison went to speak, but she was lost for words and began to laugh instead at the whole incident.

'Why would I want to go to the hospital? I'm not sick. There's nothing wrong with me,' Still laughing, Alison headed for a concrete wastebasket holder to have a cigarette.

* * *

As Alison neared the wastebasket, there was a massive flash and a roar of an explosion. The container exploded, sending dagger-like shards of concrete into Alison's body.

As she was launched across the ground, the nurse ran over but stopped abruptly upon seeing Alison's angry wounds. Especially the long spear-like shards that had punctured Alison's eyes.

Other hospital staff ran out carrying trauma packs, and two others pushed a gurney. Two doctors looked down at the fresh blood flowing from the deep wounds and being washed away by the pouring rain ... along with any evidence.

Screams from passers-by dulled the sound of the rumbling thunder.

* * *

A figure stood on East 68th Street, next to the sign for the Rockefeller University. Clad all in black, with a long black coat and a black hood. The stranger did nothing; they just watched the scene unfold. The assassin had waited for such a night; sure, there had been plenty of other contingency ideas, but this one felt right.

A bus pulled past, followed by flashes of blue from the police cars behind it. When the bus drove away, the figure had gone.

Chapter 9

The Yukon SUVs stopped, and the agents got out all at once. Steel joined them and stretched off as if he had been sleeping, taking time to bask in the warmth of the sun before following Dorson and Kitty into the CIA building at Langley.

Steel felt eyes on the other end of the many surveillance cameras watching him, like beady hawk eyes assessing prey. Steel smiled and waved to let the person know they were there.

As they passed through a metal detector, an agent stopped Steel and placed a small grey plastic basket on a counter next to him. 'All metal and electronic devices must be put into here, sir,' said the agent.

Steel smiled at the medium-built man and placed his wallet, phone, watch and everything, less for his glasses, into the basket.

'Your sunglasses as well, please, sir,' insisted the agent.

Steel stared at the man. 'Oh ... I think it's best if I keep them on.'

'Glasses in the basket *now*, please, sir!' The agent attempted to assert authority.

Dorson stopped. Curious about what would happen next, Kitty stopped and looked at Dorson.

'What are you doing?' she asked. 'Leave him. Steel will be okay or arrested, or maybe we'll get lucky, and they'll shoot him.' She laughed.

'I just want to see what happens next, see if the rumours are true,' Dorson said eagerly.

Kitty looked at him, confused.

As they watched, Steel took off his glasses, his face down as though he was looking at the tray. Slowly, Steel brought up his head, so their eyes were level, but his eyes were closed. Then, slowly, Steel opened his eyes and gazed at the agent.

Frightened, the security agent stared into the cold, soulless green eyes. He wanted to look away but couldn't.

Steel smiled and closed his eyes again. He was feeling a little childish pleasure at the man's discomfort.

The agent backed off and insisted he put his glasses back on, but Steel had already done so.

'Thanks very much.' Steel's words rang with satisfaction.

Dorson grinned as if he'd just won a bet. His calculated eyes fixed on Steel as he walked through the metal detector and began putting items back into his pockets.

Steel looked over at Dorson, feeling the man's gaze on him. As if Dorson were studying him. Watching to see what Steel did next, like a scientist observing a rat in a maze. He ignored Dorson and walked on. It had been a while since he had been in the building, but it felt like yesterday. Despite a few minor changes and upgrades, it was the same as he'd remembered.

Kitty caught up with Steel and walked next to him. She said nothing at first. Steel had the idea she just wanted to get away from Dorson, which was understandable. The man creeped out even Steel, which was saying something.

Dorson walked past them both as if he were showing them the way. They took the elevator to the third floor, then followed the corridors to the west wing and Stanton's office. Steel smiled as they headed towards a large wooden door with a brass plaque. Nothing had changed: the same office, the same door, the same secretary.

'Hello Brenda, good to see you again.' Steel leaned down to give the woman a peck on the cheek. Brenda Woods had been Stanton's secretary back in the day; she had been a sexy thirty-something then and was now an elegant forty-something. Luckily, she abandoned the skimpy clothes and revealing tops, swapping them for more attractive skirt suits. But, of course, she was still a beauty, and the years had been kind, which was more than could be said for Stanton.

Steel remembered Stanton as a bear of a man, a brown flat-top with razored sides, broad shoulders, square jaw, and a quarterback body. Now, his double chins had double chins and a gut held in by a buttoned jacket. The flat top remained, but now it was grey and didn't suit him. Steel could see success had bitten him in the rear. 'If it's not broken, why change it,' Stanton used to say when an agent was too good at his job. It was a polite way of saying, 'You're good at what you do, and we can't be bothered to train someone to take your place.'

Stanton and Steel exchanged nods. Each man seemed to hold a distance they felt comfortable with as if this were enough for them instead of hugs and handshakes.

It was an odd display to the others, but they knew Stanton wasn't the hugging type and Steel, well, they figured he was the same.

'Glad you could make my boy,' Stanton said in a gritty southern accent.

'Oh, just seeing you made it worthwhile,' Steel said sarcastically.

Next to Stanton stood another man, director Frank Headly. The man was at least six-three, with broad shoulders and a crewcut greying on the sides.

'Steel, you remember the director?' Stanton motioned. He waited for the two men to shake hands and exchange pleasantries.

'Last time we saw each other, you were section chief, sir; congratulations,' Steel said. He had known Headly for a time and had a lot of respect for the man.

'Thanks; well, I'm glad they convinced you to come along; we're in a real jam with this, and it couldn't come at the worst time.' Headly pointed to a flat screen in the corner.

'How do you mean?' Steel asked, and a look of sudden concern crossed his face.

'The Vice President is talking about running for President; the guy is an idiot and a pain in the ass for us, *all* of us,' Headly explained.

'Shall we?' Stanton asked before making his way down the corridor.

Steel and Headly shook hands once more and said their farewells; then Steel lagged behind.

The group followed Stanton down another corridor and a row of glass-walled offices. Each had spartan amounts of furnishings, a desk computer, filing cabinets, and an office chair. But all were empty and had been for some time from what Steel could tell.

'Budget cuts, can you believe it? They want us to catch bad guys but won't pay the agents to do it. Too busy spending the cash on promoting themselves in elections or pointless crap nobody wants,' Stanton complained as he pointed to the row of empty offices.

Steel followed, still not sure why he was there—apart from the fact he was cheap labour as far as Stanton was concerned. They stopped in front of a large conference room; the doors were made of frosted glass and aluminium fittings.

'Steel, my boy, we have a problem. Actually, *you* have the problem,' Stanton said and smiled as he opened the door.

The room was large, around twenty-by-twenty, with white walls and a single window which probably didn't open. A long conference table with six chairs was in the centre of the room. Four of the seats were occupied by agents Steel didn't recognise. Judging by the half-empty water bottles in front of them, they'd been waiting a while for him.

'These are some of the other agents who will be on the case. Agents Karl Simms, Trish Edwards, Mark Dutton and Alex Brown,' Stanton said, indicating to each person as he introduced them.

Steel nodded a greeting to the group, then turned his attention to six murder boards that had been set up. Each had a map and photographs pinned to the board.

'Very impressive, so who's the lead agent?' Steel asked. Hoping desperately it was someone good and not Brena.

'You are,' Stanton replied bluntly as he took a seat at the conference table.

'I don't understand. What do you need me for?' Steel asked. Looking over each of the agents individually. 'Whoever put this room together seems to have things under control.'

'There have been two murders so far. The last one was last week. Before each killing, we were sent a postcard. That was the latest one we got,' Stanton said, pointing to the second board.

Steel walked over to an enormous whiteboard held on a wheeled frame. Steel took note of the collage of notes and photographs. Amongst them was a postcard in a small evidence bag. The picture was of the New York Superior Court.

Steel took the postcard from the board and turned it over. On the back was writing, but someone had used a computer to type the script. *The small in German must pay a debt. When stormy weather comes, the sick will seek poison air and splinters of made stone will find them.*

'Thoughts?' Stanton asked. A smile crossed his face as he could see Steel in that place in his mind.

Kitty and Dorson watched, and Steel began to look at the rest of the board. The map, the pictures. The puzzle started to unfold in his mind.

Steel knew this was a test. Stanton was testing him to see if he could work out a murder that had already taken place. But he didn't care; it was exhilarating. He didn't want to play a game but felt compelled to participate.

In truth, Steel wanted to be back on the beach in Barcelona; he wanted to wake up late and go to bed even later. He didn't want to have another case that ended like that one.

'The killer is playful, intelligent, patient,' Steel stated.

'Patient?' Dorson asked, puzzled.

'The killer says when it's going to happen, a stormy day, which means a plan has been in play for a long time. They just required the right element, a storm perhaps,' Steel answered, his focus never leaving the board.

'The name of the victim?' Stanton leaned back in the chair and waited for the mind step to kick in.

'It speaks of a small German, so we are looking for a tourist, right?' Dorson spoke up as if he'd solved the whole thing.

Steel shook his head, his hands moving across the board as if he were looking for something specific. 'No, it said "a small in German" and not "a small German",' Steel said, pondering the board. Suddenly, he stopped and eyed the picture on the postcard. The picture of the courthouse. 'We are looking for a lawyer, a good lawyer.'

'A German lawyer?' Dorson asked, surprised.

Steel turned to Dorson with raised eyebrows as if surprised by the stupidity of the answer.

'How do you know it's a lawyer?' Stanton asked.

'The picture of the courthouse, and not just any courthouse, it's Superior Court,' Kitty said, taking the postcard from Steel.

Steel smiled. At last, he got a playmate.

'We are looking for someone called Klein or Kline,' Steel added.

Dorson went to ask a question, but Steel stopped him with a shake of his head. 'Klein is small in German, so it—'

'Would be Klien or Kline, right?' Stanton said with a smile.

Dorson shot Steel a confused look as if what Steel had said made no sense. Yes, the name and the postcard made sense, but the *profile* of the killer? Dorson didn't buy it.

'Our killer doesn't so much stalk his victims as he observes them. So, it wouldn't surprise me if there was a dossier on the victims,' Steel stated solemnly. 'Favourite restaurants, how they get to where they are going, be it taxi, car or subway.'

He turned back to the board; the map was held by six-round magnets. A red arrow showed the location of Alison's home; a blue one was her place of work. There was another marker, a white one, next to a hospital.

Steel turned to Stanton and looked at the man as he sat in the chair. 'When was she killed?' Steel asked.

'Last weekend. We only got the case because of the—'

'Bomb. They blew up something concrete, something that would splinter,' Steel finished for him, looking at the words on the postcard again.

Dorson's mouth fell open as he watched Steel pull everything together.

'It was a wastebasket container; a cab had taken her to the hospital after Dispatch gave the wrong address to go to. She went for a smoke, then boom,' Stanton said, making grand arm gestures.

'Small device, shape charge, I take it?' Steel returned his gaze to the board.

Stanton nodded but said nothing. He didn't want to disturb Steel's train of thought.

Steel stood transfixed by the clues on the board. But the more he looked, the more he felt something was missing, almost as if Stanton had left something out on purpose. Steel's eyes followed the lines of every street, noted every notation on the board, the black line of the timeline, and space for a time or date to be filled in. It was almost as if the board had been set up purposely with as little information as possible. As if the murder hadn't taken place yet. But it had. That meant Stanton was holding back.

'Are you testing me, Stanton?' Steel asked.

'Perhaps,' Stanton answered calmly.

'So, where's the real murder board?'

Stanton laughed out loud and clapped his hands. 'Oh, my boy, you never disappoint.' He heaved himself out of his chair and walked over to the board, and turned it around to reveal the completed murder board. With crime scene photos, reports, and diagrams, the timeline at the bottom had been filed out, ending at one o'clock in the afternoon, the time of death.

Steel looked at the new evidence with great care, like a curator took in the beauty of an old piece of art.

Dorson remained seated and looked around the room like a kid at a birthday party he didn't want to be attending. He had read up on Steel. Even managed to get the redacted copies of his file. The man was a legend to him, but this man before him was lost and broken. The man before him was nothing more than a profiler, not the John Steel he had heard about.

Steel turned to face Dorson, busy looking into nothing in the corner.

'You seem disappointed at something,' Steel said calmly, already knowing the answer.

'You … you're ….'

'Not the man you expected me to be,' Steel smiled and looked back at the murder board. 'That's the problem with stories; they get blown out of proportion, make you into something you are not … judge me by my actions, not what you have heard.'

Dorson thought for a moment and stood up and walked towards the board. 'So, what have you found?' he asked, finally taking notice.

Steel pointed out the wastebin; the front was missing, but only partially, and a large round hole sat in the centre of the concrete mass. However, the rest of the container was intact.

'This was the work of a professional, possibly police or military, an engineer or bomb squad,' Steel said.

'Why serving personnel? Why not retired or injured?' asked a voice behind them. Everyone turned to see Brena walking in. His mood was surprisingly sombre.

'I see you made it back OK,' Steel said sarcastically.

'No thanks to you,' Brena said, giving both Steel and Kitty an unpleasant look.

'Don't blame the girl; she was unconscious all the way, a little something in the water to help her through a difficult flight,' Steel said, covering for Kitty. Steel felt it was the least he could do, considering it was his fault, after all. And he felt he needed to take her out of Brena's sights for a while.

Steel figured Brena was a vindictive man, someone who would throw you under the bus if it meant making his life more comfortable or better. Steel had seen his sort before, driven with no regard for others.

As Brena approached the board, Steel offered a handshake.

Brena didn't even look at the offer; he just strolled past and looked at the board.

Steel smiled and shrugged before walking to the long table, grabbing a water bottle from the centre, cracking it open, and drinking.

Kitty raised an eyebrow at the macho display, which didn't seem to faze Steel one bit. If anything, Steel found it amusing. But Stanton didn't, his face went red at the display, but he held in his anger.

'So, Agent Brena, your thoughts?' Steel asked, watching the man make a display by rubbing his hands and rolling his neck.

'I think our killer is ex-forces, someone who feels the system has let them down somehow, a person who is trying to put right a wrong. Maybe the guy got blown up in Afghanistan and is looking for compensation. But, unfortunately, our lawyer got it tossed out,' Brena said confidently.

Steel nodded as if agreeing with Brena, who smiled when Steel smiled to confirm his assessment.

'Good, so you agree, Mr Steel?' Brena asked.

'Oh, only what the others are thinking, Brenda,' Steel said, standing up and heading for the door.

'It's *Brena*, wise-ass limey, and where the hell do you think you are going?' Brena shouted as if he were in charge.

'Well, *Brenda*, I'm off to find a decent hotel. Settle down for the morning. Have some breakfast.' Steel turned to Stanton and smiled. 'Avery, any chance you can send over the files of the two murders to my hotel? I'll let you know where as soon as I find a place. Thanks.' Steel waited for Stanton to respond.

He nodded. 'Agent West, copy all the files and take them to whatever address Mr Steel gives to us,' Stanton said.

'Yes, sir,' Kitty said.

Stanton left the room, leaving Brena, Dorson, Kitty, and the rest of Brena's team.

'So, what's the plan?' asked Agent Karl Simms.

'We don't need this Steel guy; we can solve this ourselves,' Brena said confidently.

Dorson shook his head in disagreement. Sure, Steel had pissed him off before, but something told him once Steel was out there, he would see what all the stories had been about.

'You disagree, Dorson, so what's your plan? Join up with your hero and sit around?' Brena laughed.

'I hear he didn't just give you the slip off a mountain, but he also stole your ride home. So, yeah, I think teaming up with Steel is the best bet. At least he does his research and doesn't just rush into a situation,' Dorson scoffed.

Brena scowled, unable to reply.

Kitty headed for the door; she'd had enough of this testosterone fight.

'Where are you going?' Brena asked harshly.

'Off to get copies of the files, like the chief asked,' Kitty replied.

Brena's eyes squinted with distrust. 'Make sure I get a copy also,' he ordered and waved his hand like a headmaster dismissing a pupil.

Kitty walked away. As she turned the corner, she stopped and hugged it, listening to Brena as he briefed the team.

Chapter 10

Agent Karl Simms was chosen by Brena to watch Steel. Simms didn't mind, but he got the feeling Brena was just trying to keep him out of the way. Simms was the first black guy from his street in Detroit to join the CIA. His dad wanted him to be a basketball player, but his knee injury at college changed that. Nevertheless, Simms was a bright guy with a real future. He'd studied law at Yale, then worked in the Philidelphia office, which was where the Bureau had poached him, or more accurately, Stanton had.

Karl Simms was six-one with a slender build. Even though he didn't look like much, he could chase down a cheetah. He knew if Brena had taken him along to the meeting instead of having him watch the cable car station, they would have caught Steel before he'd had a chance to bolt. But that was Brena all over.

Simms didn't know much about Steel, only what Brena had on file. Still, as Dorson had pointed out, Brena didn't research unless necessary. Even then, he'd get someone else to do it, someone like Kitty.

Simms had followed Steel to McLean, a small town of around fifty thousand, most of which were politicians, diplomats, and government officials. It had bars, restaurants, coffee shops, supermarkets, and everything a regular town had.

Karl Simms watched as Steel's taxi pulled up outside a hotel. Quickly, Simms pulled the Dodge Challenger into the parking lot and waited. He recognised the place alright. It was about the only place in town to get a room. They mostly did suites, but they were comfortable enough.

Simms put the Challenger into park and took his to-go cup out of the cupholder. He blew on the small opening, then sipped fresh coffee.

Kitty said she would bring him something to eat when she dropped the files to Steel. She was one of the good ones, maybe too green and shy for the moment, but she was eager. Simms looked at his watch. It was a German military brand with luminous dials and a picture of an eagle just below the hands. It was now ten in the morning, and his stomach told him so.

Karl Simms figured Steel had phoned Stanton with the location, and Kitty was on the way. The trip would take around an hour, plus time to get something for him at the cantina or a fast-food joint. Two hours at the most. Simms' stomach growled again. He feared that it would be too late.

Chapter 11

Steel was checked in by a small woman in her late twenties. She had black hair and huge blue eyes. She wore a black skirt and a white blouse that barely held her oversized chest. The woman, or Irene as the name shield on her shirt stated, was charming and helpful.

'Sorry, all the rooms are booked apart from the main suite,' Irene informed Steel.

'That's fine,' Steel assured her.

Irene filled out the booking on the computer and then looked for the key card. 'You're lucky; with this conference happening, all the rooms have just about gone.' She smiled and passed the key card to Steel.

Steel thanked her and headed for the elevator, leaving Irene to lean on the counter and watch him walk away. Her eyes were captivated by what they saw, and her thoughts roamed elsewhere.

Steel unlocked the door to the suite and entered. It was spacious with a sitting area, kitchenette, and a bedroom with an en-suite bathroom. The whole place was a tasteful mix of black and white. The fully stocked kitchenette had all the necessary appliances: a coffee machine, microwave, double refrigerator, and freezer. It was a tiny home away from home, and he hoped the coffee was decent for what it was costing.

Steel explored the rooms, making sure the suite was to his liking, but then he would have been comfortable with a wooden cabin in the middle of nowhere. He tossed his suitcase on the bed and hoped the team had gotten everything from the room when they packed for him. But then, he never took that much with him when he left for his little getaway.

Steel went to a small writing desk. In the corner was a folder with information on the hotel and the surrounding area. But all he needed was a good dinner and a proper breakfast. He had noticed a Chinese restaurant just over the road, as well as a steak house and a coffee shop. The options were there. The thought of a good steak and a bottle of Châteauneuf-du- Pape with the evening meal made him feel all the more hungry.

He opened the suitcase and looked through the pile of clothes, and closed the lid angrily. His expensive clothes had been shoved into the case as if they were a laundry hamper. He picked up the phone and dialled 1 for reception.

Irene answered in a chirpy voice, possibly because she'd noticed the room number that came up on display. Steel asked about dry cleaning and good restaurants. She explained about their one-day laundry system and gave a list of decent places to eat, and also offered to take him to one of them if he wasn't busy that evening.

Steel thanked her and asked for a rain check, knowing full well he would never take her up on it. Probably. Still angry about his clothes, Steel decided to shower and go to the coffee shop for a snack. Kitty wouldn't be there for ages, giving him time to freshen up.

* * *

Kitty was outside Simms car in forty minutes. The weather was bright and sunny, with cloudless blue skies. A perfect day for driving. Of course, getting as far away from Brena as possible. And as quickly as possible, it had nothing to do with it.

She had brought Simms a double-cheeseburger menu and a diet Coke. His eyes had lit up like a kid at Christmas when he saw it, which made it all the more worthwhile.

'Is he still in there?' Kitty asked, looking at the hotel.

Simms nodded as he took another bite of the burger.

'Enjoy your breakfast Karl,' Kitty said, patting him on the shoulder.

Simms just nodded the best he could with a mouth full of food and ketchup dripping from his mouth and along his chin.

Kitty walked into the lobby and headed for the elevator. Irene gave her a quick glance and thought nothing more of it, guessing Kitty was a guest. Steel had already given the room number in case of emergencies, so Kitty knew where he would be. The room was on the top floor with the other grand suites.

Kitty knocked and waited. She tried again but to no avail. Luckily, a woman from housekeeping walked past, and Kitty hatched a plan. 'I'm sorry, I appear to have locked myself out. I went to get something from the desk, and I forgot my key, but my husband is in the shower,' Kitty explained. Putting on the best performance of her life.

The maid opened the door, heard the shower running in the background, and let Kitty in. Kitty thanked the woman and gave her a ten-dollar note for her trouble. She snuck in and headed for the desk where she would leave the files. A simple in and out. Steel wouldn't even know she had been there.

Suddenly she froze as she heard someone cough behind her. Kitty turned slowly to find Steel standing with just a towel wrapped tightly around him. She blushed as she found herself in a familiar position.

'You know, I'm beginning to think you like seeing me in a towel,' Steel joked, pulling on a bathrobe he grabbed from the wardrobe next to him.

'I-I brought you the files. Sorry, didn't want to disturb your shower. In fact, when you didn't answer, I thought you were sleeping,' Kitty stumbled on her words, unable to look him in the eye—or rather, the sunglasses he'd put on earlier.

'Oh, so you wanted to catch me in bed this time,' Steel joked, causing her to blush even more.

'I have to go. Lots to do back in the office,' Kitty started to back towards the door.

'No problem. Can I get the files first, though?'

Kitty looked at him, puzzled for a second, before realising she still held the files. Quickly, she placed them on the coffee table in front of the couch and rushed off.

'Would you care to join me for lunch?' Steel called behind, tightening the belt on his bathrobe.

'I don't know … I should get back,' Kitty said, stopping at the door and trying to avoid looking at him.

'What? To Brenda? He probably doesn't even know you're not there. Come on, have lunch … you can let Simms know he's invited as well,' Steel said, heading into the bedroom and closing the door behind him.

Kitty looked at the door in wonderment. How the hell did he know Simms was here?

She went downstairs to give Simms the bad news; he was blown. Somehow, Steel had made him. But it didn't matter now.

Steel came down and handed Irene a bag with all his suits and other clothes that needed dry cleaning. As he left the hotel, the warmth of the day surprised him. Steel stood for a moment and enjoyed the sunshine and then headed towards Simms's car. He had already gotten out of the car and leaned against it with Kitty standing next to him.

'So, what's up, doc?' Simms joked.

'First breakfast, then we talk,' Steel said with a grin.

Kitty gazed at Simms, looking at her for the same response. They both shrugged and followed as Steel headed for the deli on the other side of the street.

The deli was a five-minute walk away from the hotel. A quaint-looking place with red and white striped overhangs and umbrellas for outdoor seating. Steel preferred to walk, knowing how much one missed such things when one drove—taking note of where the nearest store or decent-looking restaurant was. Kit and Simms had caught up but remained silent.

The three walked in and waited to be taken to a table. A server called Joan, a small woman with bleached-blonde hair and too much lipstick, showed them to a corner booth.

Steel took the chair facing the doorway while the others made do with their backs to the open walkway. Joan passed out their menus and took drink orders. Two coffees and a cup of English breakfast tea.

The squeak of white plimsolls on a vinyl floor signalled Joan's return.

Kit and Simms had the coffee, both black with no sugar. Steel took out the teabag before it spoilt and dropped in a bit of honey instead of milk or sugar.

Joan didn't ask for order straight away; she'd gotten the idea they needed more time the way the young woman was scanning the card and then looking at the food in front of people, so she left them alone. Hopefully, they'd find something before the end of the shift that night.

There was silence while each chose their orders. To Steel, everything looked good. Kitty spent more time observing what everyone else had, possibly to get an idea of portion size. Simms had known what he wanted before he'd left the car.

'So, Brenda sent you to watch me?' Steel asked Simms, breaking the silence.

'Brenda—oh, you mean ... yeah. He doesn't trust you,' Simms said, laughing at Steel's play with Brena's name. 'You're not gonna tell him about this, are you?'

'Your secret is safe with me,' Steel smiled as he called Joan over from the end of the counter. Making Kitty look up as she saw Joan's approach.

'Why did you do that? I haven't found anything yet?'

'Well, I'm hungry, so is Karl, and I bet he even had an idea of what he wanted before he'd stepped out of the car,' Steel said.

'How did you know that?' Simms asked, a look of surprise on his face.

'Because even though you were looking at the menu, you were just being polite. You looked at each page for three seconds,' Steel said with a shrug.

Simms laughed, unaware Steel was already profiling him.

'So, what will it be, folks?' Joan asked in a bubbly voice.

Simms got pancakes and bacon, Kitty requested the BLT, and so did Steel, but he'd asked for turkey bacon.

He watched Joan walk back to the counter to place the order. Her shoes still squeaked as she went. 'So, two murders you guys didn't even know about? Who was in charge of the cases?' Steel asked as he blew on his tea.

'You have the files. All the information is there,' Kitty said, feeling slightly bitter at having been the errand girl.

'OK, no Cliff Notes, fine. But why were you guys sent to get me like a criminal?'

'That was Brena's idea. He was told to bring you in. He had heard some of the stories and decided to use the heavy approach if you caused problems,' Simms replied, feeling embarrassed.

'What is his deal anyway? Daddy didn't get him a pony when he was a little girl or what?' Steel asked, his eyes searching the room for anything out of the ordinary.

'Brena is … well, Brena. For some reason, he wants to prove himself, stand out, be the man,' Simms said, taking a sip of coffee.

'So, in other words, he wants to solve this case, even though it has nothing to do with him. Stanton brought me in on this.' Steel said.

'The way Brena sees it, the moment he was sent to get you, he was on the case,' Kitty said, waving to get Joan's attention.

'So, what's the plan, Mr Steel?' Simms asked, his eyes lighting up at the approach of Joan and his breakfast. The conversation stopped as she placed the plates down and got Kitty's order for orange juice.

'Well, I was going to have this, then head off to the market over the road and get some items for the suite. Then, go back to my room and look at the files. But, unfortunately, you'll have to sit in the car. And Kitty will have to drive back and listen to Brena and his foolish ideas,' Steel said as soon as Joan had gotten out of hearing range.

He noted the sombre expressions of the two agents.

'Or, we could all got to the market, stock up on food and drink, then work on this together in my suite,' Steel suggested with a shrug.

'You got cable in the room?' Simms asked, his eyes squinting as if he was going to be disappointed.

'Is there a ball game on?' Steel asked.

Simms smiled and shrugged, then took a bite of his bacon.

'My place it is then,' Steel said with a smile.

Chapter 12

Stanton sat in his office. The meeting hadn't gone well, primarily due to that arrogant son-of-a-bitch Brena. Stanton knew it had been a mistake bringing him in on it, but then Brena would have found a way anyway. But Stanton felt more at ease now Steel was there. Sure Steel was an immense pain in the ass, but he got results.

Stanton looked over to a picture he had hung on his wall; it was a group photograph of him and several others, including Steel. Stanton cracked a smile as he thought back to those good old days. He remembered back to when he had pulled Steel out of the SEALs to work for them, a job that proved to be beneficial to both of them. Stanton remembered the day Steel's team was ambushed and how Steel blamed himself for letting his guard down.

The funny thing was Steel hadn't been on the operation; he had another mission to take care of. Steel was working for MI8 at the time. A mission that would later get him brought into the fold of the British Secret Service.

Stanton had to admit he'd never seen anything like Steel and had never seen the like since. Most people are driven by money, power, love, or lust. Steel was motivated by one thing; the problem was Stanton still didn't know what it was, or he could have used it to his advantage. A knock at his door made Stanton look up. In the doorway stood a stone-faced Brena.

'What can I do for you, Martin?' Stanton said, seeing Brena.

'Sir, I would like to know what the hell is going on: why did you send us to get Steel, and why is he on this case?'

Brena's words rang with composure, but Stanton knew he was ready to burst out of his skin.

'Sit down, Martin,' Stanton ordered, pointing to the chairs facing his desk. Black leather swivel chairs that felt as uncomfortable as they looked.

Brena sat down; his bottom lip pulled up so far he could have swallowed himself whole. 'I won't lie to you; I brought Steel in because he is the best I've ever seen. The man is a machine and definitely not to be fucked with, but he is also expendable if things go wrong. Believe me, Martin, this is one case you do not want. Hell, I didn't want it, but we got it. Besides, I had to bring him in,' Stanton admitted, his voice almost choked by the secret.

'Why, what's wrong, sir?' Brena asked, almost *not* wanting to know the answer from the look on Stanton's face.

Stanton pulled a postcard from out of his drawer; it was in an evidence bag. The picture was of Berlin. Brena took the postcard and scrutinised it before turning it over. The colour drained from his face as he read what was on the back: Detective John Steel, 11th Precinct Police Department, New York City.

* * *

Steel, Kitty and Simms had gone back to start their investigation.

Simms sat on the bed and grabbed the remote while Steel began to prep the coffee machine. There was a blare of noise when Simms switched on the TV, not knowing the last tenant liked his television loud and had left it on the news channel.

'Oh great, this guy,' Simms moaned, pointing at the television with the remote.

'Who, the Vice President?' Kitty asked, confused at Simms's issue with the man.

'Senator James Freeman. Now there is one mother who has a silver spoon up his ass,' Simms groaned before changing the channel to sports.

'Not a fan, I take it?' Steel smirked, emptying the grocery bag onto the table and spilling the items onto the table.

Simms said nothing, just shot Steel a look that spoke a thousand words.

While they were out getting breakfast, Steel had arranged for three whiteboards to be brought up from the hotel's conference room to be set up in his suite. He also got other items, including minicams, markers, sticky tape, maps, and Post-it Notes from the local store.

Simms had made the coffee and found a ballgame while Steel arranged the boards, so they stood against an empty wall near the bathroom, then suggested using their files to create two murder boards.

He took Alison Kline, and Kitty was working on Mark Trent. Mark Trent had been the first murderer. He had been a security officer at the Manhattan Mall. Trent had died when his computer screen blew up, and he took glass shards to the face and throat.

Kitty and Steel's boards were almost similar in an arrangement. With a map showing where the victims lived and worked and Post-its with information stuck onto relevant points, only Steel's had a timeline.

Trent was killed at home on his day off, where Kline was on her way to City Hall.

Steel stood back and compared the two, hoping for a link, a possible connection between them, but he had nothing.

Trent worked for a security firm, so he moved around, working in different locations. On the other hand, Alison Kline was a high-powered lawyer. She dealt with everything from movie stars stealing jewellery to Daddy's little son getting off a hit-and-run while under the influence. In Steel's eyes, they couldn't be any more different if they came from different planets.

'Got anything?' Steel asked, hoping for her fresh eyes to have spotted something.

'No, not really, just the need for more coffee,' Kitty joked as she headed for the kitchenette.

Steel followed and noticed Simms engrossed in the game and eating a bag of popcorn.

'When did you get popcorn?' Steel asked. Impressed at the man's lax attitude toward Brena's orders.

'Never mind that; Brena wants us back at the office,' Kitty said, showing a text she had just gotten.

Simms stood up, grumbling under his breath at having to miss the rest of the game.

'You coming, Steel?' Simms asked.

Steel shook his head. 'I don't think that I'm meant to be there. Don't forget, you're not supposed to be here. You're watching me from your car,' Steel explained.

Simms nodded in agreement; it would look strange if Steel turned up with them. They all turned as Steel's cell phone when began to vibrate loudly across the small breakfast bar of the kitchenette.

'Who is it?' Steel asked as Kitty picked up the device to check the caller ID.

'It's Stanton.' She tossed the phone over.

Steel swiped the answer icon on the glass screen and held the device to his ear. 'Avery, to what do I owe this honour?'

He listened to what his old boss had to say. 'I'll be there as soon as I can.' Steel disconnected and picked up his jacket from the couch. 'OK, I guess I will take that ride after all.' He pulled on his jacket.

* * *

Brena had left Stanton's office and headed back to his. He had plans to make. He knew now where the killer's next target would be; he just didn't know who. For Brena, it was a race against time, not just to save this latest victim but to beat Steel to the punch.

As Brena left the office, Stanton began to have reservations about Brena's motives. This case had the makings of an international incident, especially if the killer was going abroad— that was INTERPOL's backyard, and Stanton didn't need that sort of heat. Straton rocked in his office chair, pondering what to do next. Forcing Steel and Brena to work together was a bad idea. Steel was a lone wolf, always had been, and Brena was a glory hound. Their working together would create more problems than it would solve. If he ordered Brena off the case, he would find a way to get back onto it. No, there was only one solution to the problem, and he didn't like it. They would both work the case, but Brena would be under the impression Steel was out.

Stanton didn't like the plan because that made Steel leave last time.

* * *

Steel sat in the back of the Challenger, his thoughts elsewhere. Simms had the game on the radio. By the sound of things, it would be a close one. Steel never really understood the game; for him, it was like a game he had played as a child back in Britain. Simms was rooting for the Tigers; Steel guessed it was his local team from Detroit. Steel hadn't caught the other team's name. To him, at that moment, it was just noise. A sound that faded into the backdrop and became a hiss, like white noise, as he began to process things in his mind. Not just about the cases, but about Brena and Stanton, about Kitty and Simms. To Steel, something was off, and he didn't know what it was. Then the memory of his last case started flooding back, filling him with anger.

Simms let out a loud 'yes', punched the air, and briefly swerved the car into the other lane.

The noise brought Steel back to earth with a start, and he was slightly disoriented by it all. 'What happened?' Steel asked, looking around.

'His team won,' Kitty explained, holding on to her seat belt out of fear of Simms's driving.

'Do you always celebrate by trying to kill people?' Steel joked.

Kitty smiled at Simms, who said nothing, just drove with a broad smile on his face.

* * *

After showing their IDs at the gate, Simms parked, and they all got out. Their cover story for Brena was simple: Steel had found them in the hotel parking lot and asked them for a lift. So, there was no need to mention the breakfast or them all in Steel's hotel room.

They entered the lobby and passed through a security checkpoint, bag checks, and metal detectors. Steel caught up with Simms and Kitty, and they took the elevator up to the third floor. The ride up was quiet, so quiet Steel felt the need to start whistling just to break the silence but fought the urge. Finally, the doors slid open, and they got out. Steel headed left and the others right. Each said nothing to the other, almost as if the past few hours hadn't happened.

Steel headed towards Stanton's office, where Brenda was waiting for him with a huge smile.

'Go straight in, John; the old man is expecting you.' Her words were soft and seemed to float on air. Steel thanked her and knocked before entering.

'Come in, Steel, my boy, come in,' Stanton said while pouring two glasses of whiskey.

'A bit early for that, don't you think?' Steel smiled, accepting the glass.

'Son, I've seen you are drinking much worse in Bosnia, a lot earlier than this,' Stanton laughed.

The two men clinked glasses and took a seat.

'So, what's up, Avery? You pulling me from the case?' Steel saw the look of awkwardness on the old man's face as if he were trying to find the right words for the bad news.

'I am sending you to Berlin; see if your hunch was right. Brena will remain here and look at another angel,' Stanton started to explain.

Steel felt that he was being sent away for another reason.

'Look, Steel, I didn't bring you in on this. But, unfortunately, he did,' Stanton growled, pulling the postcard from his desk drawer and handing it to Steel. 'The killer wants you on this, and I'll be damned if I know why, but it doesn't matter. You and Brena are working on it, together or apart.' Stanton downed his whiskey and moved to pour another.

Steel looked at the postcard, the picture of the Brandenburg Gate, and the writing on the back. Nothing more than Steel's name, no clues to the next victim.

'The next clue is in Berlin; why does he want me in Germany?' Steel asked, downing the contents of the glass.

'Your flight leaves in an hour. So, don't be late,' Stanton took a sip from his fresh drink. 'And Steel?'

Steel stopped as he started to leave and turned to face Stanton, his face expressionless.

'Be careful and watch your back with Brena,' Stanton warned him.

Steel nodded. 'I hope you gave him the same advice about me.'

'Something like that, yeah.' Stanton shrugged. 'Now, get your ass outta here; find this son-of-a-bitch before he kills someone else.'

As Steel left, Stanton looked out his office window and sighed deeply.

Chapter 13

Steel made the hotel reservations himself, just in case Brena checked. But, as far as anyone was concerned, Steel was in Berlin attending a trade conference as spokesperson of his family's company.

The long flight allowed him to catch up and ask for some equipment to be dropped off at his hotel. For Steel, the Regent Hotel seemed a perfect choice. Sure it was a little over the top, but he was working undercover.

Steel had booked one of the suites, hoping it would draw attention, knowing Brena would be all over Steel's movements. Still, more than that, he was hoping the killer would also be watching. After all, that was what he was good at what he was doing.

The killer wanted Steel in Berlin. Why? Nobody knows? Perhaps Steel was next, and it was a trap, something Brena would love, but Steel had the feeling there was more to it. Apart from the first killing, the killer had sent a postcard giving a clue. Steel paused to think for a moment. Why hadn't the killer sent a card for the first murder? Was this person relevant? Or maybe a test run to see if they could get away with it?

Steel looked at his watch; they still had another eight hours to go. Finally, he put away his notebooks and settled down for the night. After several complimentary drinks and a meal, Steel closed his eyes and hoped the nightmares didn't return. Not tonight, not ever.

* * *

Brena sat in his office looking at the files Kitty had brought him earlier, a large, cat-like smirk on his face as he remembered the news; Steel had been sent to Berlin to follow a lead. Of course, Brena had one of his minions track Steel's whereabouts, but regardless, the case was his. He'd asked Stanton for the postcard. After all, it was evidence.

Stanton had sent it down to Brena an hour later, and now it was on the board with a collection of Post-its and scribbles.

'So, where are we with this postcard?' Brena shouted, hoping for some lightning-fast answer that would solve the case.

'The lab found no fingerprints. The ink is regular black Biro, the person is a righty, and it was hand-delivered,' Simms answered with a steaming cup of coffee in one hand and his phone in the other.

'So, what is he trying to tell us? What is it wants us to see?' Brena walked up to the near to empty board and stared at the picture on the postcard.

'Maybe the next clue is in Berlin; perhaps it's a game, a see-how-smart-you-are sort of thing,' Kitty added.

Brena shook his head, dismissing the idea, probably because she had spotted it.

'No, the other killings had taken place in New York. So, there must be something there to do with Germany or Berlin,' Brena said, trying to hide his disappointment in himself.

'Maybe it's to do with a piece of the Berlin Wall that was brought back?' put forth Trish Edwards. Trish was wearing jeans and a white blouse instead of a nun's habit.

Brena's eyes lit up. 'Good, find out how many pieces were shipped to the States and where they are now,' Brena ordered excitedly.

There was a hurried sound of typing as the agents got busy with their searches—all but Simms and Kitty, who knew this was a wild goose chase.

Kitty had found Steel and raised an eyebrow when she saw where he was staying. She cracked a smile, knowing he'd had the same thought as she'd had. It was a pity Brena was too full of himself to see the truth.

'Got it,' Trish cried out like a schoolgirl, making Simms roll his eyes.

'There are several pieces all over the US, but there are five in New York. Madison Avenue, Kowsky Plaza, The Intrepid Museum, Ripley's, and the last is at the UN building.'

'Right people, grab your gear! We're off to New York,' Brena yelled like a drill sergeant.

Everyone stood up and grabbed their IDs and guns from their desk drawers. Brena went to walk away when his phone rang; it was Stanton. Brena rolled his eyes at the old man's timing and answered it.

'Yes, sir,' Brena said, hoping the call would take too long.

'Brena, I need Simms and West in my office, special assignment,' Stanton ordered.

'Yes, sir, no problem,' Brena said with a grin. Suddenly, his day was getting better, he had a lead, and he was getting rid of two of his worst agents.

'Simms, West, the boss wants you upstairs now,' Brena said with a smirk. The words 'special assignment' was usually coded for an outstation in Siberia. Simms and Kitty watched as their team left, each member wearing a grin of satisfaction.

'You two,' said a voice from behind.

Surprised, Kitty and Simms spun around quickly to see Stanton standing with a grin of his own.

'Grab your gear; you're going on assignment,' Stanton said with a mischievous grin.

'But sir, we are on this case,' Simms started to argue, suddenly feeling like he'd been kicked in the balls.

'Sorry, you two, something has come up. It looks like a British businessman also happens to be part of the aristocracy. He requires *two* bodyguards, it seems,' Stanton smiled and tossed two brown document envelopes onto Kitty's desk, then turned and walked away.

Both of them stood for a moment, mouths gaping open like carp. Disgruntled, Kitty began to read her orders. Suddenly, the frown was replaced by a huge smile.

'How's your German, Karl?' Kitty said, watching Simms read his.

'*Sehr gut*,' Simms laughed.

Steel's flight landed around two in the morning the next day. The eleven-hour flight had only been disturbed by the transfer flight in France. He'd gotten about two hours of sleep, which was enough to recharge his batteries.

As he walked through the airport to the exit, he couldn't help feeling a little disappointed. He had been in the Army in the nineties, and he'd never managed to see Berlin as it once was. Many of Steel's Army colleagues had visited the city for a long weekend. Others had been stationed there on a tour of duty. But for Steel, this was his first time.

Steel collected his bag from the baggage carousel and headed through the exit. As he made it through the automatic doors, he saw a man in a black suit holding a large sign with Steel's name on it.

Steel walked over to the driver, who was in his late twenties. The man was tall and slender, and his tar-black hair was styled with a military cut. Steel figured he was an ex-marine or other special operations unit. The man definitely wasn't in the forces now, despite having that military look about him.

'I'm John Steel,' Steel said with a mix of suspicion and curiosity.

'I am Daniel Jones. I'm here to take you to the hotel, sir,' said the man with an American accent.

'I never ordered a car,' Steel said, eyeing him closely.

'The managing director sent me, along with your lost luggage,' smiled Daniel.

Steel nodded and beckoned the man to lead the way. He loved the way the Secret Service used aliases for their people. For example, in the MI8, CO was called Managing Director, and the quartermaster was known as Boots and Socks.

All the way to the limo, the conversation was mute at best. Neither of them felt the need to speak, meaning no awkward silence.

The car was a blacked-out Mercedes-Benz Rolls-Royce Edition limousine. Steel looked at the seventeen-foot monster and shook his head in disbelief.

'What's wrong? Couldn't find anything bigger?' Steel joked.

'Sorry, the *USS Ronald Regan* was on manoeuvres,' the driver laughed. He opened the rear passenger door for Steel, who looked inside and shook his head before getting in.

* * *

Even at two in the morning, the traffic was pretty heavy. Finally, they pulled up outside the hotel, where the doorman was waiting to open the car door for Steel. The driver got out and started taking the bags from the trunk just as a porter came with a brass luggage trolley. Steel got out and inhaled lungs full of city air.

'*Guten Morgen, mein Herr*,' greeted the doorman.

Steel guessed the man must have been six-six at most, with slim features and short sable hair. His white-gloved hands were the size of shovels.

Steel followed the porter inside while the driver hurriedly got back into the car and disappeared into the traffic. The inside of the hotel lobby was filled with red marble and luxurious fittings. As Steel looked around, he felt he was in another time. This was a five-star hotel, earning them all from what he could see.

Steel made his way to the reception desk and pulled out his passport, ready for the check-in. Behind the desk were two women, a blonde and a brunette. Each was attractive and wore little in the way of makeup.

They were dressed in hotel uniforms: an onyx-black blazer with a skirt and egg-white blouse. Steel took the time to study the lobby as he waited for one of the women to be free to check him in. Steel noticed the cue for the brunette move, and an angry German couple stood next to be served. Finally, a spot became free at the blonde receptionist, and Steel hurried into the spot before the place was taken.

'Hi, John Steel. I believe you have a reservation for me?' Steel said, placing his passport on the desk.

She smiled and took the passport, then checked for Steel's name on the computer.

'Ah, yes. Herr John Steel. We have you down for the superior suite.' Her eyes widened, and the smile broadened as she passed Steel the slip of paper with the check-in details.

Steel thanked her, took the key card, and headed for the elevators.

* * *

The suite was spacious with a sitting room, two bedrooms, and a bathroom most could only dream of having in their homes. Double windows in the sitting area showed a spectacular view of the city; its lights twinkled like embers of a fading fire. Steel stood for a moment, looking across the magnificent view while the porter unloaded the bags from the trolley.

'Will that be all?' asked the man.

Steel turned to see the man waiting at the door. He smiled and reached into his pocket to find the ten euro note he'd been keeping for such an occasion.

'*Danke*,' Steel said, shaking the man's hand while discreetly palming the cash.

The man bowed slightly as a thank you and left the room. Steel turned back to regard the city and sighed. How he wished he had brought his wife, Helen, here—before that fateful day when everything had changed. Steel glanced at the two black pieces of luggage. One was an armoured suitcase for all your international spying needs and the other a canvas suit carrier.

Steel picked up the suit carrier and was shocked at the weight of the thing and took it to the wardrobe to hang it. He figured there were new suits in there. By the heft of it, he thought there must be at least ten. As he opened the zipper, Steel gasped with surprise. Inside were four new black suits. Five shirts: three black, a dark blue, and deep burgundy. And a special Kevlar-and-titanium vest that was as thin as one of the shirts but had the strength of armour plating. Steel smiled and turned to the suitcase, wondering what possible toys lay within after seeing what was in the suit carrier.

* * *

Kitty West and Karl Simms searched for their seats in economy class.

She found her seat between two large, sweaty men and Simms was seated next to an attractive woman and an empty seat.

Simms shrugged and smiled sympathetically at Kitty before taking his seat. Kitty looked at her place and hoped the guy with the aisle seat would move and let her in. But the man just smiled at her and waited for her to squeeze past.

Oh great, this is going to be a very long flight. Kitty sighed and stuck her bag into the hold above the man's head, with him still not moving, letting her brush up against him.

'Miss West?' asked a male flight attendant.

'Yes?' Kitty replied with a pissed-off look.

'You and your colleague have been upgraded to first-class,' he informed her.

Kitty looked over at Simms, laughing and joking with the woman.

'You can ask him, but I'm pretty sure he won't want to go,' Kitty said, taking her bag down, making sure her CIA badge showed to the man below her. As their eyes met, she smiled. 'Don't worry, it's not like we know where you live,' she joked, hoping the man pissed himself.

The flight was long, for Simms anyway, as he had ended up meeting the woman's husband, a trainee quarterback for the Chicago Bears. While he sat in silence, Kitty was enjoying the comforts of first class. She didn't know who had paid for the seats, but she was glad they had. In fact, only a complete idiot would give it up—and he was sat in coach with a huge monster of a guy and his hot wife that Simms dared not look at.

Chapter 14

Steel had unpacked. He had a disappointed look on his face as the suitcase contained only clothes and toiletries. He decided to get some sleep before breakfast, as there was nothing he could do until the daytime. He'd asked for a morning call at seven o'clock and ordered room service and a map of the city.

At seven sharp, there was a knock at the door, and a woman informed him it was room service. Steel yawned and stretched off, almost unwilling to leave the comforts of the bed. He walked over and opened the door. Before him stood a man dressed in a hotel uniform with a service trolley—and, most importantly, breakfast.

He let the man in and tipped him on the way out. The cart was packed: a silver coffee pot and china cup and saucer, mixed fruits, bread, jams, and under a stainless-steel domed canopy were two eggs on toast with bacon.

By eight o'clock, he had eaten, showered, and changed into one of the new suits. The weather outside was warm and inviting, but he feared he wouldn't have much time to see the sights. So, he took the elevator down and decided to hit the streets.

Steel's first port of call was the Brandenburg Gate. He thought it was too obvious a clue to send a postcard with a picture of where the clue actually was, but Steel feared the clues would get more challenging. Whoever the killer was, he wanted them to work for the answers.

Steel stood outside the hotel; he had memorised the street names he needed. Along Charlottenstrasse and then left onto Bundesstrasse 2. Which was a fifteen-minute walk at most.

Steel turned left and followed the street, his mind switching into the zone. He was on the hunt for a killer who was *very* focused. One that had the patience of a sniper and the skill of an EOD tech. Steel was used to track maniacs and terrorists, but this was something new and deadly. But Steel didn't know what scared him more: facing this killer or the fact he was beginning to like the game.

* * *

Steel arrived at the Gate, a vast sandstone construction with an almost pantheon feel. Twelve towering pillars topped by a decorative hood of copper and stone, crowned by a statue of a woman riding a chariot. Once a symbol of peace and then one of victory.

He walked around the majestic gateway. Looking for a clue or even a hint of why he was sent there. There were plenty of tourists and people going about their business. But nothing out of the ordinary. Steel looked at his watch. It was nearly nine o'clock. He peered around again, ensuring he hadn't missed something. Nothing.

Steel took out the copy of the postcard and examined it again. It was a night-time scene of the Gate in full illumination. He turned the card over. The only thing written on it was Steel's name and the address. There was something about it all that didn't fit, and if he was meant to be there to get the next clue, where was it?

Feeling slightly annoyed and somewhat deflated, Steel headed for the nearest coffee shop. He found a nice restaurant not too far from the Gate and decided to take a seat with a clear view of it, just in case he had arrived too early.

A waiter came and took his order. Small cappuccino. People came and went. Still nothing unusual. Steel pulled out his cell phone and checked his messages, taking advantage of the restaurant's free WI-FI.

He had plenty of missed messages but none from the 11th Precinct. One was from Stanton informing him of Simms and Kitty's departure. Before he'd caught his flight, Steel had phoned Stanton, suggesting that Simms and Kitty would be useful in the investigation. Stanton had agreed and sent them to meet him using a later flight. He'd then gotten back to Steel, giving him the flight number, just in case he wanted to meet them when they arrived. Playfully Steel had upgraded them from coach to first-class; he guessed he did it to rub Brena's face in it. Two of his staff flying first-class would sting, or at least he hoped it would. Steel was surprised that Brena hadn't tried to stop it, or at least tried to send one of his lackeys as well. But then, he didn't like Simms too much, and he most certainly had no love for Kitty.

Their plane would be in around four in the evening. A fifteen-hour flight with one stop-off. Naturally, they'd stay in Steel's suite; after all, they were his security on the trip, or that's what their cover was. A simple ruse enabled them to show their IDs in public without raising suspicion. Steel found it amusing that their jobs would be their cover story, but not half as funny as when they found out he was an actual Lord.

The rest of the messages were spam or people he had no interest in talking to at that moment. The last text message was from his man in his father's company—the man who had sent the new clothes. Steel just referred to him as The Tailor, something that someone had once called the man, and it just stuck.

Steel looked up as the waiter returned with the coffee. Steel thanked him and paid straight away. He figured five euros was enough for the drink and a tip. He sat and watched the stone gate and sipped. It was half nine, and he had nothing. The thing Steel didn't like about this game: he didn't know the rules.

Steel looked at the postcard one more time. Something about it bothered him, but he couldn't put his finger on it. The CSU Department had done every test to ensure there were no hidden messages. Used everything from blacklight to testing with lemon juice but found nothing. Steel figured the message was less complicated than expected, possibly so simple overthinking would draw a person past it.

Steel picked up his cell phone and dialled Stanton's number, figuring that Stanton would be spending a lot of time at the office because of the case, and he'd told Steel his in-laws were over for a visit. The phone rang several times before a groggy-sounding Stanton picked up.

'Hi Steel, any news?' Stanton asked moodily.

'No, I didn't find any messages. So, maybe it's all a big ruse to get us out of the country,' Steel said, disappointed.

'Maybe, but keep on it. Brena is checking out New York; he figures that the Berlin postcard could refer to a piece of wall that had been brought back Stateside.'

'It's possible, doubtful, but possible. I'm going to check out a few more ideas before I pick up my security detail,' Steel laughed.

'OK, watch yourself, Steel; if the killer is there, he's dangerous and smart,' Stanton said.

'Oh, Avery, before I forget, how did the 11th Precinct know to send the card to you?' Steel asked quickly before Stanton had time to hang up.

'They didn't. It was hand-delivered.' Stanton's voice trembled with confusion.

'It was hand-delivered to Langley, but it had my New York address on it?' Steel didn't wait for an answer. He ended the call and placed the phone back in his pocket.

Once again, he looked at the postcard and realised *that it* was the missing piece. He was too early. The message said Brandenburg Gate at eleven that evening. Steel smiled smugly, finished his coffee, and stood to leave. He had solved the puzzle. The question now was, where would the next one be, and could he solve its mystery in time?

* * *

Stanton slammed the receiver onto its cradle. He hated when Steel did that. Having thoughts and not sharing. Stanton finished the glass of Scotch that sat on his desk. He had meant to finish it earlier, but the wait was exhausting, and he'd dozed off on the couch in his office. The dash across the room to his phone had woken him up slightly, but not that much. He couldn't slip back into the dream he was having. A sixty-footer on a pale blue ocean and not a care in the world, and definitely *no* Steel.

Stanton forced himself back to the couch and settled himself for the rest of the night. The smell of Chinese takeaway filled the room with a musty aroma. But he didn't care. He was eating junk food and drinking eighteen-year-old Scotch, and there was no wife to get on his back or kids to argue with, and the most important thing, no in-laws to tell him how he was doing everything wrong. He worked for the CIA as a section chief, and what was his son doing? Twenty-five to life for armed robbery.

Stanton snuggled down, closed his eyes, and pulled the blanket over him. He was warm, fed, and comfortable. All he wanted now was a little time to himself.

Suddenly Stanton's eyes shot open, and he sat up.

'It was hand-delivered, so why did they address it?' Stanton said to himself as he stood up quickly and raced to the war room.

He had left his shoes in his office, but he didn't care, not right now. Stanton searched for the postcard amongst the mass of photographs and Post-its. His hand froze over the thin card. What if he was wrong? What if they both were? Stanton took the pictured card from the board and turned it over. *11th Precinct.*

'It's eleven o'clock at night, that's what it means, goddamn eleven at night,' Stanton muttered, exhaling the breath of air he'd been holding. Stanton reached for the phone on the conference table and dialled the switchboard.

'This is Section Chief Stanton. Get me Agent Brena in New York.' Stanton waited while the call was put through to the phone in the safe house Brena and the team was using. Stanton listened to endless rings. He wondered where they could be. There should be at least one person there to answer any calls.

Finally, there was a click and then a pause.

'Yes,' a woman's voice quietly answered.

'It's Stanton. Where's agent Brena?'

There was a pause again. Then the woman replied, 'Sorry, sir, Agent Brena isn't here. He's gone out for recon.' Her voice suggested uncertainty.

'Get him to call me as soon as he gets in,' Stanton ordered, looking at his watch. Where the hell was he at three in the morning? And a recon mission on a wall outside of a secure building? Something didn't feel right about the whole tale. If she had said he was out getting drunk or laid, possibly, but that story he didn't buy.

Stanton put down the receiver and headed back to his office. He needed time to think. Twelve hours was a long time to sit and wait but a perfect amount of time to think and plan.

* * *

Agent Trish Edwards smiled as she put down the phone. She knew where Brena had gone, but it had been their secret, all of them, and she wasn't about to be the one who told. Sure, it wasn't right. But the others had agreed to go along with it regardless. They trusted his judgment.

'Who was that?' Brown asked.

'Stanton. He wanted to talk with Brena. He's got to call the old man back as soon as he gets in before someone suspects anything,' Edwards said sternly.

Brown nodded as if taking in the order.

'Any word on Simms and West?' Trish asked.

'Not much. Heard they got a babysitting detail out of the country.'

'That'll make Brena happy if they're out of his hair,' Trish smiled.

'What will make me happy?' Brena asked as he walked into the room, tossing a long hooded black coat onto the couch.

Edwards's eyes shot over to the coat, one she had never seen him wear before.

'Simms and West have been reassigned, a babysitting gig,' explained Brown, and Brena smiled and nodded. 'Oh, Stanton called. He wants you to contact him ASAP.'

The smile on Brena's face fell away; this news was not so good. 'When did he call?' he asked Brown, but his gaze fell onto Edwards, eyeing his coat.

'A couple of minutes ago.'

Brena said nothing. He stood there thinking, forming a plan.

'Get some rest; we'll start again in the morning,' he finally ordered. He walked over to the coat and bundled it into his arms, so it was unrecognisable. But Trish Edwards had seen it, and now she wondered not just about the coat but where Brena had been all night. He had told them he would see an old friend, a female friend, and he had some catching up to do.

Edwards had thought it unusual, not just the request for them to keep it quiet but the fact Brena had a friend. Brena was the most extraordinary agent. Straight down the line kind of guy. One that would do what was needed to get their man, but sneaking off and breaking protocol to see a woman? This wasn't the Brena she knew.

Edwards watched Brena disappear into his room. Maybe she was wrong; perhaps there was another side to him after all. Everyone should have love in their lives at least once. Trish had known at once. A great love, but that had gone, and all she had were memories and feelings deep in her heart.

Chapter 15

The flight arrived in Berlin on time. Kitty walked onto the connecting gantry with a spring in her step. Simms looked tired and worn out and hoped that the hotel wasn't a dump full of crack addicts and hookers. After a trip from hell, he needed a long bath and a good night's sleep.

They waited at the carousel for their luggage. One suitcase each. Travelling light seemed to be the best option, just in case, there was trouble. In fact, Kitty was impressed with how Steel had moved. *Just buy what you need; everything else is expendable.*

They didn't have to wait long before the convoy of bags traversed their way along the snaking rubber belt. Kitty and Simms stood at either end, so if one missed them, the other had a chance to grab the cases.

Simms looked over with sleepy eyes to where Kitty had stood. He rubbed the tiredness from his eyes to wipe away his blurred vision. Then, as Simms opened them, he found she was gone. Suddenly, Simms was awake. Had someone taken her? Had she left already, thinking he had gone out? His heart began to race. Simms didn't know if it was the overload of coffee on the plane or the fact he'd hardly slept in fourteen hours.

'Karl, are you OK?' asked a familiar voice behind him. He turned to find Kitty with both bags at her side.

He let out a sigh of relief and nodded with a wavering smile.

'No more coffee for you,' Kitty stated, taking control of both bags and wheeling them out.

Simms was close behind, shaking his head and praying someone had sent a car for them.

Outside, the sky was bright but overcast. The odd beam of sunlight was warm as it broke through the clouds. As if playing peekaboo with the people below. Kitty stood for a moment and inhaled deeply. Taking in the scent of a new city. Simms just looked around for a place to light up a much-needed cigarette.

'You ever been here before?' Kitty asked Simms, who had spotted people walking around with cigarettes in no-smoking zones.

'No, you?' He shot back the question while sparking up and taking a long draw on the Marlborough. Simms closed his eye as he felt that sweet nicotine fill his lungs. So engrossed was he, in fact, he never registered her answer or the car that had pulled up to pick them up.

The extended black Mercedes Rolls-Royce Edition limousine glistened in the passing breaks of sunlight. Kitty smiled as a driver in a black suit and hat got out and opened the door for her.

'Simms, shake your ass. We're leaving,' Kitty shouted, making people turn to look.

Simms opened his eyes, and his mouth fell open at the sight of the expensive car. 'Oh, thank you, God,' Simms said, crossing himself twelve times before getting into the car.

There were gentle thumps behind them as the driver loaded their suitcases. Then the driver's door opened, and their chauffeur slipped into the seat and buckled up.

'So, where are we going?' Simms asked, somewhat suspicious of this man.

The driver didn't answer. He put the car into drive and pulled out, and followed the signs for the Autobahn. Simms was about to ask again when the car phone next to the fully stocked bar rang. Kitty looked at Simms and then back to the phone.

'Do you think it's Stanton seeing if we landed OK?' Kitty asked.

Simms scowled at her and picked up the cordless receiver.

'Yes,' he said, not wanting to give his name away.

'Oh good, you got picked up alright. I'll see you both in about two hours,' Steel's voice boomed from the phone's speaker.

Simms looked at the receiver and shook his head as the line suddenly went dead.

'I'm starting to not like this guy,' Simms said, placing down the handset. He looked over to Kitty and saw she was already asleep. He smiled and decided to do the same. After all, they had plenty of time.

* * *

Steel sat in the sitting room of the suite. He looked up at the two murder boards and a third he had just constructed. The new board held as many details as he knew on the present case, which he had to admit were very few. The timeline was blank; there were no pictures, less for the postcard. Steel stared at all three while swishing the fifteen-year-old whiskey around in the crystal glass in his hand. If this were a serial killer, there would be a pattern. Someone this complex would have an end game. Steel took a sip of the Johnnie Walker Green.

To The Sentinel, this was a game he wanted Steel to play. This led Steel to believe that The Sentinel was a narcissist, playing a game of Catch Me if You Can.

Steel looked at the first board, the security guard. By all accounts, Mark Trent was an average guy who liked what he did. Trent lived alone. He had no pets or friends to speak of. Both parents had died years ago, leaving him the house he lived in.

Then the second board. Alison Kline. Single, lawyer, a good one at that. No record. Fancy place on 81st Street. No boyfriends, just brief acquaintances to scratch that itch. The two had no ties of any kind. He lived in Queens, and she Manhattan. He'd never done jury duty or been arrested. Steel's eyes drifted to the third board. A blank slate just waiting to be splashed with colour. Steel took another sip of his drink and looked at his watch. Simms and Kitty should have touched down by now, and the driver ready to bring them to the hotel. Steel took another sip of Johnnie Walker, and his gaze tracked back to the empty board.

If there was a pattern, he didn't see it … not in time to save the next victim. That was the other thing: there was never any timescale given. Usually, it was a case of 'solve this in twelve hours or else.' But this time, there was nothing. It was five o'clock and six hours to go before the meet. Steel had several options to bide the time, but he had to wait for Simms and Kitty. He had no doubt they would each have one suitcase containing only one colour and no style whatsoever. Then, there was a ping on Steel's cell. It was the driver; they'd arrived.

* * *

Brena had eyes on the pieces of the wall outside the UN building, and Ripley's Believe it or Not, Ordertorium. There were three others, but given the killer's need for the elaborate, the parks and museums didn't seem right. The others had gone to get some shut-eye; he'd volunteered to take first watch. He was good, he'd got his sandwich from the deli, and there were two pots of coffee on the go. Brena prided himself on not sleeping during a stakeout; he'd let the others rest, but he'd stay awake. Brena had a fear of missing something if he closed his eyes.

Several monitors showed a feed from the UN and the Ordertorium. There were hidden cameras that picked up anyone who approached the walls. A good idea by all accounts. The great idea, however, was getting rid of Steel and sending those two idiots Simms and Kitty on babysitting duty. Brena smiled to himself.

Brena knew that Stanton hadn't gotten rid of his star quarterback. He would have been suspicious if he had. But it didn't matter, Steel was far away, and that was all that mattered. As for the other two, Brena's imagination conjured painful ideas of what they were doing while he solved the case of the century. Stanton had Simms and West watching some wealthy Brit who probably treated them like trash and made them sleep in the basement. As for Steel, he was likely stuck in Berlin, chasing false leads and stirring up trouble. Brena smiled again. Life was good.

* * *

The special edition limo stopped suddenly, giving the two a gentle jolt to wake them.

'Hey buddy, easy on the brakes,' Simms complained as if trying to mask the fact he'd been sleeping. 'So, which shit-hole hotel have you brought us to?'

The door was opened by a tall man, but that was all either Simms and Kitty saw. The bright light and their sleepy eyes made everything blurry.

'Welcome to *der Regent Hotel*,' said the guy at the door.

As the two stepped out, they hid their eyes from the sun until they could refocus.

'You gotta be shittin' me,' Simms said, as he was the first to look around.

'Is it bad?' Kitty asked, more unwilling to look.

'Oh yeah, it's a real dump,' Simms laughed.

Kitty opened her eyes and looked up. Her mouth fell open.

'Oh yeah, a real dump.' She laughed as they both headed in through the main doors like a couple of teenagers on their first vacation. The lobby was vast, with red marble floors and antique-styled furnishings. Kitty thought it was a mistake or a practical joke made by Steel to get his own back for Barcelona.

'*Guten Tag*,' said a man behind the main desk. He was an older man in an ash-grey suit.

Simms started to say, 'Yes, we're here to see—'

'Ah, yes, the two Americans *für* Lord Steel,' the man said, beckoning them over. He produced two key cards, which they took, and put away in their pockets. 'I will see language is sent up to your room,'

'Room ... you mean rooms?' Kitty asked as a look of fear came over her face. She had seen how Simms lived, and he snored. There was no way they were sharing.

'Yes, you're all in the Presidential suite with Lord Steel, as per his request,' the man said, somewhat confused.

'Oh, yes, that's right, he did mention it. Sorry, long flight,' Simms said, backing away and heading for the elevator before there was a mistake or he woke up.

'Americans,' the man murmured, shaking his head and returning to what he was doing on the computer.

'Oh, my God,' was all that Simms said once they were in the suite.

Steel was amused the first time, but by the seventh time, it had worn thin. He tipped the man for bringing up the bags and waited until the man had left before talking.

'Oh, my—'

'Simms, I swear if you say that one more time, I'm sending you back to Brena,' Steel said, rolling his eyes behind his sunglasses.

Simms calmed down, and he and Kitty followed him around as he gave a tour of the suite. It was a vast multi-bedroomed suite with a dining area and a fireplace in the sitting room. Kitty could see this was meant for a family rather than a British cop pretending to be royalty and two CIA agents. Regardless, she was in heaven.

'OK, you've had a long flight, and we have time until twenty-three hundred.' Steel looked at his watch.

'What happens then?' Kitty asked, picking up her suitcase in preparation for finding the correct room.

'I'll explain everything during dinner,' Steel said as they passed the first bedroom. It was a big room with a king-sized bed and an ensuite bathroom.

'Damn, this room is bigger than my apartment,' Simms declared, checking out the complimentary toiletries in the bathroom. They moved out of that room and headed to the second. Kitty spotted the view as they entered the next bedroom and shouted, 'Dibs!' She tossed her suitcase onto the bed.

'You know I could call seniority over you?' Simms growled.

Kitty smiled and shut the door behind her. Simms looked at Steel for assistance but found him grinning and unhelpful.

'If you want to come between a woman and a view, be my guest but remember, she's the one who's got your back,' Steel said, walking away.

Simms nodded, realising Steel had a point.

Steel picked up the house phone and spoke to the concierge, and asked if it was possible to make reservations for dinner at eight o'clock at the *Esszimmer*, a restaurant he had seen earlier that morning near the Brandenburg Gate. By all accounts, a great-looking place that appeared more turn-of-the-century than the twenty-first century. An excellent place to dress up rather than sporting jeans and a T-shirt over a cheeseburger.

Steel set down the receiver and looked over to Simms, who had left his bedroom door open, just in case he was needed urgently. Steel watched Simms, who was pulling a cheap black suit from his case.

'I take it you had to pack quickly?' Steel shouted from his chair all the way across the sitting room.

'No, why?' Simms shouted back.

'Because your suits are ... disappointing,' Steel replied as he appeared behind Simms, causing Simms to jump.

'Jez, you scared the shit out of me.' Simms held his heart. 'What? Are you a ninja or a friggin vampire?' He laughed, hanging up a suit.

Steel felt the sleeves of the jackets, and a cringing look crossed his face.

'What's up with my threads, man?'

'Nothing for a field agent. But a bodyguard ... well, that's a different matter,' Steel smiled. 'Kitty?'

'Yes, what?' she replied while walking out, holding a hand full of sexy underwear.

Steel raised an eyebrow and smiled at her innocent pose. 'Grab your coat; we're going shopping.'

Kitty smiled and disappeared back into the bedroom.

Simms just looked at his suit and stuck out his bottom lip. 'Ain't nothin' wrong with my suits, man. Dude's got a stick up his ass,' Simms mumbled under his breath.

* * *

At seven-forty-five, the three of them stood in front of the restaurant. Kitty wore a red satin dress with a slit on the left leg and a single strap on the right shoulder. Her Stuart Weitzman pumps glistened with the diamonds encrusted around the heels. Simms stroked the arms of his new Givenchy suit. The lights from the restaurant reflected against the material, giving it a satin sheen. His size-twelve feet were tucked nicely into a pair of Bally dress shoes.

Steel gazed at Simms, who had a smug look on his face. Simms felt Steel staring and turned to him, his hands dropping to his sides quickly as if he had done something wrong.

'OK, your suits are better, and mine are basically crap,' Simms admitted begrudgingly.

'*Were* crap,' Steel said with a smile and proceeded to walk in, followed by Kitty.

Simms froze where he stood for a moment, working over what Steel had just said. 'Were … what do you mean, *were*?' Simms replied in a high-pitched, alarmed tone.

* * *

Trish couldn't sleep. It seemed like hours since Brena had sent them into the other room to get some rest. She knew everything was mission ready. They had teams all over, and surveillance cameras were watching and recording. Brena had everything under control; he liked it that way. He loved to be in charge. Trish thought back to Brena's trip off the reservation. It wasn't like him at all; he was a by-the-numbers guy, yet he had slipped away for a private rendezvous.

Her stomach gave a rumble. It was two in the afternoon, and nobody had eaten. Trish stood up and made her way out of the room.

Brena looked up as she sneaked out of the bedroom. 'Where are you going?' he asked as he watched her put her coat on.

'We need food to soak up the coffee, if anything,' she joked, but she just needed to be away from them, if only for a brief moment. She had worked with Brena on more than a few missions, but this time it was different. *He* was different.

'What you going for?' Brena asked, rubbing his stomach.

'What you want?' Trish asked, sounding like she cared.

'I saw a Chinese place down the way; grab some menus,' Brena suggested. Trish nodded and headed out the door. Brena's eyes squinted as the door closed, a look of distrust painted on his face. Brena could feel something was wrong. They had menus from all the local takeaways in a drawer; she knew that. He closed his eyes and shook his head as the sound of loud snoring emanated from the room she had just left.

'Yup, now I get ya, kid,' Brena said with a smile, shaking his head at the volume of Brown's snoring.

Chapter 16

Dinner had finished with coffee. The waiter had insisted they should try the brandy, but Steel had to decline, to his disappointment. The night sky was clear, and the cloudless heavens displayed a vast sky with a blanket of stars and a full moon, which painted everything with a blue tint. The three left the restaurant and headed for the Gate.

'A beautiful night for a stroll, isn't it?' Steel asked as they stepped out into the chilly night air. He looked over at Kitty, who was beginning to shiver. He took off his jacket and placed it on her shoulders.

Kitty looked at Steel and smiled gently.

'Nice night, my ass,' Simms complained. 'I'm freezing my butt off.'

Steel smiled and looked at the heavens. The north star seemed exceptionally bright, as its sparkle seemed to wink at him.

'All I ask is a tall ship and a star to steer her by,' Steel stated.

'That's beautiful. Who said that?' Kitty was impressed at Steel's love for the classics.

'Captain Kirk,' Simms said proudly as he walked past them.

Steel smiled and shook his head in disbelief.

Kitty rolled her eyes and followed behind.

It was a two-minute walk to the Gate. Steel didn't want to rush or seem eager. He knew if the next clue was there; it had been dropped a while ago, possibly before they left the hotel. Kitty had made sure there were cameras nearby to catch a glimpse of the person making the drop—hopefully. Steel knew that whoever it was, they were there just for show. In fact, they probably didn't even know what they were bringing to the Gate. The sound of nearby traffic hung in the air like the sound of the ocean.

The plaza near the Gate was empty, less for the odd couple out for a walk or taking the dog for exercise.

'We stick together, no matter what,' Steel affirmed, looking at the structure.

Simms looked over at Steel with a frown. 'Really, you think something is gonna happen to us here?' He laughed with disappointment. 'You disappoint me, Steel; I figured you were good. Now, I find that you're just paranoid.' Simms shook his head and headed for the carved stone edifice.

But Steel had the feeling something was off. Almost as if someone was watching them.

'You're right,' Steel shouted to Simms, hoping to make the man stop and turn around.

'About what?' Simms asked, toying with Steel, knowing what Steel was apologizing for.

'About me. I do get a little like that sometimes, you understand?'

Simms stopped and looked at Steel, a look of amazement on his face. 'So, what you are saying is I'm—'

Simms never got to finish the sentence. Black SUVs pulled up, and men in black tactical gear leapt out. There was a scream for help as the team dragged a man away. The men screamed orders for him to shut up and piled him into the back of a black transit van before it sped away.

Simms stood open-mouthed.

'Anyway, you were saying I was what?' Steel asked smugly as he walked up to one of the columns. Simms and Kitty followed, wondering who the men had been and what they wanted.

'Who was that?' Kitty asked, looking about, just in case, there were more hidden in the shadows.

'Lady and Gent, you just witnessed INTERPOL at their finest.' Steel searched the left wall of the centre archway. The walls were smooth to the touch, possibly due to a cosmetic touch-up after the wall had fallen. There was nothing to be seen, such as a hiding place to contain the next clue. Steel ran around, checking the other walls, but found nothing. He sauntered back to Simms and Kitty, waiting at the first wall.

A look of confusion was on his face. 'I could have sworn it would be here ... so that's what the message meant, I'm sure of it,' Steel said, puzzled.

'Are you sure that's what the message said?' asked Kitty, resting a consoling hand on his shoulder.

'What do you mean?' Steel asked, glancing at where the man had been snatched.

'Aren't you a little curious that INTERPOL turned up at just that moment we should have been there?'

Steel thought for a moment and then nodded in agreement. Their being there simultaneously was too much of a coincidence.

'What's the plan now?' Simms asked, hugging himself as he attempted to keep warm.

'Go back to the hotel, get some rest, and start fresh tomorrow.' Steel's words were hard, almost angry.

The walk back to the hotel was silent. Simms and Kitty dared not speak, especially to Steel, who had the look of a man ready to do damage.

* * *

Trish lay awake, her eyes mapping out the marks on the ceiling as if they were some filthy constellation. She couldn't sleep. It was in the middle of the day, and she didn't want to confuse her body's clock. Besides, something was eating at her. Where had Brena been the night before, and where had the coat come from? She wondered about Simms and Kitty. Trish had passed on the message that made Brena extremely happy; they were on babysitting duty for some Lord. On the other hand, something inside her felt sad, almost disappointed, jealous even. They were on a job that could lead to other things, Whitehouse things.

Working on this case was a golden opportunity for Brena. She knew, first chance, his name would be all over the report, possibly his face in the paper, whereas the rest of the team would be lucky if they were a footnote. Brena was an excellent agent, but he looked after only one person: himself. Trish had seen him ruin careers because of anything or anyone that might make him look bad—and lucky her, she was the guy's replacement.

Trish sat up and reached for the bottle of water that sat on the floor next to her bed. The ice-cold condensation on the bottle tickled the skin of her hand as the droplets rolled over her fingers. Finally, Trish cracked the top and took a mouthful.

The room's air conditioner was busted, so the humid air was thick and warm. Outside, it was in the high twenties. Inside, the room felt like a South American jungle, except the jungle probably had fewer bugs.

Trish got up and headed for the bathroom. White-tiled walls and floor made the whole place look like a butcher's work area. Pockets of a black mould formed in the corners, and the mirror were made from polished metal instead of glass.

It wasn't the Ritz, but it was the only place close enough for the teams to be near the UN building. Trish ran the water until the colour resembled something clear, then splashed water on her face.

Trish looked up at her reflection in the metal; she hoped this all worked out. She hoped they find the killer. But most of all, Trish hoped Simms and Kitty were having a really shitty time.

* * *

Simms and Kitty went back to the suite while Steel headed for the bar. It had been a long and fruitless day, and he needed a drink. A martini, two shots of Blue Sapphire gin and a lime wedge. He had acquired the taste for a simple drink. Tonight wasn't a night for whiskey. He needed something with a bit more kick.

Steel ordered the drink and waited while the server mixed the concoction. She was a young blonde with long legs and a happy smile. Her uniform fitted her well, unlike some places where they expected the waitress to serve wearing high heels and scanty clothes that barely fit them.

'Is it your first time in Germany?' she asked, sliding over the drink.

'No, I was here a long time ago, with the Army.' Steel smiled as if a fond memory had just crept into his mind.

'So, you're here on holiday?' she asked, checking his fingers for a ring.

Steel smiled. The attention was a welcome distraction. 'Something like that, and have you worked here long?' he asked, observing her eye movements and gestures with her eyebrows, mouth, and hands. This was a definite come-on; he just didn't know why. Possibly for better tips, places did that, but then she was dressed wrong for that. The attraction couldn't be ruled out, be he had just come in.

Steel paid for the drink using small change and gave her a tip with more change. She thanked him and stayed to talk while she polished her glasses. Steel looked up at the mirror behind the bar to see two other men walk in and sit down at the far side of the bar, and two others sat in the chairs to his far left, near a window. All four men were big and looked like they could handle themselves. Steel sipped his drink. Not wanting to risk getting poisoned. Not on the first night, anyway.

The server, whose name tag said *Brigit*, walked over to the two men at the bar and began to talk in German. Steel could tell the small talk was as fake as the covers. Steel re-checked the mirror. The two men sat, pretending to look at bar menus. Steel began to have that feeling again. He knew this setup. Hell, he had shown it to her. The question was, where was Agent Sabine Boese of INTERPOL?

Brigit came back, wearing her wide white smile. They probably chose her because of her bubbly personality and good looks, hoping to lure Steel into a deadly nightcap.

'So, where are you from?' Brigit asked, picking up a glass and cleaning it with a cotton cloth.

'The UK … just here on a spot of business and to see the sights,' Steel answered with a charming smile.

'Oh, I love London,' she said with a dreamy look on her face.

'So, you've been to London?' Steel asked, waiting for some sort of brief but made-up account.

'No, I've never left Germany,' Brigit responded with a smile and a shrug.

'Oh, that's a shame. You should ask your boss if you could go.' Steel sat back on the barstool.

'What, Herr Franks?' Brigit asked, looking over at a small, white-haired man on the other side of the bar, checking menus.

'No, Agent Sabine Boese,' Steel said.

The smile dropped from her face, and the men stood up to surround him. Steel just sat and enjoyed his drink, waiting for her to arrive.

***

A woman stepped into the bar and stopped at the entrance. She was in her late thirties, with long legs and an hourglass figure. She had short-cut hair with no particular style, her skin was smooth, and her blue eyes sparkled like the jewels in the chandeliers. Sabine was of African-American-German descent. Her father had been an American MP stationed in Berlin. Her mother had worked in a bakery down the road from the barracks.

Steel had almost forgotten how stunning she was, with a smile that could put a rainbow to shame for its natural beauty.

Sabine spotted Steel and smiled. She knew he was watching in the mirror. 'Old habits die hard,' she thought as she sat down on the empty seat beside Steel.

'Good to see you again, John.' Her words were like silk, soft but with a hint of strength.

'And you are looking as fantastic as ever, may I say,' Steel replied, spinning on his chair to take a better look at her.

'As do you, John; I see you've bulked up a bit since last we met … still training like a madman, I see,' Sabine joked, giving Steel the once-over. 'What are you doing in Berlin?'

'That's what I've always loved about you, Sabine, always straight to the point, no foreplay. I'm on vacation, just thought I'd pop over to see the city I kept meaning to get to but never found the time for,' Steel replied before taking another sip of the poorly made drink.

'And the agents, why are they here?' Sabine asked.

'Bodyguards,' Steel said with a flippant tone.

'Bodyguards, Including the girl?' Her face was screwed up in anger.

'Yes, you never know when I may get attacked. But, unfortunately, it does happen,' Steel shrugged.

'John, of all the people I know, you are the last person who needs a bodyguard. And the only person who may attack you is me,' Sabine growled.

'Interesting, but you're going to have to buy me dinner first,' Steel said with a grin.

Sabine looked away, trying to force a smile from her face before she turned back. Her hands gripped the bar before she found them around his throat.

'You still like Italian, right?' Steel placed a hand on hers.

Sabine looked at him; her eyes were wide and glassy, a mixed look of happiness and anger swirled in the pale blue pools. 'You can't turn back time Steel; what happened, happened, and you can't change that,' Sabine said flatly, pulling her hand away and standing up. 'Be on the next flight home; your trip is over,' she ordered.

'I can't do that, Sabine; I'm sorry.' Steel stood and looked at his watch. It was more early than late.

'Why are you here, John?' she asked again, her tone harder.

'Speak to Stanton. He'll explain. In the meantime, I'm tired. It's been a long day.' Steel leaned forwards and gave Sabine a small peck on her cheek.

Sabine closed her eyes at the warmth of his breath and the smell of his skin and cologne. All the memories came back to her, and not only did he look as good as ever, but he smelled even better as well. Sabine felt her knees buckle slightly as he whispered something into her ear.

Steel stepped back and smiled. 'We really must do lunch or something, perhaps dinner, tonight?'

Before she could answer, Steel had turned away and left, leaving her standing at the bar. All her emotions tangled in a knot.

'What do you want us to do?' asked one of the men at the bar.

'Keep tabs on them. I want to know every move they make,' Sabine ordered as she turned and picked up Steel's drink and downed it in one gulp. Her face cringed with discomfort. She slammed the glass on the bar. 'Jez, Steel, have you got any liver left?' She winced at the taste of the drink.

The men hurried out of the bar, with Brigit close behind. Sabine pulled out her cell phone and dialled a number on her speed dial.

The phone rang for a short while before a voice answered on the other end. 'Stanton here.'

'Avery, it's Sabine Boese.'

'Sabine, it's been a long time. What can I do for you?' Stanton replied with a joyful tone.

'You can tell me why John Steel is in Berlin.' Sabine's voice almost purred; she was hoping he was there for one purpose. The postcard killer who called himself The Sentinel.

Chapter 17

Stanton looked out of his office window. Black, foreboding clouds had brought the rain that came down in sheets. He rested a massive sprayed hand on the cold glass as he stared out onto the car park and the flashes of light from the heavens. Stanton didn't know if it was a bad omen that the weather had changed just after Sabine had hung up. He didn't believe in such things, but the irony of the situation was only brought out in movies. As far as Stanton was concerned, the woman was trouble. In fact, she was a female version of Brena. Stanton smiled at the thought of those two getting together.

Steel had known her for a long time, but the last time they met, it didn't end well, not for Steel anyway, nor for Stanton. Sure, she was a good agent, but she was also a massive pain in the ass and someone he could do without. Stanton had told her why Steel was there; she seemed happy to hear about it and was probably ordering a new suit for the press conference.

Stanton turned to his desk as his phone began to ring. The caller ID said it was an unknown number. Cautiously, he picked up the receiver and answered with a simple, 'Yes?'

'It's Steel. I ditched my phone, and I got the others to do the same. I'll have new numbers for you by morning,' Steel explained, but Stanton didn't answer. 'Why is she on this case, Stanton? What aren't you telling me?' Steel asked from the public phone.

'She said she got a tip, a postcard which was identical to the one we have,' Stanton explained, hoping Steel wouldn't bail because of her. 'I told her we have a point. So far, there has only been an incident on US soil, so she doesn't have jurisdiction.'

'I don't want her on this, Stanton; she better stay out of my way,' Steel growled, making the man at the next booth turn away, scared by Steel's tone.

'I know Steel, but that is out of my hands. Just try and stay out of her way, solve this and come home,' Stanton said calmly.

There was a click to signal Steel had put down the phone, but Stanton stood still, frozen.

'I hope to God she stays out of this one, for all our sakes,' Stanton said, falling into his office chair, the receiver still in his hand.

* * *

Steel walked back to the room from the street. He had used a payphone he had found in a nearby restaurant. He was lucky; he thought things had all gone due to cell phones, but he had faith in people's needs to stay in touch. Steel knew it wouldn't be long before Sabine had tracked down the phone and traced it back to Stanton, but that didn't matter. He had passed on the message. That was good enough for now.

Steel had another problem. If the killer was going to drop off another clue, her little stunt hours before might have spooked him, and now he was in the wind, or worse, The Sentinel thought Steel had brought her in. As Steel neared the hotel, a man in a long hooded coat bumped into Steel.

'*Entschuldigen Sie,*' a gruff male voice said before continuing on his way.

Steel quickly patted himself down. Good, everything was there. Steel felt something in his coat pocket. Slowly, he placed his hand in and pulled out a piece of a card. Steel's eyebrows raised, and he tucked the card back into his pocket. He looked back down the street, but the person was gone. Turning, he headed inside the hotel. He had much to tell the others about Sabine Boese and the card the killer had just slipped into his pocket.

'That was quick,' Simms said, looking at his watch. 'Thought you Brits liked to drink?' he joked.

But Steel didn't laugh. His face was expressionless and cold. Steel looked around the suite. 'Where's Kitty?' he asked, expecting her to be lounging on the couch or at least in bed, catching up on her sleep.

'She just went to a local garage to get a drink. Apparently, the mini bar has bugger all, and I was being polite compared to what she had said,' Simms laughed.

Steel remained stone-faced and unamused, but it was more due to the situation than Simms's attempt at humour. There was an electronic beep and a click as the suite card was used. The door opened, and Kitty stood at her door, holding a carrier bag full of bottled water and chips. She saw something was wrong. Something had changed.

'What is it?' Kitty asked, stepping out into the sitting area and placing the bag on the carpet next to her seat.

'I met with INTERPOL, or rather they tracked me to the bar downstairs. I spoke with the lead agent, Sabine Boese,' Steel began as he crossed the floor to the drinks cabinet and poured a Treble whiskey neat. 'It appears they are also on the case because the killer also sent them the same card as what we have.'

Kitty and Simms gave Steel a look of shock and puzzlement.

'So, our killer has a sense of drama or weird humour, his making us fight for the right to catch him, pitting us against INTERPOL?' Simms snarled.

'What happens now?' Kitty asked, sitting down on the couch and picking up a water bottle from the plastic carrier.

'I've spoken with Stanton. He wants us to carry on. So far, INTERPOL has no case. The killings have only happened Stateside,' Steel explained, his face cold and unfeeling.

'I mean about the next clue; this Sabine chick probably scared off the killer with that circus earlier this evening,'

Steel smiled grimly and shook his head.'I think the first postcard was a test to see who would do what,' he said, sitting opposite Kitty.

'So, who won?' Simms asked, hoping this Sabine Boese had dropped the ball.

Steel smiled and pulled out the card using the tips of his index and middle finger. 'Don't pack your bags. The game is still on,' he said with a wicked smile.

* * *

The following day was cloudy with a stiff breeze. People filled the streets, going to that job they had to endure to pay the bills, or tourists escaping the life they'd left behind, if only for a little while. All of them were stuck in that rut, oblivious to the killer who watched them from afar. But none of them were The Sentinel's targets. Instead, his foes hung on several whiteboards and were shown on monitors. Their lives are mapped out and on display.

The Sentinel sat at a special workbench full of bits of metal, fine adjustment tools, and watchmakers' magnifying glasses fixed to the bench. Boxes of wires and solder sat next to a precision soldering iron.

As The Sentinel worked on a small circuit board, 'We Have All the Time in the World' played in the background from a CD player. The haunting voice of Louis Armstrong echoed throughout the apartment.

A clap of thunder was followed by a low rumble, signalling the storm had arrived. The woman on TV had predicted it days ago. A low front from the south was meeting up with a high from the east. It was bound to have happened at some point; they'd had days of sweltering heat, and now it was about to break.

Another clap of thunder followed by a brilliant flash filled the room. The noise was like an explosion. The Sentinel rocked in the chair and watched, finding the storm calming as the rumbles grew louder.

* * *

Steel had made a photocopy of the postcard and shipped the original back to Stanton in Virginia. Steel suspected Sabine wouldn't get another card; she hadn't played nice, after all. However, he understood this was a game and, like most games, there were rules. The problem was no one knew what these rules were. Steel pinned the copy onto the board and stood back.

'So, what does it mean?' Simms asked as he stared at the photocopies of the front and back of the card. The front picture was of an eagle with the Manhattan skyline in the background. 'To detective, John Steel 425 Precinct' was written on the back in bold letters and had no characteristic handwriting pattern.

'Well, in all of these, the killer has used a thick pen and not printed them, meaning he is mobile or he's smart enough to know each printer can be traced. The pen has been held straight up, like how a child uses a pen; this means it will be hard to say if we have a lefty or righty here. We now know that the address means time, but it's the picture that is always the puzzle,' Steel said, staring at the pictures.

'Well, it seems to me like he's sending us back Stateside,' Simms said.

Steel shook his head. 'Then why bring us all the way here? No, there is more to it than that?' Steel's face was filled with a strange excitement.

'Maybe we should look at this as if there are two pictures, not one,' Kitty said, holding a copy of the postcard.

Steel looked over at her and smiled.

'How do you mean?' Simms asked, holding the A4 copy up to the light.

'What if each piece in the picture was a clue in itself, like the eagle and the New York backdrop, two completely different clues?' Steel suggested.

'Exactly, we just got to figure out what they mean before four-twenty-five tomorrow afternoon,' Kitty shrugged.

'OK, it's midnight. I want everyone to get some rest, with fresh eyes tomorrow,' Steel ordered.

Simms and Kitty nodded and said their goodnights. As Steel watched their doors close, he knew there was no chance he was sleeping, not with the clock ticking on a person's life.

He phoned down to room service and ordered a fresh pot of coffee, and told them to put it into a Thermos jug. It was going to be a long night, but his adrenaline was pumping. Steel opened his laptop and got to work. He had to find who was known as The Eagle or the *Der Adler*. The picture of Manhattan was also part of the clue. The question was, how?

The coffee arrived ten minutes later, along with a turkey-bacon sandwich to tide him over. Steel was hoping that Stanton was on the same wave of thinking; if not, the note Steel had included in the overnight delivery would give him a push.

Steel poured himself a cup of coffee and picked up half the sandwich. His mind sifted through streams of data and possibilities. They were in Berlin for a reason; a person would be chosen, given the killer's MO. They knew that The Sentinel found public places to assassinate people. Given that they had travelled halfway across the world, the idea of a random killing was out.

Steel looked at his laptop, hoping to get more than ornithologist sites and pictures of birds. The Sentinel wanted him to search for someone called The Eagle. That was the clue. He was sure of it. The internet was a bust. Steel had inspected birdwatchers and *Wikipedia* information sites that came up in the search. Steel tried *Der Alder* and got the same but in German.

Steel's fingers danced on the keyboard with just the right amount of pressure to make a sound but not enough to enter a letter. He was missing something. A bit of information stuck in the back of his mind. Steel finished the coffee and then poured another one before using the search engine to look for the type of bird of prey in the picture, hoping that was the big break. Unfortunately, the search revealed nothing more than a thousand pages of birds of prey.

Steel downed the rest of the coffee and placed the cup by the side of the computer. Steel didn't know if it was frustration or tiredness, but he found it hard to concentrate. It had been a long day, and a little sleep would help him think clearly. He closed the laptop and headed for his room. There was nothing more he could do for now. Fresh eyes, a fresh start in the morning.

As Steel shut off the lights and closed his door, a figure crept out of one of the bedrooms. It moved quickly but quietly across the floor and out of the suite.

* * *

It had gotten dark early in New York. The blackened clouds remained, but the storm had passed over hours ago, leaving lakes on the streets and roads. Brena looked at his watch: seven o'clock. They had been sitting in the safe house for hours, watching the footage but with no results. Brena could feel the veins in his forehead twitch and his blood boil. He had been made to look a fool, but the worst thing was that it was his own doing, but he couldn't take the blame. Brena looked over at Trish and the other team members with a look of callous intent. He needed one of them to botch the mission so they could all go home.

Brena looked back at the monitors and hatched a plan; the question was, who was getting thrown under the bus?

Trish caught Brena's reflection in the window; she saw the look of cold calculation. He was plotting something, and it involved them. She carried on working, checking the computer for any updates on the bombing in New York, but the tests would take time.

Trish changed her search for information on the first victim, Mark Trent, the security guard. The guy had no web history; he didn't even come up on Google. For all purposes, he was a nobody. So, why kill someone like that with such vicious intent? By all accounts, the two victims had no history together, nothing. Trish looked at the window again and caught Brena's reflection once more. Now, he looked smug, almost as if he had found a solution. But she feared who the plan was for: the killer or them?

* * *

Steel had woken early and was already pounding out an eight-mile run. Outside was dark with a bitter chill. But that didn't concern him; if anything, the cold air against his skin was refreshing and stimulating. He had let the other two sleep. They'd had a long day, and today would probably prove to be just as challenging.

He headed for the Brandenburg Gate with the hope that seeing it again with fresh eyes might jog something in his mind. Steel thought back to the stranger who had passed the message to him. He had been shorter than Steel, had a long black hooded coat, and … a scent. The man had smelt of something that Steel recognized but couldn't quite place.

The sound of Steel's footsteps echoed in the plaza. The sound of his heart was in his ears, mixed with every steady breath. Why had the message been passed that way? A possible signal to say 'I can get close to you or even a warning to confirm he is being watched?

Steel stopped at the Gate and looked up at the grand structure. Why had he been brought here? Of all the landmarks in Berlin, this was the most prominent, yes. But surely others, such as the Cathedral or Checkpoint Charley, would have done just as well?

The chatter of birds grew louder, as did the sound of traffic as it began to build. Steel hoped that Stanton had come up with something on the name Adler or Eagle, but he wasn't confident that would have happened. He walked along the stone walls of the massive gateway, his fingers brushing the cold smoothness as his mind wandered and calculated.

The picture was almost certainly that of an eagle. The background was undoubtedly New York, so what did they both mean? Steel checked his phone; there were no new messages. He tucked the cell into his pocket and ran back to the hotel. Time was running out, and he had nothing to work on.

By the time he got back, the sky was light purple. It was going to be a beautiful day, but they wouldn't have a chance to enjoy it. Steel headed up to the suite and stretched off in the empty elevator. What he needed now was a shower, a cup of coffee, a good breakfast, and a lead on who they were searching for.

On the fifteenth floor, an old married couple shuffled into the elevator. Steel smiled and nodded a greeting. The couple returned the gesture and waited for the doors to close. Steel said nothing. He just looked into space and listened to the old couple's conversation. Steel figured they were from the south, possibly the Munich region, given their accent. Most of the chatter came from the old woman, complaining about the flight they had taken and about the customs officer who had pulled them over for a baggage check.

'As if I could smuggle anything in those old suitcases of ours,' she complained, her husband nodding without interest, just to keep her amused.

Steel smiled to himself, not just because of the old couple's conversation but because she had just given him a clue to the identity of the person they were looking for.

* * *

Steel burst through the suite door to find Simms and Kitty enjoying breakfast. Kitty looked over to Steel with half a croissant sticking out of her mouth; Simms had a cappuccino moustache.

'The man we are looking for is called The Buzzard, not Eagle or Adler,' Steel said eagerly.

'How do you know?' Simms asked, wiping the foam from his top lip.

'A while back, we uncovered a weapons smuggling operation in New York—'

'The ship in the harbour?' Kitty interrupted.

'Yes, the ship in the harbour. Anyway, we discovered most of the people involved, and the name The Buzzard came up; I believe that's who we are looking for,' Steel explained.

'What makes you think he's here?' Simms asked, unconvinced.

'Because his name is Karl Falkner, and he lives in Berlin,' Steel replied with a smile. 'The only problem is, that information is *years* old, and we don't know where he is now,' he admitted, the smile falling from his face.

'So, how do you know he's still here? He could have moved. He's probably in Frankfurt or bloody Australia by now,' Simms exploded.

Steel nodded. He had to admit that was a possibility. 'True, but you're forgetting one thing.' Steel walked over to the boards. 'The Sentinel sent us here,' Steel said, tapping the first postcard.

'So, how do we find him?' Kitty asked before shoving in another mouthful of the croissant.

'We could cross-reference all known criminals with travel arrangements, get onto the German authorities, and see if they have a possible location,' Simms put forth excitedly.

Steel poured a coffee and picked up the phone, and waited for the front desk to answer.

'We could check the FBI, CIA and Homeland database to check for last known locations or alias,' Kitty added, her heart racing at the sudden thrill of the chase.

'We could do all that, I suppose …' Steel paused and raised a hand as the front desk picked up the phone, 'Good morning, Lord Steel here. I wonder, do you have a phone book I could borrow?' Steel requested smugly.

Kitty looked over to Simms and shrugged, 'Or we could do that, I suppose,' she said with an awkward grin.

Chapter 18

It was ten to six when Trish made it to the piece of the Berlin Wall at the UN building. She didn't know what she was there to do; they already had cameras on the place in the hope of catching a picture of the killer. But Brena had sent her anyway. An agent called Mark Dutton had gone to Ripley's to do the same. Dutton was a new agent fresh from the farm. He was a tall, thin-looking guy in his mid-twenties. A crew cut shaped his soot-black hair. He was green but a quick learner and capable, from what Stanton had seen.

Their orders were simple: observe and report. A simple task for sure, but if anything stupid was done, if this killer were that smart, he would be able to spot an agent a mile off. That's when it hit her; they were there to mess things up. It all made sense now. The operation had been a bust from the start, but Brena didn't have the balls to admit it had gone under—too much of a spotlight for him to fail, so he had to send someone who could be blamed if it went sideways.

Trish sat in an old beat-up Ford transit van, which smelt of greasy food, BO, and cheap air fresheners. Another agent had driven the van. Ensuring that it was parked away from any street lamps on East 45th Street at the beginning of the operation.

It was just a guy parking his van, a great disguise, she had to admit to the casual observer. The side-panel windows were blacked-out, allowing enough room for the monitoring cameras to get full shots. Trish was glad she had gotten the UN building; less chance of things going sideways. Ripleys was too confined and had nowhere to hide out. But still, she had to be on her guard even though this was an 'observe only' task, one slip-up and Brena would say it was her fault and scrub the mission.

Trish took out her tablet and opened it. The images were broken down into six smaller screens, each live stream. Placing the tablet onto its angle rest, she cracked open one of the bottles of water she had brought in her away bag and began to take small sips while she watched.

Outside the van, it was quiet and dark. The section of wall was on the grounds behind the UN building, making a line of sight impossible from the road. The UN security was on standby to apprehend anyone as soon as she gave the word. The other observation team had gone, leaving her with the next eight hours. Trish just loved shift work, especially in the back of a cramped van. She wasn't surprised to see she was on this by herself, even though regulations stipulated there should be more than one at any given time. Trish knew why she was alone, but she didn't mind. In fact, she welcomed it. If perchance, she did catch the killer, it would be her alone who had done it.

Trish took another sip of water. Her gaze switched between those on the tablet and the ones on the monitors. She smiled as she watched the images on her tablet. Black and white pictures of a man in a bedroom, working on his laptop.

* * *

Steel had showered and changed before feasting on a hearty breakfast. He was on his second cup of coffee when he contacted a friend in an agency, asking if they had or could get Falkner's location. The phone book idea would have been a good one. However, Steel hadn't counted on so many Karl Falkners in Berlin.

Kitty West decided to shower while they waited. She knew as soon as they had a lead, Steel would be out of the door in seconds. Karl Simms decided to wait it out and finish his breakfast while he did something on his tablet.

Steel watched Simms as he flicked through images on his device, images from what appeared to be security cameras. Steel's sunglasses hid his eyes, ensuring his gaze was unnoticed, making a perfect cover to catch a look at the tablet as he walked over to the boards. However, idle curiosity and Steel's trust issues played a significant role in his actions. He decided to stroll past Simms.

Simms watched Steel walk his way, pulled his tablet close to his chest, and waited for Steel to be at a safe distance before continuing his work.

This made Steel smile at the man's evasive actions. He stood in front of the whiteboards and checked the copies of the postcards. Looking to see if there were any similarities in how they were set out.

Two of them had pictures of New York, each with different times of day, whereas the new one was of Berlin at night. Each address gave a different precinct number that didn't exist, which they had worked out to be a particular time. The killer was playing a game, leaving clues, breadcrumbs, that others had failed to see. If they had, the other people wouldn't have been killed.

Steel crossed his arms in contemplation as he stared hard at the boards. Something about the first two seemed different, as if something was missing. Then, feeling that someone was behind him, Steel turned and found Kitty close by. She wore a bathrobe with a towel wrapped around the top of her head.

'Found anything yet?' Kitty asked, looking hopeful at the prospect.

'No, not yet,' Steel replied, shaking his head, his eyes fixed on the problem. 'Did we get copies of everything?' Steel finally realised what was bothering him.

'Yes … I mean, I think so. Why?' Kitty asked with a confused look.

'Something was bothering me about the boards, a nagging feeling something was missing.' He pointed to the three boards.

Simms put down his tablet and moved over to join them.

'What's missing from the other boards?' Steel asked while a smile cracked the side of his mouth.

'Well, there are postcards, each one different; there is a map,' Simms said, his eyes failing to see Steel's noticed problem.

'Before each of the previous murders, the killer sent a single postcard, but this time he sent two. Each postcard had hidden within it a location and time. But the latest has a time and a name.' Steel pointed to the most recent card on the board.

'So?' Simms asked, failing to see the point.

'My point is, why didn't he do it the other times, and if he did, where are the other postcards?'

Simms' eyes widened. If Steel was correct, there should be more somewhere. If so, that could help break the code that could help find the victim and hopefully locate the killer!

Karl Simms picked up his cell phone and pressed the speed dial for Stanton's office.

Steel and Kitty looked on as Simms waited for someone on the other end to answer.

It would be about four in the morning in the States, but Simms knew Stanton would be at the office to see this through.

'Sir, it's Simms. Yes, everything is fine, apart from we don't seem to have all the copies of the postcards from the previous murders,' Simms said, looking at Steel, who was still staring hard at the boards.

'Yes, sir, I understand. I'll let him know,' Simms acknowledged Stanton and hung up the call.

'He told you we had everything, didn't he?' Steel asked, still taking in the information before him.

'Yes, how did you know?' Simms asked, amazed.

'I don't think there were any more. In fact, I believe our friend here didn't start sending second clues until I was brought in,' Steel said, taking the new postcard from the board.

'So, this is about you?' Simms asked, a tone of anger in his voice. 'That's a bit self-aggrandizing, don't you think?' He took a seat next to Kitty.

'Possibly, but looking at this whole thing, I believe he wants us to find these people first,' Steel explained as he put the card back on the board.

'People?' Kitty asked, almost scared at what Steel would say next.

'This killer studies his victims. Knows their schedules, routines, their lives inside and out. For someone to do that, they don't usually do this once or twice,' Steel explained. 'We are looking at a serial killer, and he won't stop until we figure out his game and stop him.' He picked up his cup and downed the last of the cold coffee.

There was a low buzz as Steel's cell vibrated in his pocket. He took the phone and opened the new message: one hour, the café on Friedrichstrasse.

Steel smiled at the text and tucked his cell back into his pocket.

'What's our next step?' asked Kitty, her eyes wide with both fear and excitement.

'We try and find Karl Falkner, and fast,' Steel stated as he placed down his coffee cup and headed for the door, grabbing his coat from the back of an armchair in the sitting room.

'Where are we going?' Kitty stood quickly, ready for action.

'I'm off to see …a friend. You two stay here and try and figure out what Falkner was doing in New York recently,' Steel ordered.

'What makes you think Falkner was in New York?' Simms asked, angry at being left behind.

'The postcard shows a bird and the Manhattan skyline; he was there, and something happened when he was,' Steel said, pulling on his coat and pulling open the door. 'There is more to these postcards than just the name of the victim. I can feel it.' Steel looked at the two and smiled gently. 'You can do this.'

And with that, he was out of the door and heading for the elevators. Simms looked over at Kitty, who wore the same concerned look he did.

'Do you think he's right?' Simms asked.

Kitty nodded. A serious look crossed her face. 'Yes, and that's what scares me. What terrifies me more is Steel's involvement in all this.'

'What? You think Steel is part of this?'

'No, I believe he's the last one on the killer's list,' Kitty said with glassy eyes and a tremor in her voice.

* * *

Stepping out of the hotel, Steel was greeted by the warmth of the morning sunshine. White clouds sailed past a light-blue backdrop. High above, the vapour trails from aeroplanes left their marks. The street was busy with townsfolk and tourists. Taxis shuttled their fares, and the odd police vehicle drifted by as they made their patrols. It was a warm day with no signs of turning.

He stood for a moment to get his bearings, taking note of places anyone could watch from or possible snipers nest. Steel knew that vans were a favourite for reconnaissance vehicles, so he looked for transit vans, especially those that appeared like they had been there a while. Steel knew he was being watched, but by whom was a different matter. If he were a betting man, he'd say it was INTERPOL, but he couldn't be sure.

Closing up his coat, Steel took a right and headed north towards the local stores. He could feel eyes on him, but he didn't care. After all, they weren't after him. Steel walked a few more blocks, ensuring he made as many turns down side streets and went inside as many stores as he could. If there was a tail, he wanted it to be as tedious as possible for them.

As he passed a parked car, Steel noticed the person following him in the vehicle's windscreen, which was as good as a mirror.

The man was an average-looking guy with brown hair and sunglasses. He wore blue jeans and a white T-shirt, almost covered by a blue fleecy bomber jacket. The man tried to look as ordinary as possible—no earbud cable hanging down or talking into his wrist while pretending to cough. No, this guy blended in OK, apart from his stature, which screamed ex-Army, the stiff posture, and the way he tried not to swing his arms in time with each step. It had taken Steel years to lose that look, but he knew it crept back from time to time.

Steel headed into a clothes store with tailored suits and overpriced shoes from Italy. A bell's chime alerted the storekeeper to Steel's presence, forcing a tall senior man out of the back room.

'*Guten Morgen*,' the tailor greeted Steel with a warm smile. He wore pressed grey trousers and a white shirt with pink stripes; a yellow tape measure hung loosely from his neck. Gold-rimmed glasses sat perched on a Roman nose, his wavy grey hair styled with a side parting.

'*Guten Morgen*,' Steel responded with a nod and smile.

'*Engländer?*' asked the gentleman with a hopeful expression.

'Yes, sir, on holiday,' Steel replied.

'Ah, very good. Is there anything special you are looking for?'

'No, just looking for the moment. *Danke*,' Steel said.

He smiled and left Steel to his own devices. Outside, the man stood for a while, pretending to check a paper map and orientate himself to the location. Steel smiled and checked out some of the London suits on display. He picked out several outfits and headed for the changing rooms at the back of the store.

The older man followed Steel with an interested gaze. It was a good sale at nearly a thousand euros per suit if they were all to go.

The man following Steel looked inside the store, hoping to maintain his observation. Suddenly, a look of panic crossed his face; Steel had gone! Quickly, he entered the store and rushed towards the changing rooms, hoping Steel was there and hadn't slipped past him.

The tailor spoke to the man but was dismissed with a quick show of the man's INTERPOL badge. He backed away and left the agent to his search.

As he drew back each curtain, he found only an empty cabin. Reaching the last one, the man held his breath, hopeful of finding Steel trying on something. Quickly, he jerked back the curtain and cursed as he saw an empty changing booth, less for the six suits that hung neatly on the hanger and a note: I'll take all these. Please charge them to my account, ask the poorly dressed man who I am and where to find me.

The INTERPOL agent cursed and turned to find the older gent immediately behind him; he smiled.

'*Bitte*,' he said with a broad grin and passed him a pen and paper.

* * *

As the agent had made his way to the back rooms, Steel had hastened past a row of suits on high racks, which hid his escape. He headed out the door.

He was counting on the man's sudden panic to blind him from what was happening, a risk that paid off. Steel made his way back the way he came, all the while alert to the possibility there was a second or third agent waiting to take over just in case the first man failed to keep track of their target. It was, of course, an old trick that he had used himself many times. He was alone, but he wasn't about to risk it as far as he could tell.

Steel winded through the busy streets, keeping the same evading tactics, following no particular route. But with one final destination in mind, a café, where he hoped a contact would be waiting.

* * *

Simms had showered and put on fresh clothes. At the same time, Kitty searched for Falkner's recent movements, particularly those to the US. Steel had a theory, and they were enabling his hunch while he went off to do something secretive. Simms played along for the simple reason Steel had once worked for the agency and had gotten a reputation for getting the job done. But now, he was a hidden asset. Simms could imagine Steel behind double plate glass with a sign saying, 'Smash glass if you're in the shit and there's no other option.'

So far, Simms hadn't been impressed by what he'd seen of Steel; sure, he pulled off the whole badass look with those all-black suits and mask-like sunglasses, but work-wise, he hadn't seen anything that compared with the stories.

He poured himself and Kitty another coffee, then joined her in the sitting room.

'Anything?' Simms asked, handing Kitty the cup of fresh coffee, white with two sugars.

'He's made a lot of trips, especially to Miami, but six months ago, he visited Philly,' she said with a grin.

'But nothing to New York?' Simms asked, hoping Steel's theory had paid off.

'He flew into Philly but bought a train ticket to Grand Central two days later; he was trying to cover his tracks, but he used a credit card that popped. Steel was right; the bastard was in the city. The question is, why?' Kitty took a sip from the cool coffee.

'And what the hell is the killer's beef with the guy?'

They both stared at the board and the colourful picture of the sun-kissed Manhattan skyline with the eagle head looking to the side majestically.

* * *

Steel had entered *Café Braun* after going through side streets and even a market. He was confident he hadn't been followed, but then Steel was always wary of the fact the opposition was intelligent and had contingency plans in place. Steel walked into the busy café and sat down next to a blonde woman in an ebony skirt suit.

The woman was in her late forties, with a perfect complexion and tortoise-shell wide-brimmed sunglasses. Her golden locks hung naturally over her shoulders and across her back. Red lipstick glistened on a full set of lips. Long talon-like nails sparkled with red nail varnish. She was a looker for sure and most certainly a panther in the sack, but that was her forte. Most called her Killer Cougar, a slightly distasteful name for such a passionate creature, but that's what she was. Nastassia Petrov was the best at what she did, and that was to kill using sex, or rather the build-up to it. Nastassia could make it look like an accident or—as some clients preferred to say—messy.

Steel and Nastassia had been friends for a long time—ever since she had tried to kill him in Cuba.

Steel had spared her life, feeling she was only doing her job and it wasn't anything personal. And, after a lobster dinner with a bottle of Dom Perignon '75, they ended up together that entire weekend.

'Nastassia, you're looking as fantastic as ever,' Steel cooed.

'Steel, you are looking … well, the same, actually … perhaps a little bigger,' Nastassia smiled.

'Well, lots of time to hit the gym recently.' Steel replied with a smile.

'So I heard, but not what I meant.' Nastassia displayed an almost cat-like grin.

Steel felt himself become warm under the collar and quickly called the waitress over to distract himself from the enchantress next to him and ordered two glasses of the *Sekt*.

'I got your message.' Nastassia spoke with the tone of an angel.

'And, where is he?' Steel asked, curiosity ringing in his voice.

'Not so fast. What's your hurry?' Natassia purred.

'Someone wants to kill him, and soon,' Steel explained.

'Let them; the little shit sells death to children.' Her tone had soured; the smile was now venomous.

'Unfortunately, he may have the answers I need to catch a serial killer who is killing innocent people. After that, the killer can have him,' Steel said to oppose her need to see Falkner strung up. But he needed answers and fast.

'You'll find him at this address,' she said, handing Steel a folded note. Steel went to take it, but she held the other side tightly.

'And the price?' Steel asked with a flirtatious smile.

'Dinner and dancing,' Nastassia replied with the same feline smile as before.

'Monte Carlo?' Steel suggested.

Nastassia purred and kissed him on the cheek. 'You know me so well. Who knows, maybe the hotel will have a whirlpool?' She grinned wildly.

Steel looked up to see the waitress standing with a small round tray with two champagne flutes and a blushing face.

He took the filled glasses from the young waitress and handed one to Nastassia. They clinked, and she toasted.

'Here's to the future. May Falkner fail to have one!'

Steel raised an eyebrow and took a sip of the German sparkling wine and found it had a bitter, somewhat hard taste to it. He took another sip, hoping it would be better the second time. No luck.

'Interesting toast. Almost sounds personal,' Steel said, placing the flute aside with a frown.

Nastassia just smiled and took a sip. 'So, who is the little one with you?' she asked.

'Agent Kitty West?' Steel replied curiously.

'West,' Nastassia said with a curious tone. 'I do not know the name, but her face seems familiar somehow.' She shrugged as if to dispel the thought and smiled. 'I guess she just has one of those faces.' She raised her glass again and laughed. 'We are lucky in that way, John. Nobody ever forgets us.'

'To dinner, dancing and whirlpools,' Steel toasted to lighten the mood.

Nastassia laughed again and clinked her glass against his before finishing the drink. Then, she stood. 'I'll let you know when I'm free, John, and do me a favour. Don't get yourself killed on this one,' she said with a wink and a kiss blown from her palm.

Steel had stood with her and watched her leave. As the door closed behind her, Steel waited before heading to the waitress to pay the bill. Something Nastassia had said was nagging at him. Did she know more than she was letting on, and if so, what?

Steel paid the bill and left a decent tip before heading out of the café. Outside, he reached into his pocket and pulled out the note.

'He's behind you in the corner,' it read.

Steel turned and gazed back into the café. He saw a man sitting alone in a grey suit with cola-brown hair and a moustache. He was drinking coffee and reading the local newspaper.

Steel opened the cell phone and pressed Simms's preinstalled number. It took two rings before he answered.

'Yes, Steel?'

'Simms, grab Kitty and get yourselves to *Café Braun* as quick as you can. We've found Falkner,' Steel said calmly, with his gaze firmly fixed on him.

The search was over. Now all they had to do was to keep him alive.

Chapter 19

It was ten in the evening when they got the call to shut down the operation. Trish was just happy to be out of the cramped van and sucking in clean air once more. She knew that Brena would be pissed, so she took her time getting back to the safe house.

Trish didn't know what had caused the enviable closedown. However, she suspected it was a call from Langley, possibly Stanton himself. Whatever it was, she was grateful.

* * *

'You're an hour late. Why?' Brana asked Trish as she walked through the front door of the safe house.

'Nice to see you too,' she responded, hoping her comeback would choke him.

'We are wanted back in Langley. There have been … developments in Berlin,' Brena said with unease as if the very words were made of broken glass.

'Did they find the next target?' asked Dutton with enthusiasm, making Brena twitch with awkwardness.

'We will be briefed when we get back. But, in the meantime, don't speculate on anything,' Brena warned. 'It's probably nothing.'

Trish smiled to herself at the thought of Brena's skin crawling because of Steel making progress. She didn't show it, but she had admired Steel for a while. She had read all about his exploits, most off the record. Steel was a man of right and wrong, regardless of the rules. MI8 had trained to think outside the box and get the job done. Something he had tried to do once before and got stung for it. A trail of thoughts that Steel had been told to ignore months ago, despite knowing the serial bomber would walk from the courthouse and kill again.

'We leave in one hour, so pack up your shit,' Brena ordered, then began to walk towards one of the bedrooms he'd claimed as his own to pack.

Trish gave a sarcastic salute behind Brena's back, then sat on the couch and checked her messages on her phone. Luckily, she'd packed before she left for the UN building, just in case this situation arose.

Brena was more of a pain than usual, which brought the worst out of Trish. She had joined at the same time as Brena, but he was the golden boy for some reason. She was as good an agent as he was, if not better.

Her mailbox was full of missed messages, most of which were of no concern, apart from one. It was a message from a friend abroad: 'Package delivered, another team is in play. Be careful.'

Trish deleted the message and looked around, ensuring no one had seen her. The side of her mouth raised slightly as she gave herself a secret smile. All was going to plan.

* * *

Steel went back inside the café and bought two coffees, one American and the other with two sugars. He'd purchased them at the counter and carried them over to Falkner's table. Falkner was busy reading *The Berlin Post*, a sizeable cumbersome paper attached to a long wooden pole.

'Coffee, two sugars,' Steel said, placing the coffee cup down in front of Falkner.

'NATO standard, as you Tommies would say,' Falkner said with a surprised smile before beckoning Steel to sit in the chair opposite. 'It's been a while,' he said, placing the paper down on the chair next to him.

'Not that we actually met, but yes, perhaps too long,' Steel replied.

'And what can I do for the NYPD? Or is it still British Intelligence?' Falkner asked with a curious expression on his face.

'I'm here for you.'

Falkner raised an eyebrow and laughed out loud at Steel's statement. 'A little out of your jurisdiction, are we not?' Falkner said with a wide smile.

'It's not like that, Falkner. I'm here with the agency, someone wants you dead, and it's happening today. I'm here to take you to a safe house.' Steel wished it wasn't a safe house but a prison he was dragging Falkner to. But Falkner was a target, not a criminal this time.

'People have tried before,' Falkener said smugly.

'This one is different; you're not the only one who has been targeted, and I don't think you're the last,' Steel admitted.

Falkner saw the look on Steel's face and knew something was gravely wrong. If Steel was lying, why would they send him, of all people? Why not a regular agent?

'Do I have time to grab some personal items?' Falkner asked.

'We need to hurry … wheels up in an hour,' came a voice behind Steel.

Falkner looked up to see a tall black guy with an expensive suit and a bad attitude.

'Falkner, Simms. Simms, Falkner,' Steel said, introducing the two men. 'OK, now that's over, shall we?' He groaned, wanting nothing more than to get Falkner to safety and then interrogate him.

'I need my laptop and some items from my apartment,' Falkner said with an urgent expression.

'Don't worry, we have an agent at your place. Just let us know what you need, and she'll get it,' Simms said, pulling out his phone, ready to send the text.

Steel turned and shot Simms a disapproving look through his sunglasses.

'Some things I need are … well, are personal,' Falkner admitted quietly.

'There is no way we are letting you out of our sight now we've found you; if you want something, my agent will get it,' Simms growled.

Falkner nodded with a look of defeat. 'My laptop is the most important thing, and my passport, which is in the top drawer of my desk.' Falkner's words sounded frail, as if he had lost everything or a dirty secret had been learned.

Simms texted the information to Kitty, who sent a simple reply: 'Roger that.'

Falkner was piled into the back of a blacked-out G wagon that Simms had rented using the company's credit card. Simms sat in the back with Falkner while Steel drove.

Half an hour later, Kitty sent a quick text saying that she was already at Falkner's place. The lock had taken her less than a minute to pick, and the alarm system took even less time. And Falkner's apartment was spacious with plenty of books and works of art, from paintings to sculptures.

Simms replied, 'Be careful.'

Kitty texted that she wondered about taking sneak peeks into drawers and a large wardrobe. Not looking for anything in particular; just interested in how an arms dealer like Falkner lived.

Simms replied, 'Get the stuff and get out; no time for snooping.'

Kitty responded with a sad-face emoji and a 'LOL.'

A little while later, she texted she had found the desk with the passport and an eighteen-inch laptop. She messaged that the computer was new and the box lay open, almost as if it had just been purchased.

Then she sent another quick text to Simms, asking if the new laptop was the correct one to bring.

'Is it the new computer, or do you have another one?' Simms asked.

'No, it's the new one,' Falkner nodded and looked glumly out the window at the streets as they whizzed past as if he knew he would never see home again.

A sudden thought caused Steel to shoot a desperate look at Simms and then Falkner.

'When did you get a *new* laptop?' Steel asked, a bad feeling running through his body.

'This morning, mine broke, so I sent off for a new one. I was surprised how quickly it came,' Falkner said with surprise.

'Simms, get hold of Kitty! Tell her to drop the laptop and get the hell out of there!' Steel growled as he pressed down his foot on the accelerator.

'Way ahead of you, Steel,' Simms said, struggling to press the speed dial on his phone while being thrown about in the back seat. It began to ring, but there was no answer. Simms shot a look in the rearview mirror at Steel, showing signs of complete control.

Due to a massive traffic build-up, they took fifteen minutes to get to Falkner's apartment. Simms parked, and they all got out and gazed at the inferno that used to be Falkner's apartment. Rubble-covered cars and windows had been blown out in neighbouring buildings. Fire trucks cordoned off the building, and firefighters on cradles unleashed sprays of water to douse the flames.

Falkner just stood and watched as his home burning, and Simms kicked the tires on the car out of anger. Steel watched the flames and the black smoke bellow skywards.

'We have to go, now,' Steel snarled as he turned and grabbed Falkner and tossed him into the back of the rental.

Simms slid into the driver's side and started the engine. 'Where are we going?' Simms asked, still in shock at what had happened.

'To get as far away from here as possible,' Steel replied with venom.

He wondered what Kitty had done. Had she disobeyed Simms and gone to snoop around just in case she found something incriminating to use as leverage against Falkner? But that wasn't the plan. Get in, find the package, and get out. That's what it was supposed to be, but it was hard to tell with this team of Brena's.

Steel had seen that they were all loose cannons and had agendas, so why were they all still working with the agency?

Stanton used to pick his people well, so what went wrong with these? The only one who showed promise had been killed. Steel knew with an explosion like that, there would be little chance of finding a body, let alone signs there had been an apartment.

Everyone sat in silence as they drove to the hotel. Words had left them. Only anger remained. Falkner stayed quiet in fear of angering Steel further. Falkner had heard stories of Steel and his time in the SEALs, and that was enough to scare him into keeping his mouth shut.

Steel was in no mood to hear a word from either of them, so he didn't provoke a conversation. Instead, Steel pulled out his phone and pressed the speed dial for Stanton. Steel wanted to tell him about it before the press splashed it all over the media. It took a while before Stanton picked up.

'Yes,' Stanton answered, his voice sounding hoarse and tired.

'Stanton, it's Steel. We have Falkner, but there's been an incident,' Steel explained.

'How bad?'

'Bad. We lost Kitty,' Steel replied, anger and pain running through his voice.

After a short pause, Stanton asked, 'How?'

'Explosion at Falkner's place.'

'Accident?' Stanton asked.

'No, too much of a coincidence. It was more likely to be a trigger activation device. Kitty was getting Falkner's laptop when it blew,' Steel said, looking into the rearview mirror to catch Simms's reaction.

'When are you leaving?' Stanton asked.

'No. I'm going to get the hotel to forward the luggage back to the States. It's too dangerous to risk going back to the hotel right now. INTERPOL will be all over it,' Steel explained.

'Won't they be at the airport as well?'

'Most probably, but what choice do we have?' Steel looked back at the rearview mirror.

'We got another postcard,' Stanton told him as if trying to change the subject.

'Do we know where yet?' Steel asked, hoping for something to take his mind off Kitty.

'Someone recognised it as the Rijksmuseum in Amsterdam,' Stanton said.

'Good, that's our next location. Can you send the jet there, and we'll send Falkner to you from there?' Steel suggested, sneaking a quick look at Simms in the mirror. As he suspected, Simms was also looking over via the mirror.

'Will do. I'll get your bags sent there as well,' Stanton said.

'No, send them Stateside. Then, if INTERPOL checks, they'll think we've gone back home,' Steel stated firmly, knowing full well that Sabine Boese would be checking where their bags were going.

'Contact me when you've got to the airport,' Stanton ordered.

'Roger that.' Steel hung up the phone and tucked the cell into his pocket.

'What's the plan?' Simms asked.

Steel looked up and smiled at Simms's reflection in the mirror.

'How's your Dutch?'

Simms and Falkner both gave Steel a confused look.

* * *

It was around seven in the morning when Brena and his team arrived back at Langley, using a Delphine helicopter from JFK to save time. Two SUVs were waiting to take them the half mile to headquarters.

None of them had any idea what the rush was, but it had to be bad.

Brena was hoping Steel had messed up, and now he would be taking over the whole operation. Trish just wished they'd caught the bastard, and it was all over.

* * *

Stanton was waiting for them at the main entrance, a grim look on his face.

'I hope you're all rested because we got another one,' Stanton said, waving a copy of the latest postcard.

'Do we know where?' Brena asked, almost drooling over the prospect of taking his team abroad.

'Amsterdam. My secretary recognised the picture. It's a museum in the capital,' Stanton explained while he walked, the team following close behind.

'Any news from Steel?' Trish asked, prompting a vicious look from Brena.

'He got the target, a man called Falkner,' Stanton replied.

'The arms dealer?' Trish was surprised at the news.

'Yes, the arms dealer, but it wasn't without cost. We lost Agent West,' Stanton said solemnly. Everyone stopped, and mouths fell open at the news, all but Brena, who carried the same uninterested expression.

'What happened?' Dutton demanded.

'An explosion at Falkner's place. The Berlin office is sending me a report as soon as they get one,' Stanton said with sadness.

'So, we're going to Amsterdam while Steel heads back here?' Brena asked coldly.

'No, Agent Brena. You and your team are working on what Falkner was doing here six months ago and what he and the others have in common,' Stanton stated gruffly, shocked at the lack of compassion for his teammate.

'What's Steel and Simms doing … don't tell me they're going to Amsterdam?' Brena cursed.

'You have your assignment, Agent Brena; I suggest you get on with it,' Stanton said, giving him a look that made him step back slightly.

As Stanton walked away, Brena watched the old man step into an elevator; he mumbled something under his breath at a sidewall of the lobby.

'We best get on it,' Trish said, hoping to break the tension that hung in the air.

'You two go up. I'll catch up with you. There's something I have to catch up on first,' Brena lied. He turned and walked into the brilliant morning sun.

'Come on, Dutton, let's find out what this Falkner guy has been up to,' Trish said, walking with the young agent to the elevators. 'Let's do it for Kitty and help catch this bastard.'

* * *

Fire crews fought hard and soon had the blaze under control. Falkner's apartment was destroyed, but somehow the surrounding ones were untouched, less for broken windows from the shockwave. Agent Sabine Boese stood with her hands buried in the pockets of her long, sandy-coloured overcoat and watched from a distance. She knew it was the killer they were calling The Sentinel, but she didn't know if the target was inside at the time.

The fire chief had said it would be a while before they could enter. Which would be pointless after all the water that had been sprayed and the fire crews that had trampled through the wreckage. All the evidence would be contaminated or washed away.

'The apartment belongs to one Karl Falkner, fifty-one-years old, unmarried. He's an arms dealer for one of the major weapons companies,' said a tall, thin man.

The man was Sabine's second in command, a ghostly-looking man with a narrow face which showed too much bone structure. His salt-and-pepper hair looked like strands of thread that had been laid on in ungenerous layers.

Agent Gant had had the unfortunate nickname The Ghoul since he was a child. A name he'd had so long it didn't hurt anymore.

'Where are Steel and his two friends?' she asked.

'They're on their way back to the States; their luggage was delivered earlier to the agency's plane. I checked the flight plan; they're headed to Washington,' Gant said.

Sabine squinted disbelievingly as she watched the smoke rise from the apartment. 'That rental car, did it get back to the dealership?'

Sabine waited as Gant went on his tablet to check.

'Yes, it got picked up at the airport around the same time they boarded.'

Sabine nodded to acknowledge the information, but she didn't believe it. Sabine knew how tricky Steel was; it was his job to disappear and not leave a trace unless he wanted to be found.

'Check with the airport; ask them to let us know when the plane arrives and how many people are aboard,' Sabine ordered.

'You think they didn't make the flight?' Gant asked, wondering where her insight came from.

'If you knew Mr Steel as I do, you'd know he didn't make that flight. The question is, did he find his target, and is he with Steel or up there with the rubble?' Sabine nodded up towards the burnt wreckage. 'Also, see if there have been any car purchases at local garages. If he's not renting, he's bought a car.'

'He could have stolen one,' Gant said, shooting off an idea.

Sabine thought for a second before shaking her head. 'No, not this time. He wouldn't want to draw attention to himself,' she said with a smile, remembering something he'd done once on a mission for INTERPOL.

'We're done here. Get the local police to send us a copy of the report, and I want to know if there's a body in there,' Sabine said, then turned and walked down the street to a waiting white BMW sedan.

* * *

Simms understood why they gave the rental back, even why he had the luggage transferred onto the plane. What he didn't get was why they had bought an old beat-up BMW M3, clearly over-priced and for which Steel had paid cash and put in a bit extra for 'no questions asked.' They were flying under the radar with a man who was a target of a killer, not what Simms expected to be doing when he woke up that morning. Still, he didn't also count on losing his partner to the killer.

Simms felt terrible. After all, he had sent Kitty in there without backup, even though he knew there was a killer planning on taking out Falkner that day.

Steel was still keeping conversation to a minimum, and Falkner wasn't talking at all. According to the navigation device, it would take just over eight hours to drive there. It would be a long and painful drive without any of them speaking.

Simms put on the radio and hoped there was constant music instead of lots of talking because he didn't understand the language. Sure, he was fluent in Italian, Japanese, and a little Russian, but not Dutch.

The navigation system Steel had bought from a local gas station indicated they had another six-and-a-half hours to go. Luckily, most of that was on the Autobahn, which meant no speed restrictions for most of the way until the Dutch border.

Simms looked back at Steel, doing something on his cell phone and frowned. He felt shut out, and he didn't like it. They were meant to be a team on this, and Steel had left them in the dark ever since they'd arrived. But now, it was worse, as if Steel blamed him for Kitty's death. It wasn't enough Simms blaming himself without Steel laying it on.

Steel caught Simms's gaze in the rearview mirror and cracked a smile. The first one he'd given for a while.

'We need to get to Amsterdam airport as soon as possible; we will get our bags there, and we can get rid of Mr Happy here,' Steel said, pointing a thumb at Falkner.

Simms nodded and looked back at the road.

'In the meantime, Herr Falkner, why don't you tell me what you were doing in New York six months ago and why someone is trying to kill you?' Steel turned to Falkner and shot him an evil grin.

'I don't know what you are talking about, Mr Steel. I'm just a businessman; I travel, so what of it?' Falkner replied smugly.

'Oh, I'm sorry, I guess I got you mixed up with some other arms dealer called Falkner. My mistake. Simms, turn the car around. We're taking Mr Falkner home,' Steel announced with a devilish smile.

'No, no, wait,' Falkner yelped in panic. 'OK. What do you want to know?' he almost screamed, hoping to convince Simms from turning around and returning Falkner to what was left of his apartment.

Simms smiled, typed the airport into the satnav, paused for the device to calculate the route and distance, and then turned down the radio. Falkner started to explain his business trip to the States and why he was in New York. A lot of it was good to know, but not what they wanted. Then Simon Townsend came up, a low-life scumbag that Steel had the privilege of putting away six months before.

Simon Townsend was your average dirtbag's dirtbag. He was the sort of guy who would sell his mother for a profit and toss in his kids to sweeten the deal.

Simms made a mental note of the name and everything Falkner was saying. Knowing full well once Falkner was on that plane, they probably would never see him again.

'So, what did Townsend want?' Steel asked.

'Explosives and detonators mostly, but not your usual low-tech stuff. Instead, he wanted digital remotes that could be set off by a specific remote,' Falkner explained, almost as if he was telling a story in a bar. Falkner was cocky, possibly a coward when it came down to it, but at that moment of feeling secure, one self-righteous bastard.

Steel knew this guy would be back on the street selling again, but this time for Uncle Sam. It made sense in a twisted way; better the devil, you know, people in high places would say.

* * *

Steel traded places with Simms and took the wheel. There were three hours to go, and Steel had noticed the man was tired, not just from the long drive but because of everything that had happened. Kitty's death weighed heavily on all of them, but Simms most of all. He had, after all, sent her to the apartment alone, a decision he wouldn't make again.

Steel looked at the pair of weary men in the back seat. 'Good, they're sleeping,' Steel thought. *The second rule: get sleep when you can. You never know when you'll do it next.* More good advice the Army had taught him.

Steel looked at the clock on the dash and then at the satnav. They would get there at around seven o'clock. *Not good enough.* He pressed down the gas pedal. They needed to shave off at least an hour; more would be better. The sooner they were rid of Falkner, the better. He was now deadweight and would slow them down in their search for the next victim. Steel drove fast but steady, weaving in and out of traffic but not so erratically that the Autobahn Polizei would pull them over.

* * *

The night air seemed cold. Dark clouds travelled quickly over a stormy sky. The city's lights were bright and inviting, unlike the busy streets with their relentless flow of people. Earlier it had rained. A heavy shower had lasted most of the evening, but now the winds were pushing the weather northeast. It was eight o'clock, and the city was starting to get busy once more. Many had finished work hours before; most were just finishing. The noise melded the sounds of car horns, bicycle bells, and people marching home.

A man walked out of a library—by all accounts, an ordinary man with nothing much about him. Average height and build, an older man in his late fifties, grey hair neatly parted to the side. His brown suit looked new, but his shoes were old yet cared for. Dark-rimmed glasses framed his face, along with stubble from two days of growth. The man held himself upright and proud, but he was just another face in the crowd to everyone. However, to The Sentinel, he was next on the list.

The man walked down the street, completely unaware of his tail. A figure dressed all in black with a black hood. The disguise blended in perfectly with a crowd of delinquents and students, and people who hated their parents for being loving. The man walked on. His mind was a thousand miles away as he moved through the multitudes of people. It would have been easy to have killed him; simply move up behind him and a quick stab through the second and third rib at an upward angle. The tightly packed crowds would carry his body along for ages until they began to thin out, and then it would fall to the curb as if it had happened there. The police wouldn't have a chance of DNA, witnesses, hair samples, or anything. But The Sentinel had other plans, something more fitting.

The man moved inside a tall white building with 1930s architecture and a new paint job. The Sentinel entered the opposite building and used the elevator, taking it to the top floor. Stopping at the twelfth floor, The Sentinel got out and headed down a long corridor to room 520. The Sentinel reached into a pocket, pulled out a key and opened the door. Inside was a cosy, fully furnished apartment, but why wouldn't it be? The owner was away on a world cruise. The pad would be empty for months. More than enough time for The Sentinel. Most of the research had already been carried out. Now, it was a case of tying up a few loose ends and ironing out a couple of contingency plans in case something went wrong with the original plan.

The Sentinel moved to a desk with a computer and several monitors, two of which had split screens that showed different images inside the man's apartment. The Sentinel pulled out a digital camera and plugged in a USB connection to the computer.

A screen with images of buildings and tram stops, and junctions started to download onto the computer. Standing up, The Sentinel moved to a far wall and a large city map; bits of different coloured string marked out the different routes the man took each day. The man was also a creature of habit. Something The Sentinel loved. It made things so much easier. The Sentinel took the other pin and stuck it into a large grey area with the name Alexanderplatz in bold letters.

The pale blue light of a street lamp illuminated the window The Sentinel was staring through. The street below was quiet. The odd car passed by, or a pedestrian on a late-night walk strolled without care. It was late. 'Some much to do and so little time,' were always words to live by. The Sentinel turned to the setup that sat on a table in the middle of the room. Four laptops showed views from different cameras, which showed the target's movements. A plan was forming. All The Sentinel needed was the perfect delivery system and the right time.

The images showed all the rooms in the man's apartment and office.

The man was in his mid-thirties with scruffy brown hair and thick-rimmed glasses that looked as if they belonged to a teacher or the late seventies. He moved about the room, pacing up and down as he spoke on his cell phone. The man held the appearance of someone who liked to be in control and had power over others through manipulation. The office was a twenty-by-twenty rental. Red fleur-de-lis on white background paper covered the walls. Expensive wooden furnishings sat upon a thick beige carpet.

Works of art hung under brass picture lights, and ornaments lay behind glass cases. This was the office of a man of distinction. A man who oozed euphoria. However, this was *not* the man in Berlin.

* * *

Trish sat at her computer. She was halfway through typing Falkner's name in the CIA's data search engine. Her fingers froze above the keys. Trish stared at the screen, unblinking. Kitty was gone, dead. She was killed by accident while she got some scumbag's things. It didn't seem fair to her that such a decent person should die and someone like Falkner should still be breathing.

Trish shook her head and got back to work. Her fingers regained movement and flew across the keys. The page she required was up in seconds. Karl Falkner: Movements and Associates. Using the information Steel had passed onto Stanton, Trish checked the dates Falkner was in the country six months ago. Where he had been and who he'd seen.

Kitty had been right. Falkner had indeed flown into Philadelphia and taken a train to New York using a card under the name of Edgar Raven. He had used the same card to rent a hotel suite at the Manhattan Hotel for six nights. After that, the trail ended until Falkner's return journey.

Tris widened the search to known associates, hoping he had met up with some. After around fifteen minutes and a lot of black coffee, the computer gave up a name: Simon Townsend.

Trish made a note of it and switched her search to Townsend.

His rap sheet was a mile long, and his favourite pastimes included underground fights and money laundering. But somehow, none of it ever stuck, so the police gave up arresting him. That was until Steel came along, and Townsend's luck ran out. Townsend had gotten twenty-five to life on a pitiful charge, but his priors caught up with him. *God bless the three-strikes rule.*

Even though the priors were before Townsend got smart, it still counted. Trish picked up her coffee mug without looking and went to take a sip. Her concentration waned from the screen when air met her lips as she tilted the cup back. She looked at the empty cup and cursed her taste buds for telling her there was one last mouthful.

She got up and headed for a long table on a far wall, which held three coffee machines, baskets with creamer in small sachets and sugar in paper sticks. There wasn't a break room; there was no need for one, as most just grabbed what they needed and then returned to their desks.

Trish filled the mug with a fresh brew and turned to head back to her desk just in time to see Brena reading what she had found on-screen and in notes. Trish froze, confused at Brena's approach to finding out what she had learned. She made her way back, hoping to remain unnoticed.

'I found your man; he got around a lot,' she said, walking up behind Brena, saying nothing or even giving an acknowledgement of her presence. 'Kitty and Steel were right. He was in New York on business.'

'With whom?' Brena asked coldly.

'A man called Townsend, a—"

'A piece of filth that should have been stamped on long ago.' Brena sneered at the very mention of the man's name.

'But Steel put the man away?'

'Far too late, far, far too late,' Brena said, walking away, 'Good work Trish; now go home and get some rest. It's been a long few days, and I need everyone rested.'

Trish watched Brena walk towards the elevators. He seemed different, calm even. She sat down with her coffee and looked at the screen. The name Townsend had sparked something in Brena—she wanted to know what it was.

* * *

The Sentinel sat in front of the desk full of monitors. The Moo Shu Pork and noodles takeaway meal from the local Chinese restaurant was almost gone. The Sentinel observed the next target, a middle-aged man in an expensive apartment. His concrete-grey suit was tailor-made, and the open-plan sitting area with the kitchen had an expansive panoramic set of windows.

The view from above failed to show the view from the window. But The Sentinel wasn't interested in that. Not yet, anyway.

The plan to get out Falkner had failed somehow, but it was no consequence. He was just a means to an end anyway. They all were. The Sentinel looked over at the time; it was almost four in the afternoon.

It would be time for stage two of the new target at eight o'clock. The new person that Steel was searching for.

All the pieces were in play. All that was needed was Steel to make the first move.

Chapter 20

Ever since they'd crossed the border with Germany, Steel had noticed the change in weather. Black clouds covered the heavens and powerful winds pushed against the car, forcing Steel to counter-steer against it.

Steel had let the others sleep; no need for them to be awake and break the comfortable silence. He'd switched off the radio a while back, just after they'd fallen asleep, in fact. Steel needed quiet to think, and unnecessary noise would hinder that.

Langley had already found the next place: a museum in Amsterdam. This was a start.

Steel and Simms now knew how to break The Sentinel's code, pictures, and address. Knowing that would make things a thousand times quicker in tracking the victims. The problem would be if The Sentinel anticipated this and started to make the codes harder, or worse, lessened the time they had to do so.

Steel checked the satnav; the airport wasn't far now, fifteen minutes at most. Soon Falkner would be safe on the jet, and Simms would be going with him. Steel knew he had to do this alone. No more dead agents, not if he could prevent it. Simms was a good man and agent, but Steel worked best alone. No baggage, no worries, no bargaining chip. Steel saw the sign for the airport, took the turnoff, and followed the road. Steel followed the signs for the different terminals and headed for Departures. Finding a spot in the parking lot, Steel parked and turned off the engine.

The two men at the back were still sleeping, unaware they had stopped.

Steel pulled out his phone and sent a message to a number Stanton had given to him.

'We're here; where is the rendezvous?' Steel typed and then pressed Send.

The reply only took a few seconds. 'Terminal A13, a man in a black suit named Rodgers.' Steel closed the cell and tucked it away in his jacket pocket.

'Wake up,' he ordered, unbuckling his seatbelt.

Simms opened his bloodshot eyes and yawned.

Falkner woke up suddenly at Simms's movement and looked around blankly, unaware of his new surroundings.

'Time to go,' Steel said, getting out of the car.

Simms followed, stretching off the stiffness in his body, and Falkner opened the door and slowly placed one foot at a time onto the ground.

Suddenly, Falkner flinched at the stench of exhaust fumes, engine oil, and burnt rubber and placed a clean handkerchief to his nose and mouth.

'Let's go. They're waiting for us,' Steel said, locking the car and moving forward at a steady pace.

'*Who* is waiting for us?' Falkner asked, concerned with his fate.

'Apparently, a man in a black suit called Rodgers,' Steel answered with a happy skip in his tone.

Simms frowned as he searched his memory for a man called Rodgers but drew a blank. He moved closer to Steel, hoping the distance between them and Falkner would add to them not being overheard. 'Steel, we don't have an agent Rodgers in our department,' Simms whispered, looking back to make sure Falkner was still behind them.

'No, he's with another section.'

'Do you know him?' Simms was surprised at Steel's knowledge of what was happening in the agency.

'No, but an old friend vouched for him,' Steel said with an almost nostalgic tone.

'What job was that?'

Steel said nothing in reply. Instead, he just smiled coldly and picked up the pace.

Simms knew what that meant; he had, after all, read all about Steel and his exploits or those they had filed, and that could only mean trouble.

Rodgers wasn't there to pick up Falkner to bring him in; he was there to finish what The Sentinel had started.

Simms imagined Falkner's flight would stop off somewhere remote, and there he would be killed or left to be killed. But, instead, Falkner was a loose end in someone's world now, which meant he was expendable.

Before leaving the parking lot, Steel had stopped and gazed at the massive airport. An enormous place with thousands of people rushing here and there. A perfect place for an unseen murder. An assassination without witnesses, a knife in the back or an unfortunate trip down the stairs. With the amount of armed police and security cameras, a sniper would be out of the question, which was at least one thing less to worry about.

Steel knew something was wrong the second the message said to meet inside, something that would never happen for the simple reasons of what was about to happen. It should have been an easy drive onto the tarmac and straight to the plane.

Simms stood next to Steel and looked at the mass of glass, concrete and, more worryingly, people.

'You know this is a trap, right?' Simms asked.

'Of course, it is. The question is, why?' Steel replied, knowing full well that as soon as they left the parking structure, the game was on. 'I need you to take Falkner to the meeting point.' His gaze was locked on the building, still assessing the possible threats inside.

'Where are you going to be?' Simms asked, staring at Steel worriedly.

'Here and there; all you have to do is follow my lead,' Steel said, pulling out his cell and attaching the headset to it. 'Keep your phone on,' he ordered as he saw his chance and walked forward quickly, disappearing from view in a large crowd of people passing by.

Simms looked over to Falkner, who was sweating bullets. In truth, he didn't know what to say to the man. Simms suspected Falkner had heard most of the conversation and was now wondering who would kill him first: The Sentinel or the agency?

'Come on, let's get you on that plane,' Simms said with an expressionless look.

Falkner nodded, then swallowed hard as Simms strolled out of the parking structure. Simms felt the sweat beading and crawling down his back. He was nervous, without a doubt, but he had to appear calm for Falkner's sake. If all the operations reports on Steel were to be believed, they were in good hands. All Falkner had to do was stay calm and follow Simms's lead, which in itself was a disaster waiting to happen.

Falkner was arrogant and self-absorbed, but he was a coward most of all. He'd probably been in too many situations where his end was nigh, or maybe he was just born that way. Whatever the case, he could blow apart the whole plan in seconds and get them all killed.

* * *

Simms walked casually through the crowds with Falkner by his side, like two guys picking up someone from the airport. Simms was strong and confident. Falkner was not. His head spun around as if trying to spot a threat.

'Stop looking around and drawing attention to yourself,' Simms said just loud enough for Falkner to hear.

Falkner composed himself and started to walk alongside Simms, trying his best not to snap his head to the side at every sound or person walking towards him.

Simms looked over to a sign pointing towards A13.

'It's that way, come on,' Simms said, dragging Falkner down a long corridor towards the meeting point.

He started to feel nervous again, he hadn't heard anything from Steel for a while, but he knew better than to break the radio silence. Simms and Falkner picked up the pace by weaving through crowds like a pair of Formula One drivers. Then Simms saw their contact. A tall, well-built man with a blonde flat-top and a government-issued suit. Simms stopped Falkner with a flat palm to his chest and forced him to sit on one of the benches that had a perfect view of the man.

'What do we do now?' Falkner asked, his eyes wide with fear, wiping his damp palms on his handkerchief.

'We wait until Steel gives the all-clear,' Simms replied, his eyes fixed on the contact.

'And what if he doesn't? What if they got him first?' Falkner asked in a panic, forcing his voice to an almost whisper.

'You said that you'd heard of Steel, stories-around-campfire stuff. Do you think they got *him* first?' Simms raised an eyebrow, unsure of those stories, but he could imagine them.

'No, you're right, but what if … ?' Falkner said in a low voice.

'Then we give him five minutes, and we split and find another way back,' Simms said reassuringly.

Steel moved quickly. He figured on a six-man team: one decoy, the contact, one spotter, most than likely in an elevated position, and four players. They would more than likely start at the four corners of the departure lounge and then converge. The spotter would use comms to give each man a movement order. He had to be the last to go. Any loss of communication and the teams would split. Steel saw the first target, a medium-sized man with a recognisable look about him. Even though he wore civilian clothes to blend in, he screamed Spec-Ops. Using a Special Operations crew for this was a smart move. They were trained to be invisible. Unfortunately for them, so was Steel.

The man wore black jeans, a striped shirt, and a dark-blue padded vest. His Hi-tec boots were also a giveaway—great boots but not the sort of thing you wore on a flight. He stood in the magazine section, pretending to read a magazine, the latest issue of *Guns Monthly*. How appropriate. Steel moved around him, keeping on his blindside.

There were too many people around to start a fight, so he had to be quick. Steel moved in carefully behind him and waited for the opportune moment. A distraction would have been perfect.

Steel picked up a magazine and rolled it tight, which formed a baton. A simple weapon, one that was effective in skilled hands. A quick blow to the back of the head where the spine met the skull would render the man unconscious for a while, enough time at least to find and dispose of the others. Steel didn't need to take them all out, just enough of them to cause enough confusion so he could get to his primary target: the contact.

Steel had picked his targets; the man in front of him and the small, stocky guy at the far end. Both lingered away from the exit, which was paramount if they had to get out quick.

Steel was counting on the over-watch to be focused on the contact and the surrounding area. Keeping constant contact with the other men would be all he needed to ensure no problems on the ground. That was fine if you were dealing with civilians, not if you were up against a former special-forces combatant.

Steel had joined the team to escape being chased by the SANTINI organisation, who had murdered his family; it seemed like the perfect hiding place. After all, he was supposed to be dead.

A friend and confidant had kept the family estate and business from going into liquidation, knowing Lord Steel would return when he was ready.

* * *

A drunken pair of men waiting for their flight provided a welcome distraction; their singing was quiet in tune but was enough to make everyone look in the wrong direction. Steel's blow was quick and laid out the man cold.

Steel slipped the magazine back onto the shelf and disappeared into the crowds. Soon, Steel was on the second target. The man stood away from the gathering crowd and leaned against a concrete post. As a security guard moved towards the confusion, a quick push to the man's head sent his domed skull crashing off the post.

'OK, Simms, move in slowly. See if you can move the contact away from that spot; use the café. It will be crowded enough,' Steel ordered.

'Roger that,' Simms replied, grabbing Falkner, who was wearing a look of disdain, and dragged him to his feet so the contact could see them.

'Stay close, and whatever happens, don't run off. The others will see you,' Simms warned Falkner, who mumbled his disapproval.

The contact spotted Simms and waved him over.

Simms stayed put and shook his head before gesturing the contact to follow them to the café, which stood on the opposite side near the main entrance.

'Just follow my lead,' Simms whispered to Falkner, who was getting tired of all the spy work.

Simms headed for the open café and found an empty table with four chairs. He and Falkner sat while they waited for the contact to join them. Across the way, the drama continued as screams for help sounded, signalling the unconscious bodies of the other men had been discovered.

'You Steel?' asked the bulky contact.

'No, the name's Simms; this is the package,' Simms said, nodding to the seated Falkner. 'What now?'

The man smiled and reached into his jacket pocket, and kept it there. Falkner's eyes widened, expecting the worst.

The noise from the crowds grew louder.

'He's got a gun,' a voice shouted. Everyone turned, including the contact, and watched as the armed security rushed towards the magazine outlet.

Rodgers face twisted into a look of annoyance as he figured out what was going on. Then, quickly, he turned back towards Simms, only to find the two men gone, and in Simms's chair sat Steel.

'Where are they?' asked Rodgers, pulling out his silenced 9mm and slipping it under the table.

'Tahiti probably, but then I hear that Croatia is nice this time of year,' Steel joked, leaning forwards as if to keep the conversation private.

'I won't ask again. Where are they?'

But Steel just smiled again and looked at his watch.

'Boarding a plane around now, if they got there, OK.'

Rodgers glared at Steel.

'What plane?' Rodgers demanded, his blood boiling, unaware of Steel loosely slipping a tie he'd taken from a stand during the commotion over the man's hands.

'Why, yours, of course.' Steel's smile faded as he grabbed the tie and pulled it towards himself with great force.

Rodger's face smashed against the hardwood table, knocking him out cold.

As people looked around to see what was happening, they saw Rodgers sitting alone with his head resting on the table's polished wood. His weapon was missing, but the tie remained over his hands and was tied to the table leg.

Steel walked out of the airport and headed for the multi-story parking lot. Even though things had gone well, he worried. Steel took out his phone and pressed the speed-dial icon for Simms's cell. It rang for a brief time before Simms picked up, his voice laboured as if he had been running.

'Are you at the plane?' Steel asked, hopeful.

'Yes, just about to load Falkner on now. I'll meet you at the car in about five minutes,' Simms yelled over the noise of the turbines.

'No, I want you on that plane with Falkner,' Steel said, slotting the tiny bit of card from the barrier into the paying terminal.

'But—'

'I need you to deliver Falkner to Stanton personally—no one else, not even Brena,' Steel ordered.

'You think whoever sent those clowns works for the agency?' Simms asked in realisation.

'I'd count on it. You and Stanton are the only ones I trust,' Steel said, paying for his exit from the structure. 'Oh, and Simms?'

'Yeah?' Simms kept an eye on Falkner as he boarded the Learjet.

'Watch your arse.'

* * *

The Sentinel sat at the desk. The light from the monitors was the only illumination in the darkened room. The only sound was whirring from the desktop computers' fans. So, The Sentinel just sat and observed the movements of the next victim. The man didn't seem like much, but his story was anything but.

Reaching forward, The Sentinel picked up the can of soda and took a mouthful before placing it back down and returning to the silent movie. The digital clock next to one of the monitors said it was nearly eight in the evening, but there had been no sign of Steel or the others.

Gloved fingers impatiently tapped the arm of the office chair. Was something wrong?

The tapping stopped as The Sentinel leant forwards. Eager eyes stared at a single monitor that showed a hotel front.

The Sentinel had predicted Steel would go for this particular hotel because it was the only hotel within walking distance of the museum. Not that Steel was easy to predict. However, this time the man wasn't trying to hide. On the contrary, it was as if he wanted to make it easy for The Sentinel to find him.

It was now a game between them, a puzzle. The Sentinel leant back in the chair and began to rock back and forth. Soon, The Sentinel would have to go; the next name on the list would need the same attention, but first, the next postcard would have to be sent to the CIA.

The Sentinel turned to the other monitors and carried on with research. This one would require a unique demise, fitting for someone as evil as this one. The Sentinel opened a giant sketch pad with several drawn blueprints for an exclusive device.

The Sentinel turned several pages until the perfect choice was found. It was a crude scribble that only The Sentinel understood. Finally, The Sentinel stood, walked over to a workbench, and got started.

* * *

The sun had set over Amsterdam, leaving cloudless, star-filled heavens. The wind had died down to a gentle chilly breeze. Steel had driven to the city of Amsterdam, happy in the knowledge both Simms and Falkner were safe.

Steel thought back on his decision to use that airport instead of Hannover. Steel knew that Sabine Boese would have had photos out to all airports and train stations in Germany. She was tenacious, for sure.

The last thing Steel needed was her interference, and that was precisely what it would have been. Steel knew, for her, it was about the job, not the victims. He also knew Sabine's only reason for being on the case was getting her name in the press and a foot closer to that top position.

It was apparent to Steel that she would figure out where he was, but it would be too late by that time. Simms and Falkner would be long gone.

The web search for a hotel revealed one within walking distance of the Rijksmuseum. A little pricey, but then why should he rough it? A beautiful place with rear hotel parking and comfortable rooms that looked as expensive as their listed rental prices.

Steel's cover was a rich guy on vacation, so this hotel ticked all the boxes.

He parked in the nearby lot and headed for the entrance. The colossal structure was a mix of old and new: the grandeur of a 1900s building and the modernistic glass framework of the ceiling. The furniture was black and chrome, giving the whole place a light and dark contrast that fitted the luxurious package.

Steel approached a long black reception desk; brass reception bells of different sizes sat in a glass display case in one corner. 'A nice touch,' Steel thought as he passed them and stood before a tall brunette with tanned skin, eyes like a tropical ocean, and short black hair with scarlet-red highlights.

The receptionist gave a glossy red smile, revealing pearly-white teeth.

'Good afternoon. I believe you have a reservation for John Steel?' he said, returning the woman's smile.

'*Einen Moment, bitte*,' she replied, forcing her gaze away from Steel and down to the computer. 'Yes, Mr Steel, we have you for five nights in the Penthouse Suite.' She raised an eyebrow as her gaze fell back onto his broad-shouldered frame.

Steel gave her his passport, which she photocopied and returned to him, along with his key card. She gave him directions to the lifts and explained meal timings and about the WI-FI. Steel took it in, along with mental measurements of the receptionist. She wore the raven-black uniform like a catwalk model and filled it in just the right places.

The suite was full of windows and the same styled black furniture as the lobby. Light-coloured wood covered the floors, and walls made of glass gave the place an open feel. Polished sandstone flooring and walls made the bathroom appear light and required little in the way of illumination during the day. The hotel was nothing short of magnificent, to be sure. Steel was sorry he wasn't there to enjoy it.

Steel wandered around the suite, checking the wardrobes and the texture of the bathrobes. As he made his way into the bathroom, his eye caught a longing glimpse of the shower. But he didn't have time. Realising he had no clothes apart from what he stood in, Steel knew he needed to go shopping.

Looking at his watch, Steel saw it was five o'clock, not much time before everything closed for the day; one hour to find new clothes. He smiled, picked up the house phone, and waited for someone to pick it up.

'Concierge, please.' Steel said after hearing the receptionist's dulcet voice.

* * *

Trish had gone back to her home in the small town of Vienna. It was a grey-tiled roof bungalow with bare-brick walls and white-painted timber. She'd parked her Cadillac SUV in the driveway and headed towards the glossy white door with a brass door knocker.

It was late, and she was tired. Trish had heard that Simms was bringing back Falkner on the Learjet. News that had somehow upset Brena.

Trish slid the door key into the slot and unlocked the triple-turn lock. Inside was dark, with a faint smell of lavender in the air. She slid her hand to the side and up the wall until she felt the light switch, and with a gentle click, the sitting room was illuminated.

It was a twenty-by-twenty beige-walled room with an open-plan kitchen. Varnished wood slats zigzagged along the floor and down the hallway. She would have preferred carpet, but her beloved black-and-white cat left clumps of unwanted fur all over anything.

Dragging her suitcase inside, Trish shut the door behind her and pulled on the door chain before putting the triple lock back on. It was a safe enough neighbourhood, and she was armed, but why invite trouble, she always thought.

What she wanted was a shower, a glass of red, and to sleep until Christmas. The past couple of days had been insane, and she still had no idea why Stanton had brought in this Steel guy. Sure, he'd been some hot shit back in the day, but what was he now? NYPD? Not exactly a step up by any means.

As she went, she ripped off her clothes as if they were covered in acid, letting them fall to the floor. Finally, she stood in her kitchen, wearing nothing but her underwear, and undid the screw cap on the wine. She took a clean wine glass from the dishwasher and filled it with cheap Merlot. She took a small mouthful and then headed to the bathroom.

The sound of her bare feet pattered on the wooden floor as she went. She was eager to feel the cleansing water on her skin. She took another sip from the glass as she turned on the water and let it run, allowing for the steam to build up.

Trish liked the feel of the heat on her skin.

Placing the wine glass next to the basin and toothbrush holder, she stripped her underwear and opened the hard plastic door to the cabinet, releasing a vaporous cloud of steam that filled the small bathroom. Trish felt the hard, scolding spray of water against her skin upon stepping inside. For her, it was soothing, therapeutic even. She took the bar of milky soap and rubbed it onto her body until it produced a creamy-white lather that covered her pink skin.

Trish tilted her head back, letting the water cascade over her head and flow through her hair. She felt happy and content as the lather washed from her body.

Trish rested her back against the white-tiled wall and thought of nothing. Suddenly, her eyes opened, and she jumped out of the spray. Trish had that uneasy feeling that she wasn't alone. Someone was in the house with her. But she'd locked the door and put the chain on … hadn't she?

Trish stepped out of the shower but kept the water running, hoping the noise would make the intruder think she was still in the shower.

Taking the fluffy pink bathrobe from the back of the door, she slipped it on and slowly moved out of the bathroom. She needed to get to her bedroom and the backup Glock 42 compact pistol. The hollow point rounds would make sure the perpetrator went down.

Trish moved silently across the floor, using a towel to cover the sound of her wet feet. Even though she could feel her heart slam against her chest, Trish was calm. All her training and years of fieldwork kept her in control.

At that moment, she didn't have time to feel scared. That would come later. Trish reached the bedroom; the door was partially open but not enough to see inside. Slowly, she nudged the door open with her foot, inching it open until she had a clear view inside.

Everything seemed as if she had left it. The furniture appeared to be untouched, and the covers lay undisturbed on the box-spring double bed.

Trish moved in slowly. She was making sure her back was to the wall, preventing anyone from coming up from behind. She could feel the veins in her neck start to pulse with every heartbeat.

Reaching the bedside drawer, she began to slide it open, only to find the weapon missing. Now, fear took hold of her. Trish's only other gun was on the couch in the sitting room, and the other was in the hands of the intruder.

A sudden breeze rushed past her. Trish froze at the quick waft of air. The intruder had gotten in through a window and left it open, possibly for a quick exit, after doing whatever they were there to do.

She moved into the bedroom and shut the door before locking it behind her. Her only hope was to place a barricade between her and them, and the door would do just fine for now. Rushing over to the other side of the bed, Trish picked up the house phone. The lack of a dial tone meant the line had been cut.

She looked back towards the door, her eyes wide and expectant.

Trish cursed herself for being in such a rush to get undressed and leaving her clothes in the sitting room. Usually, everything would be folded and placed on the armchair in the bedroom corner. The first time she'd ever broken that routine, and it had bitten her in the ass.

A sound of squeaking metal caused Trish to look over at the door, just in time to see the door handle slowly turn back and forth as the intruder tried the door.

'Just so you know, I've called the police,' she bluffed, hoping to catch the intruder off guard and possibly scare him off. 'They'll be here soon.' Trish rolled her eyes at the attempt, realising whoever was there would know she'd had no phone to make that call. But she had to try something.

The door handle stopped moving. Trish moved slowly towards the door, hoping to catch the sound of footsteps walking away and down the corridor, but she heard nothing. Only the sound of her heartbeat in her ears.

Nervously, she stretched a sweaty palm towards the door handle. She didn't know if the intruder was gone, but she had to find out. She was a CIA agent, not some scared little girl. She'd fought off more significant threats.

Trish composed herself and took a deep breath before unlocking the door and slowly opening it. As the door cracked open, a great force swung it fully open. Trish's eyes widened as she saw the person in front of her.

A look crossed her face. It was a mix of terror and confusion.

'You? What are *you* doing here? I thought that you were—'

Trish's sentence was cut short by a forceful shove to the sternum. She fell back, and the bedroom door slammed shut behind them.

Chapter 21

Steel felt tired, even after he'd gotten around three hours of sleep. But, of course, that was before the nightmares woke him. Still, the memories from the mall explosion continued to haunt him as if his consciousness were trying to tell him something. Steel almost missed his old nightmare. At least there, he could see his beloved Helen again.

Steel changed into the new onyx-black suit he had bought the night before; the old garments had gone to the laundry in the hope of removing the smell of Falkner's burning apartment. Steel sat down to breakfast at the dining table designed to seat eight. He took the breakfast items off the polished brass trolley and laid them out. He poured himself a cup of black coffee, placed down a file he had made on The Sentinel, and spread out the contents. Steel had work to do and not much time.

Stanton had sent Steel an image of the new postcard via a download to his cell phone. Two photographs: one of the front and one of the rear. The address was the same, less for the precinct. This time it was blank. Steel looked at it with a puzzled look.

Was The Sentinel stepping up the game and making the clues harder? Or was it a simple case of 'I get there when I get there?

Steel knew the next clue was at the museum, but the time was frustrating. He took out his phone and looked up the museum on an internet map search. Gauging by the entrance, Steel figured the picture was taken from the south of the building. He then checked at what time sunrise and sunset were. He smiled and sipped coffee.

Steel knew by looking at the postcard—judging by the shadows made by the lampposts and the people—it was possibly around noon.

It was half six in the morning. Five hours to do reconnaissance on the museum. Entrances, exits, where CCTV cameras were, nearest subway. Nearby parking and public transport. Steel needed to know every means of escape that The Sentinel could use.

After breakfast, Steel took his time getting to the museum, making the most of the bright sunshine that was just starting to give off warmth. People on bikes travelled here and there, and dog walkers went about their daily routine. The volume of pedestrian and road traffic was still low, but then it was seven in the morning, and the rush had not yet started. Steel imagined the town centre was chaos about now as people headed off to their jobs.

But Steel was too busy enjoying the calm of the morning to worry about the city. At that moment, he had time and a peaceful walk to allow him to think and plan.

* * *

Steel stood on Museumstraat, a busy walkway of zigzagged paving stones filled with tourists and cyclists. At the end of this stood the magnificent red-brick colossus—the Rijksmuseum. Built-in the

1800s and filled with treasures beyond belief... and now the first clue to stopping a murder. Behind him were the electric whirs of trams as they hurried by, carrying commuters to and from the city. Steel looked around, pretending to be a tourist, which wasn't far from the truth. He used his cell phone to take pictures of nearby attractions and security cameras.

Steel moved around, acting like a tourist should, even to the point of making a quick stop at a nearby café and grabbing a coffee-to-go before heading for the museum entrance. He paid the entrance fee, finished the small coffee, and headed to the museum.

Inside, a spectacular glass roof of the atrium provided illumination, showing off the red brick of the walls and the white marble of the floor. A medley of old and new, coming together in a unity of splendour. Rooms filled with artwork from Rembrandt and Van Gogh hung on dark walls to make the vibrant colours stand out.

Steel checked the image of the postcard on his cell again. There didn't seem to be anything out of the ordinary about it. Not like the previous ones that screamed out, 'I'm here!' But there was something slightly off about it that Steel couldn't quite work out. Apart from being in black and white, while the others were in colour, nothing stood out.

As Steel moved further inside, he noticed a board with pictures and drawings of what the museum used to look like when it first opened.

He leant forwards with interest. And then he saw it, the same image as what he had viewed on his phone. It was a picture of the museum before the refurbishment. Steel looked around, excited. The first clue.

Steel spotted a tour guide speaking to her group and hurried towards her.

'Excuse me, I have a question,' Steel said, interrupting the woman halfway through her sentence.

The woman scowled at the interruption and turned towards Steel. Her eyes changed from thin slits to full gazes. Her brown eyes grew large, and her frown turned into a bite of the bottom lip.

'Sorry to bother you, but is there an old part of the building still intact?'

The guide put on her tortoiseshell-rimmed glasses and flicked her long brown hair. 'Oh, that's alright,' the woman said with an alluring smile while straightening her petrol-coloured skirt suit. 'How can I help?'

'During the refurbishment, did any of the original rooms remain as it was before?'

The guide thought for a moment and looked around as if searching for something. 'Possibly the Renaissance exhibit,' she finally said, turning back to face Steel with dreamy eyes. But he had gone.

Steel's quick thank you had been drowned out by the noise of the crowd. The woman looked around, trying to catch a glimpse of where he had gone. Her heart fluttered at the romantic-novel situation of it. Then, realising the tour group was staring at her, she coughed and straightened and resumed talking to her tourists.

Steel made his way through the crowds of people and groups of schoolchildren. He was hoping his hunch was correct, but even then, he had no idea what he was looking for.

The last time he had been lucky because they had received the postcard directly and not through the mail. Perhaps that was why there was no time on this one; The Sentinel had no idea when he or Steel would get there.

Either way, Steel was early.

He needed to know the layout of possible entry and exit points where the killer could come and go. Steel was there alone, just the way he liked it. Partners got in the way, a distraction, a tool the bad guy could use against you.

Steel made his way through the different exhibits laid out in chronological order. Works of art from centuries past hung in gold frames, and trinkets lay behind glass cases. Steel headed to the first floor and then the second. He needed to know what was on every level. How many stairwells and elevators, security cameras, and even toilets as there was a no better place to duck into and hide.

As Steel moved through, he heard one of the guides direct his group to a painting at the end of one room.

'And over here, we have *The Night Watch* by the master, Rembrandt.' The guide walked over to the enormous painting with the Civic Militia guard members. He wore a brown suit with a light-blue shirt and a red paisley bowtie. Steel noticed how passionately the man spoke about each subject, but Steel did not need history lessons; he'd had enough of those at Oxford.

Steel waited until the group moved away, and then he moved closer to the painting. There was something about the picture that intrigued Steel. *The Night Watch* was about striking back for justice and taking up arms to fight for what was right. And if Steel was correct, this was where he had to be at twelve.

It was now half-past nine; he had time to kill. He needed coffee and a place with good cell reception.

Chapter 22

The Sentinel sat in a darkened room with only the desk lamp and computer monitors to illuminate the apartment. The Sentinel had to hold up the illusion nobody was there. The family would be away on vacation for at least another week.

The Sentinel had set up a smaller room with no view from the busy street below. This way, the rest of the house could remain with open curtains. Of course, the noise neighbour from across the road would spot anything amiss. But that was just one of the things The Sentinel had considered when doing recon on the apartment.

The monitors showed the apartment of the dark-haired man and his expensive lifestyle. He hadn't left his abode for hours.

The Sentinel picked up a bottle of water and took a mouthful. Staring at monitors for a length of time could dehydrate you … as The Sentinel had learned a while back and paid dearly for due to massive headaches.

The dark-haired man sat at his computer, rocking back and forth, and he spoke on the house phone. The Sentinel thought the caller must have been a woman due to the man's body language. He was laughing and joking in between, taking mouthfuls of the whiskey in a crystal glass in his hand.

The Sentinel made a note on the A4 pad, circled it as if the detail was necessary, then took another mouthful of water and rocked happily in the office chair.

The man on the monitor went to take another drink, but something stopped him. He froze for a second before sitting bolt upright. He'd seen something on the television.

The Sentinel slowly sat up.

Something was wrong. Something had spooked the man.

Suddenly, The Sentinel leant forwards and began to check all the camera angles to see what the man was watching. Then, The Sentinel saw it in a reflection from a picture frame. The man had the local news on television. Hurriedly, The Sentinel searched the internet for the same broadcast. It had been a special report on the bombing in Berlin and how a man called Falkner was supposedly inside when it exploded.

A possible gas leak had been the initial story, but the counter-terrorist police unit that stood in the background advised otherwise.

The Sentinel leant back and looked on as the man began to panic.

Jotting something on the pad, The Sentinel underlined it several times.

Plan B.

* * *

Steel sat in the museum's café and sipped his cup of Coffee American. The open-air picnic ground was getting full, mostly with school kids on day trips. Steel looked at his watch. It was quarter-to-twelve. He'd spent the rest of the time walking around the museum, checking the escape routes the killer might take after dropping off the next clue. But he had to admit, choosing such an enclosed venue to stage the drop-off was ballsy … or just plain psychotic.

The museum had minimal exit points, possibly to deter thieves. Because of this, the killer would have to get past security at the exit. He would also have to avoid all cameras and, most of all, avoid being seen by Steel.

Steel got up and made his way back to the painting. He wanted to get a good vantage point, away from the painting, to see who dropped the postcard. He found a good vantage point some ten feet away, near the entrance to the Rembrandt exhibit. It was a perfectly straight line of sight to the dropoff point. But, of course, that was only if Steel was correct about it all.

Steel was working on a hunch. He'd seen everything else in the museum, and this was the only piece of art that felt right, the painting called *The Night Watch*. Steel felt it was a fitting name for what he was seeking.

Groups of people came and went, including the several school tours he had seen. Steel had an idea in his head about what kind of person The Sentinel might be. Male, in his late thirties. A loner, but someone who would blend in. Average height and build, possibly dressed in black with something that covered the face, like a hat, hoody or sunglasses. Steel smiled as he realised he had just profiled himself. Then a shiver ran down his spine at the thought of the similarities.

Another group of school children went past with four teachers in tow to keep the eight-year-olds in check. Finally, one male teacher and three attractive colleagues herded the kids along, telling them not to touch anything.

Steel smiled at the group as they moved towards the colossal masterpiece at the end. His mischievous eyes checked out the teachers. The two blondes and long-haired brunette were in their twenties with that girl-next-door look about them.

Steel shook off his indecent thoughts and got back to looking for his mark. He glanced at his watch; it was dead on noon, and no sign of the killer. He convinced himself to wait another ten minutes, just in case. After all, no specific time had been given.

John Steel used the artwork as an excuse to move slowly down the isles. But he knew he had to keep moving, or he would look suspicious, not only to the other people but security. The last thing he needed was to get grabbed and questioned while the killer made his move.

'Ten more minutes, and then I'm out of here,' Steel promised himself, getting sick of the games this killer was playing.

* * *

The ten minutes had gone, and then some. It was nearly a quarter past when Steel decided to call it a day. As he turned to leave, he saw a man in a grey hoody and black leather jacket. Black sunglasses hid his eyes.

Suddenly, Steel got that gut feeling and turned to follow the man who fitted his profile of the killer. The man walked towards the picture and stopped. His hands slid into his pockets while he stood and looked at the masterpiece. Almost as if he was waiting for something … or someone.

He waited for a moment on the off chance he wasn't who Steel thought he was. The man took out a cell phone from his pocket and checked a message before returning the device to the outside zippered pocket. Steel watched the man as he walked away. He moved as if he was disappointed by something.

Steel waited until the man had gone, then sauntered towards the painting as if he was just another tourist taking in art. As he walked up to the painting of *The Night Watch*, he noticed something on the ground in the alcove where the painting hung. So, he walked up and knelt down and found a postcard.

Steel took out a handkerchief from his pocket and picked it up. On the front was a picture of Fifth Avenue in New York. But all the flags had been changed to a red lion on a gold background. Steel turned it over and read what The Sentinel had written. 'Raindrops will consume the red lion, but the sins cannot be measured, but are seen through the eyes of false. John Steel 2330 Precinct.'

Steel's brow creased as he read it. Another riddle, another time set. He looked at his watch again. It was twelve-thirty, which gave him eleven hours to find the next victim.

Steel slid the postcard into a self-sealing plastic bag he'd brought with him, just in case it was required. But, first, he'd have to make a copy and send the original back to Langley via the American Embassy.

As he left the museum, Steel wondered when the killer had left the postcard.

* * *

The morning weather over Virginia was bright, with a few clouds drifting across a deep purple backdrop. A fresh westerly breeze had a chill to it. Still, the weathergirl had promised a beautiful day with temperatures into the high fifties.

Brena had gotten in early. He'd picked up a coffee and a Danish on the way. Breakfast on the go was all he could afford to have at this stage in the game. So, Brena had gotten home around one in the morning, slept very little, and was up at four. Stanton had sent him a message that Steel had sent another postcard via the US Embassy in Amsterdam.

Brena was both angry and excited. Angry because he should have been sent to Amsterdam, not Steel. After all, Steel had gotten a member of his team killed. However, the thought of a new clue brought him down to a simmer, not a boil.

* * *

Brena swiped in at the security desk and passed through the metal detector. He was bored with the routine but was simultaneously glad to have it in place. Brena expected his team to be there already, working hard on cracking the new code. But he knew they would have gotten the same text at the same time he had. Brena was purposely a couple of minutes late; he loved walking into the room and saying, 'Right, what we got?' The feeling of power as he walked in was intoxicating to him.

Brena headed into the war room that held his team and the murder boards Stanton had shown to Steel. A fourth board was made up of a map of Amsterdam, the postcard, and at the bottom was a thick black line for the timeline.

The first timing was twelve o'clock when Steel had gotten the postcard; the last was twenty-three-thirty. The time The Sentinel had given.

'Right, what we got, people?' Brena asked with an authoritative voice.

Dorson turned around and shot Brena a distasteful look.

'You're late, twenty minutes late,' Dorson said, not knowing what was worse, working with Brena or him thinking he was section chief and he could saunter in and ask for updates like that.

'I was stuck in traffic, not that is your concern. Agent Dorson,' Brena said scornfully.

Dorson, like Trish, had gotten into Langley at the same time as Brena. For Dorson, Brena was just like the rest of them; the only difference was his mind. Sure, the old man put him in charge a few times, but Dorson was sure that was to shut him up.

'So, any ideas yet?' Brena barked, ignoring Dorson.

'Forensics got nothing, no surprise there. We know our boy is careful. The new picture is a puzzler, though. The flags on the postcard don't represent any country. However, we are still looking at other options,' said Agent Rachel Turner.

A fresh face was brought in to pick up Kitty's slack. She was an average-looking woman with short mousey hair, dull brown eyes, and a dull black suit.

'And Steel's location?' Brena asked with his hands on his hips; as if trying to show some sort of authority.

'He said he was going to check out a book from the library,' she replied and shrugged.

Dorson saw the confusion in Brena's eyes and smiled to himself.

Brena moved to the new board and began to glide his fingers across the map, mumbling to himself.

Dorson realised he was calculating Steel's next move instead of the killer's. This made Dorson nervous because Brena was making this personal, and he was coming undone. Their jobs were to help find the next victim and connect them. Steel was in the field alone while Simms had brought Falkner back on a stolen jet. No doubt a stunt that would go down in Steel's history files.

'I'm off to see the old man. Let me know when you have something,' Brena said with a nod. Brena headed out the door. He didn't need to be there for the footwork. That was their job.

As Brena left, Dorson looked around with a puzzled look on his face.

'What's wrong?' asked Rachel, who followed his gaze around the room.

'Brena is twenty minutes late, and Trish isn't here. He's never this late, and she never takes off, especially for cases like this.' Dorson did another check, just in case he was mistaken and Trish was sitting in a corner somewhere.

'Maybe she is on special assignment for Brena,' Rachel suggested, trying to reassure Dorson.

But Dorson could feel something was wrong, and he feared the worst for Trish.

Standing, he pulled his jacket from the back of his chair and slipped it on.

'Where are you going?' Rachel asked, surprised that he would abandon them.

'Need a quick smoke. Something tells me we won't get a break for a while,' Dorson lied. He made his way out the door and turned left, not right. He made his way to Brena's office, which he shared with Trish and Simms.

* * *

Brena placed the paper coffee cup down next to the Danish on his desk before easing himself down in his leather chair. He wore a broad grin, like a child who'd just won a bowl full of candy. Brena was pleased with himself; things were starting to happen, and they were all good. For him, anyway.

Brena picked up the pastry and took a bite. His perfect teeth sunk into the crusty outer shell and the soft centre. Brena rocked back and forth in his chair, contemplating his next move before taking a mouthful of hot coffee to wash down the Danish.

He picked up the receiver of his desk phone and dialled a number written down on a Post-it. Brena coughed as a flake of pastry clung to the back of his throat. He took another mouthful of coffee while the sound of ringing emitted from the handset.

Suddenly, a woman's voice answered with a simple, 'Yes?'

'It's Brena. I know where Steel is, and I know who he's after next.'

Dorson stood outside Brena's office, his back cemented to the wall, his ear close to the door. His mouth fell open in a gasp. Who was he speaking to, and had it anything to do with Trish … or worse … Kitty?

Chapter 23

An easterly wind brought dark, looming clouds and the chance for a downpour at one o'clock. People had already started rushing about in the streets, searching for a place to have lunch in the Dutch capital. Steel had grabbed a couple of Dutch frikandel and french fries, or *Pommes Frites*. He'd first experienced the strange-tasting sausage in Bosnia at Split North Port, a small base for soldiers to wait for their flights.

Steel headed for a web café. He needed a computer and fast. The hotel was too far away to head back to. Besides, he needed to be close to the city when he got a break. Sure, he had plenty of time. The Sentinel had said twenty-three-thirty.

Steel found a place next to a coffee shop and a fast-food place. Steel walked in and looked around for a free machine. He smiled as one became available but died as a spotty kid with strawberry-blonde hair and a face full of piercings took the slot. Steel said nothing. He just waited and hoped the next freed-up computer was close to him.

Steel looked at his watch impatiently and looked around for more empty seats. That's when he saw the kid who had taken the empty slot from him. The kid was talking to a girl who was on the next computer. However, the chair thief wasn't using the computer. He was just sitting there chatting with a girl who looked around nervously as if trying to catch someone's eye to help her. Steel walked up to the owner, paid for his time, and threw in a bit of extra.

'It's too much,' said the man behind the counter, waving the hundred euro bill.

'It's for any damages,' Steel replied, marching over to the kid, who was laughing and joking, trying to make a move on the girl. But he only succeeded in making her feel uncomfortable.

'Damages … what damages?' the short man asked, standing and looking at the kid taking up the computer slot. 'Oh, dear.' He sat back down, hoping for not too much destruction.

'Excuse me, can I get to this machine? It's important,' Steel said calmly.

The kid spun around in the chair, gave Steel a once-over, sucked his teeth, and spun back around.

'Hey, kid, you're blocking the computer. Do you mind?' Steel asked, his voice slightly raised, the knuckles of his clenched fists white.

'I'm busy, fuck off, and drink some tea, English prick,' the kid laughed and produced a flick-blade.

Steel grabbed the kid's wrist and twisted it, then forced the kid backwards, so his head was on the desk. Next, Steel grabbed the knife and pinned the whelp to the desk. The blade dug deep through the kid's earlobe and into the compressed wood of the workspace, holding the kid down.

'If you move, it's going to hurt. So, be a good lad, stay still, and shut up,' Steel said calmly.

At first, people moved away but then started taking photos with their cell phones. Steel ignored the screams from the impaled youth and began to do web searches on the flag in the postcard. The owner brought over cups of coffee for Steel and the girl, who was in her mid-twenties. She smiled at the man and placed her attention on her knight in the black suit.

'Thank you,' she said in a sweet whisper of a voice. Her large blue eyes and small pouting mouth had that Betty Boop look. Long golden locks framed her blushing face and shoulders.

'You're welcome. Something tells me it's not the first time he has hit on you,' Steel said, blowing on the coffee and taking a sip.

'No, he's always in here. If it's not me, then it's another girl. But no one will touch him; he is a pig.'

Steel smiled and got back to his search. I hardly knew where to start at first.

'What a strange postcard,' the girl said with a curious tone.

'Yes, a friend sent it to me; he likes to send me pictures, and I have to figure them out,' Steel said, a tiny white lie.

'So, what does this one mean?' she asked, excited.

'I'm not sure; I just have to figure out what this flag is,' Steel admitted, shrugging as the search gave him lots of information, but none of which he was looking for.

'That is the crest for ours for … what do you call them? Um … counts, that is it. Like Dracula,' she said in broken English, grinning broadly.

Steel raised an eyebrow at the revelation.

'So, tell me …?' Steel paused as if silently requesting her name.

'Anna, my name is Anna,' she said.

'So, tell me, Anna, what's Dutch for Count?' Steel asked curiously.

'It's *Graaf.* Why?' she said with a confused look on her face.

Steel leaned over, kissed the girl on the forehead, and thanked her before hurrying out.

Anna sat dazed. Suddenly, a huge smile came over her face, and she melted back into her seat.

Steel rushed along the street. Pulling his cell phone from his jacket pocket, he pressed the speed-dial for Stanton. He heard the rings that emitted from the device as he gazed at his watch; it would be around seven in the morning in the States. The rings continued. After a while, Steel stopped and looked around. He was alone in a strange city with no backup.

A smile crossed Steel's face. But that's how he preferred to be: alone. He placed the cell phone back in his pocket. Steel knew who he was after. A low-life smuggler called Thomas Graaf. He could arrange transport for anyone and anything—for a price, of course. The agency had used him once or twice, that was until they found out he was part of a human trafficking ring, especially kids to predators.

Steel had never met the man, nor did he particularly wish to, let alone save the man's life. But that was the game, and to find the answers, Steel had to play.

Stanton stepped out of the shower. A white towel straining at his waist and another he used to dry off his hair. He'd gone home to get something decent to eat and a much-needed shower to wash off the days of sleeping in his office. The ripe smell coming from his shirts had signalled the need for a quick break from the case. Besides, there was nothing he could do at the moment. There were good people on the case doing research, and Steel was in the field.

Stanton sat on the kingsize bed and took the towel from his head. The television was on the news channel. A report from Berlin was on. The reporter was coving the explosion at Falkner's apartment. There were still crowds of people taking photographs, using cameras and cell phones.

'Goddamn civis,' Stanton growled under his breath, cursing the people as they laughed and took selfies. As if the death of another human being was a joke. If it was up to him, he'd lock them all up.

The reporter, Emily Josh, couldn't give much information, less for the owner's name. She said that the investigation was ongoing and more details were to follow. This usually meant the cops had politely told them to fuck off. Stanton smiled to himself. It was precisely what he would have done if he'd been there.

Suddenly, ding-ding-ding from Stanton's cell let him know he had a missed call. He picked it up and swore out loud for his bad timing. The alert told him that Steel had tried to call several times, the last one being as he was walking out of the bathroom. Quickly, Stanton checked his messages and email, seeing if Steel had left anything. Nothing in either. Tapping the cell on his chin, Stanton thought hard. He knew Steel wouldn't contact Brena unless there was something Steel couldn't handle, which was unlikely to ever happen.

Steel's other option: go it alone and give a briefing later. Steel had done it before.

Stanton placed down the cell phone, then headed for the drinks cabinet to pour a generous two fingers of whiskey. As he tilted the mouth of the bottle over the glass, he stopped. Furious with himself, Stanton slammed down the bottle and screwed the cap back on.

'No, you dumb bastard, not now.' Cursing himself at his weakness. Too often, he had hit the bottle when things had gotten rough. And the past couple of years, they had been rough. His wife's battle with cancer had finally taken its toll, and he sought refuge in the bottle. Stanton's kids were both in their twenties and had left home years ago, but his demise drove them further away, and now the odd phone call had turned to silence. As he raised a shaking hand, Stanton knew things had to change. Stanton gritted his teeth and made a fist out of the trembling hand, gathering all of his strength and will.

* * *

Stanton changed into a slate-grey suit and shined his shoes. Of course, he had to bring his A-game. Steel was relying on it, on him. Simms was on the way back with Falkner, and it was up to Stanton to put the man in a room and get whatever information he could out of the man.

Stanton still had no idea why the backup team didn't make it back with Simms, but that could wait. For now, he had to get back to the office and do some work instead of sitting on his hands and letting Brena run the show. Stanton knew that everyone respected him, but the fear had gone. Years before he crawled into the bottle, people trembled at the very mention of his name. Now, it was just a curious *bossman* feeling. It was time the old Stanton returned.

* * *

The weather over Amsterdam had broken. Torrents of rain came down from angry black clouds that had been hurried along by a fierce easterly wind. Steel had made it inside an Irish bar not too far from the museum. A traditional-looking place with outside seating and an authentic Irish wood-and-stone bar inside. The place itself was actually owned by an Irishman called Patrick Callaghan. He was a bruiser of a man with fiery red hair.

He had made a few enemies back in his home country, which had forced him to relocate. Now, Callaghan was a respectable businessman and pub owner, or as respectable as the old fox could ever be. At least, that was what people thought. But, in fact, he was still doing deals of questionable legality on the side.

He had met the man some time ago when Steel was in the British Army stationed in Ireland on a six-month tour in Armar. Steel's company had arrested him doing gun-running for some less than savoury people. But, of course, money talked, and Patrick walked. Steel had kept track of Callaghan, just in case, he became useful. That was until 1996, when the cease-fire was called, and Callaghan became a liability to his once so-called friends.

Steel approached Callaghan via a colleague and offered him a new life in Europe. All he had to do was be prepared to be Steel's man in whichever region Callaghan settled. Now, it was time to collect.

Steel walked into the bar and looked around. The place was packed, even at two in the afternoon. He ambled up to the bar and found a gap next to a couple of Dutch bikers, possibly part of a chapter looking at doing some dealings. The two huge men, who wore denim and sleeveless biker jackets with their colours sewn onto the backs, turned and looked at Steel and grunted disapprovingly.

'We don't like your kind here,' said the bigger one with a shaven head and tattoos all over his arms and parts of his head.

'You mean devastatingly handsome with a full head of hair?' Steel joked sarcastically.

The man gave Steel an angry look and stood, making his friend react in kind.

'Oh, lads, I don't think you want to pick a fight with Mr Steel here,' said a familiar voice.

'Why's that? The man shouldn't be here,' said the biker.

'For two very good reasons. One, he is ex-SAS and Navy Seal, which makes him as nuts as anyone here and two, if it wasn't for this British gent here, I wouldn't be here now, tellin' you all this. So, leave the man alone and let me buy the bastard a drink,' Callaghan said with a yell, which was followed by the rest of the bar letting out a resounding roar.

'Oh, great,' Steel said, rolling his eyes behind his sunglasses. 'Drinking time.'

The giant Irishman placed down two whiskey glasses and half-filled them with Irish whiskey.

'Too old times and the hope they don't come back to bite you in the arse,' Callaghan toasted.

Steel raised his glass, and the two men downed their drinks in one gulp. Both men winced as the alcohol hit home. Callaghan roared with laughter, and the bar joined in. As Callaghan went to pour another, Steel placed a hand over the glass, startling Callaghan and the others.

'You refusing a drink from an old friend, are yeh?' Callaghan growled, the rest of the bar rising from their seats, ready to pounce.

'Not at all, it's just I want to share a drink with all my new friends as well. So, drinks are on me,' Steel declared loudly, taking the bottle from Callaghan and raising it up.

The bar roared once more, and the live band that had been getting ready to perform began to play.

Steel sat down and leant forward to speak to Callaghan. 'Want to pay that debt?'

Callaghan smiled and nodded, then disappeared behind the bar to serve the rest of the restless band of reprobates, bikers, thugs, and locals that liked spending time there.

Steel leant over the bar and grabbed a bottle of Johnnie Walker Red that he'd spotted near the rinsing sink. He poured himself two fingers worth and sat back as the bar exploded into joyful song and laughter.

Steel smiled. Now he had some new friends he could call upon, and something deep down told him he might just be doing that.

* * *

'The police are still not saying what caused the blast in Berlin later today,' said the female news reporter.

The dark-haired woman sported a red jumper and grey skirt. The lettering at the bottom of the screen said Sarah Greenthorn, BBC News. The reporter gave precisely the same statement as all the other countries—that the police were still investigating and as soon as something official was received, they would let viewers know. This was universal language for the cops who have revealed jack, but it's something bad.

The Sentinel sat and studied the feed while setting up several laptops and monitors in a different room. The apartment was spacious, with signs of people with expensive taste. The furniture in the sitting room alone was worth over fifty grand. The thick velvet curtains were perfect for keeping the light in, the little light The Sentinel would emit via the computer screens.

After the final screen had been set up, The Sentinel sat back and studied the latest name on the list. This was a tall, thin man with a bad taste in clothing, mostly corduroy trousers and blazers with padding on the arms. The man had an air of a professor or wealthy landowner about him.

The Sentinel gazed longingly at the monitor, observing the man who had walked into a vast office and sat in a leather office chair. The office had the 1900s feel to it, complete with a drinks globe in the corner. The man had some bearing, but The Sentinel sensed this had been bought rather than bred into.

The Sentinel's gaze slipped back to the story on the news. Behind the reporter stood Sabine Boese. She had just received a phone call, one that made her excited enough to usher her colleagues back into the car and take off. She had received news of something.

The Sentinel stared at the screen as the vehicle took off, curious at what had made the INTERPOL agent leave like that.

The Sentinel stood up and moved to the partial set-up workbench. Several plans and roughly drawn blueprints of devices were pinned to a board next to it. The Sentinel looked through them and stopped at one, then tore it from the board. The Sentinel had the how; now, it was just a case of when and where.

Chapter 24

Steel had followed Callaghan into a backroom office, which was a small but cosy place. It had a secondhand desk Callaghan had probably gotten from one of the antique places scattered about the city. Photographs of Callaghan and his adventures hung on the walls in cheap gold frames. Since settling down to a new life, Callaghan had married and had several kids.

'So, Johnnie boy, what do ya need?' Callaghan asked, pouring two cups of coffee from the machine next to a printer.

'I'm looking for someone who lives in Amsterdam. I need to find them quickly, and I know you have eyes and ears all over the city,' Steel said with an impressed smile on his face.

Callaghan gasped, his eyes wide with surprise.

'Oh, come on, you old sod, you're an old dog who knows too many old tricks to try and learn pointless new ones,' Steel said, taking the black coffee.

Callaghan laughed and nodded.

'That I am, Johnnie boy, that I am. So, who's the poor sod ya lookin' for?' Callaghan asked before taking a mouthful of coffee.

'Thomas Graaf.' Steel moved just in time.

Callaghan sprayed the coffee where Steel had stood.

'What do you want with that piece of shit? To kill the bastard, I hope?' Callaghan boomed with an angry voice.

'To save his life, actually,' Steel said with a shrug.

'Now, what would ya want to do dat for? The man is evil, pure friggin evil.' Callaghan took another mouthful of coffee.

'I got questions; he's got answers. After that, the killer can have him.' Steel smiled and shrugged.

Callaghan looked over at the small portable TV on his desk; the news report was about the bombing in Berlin.

'Is it about that?' Callaghan nodded to the TV.

Steel nodded and took a sip of the lousy coffee. 'I believe he is next. I want to know why,' he said, his voice low and angry.

Callaghan frowned as he knew that look. 'You lose someone on this?'

Steel simply nodded. His expression said the rest.

'Consider the bastard found,' Callaghan said, standing from his ageing leather office chair. 'Where you stayin?' he asked, knowing it wouldn't be a YMCA.

Steel passed over a flyer he'd taken from the desk, just in case he needed to get a cab back to the hotel.

'Oh, roughing it, I see Johnnie boy,' Callaghan laughed.

The two men embraced like brothers, and Callaghan walked Steel to the door.

'Thanks, Pat, that's our square,' Steel said.

'No, this is on the house. Just catch the bastard that got ya partner, and if darlin' Graaf gets his on the way, well, that will be a nice bonus,' Pat said with a wink and a smile.

He saw Callaghan get on his phone as he turned to leave; the search had already started. The question was: who would get there first? Steel looked at his watch. It was three in the afternoon. Eight hours to go. Steel hoped it would be enough time to find him.

* * *

When Stanton arrived back at the office, heads turned as he got off the elevator. Stanton was looking sharp and confident. *He was back.*

As he walked into the war room that Brena's team were using, heads shot around, and nods of approval made him feel good. But he kept the warm glow inside and maintained a stiff-upper-lip look.

'Where are we at, people?' he barked. The old gravelly voice had returned also.

'We are trying to ascertain what the flags represent,' said Rachel.

'It's the flag of a Dutch count or earl,' Dorson yelled out as the web page spat out the answer.

'So, we are looking for Dutch royalty, are you sure?' Stanton asked, unsure of the sudden outburst.

'Why is he targeting a Dutch count?' Dutton asked as he worked on Steel's location.

'Or earl?' Dorson added, walking over to where Stanton stood near Rachel's chair.

'OK, check any affiliations with Dutch royalty and New York, see who has been there recently and what they were doing there. If you are right, this could be something a whole lot bigger than just killing security guards and lawyers,' Stanton said, fearing the phone call he would have to make if they were right. Stanton hoped to God they weren't.

* * *

Steel headed back to his hotel. His hopes rested with Callaghan. Steel knew if anyone could find Graaf, it would be him. However, Steel was still slightly reserved about bringing Callaghan in on this. After all, he and Graaf had a falling out some time ago. One that Callaghan never forgot nor forgave. Steel just hoped that Callaghan would leave him alive long enough to get answers. After that, all bets were off.

Steel entered the immense lobby and checked at the front desk for messages. He didn't expect any, not so soon anyway, but he could also see if anyone had been looking for him as well. The shift change had denied Steel from seeing the blonde he had seen before. Instead, this time he spoke to a raven-haired beauty with eyes the colour of a Mediterranean sky and a body that fitted the uniform in just the right places. Steel noticed her name tag read Sarah Angel, causing him to smile.

'Sorry, sir, no messages.' Her voice was low and had a gravelly substance to it.

'Oh, that's quite alright, Sarah, but if you could send a bottle of Dom Perignon 2006 to my suite, that would be fantastic,' Steel said with a seductive smile.

'Will that be *two* glasses, sir?' she enquired. Her eyes sparkled as much as the ruby-red lipstick that covered her pouting lips.

'All depends on the company, but it's a shame to waste such a good vintage drinking alone, wouldn't you say?' Steel smiled and headed for the elevators.

Sarah's eyes followed him as she leaned on the front desk. Thoughts ran through her head, and none of them was decent. Sarah smiled and picked up the phone, and dialled for room service.

'Hi, this is Sarah at the main desk. A bottle of Dom 2006 to the Penthouse Suite.' She nodded. 'Yes, two glasses.'

* * *

Brena entered the war room and looked around as everyone was too busy to acknowledge he'd even walked into the room. 'What's going on?' he asked as he moved up to Rachel.

'We may have a lead with the next one. We're looking for a Dutch count, earl or royalty,' she replied without taking her eyes off the screen.

'We think this Sentinel is going after royalty now?'

Rachel said nothing. She just nodded and furthered her search into Dutch nobility and possible movements to New York or neighbouring places.

'Any word from Steel?' Brena asked quietly, looking around the room as if he didn't want to be overheard.

'Stanton had a missed call from him earlier. After that, nothing. Looks like he's gone to ground, or he's working on something,' Rachel explained as her fingers skipped over the keys of the keyboard.

Brena stood up straight and nodded to himself, self-reassurance that everything was under control and Steel was possibly in trouble.

'Let me know if anything comes up,' he instructed Rachel.

'Will do,' Rachel replied, her gaze still locked onto the computer screen.

Dorson watched Brena out of the corner of his eye. To him, Brena seemed nervous and edgy, but why he didn't know. He observed Brena slowly cross the floor and stare at the elevator, almost as if he was uneasy about going up to see the old man. Which in itself was strange. If Brena were kept out of the loop about something, he'd head straight up there.

However, this time it was different; he was different. It had started when they learned Simms was bringing Falkner back for questioning.

Brena checked his watch, spun on his heels and headed back the way he came. Dorson spun in his chair and watched as the man took the other elevator back down towards the lobby.

'I wonder where he's off to,' Dorson said softly.

Rachel looked up for a second, catching the numbers on the elevator display board, and shrugged. 'Who knows, who cares? All I do know is he's not here, breathing down my neck,' she said, shivering at the thought of Brena looming over her with his bad breath and cheap aftershave.

Dorson checked his watch. Trish still wasn't back, and it was getting late in the day. It wasn't like her to be late, not unless she had said she was going to be. Suddenly, Dorson had a bad feeling and stood up.

'Where you going?' Rachel asked, surprised at what seemed like a lack of commitment to finding the killer.

'Trish still isn't back. So, I'm just gonna check her place, make sure she's OK,' Dorson said, pulling on his jacket.

'Why don't you try calling first?' Rachel suggested.

'Tried that, went straight to voicemail,' Dorson explained.

Rachel thought for a second, then nodded. In truth, she had only noticed Trish's lack of appearance when Dorson had mentioned it. But then Dorson had always had a thing for Trish, but rules got in the way of him acting on those feelings. 'Go on, I'll cover for you; say you had to do some research elsewhere,' Rachel told him with a half-cocked smile.

Dorson smiled a thank you and hurried to the elevators. R

Rachel looked at her watch; it was ten in the morning. A smug smile broke over her face, like a child with a dirty secret.

* * *

Dorson drove the Challenger as if his life depended on it. All the government training with evasion driving technics kicked in as he weaved in and out of the morning traffic. Trish's house was a good twenty minutes away, and he needed to make it in fifteen at the very least. Dorson wished this wasn't an unmarked vehicle; he envied cops with their warning lights. Nothing screamed 'get the hell out of the way' like red-and-blue in your rearview.

Fourteen minutes and thirty seconds. An excellent time, but Dorson hoped it was soon enough as he pulled up outside Trish's place.

The street was quiet; school buses and busy parents had already gone to work. So now, there were only dog walkers and postal delivery trucks. A guy who lived over the road was on his lawn raking up leaves, but Dorson just reconned the guy was on a pension, and he loved to watch the world. The pure form of the nosey neighbour. No sitting next to the window and looking out from behind curtains for this guy.

Dorson paid the man another quick glance and thought nothing more of it. He knew the type. They saw everything but didn't want to share what they'd seen.

He made his way up the path. A biting easterly wind stung the side of his face, forcing him to close one eye for a second. After that, he moved steadily forwards, his hands by his sides so he could get to his Sig Sauer resting in a holster at the small of his back. From the outside, everything seemed normal. There were no lights on, and her car was in the driveway. He had the thought that she had slept in or her alarm had failed to go off. It happened. In fact, it had recently happened to him a couple of times.

Dorson tried the front door. Locked solid. He made a quick inspection of the door and the Yale lock. No scratches or signs of forced entry. Reluctantly, he moved around the side to the rear of the house. There was a small white gate under a rose-bush archway. He clicked the latch and slowly pushed around. The grounds seemed quiet, too quiet.

Dorson slid his hand to his belt and back towards the polymer holster and the grip of the 9-mm.

Everything felt wrong. The car in the drive, the lack of movement inside, and the eerie silence of the backyard. Trish had once asked his advice on getting a dog, just something to come home to. He remembered telling her it would be cruel because of all the time away and late nights. She'd agreed and decided against it. Now, he wished she had gotten the damn mutt which would prove an excellent early warning system, letting you know if someone was there or something was wrong.

Dorson promised himself if he found her alive and well, he'd take her to the pound and buy her one himself.

Beads of sweat began to form on his forehead, and he could hear the sound of his racing heartbeat in his ears. Adrenaline was pumping through his veins, but his breathing was steady, his muscles tense yet ready for action.

The backyard was a thirty-by-thirty square with a patio and a couple of trees surrounding a grassy area hidden under a blanket of gold and brown leaves. A large bay window looked straight into the dining room, an office. Next to this was a long window and a door to the kitchen area. Dorson tried the door, but that, too, was solid. He stepped back and checked the windows, but nothing seemed out of place.

Finally, frustrated, Dorson headed back to the front of the house. He'd try the doorbell and hope she'd answer with messed-up hair and bleary eyes. He looked over at the neighbour, who was still working on leaf clearing and waved. The man quickly turned away as if doing so would make him somehow invisible. Dorson smiled to himself and shook his head. Then, raising his hand, Dorson extended a finger and pushed the bell. There was a faint sound of an electronic ding-dong and then silence. Dorson bounced on his heels while he waited. He'd give it two minutes before he tried again.

After the two, Dorson tried again. The same faint tone and then nothing. She was either in the shower or still sleeping if she was home. Dorson hammered on the door with his fist and yelled through the door. To no avail. Mixed feelings of fear and confusion poured over him. Something was definitely wrong.

Pulling out his cell, Dorson dialled Rachel's number. He needed to report this fast. As he listened to the ringing in the handset, he made his way around the house to try every window and door once more. He discovered all the curtains were open and doors and windows locked. Trish wasn't there, and her car was in the drive. Dorson could only come to one conclusion: Trish had been abducted.

'Did you find her?' asked Rachel's voice over the speaker.

'No, her place is empty, and her car is here in the driveway. Something is wrong; I think Trish has been taken,' Dorson admitted, nervousness sounding in his voice. 'We need to tell the old man.'

There was a pregnant pause, and then a new voice came over the speaker.

'Agent Dorson, why are you at Trish's place?'

A cold shiver ran down Dorson's back as he heard the angry tone in Brena's voice.

'Trish didn't come in today. I was worried. I believe something has happened to her because her place is empty and—'

'Trish is taking some time off … a personal matter. She phoned and asked me for the time off last night before she left work. Nothing to worry about, so you can get your ass back here and do your job before you don't have one.'

Dorson froze as the phone went dead.

Brena was mad. But Dorson wondered why. Was it because Dorson had slipped out, or was it something more sinister?

Chapter 25

A knock on the suite door disturbed Steel from his work at the murder board he had created. The magnetic whiteboard the concierge had arranged to bring up from a conference room was perfect for what Steel needed.

Steel answered the door with his shirt half undone and untucked. It was Sarah from the reception desk. She stood next to a brass waiter's trolley supporting two glasses, the bottle of Dom on ice in a champagne bucket, a big bowl of fresh strawberries and a small pitcher of cream.

'I didn't think it was coming,' Steel said with a raised eyebrow, noting the hungry look in her eyes.

'Sorry for the wait, sir; the timing wasn't right,' Sarah explained with a cheeky smile.

'For the champagne?'

'No, the end of the shift,' Sarah purred, pushing the trolley into the suite and closing the door behind them.

* * *

Two hours later, the ice had melted, and the champagne had lost its chill. Sarah lay curled up with a satisfied look on her face. This cat had definitely gotten her cream. Steel was up and about. He didn't have time to sleep. He hoped Pat would call with news of Graaf's location any minute. But so far, nothing.

Steel walked to the next room, where the whiteboard stood and picked up the blue marker. The name Thomas Graaf was circled four times. What did Graaf and all the others have in common? As far as he knew, nothing. Graaf and Falkner, he could understand, but the others?

Steel turned slightly as he heard a low moan from the bedroom. Sarah was dreaming. She had been a pleasant surprise and an exciting distraction. As well as exceedingly nimble.

Steel headed into the kitchenette and pressed the button on the coffee machine for black coffee. He needed a shower and to get the alcohol out of his system. Taking the coffee from the drip tray, Steel headed for the shower.

Steel hoped the noise from the running water would wake his guest, and she would scamper away like a thief in the night. He turned on the water and let it run for a while, allowing the water to reach the perfect temperature.

Stepping under, Steel closed his eyes and placed his hands against the back wall. The rainshower felt great, cascading water washing over his body. His mind was a million miles away, so he never heard the patter of naked feet on the bathroom floor or Sarah's naked body pulling up close behind him until the last second.

Steel turned and saw her fantastic figure standing before him.

No words were spoken or necessary. Steel pulled her in close, and they embraced; he pulled her up so her legs were wrapped around his muscular middle.

She groaned loudly as he pushed her against the wall, forcing her close to him. Her long fingers clawed at his back and ran through his hair. Sarah screamed as she felt him once more.

* * *

It was another hour before Sarah left. The timing was perfect.

As they said their farewells at the door, Steel saw Pat stepping off the elevator with a sad-looking man in a torn suit and a bloody lip and nose.

As Sarah moved past the two men, she looked back and wondered if this was the man whose name was on the board and what Steel was going to do with him. She had worked out that Steel was a cop or at least working for some agency. She had seen the whiteboard and realised he was in Amsterdam on an investigation. Then her thoughts on the bombing in Berlin. Was he there in search of the bomber? Was there a terrorist in Amsterdam? She looked back again to see the door closing, and all she could wonder was whether the man they had just brought in was the bomber himself.

* * *

As Steel closed the door to the Penthouse Suite, he noticed the look on Sarah's face and that cold chill he often got running down his spine. A tingling feeling that things were about to go sideways and fast.

'Why did you bring him here?' Steel asked, angry that the cover he was maintaining had just been blown.

'Well, that's thanks for ya,' Pat said, a tone of disappointment in his voice.

'I'm grateful you found him so quickly, but did you have to bring him to my hotel? Couldn't you have phoned or something?' Steel asked, pulling Graaf with him and heading for the bedroom to pack.

'So, you're the cop?' Graaf said, giving Steel a once-over.

'Did Pat explain why you're here?' Steel asked him.

'Someone wants to kill me, and you're here to save me. How noble,' Graaf snickered.

'Not quite, but close,' Steel smiled and gave a quick look around the room to make sure he hadn't hidden anything significant.

'Leaving so soon?' Pat said, watching Steel as he stuffed his clothes into a canvas travel bag.

'Did you see that woman in the hallway?' Steel said with a disappointed tone.

'Yeh, lucky bastard,' Pat grinned and nodded with approval.

'Well, she works here, and it wouldn't surprise me if she were phoning the cops as we speak.' Steel grabbed Graaf and the bag and headed for the room with the murder board.

'Where were you thinking of going?' Pat asked, suddenly feeling the situation that was about to unravel was his fault.

'For the moment, it's best if you didn't know. INTERPOL will undoubtedly be here soon once the police are informed. Steel admitted that there was an agent hot on his trail in Berlin.

He decided to get passage on the Hook of Holland to Harwich ferry. He could hide Graaf back in Britain until it was ready to hand him over to the agency. The less Pat knew, the better it was for both of them. Steel knew that Sabine Boese would be on her way if she weren't already.

Steel thought about telling Stanton of his plan, but he decided against it. Instead, he would secure Graaf and then let MI8 handle it.

'Can you take Graaf to Hoek van Holland Ferry Port? I'll meet you there,' Steel requested. A plan was forming in his head.

'You expecting trouble?' Pat asked with a hungry grin.

'You know me, Pat, I always expect it. That's why I'm still breathing. The trick is how to avoid it.' Steel smiled back and slapped his friend on the arm for good luck. 'Take him there and wait for me if I'm not there by,'—Steel checked the ferry information on his phone—'the next ferry is at nine.'

He calculated every eventuality. 'If I'm not there by half eight, get going and call this number.' Steel wrote down Stanton's number on a piece of paper and handed it to Pat. 'Only speak to a man called Stanton, *nobody else.*'

Pat looked at the bit of torn-off piece of paper and nodded.

'Right you are, boss,' Pat roared and gave Steel a big hug. 'Just make sure you're there.' He stuffed the piece of paper into his pocket and grabbed Graaf by the arm. 'Come on you. Looks like we're gonna spend some more time together,' Pat laughed.

Graaf said nothing. He just stared at Steel with an unamused look before being dragged towards the suite entrance.

Steel watched them leave, and a sudden feeling of relief came over him. INTERPOL and The Sentinel would be following him, not Pat. All Steel had to do was get to the ferry and return home. He had already secured two of the targets, but still, he had the feeling that The Sentinel didn't want them dead. If that were the case, they would have been killed without all of this drama.

No, The Sentinel wished to be found and wanted them to talk.

Steel grabbed the bag and made his way from the hotel suite, hoping that the device, or whatever The Sentinel had planned, would now be deactivated. But the target was out of play.

The Sentinel's MO was to scare the target. But if he was right, that didn't explain why Trent was killed at his apartment, then Alison in a quiet spot by a hospital, and Falkner's apartment was blown to pieces. Unless, of course, there was *someone else* who wanted to silence them.

This was no psychopath they were chasing. This was someone out for revenge. One of the purest reasons for what The Sentinel was doing. With Graaf gone, Steel had breathing room to work out what was going on. The deadline for Graaf was twenty-three hundred, or eleven, that evening.

Steel believed Graaf was now safe from the killer. That was the game: *find them or lose them.* Graaf had been found.

Steel had until eleven until the next card came in, but he would be at the ferry at nine. Five hours to find out as much as he could, then six hours on the ship sweating the truth out of Graaf.

Steel pulled the door shut and headed for the elevators. He had to disappear, but before he did, he'd have to speak to Sarah. If she had called the cops, they would have been asking them questions, and he didn't want her involved. He pressed the button and waited. Steel looked at the digital display, which showed the elevator was all the way down in the lobby. The numbers clicked off, unhindered. Steel knew the elevator would get to his floor in two minutes and eighteen seconds. He also knew he could make it down using the stairs in four and a half.

The display registered it was now on the floor below, and it had stopped. Steel scowled. That tingling in his spine told him there was trouble coming. Steel forced open the doors to the elevator and climbed in, using the side near the counter-balance to climb up. He'd wait until the elevator was on his floor and then climb on top of the metal box.

If he was right, even if Sarah had called the police, they wouldn't have gotten there or been able to form a tactical response team that fast. No, this was someone else, and he could imagine who. This was Sabine's doing, and there was a Special Armed Response Unit downstairs at the stairwell and another heading for his suite.

Steel hoped he was wrong. Hoping that it was just a guest going to their room down below. But that 'feeling' had never been wrong or let him down—well, not severely, at any rate. There was a clang of metal as the brakes on the elevator was released, then a whoosh as it flew upwards to the suite.

Steel carefully clambered onto the elevator roof and inched the emergency hatch open. Inside, several members of the Armed Response team were already out of the elevator and moving into position, waiting for the rest to form up.

The men wore protective body armour over civilian clothing and carried various weapons. Steel lost sight of them as they moved down the corridor. But one thing he was confident of: Sabine wasn't with them. She would be downstairs where it was safe. Besides, it wasn't her country, and she wouldn't have gotten authorisation to take over that quickly.

The standard protocol would be to seal off the area, restrict elevator usage, and cover all exits. That meant Steel's method of escape couldn't be through the front door as he'd planned. He smiled as he thought about all this. Wondering what story she had told the Dutch police to have gotten all this arranged.

Steel knew there would be hell to pay when they found out she had misled them. There was no way they would send an armed police team to arrest a British Lord on holiday or an NYPD detective; the scandal would be unthinkable.

They likely thought Falkner was with Steel and that Falkner was the bomber.

There was a gentle ping, and the elevators slid shut. Steel couldn't risk jumping inside; the security cameras would pick him up. Besides, why should he make it easy for them or her? Steel imagined Sabine biting those long painted talons she called nails. Nervous about the outcome.

What if it went wrong, and a twitchy cop shot Steel? The thought of it backfiring sounded more delicious to Steel.

The elevator moved down to the lobby. This time to pick up new guests. Steel climbed down while guests shoved their way in, then he used the elevator support structure to climb down to a safe location and waited for it to ascend.

Below would be a maintenance door. From there, Steel would have to feel his way around and eventually step out into the world. A clang of metal and the sound of air being released. The elevator flew up the shaft towards the second floor. Steel jumped down and looked around. He slowly opened the maintenance door, smiled, and hurried through. Now all he had to do was get out of the building.

* * *

Brena was pacing up and down in the men's room. He was nervous. Steel's investigation was moving too quickly, and now he looked bad. To make matters worse, the old man had found a new lease on life.

He needed a cigarette. He also required Steel out of the way or at least discredited or slowed down. Sure, he had called Sabine Boese and given Steel's location, he'd even lied and said that Falkner was with him and that Falkner was responsible for the explosion.

Also, Simms was a problem. It wouldn't be long until he landed and walked in with Falkner. For the agency, it was a win; they had gotten one back alive, but it hadn't been Brena that had done it.

Brena stopped pacing; someone was coming. He could hear their shoes tapping on the tiled floor. As an agent burst through the door, he knew it was time to leave. The two men exchanged pleasantries, and Brena left. He could almost taste the nicotine in his mouth.

Brena headed out through the security check and the main doors. He moved around the side of the building and pulled out a pack of cigarettes, removing one with his teeth. As he lit the end with the electronic lighter, Brena inhaled and closed his eyes. Heaven.

Things were going wrong. The plan wasn't meant to move this quickly.

Brena had heard the whispers about Steel and brushed them off as a rumour, Chinese whispers, stories around the campfire. But now he knew the stories did this guy no justice. This John Steel was worse than what the stories had said. This guy was a nightmare incarnate.

Chapter 26

Steel had made it out of the building using a tradesmen's entrance the cops had evidently forgotten about. He just strolled through the kitchen like he belonged there, and no one questioned him. Confidence was a significant part of blending. 'If you look like you don't fit in, chances are you don't,' he was always told by one of his teachers at the agency. Luckily, most of the waiter staff were wearing black, so Steel blended in nicely.

He walked into the prickly air. The temperature had dropped to around four degrees, causing his breath to turn to mist. His plans had soured but were not wholly ruined. 'Always have a Plan B,' his instructors used to say. So, Steel had learnt to have a Plan C and D, just in case B failed.

As he'd moved through the hotel, he'd spotted Sabine in the lobby; she was pacing about in a small area, concern on her face. Sabine had been weighing all the things that could go wrong while she was downstairs and out of the way. All the options he had thought of earlier, no doubt.

Steel smiled cunningly. Plan E just came into his head. Sure, it was risky, but where was the fun in no risk? Besides, he would have an ally, not a hindrance, if it worked. Calmly, Steel entered the lobby and coolly walked up to Sabine, who was chewing on the nail of her left index finger.

'Well, this looks exciting. Looking for someone special?' Steel asked jokingly.

'Buzz off, pal, we're busy …' Sabine stopped mid-sentence. Her eyes widened, and her mouth fell open.

'Really, Sabine, that's not a look for you,' Steel said, closing her mouth by gently pushing her chin up with two fingers.

'What are you … you should be …' Sabine fought to get out the words.

'Yes, I know. But what I need to know is who told you I was here?' Steel's smile changed to a look of anger, forcing her to step back slightly. 'Call off your dogs, Sabine. Let's talk about this before one of us gets hurt.'

'You're worried about yourself or your friend?' Sabine asked with an angry look and bitter tone.

'Actually, I was thinking about your career, and what friend? I'm here alone … ah.' The penny had dropped. 'Brena?' he asked.

Sabine nodded, shocked at his deduction but not surprised. The head of the operation stood two feet away, talking to his men, requesting updates.

'The room is clear; he's not there, and no sign of anyone else was there—well, a male, someone that is. They did find a woman's panties, though,' said the commander to Sabine.

'Sorry, I would have cleaned up, but I wasn't expecting guests,' Steel joked.

The commander turned to face Steel. His eyes widened at the sight of the man they were hunting. The man's hand went for his gun and raised it. Sabine rolled her eyes as she knew what was coming.

In the blink of an eye, Steel had taken the weapon and then handed it back with the top slide removed from the lower body, the magazine in his other hand.

'Now, can we chat?' Steel growled.

The force commander's eyes were glued to the stripped weapon in Steel's hands.

'Buy you a drink?' Sabine asked, walking to the steps leading up to the fancy-looking bar.

'Thought you'd never ask,' said the commander.

Steel shook his head and followed them.

The commander called back his teams and closed down the operation. The guests that were hanging around, looking alarmed and confused, took pictures with their cell phones. As

Steel couldn't help but think of the boosting the hotel's ratings would get. Who didn't like a little drama while on holiday? As the team dispersed, Steel stood at the top of the stairs.

'Ladies and gents, sorry for any distress, but what you just witnessed was a combined exercise by the brave police department and INTERPOL and the hotel. Displaying their willingness to always put your safety first,' Steel announced, prompting people to clap and applaud. Steel turned to the man behind the bar and called for glasses of champagne for everyone in the lobby.

The man began preparing while Steel wandered to where Sabine and the Commander sat.

'Nicely deflected,' Sabine said with a grin.

Steel handed the weapon parts back to the commander. 'No hard feelings.'

The commander was still confused about how Steel had gotten out of the building and taken the weapon so quickly.

'Don't worry, commander; it's his job to make people miserable,' Sabine said, noting the look on the man's face.

'Only yours, Sabine, and bad guys.' Steel said with a smile.

'Yes, talking about bad guys—'

'He flew back to Langley using the jet of the spooks the police picked up at the airport. I believe Brena's men,' Steel said, looking at the bar staff who were quickly distributing the complimentary champagne and waving one of them over.

'Steel, what the hell is going on?' Sabine asked.

'You know about the killings in the States?' Steel asked as the drinks arrived.

'The security guard and the lawyer?' Sabine nodded in reply as she took two glasses and handed one to the commander, sitting opposite.

'This postcard killer calls himself The Sentinel; you know this already because you got a card from him last time, correct?' Steel asked, to which Sabine reluctantly nodded.

'This guy has been bouncing me around, looking for his victims.' Steel admitted.

'Why? If you find them, doesn't that defeat the objective if he wants to kill them?' Sabine asked before taking a sip.

'I don't think he does; I think he wants them found. They all connect somehow. They all tell a story that The Sentinel wants to be told. I think the reason the others died was that somebody else was trying to shut them up. I think that is why The Sentinel brought me in on the case; he knew I'd do something before they were all gone,' Steel explained.

'That's a bit of a stretch, don't you think, and slightly self-aggrandizing?' Sabine asked, giving Steel a strange look.

'Okay, so just say that I'm right. That this killer is out for revenge … one way or the other, we save them, and we find out the story. They die, and we investigate, but we don't find out the story. The Sentinel wants the truth to be found,' Steel said, calling the bartender over.

'What truth?'

'Exactly?' Steel said with a childish grin. 'You want a big case, fine. Work with me on this, and you'll have it. CIA and INTERPOL working together.' Steel suggested.

'Don't tell me. All you want is to be left out of this at the end?' Sabine asked, a look of calculation on her face.

'I was never a part of it, merely a passer-by,' Steel said, raising his glass.

The commander did the same but had been lost in the conversation.

'Oh, one more thing.'

'Yes?' Sabine asked, rolling her eyes at the prospect of what was coming next.

'You may have to explain to the commander; I think we lost him about ten minutes ago.' Steel smiled and stood up just as the barman arrived with the bill. Steel billed it to the room and gave the man a twenty euro note for his trouble.

'Right then, things to do,' Steel said, hurrying back to the elevator.

'Like what?' Sabine called out.

'Find out what the killer wants us to find before eleven o'clock tonight,' Steel called back.

'Why? What happens at eleven?' Sabine asked, puzzled and a little afraid.

'That's when the new postcard should be delivered.'

The elevator doors closed.

* * *

Dorson returned to the office and was busy checking for anything The Sentinel's targets had in common. The good news was the more targets, the narrower the search. They'd still had no word from Steel, alive or otherwise, which Dorson felt was reassuring. But, of course, no news was good news where a man like Steel was concerned.

Upon his return, Dorson had shot Rachel the evil eye. He knew she had purposely informed Brena of what he was doing. And the fact Brena was there when he'd phoned Rachel spoke volumes. Rachel had always been one to seek favour with people. That was how she chose to move up in the world. But Dorson never knew it would come to dropping her friends into the grinder just to get a foot up.

Dorson remembered jumping at the chance to work with this newly designed team. This was the brainchild of Stanton. Which worked well initially … until Brena showed up, and then it all went to hell. The people at the top gave this project two years to run. One and a half were already up. After which, they would decide to keep it or scrap it, which meant everyone would be reassigned. Dorson couldn't wait for it to flop, but at the same time, he felt terrible for the old man. If this whole operation went under, he went into retirement.

* * *

Dorson had spent a good hour checking and rechecking. Nothing. The people couldn't be more unlike or have so little contact with one another. The only thing they had in common was the sixteenth of September. On that day, they were all in New York or a nearby city. Which was a little odd, sure, but when Dorson rechecked, he found none of them was in the same area at the same time.

Dorson looked at the empty coffee mug on his desk and thought about moving. But the sudden appearance of Rachel at the refreshments table turned his stomach and made him lose the urge. He turned back to his work and decided to dissect each person's life, starting with the security guard.

Dorson noticed Rachel's reflection in the monitor, standing behind him, watching what he was doing. He didn't turn or acknowledge her presence. As far as he was concerned, she was just someone he had to work with, nothing more. Any trust had gone, along with any ideas of friendship. She was Brena's pet, and that meant to keep away, or you were going to get burnt.

Dorson looked back at the reflection; she had gone. He turned and saw she was again at her desk. He smiled and picked up his coffee mug. 'Now, I'll get that coffee,' he said to himself, hoping she'd stay at her desk and away from him.

'Find anything?' asked Brena, who suddenly appeared behind him.

Dorson jumped and spilt coffee onto his hand, causing him to cringe with pain; he placed down the cup and flicked the liquid from his hand.

'Jezus Brena,' Dorson cursed as he grabbed a paper towel and mopped up the coffee from the floor and table.

'Well?' Brena asked, grinning as he took particular pleasure in what he had just done.

'Not much. Any report on Trish yet?' Dorson asked, standing up straight and looking Brena in the eyes as he posed the question. Hoping to see something in the man's intense grey-blue eyes.

'Well, keep on it, and Trish is fine, I'm sure. Now, get back to work.' Brena's voice was raised, and his pupils dilated.

Brena was hiding something, and Dorson wanted to know what. But he knew he'd have to be careful; his trust issues were getting worse. However, there was *one* person he could trust, and he just walked through the door with Falkner in tow.

* * *

The Sentinel was glad that the British weather had turned for the worse. That meant wearing the hood didn't look out of place. It had been the second day of constant rain, but today was a light shower, a fine drizzle like powdered water in the air.

Red double-decker buses hurried down the street, past Parliament and Big Ben, heading both ways over the Westminster Bridge. Despite the rain, it was a bright day, with patches of blue breaking through stone-grey clouds as they drifted above. The Sentinel moved down Birdcage Walk and headed for Constitution Hill.

The Sentinel strolled along, head slightly down with the coat's hood pulled forwards, The Sentinel's face hidden in shadow. There was no hurry; The Sentinel had time. There was always time.

That was part of the game. Giving the hunter time to work out everything. The new player, Steel, was not a disappointment. The only one who took this seriously, the only one without an agenda. Agent Brena and Sabine Boese were in it for the glory, a step up in their evolutionary scale. But Steel was looking at the story, rescuing the targets, giving them a chance to fill in the blanks.

At each tourist trap, the streets began to swell with people. Worse still, people with cameras. Something The Sentinel had wanted to avoid. Even though nobody had any idea what The Sentinel looked like, why take the chance? Even though Steel was a worthy adversary, he was dangerous. Smart and experienced. If anyone could pick out The Sentinel from a crowd, it was him.

The Sentinel stopped and leant against the wall of a building. Looking around quickly, The Sentinel pulled out a cell phone and checked the feed coming from several cameras. This included a new one. This time a woman came into the frame.

She was a tall thin woman in her late forties. Her long mousey-coloured hair was unstyled but fell about the shoulders of her white blouse, which was matched with a light grey skirt. The clothes hugged her figure enough to compliment her form, making her appear to be all business.

The Sentinel noticed she had an air of someone in charge.

The room was spacious, with rosewood furniture, white walls, and a wooden floor. The view from the window was obscured, but The Sentinel wasn't interested in that. The only necessary view was of the next target.

Tucking the cell back into the jacket pocket, The Sentinel continued down the street. There was still some way to walk before reaching the next safe house, but The Sentinel didn't mind. It was a beautiful day for a walk, and the fresh air helped The Sentinel think. Judging by Steel's rate of finding the targets, it wouldn't be long before he was in London once the next clue had been delivered.

The Sentinel had the decision to make. The next postcard hadn't been sent yet; it was too early. But Steel had already secured Graaf. So no, the postcard must be posted on time, at eleven that evening, or all the timings and preparation would have been for nothing.

The Sentinel hadn't anticipated Steel would be this good. But no matter. The extra time would give Steel time to dig into the targets' lives. Finally, somebody was paying attention. It would soon be over, but there was still much to be done. Two more targets to go. The Sentinel would have revenge, and those responsible would pay. One way or the other.

Chapter 27

Steel had gone back to the room and showered before putting some fresh clothes on; INTERPOL's little surprise visit had prevented him from doing so earlier. He packed and was ready to check out of the hotel, but not yet. He would be leaving for the ferry in a few hours and meeting up with Pat and Graaf in Hoek van Holland.

He had already booked passage on the ship with two rooms because he figured Graaf wouldn't want to share with a man who had violent nightmares. Besides, once Pat had told Graaf what was going on, the man wouldn't want to leave Steel's protection. No, Graaf would want to be as close to Steel as possible. If he was smart, that was.

Once Steel had all the information he needed, Graaf was useless. As far as Steel was concerned, Graaf could stay on the ship afterwards. He didn't care. Graaf was scum, and someone wanted him dead. No big deal, but until Steel knew why Graaf was significant, he was useful.

Steel set up his laptop in the dining area. It was a larger space to work in, and the coffee machine was just behind him. Steel had ordered a mushroom and pepper omelette from room service. The protein would do him good, and he was starving from the chase, not to mention the few hours before with Sarah. Before sitting, Steel placed down an A4 legal pad and a fresh cup of coffee, then logged into the Hotels WI-FI and began his search. He wanted to know everything about the victims. And to do that, he needed help from a friend.

Steel contacted The Tailor. He gave the man all the details he needed for the search. Meanwhile, he would do some digging using his computer. He started with Alison Kline. There was something that tied them all together. They all had postcards warning what would happen, all except the security guard.

Steel looked at his watch and smiled. He knew Simms would have landed about now and was in Langley with Falkner.

Steel wished he could have been there just to see the angry look on Brena's smug face. But now Falkner was Stanton's problem; Steel had enough of his own. Sabine's little welcome had not been a surprise; in fact, he would have been disappointed if she hadn't shown up. But Brena had tipped her off and lied to her about Falkner. To Steel, that was unacceptable. Wrong information could get people hurt or killed. Steel had no love for the man before; now, Steel wanted to rip out his spine and beat him to death with it.

He sipped coffee and looked through his notes. There was something in those notations, a silent clue. He flipped back and forth through the pages, but there was nothing that stood out.

Frustrated, Steel tossed the pad onto the table's polished surface, and it skidded off and onto the floor. For a second, he found it amusing. But the feeling subsided, and he forced himself from his chair and walked to the other side of the table to retrieve the notepad. The pages had landed awkwardly, displaying the different locations and dates. Steel's hand froze just above the pad, taking in this new perspective.

'How the hell do you move about so quickly, Mr Watcher?' Steel said with a smile as he picked up the pad and raced back to his computer.

Finally, at last, something he could work with. Now, they had something in common: the killer wanted them to tell a story. A story they all played a part in. All of the targets had done something or had been a part of an incident. A cover-up or just in the wrong place at the wrong time. Either way, they knew something, and The Sentinel wanted the world to know.

Steel took a blank sheet and started to write down the dates, locations, and names of the people.

Mark Trent - New York Nov 7st
Alison Klien - New York Nov 9th
Karl Falkner - Berlin Nov 16th
Thomas Graaf - Amsterdam 18th

Steel looked at the list with puzzled eyes. To start with, there had been a constant week break between the postcards and attempts. But then everything started to move quicker, with only a few days between The Sentinel's deadlines.

Why the change?

What had happened to make The Sentinel move up his schedule?

Steel had.

Since Steel's integration into the case, The Sentinel had started to pick up the pace.

He shook his head, dispensing with the notion of his involvement enhancing the killer's time frame. No, this killer had everything planned, even down to the weather. The Sentinel would have anticipated Steel's movements.

Steel smiled as a thought crossed his mind. 'That's why you brought INTERPOL into this. You wanted to know exactly where they were and who the players would be.' Steel nodded at the brilliance of the plan. The Sentinel probably brought in Steel because Brena was too volatile and unpredictable. Not that Steel was, apart from one flaw.

His needed to find the truth and bring the correct people to justice. Brena didn't care about that; he just wanted his name on the front page and a larger office.

Steel took another sip of coffee. There was something else. The Sentinel had observed these people, possibly for some time. That meant a base of operations near the target's home, plus travel and funding. Steel stood up and grabbed his jacket. He needed to see Graaf's apartment.

Chapter 28

Falkner sat in a tiny grey room. It was furnished with a metal table, two chairs, and a two-way mirror. Microphones and cameras were in the corners of the room to pick up every twitch and every whisper.

Falkner was starting to sweat. He rubbed his clammy hands on his trousers and wiped his brow on his sleeve.

They had thrown him in there an hour ago with only a cup of water and a simple order. 'Sit down, shut up, and don't move.' Falkner obeyed, but he needed the bathroom and was afraid to ask. He'd been in situations before and had just laughed them off, but this was serious. He couldn't call a lawyer because he was not under arrest for his protection, yet they treated him like a criminal.

Falkner looked at the empty clear plastic cup from the water cooler. He thought about using it to piss in, but they'd probably throw it at him. Falkner rocked back and forth. Then, finally, he couldn't take the silence or the need for the bathroom anymore.

'Hello, is anyone there?' Falkner yelled, not expecting a reply anytime soon. 'Hello, I need to go the bathroom,' he yelled once more.

'What?' shouted a massive man who was guarding the room.

'I need the can,' Falkner said, trying to sound authoritative.

The guard growled, showed his teeth, and then gave Falkner a disgruntled wave, beckoning for him to follow.

***

Simms stood outside Stanton's office like a pupil waiting to go to see the headmaster. He could hear Brena inside, yelling at Stanton about his displeasure at the whole situation. First, Stanton had misled him into thinking Steel was off the case, and then Simms turned up with Falkner alone because Kitty had been killed following Steel's orders.

Simms could catch every word, almost as if Brena was shouting extra hard so everyone could hear. But the only voice Simms could make out was Brena's. Had the old man gone soft? Was he just sitting there, taking this abuse from a subordinate?

And that was when he heard it. Stanton's roar almost broke the glass of the office window. He had merely been biding his time, letting Brena vent before he bit back, and he was going to take a big bite.

'Agent Brena, who the fuck do you are talking to? The last time I looked, it said Section Chief on *my* door, not yours. How I choose to run *my* operations is *my* business, not yours; you just do as you are told. As for the unfortunate matter of Agent West, it was the killer who was responsible, not any of *my* agents.'

Simms could only imagine the look of fear on Brena's face, and Simms loved it.

For too long, the old man had let things go by like he knew he was due to go to pasture, so why bother?

'Now, Agent Brena, we have a witness downstairs who is ready for questioning. Do you think you can do that, or shall I get someone else to do it?' Stanton growled like a vicious beast.

Brena nodded, then turned to leave.

'Oh, one more thing, Agent Brena,' Stanton barked.

'Yes, sir,' Brena said, his words slight and boyish, like a scolded child.

'I'm not going anywhere,' Stanton said, standing up straight and folding his arms, showing his full height and powerful frame.

Brena didn't speak. There was nothing more to say. He stormed out and glared at Simms as they passed in the corridor.

Simms just smiled and walked through the open door.

'Simms, get your ass in here now,' Stanton roared with a smile, enjoying his revitalisation.

Simms walked in with a sheepish look.

'Shut the goddamn door and sit down,' Stanton said, crushing himself into his leather armchair.

Simms did as ordered. His mouth was nailed shut, fearful of speaking after what he had just witnessed.

'So, you brought Falkner back with you?' Stanton asked, his voice having dropped a million decibels.

'Yes, sir,' Simms replied.

'And Steel?' Stanton asked, picking up a glass of sparkling water from his desk.

'Amsterdam. He thought I should go with Falkner, make sure he gets here safely,' Simms answered.

'But that is what the team is there for. So the question is: why did Steel take them out?' Stanton asked, almost not wanting to hear the answer.

'They were a kill team, sir, not an escort. Steel recognised one of the men. He said he was the man who had replaced him,' Simms explained.

Stanton had a sudden look of panic on his face.

'Sir, who arranged the transport and pick up?' Simms stood.

Stanton rushed for the door, and Simms followed.

'Brenda, get hold of the interrogation wing; get them to close it off, nobody in or out,' Stanton ordered as he and Simms rushed for the elevators.

'Sir, who was it?' Simms asked again as they jumped into the elevator just as the doors began to close.

'Keep your mouth shut and follow me,' Stanton ordered, patting his side as though he was checking that his gun was still there.

As the elevator doors slid shut, Simms swallowed hard. Who were they after, and why did they want Falkner silenced?

* * *

Steel arrived at Graaf's apartment. Pat had texted Steel the address and the alarm code and then requested an update. Finally, Steel could say, 'All was well, and the dogs were no longer hunting.'

The building was pre-war 1930s, possibly older. The exterior had had a significant facelift, but the character of the place was restored rather than ruined. Graaf had the suite on the upper level. White walls and a red carpet greeted Steel as he entered the main entrance. He'd gotten in through the main door just as a stunning blonde was on her way out. Steel had held the door open as she exited, and he casually entered as though he lived there, then used the stairs to avoid anyone seeing him.

Steel moved with casual urgency, trying not to draw attention to himself. Then, when he reached the top floor, he took out his lock picks and worked the lock. A gentle click sounded, and he was in.

Steel moved quickly, closing the door and typing in the deactivation code on the keypad next to the door. A small green LED blinked on, and he was safe.

Steel looked around at the spacious pad and smiled.

The man had a taste for sure. The decor was laid out in a Victorian style, with matte white walls and decorative ceilings and borders. Rosewood furniture sat upon bare wood floors and held Turkish rugs. Works of art hung in gilded frames. Chesterfield accent chairs and couches broke up the centre of the sitting room, and cast-iron and marble fireplace were situated in the centre of the right-hand wall.

Steel walked around; his eyes scanned the room, taking in the splendour. He moved up to a large globe and pulled back the top half to reveal an impressive drinks cabinet. He picked up a limited-edition Johnnie Walker Gold and cracked the seal. The scent of the golden liquid was intoxicating.

Steel went to pour himself a glass, but something stopped him. The Sentinel was trying to kill Graaf. The others had been by explosive devices, but nothing suggested The Sentinel had a particular method. Only the outcome remained the same: be found or be killed. Quickly, Steel screwed the cap back on and put the bottle back.

He turned and faced the room, scanning it for anything that might hold an explosive device. Steel figured that The Sentinel had everything planned, so he knew their routines and habits. For this to happen, you needed solid intelligence. This meant reconnaissance, cameras, microphones, and wiretaps. Steel walked up to a statue of a woman, a water jug held on her left shoulder as if she was pouring water from it; only a toga concealed her half-naked form. Steel looked inside the water jug.

Inside, a micro-camera lens winked as the light from the chandelier above reflected in it. Steel smashed the statue against the fireplace and searched through the debris for the camera.

The device was no smaller than the nail on his little finger but efficient. He searched the rest of the apartment, knowing full well there would be more.

Graaf's office was the place that held the most devices. Steel assumed this was where Graaf did most of his business rather than an office somewhere. It made sense; no utilities for a place you hardly used.

He walked over to the window and stared across the view. It was a fantastic sight and well worth every penny of the blood money. But Steel was looking for a perfect place for a good observation site.

He searched for the residence that The Sentinel had used for his data collecting. Steel's eyes stopped at a building directly opposite. All the other tenants were starting to put on their lights, except one, which lay in direct line of sight with Graaf's apartment. It was a long shot, but Steel had a feeling about the place.

Leaving Graaf's apartment, Steel hurried across the street to the building he had observed. He knew roughly the position of the apartment, which made checking the names off easier. There was only one resident on the top floor; the other was empty. So Steel knew it would be the one that was occupied. It made sense; if any lights went on, people would put it down to someone being home or one of those security timers to make it look as if someone was home.

He ran his finger down the call buttons to the apartments in the hope someone would buzz him in. There was an electronic buzz, and the door latch was released. Steel rushed in before the bolt could reactivate. Knowing a second time would cause suspicion.

The main entrance was polished wood floors, bannister rails, and picture frames. All are complemented by coloured walls and brass fittings. Steel made his way up the wooden stairwell and towards the top floor. He bumped into a man in a blue boiler suit and brown-rimmed glasses on the way there. The man was in his early fifties but had a good build and long hair tied into a ponytail. Flashes of silver highlights gave his hair a distinguished look.

'Can I help you?' asked the man, startled and suspicious of this strange man in his building.

'Are you the *Hausmeister*?' Steel asked, somewhat hopeful but at the same time reluctant to ask.

'*Ja*, and you are?'

'My name is John Steel; I'm working with INTERPOL. The room at the top, do you know if the occupants are at home?' Steel flashed an ID badge he had stolen from one of the INTERPOL agents in Berlin.

The man looked at the badge and shook his head.

'No, they are on vacation … have been for the last three weeks. Why?' the man asked, suddenly panicked.

'I need to see inside their apartment,' Steel insisted, beckoning the man forwards with an open flat palm towards the stairwell.

The man nodded, and they hurried towards the top floor.

'Are they in trouble?' asked the man, having sudden terrible thoughts about the couple who lived there.

'No, but I believe someone has been staying there while they have been away,' Steel said, trying to make a case for the unfortunate occupants.

They stopped at the door, and the *Hausmeister* took out his master key and opened the door.

'Could you wait here and, please, don't come in,' Steel insisted, knowing the man would mess up any potential evidence by touching things. He moved in and used a handkerchief to close the door behind him.

There was still enough light coming through the windows to illuminate the apartment without needing to switch on the torch he had or turn on the lights. The apartment was primarily open-plan with plenty of modern furnishings. Pictures of the couple hung on walls and sat on shelves. Fresh-faced and happy.

Steel walked around carefully, heel-to-toe, in a straight line and, most importantly, avoided touching anything. He knew the place would be clean. There wouldn't be any fingerprints or fibres. Nothing. The Sentinel was careful. But Steel could now see a profile coming together on The Sentinel. Even cautious people left something. A type of cleaning agent, how they cleaned, and where they cleaned. When something was removed, it then created a pattern.

Steel checked the rooms and found nothing. That was until he entered the owner's office. Steel stood open-mouthed at the array of rigged-up computer monitors and computer systems. The screens showed all the live feeds at Graaf's home and several unknown locations Graaf frequented.

Steel pulled out his cell and pressed the speed-dial. As he did so, he backed out of the apartment using the same line he'd come in on. The sound of ringing was cut short, and a female voice answered.

'Yes, Steel, what do you want?' Sabine answered.

'Sabine, you still want in on The Sentinel case?' Steel asked.

'Yes, why, what you got?' She suddenly sounded interested.

'Well, you'll need a warrant to search an apartment, and your word you'll keep me in the loop,' Steel said, closing the front door.

'Where are you?' Sabine asked, struggling to find a pen that worked. Her heart was racing in anticipation.

Steel gave her the address and the name of the occupants.

If she couldn't get the warrant, asking permission from the owners would work just as well. Steel had passed his cell phone over to the *Hausmeister*, who gave all the relevant information to Sabine.

'That's great, thank you, sir,' she said. 'Now, can you give me back to Agent Steel?'

The *Hausmiester* looked around, and first, a blank expression came over his face, then one of confusion. 'I'm sorry he has gone.'

The phone went dead, and the *Hausmeister* stood for a second, looking around. As if waiting for the man in black to reappear. But he stood alone. The man smiled fleetingly, shrugged, and put the expensive cell phone into his pocket.

* * *

Sabine had hung up on the man. He was no more use to her, not over the phone anyway. She'd gotten the occupants' names and where they had gone. They were on a trip to New York to see the lighting of the Christmas tree at the Rockafeller Center and do some Christmas shopping. She looked up the hotel they were staying in on the internet for the phone number.

It would be around eleven o'clock in New York, so there would be little chance the apartment owners would be at the hotel. Sabine only hoped to leave a message and hoped the hotel would pass it on in time.

She knew she wouldn't get a warrant to search the apartment; what would she say? 'Oh, an NYPD detective broke in and told me there was evidence.' She would be laughed out of the courthouse or arrested for aiding with a crime. No, the owners were the only hope. Even then, that conversation would be awkward, but she could handle people better than lawyers or judges.

Sabine found the number for the hotel and began to dial. The phone rang for several seconds before being answered by George. Sabine explained who she was and the situation back at their home. George took down the message and assured her he would pass it on.

They exchanged thank yous and farewells before hanging up. Sabine didn't seem hopeful of hearing back anytime soon. After all, the couple was in New York; they could be out for hours.

Sabine rocked in her chair. The frustration was unbearable for her. She was close to getting some evidence but still too far away from it. She wondered about Steel's next move. If Steel had been alone in the hotel, where was Falkner? Then she remembered the two agents from Berlin. Had they gone back to the States with Falkner? If so, where was the new target Graaf? He wasn't at the hotel?

Sabine looked at the phone on her desk and contemplated talking to Brena. After all, he had tipped her off as to where Steel had been. But then he had also lied about Falkner. The man had proven to be an untrustworthy source. He had burned Steel to get him out of the way, possibly worse. The man was dangerous; Steel had told her as much.

Sabine's fingers danced above the device as if it was too far for her to reach. Finally, she growled and lost the battle with herself. She pressed a number in the dial history when she picked up the phone. It rang for a while and then went to voicemail.

'Hi, it's Sabine Boese from INTERPOL. We spoke the other day. I believe Steel has the next target and is leaving Amsterdam, possibly returning to the States. Can you call me back? You've got my number.'

As she placed down the phone and sat back, a sudden terrible feeling ran down her spine. The feeling she hadn't accomplished anything apart from making things worse.

* * *

Steel headed back to the hotel using a flagged taxi outside Graaf's place. Visiting the apartment had given Steel some clarity on a few things.

One of them was that The Sentinel had planned this for some time. This wasn't just a spur-of-the-moment thing. Using the taxi gave Steel time to think. They weren't just looking for someone with a vendetta against these people but someone who had the funds and skills to carry it out.

The taxi pulled up outside the hotel, but Steel was too busy thinking to notice.

'Hey, Englander, we are here,' said the cabby impatiently.

Steel said nothing; he just gave the man a cold stare. But even with his sunglasses on, Steel's glare gave the man a cold shiver down his spine.

Steel looked at the meter. 10.00 was lit up on the digital display of the meter. Steel passed over fifteen and got out without a word. The man thanked Steel nervously and went to make change, but Steel had already jumped out of the taxi and was heading into the hotel.

The cabby took off, mumbling to himself while wiping the sweat from his brow, almost as if he'd had the Grim Reaper himself in the back seat of his taxi.

Steel took the elevator up to the room and grabbed his bag. It was time to leave. He was meeting Pat at the ferry port for the six-hour trip home. Steel would leave the investigation into the borrowed apartment to Sabine. It was the least he could do, for old times' sake. Besides, he had gotten all he needed for the moment; the rest would be made clear by Sabine's report.

Steel entered, walked to the couch, and grabbed the canvas travel bag, unlocking the door. He had to go now. Hit the road and get Graaf. Steel hoped the man was in a chatty mood because Steel had lots of questions.

He closed the door to the suite and made his way downstairs to the lobby to check out, then got on the road.

According to his cell phone route planner, the trip would take just over an hour, but Steel knew to add a few minutes for traffic. It was now six-thirty.

The check-out was swift, with no sign of Sarah. Steel thought she wouldn't be there, possibly for the best.

'Oh, a letter came for you while you were out,' said the pretty blonde behind the desk. She handed a small white envelope over to Steel with a smile and watched him open it.

Steel frowned as he pulled the postcard from the envelope.

'Did you see who delivered this?' Steel asked calmly.

The woman shook her head. 'Sorry, it was in with the mail,' she replied.

Steel turned it over and looked at the front. His name was typed out in Times Roman font, but no stamp crowned the corner. This was hand-delivered and snuck into the regular post. A bold move. The timing had to be perfect unless, of course, the killer was dressed like the mail courier.

Steel smiled at the thought but shrugged off the idea. It was more than likely that the killer had snuck the card in there after a misdirection. He had probably used the old trick of bumping into someone and helping them pick their items off the floor. An old method, but it is effective.

Steel made his way out the main entrance and around the parking lot. Moving to the BMW, he pulled out his phone and checked for missed calls or messages. There was nothing of importance, so he tucked the phone back into his pocket and unlocked the car. He opened the trunk and placed the bag inside.

He started the engine and let it tick over for a while, letting the engine warm up. The fuel gauge read half-full. He'd have a chance to fill up before the ferry port; there was a gas station near the German-Dutch border he had used when he was stationed in Germany.

Steel set the satellite navigation for the port and set off. The car was quiet. No music or broadcast from the radio. Steel needed silence to think, to plan. Sure, he could have handed Graaf over to Sabine, but Graaf had answers, and he wasn't about to spill them to INTERPOL, but he might tell his story to the man who just saved his life. Besides, if Graaf didn't give anything useful, Steel would just throw the man overboard and do the world a favour.

Chapter 29

Stanton and Simms stood at the door of the men's restroom, looking down at Falkner, who lay in a pool of his own blood. Deep red filled the gaps in the floor tiles like small canals in a white landscape. By the bloody marks on the third sink in a row of six, Falkner smashed the mirror, then offed himself by cutting his throat. The ghastly signs of arterial spray started at the broken mirror and traversed up the wall and onto parts of the ceiling.

The whole place looked more like a slaughterhouse than a men's bathroom.

The agent who had found him stood outside, shivering. He was a new guy fresh out of the farm. It was his first week there, and he'd had his first look at a dead body.

'Why the hell wasn't someone watching him?' Stanton growled at another agent. His face was almost purple, and the veins in his forehead began to throb. 'I want to know who brought him here.' Stanton wasn't happy a witness had died on his watch and even less so, the fact it was in the building.

The new agent nodded and hurried away.

Simms stood next to Stanton, and they just looked at the bloody mess before them.

'What did he know?' Stanton asked.

'Well, whatever it was, he was scared to open his mouth about it,' Simms replied, shaking his head in disbelief.

'He must have said something on the flight?' Stanton asked, hopeful of a piece of information that could string the case altogether.

'Nah, the man didn't say much about anything.' Simms told him that the man was too full of himself to talk to anyone, remembering Falkner's incessant whining about how his apartment had been blown up. Simms had slipped Falkner a couple of sleeping pills and spent the rest of the flight in sweet silence. Something he'd dare not share with Stanton, not now.

No one was allowed in the men's room; it was now a crime scene, as though Stanton didn't have enough on his plate. Steel had gone silent, INTERPOL was asking questions, and now this.

'I want this place sealed and two guards on this door at all times. Only people in are the investigation team, no one else,' Stanton explained to two agents.

The men nodded and took their posts on either side of the door.

Simms looked up at the security cameras in the corners of the corridor. 'I'll check the feed, see who brought our man here.'

Stanton shook his head and put a sturdy hand on Simms's arm. 'No, that's for the investigation team to do. We have a case of our own. Go upstairs and find out where the hell Steel is,' he ordered.

Simms nodded and hurried towards the elevators.

Stanton stood for a moment with his clenched fists resting on his hips. He didn't believe for a second that Falkner had taken his own life. He needed to speak to the person who had arranged for the pick-up in Amsterdam. Also, he wanted to know why there was a kill team and not an extraction team at the airport—but most of all, he wanted to know why Trish had arranged for those things and on whose orders.

*　*　*

Brena stood over a group of monitors that showed the corridor was now a crime scene. His motionless body stood as straight and as still as a statue. He said nothing as he watched the events unfold. The forensics team turned up along with the agency's medical examiner. All the while, Stanton stood close by, taking everything in.

A buzzing sound from Brena's pocket alerted him to a new message on his cell. He took the device from his pocket and checked the text: Steel has left the hotel alone. No new target in sight. Location is unknown.

Brena ground his teeth and closed down the cell phone before placing it back in his jacket. So far, Steel had proven to be more resourceful than he'd expected. But he was still a threat to Brena's plans.

The men's room incident was only the start of Stanton's downfall, and Brena would be there to pick up the pieces and sit in his rightful place.

So far, everything was proceeding to plan.

Brena looked down at another monitor and saw Simms heading for the war room. He, too, was becoming tiresome. Another bug that needed treading on.

*　*　*

The sound of traffic woke The Sentinel from a troubled sleep. The Sentinel checked the time on the cell phone display, then stood and headed for the kitchen.

Unfortunately, the McDonalds hadn't stocked the refrigerator before their trip, but then they weren't expecting house guests. The interior was lit by fading sunlight through the thin fabric of the white curtains. It was six in the evening, and the sun had begun to set.

The street outside was quiet, a long stretch of houses full of expensive cars.

The Sentinel picked up the electric kettle and tested the weight, ensuring there was enough water for a coffee. Next to the kettle was a pricy-looking coffee machine, but using it would mean cleaning it afterwards. That meant leaving evidence someone had been in the apartment, and that would mean cops. The Sentinel prepared the hot drink. Coffee, milk, no sugar. Then waited for the water to boil. Eyes glued to the feed displayed on a monitor in a small office.

The sound of water boiling drew The Sentinel away from the screens and into the kitchen. The Sentinel poured water into the mug and headed back to the office. There wasn't much happening. Not yet. But The Sentinel was patient. Sitting down, The Sentinel grabbed the notepad and eased back into the chair. Making notes, sketches, and plans.

All The Sentinel needed was a how; when would follow that.

The image on the laptop that sat next to the monitor showed the man in his 1900s office. His feet were up on the desk. The man sat back and watched the latest news report, this time from Amsterdam.

The reporter stood in front of a hotel and talked about a unified anti-terrorist exercise involving the Dutch police and INTERPOL.

The man drank his whiskey and rocked back and forth in the chair. Finally, the man pulled himself forwards and put his glass down before dialling a number on his cell.

'Yes, it's me. Look, this whole thing is going sideways. I need a meet. How quickly can you get here?'

There was a pause as the person on the other end checked their diary.

'Two days' time? OK, OK, I understand,' the man said, tapping his fingers nervously. The Sentinel wrote 'two days' and circled it twice. This was the time frame. Now all The Sentinel required was the when.

* * *

Steel thought back to the new postcard and how it had been slipped into the mail. Sure, a sleight of hand or even the helping-to-pick-up-items trick. But it had been hand-delivered, just like Berlin. The picture on the card was of the Marble Arch in Hyde Park, London. Again it was a nighttime scene. Steel felt uncomfortable bringing Graaf to Britain; now, he knew that The Sentinel was there.

Earlier, Steel had spoken to someone in his agency and arranged for Graaf to be picked up at the port. At least he'd be safe with the Secret Service.

Steel was driving at a steady seventy kilometres an hour, the most the Dutch would allow in that region. But the roads were almost empty, leaving him space to keep the speed constant, giving him time to think.

It had been years since Steel had been to the Arch. Years since, he had watched his friend get gunned down.

Steel felt his grip on the steering wheel tighten at the thought of that night. But this was just a meeting point, like the rest of them. He looked up in time to see a sign for the Euroferry. He was early, but that made no difference.

That gave him more time with Graaf. Steel followed the route the satnav was showing him. Steel sighed heavily. He was nearly at the port.

He was nearly home.

Chapter 30

Simms walked into the elevator and pressed the call button, then wiped his sweaty palms on the legs of his trousers. He was starting to get nervous. Ever since he'd started this case, he'd been on edge. But this wasn't like the other times; there was something more deadly. A hidden enemy—and worst of all, one who wasn't just playing them, but using them as puppets.

The elevator stopped on two, and the doors slid open. Simms looked up to see Dorson with a panicked expression on his face.

'Hey man, you OK?' Simms asked, concerned about his colleague.

'Meet me at the smoker's corner, ten minutes, tell no one,' Dorson said quickly before stepping back and letting the doors close.

Simms stood there for a moment, open-mouthed and confused. What the hell was going on? First, the guys at the airport, then Falkner got killed, and now Dorson acting all mysterious. Simms waited until the elevator stopped on the third floor, then pressed the button for the lobby. Something was going on, and Simms hoped that Dorson had the answers.

* * *

Simms found Dorson at the arranged place. A quiet spot where the agents liked to come to smoke and forget about their jobs for five minutes. Dorson looked nervous, on edge, a man holding on to too many secrets, and it was eating him up inside.

'Hey, Dorson, what's up, man? I got to find Trish, find out what she knows about the death of my witness,' Simms grumbled. He didn't have time for this man's problems.

'Simms, Trish is missing. I tried looking for her earlier, but she wasn't home,' Dorson said quietly.

'Maybe she had something on today, a doctor's appointment or something?' Simms said.

'Yeah, that's what Brena told me, just before he told me to stop looking for her,' Dorson replied flatly.

Simms shot Dorson a puzzled look but said nothing.

'Look, man, something's going on here; something ain't right. I need your help to figure out what,' Dorson said, grabbing Simms's shoulder.

Simms shot Dorson an uneasy look. 'Why me, man?'

'Because you have been out of the country while these things have been going on. Because Steel trusts you, and most of all, you have no love for Brena,' Dorson whispered.

Simms stared with a distrustful scowl. 'What the hell are you talking about, man? We saw who sent that kill team for Falkner and me. I saw who gave authorisation for the jet that picked us up. Trish, that's who. So, you're tellin' me someone used her name to do all this. Why?' Simms growled. He was getting pissed off about not knowing what was going on.

'To throw us off, make us look one way when we should be looking in another, who knows? All I *do* know is Trish is missing, her car was on the driveway, but the house was empty. Someone isn't just killing your witnesses. They are killing our agents as well,' Dorson said, a tremor in his voice. The man was scared, not just for his life, but because he might have an idea who it was.

'So, who we lookin at?' Simms asked, looking around to make sure they were alone.

'No ... not yet. I need proof first. But I'm glad you're looking for Trish. Brena can't stop your investigation into her,' Dorson said with a strange smile.

'What is it?' Simms asked, sensing a sudden conflict of emotion.

'Why stop me from finding her? Then kill your witness, knowing full well the investigation will come back to her? It makes no sense,' Dorson said, puzzled.

'I need to find Trish ... if she is alive. She has some questions to answer.' Simms said, glancing at the main building.

'And if she's dead, that leads to a whole lot of different questions,' Dorson nodded. He wished he could help Simms, but he needed to carry on as if nothing had happened and do Brena's bidding. Besides, if Brena knew Dorson was helping, it could hinder the investigation. No, Dorson knew he had to carry on as usual and hoped he could find the proof he was looking for. 'Look, I got to go. Brena will be wondering where I got to. Check out Trish's place; try and find out what happened to her,' Dorson suggested.

Simms thought for a moment, then nodded.

'Oh, Simms, one more thing,'

'What?'

'Watch your ass. There is someone out there who *doesn't* want us to find out what these witnesses know,' Dorson warned him as he started to head back to the main entrance. 'No phone contact, only face-to-face like this,' he insisted.

'Roger that, and watch your six as well, Dorson,' Simms said, then watched him hurry away before heading to his car. He pulled out his cell and pressed the speed-dial on his phone for Stanton.

The phone rang for a couple of rings before Stanton's voice boomed over the speaker.

'You found Agent Edwards yet?' Stanton growled.

'Not yet, sir. I'm just about to check her place, see if she left anything for us,' Simms answered as he moved towards his car.

'OK, but watch your back. She's already a suspect in the murder of Falkner—don't need a dead agent as well.' Stanton's voice was filled with anger, and who could blame him?

'Copy that, sir; I'll call you later with updates.' Simms closed down the cell, then put the phone into his jacket pocket and took out his car keys.

* * *

The drive to Trish's house would take a good hour with traffic, but Simms didn't mind. It got him away from the chaos. Stanton had handed over the investigation into Falkner's death to the investigation team. Simms knew that must have stung Stanton to have done that, but it was regulations.

Simms got into his car; the sun had warmed it through the windshield, making touching the steering wheel virtually impossible. He let the engine tick over and opened the windows, allowing the cold air in, hoping to bring down the temperature. As he sat there, Simms thought about Steel. He had no idea whether their efforts to bring Falkner back were in vain. That Kitty had died for nothing, which hurt the most. Simms slammed his palms against the steering wheel and silently cried out in anger. Why had he sent her? Sure, the plan was to snoop around, see if she could have found something, anything to incriminate Falkner, hoping to use that to make him talk. A good plan, but the wrong agent went. She was new and inexperienced. But that wasn't what got her killed.

Nobody could have foreseen a bomb in the laptop. Nobody but Steel. They were right. He was good, but now Simms saw why Steel preferred to work alone. Any mistakes, and it was your ass and nobody else's. Some might say that was the easy way, a cowardly way. The method of a person who didn't want to take responsibility. But it was also the smart way. No one to worry about when the shit hit the fan, no one that could be used against you if things went wrong.

Kitty had died because Simms hadn't wanted to be left out of what was going on. They could have both gone to pick up Falkner at the café, but Simms was impatient. He wanted to take Falkner in, and he wanted the evidence.

'Sorry Kitty, I let you down,' Simms murmured, almost as a prayer, just in case she was listening. He tested the warmth of the leather on the steering wheel before putting the shift into drive and taking off.

* * *

Simms pulled up outside Trish's house and sat for a moment. He stared out the side window of the Dodge Challenger, taking in the surroundings and parked cars. Dorson had said that everything looked normal, and her car was in the driveway when he got there earlier that day. Nothing had changed as far as Simms could see, but then he wasn't a white-picket-fence kind of guy.

The street was clear, apart from a delivery van and a couple of parked cars further down the street. Simms looked over at the house on the other side. A man stood slowly, raking the leaves on his front lawn. Simms gave the neighbour a quick nod, forcing the man to look the other way. Simms smiled and got out of his car. At least he knew who to talk to when he needed information.

He walked over to Trish's car and looked inside. The interior was empty, less for a jacket on the backseat. And after trying the door handle and finding it locked, Simms headed to the house. The front showed no signs of a struggle or anything that would indicate she had been abducted, but Simms couldn't rule anything out. He knew there were more ways to take someone away without the old chloroform-on-a-rag trick. Besides, chloroform took a while to take effect, unlike in movies, where it took seconds. Enough time to make a mess, anyway. If someone had taken her, it had likely been quick, possibly with the use of a taser.

Simms walked around the property, ensuring to check the windows and backdoor for signs of tampering. The house looked secure, and the view through the windows revealed nothing untoward. A confused look crossed Simms's face. Trish's car was there, but she was nowhere to be seen.

He made his way back to the front and stared over at the neighbour in the garden. If anyone had seen something, he had. As Simms approached the man, he scanned the house for security-system cameras. In the window was a sticker that read, 'Protected by the neighbourhood watch.' A black sticker with red writing, about A4 size.

Simms knew straight away this man had hidden cameras and possibly footage from when Trish came home.

'Hello there,' he said, giving a friendly wave with the greeting.

'You with the agency too?' the man asked, leaning on the handle of the rake.

'Yes, sir,' Simms said, showing the man his ID.

The man looked at it and nodded as if confirming he believed the credentials were real.

'You here about the woman from over the road?' the man asked, nodding towards Trish's place.

'Yes, sir. Have you seen her recently?' Simms asked, slipping his ID back into his pocket.

'She came back last night, kinda later. Didn't see anybody until this mornin'. Another fella was tryin' her door just like you,' he explained.

'White guy, six-feet, black hair, Italian looking?' Simms asked, knowing the man was going to confirm Dorson's description.

'Nah, that guy came later. The other man was kinda stiff, lookin' like he had a giant stick up his ass. Kinda unfriendly fucka. He musta got here around two in the mornin', just after she'd got home, in fact,' the man said, looking up into the air as if he remembered the situation.

'So, you saw this man?' Simms asked with interest.

'Only on TV, son,' the man laughed, pointing to a twelve-inch panda statue on his front porch. 'But he must have a key or somethin'. Probably snuck in a back way so nobody would see. Stop the neighbour's natterin'. Figured they done the old tango, and then it was time to leave while everyone was sleep.' The man smiled and winked.

'You know you're not supposed to film other people's properties?' Simms returned the smile.

The man raised his hands in a stop motion. 'Hey, slow down there; the lady asked me to. She'd come and get the CDs off of me once a week. Got twenty bucks for it,' the man told him with a shrewd look.

'Twenty, you say? Seems kinda steep?' Simms said, pulling a crisp note from his wallet.

'Hey, she set the price … take it up with her when he brings her back, that is,' the man said, plucking the note from Simms's fingers.

'So she left with him, the man at two?' Simms asked angrily.

The man looked shocked at Simms's outburst.

'I … I don't know. I just, uh, saw them with someone … with him in a long coat or somethin',' the man replied, stumbling over his words.

'Get me those CDs now before I arrest you for obstruction,' Simms barked. So Trish was in trouble, and this asshole was trying to make a buck out of spying on people.

The man rushed inside his house, hoping that Simms wouldn't take him in.

Simms rushed over to Trish's house and tried the front door. It was locked and secured. But the man, the neighbour, had described that someone had gotten into the house, somehow, after Trish had arrived?

Simms checked the lock for signs of it having been picked, but the Yale lock was clean. He headed over to the garage but found that also secured. Simms was stumped. The only other choice would be that the guy had a key—but she lived alone.

The sheepish-looking neighbour came back holding several CDs in cases. Simms regarded him, noting the man's laboured breathing.

'Here you go, that's all of them,' the man said, stepping back an arm's length, just in case.

Simms took the disks, his mind searching for answers.

'So, how long have you been in the surveillance business?' Simms asked casually, not really expecting a reply.

'Oh, I'm not. Trish set all this up; she's a genius with hidden cameras and stuff,' the man said, backing off and heading back home as quickly as he could.

Simms watched him cross the road, his mouth wide open. Had they been looking at this all wrong? Was she indeed involved in the death of Falkner?

Then another thought crept in. Was *she* The Sentinel?

Chapter 31

Sabine had waited over an hour for an answer from the apartment owners. Another half an hour to convince them and another half hour to get the CSU teams in. Finally, Sabine had a call from her boss; this took only five minutes and a lot of shouting. The teams needed to find something that proved her intel, or she would be manning an office in the Alps, or worse.

She sat in her car and sipped the coffee she had gotten from a fast-food restaurant down the road. She knew better than to go in and contaminate the scene. But she needed clear/clean evidence. Ever since she'd gotten that postcard, she had been like a pit bull.

She had never suspected the CIA would be part of the investigation or that they would bring in Steel. However, that was the game that The Sentinel was playing. The big question: what were the rules?

The Sentinel was leaving clues, as Steel had told her, but why bring her in on this? If this individual wanted these people found, why not offer clear signs and less of the cat-and-mouse game? Or maybe it had to be this way? It was one sure way of sparking interest; plus, it had the added bonus of scaring the hell out of the targets.

Steel was on a ferry heading back to Britain, and he'd probably hand Graaf over to his agency. It made perfect sense. Graaf would be secure, and that agency did have a way of getting people to talk.

Sabine Boese looked over the street at the building opposite her. It was a tall building, built in the 1800s, and wore a recent paint job.

Her mind wandered to thoughts of how much an apartment like that would cost. Then, a sudden tap on the car window made her jump, and she praised her decision to go with the carry-out top for her cup.

'You can come up now,' said one of the techs when Sabine wound down her window.

She nodded and raised the window before getting out and locking her car. She walked up to the top floor, taking in the view at every level, walking in the footsteps of a killer, as she would call it. She knew The Sentinel wouldn't use the elevator—too much risk in being seen. No, the stairs were safer. Her gloved hand swept over the wood of the balustrade and bannister, the latex of the surgical glove gently rubbing over her fingers.

When Sabine reached the doorway, she saw the CSU techs busy at work, dusting for prints and taking photographs.

'Got anything?' Sabine asked, hopeful of something.

'Nothing, the place is clean,' said one tech with a smile and an excited look.

'Well, I'm glad *you* are happy. I have no idea what I'm going to tell the chief,' Sabine sighed.

'No, Agent Boese, the place is clean. No prints, fibres, nothing. Someone has wholly sterilised the apartment. They even emptied the hoover and took the bag with them,' the tech said, his smile even wider.

'I'm so glad you are enjoying this, but we have nothing.' Sabine hoped the man would stop smiling before she shot him.

'Agent, they took the evidence with them. That means they knew we would check the garbage for any signs of vacuumed trash. The person who did this knows our playbook.'

Sabine regarded the tech as he rushed off to another man who had called him over. Her eyes were wide with excitement. She didn't know whether to be happy or distraught about the news.

Was the killer a cop? Or had it been one?

She strolled to the balcony. Her face began to tingle from the cold breeze which was brushing against her. She closed her eyes and let the wind brush against her, hoping it would clear away her troubles.

Sabine opened her eyes and looked directly across the apartment across the street. Unfortunately, she couldn't see much due to the lack of light within. Nevertheless, her imagination took flight as she dreamed of what the place looked like within.

She let out a sigh and went to turn, but something stopped her. The rail was sticky as if some kind of adhesive tape had been used to hold something onto it. She called over one of the techs to take a closer look. It could have been for decorations, but there was only one patch.

Sabine looked over the street. She had wondered why Steel had sent her to that particular apartment. A chill ran down her spine as an idea sprung to her mind. She raced down the stairs and headed for the opposite building.

Reaching the front door, Sabine started to check the names of the tenants. And one name stuck out: Thomas Graaf.

'Steel, you tricky bastard. No wonder The Sentinel likes you,' she said, shaking her head. Sabine pulled out her cell and pressed the speed-dial. She needed to talk to Stanton and fast.

* * *

Stanton answered on the sixth ring. Sabine didn't presume to ask what had kept him; after all, the man probably had enough on his plate as it was. Stanton sounded tired but, at the same time, alive. There was a ring to his tone that Sabine had remembered from years ago, before his wife's passing. Back when he gave a shit. Now, that sound was there again. Sabine smiled as she heard him ... a smile that soon faded.

'Avery, has Steel contacted you?' she asked, hoping that he had.

'No, I haven't heard from him since the fuck up in Amsterdam. Why?' His tone was deep. He paused before the question as if he was afraid to ask but knew he had to.

'Steel is heading back home with Thomas Graaf; he also led me to Graaf's place and…' Sabine stopped. Suddenly remembering what Steel had warned her about: Brena.

'And?' Stanton asked, hoping she wouldn't give lousy news about Steel. That Steel had blown something up or crashed something, or Graaf was dead.

Stanton somehow knew it wouldn't be her reporting Steel's death. The man had more lives than a room full of cats. He had once said that Steel was only hard to kill because he'd cause trouble in Hell.

'And, well, we are waiting for a warrant to search it,' she lied. She listened; the pregnant pause of Stanton's was unusually long.

'Thanks for letting me know, Sabine; I'll get some people on it,' he finally said softly, as if the news was painful to hear.

'I'm sure Steel has everything under control. You know Steel, Mr Organised?' Sabine joked, hoping to hear a laugh at the other end of the phone. But her words were just met with a grunt, and then the call ended. She looked at the cell and wondered what was wrong, what had happened to change Stanton's mood.

Sabine understood she had that effect on people, but this was different. Something had happened at Langley; what she didn't know, but it was enough to piss off Stanton.

Sabine tucked the cell back into her pocket and looked up at the building. She knew she had no grounds to go into Graaf's apartment, and asking him would be out of the question as she had no contact with Steel.

She knew she had to get inside, and the threat of an explosive device inside would be grounds enough. So, Sabine took out her cell and called the police tactical squad. They would have to make the entry, and EOD would take care of finding the bomb.

The only grounds she had to base her hunch on was that Graaf was on The Sentinel's list. Nobody wanted a recurrence of what happened in Berlin. So, she spoke with the operations commander, a man called Joseph Wolf.

'We'll be there in fifteen minutes. In the meantime, get everyone out of the building,' Wolf ordered.

As Sabine ended the call, she looked back at the policemen guarding the other building.

'Hey, you two,' she shouted, 'I need this building emptied and a cordon set up. Nobody in until the EOD and tactical teams get here.'

The two officers nodded and ran over, one of them relaying the orders to the others inside the building. Sabine stood and watched, directing the officers where they should go. But, first, the other building would have to wait.

Then, naturally, two cops would have to make sure nobody entered the apartment after CSU had finished. Still, the primary objective now was securing Graaf's apartment and ensuring the block was safe for the other tenants. Sabine looked at her watch; it was twenty-one-thirty, and Steel would be soon on his way with Graaf. She cursed Steel under her breath. He had left her with a ton of crap to sort out, and he had the only witness.

She began to regret her decision to help him, wishing she had locked him up until he gave up Graaf. Still, he didn't trust anyone, especially Brena.

What was it about the man that got Steel all riled up? Well, one thing was sure; if Steel didn't trust him, there *must* be something, and she should be careful what information she gave him or Stanton.

As another cold wind swept past her, Sabine shivered, pulling her coat tightly around her.

Chapter 32

Arriving at the port, Steel found Pat and Graaf sitting in a car park near the entrance to the terminal and pulled up close to Pat's car and got out, leaving the Bimmer's engine idling.

'Any problems?' Steel asked, knowing there wouldn't have been. If there were, Graaf would have been in the trunk.

'Nah, the man might be a monster, but he's alright,' Pat said with a grin.

Steel didn't even want to know what they had chosen to discuss on the journey down to the port, but whatever it was probably wasn't legal.

'Come on, Graaf; we've got a ferry to catch,' Steel said, leaning on the open window of Pat's car.

Graaf grumbled, got out, and walked towards Steel's BMW.

'Thanks, Pat; I'll catch you around. And stay out of trouble,' Steel said with a laugh, shaking his friend's hand.

'Hey, Johnny, try not to kill him. We've got some business to discuss when this is all over.' Pat laughed out loud, and, with a rev of the engine and a spit of gravel, he was gone.

Steel watched Pat's car disappear into the distance, then turned his attention to Graaf, standing next to the passenger door.

'OK, come on, let's go,' Steel insisted, getting into the driver's side and making himself comfortable.

Graaf got in and turned to Steel. 'Just so you know, I'm not saying a word,' Graaf said sternly.

Steel just smiled and put his foot down on the accelerator.

* * *

After boarding, Steel hurried Graaf along to the cabins, searching for their rooms. Steel looked at the ticket for the room numbers and followed the plan on the wall but made sure he was walking behind Graaf, giving him instructions on which way to go.

'So, here we are,' Graaf said, pointing to the room number Steel had told him to look for.

Steel opened the door, and the two men walked in.

Graaf's eyes widened as he saw only one double bed in the middle of the cabin.

'I like to cuddle in the mornings. How about you?' Steel joked, causing Graaf to shake his head. 'Don't worry, this is your room. Mine is next door, just in case you get scared.' Steel laughed, slamming Graaf's boarding pass against his chest. 'We have reservations for the buffet at half-nine, don't be late.' Steel shut the door behind him.

Graaf sighed with relief at not sharing the room. But the thought of ferry buffet food turned his stomach.

* * *

Steel had showered and headed for the restaurant, where he found Graaf wearing a glum expression.

'Oh, good … you made it,' Steel said with disappointment.

'I can stay in my room if you wish. After all, I am your prisoner.' Graaf spoke with discomfort at the thought of the cabin and possibly catching something from the food.

'Oh, my dear Graaf, and miss that charming smile of yours? Besides, we have so much to discuss.' Steel's smile changed to a sneer.

Graaf stepped back slightly, a shiver running down his spine.

As the restaurant line moved forward, a man at a small desk asked to see their tickets.

Steel smiled and showed him, and Graaf followed suit.

Steel and Graaf were ushered towards a table near the window. All the tables had white cotton tablecloths and sparkling cutlery. They finished with wine and water glasses, which made Graaf raise an eyebrow.

'What were you expecting? A burger and fries joint?' Steel smiled, ensuring his seat faced the doorway.

As Graaf sat, they were greeted by another waiter who was ready to take their drinks order. Steel chose a glass of Merlot and Graaf went for Chardonnay.

As they waited for the wine, Steel leant back and sized up Graaf. The man wore a tweed suit and dark-rimmed glasses. He held himself like a position man, possibly taking his name too literary.

'And what now, Mr Steel?' Graaf tried to appear unnerved.

'Well, once we get the wine, I was thinking of going for a side salad and possibly some curry I saw when we walked past the buffet,' Steel joked, knowing precisely what Graaf meant. Still, he wanted to get some alcohol into the man before they started.

When the waiter returned with their orders, he thought about the best truth serum ever made: alcohol.

* * *

Steel and Graaf had dinner in silence. He didn't want to jump straight in with the questions; he wanted Graaf to sweat for a bit. Besides, he didn't want to ruin his appetite. So Steel was on his third helping while Graaf played around with the roast beef he'd gotten from the carvery on his second time around.

The two men agreed the meal was over by nudging their plates away. After settling the bill for the wine, Steel headed for the exit and then for the bar. Graaf followed like a punished child.

Graaf wasn't happy about being abducted and shoved on a ferry to Britain, but the alternative seemed less appealing. He'd heard about the two killings in New York and the bombing in Berlin.

If Pat had been correct, he was better off with Steel. Pat had explained he wasn't under arrest, more under protection. However, he had to give something in return to get that protection: answer any questions Steel asked.

Steel found a seat next to a window away from the bar and stage. Steel didn't want to yell over a live band or loud chatter from the bar if they were to talk.

A steward came over to get their drinks order. Steel asked for a classic vodka martini with two shots of gin and a lime wedge on the side. Graaf opted for a beer.

Steel looked around at people who wandered by. Some headed for the duty-free shops, and others for the games and slot machines. The ferry was an hour out of port and cruising along steadily. As he looked out of the window, he could only see the reflection of the lounge. Outside was pitch black, with the lights from the port far behind.

The drinks arrived, and Steel paid straight away and tipped the man.

'Do you realise how difficult it is for some people to make this? A simple martini with gin? They have the same ingredients, but somehow, the drink has a different taste each place I go. Weird,' Steel said, causing Graaf to shoot him a puzzled look. 'And that's the puzzler. The same things in it, but each time something new. It's a bit like this case. We get postcards, each one a clue to the person and the place, but always people who have no connection to one another. So, a different taste, a different spin.' Steel leant forwards and placed down his drink.

'But you know what I think?' he asked with a crooked smile.

'No, Mr Steel, what?'

'I don't think they're that different after all; there are merely different ways of mixing them, just like these people who are connected. We just haven't found the right mix yet,' Steel smiled.

Graaf did not.

Steel stared into Graaf's eyes. Graaf's left eye twitched, and immediately he knew Graaf knew something.

'Oh, my dear Thomas, I hope you don't play poker because you have a lousy poker face,' Steel grinned as he took another sip. 'So, what do you know, Thomas? Why is this person after you?'

* * *

Steel listened to Graaf tell his life story. Three beers and six shots of whiskey were all it took to get Graaf in a talkative mood. Steel had gone to the bar to get the drinks rather than have Graaf overhear what he was ordering; he himself had been on apple juice most of the night. In Graaf's state, he'd have no idea which suited Steel fine.

'So, when were you in New York last?' Steel asked bluntly.

'New York ... a fantasy city. Love New York,' Graaf said before bursting into his Sinatra impression.

'Graaf, why were you in New York six months ago?' Steel plucked a random time out of the blue, hoping for a response.

'Wow, how do you know I was there ... here.' Graaf peered around, all confused, 'Where are we?'

'Graaf, New York, six months ago?' Steel asked again, urging him to stay on track.

'Yes,' Graaf said with a smile.

'New York, you, why?' Steel growled, thinking the drinking thing wasn't proving such a great idea. It was obvious Graaf's thoughts were elsewhere.

'Meeting with someone ... yes, that's right. I was smuggling some diamonds for someone from South Africa, but don't tell anyone.' Graaf laughed and put an index finger to his lips, and whispered, 'Shh-hoosh.'

'With who? Who was the buyer?' Steel asked insistently.

'It was ...' Graaf stopped and put a hand over his mouth.

Steel rolled his eyes and grabbed him, pulling him towards the toilets.

'Graaf, I swear, you throw up over this suit, and I'm chucking you overboard,' Steel declared, unhappy with Graaf's weak constitution. He dragged him into one of the stalls and left him leaning over the bowl while waiting outside.

As Steel stepped out, a man smaller than Steel moved out of the way, allowing Steel to pass. 'Thanks,' Steel smiled.

'No problem,' said the man as they passed each other. Then, as the door closed, Steel leant against the wall and contemplated how long he would give Graaf before he checked on him.

He let out a sigh of disappointment. Getting Graaf to talk hadn't been the hard part. Getting him to talk about what Steel *wanted* him to was the hard part.

Suddenly, Steel turned to face the door. There was something familiar about the man he had just passed, but he couldn't put his finger on it. He had seen the man recently, but where? His eyes turned into thin slits displaying anger as it came to him.

The man had been a member of the kill squad, the man from the magazine store.

Steel burst into the men's room just in time to see the man trying to drown Graaf in the toilet. He grabbed the man and pulled him out of the stall, smashing his back on the sink behind him.

The man yelped in pain as he arched his back from the impact.

Steel swept his legs, causing him to fall and smash the back of his head on a porcelain bowl. The man immediately recovered and stood up straight and ready to fight. The assassin threw a punch with his right and then his left. Each blow was dodged or deflected, then countered with quick jabs to the man's torso. The man grunted with every hit he received but kept on attacking.

The man was good, but Steel was better.

Graaf went to get up but was knocked back down as the man fell on top of him with Steel's hands around his throat.

Graaf fought desperately to hold his breath as the two men struggled on top of him, his head partially submerged in toilet water.

Steel dragged the assassin out of the stall and smashed his face against the tiled wall of the restroom. The man kicked back, almost catching Steel off guard, but it was enough for the man to break free and take flight. Steel followed the man out and up the stairwell; the man was heading outside.

Graaf crawled out of the stall, covered in water and looking battered, as two British students walked in and saw him.

'Bloody hell, I'd lay off the booze, mate. It looks like it tried to kill ya,' joked one of the young men and headed for the urinals.

Graaf sat for a moment, catching his breath and nodding in agreement. 'No more drinks, no more ships, and hopefully, no more Steel.'

* * *

The assassin slid open the door to the outer deck. Wind and seawater slapped him in the face, forcing him to close his eyes for a second.

A second distraction was all Steel needed.

He launched himself at the man, sending both of them out into the cold wind of the night. The man slammed against the safety rails and let out a lungful of air.

The man sent an elbow backwards, which contacted with the side of Steel's head, sending him back. Steel came back with a kidney punch and smack to the back of the head. The man yelped as his head contacted the lighting pole in front of him.

Punches and kicks were exchanged as the two men fought on the side deck. The passengers within were oblivious to the fight.

The man used a mix of jiu-jitsu and aikido, while Steel favoured Krav Maga for this situation.

The wind howled like a wounded beast. The waves crashed against the side of the ship, muffling the sounds of combat. But Steel was oblivious to the noise or the foamy spray; he was fixed on the man sent to silence Graaf. Steel would have preferred to keep him alive and get answers to questions, but this guy was a professional. He would rather die than give up anything.

The man's face was bloody, his nose broken, and a nasty gash ran along his forehead. But he still kept coming. Finally, the man lets loose a volley of kicks and punches. Even though both men had lost some energy, Steel was faster and countered every one of his foe's moves, followed by several hits of his own.

* * *

Thomas Graaf had gone back to his room and changed clothes, thankful that Pat had allowed him the pleasure of packing a bag, then returned to his seat in the lounge to wait for Steel.

As Graaf sat quietly, sipping old sparkling water he'd just ordered, he looked out the window, hoping to see something other than darkness. Instead, tiny lights in the distance danced about in the blackness like fireflies following each other.

Graaf reckoned it must be a fishing vessel or small boat. As he put his face against the glass to get a better look, another face met his before sliding into the night. Graaf stumbled backwards and fell onto the floor just as the two Brits walked past.

'Seriously, mate, have something to eat and lay off the booze,' laughed the young men as they walked towards the games room.

Graaf stumbled back to his chair and sat, his hands shaking with fear at what he had just seen … or thought he had seen.

'I'll tell you one thing, that weather out there is an absolute killer,' joked Steel as he suddenly appeared from nowhere.

Graaf jumped and hugged his water glass for comfort.

'You OK?' Steel asked, spotting Graaf's strange demeanour. 'I don't know about you, but I'm famished.' Steel looked around to see if they made bar snacks.

* * *

Steel dragged a hysterical Graaf to a café that sold sandwiches and strong coffee and stuck him in a corner while he got refreshments.

He returned with two large coffees and two lunches. He figured Graaf needed something to soak up the alcohol, and a BLT seemed about right.

'What happened to the other man?' Graaf asked, sipping the black coffee.

'Possibly the same thing he had intended for you, but more dignified,' Steel replied as he ripped open the packaging on the sandwich and inspected the contents.

'Who was he?' Graaf asked, looking around to see if there were more.

'Who can say? But I've seen him before, in the airport in Amsterdam.'

'Was he … ?'

'The Sentinel? No, more likely a guy on a payroll. Which clears one thing up,' Steel said, biting into the BLT on white bread.

'Clears what up?' Graaf asked, taking another sip.

'How The Sentinel can move about so quickly,' Steel said with a crooked smile.

'So, he was the one who was planting all the bombs?' Graaf asked, leaning forwards.

Steel thought for a second and then shook his head.

'No, I think that was The Sentinel, but you can bet whoever sent this guy was someone who doesn't want you breathing.' Steel paused as if going through things in his head before speaking. 'The Sentinel is all about seeing what unfolds, even if he's not there. The Sentinel is responsible for making the devices; chances are The Sentinel was in those countries days before I was to set up everything. The pleasant chap we just met was there to make sure things happened.'

Thomas Graaf looked into space while he sipped, his brain working out the information. It all made sense, apart from who wanted him dead. Sure the list was long, but none of those people would go to these lengths. Graaf's ordeal had sobered him up in more ways than one.

Steel needed answers, and he hoped Graaf could give them to him. Falkner had given him nothing, but hopefully, Simms had had more luck. Steel checked his watch; it was ten-past-ten local time, which meant it was four in the afternoon in Langley.

Stanton probably had Falkner in a six-by-six by now and was sweating the truth out of him. The thought made Steel smile, unaware that Falkner was dead and had said nothing to Simms or Stanton.

'So, what happened in New York?' Steel asked bluntly, hoping to catch Graaf off guard.

'When?' Graaf seemed confused at the question.

'Cut the crap, Graaf, you know when,' Steel growled, his patience wearing thin.

'OK, I was there but not six months ago. It was more like a year ago,' Graaf said, remembering the man's face at the window.

'Doing what? I swear if you say sightseeing, you'll be swimming after your friend,' Steel stated grimly.

'I was meeting a buyer, a man called Falkner. He was getting diamonds off of me,' Graaf admitted.

Steel sat back, a confused look on his face.

'But Falkner was an arms dealer. So, what was he doing buying diamonds off you?' Steel asked, then took a bite of his sandwich.

'He wasn't so much buying as collecting, a down payment if you will.' Graaf's words were a whisper as if he didn't want to be overheard.

'Down payment for what … or rather for who?' Steel sat back in his chair, realising this was a trade-off; nobody knew who the goods were for. All the players knew each other, but the brains of the operation would be invisible.

'More for who, and before you ask, I have no idea. My policy is discretion, Detective Steel, no questions asked or answered.'

Steel had heard that about Graaf. He found that plausible; deniability was more like a safety net for all concerned. 'Where was the meet and when?' He hoped for something he could check on later.

'Central Park, by the statue of Alice in Wonderland, midday, I believe,' Graaf answered with a smile, knowing full well Steel wouldn't be able to check on it.

'How much are we talking?'

'One million in uncut blood diamonds,' Graaf said, still smiling as he knew Steel wasn't getting the answers he wanted.

However, Steel was getting more than he had expected, and, in truth, he was surprised Graaf was still breathing. 'So, if the diamonds were payment for something, who footed the bill, and don't say you don't know,' Steel warned.

'I get a job through a sight on the dark web, a dropbox if you will. One million in diamonds, untraceable, and for my trouble, I get a painting.' Graaf offered a broad smile.

'Don't tell me that was your Renoir that went on auction two days ago?' Steel asked, looking through the scam.

'Payment by cash is dead; some use these Bitcoins, but I find that vulgar. I appreciate art much more. Besides, it only goes up in value with art,' Graaf said smugly.

Steel had to admit it was a brilliant way of moving money without it being traced. However, even art left traces, especially an expensive paintings.

'When did you get the job?' Steel asked.

'Uhm, a year ago. Whoever it was called themselves Mr Nuntius.'

'Nuntius … that's Latin for messenger,' Steel said, puzzled.

'Excellent, Mr Steel; nice to see the Army didn't beat everything out of you.' Graaf grinned before taking a bite of his sandwich.

Steel searched his memory for anyone who had called themselves that but came up empty. 'And *after* the exchange?' Steel pressed further.

'We went our separate ways, first time and last time I ever met the man,' Graaf explained. 'But he did speak with someone on his cell as he was leaving, telling them the job was done.' Graaf shrugged as if it meant nothing, but to Steel, it could mean everything. At last, Graaf had said something worthwhile.

'Who was the wire transfer from?' Steel leant forward intently.

'I can't remember,' Graaf shrugged, his expression showing he hadn't thought about it or cared to think about it.

'Try,' Steel growled.

'Look, it was some time ago, OK. I have all that stuff in files, so I wouldn't have to remember,' Graaf explained as he leaned back in his chair. 'It's in a draw on my desk.'

Steel pulled out his cell and hoped he had enough bars to make a call back to Sabine. It was a lead or possible dead end, but it was something.

Steel listened as the electronic ring came from the speaker. He let it ring until it went to voicemail. Suddenly, he had that bad-feeling sensation again, and the hairs on his neck stood up.

Steel quickly searched for a new number on his speed-dial. It was Stanton's. After several rings, a familiar voice picked up.

'Chief of Operations, Stanton's office, Agent Brena speaking.' Brena's voice was smug and had a sickly tone to it as if he had been practising that answer for a long time, but with his name at the end, not Stanton's.

Steel hung up and tapped the cell phone on the metal table. His gaze swept the room, but he saw nothing except the faces of those he could call. He stopped tapping and searched his call logs again. Finally ... *finally*, there was one other person he could speak to.

Steel just hoped Pat wasn't drunk yet.

Chapter 33

On the second retry, Pat picked up. The man was tipsy but not entirely juiced. 'Steel, what's up?' Pat laughed, thoughts of the two men on the same ship bringing all sorts of images. 'Oh, you didn't kill the little bastard, did ya?' he asked, panic in his voice.

'No, he's fine. But look, can you do me a favour and go to Graaf's apartment and speak to Agent Sabine Boese? She's with INTERPOL. I need to get in contact with her. It's urgent,' Steel said, his voice solemn.

'Graaf's place, ya say? Oh, sorry, Johnny boy. That place is ashes. That bomber ya after, he just took out Graaf's apartment. Nice job, too. Could have used the bloke back in the day,' Pat said, forgetting Steel had been on the other side of the wire at the time. 'Oh, sorry,' he apologised, then took another swig of Irish whiskey.

'Pat, you need to get down there. I need to know she's OK,' Steel said with some urgency. He hung up and hoped Pat could still walk, never mind, drive. A feeling of guilt shot through his veins. He had led Sabine to the apartment; if anything had happened to her, it was because of him. Now Steel knew how Simms felt after Kitty's death.

He stuck the cell phone hastily back in his pocket before he hurled it at the wall. He took a deep breath, hoping to suppress his anger. The Sentinel was setting up devices and not disarming them; innocent people were getting hurt, which didn't wash with Steel.

Graaf looked over at Steel, gritting his teeth and trying not to put his fist through something. 'What is it?' A sudden feeling of terror ran through his spine.

'The Sentinel just blew up your place,' Steel said grimly.

'Was anyone inside?' Graaf asked, genuinely concerned, but Steel figured it was more for his apartment than possible casualties.

'I don't know yet … waiting on Pat to find out.' Steel picked up the coffee cup and looked at his reflection in the black liquid.

Steel gazed at himself for several seconds. His thoughts started to wander. He thought about his wife and family, about the day the kill team came and took everything from him. Then, the images in Steel's head changed. He was standing in the mall, and everything was still. The people were frozen in place as if someone had pressed the pause button. Steel looked around and saw King holding the kill switch wrapped tightly around his hand with the bandage. There was a small explosion from behind him, and the window shattered. Then a flash from the device, followed by the shockwave. Everything was in slow motion, everything but him. Steel shouted to the people to get out, but everyone stared at him with blank expressions. He yelled louder, but no words came out. His feet could not move; it was as if he were glued to the marble floor.

Steel looked up in time to see the blast wave lift everyone off their feet, then watched them burst into flame. He tried to move, but his legs were like stone. He watched in horror as the people were blown apart, but he was untouched.

A little girl walked up to him; she was around six years old. The flesh on her face was blackened and burnt, her piercing blue eyes wide but somehow calm. She took Steel's hand and smiled.

'Why are you sad? It's OK. Someone will always clean up the mess,' the child said before letting his hand go and stepping into the flames.

Steel's screams were muted by the blast wave, which lifted him off his feet and sent him crashing through the window.

With a start, Steel woke from the daymare. The crashing sound he had heard was the coffee mug smashing on the floor. He looked around to see people looking over at him but then turning back as if nothing exciting was going on.

Steel turned to Graaf, who was glued to his seat, his eyes wide with fear.

'Wow, no more coffee for you,' he said, shuddering.

Steel had never had an audience for his dreams before; he usually woke up with a broken whisky glass on the floor. 'Sorry, my mind wandered off for a second,' Steel said, kneeling down and picking up a broken piece of the porcelain mug. 'We need to get some rest. Got a long day tomorrow,' Steel lied.

In truth, Steel needed time alone to think, and he couldn't do that with Graaf hanging around. But Graaf had agreed; it was late, and after the day he'd had, hitting the sack sounded like a good idea. A good night's rest and a full breakfast the next day were just what they both needed. Besides, Graaf thought he'd be safer in his cabin with a locked door between him and the world.

Thomas Graaf headed to his cabin, leaving Steel to grab a bottle for someone from the duty-free shop. Steel had no intention of turning in just yet. He had too much to do; besides, he was waiting for a call from Pat.

Steel returned to the lounge with a bottle of Johnnie Walker Green and waited for a steward to take his drink order. It was now quarter to eleven, and the place was filling up. The live entertainment was already in full swing, but nobody was drunk enough to be singing along.

Steel sat in a corner booth and waited to be served. Stewards rushed here and there serving the many new arrivals, but Steel had time. The steward who had served him and Graaf before spotted Steel and headed for him with a broad smile.

'Large Johnnie Walker Green, no ice or water.'

The steward nodded and hurried away. Steel had no intention of sleeping, not yet. He had too much on his mind, like what had become of Sabine. That was at the top of the list.

* * *

Simms went to Trish's home to review the footage on the disk. It was too dangerous to take back to the agency. Not with Brena about.

If Dorson was right, Trish had been taken; why, however, was unclear. But one thing *was* clear: Simms didn't know who he could trust, not even Dorson.

Simms wished he had stayed with Steel, but he had to make sure Falkner arrived safely, which he had done.

However, he was now stuck finding Falkner's killer and tracking down Trish. Simms started by checking her computer for any unusual activity or files. Then, reviewing the web history and any hard drives or data sticks she had. He waded through her data and saved documents, hoping to find something that would explain her disappearance, but found nothing of interest. Trish's emails were spam or messages from her family back home, as well as a load of reminders of posts she had on social media. The hard drives held pictures from holidays that she had been on with her girlfriend, but nothing racy enough to copy, not that he would have.

A gentle buzz emanated from his jacket pocket. Pulling the cell from his jacket, he checked the new message. It was Dorson. 'The explosion in Amsterdam, Thomas Graaf's apartment. Police are investigating a couple of casualties, including Agent Sabine Boese of INTERPOL. No word on the condition. Brena is asking where you are. Watch your ass and silence your phone.'

Simms knew what that meant straight away and grabbed a paperclip from Trish's desk. He had to get the sim card out, toss it, and then get rid of the phone. A few years ago, it would have been simple, take out the sim card and drop the cell down the toilet; let the water fuse the electronics. But he had to be flash and get one of those damned waterproof jobs. Good for thirty meters. Usually a great idea, but not this time.

Simms looked outside and saw a removals van parked a few doors down, four burly men with sweaty, red faces and an apparent liking for fast-food loading the truck. The idea came to him in a blink; toss the phone in the back and walk away.

It would be a brilliant plan if he didn't get caught.

Simms headed out the front door, ensuring he didn't close it completely. As he moved closer, he noticed the men were all inside. Simms smiled at his good fortune and went to hurl the device in the back. Suddenly, another man appeared from behind a wardrobe, causing Simms to pull his arm down quickly and rethink the plan.

'Howdy,' the man said, wiping the sweat from his brow with a white and blue striped handkerchief. The man was six feet each way, but mainly around the middle. His round head held strands of brown hair that he probably couldn't bring himself to get rid of.

'Hi there,' Simms replied, waving a greeting with his empty hand. 'Had no idea the neighbours were moving.'

'Yeah, last-minute thing, apparently. Poor bastard's off to Alaska,' the man laughed but then stopped and looked around to see if he'd been seen.

'Alaska, wow, who did he piss off?'

The two men laughed, making the man cough like a horse and reach for the couch to steady himself.

'You OK?' Simms asked, feeling bad about nearly killing the man.

'Yeah, doctors say I should quit smoking, but what do they know?' The man sparked up a cigarette and inhaled a lung full of nicotine.

Simms watched the man have another cough attack, but he lost the contents of his top pocket this time. A pack of cigarettes hit the tailgate along with his wallet and a stainless-steel Zippo lighter.

Simms helped the man retrieve his items and waved the phone in his face. 'Hey, don't forget your phone.' Simms hoped he'd take the bait.

'Oh, yeah, thanks.' The man gave a broken smile and tucked the items away, including Simms's phone.

'Well, safe journey,' Simms said, giving the man a friendly wave before making his way back to Trish's house.

The man waved back and called Simms a 'sucker' under his breath as Simms disappeared into the house.

Simms would have felt bad for the man, but he caught the insult on the downwind. The man would have some explaining to do, but hey, he took the phone.

He was hoping they wouldn't catch up to him until the Alaskan border, but then Simms wasn't that lucky. He figured he had around thirty minutes tops until the other agents would be knocking on the door, asking questions. Questions he probably didn't have the answer for. And if Brena had sent them, he might have filled their heads with the thought that Simms had done something with Trish; after all, he was in her house, and she wasn't there.

Simms grabbed Trish's laptop and the hard drives he hadn't checked and hurried out of the door. As he was leaving, he saw the old man, who was back in his garden, this time watching the removal men. Simms walked over and waved a quick hello.

'You got what you need, son?' the old man asked.

Simms tapped the laptop and nodded.

'Look, some other men will be coming soon. These men will be pretending to be agents; chances are they're the ones who hurt Trish. So, I need you to stay inside and keep away from the windows. Can you do that, sir?' Simms asked with a look of concern for the man's safety.

'Don't worry, son, I'll keep out of their way, don't you fret,' said the old-timer.

Simms shook the man's hand and walked back to his car. He unlocked the car and got in, but as he shut the door, he looked over at the old man, and the more Simms stared, the more he had the feeling that was the last time he was going to see the fellow alive.

* * *

Big Ben chimed twelve. Alerting the people of London Town of a new day. The rain had stopped hours ago and was replaced by a blanket of stars that winked down at the world from a clear sky. The Sentinel had been woken by a passing police car. Sirens wailed as they headed down the street, followed by intermittent flashes of blue that filled the room.

The Sentinel sat up and stretched off before heading to the kitchen to make coffee. It had been a long day and an even longer night.

The Sentinel knew Steel had Thomas Graaf and had travelled back to Britain.

Everything was going to plan. Soon, the truth would be revealed. Soon, they would all pay. Soon, The Sentinel would have revenge.

Walking into the kitchen, The Sentinel poured coffee from the glass pot, then placed it back into the machine. The aroma of hour-old coffee filled the air, but The Sentinel didn't mind. Coffee was coffee.

Taking the brew back to the couch, where The Sentinel had crashed hours before, The Sentinel looked over at the one monitor that was still covering Graaf's apartment. The small screen showed only static snow as the feed had been cut or the camera had malfunctioned. The Sentinel sat up.

Something was wrong.

Perhaps the police had found the camera and taken it out?

Quickly, The Sentinel rewound the recording to the point the transmission had failed. Then, leaning forward, The Sentinel observed the feed.

A police tactical team smashed through the door and began their room-to-room search but found nothing. Then an EOD sweeper team followed with a small military robot. The tracked device wheeled in and started the search, starting with Graaf's computer, but found it safe.

After an hour of searching, the teams called the all-clear. Then Sabine Boese and the cops came into view. The scene was now cleared for them to start investigating.

On the way up the stairs, a phone began to ring. Sabine stopped the cops behind her as the sound of the call made her nervous somehow. The chimes started once, twice … before the answering machine kicked in. Then, Sabine launched herself at the officers, knocking them back down the stairs.

There was a massive explosion that shook the building.

Then the camera went dead.

The Sentinel stood up in shock. A device had gone off, but it wasn't the one The Sentinel had put in. In fact, The Sentinel's explosive wasn't even in the building; it was somewhere else, and a disarm code had been sent.

Someone else had done this, just like at Falkner's place. Someone was silencing the witnesses. They were covering their tracks and making sure The Sentinel got the blame.

The Sentinel began to pace up and down. The new target had to be found and secured; Steel already had two, so the third was as good as safe. That just left the real killer.

The Sentinel stopped pacing. A new plan had come to mind. A risky and irrational plan. The Sentinel *had* to work with Agent John Steel.

Chapter 34

It took about an hour for the agents to find the truck and stop it outside Warfordsburg. They tracked the cell to a diner but only found the removal men instead of Simms. The lead agent phoned Brena to update him on the situation. A phone call that didn't go well. Brena had hung up the phone, and the agents left the diner with Simms's cell phone, leaving the three men shaken.

The three Yukon SUVs pulled up outside Trish's house, and twelve agents scatted information. Six went to the front, six to the back and waited for the order to breach.

The command came over the earpiece of each team leader, followed by a loud crash as both doors were kicked in. The teams moved in close, single file; this was followed by cries of 'room clear' as they searched for any signs of Simms or Trish.

Minutes later, the teams filed out; the lead agent pulled out his cell once more to make a call to Brena. As he stood on the front lawn, he held the cell phone up, so the glare of the sun didn't reflect on the gorilla glass screen. Suddenly, something caught his eye. A curtain had moved from the house over the road. They were being watched. The agent smiled and tucked the cell back into his pocket.

He left orders for the men to search the house for anything that may lead to Simms or Trish. The agent then called one of his men over, a giant of a man with a stern face and hands like bulldozer shovels, and they walked over to the house.

'Let's see if the neighbours saw anything,' said the agent as he pulled on his leather gloves.

* * *

Steel woke up around five with a bad taste in his mouth and the need for coffee. The bed had been comfortable, but then he could sleep on a razor blade if he had to. Steel showered and pulled on a black suit. He imagined Graaf had slept with one eye open; that was, if he had slept at all, given the attempt on his life the night before. He pulled on his jacket and slipped on his sunglasses even though he had put on his blue contacts … just in case border control asked for the glasses to be removed while they checked passports.

* * *

Steel left his cabin to check on Graaf, if only to annoy the man and than be concerned about him.

'Graaf, are you up? Time for breakfast and then departure,' Steel said after giving three quick knocks on the door.

There was a thumping sound, as if something had fallen on the floor. Steel looked around anxiously. Was there someone in there with him, possibly another assassin?

He hammered on the door again while trying to find a way to pick the lock. But there was no way in that he could see, not with the equipment he had. Which led to the question: how did the assassin get in?

Finally, the door sprung open, and a dazed and confused Graaf stood before him; his hair was a mess, and he looked as if he'd had a rough night.

'Seasickness?' Steel asked with a sympathetic smile.

Graaf nodded while holding his stomach.

'Oh, well, never mind, breakfast is on,' Steel smiled.

Graaf slammed the door and ran to the toilet.

'I'll meet you at the restaurant; I'll get you a full English that will settle your stomach,' Steel grinned as he heard Graaf retch in the bathroom.

* * *

Graaf appeared at the restaurant looking pale and dehydrated. Steel was already on his second helping of a fried breakfast and his third coffee. Graaf sat hard in the chair opposite Steel. He sneered at the sight of the food in front of him.

'You feeling better?' Steel asked as he stood.

Graaf said nothing, just shook his head and turned his head away from the sight of Steel's breakfast.

Steel wandered off, leaving Graaf to drink the coffee Steel had gotten for him half an hour ago. It was lukewarm but wet. Steel returned and placed down a plate of English breakfast in front of Graaf and a glass of milk.

'I can't eat this,' Graaf complained, pushing the plate away.

'Get it down your throat, Graaf; it will line your stomach, which is now empty,' Steel explained.

Graaf looked at the glass of milk and shot Steel a look. 'What, I am I? six years old? They have no orange juice?' he complained.

'Yes, you've been a big baby. Look, the milk is better for you; OJ is mainly acid; you drink that on an empty stomach, yeah, then you're gonna be poorly,' Steel explained. A lesson he'd learned in the Army after going on an all-nighter. When you got back to your bunk, they taught you to drink lots of water; that way, you wouldn't dehydrate and were likely to wake up without a headache. What they didn't tell you was when you'd been throwing up all night, how to get rid of that bad feeling.

The sergeant had taught him a lot. Everything except how to deal with your family's loss to a bunch of mercenaries.

Graaf pushed the plate away, and Steel pushed it back.

'I know to you it looks like a dog's dinner, but trust me, you'll feel better,' Steel insisted.

Graaf nodded reluctantly before slowly tucking into the bacon, sausage, and mushroom feast. Steel sat back and enjoyed his coffee while he watched the Dutchman eat and smiled to himself. Not because he was nearing home but because Pat had finally called. He told Steel that Sabine was fine, with only a few cuts and bruises; she'd probably have ringing in her ears for a while, but she was safe. She had saved the life of the other officers and would probably get a commendation for her actions, or so his contact had said.

Sabine was a good agent, a pain in the ass, but a good agent. Even though people thought it, she and Steel had never slept together, even though they had chemistry. No, Steel made it a rule never to get close to a partner; in fact, the rule applied to anyone. He had lost someone before, and he didn't want to go through that pain again. It was simpler not to feel that than to let people become distractions.

Steel sipped coffee and looked out through the windows to the side. The weather looked grey and uninviting, but he was sure it would brighten up later.

* * *

The call for the passengers to their vehicles disturbed Graaf and his third helping of breakfast. Steel was almost impressed at the Dutchman's recuperation; he just hoped he wouldn't get car sick after all the food.

A rendezvous with an MI8 agent had been set up, and a place and time arranged. Eight o'clock at an inn at a place called Horsley Cross. There would be four SUVs; after the pickup, each would take a different route to throw off any tails. Steel knew how this worked; he'd done it plenty of times with the agency. A simple tactic that dated back centuries, the art of misdirection was an agent's best friend in sticky situations.

Steel and Graaf finished their breakfasts and collected their belongings before heading to the car. At the docks, another vehicle would be waiting for them, and the BMW would be disposed of, just in case, someone was looking for it. If someone were following Steel and Graaf, the agency would make it as difficult as possible for the trackers. Finally, Graaf would be heading to London and Steel back to the family estate in Buckinghamshire.

The two men got into the car and waited for the vehicles in front to move. It had been a long couple of days for both of them, more so for Steel, but Graaf's ordeal was almost at an end. Steel's was to continue. The Sentinel was still out there, and the next target had been identified as being in Britain. Steel was glad to be going home; he missed it, even though it brought back bad memories.

He made a point to spend as much time back at the estate as possible or as work would allow. He had also inherited the family business, a multi-billion dollar company that made everything from children's toys to military equipment. His great-grandfather had created a company and was now a legacy along with the title.

Steel had joined the Army Cadets at sixteen, then later joined the regulars at seventeen and a half. Finally, at twenty, he had been picked to go on an exercise to play enemy against the special forces. He was spotted and poached by the SAS for his skills and attitude.

At thirty-two, his life changed, and his world fell apart. Steel had come home after a tour of Bosnia. But instead of a welcome-home party, Steel found a massacre. Mercenaries had invaded his home and had killed most of his family and friends—the grass was painted red with the blood of those he knew. Suddenly, the soldier kicked in, and he went hunting for those responsible. Taking them down one by one, leaving none alive.

The last thing Steel remembered from that terrible day was the laughter of the shooter and the footsteps that crept away. Then, as he began to lose consciousness, he was aware of someone else in the room. The man grabbed Steel and pulled him out of danger. The man was the family gardener, a Japanese guy who had worked for Steel's father for years, or so he had thought.

The man had nursed Steel back to health using old medicine. Steel knew the people would have done this would be after him, so he needed to hide; he had hidden at his family's cabin in Alaska. Unfortunately, his plan to stay out of sight hit a snag when a tour plane crashed. Aboard was his new boss, the head of the SEAL teams.

'They're going,' Graaf said, waking Steel from his dream-like memory.

Steel said nothing, just grumbled and put it into gear and moved forwards towards the ramp.

'So, what were you thinking about?' Graaf asked, interested in what nightmares this guy was haunted by.

'When?' Steel shrugged, hoping Graaf would shut up and let him drive in peace.

'Just then, you kind of looked into space and fazed out. Whoever pissed you off, I hope they had a big enough hole,' Graaf laughed.

The look on Steel's face almost made him wet his pants. This guy was broken and hurting, and worst of all, deadly. A great combination, just as long as you were on his side.

'Just stuff … memories,' Steel said quietly.

'Like what?' Graaf asked, insistently curious.

'Graaf.'

'Yeah?'

'Shut up, or I'll put you in the trunk,' Steel said without looking at the man.

Graaf nodded as they drove in silence.

Finally, Steel headed for the motorway and the meeting point.

* * *

In the morning, Simms headed for a motel not far from his apartment in Arlington. He decided not to head home. If the agents were looking for him, they would look in the first place. It was a cheap place, twenty dollars a night, but it had a bed and a shower and a diner not too far away.

Simms wanted to go back to the agency and tell what he had found, but so far, he had only snippets of information and nothing solid. All he did know was Brena was a threat, Falkner was dead, and Trish was missing. He'd gotten a burner cell from a store and had slipped in a new sim card. Luckily, he had a head for numbers and put Steel's cell number into the memory, along with Stanton's.

Simms sat on the bed, looked at the cell, and then turned his gaze out of the window. He felt alone and lost in his pursuits. Men were after him, *his* men. Like Stanton would do, Brena probably gave the agents as little information as possible. 'Bring me, Agent Simms, at any cost,' was probably all they got, as well as the added news of Falkner's death and Trish's disappearance. As far as the agents were concerned, by the time Brena had finished briefing them, Simms was a fugitive, without Brena actually saying that. That way, if Simms wound up dead, Brena had full plausible deniability and would put it down to misinterpretation.

Simms had to find who had killed Falkner and Trish. He prayed that she was alive, pain in the ass or not; she was one of the good ones. Simms headed over to a small desk in a corner and started the laptop. As he waited for it to boot up, he arranged the hard drives and the disks that he had gotten from the house and from the old man. If the old guy had been filming Trish's home for her, she might have transferred the data from a disk to one of the hard drives. Something had spooked her for her to take such measures.

As the home screen opened, it asked for a password. Simms growled at the screen and sat back. Trish was careful, so her password wouldn't be 'Password' or '12345.' Simms tried her birthday and came up with nothing, then tried her girlfriend's name, which also came up short. He closed down the computer and lay back on the bed. What he needed was a hacker … or at least a computer genius.

Simms smiled. He had just the man: Dorson.

* * *

Graaf slept in the backseat of the new car as Steel drove to the inn. Just outside the port was a filling station for those who needed to fill up before their long drive. Steel had met with two other agents to drop off the new vehicle and get rid of the BMW.

He looked at the blacked-out Jaguar F-PACE SUV and smiled. 'That will do' Steel brushed his fingers over the polished paintwork.

Graaf just yawned and climbed into the back as if it was a car from the airport rental service.

'Oh, don't mind him; someone tried to kill him,' Steel explained to the two bruisers. 'And someone still might if you get the seats dirty,' he yelled through the window so Graaf could hear him.

A gentle tap on the smoked privacy glass let Steel know he understood.

Steel shook hands with the men and made his way to the driver's side while the men got into the BMW. As the two cars got underway, Graaf curled up and closed his eyes. They were safe for now; all Steel hoped was that the handoff went well.

It was still some way before they got there, and Steel was enjoying the silence. He thought about putting the radio on, but he didn't want to disturb Graaf, not because he was being kind, he just didn't want to talk to the man just now. Once the agency had Graaf, someone would interview him to get more out of him than what Steel already had. Any bit of information would be crucial in trying to figure out who was doing this and why. But Steel was on the clock; he had to get to the Marble Arch at Hyde Park that evening. The journey would take two hours if the traffic were terrible.

Steel smiled to himself as he enjoyed watching the scenery blur past. The green roaming fields, trees, and wall-like bushes were fence lines. Steel couldn't wait to see the old place again, even for a short while. He had business there and also needed to pick up a few things. He had called ahead, so the head butler knew of his arrival. He still found it amusing that he had a butler, but then Jamerson also looked after the estate while he was away.

Steel had allowed it to be open to the public and permitted it to be used by film companies. All the revenue made went back into the house and gave a bonus to the staff. Steel preferred it that way; at least it was used and not left to fall into decline like some other places he had heard about that had been bought and turned into hotels or golf resorts.

The estate was still his home, and despite everything, he would never give it up. But it was more than a home; it was somewhere he could talk to his family. Although most chose to do this at a graveside, his family were still part of the Hall for him.

* * *

The built-in navigation system alerted Steel of the turnoff he had to take to get to the inn. He saw a huge roundabout upfront and turned to his right-hand side. He followed the satnav's instructions and pulled into the car park, following the roundabout. The inn was a quaint place in the middle of nowhere, with food, drink, and accommodation signs.

Steel parked the car but left the motor running. Looking around, he saw the parking lot was virtually empty, less for a couple of cars and a motorcycle. He checked the time on the vehicle head-up display. He was ten minutes early, but then the roads had been kind.

Steel switched off the motor and got out. The fresh British air smelled of the countryside. Grass, cows, and car fumes. He sucked in a lungful of air and closed his eyes. The inn looked tempting. One quick pint of the best British beer, but he needed his wits about him if something were to go wrong.

A blacked-out Land Rover Discovery pulled up, and a man got out. Dressed all in black, with a shaven head and a goatee. 'What's the password?' asked the man.

'Doesn't matter; you would have forgotten it anyway,' Steel replied.

The two men laughed out loud and embraced like brothers.

'I hear you're causing trouble again,' said the agent.

Steel shrugged and moved his hand in a rocking motion.

'Where is he?' asked the agent, looking around. 'He's not in the trunk. But Steel, you know you can't keep doing that,' laughed the man.

'Relax, he's in the back seat. And believe me, once he starts talking, I bet you'll think about it.' Steel nodded to the rear of his vehicle.

The man nodded, then spoke softly as if to himself. Suddenly, three other cars drove up, each one identical to the other, including the same licence plates.

'Showtime,' the man announced, making sure the cars lined up with their tails to the wall, then all four opened their rear passenger doors.

Steel went to Graaf's sleeping body and opened the door, completing the wall.

'Graaf,' Steel said, shaking the man to wake him up.

Graaf woke with a start. But Steel's hand muffled the cry out for help.

'Shut up and listen. You are going with these agents. You need to cross over from one vehicle to the other without touching the floor. You follow their instructions to the letter. Nod if you understand,' Steel said with a quiet but firm voice.

Graaf nodded, more out of fear than anything.

'Do it now, and do it slowly,' Steel ordered.

Graaf turned around and inched himself over until his feet were just inside the door of the other vehicle before dragging himself over. The driver inside the first vehicle told Graaf to keep going until he was in the third car. Again, Graaf said nothing, only obeyed. Steel watched as each car shut its doors and took off in different directions before getting in the Jaguar and, with a smile, putting the radio on.

Chapter 35

After a two-hour drive, Steel pulled up to the gated entrance of his home. The sound of the tyres crunching the in a gravel driveway as he approached the hall. The grounds looked empty, less for Jamerson, who stood at the main entrance. Jamerson was a tall, stocky man with greased-back grey hair and a proud look about him. Steel switched off the engine and got out, wearing a broad smile.

'Good morning, sir; I hope you had a sound journey without further incidents,' Jamerson said in a deep baritone voice.

'Morning Jamerson, yes, it turned out alright in the end, and how have you been?' Steel asked, moving towards the man and shaking his hand.

'As well as can be expected, sir. Thank you for asking.' Jamerson's mouth curled into a crooked smile.

'Your leg again?' Steel asked, shrugging slightly as if to say it was nothing. 'Maybe this will help?' He took his canvas bag out of the trunk.

'Oh, sir, you shouldn't have,' Jamerson jibbed, holding the bag.

'Ha-ha, very droll. The bottle and cigars are inside,' Steel said with a grin.

'And will sir be joining me in a nightcap?' Jamerson asked with a curious look.

'I'm afraid not. Got a killer to catch,' Steel said, looking at his watch and thinking about what he had to do. 'Cup of tea and a bacon sandwich would be great, though,' Steel grinned.

Jamerson smiled and shook his head. Even though Steel carried a title, he was foremost a soldier, like himself, and nobody could take that away from him.

* * *

Steel had taken a long shower while he loaded the updates on his new phone, watch, and unique sunglasses. The water was like tiny balls bombarding his skin. The steam filled the vast bathroom, fogging up the mirrors. Steel leant forwards, his hands resting on the polished sandstone walls, and let the boiling water wash over him.

He had lost track of time and hurried out of the shower, wrapping a towel around him and stepping into his bedroom. Jamerson sat in one of the two Chesterfield armchairs and sipped tea. He looked up at Steel and gasped. Steel's body was taut with muscle as though he had overdone his training.

'I see you've put on weight,' joked Jamerson.

Steel laughed and dropped down and pushed out a hundred push-ups.

'I remember when you couldn't do one of those bloody things without crying about it,' Jamerson winked, taking a bite of his sandwich.

'Practice makes perfect,' Steel replied, sending the mockery back.

'Touché,' Jamerson replied, raising his china teacup.

Steel finished his exercise and stood. The smell of the turkey-bacon sandwich was more than a reward for his effort.

'So, what is it this time, and how can I help?' Jamerson asked, filling Steel's cup with the fresh brew.

'You heard about the postcard killer?'

'The Sentinel, I believe he calls himself, yes. Nasty bugger,' Jamerson said, handing over the teacup and saucer.

'Well, he has been sending me clues to find the targets,' Steel explained before taking a sip.

'That's a new one, a killer who wants you to find the victims.' Jamerson shook his head, unable to fathom the reasoning.

'I think The Sentinel wants them found; he wants them to talk. Why I don't know yet, but someone *else* doesn't want them to.'

'Did you find any … alive, that is?' Jamerson asked, remembering the blast in Berlin that was all over the news.

'Two so far. I'm off to get the next one tonight,' Steel said before he dug his teeth into the thick fluffy white bread and closed his eyes before giving a moan of appreciation. 'Oh God, that's heaven.'

Jamerson laughed and refilled his cup. 'So, where is this little meet and greet?'

'Marble Arch, Hyde Park, midnight,' Steel answered, his voice low as if just saying the name brought him pain.

'You're joking?' Jamerson sat back. ' Have you been back since—'

'Since they killed Thomas at Speakers' Corner? No, I've tried to avoid it,' Steel admitted. Nevertheless, the thought of that night sprang back into his memory. How he had been too late to save his friend.

'So, what are we going to do?' Jamerson smiled.

'*We?*' Steel asked, surprised at the presumption of helping.

'You don't think you're getting all the fun to yourself this time, do you?' Jamerson stood.

'No, Sarge, I guess I'm not.' Steel stood, and the two men shook hands.

Now, all they needed was a plan that wouldn't get anyone killed, especially themselves.

* * *

Simms woke and turned to face the alarm clock. The red digital display read five-past-five. Simms sat up and rubbed his eyes with his palms while letting out a yawn. He'd only gotten a few hours of sleep, but it had been deep, and he felt better for it. The bed was comfortable, possibly too much, as he fought to roll out from between the sheets and head to the bathroom to take a leak.

Simms had no plan; he just knew he had to somehow get in touch with Dorson. He could call, but Simms knew as soon as the man had told him to ditch his phone, he'd probably done the same. He flushed and headed for the shower. His usual routine was to take a long run, but that was out of the question. Instead, he would shower, change, and head for breakfast at the diner. Not much of a plan, but it was a start.

Dorson lived on the other side of Arlington from Simms's apartment, a five-minute drive at most. But the chances of Brena having agents watching Dorson's place were high. Moreover, Brena knew that Dorson had been looking for Trish earlier and that Brena was a red flag. So, Simms had to get a message to Dorson somehow. Sure, they were trained in this kind of stuff, but so were the people looking for him. Simms almost wished Steel was there; he would have found a way to do it. But he wasn't there; Simms was alone.

After a hearty breakfast and a lot of coffee, he drove close to Dorson's street but avoided the turn. Instead, he took the next road, parked between two parked cars, and waited. It was quarter-to-six and still dark. The one thing Simms had in his favour.

Simms gave it five minutes before getting out and walking to the house that sat opposite Dorson's. Trees lined the streets, and ever-green bushes acted as fences.

Simms had to admit Dorson had done well for himself. But he knew that Dorson had inherited it after the death of his parents six months ago when they had been killed in an accident while on a trip to New York.

Simms wore stuff from a thrift store he had found: jeans, a red and blue chequered shirt, and a baseball cap. Not much of a disguise, but then he was on a budget. He walked with his hands in his pockets and his shirt hanging out. The sunglasses were a nice touch, along with the dog he had offered to take for a walk. The hotel owner was sceptical at first, but then, she knew where he lived. Room 12.

Simms walked down a side road that split the block into two, more of a dirt track used as a shortcut, but it had one quality: it ran along the back of Dorson's house.

Simms knew that Dorson would have left hours ago; he was conscientious like that, so knocking on the back door was out. So, instead, Simms wrote out a note on a paper napkin earlier at the diner. 'We need to talk; I have something, Trish's computer. So urgent.' That was all it said, besides his new cell phone number. He hoped those few words would be enough to get Dorson's attention. The idea was to slip it into the mailbox, but then it would look suspicious; some guy walking up and dropping something in someone's mailbox. And breaking in would be out. Dorson was a gadget freak and security nut; the chances were he had cameras all over the house and garden. And that was what Simms was counting on.

Simms had also bought a dog's squeezy ball and slit it so that he could place the napkin inside with enough of it sticking out for Dorson to notice. If he were right, the moment the ball went near the house, a silent alarm would go off, and Dorson would return home to check. Simms had to admit it wasn't the best plan, but he was working against the clock with no other way to communicate with Dorson. So, Simms held up the pink toy, causing the chihuahua to look at the thing and tilt its tiny head.

'Oh well, here goes nothing,' Simms said, tossing the toy.

The dog let out a displeased 'woof' as the toy sailed over the fence and hit one of the windows. Simms hurried off, making sure he wasn't seen. Stage one was complete. Now for the hard part: setting up a meeting.

* * *

A text message from the lead agent informed Steel that Graaf had gotten to the HQ in one piece. Steel nodded as if to reassure himself he could now breathe easy.

Two targets had been secured.

Steel wondered about Falkner and what he had told them. Stanton was a good interrogator. He'd done it as a young Lieutenant in Vietnam and in Gulf conflicts and Bosnia again.

Steel placed down the cell and looked over to the three murder boards he had re-created in the study. It was still early, and there was no point rushing into London just to sit about. The picture of the Arch had been another nighttime scene, and the address had been '2359 Precinct.' Steel perched himself against the edge of the desk and crossed his arms as he stared at the boards. Finally, there was the other board, but this held information that Graaf had told him, along with names and dates.

Steel knew that something or someone connected them all but couldn't see how. However, there was one thing for sure: they were all in New York at the same time for one reason or another. Steel rubbed his unshaded eyes and rolled his neck and shoulders. He was beginning to feel the effects of not training for a while.

There was a gym in the house, however, and the distraction might be good for him. Steel pushed himself off the polished oak desk and headed back to his room to change. He needed to train until his body hurt, hoping the rush of blood would kick-start his brain.

* * *

Steel's rigorous workout involved running ten miles with weights and finishing with a sparring session. All of which took around two hours. The time he didn't have time to waste but thought it necessary; after all, he hadn't done anything for the two weeks he'd been off.

Sweaty but refreshed, Steel returned to the study with a large smoothie he'd made with vegetables and fruit he'd found in the kitchen. Steel sipped the healthy drink as he returned his attention to the boards. The information was still blotchy, and he hoped that Stanton's interview with Falkner would fill in some of the gaps. He looked at the ornate Victorian metal clock; it was eleven in the morning, which meant it was around six in the morning in Langley.

Steel pressed the speed dial on his phone, knowing Stanton would be at the office, that is if he'd actually left since this whole thing started.

He listened to the rings while he continued to drink the tasty sludge from the plastic sports cup, his eyes scanning the boards to make sense of it all.

'Morning, John,' said a tired Stanton.

'Morning, Avery,' Steel replied, his eyes locked on the one board.

'Now the pleasantries are over; where the fuck are you?' Stanton barked.

'Nice to hear your voice too,' Steel said, nearly losing a mouthful of the drink from the shock of Stanton's outburst. 'I take it things are not well at your end?'

'You could say that. Falkner is dead; they are calling it suicide,' Stanton told him.

'But you're not?'

'Hell no. Doesn't make sense. Him offing himself. He was safe here, or so we thought.' Stanton's voice calmed the more he spoke, but there was something in the tone that had Steel wondering.

'And, what else? Come on, Avery, I can hear it in your voice.'

'Trish is missing, and Simms has gone to ground after I sent him to try and find out what had happened to Falkner. So, something is happening in my own backyard, and I don't know what.' There was a brief pause from both sides as they took in the information. 'Tell me Graaf is OK?'

'He's in London at the head office; they are speaking with him now,' Steel reassured his friend and, puzzled, asked, 'So, why would Simms leave the building if he was looking for someone on the inside?'

'Beats me. I guess he got a lead that took him outside. Besides, I have Brena looking for them both; they'll turn up. Hell, we'll probably find out that they were shaggin' each other,' Stanton laughed.

'Doubtful. Trish was gay,' Steel said, sipping.

'What, Trish? Nahhhhh,' Stanton declared, unconvinced at Steel's theory. 'What makes you come up with that?'

'I could see it in the way she carried herself, how she looked at women and men,' Steel said with an almost patronizing tone.

'You came on to her, and she shot you down, didn't she?' Stanton chuckled.

'The pictures of her girlfriend pretty much sealed it … nice looking couple.' Steel laughed.

'So, where are you?' Stanton asked.

'I'm back home and off to London tonight.' Steel explained that the latest postcard showed Marble Arch in Hyde Park, a nighttime scene.

'Yes, we got it from a courier from the embassy. It arrived a couple of minutes ago. The lab is running it now,' Stanton said, looking at a photocopy on his desk. '2359, midnight.'

'The Sentinel wants these people found, Avery. He doesn't want to kill them.' He placed down the cup and walked over to the boards. 'He wants these people to talk, not die.'

'So, why kill them? Two apartments were destroyed because of this lunatic, and two good agents were injured or killed in the process. As far as I can see, this loon will stop at nothing to get rid of these people, not make them talk,' Stanton argued.

'So, how do you explain Falkner?' Steel asked, not convinced by Stanton's mindset.

'The Sentinel probably had something on one of my agents, threatened their family. We are dealing with a highly skilled person that uses surveillance on people. Hell, the nut job probably had this in a contingency plan if things went wrong. Bastard probably had this whole thing planned for months,' Stanton said, his tone suggesting respect for the killer's tenacity.

Suddenly, Steel's eyes widened. Something Stanton had said had filled one of the missing pieces. 'Avery, something has come up. I'll call you later.' He hung up before Stanton had time to respond.

Steel realized something, a clue he had overlooked that was there all this time. He had been looking at the wrong timeline. He had been so focused on when the targets had been in New York that he had forgotten one thing: *when* The Sentinel had started.

The first killing was of the security guard a week ago. However, how did The Sentinel get everything on him? The surveillance took weeks, maybe months. Steel could feel a theory on the tip of his tongue, but there was still something eluding him. The houses in Berlin, Amsterdam, and now London. These nests didn't just happen overnight; they took severe planning to arrange ... movement of equipment and time schedules. The Sentinel knew when these people would be away and for how long.

Steel raced over to the computer and started to look into any records of investigations into Graaf and Falkner, precisely where the surveillance on them was carried out. Steel rocked in the chair while the agency database compiled the information.

Jamerson stood in the doorway with a tray of coffee, but he dared not enter. He could see the look on Steel's face. He had seen it before. And it always ended one way, with someone paying for what they had done.

* * *

The nightmare he'd just had seemed real, too real. It had been hours since Simms had returned from Dorson's place. He figured that he would get more research done while he was awake.

Unfortunately, the lack of sleep the night before had caught up with him, and he woke up in his hotel room with a start, his head against the keyboard of his laptop. Simms stretched off and wiped the drool from his mouth.

With blurry eyes, he checked the time. It was ten minutes to ten.

He grumbled at the thought of the lost time, but then he did feel better for the nap, less for the markings on his face and the millions of zzzzzzzs written on the screen. He found it curious the only key he'd hit was the 'z', which was basically the letter associated with sleeping. Simms smiled and stretched off again. His mouth was dry, and his stomach empty.

The early breakfast had been burnt off hours ago, and now, like an angry beast, his belly was reminding him of it.

Simms agreed there wasn't much he could do until he heard back from Dorson. He needed to know what was on that computer. The hard drives were mainly work-related, and he hadn't had time to go through them all. One file was about some rich guy in New York that the cops and the agencies had been after. Apparently, she had been on a task force before being assigned to Langley and Brena's team, or that was what he liked to call it. The truth was that he was the same as the rest, apart from getting chosen to take on this case. Before that, Trish was in charge. They all took turns. That was how Stanton liked it. But Brena had visions of grandeur and a stick up his ass.

Each team member had been picked from different offices around the country. Still, only Brena, Trish, Dutton, and Kitty had been to New York and Boston. Everyone else had been from Washington, Chicago, and other cities in various states. Kitty had been there six months; the others nearly a year.

Simms had left a contact number on the back of the napkin, so Dorson had a way of reaching him. However, he had no idea if Dorson had gotten the message or had even been back to his place to check the alarm. The worst case was that Brena hadn't let Dorson go but had sent one of his goons instead. If that were the case, this whole thing could be over in no time, and Simms would be in front of Stanton or the director.

Simms had disappeared, and it looked bad, especially considering he was supposed to be looking for Falkner's killer. It had 'guilty' written all over it. Plus, Trish was missing. Simms couldn't go back until he had proof that Trish had been taken, and hopefully, that was the same person who had killed Falkner.

Simms's belly growled once more, this time with more vigour. He was hungry and tired and had no leads for either of his assignments. He looked at the other hard drives that sat next to his laptop. There was still plenty more to look through, including the rest of the files on the three-terabyte drive. Simms packed the drives and the computer into his sports bag and walked over to the air vent near the floor.

Taking out his knife, Simms flicked open the blade and undid the screws that were holding the vent cover in place. A perfect hiding place, he thought. Better than under the bed or stuck in a draw for any snooper to find. Simms was careful not the make any scratches or marks that would indicate the cover had been taken off.

Simms stood and headed for the door.

He slipped the 'do not disturb' sign on the handle and headed for the stairs as he closed it behind him. His stomach growled yet again as the stairwell door closed behind him. He was hungry, thirsty, and sick of being kept in the dark.

Chapter 36

Stanton sat in his office and stared out of the panoramic window that overlooked the grassy area and the other buildings on the grounds. The sun was high, but passing clouds blocked out the brightness and the warmth.

He watched people walking here and there, coming and going, oblivious of the chaos that was unfolding in Stanton's world. He would turn and look at his desk phone every so often, waiting for it to ring. He was expecting two calls. One was from Steel, and the other was from upstairs. No matter how this played out, Stanton knew his career was over, had been for some time. He was just treading water until it happened. He was a dinosaur, a remnant from the old ways, the Cold War days. They were looking for someone new in this modern age, someone like Brena.

A knock on his door caused Stanton to turn and face the door. It was Brena, and he was wearing the look of a lost child.

'What is it?' Stanton asked, expecting more bad news.

'The investigation team has finished. Although they are calling it suicide, there were no markings on Falkner that would indicate he had been in a fight or subdued, and no chemicals in his system. The only marks were on his fists, telling us he punched the mirror several times before it broke,' Brena said, almost disappointed at the finding.

'So, we are not looking for a killer. So, why have you got your dogs hunting Simms like he'd done it himself?' Stanton growled, angry at Brena's heavy-handed approach to his own people. 'I thought I told you to tell him to come in, not track him like mass murder. Fix it, now,' Stanton barked before turning around and returning to his view of the grounds.

Brena went to speak but decided it was best to keep silent and just walk away. He knew that Stanton was right, but he enjoyed the chase too much, regardless of who it was on the other end. Of course, Steel remained the best query he'd had and possibly ever would.

Brena stood by the elevator and pressed the button for the second floor. A flurry of thoughts raced through his mind while he waited. Like how had it gone so wrong?

Kitty was dead, Trish was missing, and Simms had gone to ground. This, for him, was a career disaster. He was the lead agent on this, and somehow it had all fallen apart. Of course, he wanted to blame Steel, but the man had a reputation that couldn't even be scratched.

The doors opened, and the button illuminated the second floor.

Brena stepped out and headed for the war room. He still had five agents, including Dorson, when he got back from checking his house alarm, that was. Brena had only let him go because he was sick of looking at the man's angry expression every five minutes.

Brena had grounded him for looking into Trish's disappearance. But little did Brena know that Dorson had been right. Trish had gone, and nobody had any idea how or where she had gone too.

Brena's agents had spoken to a neighbour, but that had proved fruitless, apart from scaring the man half to death and landing him in hospital.

Nobody looked up as Brena entered the room. They were too busy checking for a pattern between Graaf, Falkner and the two victims. They knew that New York was a significant piece of the puzzle, but the rest was a mystery. There, one lead was in the morgue, and the other was in London. The new postcard Steel had sent was clean, just like the others. They were at a dead end, with the clock ticking. Their only hope was that Steel could get the next target before The Sentinel.

Brena walked past each desk, checking on their progress but ensuring he didn't disturb their trail of thought. Each had a different task to research. One had the New York angle, and another had background checks on all the targets. Another was to determine anything The Sentinel may have done previously, just in case this wasn't a singular occurrence. The last was tracking Steel or the best he could. Somehow, Steel had the knack of disappearing, almost as if he had vanished entirely. Stanton had told Brena that Steel was good, but he hadn't appreciated just how good, until now.

Brena walked over to Kitty's desk and sat down. His fingers danced over the keys with a light touch, but not enough to activate them. Her desk was pristine. Everything had a place and purpose. Brena leant back in the chair and swivelled it side to side, his thoughts a million miles away. He started to open drawers and look inside, more out of boredom than actual interest in the contents.

Brena picked up a notebook and flicked through the pages. He knew there wouldn't be anything interesting or prudent to this case, but he wanted to know the thoughts of one of his agents. Most of the notes were of things to do or other equally nonwork-related stuff. Finally, Brena came across a woman and a man with a baby photograph. The couple couldn't have been more than twenty-seven, and the baby was just an infant.

Brena figured it was a picture of her birth parents that she had lost at an early age, but he found it curious there were no pictures of her adopted parents.

Brena shrugged it off. He wasn't interested enough to care about her way of dealing with personal things, only how she reacted in the field. She had done OK; she wasn't the best or the worst. His only regret was she wouldn't have the chance to grow or experience life, which had been taken from her. Brena put the notebook and photographs back and closed the drawer.

'Do you want to send some agents to London?' asked Rachel.

Brena smiled and shook his head. 'No, it's OK. We have someone already there,' he replied. 'From the London office.'

Rachel smiled and nodded as if accepting the explanation.

* * *

Jamerson had insisted Steel shower and change, almost as if he was afraid the smell of sweat would seep into the furniture and would never come out. Steel had seen his point and done just that. He found the water soothing and good stimulation for the grey cells.

He used his parent's old shower because the one in his room held too many memories. A distraction he couldn't afford to have at that moment. His mind was focused on the problem at hand. How did The Sentinel research all those properties so fast?

* * *

Steel returned to the study with fresh clothes and smelling clean but no new ideas. There was a pot of fresh coffee on a silver tray, along with his favourite mug with the SAS insignia on it. Jamerson had left Steel to it; he understood that he should be left alone when Steel was in the zone.

Steel checked the progress of the database and found what he needed. The apartment opposite Graaf's had once been empty, and INTERPOL had a surveillance team watching Graaf from there. When they came up empty, the place was sold off. It was also the same for Falkner's apartment. The place across the street had the same history.

He checked with London to see if there had been any agency surveillance on anyone in the area. One name popped up: Christian Dollman.

He was the worst kind of human being, a 'fixer' to Steel. Predominantly juries, not that it could be proved. If you have enough money, this man could make sure a jury swung in your favour.

Steel rocked back and forth in his chair, pondering whether he should track down and save him or leave the bastard to The Sentinel. Finally, Steel stood up, walked over to the coffee table next to the two Chesterfield armchairs, and poured himself a black coffee. The smell of the Jamaican Blue Mountain coffee was intoxicating.

Steel took a sip and walked back to the desk. Still not entirely convinced he should save Dollman, Steel had questions, and Dollman had the answers. On the way to the desk, Steel passed the boards. He stopped for a moment and took another look at the fourth board. It was still full of gaps, but there was still some useful information. Taking another sip, he headed for the desk. He had work to do. He had to find Dollman's location before midnight tonight before the next postcard came. He opened up the database once more; he needed an address, if not Dollman's, then that of the nest, knowing Dollman's place would be right opposite.

Steel soon found the nest's address, an apartment near the US Embassy in Mayfair. He knew the area, possibly all too well. He thought back to the Christmas market they had in Hyde Park, the sounds of people, the smells from the food vendors, and the bright lights.

True, it was a fantastic sight to behold, but he had not returned to the park since his friend's murder, not even for the market.

Dollman was a smug son-of-a-bitch who needed to be taken off of the planet. He had used his influence to get some real scum from doing time, and he didn't care as long as the paycheck was right. Steel knew plenty of detectives who had their perps dead to rights, but somehow they walked free. He started to take another sip of his coffee but stopped. Suddenly, he stood up and looked at the fourth board.

'Dollman got them all off. They all walked free,' Steel said to himself, or so he thought.

'Who walked free?' asked Jamerson, who stood in the doorway.

Steel didn't answer; he put down his coffee mug and ran out of the door past a confused Jamerson.

'God, I hate it when he does that,' Jamerson said to himself, hearing the front door slam.

Steel had jumped into the Jaguar and drove to Dollman's apartment. He didn't have time to mess about it, he had an address, and he would get him and bring him in. Steel pressed the button with the telephone icon and scrolled down to the contact that read 'Office.' Steel clicked on it and waited for the ringing to start.

'Yes, Steel?' came a woman's voice over the surround-sound speakers.

'I'm on the way to Mayfair. The next target is a man named Dollman, Christian Dollman,' Steel said as he took corners like a rally driver.

'Are you sure?' said the voice, alarmed at the news.

'Positive, why?' Steel asked, suddenly having one of those bad-feeling moments.

'Because he isn't in Mayfair; he's having lunch with Charles Benetton at The Connaught.'

'The billionaire?' Steel asked.

'Yes, the very one.'

'Can't you send a team to secure him? say he is a threat to Benetton because he's got a killer after him?' Steel requested, throwing the car across the road, past vehicles and avoiding oncoming traffic.

'I don't think he would see it that way. Besides, what proof do we have?' the woman asked.

'I guess gut feelings don't wash,' Steel laughed. Not expecting an answer. 'Right, I'm off to The Connaught then,' he said before disconnecting the call. A cold smile crossed Steel's face as he gripped the steering wheel and pressed down the gas pedal.

* * *

Steel parked his car in front of the restaurant and got out. A chilly wind brushed against his face, making the skin tingle at nature's touch. Steel straightened his suit jacket and entered the building.

There was a gentle buzz of conversation and the soft clatter of silverware against bone china. Steel stood at the greeting point and looked around but saw no sign of Dollman.

'Can I help you, sir?' asked a smartly dressed man in his late fifties. The *matre d'* smiled and waved a waiter across to show Steel to a table.

'Is Mr Dollman here?' Steel asked, hoping for a quick answer and no fuss.

'I'm sorry, sir, I'm unable to answer—'

'Never mind, I've got him,' Steel had already spotted him in a corner, next to a window. Grinning, he walked on to the dismay of the man.

Steel found Dollman and Benetton in a discussion about something; their whispers and glances around the room made them look guilty of something, which they probably were.

'Christian, my goodness, good to see you. Well, actually, I'm not, but then I'm just being nice for the moment,' Steel said, grabbing a chair from another table and joining the two men.

'Sorry, whoever you are, this is a private meeting, so I'll kindly ask you to leave,' Bennetton said, nodding at a man in the corner. The bruiser walked over, his Armani suit adding to his size.

'Don't worry, David, this is Detective Steel of the NYPD. He's probably come all this way for nothing,' Dollman laughed.

The bruiser placed a massive hand on Steel's shoulder as a first warning.

'Friend, move it or lose it,' Steel warned the goon.

Dollman sat back and waited. There was a quick movement from Steel, and the man dropped to the floor in pain, holding his hand.

'I'm here to bring you in, Christian, I'm afraid,' Steel said, hiding the real reason for his appearance.

'You've got nothing on me, so scurry back to your hole in New York,' Dollman said, picking up a half-filled champagne flute and sipping.

'Unfortunately, it's not like that; I'm here to save your life. It appears someone is out to get certain people. You heard about the bombs in Berlin and Amsterdam?' Steel asked as he poured himself a glass of the Bollinger '75 and took a sip.

Dollman nodded as though he had little interest. After all, that was there; he was far away from that trouble.

'Well, it appears you are on that list. Now, believe me, I would much prefer to let the killer do his thing where you are concerned, but unfortunately, you have the information I need, so …' Steel stood, raising an arm as if ushering Dollman to the door.

'Your concern is touching. However, I must decline your kind offer. I think I will be fine,' Dollman said smugly.

'Oh, I'm sorry, you misunderstood. I wasn't asking,' Steel said sternly.

Suddenly, the beast of a man came up behind Steel and locked his massive arms around him in a bearhug.

Steel bared his teeth in anger and scraped the side of his shoe down the man's shin bone, then shot his head backwards, catching the man full in the face. He whirled and jabbed the man in the throat with a quick jab.

The bodyguard released his grip. Unable to breathe, he stumbled back, straight into a couple's table, then fell through it.

Steel turned to Dollman, who sat with a smug look.

He turned to see two more men quickly approach. Both attacked simultaneously, but Steel was quick and countered many of the blows, giving as good as he got.

One of the men threw a punch towards Steel's head, but he caught the fist, twisted the man's arm, and sent the man crashing into the other, just in time to stop the man from reaching for a knife from the table. Both men fell backwards, collapsing on top of two empty tables.

'Dollman, call off your dogs before they get hurt,' Steel said, preparing himself for the next volley of punches.

Dollman sat sipping his champagne while he enjoyed the show.

The guerrilla returned, rushing at Steel like a quarterback. But Steel moved quickly, tripping the man as he shot past. There was a loud crash when the big man sailed through the window. The sound of glass echoed through the building, and people ran for cover.

The other two men also rushed at Steel, hoping at least one of them would catch him off balance so the other could finish the job. Steel's movements were fluid, almost like a dance, as he countered and landed several strategic hits to the men's bodies. Each let out muffled cries of pain as straight-hand punches landed on specific pressure points.

The men went down, unconscious. And that was when Steel heard the click. The sound of a pistol hammer being drawn back, ready to fire. Steel spun around and jabbed Dollman in the side of both upper thighs, causing him to crouch forwards.

Steel landed an uppercut to the man's jaw as he leant down, sending Dollman into the air and out the window. Steel caught the revolver, put the hammer back, and spun out of the chamber before emptying the cartridges into his hand and tossing the weapon onto the table.

Steel leapt out the window and landed with a roll. As he stood up, he grabbed Dollman by the scruff of the neck and dragged him to the Jaguar.

'Quick, someone calls the police,' a man yelled.

'Don't worry, I *am* the police. He didn't pay for parking,' Steel said as he watched partons scrabble to get change for the parking meters.

Benetton stared out the broken window and watched Steel drive away. As he did, he took out his cell and made a call. 'Yes, it's me. We have a problem.'

Chapter 37

It was twelve-twenty when Simms got the call from Dorson. No idle chit-chat, only a one-way conversation. 'Your hotel room, 13:00 hours.'

The call was brief, but at least he got hold of his only ally.

Simms had gotten fresh coffee and some sandwiches. He figured if they were going to be there for some time, they might as well be comfortable. He hoped that Dorson would crack the password on Trish's computer. The three terabytes were useless, just lots of work, nonsense related to an old case in New York, which had been months back. The others he hadn't had time to check.

After his second breakfast, Simms used the time to check up on Graaf's file, which, oddly enough, Trish had on one of her drives.

He had to admit Graaf was a scumbag of enormous proportions, and he had no problems trying to figure out why someone would want to kill him.

A knock at the door made him jump. Slowly, he calmed himself down, headed to the door, and looked through the peephole.

There stood Dorson, dressed in a black hooded jogging outfit. He opened the door, greeted Dorson with a hearty handshake, and let him in.

'I got your message. It sounded important,' Dorson said with a serious face.

'You were right. Something did happen to Trish,' Simms said, leading him over to the desk that also held the small flat-screen television.

'I knew it. So, what did you find?' Dorson waited as Simms poured two cups of coffee.

'I got her laptop and a couple of hard drives.' Simms pointed to the devices that lay next to Dorson.

'Anything on them?'

'I haven't checked all of the drives because her password is proving to be a bitch to crack,' Simms admitted.

Dorson took hold of the coffee mug that Simms offered him and took a sip.

'The neighbour was filming her place and kept the disks,' Simms explained, causing Dorson to raise an eyebrow.

'So, the neighbour is a perv, stalker, or something?' he smiled.

'No, get this. Trish *asked* him to do it. She was nervous about something ... or someone.' Simms sat down on the bed and cradled his coffee mug in both hands.

'And you got the footage?' Dorson asked with interest.

'I don't know. The drive she was using was encrypted. It can only be played using her laptop, I think.' Simms shrugged.

Dorson nodded. If Trish were that concerned about her security, he could understand she would have done just that. Like him, Trish was a computer whiz and gadget freak. That was why she was good at surveillance, wiretaps, and hidden cameras.

Dorson spun, lifted the lid on the laptop, and got to work. Simms watched patiently as he got to work. All the while, his mind went back to Falkner and his mistake of not questioning him on the flight over.

'This may take a while, so if you have something else to do, now is the time,' Dorson told Simms.

'I got nothing but this for the moment. I'm betting whoever grabbed Trish killed Falkner.' Simms rested his back against the headboard.

Dorson smiled and nodded once as if to say he understood, then returned to the computer. Simms sat and watched. Feeling useless as he sipped his coffee and let his mind wander, trying to piece everything together in his head.

* * *

Steel drove like he stole the Jaguar. The muffled sounds of Dollman whining and sliding around in the trunk. Steel ignored him and continued his journey, hoping the uncomfortable travel arrangements would loosen Dollman's tongue for their little chat later. Steel was heading home, which was a good hour away. He had informed the agency that he had Dollman and where he would take him, which gave him roughly half an hour before they came, and his talk with Dollman would be interrupted.

Steel hoped that they wouldn't be complete arses and send a helicopter, which would be there to greet them.

He threw the car about on the road, even when there was no traffic to be overtaken. He wore a broad, satisfied grin as he did so, enjoying every bang, bump, and groan from behind him.

* * *

It was two o'clock when Steel returned home with his guest. Jamerson waited at the front door with his hands behind his back, his chin raised, and his chest out. Steel pulled up the entrance and switched off the car before getting out.

'Can you see our guest to the library?' Steel rushed inside to make a quick phone call.

Jamerson shot Steel a puzzled look. 'But there's nobody … oh, you didn't?' A series of thumps from the trunk made Jamerson look up and shake his head. 'Of course you did.' He opened the trunk and looked down at a bruised and frightened Dollman.

'Good afternoon, sir. May I offer you some assistance?' Jamerson asked, offering a hand.

'Wh-what?' Dollman asked, confused.

Jamerson rephrased the question. 'Can I help you get your fat arse out of the car … sir?'

Dollman looked at the massive butler with a blank expression.

Jamerson mumbled something and ripped Dollman from the trunk as if he were nothing and showed him into the library, a large room with two floors of books shelved on oak shelving. Stained-glass windows and a high ceiling and archways gave the place an aesthetic look and feel.

Jamerson ushered him to two red leather Chesterfield armchairs and beckoned him to sit. Dollman sat and looked around, marvelling at the room, which had to be at least two hundred years old.

As Dollman sat there with his mouth open, Jamerson went to pour him a large brandy from the drinks globe. 'I believe this should settle your nerves, sir,' he said, offering a drink on a silver salver.

Dollman took the brandy bowl and downed the eighteen-year-old brandy in one loud gulp, to Jamerson's annoyance.

Steel returned holding an electronic tablet and a large brown file.

'My lawyers are going to have a field day with you, and all this will be gone,' Dollman laughed, gesturing the room.

Steel just smiled, sat down in the other chair, and waited for Jamerson to bring the second round of drinks.

'Dollman, shut up and pin your ears back. Someone is out to get you. Now, personally, I don't give a damn, but you have information that this killer wants to suppress,' Steel explained. 'So, tell me about New York. Why were you there about six months ago?'

'Six months ago?' Dollman looked into space while he searched his memory for specific appointments that would warrant someone trying to kill him. After a while, he shook his head. 'Nah, nothing comes to mind. I was in New York a lot during that period ... lots of clients.' He laughed. But Steel didn't.

Steel handed the tablet to Dollman and told him to press the file icon. As Dollman watched, he saw pictures of the crime scenes.

'So, what's this?' Dollman asked, raising the tablet.

'Crime scene photos from The Sentinel file.'

'The Sentinel? Is that meant to mean anything?' Dollman asked quizzically.

'No, not really, he's just the bloke who wants to kill you. These are the other people who were on his list,' Steel said, cracking a smile.

Dollman's eyes widened as the severity of his situation kicked in.

'Now, like I said, I'm here to protect you, but if you don't need protection, then be my guest and go. In fact, I will drive you back myself. But be assured you will not see tomorrow.' He sat back in his chair and sipped his brandy.

Dollman looked at the pictures as they automatically swept through via a slideshow setting.

'Charles King. I got Charles King acquitted,' Dollman said, shaking with fear.

A new set of pictures appeared at a different crime scene.

'What's this?' Dollman asked, holding up the tablet so Steel could see.

'King's handy work, courtesy of you,' he growled, fighting the urge to smash the man's head against the marble fireplace.

'You knew?'

'I suspected. I just needed you to admit it,' Steel replied coolly.

'It won't stand up in court,' Dollman said smugly.

'And neither will you,' Steel grinned.

Dollman began to sweat, afraid of what he meant.

'A recording of this conversation will be sent to the press; everyone will know who you are and what you've done. You're finished, Dollman.' Steel stood just as two men in dark suits appeared in the doorway.

'Are you done?' asked one of the agents.

Steel nodded and turned his back. As the agents began to drag the dazed Dollman away, he turned. 'Dollman, how much did King give you for getting him off?'

'It wasn't Charles who retained my services. It was Edward, his father,' Dollman answered as he was quickly pulled through the door.

Steel shot Jamerson a look of desperation.

'The next target will be New York. After that, The Sentinel will be going after Edward King next,' Steel said, running full pelt to the study to call Stanton.

* * *

Simms was woken by the sound of the bathroom door closing. He opened his eyes and looked around for any sign of Dorson but found the chair he had been working at empty. He sat up and rubbed his eyes. He couldn't believe that he had fallen asleep. Still, the monotony of just sitting there, especially on a bed, could inspire slumber.

He figured Dorson had gone to take a leak; after all, he had put away a lot of coffee before Simms had crashed into a deep sleep. He looked over at his coffee cup sitting on the nightstand and let out a disappointed groan at the empty vessel. Dragging himself to his feet. He headed to the coffee machine. The strong scent of the coffee was helping him wake up as he filled his mug with the steaming liquid.

Simms walked back to the bed via the desk. He was curious about Dorson's progress and whether he had been able to crack Trish's password. As he neared, he saw the computer was unlocked, and he was staring at an image from the old man's garden camera. He rubbed the sleep out of his eyes and sat down, wondering how long ago Dorson had cracked the code and why he hadn't woken him after he had. But then, he knew he'd probably have let his colleague sleep as well if the roles had been reversed.

The image was of Trish's house at night. The front was clear, and the driveway was empty. Simms leant forwards and checked the time stamp. It was ten o'clock the evening before. Simms went to press the play icon but snatched his hand back. Dorson had cracked the code; he should be here to watch it as well. After all, they were in this together.

He felt a rush of excitement at the prospect of bringing this all to an end or being able to go back to Stanton and say 'it was him' or 'her', respectively. The cursor hovered over the play button. He felt selfish, but then what would it hurt? After all, they could play it again, and he had earned it.

Simms nodded and pressed the button. The video played out. First, Trish's car arrived and parked in her driveway. Then, after a few moments, she got out and headed for her front door. He was impressed with how clear the image was, even though it was night. Simms sat and watched as it played through, with no other vehicle stopping but several driving past. A couple of strollers and dog walkers walked by, but none of them stopped.

As Simms took a sip, he was beginning to feel bad about bringing Dorson all that way; the footage showed nothing.

Suddenly, as the clock on the screen showed ten past ten, a dark-coloured SUV pulled up, and a man got out.

Intrigued by this new development, Simms leant forward to better view the screen. Unfortunately, all he could see was that the fellow was tall and dressed all in black with a hoodie. Simms was engrossed in the footage like it was a gripping movie on TV. Trish suddenly came into view with the man behind her. She seemed scared, but she followed whatever instructions he was giving her. Finally, Trish got into the car; the man opened the door and looked around. Simms's mouth fell open as the man's face was revealed; it was Brena.

Simms never heard Dorson step out of the bathroom. The man was as quiet as a mouse in a room full of sleeping cats. But Simms caught Dorson's reflection in the laptop's display. He went to say something, but that was when he saw the gun pointing at his head. The silenced GLOCK SF 30 was Trish's favourite backup weapon. It was a 45 Auto calibre. A favourite for undercover law enforcement members or special forces groups. It was a perfect choice with a ten-shot magazine and a weight of 745 grammes.

Dorson probably used his time in the bathroom to place the suppressor on.

'You know, if you'd stayed asleep, I could have just wiped the drive, and nobody would have been the wiser, but of course, you had to wake up and start watching,' Dorson said angrily.

Simms looked confused. Why the hell did Dorson have a gun pointing at him if Brena was the one they were after? But then, as the video played on, he saw why—when a dark van pulled up around midnight, and several men got out and broke into Trish's place. After ten minutes, they returned, angry at the house's emptiness. As two of the men came into view, Simms's eyes widened. One of them was the man from the Amsterdam airport, and the other was Dorson.

Simms felt a burning rage well up from deep inside of him. All of this time, he had been played, lied to by his colleagues, and made to think everyone else was the enemy.

'Why?' Simms demanded.

'Because the pay is so good,' Dorson replied with a smirk.

Simms caught his reflection again; he was looking at his watch. That was never a good sign. Not even in the movies.

'Wait,' Simms said, hoping to buy time.

'Uhm ... no.' Dorson chose the back of Simms' head as a point of aim. There was a gentle thud, and blood splattered over the screen of the laptop and the wall behind it. Pieces of brain matter and skull clung to the wallpaper in small lumps and fragments. Then, a noise like a sack of potatoes hitting the floor resounded through the room. Followed by the sound of a door opening and a set of footsteps.

Chapter 38

Steel had caught Stanton in the middle of his lunch, a roast beef sandwich on wholemeal bread from the cantine. He had explained the situation and who he believed the next target to be. Stanton had rushed out of his office and headed down to the war room with Steel still explaining on the cell phone.

'Get your shit together; we know who the next target is,' Stanton said, bashing through the war room doors.

Brena looked up excitedly. At last, progress.

'I want Edward King secured. The Sentinel is going after him next,' Stanton ordered, and the agents grabbed their gear and hurried out.

Brena stayed behind for a moment, curious at the new development. There wasn't due to be a postcard for hours yet, but Stanton seemed to have the information now.

Then it clicked.

Stanton was on the phone with someone.

Steel. Of course, it could only be that interfering Brit.

Stanton looked at Brena, who stood before him, wearing a confused look, and hung up the phone.

'Yes, Martin?' Stanton asked, 'Ah, you want to know how we got it. Steel managed to get hold of the next target in London, a man called Dollman. He gave us King. Dollman got King's son off that bombing charge by influencing the jury,' Stanton explained.

'King, as in Charles King … of the mall bombings six months ago?' Brena's eyes opened wide with surprise as the pieces began to fit into place. The Sentinel was seeking revenge for the mall bombing. 'And he figures Edward King is the last target?' Brena asked with a hopeful look.

'It looks like it. Now, go and bring King in. He's got some explaining to do,' Stanton ordered.

Brena nodded and raced out after his team.

* * *

Steel watched as the helicopter carrying Dollman and the agents took off and headed south. Even though he'd gotten the information, He still felt something was wrong, missing even. For him, the puzzle still didn't fit together.

'I take it now that Dollman is secured, you'll be heading off to New York?' Jamerson asked as he stood next to Steel, watching the black AgustaWestland AW139 disappear over the tree line.

'No, I still have a meeting to attend at midnight,' Steel said with a low, gruff voice. Then he walked away, heading back to the study. He had plans to make.

'Right then, better get the coffee on,' Jamerson said with a shrug and proceeded to the kitchen.

Steel went back to the boards. There was still something bothering him besides the unknown identity of The Sentinel. He couldn't figure out why the killer set off the devices, knowing that the people had been taken into custody. It was likely that the devices didn't have a remote safety switch; they had to be disarmed at the source. But that made no sense. The Sentinel was thorough, so a device without an off switch went against Steel's profile of The Sentinel.

The Sentinel only wanted to hurt the targets, not innocent persons. So, why was Kitty killed and Sabine Boese injured?

Steel hoped his next theory would be correct. He would soon find out at midnight.

* * *

The Sentinel had seen the footage of Steel at the restaurant, which Dollman often frequented, as it was only around the corner from where he lived. After Steel had left with Dollman, The Sentinel continued observing.

Charles Benetton had made a call, and he didn't seem happy that Steel had snatched up Dollman.

The Sentinel cursed the small surveillance camera for not having audio, but it didn't matter. The Sentinel typed a few keys on a laptop, and the lipreading software kicked in. The electronic voice sounded almost human as it repeated what Benetton had said.

'We have a problem; some damned policeman just grabbed Dollman. His name? He called himself Steel if that means anything to you.' There was a pause as if Benetton was receiving instructions. 'Yes, I'll get right on it, certainly, Mr Williams.' Benetton's voice seemed to tremble at the very utterance of this man's name.

The Sentinel turned and took notice of the other monitors. One of them showed a man in his early sixties. He wore a thousand-dollar suit and sat with a Manhattan skyline in his office. It was Edward King. Next to the image of King was another: the judge that had let Charles King go free. In The Sentinel's eyes, the judge was just as guilty and needed to be 'judged'.

The Sentinel picked up a postcard that had been specially made as a clue for King: a picture of George Washington coming off Mount Vernon. As The Sentinel was starting to fill out the address for Steel, the image of King's office caught The Sentinel's eye. Several agents moved in and snatched up King, telling him he was in danger and he had to come with them. The Sentinel laughed and clapped. Amused at how resourceful Steel had been. Steel had exceeded all of The Sentinel's expectations. He was the best and could understand why Stanton liked him, and why Brena hated him.

The Sentinel finished filling out the card, but the address was different this time: Christ Church Spitalfields 0100. Come alone.

The Sentinel knew it was time. Eventually, Steel would work it all out, but now, The Sentinel needed Steel's help reel in one more fish.

* * *

Steel sat in the study at the computer. He wanted to know every detail of Charles King's life before his death. Associates, friends, and girlfriends, with whom he had breakfast and even when he changed his underwear. The bombing at the mall was the key to this whole thing. The Sentinel wanted payback, revenge. The question: who had The Sentinel lost in the bombing? Steel had his old notes on King on a hard drive. Nearly five hundred gigabytes on the bastard. Photos, documents, files. All of which proved that man was a psycho nut case and a self-absorbed dick.

Charles King was in trouble from day one, probably because of Daddy's money. The rich always seemed to get off doing stuff they shouldn't. So, at fifteen, he was arrested for being drunk and disorderly, and at seventeen, he got a DUI. Twenty-one, he got off on a hit-and-run charge due to a lack of witnesses or evidence.

At twenty-eight, he got pinched for beating up a hooker, which again disappeared, including the witness. Finally, at thirty, King got MI8's and Steel's attention.

The bombings happened all around the city, mostly in isolated places. The FBI was investigating because bomb nuts were their domain. That was until seven homeless people got a building dropped on them, and then that became NYPD's problem, so Steel made it his problem.

It took months of investigative work and months more to build a case. Steel remembered the look on King's face when the judge said he was a free man. But Steel knew he'd do it again; he couldn't help it.

He liked it too much.

Steel pulled up the file on the bombing. There were crime scene photograph

statements from the witnesses. One even mentioned the homeless guy who had saved their life. Steel smiled, always amused by how his costumes fooled people, but that was the idea.

Steel found the list of casualties and the dead. Thirty-two in total; thirty-two too many for Steel's liking. Steel saw his name on the list, and it made him scowl. He didn't deserve to be on the list; he most certainly didn't deserve the medal they wanted to give him, the Medal of Honour. Steel had refused it, but Captain Brant and the Mayor had other thoughts on the matter.

Jamerson walked in with a silver tray supporting coffee and Marmite on toast. Most people hated the brown paste, but Steel had learned to appreciate the stuff. After a cold march on a night-nav exercise, a cup of hot water and a spoon of the thing were welcome. It tasted like crap, but it had all the nutrients and minerals to keep your body going for a while.

Steel smiled and nodded a thank you to his old sergeant.

Jamerson wasn't a butler to Steel. He was a comrade in arms.

A man who had been failed by the system after he had left the forces. So, Steel offered him a position as head of the house when Steel was away. The butler thing was more Jamerson's idea of blending in. Besides, he had a thing for the cook, and she thought the uniform was sexy. Steel found the cover amusing; who would argue with a butler that was ex-special forces?

* * *

The list was hard to read, as each name came with age. But as Steel read each name, he could swear he could see a face to go with the name. That was when he got to a name of a little girl, the girl from his nightmares. She had perished with her grandparents. Steel's eyes froze at the names. If she was the daughter and they were the grandparents, where were the parents? Henry and Alice Siar and Lilly Marks.

Steel went into the database and looked up Henry Siar.

Henry Siar was Irish, born in Dublin in '68, moved over to the States after leaving the Irish Rangers, and served with NYPD for twelve years. He opened an Irish bar on 35 street. He was married to Alice for thirty-five years and had two daughters, Mary and Cara, and a son, Patrick.

The little girl, Lilly, was eight years old; her parents were Cara and Martin Marks. Martin was a Forces Recon Sergeant, but he was killed by an IED attack in Kabul two years before. Cara was also Forces Recon, but she was back home teaching recruits.

The son, Patrick, had gone into the US Army Rangers, and the other daughter Mary joined the Boston Police Department and was in HRT.

The family were all specialists and had enough training to be The Sentinel. Still, Steel was sure that only one of them was the person they were tracking. So, he rechecked the database for real-time locations on the two girls and the son but came up empty on the son and one of the daughters; the other was laid up in bed, six months pregnant.

A good alibi if ever he heard one.

Could The Sentinel be both of them? It would make sense; they were both qualified, but he shook off the idea. Not as being improbable, but more as unlikely. The Sentinel was a loner, someone who wasn't just hurting but wanted justice. Steel had already ascertained that The Sentinel was intelligent, thorough, and well-trained. Most people would have done something rash, but everything The Sentinel did was meticulous.

Steel bit into the cold toast and sipped the coffee while he absorbed all the new data, and Jamerson sat nearby and played Candy Crush on his cell phone.

Steel studied the boards. Each of the targets had something to do with King; each played a part in his bombing scheme without knowing. Graaf paid off Falkner with imported diamonds to pay for the explosives he had smuggled in from Berlin. Dollman had gotten the jury to vote not guilty, and Alison Klien was the lawyer for the prosecution. She must have taken a bribe to do as little as possible but not enough, so it looked like she was taking a dive.

But that left the security guard. What the hell did he have to do with it? Steel checked the files to see where Mark Trent was working. His eyes widened as he went to bite into another piece of toast. Mark Trent was in charge of the security cameras at the mall at the bombing. So, that would explain why there was no footage of King up until he had been caught by security. After that point, Trent went on a break, a very long break.

Steel sat back in his chair and began to rock back and forth. The more he looked at it, the easier it became to understand. He eyed the boards again and nodded; he was happy with his investigation. But when he looked again, his smile faded away.

'What about the judge?' Steel suddenly straightened, scaring Jamerson enough for him to lose his game.

'Oh, bollocks,' Jamerson said, shooting Steel a look of irritation.

'Quite,' Steel replied, picking up the phone and pressing the redial number.

Jamerson's looked confused.

'Avery, do you have King? Good, don't forget about the judge who presided over the King case. I think she will be next,' Steel explained before putting down the phone.

Steel looked up at the time. It was nine o'clock. He had around an hour and a half trip, and he could probably do it in less, but he definitely had time.

* * *

Stanton sat in his office. He'd had a long day, and it was only four o'clock. He'd informed Brena to swing past the courthouse and pull in the judge. He'd told him of Steel's theory. Surprisingly, Brena had agreed Steel was on to something. In fact, Stanton was so shocked he'd choked on his coffee.

He got up and headed to the war room, which was virtually empty, less for a few agents who were finishing background checks. Another was checking the data Steel had sent them via email. This was more of a report, divulging his theories and the evidence to back them. How everything fits together around King, the bombings and his father.

Stanton walked over to the young agent, busy checking and rechecking Steel's theory. 'What you working on, son?' Stanton asked, looking over the man's shoulder.

'Oh, just the report from Agent … sorry, Detective Steel.'

'Very well. Make sure I get this as soon as you are done.'

The agent just nodded and got back to work.

Stanton put his hands behind his back and headed back to his office. They were all a good team and didn't need him looking over their shoulders. Besides, there were other things to take care of.

Chapter 39

Steel had arrived at Hyde Park with plenty of time to spare. His military-style watch said it was ten-fifteen. Steel found a fast-food restaurant that was still open and ordered coffee. The place was full of teenagers and people who had just finished work and needed a quick fix before heading home. The server was a spotty teenager called Tom; his jet-black hair stuck out from under his cap, and his black-rimmed glasses kept sliding off of his nose due to sweat.

Steel paid for the coffee and put the change into the staff tips box. He found a seat that faced the door. An old habit he had picked up in the Army; that way so he could see what was coming so he could react to it. The coffee was strong, way too strong as if they had emptied a week's worth of coffee packets into the machine. The smell of greasy burgers and body odour filled the air, reminding Steel why he didn't frequent these places unless he had to.

The door sign had said the place was open until twelve. Perfect, at least he would be in the warm and dry, with plenty of people around if something happened.

Steel had no idea if the next postcard would be delivered. After all, The Sentinel would have seen that both Dollman and King had been picked up. But he was curious to see what was going to happen next.

Of course, by now, the CIA had picked up the judge as well. Steel smiled at the thought of Stanton sitting in his office, fending off phone calls from lawyers and people in high places. But then, they were there for their protection, not under arrest, not yet anyway. All it would take was one of them to crack to bring down the whole circus.

Steel sipped the coffee but tried to avoid smelling it if he could … failed on many occasions, causing him to push the cup away.

* * *

At twelve-fifty, the staff closed up after Steel had been the only customer for an hour, and he still had the same cup of coffee. Steel thanked them and said goodnight before stepping into the bitter chill of the night. The small park area where the Arch stood seemed deserted.

A couple of cars passed every few minutes; commuters and taxis headed to or from home. Steel was fifteen minutes early, but there was nowhere else to wait at that hour. So, he strolled over to a bench that wasn't too far from the Arch and sat it out. He figured, rather than stand around looking suspicious, he could do that sitting down.

Steel pulled back the sleeve of his jacket and looked at the luminous dials of his watch. It was five-to.

As he rolled the sleeve back, he spotted kids heading his way. Each one must have been nineteen and was badly dressed. Two of them had trousers that hung around their waists as if the garments were too big for them; the others had named jackets and baseball caps, along with gold chains and big watches.

'Nice watch, pops. Can I have a look?' asked a tall, thin kid whose sunglasses were stuck on top of the brim of his cap.

'Sure, you can tell the time?' Steel responded, knowing what was coming next.

Four against one. Each kid had long arms, meaning a long reach, which was only good if you knew what you were doing.

Steel was easily an inch taller than the tallest of the crew, and he had more muscle and experience. These were street punks after their next payday. But today, all they would get was a good thrashing and sent home whimpering to their mothers.

'Watch, wallet, and cell phone,' said another. This kid was shorter than the others but stockier; he was probably the muscle. He figured his size would intimidate. To Steel, he was just sport.

'Look, the guy's pissed off; I've had a long day, and I'm waiting for someone,' Steel said flatly, unwilling to move, especially for them.

'I said watch, wallet and cell phone, mother fucka,' said another one, who was getting brave while he stood behind the other two.

Steel just looked at them and shot a look that said one thing: get lost, or I'm going to hurt you.

'I said *now*,' said the stocky guy and reached for Steel's jacket.

Wrong move, number one. There was a crack, and a scream as Steel grabbed the kid's hand, then twisted, popping his shoulder out of its socket. He stood and caught the foot of the next brave soul who thought he knew kung fu. Mistake number two sent the boy to the ground with a swift kick to the groan and one to the other kneecap, resulting in him yelping on a higher note than he thought possible. The leader pushed the other kid into the ring and told him to mess up Steel.

The kid got brave and angry. He yelled out a war cry and charged. Steel sidestepped him and kicked him in the small of the back; the force hurled him forwards into the two screaming accomplices. Steel looked at the leader, the "big man", who'd just turned tail and headed in several directions before focusing on one.

Steel thought he looked like a scared rabbit ... but a rabbit knew from the start when to quit.

He reached down to the one with the popped shoulder and grabbed his arm to check the time. The kid let out a shriek of pain, making Steel smile.

'Thanks, brother,' Steel said mockingly.

It was twelve o'clock; he had been distracted. Steel stopped after taking a few steps in the direction of the Arch and looked at the three men.

'Did someone pay you to rob me?' Steel yelled.

He got nothing but moans and groans.

'If I come over there, I won't be asking nicely,' Steel said in a fake angry voice.

'Yes, yes ... just chill, man,' begged the big kid.

'Who?' Steel asked.

'Don't know ... some dude in a long black coat with a hood ... looked kinda cool,' the kid replied.

Steel thought for a moment, then worked on a hunch. 'This dude, did he give you something for me?'

'Yeah, how'd you know?' said the other kid holding his balls with one hand and his knee with the other.

'I'm psychic,' Steel snarled, walking over to them.

'Really?' replied one of the kids.

'Yes, I foresee if you don't give me the postcard, I'm going to rip an arm off and beat you to death with it.' Steel rolled his eyes at the stupidity of the question.

'Wow, how did you know it was a postcard?' asked another kid, handing over the newest clue.

'It's what they teach us at the police school, numbnuts; I'm a cop,' Steel showed his ID. Leaving the kids to 'wow' at being beaten up by an NYPD cop.

* * *

Steel took the card, headed back to his car, climbed into the driver's seat, and shut the door. He started the engine, pulled out the postcard, and read the note.

'Christ Church Spitalfields 01:00. Come alone.'

He looked at his watch. It was five past twelve, and it was a thirty-minute drive, depending on the traffic lights.

Steel put the car into drive, took off down the street towards Glouster Place, and then right onto the A501 towards Whitechapel. It had been a while since he had been down that part of town, but he was confident he would find it without the satnav sending him all over the place.

Steel drove in silence. There wasn't much on the radio that interested him at that time in the morning. Even the Radio 2 programmes he liked weren't on yet.

The streets were relatively clear, and the traffic lights seemed in his favour. The only sound was from the three-litre engine, which growled like its namesake. Steel had always been a fan of British cars. The Aston Martin, the old Rovers, Jaguar, and not forgetting the beasts, Land Rover and Range Rover. The British automotive system had reached a peak until the VW group brought out the Golf. After that, the thing went downhill from there. Some would argue it happened earlier.

Steel was concerned that if they were made in Britain, they were British regardless of who paid the bills.

Soon, he found a parking space down the road from a church next to a clothing store. Over the way was a traditional-looking pub, with an old painted sign above the door and decorative iron surrounding the door. The only things that spoilt the traditional aesthetic look were the large glass windows and the overhangs advertising cocktails.

Steel walked towards the church. Its white stone walls and impressive two-hundred-and-twenty-five-foot steeple loomed over Steel as he stood at the gates. It had stood there since the 1700s and had stood the tests of time.

Steel looked at his watch. It was nearly one; he'd made good time. But unfortunately, the temperature change had brought a mist that didn't help with where he was standing.

Steel felt a chill run down his spine, more of a primaeval fear than anything. One of those feelings you get after years of horror movies and novels. He was standing outside an ancient church with a crypt, and it was foggy. Sure, he felt something—his imagination kicking in.

He smiled at his childish foolishness, but he felt happy he could still feel that fear.

Steel pulled up the collar of his jacket but left his hands out of his pockets. It would take too long to react, seconds pulling his hands out instead of being raised up. Seconds that could make all the difference. Steel wondered about the meeting. Had The Sentinel decided to give himself up now that everyone had been taken in … or most at any rate?

But Steel had the feeling there was more to this than just a meeting. The Sentinel wanted something. He was desperate; something had not gone to plan, and he was stuck. It was a hell of a risk, asking the person chasing you for a favour. It was that, or Steel was the next one and the last on the list. He had, after all, caused the bomb to go off. If he hadn't been there, King might have just walked out and blown something else up. Steel shook his head. No, there was only one person responsible for the bomb going off: King.

Steel cupped his hands and blew warm air on them before rubbing them together. His long black coat reached down to the back of his ankles, but the wind had carried it up, so it flapped in the wind.

Then, taking out his gloves from his pocket, Steel slipped his hands inside and pulled them tight; warm lining met with flesh without a gap.

The sudden chimes of the church signalled it was one o'clock, but Steel stood alone. He would wait five minutes before heading off.

At ten past, he gave up after waiting for an extra five, just in case. Steel walked towards the car, all the while thinking he had been played or distracted from something happening somewhere else.

Steel froze.

The hairs on the back of his neck stood to attention like he'd just been electrocuted. He turned to see a hooded figure standing by the church entrance in a long black coat.

So, naturally, The Sentinel had waited and done what The Sentinel did best ... observe.

* * *

Steel had walked up to the gate, then up the stone steps that led to the church.

The Sentinel was standing at the main entrance with crossed arms and leaning on the entrance wall.

He made his way by jumping around one of the walls next to a pillar. He found it strange that he didn't fear for his life, no feeling of concern or the need to watch his back. A situation he had never found himself in before.

'I take it you want something?' Steel asked as he approached the hooded figure.

But The Sentinel remained silent, as if unsure whether speaking wouldn't give away the hidden identity.

'Well, you're not here to kill me, that's for sure. If you were, I think I'd be dead,' Steel added.

The Sentinel's hooded head rocked from side to side as if to say, 'Pretty much.'

'And you're definitely not here to talk me to death,' Steel joked.

The Sentinel remained still this time, possibly not finding the pun amusing.

'So, tell me, what is it you want? All the targets are either caught or dead, thanks to you, including some agents, I may add ... sorry agent,' Steel said, correcting himself.

The Sentinel straightened as if displaying an act of defiance against the allegation.

Steel smiled and turned to face the building in front.

'You know, there used to be a street down there, Dorset Street it was called, back in the 1800s. A woman was murdered there, Mary Jane Kelly,' Steel said. 'The last victim of the Ripper, or Jack as he had come to be known. One of the greatest crimes ever committed because, even to this day, the killer is unknown. Sure, people have speculated, but no one has come forward with actual proof.'

Steel turned to face The Sentinel.

'But that is what you've been after all this time, proof. Proof of a crime that was committed that went unpunished. A crime against you,' Steel said with a sympathetic tone.

'So, what is it you are after now, I wonder. There is nobody left. Even the judge has been picked up. So, who have we missed?' Steel asked, not just The Sentinel but himself.

He waited a few seconds, then growled, 'I swear if you don't start talking, Kitty, I'm out of here.'

Kitty drew back the hood and wore an impressed look. 'How long have you known?' she asked, walking over to him.

'I suspected, but it didn't hit home until I checked out the list of victims. Siar, it's Irish for West. Nice touch. So, I take it you are Cara because you don't look six months pregnant,' Steel said.

She clapped as if to congratulate him on his deduction, 'I prefer Kitty, but either will do.'

'But how did you get into the CIA, past all the vetting paperwork?' Steel asked, 'They don't just grab people off of the street, plus you would have had to have done the farm, so how'd you do it?'

Steel was impressed at the infiltration by Kitty. But he had gotten help getting into the SEALs, so Steel believed she also got a boost. Someone was helping her.

Steel thought back to the list of victims. But the only family who stuck out were the Siar's. He smiled. He remembered reading that Cara, or Kitty, had a brother who was supposed to be killed in action, or KIA. So what if the CIA recruited them for their skills? After all, Forces Recon would be the perfect skillset for the CIA Black Ops programmes.

Steel stopped as a thought came to him.

Something was wrong; suddenly, the math didn't add up. So, how was it that they had both been recruited before the bombings, just in time for The Sentinel to appear?

Steel smiled again, 'The Sentinel, it's not a nickname; it's a call sign, a programme. You and your brother are part of it,' He thought hard again. 'A programme like this would have to have a mission set; they wouldn't just be a rogue call sign setting their missions. Please don't tell me your brother is Brena?' Steel asked, the identity of the second member suddenly coming into his head.

'No, my brother is dead, killed by an IED, but it wasn't one of theirs. It was one of ours. Someone killed him because of an operation he'd been involved in out there. One someone wanted to keep quiet,' Kitty explained. 'But I believe you know my sister, Trish. And no, she's not pregnant. She lost the baby through complications after the bombing that killed our parents. You see, we were also meant to be at the mall that day, but something had come up at the agency. The bomb was intended for us, Mr Steel,' Kitty said with a tearful look on her face.

'After our brother was killed, we were approached by a man in the agency. He explained The Sentinel programme, entirely off the books so nobody would know our real names or what we're doing. We could be inserted anywhere. We were brought into Stanton's section because of you, John Steel; your investigation into King brought more to the surface than what you thought,' she continued solemnly. 'But you failed to see the big picture because you were too focused on Charles King.'

Kitty moved up to Steel and looked into his blue contact lenses.

Her scent was intoxicating, a sweet perfume he only noticed when he was up close to her. Steel's eyes widened. He knew that scent; it was the same as what he had smelt before going into the hotel. It had been her that had made the drop-off in Berlin.

'So, what *is* the bigger picture?' Steel said calmly as he stared at her.

Her eyes were large and sultry. Her cheeks had a faint tint of red as the wind brushed against her bare flesh.

'Charles King was blowing up properties, but they were empty, so nobody really took that much notice apart from you. You didn't see that the buildings were all owned by the banks. However, that was on paper; the real owner was Edward King. The buildings were worthless, but ….'

'The land, it was the land that was worth a fortune,' Steel said, looking away for a second, realising his mistake was in not digging deeper into the owner and just concentrating on bringing King down.

'Correct. However, Edward was just a pawn in this; a bigger brain had organised everything. You don't think that Edward King was the sort of person who ran in the circles of smugglers and arms dealers, do you? No, there was someone higher up in the food chain,' Kitty said, pulling the coat tighter around her as a howling breeze shot past them.

'Let's talk in the car, out of the wind,' Steel said, knowing that Kitty had walked there and not driven.

She nodded in agreement as she began to shiver from the last blast of cold air.

'Nice to see you still keep up appearances,' she said, climbing into the passenger side of the Jaguar.

'I borrowed it from … a friend,' Steel said, pausing midsentence as if trying to find the right words.

'Nice friend. You must introduce me sometime,' Kitty laughed.

Steel smiled and nodded as he started the engine. The beast roared as he touched the gas pedal slightly. 'We'll see,' he replied, putting it into gear and pulling away from the curb.

'Where are we going?' Kitty asked with a sudden look of panic.

'Well, we could talk on the street all night, or we could talk at my place; besides, I'm hungry,' Steel answered as he put his foot down and raced through the empty streets.

'So, this house of yours, is it far?' She wriggled about on the leather seat like a cat trying to find a comfortable spot to relax in.

'About an hour, just a little place in the country; it's not much, but it's home,' Steel replied, trying to look humble. 'Try and get some sleep; you're safe ….'

Steel stopped; she had already succumbed to the warmth and comfort of the car and was fast asleep. Steel smiled as he watched the sleeping 'Cara', but to him, she would always be Kitty, the shy and innocent agent.

He turned his gaze back to the road, and the smile faded. Kitty was investigating a big fish, as she called it. But it wasn't a fish; it was a shark, a shark that apparently worked in the CIA.

That was why she and Trish were there. They were looking for someone in their own department, and Steel had an idea who it was. His gut would say it was Brena—or not so much gut feeling as a need for him to be the one. If Kitty was right, this wasn't just some guy in an office; this was top brass.

Steel looked over at the sleeping woman again and smiled. He was glad she had made it, glad she was in his car. He searched the telephone list on the car's media centre; he thought about calling Stanton to let him know Kitty was alive but would leave out The Sentinel details. The highlighted box with Avery's name flashed, but Stanton scrolled up to Jamerson's number.

After a couple of rings, he picked up. 'Yes, John?' the gruff-sounding man asked.

'We have a guest. Can you get the cook to rustle something up? Nothing too fancy,' Steel requested, knowing the cook would probably go overboard with the food.

'I'm sure she would be delighted to make something other than steak and chips,' Jamerson said mockingly.

Steel smiled and shook his head, and tried to keep his voice even. 'Oh, one other thing, I need to speak to HQ; we have a problem.'

Jamerson replied, 'Right you are, boss.' And hung up. Leaving Steel to power on down the street until he hit the A1 and followed that until the M1 Northbound.

As he drove in silence, his mind sorted through facts, trying to leave personal feelings out of it, considering they could always cloud a detective's judgment.

Someone in the CIA had been helping Edward King and making money, and a lot of it. The only questions now were, who was it and were the new targets in CIA custody safe?

Chapter 40

Simms looked up as he lay on the floor. He was covered in blood and brain matter, but it was Dorson's. The shot had come from the doorway; someone had come in at the last second and taken out Dorson. Simms tried to wipe the blood from his eyes, but his hands were also covered. The round had hit the right spot, taking most of Dorson's head off and making a mess of anything in front of him. Suddenly, Simms felt a tug on his arm, and he was being led somewhere in the room. Then the sound of running water.

Was it a shower in the bathroom?

The other person said nothing; they just shoved him into the stall and under the running water. Simms raised his hands as if to shield himself from any bullets, even though he knew it was pointless. The shot had been silent, which meant a suppressor. Dorson never heard them come in; that said, military training, possible black ops and special forces.

As the water ran over his face, it washed away the caked blood from his eyes. Simms blinked several times, allowing his eyes to adjust to their freedom. He leaned back and looked up. His face changed from a look of fear to one of relief.

'I was wondering when you were going to get here; bastard nearly had me,' Simms said, trying not to show he had nearly pissed his pants.

'Sorry, traffic,' replied a voice from outside the bathroom.

'What traffic? The route was clear,' Simms yelled back, feeling the shooter was playing with him.

'You're alive; he's dead. What's the problem?'

Simms struggled out and headed back into the main room.

'What now?' Simms asked, looking at Dorson's body. The entry wound was around three millimetres in diameter, and the exit was the size of a quarter. The bullet had entered through the right side of the back of his head. It exited through the left front, just above the eye, before finally embedding itself into the brick wall.

'We hang up a "do not disturb" sign on the door and come back later; in the meantime, grab your shit.'

Simms looked over at the bed. There sat Trish, unscrewing the six-inch suppressor from the pistol. Simms looked at the weapon. The sleek black polymer weapon looked more space-age than the conventional armaments he used. Even the bullets were special. 5.7x28mm 40gr armour-piercing rounds resembled miniature rifle rounds more than the standard 9mm bullets he was used to. The clip was a twenty-round mag. It was a nice little number that made a lot of mess.

Simms walked over to Trish and watched as she tucked the pistol into the holster at the small of her back. She stood and smoothed her tight blue jeans and rearranged her quarter-length leather jacket; her white blouse complemented the look, along with the ankle-high boots.

'Come on, let's get you cleaned up. Don't worry about the computer and stuff; the team will take it back to the lab,' Trish explained, but Simms wasn't worried. It was nearly over, and he could get his life back again, or at least the new one the agency would have for him when the case was over.

* * *

Kitty woke suddenly. The sound of the beach crept into her dreams. She looked around, confused and disorientated. There was no beach, only a gravel path which led to a massive turn-of-the-century stately home. Kitty rubbed her eyes and tried to read her watch, but she hadn't fully awoken yet, and everything close was a blur.

'Where the hell are we?' Kitty complained as she took in the view before her.

The path was lined with tiny lights guiding the way like a landing strip. The hall was a three-story wonder that she had only seen the likes of on TV. Spotlights from the gardens illuminated the outside, giving it a mysterious look. Four stone pillars marked the entrance, and a statue fountain to the front acted as a turning circle for visitors.

'Home,' Steel said with a smile.

Her eyes widened as they drew near. She had seen big houses and mansions in the States, but nothing like this. 'Wow, whose house is it anyway, and do they know we're coming?' Kitty asked, her mouth agape.

Steel laughed to himself. 'They have a fair idea,' he said with a childish grin. As he brought the Jaguar to a gentle halt, Jamerson opened Kitty's door and stepped to the side to allow her room to exit the vehicle.

'Good morning, miss; I hope you had a pleasant journey?' Offering his most Oxford accent, Jamerson bowed slightly.

Kitty swung out her legs and pulled herself out, all the while her gaze captured by the front of the hall. She had to admit it was the grandest place she had seen, less for hotels, but an actual stately home; she had never had the pleasure.

'Chef has laid on a small snack for you and the lady in the dining room, sir,' Jamerson said, trying to seem pompous.

'Thanks, Sarge, and you can drop the act; we're working,' Steel said, racing around the front of the car towards the entrance.

Kitty's eyes widened as she looked at Steel, realising his Lord status wasn't a cover at all; it was real.

'Are you really—'

'Hungry, thirsty, in need of a stiff martini with gin, yes.' Steel grabbed her by the arm and dragged her inside. There was no time for sightseeing or explanations; they had work to do. 'Can you …?' Steel asked with a desperate look at Jamerson.

'Certainly can, boss,' Jamerson said with his broad London accent.

They passed through the dining room first to grab a snack before getting to work. Steel opened the double doors and stood there for a few seconds.

'I see Chef has gone slightly overboard again,' he said at the sight of the banquet before them. Steel turned to apologise, but Kitty had already rushed forward and filled her plate.

'I guess it beats MRE meals?' Steel strolled past the stack of plates and started to fill one with roast chicken, salads, and miniature sausage rolls. Chef had indeed surpassed herself, but Steel suspected she knew he would send the remaining food to the shelters and soup kitchens. But he didn't mind; most of the folks at the shelters were ex-servicemen who had fallen on hard times. He sometimes employed street people as informants and infiltrators, as he liked to call them. He would pay them well, but most of all, he was giving them a purpose and not charity.

'Kitty … Cara,' Steel said, shooting her an apologetic look.

She just smiled and shrugged as if to say either name would do, unable to speak due to the lobster claw in her mouth.

'We need to come up with a plan before we go back to New York.'

She shot him a puzzled look. 'New York? Don't you mean Langley?' Kitty asked after swallowing.

'King and the judge will be in New York; that is where they will have their accidents. Whoever this is can't afford another death on the grounds. Falkner looked like a suicide, another two, and you have a killer on base … no, they are there, and my guess is whoever is running the show will be there to watch or do it themselves,' Steel explained.

Kitty thought for a moment and nodded in agreement. Steel had a point; the question was, did he have a *fast plane*?

Steel knew they had very little time before they had to leave.

Kitty followed Steel into the study and watched him exchange his contact lenses for a pair of sunglasses that had been plugged into a special loading station. He grabbed a laptop and a cell phone and then hurried back towards the door. Kitty watched with interest and a moderate amount of confusion at what he was doing.

Steel darted here and there, gathering items she didn't quite see before they disappeared into a black military-style canvas carrier.

'Come on,' Steel ordered, and they headed back to the car.

'Where to? We just got here, and …' Kitty held up her plate.

Steel lifted his arms in a show of annoyance at her display.

'Right, bring it with you; I'm driving anyway,' Steel tossed the bag onto the back seat and then opened the driver's side and climbed behind the wheel.

Kitty hurried into the car; her plate and mouth were still full. She hadn't had real food for days, and this was definitely making up for it.

'Where we goin'?' Kitty asked before popping another sausage roll into her mouth.

'The airport. We have to try and get to New York before your targets get a visit,' Steel said, pulling over his seat belt and fasting it. He knew it would be close, but he had to try. Jamerson would be phoning the pilot to tell him to get the plane ready. The aircraft would be ready in minutes as the pilot always did regular pre-checks when Steel was in the country for just such reasons.

Steel pressed the starter button, put it first, and raced down the driveway towards the gated entrance. It would be a thirty-minute drive to the airport. Enough time for Kitty to finish her banquet on a plate. All Steel could hope for was good weather, them being on time, or better still, something stalling the agents who would be leaving for New York.

* * *

The London Oxford Airport was an old airfield established in 1935. By 1968, it had flourished to become one of the busiest in Britain. It was primarily used by smaller aircraft such as Seneca and Gulfstreams and, of course, Steel's Cessna Citation X private jet.

He pulled onto the small airfield and found a parking space near the Aviation Academy. He and Kitty ran from the lot and headed for the jet that Steel had indicated they were using with an outstretched arm.

There was a low whir as the turbines warmed up and a stream of light from the cabin showed the open doorway, ready to receive them.

'Hope this is a fast plane,' Kitty yelled over the noise.

Steel didn't reply; he just urged her to hurry up. A young woman greeted them and helped them aboard when they reached the steps. As Steel got on, the woman pulled the doorsteps up, sealing the aircraft. The co-pilot looked around at her, and she gave the thumbs up. Steel strapped in, and Kitty did the same. It was all done with perfection, almost with military precision. They were in the air and en route to New York minutes after parking on the tarmac.

Kitty had to admit; she was impressed. The house, the jet. Whomever Steel was working for was connected.

'So, I take it you're not really NYPD, not with a pad like that for a cover,' Kitty said as she finished off the last of the food. 'You British Secret Service or something... you know, the whole Bond thing?' The question had only just popped into her head, but the more she thought about it, the more sense it made. It would explain the house and the company jet. The great hall was probably the headquarters.

She thought back to Steel's file, and Kitty couldn't remember reading anything about his childhood. Just that he went to Oxford; his father was a minister in British Intelligence and a businessman who owned a massive family company. Steel's mother had been a nurse before getting pregnant with him. But then, his whole past was vague. He'd joined the Army at a young age, where he had joined the Royal Tactical Combat Engineers as a private, not an officer. Later, after his third year and first stripe, he was picked by the regiment for selection with the SAS; he passed with flying colours and served with them for several years.

The subsequent note stated that he had joined the US Navy SEAL team. Why was it a mystery, but some army guys just like a challenge? She had heard a tale about one British soldier who went through every special forces selection. But on completion, he turned down the chance to join because he just wanted to do a selection to see if he could pass it.

'Who else have you got inside, apart from your sister?' Steel asked as he swivelled the cream leather chair to face Kitty.

Kitty tried to look shocked at the insinuation, but Steel just shot her a come-on look.

'Just two more people, and that is all you need to know,' Kitty said sternly.

Steel smiled and nodded. He could understand she wanted to keep the other person's identity secret, but Steel needed to know whom he could trust. Then Steel thought for a moment; there was only one possible choice out of all the people he had met. Steel cracked a smile and sat back in the chair.

'So, how long have you and your sister worked with Dutton and Simms undercover?' Steel questioned, causing Kitty to stare at him with a look of surprise.

'What gave them away?' Kitty asked with a smile.

Steel looked behind him as the young stewardess brought two glasses of champagne on a silver salver.

Kitty took hers first after Steel beckoned her, then he took the remaining glass and thanked the woman before she returned to the back of the plane.

'It was the way you all acted around each other,' Steel said. 'As if you had been through a lot together, even though you had just started. I've seen it before, back in the Army. People learn to know each others' moves and thoughts. This takes time and experience, which neither of you has had with each other,' Steel explained.

He didn't want to admit that it had been a complete fluke—that he had just guessed, given the way the others treated her, Dutton and Simms seemed the most likely of candidates to have worked with her.

Trish had been harder to read. He had only seen her a couple of times, and then it was for a few minutes, so he couldn't get an accurate reading of her.

'It makes sense, really; you needed Simms to cover for you in Berlin. I thought it strange he would have sent you to a target's apartment alone,' Steel said with a smile as if it were all coming together.

'So, when did you leave for Amsterdam? The minute I went to the meeting at the cafè with my contact, or later?' It was the one piece of the puzzle he couldn't get.

'After you left, sure, it was a big risk, but as you said, Simms was there to cover for me.' Kitty smiled as if to congratulate him on his deduction.

The flight would take around four hours at the present speed. The Cessna Citation X had been voted the fastest private jet in the world, which was probably why Steel wanted one. The flight would land around midnight at JFK Airport. It would be close, to be sure. Steel had arranged for a delay of the team's departure from Langley by having another postcard sent; this, of course, had a double effect. The first would, of course, have the team running over themselves to try and break it; on the other hand, the person they were after would know it was a fake and would try and get out of wasting time. Steel figured whoever made it to New York had to be part of the cleanup operation.

It was just over an hour's flight from Washington to New York. Steel would have preferred they drive; however, flying was quicker, and they were running out of time. Steel had no doubt that word had gotten out he was on his way.

He sipped his drink and looked out the window. It was a seemingly pointless act due to the lack of visibility in the dark of the night, but he found it comforting. Next, he needed to gather his thoughts to formulate a plan. If they were going up against someone in the agency, that meant they had to get it right, or they could be classed as the enemy.

Steel pulled out his phone and started to make calls to people back in New York. They would land in two hours, which gave his people plenty of time to get the ball rolling.

Chapter 41

Avery Stanton sat in his office chair with a broad smile on his face. He'd just had a phone call; Steel was on the way back to the US, specifically New York. For Stanton, this meant one thing: it was almost over, his boy was coming back, and they had most of the targets safe and sound. The London office would be flying the others over early in the morning. Stanton had made it clear to the top brass that he didn't feel comfortable with them all meeting in New York. Still, Director Headly thought it best, considering the loss of Falkner.

Stanton had voiced his reservations; he didn't know anyone in the New York office. Sure, he had met a few at conferences but didn't know any of them. The ones he had been friends with had all retired or moved to greener pastures.

* * *

The new postcard had come in around eight o'clock that evening, and it had gotten everyone giddy but not Stanton. In fact, he was getting bored of it all, bored of playing this killer's game. All he wanted was to go home, eat a TV dinner, and watch sports.

He'd left Brena with the postcard while he flew to New York, even though Stanton still felt something amiss about Brena, but then there were no other agents he could call on. Trish, Simms, and now Dorson were missing. Someone he had definitely gotten their ass chewed for from upstairs because the word came down that Headly wanted results and fast. Stanton remembered how much Headly had opposed bringing Steel in on the case—called Steel a loose cannon. Stanton had smiled at the description; of course, he was, and that was why Stanton needed him.

He went to a small safe and took out his passport, a long brown leather wallet, and an HK SFP9 pistol with a polished steel top slide and placed them into a metal briefcase. Stanton closed the case and headed for the door. He stopped and smiled at his secretary as he walked out but said nothing. She smiled back and nodded slightly. Stanton returned the gesture and headed for the elevator. As Brenda watched him leave, a solitary tear rolled down her face as if to say goodbye.

* * *

Brena moved about frantically, yelling orders and trying to get ahead of the task. Find out who the latest target was going to be. He didn't want to be there; he wanted to be on the plane with Stanton, but Headly had insisted someone should stay and oversee the investigation regarding the latest clue. Usually, Brena would have been proud to have been chosen for such a task of leadership, but to him, this was just a numbers game. He was the only one left. All the agents with him were either new or too inexperienced to carry out the task.

Brena was annoyed he wasn't heading up the investigation into the disappearance of the three agents, but that was another department's baby. He was just tidying up an almost-finished case. To Brena's disappointment, they had all of the Sentinel's targets, and Steel had broken the case wide open.

They had King and were building a case against him with the help of the 11th Precinct and Captain Brant's homicide division; after all, it was they who had tried to indict King's son. So, with the fixer being out of the way, King was going down for a long time, his co-conspirators along with him.

Brena felt his throat grow raw from the shouting and picked up his coffee mug. A disappointed look crossed his face as he stared at the empty vessel. He walked past the busy agents and went to get a refill. It was nearly twenty-two hundred, and this wasn't the thing he was hoping to be doing at ten o'clock on a Friday night. Nevertheless, the thought of Steel returning late in the afternoon the next day amused Brena. Sure, Steel would have solved the case, but it would be Brena's face on the front page of the newspapers for being the agent in charge.

He topped up the blue mug with the CIA badge on both sides. He preferred it black, with no sugar. A proper cup of coffee, or so he would say. Brena walked back to check on the team's progress.

One agent was doing background on King, tying up loose ends for the NYPD and the DA. Another was finding anything to reference the picture on the postcard. It was of a wild bird, a goose or swan of some kind, with a background of an aerial photograph of an ancient hill site for a castle or village.

The female agent was busy with location software that would identify the site. But Brena didn't seem hopeful; in fact, he was confused about why there was another card. Undoubtedly, there wasn't anyone else left to catch, was there?

Brena sipped his coffee and paced about impatiently, like a child waiting for Christmas presents. To him, this was torcher. He had to be on a plane to New York; it was, if anything, imperative. But Stanton was taking the company jet; if Brena were to go, it would be by a civilian airline. He thought about helicopters, but he'd never get clearance, not from Headly anyway. Brena sat down at Trish's terminal and looked up flights to New York using an airline site. There was a Delta flight leaving Ronald Reagan Airport in the next hour. Brena stood up and walked over to the female agent.

'I've just got to go off base for a while, something I have to check out to reference the case,' Brena lied, but he was her superior, so she didn't need to know the ins and outs. She nodded and went back to work. Brena smiled and looked at his watch. The airport wasn't that far. Time enough to get there, get a ticket, and check in. He didn't need much, just his ID and his gun.

* * *

The Cessna Citation X landed at JFK. A storm had just hit, bringing a rain of biblical proportions. Steel and Kitty hurried off the plane and into a waiting vehicle a friend had sent to pick them up. As soon as the rear passenger doors had closed, the blacked-out Yukon SUV powered off the tarmac and headed for the exit. Traffic on the Brooklyn Bridge was backed up halfway down the Brooklyn-Queens Expressway.

'Nick, who arrived from the Langley office?' Steel asked the driver.

Nick was a big man, with around two hundred pounds of muscle from too much time in a prison gym. His tattoos were barely visible on his dark skin. He was of Jamaican descent and had a nose for sniffing out information.

Nick stroked his goatee and looked around at the traffic to see if there was any sign of moving forward. 'Nobody yet, but I got feelers out.'

'Are they secure?' Steel asked, looking at the time ticking away.

'Yes, they separated them and put them into safe houses, as you suggested. I think the knowledge about what happened in Langley had convinced them to agree with you,' Nick said, pulling into an open space and then waiting for the next gap to appear.

The traffic was slow and was beginning to annoy Steel. His plan was perfect, but it would be for nothing if they couldn't get to the meeting point in time.

'Are they OK with the second phase?' Steel asked, leaning forward, so his head was almost through the gap between the two front seats.

'They were not happy, but after your friends convinced them it was you who was taking the blame if it went wrong, they agreed,' Nick said with a chuckle in his voice.

'Oh, lovely. No pressure then,' Steel said, raising an eyebrow.

'Phase two? What was phase one?' Kitty asked, puzzled at what they were heading into.

'Well, phase one was getting everyone together. Step two—oh, you are going to love phase two,' Steel said with excitement.

He spent the next half hour breaking it down for her and requesting her assistance and that of her colleagues.

Kitty took out her cell and pressed the speed-dial icon for Trish.

'You're out of your mind; you know that, don't you?' Kitty said to Steel while she waited for Trish to pick up.

Steel just shrugged and checked the time on his watch again. The meeting was at two o'clock; it was now midnight. Steel looked over to Kitty and began to speak with the cell on loudspeaker, so Steel could hear.

Trish had picked up and explained what had happened with Dorson and Simms.

Kitty shook her head in disbelief; she never figured Dorson was capable of that, not him. She could have imagined most of the others in the team but not him.

'Where are you now?' Steel interjected.

'We're heading to New York; we are just outside the Philadelphia border crossing,' Trish replied with a curious tone.

'Where is Dorson's body?' Steel pulled out his cell and prepared to send a text.

'The Fairway Hotel, Arlington, Room 213,' Simms said with a regretful tone.

Steel sent a quick text to someone and placed the cell back into his pocket. Kitty gave Steel a curious look. 'Why do you have a cleaning crew on speed dial?' Kitty asked, stopping Trish from speaking.

'The question is, why don't *you*?' Steel replied with a straight face.

Nick laughed out loud and shook his head.

'When you get to New York, head for this address,' Steel ordered Dutton and Trish. He gave them the time and place and what they were meant to do when they got there.

Dutton and Trish said they understood and hung up, leaving an awkward silence in the car.

Kitty stared at Steel, trying to make him out. 'So, why do this? I have my reasons, but what have you got against this guy, whoever he is? Is it a justice thing that you want to bring him in?'

'You brought me in, giving me clues to prove what you had already discovered. But you couldn't do anything, not without proof or indeed blowing your cover. So, you needed someone to investigate,' Steel explained.

Kitty raised her eyebrows in astonishment at his investigative mind.

'But you never counted on a killer cleaning up his mess. Okay, you built devices that would cause damage, but those were meant to go off when the people weren't there, hence the minimum of destruction. But someone cottoned on to your plan and decided to use that to hang you; sure, if you were caught and nobody got hurt, you might be able to sway the jury. But if people died, that would be a different story. So, you go to jail, and the killer goes free,' Steel continued as he looked out the smoked glass.

'What drives me, you asked. At first, it was a challenge, but now it's for whole other reasons … that day, I saved over thirty people by securing the device. Someone else set off the bomb. I watched as those people were engulfed in flames or ripped to pieces. Yes, I want justice, but this time the bastard isn't going to walk; I'll make sure of that,' Steel promised grimly.

'Fine words, Mr Steel, but until you have lost someone, I'll take the whole justice speech with a pinch of salt,' Kitty said angrily.

Suddenly, she caught a look that Nick shot her, a look of contempt over something she had said. As he went to speak, Steel interrupted. 'You are right, of course; I can't imagine what you are going through; I apologise,' Steel said humbly.

Kitty smiled softly, feeling she had been too harsh. After all, he was helping her, and as he said, he had witnessed everything, including those being injured.

'We need to get out of this,' Steel said, looking around at the stationary traffic. 'We need to run.' He got up and headed to the trunk to retrieve a long canvas bag. 'Nick, meet us when you get there; you know what to do.' He caught his friend's reflection in the rearview.

As he slammed the trunk shut, Kitty stepped out and followed Steel as they weaved in between vehicles until they reached the bridge's footpath. Nick leant back into the seat of the SUV and rubbed his face with his massive hands out of frustration. He knew he would be there for hours and he would miss the party.

* * *

It was a fifteen-minute walk to Brookfield Place and around eight minutes to run there. For Steel, this was where it all began, and he would make sure that was where it would come to an end. The plan was in motion; Steel just hoped everyone played their part, or this could go south real fast.

As they approached the mall, Steel stopped on Vesey Street and looked across at the renovated structure. To Steel's annoyance, they found that the front was cordoned off by fencing while continuing the construction, meaning they would have to go to the underground parking structure. In addition, the blast from King's bomb had done significant structural damage. Still, the architects thought it was also a good time to iron out issues they had discovered while it was open.

Steel gave the structure another once-over before rushing forwards and over the street with Kitty close behind. All the while, she was hoping his plan would work and they would flush out the real killer.

Brookfield Place wasn't just a building; it was several different structures combined over a shopping mall; this meant many entrances, but they just needed one. Steel pulled out his phone and went to a city map, notably over the mall. He needed to know alternative entry points. Steel smiled, tucked the cell back into his pocket, and started down West Street towards Liberty Street and Pumphouse Park.

There was an entrance out of sight from the street, with trees and bushes in the park giving perfect cover. All he had to do was break in.

The park was quiet and shrouded in darkness. It was half one in the morning, with a biting chill in the air. As Steel worked on the lock, Kitty kept a lookout.

'Why are we breaking in if they are expecting us?' Kitty asked, confused and cold.

'They are expecting me, not you, and they definitely aren't expecting me so soon. Don't forget; we just travelled from the UK; that was an eight-hour flight,' Steel said with a grin.

Kitty stared at him as he finished the final tumbler. 'So, why set the meeting for now?'

'A, it gives everyone time to get here. B, it allows the agencies to set up their men that they think they will need,' Steel explained as he inched open the door, allowing Kitty through first and then himself.

'What do you mean they think they will need?' Kitty asked, confused as ever. Sure, Steel had explained his plan, but by the sounds of what he was now saying, he'd left out some details. Steel said nothing; he just gave a quick smile before racing down the expansive ground floor of the mall's south side. Empty glass window fronts reflected their images as they moved quickly to the spot that Steel had chosen to be the meeting place. However, they weren't going there; they were going to the first floor above.

They used the motionless escalators to reach the level above. All the while, Steel shifted his gaze to pick up any movement or anything that might cause him concern but found the way clear. There were blank spaces where the 360-degree view security would eventually go. This was both a good and a bad thing. It was great that nobody could see their approach, but on the other hand, if something were to happen, it wasn't captured on tape.

Kitty followed Steel, keeping low but moving quickly across the dusty stone floor. Seeing the empty stores saddened Kitty as she remembered what it used to look like. She had visited the scene sometime after the explosion. Her CIA credentials had seen her pass security without too many questions. That and a friendly smile could always open doors for her.

'How do you know they will all show?' Kitty asked with a look of doubt.

'Simple, I told them I knew who the real killer was,' Steel said with conviction.

'And *do* you?' Kitty asked, grabbing Steel's arm and holding him fast in place.

Steel stopped, looked down at her hand on his arm, and then noticed her tearful blue eyes.

'In truth, I won't know until we get to the meeting. I know you want your revenge, and I know you also want to be the one who brings him down; just be patient,' Steel said, resting a large hand on hers.

Kitty smiled and nodded. She knew if anyone could find the real killer, it would be Steel.

Smiling, he nodded over to the balcony that overlooked the ground floor, the exact place where he had been months ago. Kitty looked over to the glass railings and then let go of his arm. 'Shall we?' Kitty asked calmly.

'*I* shall. I need you to do something else,' Steel said solemnly.

'Do what?' she asked sternly, having the feeling he was trying to keep her out of the way.

'I need you to find a bomb,' Steel said with an expressionless face. His mood had suddenly changed. He had cut off all feelings and had slipped back into the mindset of his old cold agent self.

'Where should I start?' Kitty's voice held a hint of fear. She had never seen anything like him before, not like this. It was as if he were a completely different person.

'My guess is the parking garage. Pack a van with explosives, and you would bring the whole building down,' Steel replied, looking back at the balcony. Flashes from the past blurred with the present like two films overlapping each other on the same screen. Thoughts started to run through his head ... and questions.

'What was the bomb for?'

Kitty looked over at Steel, who wore a puzzled look.

'Probably to level the building and kill us all, I suppose. Who cares? I'll find it and stop it,' Kitty asked, perplexed.

'No, not the one now ... if there is one, and I'm quite certain there is. I mean the one King had. It was a single device meant to cause devastation but not big enough to "level" this place, as you colourfully put it. He wasn't here to kill anyone because that wasn't his MO. By all accounts, he was a coward who hid behind his father and his money, but a killer he wasn't; he didn't have the balls for it. So, what was it for?'

'Who knows, and who cares? The sick bastard is dead, and now we have the chance to get rid of another killer and stop his bomb,' Kitty stated, looking confident.

Steel nodded, and his expression changed again as he put on his cold, game face. 'Let's go,' he said coolly.

Kitty turned and headed towards the lower levels.

'Kitty?' Steel called out suddenly, forcing her to turn around.

'What?' She hoped for something inspirational from him.

'You're going the wrong way; it's over there,' Steel said, pointing over to the north.

Kitty quietly scratched her nose with an extended middle finger. Steel smiled as he got the message, and they went their separate ways.

* * *

Steel moved to the spot where he had observed King on the day of the explosion. Not much had changed as if they were rebuilding using the same reference to the former building.

Below, the targets had gathered along with the agents from the justice department playing babysitters. The targets looked worried, the agents on edge. Both with the same idea: had they just walked into a trap? Steel would give it a few minutes and wait for the rest of the party to show up. He did not doubt that Graaf and Dollman would not be too far away, and neither would whoever was coming from Langley.

Steel checked his watch as two more agents arrived, along with Dollman and Graaf in tow.

'So, what's this all about anyway?' Dollman yelled as if to make himself seem superior to the rest of them.

'It's about all of you,' Steel said, his voice echoing around the empty building. 'It's about all of you being part of a plan to bomb the city.'

All the targets started to talk at once, and the volume of voices grew louder as they started to compete with one another.

Steel yelled, causing them to become silent and look at him as he walked down the stationary escalator. 'Most of all, it's about you all being loose ends.' Steel had a stern, displeased look on his face. 'Now, personally, I don't care if someone is taking you guys out; they're doing the world a favour by all accounts. But I do care about the innocent people who died in this very spot to cover up what you people helped do all those years ago. So, now I was wondering what all of you had in common—yes, you all did things to help dear little Charles get off of death row, but there was something more, something I couldn't put my finger on at first.' Steel moved about the massive mall lobby.

'You all had one specific thing in common on one particular day. Now, agents back in Langley had been researching your movements before the bombing to try and put you and Charles King together. And at a stretch, they had, but all these meetings happened separately, weeks apart. But then I got to thinking about the bomb that went off here. It wasn't large enough to bring down a building, but it would cause some serious damage if it were in, say … a parking garage. I bet that all of you were downstairs waiting for a meeting that was never going to happen; in fact, I bet the killer even went as far as to tell you all where to park?'

Looks of realisation washed over their faces as they understood they had been set up that day, that the bomb was meant for them.

'Well, if it was meant for us, why was it up here and not down there?' Graaf asked, wiping the sweat from his brow with his handkerchief.

'When I saw King leave his building, he didn't have a bag; the next time I saw him here, he had a long heavy-looking canvas bag. King had gotten the bomb from in here, and he was probably told to drop it off in a certain location, namely where you were all parked,' Steel stated, taking note of all their expressions.

'But he set it off up here, not downstairs,' Dollman said, his arms flapping about.

'King was on his way downstairs when he saw security; he thought they were after him when they were after a homeless man,' Steel explained.

'A homeless guy?' Graaf repeated, his brow furrowed.

'Well, actually, it was me in disguise. But the point is Charles King panicked. He had a bomb. The cops were coming, so he did the only thing a spineless sod would do; he dropped the bag and made a hostage situation,' Steel said, looking over at Edward King.

He was saying nothing or making eye contact.

'Someone sent Charles there, not just to set up the bomb, but to die with it also. A great plan by all accounts. The killer got rid of all loose ends simultaneously. With what was in the device, the corner of CSU wouldn't be able to get anything to identify the bodies,' Steel said, walking up and down, his gaze fixed on the targets. 'But Charles had to go; whether it was downstairs or right here, he had to go. He knew too much. He had already dodged the bombing bullet, but what if someone found something else? No, he was a liability, so they killed him along with thirty other people.' Steel's voice was calm.

'But in your report, you said you had secured the kill switch by wrapping a bandage around his hand, so what happened?' asked a familiar voice.

Steel looked behind the line of people and saw Brena standing there with his agents.

'Just before the explosion, I remembered the window being broken in one specific place,' Steel answered. Walking over to the replacement pane of glass, he touched it where the small spiderweb shape had appeared in his memories.

'A gunshot?' Brena asked.

'A sniper, to be more precise, from over there,' Steel said, pointing at the river.

'So, what are we thinking, Mermaid or Sponge Bob?' said one of the agents from justice.

'I'd say boat. The shot is too far away to come from over the other side unless it was a highly trained sniper. It's too high for it to be shot from the grounds,' Steel answered as he pointed back at the view.

'They shot the bag?' Brena was unconvinced. 'Sure, you're not saying that to cover your ass?' S

Steel didn't move; he just continued to stare out of the window. 'You are right, of course; I could be lying or mistaken.' Steel said, causing Brena to smile and the others to gasp. Steel reached out a congratulatory hand.

Brena smirked and took the handshake to mean he had won. Brena was on the floor in seconds. Steel had grabbed his hand, put him into a lock, and rapidly handwrapped a bandage around his hand. Steel stood up, and Brena clambered to his feet.

'So, Brena, did I drop the ball?' Steel asked after proving his point.

Brena sulked in defeat and struggled with the bandage around his hand.

'I believe the sniper was a contingency plan in case something screwed up. All of you could go later, but he had to go then. With Charles dead with a bomb in his possession, the business could continue, and every past deed would be forgotten,' Steel added.

'Business, what business?' Dollman asked, a look of concern on his face.

'Edward King was making money from the bombings. The buildings would be damaged beyond repair. His firm would be contracted to clear the site and build whatever monstrosity was on the drawing board,' Steel explained. 'Clearly, when Charles was arrested for being the bomber, your business took a dive; people were adding things together. But after he had been cleared, there was a doubt, but business was coming back,'

Steel moved about as he spoke. ' So, what to do? Well, it would be simple, if your son was killed in a bomb attack, you would get the sympathy vote, and business would boom again. Unfortunately, someone had left the bomb in the public lockers for him to pick up. Leaving the bag downstairs was too risky; someone might see it. So, all he had to do was pick it up and drop it off,' Steel stared at Edward King, his expression condemning.

'And he couldn't get that right,' King said, rolling his eyes and crossing his arms.

'You sent your own son on a suicide mission?' Graaf asked a look of disgust on his face. 'And they call me an evil bastard?'

'OK, so where is your proof?' King said with a knowing grin.

'In truth, it's all theory. In time, we will fit it all together, but for now, we have nothing,' Steel said with a broad smile and raised his arms as though he were tossing something in the air, making King's smile grow. 'But I don't need any; you are all dead anyway. The killer is after you, and I've no doubt he will find you.'

'What, this Sentinel person?' King continued wearing his smug look.

'No, The Sentinel wanted you found so you could tell the truth; someone else wants you guys dead,' Steel explained with a strange sense of enjoyment.

'Who then?' Brena asked, confused at where Steel was going with this.

'Good question,' Steel said, looking in Brena's direction.

Chapter 42

Kitty crept down to the parking lot, sticking to the shadows and avoiding anything that could give off light. She had no idea what she was looking for, but she knew it had to be big to bring the building down on top of them.

As Kitty exited the stairwell and stepped onto the lot, she found nothing unusual at first. A few parked cars were there, but she put that down to the justice department and the Feds. She walked further in, but nothing stuck out, no big trucks or vans. Eighteen-wheelers would have to go elsewhere as the ceiling was too low for them to enter.

Kitty turned to walk back and report Steel's theory was wrong.

That was when she stopped and looked around again. Besides the typical blacked-out Yukon SU's, there were twelve cars parked at irregular intervals, some of which was next to the roof supports. Carefully, Kitty walked over to one of the cars and looked inside. The whole interior had been stripped, and it was filled with explosives. If one of these went off, it would be devastating; if all went off, it would be catastrophic.

Kitty backed off slowly but then picked up speed. She began running for her life and those upstairs.

* * *

Kitty pulled out her phone and pressed the speed dial for Steel's cell. She needed to tell him, warn him.

'Yes, what's up?' Steel asked, shocked she was calling so soon.

'You were wrong about the bomb,' Kitty said, trying to sprint and talk simultaneously.

'Really, that's odd; I'm usually quite good at things like that,' Steel said arrogantly.

'There's not one! There are at least twelve! And they are all car bombs, and I do mean *car bombs*,' Kitty declared.

'Kitty, I want you to get out and find a cop as soon as you can. Let him know, but I want you away from this building, do you understand?' Steel growled.

'Yes, but what about you?' Kitty asked, heading for the nearest exit.

'We'll be fine; you just get yourself away,' Steel said before hanging up and pocketing his phone. Steel turned to the others. An unsurprised look crossed his face. 'So, who told someone where we were meeting?'

Everyone looked around, surprised at the question.

'No one, why?' Dollman spoke up, pushing his chest out as if taking the question as an insult.

'Well, unless someone just left twelve cars packed with explosives here overnight before they took them further, I would say we were blown. So, who talked?' Steel asked again.

The men in front of him began to panic. Agents got onto their radios and cell phones to call for backup, but all the while, Steel just stood and stared at the chaos before him.

'Aren't you going to do anything?' Dollman turned to Brena.

'Like what? There are twelve devices, and I'm not trained for that shit,' Brena said with a tone of alarm in his voice.

'Well, I suggest we leave, possibly through the north entrance,' Steel put forth.

'Why? Is it further from the blast?' asked Graaf.

'Yes, and there is a coffee shop with fantastic pastries just outside,' Steel said with a surprised tone in his voice.

* * *

Steel made his way to the north entrance on Vesey Street. The targets and their keepers followed. The team leaders talking on their wrist mics, giving HQ updates.

'I don't understand why we don't just go back to the vehicles,' Graaf said, his voice filled with fear.

'Be my guest, but can you make sure I'm out of the building first? I've been blown up here once before; I don't want a repeat performance,' Steel said as he scanned the area for anything out of place. As he walked, he had that feeling that something wasn't quite right.

Steel stopped and raised a clenched fist; for him, it was second nature to give the military sign for stop and don't move, something the others weren't aware of.

'What is it?' asked one of the agents, grabbing Graaf's collar to stop him from moving.

'You know when something is too easy?' Steel asked as he crouched down and looked across the open floor.

'What are you thinking, Steel?' asked the agent as he followed suit.

'I was thinking about the bombs downstairs; if nobody said anything about the meet, that means they had been here for some time. If that is the case, for what?' Steel's gaze fixed on the floor as if he were expecting something to appear.

'Mr King, when was this meant to open?' Steel asked without moving from his position.

'Around two days from now, why?' King answered, confused by the question.

'Anyone special meant to be here?'

'Myself, the governor, the mayor, a couple of investors,' King answered, still failing to see a point.

'And no one else? A top name you are hiding so you don't ruin the surprise?' Steel pressed, feeling King wasn't entirely forthcoming with his answer.

'OK, the Vice President was asked to come and cut the ribbon,' King said with a disappointed tone.

Steel and the agent turned around slowly and stared at King with raised eyebrows.

'And you didn't think that was important enough to tell us?' the agent asked, suddenly getting onto his sleeve microphone.

Steel walked up to King, grabbing him by the epaulettes of his thousand-dollar suit and lifting him off the floor before slamming his back against one of the store windows. The glass shook but held. 'What's the connection between all this and the Vice President?' Steel growled.

King looked around, hoping someone would help him, but the rest held the look of people who would enjoy watching Steel tear him apart.

'Nothing, he has nothing to do with this,' King cried out.

Steel snarled, spun around, and launched King at the opposite window. There was a massive crash of glass as King flew through the display window and lay in broken glass and blood from the scratches he'd just endured.

Steel reached down and grabbed King again. 'Talk,' Steel ordered with bared teeth.

'I don't know anything,' King said between gasps of breath.

'That's OK; it's a big mall with lots of windows. Starting with this one,' Steel said, tossing King through the window he had just been forced against. The sound of breaking glass and yelps from King filled the walkway.

The other targets looked on with worried looks as if they knew they would be next if King died.

Steel walked over to King, dragged him out of the store, and tossed his bloodied body to the ground. King crouched on all fours, gasping to take in air like a runner after a marathon.

'No more, please, no more,' King begged, raising a hand to halt Steel's advance.

'So, what is the connection?' Steel asked again.

'Before he got where he is, he was a senator in New York, in charge of housing and refurbishment plans. You know what goes where, how much, and who gets the contract,' King started to explain as he lay on his side. 'He was doing OK, lots of work for the city, but then things started to dry up. The economy was taking a dive; fewer buildings were commissioned to local firms because they cost too much. So, we needed an edge.'

A look of anger crossed Steel's face as he figured out what was going on. 'So, if there were a crazy bomber, it would push out the competition, and your firm could move in, and the senator would get a cut,' Steel said, nodding as everything started to make sense.

'But, what's with the bombs downstairs?' asked the agent with a bemused look.

'If this place goes up, they could say that the police were wrong all of this time and that the bomber was still at large. And there would be the added bonus of getting rid of the senator, who I have no doubt was asking for more money, or he would blow the whistle,' Steel said with a smile. 'You wanted to shut up shop, but he wanted to keep going, knowing there was no trail to himself?'

'Pretty much,' King replied with a grim laugh. 'The greedy bastard said he had kept proof of everything; he would send it to the police and media if we didn't give him more money. A contribution to his run for President, he called it.'

'But that doesn't explain who was clearing house, why The Sentinel was after us,' Graaf said, shrugging.

'The Sentinel wanted revenge, The bombing here robbed The Sentinel of family, mom, dad, sister; you get the idea. So, The Sentinel tried to frighten you into giving up the details of all of your connections with Charles King, how he got the bomb used, and how he got off going to prison. The Sentinel wants you to talk, not to die. But yes, that does leave the question of who is trying to keep you silent.' Steel looked down at King, who simply shook his head as if to say he had no idea.

Steel turned back to the floor leading to their exit.

'So, why don't we just go?' Graaf said, pointing to the glass doors.

'I think this whole place is wired. When we broke in, it activated something,' Steel said, kneeling down again and grabbing a handful of dust and dirt from the floor. Steel looked at the secret service agent who had rejoined him.

'Do it,' said the agent, switching his gaze from Steel to the ground in front. Steel tossed the dust into the air as far as it would go and waited for it to float gently down. Thin green beams of light stretched from one side to the other.

Steel and the agent stood up and looked at each other.

'I believe the term you are looking for is "oh bugger,"' Steel said with a dry smile.

'I was going for something a little stronger, but yep, that sums it up,' replied the agent.

'What is it?' Dollman asked, unsure of what they had seen.

'Laser tripwire, probably one on each exit as well,' explained the agent before walking to the side and giving HQ an update.

'So, in other words, we are trapped here?' Graaf asked with a note of hysteria as he began to wander around in a circle.

'Someone wants you dead ... *all of you.* One of you knows who it is,' Steel said, looking at his watch.

All eyes fell on King, who was nursemaiding his wounds, until he felt everyone's staring eyes on him.

'Hey, don't look at me! I told you all I got,' King bleated, waving a bloody hand.

Steel looked around at the group of people, agents and targets together in a shitty situation. But there was something else bothering Steel as he looked closer at the crowd. Suddenly, his gaze landed on Brena.

'Why are you here, Brena?' he asked cautiously.

'We got the word about the meeting, and I thought I should be here because it's my case, remember?' Brena barked.

It was true, someone from the section was expected, but it wasn't Brena he was waiting for.

'So, where is Stanton?' Steel asked, his tone monotone and unfeeling, as though he was preparing himself for the bad news.

'What you asking about him for? He's probably back in his office, drinking himself to death.' Brena shrugged.

'Because I sent a message to Stanton to let him know about this. I told him to tell no one but leave the address written down somewhere on his desk; it's funny you should show, though,' Steel admitted in a disappointed tone.

'Why is that then?' Brena asked as he began to nudge his jacket to the side, feeling the walkway walls starting to close in as all eyes began to stare at him.

'Because you are here. If you had anything to do with all this, you would have stayed away; I'm sorry to say I was wrong about you, Brena. I thought it was you,' Steel said with an angry look.

'Happy to disappoint you,' Brena said, taking Steel's look as a sign of defeat. A broad smile crossed his face.

'I'm disappointed, but it's not because of you; it's Stanton. So, either it's him we are looking for or ...' Frowning, Steel paused as if he could not complete the sentence for fear of it being true.

'The killer got to him,' Brena said, filling in the missing words. Brena had had suspicions that something was amiss when he'd arrived, and Stanton was a no-show.

Steel looked over at Brena, his anger still welling inside of him like a volcano ready to erupt.

'Get some people over to Stanton's place, check all flights out of Ronald Reagan, and make sure Stanton doesn't leave the state,' Steel ordered.

Brena nodded and complied; he didn't wasn't to get on Steel's bad side while he was still volatile.

Suddenly, Steel's phone let out three electronic beeps, signalling an incoming text. Yanking the cell from his pocket, he opened the message and read it. His look of anger seemed to double as he tucked the cell into his pocket.

'Bad news, I take it?' Brena asked, hoping to get more information than Steel's usual evasive shrug.

'The worst,' Steel answered before he started to walk down the walkway towards the door; everyone looked at him with confusion and fear.

'What are you doing—the tripwire, the bombs!' yelled Graaf as he grabbed King and hid behind him.

King shrugged off Graaf's weak grip, stood, and joined the others.

As Steel approached where the laser had been seen, he knelt down and picked up a laser pointer and stuck it into his pocket. The others watched with anger at the deception.

'And the bombs?' Brena asked, walking towards Steel.

'Ah, that would be our doing, but it's his fault,' said the secret service agent with a half-cocked smile. 'Steel asked us to place stripped-out vehicles in the parking lot, dress them up like there were bombs inside. He said we would get a confession, and oh boy, was he right,' he explained, grabbing King and slapping handcuffs onto his wrists.

'So, this was all an elaborate setup; who else was part of this?' Brena asked.

'We were,' said familiar voices in unison. Brena turned to see Trish, Dutton, Simms, and Kitty standing before him. His mouth fell open from shock.

'You're—'

'Alive, very much so,' Kitty finished his sentence with a cat-like smile.

'Gentlemen, I'd like you to meet the team who was responsible for saving your worthless hides from The Sentinel and the killer.' Steel lied, knowing telling their actual involvement would jeopardise what they had been working on for so long.

'You were in on this?' Brena asked, shocked and angered nobody had told him.

'Yeah, sorry about that. They need to know that what they were doing was way past your pay grade. They had to act as they did to make the killer seem comfortable and make mistakes, and he did,' Steel continued matter-of-factly.

Brena shot him a confused look. 'How?' Brena asked as they stood on the walkway.

'He sent his assassin to take me out; as you can see, the mother failed, and he got his,' Dutton said with a grin.

Trish looked over at Dutton and gave him a look. Dutton's smile faded, and he stood cross-armed and moody.

'Assassin?' Brena asked, still trying to take it all in.

'Dorson … real name Derick Abbot, ex-special forces Delta,' Steel answered.

Brena leant a hand against the concrete wall and tried to digest the information he had been thrown.

'And all this was Stanton's doing?' Brena asked slowly, 'He was this brains of the operation you were talking about?'

Steel smiled and shrugged before walking away, followed by Kitty and the rest of The Sentinel group. Brena watched them leave while the agents arrested the targets and led them downstairs. Brena stood up and put his hands on his hips as he looked around at the empty mall. Confusion and the fear of not knowing what he was supposed to do next swept over him. Finally, he let out a massive yell, kicked a wall, and ran after Steel and the team.

Chapter 43

A full moon hung in a blanket of a billion stars. The midnight air was warm, with an occasional cool breeze that swept away the heat for a few seconds. The Cuban Hotel was lit up, giving it a grand appearance. The sound of crashing waves was dulled by the traditional music playing in the bar.

The door opened to room 120, and the drunken silhouette stumbled into the suite and headed for the bathroom. Brief grumbles and groans came from the unlit bathroom. The guest hadn't placed the room card into the slot to turn on the power. But he was too drunk to notice or care. The sound of him relieving himself echoed from the marble-fitted bathroom. Followed by another groan and mumble as he stumbled out and made his way to the bed.

There was a loud crash as the man's colossal body hit the bed like a dead weight. Then silence. The only sound was the muffled music downstairs and couples walking along the corridor. The man scratched himself and rubbed his gut, forcing the short-armed shirt bottom to come up over his navel. The drink and heavy meal had taken their toll and made the man tired and weak … or possibly it was the cocktail of drugs that a quick hand had slipped into his drink at the bar.

As the man lay there, a figure slipped out of the shadows and moved carefully up to the man. A gloved hand went over his mouth to prevent any crying out. If the drugs had taken effect, the man would be unable to move, which would make the assassin's life easier. But, instead, the man's eyes opened as the gloved hand slipped over his mouth.

Director Frank Headly froze in place. Mostly out of fear, as well as the cocktail starting to take effect. He looked up at the masked figure. The suit was of a strange neoprene composition and a full-headed mask with two dark glass eyelets. Headly went to scream, but his vocal cords were frozen by the drug.

The assassin stood over Headly and took a syringe from a leg pouch. Headly began to sweat and tried to cry out. The drug had entirely kicked in, and the assassin would only have a short window before it wore off and disappeared from Headly's system.

The assassin took the safety cap off the needle and knelt over Headly but didn't tap the syringe to remove air bubbles. After all, Headly was going to die anyway.

The assassin moved the needle over Headly's navel and found a perfect spot in a crease of skin where a mosquito had gotten there before him. The assassin struck the needle in slowly but didn't inject the contents, not yet. The assassin wanted to look Headly in the eyes, to watch the life drain out of him before slipping away into the shadows.

The assassin pressed the plunger and watched. At first, there was nothing. Then, after several seconds, Headly started to convulse.

The assassin stood and moved back, knowing exactly what would occur. Vomit spewed from Headly's mouth, but he was powerless to do anything. Then the gurgling came as the vomit began to seep back into the trachea. It wouldn't be long now. The assassin could have left but decided to stay and watch the man who had ruined so many lives for profit choke.

The assassin didn't check to see if Headly was dead; if he weren't now, he would be later. Instead, the assassin headed to the balcony window and slipped out into the night.

* * *

The hotel bar was packed with tourists. The music was loud, but the roar of conversation was even louder. Kitty leant on the bar and ordered a drink … six glasses of tequila. She smiled at the handsome young barkeep, then took the drinks that he had placed on a small tablet for her.

Kitty spotted a table in a quiet corner and made her way there. Her short black dress hugged her curves and complemented the black high heels. She placed the tray down, took a glass, and raised it as if to make a toast.

'To those, we have lost, and to those, we have gained,' Kitty said. There was a noise from behind her, but she didn't look.

'A bit selfish, starting without us,' Dutton said, sitting down beside her.

'She always was a little selfish, keeping all that stuff to herself about Steel,' Trish said, moving in close and giving her sister a loving peck on the cheek.

'What now, now it's all over, I mean?' Dutton asked, picking up his glass and raising it to salute the toast before downing it and sucking on the lime wedge.

Kitty and Trish stared at each other, almost as if hoping the other had the answer.

'Well, we are still active, so we can still do missions for the agency,' Kitty admitted.

Trish shrugged and nodded as though agreeing with the plan.

'I'll drink to that,' Dutton said, picking up another glass and raising it up above his head. He looked around, puzzled for a moment as the glass was picked from his hand.

'Not if that's my drink, you're not,' said Steel, appearing from nowhere. He raised the glass and downed the liquid in one swallow before taking his seat.

Kitty looked at Steel and smiled.

'So, why are we all here?' she asked, puzzled but also happy at the location.

'Well, I figured you could all do with a vacation and possibly a new prospect,' Steel said, leaning back in his chair.

'What do you mean, prospect?' Dutton asked.

Steel looked up as a tall, thin man in his late fifties approached. He looked out of place in his white suit, but the white straw fedora made it work.

'Whose that? The guy from the 70s Bond movie?' Dutton asked.

Steel smiled and stood and said, 'He's your new employer. Meet Staff.'

The others looked at Steel, shocked.

'But we have an employer,' Kitty declared.

'Not anymore, you are still dead, and your two counterparts will be found in a burnt-out building; I'm afraid you were both killed on the last mission,' said Staff as he took Steel's seat.

'Right, Staff, I'll let you get acquainted,' Steel said, nodded at him and gave a strange smile before walking away slowly without so much as a goodbye.

'Wait! What happened to Headly and Stanton?' Kitty asked while Steel was in earshot.

'Stanton … I'm afraid … was found at the bottom of Potomac River. His car had come off the road. Well, that's the official story; he is actually head of our Bermuda office,' Staff smiled. 'As for Headly, who knows? Maybe he finally choked on his own greed.'

Steel smiled at the thought that justice had been served, but he couldn't shake the feeling that something still needed to be done.

Kitty excused herself from the table and ran after him. 'Hey, wait!'

Steel turned. 'What is it?' he asked with that cold stare he gave when detached from his feelings.

'You can't just go without saying goodbye,' Kitty said.

A thought slipped into Steel's head. He knew now what it was that he had to do. He reached forwards and cupped Kitty's face in his hands before placing a gentle kiss on her forehead.

'You'll be fine, all of you,' Steel said with a warm smile.

'And you?' Kitty asked with a concerned look.

Steel looked into the horizon and shrugged. 'I have to go. I'm wanted back in London; they have a new assignment for me.'

Kitty nodded. 'Until next time, then.'

'I can't wait' Steel smiled. He turned and walked away.

Kitty watched him disappear into a crowd of people. She sighed and turned towards the table and the group waiting for her. She whirled, taking one last glance at where Steel had been standing in time to see the police rushing into the hotel and a hysterical maid being led downstairs.

'What happened?' she asked one of the waiters taking fresh drinks to her table.

'Oh, some guy in one of the suites was found dead, choked on his own vomit they said. He was American, some guy named Hatley or something,' the waiter said before heading to the table.

'Headly. His name was Headly,' Kitty said with a satisfied smile.

About the Author

Stuart Field is the author of the John Steel thriller series.

He's born in the West Midlands, Great Britain. Later, he joined the armed forces where after 22 years of fun and adventure, he left to start as a writer. Married with a daughter, he still hasn't grown up, which helps with the imagination. He loves to travel and experience other cultures. He loves to love life.

***

To learn more about Stuart Field and discover more Next Chapter authors, visit our website at www.nextchapter.pub.

John Steel Collection - Books 4-6
ISBN: 978-4-82417-566-3 (Paperback Edition)

Published by
Next Chapter
2-5-6 SANNO
SANNO BRIDGE
143-0023 Ota-Ku, Tokyo
+818035793528
28th April 2023